# THE YEAR'S BEST

# Fantasy & Horror

## Also Edited by Ellen Datlow and Terri Windling

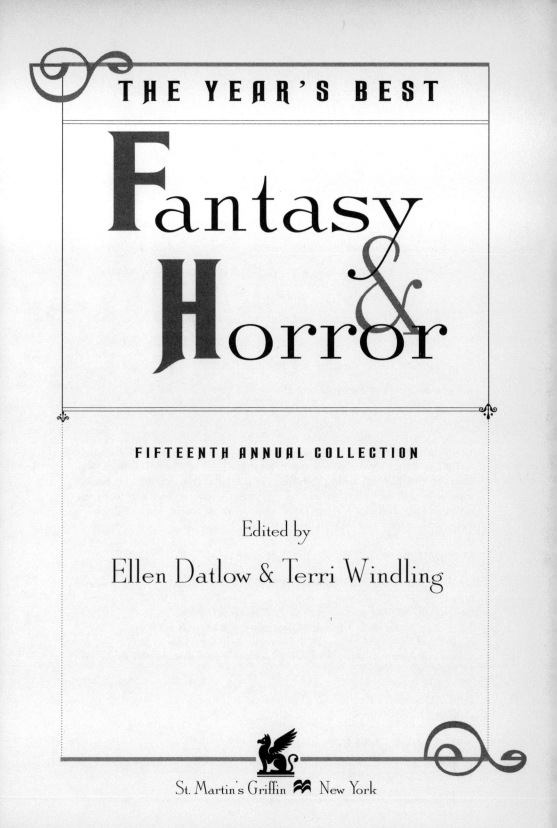

# THE YEAR'S BEST

# Fantasy & Horror

## FIFTEENTH ANNUAL COLLECTION

Edited by

Ellen Datlow & Terri Windling

St. Martin's Griffin ❧ New York

www.stmartins.com

ISBN 0-312-29067-5 (hc)
ISBN 0-312-29069-1 (pbk)

A Blue Cows—Randall Vilas Production

First Edition: August 2002

10  9  8  7  6  5  4  3  2  1

We dedicate this volume to Jenna Felice (1976–2001), colleague and friend, who was a lover of the fantastic and a champion of short fiction.

—E.D., T.W., and J.F.

# Contents

# Acknowledgments

Once again, I am grateful to all the publishers, publicists, editors, writers, artists, and music companies who sent review material to us in 2001, as well as to all the folks who passed on recommendations. *Locus Magazine* and *Publishers Weekly* were, as always, particularly valuable reference sources, both for publishing news and insightful reviews. The following people deserve special thanks for providing various help in 2001: Ed Bryant, Charles de Lint, Gavin Grant, Patrick Nielsen Hayden, Tappan King, Ellen Kushner, Kelly Link, Beth Meacham, Joe Monti, Steve Pasechnick, Delia Sherman, Midori Snyder, Charles Vess, Joan Vinge, and Jane Yolen.

The fantasy half of this book would not exist without the hard work of assistant editors Richard Kunz and Mardelle Kunz, whose dedication to this project goes far above and beyond the call of duty each year. The deepest thanks to you both. Thanks are also due to series creator/packager Jim Frenkel and his assistants, Jesse Vogel and Steve Smith; to our St. Martin's Press editor, Marc Resnick; and to my terrific co-editor, Ellen Datlow. And to Tom Canty, who never fails to come up with gorgeous cover art for us.

For information on submitting fantasy material to future volumes of *The Year's Best Fantasy and Horror*, please visit the FAQ page of the Endicott Studio of Mythic Arts Web site: www.endicott-studio.com.                           —T.W.

*The Year's Best Fantasy and Horror* requires the cooperation of a number of people. I'd like to thank the publishers, editors, writers, and readers who send material and make suggestions every year. This year I'd particularly like to thank Gene O'Neill, Lawrence Schimel, and Bill Congreve for their recommendations and help. Also, an extra special thanks to Kelly Link for helping me out during the year.

Thanks to Jim Frenkel, our hardworking packager, and his diligent assistant, Jesse Vogel; also, to Tom Canty for his fertile visual imagination. Finally, thanks to my co-editor and friend, Terri Windling, for inspiring me to go the last mile on this thing just by being there so that I know that I'm not alone in the task.

The following magazines and catalogs provided invaluable information regarding material I was unable to find: *Locus, Science Fiction Chronicle, Publishers Weekly, Washington Post Book World, The New York Times Book Review,* Dream-

haven's catalog, *Hellnotes*, the *DarkEcho Newsletter*, and *Jobs in Hell*. And thanks
to the magazine editors who made sure I saw their magazines during the year.

—E.D.

In this strange, traumatized year, many, many people pulled together to create
this year's anthology: Ellen and Terri, our brilliant and intrepid editors, Ed Bryant and our new columnists, Charles Vess and Joan D. Vinge, Tom Canty, for
another eye-catching package, Jessi Frenkel, for the cover concept, and all the
contributors and others who cooperated in letting us reprint materials.

Thanks also to my assistants, Jesse Vogel and Stephen Smith, and to our
interns, Anne Jensen, Hannah Pardee, Andrea Reber, and Natale Zimmer, without whom this book would be later, and not as well, produced.

And special thanks to Marc Resnick, our St. Martin's Press editor, who, aided
by assistant Rebecca Heller, has manfully weathered the storms that buffeted
this production. —J.F.

# Summation 2001: Fantasy

## Terri Windling

Welcome to the fifteenth edition of *The Year's Best Fantasy and Horror*, an anthology series created as an annual celebration of magical literature in all its guises—from high fantasy (à la J. R. R. Tolkien) to magical realism (à la Gabriel García Márquez), from mythic fiction to surrealism, from ghostly stories to darker fantasias. For the purposes of this anthology, our definition of "fantasy" is broad and inclusive, covering all the various kinds of magical fiction that come into print each year, whether published as genre fiction, mainstream fiction, or children's fiction. Thus you'll find each of these areas represented in this volume, demonstrating the rich diversity of fantasy and horror fiction being written and published today.

Ellen Datlow and I consider fantasy and horror to be sister fields that share certain traits, enriching each other when viewed side by side—but for readers who have a strong preference for one kind of story over another, the horror selections carry Ellen's initials after the introduction, the fantasy selections carry mine, and works that fall into the shadow realm between the two list both our initials, with the acquiring editor listed first. For those new to our series, I should explain that the following Summations provide an overview of fantasy and horror publishing in the year just past, with lists of recommended novels, story collections, anthologies, children's books, art books, nonfiction, etc. Separate Summations cover fantasy and horror in comics and in media arts, in animé and manga, followed by an Obituaries section noting the passing of people who have contributed to our field.

In 2001, the biggest fantasy news came from the film world, of course, with the huge success of the Harry Potter movie and Peter Jackson's rendition of *The Fellowship of the Ring*. We've already seen the effect that the Potter phenomenon had on children's book publishing, an effect that can only be increased by the popularity of the film. Thanks to Rowling, fantasy novels for young-adult readers are more numerous these days, and are enjoying better promotion and visibility than they have for many years past. In 2001, two promising new lines were created specifically for YA fantasy and science fiction: Viking's Firebird, edited by Sharyn November, and Tor's Starscape, edited by Jonathan Schmidt.

Both lines are reprinting wonderful books in YA trade paperback editions by the likes of Jane Yolen, Lloyd Alexander, Nancy Springer, Midori Snyder, Pamela Dean, Will Shetterly, and will feature original titles as well.

As for *The Lord of the Rings*, the broad success of this film with mainstream audiences certainly means we'll be seeing more fantasy films in the future, but will it also boost fantasy publishing? As of this writing, it's still too soon to say. Certainly the film has prompted people to go back and read J. R. R. Tolkien's trilogy, rediscovering (or, in some cases, discovering) the pleasures of journeying through imaginary lands. I've personally noticed a sharp rise in requests for recommendations of other good fantasy books, often from people who've shown little interest in the genre before. Whether this interest will last, or will extend beyond imaginary-world novels to other kinds of fantasy, still remains to be seen. As for now, Jackson's film (with two more films in the sequence still to come) has put fantasy back on the pop-culture map as something of interest to viewers and readers beyond its core audience.

Good imaginary-world novels in 2001 ranged from grand high-fantasy epics to entertaining, fast-paced adventure tales, the best of them from Jeffrey Ford, Sean Russell, Elizabeth Haydon, Robin Hobb, Steven Brust, and Storm Constantine in adult fiction, from Garth Nix and Meredith Ann Pierce in children's fiction— with the highlight of the year being not one but *two* new "Earthsea" books from Ursula K. Le Guin. Contemporary fantasy made a strong showing in 2001 with new books from some of our field's best writers, including Jonathan Carroll, Jack Cady, Nina Kiriki Hoffman, and Charles de Lint. Historical fantasy had a banner year with fine new books by J. Gregory Keyes, Judith Tarr, Thomas Harlan, Kara Dalkey, and the talented newcomers Chris Adrian, Jane Alison, and Suzanne Allés Blom. One of the strongest areas of all, suprisingly, considering the gloom-and-doom rumblings one hears from the publishing industry, was in First Novels. The number and quality of debut novels was sharply up this year, with magical, innovative, remarkably accomplished books turning up both in the fantasy genre and in mainstream fiction. Another trend I noticed was the number of wonderful books coming out of Australia, by the likes of Jack Dann, Paul Brandon, Cameron Rogers, Sean Williams, Sara Douglass, Isobelle Carmody, and Cecilia Dart-Thornton.

Two thousand one was a strong year for short fantasy fiction in genre magazines, slightly less so in mainstream journals. In both venues, there was a marked preponderance of ghost stories this year. (And in literary journals, for some darn reason, a plethora of poems about crows. Go figure.) Small publishers such as Small Beer Press, Edgewood Press, Subterranean Press, Coffee House Press, and Golden Gryphon picked up the slack from the larger publishers by producing good single-author story collections in attractive editions. There was, in general, a dearth of good anthologies of original fiction in 2001, both in genre and mainstream publishing, with a very few sterling exceptions discussed in "Anthologies" below.

Among reprint anthologies, the most important news of 2001 was the launch of David G. Hartwell and Kathryn Cramer's mass-market sized *The Year's Best Fantasy* annual, a book that takes up the reins from the wonderful old DAW Books collections of that title edited by Lin Carter and Arthur D. Saha. Hartwell and Cramer, like Carter and Saha before them, have set themselves the task of collecting the best stories published each year within the established boundaries of the fantasy genre. It's a different mission than the one Ellen and I have in this anthology, where genre fiction is but one of several areas of magical literature we cover, and where a large part of my job is to gather, under one cover, magical works published in other places that readers might otherwise miss. For the fifteen years I've been doing this, however, there has been one segment of the fantasy readership clamoring for an entirely different book—one that devotes its pages to genre fiction, as the Carter-Saha volumes did. My answer to them has always been: "Yes, I agree, that would be a fine book indeed. But it's not *this* book. Perhaps someone else will take up that worthy task." Now, finally, someone else has. David Hartwell, with his years of editorial experience, is a proper successor to Carter and Saha, and judging by the first volume of the Hartwell & Cramer annual, those gentleman would be pleased. I confess that I find myself impatient with critics who insist on seeing these two separate annuals as being in conflict with each other. Rather, I see them as part of a chorus of voices, demonstrating once again how rich and diverse the fantasy field truly is, and has always been—supporting not only a variety of authorial voices, but of editorial ones. Fantasy readers are the winners here, presented annually with the treasures provided by two anthologies, each covering somewhat different ground. For the sake of truth in advertising, should these books be titled *The Year's Best Fantasy According to Hartwell & Cramer's Editorial Bias and Critical Ideas about Genre Fiction* and *The Year's Best Fantasy and Horror According to Windling & Datlow's Editorial Bias and Windling's Magpie Gleanings of Stories from All Over the Damn Place?* Well, yes. But readers have always known that. Myself, I intend to support our genre's new annual by buying it, recommending it, and enjoying the stories therein. *Vive la différence.*

Now let's go on to some recommendations, drawn from the books that my hard-working assistants, Richard and Mardelle Kunz, gathered for review last year—over five hundred titles in all. We think we've found some real gems among them (I'm not going to tell you about the stinkers!), and I hope that you'll agree.

## Top Twenty

The following books from 2001 are ones no fantasy lover should miss. As a group, they demonstrate the sheer diversity of modern magical fiction, drawn from the "subgenres" of imaginary-world fantasy, alternate-history fiction, dark fantasy on the borderline of horror, magical realism, and young-adult fiction. In alphabetical order by author:

*Gob's Grief* by Chris Adrian (Broadway Books) is an historical fantasy novel in which the poet Walt Whitman teams up with the (imaginary) son of the (real) feminist Virginia Woodhull to create a machine that will bring the Civil War dead back to life. The evocation of the period is first-rate in this absorbing, fascinating, and beautifully penned first novel.

*The Kappa Child* by Hiromi Goto (Red Deer Press) is another astonishingly good first novel—so good, in fact, that it won the Commonwealth Writers' Prize and the James Tiptree Jr. Award. This highly original book is a contemporary fantasy about a Japanese-Canadian girl growing up in rural Alberta, wound through with Japanese "Kappa" legends about a water imp and trickster, benevolent and malevolent by turns.

*Mother of Kings* by Poul Anderson (Tor), the last novel by one of the greats of the fantasy field, is a vigorous historical fantasy rooted in Norse history and myth, recounting the life of Gunnhild, Queen of England and Norway in the tenth century. Vast in scope, Anderson depicts a violent world where the old gods stand before the challenge of the new god of Christianity. The author brings rich characters to life against a harsh and yet beautiful backdrop.

*Leaving Tabasco* by Carmen Boullosa (Grove Press), translated from the Spanish by Geoff Hargreaves, is Mexican magical realism—a coming-of-age novel about a girl growing up among witches, ghosts, and miracles. By turns funny, touching, and horrifying, Boullosa's account of a childhood in a small Mexican village is brimming with folklore and fantasy, yet grounded, too, in her country's politics of the 1960s.

*Swim the Moon* by Paul Brandon (Tor) is another remarkably assured first novel, this one a contemporary fantasy set on the far north coast of Scotland. It's a darkly romantic story, wound through with Celtic music, selchie legends, and family secrets—well crafted, deeply mythic, and marking Brandon as a writer to watch.

*The Hauntings of Hood Canal* by Jack Cady (St. Martin's Press) is a fine contemporary fantasy tale concerning three small towns in rural Washington State and the canal that links them, which is suddenly claiming more than its share of drownings and road accidents. It's a dark tale with occult elements, straddling the border of horror fiction, using supernatural and folkloric themes to illuminate real life in the American Northwest.

*The Wooden Sea* by Jonathan Carroll (Tor) is yet another good contemporary fantasy, this one set in upstate New York, involving a mysterious three-legged dog, the nature of time, and a small-town cop on whom the fate of the world suddenly seems to depend. Once again, the iconoclastic Mr. Carroll delivers a fast-paced story that is harrowing, funny, poignant, mysterious, confounding, and astonishingly wise. This excellent tale is one of his best.

*Counting Coup* by Jack Dann (Tor) is a supernatural "road novel" about an ex-janitor down on his luck and an alcoholic Indian medicine man fleeing "bad medicine." Dann's story follows these two across the back roads of America—through car thefts, burglaries, drunken binges—exploring the dark side of the American Dream, and finding a kind of transcendence by journey's end. Previously published in Australia under the name *Bad Medicine*, this is the first U.S. publication of an exceptional novel.

*The Onion Girl* by Charles de Lint (Tor) is the latest in de Lint's long-running "Newford" saga: mythic fiction set in an imaginary, contemporary city somewhere in North America. Artist Jilly Coppercorn has been one of the major recurring characters in the Newford tale—a winsome young lady whose dark past has only been hinted at previously. With this novel, Jilly takes the spotlight in a hard-hitting story about families and secrets and the magics that can save or destroy us.

*The Eyre Affair* by Jasper Fforde (New English Library, U.K.—Viking, U.S.) is a fantasy/satire/detective/time-travel/alternate-history novel, set in literature-obsessed London in 1985, in an alternate world where the Crimean War has never ended. The story involves the dastardly Acheron Hades, intent on kidnapping the fictional character Jane Eyre, and Thursday Next, the dashing literary detective whose business it is to foil him. Fforde's wacky book is a first novel, and a complete delight from start to finish.

*The Beyond* by Jeffrey Ford (Avon Eos) is the third and final book in a sequence that began with his World Fantasy Award–winning novel *The Physiognomy*. Now he brings the trilogy to a satisfying close, just as powerfully as he started. In this richly imagistic, allegorical fantasy, Ford's protagonist, the former "Physiognomist," must travel to the sentient wilderness beyond the rubble of the Well-built city. This trilogy is simply brilliant, and constitutes a modern masterwork of fantasy.

*American Gods* by Neil Gaiman (William Morrow) is an ambitious, tour de force of a novel about contemporary American life—about the old gods who live at the margins of it and the new gods emerging from our restless culture, fighting the old gods for turf. Gaiman's protagonist, an ex-con named Shadow, becomes embroiled in this lethal rivalry, setting him off on a hero's journey across the U.S. in a richly panoramic book that is dark, and deep, and occasionally even profound. It's a remarkable work.

*Destiny* by Elizabeth Haydon (Tor) is high-fantasy adventure of the best sort—a page-turner of a tale that is also well crafted, intelligent, and grounded in a broad knowledge of myth and history. Haydon's sweeping tale of magic and intrigue, set in a richly imagined secondary world, is the concluding book the "Child of the Sky" trilogy that began with *Rhapsody*. This new writer's work invites comparison to Guy Gavriel Kay or C. J. Cherryh, and that's praise indeed.

*Past the Size of Dreaming* by Nina Kiriki Hoffman (Ace) is the sequel to Hoffman's contemporary fantasy novel *A Red Heart of Memories* (short-listed for the World Fantasy Award) about a homeless young woman who communicates with inanimate objects, and her companion, a male witch. These terrific books are contemporary fantasies of the Charles de Lint or Alice Hoffman sort—character-driven, psychologically acute, mystical, and vastly entertaining.

*Celtika* by Robert Holdstock (Earthlight, U.K.) is the first book in the new "Merlin Codex" series, loosely related to Holdstock's previous "Mythago Wood" sequence. This one is a blend of Greek and Celtic myth, with the figure of Merlin at its center, involving Jason and Medea and a "Land of Heroes" where time flows differently. These ingredients make for a fine tale indeed, with all the familiar Holdstock themes: explorations of myth, history, and twisted family relationships.

*The Otherwind* by Ursula K. Le Guin (Harcourt) is Le Guin's first "Earthsea" novel in a decade, and a powerful addition to that canon indeed—a tale of magics both great and small, of wizards and dragons, farmers and "menders," thrilling and thought-provoking in equal measure. Just as Tolkien's "Middle-earth" was the primary fantasy creation of the mid–twentieth century (even over such fine creations as Narnia and Gormenghast), it is my firm belief that "Earthsea" is the primary creation of our time—from its origins as children's fantasy in the late sixties/early seventies, to the mature reenvisioning of her world that Le Guin has accomplished here. This satisfying fantasy has my vote as the best book of the year.

*Lost* by Gregory Maguire (HarperCollins) is a wonderful dark fantasy set in contemporary London but deeply bound up with the Victorian world of Charles Dickens and Jack the Ripper. It's a literary mystery of sorts, about books and ghosts and family secrets—a delicious read, and the best novel yet from a remarkably talented writer.

*The Dreamsmith's Daughter* by Michael Moorcock (Warner Aspect) brings two of Moorcock's great fictional creations together: the albino warrior and sorcerer Elric of Melniboné, and Count Ulric von Bek, last of a mystical German family, serving as guardian of mythic objects of power during World War II. As usual, Moorcock's fantasy is multilayered and fiercely intelligent, rich with historical detail, panoramic in scope, dazzling in vision, language, myth, and magic.

*Lirael: Daughter of the Clayr* by Garth Nix (HarperCollins) is splendid high fantasy for young adults, deep, dark, and complex enough to be of interest to adult readers as well. It's the continuing saga of the "Old Kingdom," a Gothic land of necromancers, seers, and elementals, where a Third Assistant Librarian named Lirael, along with her mysterious companion "Disreputable Dog," becomes an unlikely hero in the ongoing battle against dark powers. (Be warned: it's the middle book in a series that began with *Sabriel*. Readers who don't like cliff-hanger endings may want to wait until the third volume, *Abhorsen*, is released.)

*The One Kingdom* by Sean Russell (Little, Brown), Volume I of the "Swan's War" series, is high fantasy of the Tolkien sort, using standard tropes of the form—but Russell is too darn good of a writer to be merely derivative. Instead, he's created a magical adventure that is fresh, skillfully plotted, rich in landscape, language, and nuanced characters. Russell is one of our field's hidden treasures, and deserves the wider readership this book will surely bring him.

## First Novels

There were a number of impressive debuts in the fantasy field this year, as well as several magical mainstream novels that are worth your attention. To start with the genre titles, the best first novels of the year were three stories with highly personal visions. First, there was Paul Brandon's contemporary fantasy *Swim the Moon*, listed in the Top Twenty above. Second, I recommend Jacqueline Carey's imaginary-world fantasy *Kushiel's Dart* (Tor), a trangressive tale of court intrigue set in a kingdom that is decadent and deadly, following the life of a young woman sold into servitude, trained as a courtesan and spy. This ambitious, darkly erotic novel won't be to every reader's taste—I admit that the sadomasochistic themes in the book were not to mine, and in a lesser writer's hands would have put me off, but the author won me over with the breadth of her vision and the assurance of her craft. *The Music of Razors* by Cameron Rogers (Penguin, Australia) is another innovative first novel: dark, stylish, and unique. It concerns a little boy who is trapped, along with his "guardian monster," inside the shell of his comatose body, wandering a world of monsters and fallen angels while trying to protect his sister from the same menace that put him in this state. This highly unusual fantasy is not flawless, but when it works it *really* works, and is well worth seeking out.

Other first novels of note: *Ill Met by Moonlight* by Sarah A. Hoyt (Ace) is a captivating book starring the young William Shakespeare in a world of faery intrigue and treachery. *Children of the Shaman* by Jessica Rydill (Orbit, U.K.) is a thoughtful coming-of-age fantasy that is indeed about the children of a shaman, set in a magical version of our far future after an apocalyptic ice age. *Mother Ocean, Daughter Sea* by Diana Marcellas (Tor) is another coming-of-age novel about a young woman with magical powers, this time in a land where witches like herself have been brutally persecuted. The author transcends the potential clichés of her material to produce a satisfying tale. *The Ill-Made Mute* is the first volume in the "Bitterbynde" series by Australian writer Cecilia Dart-Thornton (Macmillan, Australia). The breathless quotes on the back compare the book to Tolkien, which raises reader expectation way too high—but if such comparisons are avoided, this lyrical, quest-style fantasy, rich with folklore, does show promise. *Enemy Glory* by Karen Michalson (Tor) is a magician-in-training-type fantasy concerning a young man born into a world of political, religious, and magical conflicts. Darker than most similar novels (indeed, almost relentlessly so), it's a memorable and interesting book that raises interesting questions. Terry McGarry's *Illumination* (Tor) is another mages-and-magic fantasy that's a cut above other books of the type. It is the first of a projected series, imbued with a fine sense of mysticism. *Circle of Nine* by Josephine Pennicott (Earthlight, Australia) draws on an oddly mixed bag of Celtic, Greco-Roman, and other myths in a contemporary, unabashedly pagan fantasy about a young woman artist drawn into a world of goddesses and fallen angels.

On the mainstream shelves, I highly recommend the following: *The Nature of Water and Air* by Regina McBride (Scribner) is a wonderful Irish novel about a young girl trying to come to terms with her mother, a tinker (the Irish term for gypsy). Like Paul Brandon's *Swim the Moon*, this book is stitched together by the skillful use of selchie myths. Equally good is *The Complete Tales of Kezia Gold* by Kate Bernheimer (Black Ice Books), a marvelous novel with a fractured, prismatic structure that uses fairy tales and Jewish folktales to illuminate what could be called a postmodern coming-of-age story. If you like your fiction on the cutting age, Bernheimer's story is truly memorable. *Staircase of a Thousand Steps* by Masha Hamilton (BlueHen) is another gem of a book with a coming-of-age theme, this one about a young girl in a Jordanian village in the 1960s, providing a fascinating portrait of Middle Eastern landscape, culture, and mysticism. *The Love-Artist* by Jane Alison (Farrar, Straus & Giroux) concerns the Roman poet Ovid and the mysterious witch-woman who becomes his muse, in a skillful, stylish tale that speculates on how the poet's version of *Medea* came to be lost to history.

Also of note: *Inca* by Suzanne Allés Blom (Forge) is an engrossing, beautifully crafted work of alternate history, reimagining the Incan Empire at the time of the Spanish Conquistadors. *In the Company of Angels* by N.M. Kelby (Theia/Hyperion) is a book by turns poetic (sometimes overly so) and unflinchingly horrific. Set in Belgium during the Holocaust, Kelby's magical realist tale concerns two nuns with complicated pasts, an orphaned Jewish girl, and the nature of faith. *The Third Witch* by Rebecca Reisert (Washington Square Press) is an historical fantasy set in eleventh-century Scotland, based on the story of Macbeth as viewed through the eyes of one of the three witches: cast here as a vengeful young woman who disguises herself as a boy and becomes a servant in Macbeth's castle. While it has some first-novel flaws, it's an enjoyable story, well grounded in period detail. *Observatory Mansions* by Edward Carey (Crown) is more Gothic than overtly fantastic, though it's certainly a fantasia of sorts. This very British novel concerns a group of eccentrics living in a once-elegant mansion that is now a collection of crumbling flats. Though dark in tone, there is light and redemption at the core of Carey's quirky book.

## Imaginary-World Fantasy

For "high fantasy" of the Tolkien sort, the best books were the three by Ursula K. Le Guin, Garth Nix, and Sean Russell listed in the Top Twenty. Otherwise, worthy books of this sort were light on the ground this year. When we turn to adventure fantasy, however, the list of good reads grows longer. I particularly recommend: *Fool's Errand* (Bantam Spectra), in which Robin Hobb takes the hero of her "Farseer" books and places him in a new trilogy set fifteen years later in his life. Like Le Guin, Hobbs is particularly skilled in creating nuanced characters and exploring themes of middle age while still telling a rousing good tale. *Issola* by Steven Brust (Tor) is the latest volume in this author's witty, smart, surprisingly philosophical "Vlad Taltos" series about a magical assassin. Reminiscent in all the right ways of Roger Zelazny's "Amber" books, this novel is a strong addition to a series that is not only fun but wickedly subversive. Equally subversive, but more Gothic in tone, is *Crown of Silence*, Book #2 in "The Chronicles of Magravandias" by Storm Constantine (Gollancz, U.K.)—a dark and passionate book about war, wizardry, and their consequences. Also from England, *Rebel's Cage* by Kate Jacoby (Gollancz, U.K.) is another intelligent, fast-paced tale of magical political intrigue, the sequel to her strong debut novel *Voice of the Demon*. *The Curse of Chalion* by Lois McMaster Bujold (Avon Eos) is a romp of a story by an author better known for science fiction tales. This novel, rooted in Spanish history, is clever, romantic, and colorful. *BattleAxe* and *Enchanter* by Sara Douglass (Tor) are the first U.S. publications of Books #1 and 2 in "The Wayfarer Redemption," an epic fantasy series that has proven a big hit with Australian readers. The first two books are page-turners—long on adventure, shorter on characterization. For those more interested in the latter, stick with this series—it gets richer as it goes. Strong characterization has always distinguished the books of Lyn Flewelling's "Nightrunner" series. *The Bone Doll's Twin* (Bantam Spectra) is a "prequel" to the other books, and the strongest yet from this writer—a page-turner of an adventure tale, skillfully written. *Through Wolf's Eyes* by Jane Lindskold (Tor) is a feral-child tale about a wolfgirl in a magical world. Though the fantasy elements are standard ones, the author's portrayal of wolf life and lore makes for enchanting reading. *Once Upon a Winter's Night* by Dennis L. McKiernan (Roc) is a novel inspired by the fairy tale "East of the Sun, West of the Moon." In this old-fashioned Romance, a young woman is carried away by a big white bear to marry a prince of Faery. It's a charming conceit, more intimate in scope than McKiernan's better-known epic fantasy.

Also of note: *Summers at Castle Auburn* by Sharon Shinn (Ace), a coming-of-age fantasy with surprising twists; *The Way of the Rose* by Valery Leith (Bantam Spectra), the final volume of Leith's complicated "Everien" trilogy; *Summerblood* by Tom Deitz (Bantam Spectra), Book #3 in his "Tales of Eron" series, inspired by Celtic and Native American myths; *The Queen's Necklace* by Teresa Edgerton

(Ace), a quick-paced swords-and-intrigue novel with an eighteenth-century feel; *Corsair* by Chris Bunch (Warner Aspect), a sprightly tale for those who like their adventure set on the high seas; and the continuation of three epics that are better than the usual: *Sea of Sorrows* by Michelle West (Daw), Book #4 in the "Sun Sword" series; *The Golden Sword* by Fiona Patton (Daw), Book #4 in the "Branion" series; and *Revelation* by Carol Berg (Roc), the sequel to *Transformation*.

## Contemporary Fantasy

This category consists of contemporary tales in real-world settings infused with magic, including urban fantasy, and magical realism published within the fantasy genre. The best books of this kind were the Jonathan Carroll, Jack Dann, Charles de Lint, Neil Gaiman, and Nina Kiriki Hoffman books listed in the Top Twenty. In addition to these, I recommend the following: *Tattoo Girl* by Brooke Stevens (St. Martin's/Griffin) is a mesmerizing dark fantasy about a silent young girl covered in fish-scale tattoos who is found abandoned in an Ohio mall, and the woman who adopts her, a former circus fat lady. Drawing on myths ranging from Icarus to the Fisher King, Stevens has created a suspenseful novel that is heartbreaking, frightening, and luminous by turns. *Bloodtide* by Melvin Burgess (Tor) is a dystopian novel that falls in the interstices between young-adult and adult fiction, between science fiction and fantasy. Set in a near-future version of London, a ruined city of street gangs and shapeshifters, it's an unflinching story of love, blood, and revenge, with fourteen-year-old protagonists—inspired by the Volsunga Saga, the great epic of Icelandic folklore. Francesca Lia Block is another writer of "noir fantasy" that falls somewhere between adult and young-adult fiction, with large followings among both audiences. Readers who've complained that Block's fiction has been a bit trendy or self-indulgent of late will be glad to discover that she's back on form with *Echo*, a coming-of-age novella that covers her usual turf (a troubled young woman living in a magical version of L.A.) but does so with three-dimensional characters as well as style. There have been so many novels in the past two decades in which magic suddenly intrudes upon our modern world, usually after a natural or man-made disaster, that these books could practically become a genre of their own. *Magic Time* by Marc Scott Zicree and Barbara Hambly (HarperCollins) is yet another magical postdisaster novel set in New York City. This book apparently started as a media project, which shows in the overly episodic pacing, but likable characters save the story and lift it above cliché. *The Dragon Charmer* by Jan Siegel (Del Rey) is another book that strays close to fantasy clichés, but nonetheless has its strengths. The story's protagonist moves between modern-day London and a hidden magical world in this entertaining sequel to Siegel's coming-of-age fantasy *Prospero's Children*.

## Historical and Alternate-History Fantasy

Fans of historical fantasy had a wealth of books to choose from this year. In addition to the Chris Adrian book listed in the Top Twenty, and the Jane Alison and Suzanne Allés Blom books listed in First Novels, here are five more that should not be missed: *The Shadow of God* is the fourth and final book of J.

Gregory Keyes's "Age of Unreason" series (Del Rey), depicting an alchemical version of the eighteenth century. Ben Franklin, King Phillip, Tsar Peter, and Voltaire all have a hand in this satisfying conclusion to Keyes's smart, inventive saga. *Pride of Kings* (Roc) is another tour de force by Judith Tarr, who has long since proven herself to be one of the fantasy field's best writers. Here she turns her attention to Richard the Lionheart, his brother John, and an unusual version of Robin Hood, in a sorcerous, ingenious tale rich in character and imagery. *The Storm of Heaven* by Thomas Harlan (Tor) is Book #3 in his sweeping "Oath of Empire" series, set in a version of the seventh century where the Roman Empire still stands. There's more of an emphasis on action than character this time, which will probably delight as many readers as it disappoints, but Harlan's command of history and period detail remains first-rate. *Point of Dreams* by Melissa Scott and Lisa A. Barnett (Tor) is another kettle of fish altogether—a sly, wry, sparkling mystery novel set in a magical Renaissance-style city full of swordsmen, astronomers, playwrights, and ghosts. For something different again try *Genpei*, the beautiful new novel by Kara Dalkey (Tor). Set among the warrior clans of Japan in the twelfth century, it's an epic both finely drawn and gripping, as rich in folklore as it is in warfare.

Also of note: *Son of the Shadows* by Juliet Marillier (Tor) is intelligent historical romance set in a magical version of early Ireland, involving the daughter of the heroine of Marillier's last book: the lovely fairy-tale novel *Daughter of the Forest*. *The Angel and the Sword* by Cecelia Holland (Forge) is another good novel, like Marillier's, exploring the conflict between Christian and pagan beliefs—this one concerning a young woman in a magical version of ninth-century Paris. Though Holland is best known as the author of straight historicals, her fine new book indicates she's no slouch at fantasy either. *The Burning Times* by Jeanne Kalogridis (Simon & Schuster) is yet another novel about a young pagan woman—this time among the witch-burners of fourteenth-century France. As an historical novel (touching upon the myths of the Knights Templar, the Black Death, and the Hundred Years War) Kalogridis's book makes for interesting reading, but as fantasy (the heroine is a reincarnation of the Goddess) it's a little fuzzy-headed. *Leopard in Exile* by Andre Norton and Rosemary Edghill (Tor) is the second book in the "Carolus Rex" series, magical mysteries (with a good dollop of romance) set in an alternate version of the eighteenth century. This one casts the Marquis de Sade as a black magician aiding Napoleon's march across Europe. It's lightweight, but good fun. For a deeper immersion into the past, try *The Mystic Rose* by Stephen R. Lawhead (Morrow), the final volume of a trilogy that follows two generations of a Scottish family on the Crusades; and *The Destruction of the Inn* by Randy Lee Eickhoff (Tor), Book #4 in his "Ulster Cycle," based on eleventh-century Irish texts. For fans of time-travel fantasy there's *Knight Errant* by R. Garcia y Robertson (Forge), a fast-paced tale about a contemporary American woman who finds herself in Renaissance England; and *Son of the Sword* by J. Adrian Lee (Ace), about a young American man in a magical version of medieval Scotland. *Call Down the Stars* by Sue Harrison (Morrow) is the final book in her "Storyteller Trilogy" set in prehistoric Alaska. Harrison wraps this highly atmospheric novel around the "Great Sedna" myth. *A Feast in Exile* by Chelsea Quinn Yarbro (Tor) is the latest in this author's long-running "Saint-Germain" series of vampire historicals. This volume brings the immortal Count Saint-Germain to the streets of fourteenth-century India.

For Arthurian fiction, the most interesting book of the year was *Lancelot du Lethe* by J. Robert King (Tor), a fey and very unusual take on the Lancelot-Guinevere legend. Other titles of note: *The Child of the Holy Grail* by Rosalind Miles (Crown), Book #3 in the "Guinevere" series, is an intelligent, insightful look at this mythic queen and other women of Arthurian legend, well-grounded in mythic scholarship. For something a little more testosterone-driven, try *Uther* by Jack Whyte (Forge), Book #7 in Whyte's popular "Camulod Chronicles"— a grittier look at the mythos, also rooted in sound scholarship. *The Merlin of the Oak Wood* by Ann Chamberlin (Tor) is Book #2 in the "Joan of Arc Tapestry" series, which combines the Joan of Arc legend with Arthurian and Celtic myths and somehow makes it all work. For something completely different try Irene Radford's fast-paced "Merlin's Descendants" series: *Guardian of the Balance*, *Guardian of the Trust*, and *Guardian of the Vision* (DAW), which begins with the Arthurian mythos, moves to the time of King John, and then on to Queen Elizabeth I. The oddest Arthurian book of the year might be Phyllis Ann Karr's *The Follies of Sir Harald* (Green Knight Publishing), a Camelot comedy about a knight equally hapless in love and adventure. Or it might be *Code of the West* by Aaron Latham (Simon & Schuster) which transplants the myth to the Texas frontier. In this Western novel, Arthur is a boy raised by Comanches, Lancelot is a handsome cowpoke with remarkable horse skills, and Guinevere is a rich man's daughter rescued from an outlaw's clutches.

## Humorous Fantasy

In addition to the Jasper Fforde book listed in the Top Twenty, Terry Pratchett's work is once again at the top of the list for humorous fantasy with the latest book in his vastly popular "Discworld" series. Volume #26 is *Thief of Time* (HarperCollins), a tale about the "History Monks" of Discworld who are charged with keeping time running straight. Pratchett also graced us with a "Discworld fable": *The Last Hero of Discworld* (HarperCollins), the adventures of the aging hero Cohen the Barbarian, in an edition extensively illustrated by Paul Kidby. He also published a Discworld book for younger readers, listed in Children's Fantasy. *Stolen From Gypsies* by Noble Smith (Aubrey House) is another book that has gotten a lot of attention—a bawdy picaresque novel about a frail nineteenth-century nobleman and the magical story recounted to him by a mysterious gypsy in Tuscany. The book's zany style has been alternately compared to William Goldman's *The Princess Bride* and Monty Python.

Also of note: *Plumage* by Nancy Springer (Morrow) is a strangely wonderful novel about middle age, cross-dressing, magical mirrors, and parakeets. *Mimi's Ghost* by Tim Parks (Arcade) is a blackly comedic mystery about a man haunted by the ghost of a woman he loved, and kidnapped, and murdered. *Turning on the Girls* by Cheryl Bernard (Farrar, Straus & Giroux) is a near-future novel depicting a world that has been taken over by women—a satire of gender politics and political correctness that remains, nonetheless, feminist at its core. *Casual Rex* by Eric Garcia (Villard) is an oddball novel about a dinosaur detective living in human disguise in Los Angeles. It's the sequel to Garcia's well-received comic thriller *Anonymous Rex. Baccarat* by Mark Broderick (Creative Arts) is a frenetic little novel in which Greek gods and mortals come together to gamble (for the prize of Creator) aboard a ship on the eve of the New Millennium. *Sir Apropos of Nothing* by Peter David (Pocket) is satirical fantasy about a thief who becomes a hero.

## Fantasy in the Mainstream

Magical novels published as mainstream fiction are harder to spot than those labeled as fantasy, so each year we make a special effort to identify books that you might otherwise overlook. One of the most unusual of these that I encountered in 2001 was Hayden Middleton's slim novel *Grimm's Last Fairy Tale* (St. Martin's). The volume is evenly divided between an historical story set in mid-nineteenth-century Germany involving the niece of fairy-tale collector Jacob Grimm, and a fantasy narrative reworking the familiar story of Sleeping Beauty. I adored this novel for its lyrical prose and fairy-tale symbolism—but other discriminating readers of my acquaintance have found it much less engaging. (The heroine *is* awfully prim.) If you're a fan of fairy-tale fiction, give it a try and decide for yourself. For fans of mythic fiction, don't miss the latest novel by myth and folkore historian Marina Warner, *The Leto Bundle* (Farrar, Straus, & Giroux), a rich, shrewd, fantastical story about Leto, the Titan who is raped by Zeus and gives birth to twins with no navels. Warner's novel reminds me of A.S. Byatt's work, cleverly mixing myth and history as she follows Leto back and forth through time and into modern-day London. Another fine book with strong fantasy elements is *The Fairest Among Women* by Israeli writer Shifra Horn, translated by H. Sacks (St. Martin's)—Jewish magical realism following the life of a Jerusalem woman born at the same time as her country. It's a tale full of magic, miracles, colorful characters, and startling imagery, well worth a read even if it doesn't quite soar to the heights of Horn's previous book, the award-winning *Four Mothers. The Bonesetter's Daughter* by Chinese-American writer Amy Tan (Putnam) is a novel *about* fantasy and storytelling rather than being fantastical itself . . . but this fairy-tale-like saga of ghosts and curses, concerning three generations of Chinese women, contains enough magic around the edges to warrant the interest of fantasy readers. Tan is one of America's finest writers, and this is one of her best. *The Last Report on the Miracles at Little No Horse* by Native American writer Louise Erdrich (HarperCollins) is another book with magic around the edges—less overtly fantastical than her World Fantasy Award-winning novel *The Antelope Wife*, but connected to that book, with elements of myth and mysticism that shine through the gorgeous prose. Set on the fictional Ojibwa reservation that the author has explored in previous novels, it's the story of Father Damian Modeste, an elderly priest who is a woman in disguise. *The Songcatcher* by Sharyn McCrumb (Dutton) is the latest book in this author's "Ballad" series of novels set in the Appalachian Mountains, inspired by old folk ballads. In this entertaining volume, the song of a shepherd girl who witnesses the dead rising from their graves binds together a contemporary tale of a country singer returning to her home in North Carolina and a historical tale about a boy kidnapped from the Scottish island of Islay.

*Sputnik Sweetheart* by Japanese writer Haruki Murakami, translated by Philip

Gabriel (Knopf), is yet another wise and witty novel from this irrepressible writer—a magical, slightly surreal tale involving two college classmates in Tokyo, a mysterious disappearance, and the "Sputnik" space program. It's a wonderful book from an author who could be considered Japan's answer to Robert Olen Butler. *Dark Back of Time* by Spanish writer Javier Marías, translated by Esther Allen (New Directions), is a wicked little novel set in Oxford, England, exploring the division between fiction and reality, involving the ghosts we create, academic politics, and characters from Marías's previous Oxford novel, *Old Souls*. There is no short description that can do justice to Marías's clever puzzle of a book. *Monstruary* by Spanish writer Julián Ríos, translated by Edith Grossman (Knopf), is a stylistically inventive dark fantasy novel about the European art world, saturated with mythology and monster legends from Melusine to Dracula. This one's for readers who like their fantasy Gothic, and on the cutting edge.

*In the Shape of a Boar* by Lawrence Norfolk (Grove Press) is a challenging but powerful mythic novel that binds a harrowing tale of World War II to the legend of a king trying to rid his land of a plague of supernatural boar sent by the goddess Artemis. *Hermes in Paris* by Peter Vansittart (Peter Owen, U.K.) is another mythic tale—sly, smart, and stylish. In this one, the trickster god of Greek myth dallies in Paris in the days leading up to the Franco-Prussian War. Although he's on vacation, Hermes can't quite resist meddling in the affairs of politicians, businessmen, and Left Bank intellectuals in a book that uses fantasy to illuminate the real history of a fascinating era. *Undercurrents* by Marie Darrieussecq (The New Press), one of France's best young writers, is a short, surrealist novel about the mystery surrounding a young girl who has been kidnapped by her mother. *The Committee* by Egyptian writer Sun'allah Ibrahim is another short but haunting novel—a chilling allegory loosely inspired by Kafka's *The Trial*. This timely fantasy comes from one of the great writers of the Arab world. *The Death of Vishnu* by Indian writer Manil Suri (W. W. Norton) brings to life the various denizens of an old apartment house in Bombay. Wound through with Hindu and Islamic mythology, it's a book rich in character and atmosphere.

*Still She Haunts Me* by Katie Roiphe (The Dial Press) explores the complicated relationship between Charles Dodgson (a.k.a. Lewis Carroll) and Alice Liddell, the child who inspired his "Alice" fantasies. It's an intriguing subject, and the book (which contains appearances by other eminent Victorians, such as Dante Gabriel Rossetti) is an enjoyable one, though the story occasionally gets buried in the author's overly stylized prose. *Black Oxen* by Elizabeth Knox (Farrar, Straus & Giroux) is the latest from the author of the sensual fantasy novel *The Vintner's Luck*. This one is equally fantastical and original—yet more frenetic in style and somehow less engaging. Set in the near future, Knox's novel tells the story of a woman trying to come to terms with her charismatic, not-quite-human father—moving from a therapist's couch in California to memories of black magic and revolution in South America. *Erased Faces* by Graciela Limón (Arte Público Press) is a hard-hitting, moving book that weaves Mayan myth and history together into a contemporary tale about Mexico's Chiapas uprising, as seen through the eyes of women. *Our Lady of the Lost and Found* by Diane Schoemperlen (Viking) is the story of a modern woman who becomes friends with the Virgin Mary, pictured here as an exhausted woman in a raincoat, resting between spiritual obligations. As a novel, it doesn't quite work, but as a look at

"Marion" legends from around the world, it's intriguing. *Only Human* by Jenny Diski (Picador) is a wonderful exploration of the biblical story of Sarah and Abraham, recounted with wit and wisdom. Though Diski is billed as a postmodern writer, don't let that put you off—this is a very accessible read, and a memorable one.

## In Other Genres

Each year there are books published in the horror, science fiction, and mystery genres that fantasy readers might also enjoy, as well as works of "interstitial fiction" that cannot be easily pinned down with genre labels. Among those I read in 2001, I particularly recommend the following: *The House in the High Woods* by Jeffrey E. Barlough (Ace) is Volume II in his "Western Lights" series, an extraordinary work I've only just caught up with this year, set in an alternate (extremely alternate!) version of nineteenth-century England. These books fall into the shadow realm between horror and dark fantasy, with a bit of mystery and comedy thrown in for good measure—written in a fine literary style that invites comparison to Dickens. *Bold as Love* by Gwyneth Jones (Gollancz, U.K.) is a new interstitial work that falls somewhere between near-future science fiction, fantasy, and alternate history. Set in England in 2007, a land much altered by environmental and economic collapse, it's a story of politics—both traditional politics and those of the counterculture, filtered through the world of rock and roll. This terrific book is the first of a projected series, and highly recommended. *Sea of Silver Light* by Tad Williams (DAW) is the fourth and final volume of his massive, impressive "Otherland" sequence, set in a world "made of numbers and light" that coexists with our own. These books blend science fiction with quest-style fantasy, myth, folklore, even nursery rhymes, and are recommended to fans of epic fantasy looking for something a little different. *Coldheart Canyon* by Clive Barker (HarperCollins), subtitled "A Hollywood Ghost Story," is a fascinating book that stands in the shadow realm between dark fantasy and horror. Barker uses tropes from both genres to underscore a contemporary story about Hollywood past and present, and lives lived in the shadow of celebrity. *Shadows Bite* by Australian author Stephen Dedman (Tor) is billed as a "magical noir thriller." It's the story of a man who receives a mysterious key that gives him the power to heal the sick—but embroils him in a dark adventure involving vampires, the Japanese Mafia, and murder. This one's dark, and beautifully written. *Silence and Shadows* by James Long (Bantam) is a mystery about a retired rock star who takes up archaeology and moves to Wales, where he finds mysterious connections between an old folktale, his dead wife, and a colleague who resembles her. It's a lightweight, atmospheric read. *Grandmother Spider* by James D. Doss (Morrow), is the author's sixth "Charlie Moon" mystery, involving a Ute tribal policeman and his feisty shaman aunt Daisy. Although his books are inevitably compared with Tony Hillerman's Navajo mysteries, Doss has developed a voice of his own in books that are entertaining, suspenseful, and mystical. This one involves a murder (of course) and the legends of "Grandmother Spider."

## Oddities

The "Best Unusual Book" distinction this year goes to *Hippolyte's Island* by Barbara Hodgson (Chronicle), an illustrated book in the Nick Bantock style, but with a more substantial text than one finds in Bantock's better-known "Griffin and Sabine" series. Hodgson's novel follows the quest of a travel writer and nature historian named Hippolyte Webb as he goes in search of South Atlantic islands that have the disconcerting tendency to disappear—cheered on, with misgivings, by the New York editor who plans to publish an account of his journey. The book starts off slow but rewards the reader with a suspenseful, romantic story, rich in imaginary detail. Like Webb's editor, I started off with doubts, but was charmed in the end. Nick Bantock himself weighs in this year with *The Gryphon* (Chronicle), a new "mysterious correspondence book" for people who like to read other people's mail. This one is told in the form of letters and postcards going back and forth between a young archaeologist in Egypt and his girlfriend back in Paris. It's the beginning of a new trilogy directly connected to *Griffin and Sabine*.

Another odd but recommended book is *The Little Girl Who Was Too Fond of Matches* by French writer Gaétan Soucy, translated by Sheila Fischman (Arcade). This one is a short, dark fairy tale of a novel written from the point of view of a girl who, with her brother, has been raised in isolation on a country estate—until the death of their father brings them into contact with the world beyond. It's a magical and brutal book—brilliant, but it won't be for every reader. Fans of fairy tales, linguistic invention, and surrealism should seek this one out.

## Briefly Noted

The following fantasy novels hit the various best-seller lists in 2001. Beloved by large numbers of readers, they deserve mention: *Priestess of Avalon* by Marion Zimmer Bradley and Diana L. Paxson (Viking), *The Redemption of Althalus* by David and Leigh Eddings (Del Rey), *Wizardborn* by David Farland (Tor), *Krondor: Tear of the Gods* by Raymond E. Feist (Avon Eos), *Winter's Heart* by Robert Jordan (Tor), *The Fire Dragon* by Katherine Kerr (Bantam), *The Serpent's Shadow* by Mercedes Lackey (DAW), and *Beyond the World's End* by Mercedes Lackey and Rosemary Edghill (Baen).

Wildside Press has begun publishing a series of classic works that will be of interest to fantasy readers. It's good to see someone doing the worthy job of bringing these tales back into print, though the editions could be improved with better packaging. These publications included *The Wood Beyond the World's End* by William Morris, *The Witch of Prague and Khaled* by F. Marion Crawford, *Kai Lung's Golden Hours* by Ernest Bramah, *Some Chinese Ghosts and Fantastics and Other Fancies* by Lafcadio Hearn, and *The Enchanted Island of Yew* by L. Frank Baum.

## Children's Fantasy

While Garth Nix's *Lirael*, listed in the Top Twenty, was the most impressive work of children's fantasy published in 2001, there were a number of other books for young readers that should not be missed. I recommend: *Treasure at the Heart of the Tanglewood* by Meredith Ann Pierce (Viking), a deeply mythic fantasy (drawing on the Demeter-Persephone legend) that follows a young woman's quest through the heart of the woods on a journey of self-discovery. Pierce takes standard fantasy ingredients and weaves them into a lyrical tale that bears comparison to Patricia A. McKillip's fine books. It's the author's first novel in five years, and proves worth the wait. *Heaven's Eyes* by David Almond (Delacorte) is the latest from the extraordinary author of *Skellig* and *Kit's Wilderness*, and it, too, does not disappoint. This novel follows the adventures of three children who run away from an orphanage on a river raft. By turns dark and bright, it's a powerful story, mysterious and thought-provoking. *The Stone Mage and the Sea* by Sean Williams (Voyager/HarperCollins Australia) is Book 1 of "The Change," epic fantasy set in an imaginary world inspired by the coastal landscape of southern Australia. It's a coming-of-age story about a young boy with a talent for magic, lifted above genre clichés by its vivid, unusual setting.

*Troy* by Adele Geras (Harcourt) is an engrossing mythic novel based on the *Iliad*, viewing the events of the fall of Troy through the eyes of Trojan women. *I Am Morgan Le Fay* by Nancy Springer (Philomel) is a lucid retelling of the Arthurian myth from the point of view of Arthur's sorcerous half sister. This book is a "prequel" to Springer's equally good novel *I Am Mordred*. *Labyrinth* by John Herman (Philomel) is a dark, suspenseful story about a boy whose dreams are pulling him into another world, away from harsh reality, where his father has committed suicide. The secondary world proves no less challenging, however, in a tale inspired by Minotaur myths. *Aquamarine* by Alice Hoffman (Scholastic) is a charming, very short book about two contemporary girls and a mermaid, drawing loosely on the Little Mermaid fairy tale. Hoffman is one of the best adult fiction writers in America today, and here she works her potent magic for young readers. *The Wizard's Dilemma* by Diane Duane (Harcourt) is a strong new volume in Duane's pre-Potter "Young Wizard" series, deepening the characters of her teen wizards and upping the ante on the challenges they face, both magical and mundane.

*Witch Child* by Celia Rees (Candlewick Press) is something of a gimmick book, purporting to be a recently discovered American colonial diary. Ignore the gimmick, however, and it's actually a reasonably good historical fantasy of a girl who runs from the witch burnings of England and hides herself in Puritan New England, where she encounters Indians, and finds that safety is illusive. *Wolf Star* by Tanith Lee (Dutton) is another book written in the form of a diary by a strong-willed young woman. This is fast-paced imaginary-world fantasy, Book #2 in Lee's "Caidi Journals" series. Kevin Crossley-Holland's new Arthurian novel, *The Seeing Stone* (Arthur A. Levine/Scholastic) is another book told in the form of a diary—this time, the journal of a thirteen-year-old boy named Arthur living in an English manor house in the twelfth century. The boy's story is entwined with that of the legendary Arthur, glimpsed by means of a magical stone, in this handsomely packaged book that's rich with period detail.

*Firebird* by Mary Frances Zambreno (Random House) is Book #5 in the "Voyage of the Basset" series, set in a land where myths are real, based on the art of James C. Christensen. It's an enchanting tale involving a magical lighthouse and the phoenix legend. *Street Mage* by Tamora Pierce (Scholastic) is Book #2 in this always-capable writer's "The Circle Opens" series. It's standard fare of mages and magics in an imaginary world, but well crafted and enjoyable nonetheless. *Among the Imposters* by Margaret Peterson Haddix (Simon & Schuster) is a strong sequel to *Among the Hidden*, about a third-born child in a world where having more than two children is against the law. *Eccentric Circles* by Rebecca Lickiss (Ace) is a romantic story about a young would-be fantasy writer whose grandmother's cottage is the gateway to magic. Filled with wizards, fairies, dwarves, and elves, it's a light but enjoyable read. *The Hob's Bargain* by Patricia Briggs (Ace) is a somewhat darker tale, but another one that will appeal to younger readers, about a young woman whose family has been killed by raiders and a Hob, a magical creature from the forest, the last of his kind. *Touching Bear Spirit* by Ben Mikaelsen (HarperCollins) is the memorable contemporary tale of a troubled young man who chooses banishment to a remote Alaskan island in the place of prison, where his life is changed by an encounter with a bear. This unflinching story of anger and redemption draws on Native American myth. *Raven of the Waves* by Michael Cadnum (Orchard) is a well-crafted, vigorous, historical novel about a boy among Viking warriors. *Tartabull's Throw* by Henry Garfield (Atheneum) is a suspenseful dark fantasy novel about werewolves, time travel, baseball, and the power of friendship.

Good books for younger adolescents: *Odysseus in the Serpent Maze* by Jane Yolen and Robert J. Harris (HarperCollins) is a magical fantasy adventure imagining the life of a boy who will grow up to be the great hero of Greek legend. *Straw into Gold* by Gary D. Schmidt is a fine fantasy adventure that reworks the fairy tale Rumplestiltskin in fascinating ways. It's a story of magic, and riddles, and a boy whose life depends on answering them. *Goose Chase* by Patrice Kindl (Houghton Mifflin) is an enchanting novel that draws upon various fairy tales to relate the wry story of the headstrong Goose Girl and her twelve feathered companions. *The Two Princesses of Bamarre* by Gail Carson Levine (HarperCollins) is an original fairy tale about two princesses, following the adventures of the younger, less courageous sister when her sibling falls ill. It's a charming, funny, bittersweet story. *Knockabeg: A Famine Tale* by Mary E. Lyons (Houghton Mifflin) is an enchanting short book about fairies and the Irish potato famine.

*Tree Girl* by T. A. Barron (Philomel) is a mystical, thoroughly magical fable about a young girl drawn to the dark of the woods, seeking answers about her parentage. It's a slim volume, really a long short story, but a beautiful and deeply mythic one. *Rowan Hood: Outlaw Girl of Sherwood Forest* by Nancy Springer (Philomel) is an engaging little story about a girl (disguised as a boy) who is actually Robin Hood's daughter. *Rowan of Rin* and *Rowan and the Travelers* by Emily Roda (Greenwillow) are the first U.S. editions of Books #1 & 2 in a popular Australian fantasy series. It's imaginary world fantasy of the Tamora Pierce sort.

Fans of animal fantasies, and mice in particular, have several works to choose from. *The Sands of Time* by Michael Hoeye (Terfle Books) is the sequel to *Time Stops for No Mouse*, a sprightly detective mystery with a mouse for a hero. Grittier than the Hoeye book is Robin Jarvis's *The Dark Portal* (Books of Wonder/SeaStar), Book #1 of the "Depford Mice" trilogy in a new reprint edition. This is epic fantasy about the complex society of mice below the city of London. The best of them all, however, is *Teggerung* by Brian Jacques (Philomel), the latest in his long-running "Redwall" series. Once again, Jacques delivers an action-packed, swashbuckling animal tale that is thrilling and convincing. I don't know how he manages to keep this series fresh and lively, but he does. Jacques also published an unrelated novel in 2001, *Castaways of the Flying Dutchman* (Philomel). This stirring adventure fantasy set on the high seas, inspired by the Flying Dutchman legend, proves that Jacques is as adept at creating human characters as he is at rodents.

Young fans of humorous fantasy also have a number of good books to chose between. First, there's Irish writer Eoin Colfer's best-selling novel *Artemis Fowl* (Hyperion), which the author describes, aptly enough, as "*Die Hard* with fairies." The story involves the twelve-year-old criminal mastermind Artemis Fowl and a tough-talking female police officer from the fairies' LEPrecon Unit in a pun-saturated adventure. As black humor goes, it's pretty good. Lemony Snicket continues his Edward Gorey–like account of the ill-fated Baudelaire orphans in *The Ersatz Elevator* and *The Vile Village*, Books #6 and 7 in his "Series of Unfortunate Events," illustrated by Brett Helquist (HarperCollins). The books remain wickedly inventive, and though adult readers may feel that the joke is wearing thin, kids are eating up these subversive little novels and demanding more. *The Amazing Maurice and His Educated Rodents* by Terry Pratchett (HarperCollins)—ah, those mice again—is a "Discworld" book for young readers, a fractured fairy-tale version of the legend of the Pied Piper. *The Monsters of Morley Manor* by Bruce Colville (Harcourt) is a fast-paced little adventure about monster figurines that come to life and two children who save the universe in the course of their adventures.

Children's fantasy reprints of note: *Wet Magic* by E. Nesbit is nicely illustrated by H. R. Miller in a new edition introduced by Peter Glassman (Books of Wonder/SeaStar). *The Magician's Nephew* by C. S. Lewis has been reprinted in an edition containing the classic Narnia illustrations by Pauline Baynes (Harper-Collins). *Pinocchio* by Carlos Collodi has been reprinted in a very handsome edition that brings together illustrations by a host of fine artists from the late nineteenth and early twentieth centuries, compiled by Cooper Edens (Chronicle). And *Peter Pan* by J. M. Barrie has been released in a lovely new edition with illustrations by Trina Schart Hyman (Atheneum).

## Single-Author Story Collections

2001 was an exceptionally good year for story collections. At the very top of the list is the brand-new "Earthsea" volume by Ursula K. Le Guin, containing four new stories set in that land, two original to the book, and each one of them exquisite. High fantasy just doesn't get better than this. Next on the list are collections by two of the best new writers in our field: Nalo Hopkinson and Kelly Link. *Skin Folk* by Nalo Hopkinson (Warner Aspect) is a splendid volume of richly colorful, magical tales that range, to quote the back cover, "from Trinidad to Toronto." Hopkinson is a Caribbean writer who now makes her home in Canada, writing interstitial fiction that borrows tropes from fantasy, science fiction, horror, and Caribbean folklore. The book consists of ten reprint stories and five originals. *Stranger Things Happen* by Kelly Link (Small Beer Press) is a very handsome small press edition that mixes reprinted and original stories, including Link's Tiptree Award–winning "Travels with the Snow Queen" and her World Fantasy Award–winning "The Specialist's Hat." This, too, is an interstitial collection that defies strict genre classification, drawing from fantasy, horror, detective fiction, surrealism, ghost stories, and more. If you want to see the cutting edge of the fantasy field, pick up the Hopkinson and Link collections—along with two more brilliant books from a pair of writers in southern California: *Night Moves and Other Stories* by Tim Powers (Subterranean Press) and *Thirteen Phantasms* by James P. Blaylock (Edgewood Press). Between them, these two gentlemen are quietly (or not so quietly, in Powers's case) redefining the boundaries of the fantasy story.

Also highly recommended: *City of Saints and Madmen: The Boots of Ambergris* by Jeff VanderMeer (Cosmos/Wildside) is an attractive small-press edition collecting four novellas set in the imaginary city of Ambergris, including the author's World Fantasy Award–winning story "The Transformation of Martin Lake." VanderMeer's dark, sly, dreamlike, surrealist style defies easy description. One can point out the literary influences (Kafka, Lord Dunsany, Mervyn Peake, H. P. Lovecraft, Jack Vance, and M. John Harrison, just for starters), yet VanderMeer's voice is still uniquely his own as he creates his textured, multi-dimensional city in story after story. A second Ambergris "publication" will give you a sense of VanderMeer's world: "The Exchange" is a short story purportedly written by Ambergis author Nicholas Sporlender, from the Ambergris publisher Hoegbotton & Sons. It comes in a handsome little black box produced for the city's Festival of the Freshwater Squid, along with a votive candle, a "memory capsule," a poison mushroom, and its antidote. (For more information: www.vandermeer.redsine.com.) *Meet Me in the Moon Room* by Ray Vukcevich (Small Beer Press) is only slightly less mysterious. This excellent, beautifully produced collection of largely surrealist tales contains thirty-three unusual, memorable stories, five of them original to the volume. *My Mother's Erotic Folktales* by Robert Antoni (Grove Press) is yet another unusual but wonderful collection. This one consists of lusty, lively interlocking stories rooted in Caribbean folklore, set on an island in the Bahamas during World War II, as recounted by a ninety-six-year-old woman to her grandson. *The Man Who Swam with Beavers* by Nancy Lord (Coffee House Press) is a collection of colorful stories set in Alaska, largely realist in nature, but wound through with Native Alaskan legends. (The title story is particularly enchanting.) *The Devil's Larder* by Jim Crace (Farrar, Straus & Giroux) is an oddly bewitching little collection of short-short tales, some surrealist in nature, on the subject of food. *The Ghost of John Wayne and Other Stories* by Ray Gonzalez (University of Arizona Press) mixes magical realism into brief, vivid tales of life on the Texas-Mexico border. It's terrific.

For those who like their short fiction in a more traditional vein, there are also several good books to choose from. *The Uncharted Heart* by Melissa Hardy (Alfred A. Knopf, Canada) is a splendid collection of tales both realist and magical, both historic and contemporary. For fantasy readers, her stories "The Uncharted Heart" and "The Bockles" (the latter reprinted here) are particularly recommended. *Transfigured Night and Other Stories* by Richard Bowes (iPublish) is an excellent volume available in a reasonably attractive print-on-demand format, collecting the urban fantasy stories of another World Fantasy Award winner. These are stories about growing up the hard way in the urban Northeast in the fifties and sixties. Bowes is one of the best writers in our field, and this one's worth seeking out. *Quartet* by George R. R. Martin (NESFA Press) is a small-press edition with art by Charles Vess, containing three strong fantasy and mystery novellas, as well as a television screenplay. *Stories for an Enchanted Afternoon* by Kristine Kathryn Rusch (Golden Gryphon) is a small-press edition with art by Thomas Canty, collecting eleven stories by this talented, prolific writer, consisting of fantasy, science fiction, and historical tales. Another good reprint collection that mixes science fiction and fantasy tales is *Other Voices, Other Doors*, by the always-excellent Patrick O'Leary (Fairwood Press).

Also of note: *Strange Mistresses: Tales of Wonder and Romance* by James Dorr (Dark Regions Press) contains lyrical dark fantasy and horror, consisting of two original stories, twelve reprints, and poetry. *Winter Shadows and Other Tales* by Mary Soon Lee (Dark Regions Press) contains an interesting mix of genre stories, consisting of fifteen reprints and four originals. *Dossier* collects the unusual, surreal short stories of Stepan Chapman (Creative Arts). *Redgunk Tales* is a collection of interconnected contemporary fantasy stories by William R. Eakin (Invisible Cities Press). *On the Fringe* contains magical tales on the game of golf by Gregory G. Barton (Triple Tree Publishing). *The Other Nineteenth Century* by Avram Davidson, edited by Grania Davis and Henry Wessells (Tor), is a welcome edition collecting long-out-of-print stories by this master fantasist, focusing specifically on the author's historical fantasias. *Dust Returned* by Ray Bradbury (Morrow) is a fine collection of the author's early "Elliot family" stories about vampires and their odd kinfolk who live in a Victorian castle in Indiana. *The Merriest Knight* by Theodore Goodridge Roberts, edited by Mike Ashley (Green Knight Publishing), collects Roberts's "Sir Dinadan" stories, a cycle of humorous Arthurian tales first published in the fifties.

Story collections for younger readers: *Being Dead* by Vivian Vande Velde (Harcourt), contains seven original contemporary ghost stories. *Beauty and the Serpent* by Barbara Ann Porte, illustrated by Rosemary Feit Covey (Simon & Schuster) contains thirteen original stories about magical animals.

## Anthologies

I was about to write that 2001 wasn't a particularly good year for anthologies, but then I looked at my notes and saw that there were actually four very good ones last year that certainly deserve your attention and support. *Starlight 3*, edited by Patrick Nielsen Hayden (Tor) is the latest volume in this World Fantasy Award-winning series dedicated to speculative fiction. This edition contains original fantasy stories by Ted Chiang, Colin Greenland, Andy Duncan, Susanna Clarke and Jane Yolen (the latter two reprinted here), all of them top-notch. *The Year's Best Fantasy*, edited by David G. Hartwell and Kathryn Cramer

(HarperCollins) is the first volume in a new annual celebrating genre fantasy fiction, in the tradition of those old, much-missed Lin Carter/Arthur Saha fantasy annuals. It's a first-rate collection, containing memorable tales by George R. R. Martin, Michael Swanwick, Brian Stableford, Charles de Lint, Nalo Hopkinson, and many others. *Jewish Fabulist Fiction*, edited by Daniel M. Jaffe (Invisible Cities Press) contains a mix of wondrous tales from Jewish writers around the globe. I particularly recommend the contributions by Ruth Knafo Setton, Deborah Shouse, and Daniel Ulanovsky Sack (the latter is reprinted here). *Dreaming Down Under*, edited by Jack Dann and Janeen Webb (Tor) is a speculative fiction anthology out of Australia, containing some very good fantasy, both dark and bright, by the likes of Lucy Sussex, Paul Brandon, Jane Routley, and Sara Douglass, among others. Published in Australia in 1998, this is the first U.S. edition.

Also of note: *Sword and Sorceress XVIII* (DAW) is the last book in this series to be edited by Marion Zimmer Bradley, finished by Elisabeth Waters after Bradley's death. This volume is distinguished by a strong story from newcomer Susan Urbanek Linville. *Out of Avalon*, edited by Jennifer Roberson (Roc), billed as "an anthology of old magic and new myths," contains a particularly fine story by Judith Tarr, and poetry from Nina Kiriki Hoffman. *Oceans of Magic*, edited by Brian M. Thomsen and Martin H. Greenberg (DAW), contains a range of seafaring stories, including good contributions from Rosemary Edghill and Tanya Huff (the latter reprinted in this volume). *Single White Vampire Seeks Same*, edited by Martin H. Greenberg and Brittiany A. Koren (DAW), a volume of stories about magical romance, contains a delightful "Newford" story by Charles de Lint (reprinted in this volume) and a strong tale from Tim Waggoner. *A Constellation of Cats*, edited by Denise Little (DAW), contains thirteen magical tales about felines, with good contributions by Nina Kiriki Hoffman and Kristine Kathryn Rusch; while *Creature Fantastic*, also edited by Denise Little, spread its range to all manner of beasties, with a memorable story from Gary A. Braunbeck. *The Best Alternate History Stories of the Twentieth Century* (Del Rey), a fat reprint anthology edited by Harry Turtledove and Martin H. Greenberg, contains worthy stories by Poul Anderson, Greg Bear, Kim Stanley Robinson, among others. *The Treasury of the Fantastic Romanticism to Early Twentieth Century Literature* edited by David Sandner and Jacob Weisman (Frog, Ltd. and Tachyon Publications) is an even fatter volume, this one reprinting classic fantasy tales from the Romantics to early-twentieth-century writers. On the mainstream shelves, I recommend seeking out *Hohzo: Walking in Beauty*, edited by Paula Gunn Allen and Carolyn Dunn Anderson (Contemporary Books), an anthology of stories by Native American authors, containing fine mythic fiction mixed in with equally fine realist tales.

In young-adult fiction, the best anthology of the year was *Half-Human*, edited by Bruce Coville (Scholastic), containing stories of half-human and half-mythic or animal beings. Coville, Tamora Pierce, Janni Lee Simner, Nancy Springer, Jane Yolen, and Gregory Maguire contributed good tales to the book (the latter is reprinted here). *The Color of Absence*, edited by James Howe (Atheneum), is an anthology of stories about death and loss, notable here for a great new vampire story by Annette Curtis Klause.

# Magazines

The best sources in America for fantasy fiction continue to be the big three genre magazines: *The Magazine of Fantasy & Science Fiction*, edited by Gordon Van Gelder, maintained its high quality of fantasy selections in 2001. Three stories reprinted in this volume were drawn from its pages, as were numerous Honorable Mentions. *Asimov's Science Fiction*, edited by Gardner Dozois, is also excellent but seemed more focused on science fiction than fantasy in the year just past. It, too, is represented in the Honorable Mentions selections. The quality of stories in *Realms of Fantasy* has gone up noticeably, with praise due to editor Shawna McCarthy. Two stories are reprinted from its pages this year, and the magazine also makes a good showing in Honorable Mentions. In England, the best fantasy can be found in the always-excellent *Interzone*, edited by David Pringle. In Australia, the best source is *Aurealis*, edited by Stephen Higgins and Dirk Strasser. The Australian journal *Eidolon* was, unfortunately, on hiatus in 2001.

The following magazines, large and small, provided fantasy stories and poems for our volume this year: *The Atlantic Monthly, Descant, Lady Churchill's Rosebud Wristlet, Calyx, The Louisville Review, Quarterly West, Poetry Review, The Beloit Poetry Journal, The American Poetry Review*, and *Poem*. In addition, the following magazines published fantasy stories and poems listed as Honorable Mentions: *The New Yorker, The New York Quarterly, Minnesota Monthly, The Missouri Review, The Colorado Review, The Indiana Review, SouthWest Review, The New England Review, Texas Review, The Antigonish Review, The Antioch Review, Cumberland Poetry Review, TriQuarterly, Pleiades, Dark Regions, 3rd Bed, Wicked Words, Facts*, and *New Genre*. Other magazines regularly covered for this annual include *Black Gate, The Third Alternative, On Spec, Amazing Stories, Adventures of Swords and Sorcery, Fantastic Stories, Indigenous Fiction, Dreams and Nightmares, Talebones, Scheherazade, Tales of the Unanticipated*, and *The Magazine of Speculative Poetry*. For book reviews and news about the fantasy field, *Locus* magazine is a particularly invaluable source, along with *Publishers Weekly, The New York Times Book Review, The New York Review of Science Fiction, Science Fiction Chronicle, The Hungry Mind Review*, and *The Women's Review of Books*. For myth and folklore material, I recommend the journals *Marvels and Tales: The Journal of Fairy Tale Studies* (Wayne State University Press) and *Parabola*. For folk music, try *Folk Roots* (out of the U.K.) and *Dirty Linen*.

As for Internet fiction, this year we've reprinted fantasy stories and poetry from the following Web journals: *SCIFiction* at *SciFi.com*, edited by Ellen Datlow (www.scifi.com/scifiction/) *Strange Horizons* edited by Mary Anne Mohanraj (www.strangehorizon.com); and *Dark Planet*, edited by Lucy A. Snyder (www.sfsite.com/darkplanet/), all of which are recommended to fantasy readers. (*Dark Planet* is on hiatus as of this writing, but its archives are accessible.) For book reviews, essays, interviews, and news about the fantasy field, try *The SF Site* edited by Roger Turner (www.sfsite.com), *The Fantastic Metropolis*, founded by Gabe Chouinard and edited by the FM board: Michael Moorcock, Luís Rodrigues, Jeff VanderMeer, Paul Witcover, and Zoran Zivkovic (www.sfsite.com/fm/); *The Green Man Review* edited by Cat Eldridge (www.greenmanreview.com); and *Rambles* edited by Tom Knapp (www.rambles.net). For children's books: *The*

*Children's Literature Web Guide* (www.acs.ucalgary.ca/~dkbrown/index.html) and *Achuka* (www.achuka.com). For myths and fairy tales, the best site out there, hands down, is *The SurLaLune Fairy Tale Pages* edited by Heidi Anne Heiner (www.surlalunefairytales.com). For fantasy art, try *The Fairy Tale Illustration Gallery* edited by Heidi Anne Heiner (http://surlalune.tripod.com/illustrations/index.html), and *ArtMagick*, edited by Julia Kerr (www.artmagick.com). The second annual "Best of the Year" mention for a writer or artist in the fantasy field with the most interesting Web site goes to Jane Yolen this time, www.janeyolen.com.

## Art

At the top of the list of art books in 2001 are three that celebrate the work of three of the fantasy field's finest artists: Michael Kaluta, Phil Hale, and Dave McKean. *Wings of Twilight: The Art of Michael Kaluta* (NBM) and *GOAD: The Many Moods of Phil Hale* (Donald M. Grant) are two beautifully produced volumes celebrating the work of two enormously talented painters. *Pictures That Tick* by Dave McKean (Hour Glass/Allan Spiegel Fine Arts) is an anthology of "short sequential stories" by McKean, told through minimal text and page after gorgeous page of his distinctive art. Also from Allen Spiegel Fine Arts comes a fine collection of stories and art titled *Bento: Story Art Box*. This handsome edition contains short-short stories by Jonathan Caroll, Neil Gaiman, Rachel Pollack and others; art by Dave McKean and a host of other talents (www.allenspiegelfinearts.com).

Jim Vadeboncoeur, Jr. began publication of a new art magazine called *The Vadeboncoeur Collection of Images*, featuring art from his extensive collection of classic illustrations (works published prior to 1923). The first issue focuses on Heinrich Kley, and also contains art by Maxfield Parrish, Arthur Rackham, and others. You can find more information on the Bud Plant Illustrated Books web site (www.bpub.com). Cathy and Arnie Fenner have edited a new edition of their annual juried survey of fantasy art and illustration: *Spectrum 8: The Best in Contemporary Fantastic Art* (Underwood Books), as well as a new book on Frank Frazetta: *Testament: The Art and Life of Frank Frazetta* (Underwood). Art Spiegelman and Françoise Mouly have published a second volume in their wonderful "Little Lit" series, following up last year's *Folklore and Fairy Tale Funnies* with *Strange Stories for Strange Kids* (RAW/Joanna Cotler). This volume contains work from Maurice Sendak, Barbara McClintock, Jules Feiffer, Kaz, and others, and it's a hoot (www.little-lit.com). *The Witches and Wizards of Oberlin* by Suza Scalora (Joanna Cotler Books) is the sequel to *The Fairies*, her volume of stylish "fairy photographs." This one contains pictures and text about wizards and witches tied to the four elements: earth, air, wind, and fire. Published in a smaller, busier format than the previous book, it's rather difficult to read. A better-produced volume is *The Red Tree*, from the World Fantasy Award-winning artist Shaun Tan (Lothian), a very moving tale on the subject of depression, beautifully illustrated.

*Fantasy of the 20th Century: An Illustrated History* by Randy Broecker (Collectors Press) is an historical overview of the fantasy field, illustrated with magazine and book illustrations from the pulps to modern paperbacks. *Pulp Culture:*

*The Art of Pulp Fiction* by Frank M. Robinson and Lawrence Davidson (Collectors Press), winner of the Pop Culture Book of the Year Award from Independent Publishers, goes beyond fantasy and science fiction to look at all the genres of classic pulp magazine tales in this lavishly illustrated edition. *The Great American Paperback* by Richard A. Lupoff (Collectors Press) looks at the growth of the paperback industry from its early days to the present. It's a fascinating history, extensively illustrated with classic paperback art. For Hildebrandt fans, *The Tolkien Years* by Greg and Tim Hildebrandt (Watson-Guptill) collects their Middle-Earth illustrations. *Animerotics: A Forbidden Cabaret in 26 Acts* by David Delamare (Collectors Press), is an alphabet book of sorts, consisting of surrealistic, erotic paintings of women, mythic creatures, and animals.

For fans of surrealist art, *Surrealism: Desire Unbound*, edited by Jennifer Munday (Princeton University Press), is a must-have book of essays published to go along with last year's excellent Surrealist exhibition at London's Tate Gallery. *Surrealist Painters and Poets*, a collection of imagery and text compiled by Mary Ann Caws (MIT Press), is also recommended. My favorite surrealist book of the year, however, was *Between Lives: An Artist and Her World* by Dorothea Tanning (W.W. Norton). This is a memoir, recently expanded by Tanning (she's now in her nineties), reflecting on her life, her art, and her marriage to Max Ernst. Also of note is *Yves Tanguy and Surrealism*, edited by Karin von Maur (Hatje Cantz Publisher), which provides an insightful overview of this French artist's magical work. For fans of Pre-Raphaelite art, Pamela Todd's *Pre-Raphaelites at Home* (Watson-Guptill) is a lovely edition, looking at the interconnected lives of these painters and poets, illustrated with art and photographs. *Jane Morris: The Pre-Raphaelite Model of Beauty* by Debra N. Mancoff (Pomegranate) is an autobiography of Rossetti's favorite model (and William Morris's wife), as well as a look at the idea of beauty in Victorian society. *The Blue Bower: Rossetti in the 1860s* by Paul Spencer-Longhurst (Scala Books) is an examination of the artist's life and work during this time period.

## Picture Books

Here are ten of the best picture books that came across my desk in 2001, all with magical stories and wonderful art. Don't miss the following, listed in alphabetical order by author:

*Petite Rouge* by Mike Atell, illustrated by Jim Harris (Dial) is a Cajun version of the Red Riding Hood story, a sassy little rendition in which a young duck named Petite Rouge sets off across the swamp to visit her grandmère with a basket full of gumbo and boudin.

*The Wolf of Gubbio* by Michael Bedard, illustrated by Murray Kimber (Stoddard), is my personal favorite of the year, a quietly powerful story about a boy in an Italian hill town, a wolf, and Saint Francis of Assisi.

*Children of the Dragon: Selected Tales from Vietnam* by Sherry Garland, illustrated by Trina Schart Hyman (Harcourt), presents little-known tales in a volume charmingly adorned by Hyman's distinctive watercolor paintings.

*The Adventures of Tom Thumb* by Marianne Mayes, illustrated by Kinuko Y. Craft (SeaStar), provides a fine retelling of this traditional story, but the real reason to buy this book is for Craft's gorgeous illustrations.

*The Dog Prince* by Lauren A. Mills and Dennis Nolan (Little, Brown) is a marvelous collaboration by this husband-and-wife team, telling the story of a bored young prince who finds himself transformed into a bloodhound.

*Puss in Boots: The Adventures of That Most Enterprising Feline* by Philip Pullman, illustrated by Ian Beck (Knopf), is a hilarious rendition of this classic story, written by an author who is (or should be) well-known to fantasy fans for the brilliant "His Dark Materials" trilogy. Beck's illustrations are a treat too.

*Cinderella: An Art Deco Love Story* by Lynn Roberts, illustrated by David Roberts (Abrams), is a witty version of this fairy tale adorned with pictures in comic "art deco" style, rich with period detail.

*The Golden Mare, the Firebird, and the Magic Ring* by Ruth Sanderson (Little, Brown) is a sumptuously illustrated version of a classic Russian folktale, beautifully retold.

*A Small Tale from the Far, Far North* by Peter Sis (Farrar, Straus & Giroux) is an enchanting book that chronicles the life of Czech folk hero Jan Wetzl on his journey through the arctic seas. Prose and pictures alike are wonderful.

*The Three Pigs* by David Wiesner (Clarion) won a well-deserved 2001 Caldecott Medal. It's an exuberant tale with fantastic pictures that follow the three pigs right out of the pages of their own story and into other storybooks.

Also of note: *The Wolf Girls: An Unsolved Mystery from History* by Jane Yolen and Heidi Elisabet Yolen Stemple, illustrated by Robert Roth (Simon & Schuster), recounts the story of two wild girls found in India in 1920, complete with clues to help young readers puzzle out the mystery for themselves. *Storm Maker's Tipi* by Paul Goble (Atheneum) is a stylish volume that looks at tipis (complete with diagrams for their construction) and recounts a traditional Blackfoot tale about how tipis first came to the People. *The Pot of Wisdom* by Adwoa Badoe, illustrated by Baba Wagué Diakité (Groundwood/Douglas & McIntyre), collects trickster tales of Ananse the Spider from the African folk tradition. *Fiesta Femenina* by Mary-Joan Gerson, illustrated by Maya Christina Gonzalez (Barefoot Books), is a lively collection of stories celebrating women in Mexican folktales. *The Lady of Ten Thousand Names* by Burleigh Mutén, illustrated by Helen Cann (Barefoot Books), is a handsome collection of Goddess stories from many different cultures. *Sacred Animals* by Kris Waldheer (HarperCollins) looks at animals, both real and mythic, in folktales from around the world. I should also mention *The Winter Child*, a fairy story set in an old oak wood in the west of England, for which I wrote the text, while the enchanting pictures are by dollmaker Wendy Froud (Simon & Schuster).

## Nonfiction

Several good new volumes on J. R. R. Tolkien's work came out in 2001. The best of them, hands down, was Tom Shippey's brilliant new study of Tolkien's life and art, *J.R.R. Tolkien: Author of the Century* (Houghton Mifflin), which is the most insightful and informative book on this fantasy master that I've yet read. Two new books that will be of interest to Tolkien scholars are *Lord of the Rings: The Mythology of Power*, which places Tolkien's work in the context of the author's life and times, and *Tolkien's Art: A Mythology for England*, which examines Tolkien's source materials, both by Jane Chance (The University Press of Kentucky). *Meditations on Middle-Earth* edited by Karen Haber, illustrated by John Howe (St. Martin's), is a less-scholarly proposition, aimed at general readers, containing essays on Tolkien and his influence by a number of writers from the fantasy field, including Ursula K. Le Guin, George R. R. Martin, Esther M. Friesner, Charles de Lint, Robin Hobb, Lisa Goldstein, and a host of others. The contributions by Le Guin and Michael Swanwick are worth the cover price alone. *Hobbits, Elves, and Wizards: Exploring the Wonders and Worlds of J.R.R. Tolkien's The Lord of the Rings* by Michael N. Stanton (Palgrave/St. Martin's) is a guide to the characters, landscape, and history of Middle-earth, and might be particularly useful for younger readers. *The Fellowship of the Ring Visual Companion* by Jude Fisher (Houghton Mifflin) is basically a picture book with stills from the movie and brief descriptions of its major characters and motifs.

The other big fantasy media event of 2001, of course, was the Harry Potter film, and there were several book publications tied to its release as well. *Exploring Harry Potter* by Elizabeth D. Schafer is part of the "Beacham Sourcebooks" series for teaching young-adult fiction (Beacham Publishing), with sections aimed at teachers, librarians, students, and researchers. *The Sorcerer's Companion: A Guide to the Magical World of Harry Potter* by Allan Zola Kronzck and Elizabeth Kronzck (Broadway Books) is an alphabetical compendium to the series, listing characters, places, magical objects, etc. *Kids' Letters to Harry Potter from Children Around the World* compiled by Bill Adler (Carroll & Graf) is a slim, not very interesting book that I truly don't see the point of. All three of these titles are unauthorized editions, and only the first has any claim at all to being anything but an attempt to cash in on Pottermania. Also in the "Beacham Sourcebooks" series, *Exploring C.S. Lewis' The Chronicles of Narnia* by Kirk H. Beetz, explores Lewis's life and art in a volume aimed at teachers and their students.

The very best (and most provocative) book on children's literature last year came from Jack Zipes: *Sticks and Stones: The Troublesome Success of Children's Literature from Slovenly Peter to Harry Potter* (Routledge), in which Zipes argues against the limitations of children's fiction as it's currently defined and published. I also highly recommend *Tales, Then and Now: More Folktales as Literary Fictions for Young Adults* by Anna E. Altmann and Gail de Vos (Libraries Unlimited), the second volume in their examination of contemporary fiction (including works from the fantasy genre) based on classic folklore themes. In this edition, they discuss Beauty and the Beast, Tam Lin, Thomas the Rhymer, and several Hans Christian Andersen tales, among others, as well as novels, stories, poems, plays, films, and theatrical presentations based on them. It's an excellent guide. Also of note: *Mystery in Children's Literature: From the Rational to the Supernatural*, edited by Adrienne E. Gavin and Christopher Routledge (Palgrave), contains interesting scholarly essays on *The Secret Garden, The Little Princess*, and other classics. *Alternative Worlds in Fantasy Fiction* by Peter Hunt and Millicent Lenz (Continuum) is part of the "Contemporary Classics in Children's Literature" series. This volume looks at the fiction of Ursula K. Le Guin, Terry Pratchett, and Philip Pullman.

*Fantasy Literature: From Dragon's Lair to Hero's Quest*, edited by Philip Martin (The Writer Books), is a "how to" book for aspiring fantasists, published as part of "The Writer's Guides" series from *The Writer* magazine. This is a useful, well-written book, interspersing nuts-and-bolts information (how to revise your work, how to submit manuscripts for publication, etc.) with very interesting essays by Patricia A. McKillip, Donna Jo Napoli, Elizabeth Hand, Midori Snyder, Jane Yolen, Ursula K. Le Guin, and other top practitioners of the craft. All and all, it's a welcome and worthwhile volume. *Rewriting the Women of Camelot: Arthurian Popular Fiction and Feminism* by Ann F. Howey (Greenwood Press) looks at the works of writers like Mary Stewart, Marion Zimmer Bradley, and Gillian Bradshaw. *The Hidden Library of Tanith Lee: Themes and Subtexts from Dionysos to the Immortal Gene* by Mavis Haut (McFarland) examines the themes and subtext in the work of this British fantasist. *Snake's-hands: A Chapbook About the Fiction of John Crowley*, edited by Michael Adre-Driussi and Alice K. Turner, with a preface by Harold Bloom (Sirius Fiction), is a short but informative collection of essays on this important American author. *On Histories and Stories*, a fine new collection of essays by A. S. Byatt (Harvard University Press), is of interest here for Byatt's thoughts on fairy tales and fantasy themes in the works of authors ranging from Salman Rushdie to Terry Pratchett.

*The Queen's Conjurer* by Benjamin Wooley (Holt) is a fascinating new biography of Dr. John Dee, the famous sixteenth-century scientist, magician, and advisor to Queen Elizabeth I. *Final Séance* by Massímo Polídoro (Prometheus Books) examines "the strange friendship between Houdini and Conan Doyle," including Doyle's involvement with spiritualism and the Cottingley fairy photographs. *I, Toto* by Willard Carroll (Stewart, Tabori, & Chang) is the autobiography of Terry, the dog who was Toto in the *Wizard of Oz* film. (No, I'm not making this up.) *The Gentleman from Angell Street: Memories of H. P. Lovecraft* by Muriel E. Eddy and C. M. Eddy, Jr. (Fenham Publishing) is a slim memoir written by two friends and colleagues of H. P. Lovecraft's.

## Mythology, Folklore, and Fairy Tales

*Literature and the Gods* by Roberto Calasso, translated from the Italian by Tim Parks (Knopf), is a brilliant collection of essays examining the themes of classical myth in literature and life. Calasso is one of the world's finest mythic scholars (author of *Ka* and *Cadmus and Harmony*); these essays were originally delivered as a series of lectures at Oxford University. *Once and Future Myths: The Power of Ancient Stories in Modern Times* by Phil Cousineau (Conari Press) is a less dazzling but still fascinating look at the power of myth in modern life and pop culture. Cousineau was a disciple of Joseph Campbell; his work is Campbellian in the best sense, without being merely derivative. Another fine volume on the relevance of myth today is from Martín Prechtel (author of *Secrets of the Talking Jaguar*). In his latest, *The Disobedience of the Daughter of the Sun: Time and Ecstasy* (Yellow Moon Press), Prechtel recounts a traditional Mayan tale, then examines its layers of meaning. And yet another good book on mythology today is *SAGA: Best New Writings on Mythology, Volume II*, edited by Jonathan Young (White Cloud Press), containing essays by Jack Zipes, Joyce Carol Oates, Jean Houston, Margaret Atwood, and Matthew Fox, among others.

*Trickster Lives: Culture and Myth in American Fiction* edited by Jeanne Campbell Reesman (University of Georgia Press) is a terrific collection of essays on this subject by William G. Doty, the brilliant Lewis Hyde, and others. *Twice Upon a Time: Women Writers and the History of the Fairy Tale* by Elizabeth

Wanning Harries (Princeton University Press) is an excellent new study of this topic, ranging from the salon writers of seventeenth-century France to authors like Angela Carter, A. S. Byatt, and Emma Donoghue today. Disappointingly, however, the author seems unaware of the large number of women writing fairy-tale fiction in the fantasy genre. Also of interest is Susan Seller's study *Myth and Fairy Tale in Contemporary Women's Fiction* (Palgrave), which looks at fairy tales in the works of Angela Carter, A. S. Byatt, Sheri S. Tepper, and other modern writers. *The Queen's Mirror*, edited by Shawn C. Jarvis and Jeannine Blackwell (Bison Books), is an enchanting collection of literary fairy tales published by German women, 1780–1900. *At the Bottom of the Garden* by Diane Purkiss (New York University Press), subtitled "A Dark History of Fairies, Hobgoblins, and Other Troublesome Things," is a fascinating examination of fairy lore through the ages, and ought to be required reading for fantasists who use these themes. *The Arthurian Companion: Second Edition* by Phyllis Ann Karr (Green Knight Publishing) is a useful compendium of Arthurian information published in an encyclopedic format. Two other good volumes for the reference shelves are: *The Meaning of Herbs: Myth, Language, and Lore* by Gretchen Scoble and Ann Field (Chronicle); and *The Language of Flowers: Symbols and Myths* by Marina Heil-meyer (Prestel U.S.A.).

The most important folktale collection to appear last year was *Latin American Folktales: Stories from the Hispanic and Indian Traditions*, edited by the excellent John Bierhorst and published in the Pantheon Fairy Tale and Folklore Library (Pantheon). This volume is one that no good folktale collection should be missing. Also, Thomas Crane's *Italian Popular Tales* was finally brought back into print in an attractive new edition introduced by Jack Zipes (ABC-Clio). This was one of the first books to call attention to Italy's rich fairy-tale tradition. Other good collections: *The Fish Prince and Other Stories: Merman Folk Tales*, a lyrical volume by Jane Yolen and Shulamith Oppenheim (Interlink); *The Orphan Girl and Other Stories: West African Folktales* charmingly retold by Buchi Offodile (Interlink); *Holy Archer and Other Classic Chinese Tales*, seven classics retold by Shelley Fu (Linnet Books); *One Thousand and One Papua New Guinean Nights: Folktales from Wantok Newspapers*, Volumes 1 & 2, an exhaustive collection edited and translated by Thomas H. Slone (Masalai Press); *Our Voices: Native Stories of Alaska and the Yukon*, a truly gorgeous collection edited by James Ruppert and John W. Bernet (Bison Books); *Hopi Stories of Witchcraft, Shamanism and Magic*, an unusual collection by Ekkehart Maltoki and Ken Garey (University of Nebraska Press); and *On the Trail Made of Dawn: American Indian Creation Myths*, a nice overview volume, covering thirteen tribes, by M. L. Weber (Shoestring Press). *Creation Myths* by Louise-Marie von Franz (Shambala) is a terrific new collection of essays on the subject from a major Jungian scholar. *The Quest for the Green Man* by John Matthews (Quest) is an introduction to and meditation on this mysterious icon. *The Dybbuk and the Yiddish Imagination*, edited and translated from the Yiddish by Joachim Neugroschel (Syracuse University Press), examines myths of the dybbuk in folklore and follows its appearance in literature from the sixteenth century to the present day. *Journey to the West* by Wu Cheng'en (Foreign Language Press) is a classic Chinese mythological novel based on traditional folktales, written in the Ming Dynasty. This four-volume edition is translated from the Chinese by W. J. F. Jenner.

# Music

Traditional music is of interest to many fantasy lovers because it draws on the same cultural roots as folktales and other folk arts. There is such a wealth of traditional music available these days that we have room to mention only a handful of favorites from 2001 here. For further recommendations, check out reviews on the following web sites: The Green Man Review (www.greenman review.com) and Rambles (www.rambles.net).

*The Merry Sisters of Fate* by Lúnasa (Green Linnet) and *In Good Company* by flutist Kevin Crawford (Green Linnet) were my favorite CDs of traditional music from Ireland released in 2001, while from Scotland came *Fit?* by Old Blind Dogs (Green Linnet) and *First Frost* by Whirligig (Lochshore). For those who like their Celtic music fused with jazz and other world rhythms, try *Seafaring Man*, the lovely new CD from Mouth Music (Nettwerk) and *Out of the Bag* from Bag o' Cats (Greentrax). *Wee Blue Man* by Celtic Soul mixes Celtic and Western swing to mostly good effect (Lost Resort), while *Dreaming in Hell's Kitchen* by The Prodigals (Dara) pulls out the stops for some good punky Celtic thrash.

Northside, a music company in Minneapolis, continues to bring traditional and contemporary Nordic music from Finland, Sweden, Norway, and Denmark to American shores. Among the best Northside releases this year were *Ilmatar* by Varttina; *Garmarna*, a remastered release of Garmarna's first CD; *May Monday*, acoustic music from Karen Tween and Timo Alakotila; and *Airbow*, from Maria Kalaniemi and Svan Ahlbäck, with vocal guest Susanne Rosenberg. For those who like a mix of old and new, try *Sorten Muld III* by Denmark's Sorten Muld, which turns ancient Nordic ballads into contemporary dance music.

From other parts of the world, my favorite release of the year was *Movimento* by Madredeus, featuring the gorgeous "fado" music of Portugal (Blue Note). Also of note: I *Left My Sweet Homeland* by The Ökrös Ensemble preserves the traditional music of Hungary and of the Roma people of Transylvania. *1.0* by Fiamma Fumana is an intriguing CD of roots music from Italy. *Canto* by Los Super Seven (Sony) is this band's second CD, mixing infectious traditional Mexican tunes with pan-Latin rhythms. *Baro* by Habib Koite (Putumayo) is a fabulous CD of African music from a Malian musician working in the "griot" (singer/historian) tradition. I also recommend Putumayo's fine surveys of music from around the world: *African Odyssey*, *Arabic Grove*, and *Gypsy Caravan*. For Native American music, try *Edge of the Century*, a cross-cultural collaboration between the Ute/Navajo flutist R. Carlos Nakai and jazz player AmoChip Dabney; *Big Medicine* by the R. Carlos Nakai Quartet (Nakai, Dabney, Mary Redhouse, and William Clipman); and *Bless the People* by Verdelle Primeaux and Johnny Mike, featuring the haunting songs of the Native American Church. (All three of these CDs are from Canyon Records.)

Finally, don't miss *Play Each Morning Wild Queen*, the delightful new CD from The Flash Girls (Fabulous Records), a duo consisting of Lorraine Garland and Emma Bull (author of fantasy novels such as *War for the Oaks*), playing a mix of traditional tunes and songs written by the likes of Neil Gaiman, Steven Brust, Adam Stemple and Todd Menton (the latter two from Boiled in Lead), in addition to Bull and Garland's own compositions.

Recommendations from writer/folklorist/musician Charles de Lint:

I'm often asked to recommend Celtic music to folks who are completely unfamiliar with it and while there are any number of fine labels out there, I usually steer them to Green Linnet, simply because their selection is so huge. Of course, then I get asked, "But which one should I get?"

Happily, I now have the perfect answer: the two CD label retrospective *Green Linnet Records, 25 Years of Celtic Music* (www.greenlinnet.com), thirty-two brilliant tracks from some of the best practitioners in the field. Certainly it only gives you a taste of each artist, but a combination of this set, and a visit to their site to get more information, should be enough to put you on the right path to some great music.

For those who already have a good familiarity with traditional music, I'd like to recommend: *The Merry Sisters of Fate* by Lúnasa (www.lunasa.ie), still one of the best traditional Celtic groups working today; *At First Light* by Michael McGoldrick and John McSherry (www.compassrecords.com), flute and Uillean pipes from players with a strong Lúnasa connection; *The Blue Idol* by Altan (www.altan.ie), Donegal fiddling and the sweet voice of Mairéd Ni Mhaonaigh; *Tin Air* by Frank Cassidy and Friends (email: tinairmusic@hotmail.com), a superb collection of music led by Cassidy's regular and low whistles; *The World Is Only Air* by Mike Stevens (www.borealisrecords.com), an incredible harmonica album—you won't believe that Stevens is only using standard-tuned Marine Bands; and my favorite of the year, the short but gorgeous *Music for a New Crossing* by Kathryn Tickell and Andy Sheppard (www.kathryntickell.com), an inspired duet of Northumbrian pipes and saxophone.

Lastly, those of you missing the music of Loreena McKennitt (and who among us isn't?) might be interested in *Celtic Heartland* by Ron Korb (www.ronkorb.com), the flautist from McKennitt's band. It's an intriguing mix of original music with a heavy Celtic and Middle Eastern influence, featuring appearances by the likes of cellist Caroline Lavelle, Uillean piper Stéphan Hannigan, and harpist Sharlene Wallace (all wonderful recording artists in their own right). For a touchstone, think of a McKennitt album without any vocals.

## Awards

The World Fantasy Convention was held in Montreal, Quebec, Canada last year. The guests of honor were Fred Saberhagen, Joel Champetier, and Donato Giancola, and the toastmaster was Charles de Lint.

The 2001 World Fantasy Awards (for works published in 2000) presented at the conventions were: Lifetime Achievement: Philip José Farmer and Frank Frazetta; Best Novel (tie): *Declare* by Tim Powers and *Galveston* by Sean Stewart; Best Novella: *The Man on the Ceiling* by Steve Rasnic Tem and Melanie Tem; Best Short Fiction: "The Pottawatomie Giant" by Andy Duncan; Best Collection: *Beluthahatchie and Other Stories* by Andy Duncan; Best Anthology: *Dark Matter* edited by Sheree R. Thomas; Best Artist: Shaun Tan; Special Award— Professional: Tom Shippey for *J.R.R. Tolkien: Author of the Century*; Special Award–Nonprofessional: Bill Sheehan for *At the Foot of the Story Tree: An Inquiry into the Fiction of Peter Straub*. The judges for the 2001 Awards were Steven Erikson, Paula Guran, Diana Wynne Jones, Graham Joyce, and Jonathan Strahan.

The 2001 Mythopoeic Awards were presented at Mythcon at the University of California—Berkeley: Scholar Guest of Honor: David Llewellyn Dodds; Author Guest of Honor: Peter S. Beagle; Best Adult Literature: *The Innamorati* by Midori Snyder; Best Children's Literature: *Aria of the Sea* by Dia Calhoun; Scholarship Award for Inklings Studies: Tom Shippey for *J.R.R. Tolkien: Author of the Century*; Scholarship Award for General Myth and Fantasy Studies: Alan Lupack and Barbara Tepa Lupack for *King Arthur in America*. The awards are judged by members of the Mythopoeic Society.

WisCon was held again last year in Madison, Wisconsin. It is a forum for writers, artists, publishers, fans, and academics to explore feminism and gender roles and relationships in speculative fiction. The Guests of Honor were Nancy Kress and Elizabeth Vonarburg.

The James Tiptree Jr. Memorial Award for the best gender-bending fiction for 2001, which was presented at Readercon in Massachusetts in July 2002, went to Hiromi Goto for her novel *The Kappa Child*. The judges for the award were Suzy McKee Charnas, Kathleen Ann Goonan, Peter Halasz, Joan Haran, and Ama Patterson.

The winner of the 2001 William L. Crawford Award for the best first fantasy novel is *The Fox Woman* by Kij Johnson. The award was presented at the International Convention of the Fantastic in the Arts which took place from March 21–25, in Fort Lauderdale, Florida.

That's an overview of the year in fantasy, now on to the stories themselves. Once again there were stories we were unable to include in this volume which should nonetheless be considered among the year's best. Foremost among them was "Spirit of Place" by Gregory Feeley (iPublish.com), a beautiful work of historical speculation that was simply too long for this book. I also recommend seeking out:

"The Lady of the Winds" by Poul Anderson in the Oct./Nov. issue of *F&SF*.
"On High Marsh" by Usula K. Le Guin from her collection *Tales from Earthsea*.
"Eternity and After" by Lucius Shepard from the March issue of *F&SF*.
"The Far Side of the Lake" by Steve Rasnic Tem from his collection *The Far Side of the Lake*.
"'The Exchange' by Nicholas Sporlender" by Jeff VanderMeer, a "Hoegbottom & Sons" publication.
"Counting the Shapes" by Yoon Ha Lee from the June issue of *F&SF*.

I hope you'll enjoy the stories and poems chosen for this volume as much as I did. Many thanks to the authors, agents, and publishers who allowed us to reprint them there.

—Terri Windling
Devon, U.K., and Tucson,
U.S.
2001–2002

# Summation 2001: Horror

## Ellen Datlow

Tuesday, September 11, 2001, an event took place that influenced everyone who lived through it directly or indirectly: the attack on the World Trade Center Towers in New York City and the Pentagon in Washington, D.C. This event has had and will continue to have an impact on everyone in the world, of course, but also more specifically on creators of art, movies, and fiction.

It brings up a serious question that perhaps cannot be answered: What responsibility do artists have? Can/should they create fictional horror when a real-life horror such as 9/11/2001 has taken place?

But reading the daily newspaper to me is a *constant* horror show. I cannot pick one up without reading an article about a child being killed by its parent, about someone powerful preying on those less powerful, about corporate greed stealing from the workers without whom those corporations would not exist, about interethnic cruelty and warfare the world over. Art may be the most potent weapon we have. And horror literature is one of those arts. Use it wisely.

Back to the relatively less weighty news of the year, publishing news:

Monday, June 25, in a 7–2 majority decision, the Supreme Court upheld a September 1999 ruling by the U.S. 2nd Circuit Court of Appeals, which ruled that freelance writers have the right to control the reproduction of their works in electronic form. The ruling came seven years after freelancer Jonathan Tasini, along with members of the National Writers Union (NWU), first filed suit against media heavyweights The New York Times Company, *Newsday*, *Time*, Lexis/Nexis, and University Microfilms. This landmark decision immediately caused some of those plaintiffs to make the retaliatory move of removing hundreds of authors' works from their databanks rather than begin to pay for the work.

Phyllis Grann, one of the most influential publishing executives, resigned as president and chief executive officer of Penguin Putnam "to start a second act." Grann, who started in publishing in 1958 as a secretary for Doubleday, joined Putnam Berkley in 1976. She became chairman and CEO in 1991. Among the authors published during her tenure there were Stephen King, Tom Clancy, Amy Tan, Terry McMillan, and Nora Roberts. David Shanks, currently Penguin's

COO, will take over as CEO. Executive Vice President Susan Peterson Kennedy will succeed Grann as company president.

Simon & Schuster divided Pocket Books into two divisions. As a result of the realignment, Pocket will focus on mass market and trade paperback publishing, while hardcover titles will be released under a new imprint called Atria. Judith Curr, formerly president and publisher of Pocket Books, now heads Atria. Louise Burke, president and publisher of New American Library, was hired as executive vice president and publisher for Pocket. Carolyn Reidy, president of the S&S adult trade group, said the changes would allow each division to focus on one thing, for better results. She also predicted that PB Press will have a hardcover program that is both bigger and stronger, publishing about sixty titles a year, an increase of approximately 25 percent over Pocket's previous hardcover output.

Time Warner eliminated a hundred positions when it shut down its direct-mail division at Time-Life Books. At the same time, Little, Brown publisher Sarah Crichton was replaced by Michael Pietsch because of "a difference in philosophy" with Larry Kirshbaum, chairman of Time Warner Trade Publishing. Sources said that part of the problem was Crichton's resistance to the idea that LB adopt a publishing approach similar to that of Warner Books, although Kirshbaum asserted that he is committed to maintaining separate editorial identities for Little, Brown and Warner.

Gauntlet Press announced its expansion into the mass market field with its new Edge imprint of trade hardcovers and trade paperbacks. The first of the titles in the imprint are *Are You Loathsome Tonight?* by Poppy Z. Brite and *Ladies Night* by Jack Ketchum. They will be published in initial print runs of five thousand copies.

After more than two years as a publisher of limited-edition hardcovers, Delirium Books began a trade paperback line in August.

Ministry of Whimsy Press has been acquired by Sean Wallace's Prime Books in a deal concluded on August 31, 2001. The Ministry will remain under the creative control of its founder Jeff VanderMeer while Sean Wallace will assume the role of publisher. VanderMeer says, "The deal with Prime allows us to continue publishing unique books that readers can't find anywhere else while ensuring financial stability. You can expect our choices of material to remain joyfully idiosyncratic and of very high quality. Production values will continue to be competitive with commercial publishers."

As an imprint under Prime Books, the Ministry of Whimsy will convert to print-on-demand publishing. The first book scheduled for publication will be the third volume of the *Leviathan* fiction anthology. Forrest Aguirre will join the Ministry as an associate editor.

Scorpius Digital Publishing officially launched their spring 2001 horror lineup at the World Horror Convention in Seattle in May, announcing upcoming collections by Dennis Etchison, Jack Cady, and Alan M. Clark. Scorpius was founded in August 2000 by Bridget McKenna and her daughter, Marti McKenna. All Scorpius titles are published in the Microsoft Reader eBook format.

Paula Guran's *Darkecho* newsletter closed down with its last issue e-mailed January 26, 2001. Guran has been occasionally publishing *Daughter of Dark Echo* for readers on her mailing list.

*Jobs in Hell*, the weekly marketing newsletter published by Brian Keene, has been sold to Kelly Laymon. The change in editorship will take place in early 2002. The format will remain the same and the staff will stay onboard. Keene has been owner and editor in chief for three years but found his writing suffering as *JIH* took increasingly more of his time.

*The Spook* (http://www.thespook.com), published and edited by Anthony Sapienza as a downloadable magazine, made its debut in mid-June.

Kelp Queen Press was officially launched at the World Fantasy Convention in Montreal, November 1–4. The press plans to publish poetry and prose in chapbook and perfect-bound book form, in all genres, and will also produce specialty items such as individual broadsides, cocktail manuals, dating guides, artwork and "other things whimsical and alarming."

*Aurealis: Australian Fantasy & Science Fiction* is now edited by Keith Stevenson, who will take over the day-to-day running of the magazine from Stephen Higgins and Dirk Strasser after the October 2001 issue. Chimaera Publications will continue to publish the magazine, and from 2002 *Aurealis* will return to its regular two issues a year schedule. Chimaera Publications will also continue to run the *Aurealis* Awards.

Stealth Press continued to bring back into print horror classics like John Skipp and Craig Spector's novel collaborations and Chelsea Quinn Yarbro's St. Germain series in addition to first editions of new collections by Dennis Etchison, John Shirley, and William F. Nolan.

After publishing several new chapbooks, collections, and one novel in 2001 DarkTales Publications announced in October that it was cutting back on its production and "turning our attentions to strengthening the distribution reach for our present titles, and any future titles we do come out with, in hopes we can shore up the foundation of the company."

Shane Ryan Staley, editor in chief of Delirium Books, reported late in 2001 that the *Delirium* website has been pulled from its host server, KC Online, after receiving a complaint. Citing graphic material that was unsuitable for their web presence, the host server reviewed the site and found that the *Delirium* ezine, Gross-Out Tournament, and certain author Message Boards were unsuitable for their server. Last year, Tripod shut Delirium's website down for the same reasons.

Wormhole Books inaugurated a monthly "Contemporary Chapbook series" with a series of original or reprinted science fiction and horror stories and a novel excerpt.

Dead magazines: *Psychotrope*, closed down with Issue 9, *Indigenous Fiction* has closed down with Issue 8, *Aboriginal SF* is dead—its unpublished inventory will be published by other DNA Publications magazines.

The 2000 Stoker Awards were presented in Seattle May 26, 2001. The winners were:

Novel: *The Traveling Vampire Show* by Richard Laymon; First Novel: *The Licking Valley Coon Hunters Club* by Brian A. Hopkins; Long Fiction: "The Man on the Ceiling" by Melanie and Steve Rasnic Tem; Short Fiction: "Gone" by Jack Ketchum; Fiction Collection: *Magic Terror* by Peter Straub; Anthology: *The Year's Best Fantasy and Horror, Thirteenth Annual Collection*, edited by Ellen Datlow and Terri Windling; Nonfiction: *On Writing* by Stephen King; Illustrated

Narrative: *The League of Extraordinary Gentlemen* (miniseries) by Alan Moore; Screenplay: *Shadow of the Vampire* by Steven Katz; Work for Young Readers: *The Power of Un* by Nancy Etchemendy; Poetry Collection: *A Student of Hell* by Tom Piccirilli; Other Media: Chiaroscuro (Web site) by Patricia Lee Macomber, Steve Eller and Sandra Kasturi; Lifetime Achievement Award: Nigel Kneale; Specialty Press Award: Subterranean Press, William K. Schafer.

The International Horror Guild Awards were presented at Dragon*Con on September 1, 2001, in Atlanta, Georgia. Nominations were derived from recommendations made by the public and the judges' knowledge of the field. Edward Bryant, Stefan R. Dziemianowicz, Hank Wagner, and Fiona Webster adjudicated. The winners are:

Novel: *Declare* by Tim Powers; First Novel: *Adam's Fall* by Sean Desmond; Long Story: "The Man on the Ceiling" by Melanie Tem and Steve Rasnic Tem; Short Story: "The Rag and Bone Men" by Steve Duffy; Illustrated Fiction: "I Feel Sick" #1 & 2 by Jhonen Vasquez; Collection: (tie) *City Fishing* by Steve Rasnic Tem and *Ghost Music and Other Tales* by Thomas Tessier; Anthology: *October Dreams*, edited by Richard Chizmar and Robert Morrish; Nonfiction: *At the Foot of the Story Tree* by William Sheehan; Publication: *Horror Garage*; Art: Joel-Peter Witkin; Film: *American Psycho*; Television: *Angel*; Living Legend Award: Alice Cooper.

The 2001 British Fantasy Awards were presented on September 23, 2001, at the BFS's 30th Birthday Bash at Champagne Charlie's in London. The winners of this year's awards were as follows: Best Novel: *Perdido Street Station* by China Miéville (Macmillan); Best Anthology: *Hideous Progeny*, edited by Brian Willis (RazorBlade Press); Best Collection: *Where the Bodies Are Buried* by Kim Newman (Alchemy Press/Airgedlámh Publications); Best Short Fiction: "Naming of Parts" by Tim Lebbon (PS Publishing); Best Artist: Jim Burns; Best Small Press: PS Publishing; Karl Edward Wagner Award: Peter Haining.

## Novels

*Declare* by Tim Power (William Morrow) is a remarkably realistic depiction of cold war espionage and a vivid portrait of British traitor Kim Philby with a large, fascinating dollop of the supernatural thrown in. A young man is recruited to be part of a top secret organization within the British government. With all the deliberate flippings of his loyalties, the only thing he has to hang on to is the young woman he spent time with during one of his early missions. A brilliant entertainment. The Subterranean Press limited edition, published in 2000, won The International Horror Guild Award and was cowinner of the World Fantasy Award.

*Under the Skin* by Michael Faber (Harcourt, Inc) deftly combines horror with science fiction in a chilling and strangely moving story that begins with an odd young woman driving the roads of the Scottish highlands, trolling for suitable male specimens to "take." Gradually, what seems at first to be a simple serial killer novel veers into something even more sinister. The woman is not from around here and has been, in her own words, "mutilated" to conform to the appearance of a vulnerable human female to become a kind of Venus flytrap. While the reader follows her daily routine, she gathers a cross section of male human behavior in a very specific situation. Creepy, disturbing, and occasionally wince-producing (more for men than women, I'd think) this is a fascinating sf horror novel.

*The Wooden Sea* by Jonathan Carroll (Tor) is the author's eleventh novel and it's a doozy. From the moment a three-legged dog steps into the life of a police chief, that life is never the same. The dog drops dead, is buried, and shows up in a car trunk—and then things get really strange. The chief is a likable character who literally has to face his cocky past and make important decisions that could change the world. Compulsively readable, *The Wooden Sea* is a complex cross-genre confection combining elements of science fiction (time travel), surreal fantasy, and dark fantasy for a rich, satisfying read (disclaimer: I am Carroll's editor at Tor).

*The Ragchild* by Steve Lockley and Paul Lewis (RazorBlade Press, U.K.) is a well-rendered novel about a secret London that shelters the needy and is the soul of the London we know. An evil being that takes the form of a child does its best to destroy this fragile city by manipulating a bunch of losers to create a formidable monstrous army to do its bidding. A young runaway, a former soldier miraculously saved from certain death in WWI, and a mysterious and scarred clairvoyant are the city's only hope.

*Threshold* by Caitlín Kiernan (Onyx) is the author's second published novel. Kiernan expertly uses her knowledge of paleontology to develop a dangerous mystery about a living fossil that haunts an abandoned water tunnel. Kiernan is exceptionally good at depicting the murky malaise of young misfits with too much time on their hands.

*The Lost* by Jack Ketchum (Leisure Books) is a powerful, fast-moving, and terrifying portrait of a young psycho from the suburbs of New Jersey toward the end of the sixties. In 1965 the psycho murders two young woman at a campsite. For the next four years he confounds the two cops who suspect him and holds in thrall two friends who were inadvertent witnesses to the slaughter . . . until things—and the psycho—start to crack. A limited hardcover edition was published by Cemetery Dance Publications. See below.

## Other Novels

*Voice of the Blood* by Jemiah Jefferson (Leisure Books); *Salem Falls* by Jodi Picoult (Pocket Books); *In the Face of Death* by Chelsea Quinn Yarbro (Hidden Knowledge, ebook); *The Doorkeepers* by Graham Masterton (Severn House, U.K.); *Hell on Earth* by Michael Reaves (Del Rey); *The Manhattan Hunt Club* by John Saul (Ballantine); *Dreamcatcher* by Stephen King (Scribner); *Gob's Grief* by Chris Adrian (Broadway Books); *Ambrosial Flesh* by Mary Ann Mitchell (Leisure); *House of Pain* by Sèphera Girón (Leisure); *Monstruary* by Julian Rios (Alfred A. Knopf); *A Feast in Exile* by Chelsea Quinn Yarbro (Tor Books); *Affinity* by J. N. Williamson (Leisure); *Straight on 'Til Morning* by Christopher Golden (Signet Books); *Red Moon Rising* by Billie Sue Mosiman (DAW Books); *Narcissus in Chains* by Laurell K. Hamilton (Berkley); *The Fury and the Terror* by John Farris (Forge); *The Association* by Bentley Little (Signet); *Darkness Demands* by Simon Clark (Leisure); *His Father's Son* by Nigel Bennett and P. N. Elrod (Baen Books); *Dead Love* by Donald Beman (Dorchester); *The Lecturer's*

*Tale* by James Hynes (Picador); *Teeth* by Edo Van Belkom (Meisha Merlin); . . . *Doomed to Repeat It* by D.G.K. Goldberg (Design Image Group); *Night Players* by P. D. Cacek (Design Image Group); *Dark Sleeper* by Jeffrey E. Barlough (Ace); *The Treatment* by Mo Hayder (Doubleday); *Balak* by Stephen Mark Rainey (Wildside Press); *Eternity* by Tamara Thorne (Pinnacle); *The Burning Times* by Jeanne Kalogridis (Simon & Schuster); *That Way Madness Lies* by William Rand (iPublish); *Greed & Stuff* by Jay S. Russell (St. Martin's Press); *Quincey Morris, Vampire* by P. N. Elrod (Baen); *This Flesh Unknown* by Gary Braunbeck (Foggy Windows Books/Chimeras); *The Living Blood* by Tananarive Due (Pocket); *Dark Inheritance* by Kathleen O'Neal Gear and W. Michael Gear (Warner); *Black Oak: When the Cold Wind Blows* by Charles L. Grant (Tor); *Necroscope: Avengers* by Brian Lumley (Hodder & Stoughton, U.K.); *Fright Train* by Paul Stewart (Scholastic, U.K.); *A Feral Darkness* by Doranna A. Durgin (Baen); *Evil Whispers* by Owl Goingback (Signet); *Wire Mesh Mothers* by Elizabeth Massie (Leisure); *In the Blood* by Stephen Gresham (Pinnacle); *Bound in Blood* by David Thomas Lord (Kensington); *Amnesia* by Andrew Neiderman (Pocket); *The Beast That Was Max* by Gerard Houarner (Leisure); *The White Room* by A. J. Matthews (Berkley); *The Songcatcher* by Sharyn McCrumb (Dutton); *Vampire Vow* by Michael Schiefelbein (Alyson); *Nailed* by Lucy Taylor (Signet); *Night Blood* by James M. Thompson (Pinnacle); *The Ancient* by Muriel Gray (HarperCollins, U.K.); *Night in the Lonesome October* by Richard Laymon (Headline, U.K.); *The Evil Returns* by Hugh B. Cave (Leisure); *More Than Mortal* by Mick Farren (Tor); *The Last Vampire* by Whitley Strieber (Pocket); *Candle Bay* by Tamara Thorne (Pinnacle); *Bitten* by Kelly Armstrong (Viking); *Night of the Triffids* by Simon Clark (Hodder & Stoughton, U.K.); *Mutant: Hair Raiser* by Graham Masterton (Scholastic, U.K.); *Ghostkiller* by Scott Chandler (Berkley); *Blood Games* by Lee Killough (Meisha Merlin); *Fireworks* by James A. Moore (Meisha Merlin); *Hangman* by Michael Slade (NAL); *The Vampire Vivienne* by Karen Taylor (Pinnacle); *Night of the Bat* by Paul Zindel (Hyperion); *Là-Bas: A Journey into the Self* by J. K. Huysmans, newly translated from the original French (1891) by Brendan King (Dedalus, U.K.); *Mean Spirit* by Will Kingdom (Transworld/Bantam, U.K.); *Canyons* by P. D. Cacek (Tor); *The Haunting of Hood Canal* by Jack Cady (St. Martin's); *The Infinite* by Douglas Clegg (Leisure—first hardcover by the company); *Deep Midnight* by Shannon Drake (Zebra); *The Altar Stone* by Robert Hackman (Goodfellow Press); *Black House* by Stephen King and Peter Straub (Random House); *Running on Instinct* by N. M. Luiken (Forge); *Gargoyles* by Alan Nayes (Forge); *Frankenstein: The Legacy* by Christopher Schildt (Pocket); *Night of Dracula* by Christopher Schildt (Pocket); *Black Dawn* by D. A. Stern (Harper/Torch); *Coldheart Canyon* by Clive Barker (HarperCollins, U.K.); *Hamlet Dreams* by Jennifer Barlow (Aardwolf Press); *Chelsea Horror Hotel* by Dee Dee Ramone (Avalon); *Crimson Kiss* by Trisha Baker (Pinnacle); *The Nature of Balance* by Tim Lebbon (Leisure); *A Lower Deep* by Tom Piccirilli (Leisure); *Lost* by Gregory Maguire (ReganBooks/HarperCollins); *Last Day* by Richard Sears (Forge); *Darkness* by Sam Siciliano (Pinnacle); *The Eleventh Hour* by Brian Stableford (Cosmos Books/Wildside Press); *Swimmer* by Graham Masterton (Severn House, U.K.); *Feather & Bone* by Gus Smith (Big Engine, U.K.); *Wringland* by Sally Spedding (Macmillan, U.K.); *Skeleton Man* by Joseph Bruchac (HarperCollins [YA]); *Pact of the Fathers* by Ramsey Campbell (Forge); *Shadows*

*Bite* by Stephen Dedman (Tor); *Bone Walker* by Kathleen O'Neal & W. Michael Gear (Forge); *Prowlers: Predator and Prey* by Christopher Golden (Pocket Pulse); *Blood and Gold* by Anne Rice (Alfred A. Knopf); *The Surgeon* by Tess Gerritsen (Ballantine Books); *The Savage Girl* by Alex Shakar (HarperCollins); *Skimming the Gumbo Nuclear* by M. F. Korn (Eraserhead Press); *Northern Gothic* by Nick Mamatas (Soft Skull Press); *From the Dust Returned* by Ray Bradbury (William Morrow); *EarthCore* by Scott Sigler (iPublish); *The Muse Asylum* by David Czuchlewski (Putnam); *American Gods* by Neil Gaiman (HarperCollins); *The Pariah* by Paul Pinn (Time Bomb Publishing, U.K.) [2000]; *The Horizontal Split* by Paul Pinn (Time Bomb Publishing, U.K.) [2000]; *Chemical Pink* by Katie Arnoldi (Forge); *Listen to the Shadows* by Danuta Reach (Morrow); *A Flock of Crows Is Called a Murder* by James Viscosi (DarkTales Publications); *Too Late Now* by David Sparks (City Contrasts Publications); *The Pig Punch* by Louis Maistros (XLibris); *Ordinary Horror* by David Searcy (Viking Press); *Naomi* by Douglas Clegg (Leisure); *The Book of the Dark* by William Meikle (Greatunpublished.com); *Dead Until Dark* by Charlaine Harris (Ace); *Dead Ground* by Chris Amies (Big Engine, U.K.); *Blackrose Avenue* by Mark Shepherd (Yard Dog Press); *The Haunting of Hip Hop* by Bertice Berry (Doubleday); *One Door Away from Heaven* by Dean Koontz (Bantam); *Spirit* by Graham Masterton (Leisure); *Riverwatch* by Joseph M. Nassise (Barclay Books); *Domain* by Steve Alten (Forge); *Moontide* by Erin Patrick (Wildside); *A Crown of Lights* by Phil Rickman (Macmillan, U.K.); *The Cure of Souls* by Phil Rickman (Macmillan, U.K.); *Death's Door* by Michael Slade (Penguin Books Canada); *Answer Man* by Roy Johansen (Bantam); *The Girls He Adored* by Jonathan Nasaw (Pocket); *Awash in Blood* by John Wooley (Hawk); *Smoking Poppy* by Graham Joyce (Pocket, U.K.); *Once* by James Herbert (Macmillan, U.K.); and *Hosts* by F. Paul Wilson (Forge).

## Collections

Single author collections have been given a giant boost with the advent of print-on-demand book-publishing technology. This technology enables smaller numbers of books to be printed at a lower cost, making publication possible for writers who can't get a book deal from either the big or even small press genre publishers. Often the P.O.D. publishers don't pay an advance, but pay royalties on copies sold. They're usually done as trade paperbacks with minimal or no marketing. Depending on the publisher, the books might be indistinguishable in look and feel from traditional publishing ventures or they might, at the other extreme, look downright amateurish. The downside of this new technology is that not all print-on-demand publishers realize that distribution and publicity effort—at least sending out copies of books to reviewers—is a necessity of doing business. Far too often I only discovered the existence of a P.O.D. collection or anthology published in 2001 by accident and too late to consider covering the title for this anthology. So authors beware. The burden is on you to ensure that your print-on-demand books are seen and reviewed.

In 2001 the floodgates seemingly opened. Big Engine (U.K.), Wildside Press and its imprint Cosmos Books, Prime, Babbage Press, DarkTales, and the Time-Warner Book Group's short-lived iPublish program brought out dozens of collections by a diverse group of writers. Conversely, Sarob Press, Ash-Tree Press,

Tartarus Press, and Midnight House are regularly publishing attractive hardcover books dedicated to keeping the traditional macabre, weird tale, and ghost story alive. The only problem with the last group of publishers is that most of the books are pricey and are more likely to appeal to the collector than to snag an unwary potential reader. Now, if only someone would make these wonderful titles available in cheaper editions. Perhaps the print-on-demand publishers could get into this market.

*Cobwebs and Whispers* by Scott Thomas (Delirium Books) is one of the best collections of the year. More than half of the twenty-six stories are original to the collection and many of them are excellent. Its beautiful dust jacket was illustrated and designed by Colleen Crary. Two stories are reprinted herein.

*Wrong Things* by Poppy Z. Brite and Caitlín Kiernan (Subterranean Press) might be too short to be officially considered a collection but this beautiful hardcover three-story chapbook is an excellent *objet d'art* as well as a great read. It includes three original stories: one each by Kiernan and Brite, one a collaboration by the two writers. The stories use some of Brite's characters and the setting plus Kiernan's self-professed keen interest in "urban archaeology and the ruins of the machine age" in addition to her occasional journeys into Clark Ashton Smith/Lovecraftian mysteries. The dustjacket and interior illustrations are by Richard Kirk and the jacket design is by Gail Cross. Kiernan supplies an afterword explaining how the collaboration came about. Available in two editions. Also from Subterranean Press: *The Baku* by Edward Bryant collects three previously published stories and the unproduced script adaptation of "The Baku" written for *The Twilight Zone* television series. The stories are about Hiroshima and its aftermath. Bryant writes an introduction about his experience trying to sell the script to *TZ*. The handsome black-and-white wraparound cover is by David Martin. Available in two editions. *Eye* by David J. Schow is the author's fifth collection and contains thirteen of the author's most recent short stories, a few of which appear for the first time. Schow's writerly voice is one of his greatest virtues (this applies to his nonfiction, too) and some of the best short fiction in *Eye* is unclassifiable but compulsively readable. The gorgeous jacket photography and design is by the author (except for the photo of an eyeball by Carlos Batts), the endpapers and signature page illustrations are by Grant Christian, and the interior design is by Tim Holt. Available in two hardcover states.

*Second Sight and Other Stories* by Chico Kidd has four original yarns about Captain Da Silva, a sea captain who lost an eye to a demon and gained the ability to see ghosts. These are charming traditional stories of "ghost-finding." For information: http://www.chico.nildram.co.uk/

*Cold Comforts and Other Fireside Mysteries* by Peter Crowther (Lone Wolf Publications) is a CD-ROM with eighteen of the author's crime and mystery stories. Crowther provides an introduction. Cover photo is by Gerard Houarner. There don't seem to be any first publication credits included.

*The Whisperer and Other Voices* by Brian Lumley (Tor) has eight stories and one short novel by the author of the "Necroscope" series.

From DarkTales Publications: *Six Inch Spikes* by Edo Van Belkom has sixteen erotic horror stories by the award-winning author, including four original to the collection. With a foreword by Michael Rowe and an afterword by the author. *Dial Your Dreams & Other Nightmares* by Robert Weinberg is a collection of fourteen stories, most previously published in anthologies during the 1990s. Two of the stories are original to the collection. There is a foreword by Richard Gilliam, an afterword by Mort Castle, and commentary on each story by Weinberg. Cover illustration is by Virgil Finley. *Cold Comfort* by Nancy Kilpatrick contains twenty-seven stories, four of them original to the collection. The other stories are from a variety of small-press publications and some higher-profile anthologies, and range over a ten-year period. With an introduction by Paula Guran.

From Wildside Press: *These Words Are Haunted* by Scott Edelman is the author/editor's first collection, and it's worth the wait. Thirteen stories published between 1983–2001 in a hard-hitting package (the jacket art takes a detail from Goya's grisly painting *Saturn Devouring His Children*). Introduction by Adam-Troy Castro. *Nasty Stories* and *Even More Nasty Stories* by Brian McNaughton are two collections of the author's short-shorts with a few longer stories included. A handful are published for the first time. They're entertaining and lightweight but few of them are as striking as his stories about ghouls collected in *The Throne of Bones*. *Fluid Mosaic* by Michael A. Arnzen collects thirteen horror stories, one original, with notes by the author about how each story came to be written (2000-published title, seen for the first time in 2001). *The Unspeakable and Others* by Dan Clore is a collection of forty-seven weird stories and sketches in the Lovecraftian tradition. Introduction by S. T. Joshi. A *Desperate, Decaying Darkness* by Adam-Troy Castro is a 2000 print-on-demand title seen for the first time in 2001. The thirteen stories, some original to the volume, range from the very short grotesquerie "Toy" to the dazzling surreal novella "The Juggler." *The Last Trumpet* by Stephen Mark Rainey has thirteen stories, mostly Cthulhu-mythos-related which take place in the fictitious locale of Sylvan County, Virginia.

From the Cosmos Books imprint of Wildside Press: *Through Dark Eyes: Glimpses of Terror and Torment* by Derek M. Fox is the author's second collection and has very effective dark cover art by Rose Mafrici designed by Garry Nurrish. Several of the eighteen stories in the book are original to the collection. Fox is a writer whose work bears watching. *City of Saints and Madmen: The Books of Ambergris* by Jeff VanderMeer is a terrific collection of four surreal novellas. Introduction by Michael Moorcock. *Similar Monsters* by Steve Savile collects fifteen stories, five original to the collection. The beautiful cover art is by Geoff Priest, designed by Garry Nurrish. *The Great World and the Small: More Tales of the Ominous and Magical* by Darrell Schweitzer is a collection of sixteen weird stories with cover art and illustrations by Jason Van Hollander.

Kicking off Delirium Books's new trade paperback line was Greg F. Gifune's *Heretics*, with a limited run of 250 signed, numbered trade paperbacks and 50 signed, numbered hardcovers. The cover art is by Keith Minnion. Brian A. Hopkins provides the introduction. *I'll Be Damned* by Shane Ryan Staley (Delirium) collects thirty stories/vignettes (some original to the collection) by the publisher of *Delirium* magazine and Delirium Books. The dust jacket bears art by R. S. Connett. The introduction is by Brian Keene. Other titles from Delirium included: *Tales of Love and Death* by W. H. Pugmire, a chapbook featuring sixteen Lovecraftian tales (two original) published between 1986 and 2001. Pugmire, like Thomas Ligotti and William Browning Spencer, creates something fresh from the Cthulhu mythos. The cover and interior art is by Mark McLaughlin.

This is unfortunately not one of Delirium's better productions—the cover art is poorly reproduced and the staples holding my copy of the chapbook together were out of place, making the whole chapbook misshapen. Wait for the hardcover coming out in 2002.

From Stealth Press: *Dark Universe* by William F. Nolan is a collection of forty-one stories chosen by the author from throughout his career 1951–2001. Preface and story introductions by Nolan. *Talking in the Dark* by Dennis Etchison is an overview of the career of one of the best writers of short dark fiction today. The twenty-four stories (one published for the first time) include several award winners. *Darkness Divided* by John Shirley collects twenty-two pieces, mostly previously uncollected stories, and three originals. The book is divided into two sections: past/present stories and stories about the near future (science fiction). There's an introduction by Poppy Z. Brite. The complete *Books of Blood* by Clive Barker is a hardcover, and there's a special limited edition that includes a nude photograph of the author.

*The Thing on the Doorstep and Other Weird Stories* by H. P. Lovecraft (Penguin Twentieth Century Classics) collects twelve weird stories, with introduction and notes by S. T. Joshi.

*The Compleat Adventures of Jules De Grandin* by Seabury Quinn (Battered Silicon Dispatch Press) is the first of three volumes. This first volume is over 430 pages and has an introduction by Robert Weinberg. The full-color dust jacket depicts eleven *Weird Tales* covers.

From Sarob Press: *Can Such Things Be? & By the Night Express* by Keith Fleming contains the short novel *Can Such Things Be?* plus the three novellas that comprised *By the Night Express*, first published in 1889. Introduction by John Pelan and afterword by Richard Dalby. With cover and interior art by Randy Broecker. All Sarob Press books are limited editions. *The Haunted River & Three Other Ghostly Novellas* by Mrs. J. H. Riddell, edited and introduced by Richard Dalby, originally appeared as seasonal "Routledge Christmas Annuals" and are traditional Victorian ghost stories combined with a murder mystery. This is their first appearance in one volume. They are accompanied by the original illustrations by Randolph Caldecott, A. Chantrey Corbould, and D. H. Friston. *The Sistrum and Other Ghost Stories* by Alice Perrin edited and introduced by Richard Dalby is the fifth volume of the editor's "Mistresses of the Macabre" series. The book contains fifteen of Perrin's best ghostly weird tales from various collections on the occasion of the centenary of her debut collection *East of Suez*. Interior illustrations and dust jacket art are by Paul Lowe. *A Ghostly Crew: Tales from the Endeavor* by Roger Johnson contains fifteen ghost stories published in various British magazines and anthologies from 1984 through 1995. Included is an introduction by David G. Rowlands; dust jacket and interior art is by Paul Lowe.

*No Rest for the Wicked* by Brian Keene (Imaginary Worlds) is an attractive-looking but poorly produced (no page numbers) first collection by an up-and-coming young writer of literate visceral horror. Most of the twelve stories were published since 1996. The book includes a rousing original novella and one original collaboration with David Niall Wilson. The introduction is by the late Richard Laymon; the jacket art is by Paul Siberdt.

*Escaping Purgatory: Fables in Words and Pictures* by Gary A. Braunbeck and

Alan M. Clark (IFD Publishing) is a beautiful hardcover graced with pullouts of full-color art by Clark at the front of the book, and black-and-white illustrations for each of the five stories and novellas, and framing vignettes. Two of the stories are by Braunbeck and Clark, three are by Braunbeck. All are worth reading.

*The Mountain King* by Rick Hautala (Leisure) contains a short novel and three short stories.

From Silver Lake Publishing: *Aliens, Minibikes and Other Staples of Suburbia* by M. F. Korn reprints eight short-shorts and one novella, and includes a brief introduction by Sherry Decker. *Confessions of a Ghoul and Other Stories* by M. F. Korn is a trade paperback of six, mostly slight, stories and one novella. There is an introduction by D. F. Lewis. Good-looking cover art.

*Dregs of Society* by Michael Laimo (Prime), the author's second collection, concentrates on fifteen stories of psychological horror, one original to the collection. There's an anti-introduction by Gary A. Braunbeck and an "outre" by Gerard Houarner. The cover art is by Ron Leming.

*A Pound of Ezra & Other Units of Gothic Measure* by Gregory R. Hyde (Cyber-Psychos AOD) is an impressive first collection with an introduction by Edward Bryant and illustrations by Steve James. The six stories, all published for the first time, ranging from the graphic/horrific-erotic to science fiction, are varied and well written.

*The Man with the Barbed Wire Fists* by Norman Partridge (Night Shade Books) is the third collection by this talented writer. The book has twenty-four stories, two original (and one reprinted herein). The introduction by the author explains how drive-in movies inspired him to become a writer. Two editions available. Also from Night Shade Books comes *The Devil Is Not Mocked* by Manly Wade Wellman, a collection of twenty-eight stories, the second volume in *The Selected Stories of Manly Wade Wellman*, a projected five-book series. There is an introduction by Ramsey Campbell. Illustrations by Kenneth Waters. The third volume, *Fearful Rock and Other Precarious Locales* also came out in 2001. It contains eight stories (including a "lost classic" reprinted here for the first time since its original publication in 1939) and an introduction/reminiscence about Wellman by editor Stephen Jones.

*Cat Stories* by Michael Marshall Smith (Earthling Publications) is a chapbook of three stories, two previously published (one reprinted in an earlier volume of *YBFH*)—the original is science fiction rather than horror. Available in paperback or hardcover.

Quantum Theology Books brought out three chapbooks by the very talented Gemma Files: *The Narrow World* is a five-story chapbook with one original story, and The International Horror Guild Award–winning story "The Emperor's Old Bones," which was reprinted in an earlier volume of *YBFH*. Introduction by Michael Rowe. *Narukh: Chaos Engine* contains four reprints. *Heart's Hole* has five reprints and an introduction by Thomas M. Deja. Cover design and illustration for all three titles are by Dale L. Sproule and all three have bibliographies.

From Midnight House: *Return of the Soul and Other Stories* by Robert Hichens is the first of a two-book set that will present a comprehensive collection of his supernatural tales. The eight stories in this volume were originally published between 1896 and 1905. This collection was edited and contains an introduction by S. T. Joshi. The handsome book has artwork by Allen Koszowski. *Sesta &*

*Other Strange Stories: The Horror Fiction of Edward Lucas White* is the second of a two-book series of this author's work. More than half the stories are published for the first time and are certain to be of interest to fans of weird fiction. The book is introduced by Lee Weinstein, who also supplies short notes for each story in the book. Dust jacket art is by Allen Koszowski. *The Black Gondolier and Other Stories* by Fritz Leiber is the first of two volumes intended to bring back into print the best short fiction of this master. John Pelan has contributed an introduction, and Steve Savile supplies an afterword. Oddly for Midnight House, there's no first publication information for any of the eighteen stories. *The Scarecrow and Other Stories* by G. Ranger Wormser was edited and contains an introduction by Douglas A. Anderson. This collection is expanded from the original 1918 edition of *The Scarecrow*, and includes five additional tales, making this book the complete repository of the author's weird and supernatural fiction. Cover art and interior portrait are by Allen Koszowski.

From Ash-Tree Press: *Where Human Pathways End* by Shamus Frazer is the first collection of all this late author's short stories. His first five stories were published in his lifetime and at the time of his early death from cancer in 1966 he had hoped to collect those stories with five unpublished stories and one poem, all of which are included in the current volume. All the new stories are very readable although not all of them are horrific. *The Five Quarters* by Steve Duffy and Ian Rodwell is an entertaining collection of five stories (one of which was chosen for *YBFH 14*). The conceit is that five professional men meet quarterly to tell each other scary stories. Duffy and Rodwell bring it off brilliantly, in a rousing update of a literary tradition. The creepy cover painting is by Paul Lowe. *Couching at the Door* by D. K. Broster, edited by Jack Adrian, brings back into print for the first time in sixty years the entire collection *Couching at the Door*, the weird tales from Broster's collection *A Fire of Driftwood*, and a previously unpublished story. The introduction, by Jack Adrian, explores what little is known about the private life of this prominent novelist of the 1930s. Jason Van Hollander has created eerily evocative jacket art. *The Floating Café* by Margery Lawrence contains twelve stories of the weird, fantastic, and the supernatural originally published in 1936 and not seen in print for fifty years. This is the third collection of Lawrence's to be published by Ash-Tree; more are to follow. There's an introduction by Richard Dalby; cover art by Paul Lowe. *Mystic Voices* by Roger Pater is a collection of stories supposedly told to the author by the fictional Rev. Philip Rivers Pater. Roger Pater was itself a pseudonym for Dom Roger Hudleston, whose contemporary obituary is provided at the end of the collection. Fourteen stories and "a biography of the author's cousin Philip." Introduction by David G. Rowlands and preface by Roger Pater. Dust jacket art by Paul Lowe. *After Shocks* by Paul Finch is the first collection of short fiction by this British writer. It includes eighteen stories, including the excellent story published in 2000, "The Punch and Judy Man"; three of them are original to the collection. Most of the previously published stories first appeared in the U.K., in small-press magazines. *The Far Side of the Lake* by Steve Rasnic Tem collects over twenty years' worth of the quieter, more supernatural stories of the author from 1983–2001 (in contrast to last year's *City Fishing*). The title story is original to the volume, and for the first time Tem's "Charlie Goode" stories are collected in one place. *A Pleasing Terror: The Complete Supernatural Writing of M.R. James* includes thirty-three complete ghost stories from *The Collected Ghost Stories*, three other stories, seven story drafts left among the author's papers, twelve medieval ghost stories discovered and published by James, various articles, including prefaces and introductions to his various collections. An important addition to any horror library. *Spook Stories by E.F. Benson: Mrs Amworth* is the third and final volume of the series that brings together all the known supernatural and weird stories of the author. The series was edited by Jack Adrian, who edited and introduced each volume. Sixteen stories are included in this one. The creepy black-and-white front and back cover illustrations are by Douglas Walters and the lettering is by Rob Suggs. *The Shadow on the Blind and Other Ghost Stories* by Mrs. Alfred Baldwin brings together all nine stories from the collection originally published in 1895, adding one tale never before published in book form. Also included are seven of J. Ayton Symington's illustrations from the first edition. The dust jacket illustration is by Allen Koszowski, the introduction is by John Pelan and Richard Dalby. *The Golden Gong and Other Night Pieces* by Thomas Burke is edited, and with an introduction by Jessica Amanda Salmonson, who has brought together twenty-one of Burke's tales of the weird and supernatural. The color dust jacket illustration is by Paul Lowe. Burke's publisher Grant Richards provides an afterword. Most Ash-Tree covers are designed by publisher Christopher Roden.

*Dreadful Tales* by Richard Laymon (Hodder Headline, U.K.) collects twenty-five stories, one original. Along with two earlier volumes of stories: *Out Are the Lights* and *Fiends*, this book collects the late author's adult short stories up through 1997.

*Being Dead* by Vivian Van Velde (Harcourt) is a YA collection of seven dark fantasy stories of ghosts and the undead (not seen).

*Tales of Devilry and Doom* by John B. Ford (Rainfall Books, U.K.) has ten stories and four poems. Introduction by Michael Pendragon. Cover art is by publisher/artist Steve Lines.

From Gauntlet Press: *Through Shattered Glass* by David B. Silva is the first collection of stories by this author, who was the editor of *The Horror Show*, coeditor of two anthologies with Paul F. Olson and currently coeditor of *Hellnotes* with Olson. The stories were all published between 1985 and 1999 and include the Bram Stoker Award–winning story "The Calling," which was reprinted in an earlier volume of this series. The haunting dust jacket art is by Harry O. Morris. Dean Koontz provides a humorous and gracious introduction. Available in two limited states. A *Life in the Cinema* by Mick Garris (2000) collects eight stories (one original) and a screenplay based on one of the stories. There is an introduction by Stephen King, and an afterword by Tobe Hooper. The jacket art is by Clive Barker. Ray Bradbury's classic collection *Dark Carnival* comes in two editions, with cover art by Bradbury and an introduction by Clive Barker. This is one of the "classics revisited" series.

*Bad Seed* by Harry Shannon (Medium Rare Books) brings together the first fifteen noir and horror stories the author ever published. Cover and interior art by John Turi.

*The Essential Ellison* by Harlan Ellison (Morpheus International) and edited by Terry Dowling, Richard Delap, and Gil Lamont is a revised and updated edition of the 1987 Nemo Press edition, including seventeen additional new items and a new preface.

From Tartarus Press: *The Collected Macabre Stories* by L. P. Hartley contains thirty-seven of Hartley's best tales, ranging from his well-known, traditional ghost stories through his darkly humorous ones and the Aickmanesque "The Pylon." These encompass a wide range of settings, from English country houses to Venetian palaces. There is an introduction by Mark Valentine and the author's own introduction to *Lady Cynthia Asquith's Third Ghost Book*. *Dromenon: the Best Weird Stories of Gerald Heard* contains nine stories from the 1940s that range from science fiction to fantasy, ghost stories, and psychological fiction. Included is an extensive introduction by John Cody.

*Odd Lot* by Steve Burt (Burt Creations) is a trade paperback collection of nine stories, one original to the collection. The attractive cover art is by Jessica Hagerman.

*Walter de la Mare: Short Stories 1927–1956*, edited by Giles de la Mare (DLM) is a follow-up to *Walter de la Mare: Short Stories 1895–1926*, published a few years ago. The new volume collects stories from *On the Edge: Short Stories*, *The Wind Blows Over*, and *A Beginning and Other Stories* plus four uncollected stories and four never previously published.

*Alone in the Dark* by Paul Kane (BJM Press, U.K.) is a collection of twelve horror stories from small press magazines.

*The Three Impostors and Other Stories* by Arthur Machen (Chaosium) is a collection of three stories and the title set of linked stories. First volume of a projected *The Best Weird Tales of Arthur Machen*.

*Exit into Eternity: Tales of the Bizarre and Supernatural* by C. M. Eddy Jr. (Fenham Publishing) is a reprint edition of a collection of five weird tales (one unfinished) by a friend of H. P. Lovecraft. The collection was originally published by Oxford Press in 1973.

*Beneath the Skin and Other Stories* by Matthew Sturges (Clockwork Storybook) has some interesting stories by a new writer.

*The Raven and Other Poems and Tales* by Edgar Allan Poe (Little, Brown/Bulfinch Press) includes illustrations by Daniel Alan Green.

*Painted Demons* by William Rand (iUniverse) is a collection of nine linked horror stories about a man and a priest confronting a demon.

*Nocturne: Thirteen Ghost Stories* by Michael M. Pendragon (Malleus Maleficarium Press) is a collection of traditional ghost stories by the editor of *Penny Dreadful*. Five of the stories are original to the collection.

*Desecration Day* is a two-story collection by Paul Finch (Dream Zone) with an additional story by Simon Logan.

From Scorpius Digital: *Fine Cuts* by Dennis Etchison, *Vermifuge and Other Toxic Cocktails* by Lorelei Shannon, nine original stories, and *Hemoglobins* by Alan M. Clark, three original stories in ebook format.

From Electric Story: Suzy McKee Charnas's *The Music of the Night* and two collections by Lisa Tuttle, *Ghosts and Other Lovers* with thirteen stories and *My Pathology* with sixteen stories, both in ebook format.

*Halloween Candy* by Thomas M. Sipos (1st Books Library) is a miscellany of stories, essays, and a screenplay.

## Mixed-Genre Collections

In six short years, the talented Kelly Link has established herself as one of the major short story writers of her generation with her dreamlike prose and touches of surrealism. Her first collection, *Stranger Things Happen* (Small Beer Press) showcases most of her output to date, including the World Fantasy Award–winning "The Specialist's Hat" and the James Tiptree Jr. Award–winner, "Travels with the Snow Queen." Also included among the eleven fantasy and horror stories are two published for the first time. Also, from Small Beer Press comes *Meet Me in the Moon Room*, the first collection by the very strange writer Ray Vukcevich. Surreal, playful, funny, and occasionally creepy, these thirty-three very short stories, six original to the collection, are all over the place and very enjoyable. The gorgeous cover art is by Rafal Olbinski; *Wondrous Strange* by Robin Spriggs (Circle Myth) contains twenty-five sf/f/h stories and vignettes, more than half original to the collection; *Stalking Midnight* by Paul Collins (with several collaborations uncredited in the body of the book (but mentioned in the "publishing history" on the final page) (Wildside Press/Cosmos Books) contains mostly sf but includes a few notable horror stories; *Night Moves and Other Stories* by Tim Powers (Subterranean Press) is a slender collection of six stories, representing all the author's short fiction. The book includes an introduction by James P. Blaylock, who coauthored two of the stories, story notes by the author and a bibliography. It is available in two editions. Jacket art is by Phil Parks; *Jubilee* by Jack Dann (HarperCollins, Australia) provides an overview of Dann's short fiction 1978–2001 with a fine mixture of science fiction, fantasy, and horror; *Masque of Dreams: Tales of Illusion and Identity* by Bruce Boston (Wildside Press) is a collection that ranges over thirty years and contains twenty-one stories and fifteen poems. It has one original story in it; Brian A. Hopkins had two collections out in 2001, with no overlap in stories: *Salt Water Tears* (Dark Regions Press) with ten stories published between 1995 and 2001, including his Stoker Award–winning "Five Days in April" and one story original to the collection. Gary A. Braunbeck provides the introduction. And *These I Know by Heart* (Vox 13 Publishing) collects seventeen stories, one original. The introduction is by Yvonne Navarro. The volume has beautiful cover art by Matt Harpold and is designed by Judi Rohrig; Nalo Hopkinson's impressive debut collection, *Skin Folk* (Warner Aspect) is an entertaining mix of science fiction, fantasy, and horror—Hopkinson often uses Caribbean folktale, dialect, and sensibility to excellent effect. *Flaming Arrows* by Bruce Holland Rogers (IFD Publishing, 2000) collects the author's short-shorts from a variety of magazines and anthologies and concludes with an afterword by the author about the writing of the short-short. The book is illustrated by Jill Bauman and Alan M. Clark, and is introduced by Kate Wilhelm (available in hardcover and trade paperback). There are two stories in it published for the first time. *Bad Timing* by Molly Brown (Big Engine, U.K.) contains twenty-one stories, most from *Interzone* and some of them horror, including "The Psychomantium," which appeared several years ago in an earlier edition of *YBFH*. One story is original to the collection. *Transfigured Night and Other Stories* by Richard Bowes (iPublish) is the first short collection of this talented writer of science fiction and dark fantasy. The novella "Streetcar Dreams" won the World Fantasy Award and became the basis of the Lambda

Award–winning novel, *Minions of the Moon*. The book also includes an original novella. *Winter Shadows and Other Tales* by Mary Soon Lee (Dark Regions Press) is a good introduction to the author's work. Several of the twenty stories of science fiction, fantasy, and horror appear in this debut collection for the first time. *Strange Mistresses: Tales of Wonder and Romance* by James Dorr (Dark Regions) is a fine collection of this fantasist's poetry and prose. Two stories and a poem original to the collection are excellent dark fantasies; *Idiopathic Condition Red* by Paul Pinn (Time Bomb Publishing), the second self-published collection by the author, contains fifteen stories in various genres, one published for the first time. Two are collaborations. The good-looking cover art of this trade paperback was designed by the author but there are no running heads in the book, making it difficult to flip through and find a story; *Strange Days: Fabulous Journeys with Gardner Dozois* (NESFA Press) is a lovely tribute to Dozois on the occasion of his being Editor Guest of Honor at the 2001 World SF Convention in Philadelphia, his hometown. Although today better known as an editor, when Dozois was at the top of his writing form he was one of the best short story writers in the field. The book contains twenty-three stories (many of them dark) with introductions by his fellow writers; and also some of Dozois's trip reports; *Other Voices, Other Doors* by Patrick O'Leary (Fairwood Press) collects eight stories, nine essays, and twenty-eight poems. This volume contains a foreword by Gene Wolfe; *Supertoys Last All Summer Long and Other Stories of Future Time* by Brian Aldiss (Little, Brown/Orbit, U.K.) collects fifteen stories, the title story having been the inspiration for Steven Spielberg's movie *AI*. The foreword describes Aldiss's involvement in the moviemaking process with Stanley Kubrick and Spielberg; Harlan Ellison has a new collection of older stories out called *Troublemakers* aimed at the YA market (ibooks). It includes a new foreword and story notes by Ellison; *Journeys into Limbo* by Chananya Weissman (InfinityPublishing.com) has fifteen mixed-genre stories, most original; *Ghosts, Spirits, Computers and World Machines* by Gene O'Neill (Prime) is a brief (eight stories) but excellent introduction to this writer's work in various genres. It contains an introduction by Kim Stanley Robinson and an afterword by Scott Edelman, and sports a great cover with art by Geoff Priest, designed by Garry Nurrish; *Love in Vain* by Lewis Shiner (Subterranean Press), the long-overdue first collection of an author who writes sf/f/h and mainstream fiction, is a beautiful book with a stunning dust jacket. My only caveat is that there is no introductory material by the author, to place the stories in context; the prolific Joyce Carol Oates had a new collection out from HarperCollins called *Faithless: Tales of Transgression*, with twenty-one intensely dark stories of love in all its obsessiveness that only she could have written; *The Other Nineteenth Century* by Avram Davidson (Tor), edited by Grania Davis and Henry Wessells, brings back into print twenty-three stories of one of the twentieth century's great fantasists; *Dossier* by Stepan Chapman (Creative Arts) contains seventeen of the author's quirky stories, most reprinted from a Ministry of Whimsy chapbook or from various small genre and literary magazines; M. Shayne Bell's first collection *How We Play the Game in Salt Lake and Other Stories* (iPublish) consists of sixteen stories spanning the last twelve years of his career; although most of the stories are science fiction, there are a couple of horror stories snuck in; *Dreams, Demons and Desire* (Peter Owen, U.K.) is British author Wendy Perriam's first collection and it's a doozy. She writes with wit and viciousness about obsession, anger, and various kinds of nuttiness.

## Poetry Chapbooks, Collections, and Magazines

*White Space* by Bruce Boston (Dark Regions Press) is a mixed-genre collection by one of the fantastic fiction field's most lauded poets. Ten of the thirty-eight poems are original to the collection. The cover illustration is by Larry Whitney.

*Consumed, Reduced to Beautiful Grey Ashes* by Linda D. Addison (Space and Time) is an excellent mixed-genre poetry collection with some poems appearing for the first time. The cover art is by Colleen Crary and the interior illustrations are by Marge Simon. The book includes an introduction by Charlee Jacob.

*The Worms Remember* by Ann K. Schwader (Hive Press) has cover art by publisher Ken Withrow and an introduction by Robert M. Price. The 118 pages of poetry are mostly Lovecraft-influenced. Sixteen are original to the collection.

*Ancient Tales, Grand Deaths & Past Lives* by Colleen Anderson (Kelp Queen Press) includes twenty sf, fantasy, and dark fantasy poems, a few published for the first time. Cover art by Kristy-ly Green. From the same publisher comes *Cities of Light and Darkness*, five mostly mainstream poems by David Niall Wilson, in attractively presented sheets that can be framed, all originally published in *Chiaroscuro*. The cover art is by Lisa Snellings and interior images are by Helen Waters.

*The Ancient Track: The Complete Poetical Works of H.P. Lovecraft* (Night Shade Books) is edited with extensive notes and an introduction by S. T. Joshi. It collects all of Lovecraft's known poetry—over 350 poems and fragments, and a play. It's illustrated by Thomas N. Brown, Jason Eckhardt, Allen Koszowski, Robert H. Knox, and Joey Zone. The volume is available in hardcover and paperback editions.

*Rough Beasts*, edited by Sandra Kasturi (Lone Wolf Publications) features fifteen poems by poets including Linda Addison, Melanie Tem, Charlee Jacob, Steve Rasnic Tem, and others. Its form is a limited-edition CD-ROM with art by Nelly Chichlakova.

Perihelion Broadside Series, Miniature Sun Press published by artist Brandon Totman, brought out three volumes and each is a gem. *Skin* by Charlee Jacob, *Hallucinating Jenny* by G. Sutton Breiding, and *The Lesions of the Genetic Sun* by Bruce Boston. All three items are designed by and decorated with the collage art of Totman. Editions are limited to 200 copies, 125 signed and numbered by the author. Consider buying them as gifts for the poetry lovers in your life. Jacob's "Skin" is reprinted herein.

The press also publishes the Aphelion Signed Limited Edition Book Series. Bruce Boston's long poem, *Pavane for a Cyber-Princess* is the first in the series. *Quanta*, Boston's collection of twelve award-winning poems is the second. In addition to the poems, *Quanta* provides a bibliography, extensive notes on the poems themselves, an essay on "The Making of a Speculative Poet," and an introduction by Andrew Joran. The third volume in the series is *Taunting the Minotaur* by Charlee Jacob, a limited edition of seventeen mostly dark poems, several original to the book. Cover collages are by Totman.

A *Dark Ride* by Corrine de Winter (Black Arrow Press) has over thirty short poems, some of them published for the first time in 2001.

*Songs of Sesqua Valley* by W. H. Pugmire (imelod Publications) has forty-three Lovecraftian poems illustrated by Marc A. Damicis and Peter A. Worthy. Two were previously published. There's an introduction by Worthy.

Flesh & Blood Press, edited by Jack Fisher, brought out *What the Cacodaemon Whispered* by Chad Hensley, with thirteen poems and cover and interior art by H. E. Fassl. The attractive book design is by David G. Barnett. One poem was published in 2001. Also *Deadly Nightshade* by Jacie Ragan collects thirteen of her poems. The cover art is by Keith Minnion.

*Mythic Delirium* edited by Mike Allen is a better than average poetry magazine. $10.00 for one year (two issues) payable to DNA Publications, P.O. Box 2988, Radford, VA 24143-2988.

*Dreams and Nightmares* edited by David C. Kopaska-Merkel is possibly the longest regularly published poetry magazine specializing in horror and the fantastic. A subscription is $12.00 for six issues payable to David C. Kopaska-Merkel, 1300 Kicker Road, Tuscaloosa, AL 35404.

*Frisson: Disconcerting Verse* edited by Scott H. Urban is another long-running poetry magazine. It's available by the single issue for $2.50 or $10.00 per year payable to Skull Job Productions, 1012 Pleasant Dale Drive, Wilmington, NC 28412-7617.

*The Magazine of Speculative Poetry* edited by Roger Dutcher is available by the single issue for $5.00 or by a four-issue subscription for $19.00 payable to MSP, P.O. Box 564. Beloit, WI 53512.

*The 2001 Rhysling Anthology* edited by David C. Kopaska-Merkel (Science Fiction Poetry Association) serves as the ballot for the Rhysling Awards for best science fiction, fantasy, or horror poetry of the year. It contains thirty-five poems.

*Star*line* edited by David C. Kopaska-Merkel is the journal of the Science Fiction Poetry Association and is one of the benefits of membership in the organization. In addition to publishing poetry, the journal also has market reports and small-press reviews. Membership is $15.00 a year in the United States, $18.00 for Canada or Mexico, $21.00 other places. Check out the Web site for more information: http://www.dm.net/~bejay/sfpa.htm

## Anthologies

2001 was a disappointing year for original horror anthologies. The few published were mostly of uneven quality from small-press publishers with limited distribution.

*The Museum of Horror*, edited by Dennis Etchison (Leisure Books) is an all-original anthology of horror stories presented under the aegis of The Horror Writers Association, and it's one of its best efforts, although the loose theme might have better served the contents by having been dispensed with altogether. There are some very good stories in the book, particularly S. P. Somtow's "The Bird Catcher," reprinted herein.

*The Mammoth Book of Vampires Stories by Women*, edited by Stephen Jones (Robinson, U.K./Carroll & Graf) is a mixture of original and reprint stories ranging from classics by Edith Nesbit and Elizabeth Braddon and more recent reprints by Chelsea Quinn Yarbro, Pat Cadigan, and Elizabeth Hand to fourteen original stories including works by Melanie Tem, Roberta Lannes, and Caitlín Kiernan. One, by newcomer Gala Blau, is reprinted herein.

*Haunted Houses and Family Ghosts of Kentucky* by William Lynwood Montell (The University Press of Kentucky) collects chilling folk tales representing experiences from around the state; *Real-Life X-Files: Investigating the Paranormal* by Joe Nickell (The University Press of Kentucky) investigates supernatural mysteries of all kinds from reports of alien abduction to the Shroud of Turin.

*Best of Horrorfind*, edited by Brian Keene, is a selection of eighteen stories that were originally published on the horrorfind.com Web site. The first edition of this attractive trade paperback is numbered, and limited to five hundred copies. Murder, mayhem, and insults to bodily integrity are the rule. Some of the contributors are John Pelan, Tom Piccirilli, Mark McLaughlin, Gerard Houarner, Michael Oliveri, Geoff Cooper, and Gene O'Neill.

*The Rare Anthology*, compiled by Brian Knight (Disc-Us Books), has sixteen original horror stories by newer writers.

A *Darker Dawning* (Dark Dawn Industries) is a minianthology of seven original stories (some ultraviolent) by newer writers best known so far in the horror small press. Cover art by GAK.

*Wild Things Live Here*, edited by Don Hutchison (Mosaic Press), is an excellent anthology featuring sixteen of the best stories culled from his multivolume original anthology series, *Northern Frights*. A number of them have appeared in earlier volumes of *YBFH*.

*4x4* by Michael Oliveri, Geoff Cooper, Brian Keene, and Michael T. Huyck, Jr. (Delirium Books) includes all-original collaborative and solo stories by these up-and-coming writers, showing them at their best. Introduction by Ray Garton with artwork by GAK. Available in hardcover and trade paperback.

*Triage*, edited by Matt Johnson (Cemetery Dance Publications), contains novellas by Richard Laymon, Edward Lee, and Jack Ketchum—all taking off from the same premise: a mysterious stranger walks into a place of business and opens fire. The Laymon is fast-moving, sexually and violently graphic, the Lee is a space opera with splashy mayhem and a horrific overtone, and the Ketchum is a darkly humorous story of a few days in the life of a would-be writer having a really bad time of it. Dust jacket art and design are by Gail Cross. Available in two signed hardcover states, one numbered and one a deluxe-lettered edition.

*Poddities*, edited by Suzanne Donahue (Day Off Publications), is an unexpected treat: a tribute to Jack Finney's novel *The Body Snatchers* that features five original stories and eleven short pieces of commentary about the novel and the three film versions it inspired.

*Brainbox II: Son of Brainbox*, edited by Steve Eller (irrational press) is a good original anthology of seventeen stories, most of them horror, with a few fantasy stories thrown into the mix. Each story is accompanied by the author's personal essay about how it came to be written. It sports great cover art by Shannon Hourigan.

*Blood & Donuts*, edited by Tina L. Jens (Twilight Tales and 11th Hour Productions), is a batch of eighteen entertaining stories, mostly original, about private eyes and cops. From the Twilight Tales Presents series.

*Bubbas of the Apocalypse*, edited by Selina Rosen (Yard Dog Press), is about zombies and rednecks hit by a plague in 2025. The nineteen stories and poems could all have been written by the same hand, judging from the similarity of voice. Let's just say the anthology is in the tradition of, "hey, why don't we put on a show in this ole barn and invite some of our friends?"

*Acolytes of Cthulhu*, edited by Robert M. Price (Fedogan & Bremer), is a reprint anthology of twenty-eight Lovecraftian stories, one in a new translation, taken from the 1930s–1990s. Dust jacket art by Gahan Wilson. Included are stories by Joseph Payne Brennan, Edmond Hamilton, Jorge Luis Borges, S. T. Joshi, and Neil Gaiman.

*Song of Cthulhu: Tales of the Sphere Beyond*, edited by Mark Stephen Rainey (Chaosium), has nineteen mythos tales, mostly original, by some good writers including Fred Chappell, Caitlín Kiernan, and Thomas F. Monteleone.

*Extremes 2: Fantasy and Horror from the Ends of the Earth*, edited by Brian A. Hopkins (Lone Wolf Publications), is a beautifully produced CD-ROM created to be read in Adobe Acrobat format, allowing for a great variety in presentation: there are videos of Hopkins and of the artist, Margaret Baliff Simon, biographies of each author, and the occasional audio presentation. Illustrated throughout. The CD includes twenty stories and poems. In addition, two songs by Scott Nicholson, a musician as well as writer, are included. The idea is for the stories to explore different geographical areas of the world.

*Extremes 3: Terror on the High Seas*, also edited by Hopkins (Lone Wolf), has a title that's self-explanatory and twenty horror stories. Again, this is a nicely produced audio-visual-textual package. The art is by Thomas Arensberg.

*Bloodtype*, edited by Michael Laimo (Lone Wolf), is a very good non-theme anthology of fifteen stories—some pretty extreme. What the stories lack in subtlety they make up for with the high quality of the writing. Some of the better known writers are P. D. Cacek, Gerard Houarner, and Edo Van Belkom. Another nicely produced multimedia CD-ROM.

*Trick or Treat: A Collection of Halloween Novellas*, edited by Richard Chizmar (Cemetery Dance Publications), contains five novellas by Gary A. Braunbeck, Nancy A. Collins, Rick Hautala, Al Sarrantonio, and Thomas Tessier. Available in three states. Dust jacket art by Alan M. Clark.

*The Bible of Hell*, edited by Michael M. Pendragon (Pendragonian Publications), has no copyright page, unclear credits, and minimal cover design, but despite these lapses the poetry and prose within, modeled loosely on the selfsame lost or nonexistent text by William Blake, is surprisingly well written and entertaining. The editor has created twenty-one sections or books from *The First Fall* through *The Apocalypse*, and the contents range from excerpts of *Moby Dick* and poetry by Shelley, Poe, Milton, and Blake himself to contemporary writers such as Charlee Jacob, James Dorr, Ann K. Schwader, and Scott Urban. The interior illustrations by Gerald Gaubert are very good.

*The Dead Inn*, edited by Shane Ryan Staley (Delirium Books), contains twenty-five stories, mostly original, in a hardcover with jacket art by Jamie Oberschlake and book jacket design by Colleen Crary. I can't discern a theme although the introduction implies that the stories all take place in the haunted establishment named the Dead Inn (they don't).

*Urban Gothic*, edited by David J. Howe (Telos), is a trade-paperback anthology of six stories taking place in the dark, horrific London created by Tom de Ville as a television series. Half of the stories are based on scripts written by de Ville and half are original stories by Christopher Fowler, Simon Clark, and Graham Masterton. Also included are a note by de Ville about the world he created, and a couple of behind-the-scenes articles. Very effective, even without having seen the series (which I haven't). Also available in a hundred-copy hardcover edition.

*Single White Vampire Seeks Same*, edited by Martin H. Greenberg and Brittiany A. Koren (DAW), is an amusing assortment of mostly lightweight vampire stories with a bit of horror.

*The Night the Lights Went Out in Arkham*, edited by Cullen Bunn, (Undaunted Press), is a short anthology of five original Lovecraftian stories set in the 1970s. Cute but not very scary.

*Scars*, edited by Gina Osnovich (Fall Reaching Productions), was quickly put together by members of the New York chapter of the Horror Writers Association. All proceeds go to the American Red Cross, earmarked for victims of the World Trade Center attack. The nine pieces of fiction (most original) by writers such as Jack Ketchum, Linda Addison, and Gerard Houarner are interspersed with essays about experiences on September 11, 2001. Cover artwork is by Marco DiLeonardo and Joseph Milazzo. Information on purchasing this worthy effort can be found at the Web site of the NY Chapter of the HWA: www.horror.org/nyc.

*Bending the Landscape: Horror*, edited by Nicola Griffith and Stephen Pagel (Overlook Connection Press), is the third and last volume in this series featuring gay and lesbian stories. Although billed as horror, some of the stories are not. Those that are, however, are pretty good, particularly Mark Tiedemann's powerful and disturbing entry.

*The Ash-Tree Press Annual Macabre 2001*, edited by Jack Adrian, collects thirteen stories from weekly or monthly fiction magazines popular between the 1920s and 1939. All but one were never before published in book form. Cover illustration is by Rob Suggs.

*Darkness Rising, Volume One: Night's Soft Pains*, edited by L. H. Maynard & M.P.N. Sims (Cosmos Books/Wildside Press), is an original anthology, but I have no idea if it has a theme or not. The subtitle seems to indicate that it does but the brief introduction by Hugh Lamb does nothing to illuminate the contents. The stories are readable, but only a couple stand out.

*Darkness Rising Volume Two: Hideous Dreams*, second in the same series, has a higher percentage of notable stories.

*The Gauntlet Press Sampler* is a twenty-four-page chapbook of four interesting short stories by Richard Matheson, Rain Graves, Richard Christian Matheson, and Barry Hoffman, and a brief poem by Clive Barker. The illustrations are by Harry O. Morris and photography is by David Armstrong.

*The Midnighters Club: Tales from the Harker House Collection*, edited by Ron Horsley (InfinityPublishing.com) is a selection of original tales by newer writers in the genre.

*Masters of Terror 2001*—Anthology is a web anthology edited by Andy Fairclough, publisher of the Masters of Terror Web site. http://www.horrorworld.cjb.net.

*The Book of All Flesh*, edited by James Lowder (Eden Studios) is an outgrowth of a role-playing game called *All Flesh Must Be Eaten*. What more can one say? If you're into flesh-eating zombie stories, this anthology's for you. It's better than it might have been, with some tasty treats that go beyond the eat, eat, and be merry of the zombie set.

*Night Visions 10*, edited by Richard Chizmar (Subterranean Press), is a continuation of the well-regarded Dark Harvest series. Three writers are showcased, presenting original fiction: the new volume contains novellas by Jack Ketchum and John Shirley and five stories by David B. Silva. The surreal jacket art is by Alan M. Clark.

*The Ultimate Halloween* edited by Marvin Kaye (ibooks) is a combination of original stories and reprints about the holiday that most celebrates the macabre.

*Isaac Asimov's Halloween*, edited by Gardner Dozois and Sheila Williams (Ace), reprints stories originally published in *Asimov's Science Fiction Magazine*.

*The Treasury of the Fantastic: Romanticism to Early Twentieth Century Literature*, edited by David Sandner and Jacob Weisman (Frog, Ltd. and Tachyon Publications) is a hefty tome of almost 750 pages. Many of the stories and poems will be well-known to readers and others, as Lucy Lane Clifford's "The New Mother" should be. More than half the stories are in the darker range of fantasy and so should be of interest to readers of horror. Peter S. Beagle has provided a short foreword. The only element missing is author biographies, but at $27.50 it's still a good buy.

*Into the Mummy's Tomb*, edited by John Richard Stephens (Berkley), is a reprint anthology of eighteen fiction and nonfiction pieces by Ray Bradbury, Louisa May Alcott, Agatha Christie, Tennessee Williams, Egyptologist Arthur Weigall, Rudyard Kipling, and many others on mummies, their curses, etc.

*Meddling with Ghosts*, selected and introduced by Ramsey Campbell (The British Library), brings together some of the best stories written in the M. R. James tradition, including those by predecessors such as Sheridan Le Fanu and Sabine Baring-Gould, his contemporaries such as T. G. Jackson and Mrs. H. D. Everett, and his successors Fritz Leiber, T.E.D. Klein, Sheila Hodgson, Terry Lamsley, and Ramsey Campbell, among others. Rosemary Pardoe has expanded "The James Gang," a booklet originally published by the Haunted Library in 1991 into an invaluable checklist that should keep aficionados of supernatural fiction busy for quite a while.

*Medieval Ghost Stories*, edited by Andrew Joynes (Boydell & Brewer, U.K.), provides a sampling of tales from the Middle Ages that were written down in some of the earliest printed literature.

*The Mammoth Book of Best New Horror, Volume Twelve*, edited by Stephen Jones (Robinson), overlapped with *YBFH* on four stories. Jones's volume has a necrology and summary of the year.

*Hours of Darkness*, edited by Lorelei Shannon and Marti McKenna, Scorpius's first horror anthology, features reprinted tales of the darkness within and without by a lineup of stars and newcomers such as Ramsey Campbell, Simon Clark, Peter Crowther, Dennis Etchison, Christopher Fowler, Rain Graves, Joe R. Lansdale, Elizabeth Massie, Richard Christian Matheson, Yvonne Navarro, and others.

Other anthologies with some horror: *Redshift*, edited by Al Sarrantonio (Roc), was billed as speculative fiction but had at least three stories that could be considered horror, particularly Elizabeth Hand's marvelous novella "Cleopatra Brimstone" and a Koja-Malzberg collaboration, both reprinted herein; *Strange Pleasures*, edited by Sean Wallace (Cosmos/Wildside), with fourteen stories, all but one original to the book. There are a few stories in it that might be of interest to horror readers, although most are sf or fantasy; *Starlight 3*, edited by Patrick Nielsen Hayden (Tor), has a few dark stories, including one excellent horror story by Susan Palwick, reprinted herein; *The Best American Mystery Stories 2001*, edited by Lawrence Block (Houghton Mifflin), included stories by such diverse writers as Russell Banks, T. Jefferson Parker, and Joyce Carol Oates; *A Century of Great Suspense Stories*, edited by Jeffery Deaver (Berkley Prime Crime) has thirty-six stories by everyone from Mickey Spillane to Stephen King; *The World's Finest Mystery and Crime Stories: Second Annual Collection*, edited by Ed Gorman and Martin H. Greenberg (Forge), takes a number of its stories from *Ellery Queen's Mystery Magazine*, some from *Alfred Hitchcock's Mystery Magazine*, others from various mystery anthologies, a couple from the pages of *Playboy*, one from *The New Yorker*. Surprisingly, *Crime Wave*—to me, the best of the mystery/crime magazines currently being published, is ignored. The Honorable Mentions section is thin, and has at least one story that was first published several years earlier; *Historical Hauntings*, edited by Jean Rabe and Martin H. Greenberg (DAW), is a so-so original anthology with a few strong stories; *Dracula in London*, edited by P. N. Elrod (Ace), is a mostly nonhorrific anthology of hohum Dracula stories, with a few exceptions; *Dead on Demand: The Best of Ghost Story Weekend*, edited by Elizabeth Engstrom (Triple Tree Publishing), contains twenty original stories of mostly fantasy and dark fantasy produced during an annual weekend on the coast of Oregon; *Nor of Human: An Anthology of Fantastic Creatures*, edited by Geoffrey Maloney (CSFG Publishing, Australia), representing the Canberra Speculative Fiction Society, has a few darker stories in it; *The Clockwork Reader*, Volume 1 (Clockwork Storybook) showcases stories and excerpts from forthcoming novels of the four founders of an sf/f/h Web site. Nancy Kilpatrick edited an ambitious and beautiful multimedia CD-ROM to accompany Montreal's 2001 World Fantasy Convention Program Book. The CD-ROM features themes of all twenty-seven World Fantasy conventions and contains fiction, poetry, articles, a video, music by Lia Pas, and an art gallery all focusing on Canadian writers, artists, and cultural institutions. This is a marvelous overview of the Canadian fantastic; *Villains Victorious*, edited by Martin H. Greenberg and John Helfers (DAW) is self-explanatory—a couple of the stories are very dark; *The Ant-Men of Tibet, and Other Stories*, edited by David Pringle (Big Engine, U.K.), is an anthology of ten stories from *Interzone* magazine.

## Artists

The artists who work in the small press toil hard and receive too little credit all too often (and even less money). I feel it's important to recognize their good work. The following artists created art that I thought was noteworthy during 2001: Ciruelo Cabral, Poppy Alexander, Jon Foster, Tony Di Terlizzi, Stephen Johnson, Bernie Mireault, Allen Koszowski, Jason Van Hollander, Chuck Demorat, John Picacio, Dominic E. Harman, Ian Brooke, Deirdre Counihan, Paul

Lowe, Menglef, Mike Bohatch, Chris Nurse, Steve Bidmid, Rob Middleton, Roddy Williams, Dallas Goffin, Louis de Niverville, Douglas Walters, Frank Wu, Andrew Wiernicki, Bob Hobbs, Keith Boulger, Nigel Potter, Cathy Buburuz, Shikhar Dixit, Deborah McMillion-Nering, Darren Floyd, Robert Pasternak, Peter Loader, Donna Johansen, Russell Morgan, Jeffrey Thomas, June Levine, Kenneth B. Haas III, Rhil Renne, H. E. Fassl, Eric M. Turnmire, Catriona Sparks, Trudi Canavan, Michael Georges, Russell Dickerson, Mitch Phillips, Gerald Gaubert, M. Parker, Sophia Kelly-Schultz, Augie Wiedemann, Terry Campbell, Marshall Browne, Brian Jordan, Bob Covington, Jason Eckhardt, Robert H. Knox, Dee Rimbaud, Lara Bandillo, Sarah Zama, and Steve Lines.

## Magazines and Newsletters

Small-press magazines come and go with amazing rapidity, so it's difficult to recommend buying a subscription to those that haven't proven their longevity. But I urge readers to at least buy single issues of those that sound interesting. Unfortunately, there isn't room to mention every magazine publishing horror. The following handful are those that I thought were the best in 2001.

Some of the most important magazines/webzines are those that specialize in news of the field, market reports, and reviews. With *Necrofile* and *Darkecho* gone the field is left with *Hellnotes*, *Jobs in Hell*, and two major zines that specialize in reviewing short stories: *Tangent Online* and *The Fix*. *Locus* and *Science Fiction Chronicle* also cover horror but not as extensively.

*Hellnotes* is a weekly newsletter edited by David B. Silva with Paul Olsen. It regularly opens with a thoughtful, lengthy editorial about the nature of horror and the horror field and provides news in literature and film, short horror reviews by various people, and market reports. *Hellnotes* is subscription-based and is published fifty-two times a year by Phantasm Press. E-mail subscriptions are available for $21 per year ($40.00 for two years), and $55.00 a year for a hardcopy subscription ($105.00 for two years). To subscribe by credit card, go to: http://www.hellnotes.com/subscrib.htm. To subscribe by mail, send a check or money order (made out to David B. Silva) to: Hellnotes, 27780 Donkey Mine Road, Oak Run, CA 96069.

*Jobs in Hell*, edited by Brian Keene (recently sold to Kelly Laymon) is a newsletter and market report with attitude. Keene is irreverent, bitchy, and passionate. He regularly runs opinionated commentary written by himself or other horror writers and often publishes letters in reaction to the commentary. A one-year/fifty-two-issue subscription to *JIH* is $20. Payments should be made to Brian Keene, *not Jobs in Hell*, and mailed to Brian Keene, 10A Ginger View Court, Cockeysville, MD 21030. Include your e-mail address. To order a subscription from the web site using a credit card, bank debit card, or personal check, go to http://home.earthlink.net/~jihadpubs/.

*The Fix* edited by Andy Cox is a new nonfiction magazine specializing in short fiction. It evolved from his *Zene* and the first two issues are quite impressive. They possess the same high production values of Cox's other magazines, *The Third Alternative* and *Crimewave*, with powerful black-and-white cover art by Mike Bohatch. In addition to reviews, the magazine has a feature called "The

Story of My Life" in which "short story junkies reflect on their favorite or most inspiring story, collection, or anthology," plus interviews with editors, publishers, and writers influential in the world of short stories. The first issue had an interview with Gordon Van Gelder, publisher/editor of the *Magazine of Fantasy & Science Fiction*. The second has one with me. Cox hopes to be bimonthly in 2002. You can buy a single issue for $7.00 or a subscription for $33.00 (six issues) or $66.00 (twelve issues) payable to TTA Press, 5 Martins Lane, Witcham, Ely, Cambs CB6 2LB, UK or TTA Press, P.O. Box 219, Olyphant, PA 18447, U.S.A. Subscriptions can also be purchased by credit card on-line at: http://www.ttapress.com/.

*Tangent Online* edited by Dave Truesdale is on the web and regularly reviews all the short fiction from professional magazines and webzines plus fiction in anthologies and collections. New reviews come out several times a week. Only $5.00 for a year's subscription through the Web site at: http://www.tangent online.com/.

*The Fix* and *Tangent Online* are currently the only magazines or webzines that exclusively cover short fiction. Although they both specialize in science fiction and fantasy more than horror, they *do* cover some sources of horror.

Although it wasn't available in print for much of 2001, Kathryn Ptacek's *Gila Queen's Guide to Markets* is providing e-mail updates. For more information, contact her at: GilaQueen@worldnet.att.net.

*Scavenger's Newsletter*, edited by Janet Fox covers small-press markets on a monthly basis. $12 for a six-issue subscription in the US, $11.50 Canada, $14.50 overseas airmail payable to *Scavenger's Newsletter*, 833 Main, Osage City, KS 66523-1241. This always useful, long-running market newsletter unfortunately ceases publication January 2003.

*Video Watchdog®*, edited by Tim and Donna Lucas, is the best magazine for up-to-date information on various cuts and variants of all kinds of movies, available on video. This digest-sized monthly is always entertaining with its coverage of fantastic video and is a must for anyone interested in quirky reviews and columns. Highlights in 2001 were features on the bootleg work print of Timothy Dalton's 007 debut, *The Living Daylights*, and on the restoration of Willis O'Brien's *The Lost World*, an article on the Beach Blanket movie series, and coverage over two issues of Universal's *Alfred Hitchcock Collection*. $48 for twelve issues (bulk mail), $70 (first class) payable to *Video Watchdog*, PO 5283, Cincinnati, OH 45205-0283.

*Fangoria*, edited by Anthony Timpone, covers all the big Hollywood horror films and the occasional movie from another culture or independent. There was a look at Japanese horror and anime movies and an issue highlighting Italian splatter films. On the downside, *Fango* doesn't go out of its way to cover smaller, more interesting horror fare. Does the reader really need three features on *Jurassic Park III*, three on *Ghosts of Mars*, and two each on *Tremors 3* and *Bone* in six months? On the positive side, the magazine ran a profile of writer Kim Newman and a survey by Douglas E. Winter of classic Italian splatter flicks. Also, the monthly video and book columns are well worth reading.

*Gauntlet: Exploring the Limits of Free Expression* is a semiannual, published in May and November and edited by Barry Hoffman. $16 a year, payable to *Gauntlet*. Both issues covered independent films and the second issue had an interview with John Landis by Mick Garris. There's also a fiction reprint by Garris.

*Crime Time*, edited by Barry Forshaw, is an excellent British quarterly in trade paperback format. *CT* provides fine coverage of the field and is chock-full of articles, columns, book and film reviews, interviews, and brief novel excerpts. £30 sterling for four issues payable to Crime Time Subscriptions, 18 Coleswood Road, Harpenden, Herts. AL5 1EQ, England.

*Lovecraft Studies* and *Studies in Weird Fiction* are both edited by S. T. Joshi. *Lovecraft Studies* is published twice a year and has for twenty years been devoted to the scholarly study of H. P. Lovecraft and his works. The journal includes articles analyzing individual stories, overall themes, reviews, etc. It's a rich source of information for aficionados of Lovecraft. *Studies in Weird Fiction* is "designed to promote criticism of fantasy, horror and supernatural fiction subsequent to Poe." The 42–43 double issue of *Lovecraft Studies* is $12.00 and a single issue of *Studies in Weird Fiction* is $6.00 payable to Hippocampus Press.

*Crypt of Cthulhu*, edited by Robert M. Price, is the perfect fictional complement to the two journals above. The most recent issue is #104 and it can be ordered for $6.00 from Mythos Books.

*Horror Garage* #3 disappointed in the fiction department in 2001 but had an interview with China Miéville and an excerpt from his Arthur C. Clarke Award–winning novel *Perdido Street Station*.

*Penny Dreadful*, edited by Michael Malefica Pendragon, brought out one big 217-page double issue in 2001. Its specialty is dark fantasy, and the poetry that makes up the bulk of the issue is generally better than the tales, most of which are not meaty enough to create much of an impact. Pendragon also published *Songs of Innocence*, specializing in lighter fantasy. Each is $10.00 payable to Pendragonian Publications, P.O. Box 719, Radio City Station, New York, NY 10101-0719.

*Dark Regions*, edited by Joe Morey, is published twice a year. The two issues that came during 2001 were pretty good, with some notable darker stories and poetry in each. Single-issue price is $4.95 plus $1.25 postage. A two-issue subscription is $8.00 payable to Dark Regions Press.

*Bare Bone* #1, edited by Kevin L. Donihe, made an auspicious if later-than-promised debut. Announced as a triannual, the first issue was very very late. If you want to check it out I'd buy a single issue for $5.25 payable to Kevin L. Donihe, 1742 Madison Street, Kingsport, TN 37665.

*Flesh & Blood*, edited by Jack Fisher, has fiction, poetry, and the occasional interview. There were two issues in 2001 and they each had some excellent horror poetry. Single copy is $4.00. A three-issue subscription is $11.00 payable to Jack Fisher, 121 Joseph Street, Bayville, NJ 08721.

*Dark Horizons*, edited by Debbie Bennett, is the biennial fiction magazine that comes free with membership in The British Fantasy Society. It's usually quite good and recommended to readers interested in traditional supernatural fiction. The British Fantasy Society is open to everyone. Members receive the informative bimonthly newsletter, *Prism*, in addition to *Dark Horizons*. The society organizes Fantasycon, the annual British Fantasy Convention, and its membership votes on the British Fantasy Awards. Subscription rates are: £20 UK, £25 Europe, £40 U.S.A. and elsewhere. Payable only in pounds sterling or by credit card on-line. For information write The British Fantasy Society, the BFS Secretary, 201 Reddish Road, Stockport SK5 7HR, England. www.britishfantasy society.com.

*Cemetery Dance*, edited by Richard Chizmar, published three issues in 2001, and all had some outstanding fiction. There were also interviews with Peter Straub, Simon Clark, Bentley Little, and Douglas Clegg and columns by Poppy Z. Brite, John Pelan, and others, including the return of Thomas F. Monteleone's usually provocative "The Mothers and Fathers Italian Association." One-year subscription (six issues) $22 payable to Cemetery Dance Publications. Be aware that in the past several years, the magazine, meant to be bimonthly, has been intermittent in publication, although Chizmar is trying to return it to a more regular schedule.

*The Third Alternative*, edited by Andy Cox, is a quarterly with a cross-genre mix. Of all the magazines that I regularly read *TTA* provides the most consistently literate, challenging and entertaining fiction, even though it's rare that the magazine publishes anything resembling a traditional piece of horror fiction. A single issue is $7.00, and a six-issue subscription is $33.00 payable to *TTA* Press, PO Box 219, Olyphant, PA 18447.

*Crimewave 5: Dark Before Dawn*, edited by Andy Cox, is another excellent issue of this well-designed magazine of crime fiction. Slick covers and clean interior design makes this the best-looking genre magazine around. In this issue the striking cover photograph by Larrie Thomson is carried through as the interior illustration for each story and it works. More important, there are some very good stories by writers such as Sean Doolittle, Brady Allen, and Christopher Fowler, the latter of which is reprinted herein. A single issue is $12.00 and a four-issue subscription is $40.00 payable to *TTA* Press.

*Roadworks: Tales from the Hard Road*, edited by Trevor Denyer, is a biennial magazine from England. There were at least ten notable horror stories, making this a magazine to watch and support. Single copies are $8.00 and four issues are $30.00 payable to T. Denyer, 7 Mountview, Church Lane West, Aldershot, Hampshire, GU11 3LN, England.

*The Spook* (http://www.thespook.com), edited by Anthony Sapienza (with Paula Guran consulting), has been showcasing some of the most recognizable names in horror such as Joyce Carol Oates, Jonathan Carroll, John Shirley, Ramsey Campbell, Poppy Z. Brite, Jack Ketchum, Norman Partridge, and Dennis Etchison, but overall, while consistently good, few stories from its first year stood out as great. This free, downloadable webzine also features articles and book reviews related to horror and suspense. The nonfiction has become progressively less related to the fiction.

*Weird Tales*, edited by George H. Scithers and Darrell Schweitzer, is a quarterly now in its seventy-seventh year. Under DNA's publishing umbrella the magazine has finally kept to its schedule and brought out four (or five if you count the winter 2001–2002) issues in 2001. The magazine's fiction generally provides a who's who in dark fantasy/horror. During the year there was an excellent novella by Tanith Lee and typically strange stories by Thomas Ligotti. S. T. Joshi writes a regular column. The cover art varies in quality and effectiveness. Subscriptions are $16.00 for four issues payable to DNA Publications, Inc., PO Box 2988, Radford, VA 24143-2988.

*Nemonymous*, edited by D. F. Lewis, is an unusual experiment to publish sto-ries without author credit until the subsequent issue. Some of the stories were even submitted anonymously. The first issue is an elegant ninety-six-page perfect-bound magazine with a beautifully spare color cover and sixteen literate stories ranging from the surreal to the deeply disturbing and darkly menacing. A highly recommended debut. A single issue costs $10.00 including postage. Contact Nemonymous@hotmail.com for address.

*Lady Churchill's Rosebud Wristlet*, edited by Gavin J. Grant, is a consistently excellent cross-genre magazine that comes out a few times a year and showcases a variety of short fiction, poetry, and the occasional nonfiction piece. $4.00 for a single issue; $12.00 for four issues payable to Gavin Grant, Small Beer Press.

*Aurealis*, edited by Stephen Higgins and Dirk Strasser for ten years, changes editorial reins in 2002. Although this Australian magazine has traditionally pub-lished more sf than fantasy or horror, there is occasionally a dark fantasy or horror. Only one issue came out in 2001, but it was a hefty one, with 264 pages in a combined #27/28. A four-issue subscription is $38.50 (AU). Single issues for $12.50. P.O. Box 2164, Mt. Waverley, Victoria 3149, Australia www.sf.org.au/aurealis. Unfortunately, *Eidolon*, the other Australian magazine has been on hi-atus during 2001.

*Talebones*, the quarterly edited by Patrick and Honna Swenson, usually has at least a few dark fantasy stories in its eclectic mix. There's also nonfiction by Edward Bryant, lots of mini reviews, and a few in-depth reviews. Peter Straub was interviewed in Issue #21. The art was exceptionally good throughout 2001. Single issues are $5.00. A subscription of four issues is $18.00 payable to Tale-bones, 5203 Quincy Avenue SE, Auburn, WA 98092.

*All Hallows: The Journal of the Ghost Story Society*, edited by Barbara and Christopher Roden, is an attractive perfect-bound magazine published thrice yearly and available only to members of the Ghost Story Society. It is an excellent source of news, articles, and ghostly fiction. But another good reason is the support of an organization dedicated to providing admirers of the classic ghost story with an outlet for their interest. The Ghost Story Society's subscription year runs from 1 April to 31 March, and includes three issues of *All Hallows*, which are published at the end of June, October, and February. The society accepts payment by personal checks in Canadian and U.S. dollars and pounds sterling; by International Money Orders (in Canadian dollars only); and by cash (this sent at sender's risk). Make checks payable to the Ghost Story Society. Membership fees for the 2002-3 subscription year are as follows: United States: U.S. $28.50; Canada: Cdn $35.00; Rest of World (airmail only): £19.00 / U.S.$33.00/ Cdn $45.00 payable to: The Ghost Story Society, P.O. Box 1360, Ashcroft, British Columbia, Canada V0K 1A0. For more information visit the Ash-Tree Press Web site http://www.Ash-Tree.bc.ca/gss.html.

*Ghosts & Scholars*, edited by Rosemary Pardoe, is an excellent biannual mag-azine devoted to continuing the M. R. James tradition of ghost stories. Its com-bination of original and reprinted stories, book reviews, and scholarly articles make it a must for any reader interested in the traditional ghost story. Unfor-tunately, publication ceased with issue #33 at the end of 2001.

Readers can often find excellent short horror fiction in publications that are better known for other kinds of fiction. In 2001 there were excellent horror stories in *The New Yorker*, *Interzone*, *The Magazine of Fantasy & Science Fiction*, *Asimov's Science Fiction* magazine, *Conjunctions*, *Realms of Fantasy*, *On Spec*, *New Genre*, *Ellery Queen's Mystery Magazine*, *Alfred Hitchcock's Mystery Magazine*, and the sf Web sites: *SCI FICTION* (for which I work), *Fantastic Metropolis*, and *Strange Horizons*.

The Internet has been evolving into an important publisher of horror stories and although there's a lot of dreck out there, some of the best Web sites for fiction are:

*Gothic.net*, edited by Darren McKeeman, is run by subscription of $15 a year. http://gothic.net/

*Horrorfind.com*, edited by Brian Keene, ran some very good fiction during the year. http://www.horrorfind.com/

*Frightful Fiction*, edited by Thomas Deja, is a new area of the *Fangoria* web site. http://www.fangoria.com/tpage/frightful_fiction/frightful_index.htm

*Chiaroscuro*, a quarterly edited by Patricia Lee Macomber, with fiction edited by her, Brett A. Savory, and Steve Eller and poetry edited by Sandra Kasturi. It won the Bram Stoker Award in the Other Media category in 2000. http://gothic.net/chiaroscuro/chizine/

## Nonfiction Books

*The Essential Stephen King* by Stephen J. Spignesi (Career Press/New Page Books) is a reference guide ranking King's 101 greatest, novels, stories, movies, and more. It also contains five brief articles about King and an index; *The Cinema of Nightfall: Jacques Tourneur* by Chris Fujiwara (Johns Hopkins University Press). According to Fujiwara, producer Val Lewton is generally given complete credit for the look and feel of Tourneur's movies. Instead, Fujiwara argues persuasively for the auteurship of the director of *I Walked with a Zombie*, *Cat People*, *The Leopard Man*, and other dark films. Fujiwara provides a detailed film-by-film analysis of Tourneur's work. The book includes a foreword by Martin Scorsese; *Dark City Dames: The Wicked Women of Film Noir* by Eddie Muller (Regan/HarperCollins) is a follow-up to his earlier *Dark City: The Lost World of Film Noir* and focuses on the women, played by Marie Windsor, Colleen Gray, Jane Greer, and others. Muller reports on these actors today, interviewing his subjects and providing an analysis of the social, political, and economic pressures of the industry; *The Modern Weird Tale* by S. T. Joshi (McFarland & Company), is the long-awaited sequel to the author's *The Weird Tale* and includes essays on Stephen King, Clive Barker, William Peter Blatty, Shirley Jackson, Ramsey Campbell, Robert Aickman, Anne Rice, Thomas Ligotti, Peter Straub, Thomas Tryon and T.E.D. Klein; *Starlight Man* by Mike Ashley (Constable, U.K.) is the first full-length biography of Algernon Blackwood and contains previously unknown information about Blackwood's life through letters, newspaper reports, and archives; *Creepshows: The Illustrated Stephen King Movie Guide* by Stephen Jones (Titan, U.K.) is an illustrated guide to every Stephen King movie, sequel, or spin-off. Illustrated in color and b&w with rare posters, photographs, and book covers; *The Satanic Screen: An Illustrated History of the Devil in Cinema* by Nikolas Schreck (Creation Books) claims to be the first comprehensive study of the Devil in cinema, covering over a century of film; *Sacred Pain: Hurting the Body for the Sake of the Soul* by Ariel Glucklich (Oxford University Press) explores the religious uses of pain, from the perspective of the practitioner and from the scientific standpoint, ranging over a broad spectrum of cultural and historical contexts; *The Stephen King Universe* by Stanley Wiater and Christopher Golden with Hank Wagner (Cemetery Dance Publications) is a guide to all of King's fiction through *Blood and Smoke*. Available in two limited editions; *Atomic Bomb Cinema: The Apocalyptic Imagination on Film* by Jerome F. Shapiro (Routledge); *The Witchcraft Reader*, edited by Darren Oldridge (Routledge), provides a wide selection of historical writings on the subject; *The Ghastly One: The Sex-Gore Netherworld of Filmmaker Andy Milligan* by Jimmy McDonough (ACapella) is about the creator of such movies as *The Naked Witch* and *Monstrosity*; *An H.P. Lovecraft Encyclopedia* edited by S. T. Joshi and David E. Schultz (Greenwood) has entries for individual stories, an essay-length entry on the Cthulhu mythos, and entries on the author's juvenilia, letters, and travels. It does not include a separate entry on Lovecraft's philosophy as, according to the editors, "the topic is too complex for succinct discussion"; *The Great Fairy Tale Tradition: From Straparola and Basile to the Brothers Grimm*, Selected and Edited by Jack Zipes (A Norton Critical Edition), is based on new scholarship. Zipes challenges conventional wisdom regarding the origins of the Grimm fairy tales, which holds that they collected their tales from the oral traditions of peasants. Instead, according to Zipes, they took most of their tales from literary sources, rewriting them again and again; *The Ingrid Pitt Book of Murder, Torture and Depravity* by Ingrid Pitt (Batsford); *Buried Alive: A Terrifying History of Our Most Primal Fear* by Jan Bondeson (Norton) includes the literary and actual history of the notion of premature burial; *Vampire Legends in Contemporary American Culture* by William Patrick Day (The University Press of Kentucky) examines how vampires stories—from Stoker to *Blacula*—have become part of our ongoing debate about what it means to be human; *Religion and Its Monsters* by Timothy K. Beal (Routledge) is about the monsters such as Leviathan and Behemoth that lurk in religious texts, and how monsters and religion are irrevocably entwined. The author explores the religion lurking in the modern horror genre from Dracula and Frankenstein to the works of H. P. Lovecraft and Clive Barker; *Eaten Alive!: Italian Cannibal and Zombie Movies* by Jay Slater (Plexus Publishing) explains how the myth of the Haitian walking dead merged with the legends of third-world cannibalism to create such zombie cult films as *Cannibal Holocaust* and *Day of the Living Dead*; *The Attempted Rescue* by Robert Aickman (Tartarus Press) is a reprint of Aickman's 1966 memoir, a chronicle of the great ghost-story writer's childhood and youth, and in particular his relationship with his eccentric father. With a foreword by Jeremy Dyson; *Ray Bradbury*, edited by Harold Bloom (Chelsea House), contains nine critical essays on Bradbury's work. It's part of the "Modern Critical Views" series. An index and bibliography are included; *In Search of Dr. Jekyll and Mr. Hyde* by Raymond T. McNally and Radu R. Florescu (Renaissance Books) is a critical examination of historical events that inspired Robert Louis Stevenson, and the novel's cultural impact. With a bibliography, filmography, list of Web sites, a chronology of Stevenson's life, and a travel guide; *Mary Shelley's Fictions: From Frankenstein to Faulkner*, edited by Michael Eberle-Sinatra, collects fourteen essays on Shelley, all but three original; *The Hidden Library of Tanith Lee: Themes and Subtexts from Dionysos to the Immortal Gene* by Mavis Haut (McFarland & Company) is a critical exploration of recurring themes and references in Lee's works. With index, notes, bibliography, and an interview with the author; *A Dreamer and a Visionary: H.P. Lovecraft in His Time* by S. T. Joshi (Liverpool University Press, U.K.) is a critical biography of Lovecraft with notes and an index; *Ramsey Campbell and Modern Horror Fiction* by S. T. Joshi (Liverpool University Press, U.K.) is a critical analysis of Campbell's work with a memoir by Campbell and bibliography; *The Gentleman from Angell Street: Memories of H.P. Lovecraft* by Muriel E. Eddy, and C. M. Eddy, Jr., edited by Jim Dyer (Fenham Publishing), is a collection of essays and poems in personal remembrance of Lovecraft; *American Horror Writers* by Bob Madison (Enslow Publishers) is a YA edition of the "Collected Biographies" series with brief biographies of ten authors including Poe, King, and Lovecraft; *Femicidal Fears: Narratives of the Female Gothic Experience* by Helene Meyers (State University of New York Press) is a critical examination of feminism and female fears as reflected in contemporary, nonsupernatural Gothic literature, concentrating on the works of Angela Carter, Joyce Carol Oates, and Muriel Spark; *Guide to First Edition Prices* 2002/3 by R. B. Russell (Tartarus) is the fourth edition of this useful title. More than five-hundred British and U.S. authors and artists are covered; *The Horror Movie Survival Guide* by Matteo Molinari and Jim Kamm (Berkley Boulevard) is a tongue-in-cheek guide to the most basic monster clichés in the movies. Neither as useful or as funny as it thinks it is; *Shots in the Dark: True Crime Pictures* by Gail Buckland (Bulfinch), with commentary by Harold Evans, is a tie-in to a tenth-anniversary *Court TV* special of the same name. This is one of the better books on the subject. The text, for once, is as detailed as it needs to be, providing context for the photographs, which range from mug shots, mob assassinations, and lynchings, to just plain murders; *Wild Hairs* by David J. Schow (Babbage Press) collects columns written by the author about movies, books, and the horror field in general over the past twenty-five years. The columns, most of which were originally published in *Fangoria*, are irreverent, opinionated, and often hilariously on target. It's a beautifully designed gorgeous and sturdy trade paperback; *AntiCristo: The Bible of Nasty Nun Sinema & Culture* by Steve Fentone (FAB Press) is an exhaustive overview of heretical nuns from Italian exploitation titles to *The Flying Nun*. The book includes 170 pages of detailed filmography, an index of themes, and, of course, lots of photos; *Art of Darkness: The Cinema of Dario Argenti* edited by Chris Gallant (FAB) has five essays by the editor, then reviews by each of eleven writers (including Kim Newman) of one of his favorites of Argenti's fourteen films. The book has an extensive filmography. Not for the casual reader, and according to one reviewer it's mandatory to view each film before reading the accompanying essay. Lavishly illustrated throughout with b&w and color movie stills; *The Gorehound's Guide to Splatter Films of the 1960s and 1970s* by Scott Aaron Stine (McFarland & Company) gives a history of gore films, provides copious reviews of relatively obscure movies in addition to the better-known titles, and is illustrated throughout with old VHS covers; *If Chins Could Kill: Confessions of a B Movie Actor* by Bruce Campbell (St. Martin's) is the autobiography of the actor who starred in *The Evil Dead*. It's filled not only with his own experiences in the industry but with useful information for those aspiring to get into the movie business; *Memoirs of a Wolfman* by Paul Naschy and translated from the Spanish by Mike Hodges (Midnight Marquee Press) is a memoir by this Spanish actor/director, and scriptwriter; *The Peter Cushing Companion* by David Miller (Reynolds & Hearn) encompasses Cushing's whole working life as an actor, including Cushing's stage, radio, and television credits; *The Mummy Congress: Science, Obsession, and the Everlasting Dead* by Heather Pringle (Theia/Hyperion) tells of the author's experience attending the Third World Congress on Mummy Studies, a little-known gathering of about 180 mummy experts in a remote city in northern Chile. Africa is beloved by those passionate about mummies because of its climate—which is perfect for the preservation of human corpses into mummies. It might be considered the mummy capital of the world. This is an extraordinarily entertaining book that brings to life a somewhat arcane expertise. Included are several pages of color photographs; *Cemetery Stories* by Katherine Ramsland (HarperEntertainment) is an entertaining if occasionally disturbing discourse on all aspects of the way we die now, as the book follows the author as she talks business with an embalmer, attends an undertakers' convention, witnesses an autopsy, and otherwise explores the business of death; *Ascending Peculiarity: Edward Gorey on Edward Gorey* (Harcourt), edited by Karen Wilkin, is a collection of interviews with the late artist, arranged chronologically, and illustrated throughout. Some of the illustrations are reproductions of previously unpublished drawings by Gorey. This charming book includes a bibliography, notes, and an index; *Demons of the Modern World* by Malcolm McGrath (Prometheus) compares contemporary Satanic cult fears with the seventeenth-century witch-hunts and views Satanism scares as related to mass hallucination; *Roger Corman* by Beverly Gray (Renaissance Books) is an unauthorized biography by someone who worked as Corman's personal assistant for two years and as his story editor for eight years; *Wes Craven: The Art of Horror* by John Kenneth Muir (McFarland & Company) covers every aspect of Craven's career; *Screams & Nightmares: The Films of Wes Craven* by Brian J. Robb (Overlook Connection Press) is more of a coffee-table book; *The Haunted Screen: Ghosts in Literature and Film* by Lee Kovacs (McFarland & Company) is an analysis of "the romantic ghost film"; *Vampire Over London: Bela Lugosi in Britain* by Frank Dello Stritto and Andi Brooks (Cult Movies Press) is about the six-month-long tour of Britain by Bela Lugosi in the play *Dracula* in 1951— his last performances in that role; *Hitchcock Becomes "Hitchcock": The British Years* by Paul M. Jensen (Midnight Marquee Press); *Ridley Scott—Close Up: The Making of His Movies* by Paul M. Sammon (Thunder's Mouth Press) chronologically documents Scott's career up to but not including the making of *Gladiator*; *See No Evil: Banned Films and Video Controversy* by David Kerekes and David Slater (Headpress Critical Vision) is a case-by-case study of seventy-four unredeemable "video nasties" singled out by the U.K.'s Director of Public Prosecutions as a result of the Video Recordings Act (1985) that required all new video releases to be submitted for approval by the British Board of Film Classification; *A History of Exploitation Films, 1919–1959* by Eric Schaefer (Duke University Press); *Uneasy Dreams: The Golden Age of British Horror Films: 1956-1976* by Gary A. Smith (McFarland & Company); *Personal Demons* edited by Garrett Peck and Brian A. Hopkins (Lone Wolf Publications) is a powerful CD-ROM with essays by forty-two writers about real-life events in their lives that have influenced them as horror writers; *Ten Years of Terror: British Horror Films of the 1970s* edited by Harvey Fenton and David Flint (FAB Press) is a coffee-table book encompassing more than 140 films; *Guilty But Insane* by Poppy Z. Brite (Subterranean Press) is an entertaining collection of the series of titular columns Brite wrote for *Cemetery Dance* plus essays written for other venues between 1996 and 2000. The book is gorgeous inside and out, with a dust jacket illustrated by J. K. Potter and designed by Desert Isle Design, LLC., and interior design by Tim Holt; *Heart of Shadows: Lord Byron and the Supernatural* by Derek Fox and Mike Vardy (Blackie & Co. Publishers, U.K.) is an exploration of Lord Byron's life through his poetry and his relationships with women. Given access to Newstead Abbey, Byron's home, along with his coauthor and photographer, Vardy, Fox was allowed to interview staff concerning their ghostly experiences; *The Supernatural in Modern English Fiction* by Dorothy Scarborough (Lethe Press) was originally published in 1917; *Close to Shore* by Michael Capuzzo (Broadway) is nonfiction but reads like a novel. In the summer of 1916, just before the United States entered World War I, a new leisure class was springing up and going to the beaches for entertainment for the first time. Swimming in the ocean, relaxing on the beach. Over the July 4 weekend and a week after, a lone great white shark, out of its element as a result of the convergence of unusual circumstances, roamed and preyed along the New Jersey coastline, becoming the first shark to attack humans in U.S. history. Alternating chapters provide the reader with glimpses of the age of innocence and the culture surrounding that era and speculate (without anthropomorphizing the shark) on the circumstances that caused the shark, against its instincts, to move farther and farther from the sea and its natural environment. *In Harm's Way* by Doug Stanton (Henry Holt & Company) is the horrific account of the USS *Indianapolis*, torpedoed by a Japanese submarine near the end of World War II. Nine hundred of the twelve hundred men on board survived the initial assault and went into the water. Exposure and sharks killed all but 321 survivors.

## Chapbooks and Other Small Press Items

*The Exchange* by Nicholas Sporlender, illustrated by Louis Verden, is a wonderful little gift box containing a story booklet, "published by Hoegbotton & Sons in celebration of the 300th Festival of the Freshwater Squid" plus useful items that are meant to enhance the festival experience including dried mushrooms, a votive candle, a memory capsule, etc. The story is fun, the illustrations terrific. Just the booklet in the envelope is $6.99 postpaid. The deluxe version (the gift box) is $20.00 postpaid U.S., $23.00 postpaid outside the U.S. For information: http://www.vandermeer.redsine.com/.

A *Game of Colors* by John Urbancik (Yard Dog Press), illustrated by Peter Bradley, is a short story about a young woman who becomes an initiate into a coven in order to find her sister.

Electric Story brought out Suzy McKee Charnas's novel *The Vampire Tapestry* in ebook format.

From Midnight House: *Dark Sanctuary* by H. B. Gregory, edited with an introduction by D. H. Olson, is a new edition of one of the rarest novels of supernatural horror in the twentieth century. Artwork is by Allen Koszowski. *The Beasts of Brahm* by Mark Hansom, with dust jacket art by Allen Koszowski and an introduction by John Pelan, examines the mysterious disappearance of the author, who vanished after writing a string of highly successful supernatural thrillers.

*Deadliest of the Species* by Michael Oliveri (Vox 13) is the author's first novel. It's published in three editions, with an introduction by Tom Piccirilli and dust jacket art by publisher Kenneth Waters.

Arkham House published *The Book of the Dead* by E. Hoffman Price, a book of essays adapted from his diaries of visits to friends, many of whom were fellow pulp writers. Some of the essays were published in fanzines. The book includes additional essays by and about E. Hoffman Price, and an E. Hoffman Price bibliography by Virgil Utter. Included are sixteen pages of rare photos, and a special introduction by Jack Williamson.

The debut book from Earthling Publications is the impressive *Simon Clark: A Working Bibliography & A Trip Out for Mr. Harrison*. In addition to a full bibliography with black-and-white illustrations of each book jacket, this thirty-five-page chapbook provides an introduction by Tim Lebbon plus one by Clark describing the sale of his first published story in 1978, a facsimile of the original marked-up manuscript and the story itself. The cover illustration is by Fredrik King. Published in two editions.

Dark Muse Productions published a chapbook of *Funkytown*, a story by Gene O'Neill. Artwork is by Rob Mansperger.

RazorBlade Press brought out Gary Greenwood's second novel, *The King Never Dies* with attractive cover art and design by Chris Nurse.

ShadowLands Press published Tom Piccirilli's novel *The Night Class*, in two editions, with provocative dust jacket art by Kenneth Waters.

PS Publishing brought out its first novel, Tracy Knight's *The Astonished Eye*, with an introduction by Philip José Farmer, and cover art by Alan M. Clark.

*Eden* by Ken Wisman (Dark Regions Press) is really a science fiction story, but this chapbook might be of interest to horror readers. Cover art is by A. B. Word.

*Common Ectoids of Arizona* by Stepan Chapman (Lockout Press/Four-Sep Publications) is a chapbook collection of illustrations, purportedly a set of field drawings and notations of ectoplasmic entities (not seen).

Prime published Brett A. Savory's slapstick version of hell in a chapbook called *The Distance Travelled*. Cover art is by Herod Gilani and the cover design is by Garry Nurrish. It includes an introduction by Philip Nutman and an afterword by P. D. Cacek. Also included is a short story written when the author was eleven years old.

Chapbooks from DarkTales Publications: *Holy Rollers* by J. Newman, a creepy story about two mad religious fanatics who take a couple prisoner in their own home in order to "bring them to Jesus." *Natural Selection* by Weston Ochse is a powerfully told tale about a bouncer for a club of the damned, a woman attracted to the club's danger, and their encounter with a strange boy. With an introduction by Richard Laymon. The cover is designed by Natalie Niebur. *Filthy Death the Leering Clown* by Joseph Moore and Brett A. Savory, about a psychopathic murderer. Chad Savage did the colorful and demented cover art. *Dead-fellas* by David Whitman is an amusing novella about hit men fighting off zombies and doubles of themselves. It's got a great cover design by Keith Herber.

Overlook Connection Press brought out *Graven Images* by Gary Raisor, the first of four horror novellas in the "Sinister Purposes" series. Introduction is by Edward Lee and cover art by Colleen Crary. Published in three editions, all signed.

*The Temporary King* by P. K. Graves (Flesh & Blood) is a dark fantasy produced as an attractive chapbook, with cover art by Julia Morgan-Scott.

Chapbooks from Subterranean Press: *Black Dust* by Graham Joyce is a two-story chapbook with wonderfully expressive black-and-white cover art by John Picacio and excellent interior design by Tim Holt. The title story about the bleak life of coal miners and their families appears for the first time. The second story, "The Apprentice," is a reprint from 1994. "Black Dust" has been reprinted by *The Magazine of Fantasy & Science Fiction* and also appears herein. *Together Again* is a charming tale by Michael Cadnum about poor Humpty Dumpty, with cover and interior art by Keith Minnion and attractive interior design by Tim Holt. *On Pirates* by William Ashbless contains an unpublished short story and a lengthy pirate poem. Included are an introduction by Tim Powers and an afterword by James P. Blaylock. Cover and interior illustrations are by Gahan Wilson. Published in three editions. *Blackburn's Lady* by Bradley Denton is a novelette published in two editions.

Novels from Subterranean: Joe R. Lansdale's weird sf/horror/Western novel *Zeppelins West*. The book was published in two limited editions. Jacket art is by Mark A. Nelson. Also by Lansdale, a new Hap and Leonard adventure *Captains Outrageous*, with cover art and design by John Picacio and lovely interior design by Tim Holt. *Sex and Violence in Hollywood* by Ray Garton, a thriller published in two limited editions with dust jacket art by Gail Cross. The limited includes an extra novella-length scene cut from the novel. *Dark of the Eye* by Douglas Clegg comes in one limited edition with dust jacket art by Gail Cross. The limited-print edition of Clegg's successful e-publishing experiment—the first e-mail serial novel, *Naomi*, is now a beautiful hardcover with dust jacket art by Gail Cross. The novel was published in two editions. *The View from Hell* by John Shirley is a short horror novel published in two limited editions. Dustjacket and all interior illustrations are by Jill Bauman.

PS Publishing continued its novella program with "Nearly People," an excellent sf/horror story by Conrad Williams with an introduction by Michael Marshall Smith and cover art by Wieslaw Walkuski. The novella is a harrowing, well-told story about survival and self-exploration in a frighteningly ugly future. The press also brought out "A Writer's Life," an eerie and chilling ghost story by Eric Brown. Paul Di Filippo has provided the introduction, and the effective cover art is by Julian Flynn. Both titles were released in numbered limited hardcover and paperback editions.

Wormhole Books inaugurated a "Contemporary Chapbook series" with signed and numbered editions of Melanie Tem's powerful new science fiction story *Pioneers* and Edward Bryant's harrowing but moving reprint, *A Sad Last Love at the Diner of the Damned*. The Tem has a brief introduction by Nancy Holder, with attractive cover and interior art by Joann Erbach. The Bryant has an introduction by S. P. Somtow, an afterword by the author, and great cover art by David Martin. Later in the year the press published *Pink Marble and Never Say Die*, a chapbook with two very good stories by publisher Dawn Dunn, with cover and interior art by Erbach, and an introduction by Nancy Kilpatrick. Edward Bryant's vintage story "While She Was Out" was also published, with cover art by Joanna Erbach, interior photography by the author, and a short biography by Dawn Dunn. Steve Rasnic Tem's excellent original story "In These Final Days of Sales," (reprinted herein) has cover art by Joyce Abramson and an informative afterword by the author about the writing of the story. All the chapbooks are beautifully and professionally produced in heavy paper stock, with handsome interiors. They are all available in three editions.

Gauntlet Press produced a series of attractive signed and numbered chapbooks by Graham Masterton, Richard Matheson, David B. Silva, Richard Laymon, and artist/writer Alan M. Clark that were given away as premiums with orders for books bought directly from the publisher. They can also be purchased separately.

Also from Gauntlet Press: Barry Hoffman's *Judas Eyes*, third in a series was published with an afterword by Jack Ketchum and dust jacket art by Harry O. Morris. Available in an Edge edition and as a limited hardcover. F. Paul Wilson's "Repairman Jack" novel *Hosts*, with artwork by Harry O. Morris. Available in three editions. From the "classics revisited" series: *The Shrinking Man* by Richard Matheson, in two editions with ten pages of Matheson's screenplay for the original film, a new introduction by the author, and an afterword by David Morrell. Nancy A. Collins's second novel *Tempter*, reissued in a completely rewritten edition that removes the vampires and revises almost every page. Cover art is by Alan M. Clark. In two editions. Also, in trade paperback: *Richard Matheson's The Twilight Zone Scripts Vol. 1* by Richard Matheson, edited by Stanley Wiater.

From Cemetery Dance Publications: *Friday Night at Beast House* by Richard Laymon, a short novel set in the same world as *The Cellar*, *The Beast House*, and *The Midnight Tour*. Available in two limited editions. The dust jacket art is by Alan M. Clark. *Night in the Lonesome October*, with dust jacket art by Alan M. Clark is also available in two editions. *The Halloween Mouse*, a children's story by Richard Laymon, with color artwork throughout by Alan M. Clark, is available in three states. *City Infernal*, a new novel by Edward Lee with dust jacket art by Gail Cross, is available in two limited states.

*Darkness Demands* and *Blood Crazy* by British author Simon Clark, each in two limited editions. The dust jacket art for *Darkness Demands* is by Alan M. Clark, and Gail Cross did the dust jacket art for *Blood Crazy*. *The Folks* by Ray Garton is a short novel in two editions with dust jacket art by Gail Cross. *Bonny Winter*, a novella by Graham Masterton in two editions with dust jacket art by Keith Minnion. *Camp Pleasant*, a new murder mystery by Richard Matheson with dust jacket art by Harry O. Morris in two editions. *The Lost* by Jack Ketchum comes in two hardcover editions, with dust jacket art by Neal McPheeters. Tim Lebbon's short novel *Until She Sleeps* was published in two editions with dust jacket art by John Picacio.

Necro Publications brought out the first hardcover edition of Edward Lee's 1992 novel *Succubi*, adding the prologue that was cut from the earlier edition. The book was published in two limited states. Also, the two-story chapbook by Lee and Ryan Harding titled *Partners in Chyme* debuts the new Necro chapbook line. The cover art is by publisher David G. Barnett and the interior art is by Erik Wilson.

From Tartarus Press: *Uncle Stephen* by Forrest Reid, with an introduction by Colin Cruise, is a supernatural novel with time travel and magic that was first published in 1931; *The Princess Daphne* by Edward Heron-Allen and Selina Dolaro was written in the 1880s and is often described as a tale of psychic vampirism. R. B. Russell and Rosalie Parker provide context, and background in the introduction. All Tartarus books have a common jacket and interior design that makes them stand out—a photograph of the author as the frontispiece, colored endpapers, a ribbon bookmark, and the judicious and effective use of period design elements on the dust jackets and interiors; *The Thirty-Seven Parts of Albie Muensch* by Mary SanGiovanni is a nicely produced self-published chapbook with good-looking cover art by Shikhar Dixit.

Sarob Press published *Spalatro: Two Italian Tales* by J. Sheridan Le Fanu, with interior illustrations and a gorgeous wraparound dust jacket by Douglas Walters. The title story has not been reprinted since its original magazine appearance 158 years ago, when it was published without being identified as by Le Fanu.

From Babbage Press: a new edition of Dennis Etchison's classic first collection, *The Dark Country*, James P. Blaylock's Victorian fantasy *Homunculus*, a new edition of William F. Nolan's 1984 collection, *Things Beyond Midnight* (late 2000), and S. P. Somtow's *The Fallen Country*, all in attractive trade paperback editions.

Hippocampus Press brought out a new trade paperback edition of the novella *The Shadow out of Time* by H. P. Lovecraft, with corrected text edited by S. T. Joshi and David E. Schultz. The book comes with an extensive introduction and editorial notes.

*American Graveyards* by Ray Nayler, a novella, is the first *Crimewave* Special, a spin-off from *Crimewave* magazine.

From Sidecar Preservation Society: *Swedish Lutheran Vampires of Brainerd*, a funny vampire story by Anne Waltz with an afterword by Karen Taylor and art by Jon Arfstrom; *Chips & Shavings and Another Writing*, eight nonfiction pieces written by Lee Brown Coye (better known as a horror artist than writer) for the column he wrote in the *Mid-York Weekly* during the 1960s. The cover art is by Coye. A *Donald Wandrei Miscellany* edited by D. H. Olson provides a sampling of the author's fiction, nonfiction, verse, humor, and satire, some of which was first published in *Ski-U-Mah* and the *Minnesota Daily*. The cover art is by Rodger Gerberding; Hugh B. Cave's *Loose Loot*, an entertaining detective story with cover art by Tom Roberts. Flint & Silver Distributors carry all their titles. See the end of this summation for address.

From Night Shade Books: Tim Lebbon's new short novel *Face*, with dust jacket art and design art by John Picacio. Published in two editions; . . . *And the Angel with Television Eyes*, a novel by John Shirley with beautiful cover art by Matt Harpold. In two editions.

## Odds and Ends

*Dark Dreamers* by Stanley Wiater and Beth Gwinn (Cemetery Dance Publications) is a book of photographic portraits of over one hundred horror authors, artists, editors, and filmmakers, with brief comments by each, and their eclectic lists of recommended reading/viewing. Photographs are by Gwinn. There is a foreword by Clive Barker. Signed limited editions and leather-bound, lettered editions. If you want to get a look at some of your favorite horror writers and editors (yes, I'm in there) and read what they have to say for themselves, here's your chance.

*Travelers by Twilight* (Magic Pen Press) is a chapbook portfolio of artist Allen Koszowski's selected illustrations from *Weird Tales, Asimov's Science Fiction Magazine, Lore, The Horror Show, Gauntlet, Deathrealm,* and a host of other small-press magazines and publishers. Koszowski's black-and-white illustrations are instantly recognizable, with their almost pointillist style and lovingly rendered Lovecraftian monsters. Includes an introduction by Brian Lumley and an appreciation by Jason Van Hollander.

*Spectrum 8: The Best in Contemporary Fantastic Art,* edited by Cathy and Arnie Fenner (Underwood Books), is another winner in this annual series that belongs on the bookshelf of anyone interested in fine genre art. This year's Grand Master Award winner is Jean "Moebius" Giraud. The volume includes a profile of Giraud, a short survey of the year, and a beautifully designed showcase for a couple of hundred artists of fantasy, science fiction, dark fantasy, and horror.

*Fantasy of the 20th Century: An Illustrated History* by Randy Broecker (Collection Press) is a lavishly illustrated pictorial history of the modern genre fantasy, from pulps to the present. Oversize, and filled with eye-popping vintage book and magazine covers.

*Brushfire: Illuminations from the Inferno* by Wayne Barlowe (Morpheus International) is a luscious portfolio of fifteen large color plates, continuing the hellish artwork he's created since publishing his gorgeous book on Hell, *Inferno.*

*Brom: Offerings* (Paper Tiger) is a sumptuous hardcover overview of this dark fantasist's best work. High fantasy, goth, playful, erotic, disturbing, and gross, Brom's art roams the spectrum of fantasy and horror.

*Koan*: Paintings by Jon J. Muth and Kent Williams (ASFA) is a beautiful art book of these two fine artists' recent sketches and paintings. Their work often drifts from dream to nightmare. With an introduction by José Villarrubia.

## Small Press Addresses

American Fantasy Press, Garcia Publishing Services, P.O. Box 1059, Woodstock, IL 60098.

Arsenal Pulp Press, 103, 1014 Homer Street, Vancouver, British Columbia V6B 2W9, Canada. http://www.arsenalpulp.com

Ash-Tree Press: PO Box 1360, Ashcroft, BC V0K 1A0, Canada. http://www.AshTree.bc.ca/ashtreecurrent.html

Babbage Press: 8740 Penfield Avenue, Northridge, CA 91324. http://www.babbagepress.com

BBR Distributing, PO Box 625, Sheffield S1 3GY, U.K. http://www.bbr-online.com

Big Engine: PO Box 185, Abingdon, OX4 1GR, U.K. http://www.bigengine.co.uk

Black Arrow Press: P.O. Box 454, East Longmeadow, MA 01028. http://www.corrinedewinter.com

Cemetery Dance Publications: P.O. Box 943, Abingdon, MD 21009. http://www.cemeterydance.com/

Cyber-Psychos AOD: P.O. Box 581, Denver, CO 80201. http://cyberpsychos.netonecom.net/

Dark Regions Press: P.O. Box 1558, Brentwood, CA 94513. http://darkregions.hypermart.net/

DarkTales Publications: P.O. Box 19514, Shawnee Mission, KS 66285-9514. http://www.darktales.com

Delirium Books: P.O. Box 338, N. Webster, IN 46555. http://www.deliriumbooks.com

Eden Studios, Inc.: 3426 Keystone Avenue #3, Los Angeles, CA 90034-4731. http://www.edenstudios.net

Fedogan & Bremer: 3721 Minnehaha Avenue South, Minneapolis, MN 55406. http://www.charlesmckeebooks.com/~fedogan/

Fenham Publishing: P.O. Box 767, Narragansett, RI 02882. E-mail: Fenham@ids.net

Flesh & Blood Press: 121 Joseph Street, Bayville, NJ 08721.

Flint & Silver Distributors, P.O. Box 17283, Minneapolis, MN 55417-0283. http://www.flintsilver.netfirms.com

Frog, Ltd.: P.O. Box 12327, Berkeley, CA 94712.

Gauntlet Press: 309 Powell Road, Springfield, PA 19064. http://www.gauntletpress.com

Greenwood Publishing: 88 Post Road West, P.O. Box 5007, Westport, CT 06881. Phone: (203) 226-3571.

Haffner: 5005 Crooks Road, Suite 35, Royal Oak, MI 48073-1239. http://www.rust.net/~haffner/

Hippocampus Press, P.O. Box 641, New York, NY 10156. http://www.hippocampuspress.com

IFD Publishing: P.O. Box 40776, Eugene OR 97404. http://www.IFDpublishing.com/

Kelp Queen Press: c/o Sandra Kasturi, 3-334 Westmount Avenue, Toronto, Ontario, M6E 3N2 Canada. http://kelpqueenpress.com

Lone Wolf Publications: 13500 SE 79th Street, Oklahoma City, OK 73150. http://www.dm.net/~bahwolf/lwp.htm

McFarland & Company: Box 611, Jefferson, NC 28640. http://www.McFarland & Companypub.com

Meisha Merlin Publishing: P.O. Box 7, Decatur, GA 30031. http://www.meishamerlin.com

Midnight House: 4128 Woodland Park Ave. N., Seattle, WA 98103. http://www.darksidepress.com/midnight.html

Miniature Sun Press: P.O. Box 11002, Napa Valley, CA 94581. Miniaturesunpress@hotmail.com. http://www.miniaturesunpress.com

Morpheus International: 9250 Wilshire Blvd, Suite LL15, Beverly Hills, CA 90212.

Mythos Books: 218 Hickory Meadow Lane, Poplar Bluff, MO 63901-2160. http://www.mythosbooks.com/

Necro Publications: P.O. Box 540298, Orlando, FL 32854-0298. http://www.necropublications.com

Night Shade Books: 348 Pierce Street, San Francisco, CA 94117. http://www.nightshadebooks.com

Overlook Connection Press: P.O. Box 526, Woodstock, GA 30188. http://www.overlookconnection.com

RazorBlade Press: 108 Habershon Street, Splott, Cardiff, CF24 2LD, U.K. http://www.razorbladepress.com/razor/index.htm

Sarob Press: Brynderwen, 41 Forest View, Mountain Ash, Mid Glamorgan, Wales CF45 3DU, U.K. http://home.freeuk.net/sarobpress

Scorpius Digital Publishing: http://www.scorpiusdigital.com/

ShadowLands Press: Bereshith Publishing, P.O. Box 2366, Centreville, VA 20122. http://www.bereshith.com/

Small Beer Press: 360 Atlantic Avenue, PMB #132, Brooklyn, NY 11217. http://www.lcrw.net/

Space and Time: 138 W. 70th Street, New York, NY 10023-4468

Stealth Press: 336 College Avenue, Lancaster, PA 17603. http://www.stealthpress.com

Subterranean Press: P.O. Box 190106, Burton, MI 48519. http://www.subterraneanpress.com/

Tartarus Press: Coverley House, Carlton, Leyburn, North Yorkshire, DL8 4AY, U.K. http://homepages.pavilion.co.uk/users/tartarus/welcome.htm

The Design Image Group: P.O. Box 2325, Darien, IL 60561.

Underwood Books: P.O. Box 1609, Grass Valley, CA 95945. http://www.underwoodbooks.com

Wildside Press: P.O. Box 45, Gillette, NJ 07933-0045. http://www.wildsidepress.com/

Wormhole Books: 7719 Stonewall Run, Fort Wayne, IN 46825 http://www.wormholebooks.com

# The Year in Media of the Fantastic

Edward Bryant

2001 was a year in which *Shrek* not only sold enormous numbers of repeat tickets, the DVD rolled up close to ten million sales. The much-awaited openings of *Harry Potter and the Sorceror's Stone* ($93 million the first weekend) and *The Lord of the Rings: Fellowship of the Ring* garnered box office receipts totaling the estimated international cost of rebuilding Afghanistan. Seven out of ten of the top grossers for the year were films of the fantastic. The tragedy of September 11 turned out not to have profoundly altered the nature of the Hollywood beast, though it did modify some short-term commercial behavior.

Here's what you should have seen at a bare minimum in the field of the fantastic if you expect to hold your own in the right cocktail party chat circles. Or if you expect to salvage any sense of self-respect in the odder versions of Trivial Pursuit.

Let's start with feature films.

## Horror and Dark Fantasy

*Brotherhood of the Wolf* is another French production to confound purists. Is it a horror film? Monster movie? Period historical costume drama about secret societies and political intrigue? Martial arts epic featuring two blood brothers, a French Royal Naturalist (Samuel le Bihan) and a Mohawk-Iroquois shaman (Mark Dascascos) from the New World? It is, of course, all the above and more. Screenwriter Stéphane Cabel and director Cristophe Gans have stuffed an enormous amount of material into these two and a half hours of film. The naturalist and the shaman are dispatched by King Louis XV to a remote province to discover the nature of the apparent giant wolf that's terrorizing the countryside. What they discover goes beyond the mere lupine, and even the lycanthropic. It's a startling concoction created by Jim Henson's Creature Shop. There's something here for everyone. Every female viewer I've talked with was mesmerized by the hunky Iroquois. The cinematography throughout is spectacular, but perhaps most visually arresting during a wide-screen monster hunt when the camera settles in on a crimson vision in the form of the local noble ingenue (Emilie Dequenne). For me, though, the center of female power is an apparent courtesan (Monica Bellucci) who turns out to be something of a James Bondish secret agent for the Vatican. Whatever. It's all a tremendous amount of fun.

Make some effort to track down Guillermo Del Toro's *The Devil's Backbone*. In 1992 Del Toro gave us the intriguing *Cronos*, an idiosyncratic tale of a non-traditional vampire and an immortality machine. That got him a studio shot with a reasonable budget to film 1997's *Mimic*, a mostly smart and stylish thriller about large and very clever roaches in the New York subways, a script loosely based on a vintage story by Donald A. Wollheim. Now the wheel has turned again and there's *The Devil's Backbone*, a low-budget, Spanish-language eerie thriller set during the Spanish Civil War at a remote orphanage for boys. When new young boy Carlos (Fernando Tielve) is unwillingly deposited at the orphanage, he discovers there are some terrible secrets to be found. There's abuse, murder, and a thoroughly troubling revenant. The ghost scenes are genuinely creepy. The distance lent by the far-off war and the desolate, arid landscape on which the orphanage squats all add to the picture's disturbing tone.

Few would have suspected it would be Allen and Albert Hughes (1993's *Menace II Society*) who would take Alan Moore and Eddie Campbell's epic graphic novel speculation about Jack the Ripper and transform it into a sharp, nasty, socially conscious tale concerning murder, class warfare, and the general nature of modern evil. *From Hell*, filmed in Prague to evoke Victorian London, features Johnny Depp as a distracted and somewhat dissolute police detective who first uses, then falls in love with prostitute (and historical Ripper victim) Mary Kelly (Heather Graham). Clearly the Hughes brothers are eager to suggest the underpinnings of the terrible evils which will grow into the imminent twentieth century, and they're largely successful in doing so.

Early in 2001, *The Gift* was indeed that; the first good film of the supernatural for the year. Directed by Sam Raimi from a script by Billy Bob Thornton and Tom Epperson (they of the script for the crisp *One False Move*), the title refers to the psychic ability possessed by an otherwise unremarkable Southern widow played by Cate Blanchett. As usual, Blanchett's acting skills are impeccable; this Australian actress plays a Southern American with nary a screwup in accent. Anecdotal evidence suggests that Blanchett's characterization is based to a degree on triple-threat writer/actor/director Thornton's own mother. A carpenter friend of mine is also a professional psychic (though he terms his alter ego job as a "psychic counselor" on his business card), and opined that the psychic character in *The Gift* is one of the better and more accurate representations in movies of the paranormal. In any case, *The Gift* uses its Southern Gothic backdrop to solid advantage in this tale of paranormal powers and murder.

*Jeepers Creepers*, the latest feature from Victor Salva (*Powder*) was a nearly perfect summer horror movie. Filmed against the eerie backdrop of rural Florida, the story captures a nicely claustrophobic Southern Gothic feel. A brother and sister (Justin Long and Gina Philips) are driving home from college when they spot what apparently is a sinister figure stuffing sheet-wrapped corpses down a roadside drainpipe. Of course they investigate and discover an unending world of hurt. Jonathan Breck plays the Creeper, a villain who evolves throughout the plot. Is he a merely mortal psychotic killer? A vampire? A demon? An extraterrestrial weirdo? The idea is to keep the audience off-balance. For the most part, it works. And it's no accident that the song from which the film is titled plays an integral choral role in the melodrama. Once the credits roll, the tune will likely never be appreciated the same way by the audience.

Nicole Kidman nailed down a superb role in Alejandro Almenábar's *The Others*, an atmospheric ghost story set on a remote island off the British coast right after World War II. Kidman has endured the war as well as possible, protecting her two young children. The Germans occupied the island; Kidman's British soldier husband never has returned from his battles. Now she's interviewing some new servants to replace the ones that inexplicably fled the house in the recent past. The children are a bit of custodial trouble since they suffer from a rare ocular disorder that keeps them from ever enjoying natural sunlight. The house must be always closed up during sunlit hours. And Kidman enforces a rule that all who traverse the interior of the house must lock each door through which they pass before opening the next one. This is a puzzle story, but the script plays fair with the viewer as the clues begin to mount. Some in the audience will correctly guess ahead to the inevitable surprise; but most will figure out the solution at roughly the point the director and writer intend. The tone of the film is unsurprisingly Jamesian. Nicole Kidman does quite well as a woman performing her maternal duties under nearly unbearable pressure. The film achieves maximum effect through suggestion and the gradual building of tension rather than digital effects. This is a good thing, if atypical for this graphic era in filmmaking.

## On the Side

*Jurassic Park III* perhaps is not a horror movie by most definitions. Technically one could argue it's at least nominally science fiction. But particularly in this third installment in the series based on Michael Crichton's original best-seller about the downside of cloning giant reptiles, a monster is a monster is a monster. *Jurassic Park III* hews to the classic fifties monster B-movie template. It's a mere hour and a half long; apparently all the expository narrative was in the half hour that ordinarily would have been appended. The plot moves along hyperkinetically as paleontologist Sam Neill and a brave crew fly out to a mysterious island off the coast of Costa Rica to help distraught parents William H. Macy and Téa Leoni search for their lost son in jeopardy. And the onslaught of digital monsters is wonderful. The level of technology has finally reached the point where convincing special effects pterodactyls can be portrayed. But the toothy ground-based sauropods are still quite impressive. No pretense here. Label this one an unashamed guilty pleasure.

*The Mummy Returns* is another big-budget, CGI-heavy summer B-movie. It's far more palatable than *The Mummy* from two years ago, though some of us still wish Universal had gone with the Clive Barker script for a remake. Taking place in 1933 and a decade after its predecessor, the sequel gives us Brendan Fraser and Rachel Weisz as a glam married couple with a young son. The melodrama-saturated plot rapidly brings in Im-Ho-Tep's old nemesis, the Scorpion King (a barely utilized The Rock), an ancient conqueror who forged an unholy deal with the god Anubis to conquer the known world. Scarabs, scorpions, reanimated mummies both large and pygmy, a wide pool of conspirators, some reincarnated, some just along for the ride, a preposterous balloon flying machine, it all adds up to a rapid amusement with just about no nutritional value whatsoever. Brendan Fraser lends his best efforts to heroics, but his cause is not aided by a script that tries to make him even more a clone of Indiana Jones. Even the CGI effects try just a little too hard. Early on in the picture, it's disconcerting to see a panoramic crowd scene with about two zillion jackal-headed soldiers charging an enemy city. Except everyone's feet look like the rolling wheel-like locomotion of so many Warner Bros. cartoon characters.

13 Ghosts is the second remake of a William Castle fifties schlock horror classic in as many years. Unfortunately it doesn't achieve nearly the triumph of manic excess that last year's House on Haunted Hill managed. Still, it does possess a minimal number of enjoyable moments as a broken family falls for their departed uncle's nefarious plan and moves into a high-tech house haunted by a dozen ghastly revenants imprisoned in containment rooms throughout the home. "So, what did you and my dead uncle do?" "We hunted ghosts." "Goats? You hunted goats?" Maybe you had to be there.

## Science Fiction

Most of you are aware that A.I.: Artificial Intelligence is Steven Spielberg's well-intentioned attempt to bring Stanley Kubrick's long-delayed pet project to life after the latter's untimely death. As it turned out, the critical reception was mixed, the box office totals somewhat disappointing. But with original source material from Brian Aldiss and Ian Watson, the movie wasn't at all a disappointment for me. The plot's quite Asimovian as a couple despondent over their terminally ill young son (he's been placed in cryonic sleep) orders up a cybernetic duplicate of their kid (Haley Joel Osment). The parents, especially the mother, have to come to terms with their substitute child, and vice versa. But when futuristic medicine cures their boy and he returns, there's clearly one child too many in the family. By now, unfortunately for the robot son, he's got too much acquired and absorbed humanity to go back to being a mere machine. Soon he's on the run and looking for a magic means of becoming a true human boy. One of his more intriguing new allies is Gigolo Joe (Jude Law), a wonderful robot lothario. Though there are plenty of spiffy futuristic effects, one of the most effective scenes is a set piece that almost assuredly came from Kubrick's original vision. The Flesh Fair is a hideous attempt by resentful mortal humans to take revenge on the robots they perceive as on the way to replacing them. It's a viscerally compelling sequence, a horrific vision of lynchings done high-tech style. All in all, A.I. brings together what many viewers perceived as an extremely mixed message about a future alternately viewed as warm and fuzzy, and bleakly austere and edgy.

Okay, so most people aren't thinking of the Coen brothers' The Man Who Wasn't There as a science fiction drama. Of course those are the people who probably didn't think of last year's wonderful O Brother Where Art Thou? as fantasy. Well, wrong. It's true that *The Man Who Wasn't There* is a nifty dark period noir piece, replete with murder and plenty of forties atmosphere. Along with others including Tony Shalhoub, Frances McDormand, James Gandolfini, and Scarlett Johansson, Billie Bob Thornton stands out in the cast as an oddly repressed barber. But if you pay attention, it's really sf, or at least sf forms an important element. Roger Deakins's black-and-white cinematography is superb.

Tim Burton's remake (or more properly, reworking) of *Planet of the Apes* didn't exactly please everyone. But with a director as idiosyncratically distinctive as Burton, would you expect anything different? The danger of a remake, particularly one that has become something of a cult or nostalgic favorite, is that those in the original audience who are still alive cannot do otherwise but agonize over comparisons. I liked the visual aspects of Burton's version quite a lot. If truth be told, I enjoyed this more than Franklin J. Schaffner's 1968 version starring Charlton Heston. I did also enjoyed seeing Heston's cameo in Burton's film; and I particularly liked the character's speech, lines that—perhaps—indicated scripted anti-gun oratory. Otherwise, the film is effective in spite of heavy-handed (and maybe heavy-breathing as well) Fox executives ordering the film to drop a love scene between stranded astronaut Mark Wahlberg and sophisticated simian Helena Bonham Carter on grounds that "bestiality was way over the line."

Before I saw it, for whatever reason, I didn't expect much from Cameron Crowe's *Vanilla Sky*, and so was quite delighted to discover that this Tom Cruise vehicle is a mostly successful full-blooded sf melodrama about life extension and virtual reality. Based on director Alejandro Almenábar's 1998 *Abre los Ojos* (*Open Your Eyes*), *Vanilla Sky* carries over the casting of Penelope Cruz as the protagonist's primary love interest. Tom Cruise is a rich and successful young magazine publisher who wakes up one morning to discover that he and his Ferrarri are the only things moving in an uninhabited New York City. This apparently turns out to be a dream, but reality is trickily suspect for the next two hours. Once Cruise is hideously maimed in a car crash engineered by his psychotically jealous lover (Cameron Diaz), he has a series of marvelously acted sequences in which he's hidden within a disturbing latex mask. What inexorably builds is an undeniably sf scenario, much in the tradition of *The Matrix*, *eXistenZ*, and *The Thirteenth Floor*. Cinematographer John Toll's images are extraordinary. The only rub comes toward the end, when all the artful construction is brought to a screeching halt while a few minutes are devoted to the Expository Lump That Explains Everything. Too bad. *Vanilla Sky* is good, but it could have been a classic.

## On the Side

Melodramas on Mars continue to fascinate Hollywood. 2001's turn at spotlighting the Red Planet was *John Carpenter's Ghosts of Mars*. Very deliberately a John Ford tribute as the ghosts of long-dead Martians come back from the distant past to possess the bodies of future Earth colonists and eventually to besiege the final fortress of human survivors, *Ghosts* is unpretentious fun. And, just for the level of estrogen (Carpenter's future Mars is governed by tough, capable women), it outperforms the previous year's *Red Planet* and *Mission to Mars*.

*K-PAX* has the asset of terrific performances by Kevin Spacey and Jeff Bridges. But this touchy-feely tale of is-the-mental-patient-really-an-extraterrestrial-from-a-spiritually-advanced-world-or-isn't-he? also has the downside of being a near carbon copy of Eliseo Subiela's 1986 Argentinean film, *Man Facing Southeast*. If it is indeed a remake, it's not a wholly successful one, despite the acting.

## Fantasy

Off in the fantasy slipstream, an enormous audience has been building for months for Jean-Pierre Jeunet's French-language *Amélie*. Jeunet's no stranger to the audience of the fantastic—remember 1991's spectacularly over-the-top post-apocalyptic comedy, *Delicatessen*? The wondrous *City of Lost Children*? *Amélie*'s title character is played by luminous newcomer Audrey Tautou. Imagine a contemporary benign social meddler along the lines of Jane Austen's Emma, free of earlier centuries' constraints and eager to help troubled Parisians at the drop of a synchrony. It's all fun, serious and affecting beneath the playfulness, and completely freewheeling.

*Harry Potter and the Sorceror's Stone* was the first of the truly large fantasy hits of the year. It hit big, dragging in hordes of skeptical parents and dubious but optimistic kids, and making believers of most. Director Chris Columbus crafted a perfectly corporate, highly marketable, very mainstream, but still relatively faithful adaptation of J. K. Rowling's first volume in her best-selling series of novels about orphaned young sorcerer Harry Potter (Daniel Radcliffe), his rescue from a dead-end life among the mundane disbelievers in magic of any kind, and his education as a talented novice magic-worker at the Hogwarts School of Witchcraft and Wizardry. Rowling came out of British blue-collar obscurity to create a phenomenon—a series of substantial novels that brought masses of video-game- and TV-jaded youngsters back to the printed word. Four novels into the series (and presumably, grosses continuing to hold up, they'll all become movies), Harry's getting older at a reasonable rate, and is presumably about to confront sex and death fairly directly. But in the film he's still younger and wide-eyed, agog at his owl familiar Hedwig, his friends Ron Weasley (Rupert Grint) and Hermione Granger (Emma Watson), and delighted to discover his consummate skill at the F-16-paced flying-on-broomsticks competitive game, quidditch. This is solid, entertaining, empowering material, if a bit derivative. And so far, despite skepticism from conservative religious quarters, there have been no confirmed cases of the movie directing children into full-blown Satan worship.

*Hedwig and the Angry Inch* is about as far from *Harry Potter* as one could get. Solidly in the tradition of *Rocky Horror* in terms of outrageous dialogue, visuals, and infectious music, *Hedwig* is writer/director/star John Cameron Mitchell's translation of his own hit stage production. This brash depiction of a gender-confused young man victimized by a botched sex-change surgery, who then reinvents himself as a glam-rock-goddess is an unqualified triumph. It may well be the best rock musical yet.

Along with *Harry Potter Lord of the Rings* is the other major fantasy hit of the year. Director Peter Jackson (remember the astonishing *Dead Alive*? *The Frighteners*? The somber and affecting *Heavenly Creatures*?) has always loved

J. R. R. Tolkien's cornerstone of modern fantasy. At just the right moment, he got New Line and its backers to pony up nearly a third of a billion dollars to film all three volumes back-to-back, and then to release the trilogy one film at a time for three years. Some years back, animator Ralph Bakshi managed to cram two-thirds of the trilogy into a single unsatisfactory feature. Jackson faced considerable skepticism. Tolkien's epic is founded on archetypes, and has been the inspiration for more pastiches and, indeed, outright rip-offs, than anything else in twentieth-century fantasy. The tension, the suspense, the accounting department's collective ulcers all mounted. Then *Fellowship of the Ring* opened. Everything worked. The movie validated the massive pre-release Burger King toy giveaway (eighteen interlocking light-up and/or speaking figures, plus the Ring of Power! And don't forget the quartet of ruby LED light-up mugs!). Filmed in the protean landscapes of faraway New Zealand, the vistas of Middle-earth have the right look, familiar yet exotic. The effects, digital and otherwise are mostly highly accomplished. The cast is fine, ranging from Ian McKellen as good wizard Gandalf and Christopher Lee as the treacherous Saruman, to Liv Tyler as elf queen Arwen and a buff Viggo Mortenson as the resourceful and heroic Strider. Young Elijah Wood, always a good actor in the past, has gotten some static for his deer-in-the-headlights portrayal of hobbit Frodo Baggins. Skeptics may be forgetting this is a three-picture, nine- or ten-hour epic. Our hairy-footed young friend has time yet to evolve in his role as the reluctant hero off to dispose of the troublesome magic Ring of Power, right there in its one place of vulnerability, the heart of evil where it was forged. Director Jackson clearly loves Tolkien's work, understands it, and treats it respectfully. *The Fellowship of the Ring* is an epic film that deserves the apellation.

*Just Visiting* is director Jean-Marie Poire's American remake of his own 1993 French hit comedy dealing with a twelfth-century knight (Jean Reno) and serf (Christian Clavier) who get shunted into contemporary Chicago after a sorcerous mishap. The level of comedy and sharp observation in this fish-out-of-water entertainment are such that the likes of *Black Knight* and *Kate and Leopold* should bow their heads in shame. As the chivalrous knight's serf says when offered a route back to their original time: "I want to stay here, where I can eat doughnuts and wear exciting men's fashions at rock-bottom prices."

*Moulin Rouge* displays Nicole Kidman in her *other* good role in 2001. Australian director Baz Luhrmann, working from a script by him and Craig Pearce, has created a flashy, enchanting, sensual fantasy of a Paris that never was. You might think of it as the "before" side of a scenario in which *Cabaret* would constitute the perverse, decaying "after." Set close to the turn of the nineteenth century into the era of modernism, *Moulin Rouge* features Kidman as the beautiful but doomed star of the infamous Paris club, with Ewan McGregor as the young writer fated to fall in love with her. The supporting cast is wonderful, particularly Jim Broadbent, Richard Roxburgh, and John Leguizamo as Toulous-Lautrec. Donald McAlpine's dreamlike cinematography, particularly that of a nighttime fantasy Paris, is striking. The music throughout is eclectic, drawn from the entire twentieth century. A surreal effect? That's the idea.

On the surface, *Sexy Beast* is about retired British gangsters and their wives hoping to live out satisfactory lives on the sun-drenched Spanish coast. But weirdness gets in the way of the whole notion of peaceful declining years. In the first scene, Ray Winstone's character has to deal with the synchronicity of an enormous boulder rolling down the hillside, bouncing over him in his chair at poolside, and splashing down dead center in the swimming pool. But things get stranger. Ben Kingsley's a remnant of the Bad Old Days in the U.K., a vicious and psychotic gangster who's been dispatched to lure Winstone back to England for one last heist. Other critics have referred to Kingsley's role here as the anti-Gandhi. That's accurate. Kingsley could indeed be the titular "sexy beast." Or that might refer to the demonic figure who periodically appears to Winstone as perhaps a one-creature Greek chorus, or more likely a Satanic voice offering suspect advice in Winstone's ear. Whichever. Ultimately the primary gift of the film is watching increasingly uneasy citizens (decent enough, for former crooks) attempting to deal with a genuine monster; Kingsley is filled to the bursting point with escalating craziness.

Okay, you say, how does Lasse Hallstrom's adaptation of E. Annie Proulx's long and complex Pulitzer Prize–winning novel qualify as fantasy? There's not a mountain troll in sight. Maybe not, but the location shooting in Newfoundland would do justice to the New Zealand locations for *Lord of the Rings* in terms of looking simultaneously familiar and exotically alien. Also it's got a pivotal role by Cate Blanchett. But unlike the ethereal Galadriel, here Blanchett plays the ultimate trailer-trash tramp Petal, a cunning woman who seduces the hapless Quoyle (Kevin Spacey) into marriage, also giving him an accidental daughter. After Petal dies in suitably grotesque fashion, water-hating Quoyle and his daughter are inveigled into migrating back to their ancestral Newfoundland by a long-lost aunt (Judi Dench). In the stark and beautiful north country, our hero deals with what turns out to be a grotesque family history (including mass murder and mutilation), and attempts to build a new life. So where's the fantasy? Quoyle and his people are riddled with ghosts, perhaps metaphorical, maybe literal. The bulk of the film is about exorcism in one form or another. And there are demonstrations of psychic abilities. Call it magic realism if you wish, but *The Shipping News* is both a satisfying work of humanity and of the imagination.

So what would most viewers have expected director Robert Rodriguez to tackle after executing the consummate ultralow-budget martial arts/Mexican music/noir crime melodrama *El Mariachi,* the upper-scale studio remake of same, *Desperado,* the Quentin Tarantino epic *From Dusk Till Dawn,* and the better of the four segments of Tarantino's unbearable *Four Rooms?* Well, probably not an astonishing, amusing, and totally charming thriller for kids and older viewers as well, *Spy Kids. Spy Kids* really is a James Bond fantasy in which the resourceful young offspring (Alexa Vega and Daryl Sabara) of a married pair of abducted international secret agents (Antonio Banderas and Carla Gugino) take off to rescue their parents when other avenues fail. The movie possesses warmth, cleverness, and wit. Teri Hatcher, Robert Patrick, Alan Cumming, and Tony Shalhoub make a wonderful bunch of crazed antagonists. Imagine *Austin Powers* without wretched excess.

## On the Side

With direction from Scott Hicks and a script by William Goldman, the film adaptation of Stephen King's *Hearts in Atlantis* had a fighting chance. The result is a draw. One problem for extracting a script from King's lovely book is that it's a collection of tales, all related, but mostly diverse in tone and subject matter, one from the next. The filmmakers opted to fiddle with the plot from the largest of the stories, an atmospheric tale of a young boy living with his unhappy single mom (Hope Davis) when a somewhat eccentric older lodger (Anthony Hopkins) moves in upstairs. The story in print form was essentially a *Dark Tower*–related fantasy in which boy and old man forge a solid friendship as it becomes apparent that some formidable and terrible supernatural foes are in pursuit of the adult. The movie keeps the relationship but downgrades the melodramatic pursuit to a rather less fantastical plot about cold war paranoia, government plotting, and psychic warfare. The acting's all good, and Hopkins, as ever, is capable of carrying the script. But the script staggers, and the story will still be a disappointment for any fan of King's.

*Josie and the Pussycats*, adapted from the *Archie* comic book, has all the substance of low-fat meringue, but it manages to balance, for the most part, on a knife edge of sweetness evenly dividing light entertainment and pure nothingness. Rachel Leigh Cook, Tara Reid, and Rosario Dawson are the naive young girl rock band; Parker Posey and Alan Cumming do their best to represent the forces of Big Record Business and Big Government conspiring to create Big Evil.

*A Knight's Tale* isn't a bad nonrealistic romantic melodrama of a courtly time that didn't exactly exist the way it's portrayed here. (Now a bad example would be Chris Rock's unfortunate but fortunately uncredited rerun of Twain's *A Connecticut Yankee*, *Black Knight*.) One guesses it was something of a self-indulgence for director Brian Helgeland (*L.A. Confidential*). Heath Ledger's a peasant-level squire to an undistinguished knight who, upon his master's death, flouts law and custom to reinvent himself, with the help of his friends, as a hot young knight from a distant land. This was another fantasy film that utilized anachronistic music for its score, in this case, hits of the seventies, and wove that into such bits as medieval audiences inventing the stadium "wave." Some amusements such as a walk-on role by Geoffrey Chaucer (Paul Bettany) were pretty entertaining. But ultimately, the viewer has to learn to love jousting about like viewers of *The Fast and the Furious* had to dig street-racing.

Okay, so no one will mistake *Tomb Raider* for *A Beautiful Mind* or *Iris*. I merely mention this visualization of the enormously popular video game because Angelina Jolie performs a mainly bang-up job as Indiana Jones–ish Lara Croft, an orphaned young woman adventurer both lethal and lovely. The movie's smart, quick, and occasionally deliberately funny, though God only knows how the Illuminati get dragged, kicking and screaming, into the plot. This is another ideal rental entertainment.

In *Cats & Dogs* the conceit is that cats and dogs are both highly intelligent species that have been battling for control of the world since time immemorial. The canines are presented with a great deal of sympathy—and they are also presented as the species that has cozied up to *Homo sapiens* as a protective ally. Not so the arrogant and evil felines. I'll admit from the git-go that the politics here grated on my sensibility—and that of my two furred masters here at home. But more objectively, there was the matter of tone—this interspecies battle depends so heavily upon slapstick rather than wit, it is another reminder that the Three Stooges' heritage has fallen upon hard times indeed.

## Dark Suspense

I thought Thomas Harris's most recent installment in the "Hannibal Lecter" cycle of novels was a qualified success. I loved the ending, but wondered how on earth the inescapable major film adaptation would handle the truly disturbing material. The answer turned out to be simple; ignore it and fabricate something sobering, but less trauma-inducing. In Ridley Scott's version of *Hannibal* Anthony Hopkins is again superbly creepy as the eponymous art-loving, gourmet cook and sociopathic killer. Jody Foster declined to repeat as Lecter's intellectual adversary and ambivalent kindred spirit, FBI agent Clarice Starling. Julianne Moore adopts the role well. *Hannibal*'s full of color (all that location shooting in Florence) and kinetic movement, and manages to retain some of the over-the-top feel of the novel. But it will still allow the viewer to eat supper afterward in peace.

Newcomer director Christopher Nolan's *Memento* is an absolute triumph. With a script based on his brother's short story, this is a technical tour de force about a damaged insurance investigator (Guy Pearce) in search of his wife's murderer, a man whose quest is made a touch difficult by possessing no faculty for long-term memory. Psychologically he's obliged to live in an approximately two-minute window around the present moment. To make things more challenging for the viewer, the plot is told sequentially backwards, starting with the ending and moving inexorably back in time, each scene shedding illumination on what we've already watched. What's accomplished is a tricky examination of memory and identity in which the writer/director plays completely fair. Everything's here, as one realizes after the final scene. I wouldn't hesitate to use *Memento* as a good example of ambitious plotting in any writing class.

David Lynch's *Mulholland Drive* was roundly beaten about the head and shoulders by a large chunk of critics when it opened. Incomprehensible, they said. Incoherent. No, just a touch challenging. Slowly, in its darkly glittering and surreal way, the film's found its audience with time. A meditation on reality and identity, *Mulholland Drive* features Naomi Watts as a young and wholesome Canadian woman lately arrived in Hollywood to seek success and fortune in the movies. After discovering an amnesiac young woman (Laura Elena Harring) in her aunt's home, she's apparently drawn into ring within ring of concentric levels of conspiracy, violence, and madness. Ultimately the story may or may not be the compressed life of a suicide expanded in the split second after pulling the trigger. Or maybe it's something else. In any case, Lynch's movie draws together coherent thematic and emotional sense.

## Animation

*Atlantis: The Lost Empire* got betrayed by its parent, as the studio decided to sink its animation awards–lobbying cash into the more hugely successful *Shrek*. In any case, don't overlook this period pulpy adventure of a nineteenth-century expedition to a strange world beneath the ocean floor. It's a kids movie with endless adventure, exotic scenery, and an atypical recognition that even characters can die in the course of the plot. What the movie finally evoked in me was the sense of capturing the whole taste and tone of one of Jack Williamson's 1930s sf adventure magazine serials.

The reputation of being based on a video game is enough to sink most such movies for the adult viewer. *Final Fantasy* rose above that. The plot was adequate: refugee phantom aliens wreak holy havoc on a largely ruined Earth, even as high-tech human survivors seek both the meaning of the alien onslaught and a means of turning the tide. The real attraction here is the level of animation. Prolonged sequences won't fool the eye, but in the quick cuts used the first time I saw *Final Fantasy*'s trailer, I really did think I was watching actual human actors. Scary. I understand the Screen Actors Guild is already working out strategy for incorporating and dealing with digital animation based on flesh-and-blood players.

*Monkey Bone* got a bad rap. Beautifully and hyperkinetically filmed as a hybrid live action and animated feature, the film is a feast for the eye and brain both. Based on the eponymous graphic novel by Kaya Blackley, *Monkey Bone* features Brendan Fraser as the creator of the cartoon in question, whose untimely coma shifts him into the animated world where the character Monkey Bone schemes to escape into our physical reality. That internal world is a magical place featuring all manner of astonishments ranging from Whoopi Goldberg as Death to a Stephen King look-alike. The film is edgy and witty.

*Monsters, Inc.* doesn't have quite the same universal appeal as *Shrek*, but it's still a high achiever in terms of keeping a younger crowd amused. Pixar Animation Studios (they of *Toy Story*) have created some terrific visuals in this tale of the industry of childhood nightmares. It turns out that monsters labor away at a nine-to-five gig (though nocturnally, natch) scaring sleeping kids. It's the children's screams that provide the energy that powers the monsters' world. It's not as grim as it might sound. The monstrous critters are mostly likeable, particularly Sully (voiced by John Goodman) and his doofus buddy (Billy Crystal). The two friends find themselves engaged in rescuing a little human girl who has strayed into the monsters' domain, before she's discovered by the rather more problematic and nasty monster Randall (voiced by Steve Buscemi).

For my money, it's *Shrek* that shows the levels of entertainment a fine animated feature can achieve. As with all other films of universal appeal, there's something here for any age, child or adult. This fairy tale of a mildly gross swamp ogre named Shrek (voiced by a Scottish-burring Mike Myers) obliged to embark upon a royal quest to rescue an imprisoned princess from a nasty dragon is full of changes and surprises. The princess turns out to be a rather more independent and tough-minded royal (Cameron Diaz) than many fantasy fans might expect. Shrek's sidekick, a highly verbal donkey (Eddie Murphy) demonstrates how successfully low comedy can be used. And the plot's jam-packed with all manner of political jibes (the local despot forces a wide variety of known fantasy figures into refugee status, driving down the property values in Shrek's already dismal neighborhood), not to mention some choice parody of Michael Eisner and the Disney industry). DreamWorks knows where its bread is buttered. The feature's literate, amusing, and warm.

I'm going to put Richard Linklater's *Waking Life*, filmed in live action and then animated, in this section despite the fact that I found it tedious, pedantic, and sleep-inducing. But I'm apparently in the minority, so go figure. I loved Linklater's other films such as *Slacker*, and I'm willing to consider the possibility I was having a bad day. The film features a long series of dialogues about the nature of reality and most other general intellectual topics of discussion. Think an animated *My Dinner with Andre,* but with a round-robin sequence of conversationalists, most of whom have seemingly thought a great deal less about their topics and absorbed rather less maturity over the years than Andre Gregory and Wallace Shawn. Do you remember late-night dormitory bull sessions in college with a great deal of nostalgia? Then *Waking Life* may be your cup of grad-lounge coffee. Me, I'd almost rather listen to two hours of AM talk radio. Almost.

## On the Side

I'm from the generation that learned much about science and human physiology from animated science features, many of which, I seem to recall, were produced by Bell Telephone. One of my favorites was *Hemo the Magnificent,* the vivid evocation of how the human bloodstream worked. Two thousand one saw *Osmosis Jones,* a combination animation and live-action feature courtesy of the Farrelly Brothers' guiding intelligence, something like a Benny Hill remake and expansion of *Hemo.* The number of visual and audio jokes regarding human functions are a thrill for younger kids of all ages.

## Television

In the 2001 seasons on the small screen, one needed a program to keep track of all the players, though employing the services of the Oracle at Delphi might have been more productive. Shows arrived; shows departed. Shows were shuttled all over the TV scheduling map. But whatever the given chart each day, week, or month, there was plenty of material of the fantastic arriving at home via antenna, cable, or satellite. Some of it was worth watching.

New programs tended to be quick or be dead. One of the most promising was UPN's *All Souls,* which screened all of four episodes before summary cancellation. Created by Stuart Gillard and Stephen Tolkin for producers Aaron Spelling and E. Duke Vincent, this was sort of a cross-pollination of Stephen King with Robin Cook or Michael Crichton.

The setting was All Souls Hospital of Boston, founded in 1838. Rumor has it that the closed-off section beneath the tower was the site of an insane asylum. It's rumored that the spirits of the dead still hang out in this huge hospital. About eighteen hundred folks die here every year. And what about the experimental programs, including the sinister spinal injury section?

The fairly complex cast was quite promising. The protagonist was Dr. Mitchell Grace (Grayson McCouch), a bright young intern drawn to All Souls by strange forces. His father was a janitor who died at the hospital under mysterious circumstances. Clues indicate that Mitch could be the incarnation of one of the hospital's founders. Adam Rodriguez plays Mitch's best friend, a paraplegic from a motorbike accident three years before. Serena Scott Thomas is the chief of medical staff, with all the dark secrets one might expect from a hospital administrator. Irma P. Hall plays Glory, the nurse who's seen it all . . . including the knockout siren, clad all in Victorian black, wheeling a baby carriage around the corridors. Presumably the Angel of Death.

Then there are the ghosts, ranging from Lazarus, the spirit of a Civil War orderly, to the more recent spirits of the dead ectoplasmicly shambling, dancing, or resignedly tramping down the hospital corridors postmortem. Set up in quasi-serial format with a real sense of plot progression from one episode to the next, *All Souls* promised quite a lot, but never made it out of critical care.

Another four-episode run before the programming guillotine hit was NBC's *Wolf Lake* with Lou Diamond Phillips, something of lycanthropic *Twin Peaks* melodrama about a contemporary small town in the American Northwest inhabited mainly by a pack of werewolves. While it had its moments, the series was clearly struggling to establish a mythos and identity.

Less ambitious, but also less terminal, was one of the SciFi Channel's amusements for the summer, *The Chronicle*. This supernatural/sf series revolves around a contemporary supermarket tabloid, the staff of which is well aware that their subject matter is often far too real for comfort. You could call it something of a civilian version of *Special Squad* 2, or, if you wanted to be really grandiose, a twenty-first-century *Kolchak: The Night Stalker*. It isn't the last, of course. Chad Willett, as an ambitious young reporter, just doesn't have the presence of a Darren McGavin, at least not at this stage of his career. Nor do Rena Sofer as the female reporter or Reno Wilson playing the photographer. But working together as something of an ensemble company, they do generate a refreshing gestalt effect of simple pure fun. Jon Polito evokes a good newspaper editor, a guy who's far more than he first appears. And Curtis Armstrong gets points as the half-human Pig Boy, the science geek working down in the *Chronicle*'s deeply buried archives. Created by Silvio Horta, *The Chronicle* is based on Mark Sumner's fiction paperback series, *News from the Edge*.

Speaking of *Special Squad* 2, that's UPN's *Kolchak* effort. Set in Chicago, it's sort of a cop version of *Men in Black*, with supernatural creatures for adversaries. The main two protagonists are a mismatched pair of officers presumably suggestive of Mulder and Scully. The humor can best be termed broad. The musical scoring is used to obnoxious auditory effect.

In terms of proven favorites, things got complicated in the Buffyverse. At the end of the spring 2001 season on WB, it was announced that *Buffy the Vampire Slayer* would be moving to UPN in the fall. But *Angel* would stay with WB, its original network. As an intriguing segue, Buffy died at the end of the spring season. The assumption for any sensible audience member was that she'd be revived in the autumn on UPN, but how? Series creator Joss Whedon, to his credit, avoided anything so lame as the *Dallas* it-was-all-a-dream scenario.

When Buffy returns from the dead, that's precisely what happens. Her witch buddies Willow and Tara use sorcerous powers to reclaim her from the grave. And when she comes back, Buffy's a bit traumatized by the experience. As one should expect from a series as skillfully constructed and scripted as *Buffy*, the sequence is sober and affecting. The series continues to evolve in promising, even outrageous ways. Who would have thought that by the end of the year, Buffy and the long, long post-Goth vampire Spike would be having a clandestine, touching, funny, and almost seismically explosive affair?

Back at the WB, *Angel* started opting for more comedy and even a tone of domesticity as the eponymous good-guy vampire found himself unexpectedly caring for an unanticipated infant son. *Angel*'s certainly evolved beyond being a spin-off clone of *Buffy*, and I think it's all for the good.

Fox's longtime established favorite *The X-Files* is in its ninth and final season. Original male lead David Duchovny has limited his participation to very occasional cameos, and less emphasis has been placed on his female counterpart, Gillian Anderson. Taking the burden off Agents Mulder and Scully have been Robert Patrick and Annabeth Gish as Agents Doggett and Reyes. Each has done quite a creditable job establishing their roles in the series, but it's a thankless task. Obviously the great mass of the audience will settle for nothing less than Mulder and Scully, alas. *The X-Files* still cooks, but not for much longer.

*The X-Files* spinoff series *The Lone Gunmen* started promisingly enough, but died after airing about eight episodes. The amusement value of the three techie geeks didn't sustain as well at an hour as it did for cameos in *The X-Files*. Internet word is that unfinished plot business in *The Lone Gunmen* will be tied up in a projected two-episode series finale for *The X-Files* in 2002.

More death notices: *Roswell*, the aliens-among-us show for teens, most recently picked up by UPN, is lurching toward the end of its life-span. So are *The Outer Limits* and *The Invisible Man* on SciFi. Sadly Fox pulled the hapless superhero comedy *The Tick* after eight episodes.

UPN had one of its best ratings weeks when it debuted the new *Star Trek* series, *Enterprise*. Set much closer to our present time than any of the other *Trek* series, *Enterprise* sends out an early human interstellar expedition under the command of Scott Bakula. It's interesting to see the writers grappling with the concept of a comparatively technologically primitive *Trek* universe. I paid more attention to the series when I heard the radio talk show darling, Dr. Laura (an avowed Trekkie) opine that she wouldn't watch *Enterprise* because of the "trashy sex." Hmm. Innocent, rather adolescent sexuality, perhaps, but not trashy.

The WB also struck ratings gold by debuting *Smallville*, a teen series depicting the coming-of-age years for Superman, Lex Luthor, and any other DC character who can reasonably be pulled into the scenario. Michael Rosenbaum is especially intriguing as young Luthor. Right now the series strikes me as something of a one-trick pony, and is still struggling to widen the focus sufficiently to allow a variety of stories. I wish them well.

*Farscape*'s still around on SciFi to give us solid space opera; the *Heavy Metal*-lite *Lexx* continues as well. *Lexx* inexorably mutates into a haven for pure, unadulterated silliness.

Though the creative team's reshuffling, the syndicated *Gene Roddenberry's Andromeda* continues to offer solid space opera and futuristic adventure. On Showtime, *Stargate: SG-1*'s Richard Dean Anderson and his team still shuttle out to weird destinations, the plots varying wildly in ambition and execution.

And on new seasons of Fox's *Dark Angel*, young genetic superwoman Jessica Alba continues to battle all manner of repressive forces in the postapocalyptic Pacific Northwest. It still feels fresh and fun, and Alba successfully carries a refreshing cargo of charisma.

## Toys

Here's a visual medium I haven't treated before, but I'll keep it brief. Are you familiar with the burgeoning world of action figures? Think dolls for boys, at least for the most part. Sports figures, monsters, comics and media effigies, most done at a scale of one inch per one foot, increasingly elaborately designed with jointed posable limbs and all manner of costume and accessories. Right now the hottest name in action figures is Todd McFarlane Toys. Some backfill may be needed here. McFarlane is the comics artist who created *Spawn*, the project that led to popular graphic novels, a feature film, and an animated TV series. His work has made McFarlane a rich fella, so flush that he indulged the fantasy of creating his own toy company. McFarlane figures are superbly crafted with amazing detail and a high degree of articulation. While the company does well at replicating in plastic 1/12 scale sports figures and rock musicians (these days in Hollywood, it's considered a major status coup to become a McFarlane action figure), the arena in which it especially shines is the horrific and grotesque.

The *Tortured Souls* toy set represents a creative partnership between McFarlane and Clive Barker. They would seem to be made for each other. There are six figures, each one accompanied by one-sixth of a new novella by Barker. Needless to say, the story is not a tale for kiddies, and many parents would be wary about letting their more impressionable offspring place the accompanying action figures in strategically dark corners of the bedroom. Hooks, barbs, teeth, stretched skin, distorted anatomy, bondage and impalement, these toys could be used for unforgettable show-and-tell demonstrations in class.

But let's be brutally honest for a moment. Once you destroy the considerable collector's value of the six blister-packed figures by cutting them open so you can read the story, you might as well let your creative imagination run riot. Imagine the impressionable friends you can drive screaming from your presence once they see the imaginative dioramas possible when Barbie and her buds run face-to-face into Venal Anatomica and the mongroid!

There are no audio chips in these exotic creatures. You'll have to provide your own dialogue. You'll also have to do some minor homework to afford the Barker set. I found the figures priced at $8.95 at Tower Records; they're twelve bucks at Electronics Boutique; and an extortionate $15 at Hot Topic. So caveat emptor.

McFarlane Toys also produced an exemplary selection of *Shrek* items in 2001, but the Barker set is the definite prize.

## Coming Attractions

You can bet 2002 will see no drought of horror, fantasy, and science fiction on the screen. Expect more Tolkien and Rowling on the big screen. Look for Philip José Farmer's *Riverworld* epic saga on television.

Times of societal trouble and crisis simultaneously breed a desire not only for escape, but for stimulation as well. I think we're going to see a plethora of both.

# Fantasy and Horror in Comics: 2001

## Charles Vess

Luckily for the readers of this anthology the art of comic books as a storytelling medium has grown and matured into a surprisingly rich tapestry of genres, fully capable of engaging the adult mind as well as exciting the child in all of us. One has only to read Art Spiegleman's *Maus*, Al Davidson's *The Spiral Cage*, or Bryan Talbot's *The Tale of One Bad Rat* to know that comics aren't just for kids anymore. The world, too, has discovered the untapped resources of this medium, as many mainstream awards have been showered on these works, such as the Pulitzer, the Guardian Literary Award, the American Parent's Choice Awards, etc. And yet the child lying beside you at bedtime or hiding itself beneath your own cloak of wrinkles can find splendid all-ages joy within the pages of Mark Crilley's *Akiko* or Jill Thompson's *Scary Godmother* tales.

Admittedly comics are an odd medium. The stories that reside between those oftentimes brightly colored covers may appear to the layman at first glance to be too short and sometimes too crudely drawn to confront themes of any importance or depth. But you have to bear in mind that in this medium, it is words and pictures, working as integral parts of the same whole, that lead the reader through the rise and fall of the action and ultimately into the safe harbor of the story's conclusion. The drawn images of each individual panel take the place of the abundant use of adjectives and verbs that display for the reader of a prose story a specific time and place, the details of clothing and facial features, as well as the emotions of each character.

For example, a paragraph of descriptive prose such as: "Deep in the darkness of a great looming forest sits a small, thatched hut. Amongst the crude stones that make up the foundation of this cottage, intermittent blades of grass struggle ceaselessly against the hard-packed dirt of the rest of the small yard that divides house from forest eternal. Across the hardened clay earth, scattered in no particular order or pattern, are rough wooden stakes. To the top of each of these stakes is tied a skull, eerily glowing in the darkness, a darkness that seems blacker than that of the surrounding night of that deep forest, perhaps as black as the heart of the witch that waits, sitting patiently within the house, for any poor benighted wanderer that chances by and would try her hospitality" could be depicted in a single panel with one short caption.

This is the essence of the best that the comics medium has to offer. Words and pictures acting in perfect consort to achieve an effect that neither simply prose nor pictures standing alone can achieve as easily or as quickly.

Just as there are stylistic difference from one writer to another, so, too, are there stylistic approaches in the art that makes up each comic. Some are stark and stylized, as pared down in their economical use of drawn lines as any prose in a Gypsy folktale. Others will be as richly textured and fully naturalistic as a novel by Charles de Lint.

From its beginning in 1933 with *Funnies on Parade*, the comic book was quick to take advantage of the visual appeal that all the familiar tropes that folktales and fairy tales have to offer.

However it wasn't until the early 1940s that two comics appeared that are of special interest to lovers of the fantastic. The first, begun by artist/writer Walt Kelly (who later went on to create the "Pogo" newspaper strip) was called *Fairy Tale Parade*. It was crammed with short tales adapting fairy tales from all over the world, sometimes spinning new fantasy adventures out of whole cloth. At the same time the long-running *Raggedy Ann and Andy* comic started. This series (almost all drawn by the same unidentified artist) contained gentle stories populated quite frequently by characters out of your favorite fairy tales.

The initial comics' craze for superheroes was beginning to die out by the late forties to be replaced by the new kid on the block—the horror comic. These increasingly gruesome tales proved to be an instant success. The newsstands were soon flooded with all manner of violent, always garishly colored, terror tales. The zenith of these books was to be found in the output of the EC Comics group. *The Vault of Horror* and *The Crypt of Terror* offered monthly doses of short stories (often adaptations from well-known authors such as Ray Bradbury), that usually contained a macabre twist at the story's end but always with superb, atmospheric art.

By the mid-1950s comics of this ilk had caught the eye of the "watchdogs" of mainstream culture and were soon accused of being a chief reason behind that era's rise in juvenile delinquency. Horror comics in specific, and comic books in general, were blamed for every "evil" in society. Comics were blamed as the leading cause of illiteracy amongst the youth of America. Comics publishers began to self-regulate themselves by creating a Comics Code Authority (CCA). This group forbade the use of most of the elements that had made the horror comic so compelling. Companies that joined the CCA painted themselves into a desperate corner that only allowed for the most puerile product (*Casper, Archie*, etc.) to be published.

In the early 1960s the world of the comic book began to reemerge from this bland, self-inflicted shell when Warren Publishing printed at magazine size (so they could step around the iron hand of the CCA) two "comics," *Creepy* and *Eerie*. These books, using many of the same artists and writing styles that had made the EC comics so popular proved sucessful, and once again zombies, beheadings, and grisly deaths splashed across the newsstands of our nation.

The 1960s hippie phenomenon of "head shops" spread across the country and soon built a growing demand for a new type of comic, the underground. These comix (*Zap*, *Mr. Natural*, *The Fabulous Furry Freak Brothers*, etc.) displayed a wildly experimental storytelling style with hard-edged revolutionary political themes influenced in part by the free use of drugs and the breaking down of sexual taboos. A wave of young comics artists and writers fresh to the until-then-closed shops of the mainstream comic-book world were quick to make aesthetic use of this newfound freedom in the graphic arts.

Soon after, in Europe (particularly in France and Belgium) there was an explosion of sucessful fantasy-, horror- and sf-themed graphic novels (properly called albums). There the popular format called for a hardcover collection with one stand-alone story that was produced annually. Druillet, Moebius, Bilal, Hermann, Juillard, and Tardi created album after album of beautifully produced, specifically for a mature audience, full-color comic novels, most of which unfortunately have not been translated into English.

In 1970 Marvel Comics published *Conan the Barbarian*, which brought the world of sword and sorcery, long a staple of pulp fiction, into comics. It was the quickly maturing work of a young British artist, Barry Smith, that made the Conan comic a sales juggernaught, inspiring a rush of imitators. At the same time across town at DC Comics, new doors in exciting aesthetic directions began to open. Joe Kubert's adaptions of the early "Tarzan" novels, and Michael Kaluta's exquisite rendering and dead-on visualization of the "Carson of Venus" series, as well as the horror comic series *Swamp Thing* (by Bernie Wrightson and Len Wein) are prime mainstream examples of this "new" comic.

Soon another wave of artists, who didn't want their personal vision corrupted by the large corporation's desire for bland, middle-of-the-road, commercial entertainment, were attempting to produce self-published books that held true to their inner vision. The insistence on work-made-for-hire practices that attempted to strip away the rights of a creator (be they the author or the artist) to his or her own creations by these same corporations also figured prominently in this move toward self-determination.

The first of these books came out in 1977. Dave Sim's *Cerebus* (Aardvark/Vanaheim) began as a parody of the then-current craze for barbaric sword-and-sorcery fantasy. It's the story of one man's primal scream at a universe that he wants to control but never will; it's laced with acid commentary on the war of the sexes, politics, philosophy, and gender—all spouting from the small, unlikely mouth of an anthropomorphic pig. By the next year a second self-published s/f fantasy adventure comic *Elfquest* (Warp Graphics) was sucessfuly launched by Wendy and Richard Pini. Then Kevin Eastman and Peter Laird's *Teenage Mutant Ninja Turtles* followed and took the comics world—and the world at large, as well—by storm.

In the last decade the comics genre, especially within the field of smaller publishers and self-published books, has produced some remarkable work that, not incidentally for us, has relied quite heavily on themes of both fantasy and horror. Even the large comic-book corporations have become interested in this genre. DC Comics has responded with Vertigo, a new line of books that initially focused on a more mature reader, exploring themes rife with horror and fantasy. With each new work that has sought to exploit the full potential of myth, fairy tale, and horror, the genre seems to be in an ever-expanding-snowball mode that bodes well for the health of comics in general.

It's hard to believe that most comics, at least in this country, are still published as serial adventures, each thirty-two-page book coming out every month or every other month! Is it any wonder that so few comics attain the full potential that this medium has to offer? If a prose author, no matter how speedy, were to produce a novel a month, how often would there be any reading worth the cost of all those trees? When it does happen, and happen it does in the world of comics (witness Neil Gaiman's *Sandman* or Jeff Smith's *Bone*), it is cause for celebration by us all.

One final caveat before I begin. There are many *very* deserving comics being published today, but for this particular review they simply do not fit within the fantasy and horror criteria. So to all those hardworking writers and artists who labor in this field, forgive me if your work is not cited in this list.

Join me now as we celebrate the best in comics from the year 2001.

Perhaps the most auspicious event of the year was the conclusion of P. Craig Russell's fourteen-issue adaptation of Richard Wagner's *Ring* opera cycle. Weighing in at over four hundred pages, this sumptuous, handsomely drawn story is the completion of a lifelong dream on Russell's part. He has adapted many operas to the comics medium as well as three hardcover volumes of *The Fairy Tales of Oscar Wilde* (NBM), but with this series he has hit a high-water mark in his career. It comes as a set of two softcover trades from Dark Horse Comics. I cannot recommend this one enough.

For the last ten years writer/artist Jeff Smith has been drawing the adventures of the Bone cousins as they navigate the hidden world of The Valley in his self-published book, *Bone* (Cartoon Books). I eagerly await each new issue as Smith manipulates his amazing cast of characters (dragons, princesses, and strange, strange creatures) and his readers with a sure hand for moments of laugh-out-loud action balanced deftly with scenes of sheer terror. There are now seven hard/soft cover collections available. Please do yourself a favor and run right out and buy them all; you won't be disappointed.

This year also saw the conclusion of a prequel to *Bone* written by Jeff Smith and painted by me, *Rose* (Cartoon Books). I find it difficult to recommend my own work with an easy conscience, but the response to our story has been so overwhelmingly positive that I am placing it in this list. You need not have read any of *Bone* to enjoy this stand-alone fantasy adventure, which relates the tale of two sisters, Rose and Briar, and their efforts to defeat the ancient enemy of their people, the Lord of the Locusts.

*Age of Bronze* (Image Comics) is artist/writer Eric Shanower's wonderful, on-going series depicting the events leading up to and occurring in the aftermath of the Trojan War. It is vivid, historically accurate and lushly rendered, depicting fully realized characterizations of Paris, Odysseus, Achilles and, of course, Helen. A two-hundred-page trade paperback volume, *A Thousand Ships* (Image Comics) was released last summer.

Mark Crilley's ongoing bimonthly comic series, *Akiko*, is not to be missed. These whimsical, charming adventures of a twelve-year-old girl on a faraway planet, surrounded by a whacky set of characters, are always a joy to read. Besides the ongoing comic series and several trade collections (both published by Sirius), Crilley has written and illustrated a series of *Akiko* young-adult novels for Bantam Books.

If you ever wanted to know what it is like to walk around inside the psychedelic, constantly expanding universe that is the mind of Alan Moore (*Watchman*) you have but to read his ongoing series *Promethea* (Wildstorm/DC Comics). Evocatively drawn by J. H. Williams and Mick Gray, it really remains Moore's show, as he escorts the reader through his perception of magic, myth systems, and physical illusion to show how our perceptions of those elements influence and regulate all of our lives.

Begun late this year and published as an ongoing series by CrossGeneration Comics is *The Ruse*. Written by Mark Waid and beautifully drawn by Jackson Guice, it is a detective story set in an alternate world London where the gargoyles are real and magic glimmers in the dark back alleys. There is a delightful repartee between our handsome but icy-cold detective and his beautiful female associate. A real delight both in script and art.

There have been four beautiful hardcover collections of French artist/writer Michel Plessix's adaptations of Kenneth Grahame's *The Wind in the Willows* (NBM) translated into English so far. Each volume relates two of Grahame's short tales featuring his beloved characters, Mole, Rat, and Toad, as they live their lives by the great winding river or deep in the Wild Wood. This series of painted graphic novels surely is a labor of love for Plessix, and he has lavished on it an extraordinary amount of research and detail. His depictions of the English countryside awash in late-afternoon summer light are breathtaking, as is the appearance in volume #3 of the Piper at the Gates of Dawn. A wonderful treat for the eyes and for the heart.

*Castle Waiting* by Linda Medley, published by her own Olio Press, is another not-to-be-missed series, with several trade collections available. Have you ever wondered what happens after the princess rides off with the prince into the "happily ever after" ending of most fairy tales? What becomes of the cook, the maid, the stableboy? Medley's tale answers that question by populating her narrative with those who are left behind, both figuratively and metaphorically, in the castle. It's a gentle story that uses humor and pathos to develop her themes.

There are four fully painted picture books by Jill Thompson featuring her wonderful character *Scary Godmother* (Sirius). Scary lives in a splendid house, just over the edge from our world, where it's Halloween all year round, full of a diverse crew of crazy friends: BugaBoo the purple monster that lives under every child's bed, Mr. Petty Bone the skeleton, Harry the werewolf, and a host of others. Witty. Charming. Fun. Also by Thompson, *The Little Endless Storybook* (Vertigo/DC Comics) features the cast of Neil Gaiman's "*Sandman*" comic series as infants in a delightful children's picture book masquerading as a comic.

The whimsical form of the picture book proves its continued allure this year as Tony Millionaire's *Sock Monkey: A Children's Book* (Dark Horse) saw print. Millionaire's art, which is deeply indebted to illustrators of the past, looks quite handsome in the small edition, with its very quirky story.

I was very pleased that a fourth issue of Mike Kunkel's *Herobear and the Kid* (Astonish Comics) saw the light of day in 2001. Kunkel's story is about a young boy, Tyler, who discovers that he is protected by his grandfather's spirit, which inhabits a stuffed toy bear the boy inherits. And it is a delight. Kunkel has given us a rare comic of subtle charm that is a treat in a field usually smothered in exclamation marks.

In Stan Sakai's *Usagi Yojimbo* (Dark Horse) a samurai rabbit roams the world of feudal Japan encountering beasts and demons transplanted from Japanese folklore into new stories full of zest and appeal. Simply but evocatively drawn and written, it is a book for all ages.

The fifth and concluding book of Scott Morse's epic fantasy *Soulwind* (Oni Press) was released this year. This volume neatly ties up all the myriad plot threads that had tangled themselves through the five years it took to complete his tale. Morse has drawn together diverse elements from sf and fantasy backgrounds, featuring Oberon, Titania, the courts of Faerie, magic swords, and the power of story and myth that directs all of our lives. He's succeeded in giving all of these elements a fresh twist, and he's wrapped up his story with a grand flourish. The art is simple, stylized, and perfect for the journey on which he takes us.

*The Last Knight* (NBM), a greatly shortened adaptation of Cervantes's classic picaresque novel, *Don Quixote*, and *The Princess and the Frog* (NBM) from the fairy tale of the same name are by comics giant Will Eisner. Eisner has been producing cutting-edge work for over sixty years, first with his legendary *The Spirit* and later with a long string of graphic novels dealing with life in New York City over many generations. Here he works for the first time with outright fantasy motifs, and the results are quite refreshing.

For almost twenty years writer/artist Colleen Doran has been producing her grand, far-flung sf/fantasy comic series, *A Distant Soil* (Image), now collected into several trade collections. An elegantly drawn, complex cast of characters crowd through her pages and fill her multidimensional story with a complex weave of emotion and wonder.

A brilliant concept by artist/writer Batton Lash makes the series (and trade collections) *Supernatural Law* (Exhibit A Press) a fun read. Alanna Wolff and Jeff Byrd are legal counsel for every creature that goes bump in the night. Defending everything from vampires to Frankenstein creatures to hulking monsters who have inadvertently stepped on vast metropolitan cities, their legal efforts are bizarre to say the least.

Mike Mignola, on the other hand, uses full-throttle pulp horror to jump-start his powerful *Hellboy* (Dark Horse). Mignola's stylishly sleek graphics grab you by the neck and pull you into his dark narrative world of demons, Nazis, and Lovecraftian beings of primal horror, all leavened with a keenly absurd sense of humor that makes you come back for more.

In seventeenth-century Paris *The Marquis* (Oni Press), on a mission for the Holy Roman Church, strides snowy streets, staining their bleached whiteness red with the blood of those he was sent here to slaughter: demons, the filth of Satan. But can he truthfully tell reality from illusion? Are those the innocent he leaves crumpled, dead in the snow? Writer/artist Guy Davis brings his tale powerfully to life with his blend of scratchy pen lines and faith-questioning story.

Jim Woodring's *Frank* (Fantagraphic Books) is a claustrophobic, dreamlike experience. His narrative has the unexpected convolutions of a surreal nightmare that leaves us sucking at the teat on the dark underbelly of the beast that lurks in our collective unconscious as well. Here there be dragons indeed!

I have never read William Hope Hodgson's Victorian horror novel *The House on the Borderland,* so I can't say whether this graphic novel adaptation (Vertigo/DC Comics) by Simon Ravelstoke and artist Richard Corben is true to its source material or not. The story they do present is unnerving, and the plight of the brother and sister protagonists as they are beset by demons from the outer darkness in their newly rented home in the wilds of Ireland is a harrowing tale, well told and drawn. It certainly gave me a shiver or two.

Another look into the horrific side of life is *Black Hole* (Fantagraphic Books) by Charles Burns. His panels, filled with deep pools of inky black, slowly pull the reader into a horrific urban nightmare where each teenage character is undergoing some sort of strange metamorphosis. One grows a tail, another the face of a dog, yet another has a mouth appearing at the base of her throat. These and other powerful, well-conceived images sink deep into your subconsciousness to create a sense of unease and terrifying angst. Certainly not for the faint of heart.

For a slightly surreal experience you need look no further than Gary Spencer Millidge's *Strangehaven* (Abiogensis Press). After a road accident in rural England a young man is left stranded in a remote village. Following numerous unsuccessful attempts to leave the village, he slowly begins to build a life for himself there. Strange religious cults and erratic behavior by the inhabitants make his life difficult. An indefinable sense of lurking doom at the edge of each panel makes Millidge's story odd as well as compelling.

*Raptors* (NBM) is a translated European import by the team of Dufaux and Marini. Its stylish, fully painted art is easy on the eye and gives the story a strong sense of place. This is a tale of a brother and sister, renegades from a worldwide cult of vampires whom they are willing to destroy at any cost. Illuminati-like, this cabal of vampires controls all the world's top business corporations and law enforcement agencies. The reader is not yet told why this brother and sister are renegades or why they seek to destroy the cult, since they appear to be vampires themselves, but the promise of an interesting answer to this tricky question and the well-executed art easily pulls you through all three collections with more to come.

By far the book that has had me squirming most uncomfortably this year is Dave Cooper's *Crumple* (Fantagraphic Books), stunningly drawn in an old-fashioned, almost 1930-ish cartoon style. Once it has you by the throat Cooper's story shakes you unmercifully and will not let you go until long after you've finished reading this modern-day nightmare of sexual fear and gender war.

Art Spiegelman and Françoise Mouly presented the second volume in their "Little Lit" anthology series with *Strange Stories for Strange Kids* (Harper-Collins). Eight stories are sumptuously presented by master artists ranging from Maurice Sendak to Posey Simmonds. Weird and wacky, it is a delight to behold and read.

Only one issue of the exciting new fantasy anthology, *The Forbidden Book* (Renaissance Press) was released this year. At 130 pages, it's packed with a huge selection of stories featuring a diverse lineup of artists and writers at various story lengths. A color story by Colleen Doran, *Three Black Hearts* adapting a folk legend from Virginia and a short poetic meditation on blood and magic by Jeffrey Jones stand out in this collection, which includes work by Michael Cohen, Rick Vietch, Marv Wolfman, and Charles Vess.

While not strictly fantastic in nature, *The Golem's Mighty Swing* by James Sturm (Drawn and Quarterly) is an elegantly packaged original graphic novel that relates the tale of a group of Jewish baseball players who in the 1920s travel from town to town and are paid for playing whoever will join them on the field. As a publicity stunt, one of their number dons the guise of a legendary figure from Jewish folklore, the Golem. The time period is painted in the bold black-and-white strokes of the artist's brush, and his plot is full of telling details of historical interest. It is the story's use of Jewish mythology that puts such an interesting spin on the tale, and it is for this element that it was included here, as well as for its fully realized picture of an often-overlooked part of our history.

The European team of artist François Schuiten and writer Benoit Peetes has been producing a series of albums in their "Cities of the Fantastic" series for years. Now NBM has translated their latest collaboration, *Brusel,* for our reading pleasure. Lavish visualizations of an intricately realized imaginary city form the stunning backdrop for this paranoid tale of a vast government bureaucracy that is crushing all individual impulse from its citizens, slowly rendering them faceless automatons.

Now comes a collection of Bryan Talbot's *Heart of Empire* (Dark Horse), which was originally serialized in nine, forty-page installments and is a brilliant read. In an alternate British Empire of the future, a fascist monarchy rules with an iron hand. Only Princess Victoria, the daughter of a great revolutionary of the past, Luther Arkwright, holds the key to their downfall. Quite different in mood and subject matter from the artist's previous work, *The Tale of One Bad Rat*, this complex fantasy/sf adventure mixes politics, drugs, sex, and magic into a heady brew that is impossible to put down.

Other books from 2001 that are definitely worth a look are: *The Chuckling Whatsit* by Richard Sala (Fantagraphic Books), *The League of Extraordinary Gentlemen* by Alan Moore and drawn by Kevin O'Neil (Wildstorm/DC Comics), *Thieves and Kings* by Mark Oakley (I Box Pub.), *Tellos* by Todd Dezago and artist Mike Wieringo (Image Comics), *House of Secrets: Facade* by Steven Seagle and painter Teddy Kristianson(Vertigo/DC Comics), *The Hobbit,* scripted by Chuck Dixon and painted by David Wenzel (HarperCollins), and *Rodrigo* by Hermann (Dark Horse).

I also wanted to mention these books from years past that for one reason or another haven't previously made it into this column. Look for them from either the publisher or a secondhand bookstore. A few of the highlights are: *The Life and Adventures of Santa Clause* adapted from the novel by L. Frank Baum by Mike Ploog (Tundra/Kitchen Sink), *Clan Apis* (Active Synapse) by Jay Hosler, *Beowulf* (The Comic.Com) by Gareth Hinds, *The Big Book of Grimm* (Paradox Press) scripted by Jonathan Vankin and drawn by divers hands, *The Wizard's Tale* (Image Comics) by Kurt Busiek and painted by David Wenzel, *The Replacement God* (Amaze Ink) by Zander Cannon, *Kingdom of the Wicked* (Caliber Comics) by Ian Edgington and drawn by Disraeli, *The Minotaur's Tale* (Gollanz) by Al Davidson, "The Nausicaa" (Viz) series by Hayao Miyazaki, *Dinosaur Shaman* (Kitchen Sink Press) by Mark Schultz, *Concrete, Think Like a Mountain* (Dark Horse) by Paul Chadwick, *Winging It* (Solo Press) by Roberta Gregory, and the all-ages fun romp *Leave It to Chance* (Image Comics) by James Robinson and drawn by Paul Smith.

Two art books that should be of interest:

For over thirty years now one of the best-kept secrets of the fantasy art world has been the work of Michael William Kaluta. His work has mostly surfaced in the world of comic books, where he first established himself with his efforts on, among many other books, *The Shadow* and *Starstruck*. In 1980 a legendary art book *The Studio* (Dragon's Dream) was published. That book, a collection of four artists, Jeffrey Jones, Barry Smith, Bernie Wrightson, and Kaluta, who were at the time sharing a work space in Manhattan, is now a sought-after collector's edition. Twenty years later we have *Wings of Twilight: The Art of Michael Haluta* (NBM), an art book devoted solely to Michael Kaluta. The book is filled with art from many disciplines: poster art, album and CD designs, movie and TV preproduction art, the 1995 Tolkien calendar, and many, many comic-book covers. It is a rare and wonderful look at the career of an artist who deserves our fullest attention.

A benchmark in the art form of the comic strip was the splendid, full-page Sunday comic, *Prince Valiant, in the Days of King Arthur*. This was the work of one artist, who wrote and drew the strip from 1937 until he retired in 1970. In his book, *HAL FOSTER: Prince of Illustrators* (Vanguard) writer, researcher, and historian Brian Kane has done us all a huge favor and put together a collection overflowing with rare examples of this magnificent artist's work. Additionally, photographs from all periods of his very adventurous life are included, such as prospecting for gold in the Canadian wilderness, riding his bicycle three hundred miles to Chicago in search of work during the Great Depression, and sailing the fiords of Norway as he researched the PV story. No other newspaper comic-strip artist was ever able to draw a scene so naturalistically, so completely, and able to put his reader directly into the midst of the story as Hal Foster.

If you have any trouble locating any of these books through your local bookstore you might try calling the official Comic Shop Locator Service at 1-888-266-4226. Those fine folks will assist you in finding a full-service comic shop nearest you. Then, too, many of these trade collections are carried by the friendly and well-stocked Bud Plant Comic Art (www.budplant.com).

Good luck, good hunting, and happy reading!

# Manga and Anime in 2001: Through the Looking Glass

### Joan D. Vinge

*Konnichiwa, minasan!* . . . Greetings, everyone!

Yes, that is Japanese. No, I don't actually speak it. Chances are, you don't either, although I hope you are familiar with the terms *manga* and *anime*, which refer to Japanese comics and animation.

Don't stop reading. "The secret of Zen is just two words: 'Not always so!'" (*Shunryu Suzuki*)

I find I have a difficult enough time justifying, let alone explaining, why I am an *otaku* (M&A fan), even to readers of F/SF and Horror. Too many intelligent people reject the words "comics" and "animation" outright, without them being *foreign* . . . even though respected writers like Neil Gaiman and Vernor Vinge (who got me to truly appreciate animation) know what serial art can do, as well as how it has matured across its entire spectrum. Defending an interest in manga and anime is very much like explaining to "mundanes" why anyone would read— let alone write—F/SF or Horror. If you know what I mean.

Still snickering? I urge you to seek enlightenment. Read Scott McCloud's *Understanding Comics*, a much-praised book that should make you think—a lot—about how we perceive and interpret visual information. You may see serial art, and the world around you, in a whole new light.

*Got to wear shades—?* If not, leap ahead to the recommended reading and viewing. If so, here are a few (*extremely* oversimplified) guidelines to help your eyes adjust.

**Q**: What are manga and anime really like?

**A**: Manga are like ongoing comic book series; in Japan, however, anthology magazines (in black and white) are the most common way of publishing them. Each anthology runs several manga serials, usually in a variety of genres but aimed at a particular audience: *shonen* (boys and young men); *shojo* (girls and young women); and adults. It is perfectly acceptable for adults to be seen reading manga during their work commute. The individual story lines are reprinted as graphic novels; translated graphic novels are what Americans generally see, though some manga are also published as ongoing comic series.

Anime comes in several forms: animated feature films and prime-time TV series are much more common in Japan and deal with a much broader range of subject matter than do American cartoons. Anime stories are frequently based on manga, novels, or popular video games. OAVs (OVAs)—Original Animation Videos—are direct-to-video movies, or else TV miniseries. Usually an OAV has a bigger budget, a more serious theme, and better animation than a weekly series, though many are sequels (or prequels) to ongoing series.

**Q:** Why do so many M&A characters look like white Americans, when they're supposed to be Japanese?

**A:** Not all Japanese people look alike. But giving individual characters as wide a range of hairstyles, eye colors, and face shapes as possible makes them easier to tell apart, especially when the art tends to be stylized. As for them all looking like Americans, many of them actually have neon-colored hair—naturally green, purple, shocking pink. As one writer observed, "That would make Ohio a much more interesting place to live." ("Albino-white" people are usually some sort of demon in disguise, but the whiteness symbolizes the ghostly, the spirit world; it's *not* a comment on race.)

**Q:** Why all the wide, goo-goo eyes; and all the teens or "adults" who look like kids?

**A:** The eyes are the window to the soul: Wide eyes (a neotenous feature) look trustworthy and innocent. They tend to be a stereotypical feature of girls and women in M&A . . . even ones who have "magical girl" shamanistic powers, or carry swords. (Go ahead, laugh at her—once.) Eyes that are more in proportion make a character look older, more worldly, or more suspicious.

Not all M&A characters are drawn that way; the full range of art styles is quite varied. But most *otaku* become fans when they're young, like fans here (although *otaku* are about 30 percent female; just when you thought you knew your stereotypes). Young fans identify with young characters, who predominate in the comedies, adventures, and romances that teens usually prefer. The familiar-looking characters, plus entertaining plots, keep them involved while they absorb a few deeper, more mature and thoughtful life lessons—ones even adults "just relaxing" can appreciate. (Okay . . . not *always*. But then, what we discover in any story depends on what we're looking for.)

*Chibi* are a special convention of M&A: child-caricatures that adults abruptly transform into when their "inner child" is literally acting out. *Chibi* moments tend to occur in continuing series, even when the stories have serious themes; the effect can be disconcerting, especially after a big dramatic climax. But *chibi* are there to provide comic relief, accent on the "relief." It's a concept Shakespeare would have understood: a show with broader audience appeal gets pelted with less dead fish and/or cancellation notices.

**Q:** Why is there so much "T and A"—impossibly big hooters, babes in miniskirts, schoolgirls with panties showing, scantily clad space aliens . . . not to mention the "catgirls"?

**A:** It's called "fan service," and it's just what you think—*bishojo*, sexy girls, are a natural attention-getter for teenage boys. The joke's on Fanboy, however—because the reason all those shapely young girls suddenly find their lives turned upside down is not because they've grown breasts; it's because they just gained their magical powers. Japan's indigenous (and ancient) Shinto religion was originally overseen by shaman-priestesses, who gained powerful spirit-magic at womanhood. Teenage boys today may ogle the obvious; but both boys and girls are still seeing strong, empowered female role models, who make the stories popular with both sexes.

"Catgirls" may also have a secret, powerful ancestress; there is a book called *The White Tigress: Secret Writings of Taoist Women*, "ancient writings about sex, by and for Taoist women." Catgirls in M&A may seem to be fuzzy-eared twits, but they are often shapechangers who transform into weretigers, or other large ferocious cats. The *Outlaw Star* anime series contains a good example; set in outer space, it's full of Taoist magic and imagery.

(Teenage boys in M&A currently gain supernatural powers—or giant robots—at puberty, too. *Mazel tov*, y'all!)

**Q:** So what about all those delicate, beautiful young men, who look prettier than the women . . . ?

**A:** *Bishonen* ("pretty boys") are mainly "fan service" for the ladies, guys; stories featuring them are usually written and drawn by women. They are no more weaklings than the well-endowed "magical girls" are. Usually they're excellent, often deadly, fighters, with a will of steel. A dark past may haunt them, but they're loyal, tender, idealistic and . . . sigh . . . lonely. Which is much more appealing than some big bullying lout. Many *shonen* series reflect the trend these days: It not only attracts female readers (who "some days, just need to see some violence," too, as one female reviewer put it), but also reassures young males that the hero isn't always the one with the biggest muscles, or gun. . . . The *bishonen*-style hero's strength comes from the depth of his spirit, and that defines true manliness.

**Q:** But do manga and anime include fantasy and horror?

**A:** Yes! All the F/SF and horror tropes that you know and love, or loathe, exist in manga and anime. Classic myths and legends retold; sword-and-sorcery adventure; vampires; alternate worlds; genre-bending gunslinger/samurai bounty hunters on alien worlds; "mythmoshes" of angels, demons, and giant robots . . . and the entire gamut of urban anomie, from tech-noir *oni* (demons) to the monsters that sleep in the souls of ordinary humans leading ordinary lives. But when Euro-American cultural icons merge with their Asian counterparts, you get something more: a strangely parallax view of the dreams and nightmares haunting our universal subconscious. (This does mean you should expect more endings that are ambiguous, bittersweet, or even tragic; if you've seen *Crouching Tiger, Hidden Dragon*, then you have some idea.)

Good M&A trusts the viewer's intellegence: They may "send in the chibi";

but they will not spoon-feed you their themes or implications. Even the most escapist fare may get unexpectedly "real" about life; and life is not a cartoon.

So put on your thinking cap and toss the dunce cap in the garbage, where it belongs. (The motto of U.S. manga and anime distributor CPM is "World Peace Through Shared Popular Culture." Hey, it could happen. . . . )

Now you should be ready to start reading—and viewing—some of the recommended works below. Because, as the Taoist philosopher Lao-tsu said, "The Way which can be told is not the true Way." You'll have to find out for yourself.

## Recommended Manga

These are available in English translation, and in no particular order. This is a very short list, a hint at the variety you'll find when you begin exploring the genre:

*Blade of the Immortal*: beautiful art, artful writing; samurai adventure/fantasy, not for the squeamish;

*Vagabond*: ditto above, but based on the life of legendary swordsman Miyamoto Musashi; one of several translated manga series being reprinted authentically—read "back to front," reflecting the original Japanese-language version (read right to left) rather than "flopping" the art;

*Eagle*: solid art, dead-on acerbic view of American politics—alternate-world story of first Japanese presidential candidate;

*Uzumaki*: good art—spiral-horror tale guaranteed to make your flesh crawl;

*Inu-Yasha*: a comedy/horror/magic-jewel-quest by the wonderful Rumiko Takahashi, creator of *Ranma 1/2*, among others—quirky characters and demons galore in feudal Japan; anime version not available here, but should be soon;

*Akira*: apocalyptic/tech-noir/adventure/horror—entire manga series, reprinted in six huge volumes, to coincide with re-release of legendary anime on DVD, shows how much story you missed in the film;

*Lone Wolf and Cub*: reprints the famous, bloody-but-beautiful series about a revenge-seeking samurai and his infant son;

*No. 5*: a surreal tale with surreal art, set in a surreal landscape where a strange love affair is playing out between mythic figures of life and death;

*Ceres: Celestial Legend*: world-myth/fantasy/horror tale of a spirit-shape-shifter—variously seal, fox, bird, mermaid, "angel"—trapped in human form by a man who hides her "magic" skin; this contemporary retelling of the Japanese variant is a passionate drama of truth, lies, and bloody murder (warning: some "comic relief" scenes may be a big shock), by Yu Watase, creator of *Fushigi Yugi*; the anime series came out this past year as well, and *Fushigi Yugi* is also available as an anime series;

*Clover*: beautifully designed graphic novel series with art, dialogue, and poetry all interwoven; dystopian future/fantasy/romance, the latest work of CLAMP, a popular all-female group of manga creators who are probably best known for the ongoing X series (like *Akira*, the X story line lost much of its complexity in last year's *X: The Movie*, although the animation was striking);

*Dark Angel* and *Dark Angel: Resurrection*: myth/fantasy/adventure/dragons; based on Chinese mythology, like many M&A (China was to Japan what Europe was to America, for many centuries: a source of cultural inspiration, both in its traditions and innovation). *Dark Angel* is being reprinted in a series of graphic novels, in its original black and white; while the sequel has been coming out (painfully slowly) as a full-color comic book series. Creator Kia Asamiya is another manga icon, with a number of well-known titles; the anime adaptation of his tongue-in-cheek, spacey *Nadesico* series was one of last year's fan favorites.

## Who, US?

Manga and anime style have influenced American serial artists for at least the past decade; the increasing popularity of both M&A has resulted in American comic-book publishers putting out increasing numbers of books that don't just vaguely resemble, but intentionally attempt to capture the genuine look and feel of a manga series. (The creators themselves are often Japanese, or at least Asian—Korea and China also produce some manga-style series; a few, like *Storm Riders* and *Island*, are now appearing here.)

The Dreamwave line, formerly an imprint of Image, is all manga, all the time, from the sword-and-sorcery *Warlands* series to cyberpunk horror in *Dark Minds*. Image still runs other manga-style series. DC's Wildstorm line is publishing manga miniseries like *Taleweaver* and *Ninja Boy* (winner of the Ninja Screw Award for killing all the heroes in the last issue of a lighthearted fantasy/adventure, when the series was canceled: Your loyal readers suffered, not the publisher, guys). Some of DC's "Elseworlds" specials have featured manga-style Superman, the Titans, and Green Lantern. Marvel put out a Wolverine/Electra miniseries illustrated by the noted artist Yoshitaka Amano, and published "Mangaverse" (a special-event manga "take" on well-known Marvel heroes, showcasing a variety of "manga art" styles), now out as a graphic novel and also an ongoing series.

These big guns have joined Dark Horse, CPM, Oni, Viz, and other independent publishers, including the new TokyoPop and ComicsOne, which not only put out translated manga series, but works by manga-loving American creators like Adam Warren, Ben Dunn, Lea Hernandez, and Chynna Clugston-Major. New publisher CrossGen now has two manga-themed series, plus the ongoing *Scion*, a sword-and-sorcery tale with manga overtones.

## The Best Manga You May Never Have Seen:

*Usagi Yojimbo* by Stan Sakai, who has written and drawn perhaps the best damn American manga series of all, for years. In an alternate Japan, the hero, samurai Usagi Miyamoto, is a *ronin yojimbo* (bodyguard) by trade. He is also a rabbit.

His ne'er-do-well buddy is a scruffy rhino; the woman he loves (with all the unrequited passion of a true warrior) is a samurai cat, the bodyguard of a young panda *daimyo* (lord). . . . And if you don't forget inside of three pages that they aren't every bit as "human" as you are, then you aren't human. The characters are wonderful and real, the stories are filled with adventure, mystery, lore, and sly wit; the books are guaranteed to leave you smiling, and wiser for it.

## Anime: Movies

MEDIA NOTE: DVD, or not DVD—? I finally vote "yes," without hesitation. DVD players have dropped in price; so have DVDs. And for anime, it finally settles the ongoing "subtitled vs. dubbed?" debate, because as a rule, the DVD contains both, and sometimes worthwhile extra features. (AnimeWorks' "blooper reels" contain some hilarious ad-libbing.) You'll need a DVD, or at least a VCR, to see most anime—because its presence is still all too rare on TV (though its popularity has grown rapidly over the past year), and almost invisible at the movie gigaplexes.

## Recommended Movies

Perhaps the most highly anticipated event of the year was the re-release of the *Akira* anime, made in 1988. *Akira* was the first anime motion picture many fans ever saw: the work that made them fans. Its legendary reputation, plus the fact that so much of its original imagery has since been "homaged" to death, made the actual film almost an anticlimax, when I finally saw it; I do want to see it again, however, strictly on its own terms.

The best new anime films released here last year showcase some of the most awesome, beautiful, and subtle animation I have ever seen. Anime has been cutting-edge in combining computerized special effects with hand-animated 2-D cel art; but combining them seamlessly has turned out to be exceedingly hard to accomplish. A larger budget helps, which is why the best results tend to be found in theatrical movies. (Anime is boffo box office in Japan—but alas, still nearly impossible to get booked into a theater here.)

*Spriggan* is a "Young Indiana Jones vs. the Illuminati" adrenaline rush of fantasy adventure, eye-poppingly cinematic, strikingly designed and rendered. It's even more impressive when you learn (from the excellent commentary track on the DVD) that two-thirds of the movie was completely hand-animated. The story is not deep—basically it asks the question, "Who's more dangerous: a seventeen-year-old assassin with a big gun and a noble heart, or an insane ten-year-old with access to a doomsday machine?" But the nonstop action never completely jumps the rails of its context—a story of humanity lost and humanity reclaimed. Besides, not everything that mentions cockroaches has to be Kafka. Hold on to your hat, gape at the scenery, and just have a butt-kicking good time. (A 'spriggan' is a spirit-guardian of ancient ruins, in the British Isles. The movie is based on a manga, part of which appeared in translation here as *Striker*.)

If you crave food for thought rather than popcorn, try the haunting, state-of-the-art alternate-history *Jin-roh* (*The Wolf Brigade*), a film that really opens trapdoors under your assumptions about what "humanity" means. *Jin-roh* takes place in Japan after a World War II won by—Germany. It seems Hitler, once all his "real" enemies were conquered, turned on his allies and devoured them, too. But at its bleeding heart, the movie is "Little Red Riding Hood" as it might have been retold by George Orwell, and revised by Joseph Conrad. As one character cynically remarks, "Tales of a human who falls in love with a beast never end well." . . . But which is which? Who really has the biggest teeth of all? And, in the end, is anyone left alive . . . or could that whiter shade of pale signify that all along you've been watching a ghost story in sheep's clothing? It takes *Jin-roh* more than two and a half hours to surrender its answer; the questions will haunt you like lost souls for far longer. (Created by *Akira*'s Hiroyuki Okiura, and Mamoru Oshii, who also did the classic film *Ghost in the Shell* and the "Seinfeld with giant robots" police series *Patlabor*. . . . NOTE: Check out the site <www.davidson.edu/personal/nidonowitz/Werewolf_Prostitute.asp> and read the article, "Little Red Riding Hood: Werewolf and Prostitute." Then consider all the implications of lying down with wolves. . . . )

## Other Recommended Films:

(New, or newly available on DVD):
   Yoshitaka Amano's *Vampire Hunter D: Bloodlust* (and its prequel/sequel, *Vampire Hunter D*); *Blood: The Last Vampire*; *Ghost in the Shell*; *Ninja Scroll*; *X: The Movie*, and *Princess Mononoke*.

## Anime: Series

MEDIA NOTE: Most anime series have a distinct "rhythm," and a definite beginning and end. A popular one may contain evolving story arcs, and/or produce "continuing adventure" sequels, miniseries, and movies. Usually the early episodes are self-contained plots that introduce the cast members, with only a few scattered hints of the real story line—which then begins to build about midseries. It may seem like the creators only realized the story's potential halfway through; but this pattern occurs too often to be coincidental. Watching an anime series is like a relationship: time and patience may be required. If you lack one or the other, start in the middle and watch from there. If you like it, start again from the beginning. (A good series is worth viewing more than once, to fully appreciate how characters and metathemes evolve within the plot. Like *Buffy the Vampire Slayer*, many series that look like simple escapism turn out to be unforgettable journeys.)

## Series for Sale or Rent

*Rurouni Kenshin* (*Kenshin, the Wandering Swordsman*) is Joan's Addiction. It's a "what if . . ." story based on a real person, an assassin/hero (he was on the winning side) of the nineteenth-century *Meiji* Revolution who disappeared during its final days. The series' literally fantastic swordplay, high drama, and human comedy take place during Japan's actual postrevolution era of modernization following the downfall of the Shogunate. The series was very popular in Japan, and so it's very long (popular series don't get canceled there either), although the story does eventually come to a definite end, as most of them do. It builds slowly, like a long novel, and the *chibi*-relief can be jarring (though oddly faithful to how real people behave); but the series' unfolding metathemes are timeless and powerful, as Kenshin the Wanderer struggles to make peace with his worst enemy—Kenshin the Assassin. Like the nation he fought for and the people he comes to love, he takes two steps forward, one step back, on the way to the future. The characters feel like old friends to me now, quirks and all; even once-"demonic" enemies have become three-dimensional human beings, through deft plot twists sometimes only a sentence long. (NOTE: A different company distributes a two-part prequel—calling it *Samurai X: Trust* and *Samurai X: Betrayal*—and also *Samurai X: the Movie*. I recommend watching a few episodes of the *Rurouni Kenshin* series before watching the prequel; it works best if you know who Kenshin is "now," before you really see who he was before. . . . The movie fits best between volumes six and seven of the series. The anime is based on a manga series, unfortunately still untranslated here.)

## Series As Seen on TV

(They are still few and far between—check your local TV listings, or some of the anime magazines or Web sites for details.)

Probably the best anime series shown yet on American television was last year's *Cowboy Bebop* (in the new "Adult Swim" bloc of uncensored anime): a Mars-based, retro-sixties, jazz-fusion western/noir/mystery, with the hippest sunglasses-at-night antiheroes ever forced to go bounty-hunting in a cramped spaceship together. "What's money between friends? Who says they're friends—?" It has an awesome soundtrack by the incredible Yoko Kanno, "the best 'undiscovered' composer in the world."

*Bebop* has attracted enough attention that the translated manga is now out, as well as a "series guide" actually translated into English (an encouraging trend, since most guides are only available from specialty dealers, in the original Japanese).

## The Best Anime You May Not Have Seen:

*Eatman* (the first, and harder to find, of two TV series based on a manga) has a hero named Bolt Crank. Bolt Crank is not a cannibal—he's a *ronin*-like mutant on a bleak post-apocalyptic world; he eats metal and drinks cans of oil, then extrudes weapons, etc. from his hand, as needed. Sound absurd? Sure. And yet, if you're really *watching*, each sere minimalist episode can reveal depths of supernatural mystery, brooding tragedy, thought-provoking drama, and surprising compassion. Bolt Crank turns out to be profoundly human after all, and a whole lot more: "Only someone who has eaten iron while crying can know what adventure tastes like."

*Armored Trooper VOTOMS* (based on a series of novels) is the pilgrim's progress of a shell-shocked future war veteran. Chirico Cuvie seems to be unkillable, but he only feels safe—and alive—inside his robot armor, because he barely remembers how to be human. The multi-arc series is a gold mine of poignant irony about miscommunication that actually leads to salvation, "what fools we mortals be," and, above all, the inhuman nature of war. It was as popular as *Gundam* or *Robotech* (two other multiarc, giant-robots-'n'-space series) in Japan; but it got only a brief unheralded release here—even the new DVDs are subtitle-only, and they are rapidly becoming unavailable, while new *Gundam* and *Robotech* DVD releases are thriving. What fools, indeed. . . .

## Who, US?

Yes, of course, there was a big new Disney movie last year: *Atlantis*, a steampunk fantasy inspired by Verne's Captain Nemo novels. The animation was excellent, stylistically influenced by the work of comic artist Mike Mignola as well as by anime; but despite its cartographer hero, a cross-species romance, and colorful supporting characters, *Atlantis* had all the plot depth of a wading pool. The new anime series *Nadia of the Blue Water*—coincidentally featuring both Atlantis and Nemo—has everything *Atlantis* should have had, and more of it. (*Mulan*—based on a Chinese legend and featuring a female hero—is still my favorite Disney tale; probably because the studio thought it would flop, so its creators were left alone and really cut loose.)

*Final Fantasy: The Spirits Within*, a joint American/Japanese production, had amazingly good, all-CGI animation . . . but it was a box office "failure"; because once again (hello, Hollywood—?) it had almost no plot or characterization, or even any relationship to the popular video games. The twentieth-anniversary DVD of *Tron*, the first movie to be virtually all CGI, may look primitive in comparison; but you'll care a lot more about who wins the game.

## US on TV

The ever-increasing popularity of anime on television—especially the Cartoon Network with its "Toonami" anime bloc—continued to soar: Japanese imports like *Sailor Moon* and *Dragon Ball Z* have inspired American anime like *Powerpuff Girls* and the new *Samurai Jack* series; while "Adult Swim" at last allows viewers to dive off the deep end and experience the sophisticated, controversial, and/or bawdy themes and content of anime created for more mature audiences, shown without expurgation at last.

## The Best American Anime You May Not Have Seen:

You want to see a totally CGI, American-made show that won't insult your intelligence? Try *Roughnecks*, a TV series recently released on DVD; based on Heinlein's *Starship Troopers*, it reminds me more of the late, lamented (by some of us) series *Above and Beyond*.

## Other Series Recommendations

Again, only a random sample of the vast variety of series, in no particular order:

*Neon Genesis Evangelion* and *Garasaki*; *Trigun*, *Outlaw Star*, and *Lost Universe*; *Blue Sub 6*; *Big O*; *Reboot*; *Serial Experiments Lain* and *NieA under 7*;

*Harlock Saga; Utena* and *Cardcaptor Sakura; Generator Gawl; Gundam* series and *Robotech* series; *Slayers* series and *Sorcerer Hunters; Nadesico; Escaflowne* and *Magic Knight Rayearth; Record of Lodoss War* series; *Nightwalker: Midnight Detective; Tenchi Muyo* series; *Orphen* and *Arc the Lad; The Irresponsible Captain Tylor; Nadia; Jubei-Chan, the Ninja Girl; Vampire Princess Miyu* and *Boogiepop Phantom; Soul Hunter* ("*Houshin Engi*"); *Ceres: Celestial Legend; Knight Hunters* ("*Weiss Kreuz*").

## World Music

Anime soundtracks are generally good, and often exceptional. The music ranges from soaring classical to heavy metal to blues to, quite literally, music from all around the world, including traditional Japanese music played on traditional instruments. You'll rarely find its like here, since most of it only exists on import CDs from Japan, or else Hong Kong bootlegs, which are a lot cheaper . . . because the creators get no royalties. (Some original soundtracks that are out of print in Japan can only be gotten from Hong Kong.) The good news: TokyoPop, a US distributor of manga and anime, has begun to release a line of fully licensed soundtracks at regular CD prices; they have a small but growing list. I recommend anything composed by Yoko Kanno . . . beyond that, listen as you watch, and you'll know the soundtracks you want when you hear them.

## Resources: How to Find It, Buy It, Learn More About It

**Books:** *The Anime Encyclopedia* by Jonathan Clements and Helen McCarthy; *Manga! Manga!* and *Dreamland Japan* by Frederik L. Schodt; *Anime Essentials* and *The Anime Companion* by Gilles Poitras; *Samurai from Outer Space* by Antonia Levi; *Understanding Comics* by Scott McCloud; and *The Demon in the Teahouse* and *The Ghost in the Tokaido Inn* by Dorothy and Thomas Hoobler (YA fiction set in eighteenth-century Japan; recommended).

Art and "making of" books for popular anime series are mostly still imports (with 99 percent Japanese text, but the pictures . . . !). Series guides for *Cowboy Bebop* and *Serial Experiment Lain* are the first guidebooks to come out in English; *Trigun* and others are set to follow. Guardians of Order, a publisher of gaming guides, has begun a new series of anime guides—*Lain* is the first—following the popularity of its *Big Eyes, Small Mouth* role-playing book, which is also a useful resource on M&A tropes.

**Magazines:** *Animerica* and the new *Anime Invasion* cover the anime field (and usually some manga) in depth; there are also plenty of ads to guide you to anime stores and sites. *Pulp* magazine now has manga reviews and articles on the genre, along with its regular adult manga serials. (A number of American publishers are now emulating manga magazine-anthologies, and you can try a cross section of stories at a bargain price: besides *Pulp*, which is definitely for mature audiences, look for *Animerica Plus; Super Manga Blast; Smile;* and *Manga Zine* among others. CrossGen is trying the same thing with its own comics—in color.)

**Where to Buy—or Rent:** And make new friends . . . at your local independent comic shop, whenever possible. If they don't carry what you want, they're usually glad to special order it. Urge them—politely—to carry more manga and related materials. Call the Comic Shop Locator Service, if you don't know of a store: (888-266-4226. Toll free.)

If there's a good independent video store in town, it may have a lot more anime than Blockbuster has; it's a good way to find out whether you like something enough to buy it. Suncoast Video stores usually have a good selection of the latest anime for sale; they also have a new "rental service" of sorts. The clerks are nice people, which probably explains why the Sam Goody Megacorp gives them no feedback capacity whatsoever. Best Buy also carries anime, often at bargain prices.

**On-line ordering**: Specialty import stores can be few and far between, in realtime; thank god for cyberspace. Two very well stocked and very reliable sites are AnimeNation <www.animenation.com>, which has an especially good selection of hard-to-find soundtracks, along with anime and manga, and The Right Stuf <www.rightstuf.com>, which carries a lot of older anime, often at bargain prices, as well as the newest M&A. The Right Stuf's customer service is exceptional, and they publish an encyclopedic hard-copy catalog. Both sites have a variety of other merchandise too—imported (untranslated) manga, art books, T-shirts, posters, etc.—plus e-mail newsletters and links to related Web sites. AnimeNation has "Ask John"—a regular feature anwering questions about M&A and Japanese culture.

For hard-to-find back issues of translated manga, try the vast resources of Mile High Comics <www.milehighcomics.com>. They also have a great newsletter.

Amazon.com carries the latest anime, with preorder sales, as well as translated manga, reference books, and even some import soundtracks and books. Its "Z-shops" are a good resource for used and/or hard-to-find anime at lower prices. Mail-order service is generally prompt and reliable; however, their Customer Service is controlled by an artificial intelligence.

Suncoast Video has an online site <www.suncoast.com> where you can find a much wider selection of anime than in the local store, and also some new anime on sale. Their mail-order service is also good; but god help you if there's any glitch—their online Customer Service is straight out of *The Prisoner*. (I've personally spoken to Number Two.) Winner of a Ninja Screw Award "Dishonorable Mention."

*Many Thanks*! To the Westfield Comics crew: the diabolically charming Nick and Josh and Chadi, who point me at way too many terrific new works; and most excellent manager Bob, who, as Pogo would say, "allus remembers"—not only my favorite obscure F&SF TV shows, but also my favorite obscure manga series, every time. It's more than just a store, it's a happy hour. . . . To Nathan and all the funky folks at Four Star Video Heaven in Madison. . . . And to honorable Loren Hekke-san, and the members of the West High School Japanese and Anime Clubs, who took the time to help me with some nagging questions and give me their feedback on the best anime of the year; I had a great visit! *Domo arigato, minasan!*

# Obituaries: 2001

James Frenkel

As noted already, and as contemporary readers must be aware, death struck a massive blow on September 11. The rest of the year took its toll on those who create with their imagination and talent for us, and for future generations. The following talented people contributed to our culture, and their contributions live on beyond their span of years. Some of these names will be familiar; others we acknowledge though their contribution was less obvious. Perhaps you'll find inspiration in the works of those whose names aren't familiar.

**Dorothy Dunnett**, 78, wrote the enormously popular and endlessly fascinating "Lymond Chronicles" and "The House of Niccolo" novels, historical fiction with a fantasy edge. Her complex, intricate works inspired fanatical devotion in the ranks of an ever-growing readership. **Gordon R. Dickson,** 77, wrote SF, fantasy, and supernatural horror as well as mystery, songs, radio scripts, and articles. He was beloved for his Dorsai stories, which fit into his lifelong epic series, the Childe Cycle of SF. His fantasy was less prominent but quite popular, especially his series started with *The Dragon and the George.* He also wrote the "Hoka" series with Poul Anderson. He won the Hugo Award, the Nebula Award, was a founding member of the Science Fiction Writers of America, and president of SFWA from 1969 to 1971. **Poul Anderson**, 74, was the author of more than 120 books, as well as numerous novellas and short stories; winner of seven Hugos, three Nebulas; a SFWA Grand Master, inductee into SF&F Hall of Fame; Gandalf Grand Master of Fantasy. He was better known for his science fiction than for his fantasy, but wrote some fine fantasy, ranging from adventure- and magic-filled works to sword-and-sorcery action. He also collaborated with his wife, Karen Anderson, on some of the fantasy, especially Celtic-themed works. An innovator and pioneer in science fiction, he was also one of those who proved that sf and fantasy both could be written well by a single author. **Richard Laymon**, 54, was the author of over three dozen books, mostly horror. His works included *The Cellar* (1980), *Beast House Chronicles*, *A Writer's Tale* (1998), and *The Traveling Vampire Show* (2000). **Douglas [Noel] Adams**, 49, was best known as the author of *The Hitchhiker's Guide to the Galaxy* which started as a tongue-in-cheek novel, became a BBC radio series and TV series, and is scheduled to be released as a feature film this year. His other works include *The Restaurant at the End of the Universe* (1980), *Life, The Universe and Everything* (1982); *So Long, and Thanks for All the Fish* (1984); and *Dirk Gently, Holistic Detective*. **Jorge Amado**, 88, was an important Brazilian magical realist author whose books sold 30 million+ copies worldwide, in 58 countries and 48 languages.

**William Hanna**, 90, was an animator. He and Joseph Barbera first worked together at MGM's animation unit in 1937, and produced over a hundred cartoons featuring *Tom and Jerry*. In 1957, they set up their own production company when MGM shut down their animation unit. As the dominant animation house creating shows for television, they brought cartoons to prime time with *The Flintstones* and *The Jetsons*, and also developed other characters that became staples, such as Huckleberry Hound, Yogi Bear, and Scooby Doo, to name just a few. Hanna won eight Emmys. The Hanna Barbera animation technique revolutionized animation on television with its simplified movements and shallow backgrounds, fueled by the personality of its characters.

**Josh Kirby**, 73, was a British fantasy and science fiction artist best known for his hilarious paintings for Terry Pratchett's "Discworld" books, among many book jackets or covers he illustrated.

**Mary Shephard**, 90, was the illustrator of "Mary Poppins" in seven books by P. L. Travers. She was the daughter of E. H. Shephard, who illustrated *Winnie-the-Pooh* and *The Wind in the Willows*. **William Hurtz**, 81, was an animator for Disney. He worked on the dancing mushroom sequence in 1940's *Fantasia*; after WWII he joined with other animators to create United Productions of America (UPA). He worked on many other series, including the Academy Award-winning *Gerald McBoing-Boing* in 1952, *A Unicorn in the Garden*, did animated titles for films such as *Around the World in 80 Days* and *Psycho*, and in 1959 he moved to Jay Ward Productions, becoming one of the earliest directors and supervisors on *The Adventures of Rocky and Bullwinkle* and *George of the Jungle*, and also did 1992's *Little Nemo: Adventures in Slumberland*. **Gray Morrow**, 68, was a versatile artist in the field of comics, doing noteworthy work on the *Tarzan* Sunday comic strip; he was also a prolific SF and fantasy illustrator. He illustrated for such comics companies as DC, Marvel, Triangle, AG, and Atlas; in the SF and Fantasy field, he illustrated for magazines such as *Galaxy, If, Amazing, Analog, Fantastic Worlds of Tomorrow, The Magazine of Fantasy & Science Fiction* among others, and painted illustrations for hundreds of book covers. He also did work for television and movie productions as a layout and conceptual artist. One of his final artworks was a contribution to a charity anthology to benefit the victims of the September 11, 2001, terrorist attack on the World Trade Center, NY.

**Jason Robards, Jr.**, 78, was an Oscar-winning actor who starred in many fine films; he also was an acclaimed stage actor, capturing more than one Tony Award for portrayals on Broadway. **Ray Walston**, 86, was a veteran character actor. He was the devil . . . in the musical and film *Damn Yankees*. He also became well-known on television in a number of roles in series, ranging from *My Favorite Martian* to *Picket Fences*. **Beatrice Straight**, 86, was an Oscar winner, an outstanding character actress for many years in many venues. Many will recall her performance as the paranormal investigator in *Poltergeist*.

**Stanley Kramer**, 87, was a major film producer and director. Among his many outstanding productions were the 1953 fantasy film written by Dr. Seuss, *The 5,000 Fingers of Dr. T.* and 1959's *On the Beach.* **Emile Kuri**, 93, was an Oscar-winning set director, who worked on 20,000 *Leagues Under the Sea, Topper, It's a Wonderful Life, Bedknobs and Broomsticks, The Absent-Minded Professor,* and *Mary Poppins,* among many films in a long career. He was also a consultant for Orlando's Walt Disney World. **Howard W. Koch**, 84, was a film producer and director perhaps best known for *The Manchurian Candidate.* He produced a number of films with fantasy themes, including *On a Clear Day You Can See Forever, Heaven Can Wait,* and *The Keep.* **Richard Stone**, 47, was a seven-time Emmy Award-winning composer for movies and cartoon shows such as *Sundown: The Vampire in Retreat, Pinky and the Brain, Animaniacs, Freakazoid!, Taz Mania,* and *The Sylvester and Tweety Mysteries.* **John A. Alonzo**, 66, was cinematographer and actor, but much better known for his cinematography. He worked on many films, including, notably, *Close Encounters of the Third Kind, The Guardian, Cool World, The Meteor Man,* and *Star Trek: Generations,* to name a few.

**Herbert Ross**, 74, was a chorographer, director, and producer of stage, screen, and television. Among his successes was the film *On a Clear Day You Can See Forever.*

**R. Chetwynd-Hayes**, 81, was a horror writer whose full name was Ronald Henry Glynn Chetwynd Hayes. In the early 1970s he became a prolific full-time writer producing ghost stories and tales of terror, since widely reprinted. He edited numerous anthologies, and his stories were adapted in the anthology movies *From Beyond the Grave* (1973) and *The Monster Club* (1980). He was given Life Achievement Awards by The British Fantasy Society and the Horror Writers of America in 1989. He's said to have kept alive the tradition of the typically British ghost story. **Simon Raven**, 73, was a controversial British author who wrote a number of stories of horror, particularly ghost stories, at least one of which was filmed. **Catherine Storr**, 87, was a prolific British author who wrote dozens of novels, some for children, others for adults. Her most successful works included *Clever Polly and the Stupid Wolf* and YA fantasies *Marianne Dreams* and *Marianne and Mark.* **Mirra Ginsburg**, 81 or 91, depending on which of her two listed birth dates one believes, was an editor, author, and translator from Russian and Yiddish into English. Her own best-known work was children's books adapted from Russian and Eastern European folktales. **Spencer Holst**, 75, was a writer and teller of fables that drew on many cultural paradigms, and were unclassifiable except as being original and wonderfully told. His wife, artist Beate Wheller, once said that his stories, "are halfway between Hans Christian Andersen and Franz Kafka." **Mary Williams**, 97, was a British novelist and prolific writer of ghost stories (more than two hundred gathered into seventeen collections). Her literary career spanned seventy-eight years from her first book of poetry, *Dreams of England* (1922), to her final collection of ghost stories, *The Secret Pool* (2000). **Eloise McGraw**, 84, was a children's author. Her medieval fantasy *The Moorchild* was a 1966 Newbery Honor Book. **Gella Naum**, 86, was best known in the U.S. for *Zonobia;* Romanian surrealist, poet, and author of children's books, she also worked as a translator. **Evelyn E. Smith**, 77, best known for her Miss Melville detective novels, published numerous science fiction and fantasy stories between 1952 and 1969. Under the pseudonym Delphine C.

Lyons she wrote the fantasy novel *Valley of Shadows*. **Frederick A. Raborg, Jr.**, 67, wrote as Dick Baldwin. His stories appeared in Marvin Kaye's anthologies; also wrote poetry, founded a small press for international poetry and fiction magazines, *Amelia* and *Cicada* as well as *SPSM&H*, all of which he edited. **Daniel Counihan**, 83, was the author of the children's fantasy novel *Unicorn Magic*. **Peggy Kennedy**, 70, was a master costumer active at SF/F conventions since the early 1960s; she completed two fantasy novels and was working on a third in the trilogy; her first novel, *Dragon's Clutch*, was published in 2001. **Gerald Suster**, 49, was a British horror author of a number of occult thrillers (perhaps best known for *The Devil's Maze* (1979), *The God Game* (1997), and *The Labyrinth of Satan* (1997)—a loosely linked trilogy). He also wrote a number of nonfiction volumes based on his own personal interest in the occult, and contributed a regular column to the esoteric magazine *The Talking Stick*. **Tove Jansson**, 86, was a Finnish fantasy writer best known for her YA "Moomin" series about a family of eccentric trolls. **Frederick Drimmer**, 83, wrote and edited a number of books on macabre subjects. **C. Artmann**, 79, was an Austrian poet noted for his poetry, which, according to the *New York Times*, "mimicked various Viennese characters but teemed with vampires, ogres, and demons of fantasy." **Ken Kesey**, 66, was the author of *One Flew Over the Cuckoo's Nest* and other novels.

**Rayner Unwin**, 74, was a major figure in publishing in England for many years. His place in history was assured when he was ten years old, and his father, Sir Stanley—head of the publishing company, George Allen & Unwin—gave him J.R.R. Tolkien's manuscript of *The Hobbit* to read. He wrote a favorable report for a shilling; his father published the book; later, he bought the manuscript *The Lord of the Rings* and convinced Tolkien to publish it in three volumes with separate titles. The rest is history. **Clarkson Nott Potter**, 73, founder of Clarkson N. Potter, Inc., was a producer of fantasy art books until he retired.

**George P. Brockway**, 85, was an editor and then publisher of W.W. Norton & Company, a resolutely independent publisher. He was responsible for the company's current ownership structure, in which the employees own all the company's stock. **Jack S. Liebowitz**, 100, was the publisher of DC Comics. A printer by trade, he took over the foundering National Comics in 1983 and published *Detective Comics* and *New Adventure Comics* (which were the first to run regular serial adventures featuring the same character). He was also responsible for moving Superman onto television. **Fred Marcellino**, 61, was a book jacket designer and illustrator who played a large part in changing the look of books in the 1970s. **William Jovanovich**, 81, was the head of Harcourt, Brace, Jovanovich for thirty-eight years, re-creating the company in the 1960s and 1970s, moving its headquarters, acquiring nonpublishing assets such as Sea World, and invigorating the company's textbook division during his tenure. **Jenna A. Felice**, 25, was a fantasy and science fiction editor at Tor Books. She edited authors such as Isobelle Carmody, Terry A. McGarry, and Jonathan Carroll. She also was associate editor of *Century* magazine, which she published with her companion, Rob Killheffer. She started as an intern at Tor when she was fifteen, not long after she was orphaned; at twenty-one she became the youngest editor in the field. **Scott Imes**, 52, was the manager of Uncle Hugo's Science Fiction Bookstore, in Minneapolis. He worked there for twenty-five years. He also edited, for eight years, *What Do I Read Next?*, a wonderful resource published by Gale

Research. He was also a longtime fan, and expert in the ways of video, which he brought to the 1976 Worldcon, enabling a video record of MidAmericon. His encyclopedic knowledge of SF and fantasy was legendary; so was his warmth and kindly helpfulness to all. **James Allen**, 48, was president of the Virginia Kidd Literary Agency. He started as a teenager and worked his way up to become head of the firm before his death. The agency represents many fantasy and SF authors. **Keith Allen Daniels**, 45, was a poet and the publisher of Anamnesis Press, a small SF/fantasy publisher in the San Francisco Bay Area. **Jennifer Moyer**, 52, was the president of Moyer Bell Ltd., a publisher of art books and literature.

**Werner Klemperer**, 80, was a German/Jewish-born character actor ironically best known for his role as Colonel Klink in TV's *Hogan's Heroes.* He played many roles on countless television shows. **Albert Hague**, 81, was a composer and an actor. Best known for his portrayal of a music teacher in the film and television program, *Fame,* he wrote many songs, and the scores of a number of stage and film productions, including the recent film, *How the Grinch Stole Christmas.* **Jason Miller**, 62, was an actor and a playwright. Best known to audiences for his eponymous role in *The Exorcist,* he won a Pulitzer Prize for his play, *That Championship Season.* **Steve Barton**, 47, was an actor on stage and screen. His most famous role was the eponymous Phantom of the Opera, in Andrew Lloyd Weber's musical. **Jean-Pierre Aumont**, 92, was an internationally renowned French actor. **Harry Towne**, 86, was a longtime character actor, mostly on television. **Robert Enrico**, 69, directed the famous twenty-four-minute *Incident at Owl Creek,* based on an Ambrose Bierce story; the film won a Palme d'Or in 1962 in Cannes and a 1964 Academy Award. **Billy Barty**, 76, the three-foot-ten-inch actor starred in numerous films and TV series during his seventy-year career; he starred in *Bride of Frankenstein* (1935), *Alice in Wonderland* (1933), *Pygmy Island, Legend, Rumplestiltskin, Masters of the Universe,* and *Wishful Thinking,* to name a few. **Carroll O'Connor**, 76, became famous as Archie Bunker in TV's *All in the Family,* and acted in many film and stage productions. **Theodore Gottlieb**, 94, who performed in clubs as Brother Theodore, narrated the 1970 horror film *The Horror of the Blood Monsters,* and was the voice of Gollum in the animated TV films *The Hobbit* and *The Return of the King,* and also appeared in other film fantasy, including *Nocturna,* the *Jaws* parody, *Gums, The Invisible Kid,* and *The 'Burbs.*

**Jay Livingston**, 86, was an Oscar-winning composer and lyricist who, teamed with collborator Ray Evans, had many big hits. **Ralph Burns**, 79, was a composer and arranger of songs and film scores. **Joe Darion**, 90, was a lyricist who worked in venues ranging from stage to opera to screen. He is most famous for the musical and film *Man of La Mancha.* **Douglas Benton**, 75, was a prolific TV producer whose credits included the horror anthology series *Thriller,* hosted by Boris Karloff; he also produced *The Girl from U.N.C.L.E.* and *A Howling in the Woods.* **Pierro Umiliani**, 75, composed scores for over a hundred films. **Leo Gordon**, 78, was a veteran actor and screenwriter who appeared in more than seventy films and dozens of TV shows. **Nick Stewart**, 90, a black actor, starred as Lightnin' on TV's *Amos 'n' Andy,* and was the voice of Brer Bear in Disney's *Song of the South.* He was active in cultural preservation in Los Angeles for over fifty years. His Ebony Showcase Theater has been a launching pad for many performers of all backgrounds. **Ann Sothern**, 92, was a film and TV actress best known for her eponymous role in the series *Private Secretary*. **Marie Windsor**, 80, was called "Queen of the B's" for bad-girl roles in seventy-four films. *Cat Women of the Moon*, *Swamp Women*, *Abbott and Costello Meet the Mummy*, were just a few.

**Ray Lovejoy**, 58, was a highly respected film editor on such films as Stanley Kubrick's *2001: A Space Odyssey*, as well as Stephen King's *The Shining*; also *The Ruling Class*, *Ghost in the Noonday Sun*, *Krull*, *Aliens*, *Batman*, *Mister Frost*, and 1998's *Lost in Space*. **Ralph Thomas**, 85, was a veteran British film director. **Danilo Donati**, 75, was an Oscar-winning costume and set designer for films. **Julian Roffman**, 84, was a Canadian film producer and director. **Bernard Vorhaus**, 95, was a film director. **Hoyt Curtin**, 78, composed numerous animated TV show and film theme songs and scores. **Don Devlin**, 70, was a film producer and actor. **Terence Feely**, 72, was a British television writer who wrote such British series as *The Avengers*, *Arthur of the Britons*, *The Prisoner*, *Thunderbirds*, *Space: 1999*, *The Return of the Saint*, and *The New Avengers*. **Jun Fukuda**, 76, was a Japanese film director; he helmed several films in Toho's popular "Godzilla" series. **Richard Hazard**, 79, was a composer for film and television. **Ted Mann**, 84, was a film producer, and owned the Chinese Theater in L.A. at one point. **Sam Wiesenthal**, 92, film producer; worked with Carl Laemmle, Jr. on the horror film classics *Frankenstein* and *Dracula* in the early 1930s.

**Maurice J. Noble**, 91, was a film animator for *Snow White and the Seven Dwarfs*, *Fantasia*, *Dumbo*, *Bambi*, *What's Opera, Doc?* and *Duck Amuck*, directed the Academy Award-winning *The Dot and the Line*, and worked with Chuck Jones on *The Cat in the Hat*, *Horton Hears a Who*, and *How the Grinch Stole Christmas*.

**Richard Jay Shorr**, 58, was a film director and sound designer on such films as *Teenage Mutant Ninja Turtles*, *I Come in Peace*, *Highlander II: The Quickening*, *Ghosts Can't Do It*, *Shadow of the Wolf*, *Highway to Hell*, and the 1983 television film *The Day After*. **Lou Steele**, 72, was best known as announcer and host of the horror film showcase *Creature Features* at WNEW-TV in New York. **Raymond C. Sparenberg**, 72, hosted Indianapolis's *Fright Night* television show. **Evan Lottman**, 70, was a film editor. He received an Oscar nomination for his work on *The Exorcist*. Other film folk who died in 2001: **Polly Rowles**, 87; **Jane Greer**, 76; **Joseph O'Conor**, 84; **Michael Johnson**, 61; **Anthony Steel**, 81; **Nyree Dawn Porter**, 61; **Miriam Wolfe**, 78; **Rayford Barnes**, 80; **Elizabeth Bradley**, 78, a British character actor; **Alejandro Cruz**, 78, one of Mexico's leading pro wrestlers in the 1950s, starred in many Mexican horror/action films in the 1960s and 1970s; **Peter Jones**, 79, was a British actor; **Patricia Owens**, 75, a film actress in the fifties and sixties. **Arthur Friedman**, 81; **David Lewis**, 84; **Scott Marlowe**, 68; **Nancy Parsons**, 58; **Al Waxman**, 65; **Lewis Wilson**, 80; **Roman Beaumont**, 87, a British actress; **Peggy Converse**, 95; **Norma Macmillan**, 79; **Reginald Marsh**, 74; **Lancelot Victor Pinard**, 97; **John Warner**, 77; **Deborah Walley**, 57; **Linden Travers**, 88; **Pauline Moore**, 87. **Giacomo Gentilomo**, 92, was a film director. **Ken Hughes**, 79, was a film director. **Adrian Weiss**, 83, was a film producer and director. **Bobby Bass**, 65, was a stuntman in many films and TV shows.

**Seymour V. Reit**, an author and illustrator, was the creator of Casper the

Friendly Ghost and worked on various other cartoon characters, both on paper and animated; in a long career he also wrote a number of books, both for children and adults. **Faith Hubley**, 77, was an Oscar-winning animator who created a number of films with her husband, John, and after his death, with others. Her work was characterized by a deep humanism, music from many traditions, and roots in myth and folklore. **Beni Montresor**, 78, was an artist who illustrated children's books and designed costumes for operas the world over. Much of his work was fantastical, including his Caldecott Award-winning book, *May I Bring a Friend*, (written by Beatrice Shenk de Regnier). **Frederick E. Ray, Jr.**, was one of the original illustrators of the *Superman* and *Tomahawk* comics for DC Comics in the 1940s and 1950s. **Herbert Block** (known as Herblock), 91, won multiple Pulitzer Prizes for his editorial cartoons in the *Washington Post* until shortly before his death. He was also a trenchant writer; in all his work he was dedicated to exposing hypocrisy, corruption, and wrongdoing. **Dan DeCarlo**, 82, was a cartoonist for Archie Comics for over forty years. He created and drew *Josie and the Pussycats* among many comics, basing Josie on his wife. **Dave Graue**, 75, was a cartoonist best known for his work on the syndicated strip *Alley Oop* which he took over from Vincent Hamlin, the strip's creator, after years of assisting him. He also wrote the strip, and continued to write it after he stopped drawing it, in 1973. He also painted brilliantly colored, pointillistic landscapes. **Clyde Taylor** was an agent at the Curtis Brown Agency, and before that an editor at Putnam/Berkley. **Phyllis White**, 85, was the wife of the cofounder of the *Magazine of Fantasy & Science Fiction*, William Anthony Parker White, better known as author, editor, and critic Anthony Boucher; she read the slush pile from 1949 to 1954 and did other work for the magazine as well.

# ANTHONY DOERR

## The Hunter's Wife

*Anthony Doerr is the author of a stunning debut collection,* The Shell
Collector. *Born in Cleveland, Doerr has lived in Africa and New Zealand.*

*"The Hunter's Wife," set in wintery northern woods, has my vote for the
best contemporary fantasy story of the year. It's a powerful, beautifully crafted
tale about the mysteries of love, death, and forgiveness. Doerr's fine story first
appeared in the May issue of* The Atlantic Monthly. *It has won an O. Henry
Prize, it's been reprinted in* The Shell Collector, *and it is a pleasure to reprint
it here.*

—T. W.

It was the hunter's first time outside of Montana. He woke, stricken still with
the hours-old vision of ascending through rose-lit cumulus, of houses and
barns like specks deep in the snowed-in valleys, all the scrolling country below
looking December—brown and black hills streaked with snow, flashes of iced-
over lakes, the long braids of a river gleaming at the bottom of a canyon. Above
the wing the sky had deepened to a blue so pure he knew it would bring tears
to his eyes if he looked long enough.

Now it was dark. The airplane descended over Chicago, its galaxy of electric
lights, the vast neighborhoods coming clearer as the plane glided toward the
airport—streetlights, headlights, stacks of buildings, ice rinks, a truck turning at a
stoplight, scraps of snow atop a warehouse and winking antennae on faraway hills,
finally the long converging parallels of blue runway lights, and they were down.

He walked into the airport, past the banks of monitors. Already he felt as if
he'd lost something, some beautiful perspective, some lovely dream fallen away.
He had come to Chicago to see his wife, whom he had not seen in twenty years.
She was there to perform her magic for a higher-up at the state university. Even
universities, apparently, were interested in what she could do.

Outside the terminal the sky was thick and gray and hurried by wind. Snow
was coming. A woman from the university met him and escorted him to her
Jeep. He kept his gaze out the window.

They were in the car for forty-five minutes, passing first the tall, lighted architecture of downtown, then naked suburban oaks, heaps of ploughed snow,

gas stations, power towers and telephone wires. The woman said, So you regularly attend your wife's performances?

No, he said. Never before.

She parked in the driveway of an elaborate and modern mansion with square balconies suspended at angles over two trapezoidal garages, huge triangular windows in the facade, sleek columns, domed lights, a steep shale roof.

Inside the front door about thirty name tags were laid out on a table. His wife was not there yet. No one, it seemed, was there yet. He found his tag and pinned it to his sweater. A silent girl in a tuxedo appeared and disappeared with his coat.

The foyer was all granite, flecked and smooth, backed with a grand staircase that spread wide at the bottom and tapered at the top. A woman came down. She stopped four or five steps from the bottom and said, Hello, Anne, to the woman who had driven him there and, You must be Mr. Dumas, to him. He took her hand, a pale bony thing, weightless, like a featherless bird.

Her husband, the university's chancellor, was just knotting his bow tie, she said, and laughed sadly to herself, as if bow ties were something she disapproved of. Beyond the foyer spread a vast parlor, high-windowed and carpeted. The hunter moved to a bank of windows, shifted aside the curtain and peered out.

In the poor light he could see a wooden deck encompassing the length of the house, angled and stepped, never the same width, with a low rail. Beyond it, in the blue shadows, a small pond lay encircled by hedges, with a marble birdbath at its center. Behind the pond stood leafless trees—oaks, maples, a sycamore white as bone. A helicopter shuttled past, winking a green light.

It's snowing, he said.

Is it? asked the hostess, with an air of concern, perhaps false. It was impossible to tell what was sincere and what was not. The woman who drove him there had moved to the bar where she cradled a drink and stared into the carpet.

He let the curtain fall back. The chancellor came down the staircase. Other guests fluttered in. A man in gray corduroy, with BRUCE MAPLES on his name tag, approached him. Mr. Dumas, he said, your wife isn't here yet?

You know her? the hunter asked. Oh no, Maples said, and shook his head. No I don't. He spread his legs and swiveled his hips as if stretching before a foot race. But I've read about her.

The hunter watched as a tall, remarkably thin man stepped through the front door. Hollows behind his jaw and beneath his eyes made him appear ancient and skeletal—as if he were visiting from some other leaner world. The chancellor approached the thin man, embraced him, and held him for a moment.

That's President O'Brien, Maples said. A famous man, actually, to people who follow those sorts of things. So terrible, what happened to his family. Maples stabbed the ice in his drink with his straw.

The hunter nodded, unsure of what to say. For the first time he began to think he should not have come.

Have you read your wife's books? Maples asked.

The hunter nodded.

In her poems her husband is a hunter.

I guide hunters. He was looking out the window to where snow was settling on the hedges.

Does that ever bother you?

What?

Killing animals. For a living, I mean.

The hunter watched snowflakes disappear as they touched the window. Was that what hunting meant to people? Killing animals? He put his fingers to the glass. No, he said. It doesn't bother me.

The hunter met his wife in Great Falls, Montana, in the winter of 1972. That winter arrived immediately, all at once—you could watch it come. Twin curtains of white appeared in the north, white all the way to the sky, driving south like the end of all things. They drove the wind before them and it ran like wolves, like floodwater through a cracked dyke. Cattle galloped the fencelines, bawling. Trees toppled; a barn roof tumbled over the highway. The river changed directions. The wind flung thrushes screaming into the gorge and impaled them on the thorns in grotesque attitudes.

She was a magician's assistant, beautiful, sixteen years old, an orphan. It was not a new story; a glittery red dress, long legs, a traveling magic show performing in the meeting hall at the Central Christian Church. The hunter had been walking past with an armful of groceries when the wind stopped him in his tracks and drove him into the alley behind the church. He had never felt such wind; it had him pinned. His face was pressed against a low window, and through it he could see the show. The magician was a small man in a dirty blue cape. Above him a sagging banner read THE GREAT VESPUCCI. But the hunter watched only the girl; she was graceful, young, smiling. Like a wrestler the wind held him against the window.

The magician was buckling the girl into a plywood coffin that was painted garishly with red and blue bolts of lightning. Her neck and head stuck out one end, her ankles and feet the other. She beamed; no one had ever before smiled so broadly at being locked into a coffin. The magician started up an electric saw and brought it noisily down through the center of the box, sawing her in half. Then he wheeled her apart, her legs going one way, her torso another. Her neck fell back, her smile waned, her eyes showed only white. The lights dimmed. A child screamed. Wiggle your toes, the magician ordered, flourishing his magic wand, and she did; her disembodied toes wiggled in glittery high-heeled pumps. The audience squealed with delight.

The hunter watched her pink fine-boned face, her hanging hair, her outstretched throat. Her eyes caught the spotlight. Was she looking at him? Did she see his face pressed against the window, the wind slashing at his neck, the groceries—onions, a sack of flour—tumbled to the ground around his feet? Her mouth flinched; was it a smile, a flicker of greeting?

She was beautiful to him in a way that nothing else had ever been beautiful. Snow blew down his collar and drifted around his boots. The wind had fallen off but the snow came hard and still the hunter stood riveted at the window. After some time the magician rejoined the severed box halves, unfastened the buckles, and fluttered his wand, and she was whole again. She climbed out of the box and curtsied in her glittering slit-legged dress. She smiled as if it were the Resurrection itself.

Then the storm brought down a pine tree in front of the courthouse and the power winked out, streetlight by streetlight, all over town. Before she could move, before ushers began escorting the crowd out with flashlights, the hunter was slinking into the hall, making for the stage, calling for her.

He was thirty years old, twice her age. She smiled at him, leaned over from the dais in the red glow of the emergency exit lights and shook her head. Show's over, she said. In his pickup he trailed the magician's van through the blizzard to her next show, a library fund-raiser in Butte. The next night he followed her to Missoula. He rushed to the stage after each performance. Just eat dinner with me, he'd plead. Just tell me your name. It was hunting by persistence. She said yes in Bozeman. Her name was plain, Mary Roberts. They had rhubarb pie in a hotel restaurant.

I know how you do it, he said. The feet in the sawbox are dummies. You hold your legs against your chest and wiggle the dummy feet with a string.

She laughed. Is that what you do? she asked. Follow a girl to four towns to tell her her magic isn't real?

No, he said. I hunt.

You hunt. And when you're not hunting?

I dream about hunting. She laughed again. It's not funny, he said.

You're right, she said, and smiled. It's not funny. I'm that way with magic. I dream about it. I dream about it all the time. Even when I'm not asleep.

He looked into his plate, thrilled. He searched for something he might say. They ate. But I dream bigger dreams, you know, she said afterward, after she had eaten two pieces of pie, carefully, with a spoon. Her voice was quiet and serious. I have magic inside of me. I'm not going to get sawed in half by Tony Vespucci all my life.

I don't doubt it, the hunter said.

I knew you'd believe me, she said.

But the next winter Vespucci brought her back to Great Falls and sawed her in half in the same plywood coffin. And the winter after that. After both performances the hunter took her to the Bitterroot Diner where he watched her eat two pieces of pie. The watching was his favorite part: a hitch in her throat as she swallowed, the way the spoon slid cleanly out from her lips, the way her hair fell over her ear.

Then she was eighteen, and after pie she let him drive her to his cabin, forty miles from Great Falls, up the Missouri, then east into the Smith River valley. She brought only a small vinyl purse. The truck skidded and sheered as he steered it over the unploughed roads, fishtailing in the deep snow, but she didn't seem afraid or worried about where he might be taking her, about the possibility that the truck might sink in a drift, that she might freeze to death in her pea coat and glittery magician's-assistant dress. Her breath plumed out in front of her. It was twenty degrees below zero. Soon the roads would be snowed over, impassable until spring.

At his one-room cabin with furs and old rifles on the walls, he unbolted the crawlspace and showed her his winter hoard: a hundred smoked trout, skinned pheasant and venison quarters hanging frozen from hooks. Enough for two of me, he said. She scanned his books over the fireplace, a monograph on grouse habits, a series of journals on upland game birds, a thick tome titled simply *Bear*.

Are you tired? he asked. Would you like to see something? He gave her a snow-suit, strapped her boots into a pair of leather snowshoes, and took her to hear the grizzly.

She wasn't bad on snowshoes, a little clumsy. They went creaking over wind-scalloped snow in the nearly unbearable cold. The bear denned every winter in the same hollow cedar, the top of which had been shorn off by a storm. Black, three-fingered and huge, in the starlight it resembled a skeletal hand thrust up from the ground, a ghoulish visitor scrabbling its way out of the underworld.

They knelt. Above them the stars were knife points, hard and white. Put your ear here, he whispered. The breath that carried his words crystallized and blew away, as if the words themselves had taken on form but expired from the effort. They listened, face-to-face, their ears over woodpecker holes in the trunk. She heard it after a minute, tuning her ears into something like a drowsy sigh, a long exhalation of slumber. Her eyes widened. A full minute passed. She heard it again.

We can see him, he whispered, but we have to be dead quiet. Grizzlies are light hibernators. Sometimes all you do is step on twigs outside their dens and they're up.

He began to dig at the snow. She stood back, her mouth open, eyes wide. Bent at the waist, he bailed snow back through his legs. He dug down three feet and then encountered a smooth icy crust covering a large hole in the base of the tree. Gently he dislodged plates of ice and lifted them aside. The opening was dark, as if he'd punched through to some dark cavern, some netherworld. From the hole the smell of bear came to her, like wet dog, like wild mushrooms. The hunter removed some leaves. Beneath was a shaggy flank, a brown patch of fur.

He's on his back, the hunter whispered. This is his belly. His forelegs must be up here somewhere. He pointed to a place higher on the trunk.

She put one hand on his shoulder and knelt in the snow above the den. Her eyes were wide and unblinking. Her jaw hung open. Above her shoulder a star separated itself from the galaxy and melted through the sky. I want to touch him, she said. Her voice sounded loud and out of place in that wood, under the naked cedars.

Hush, he whispered. He shook his head no. You have to speak quietly.

Just for a minute.

No, he hissed. You're crazy. He tugged at her arm. She removed the mitten from her other hand with her teeth and reached down. He pulled at her again but lost his footing and fell back, clutching an empty mitten. As he watched, horrified, she turned and placed both hands, spread-fingered, in the thick shag of the bear's chest. Then she lowered her face, as if drinking from the snowy hollow, and pressed her lips to the bear's chest. Her entire head was inside the tree. She felt the soft, silver tips of its fur brush her cheeks. Against her nose one huge rib flexed slightly. She heard the lungs fill and then empty. She heard blood slug through veins.

Want to know what he dreams? she asked. Her voice echoed up through the tree and poured from the shorn ends of its hollowed branches. The hunter took his knife from his coat. Summer, her voice echoed. Blackberries. Trout. Dredging his flanks across river pebbles.

I'd have liked, she said later, back in the cabin as he built up the fire, to crawl all the way down there with him. Get into his arms. I'd grab him by the ears and kiss him on the eyes.

The hunter watched the fire, the flames cutting and sawing, each log a burning bridge. Three years he had waited for this. Three years he had dreamed this girl by his fire. But somehow it had ended up different from what he had imagined; he had thought it would be like a hunt—like waiting hours beside a wallow with his rifle barrel on his pack to see the huge antlered head of a bull elk loom up against the sky, to hear the whole herd behind him inhale, then scatter down the hill. If you had your opening you shot and walked the animal down and that was it. All the uncertainty was over. But this felt different, as if he had no choices to make, no control over any bullet he might let fly or hold back. It was exactly as if he was still three years younger, stopped outside the Central Christian Church and driven against a low window by the wind or some other, greater force.

Stay with me, he whispered to her, to the fire. Stay the winter.

Bruce Maples stood beside him jabbing the ice in his drink with his straw.

I'm in athletics, Bruce offered. I run the athletic department here.

You mentioned that.

Did I? I don't remember. I used to coach track. Hurdles.

Hurdles, the hunter repeated.

You bet.

The hunter studied him. What was Bruce Maples doing here? What strange curiosities and fears drove him, drove any of these people filing now through the front door, dressed in their dark suits and black gowns? He watched the thin, stricken man, President O'Brien, as he stood in the corner of the parlor. Every few minutes a couple of guests made their way to him and took O'Brien's hands in their own.

You probably know, the hunter told Maples, that wolves are hurdlers. Sometimes the people who track them will come to a snag and the prints will disappear. As if the entire pack just leaped into a tree and vanished. Eventually they'll find the tracks again, thirty or forty feet away. People used to think it was magic—flying wolves. But all they did was jump. One great coordinated leap.

Bruce was looking around the room. Huh, he said. I wouldn't know about that.

She stayed. The first time they made love, she shouted so loudly that coyotes climbed onto the roof and howled down the chimney. He rolled off her, sweating. The coyotes coughed and chuckled all night, like children chattering in the yard, and he had nightmares. Last night you had three dreams and you dreamed you were a wolf each time, she whispered. You were mad with hunger and running under the moon.

Had he dreamed that? He couldn't remember. Maybe he talked in his sleep.

In December it never got warmer than fifteen below. The river froze—something he'd never seen. Christmas Eve he drove all the way to Helena to buy her figure skates. In the morning they wrapped themselves head to toe in furs and went out to skate the river. She held him by the hips and they glided through the blue dawn, skating hard up the frozen coils and shoals, beneath the leafless alders and cottonwoods, only the bare tips of creek willow showing above the snow. Ahead of them vast white stretches of river faded on into darkness. An owl hunkered on a branch and watched them with its huge eyes. Merry Christmas, Owl! she shouted into the cold. It spread its huge wings, dropped from the branch and disappeared into the forest.

In a wind-polished bend they came upon a dead heron, frozen by its ankles into the ice. It had tried to hack itself out, hammering with its beak first at the ice entombing its feet and then at its own thin and scaly legs. When it finally died, it died upright, wings folded back, beak parted in some final, desperate cry, legs rooted like twin reeds in the ice.

She fell to her knees and knelt before the bird. Its eye was frozen and cloudy. It's dead, the hunter said, gently. Come on. You'll freeze too.

No, she said. She slipped off her mitten and closed the heron's beak in her fist. Almost immediately her eyes rolled back in her head. Oh wow, she moaned. I can *feel* her. She stayed like that for whole minutes, the hunter standing over her, feeling the cold come up his legs, afraid to touch her as she knelt before the bird. Her hand turned white and then blue in the wind.

Finally she stood. We have to bury it, she said. He chopped the bird out with his skate and buried it in a drift.

That night she lay stiff and would not sleep. It was just a bird, he said, unsure of what was bothering her but bothered by it himself. We can't do anything for a dead bird. It was good that we buried it, but tomorrow something will find it and dig it out.

She turned to him. Her eyes were wide; he remembered how they had looked when she put her hands on the bear. When I touched her, she said, I saw where she went.

What?

I saw where she went when she died. She was on the shore of a lake with other herons, a hundred others, all facing the same direction, and they were wading among stones. It was dawn and they watched the sun come up over the trees on the other side of the lake. I saw it as clearly as if I was there.

He rolled onto his back and watched shadows shift across the ceiling. Winter is getting to you, he said. In the morning he resolved to make sure she went out every day. It was something he'd long believed: go out every day in winter or your mind will slip. Every winter the paper was full of stories about ranchers' wives, snowed in and crazed with cabin fever, who had dispatched their husbands with cleavers or awls.

The next night he drove her all the way north to Sweetgrass, on the Canadian border, to see the northern lights. Great sheets of violet, amber and pale green rose from the distances. Shapes like the head of a falcon, a scarf and a wing rippled above the mountains. They sat in the truck cab, the heater blowing on their knees. Behind the aurora the Milky Way burned.

That one's a hawk! she exclaimed.

Auroras, he explained, occur because of Earth's magnetic field. A wind blows all the way from the sun and gusts past the earth, moving charged particles around. That's what we see. The yellow-green stuff is oxygen. The red and purple at the bottom there is nitrogen.

No, she said, shaking her head. The red one's a hawk. See his beak? See his wings?

Winter threw itself at the cabin. He took her out every day. He showed her a thousand ladybugs hibernating in an orange ball hung in a riverbank hollow; a pair of dormant frogs buried in frozen mud, their blood crystallized until spring. He pried a globe of honeybees from its hive, slow-buzzing, stunned from the sudden exposure, each bee shimmying for warmth. When he placed the globe in her hands she fainted, her eyes rolled back. Lying there she saw all their dreams at once, the winter reveries of scores of worker bees, each one fiercely vivid: bright trails through thorns to a clutch of wild roses, honey tidily brimming a hundred combs.

With each day she learned more about what she could do. She felt a foreign and keen sensitivity bubbling in her blood, as though a seed planted long ago was just now sprouting. The larger the animal, the more powerfully it could shake her. The recently dead were virtual mines of visions, casting them off with a slow-fading strength like a long series of tethers being cut, one by one. She pulled off her mittens and touched everything she could: bats, salamanders, a cardinal chick tumbled from its nest, still warm. Ten hibernating garter snakes coiled beneath a rock, eyelids sealed, tongues stilled. Each time she touched some frozen insect, some slumbering amphibian, anything just dead, her eyes rolled back and its visions, its heaven, went shivering through her body.

Their first winter passed like that. When he looked out the cabin window he saw wolf tracks crossing the river, owls hunting from the trees, six feet of snow like a quilt ready to be thrown off. She saw burrowed dreamers nestled under the roots against the long twilight, their dreams rippling into the sky like auroras.

With love still lodged in his heart like a splinter, he married her in the first muds of spring.

Bruce Maples gasped when the hunter's wife finally arrived. She moved through the door like a show horse, demure in the way she kept her eyes down but assured in her step; she brought each tapered heel down and struck it against the granite. The hunter had not seen his wife for twenty years, and she had changed— become refined, less wild, and somehow, to the hunter, worse for it. Her face had wrinkled around the eyes, and she moved as if avoiding contact with any-thing near her, as if the hall table or closet door might suddenly lunge forward to snatch at her lapels. She wore no jewelry, no wedding ring, only a plain black suit, double-breasted.

She found her name tag on the table and pinned it to her lapel. Everyone in the reception room looked at her then looked away. The hunter realized that she, not President O'Brien, was the guest of honor. In a sense they were courting her. This was their way, the chancellor's way—a silent bartender, tuxedoed coat girls, big icy drinks. Give her pie, the hunter thought. Rhubarb pie. Show her a sleeping grizzly.

They sat for dinner at a narrow and very long table, fifteen or so high-backed chairs down each side and one at each head. The hunter was seated several places away from his wife. She looked over at him finally, a look of recognition, of warmth, and then looked away again. He must have seemed old to her—he must always have seemed old to her. She did not look at him again.

The kitchen staff, in starched whites, brought onion soup, scampi, poached salmon. Around the hunter guests spoke in half whispers about people he did not know. He kept his eyes on the windows and the blowing snow beyond.

The river thawed and drove huge saucers of ice toward the Missouri. The sound of water running, of release, of melting, clucked and purled through the open windows of the cabin. The hunter felt that old stirring, that quickening in his soul, and he would rise in the wide pink dawns, take his fly rod and hurry down to the river. Already trout were rising through the chill brown water to take the first insects of spring. Soon the telephone in the cabin was ringing with calls from clients, and his guiding season was on.

Occasionally a client wanted a lion or a trip with dogs for birds, but late spring and summer were for trout. He was out every morning before dawn, driving with a thermos of coffee to pick up a lawyer, a widower, a politician with a penchant for native cutthroat. After dropping off clients he'd hustle back out to scout for the next trip. He scouted until dark and sometimes after, kneeling in willows by the river and waiting for a trout to rise. He came home stinking of fish gut and woke her with his eager stories, cutthroat trout leaping fifteen-foot cataracts, a stubborn rainbow wedged under a snag.

By June she was bored and lonely. She wandered through the woods, but never very far. The summer woods were dense and busy, nothing like the quiet grave-yard feel of winter. You couldn't see twenty feet in the summer. Nothing slept for very long; everything was emerging from cocoons, winging about, buzzing, multiplying, having litters, gaining weight. Bear cubs splashed in the river. Chicks screamed for worms. She longed for the stillness of winter, the long slumber, the bare sky, the bone-on-bone sound of bull elk knocking their antlers against trees. In August she went to the river to watch her husband cast flies with a client, the loops lifting from his rod like a spell cast over the water. He taught her to clean fish in the river so the scent wouldn't linger. She made the belly cuts, watched the viscera unloop in the current, the final, ecstatic visions of trout fading slowly up her wrists, running out into the river.

In September the big-game hunters came. Each client wanted something different: elk, antelope, a bull moose, a doe. They wanted to see grizzlies, track a wolverine, even shoot sandhill cranes. They wanted the heads of seven-by-seven royal bulls for their dens. Every few days he came home smelling of blood, with stories of stupid clients, of the Texan who sat, wheezing, too out of shape to get to the top of a hill for his shot. A bloodthirsty New Yorker claimed only to want to photograph black bears, then pulled a pistol from his boot and fired wildly at two cubs and their mother. Nightly she scrubbed blood out of the hunter's coveralls, watched it fade from rust to red to rose in the river water.

He was gone seven days a week, all day, home long enough only to grind sausage or cut roasts, clean his rifle, scrub out his meat pack, answer the phone. She understood very little of what he did, only that he loved the valley and needed to move in it, to watch the ravens and kingfishers and herons, the coyotes and bobcats, to hunt nearly everything else. There is no order in that world, he told her once, waving vaguely toward Great Falls, the cities that lay to the south. But here there is. Here I can see things I'd never see down there, things most folks are blind to. With no great reach of imagination she could see him fifty years hence, still lacing his boots, still gathering his rifle, all the world to see and him dying happy having seen only this valley.

She began to sleep, taking long afternoon naps, three hours or more. Sleep, she learned, was a skill like any other, like getting sawed in half and reassembled, or like divining visions from a dead robin. She taught herself to sleep despite heat, despite noise. Insects flung themselves at the screens, hornets sped down the chimney, the sun angled hot and urgent through the southern windows; still she slept. When he came home each autumn night, exhausted, forearms stained with blood, she was hours into sleep. Outside, the wind was already stripping leaves from the cottonwoods—too soon, he thought. He'd lie down and take her sleeping hand. Both of them lived in the grips of forces they had no control over—the November wind, the revolutions of the earth.

That winter was the worst he could remember: from Thanksgiving on they were snowed into the valley, the truck buried under six-foot drifts. The phone line went down in December and stayed down until April. January began with a chinook followed by a terrible freeze. The next morning a three-inch crust of ice covered the snow. On the ranches to the south cattle crashed through and bled to death kicking their way out. Deer punched through with their tiny hooves and suffocated in the deep snow beneath. Trails of blood veined the hills.

In the mornings he'd find coyote tracks written in the snow around the door to the crawlspace, two inches of hardwood between them and all his winter hoard hanging frozen now beneath the floorboards. He reinforced the door with baking sheets, nailing them up against the wood and over the hinges. Twice he woke to the sound of claws scrabbling against the metal, and charged outside to shout the coyotes away.

Everywhere he looked something was dying ungracefully, sinking in a drift, an elk keeling over, an emaciated doe clattering onto ice like a drunken skeleton. The radio reported huge cattle losses on the southern ranches. Each night he dreamt of wolves, of running with them, soaring over fences and tearing into the steaming, snow-matted bodies of cattle.

Still the snow fell. In February he woke three times to coyotes under the cabin, and the third time mere shouting could not send them running; he grabbed his bow and knife and dashed out into the snow barefoot, already his feet going numb. This time they had gone in under the door, chewing and digging the frozen earth under the foundation. He unbolted what was left of the door and swung it free.

A coyote hacked as it choked on something. Others shifted and panted. Maybe there were ten. Elk arrows were all he had, aluminum shafts tipped with broadheads. He squatted in the dark entryway—their only exit—with his bow at full draw and an arrow nocked. Above him he could hear his wife's feet pad silently over the floorboards. A coyote made a coughing sound. He began to fire arrows steadily into the dark. He heard some bite into the foundation blocks at the back of the crawlspace, others sink into flesh. He spent his whole quiver: a dozen arrows. The yelps of speared coyote went up. A few charged him, and he lashed at them with his knife. He felt teeth go to the bone of his arm, felt hot breath on his cheeks. He lashed with his knife at ribs, tails, skulls. His muscles screamed. The coyote were in a frenzy. Blood bloomed from his wrist, his thigh.

Upstairs she heard the otherwordly screams of wounded coyotes come through the floorboards, his grunts and curses as he fought. It sounded as if an exit had been tunneled all the way up from hell to open under their house, and what was now pouring out was the worst violence that place could send up. She knelt before the fireplace and felt the souls of coyote as they came through the boards on their way skyward.

He was blood-soaked and hungry and his thigh had been badly bitten but he worked all day digging out the truck. If he did not get food, they would starve, and he tried to hold the thought of the truck in his mind. He lugged slate and tree bark to wedge under the tires, excavated a mountain of snow from the truck bed. Finally, after dark, he got the engine turned over and ramped the truck up onto the frozen, wind-crusted snow. For a brief, wonderful moment he had it careening over the icy crust, starlight washing through the windows, tires spinning, engine churning, what looked to be the road unspooling in the headlights. Then he crashed through. Slowly, painfully, he began digging it out again.

It was hopeless. He would get it up and then it would crash through a few miles later. Hardly anywhere was the sheet of ice atop the snow thick enough to support the truck's weight. For twenty hours he revved and slid the truck over eight-foot drifts. Three more times it broke through and sank to the windows. Finally he left it. He was ten miles from home, thirty miles from town.

He made a weak and smoky fire with cut boughs and lay beside it and tried to sleep but couldn't. The heat from the fire melted snow and trickles ran slowly toward him but froze solid before they reached him. The stars twisting in their constellations above had never seemed farther or colder. In a state that was neither fully sleep nor fully waking, he watched wolves lope around his fire, just outside the reaches of light, slavering and lean. A raven dropped through the smoke and hopped to him. He thought for the first time that he might die if he did not get warmer. He managed to kneel and turn and crawl for home. Around him he could feel the wolves, smell blood on them, hear their nailed feet scrape across the ice.

He traveled all that night and all the next day, near catatonia, sometimes on his feet, more often on his elbows and knees. At times he thought he was a wolf and at times he thought he was dead. When he finally made it to the cabin, there were no tracks on the porch, no sign that she had gone out. The crawlspace door was still flung open and shreds of the siding and door frame lay scattered about as though some wounded devil had clawed its way out of the cabin's foundation and galloped into the night.

She was kneeling on the floor, ice in her hair, lost in some kind of hypothermic torpor. With his last dregs of energy he constructed a fire and poured a mug of hot water down her throat. As he fell into sleep, he watched himself as from a distance, weeping and clutching his near-frozen wife.

They had only flour, a jar of frozen cranberries, and a few crackers in the cupboards. He went out only to split more wood. When she could speak her voice was quiet and far away. I have dreamt the most amazing things, she murmured. I have seen the places where the coyotes go when they are gone. I know where spiders go, and geese. . . .

Snow fell incessantly. He wondered if some ice age had befallen the entire world. Night was abiding; daylight passed in a breath. Soon the whole planet would become a white and featureless ball hurtling through space, lost. Whenever he stood up his eyesight fled in slow, nauseating streaks of color.

Icicles hung from the cabin's roof and ran all the way to the porch, pillars of ice barring the door. To exit he had to hack his way out with an axe. He went out with lanterns to fish, shoveled down to the river ice, drilled through with a hand auger and shivered over the hole jigging a ball of dough on a hook. Sometimes he brought back a trout, frozen stiff in the short snowshoe from the river to the cabin. Other times they ate a squirrel, a hare, once a famished deer whose bones he cracked and boiled and finally ground into meal, or only a few handfuls of rose hips. In the worst parts of March he dug out cattails to peel and steam the tubers.

She hardly ate, sleeping eighteen, twenty hours a day. When she woke it was to scribble on notebook paper before plummeting back into sleep, clutching at the blankets as if they gave her sustenance. There was, she was learning, strength hidden at the center of weakness, ground at the bottom of the deepest pit. With her stomach empty and her body quieted, without the daily demands of living, she felt she was making important discoveries. She was only nineteen and had lost twenty pounds since marrying him. Naked she was all rib cage and pelvis.

He read her scribbled dreams but they read like senseless poems and gave him no clues to her: *Snail*, she wrote,

> *sleds down blades in the rain.*
> *Owl: fixed his eyes on hare, dropping as if from the moon.*
> *Horse: rides across the plains with his brothers . . .*

Eventually he hated himself for bringing her there, for quarantining her in a cabin winterlong. This winter was making her crazy—making them both crazy. All that was happening to her was his fault.

In April the temperature rose above zero and then above twenty. He strapped the extra battery to his pack and went to dig out the truck. Its excavation took all day. He drove it slowly back up the slushy road in the moonlight, went in and asked if she'd like to go to town the next morning. To his surprise, she said yes. They heated water for baths and dressed in clothes they hadn't worn in six months. She threaded twine through her belt loops to keep her trousers up.

Behind the wheel his chest filled up to have her with him, to be moving out into the country, to see the sun above the trees. Spring was coming; the valley was dressing up. Look there, he wanted to say, those geese streaming over the road. The valley lives. Even after a winter like that.

She asked him to drop her off at the library. He bought food—a dozen frozen pizzas, potatoes, eggs, carrots. He nearly wept at seeing bananas. He sat in the parking lot and drank a half gallon of milk. When he picked her up at the library, she had applied for a library card and borrowed twenty books. They stopped at the Bitterroot for hamburgers and rhubarb pie. She ate three pieces. He watched her eat, the spoon sliding out of her mouth. This was better. This was more like he dreamed it would be.

Well, Mary, he said. I think we made it.

I love pie, she said.

As soon as the lines were repaired the phone began to ring. He took his fishing clients down the river. She sat on the porch, reading, reading.

Soon her appetite for books could not be met by the Great Falls Public Library. She wanted other books, essays about sorcery, primers on magic-working and conjury that had to be mail-ordered from New Hampshire, New Orleans, even Italy. Once a week the hunter drove to town to collect a parcel of books from the post office: *Arcana Mundi*, *The Seer's Dictionary*, *Paragon of Wizardry*, *Occult Science Among the Ancients*. He opened one to a random page and read, *bring water, tie a soft fillet around your altar, burn it on fresh twigs and frankincense*. . . .

She regained her health, took on energy, no longer lay under furs dreaming all day. She was out of bed before him, brewing coffee, her nose already between pages. With a steady diet of meat and vegetables her body bloomed, her hair shone; her eyes and cheeks glowed. After supper he'd watch her read in the firelight, blackbird feathers tied all through her hair, a heron's beak hanging between her breasts.

In November he took a Sunday off and they cross-country skied. They came across a bull elk frozen to death in a draw, ravens shrieking at them as they skied to it. She knelt by it and put her palm on its leathered skull. Her eyes rolled back in her head. There, she moaned. I feel him.

What do you feel? he asked, standing behind her. What is it?

She stood, trembling. I feel his life flowing out, she said. I see where he goes, what he sees.

But that's impossible, he said. It's like saying you know what I dream.

I do, she said. You dream about wolves.

But that elk's been dead at least a day. It doesn't go anywhere. It goes into the crops of those ravens.

How could she tell him? How could she ask him to understand such a thing? How could anyone understand? The books she read never told her that.

More clearly than ever she could see that there was a fine line between dreams and wakefulness, between living and dying, a line so tenuous it sometimes didn't exist. It was always clearest for her in winter. In winter, in that valley, life and death were not so different. The heart of a hibernating newt was frozen solid but she could warm and wake it in her palm. For the newt there was no line at all, no fence, no River Styx, only an area between living and dying, like a snowfield between two lakes: a place where lake denizens sometimes met each other on their way to the other side, where there was only one state of being, neither living nor dead, where death was only a possibility and visions rose shimmering to the stars like smoke. All that was needed was a hand, the heat of a palm, the touch of fingers.

That February the sun shone during the days and ice formed at night—slick sheets glazing the wheat fields, the roofs and roads. He dropped her off at the library, the chains on the tires rattling as he pulled away, heading back up the Missouri toward Fort Benton.

Around noon Marlin Spokes, a snowplough driver the hunter knew from grade school, slid off the Sun River Bridge in his plough and dropped forty feet into the river. He was dead before they could get him out of the truck. She was reading in the library a block away and heard the plough crash into the riverbed like a thousand dropped girders. When she got to the bridge, sprinting in her jeans and T-shirt, men were already in the water—a telephone man from Helena, the jeweler, the butcher in his apron, all of them scrambling down the banks, wading in the rapids, prying the door open. She careened down the snow-covered slope beneath the bridge and splashed to them. The men lifted Marlin from the cab, stumbling as they carried him. Steam rose from their shoulders and from the crushed hood of the plow. Her hand on the jeweler's arm, her leg against the butcher's leg, she reached for Marlin's ankle.

When her finger touched Marlin's body, her eyes rolled immediately back and a single vision leapt to her: Marlin Spokes pedaling a bicycle, a child's seat mounted over the rear tire with a helmeted boy—Marlin's own son—strapped into it. Spangles of light drifted over the riders as they rolled down a lane beneath giant sprawling trees. The boy reached for Marlin's hair with one small fist. Fallen leaves turned over in their wake. In the glass of a storefront window their reflection flashed past. This quiet vision—like a ribbon of rich silk—ran out slowly and fluidly, with great power, and she shook beneath it. It was she who pedaled the bike. The boy's fingers pulled through her hair.

The men who were touching her or touching Marlin saw what she saw, felt what she felt. They tried not to talk about it, but after the funeral, after a week, they couldn't keep it in. At first they spoke of it only in their basements, at night, but Great Falls was not a big town and this was not something one kept locked in a basement. Soon they talked about it everywhere, in the supermarket, at the gasoline pumps. People who didn't know Marlin Spokes or his son or the hunter's wife or any of the men in the river that morning soon spoke of the event like experts. All you had to do was *touch* her, a barber said, and you saw it too. The most beautiful lane you've ever dreamed, raved a deli owner. Giant trees bigger'n you've ever imagined. You didn't just pedal his son around, movie ushers whispered, you *loved* him.

He could have heard anywhere. In the cabin he built up the fire, flipped idly through a stack of her books. He couldn't understand them—one of them wasn't even in English.

After dinner she took the plates to the sink.

You read Spanish now? he asked.

Her hands in the sink stilled. It's Portuguese, she said. I only understand a little.

He turned his fork in his hands. Were you there when Marlin Spokes was killed?

I helped pull him out of the truck. I don't think I was much good.

He looked at the back of her head. He felt like driving his fork through the table. What tricks did you play? Did you hypnotize people?

Her shoulders tightened. Her voice came out furious: Why can't you—, she began, but her voice fell off. It wasn't tricks, she muttered. I helped carry him.

When she started to get phone calls, he hung up on the callers. But they were relentless: a grieving widow, an orphan's lawyer, a reporter from the *Great Falls Tribune*. A blubbering father drove all the way to the cabin to beg her to come to the funeral parlor, and finally she went. The hunter insisted on driving her. It wasn't right, he declared, for her to go alone. He waited in the truck in the parking lot, engine rattling, radio moaning.

I feel so alive, she said afterward as he helped her into the cab. Her clothes were soaked through with sweat. Like my blood is fizzing through my body. At home she lay awake, far away, all night.

She got called back and called back, and each time he drove her. Some days he'd take her after a whole day of scouting for elk and he'd pass out from exhaustion while he waited in the truck. When he woke she'd be beside him, holding his hand, her hair damp, her eyes wild.

You dreamt you were with the wolves and eating salmon, she said. They were washed up and dying on the shoals. It was right outside the cabin.

It was well after midnight and he'd be up before four the next day. The salmon used to come here, he said. When I was a boy. There'd be so many you could stick your hand in the river and touch one. He drove them home over the dark fields. He tried to soften his voice. What do you do in there? What really?

I give them solace. I let them say good-bye to their loved ones. I help them know something they'd never otherwise know.

No, he said. I mean what kind of tricks? How do you do it?

She turned her hands palm up. As long as they're touching me they see what I see. Come in with me next time. Go in there and hold hands. Then you'll know.

He said nothing. The stars above the windshield seemed fixed in their places.

Families wanted to pay her; most wouldn't let her leave until they did. She would come out to the truck with fifty, a hundred—once four hundred—dollars folded into her pocket. She grew her hair out, obtained talismans to dramatize her performances: a bat wing, a raven's beak, a fistful of hawk's feathers bound with a sprig of cheroot. A cardboard box full of candle stubs. Then she went off for weekends, disappearing in the truck before he was up, a fearless driver. She stopped for roadkill and knelt by it—a crumpled porcupine, a shattered deer. She pressed her palm to the truck's grille where a hundred husks of insects smoked. Seasons came and went. She was gone half the winter. Each of them was alone. They never spoke. On longer drives there were times she was tempted to keep the truck pointed away and never return.

In the first thaws he would go out to the river, try to lose himself in the rhythm of casting, in the sound of pebbles driven downstream, clacking together. But even fishing had gone lonely for him. Everything, it seemed, was out of his hands—his truck, his wife, the course of his own life.

As hunting season came on his mind wandered. He was botching opportunities—getting upwind of elk or telling a client to call it quits thirty seconds before a pheasant burst from cover and flapped slowly, untroubled, into the sky. When a client missed his mark and pegged an antelope in the neck, the hunter berated him for being careless, knelt over its tracks and clutched at the bloody snow. Do you understand what you've done? he shouted. How the arrow shaft will knock against the trees, how the animal will run and run, how the wolves will trot behind it to keep it from resting? The client was red-faced, huffing. Wolves? the client said. There haven't been wolves here for twenty years.

She was in Butte or Missoula when he discovered her money in a boot: six thousand dollars and change. He canceled his trips and stewed for two days, pacing the porch, sifting through her things, rehearsing his arguments. When she saw him, the sheaf of bills jutting from his shirt pocket, she stopped halfway to the door, her bag over her shoulder, her hair brought back. The light came across his shoulders and fell onto the yard.

It's not right, he said.

She walked past him into the cabin. I'm helping people. I'm doing what I love. Can't you see how good I feel afterward?

You take advantage of them. They're grieving, and you take their money.

They *want* to pay me, she shrieked. I help them see something they desperately want to see.

It's a grift. A con.

She came back out on the porch. No, she said. Her voice was quiet and strong. This is real. As real as anything: the valley, the river, the trees, your trout hanging in the crawlspace. I have a talent. A gift.

He snorted. A gift for hocus-pocus. For swindling widows out of their savings. He lobbed the money into the yard. The wind caught the bills and scattered them over the snow.

She hit him, once, hard across the mouth. How dare you? she cried. You, of all people, should understand. You who dream of wolves every night.

He went out alone the next evening and she tracked him through the snow. He was up on a deer platform under a blanket. He was wearing white camouflage; he'd tiger-striped his face with black paint. She crouched a hundred yards away, for four hours or more, damp and trembling in the snow behind his tree stand. She thought he must have dozed off when she heard an arrow sing down from the platform and strike a doe she hadn't even noticed in the chest. The doe looked around, wildly surprised, and charged off, galloping through the trees. She heard the aluminum shaft of the arrow knocking against branches, heard the deer plunge through a thicket. The hunter sat a moment, then climbed down from his perch and began to follow. She waited until he was out of sight, then followed.

She didn't have far to go. There was so much blood she thought he must have wounded other deer, which must all have come charging down this same path, spilling out the quantities of their lives. The doe lay panting between two trees, the thin shaft of the arrow jutting from her shoulder. Blood so red it was almost black pulsed down its flank. The hunter stood over the animal and slit its throat.

Mary leapt forward from where she squatted, her legs all pins and needles, dashed across the snow in her parka and, lunging, grabbed the doe by its still-warm foreleg. With her other hand she seized the hunter's wrist and held on. His knife was still inside the deer's throat and as he pulled away blood spread thickly into the snow. Already the doe's vision was surging through her body—fifty deer wading a sparkling brook, their bellies in the current, craning their necks to pull leaves from overhanging alders, light pouring around their bodies, a buck raising its antlered head like a king. A silver bead of water hung from its muzzle, caught the sun, and fell.

What?—the hunter gasped. He dropped his knife. He was pulling away, pulling from his knees with all his strength. She held on; one hand on his wrist, the other clamped around the doe's foreleg. He dragged them across the snow and the doe left her blood as she went. Oh, he whispered. He could feel the world—the grains of snow, the stripped bunches of trees—falling away. The taste of alder leaves was in his mouth. A golden brook rushed under his body; light spilled onto him. The buck was raising its head, meeting his eyes. All the world washed in amber.

The hunter gave a last pull and was free. The vision sped away. No, he murmured. No. He rubbed his wrist where her fingers had been and shook his head as if shaking off a blow. He ran.

Mary lay in the blood-smeared snow a long time, the warmth of the doe running up her arm until finally the woods had gone cold and she was alone. She dressed the doe with his knife and quartered the carcass and ferried it home over her shoulders. Her husband was in bed. The fireplace was cold. Don't come near me, he said. Don't touch me. She built the fire and fell asleep on the floor.

In the months that followed she left the cabin more frequently and for longer durations, visiting homes, accident sites and funeral parlors all over central Montana. Finally she pointed the truck south and didn't turn back. They had been married five years.

Twenty years later, in the Bitterroot Diner, he looked up at the ceiling-mounted television and there she was, being interviewed. She lived in Manhattan, had traveled the world, written two books. She was in demand all over the country. Do you commune with the dead? the interviewer asked. No, she said, I help people. I commune with the living. I give people peace.

Well, the interviewer said, turning to speak into the camera, I believe it.

The hunter bought her books at the bookstore and read them in one night. She had written poems about the valley, written them to the animals: you rampant coyote, you glorious bull. She had traveled to Sudan to touch the backbone of a fossilized stegosaur, and wrote of her frustration when she divined nothing from it. A TV network flew her to Kamchatka to embrace the huge shaggy forefoot of a mammoth as it was airlifted from the permafrost—she had better luck with that one, describing an entire herd slogging big-footed through a slushy tide, tearing at sea grass and bringing it to their mouths with their trunks. In a handful of poems there were even vague allusions to him—a brooding, blood-soaked presence that hovered outside the margins, like storms on their way, like a killer hiding in the basement.

The hunter was fifty-eight years old. Twenty years was a long time. The valley had diminished slowly but perceptibly: roads came in, and the grizzlies left, seeking higher country. Loggers had thinned nearly every accessible stand of trees. Every spring runoff from logging roads turned the river chocolate-brown. He had given up on finding a wolf in that country although they still came to him in dreams and let him run with them, out over frozen flats under the moon. He had never been with another woman. In his cabin, bent over the table, he set aside her books, took a pencil, and wrote her a letter.

A week later a Federal Express truck drove all the way to the cabin. Inside the envelope was her response on embossed stationery. The handwriting was hurried and efficient. *I will be in Chicago*, it said, *day after tomorrow. Enclosed is a plane ticket. Feel free to come. Thank you for writing.*

After sherbet the chancellor rang his spoon against a glass and called his guests into the reception room. The bar had been dismantled; in its place three caskets had been set on the carpet. The caskets were mahogany, polished to a deep luster. The one in the center was larger than the two flanking it. A bit of snow that had fallen on the lids—they must have been kept outside—was melting, and drops ran onto the carpet where they left dark circles. Around the caskets cushions had been placed on the floor. A dozen candles burned on the mantel. There were the sounds of staff clearing the dining room. The hunter leaned against the entryway and watched guests drift uncomfortably into the room, some cradling coffee cups, others gulping at gin or vodka in deep tumblers. Eventually everyone settled onto the floor.

The hunter's wife came in then, elegant in her dark suit. She knelt and motioned for O'Brien to sit beside her. His face was pinched and inscrutable. Again the hunter had the impression that he was not of this world but of a slightly leaner one.

President O'Brien, his wife said. I know this is difficult for you. Death can seem so final, like a blade dropped through your center. But the nature of death is not at all final; it is not some dark cliff off which we leap. I hope to show you it is merely a fog, something we can peer into and out of, something we can know and face and not necessarily fear. By each life taken from our collective lives we are diminished. But even in death there is much to celebrate. It is only a transition, like so many others.

She moved into the circle and unfastened the lids of the caskets. From where he sat the hunter could not see inside. His wife's hands fluttered around her waist like birds. Think, she said. Think hard about something you would like resolved, some matter, gone now, which you wish you could take back—perhaps with your daughters, a moment, a lost feeling, a desperate wish.

The hunter lidded his eyes. He found himself thinking of his wife, of their long gulf, of dragging her and a bleeding doe through the snow. Think now, his wife was saying, of some wonderful moment, some fine and sunny minute you shared, your wife and daughters, all of you together. Her voice was lulling. Beneath his eyelids the glow of the candles made an even orange wash. He knew her hands were reaching for whatever—whoever—lay in those caskets. Somewhere inside him he felt her extend across the room.

His wife said more about beauty and loss being the same thing, about how they ordered the world, and he felt something happening—a strange warmth, a flitting presence, something dim and unsettling like a feather brushed across the back of his neck. Hands on both sides of him reached for his hands. Fingers locked around his fingers. He wondered if she was hypnotizing him, but it didn't matter. He had nothing to fight off or snap out of. She was inside him now; she had reached across and was poking about.

Her voice faded, and he felt himself swept up as if rising toward the ceiling. Air washed lightly in and out of his lungs; warmth pulsed in the hands that held his own. In his mind he saw a sea emerging from fog. The water was broad and flat and glittered like polished metal. He could feel dune grass moving against his shins, and wind coming over his shoulders. The sea was very bright. All around him bees shuttled over the dunes. Far out a shorebird was diving for crabs. He knew that a few hundred yards away a pair of girls were building castles in the sand; he could hear their song, soft and lilting. Their mother was with them, reclined under an umbrella, one leg bent, the other straight. She was drinking iced tea and he could taste it in his mouth, sweet and bitter with a trace of mint. Each cell in his body seemed to breathe. He became the girls, the diving bird, the shuttling bees; he was the mother of the girls and the father; he could feel himself flowing outward, richly dissolving, paddling into the world like the very first cell into the great blue sea. . . .

When he opened his eyes he saw linen curtains, women in gowns kneeling. Tears were visible on many people's cheeks—O'Brien's and the chancellor's and Bruce Maples's. His wife's head was bowed. The hunter gently released the hands that held his and walked out into kitchen, past the sudsy sinks, the stacks of dishes. He let himself out a side door and found himself on the long wooden deck that ran the length of the house, a couple inches of snow already settled on it.

He felt drawn toward the pond, the birdbath and the hedges. He walked to the pond and stood at its rim. The snow was falling easily and slowly and the undersides of the clouds glowed yellow with reflected light from the city. Inside the house the lights were all down and only the dozen candles on the mantel showed, trembling and winking through the windows, a tiny, trapped constellation.

Before long his wife came out onto the deck and walked through the snow and came down to the pond. There were things he had been preparing to say: something about a final belief, about his faithfulness to the idea of her, an expression of gratitude for providing a reason to leave the valley, if only for a night. He wanted to tell her that although the wolves were gone, may always have been gone, they still came to him in dreams. That they could run there, fierce and unfettered, was surely enough. She would understand. She had understood long before he did.

But he was afraid to speak. He could see that speaking would be like dashing some very fragile bond to pieces, like kicking a dandelion gone to seed; the wispy, tenuous sphere of its body would scatter in the wind. So instead they stood together, the snow fluttering down from the clouds to melt into the water where their own reflected images trembled like two people trapped against the glass of a parallel world, and he reached, finally, to take her hand.

# MARIN SORESCU

# The Cowardly Coffin

*Marin Sorescu (1936–1996), one of Romania's most celebrated poets, was Romania's Nobel Prize nominee in the year of his untimely death. He is the author of more than twenty collections of poems, including* The Youth of Don Quixote; Fountains in the Sea; Water of Life, Water of Death; Poems Selected by Censorship; *and* The Crossing. *His work has been translated into English by fellow poets such as Seamus Heaney, Ted Hughes, and Paul Muldoon. Sorescu also wrote plays, including* Jonah, The Verger, The Matrix, Vlad the Impaler, *and* Cousin Shakespeare. *He was the recipient of numerous prizes: Writer's Union Prizes for both poetry and drama, the Fernando Riello poetry prize in Madrid, the Herder Prize in Vienna, Le Muze prize in Florence, and the Gold Medal at Naples, among others.*

*"The Cowardly Coffin" was written for Sorescu's last collection,* The Bridge, *in the last two months of his life, as the poet was dying of cancer. It appeared in 2001 in English translation in* The American Poetry Review. *As a longtime fan of Sorescu's work, I consider it a very great privilege to be able to include "The Cowardly Coffin" in this volume.*

—T. W.

It let itself be laid carefully in the grave
By skilled, brawny men
Inured to this.
("Hold it there! A bit more to the right!
That's it, OK! Let go! No, no, not all the way.")

When I finally touched bottom in the grave
(It had to be widened, since they dug it rather narrow),
The coffin gave a sudden shudder,
A start.
And shot high above
Dragging the gravediggers along.
Caught in the straps.

The procession was astounded.
What material could the coffin be made of?
Or was there something horrifying
At the bottom of the grave?
The newspapermen required a clarification
And blamed the upcoming elections.

The coffin, which appeared quite ordinary,
Rough-planed planks nailed with 10-penny nails.
Knocked over several crosses,
Banged into the church steeple,
Swung about through the air
(The gravediggers climbed down from trees,
A plum or two in their mouths),
And after a while
Returned, contrite, to the rim of the grave.
It waited for flowers to be thrown.
And fresh earth.

The woman, commencing to weep all over again,
Filed by it.
"Let's get with it, man! Give it another try!
Play out some more rope,
And you, you hold it down.
Two of you men sit on its lid
To make it heavier.
Others of you, jump on when it touches the ground,
To counterbalance it."

A little this way, a little that way, very carefully.
It descended like lead to the other world.
Then, of a sudden, a tremor—
And with a sort of stifled moan,
The narrow end first, as if from a launching pad,
Aerodynamic it blasted off again.

As late as nightfall, with all manner of tricks,
It would not be buried.
Now it's flying crazily in the sky,
Soon to be shot down
By some rocket or another
From our missile defense.

# STEVE RASNIC TEM

# In These Final Days of Sales

*Steve Rasnic Tem's stories have been published in numerous anthologies, including* MetaHorror, Forbidden Acts, Dark Terrors 3, The Best New Horror, *and earlier volumes of* The Year's Best Fantasy and Horror, *as well as in various magazines. He has had two collections published in English,* City Fishing *and* The Far Side of the Lake. *His novel,* The Book of Days, *was recently published by Subterranean Press. Also, Lone Wolf just released a multimedia CD,* Imagination Box, *by him and his wife, Melanie Tem.*

*"In These Final Days of Sales" was originally published as a chapbook by the new publisher Wormhole Books.*

—E. D.

**M**ain thing is, you're selling something those folks need, something they can't live without.

"It's not the bang in your buck, it's the buck in your bang." At the end of the commercial the words blaze a brilliant white across the black screen, then fade. Emil remembers a time when clarity was of the utmost importance in sales, conventional wisdom being that people would not buy an unknown quantity. Of course, what they thought they were getting might not bear much resemblance to the object eventually delivered wrapped in brown paper C.O.D., but at least the transaction began with that image in mind, clear if erroneous.

Now, a certain degree of clairvoyance is required to discern what goods are actually being advertised. Emil, himself in the sales business, watches commercials in the hotel rooms along his route, trying to map out exactly what the rules are now. What troubles him most is that they seem to be not just about new sales techniques, but about a change in the human psyche itself. We have become the creatures in our dreams, he thinks, poured into pleasing and biodegradable packaging.

People want something—that has been the message behind the message in every ad or commercial. *You want something*, they remind us. The ads advertise want. They advertise need. No wonder the actual product remains in the background. At some level the advertisers have finally realized their products are merely symbolic, almost irrelevant.

Much of the mysterious advertising, Emil has finally concluded, is for various brands of pants.

After a few years, all the towns, all the countless burgs and villes line up like endless doors, opening one by one, and seem like the same town, the same Main Street with the same row of worn brick or white-washed wood on each side, the same people of pink or yellow or brown in their denims, corduroys, cottons, or polyesters, waving or not waving depending on how friendly toward strangers they are feeling on this particular day. And yet Emil, the professional salesman, has never really thought of himself as a stranger.

That was the first thing he learned in sales: you cannot act like or think of yourself as a stranger. Not if they are going to trust you. Not if they are going to *buy*. And how is buying any different from shaking a hand, giving a good how-do-you-do, getting married, kissing the kids goodnight? Not much, when you really think about it. Just another form of social exchange, value for value, you rub my back and I'll rub yours. You don't want to be left back on the shelf when everybody's buying. That's the very worst thing. You don't want to remain unsold all your life.

Sometimes Emil is so intent he is on the eventual accounting that he forgets sales is more than that. It is a matter of wishes and dreams, of planning and foresight, of frustration and expectation. After years on the road, each town is exactly what he'd expected it to be. The streets are exactly what he'd imagined; the people are perfectly familiar because they've already walked these streets in one of his countless motel daydreams.

It is as if, every day, the citizens of these tiny communities rebuild their town according to his expectations, anticipating his particular arrival. Given how self-centered human beings are, this is no doubt a common misperception. It is one of the first things you learn as a salesman, and if you are good at your job, you use it to your advantage.

Emil is not good at his job. In fact, if there is a worse salesman out there on the road Emil has not yet met him.

The man with the off-kilter eyes fills the screen with a loopy grin. A dolly back to reveal the rest of the family: the wife rubbing up against him in her new red dress, barely able to contain herself, the kids jumpy. Emil thinks the boy may have peed his pants.

They are all holding up great wads of fake cash to the camera: the portrait on one of the bills resembles Clark Gable more than any president Emil can think of. And yet these people are so thrilled to have it in their hands—they jump around as if affected by some nervous disease.

Having little tolerance any more for the manic patter of commercials he keeps the volume down as he watches the television family pantomime surprise, joy, delirium. They've gotten what they've always wanted. Failing that, perhaps they can rent it. If it's still available. If they can ever figure out what it is.

He really shouldn't make fun, he thinks. If people didn't behave this way, if they stopped looking for something to make them happy, they wouldn't buy.

Of course, people seldom buy from him in any case. In fact, Emil has come to think of himself as the anti-salesman, like some super villain with a huge gray cape and unpleasant teeth.

Emil has in his pocket a letter from an old salesman he used to meet out on the road a couple of times a year. Their paths might cross in Goodland, or in Hugo, perhaps even in Kansas City. Supposedly Walt had been quite successful in his time, but Emil knows him only as this tired-looking fellow who might have been a retired teacher or someone recently recovered from a lengthy illness.

"Emil, this is a job offer of sorts. Not for a specific job really but it is the promise of a job, a good job with regular hours and good benefits. And there's *no* travel involved. My friends and I have had this dream we've developed over years on the road, a dream built a stick at a time in hotel rooms and all-night diners, of someday having our own town, a factory outlet town where customers would come to *you* to buy the things they really needed to buy. So no sales pitches or how-many-should-I-put-you-down-fors. Why any pressure high or low would simply be out of the question! We need salesmen to run the stores of this new town, trained salesmen who have become more interested in helping people than they are in earning high commissions. . . ."

Emil has taken this letter out and unfolded it and reread it so many times it threatens to fragment into a dozen or so worn paper squares held together by a few commas and dashes.

He has never visited this new town. It just makes him feel good knowing that it is there.

Sometimes Emil fantasizes that he will find a way to sneak back and catch the residents of a town unawares. Then he will find out exactly what each of these places is really like. Perhaps at last he will discover what people really think about him. The thought is both exciting and dreadful.

Emil's career in sales hasn't always been like this. In the beginning he never knew what to expect when he arrived in a new town. It had been interesting. It had made him anxious. He never knew if he'd find hell or paradise. Most of the time it had been neither, of course, a necklace of gray towns and gray people, but at least that heady anticipation had always been there.

"The *main* thing is . . ." Jack looked around for a place to spit. Emil moved his feet out of the way. Finally the old man looked over his shoulder and spat behind him. "Main thing is, you're selling something those folks *need*, something they can't live *without*."

"I don't want to lie to anybody," Emil had said.

"*Lie?* Who said anything about lying, boy? I don't want you to *lie*, for chrissake! Who *knows* what anybody needs? I don't know what *you* need. Are you arrogant enough to tell me you know what *I* need? Do *you* really know what *you* need? I doubt it. Even occasional self-knowledge is a *rare* thing, boy. It's *luck*, pure and simple. So don't talk to me about lies. Guesses would be more accurate."

"I don't even know what I'm selling," Emil said.

"That's because I haven't *told* you yet, boy." Jack pulled an oft-creased, yellowing square of paper out of his back pants pocket. Ignoring the tiny paper slivers that flaked off and littered the floor, he unfolded it, unfolded it again. When it was about a yard square he stopped and pressed his nose against it. The paper was so worn and discolored it made Emil think of a thin layer of old skin. He could practically read Jack's expression through the huge square: the wrinkled forehead, the pursed lips, the mushy dark gray eyes like a baby's. But Emil couldn't make out any of the writing, or even if there was any writing.

"There's some difference of opinion on this." Jack's voice raised and lifted the paper as if it were a floating tissue. "But encyclopedias are best for a beginner, I suspect. You're offering them the world of knowledge, the flying carpet to distant lands, all of that for just a few bucks a month. Just gotta remember that with encyclopedias you only call on people who have kids."

"Because most adults think their learning days are over," Emil added helpfully.

"Somethin' like that. Tell me, are *you* willing to learn, or do you just want to put your own two cents in?"

"Oh, yes, I want to learn. Really." It was just to be a short-term job following graduation, something to put food in his mouth and a roof over his head until something better came along.

"OK, then. The thing about selling encyclopedias is you can convince them they need to buy a set for their kids' futures. Everybody wants to do things for the future of their kids—in this country we spoil them rotten."

Emil's own parents had begrudged him every penny. You would have thought they might have found the cure for cancer if only they hadn't had to worry about their only son.

If he ever had children, if he ever could convince a woman he was worth raising a family with, he'd surely buy them a set of encyclopedias. A whole damn library. You could not do enough for your kids.

"You'd buy your own kids encyclopedias, wouldn't you? I mean if you had any?" It was as if the old man read his mind. A good salesman, according to that first training manual, could tell when interest had peaked, when the customer was growing bored, as well as determine the particular magic phrase that might turn sales, and lives, around.

"Oh, well, of course. If I had the money . . ."

"Even if you *didn't* have the money you'd do it! You'd find a way *somehow*. Now don't tell me that you wouldn't!"

"Well, you're right . . ."

"See now, *that's* what I'm talking about. In this country we buy our kids things, especially if we have even the vaguest notion it'll give them a better life than what we've had. Something bright and shiny, and fluttering with color and motion. That's pretty much the American way."

Jack somehow found an opportunity to drop the word American into practically every conversation, his particular style of sales patter. Emil wasn't sure he himself had his own style, even after all these years, except that it involved a great deal of sitting, of daydreaming through visits in old-fashioned parlors and newly decorated living rooms, waiting for a change in the air or the light, or the order of the universe.

"You know, I've never sold anything before," Emil said.

"Sure you have. Like everybody else you've been selling all your life. The question is whether you've been giving the people good value."

Sales had been as unlikely an occupation for someone of Emil's temperament as anything he might imagine. He'd gone on very few dates, unable to sell himself to women. He'd been passed over for the simplest jobs, because he'd been unable to sell himself to employers. Whatever friends he had acquired seemed largely accidental.

He had no aptitude for closing the deal, shaking the hand, laughing at the obligatory jokes. It was the world's sense of humor that had brought him into sales after graduation—you understood that sort of thing if you were a salesman.

So it had all come down to the day he'd picked up his sample set at the warehouse, along with the brochures and studies proving how kids raised on encyclopedias had increased IQ, appetite and stamina, and set out his first time on the road using the route map the old man had given him. Instead of the usual dots or squares to represent towns and cities, there were little drawings of houses, all of them the same size, crude yet childishly cheerful, pastel yellows and blues and pinks. When he examined those tiny houses with his magnifying glass he spied children's faces in the windows of several, here and there a smiling mother or father out on the lawn, baby brother in a stroller, the shirtless neighbor watering his lawn. A tiny blotch of ink that might have been a dog or a cat.

A company-owned car was provided for his first trip out. Imagine, a company car! But he was alarmed to discover a broad scrape along the length of the passenger side, and cracks in the windows. "They want you to keep that passenger side parked away from your customers' houses at all times," the chief dispatcher informed him.

The brown dashboard had enough cracks in it to fill a dried-out riverbed. The clock was missing an hour hand (if he scrunched sideways against the steering wheel he could just see that missing hand reclining in the bottom scoop of the dial). The seat and back had even more cracks, futilely repaired with a variety of tapes that caught and pulled at his neatly pressed suit.

Out on the road he realized that major cities—New York, St. Louis, Philadelphia, Chicago—weren't even depicted on the map. "We like to leave the big places for the veterans," Jack had told him.

Now and then over the years he would come to a town that felt far more familiar than most. With a "B" name like Bennett or Bailey or Baxter, it would be a town with ambition: the main street in the process of restoration, new motels and restaurants at the outskirts, and at least one new mall. A construction sign just outside town limits advertises a multiplex. Overpriced town homes are being erected along the distant foothills.

Emil has met the desk clerk at the cheapest hotel and asks about the health of his youngest daughter. The clerk does not act surprised. At the bake sale outside the post office, the woman in the bright yellow dress sells him a small bag of ginger snaps for the eighth time this year.

In the windows of the hardware store are pictures of missing children. It is an epidemic; he wonders about the strangers who steal children out of the Baileys and Baxters and Bennetts of the world. Perhaps the kidnapper is an airline pilot, he thinks. Perhaps he is the representative of some obscure government regulatory agency. Perhaps he is a traveling salesman who is lost in the identical towns and quiet streets of America.

It never occurs to him that anyone might suspect him, anymore than it would occur to him to commit such a crime.

The automobile on the flickering screen is unlike any Emil has ever seen: so sleek, so modern, it appears to drive itself, passing without damage through tornadoes, mudslides, nuclear attacks. The message of the commercial is that a person could not die in such a vehicle. Death has always been the big mistake, the nasty trick, the unacceptable penalty. Emil believes if he just didn't have to die he might someday become a successful human being.

Now, in these final days of salesmanship, Emil is on his twenty-sixth company car. He knows this from the files of paperwork in a cardboard box in the back seat. He wonders if bad driving is one of the by-products of salesmanship, this pushing through the highways and byways of the assigned route, whatever the weather or road conditions; this nervous and careless passing, this incessant hurry to get nowhere. If it all came down to driving habits, he'd have been declared the perfect salesperson a long time ago.

But he has no talent for sales. He sometimes wonders what kind of man he must be, to spend his life dedicated to something he is so poor at. But if he has learned anything at all in his wanderings it is that life itself, for most of humanity, is this constant doing and undoing, doing poorly at what we attempt, undoing the better efforts of those who have come before us.

Still, survival requires food for the mouth, a pillow for the head, motion of the eye, and a new day's list of prospects for the brain to process.

In these last few days of salesmanship his lack of aptitude cannot be helped. In these last few days of salesmanship there are many more towns to investigate, hotel rooms to rent, long hours to spend waiting on the couches, and good chairs in the living rooms of America, meditating through the afternoons in quiet contemplation of the people who need everything and nothing. He means no criticism in this, it is simply the life we live in these last days of sales, trying not to think too much about the small tragedies or joys.

The sound at the door is more a rubbing or a scraping than a knocking. He hesitates to open it—no one knows he is here except the clerk.

A small old lady of gray flesh peers up at him beyond the dire weight of her glasses. "I just wanted to thank you for that new Bible you sold me," she tells him, and lifts her head to kiss him on the cheek, exposing the ragged hole in her throat.

He tries to close the door on her, but she shoves the shiny red leather Bible between the door and the jamb. He turns to escape and trips over his sample case. She drapes herself over him, whispering, *I just want you to sell me again,* and he is appalled to discover the erection growing like an impending purchase beneath his belt.

*Remember that there's a pit waiting for you in self-pity, so put that I in try and get back on your feet and run!*

The cheers, the applause, the feet stampings are so loud Emil is compelled to fiddle with the volume control. It takes some time for him to figure out that the dark-haired man on the screen is not a preacher, but a salesman like himself. Or not like himself, for this man is wildly successful the world over.

The man sells tapes and books, and a correspondence course of some sort, but even more clever than that, Emil suddenly realizes, the man is *selling people back to themselves*. An incredible idea—an endless supply of product with so little overhead.

There is a sadness about it all, he thinks, but who is he to say? Who is he to even have an opinion on such matters?

*That A in ambition is as high as any mountain, but climb it anyway! Don't eat the pear in despair. Remember there's no hope in dope! Take that H out of whining and you'll be winning!*

Emil cannot understand why the company has never fired him. In all his years on the road he has never once met his quota. And yet he has been allowed to continue making contacts, meeting prospects, conversing for long, leisurely days in the living rooms and on the front porches of America.

Periodically the home office sends out trainers (usually men) whose job is to sharpen the skills of the sales force. He isn't sure what their *real* job is—half the time they make no pretense of training.

Just as he suspects, their courtships of his customers are for the most part rewarded. It is amazing, sometimes frightening, to watch as the salesman nods, and the customers nod in return, as smile echoes smile and laughter echoes laughter, as the customers slowly transform into salesman doppelgangers, and a good time is had by all, except for Emil, who stands by the door and attempts to shake off his anxiety.

Many of the salesmen appear to achieve their success by means of sheer animal dominance. These are the alpha males, and although the herd of customers may mimic the salesman's gestures to the point of slavishness, they can never hope to match the salesman in strength or confidence.

Other salesmen at first glance appear to be no more impressive than Emil, but they are persistent almost to the point of their, and Emil's, humiliation. He spends one appalling afternoon camped out on a front porch, the foxlike salesman with the wired eyes refusing to leave until the elderly couple has purchased something. The husband gives in with shaking hands and cornered eyes.

A few of the men the company sends are interrogators, and they grill many of his prospects as to their needs and dreams, why they were at all hesitant to buy such a fine product. They use the customers' own hesitations and rationalizations against them.

And there are those for whom Emil can think of no better word than crazed, the ones who affect a certain delirium—dancing a jig, forcing facial spasms, singing spontaneously and inappropriately—that so troubles the customers they buy what they can in order to get rid of them.

Emil, of course, is unlike any of these salespeople. There is no good reason for the company to retain him, and yet he remains year after year, hoping for the blessed dismissal that will free him, which he cannot ask for himself, and which never comes.

---

And here he is again, the wife on the couch making polite conversation, the husband puttering around in the next room, pretending to make repairs, but whose real business is to listen in on the wife's dealings and make sure she does not spend too much of their rapidly disappearing funds. The wife has no real desire to buy except out of politeness or pity. Her real need is to have someone to talk to about the children, share her memories of the sister's dead baby, her own medical troubles, her thinly-disguised fears that her world is a precarious thing about to end, and her husband will not listen, has not really listened in years.

Outside it is a kind of Kansas, although they are miles and years from that state: sun burning the distant edges of crops, the horse moving slowly across the hill, the small boy on his bicycle struggling through mud ruts deep enough to swallow his wheels.

Soon the wife will offer her final apologies, so many unexpected expenses of late, folks hereabouts having pretty hard times, such a good product it's really too bad we don't have the money to spare, I'm afraid we can't see our way, and it's not your fault at all. . . .

And he will happily be free once again to step outside and stride to his car, relieved that he will not have to fill out all the paperwork that an actual sale entails.

"So my husband agrees we should take one, at that discount rate you said you were offering today, one time only and not to be repeated and who could pass up such a bargain, I mean, *really*."

Emil stares at the young wife as if she has suddenly gone crazy, as if she's been spitting and drooling and speaking in tongues. But in fact she is an older woman, graying at the temples and wearing an old-fashioned housecoat fading into transparency around the hem. He cannot understand—it is as if he's nodded off with the unending familiarity of his own sales spiel, and the woman's mother has replaced her in the chair. He gazes around the vaguely familiar room and sees her elderly husband slumped forward in his overstuffed chair, sleeping or dead.

"Just a minute," he finally manages to say through a rising panic, "Just a goddamn minute!" Has he really cursed a customer? "I've got my order book here somewhere. We'll get you fixed right up. Yes, indeed, you won't be sorry about *this* purchase, nomaam! It's the gift that keeps on giving, the key to a lifetime of success, the satisfaction of knowing you're doing . . . you're doing, well, what you're doing, it's the cap . . . on the toothpaste, the bridge . . ."

Emil's hand flops about in the worn-out leather satchel like a broken sparrow. He's not sure what he's seeking, in fact cannot remember the last time he'd reached into his sales valise, when his fingers seize the tattered edges of the sales book and retrieve it carefully as if it were some moth losing wing scales in frightening amounts. He spreads it open on his lap, carefully positioning the disintegrating slip of carbon paper, writes "1" as the quantity, then stops.

What is he selling this woman? He looks up at her expectantly. "You wanted one . . ." His dry tongue adheres to his bottom lip.

She smiles so broadly he thinks her mind is, in fact, gone, and he will not have to complete the order form after all. But then she nods slowly, happily, as if perfectly aware that she is doing the right thing for herself and the generations to come.

For the briefest of seconds he is unable to pull his tongue from his lip, and when finally he does it is so painful he feels a tear balanced dangerously in the corner of one eye. "One . . ." he repeats, and looks around for the sample he has been showing her, but it is nowhere to be seen.

"Deluxe edition," she finally replies, so he knows it isn't the Sports Weathervane or the Speedo pocket groomer or five of the twelve handy household helpers he sells, or used to sell. If he could only remember what it was he was selling this trip out, what he had put into his sample case, but there is nothing there, and nothing anywhere to be seen but this giant book bound in red leather she grasps so lovingly in her two trembling hands.

"I only wish our son Johnny would read this with us. So long he has been away from the Lord . . ."

"One Deluxe Bible, Red Leather, with the special painted map inserts tracing Jesus's path through our mortal world," Emil says confidently, writing *1 RB* onto the pad.

He settles back, calmed, as the elderly woman (but he recognizes her now, remembering how he had stopped here when she *was* a young bride, and realizes how much she must regret not having bought that Bible the first time he came by, when her baby was still a magical creature of hope and possibility) drones on about the sorry affairs of her son, the all-too-familiar litany of failures and small betrayals.

Gazing out the window Emil sees a small blond boy on a backyard swing, perhaps this woman's grandchild, or impossibly, her son at a better age, conjured up by her sad monologue. Emil rises from the chair—the woman does not seem to care, or notice, while the husband continues his uninterrupted rehearsal for death—and climbs out the window, strides across the bright lawn bordered in corn and sits in the child's other swing, the one reserved for playmates yet to arrive.

"It's too nice a day to be indoors," he says, both an explanation and an introduction.

"Who are you?" the little boy asks, staring up at Emil's face.

Emil gazes out over the endless and precisely aligned rows of corn. The sun glazes the leaves a green-gold, and he feels a smile travel unbidden across his face. "I'm nobody, really," he finally replies. "Just a salesman, calling on your parents with my promises and offers, my bag full of hope and secrets."

Suddenly stern, the boy says in an old man's querulous voice, "Are you going to try and *sell* me something?"

Emil is startled. He has been asked the question before, and it never fails to upset him. "No, no," the salesman in him lies. "I'm not *selling* anything today."

"Then what are you *doing* here?"

"I'm spending time here in this swing. I'm the customer this afternoon, buying myself a piece of this beautiful day."

The boy stares intently over the corn as if seeing a body hanging from the line of the horizon. When he looks back at Emil, his expression is eager. "So you've been to a lot of different places, not just here?"

"More places than I can count, son. I hope you don't mind the familiar."

"And the people in these places, they're all different in these places?"

"Well, you know it's funny that you should ask that, young man. It's been my experience that people are the same the world over, subject to the same wants and needs, accessible by the same techniques."

"No, you're lying!" the boy shouts. "Tell me that they're *different*! They *have* to be different from here!"

"Well . . ." Emil scrambles for the right words that will calm the boy, that will sell him some peaceful behavior. "We wouldn't understand each other too well, now would we, if we were all that different from each other."

"Get off my swing!" Alarmed, Emil trips getting out of the swing and sprawls on the ground. He heads back toward the open window, dusting off his pants as he goes. Behind him the boy sobs, but Emil will not let himself turn around. Customers don't like it when you watch them cry.

He climbs back through the window and slips into the chair. Spying a strand of burry weed stuck to one dress sock, he leans forward to remove it. The woman continues narrating her list of sadnesses. But it is not the same woman. This woman is younger, a brunette, and although the room is of the same style as the previous one, there are differences.

This husband is livelier than the other one. He rushes back and forth, a gun in his hand. "You hear that?"

After some delay Emil realizes the question is addressed to him. And then he *does* hear something coming from outside: gunshots and shouting, the alarmed cries of animals. "What . . ."

"It's that Wilkins boy—Johnny! He shot his ma and pa, and now he's killing all the livestock in sight!"

Emil can hear a rumbling engine between the shotgun blasts. "But he's just a boy . . ."

"Sixteen if he's a day! Old enough to blow a stranger's head off if he's dumb enough to stick his head outside! Guess he didn't read those encyclopedias you sold them ten year ago."

Crazily, Emil wonders if the Wilkinses had purchased their easy annual update volume subscription plan. It has been designed to keep your youngster apprised of all the latest developments not only in the sciences but in the arts as well.

An hour later it is all over. Emil cannot remember if this family has placed an order or not. But there is such a relief in leaving a customer's house he could care less. It is the best he ever feels.

Emil comes out of the house feeling that now would be a good time to take a walk, a relaxed stroll through a friendly neighborhood where he has lived all his married life. Their kids know his kids—they don't always get along but they play together every day—and he sees the parents at the grocery, in church, and every other Wednesday night for bowling. They aren't exactly friends, but there is a kind of comfort in these small, recurrent encounters. It is a good life, if you avoid looking too many steps ahead.

When he sees his battered black Buick parked at the curb, he recalls that he is a salesman, has never been married, and has very few friends to speak of. His key sticks and hangs, as if the lock mechanism has not been used in some time. He is careful not to strain the key too far as he manipulates it against the roughness of the internal workings, and finally there is a giving and a surprised suction as he jerks open the door.

Inside the air is as thick and cloying as the air trapped in a dead grandmother's old trunk, and the fast-food wrappers layering the floor appear to have been there for years. He sits in a bed of dust as soft and thick as another layer of upholstery.

He has no hope of starting this vehicle. This is a dead machine, designed for the transportation of the dead. He puts his key into the ignition and turns it anyway. There are no signs of electrical activity. He gets out of the car and looks under the hood. The engine appears to have been ripped out ages ago.

When he calls the main office he is too embarrassed to tell them that the car is an ancient piece of junk that has not been driven in years, because of course this would make no sense. He simply reports that his career in sales has outlived another vehicle, and that he will need a replacement. They authorize a budget and he picks a used car dealer at random from the phone book, his only criterion is that it is within walking distance.

He waits at a safe distance from the car lot and watches as people drive in, are greeted in rapid succession by eager, excited salespeople, are spirited away to the cars that will change their lives, the cars that were made for them and them alone, with bucket seats, SRS brakes, extras and more than extras, the cars that will strain their marriages and bankrupt them. Many of these customers already know the possible end result of their reasonable time payment purchases, are perhaps even determined that it not happen to them again, and yet they will be so excited, so agitated by the experience and all the grand possibilities they will be absolutely thrilled to pay more and more for less and less.

Emil has an advantage. For so many of these people a new car means a new life, transportation out of bad decisions and past mistakes. For him it is simply a continuation of the long, sad trip he has been on all of his life.

He waits until the right couple comes in driving the roughest, most battered vehicle he has seen in years. But it does not smoke, and there is no obvious wobble as it pulls in front of the dealership. An hour later they drive away in a bright blue teardrop of promise, and he walks across the street and into the sales office.

"What do you mean that doesn't include floor mats?" speaks a surprised voice out of a tiny office to his left.

"I want to buy that car, there," Emil says to the first salesman to approach him.

"Excuse me, sir?" Emil might have asked to buy a tombstone in a shoe shop. "That car, there."

The salesman glances over Emil's shoulder without much interest. "Must be a trade-in. It hasn't been worked up yet."

Emil struggles to look the man directly in the eyes. "That's the one I want."

The salesman attempts to stare him down in the friendliest possible way. "What if I told you I could get you into a better car for less money?"

"You and I both know how much it's worth," Emil says a little shakily. "Take that figure and add fifteen percent." He forces himself to pause and looks even more directly at the man. He isn't sure if he's pulled off a smile. "I'm a salesman, too. Since college—it's the only job I've ever had."

The car salesman nods, unimpressed, and Emil decides this has been a failure. "I'll have to take this to my manager," the salesman says, and for an unreal moment Emil thinks he is about to be arrested. Emil gazes after the man as he enters another office, waits anxiously as the salesman confers unemotionally with his boss who glances up at Emil only once, then down at a notepad. The boss gives the salesman a piece of paper, who carries it out to Emil and puts it into his hand. He almost expects the car to stall out as he drives it out of the lot, which would be embarrassing but survivable.

Studying the violent screen flickers of these motel room TVs, Emil has developed a theory that these sporadic discharges of light are part of an attempt to hypnotize the viewer into buying whatever product is being discussed. This sales maneuver is doubly clever because these residents are generally poor travelers who cannot afford to leave their rooms. They watch these commercials in a state of desperate exhaustion.

A collage of images impresses onto the tired and ill-used tissue of his brain: children, small tidy houses, walks in the park with the family dog, vacations at the beach. *Be A Man* floats eerily across the screen in colors muted to suggest a whisper. *What are they selling?* There is no way to determine. Whatever it is, it is certainly something he does not have.

*ARE YOU READY?* in bolder than bold type shouts at him from the screen. He waits for the kicker, the product revelation, the final sales pitch before he is returned to their regularly scheduled program. But there is no return. There is no change. The words remain frozen, oppressive, unforgiving, even when he unplugs the television in frustration.

Emil is traveling I-70 just outside Salinas when he sees the billboard "The City of Commerce" with a huge red arrow perched on top. The sign is somewhat worn, but he thinks maybe this is from the road construction he's seen in the area over the past year. He thinks of the letter folded up in his pocket, and he turns onto the access road: all black and shiny with promise.

He might quit his job this very day, call the company office and have them pick up the car and his samples if they care to bother.

He passes no cars on the road and considers the afternoon heat and thinks this must be a slow time for shopping traffic. He spies the gleaming steel tower from a couple of miles away, a variety of buildings spread about its base like flowers planted around an airport control tower. In the afternoon sun everything gleams like a nest of needles. Just before he turns onto the main street, another large sign appears. *Welcome to the City of Commerce*, with a picture of a happy little girl gesturing to the wonders behind her. *Alice in Wonderland*, he thinks, and the artist's vision of the shopping center confirms the notion—it might easily grace the cover of some edition of something by Carroll or Baum.

Emil is bewildered by the cold tears he feels leaking from his eyes. What is happening to him? He should just turn around. "City of Commerce" indeed. It almost makes him laugh.

Then he sees the bullet holes above the little girl's head almost making a halo, the torn passages through the faded backdrop of the city.

A turn onto the main street of the "City of Commerce" confirms that the place has been abandoned for some time. The finished buildings appear empty and the unfinished buildings ready to collapse beneath their architecturally unsound frameworks. He has nothing better to do—never did have—so he continues his leisurely drive past the vast fields of asphalt.

The streets appear to have been laid out with remarkable care: a perfect grid of block after block of abandoned buildings, partially finished constructions, lots full of dried-up landscaping, mounds of mysterious concrete, in one place a huge outdoor skating rink (Remarkable! Ice-skating in Kansas! the signs scream). Now it looks like a large, shallow swimming pool with no water, much less ice. Remarkable, indeed.

The abandoned construction sites in particular draw Emil's eye. Much of the time he cannot tell what the building was intended to be. Multiple girders jut out sideways in parallel like huge claws taking a swipe at the sky. Rooflines twist and turn like the skeletons of roller coasters. Giant square passages where walls might have been form windows for watching the world change color. Enormous Mondrian sculptures line up like a fleet of cubist spaceships.

He parks along one street of gravel and sand and peers through the great transparent teeth of a clownish building with round window eyes. The swirling pink and orange paint job within makes him think of an ill child after a day's overeating at the circus.

What might they sell in such places?

The fact that the buildings are relatively new, unlike those in the Western ghost towns of old, fills him with a peculiar dissonance, as if he is hearing dozens of ill-tuned chimes playing nearby.

He turns the corner and is face-to-knee with a silver metal beaver at least a dozen feet tall. Beside it, and still gigantic at half the beaver's size, is a brilliant white fiberglass baseball. The beaver's eyes are wide and staring, as if it is as surprised to see this baseball as Emil is.

He can find no specific business these statues might be attached to and therefore assumes this must be some sort of installation of public art. He wonders about what the customers must have thought of these two objects, for ever how long this place had customers.

As he walks past the rows of storefronts it occurs to him how insubstantial everything seems—the empty stores like huge display boxes having no value without their goods. The wind thunders against the expanse of glass and shiny metal. There are no indications of residences, of schools, or of any other structure where the day-in and day-out of life might take place. But, of course, this is the "City of Commerce," a container for commercials and impulsive retail exchange. Now even the signs indicating what might have gone on here are gone.

One door is slightly ajar. Emil tugs it lightly and slips inside. This one has been occupied at one time—the outlines of counters and shelving decorate the floor. Dead electrical cables dangle where light fixtures have been removed. Here and there lie a candy wrapper or a bit of a magazine, gray tracks in the dust where small creatures have roamed. There has been surprisingly little vandalism.

"You don't belong here." The dry voice speaks from behind.

Emil turns to see a man with one hand poised over a holster. "Hey, easy now," Emil says softly. "I . . . I have an invitation, I guess, to work here." He slides one finger into his front pants pocket, fishing for the paper, careful to let the guard see the rest of the hand. He retrieves the letter and extends it.

The guard shakes his head. "Not necessary—I didn't think you were the stealing type anyway. You're the salesman type. I've seen a lot of you around here, sniffing around. All of them had letters like yours."

Emil puts the paper back into his pocket. "What's to steal around here anyway?"

The guard looks around the vast room as if for the first time. "Fixtures," he says, with a hint of sadness.

Emil walks past the guard and out the door. Then he pauses. "How long?"

"Oh, about three years."

"What happened?"

The guard smiles a little. "They had a huge supply of what people didn't want."

On the otherwise unnaturally quiet walk back to his car, Emil finds himself chuckling aloud.

In these last few days of sales, generous discounts can be offered, bonus gifts pulled out of the dusty trunk and placed into hesitant buyers' hands. In these last few days of sales, he is full of compliments and important news for everyone's family. In these last few days of sales, he represents the church, the school, and a benevolent government. In these last few days of sales, he cannot remember what he is selling, nor does he recognize the odd objects in his sample case. In these last few days of sales, he cannot bring himself to ask *Which do you like best?* and *How many should I put you down for?* In these last few days of sales, he knows that sometimes a customer just wants a warm body to talk to. In these last few days of sales, he sees all the lonely people on his list, all the sad people for whom his brief visit is a major event.

He has been traveling for quite a long time. *Of course,* he thinks. *You're a career salesman—you've been traveling forever.* Towns have died during the time he has been a salesman. Local economies have been disrupted. Great masses of people have lost their definition, reduced to reading self-help volumes and watching far too many movies. Everyone he meets is desperate to sell, but so many are reluctant to buy, having been disappointed so many times, having been cheated and lied to, having been murdered for their dreams and ambitions.

The towns he passes through are painted in FOR SALE signs. People have moved on ahead of him. Those left behind in the streets walk aimlessly with eyes like dull pennies.

In these last few days of sales, he yearns to complete one last transaction. Coming upon the white-haired man out on the street thrills him as nothing has in years. He lets the man have one last swig from his bottle, then props him against the wall. The old man resembles Jack, the fellow who trained him years ago, but he resembles the guard at the City of Commerce, as well. He may resemble the salesmen who built the City of Commerce, but Emil doesn't know how they might have aged. He resembles most old men Emil has ever known. Perhaps he resembles Emil himself, who has not looked at his own face for a long time.

"You only want the best for them," he begins. "Your children. Your grand-children. And if you don't have children it's the children of others you want to thrive—is this not so? Because then you can believe that something of this life will go on, and do well, and make of itself a thing of beauty against the failing of the light. For what else is there but the spark of us carried by children into the lands where we will never travel?

"And so you buy them things, grand things your own parents could never afford. And you hand these things to them, as if you were handing down sacri-fices and offerings to some fierce and unstoppable god. 'Take these things I have given you and do well,' you say. 'Make my dreams into something capable of movement and breath. And do not damage me, make no attempt to rob me of my last remaining dignities because I swear, I only wish you well.'

"And that's the best you can do. That's the best any of us can do, in these final days of sales."

Placing his sample case on the concrete in front of the old man, he goes into the trunk of his car and hauls out box after box of Bibles and encyclopedias, grand dictionaries full of ideas he has never been able to express, baskets of outdated kitchen accessories which have lost both their utility and their names, perfumes and cleansers, small gifts for every occasion. The old man stares drunk-enly at the salesman, unable to manage even a thank you.

The salesman walks away empty-handed, leaving all the voices, all the give-and-takes and the I've-got-something-special-for-yous behind, knowing full well that he will not have to sell himself to the rain, or the wind, or the ground with its daily increase in gravity. And there is a peace in knowing that not all deals have to be closed.

From the outside, his home looks no different from all the others. This is the way he wants it—there is a comfort in the cloning of every house he has ever seen on television, the slavish duplication of columns and brickwork, the same angled roofs repeated again and again across the horizon to become a geometry of reassurance.

Emil has no reason to leave his house. The company pension provides for him quite comfortably. Why he should be receiving a pension, why they should re-ward decades of poor salesmanship, he has no idea. But then reward and pun-ishment has always been a puzzle he is unable to solve.

Groceries can be delivered relatively cheaply from the smaller stores. Items may be ordered over the phone even without a catalog: he will work from lists of merchandise but pictures of anything are forbidden in his house. He receives a daily newspaper, but pays the man next door a handsome sum to censor it for him, until the paper is like lace in his hands, beautiful in its way as shreds of celebrities and the dire news of the world allow the morning sunlight to pass through, making intricate shadowscapes on his formica kitchen table.

He spends much of his day walking around naked. He has grown increasingly uncomfortable with clothing: even the plainest garment seems to evoke one style or another, and then he feels he is wearing packaging, and cannot breathe until it is shed.

Without clothes he can clearly see the damage that wraps him. There are cracks in his lower face and left arm from hours driving directly into the sun.

There is dry and flaky skin across his chest and abdomen that no one has touched in years. There is an arthritic right hand that burns and freezes in the position of one asking for money. Several of his toes are missing. He does not remember what he did with them.

He has lost the full range of motion in his left arm. His left leg twists awkwardly inward, making it painful to maneuver up and down steps. *I didn't even sell these things*, he thinks. *I was never that good. My arms, my legs, my hands, my heart pulled and squeezed: I just gave them all away.*

His front doorbell rings. He peers out a nearby window. A small boy, staggering under the weight of a large box, looking up at Emil's closed door forlornly, as if behind it lies the only safety the boy has ever known, and yet the door must seem hundreds of miles away. Emil wraps a towel around himself and goes to greet his visitor.

The boy's eyes grow huge when he sees Emil. But he musters his courage. "Sir, I'm trying to earn extra money this summer selling these fine candies . . ."

"Son." Emil crouches next to the boy, careful not to expose himself. People are scared, they're scared everywhere he's ever been, and he doesn't want them to get the wrong idea. "Son, listen. You've got to get my *attention* first. Then you've got to pique my *interest*."

"Peek, sir?"

"Then you have to show me some *conviction*. Then you have to kindle my *desire*. And finally you have to *close* the deal. Nothing really happened here today if you can't manage that last part. It was all just a dream, one big fantasy if there's no closing. AICDC, son. Attention, interest, conviction, desire, close. Remember that."

Emil realizes the boy is staring at his belly. Poor salesmanship, drawing the prospect's attention to his own faults. "So are you gonna buy a candy bar, Mister?"

"Say I *do* buy a candy bar from you. What are you going to do with the money? Are you going to save that money, son?"

"I'm gonna go to the movies with it, if you buy a box of 'em. Six to a box. Ten dollars."

"OK, then. I'll buy two boxes."

"Do you have a wallet, sir?" the boy asks skeptically.

"I own a wallet, even a pocket in a pair of pants to keep it in. I probably even sold myself that pair of pants. I don't always walk around naked, you know?" The boy continues to stare at him. Emil stares back. Finally Emil asks, "Do I give you the money first, or do you give me the candy bars first? Anymore I'm not so good . . . at this commerce thing."

When they find him a week later only half the candy bars have been consumed. The property is on the market for several years before it finally sells, longer than any listing the local realtors can remember. In fact, the poorly-painted "For Sale" sign becomes a familiar landmark that the neighbors actually miss when it is gone.

# JUNE CONSIDINE

# To Dream of White Horses

*Some very fine fantasy indeed can be found in young-adult fiction these days—*
*not only overtly wizardly tales of the Harry Potter sort, but contemporary,*
*subtly enchanted stories like the one that follows, in which a young, free-*
*spirited stranger conjures magic with her art.*

*June Considine is an Irish writer who began her career as a journalist, and*
*now devotes her time to the writing of novels and short fiction. She has*
*published twelve popular books for children and young adults, including the*
*Luvanders fantasy series,* The Glass Triangle, View from a Blind Bridge
*(nominated for the Bistro Book of the Year Award), and* Letters to Nirvana
*(forthcoming). Her short story "Exposé," published in the* Sunday Tribune,
*was shortlisted for the Hennessy Award, and she has recently published her*
*first novel for adults,* When the Bough Breaks. *In addition, Considine*
*participates in the Irish radio program* Sunday Miscellany *and teaches writing*
*workshops. She and her husband live in Malahide, a coastal village near*
*Dublin.*

*"To Dream of White Horses" is reprinted from Gordon Snell's anthology*
Thicker Than Water: Coming-of-Age Stories by Irish and Irish American
Writers *(Delacorte Press.)*

—*T. W.*

Last night I watched a nature documentary. I saw newborn squid rising
from the bed of an ocean with nothing to protect them from the lurking
dangers floating all around them. No mother. No father. Their parents had
paid the ultimate price for their brief encounter by dying as soon as the
eggs were laid. They left nothing behind except their genetic imprint and an
inherited instinct for survival.

The documentary made me think of Zoe. The miracle baby. An orphan before
she was born. Her photograph was on the front pages of newspapers. Her birth
by cesarean operation was reported on the television evening news. A skid on an
icy road and her parents wiped out before their first child was born. Good media
material. She was still kicking when her mother's body was rushed to the ma-
ternity hospital. Even then, Zoe was a survivor.

We met in February. A cold day, the wind sharp as glass on my face. I huddled into my parka, killing time on a park bench in Stephen's Green. I'd been spending a lot of time in the park, holed up until school was over and I could safely return to the apartment. Sooner or later someone always sat down beside me. Old guys with yellow eyes and booze in paper bags. Old women with memories to spend. Mothers watching their children feeding the ducks. But, on this particular day, even the ducks were sheltering out of sight on the island in the center of the lake.

Zoe was drawing on the pavement near where I was sitting, a kaleidoscope of colored chalk scattered around her. Her concentration was absolute. I could have been invisible, even when I moved from the bench to see what she was doing. She had drawn a city. High buildings, stick people without features, crazily tilted shops, and office blocks dominated by a hulking mountain in the background. Its height seemed to drain the landscape, dimming the brighter street colors until everything appeared to lie in its dreary dark shadows. In the corner of the picture I saw a tear. A solitary shining bubble. When I looked closer, I realized there was a tiny figure curled inside it.

Zoe sighed impatiently, as if I had disturbed her, and glanced up. Her eyes were a greeny gray, like the sea on those overcast days when clouds are low and the rain is hanging in the air. I know about the sea. I used to watch it from my bedroom window when it roared toward the shore, foaming high and thrashing the rocks.

"Shouldn't you be at school instead of hanging around here flirting with hypothermia?" she asked. She began to draw again but the feverish concentration had left her. She stroked the pavement, lightly blurring the shape into the mountain with the flat of her hand.

"I should. But I'm not. End of story."

"Touchy subject?"

"No. Just a boring one. It's more educational to watch you work."

"Then we'll have to postpone your education for another day." She gathered up the chalk and stood stamping pins and needles from her feet. Her black ankle boots were scratched and covered in chalk dust. As I stood staring at her, not sure what move to make, rain began to fall. We took shelter under a tree as a sudden heavy shower swirled over the pavement, chasing the stick people and splashing off the buildings until only the dark head of the mountain remained. Then it too merged into the running colors and disappeared.

"Your drawing is destroyed," I said, wondering how she could be so calm. Hours of detailed work gone in an instant.

"So what?" She shrugged. "I can do another one tomorrow." She sounded bored. "Now it's time to eat. Like to share some hot chocolate and doughnuts with me?"

"That's the best offer I've had all day."

She allowed me to carry her rucksack to the bench. It looked far too heavy for her slight figure and, like her boots, had seen much wear and tear. We wiped off the rain and sat down. She took out a flask and a bag of doughnuts. Two ducks waddled from behind the foliage on the island. They nose-dived into the freezing water to prove there was a serious shortage of food and we rewarded them with sugary crumbs.

I had seen homeless people sleeping in shop doorways. They sat on O'Connell Bridge and held cardboard placards in front of them. Their hard, searching eyes carried the secrets of an invisible city. Drugs, alcohol, fights, loneliness, the police moving them on, the long winter nights in the open. It was difficult to connect that world with Zoe. Yet she too sought shelter in abandoned houses or slept in the basements of office blocks. She told me that she was thirteen when she went on the road for the first time, escaping from her grandparents, who smothered her with anxiety and rules that had to be instantly obeyed. She was found by the police as she was about to board the ferry at Dun Laoghaire but a year later she ran away again. By the time she was eighteen and in charge of her own life she had run away six times. "Alternative living," she called it. My father would have called it bumming around.

Now she was twenty-five. Her grandparents were dead and the hardness of the city was beginning to touch her mouth. A shadow of things to come but when she laughed and tossed her hair she was beautiful.

Sometimes she was commissioned to paint murals on the walls and hoardings of building sites. Cheerful scenes to hide the destruction going on behind them. Mostly she drew on pavements and hoped that people would throw money at her. She never stayed in the same place for long. When she grew tired of city noises, she headed for the mountains. Every mountain has its ruins, she said, and she would hole up in one of those tumbledown cottages until the streets drew her back again. Her life sounded wild and out of control. I had a sudden urge to walk away from her and half-rose from the bench, ready with excuses. She reached out her hand and gripped my wrist. "I need a squat for a few days. Don't suppose you happen to know of an empty house where no one's looking too closely?"

I didn't want to tell her about Seaview Tower. I didn't want her disturbing the spirits that rested uneasily there. I felt her grip soften as her hand slipped into mine. "A roof . . . that's all I need, Eoin. Even if it's leaking I can put up the tent inside the house."

"I know a place." I pulled her to her feet. "Come on. I'll show you."

We took the bus to Corry Pier. White horses were slanting in on the tide, sweeping away the smell of seaweed and the beached, dead jellyfish. I carried her rucksack across the road toward the embankment I'd always used as a shortcut to the house.

A tall, round tower house guarding the sea. Rosa's house. So flaky and old that only crazy people would want to live in it. My home for fourteen years. So close to the shore that sand seeped under the doors, filling corners and crevices, a gritty trail under our feet. In winter the walls wept and sprouted mushrooms. The stained-glass panes above the front door cracked at the first sign of frost. Such inconveniences, when she noticed them, never bothered Rosa, my mother. She would proudly point to the carvings on the doors and the oak floorboards in the drawing room that had once been part of a great ship, insisting I was lucky to live in a house with such character. When my father sold it to a property developer and we drove away he ordered me not to look back. "The past is a sharp corner," he said. "Once you turn it there's not a lot of sense in looking behind."

"Crazy!" Zoe stood back and gazed at the round walls. She took a chisel and mallet from her rucksack. I hammered and levered loose the planks covering the windows and front door, regretting the impulse that had brought me back here.

"I don't think this is a good idea," I said. "You'll probably be able to find somewhere much better if you look around."

"No. This is it. It's cool."

When I forced open the hall door a newspaper rose from the floor, spreading yellow wings as the wind gusted under it. Zoe kicked aside a beer can, dismissing the litter and the cold and the moldering smells. She didn't notice the ghosts.

"You won't recognize this place when you see it again," she said, and hummed softly as she unpacked her rucksack.

In the bus on the way to the apartment I imagined her moving through the rooms. She would climb the spiral stairs, the fifth step squeaking in protest when she stepped upon it. Her fingers would touch the gouged wood on the banisters where I had carved my name before leaving with my father. She would stand in my parents' empty bedroom and look down to the wilderness that was once our back garden. Under the weeds and the sucking creepers, there were snowdrops, crocuses, and daffodils. As night drew down, she would climb the attic stairs and stand in the gloom of Rosa's studio. The paints were still there. Rusting brushes in jars of cloudy water. Canvases stacked against the walls. Beyond the window she would watch the lights of Corry Head illuminate the darkness, spilling like a necklace around the lower slopes and climbing upward to the summit, glowing and winking. A golden oasis. Would she feel my mother's presence at her shoulder? Artist to artist. Her breath whispering, "See how the night shines. But it's not real, you know. There's a void beyond the glory and that's what I have to paint." How many times had she breathed those words into my ears? Our eyes fixed on the quivering headland as we tried to imagine the secrets hidden between the folds of light. No . . . Zoe would not hear my mother's whispering voice. She was a survivor. Seaview Tower would be her shelter until she was ready to move on, nothing more.

In the apartment I saw the bottle of whiskey on the coffee table. A bad sign; my father usually waited until the evening meal was over before pouring his first drink.

"You took your time today," he said when I entered the kitchen. He always made the same comment when I was late, but I'd never heard him ask the reason.

"Smells good." I sniffed appreciatively when he opened the oven door and carried a casserole dish to the table.

"How was school?"

"Oh, you know . . . same as usual."

"We began to eat. The silence was a sullen space between us. Sometimes I imagined having witty, stimulating conversations with him. But we never managed more than a few sentences before the effort of communicating exhausted us. When he sold Seaview Tower he gave the furniture away. Two men from the St. Vincent de Paul Society came and removed everything except my mother's paintings. I believed he was going to bring them to the apartment.

"No space," he said when the time came to leave. He allowed me to choose one painting, then firmly closed the door of her studio.

The painting hung in my bedroom, a feathery image of green, almost a whisper on canvas as it drifted above the strong burgeoning roots that thrust downward, forcing their way between rocks and the seething underground world of insect and animal. I was eight years old when she painted it and had been repelled by the images. "It's awful—ugly! . . . Trees aren't like that at all. You're always making everything look different."

"Ah, but think, Eoin." She always smiled when she explained things to me. "Without roots we have no trees. Can you imagine such a dead world? It's not only what we see and touch and understand that matters. The things we cannot see or touch or understand are just as important."

My father used to wink when he heard her talking like that. "It beats me what's going on in your mother's crazy, wonderful head." He'd press his lips against her forehead. A time came when he stopped calling her crazy. It became a loaded word. He described her paintings as Rosa's therapy. I can still remember the expression on her face when he said that. As if she had felt the sting of a small stone on her skin.

The property developer who bought Seaview Tower planned to build luxury apartments with balconies and glass elevators and a view. The sea shimmering in sunshine. Corry Head shimmering at dusk.

"Don't go back there," warned my father. "There'll be heavy machinery. I don't want you getting in the way of the builders."

Months later, when I did return, the house was still standing. The panes above the front door were smashed and graffiti had been sprayed over the outside walls. Cider cans, hamburger cartons, and used condoms littered the hall. Thieves had taken the wrought-iron gates. My house had become a sick joke, a hulk. I longed for a crane with a hanging ball to smash it to pieces. But the property developer was having trouble with planning permission. His apartments with a view were still on hold. Soon afterward, he had the doors and windows boarded up.

My father bought modern furniture for our new life. Streamlined, minimalist, said the saleswoman. Perfect for an apartment. A fold-up table, spring-back beds, built-in closets. A space for everything. He used one of the rooms as his office. His business card read BILL CARTER. FINANCIAL CONSULTANT.

"Working from home is the way of the future," he said.

I figured it was because he couldn't cut the morning traffic with a hangover. Before Rosa left us he used to travel all the time. New York, Boston, Sydney, Tokyo. He was always landing or taking off on planes. He brought me presents from abroad, denim jackets with American designer labels, the latest computer games, books on astronomy. He bought my mother perfume at airports and was furious when she began to throw the unopened bottles into the garbage.

We never had to talk in those days. Rosa was the conduit between us. She told me he was proud and delighted when I earned good grades, made the school athletic squad, joined the debating society. I believed in this dream figure she created and then discovered she'd left me face to face with a stranger.

He switched on the television. We watched the news and a game show. He sipped whiskey and stared into his glass.

"It's two years today." His voice was flat. "I wondered if you remembered."

"Why should I forget?"

"Are you all right . . . everything okay?"

"Sure. It's just . . . two years. It seems so long when you say it but it's not . . . is it?"

"Time passes, Eoin."

"But it doesn't heal." I wanted to shout at him but that would be real conversation so I said the words to myself and switched television channels. He made no effort to make further conversation. That was fine by me. Talking was disastrous when he was drinking. He'd start by reminiscing about his young days and how hard he'd had to work to achieve his success. Young people didn't know the meaning of hard work because everything was laid on for them. We were the wimp generation, hooked on having a good time at any cost.

"Spoiled from birth . . . that's what you are. You haven't a clue. Nancy boys, all of you." He'd thump my arm, laughing. Big joke. It's a sore spot, just above the elbow. His fist was a hard ball digging deep. I'd hit back hard and he'd hit harder and then it wasn't a game anymore but one of those stag things with the antlers rattling, both of us determined to win. I'd feel sick, unable to stop yet afraid he'd freak out and let his thoughts spill over . . . and then what would we say to each other?

The dream came again that night. White horses, a herd of them rising from the sea, pounding toward me. Their hooves drummed in my ears. I tried to move out of their way but my feet sank in sand. Then they were underneath me and I was rolling over their backs, trying to hold their flailing manes. I went under, sinking deeper and deeper into a void where there was nothing, only the dark silence of drowning. I always woke up on a scream. But there was no scream when I forced my eyes open. Just a grinding moan of relief.

My file was open on the school principal's desk when I entered her office the following morning. Notes forged with my father's signature were stacked beside it. "I must say, Eoin, you look remarkable healthy for someone who's been afflicted by so many ailments." Mrs. Parkinson glanced down at the note on top of the pile. "Your father must be quite worried about you."

"The doctor says my immune system is low. I'll be fine when it builds up again."

"How long will this buildup process take?" She made no effort to hide her sarcasm.

"Soon. I'm on multivitamins and iron tablets."

"Spare me the medical report, Eoin Carter." She handed me a letter. "Give this to your father. I want to see him in here with you on the Monday following midterm break. Then we'll discuss your immune system, among other things. . . . Is that understood?"

Across the bay Corry Head was beginning to glimmer as evening traffic twisted along the steep, narrow roads. Zoe had lit a fire in the old house and driftwood blazed up the chimney. Burning candles jutted from wine bottles. In the flickering flames she seemed to belong to the shadows that had captured the room. She was kneeling on the floor, drawing on the boards, so absorbed I had to call twice before she heard me.

"I found photographs of you in that attic room," she said. "You never told me you used to live here."

"It's a long time ago." I hunched down to examine her drawing. She had just started to work on it. White lines curling like a question mark into empty space.

"Interesting. What's it supposed to mean?"

"Whatever you want it to mean. Who owns the painting upstairs?"

"My mother. The attic was her studio."

"Cool spot. The light is brilliant . . . not to mention the view. Does she still paint?"

"No. . . . Where did you find the photographs?"

"Stuck in a press with her sketch pads. I'll get them for you."

In the grate the wood burned to find gray ash. A gas ring fluttered underneath a saucepan, chicken simmering in spices and rice. Familiar smells. I thought about the dinner parties Rosa used to hold. The laughter floating upward into my bedroom. When people stopped coming there were no more spice smells. Some days she did not get out of bed until I came home from school. Then I made sandwiches and we ate them in the kitchen. She would stare at the wall behind me. When I pushed her hair back from her face she winced as if the sun hurt her eyes. But I don't remember any sunshine. Just clouds moving slow over the sea.

"What's depression?" I asked my father.

"It's all about the power of the mind," he said. "The only thing that will make it go away is your own determination." He ran his hand over the window ledge and frowned at the smudge on his fingers.

When Rosa was happy our house was filled with music. I could never imagine the silences returning. The light in her studio burned through the night.

One summer she painted Corry Head. The gorse blazed like a fireball. Purple heather covered the rocks. She painted it with the mist falling down and hiding all the color. I wondered if that was what her life was like. Always trying to escape from behind the mist.

I stared at the photographs that charted our fourteen years together. In one of them I stood between my parents, toothy grin, my hair neatly parted to one side. "Happy families." Zoe grinned. "That's kind of cute."

"Cute?" I placed the album on the mantelpiece, no longer interested. "That's not the word I'd use."

My father was right. The past was a sharp corner. No time to dillydally on the bend.

Every day during midterm break I returned to Seaview Tower, terrified that the builders would have chased her away. The property developer had sorted out his planning problems. Work would begin soon. I imagined throwing myself in front of bulldozers or chaining myself to the front door. Instead, I gathered driftwood and shopped for food in Corrystown. Zoe picked forsythia and placed it in jars on the window ledges. Her drawing on the floor remained unfinished but she used my mother's paints to cover the walls with murals. A circus ring, children and clowns turning somersaults. Her rucksack rested near the front door. A house on a frame. So many pockets and loops, each with a purpose, a storage space, a hanging space. Within a few minutes she could pack everything she needed to exist and carry it on her back.

We were walking along the strand one morning when she told me about the accident. The birth of a miracle baby.

"My mother wanted to see the mountains in snow," she explained. "There were road warnings being broadcast. Is your journey really necessary, that kind of stuff. Why on earth did he have to listen to her? Why?"

I was startled by her anger. It came so fast, as if her breath had suddenly exploded free. Then she tossed her head. "Oh well, what does it matter now?" A question asked in the same dismissive tone she had used when she watched her chalk city float from the pavement.

"Is that why you're always running?" I asked.

"I don't know how to explain." She hesitated for an instant. "No one understands."

"I want to understand. Tell me."

"I'm searching for something I lost before I was born."

"Your parents?"

"No. I've never had to search for them." She held out her long fingers and examined them. "I have my father's fingers. Piano fingers. My mother's eyes. When I smile I look exactly like her. That's what my grandparents always said. My father's family too. They never saw me, just the reflections of their lost children." Her voice was low, a talking to herself sort of voice. "I've always wanted to take them for granted . . . but the dead don't allow it. They leave too many questions behind. My parents were just ordinary people but what happened to them made them extraordinary and they're here . . . all the time in my head. . . ."

I remembered the crush of people in her drawing. The mountain so dark and dominating. The tiny bubble figure.

"Aren't you scared being homeless and on your own all the time?" I asked.

"Does a home stop you from being scared?" She stopped and turned to face me.

"I'm not scared. What makes you think that?"

"Do you want to tell me what's wrong?"

"There's nothing wrong. . . . Everything's cool."

We continued walking by the edge of the shore, adding our footprints to the tiny bird claws and the deep hollows left by the horses from the riding school that had cantered past us. Sand blew in the wind, stinging like needles. We headed toward the beach shelter and sat together on the bench. Zoe used a tissue to remove grit from my eyes. One story borrows another and so I told her about Rosa. The first time I had mentioned her name since she went away.

"Does your father know you come back to the house?" she asked when I fell silent.

"He'd freak if he found out."

"Do the two of you ever talk about her?"

"Never."

"What would happen if you did?"

"He'd blame me . . . I see it in his face all the time."

"What if it's his own guilt you see? His own demons?"

"He doesn't have any. He says he did everything for her and she flung it all back at him."

The beach shelter was still the same. Gray pebble-dash walls with graffiti. The seeping smell of urine. I wondered if the gang still gathered there at night. Brian O'Neill played guitar with a rock band. Morgan Dunne's father was a doctor with a clinic full of pills. One night when Rosa was sleeping I sneaked out and joined them. We played music on ghetto blasters and smoked. We talked about girls and sex and football until Morgan Dunne produced a bottle of vodka. We mixed it with the pills. The sea rolled away from us and the stars streaked across the sky. Blue lights flashed. We were too stupefied to move until the squad car screeched to a halt and the cops came running. They chased us along the hard sand. One of them grabbed me in a rugby tackle.

"That's it, you little scumbag." He breathed hard into the back of my neck. "That's the end of your little game."

Rosa collected me from the Garda station. She rang my father in San Francisco and he arrived home two days early.

"See what you've done to your mother?" He shouted and lifted his fists in the air. I'd never seen him in such a temper. "I hope you're satisfied. You were supposed to look after her when I was away but all you've done is add to her problems." I was beaten for the first time in my life. "Let that be a lesson to you." His hands shook as he placed them on my shoulders. "I don't ever want to do that to you again . . . but I will if it's necessary."

My dreams changed to drowning of another kind. Drowning in Zoe's arms. I wanted to stay there forever, stroking her, kissing her. My tongue moving over her breasts until she moaned and called out my name. Such a wild cry. I woke on the sound, my body releasing its pleasure on the sheets; the spent energy of a fantasy. My skin was on fire. It seemed such an invasion, the things I had done to her without her knowledge. In the bathroom. I lit a match and burned the letter from Mrs. Parkinson. Midterm break was over. I flushed the ash down the toilet bowl.

On Monday afternoon two men arrived with tripods and stood at the foot of the embankment.

"I'll have to move on soon." Zoe glanced down at them. "It looks like the action is about to begin."

"I'm going with you," I said. "I've been thinking of nothing else for days."

"That's crazy, Eoin. You're just a boy."

"I'm sixteen. And I'm in love with you."

"Love!" She dismissed the word. "No one has ever loved me."

"Your grandparents did."

"It was never love. Just duty."

"So . . . What do you call my love? Infatuation? A mother fixation? An escape route?"

"Stop it, Eoin." She held her palm toward me, warding off my words. "I don't want to hurt you."

"Let me go with you, Zoe. I won't make demands or anything. I just want to be with you."

She gently pushed me away when I tried to put my arms around her. "There's too many people in my life already, Eoin."

"Dead people," I said. "You don't need them. You've never needed them. You're the most complete person I've ever known."

"I'm always running but I'm still in the same place. Is that what you want?" She touched my forehead with her lips. No passion. Just understanding, so much understanding. "Have the courage to set her free."

They came the following morning. Two diggers churned the front garden. The noise from the engines was overwhelming. A crane was already in position in front of the house. Men in yellow jackets and helmets stood beside it. I ran toward them, shouting. "Stop! There's someone living in there."

"Stand back, lad. There's no one in there." The foreman held out his hands in front of me. I shoved him aside and ran through the open door. Dead embers, burned-out candles. Her rucksack gone.

She had finished the drawing on the floor. In the sunshine spilling through the window the flowing lines were so sharply defined that for an instant they seemed to rise from the floorboards. White horses whirling and circling, onward, outward. An eternal journey of light and shade. Along one wall she had placed my mother's canvases.

"Are you happy now?" The foreman stood in front of me. "I told you the place was empty."

"You drove her away." My fingers locked so hard together they hurt.

"Drove who away? Talk sense, lad. The house was empty when we arrived. Off you go now and let the men get on with their work."

I picked up the first canvas. "I'm taking these paintings with me. They're mine."

He glanced at his watch and sighed impatiently. "Take whatever you want and be fast about it or you'll feel the toe of my boot up your arse."

In the city I searched for Zoe. No chalk marks on the pavement. The buskers on Grafton Street didn't know anyone answering her description. An old woman with a shopping trolley sat on the park bench and threw bread at the ducks. I asked the same question and she shook her head. It was late when I returned home.

"You took your time today." My father lifted steaks from the grill and laid them on warmed plates. "What kept you?"

"I stayed back at school to work on a French project."

"I see." His tone was even as he began to eat. After a few minutes he laid down his knife and fork and stared at me. His eyes were clear, sparking with anger. "I received an interesting phone call today from Mrs. Parkinson. Remember her? She was wondering why neither of us turned up for a certain meeting she arranged yesterday. Apparently, you were supposed to give me a letter."

"I don't remember any letter."

He ignored my reply. "She also wanted to know why you've been missing so much school lately. But first things first. We'll start with the letter. Show it to me. Immediately!"

"I burned it . . . I didn't want to worry you."

"That's very kind of you, Eoin. At least it would be if I thought you were telling me the truth. The only thing wrong with your immune system is that it's keeping you alive. What have you been doing when you were not at school . . . huh? Messing around with drugs? Shoplifting? Joyriding? Tell the truth for a change."

"It's none of your business what I do." I was on my feet, shouting into his face. Not caring anymore. "They knocked it down today. Every brick. It's all gone. Are you happy now that nothing's left?"

"I told you not to go there." He smashed his fist off the table and rose to face me. "But when did you ever do anything you were supposed to do?"

"How would you know? You're never sober long enough to notice."

"How dare you—how dare you." He hit me, his fist slamming against my chest and shoulders. No games this time. I preferred it this way.

"I'm sick of it—do you hear me?" I couldn't stop shouting. "I'm sick of your drinking and your silence and the way you look at me . . . as if I'm to blame. I don't want to go on feeling like this . . . every day feeling I don't deserve to be alive. I want her back again. Do you hear me? I want her back!"

He grabbed me again, holding me hard against his chest until I fell silent. I felt his heart thumping but then I thought . . . maybe it's mine . . . maybe it's both of us. I ran to my room and returned with one of the canvases. He was slumped in a chair, his face in his hands.

"You want to know what I did today?" I asked, my voice quiet now. I placed the canvas in front of him. "I took back our past."

He touched the canvas, his fingers tensed as if they would burn on contact. "I'm so angry, Eoin," he whispered. "Christ! I'm so angry since she went. . . ." I left him staring at her painting. Corry Head with the mist falling.

My mother was placing daffodils in a glass vase the last time I saw her. The morning news was on the radio. Northern Ireland peace process talks. She switched channels and swayed to the music. Our kitchen was filled with white light. I knew her happiness was as transient as the sunshine. I wanted no part of it.

"Hurry home from school, Eoin." She called after me and waved in the direction of the headland. "I want to paint it again. But different this time. Come with me, won't you?"

I nodded and slung my school backpack over my shoulder. I can't remember if I kissed her. I think not. But I hope I did.

After school I went into Dublin city with Morgan Dunne. We played computer games and went to the cinema. It was dark when we reached the beach shelter. Morgan had white pills. We mixed them with cider. I lost time that night. I saw shapes on the sea. A ship with lights sailing over the sand. A circling moon.

As soon as I entered the house I knew it was empty. Yet I searched every room, calling her name over and over again. Then I ran down the embankment and onto the strand. A man walking his dog had seen a woman on the rocks below Corry Head. He worried because the waves were high. A spring tide, treacherous.

I rang the police and then my father in New York. I've no memory of how we passed the time while we waited for news of her return. People called and spoke in quiet voices. Their fixed, reassuring smiles terrified me. The search lasted for three days until her body was swept ashore on an incoming tide.

The call of cormorants rose from the rocks. A shrill warning as I climbed through the barrier at the end of Corry Pier. I stood on the narrow ledge staring down into the water. Zoe had shaped my nightmare on the floorboards. White horses riding the night. Beneath the turmoil I sensed the stillness, the invisible depths of silence. I imagined my body falling like a stone, drawn down under the waves until it was floating in the timeless rhythm of tides. My heart began to beat faster. A step closer and it would be over. I swayed forward. How could she leave me with nothing but guilt to mark our years together?

Spray stung my eyes. I couldn't remember the last time I cried. My anger flowed into the sea. White horses lifted it, tossed it high, and gave it back to me, a spent force. For a dizzy instant my mother and Zoe merged and became one, moving away from me as the tide raged upward against the pier. Pictures I could not see or touch or understand flowed around me. They formed a space that I must not be afraid to enter. A space where pain had to be endured so that it could pass away. Where the waves wasted upon the sands before turning to gather strength for a new day.

The moon came out. A pale lantern shining. A room blazing with the light of many candles. I imagined Zoe trudging over mountains. Alone in an empty landscape, thinking thoughts of what might have been. My mother came slowly from the mist where I had walked since she died.

"Rosa . . . Rosa." I whispered her name. "What happened to you? That's the most awful part . . . not knowing."

No one answered. No one ever would. Some questions have no answers. White horses reared toward us, ready to carry her safely home.

Headlights swept the sea. A car braked sharply. A door slammed.

"Eoin!" My father's voice carried above the waves. It could have been a question. Or maybe it was a cry. I heard his footsteps on the pier. I turned and hurried toward the sound.

# CHARLEE JACOB

# Skin

Charlee Jacob has published some four hundred poems and two hundred stories. Her novel, This Symbiotic Fascination, has just been reprinted by Leisure Books.

Her second book, Soma, will follow in 2003. Her chapbook of poetry, Taunting the Minotaur, was recently published by Miniature Sun Press, the same company that published her broadside of Skin, which is one of the books in the Perihelian Broadside Series.

—E. D.

Suffocating by wrinkling inches,
rustling like a puppet's rebellion
   tangled in scabbed strings,
this rotting rawhide limps to an empty beat.
Poetry is the reproductive organ
but the skin is a horror story,
told lyrically with leather,
an epic epidermis the beauty of which
is shattered by wrecking ball time.
It is the integument that keeps the contents in:
a)   the heart kind to stray animals
     but stone to missing children
b)   the stomach that digests the crimes
     it devoured to conceal
c)   the brain rippled silken with religious mania,
     prophet of nightingales but apostle of butchers
d)   canals of blood that—without it—would have
     no home and nowhere to run.

Is this the skin I seek my rhymes in?

With an instinct for tyranny
a voice on the radio explains
the proper way to skin a rabbit,

pulling the hide off like a fluffy sock.
It speaks as if in a language
invented solely for usage by the teeth.
But that action is a recurring dream,
a talk show performed under starlight,
where with the twist of a blade
the universe can be turned inside out.

Is this the skin, sinister with scraping?

Melanomas sprouted while at the summit
   of the sun god's temple
where the bloodied altar and stone steps
   provide no shade.
I change my allegiance to darker rituals
—on the advice of my physician.
Shaking the tambourine of teeth,
putting lips to a flute of hollowed thigh bone,
pounding on a skull drum which doubles
    . . . when turned upside down . . .
   as a drinking goblet.
All body parts (I took as found treasures)
/none spared or wasted/
have their use in the scheme and skein.
   and skin of things.
I wear the flayed face as a mask,
a concealment or hint as to spiritual motives,
capering with the borrowed grin and grimace,
chewing moonlight I spit out as verse
   composed to a lunar deity.
That pockmarked god understands antics,
   appreciates the craters
   and loves the cross sections
where it seems a knife of night slashed down.

Is this the skin so sleek it screams?

My 'to do' list:
1. Collect all the dust my skin ever made
   as it powdered, fugitive from the wrap.
2. File down that sharp edge to infinity
   I keep cutting myself on,
   . . . because it bleeds the eye,
   strains the sex, and slows me down.
3. Hang up the neighborhood wash,
   dripping shrouds of body encasements,
   flapping on the wire-thin timeline.
4. Repeat and repeat until I perfect the syntax
   of this ragged yet eloquent fleshspeak.

My live motto: skin and let skin.

Going through the morgue, I read the toe tags
which described with finesse the quality therein.
This one was silk,
   watermarked as she drowned in her tub.
The next was crinoline,
   spinning insane in the light
   until she burned transparent.
This other was wool,
   emotions mossed thick to strange him.
This last was the velvet I needed for myself,
winter calling for a fine new coat.

Membrane mute/remote,
licking the salt from my hands and arms/
one of the few positive things about skin: it's flavor.
Is this what my soul will miss?
Is this the skin that tourniquets
   an otherwise bleeding doll?

I came in from the wars,
slamming the door on the wind
   which howled in tubercular haunting.
I headed for my bed to leave in nightmares
where pits and trenches were filled with bodies—
flesh in punctured balloons
   or shrunken in starved rind,
where battlefields were strewn
with ripped uniforms and twisted insignia,
where cellars dangled from ceilings
the manacled hopes for generations,
knickers down around ankles,
sleeves torn backward from the shoulders until
   —swinging in the dark—
they might have been mistaken for angels
trooping off to get a group rate
   from a plastic surgeon.
I came in from the wars,
   camouflaged with scars,
to ready myself for the dermis dream
by peeling away the Kanonenfutter's ruin,
mining down to raw nerve which presages
the skin graft that night weaves
to make us believe we wake up whole.

See the flesh as the shoreline
   of the human island.
Contained but isolated on the world
crowded with pain.

Sometimes the hands go up and wave to those asea.
Sometimes the hands go up to signal
to the black edge beyond horizon's rib,
begging to know:
Is this the skin sensitive to ice cubes,
      aroused by the orchid fist,
etched by fire's carefully applied disfigurement,
rippled by a razor's edge dragged sideways?
Is this the skin outraged
      in confinement by spiders,
by a poison extinct—delivered out of amber?
      Is this the skin?
Is this the frontier of what I'm made of?

# MARION ARNOTT

# Prussian Snowdrops

*Marion Arnott is a Scottish writer whose work has appeared widely in such small UK presses as* Paisley Yarns, Peninsular, West Coast, Scottish Child, Books Ireland, Hidden Corners *and* Crimewave. *She also has had a story published in the American magazine* Over My Dead Body. *She is a mother of three teenagers and teaches English and history at St. Andrews Academy in Paisley. She also runs a small creative writing group for teens and is a passionate fan of the short story in all its forms.*

*Although Arnott resists being classified as a writer of a particular genre, she appreciates the scope that the crime and horror genres allow her to explore all kinds of things in her character-driven stories. She won the Philip Good Memorial Prize for Fiction in 1998, and has been nominated for the British Science Fiction Award and for the Crime Writers' Award.*

*"Prussian Snowdrops" is a wonderful example of Arnott's character-driven stories. It was originally published in* Crimewave 4: Moon Indigo.

—E. D.

Traudl arrived with the spring, which was sudden that year. Karl was taken unaware by both, startled awake one glittering white night by the sound of the spring thaw; the river cracked like a pistol shot and, in the shivering dark, began to move through sundered ice. Karl's hot water bottles were flabby and chill as fish on a slab, and he cursed between chattering teeth: spring nights in Prussia were noisy with crashing ice and gurgling water, howling wolves and the drip-drip of melting icicles. He longed sleeplessly for the soft air of Berlin, gently gilded and scented with hyacinths.

He longed even more once he met Traudl. He was crossing the square to the inn that Sunday when he saw what looked like a bundle of rags on the stone bench beneath the statue of the Teutonic knight. He peered through fluttering sleet and saw that the bundle was a woman, ugly, lumpen, and scowling ferociously.

"Your pardon, *Gnädige Frau*," he said before he walked on, shaken both by her malevolence and a painful yearning for cheerful girls in stylish hats.

"Who was that, Ernst?" he asked when he joined the little company in the warm corner beside the fireplace.

"Traudl," the schoolmaster said, tamping down his pipe.

The postmaster nodded. "I thought she had given that up. It must only have been the winter that kept her away."

"She reminded me of that story," Karl said. "You know—'What big teeth you have, Grandma!' 'All the better to eat you with, child.' I thought, any minute she's going to spring and tear my throat out. Why is she sitting out there in the cold?"

"Waiting," the teacher said. "And before you ask what for, no one knows. She's from the asylum—quite incoherent. All she'll say is that she's waiting. Every Sunday afternoon she waits until darkness falls. And then she goes home."

The postmaster smirked into his *bierstein*. "I did hear one story. A man gave her a kind word thirty years ago and said he'd be back soon. So she waits in hope." Karl sniggered. "That face never had a hope and has always known it."

"Well, then," Ernst said. "Hopelessly ugly, therefore no story to tell, therefore not to be written about in your 'Tales from a Village.' Now who's for another beer?"

Karl was amused by the attempt to influence his articles; the teacher's status as most educated villager, and the only one who had joined the Party *before* the Führer swept to power, had gone to his head; or rather to his flat cheeks, which puffed out like a hamster's whenever he recalled that fact. He insisted that the tales reflect well on his village, and Karl made sure they did when he whiled away long Prussian nights with schnapps and purple prose. The villagers, he had written, helpless with laughter at the thought of the schoolmaster's coterie of turnip-witted farmers, were purest Aryan stock, a living link with Germany's heroic past; soul brothers of the men who had fought Roman, Turk, and Russian and poured their blood into the soil, making it theirs forever, of the same Germanic tribe admired by the noble Tacitus for virtuous beautiful women and merciless moral men.

Blood and soil and heroes made the schoolmaster's spectacles mist with emotion; Karl never knew how he kept his face straight while the tedious little man polished them clear. Even funnier, the Führer himself had proclaimed the tales inspirational, which only confirmed Karl's opinion of the Führer, and since then, the villagers had bombarded Karl with local legends of the Knights of the Teutonic Order, heroic resistance to Jew landlords, and of Aryan bloodlines untainted since the Dark Ages.

Karl put all their stories in his column. They were his living, and possibly a ticket back to Berlin, hurriedly abandoned after his coverage of the Führer's reception for the world's ambassadors. The sight of booted blackshirts displaying courtly manners and a knowledge of fine art—the Führer had issued a general order that they should—was hilarious enough, but when they got drunk, groped the French ambassador's wife and dumped her in the fountain along with her protesting husband, he lost all sense of self-preservation and reported it. Half Berlin sniggered, the other half wanted his blood.

"What you must remember," his editor said, "is that Nazis have no sense of humour. East Prussian office for you until things cool down." "But there's nothing to report there," Karl protested. "Find something," the editor said, "some-thing not funny." Karl found "Tales from the Village."

Karl sighed. The schoolteacher was telling him of his plans to revive an ancient summer solstice festival: bare-breasted blonde Valkyries holding sheaves of corn, together with bare-chested blonde Titans wielding swords, would re-enact an authentic pagan sacrifice in the water meadows. Ernst elaborated to a distressing degree until the flow of scholarly claptrap was interrupted by the arrival of the beer.

"My round, *meine Herren*," Karl beamed. The answering smiles displayed bro-ken brown teeth and cavernous gaps. The sight plunged Karl into despair: you'd think there'd be dentists, even in East Prussia. He averted his eyes, and through the sleet blooming on the window pane glimpsed Traudl, solid as a boulder wrapped in a blanket. The prospect of dozens like her displaying their all among the wheat sheaves rendered him speechless, and the schoolmaster, mistaking his silence for interest, began describing an entire calendar of pagan festivals. Karl sighed heavily.

Traudl was under the statue every Sunday. Karl always met her unwavering stare with a polite bow and a "Good afternoon, *gnädige Frau*." This was brave of him because her intensity made him nervous, and it provoked the schoolmaster to pontificate on the subject of degeneracy. He would steeple his fingers under his chin and say "And now if I may move on to matters esoteric" and serve Karl, the only man in the village with sufficient intellect to understand him, a dollop of Nazi science.

The day that Traudl first spoke to Karl the schoolteacher passed the afternoon blaming the high incidence of imbecility in East Prussia on the proximity of the Polish border. Karl struggled not to laugh as he imagined diseased Slavic wits drifting across the frontier like dandelion seeds seeking out a hapless Aryan womb in which to root. Ernst claimed that Traudl was a mongrel produced by a Polish father and a morally degenerate mother, and that in spite of the best efforts of the Party, that kind of unregulated breeding would continue to degrade Aryan bloodlines until the Führer's programme for purifying racial stock was carried out.

Karl smothered a yawn and the schoolmaster rebuked him mildly. "Some-times, Karl, I don't think you take eugenics entirely seriously."

"On the contrary," Karl smiled, "I was remembering the last time the Führer spoke on the subject. At Nuremberg. We ended the rally with the *Horst Wessel Lied*. It was most moving. You know, Ernst, we must get you to Berlin so that you can experience it all for yourself."

The teacher, who never cared to be reminded that he had never personally witnessed the Reich's ceremonies, resumed lecturing. He had devised a course on eugenics for his village pupils: responsible breeding, the duty of individuals to the race, sterilisation of the unfit and so on, and he thought perhaps that Karl might care to write a little something about his work.

Karl nodded enthusiastically, stopped listening, and thought about the rally. He and Siggi and Friedrich had been as drunk as lords and bawled out the first verse of the *Horst Wessel Lied* because it was the only one they knew; then gradually they realised that everyone else knew all the verses, every last turgid one, which seemed to them hysterically funny. "They're word perfect," Friedrich said. "No one but a man of genius could have inspired them to it. We have underestimated the Führer." Siggi said that the Führer would rise in his estimation when they could all sing in tune and as he spoke, the arc lights which blazed a cathedral's vaulted ceiling across the night sky were suddenly extinguished, and they found themselves giggling into a black void, unable to stop.

Karl looked out of the inn window to hide another grin. Traudl was out there as usual, sitting in the shadow of the knight, waiting. She could have been a statue herself, she sat so still, except that sometimes she tilted her head as if she were listening. Karl followed her gaze. She had a view along the river and the road which wound beside it; and in the far distance, the ruined church in the water meadows, its collapsed tower, its roofless walls, its screen of naked trees piercing the pale glassy sky. She was looking at nothing and listening to nothing and waiting for something to come of it all, which, he decided, made her no more feeble-witted than half of Germany.

It was night when she spoke to him. He was weaving unsteadily back to his lodgings in the thickening darkness, slithering across icy cobbles, when she stepped out of an alley and stood in his path. Her accent was coarse, her voice harsh.

"*Mein Herr*, I have been waiting for you."

She was nervous, but determined. Karl bowed, trying not to notice her troglodyte eyebrows.

"*Gnädige Frau*, it is late and very cold. Some other time—"

"A word. Only a word." Her face in the acid light of the wrought iron street lamp was yellow and surly. "A word can't hurt, can it?"

No, he thought, and a smile wouldn't either. Then, seeing the heavy bony face darken to jaundice, decided that it wouldn't help in the slightest.

"Another time. Next Sunday—"

He made to pass her by, but she seized him his arm with surprising strength.

"Not in the village. They wouldn't like that."

"Who wouldn't?"

"The schoolmaster. The postmaster."

Karl hiccoughed and reclaimed his arm. "*Gnädige Frau*, the schoolmaster may like or dislike as he pleases. It is a matter of impreme sudifference to me. Supreme indifference." He giggled and shook his head.

"Are you laughing at me?"

"Not at all. I am drunk, as you see. In no condition for a gossip. *Gnädige Frau*, good evening."

She came after him, her heavy boots thumping dully on stone cobbles.

"I have money. You can have it all."

She snatched at him, but he twisted away, fell, and lay dazed while she fumbled in a woollen stocking cap that she fished out of her pocket. She was breathing heavily and he was suddenly afraid—*what big teeth you have, Grandma*—but it was only money she pulled from the cap, wads of *Reichsmarks* tied up with string. She loomed over him, yellow-fanged and panting, trying to push the notes into his hand.

"All for you," she gasped.

Her excitement alarmed him. He had heard of women possessed by erotic fantasies; there had been a case in Berlin, a bloodied knife—

She hauled him up by the lapel of his coat. "The money," she said. "Take it. You do something for me. An easy thing."

"Please," he said, thrusting the money back at her, "there's nothing I can do for you."

"A letter. Write me a letter. That's all."

He blinked and swayed. "*Gnädige Frau*, what on earth would I write to you about?" He laughed and stepped back.

"From me. You write a letter from me."

"Why?"

"Because I can't write!" Anger flared like lightning in her dull eyes. "You write lots of things. It's not much to ask." Her voice deepened in desperation. "I can pay."

He hardly knew how he came to agree, but he did, partly from pity, partly because she wasn't going to go away unless he did, and partly from a humiliating fear of her flickering urgency. He salvaged his pride by grandly waiving payment, and then was in such a hurry to get away that he forgot to ask what kind of letter she wanted.

Karl wrote to Friedrich about the mystery of Traudl's letter: he imagined pleas to the lost lover to return, advertisements for the marriage columns ("I can pay!"), and postcards for display on the noticeboards of dubious nightclubs ("Honestly, I can pay!").

His cousin's reply was prompt and full of Berlin gossip and their friend, Siggi, who was the subject of most of it. Siggi was in "this-time-you-'ve-gone-too-far-trouble" with the editor. He had drawn the weedier Party leaders—round shouldered under the weight of masses of silver braid and death's-head insignia—demonstrating the etiquette of saluting Nazi style: the full stiff-armed salute, delivered along with a stentorian '*Heil Hitler!*', was given by inferiors to superiors; the half salute from the elbow, palm up, with a drawling '*Heil Hitler!*' was a sign of very high rank; and a half salute, palm down, was terribly, terribly sweet and greeted with whistles and cries of 'Hello, darling' from the prettiest boys in town. Respectable citizens were worried about giving the wrong impression, and Doktor Göbbels was incandescent with rage. Siggi could not see what all the fuss was about because he had, after all, shown considerable self-restraint by not drawing Göering in his Chinese silks and green nail polish.

Karl laughed at the cartoon that Friedrich had thoughtfully enclosed with his letter. The Party leaders reminded him of Ernst in his Sunday best SA uniform, self-important nonentities with an awesome talent for talking bilge. Siggi often said that listening to them was the penalty for living in the Age of the Common Man; he doubted that the Reich would last the promised thousand years, but judging by the amount of speechifying that went on, it was going to feel as if it had.

As for the troglodyte, Friedrich wrote that there was hope for her yet: the Führer had promised every Aryan female a husband and decreed that it was a civic duty to breed for Germany. Siggi was ecstatic about it: all over Berlin, patriotic women were throwing themselves at men, pleading to be impregnated.

The SS, flower of Aryan manhood, were the favoured target, and Siggi was desperate to join but didn't think they'd let him in after the saluting business.

Karl's homesickness was particularly acute all that week.

On the following Sunday, Karl waited for Traudl at the appointed place and time: at the back door of his lodgings after his landlady had gone to church. "No one must see," Traudl had said. "No one."

He led her into the parlour. She was intimidated by *Frau* Haar's brutal cleanliness and would not sit down until the third invitation, and only then after she had stretched her woollen scarf under her boots to protect the linoleum. She hunched silently on the edge of her chair, staring at her big red hands lying loosely in her lap.

"*Gnädige Fräu—*"

"I'm not married."

"*Gnädiges Fräulein—*"

Her quick upward glance revealed dull brown eyes lit by a reddish glow. "Are you laughing at me?"

"Your pardon—"

"That's how the Doktor speaks to the rich relatives. Me, I'm just Traudl."

"It was a courtesy, but . . . Traudl, if you prefer."

She stared him full in the face, making up her mind, and he was absurdly relieved when the light in her eyes faded to the colour of old stone and she resumed the study of her hands.

"You wanted a letter written, Traudl. Shall we begin?"

"I don't know how."

"What you want to say?" he said, whittling a pencil to a point with a penknife. "And where do you want to send it?"

"I don't know."

It took an hour to make sense of it all: Traudl wished to notify her former employer that her services as a laundress were still available. The difficulty was that he had decamped in the night without leaving a forwarding address, a course of action with which Karl could sympathise if *Herr Doktor* Reichardt had been often exposed to Traudl's efforts at conversation. He told Traudl that without an address, it was impossible to write to the Doktor.

"But he must be somewhere."

"He could be anywhere."

"You're clever. You could find him."

"He could be anywhere. And perhaps he doesn't wish to be found."

She shook her head. "No. He was looking for the patients. To bring them home." The mystery deepened. First, a mislaid Doktor, then mislaid patients. How careless Traudl had been!

"I think, Traudl, that if the Doktor wishes to employ you again, he will be in touch." Her heavy brow furrowed with the painfulness of thought. "How? He knows I can't read. And the telephone at the hospital doesn't work any more."

Unpaid bills, Karl decided. The good Doktor had fled his creditors.

"Perhaps you should seek some other employment until the Doktor is settled again."

"He left me in charge," she said, shaking her head. "I have to look after his dog."

"Without an address, I can do nothing," he said kindly.

Her protests turned her complexion an ugly brick colour as she repeated over and over, "But he must be somewhere. You could find him."

Her disbelief and his denials collided across *Frau* Haar's hearthrug. Traudl rocked backwards and forwards in her chair, her fists clenched in her lap. "He told me he'd be back soon!" She made a sound somewhere between a growl and a whine. The scene was becoming distasteful. Karl rose and crossed to the door. "I'm sorry, Traudl. Try the police. It is their job to find missing persons."

Her rocking stopped suddenly. "No!" She pounded her fists on her knees. "No! No! The Doktor said not to talk to them. They're bad."

"Then I don't know who can help you." Karl opened the door wider. "You must go now, Traudl. *Frau* Haar will be back shortly."

She lunged out of her chair. He sidestepped quickly, but she only swooped over the pencil shavings and scooped them up.

"She likes things tidy," she said and blundered past him to the kitchen door. He heard the heavy boots thumping across the vegetable patch, then the creak of the back gate. When he looked, she was gone.

The morning wasn't entirely wasted; it gave Karl the opportunity to tease the schoolmaster. The little man drew Karl aside as soon as he arrived at the inn.

"Karl," he said heartily. "You look well today. You have colour in your cheeks. The spring air?"

Karl nodded. "Delightful, isn't it? I didn't have to break the ice in the wash basin this morning and the electricity supply reappeared in the night. Suddenly life is full of promise."

"Karl—" The schoolmaster removed his spectacles and polished them, then folded his handkerchief neatly into his breast pocket. "The strangest story has come to my ears. Rumour has it that you were consorting with Traudl this morning."

"Consorting? What a quaint expression, Ernst."

"Of course, I said I found that hard to believe."

"That was thoughtful of you."

"An unlikely tale, isn't it?"

"If you say so."

"You're fencing with me, Karl," the schoolmaster said with a tight smile. "Is there any truth in it?"

"I don't know, Ernst. It depends what you mean by consorting."

"Then she did visit you this morning?"

"Yes, she did. I'm relying on you to keep that quiet, Ernst."

"Too late for that. People are wondering what you could possibly want with her."

"My business, surely?"

"Nevertheless, people are talking."

"There isn't much else to do on a Sunday afternoon." He took the schoolmaster by the arm and drew him over to the fire. "Except to sit in the warm and have a beer and some good conversation."

The schoolmaster returned to Traudl's visit several times, but Karl refused to be drawn and Ernst was reduced to a series of irritated harrumphs.

Karl wrote to Friedrich that night. "My learned friend was so cross that he didn't mention his beloved Valkyries and pagans once. With any luck, he's going to ban me from attending his festivals. He did give some fatherly advice about keeping bad company. And a little lesson in eugenics. Because of her Polish blood, Traudl can be violent; because of her mother's depravity, she can be promiscuous. I'm not sure whether Ernst fears most for my virtue or my life."

He had to end the letter there. The light flickered twice and went out, and he couldn't find the matches to light the oil lamp. The drumming of the river filled the room; it seemed louder in the pitch dark. So did the wolves.

His next meeting with Traudl came after he heard from Friedrich again. "Tell the troglodyte," Friedrich wrote, "that her Doktor is dead. He committed suicide in the foyer of the Ministry of Health at Tiergarten No. 4. Before he pulled the trigger, he said, 'I can't live with the guilt.' No one knows what he meant and, interestingly enough, no one wants to know. He was a respected psychiatrist and his death didn't even make the Stop Press. Siggi says the importance of a story can be measured by the silence it engenders; this silence is riccochetting round Berlin and everyone's running for cover. Even Siggi's friends, who are always in the know even when they aren't, declare to a man that they haven't heard about the very public suicide of *Herr Direktor* Reichardt or his guilt complex. They've never heard of Tiergarten 4 either. Since most of them pass it on the tram home, Siggi has concluded regretfully that they are all lying through their teeth. He is now in pursuit of what he is sure is a very nasty scandal.

"He has found a charwoman who saw Reichardt hanging around the foyer for days before he died. Every official was too busy to see him. That didn't surprise the char. She didn't approve of his unshaven appearance or his stale shirt or the way he paced up and down the foyer pushing his fingers through his hair. More than once she had to ask him to move so that she could mop the floor; he won her good opinion when he apologised charmingly for being in her way, but the poor gentleman didn't half make a mess of the marble tiles when he blew his brains out.

"Siggi wants you to quiz Traudl. He feels suicide is a massive overreaction to an unpaid telephone bill. You're to find out how he lost his patients and what was worrying him. If necessary, you're to sacrifice your virtue."

Karl knew Siggi was like a hound after truffles when it came to scandal and that he would have no peace until he found out something, anything. Accordingly, he left the inn early the following Sunday afternoon and waited in the alley, intending to startle Traudl for a change.

"Traudl!" he hissed and leapt out into the lamplight. He felt foolish when she only hesitated for a moment before walking on. He fell into step beside her. "Traudl. We must talk."

She plodded onward with a sulky bovine tread that made her chins tremble. Only East Prussia could produce such a creature, he thought; perhaps there was something to the schoolmaster's theories after all.

"Traudl, are you angry?"

"No."

"Yes, you are. No time for chat tonight."

"Nothing to say."

"You had lots to say last week."

"You didn't."

"I have now."

He could not see her expression. They had moved out of the circle of light under the lamp and the shadows had erased her features. She turned off the main street and took the narrow path down to the river.

"Where are you going, Traudl?"

"Home."

"May I come with you part of the way?"

They trudged along in silence. There were no lights beyond the village, and Karl soon lost sight of her in the icy dark. The path sloped sharply downwards and was slippery with deep sucking mind. He clung to bushes and skeletal branches to steady himself.

"Traudl! Slow down!"

Her heavy tread never faltered, but her voice floated back to him in the darkness. "Go back! I don't want to talk to you!"

"But it's about the Doktor!" The wind threw his words back at him—Doktor! Doktor!—and startled him. His foot caught on a root and he plunged headfirst down the slope into a cold slime of rotten leaves. He lifted his head and smelled the airy cleanness of open water nearby. There was a rustling movement in the inky darkness, and then Traudl was standing over him. She stooped and dragged him upright.

"Did you find him?"

"Let me catch my breath."

"Did you?" She tugged at his arm and swung him back and forth like a rag doll. He remembered big square laundress's hands which could wring blankets dry as easily as twisting a kiss curl. He could not tell her that the Doktor was dead, not out here in the lonely dark. There was no telling how she would react.

"I have news," he said. "Come to *Frau* Haar's and I will tell you."

"No, now."

"*Frau* Haar—"

"No. Not her house. Here."

"But—"

"Where is he?" she shrieked, shaking him harder.

"Berlin. He's in Berlin."

"Is it far?"

He laid a hand on hers and patted it tentatively. "Oh, yes, Traudl. Very far. And you don't know the way." He could feel her thinking, and he grew cunning, remembering Siggi's hopes of a spectacular scandal. "The Doktor's in trouble, Traudl. He needs your help before he can come home."

"The patients. Are they with him?"

"No, they're still lost."

"He said they'd be back. Like last time."

"Last time?"

"Yes. They all came back."

"But they haven't come back this time, have they?" Karl improvised wildly. "And everyone says it's the Doktor's fault." He detached himself carefully from Traudl's grasp. She stood immobile, gazing up at a black sky flecked with sparks of steel, and tilted her head as if she were listening. "Don't you want to help the Doktor, Traudl?" he asked softly.

She wrung her hands and shuffled from foot to foot. "I'm not to tell. The Doktor could get into trouble. Me, too. I helped."

Karl moved closer to her. "But he's already in trouble, *liebling*."

She cracked her knuckles in her agitation. "Do the police know what we did?"

Karl felt one of his headaches coming on and wished he knew what they were talking about. "They've locked him up," he said desperately. "He must have done something bad to the patients."

"Not him. Never."

"Well, then, tell me about it. I'll write in the newspapers that he never did a bad thing, ever, and the police will let him out."

She whirled suddenly and stumped along the path. "No, I promised not to tell." She barged down the path, arguing with herself.

"Traudl! You must help me help the Doktor!"

She halted abruptly when she reached the river bank. "Is it help if I tell about the last time? The time they all came back? That's not a secret. Everyone knows. They only say they don't."

"I think it might help, yes."

Traudl decided quickly. She flopped down on to one of the large rocks which littered the river bank. "All right," she said and chewed at the cuff of her mitten. "All right. He didn't do bad things. The hospital was a good place after he came. He wasn't angry like the one before. No hitting with wet towels. No electric wires on us."

"Oh, that was kind," Karl said, taken aback. "Now, what was the 'last time' you were talking about, the time when they all came back?"

"That was later. He let me work and gave me money for it. I learned to be tidy and wash things. Nobody made the sheets as white as me." She halted on a note of coy pride until Karl murmured admiringly. "I ironed the little cloths for his breakfast tray. I never forgot. That was the first year he came—"

"What trouble are you and the Doktor in, Traudl?"

"—he said I was his best laundress. And a good talker, too. I never talked before he came but he helped me. I don't talk to everyone. Just him and some of the patients. And you."

Karl silently cursed the good Doktor. Traudl was going to talk mountains of trivia—he knew the signs. And Siggi would kill him if he didn't listen. He gathered his coat around him and perched on the rock beside hers. She began talking and continued all through the night. He struggled to keep the story orderly in his mind, but names, events, happy-days and phone calls, Traudl's matter-of-fact recital and the shrieking wind made a whirling kaleidoscope in his head.

On his way home, he saw that dawn had turned the horizon ice pink on the far side of the river. Birch trees, black lace against the skyline, speared the new morning. What had she said? Little Heinrich was afraid of the birch trees, and she always had to hold his hand to calm him down.

---

*Frau* Haar kept a respectable house and preferred that he keep respectable hours. Karl slipped into the house through the back door. In the hall, he put out a hand and touched the silver framed photograph of *Frau* Haar's grandchildren on the dresser. This was the frame Traudl had described, silver, etched with a pattern of feathers. It was the first proof of the veracity of her story. It had been Elvi's frame, and Elvi had searched everywhere for it, crying for her mother's photograph. *Frau* Haar had been housekeeper at the hospital, and she was angry with Elvi for losing the picture the way she lost everything, the careless stupid half-wit, it was no wonder her father had had her locked up. Traudl knew all the time that *Frau* Haar had taken the frame—she liked pretty things—but she didn't say anything, because *Frau* Haar had a bunch of heavy keys, and she often hit Traudl for staring too hard or Elvi for crying and getting on her nerves.

Karl considered *Frau* Haar's love of pretty things. He tiptoed quietly to his room so as not to disturb his landlady. He didn't think that he could stomach her smiling grandmotherly reproof this morning.

He spent most of the day writing it all down for Siggi and Friedrich. Traudl's story had been like a country ramble down winding lanes and through thickets of detail, but he summarised it ruthlessly: in the summer of 1933, men came to the asylum. They were uniformed and had long boots and guns. The Doktor had argued with them for a long time in the hall, but they showed him papers. The Doktor telephoned to Berlin while the patients were being brought out; he shouted a lot until the man with the papers pulled the telephone wires out of the wall and asked which patients could work: he didn't want any dangerous or very feeble-minded ones.

The Doktor wouldn't tell, but *Frau* Haar took the men into the office where the files were kept. One of them stood in the doorway and called out names written on white cards: Elvi and Maria and Detlef and lots of others. He called Traudl's name, too, but the Doktor said she was an employee, not a patient, and the man burst out laughing. "Oh, I do apologise, *Gnädige Frau.*"

All the patients in the locked ward were left behind, but the rest were taken away. The men shouted and shoved them to make them go faster. Elvi cried and cried, and one of the men said she was a pretty little silly who should play it smart and not make herself red-eyed and ugly. Then the Major came out in his old uniform jacket with the Iron Cross on a ribbon. The man looked at his card. "What's wrong with him?" he asked. The Doktor told him the Major had shell-shock and that he was a war hero. The man with the white card saluted and told the Major to stay in the hospital because he had already done enough for Germany. All the soldiers smiled, but the Major was upset. His bad dreams came back, and he screamed all night long. The Doktor said it was because of the guns.

One other thing happened that night. *Frau* Haar said the patients wouldn't be spoiled where they were going. The Doktor slapped her face hard and told her to get out. She stood there with her hand on her cheek and her mouth flapping open. She never came back again and the Doktor let Traudl be house-keeper, but there wasn't much work. There were hardly any patients left—

Karl put his pen down and leaned back in his chair. Apart from a hiss of excitement at the telling of the slapping of Haar's face, Traudl might as well have been reciting a railway timetable. He had asked for details, but her memory was a repository for irrelevance: she didn't know the name of the man with the cards, the surnames of the patients, the date of the visit, or the name of any of the Berlin personnel that Reichardt had contacted. But Friedrich and Siggi would find out. This was going to be the Tale from the Village to end all Tales. Ernst was going to be furious! Karl picked up his pen again.

"And that's when she first started waiting,". he wrote. "The Doktor got the phone fixed and phoned Berlin. He was promised his patients back when the road-building season was over. He told Traudl they would come home soon, and all that summer on her afternoon off, she sat in the village square, watching the road for them. Little Heinrich had taken his flute with him, and she listened for him piping the others home along the riverbank. All summer she watched and listened and waited.

"They returned one frosty night in autumn in a big lorry. The Doktor came downstairs in his plaid dressing gown and opened the big front door. He had to sign bundles of papers. The patients came in quietly and stood in the corner, looking down at the floor. None of them said hello. The man with the papers said they had been good little soldiers once he'd knocked the nonsense out of them. The Doktor told him to leave, and he went out laughing.

"The Doktor didn't laugh. He walked up and down the line of patients in the corner and didn't say a word. Elvi began to cry, and the others shouted at her to stop before they all got into trouble. She stuffed a rag into her mouth and cried without noise. 'Good little soldiers,' the Doktor said, and then he sat on the stairs and cried. Then they all did."

Karl stopped writing again. Traudl had almost criticised her Doktor then. What was the use of crying? Heinrich was blue with cold without his shirt, Detlef had a broken arm, and Elvi was walking on the carpets with dirty bare feet. Traudl had to see to everything all by herself because the Doktor only cried and pulled his hair. "I can't believe that this has happened," he kept saying.

But Traudl believed. She knew the things that happened in the world. She was the first to know that Elvi and Maria were pregnant. She knew about Maria because she was sick every morning. She knew about Elvi because she sat rocking on the floor all day, saying her alphabet over and over. She thought her mother might come for her if she could prove she wasn't stupid. Traudl guessed from the rocking that she would have a baby soon, because she had rocked too when a bad thing had happened to her. She had rocked and rocked but she didn't know her letters and so she had sung a little song. That was when they put her in the hospital. The three men didn't get put anywhere, though. She had seen Karl drinking with them at the inn. No, she wouldn't say their names because they'd get her locked up again. And what did it matter? These things happened all the time. She didn't understand why a clever man like the Doktor didn't know that.

Karl chewed his pen, thinking of Traudl and her three men. She had hummed her song for him, tilting her head and tunelessly crooning a cracked counterpoint to the shrieking wind which drove the clouds away from the moon and whipped at her scarves and wrappings. He decided to censor that little tale from his letter. No one would ever believe that the Troglodyte could attract three men. He thought of the farmers he drank with in the inn—no, not even in East Prussia could any man be that desperate. This was clearly the erotic fantasy of a mad-woman, and would cast doubt on her truthfulness if it were known. But the fantasy didn't mean that she had lied about everything else. The tale of Rei-chardt had the ring of truth, was even touching in its way. And his suicide was a verifiable fact. But for the life of him, Karl couldn't think what the Doktor had to reproach himself with. "And," he wrote to Friedrich, "we may never know, because Traudl refuses absolutely to discuss the second time the patients went away."

It was a week before he heard from Friedrich. "Traudl must spill the beans," his cousin wrote, "for Siggi's sake. He has been afflicted with moral outrage. We all thought it was some new joke at first, but now we fear the case is genuine and irrecoverable. Siggi is earnest and never amusing and no one can stand his com-pany for long. He darts like a firefly all over Berlin, enquiring about forced labour and vanished lunatics; he pins T4 clerks to walls and bribes them to bring him the contents of their superiors' waste paper baskets.

"So far he has gleaned that the Ministry at Tiergarten 4 researches eugenics, fertility, and insanity. They distribute grotesque photographs of the insane to demonstrate the effects of degeneracy on racial health. Siggi produces these gross pictures without the slightest provocation, even at the dinner table. He rages that his zanies have been rounded up and put into labour camps along with politcos and other undesirables. He considers it a harrowing fate to have to dig roads and be lectured at by the politically committed.

"Certainly, some sort of forced labour programme was in operation last year, and yours is not the only report of non-return from labour duties. All enquiries are met with referrals to other departments and officials—there are dozens of them. The Führer breeds them like rabbits and they are all alike: they know nothing and they write down in triplicate the names of people who want to know. Siggi makes them spell his name aloud three times in case they get it wrong.

"He is full of high purpose. The editor refused to print his latest cartoon (he's still apologising for the saluting business), but Siggi persuaded him. You should have heard him: 'Of course it will embarrass the government! Why else are we here?' 'Someone has to worry about the poor lunatics digging roads while being preached at by socialists and trade unionists. Why else are we here?' 'The cartoon is not mocking the Party. It isn't the slightest bit funny—' "

And it wasn't, Karl had to agree when he looked at it; it was chilling. It showed the Pied Piper of Hamelin with a death's-head face and a flute at his mouth, dancing a ragged file of grotesques up a wooded mountainside. One by one, they disappeared into a narrow cleft in the rocks while the death's-head grinned and fluted. "Where are they now?" the caption underneath read.

It was a grim flight of fancy, but Karl chuckled. Moral outrage! Not Siggi! More likely he was suffering from a prolonged hangover and plain old-fashioned guilt. He had a sister confined in an institution. He had mentioned her once at the end of an evening of inventive depravity when he was reviewing his life through the bottom of a glass. "SShhh!" he said. "Today is someone's birthday, but I must not say her name. My father forbids it. She brought shame on us by being peculiar, you see, and so forfeits her place in the family and the world. All day long she hears the voices of angels and devils, all kinds of voices, but never ours. Her photographs have been removed from the mantlepiece and the lock of her baby hair from my mother's jewel box. No one remembers her. Except me." He grinned slyly and drew letters in the beer slops on the table. "You see? Her name." He rubbed it away with his cuff before Karl could read it. "SShhh!" he whispered. "Her name must never be spoken; her absence must never be noticed. Have you any idea how much effort it takes not to notice someone who isn't there? But I keep her here." He had knuckled his forehead so hard that Karl pulled his hand down and pinned it to the table.

Karl frowned. Siggi was odd sometimes. Perhaps there was a family weakness.

The schoolmaster had regained his good humour by the following Sunday. "I brought you my lesson plans," he said, basking in the rosy firelight beside Karl. "Eugenics. Perhaps your readers would be interested. Berlin should know that we are not all backswoodsmen out here."

"Very thoughtful of you, Ernst. The electricity, plumbing, and church gargoyles may be mediaeval, but the village is in the vanguard of the new science. Your influence, of course."

The schoolmaster flushed with pleasure. "I try. One likes to pass the torch of enlightenment to the next generation."

"Your lesson plans may well be of interest, Ernst. There is a Ministry in the Tiergarten entirely devoted to—"

"Oh, yes, I know. I send for all their public information pamphlets. But I believe I have refined the theories to a consistency suitable for children to digest. I have devised a programme—"

And he was off. Karl waited patiently for a break in transmission. When the schoolmaster paused for a swallow of beer, he said suddenly, "And did you ever have contact with the asylum here, Ernst? To increase your understanding of the problem?"

"Goodness, no. It's seven miles outside the village and you know these places—closed doors and no outsiders, please." He placed his empty *stein* carefully on the table. "What makes you ask?"

"I wondered if the patients were the inspiration for your studies."

"No, not really. We occasionally met the better behaved ones in the village, exchanged a good morning and so on. They were not inspiring."

"I understand the hospital is empty now."

"Yes. The *Direktor* abandoned the place once the inmates had gone."

"They're not coming back then? The patients? I believe they left once before and returned."

"Oh, they didn't exactly leave that time. They were temporarily seconded to a labour-therapy squad. The programme was successful, I believe."

"But that's not why they left the second time?"

The schoolmaster's spectacles misted over. "They didn't exactly leave then either, Karl. There was an outbreak of typhus. Most of them died, the rest went home, and the *Direktor* abandoned the place."

"The *Direktor* shot himself."

The schoolmaster blinked rapidly. "Really? How sad that is. But, you know, the man was as unstable as his patients. Ask anyone in the village."

"He had something on his mind. He said he couldn't live with the guilt."

"Perhaps he neglected the hospital drains." The schoolmaster emptied his glass. "The interesting question is, does psychiatric work attract the unbalanced, or do they become like that through contact with the insane?" He signalled to the barmaid. "Did I tell you that I am planning a trip for the children? To *Nürnberg* for the autumn rally? We are all so excited."

*Frau* Haar was even less communicative than Ernst. She said nothing about life in the asylum except that she had been like a mother to those poor souls. As for Reichardt's suicide and the fate of the patients, she knew nothing at all about what happened there after she retired. But she would pray for the good *Doktor*.

Like Siggi, Karl concluded regretfully that they were both lying through their teeth.

Wednesday's weather was milder, if not quite springlike. Karl wrapped up warmly, and with Siggi's cartoon in his pocket, set out for his tryst with Traudl. He had persuaded her to show him the snowdrops at the place where the patients had their happy-days, and the birch trees which had frightened Heinrich. He put it to her that it was the least she could do if she wouldn't tell him her story.

The air was crisp and the sky a glassy blue. Karl enjoyed the brisk walk past gardens sparkling with frost until he turned down the path that wound beside the river. It was like entering a dank tunnel. The path was overhung with branches, bushes and trailing grasses, which rotted mournfully in the mud. He took his mind off his discomfort by planning how to make her talk.

He was wet and filthy by the time he reached the little white style where Traudl awaited him, swathed in shawls and scarves. "The snowdrops are this way," she said, and without another word led the way across the water meadows. They waded knee-high through grass crunchy with frost, and only halted when they reached the birch trees which pallisaded the edge of the meadow.

She waved her mittened hand. "The birches," she announced. "The ones Heinrich was afraid of." She clearly expected a reaction. He struggled to find one. "Ah, yes," he said at last, "where Heinrich lost the race."

She nodded. "Every summer. Heinrich kept up with Detlef when they ran across the meadows, but Detlef always won because Heinrich stopped at the trees. They frightened him. He wouldn't go in the woods unless I came and took his hand." Traudl gazed dreamily into the leafless thicket.

"Is this where Heinrich played his flute, Traudl?" He had to ask her twice.

"Not here," she said at last. "He didn't like the trees whispering to him. Or Detlef running off through the woods. He could hear Detti's sandals getting further and further away—" She clapped her mittened hands together in a light rapid rhythm. "Like that. Slap. Slap. Slap." She clapped again and added helpfully, "The path is hard like biscuit in summer. Slap. Slap. Further and further away until Heinrich couldn't see him any more. 'Oh, Traudl!' he shouted every time. 'Where's Detti? Where's he gone?'

Karl was amused to find that just for a moment, he felt Heinrich's dread of the silent forest closing in over the sound of invisible running feet. Traudl was still speaking. "But," she said, "he was all right when I carried him."

"Carried him?"

"He's small for his age."

"How old?"

"Ten. But small."

"Ten? In an asylum?"

"Since always." Traudl grinned wolfishly, pushed her eyelids into a slant, and sank her chin into her shoulders. "He's funny looking. The snowdrops are this way."

The clearing was a long way into the forest. He arrived panting and overheated. Traudl was well ahead of him. "This is where the happy-days were," she said with a sigh. A tiny ruined chapel stood to one side. Birches crowded spikily upwards from inside its roofless walls. The clearing was studded with flat table tombs, each carved with a great crusader's cross, symbol of the Teutonic knights, the flower of the Aryans. Karl sat on a tomb and lit a cigarette. His feet were buried to the ankles in a carpet of snowdrops that trembled thick and white in the breeze.

Traudl tramped round the perimeter of the clearing, slapping her arms to keep warm.

"Is it pretty? Do you like it?" she called to him.

He nodded. "Very pretty. And peaceful."

"The Doktor said the snowdrops were a sign that winter was nearly over. We all—"

Karl flicked his cigarette into the snowdrops and heard it sizzle. "I have something to show you, Traudl." He held out Siggi's cartoon. "Look. My friend drew this. It's in the newspapers."

She began circling the clearing again. "Heinrich didn't like it here."

"Traudl, come and see."

Her speed increased to a lumbering trot.

"Traudl!"

She turned and ran in the opposite direction.

"Why didn't he like it here, Traudl?" He patted the space beside him. "Come and tell me all about it."

She stood still. "I told you. He didn't like the trees. Or those." She pointed at the tombs. "There's dead people in there. See? Pictures of their bones."

Karl glanced at the table tomb; it was carved with skulls and scythe-bearing skeletons, their bony fingers pointing at a Latin inscription—*Memento Mori*. Traudl came closer.

"Heinrich heard claws scratching to get out from under there."

Karl grinned. "Heinrich had a vivid imagination."

Traudl pouted sulkily. "He heard them scratching like rats." Her whisper was like the rustle of dead leaves. "He thought the trees grew out of their bones." She pointed skywards. "See their fingers? And their arms?"

The birches, naked and slick with ice, soared dizzyingly above their heads. Twigs were like fingers flexed in frozen anguish, branches like arms uplifted to Heaven, and the wet silver bark that covered them looked like rotten dead flesh. Or so a little boy might think, Karl thought with a shudder.

"Woo! Woo!" Traudl screamed suddenly. "Woohoo!" She leapt at him and he tumbled backwards off the tomb. She slapped her thighs and laughed. "The *Doktor* fell off, too. Every time. Good joke, isn't it?"

"Yes," he said, brushing wet debris off his trousers. "I can see why you call them happy-days."

"Yes. Heinrich laughed and laughed and then he wasn't frightened. He asked questions. Why do trees grow upwards? Why do snowdrops grow in circles? I didn't know, but the *Doktor* did. Do you know why?"

Karl seated himself and lit another cigarette. "I don't think I do, Traudl," he said patiently. "What did the *Doktor* say?"

She recited carefully. "Trees and snowdrops are just like people—each grows according to its nature." She pursed her lips. "That's clever talk, isn't it?"

"Yes, it is, Traudl. Wouldn't it be wonderful to have the *Doktor* back?" She nodded and dropped her eyes. "I think I know how. Will you look at my picture now?" She sidled nearer. "See, Traudl? The patients are being led away. It says, 'Where are they now?' My friend is worried about them. He would bring them back if he knew where they were."

"I don't know where."

"Did they go with the soldiers like before?"

She kicked idly at snowdrops. The smell of smashed stalks rose green in the air. "The picture's wrong," she said. "Heinrich had the flute, not the soldiers. And they didn't walk. They went in a big lorry."

"So the soldiers did come again? You know, *liebling*, if we tell about the soldiers, then the *Doktor* will be let out. And we'll make the soldiers tell where the patients are. But if we don't tell, then maybe you'll never see any of them again."

Snowdrop stalks snapped and squeaked under her boots. "I could get into trouble. I don't want to be locked up."

There was real terror in her eyes. Karl patted her arm. "Traudl, tell me about it. If it will get you locked up, then I'll keep it a secret. If it won't, then I'll put it in the papers and find the *Doktor*. Is it a deal?"

He was frozen to the marrow of his bones by the time she agreed, and even then the ordeal was not over—she insisted he accompany her to the hospital because she had to give Fritzi his dinner.

"I thought all the patients were all gone away," he said.

"Fritzi's the *Doktor's* dog," she said.

"Oh. Sorry."

She grew confidential. "Fritzi gets his dinner early or he makes a pest of himself when the patients are having theirs."

"But there are no patients."

"It's still Fritzi's dinner time."

There was no arguing with that.

It was about four miles through the woods to the hospital. Karl stumbled after Traudl while she barked amusing anecdotes about Fritzi over her shoulder. The animal was, apparently, every bit as remarkable as the *Doktor*. He gasped admiration whenever he could summon the breath and swore inwardly that Siggi was going to pay for this.

The hospital was a gracious old hunting lodge with carved wooden gables and a solid square frontage half-hidden in red creeper. He might have admired its prettiness if he hadn't been exhausted. They entered by a side door. Traudl stood by the oak coat-stand in the little hallway. "Overshoes," she chanted. "Coat. No drips, please. I polish the floors on Wednesdays."

He divested himself of wet garments while she removed layers of shawls and scarves and an old military greatcoat. Her hair, he saw, was iron grey and cut short with a side parting scraped back in an enormous diamante clasp. The effect was oddly childlike. She smiled her wolf's fang grin and touched her clasp. "Pretty, isn't it? The *Doktor* won it in the Christmas lucky dip. He said he would give it to his best girl. That's me. I'll feed Fritzi now. You can watch if you want."

The kitchen was warm and bright and the little daschund was frantic with joy. Karl restrained him while Traudl filled his bowl with meat. He pulled a chair close to the stove. "Tell me about when the soldiers came."

She said it was like the first time: the soldiers, the papers, the shouting, the lorry. Elvi was hit with a gun to shut up her screaming. And they pushed the *Doktor* to the floor when he tried to help her. The soldiers walked right over him. "My God," he kept saying, "what have I done?" But Traudl didn't tell.

Karl was bewildered. He studied the coffee pot in front of him. "But what could you have told, Traudl? The *Doktor* hadn't done anything. None of this was his fault." She was suddenly busy, mopping up a coffee splash, muttering under her breath. He waited patiently.

"They took the Major with them this time."

"They didn't before. Why did they this time?"

She polished furiously at the bass taps shining over the sink. "Because of what the *Doktor* did. And me."

She left Karl in Reichardt's office while she took Fritzi for his walk. Slowly he began to make sense of what she had told him. The phone, black and gleaming on Reichardt's desk, had rung two days before the soldiers came. A voice warned Reichardt he was about to be visited again. He shut himself in his office all that day.

Traudl knocked at the door after everyone had gone to bed and brought him sandwiches. What a mess the room was in! The drawers in the filing cabinet were open and there were little white record cards all over the desk and the floor. He was typing and Traudl asked if she should send for *Fräulein* Harkus, because typing was her job, but he said he couldn't trust her and gobbled down his sandwiches.

"But I can trust my best girl, can't I, Traudl? Not clever Harkus or my loyal nurses. Only you. You must never say anything about this, Traudl. It could mean big trouble for us both. You can keep your mouth shut, can't you?"

Karl stood in front of the desk where Traudl must have stood that night. The desk was wide and covered with green leather. There was a green shaded lamp to one side. He imagined Reichardt, pale and unshaven, in a splash of light among the shadows, peck-typing and wolfing down sandwiches. His eyes would have been bright and feverish when he told Traudl his plan. "It's a paper game," he told her. "Paper gives them power over us. We shall fight paper with paper." Traudl hadn't understood, but she'd fetched the garden refuse sacks, and while he typed, obediently shredded all the little white cards he pointed at, then filled the sacks with them.

He had a pile of new cards beside his typewriter. "What shall I say about the Major, Traudl? And Elvi—we can't let them take her, not after last time."

Traudl couldn't remember what he said about the Major and the others, but she had allowed Karl to look through the filing cabinet. Maria Barbel, Elvi Polk, Heinrich Reinke, Major Beck—according to the records, they were all suffering from multi-syllabic psychiatric illnesses, presenting as hallucinations, delusions, violent outbursts, and a total incapacity to follow a disciplined regime. In short, unfit for work.

Karl understood. The soldiers hadn't wanted the severely disordered the first time and so Reichardt had transformed his patients, working throughout the night to produce records showing false diagnoses and hopeless prognoses. Traudl kept him going with coffee and burned the old records to wisps of ash in the boiler room furnace.

Karl stood entranced, seeing it all happen by the light of a green shaded lamp, hearing the quiet flip of a card across the table, the rip as Traudl tore it to pieces, the tap-tap of the typewriter. He saw Reichardt yawning and filing his new records so that everything was in order, proper and correct.

When the soldiers came, Traudl hid in the cupboard in the hall. They were smiling and polite this time. So was the *Doktor* as he regretted that he had no patients fit for work. The soldiers were delighted to hear it. It was the unfit they had come for this time. 'What for?' Reichardt demanded. 'What use are they to you?' 'None at all,' the soldiers said. 'They are being relocated.'

The *Doktor* turned chalk white then. He said they couldn't do that, but they showed him papers and said he should be pleased to be rid of the troublesome ones. They were going to a special hospital for people like them. Reichardt fetched his coat and said he was coming, too, but the soldiers locked him in his office and told him there were enough *doktors* where they were going.

From her hiding place, Traudl saw a scene from Hell. The patients were screaming and running everywhere, trying to get away from the rifle butts. Elvi hugged her baby and cried. One soldier was kind and stroked her hair. "Do you think we are monsters, *liebling*? Would we hurt our little Elvi?"

Reichardt hammered on the door of his office, shouting that he was going to report this, but the soldiers only laughed. Traudl let him out after they'd gone, and he spent the next two days on the telephone. But it was no use. "No one can say where they are, Traudl," he said. "Due to staff shortages, the paperwork has been held up. We will be informed in due course." He laughed till he trembled. "They've been lost like parcels in the post. I must go to Berlin and see these people face-to-face. I shall make them give our people back."

When Traudl returned with Fritzi, Karl told her firmly that her story must be told. There would be no trouble. The newspapers would protect her. Once people knew what was going on, the soldiers would be in trouble and *Doktor* Reichardt and the others would be brought back home. He would be proud of his best girl and know he had been right to trust her.

"I shall send the story to Berlin, Traudl. I'll show it to you first, of course." She shrugged. "I can't read." She fiddled, frowning, with her diamante clasp.

"I'll read it to you. Would you like that?"

"I don't have much free time," she said almost coquettishly.

"You can polish the floors while you're listening," he laughed.

"Will the *Doktor* read about me, too?"

"Definitely."

He was halfway home and tramping through the snowdrop clearing before he remembered that Reichardt was dead. With a stab of pity he pictured again the pale unshaven man in the green lamplight. Karl rested on a tomb for a few minutes, thinking and smoking. Snowdrops glimmered ghostly white around his feet in the fading light; they were everywhere. His eye travelled along jagged lines of them into the long grass under the trees while he planned his exposé, and his future. There was no telling where this would end. Governments had fallen for less and the credit would be his. Reichardt had done his best and he would mention that—but for the life of him, he still couldn't understand why the man had shot himself.

There was a letter awaiting him at *Frau* Haar's. Karl sat stunned on the edge of his bed when he'd read it. Siggi was in hospital after a drunken brawl with some blackshirts. The details were sickening. Siggi had been identified by his press card, which had been the only recognisable thing about him. His friends had prayed that he would live, but now they prayed he would die, so severe was the damage to his brain, which was slopping around in his skull like mashed pumpkin.

Karl hugged his knees to his chest, sick to the pit of his stomach. Friedrich said that Siggi had been delighted by the response to his Pied Piper cartoon. At first, furious relatives of patients denied that the patients were missing—they had died of typhus and they had the medical certificates to prove it. The trouble was, there were hundreds of them, all dying of the same disease, in the same span of time in places scattered all over Germany. Now the relatives were asking hard questions about the conditions the patients were being held in. The editor had been summoned to T4 and been harangued by an official about the distress that Siggi's cartoon had caused the recently bereaved, and about Siggi's relentless badgering of T4 staff. The official was moved to question the role of the Free Press in a civilised society. The editor had apologised profusely, swore that it would never happen again, returned to the office and told Friedrich that Siggi had been right all along and they were going to prove it. Friedrich advised Karl to break the story before someone else did; for Siggi's sake, he'd added, or he'll come back and haunt you.

Karl spent the rest of the day planning how to introduce the patients to the public. He would have to make them interesting. The hard facts about their removal from care and subsequent ill-treatment would send shockwaves round the Reich. In tribute to Siggi, he would head the story "Where Are They Now?" Everyone had heard rumours about the conditions in labour camps. The Party had as good as deliberately infected the patients with typhus by sending them there. He would lead the crusade to bring the survivors home and make his reputation forever.

He laid out his typewriter, carbons and paper and began. Words had never flowed so easily before. Reichardt must have felt like this the night he changed the patients' records: no fatigue or hesitations, no stumbling after the right phrase. He worked on through the night, sealed his scoop in a large brown envelope and took it to the postbox at the end of the street.

Dawn broke as he turned back home. The river rushed noisily through crystalline light and made him think of Traudl. He considered the unexpectedness of things that happened in the world: who would have thought that a dismal night spent on a riverbank with a Troglodyte would lead to all this? He shook his head in disbelief and when he reached his lodgings, plunged straight into a deep sleep.

He woke suddenly with the crack of a pistol shot echoing in his ear. "But they don't!" he cried out. He sat bolt upright and snapped on the light, but the room was empty and quiet: no pistol shots, no sandals slapping across earth baked hard as biscuit, no flute piping off-key. Shivering, he pulled his blankets round his shoulders. Such a strange dream: bright sunshine and screams, a blue and golden summer day, and thousands of snowdrops, splashes of out-of-season frost, zigzagging through the grass towards the trees. And above the screams and shots, a child's voice, clear and sad like a flute's: 'Why do snowdrops grow in circles?'

"But they don't," he said aloud.

And they didn't. He was back in the clearing by midmorning. On one side, snowdrops formed circles like ever-widening ripples round the trees and tombs; on the other side, the ripples were broken into jagged lines, as if the earth and the bulbs clinging underneath had been disturbed. His eye followed the jagged lines and traced a pattern of grassy rectangles humped side-by-side among the snowdrop circles.

He lit a cigarette and slumped against a tomb. He saw it all now. The patients had been permanently relocated, and much closer to home than anyone had thought, right under the birches that had terrified little Heinrich. Perhaps he'd had a premonition. Maybe Reichardt had, too, when he'd turned white at that word "relocated." "What have I done?" he kept asking. Had he sensed he'd signed their death warrants? He couldn't have—such a thing was beyond guessing. But he found out somehow. Then he shot himself.

Suddenly, the rotting dead flesh of the birches nauseated Karl and he crashed through the snowdrops, out of the clearing, and went running home. He had an article to rewrite.

The schoolmaster was sipping tea from *Frau* Haar's wedding china when he arrived.

"Karl!" he called cheerfully as Karl made to slip upstairs. "I was about to send out a search party! Come and have some tea. You look frozen."

Karl took a seat by the fire; it would be a comfort to feel warm. The schoolmaster looked pointedly at his boots. "You've been walking, I see."

"Yes. I needed the exercise. I've been lazy lately."

The schoolmaster's cup chinked in his saucer. "Lazy, Karl? A little bird told me you were working all night." He stirred his tea, smiling gently. "*Frau* Haar was concerned, especially when you went out so early this morning, and then went out again without breakfast. Some tea?" He turned to Karl's landlady. "*Frau* Haar, when you're in the kitchen, tell the boys I won't be much longer."

*Frau* Haar left the room, and through the open door, Karl glimpsed three burly brownshirts sitting at the kitchen table. A finger of unease stroked his spine.

"We're on our way to a meeting," the schoolmaster said. "But there was something I wished to discuss with you first."

*Frau* Haar returned with a cup and saucer. Karl beamed warmly at her and gestured at the tray on the table. "You've been baking, *Frau* Haar," he said, "This looks wonderful."

"Then eat," she said coldly as she went out again.

Karl took a piece of *stollen* cake. He had to sit with it in his hand. *Frau* Haar had forgotten to bring him a plate.

"So, Karl. Where did your walk take you?"

"Down by the river."

"Really? Wilhelm says he saw you in the woods."

"Did he? Well, nowhere is very far from the woods around here." Karl bit into his cake, but the icing sugar clogged his tongue like sawdust and he couldn't swallow.

"You look weary, Karl. But, if you will burn the midnight oil—the work must have been very important."

Karl shrugged. "The usual, Ernst. A little Tale from the Village."

"You're too modest, Karl. The chief charm of the Tales is their variety. They dot here and there, into the distant past, the recent past, back to the present, and cover all sorts of subjects on the way. There's no telling what you'll come up with next, except that it will be vivid and interesting. That's a great gift. Come. Indulge me. What is the new Tale?" Karl swallowed hard and looked for somewhere to put his cake, which was growing sticky. He laid it on the embroidered tablecloth. "You'll see when it's published, Ernst."

"This sounds mysterious."

"There's no mystery. It's just that—oh, I can see I'll have no peace until I tell you. But you're spoiling your own surprise."

The schoolmaster's teaspoon clinked cheerfully. "Surprise?"

"Yes. The Tale concerns your calendar of pagan festivals and ancient rites—" The schoolmaster smiled briefly and nudged the leather coat that lay across the arm of his chair. There was an envelope, large and brown and addressed in Karl's handwriting. It should have been well on its way to Berlin by now.

"That was an unworthy lie, Karl." The schoolmaster laid the envelope across his knees. "And a stupid one. The postmaster is a devoted Party member. He helps me keep an eye on things. I have said it before, Karl—you don't take us seriously enough. One cannot put an old head on young shoulders, but someone of your intelligence should have a firm grasp of the realities of life. Your friend, Siggi, is another such, although I fancy he has a firmer grasp now. Don't frown, Karl. We read all your correspondence to and from Berlin." Ernst stared steadily at him through gold-rimmed glasses. "I am glad you found us all so amusing."

There was a short painful pause while the schoolmaster collected himself. He steepled his fingers under his chin and for one hysterical moment, Karl thought he was going to say, "And now if I may move on to matters esoteric," and if he does, he thought, if he does, I'll giggle and won't be able to stop.

But the schoolmaster was concerned with reality today. "Your friend stirred up a furore. He was warned several times. Did you know that? But he was stubborn and wilful and inflamed by the gossip you sent him. Oh, yes, Karl, you bear some responsibility for what has happened." He blinked rapidly. "I hope you will accept that it would grieve me should a similar unpleasantness enter your life. But there's no reason it should, is there? Your friend let emotion overrule his intellect and his own best interests. I fancy that you are not a man of that stamp."

The pause this time was longer and much more painful for Karl. It only ended when he dropped his eyes. The schoolmaster carried on gently. "A young man of your talents has much to offer the Reich, but you do need guidance, Karl." He tapped the envelope on his lap. "This article is what I would have expected from you—angry, full of appeals to popular sentiment. Well, a young man should have heart and feeling—that is to his credit. One would need a heart of stone not to feel for little Heinrich and pretty Elvi. Do you think I have a heart of stone, that I cannot feel?" A sense of grievance pursed Ernst's lips. "I thought you knew me better. If I had no feeling, would I be talking to you now like a father? Now, don't lie to me. You went to the clearing yesterday with Traudl. And you went there again today. May I take it that the secret is no longer a secret?"

Karl's heart lurched and he sat very still, uncomfortably aware of the deep rumble of brownshirts' voices in the kitchen. He pictured a brain like mashed pumpkin and felt the colour and warmth drain from his face. The schoolmaster nodded. "I thought as much. And you came racing home to write about it, full of outrage and popular sentiment." He steepled his fingers again. "Why, Karl, do you think a quiet schoolmaster like me, with some pretensions to culture, is involved with this unsavoury business? You see? I am trusting you. I admit I played my part in it. Do you understand why? These unfortunate creatures are a threat to us all, a virulent bacteria in the bloodstream of the race. Just as a doctor takes drastic action, such as amputating a diseased limb so that the rest of the body may thrive, so we take action against them. Sometimes, Karl, awful things have to be done for the higher good, things that one would shrink from if left to oneself and mere human sentiment." Ernst gazed thoughtfully into the fire. "It takes a brave man and a strong one to recognise that truth, to take action when he bears no malice, to rise above natural inclination and engage with necessity—"

"A merciless moral man?" Karl asked, and thought, my God, he believes all this. He lives according to his nature and calls it philosophy.

"That's what I admire about you, Karl, the apt word, the telling phrase. The Party has need for that talent. You must consider your future. Next week your newspaper is being bought over. In the time you have been writing the Tales, you have touched a chord in thousands of hearts and the Führer himself admires your work. People identify with the noble simplicity of your stories. A thousand texts by our philosophers and scientists could not win us the converts you have."

Something shrivelled in Karl as he listened: he knew he was complicit; knew he could never be a Siggi or a Reichardt; knew he was already considering his future. He loathed the schoolmaster for understanding these things about him.

"It is only because of your potential contribution to the Reich's success that I make time for you now," the schoolmaster said. He held up Karl's envelope and tore it in half. "Look. As a gesture of goodwill, I will destroy this." He tossed the halves on to the fire. "See? All gone. Some things are better left unsaid, unwritten and unread. Now it is your turn to show goodwill. You could write that piece you spoke of—my calendar of festivals and their importance in the Aryan tradition. Do it well enough, and you will make both of our reputations in Berlin."

Karl nodded. The schoolmaster rose and put on his coat. "Good. I shall collect the piece on the way home and post it myself." He turned in the doorway. "By the way, does Traudl know about—?"

Karl shook his head.

"All the same, she remembers more than she should. We must arrange her silence. Don't look so stricken, Karl. Nothing dreadful is going to happen. We shall organise another institution for her, one where no one will listen to her ravings."

Karl decided the wisest course was to believe him. He wrote the article and pulled out all the stops. Ernst's spectacles must be made to mist with emotion.

Traudl waylaid him in the alley the following Sunday night.

"You didn't bring my story."

Karl stared. There appeared to be two Traudls. He had drunk too much again. "*Gnädiges Fräulein*, how nice to see you **again**."

"Did you put it in the papers?"

"Oh, yes, *liebling*, that's what I do. Put things in the papers."

"You didn't read it for me." She was electric with excitement.

"No, I've been busy. But I have it here."

He produced a Party pamphlet Ernst had given him. The front page was devoted to the virtues of euthanasia and its alter ego, mercy. And it listed all the categories of people who would be better off out of their misery.

They were standing under the light that burned at the end of the alley. It was the last lamp before the path turned down to the river and the smothering dark. Karl felt as if he were standing at the edge of the world. Traudl was in her listening pose: head tilted sideways, gaze fixed on the stars above. Her woolly scarf slipped back to show her diamante clasp dazzling in the lamplight. It wouldn't do any good to warn her, he thought, because where could she go?

"The story is on the front page, Traudl." He improvised wildly. " 'The mystery of the disappearance of thousands of mental patients was solved today thanks to the courage and kindness and honesty of a woman named Traudl—' "

Traudl was radiant. He had never seen her smile before; this must be a happy day for her. He gave her his most deathless prose. It would be cruel to short-change her.

# JEFFREY FORD

# The Honeyed Knot

*Jeffrey Ford burst onto the fantasy scene with his extraordinary debut novel,*
The Physiognomy, *a* New York Times Notable Book of the Year *in 1997 and
winner of the World Fantasy Award in 1998. He followed this up with two
equally compelling novels,* Memoranda *and* The Beyond, *as well as short
stories published in* The Northwest Review, The Magazine of Fantasy &
Science Fiction, Event Horizon, Time and Space, *and* The Greeman: Tales
from the Mythic Forest. *A previous story,* "At Raparata," *appeared in* The
Year's Best Fantasy & Horror: Thirteenth Annual Collection.

*Ford lives in Monmouth County, New Jersey, where he has taught Research
Writing, Composition, and Early American Literature at Brookdale
Community College for the past twelve years.* "The Honeyed Knot," *a
marvelous work of contemporary fantasy set on a college campus, is reprinted
from the May issue of* The Magazine of Fantasy & Science Fiction.

—T. W.

About ten years ago I had a student in a composition course I was teaching who, upon my giving the class a writing assignment, raised his hand and, with a monotone voice, asked, "Mr. Ford, what if we don't have any rhymes?" I looked up to see if he was joking, but what I saw was a worn leather jacket, an ageless face, a sinister Dutch-boy haircut and eyes that stared so intently they seemed to be seeing all the way around the world to the back of his own head.

"Don't worry," I said. "We're not writing poetry. Just tell a story."

"But I have no rhymes," he insisted.

He sat there for the entire class and did nothing but stare. I didn't understand his dilemma, but it was college, he was paying, and as long as he wasn't obstreperous, I figured I'd let him sit there and work through it.

After teaching for another ten years, though, his statement eventually became clear to me. Hundreds of students and thousands of papers later, I, too, had begun to feel a conspicuous lack of rhymes. At first, I thought perhaps it was my age. Long gone were the days when the students would mistake me for one of their own. I felt out of touch at work, as if I had been hollowed out and were sleepwalking through my duties. It was eerie, otherworldly, and I had a vague presentiment that it had to do with the residual power of all those papers I'd read and the authors' minds behind them. Make no mistake, words have magic. They are contagious. In delving so deeply into other individuals' writing processes, I had come in contact with secret machinations. I had witnessed inexplicable instances of the uncanny.

I remember one woman who wrote that her husband's ex-wife had placed a Santería spell on her. She was surprised on a particular Sunday morning to find dinner plates of dry rice and human hair positioned at the four corners of the outside of her house. Under the advisement of an aunt, who was also an adept of the mysteries of that religion, she suspended a bowl of water with an egg in it from the ceiling. Three days later, when she broke open the egg, she found it contained a blood spot. This is how she discovered the true nature of the curse. Before finally going to New York and hiring a *bruja* to sacrifice a chicken for her, she met with all manner of accidents and mishaps, some of which I had seen the proof—bruises from her fall down a flight of stairs, her car dented in the parking lot, the aftermath of a fire that had started spontaneously in her pocketbook.

Another young woman, a favorite student of mine, divulged in an essay that she was a witch and, later in the semester as a favor to me, cast a spell to cure some trouble I was having with my vision. The night she worked her magic, she came to class in a pure white outfit, like a child's party dress, and white patent-leather shoes. She never said a word and left before the class was over. Three days later, my sight had improved.

I remember a young African-American student who had traced his lineage, with green crayon on a piece of cardboard, back to Leif Ericsson, the Viking explorer, on one side of his family, and, on the other, to Geronimo. He believed he was constantly being watched by the infrared eyes of satellites. Who was I to tell him he was mistaken? Perhaps even more pathetic was a girl who wrote that she had a disease that caused exotic flowers to grow in her lungs. When I inquired further about it, she said, "Like a garden. When they blossom, I will suffocate to death."

Then there was the meek, bespectacled young man who spoke only in whispers, and ended up raping and murdering a child in his neighborhood during the time he was a student of mine. All of his stories and essays revolved around a dragon named Flamer, and when I saw my student on CNN, manacled and accompanied by two U.S. marshals, I blamed myself for having failed to decipher the obscure symbolism of his tales and ward off the tragedy. That little girl's death haunted me for years.

But the most unnerving incident of my career had to do with a forty-seven-year-old woman with a metal plate in her head. Her story proved to be a prism that focused all the disparate narratives of all of my hundreds of students together into a lesson I will never forget.

Mrs. Apes came to my class in that fall semester so devoid of rhymes I had considered quitting. She was very soft spoken, and although her face was scarred and her hair somewhat spotty in front, she had a look of simple kindness about her that I immediately liked. The other students, all much younger, were at first put off by her questions and encouragements because she was unabashed in her expression of emotion and would touch them lightly on their shoulders when talking to them. By the third class session, though, they were treating her like the mother they wished they had.

Her writings were neither stories nor essays. "Visionary testaments" is the best way I can think to describe them. I hadn't seen anything like them since the dragon stories of that doomed young man, Kevin Wheast. They had no official beginning or ending, and their purpose was elusive. Birds turned into wolves that leaped into the sky to reside in a magical cloud realm where the tears they cried became a rain that washed terror out of lonely children. Deer knew the secrets of creation, crows lived inside men's minds, dogs harbored the souls of dead saints. And the loving spirit Avramody watched over this strange and complex cosmology.

I knew it was best to work with what I was given by the student at first and then try to move on to different things as the semester progressed. She was an atrocious speller, and her sentence structure was, at times, bizarre, as if she were translating from another language. Paragraphing was out of the question. When I would mention these problems to her and possible strategies to overcome them, she would laugh softly and look into the distance as if remembering the amusing antics of a long-dead relative.

Then one day, when I was having a conference with her at my desk at the front of the classroom, I asked her to write a story about some incident that happened in her life. She was silent for some time before blurting out that her husband had brutally beaten her and broken her skull. "The police had to shoot him," she said. "And when they took me to the emergency room, I came out of my body and flew around the hospital, seeing everything. I saw people's true colors, like a glowing ball of light, right here," she said, pointing to her solar plexus. "With each soul I encountered in this form, their color would shoot out a beam at my head. Finally, I met up with a little girl down in the hospital morgue in the basement who called me to her and kissed me between the eyes. She told me to return to my body and that I would live. Now I have the metal up there." And she knocked on her head as if it was a door.

"A metal plate?" I asked her.

She nodded. "My head is a magnet and a beacon. At times it is a bonus, because it allows me to see into situations, to broadcast to the world, but it also makes me forget important things I need to remember."

I knew the worst thing I could do was to dismiss Mrs. Apes's story. It was her reality, and if I wanted to help her with her writing, I had to respect it no matter how incredible it sounded. Still, I had my job to do, so I pressed her a little, hoping to find a focused topic she would be willing to write about.

"What's one of the things you have forgotten?" I asked. "For you to feel that there is something missing from your memory, you must have a vague idea what it entails."

"I had a daughter," she told me. "She was a beautiful girl, as sweet and kind as her father was a monster. Four years ago, two years after I was attacked, when she was fourteen, she was hit by a car while crossing the street in front of her school. She was rushed to the hospital and the doctors worked on her for hours, but she finally died from a traumatic head injury. I almost died from grief myself.

I've always felt I should have seen it coming, should have been there to help her," she said, but her placid expression never diminished.

I looked away from Mrs. Apes for a moment and saw the other students of the class had been listening intently. Their various facades of youthful cynicism and cool had melted, leaving their faces looking like those of a bunch of children watching, for the first time, the squadron of hideous monkeys take wing in *The Wizard of Oz.*

Mrs. Apes continued. "Anyway, my daughter was taken to the same hospital I had been taken to." Here she leaned forward and put her hand on my arm. "Do you know that because of our same last name, the x-ray technician mixed up my head x-rays with hers? When the doctor noticed from the first name that the tech had pulled the wrong pictures, he asked for my daughter's. At one point, he had a copy of each on his desk. That is when he discovered they were identical. The damage, the breaks, the fractures, were a perfect likeness of each other. I mean *perfect.*"

I shook my head.

"Think about it," she said. "I was forty-one when it happened to me and my daughter was fourteen."

"What does it mean?" I asked.

"I'm not sure," she said. "But I believe my visions are leading me to the answer."

"What is it you've forgotten?" I asked.

"My daughter's name," she said. "I can't for the life of me remember her name. I call my sister in California and ask her what my daughter's name was, and she tells me, but before I can write it down I forget it. If I'm not looking at it on a piece of paper, I can't remember. That loss of memory is agony to me."

"Could you write about that?" I asked.

Mrs. Apes turned very somber. "I'll try," she said, "but wait till you see what happens."

I took her vague warning under advisement, and wondered if I had done the right thing by trying to get her to write about something so close to her. I had learned through the years that students who dealt with very personal material could have real breakthroughs in their writing, because, very often, it was the confusion caused by the memories of these events that hampered their ability to express themselves clearly. Stories and essays don't produce themselves, and they aren't born from typing fingers. The reality of a narrative exists first in the mind.

She went back to her computer and started working. I had to address some of the questions and problems of other students, and for a while I paid no attention to her. As I made my rounds of the classroom, checking in with everyone and reading pieces of the projects they were working on, I finally came to Mrs. Apes's workstation. She was not typing but simply staring blankly at the screen. I looked over her shoulder and saw that the monitor was flashing a jumble of letters and symbols that changed with each pulsation. The background color, normally a royal blue, was now pink.

"Wow," I said. "I've never seen that before."

When she laughed the screen went completely blank, and the computer made a sound like it was dying.

"I told you," she said. "It's the plate in my head. Now it's ruined your machine."

"No," I said. "It's probably just a glitch. These machines are used by thousands of students every year. The wear and tear probably did it in. Maybe it contracted a virus along the way."

"If you say so," she said.

"Were you making any progress?" I asked.

She nodded.

"Well, before you forget what you had typed, let's switch you to another machine." I walked over to an empty workstation and got the computer up and running for her.

By the end of the class, Mrs. Apes's metal plate had beamed three machines into uselessness. She was effusively apologetic but kept telling me that she had warned me. She was the last student to leave, and I stopped her and told her not to worry about the machines, that I would have them fixed.

"Thank you, thank you," she said. "You know, I saw in my writing that you'd find a buck in the road."

"Gratuities are unnecessary," I said. "But let's hope it's a hundred."

She smiled at me and left.

Later that afternoon, I had the computer tech take a look at the machines that had gone haywire. He turned them on and they worked perfectly.

"There's nothing wrong with them," he said.

I described what I had seen and explained to him Mrs. Apes's metal-plate theory. He told me it was possible that the plate might have had something to do with it. "There's an electromagnetic field around these machines when they are on, and the body generates its own electromagnetic field. I've never heard of it happening before though. More than likely she didn't want to write and just screwed them up herself when you weren't watching."

I hadn't considered the fact that she might be sabotaging the machines consciously in order not to have to deal with her memories of her daughter. It was an interesting possibility, and it made me decide that during the next class I would have her write about something less personal. If she was going to those lengths to avoid the subject, it might be dangerous to force her to it. I had to remind myself that it was a writing class and not a psych experiment.

That night I had a late class and some time to kill beforehand, so I went over to the library and asked the librarian to do a search for me on the name or word "Avramody." I told her I suspected that it might be from some crackpot religion or cult, maybe the title of one of the myriad mediaeval demons. She promised that she would work on it and let me know if she found anything.

Then I phoned Mrs. Apes's counselor and asked what he knew about her claims of a metal plate in her head. He said she had never told him anything about it. "Look," he told me, "she seems like an ordinary middle-aged woman to me, but sometimes that ordinariness is the problem. It wouldn't be the first time one of our students has invented an interesting past for themselves. She was obviously abused by her husband, maybe she is looking for empowerment through a sense of individuality. She wants to be different and special. Maybe she is reinventing herself now that she is in school. Don't question it too deeply," he said.

My night class let out at 10:30. By the time I got to my car and began the hour and half ride home, it was almost 11:00. Instead of taking the New Jersey Turnpike, which was too fast for me, I always took route 537, a country road that passed through farmland and woods. Just after the midnight news came on the radio, I found my buck.

Weighing about 250 pounds and carrying a ten-point rack, it came charging out of a blind of cattails on the left side of the road. In an instant, I slammed on the brakes, but the car went into a skid, and I helplessly watched as the corner of my station wagon nailed the huge animal in the side. Upon impact the deer bent in toward my windshield and, for a moment, I could clearly see its eye, brimming with animal fear, looking in at me. Then it flew off my car from the force of the collision while at the same time my car stopped. The radio shut off when the car cut out and everything was dead quiet.

I couldn't open the driver-side door because the whole left front of the car was smashed back and out of alignment. Instead, I crawled across the seat and let myself out the passenger side. The buck was writhing on the side of the road, kicking only one of its back legs spasmodically. I was shaking and my mind was blank. The animal craned its neck up out of the pool of blood it lay in and looked back over its shoulder at me. That is when I noticed that one of its lower antler points had grown down and into the side of its jaw. The sight of that anomaly made me wince.

A great rasping sound came up from its chest and turned into high-pitched squeals. It was clear to me that the creature was about to die. "I'm sorry," I said aloud to it. Its cries became weaker and more breathy, and just before it went limp, the buck made a noise through its mouth that sounded distinctly like a human voice uttering a word. I swear I heard it, a word made up of only vowels. I shook my head and backed away. As soon as I crawled back into the car, I got it started, and drove slowly to the Vincent Town Diner, where I called the police to report the mishap. The officer told me he'd send someone out to fetch the animal.

For the rest of the drive home, I was jittery, waiting for something else to come dashing across the road. I prayed the car, which was in very bad shape, wouldn't crap out and leave me stranded in the dark. When I finally pulled into my driveway, I felt like crying. The first thing I did upon entering the house was go upstairs and check on my sons who were fast asleep. Their light, steady breathing diminished the trembling of my hands and put me at ease. My wife was also asleep; I undressed and climbed into bed beside her.

"I hit a deer on the way home," I told her.

"Why?" she asked from sleep.

I didn't bother to wake her. Once I told her about the accident she would be unable to sleep for the rest of the night. I just lay there in the dark, trying to get warm by thinking about a vacation we had taken to the beach the previous summer. My method of relaxation worked quite well, and I was eventually able to doze off. Somewhere in my sleep, I relived the accident, saw the wounded deer, and heard that haunting word composed of vowels. In my dream I told myself, "You've got to remember this word when you wake up." But then the morning had come and I had forgotten.

The accident had left me with a feeling of unreality, as if I had died in it and was now a spirit unaware that he was no longer alive. My wife, who was a nurse, told me to take the day off, and I decided to take the rest of the week off. It was not only that I was afraid of driving again, but more that I didn't want to leave home. I wanted to stay close to my sons for some reason. They were eight and ten, at ages where a hug had to be requested from them, but when I told them what had happened with the deer, they kept hugging me and touching my face.

After my wife left for work and the boys had gone to school, I called the college and explained that my car was wrecked, and I had been slightly hurt; although truthfully there was nothing physically wrong with me. Then I called the garage in town to come and tow the car in for repairs. While I was waiting for the tow truck, I decided to make a pot of coffee. At the kitchen sink, while running water into the pot, I looked out the window into the backyard. There, in broad daylight, I saw a deer drinking out of the birdbath. The sight of it sent a wave of fear through me. I walked to the back door, pulled it open and yelled, "What do you want?" There was nothing there.

I drank my coffee and reasoned that the deer was just a coincidence as we did live in a wooded area very close to the Pine Barrens. Still, a deer sighting in daylight was not a common occurrence. I played music, tried to grade a stack of class papers, watched television, but the entire time I kept trying to remember that word the buck had spoken to me.

That afternoon, when my older son, who rode his bike to school, did not return on time, I felt an ominous reptile uncoiling in my thoughts and I became frantic. I took the younger one, who had been delivered by the bus and, since I didn't have a car, set out on foot to look for his brother. All manner of horrors went through my mind, and don't think I didn't remember what had happened to Mrs. Apes's daughter. I walked so fast my son had to run to keep up.

After walking the length of five long blocks at a breakneck pace, we saw him at a distance coming along on his bike. I was so relieved I laughed out loud. When he reached us he told me that he had stopped with some other kids to see a deer that had come out of the woods by the lake. I told him I had seen the same one in our backyard that morning.

"The one with the weird horn?" he asked.

"What do you mean?" I said.

"It had a weird horn that grew down instead of up."

I told him the one I had seen didn't have antlers.

"Two deer in one day," he said, "good thing your car's in the shop," and then he took off on his bike. "I'll race you guys home," he called back over his shoulder.

I was in a perpetual fog for the next few days, only surfacing when the kids said they were going to do something. Then my mind focused into worry. During these days I must have filled the backs of twenty envelopes with combinations of vowels, trying to reproduce the word that eluded me. Finally, on Monday, I picked up my car at the shop on the way to work. It was a white-knuckle drive that morning even though the sun was bright and the day was beautiful.

When I arrived at work, I found in my mailbox an interoffice envelope from the librarian. Inside was a typed sheet with a yellow Post-It note attached, which said:

Jeff,

Next time, how about something a little easier, like who invented Velcro? Anyway, here's what I found on Avramody. Hope it's what you were looking for.

Jean

I took the sheet back to my office, closed the door, and read it.

Nicholas Avramody, born 1403, died 1441, lived in the village of Fornapp on the southern coast of England. He had been born into a well-to-do family and was given a classical education by his father who was a cartographer. Around the age of twenty, Avramody left home and gave up his part in his father's business. He built himself a small home in the nearby woods and began writing a book that was later published, entitled *The Honeyed Knot*. This work would eventually become a key text for the Puritans, and would figure extensively in the religio-philosophical works of Cotton Mather. The "honeyed knot" was a metaphor for the impossibly complex plot of human existence. For mere mortals, their lives and the reasons for the events in them may seem like a tangled ball of string, but this inexplicable mess is a sweet one because it is the deity's plan for us. Within the knot, all our lives touch and crisscross and bind together for good but unknowable reasons.

This philosopher-hermit eventually fell afoul of the church for another belief of his, namely the fact that animals have souls and given enough patience, one can communicate with them. Creatures all have knowledge of the plan, a knowledge we lost in the Garden of Eden. When the locals started going to him for spiritual guidance, the clergy became jealous and started rumors that he practiced bestiality with the various animals of the forest that flocked around his small home. It so happened at this time that a girl in Fornapp was bitten by a bat, contracted rabies and died. The church fathers told the townspeople that the bat had been sent by Avramody. They incited such fear and contempt of him that he was eventually attacked by an angry mob and cudgeled to death.

With this knowledge still buzzing in my head, I went downstairs to my class only to be met by Mrs. Apes. She handed me a paper and said, "I did it. I finished the piece you asked for." As soon as I was able to get all of the students working on their various projects, I sat down with her at my desk and looked at her writing. The piece had been executed very sloppily in pencil and was about four pages long. I got no further than the title, though, because *there* was the word the buck had spoken to me. I realized now that it did have one consonant, but a soft one that sounds like another vowel when surrounded by vowels.

"Ayuwea?" I said to Mrs. Apes.

She smiled, "My daughter's name."

"It's unusual," I said.

"My mother's mother was half Ojibwa Indian, and I had heard her name from my mother many times, but never saw it spelled. So when I had my daughter, I named her after my grandmother but had to invent the spelling. I knew she would be a special child and needed a special name."

"Does it mean anything?" I asked.

She shook her head and shrugged. "Something, I'm sure," she said.

"I thought you couldn't remember it," I said.

"Well, it was the strangest thing. Last week, after I had tried to write about her in class, I couldn't get her off my mind. Later that night, I was sitting in front of my television and the name just popped into my head. I remembered it just like I had never forgotten it. I'm sure trying to write about her brought the name to me."

So I read Mrs. Apes's paper about her daughter. It was a loving tribute but nothing I hadn't seen from a thousand other students who had lost someone close to them and recorded their feelings and memories in writing. As I had suspected she would, Mrs. Apes had made great strides in her grammar and spelling in that paper, but I never got the chance to continue working with her because she never returned to class after that day. The school had no phone number for her and none of the other students knew her or where she lived.

This is where I thought the story should end. In one way it seemed satisfying that my student had come to some greater understanding of herself. There were loose ends, though, and all of the amazing connections really didn't seem to add up to much. I decided to pass it off as one huge coincidence that I had somehow helped to generate through a bout of paranoia. With each class that came and went, I held out hope that Mrs. Apes would return and I could continue to work with her.

At lunch one day, three weeks after Mrs. Apes's disappearance, I saw a familiar face in the college pizza shop. She was wearing all black but looking exactly the same as when I had last seen her. I took my lunch over to her table and sat down.

"Do you think you could put a spell on this pizza and make it taste better?" I asked.

She looked up at me and shook her head. "It's dangerous to mock powers that are greater than you," said the witch and smiled.

She filled me in on what she had been doing since going on to study at the state university in graduate-level anthropology. I was always happy to hear when my students hadn't opted for a degree in business. On this particular day she had come to the college, which was near her house, to do some research on her thesis, concerning the importance of written language in magic and witchcraft.

"How are your eyes?" she asked.

"I haven't had a problem since," I told her. "It's not my eyes I'm having a problem with now, it's my head."

"Such as?" she asked.

"As a matter of fact," I said, "you'll love this." I proceeded to tell her the entire story of Mrs. Apes in all of its convoluted detail. When I got to the part about the buck I had hit and the word I believed I had heard it speak, she laughed. When I was done, I asked her, "What do you think of that?"

She looked into my eyes and her expression became serious. "You've missed something," she said.

"Like the boat?" I asked.

"It's important," she said.

"I think I was shaken by the incredible synchronicity of the whole thing," I told her.

"Listen," she said, "I'll make you a deal. If you'll read my thesis over before I submit it, I'll look into things for you."

"I'll read your paper anyway," I said, unsure if I wanted any more involvement in the supernatural.

I had to run to class after that, but before I left, she told me she would be in touch.

Weeks passed and although I had learned to keep my uneasiness at bay, it was always there, hovering in the background. At the end of the semester, I had a hard time giving Mrs. Apes an F for the course, but I was required to because she had "phantomed" halfway through the semester. She had definitely learned something, though what it was exactly I wasn't sure.

On the last day, I still had quite a few papers to read before I could make out my grade sheets. I envied all those who had fled in a mass exodus after the final class had let out. The place was as still as a ghost town while I sat in my office reading. Just when I finished and was about to enter the final grades, the phone rang. It was Jean from the library.

"I think we're the only ones left on campus," I said.

"Count me out," she said. "I'm home, but I just remembered something I had meant to tell you."

"Okay," I said.

"I thought I was done with Avramody," she said, "but I found something else."

"What's that?"

"There was a student at the library yesterday, a young woman. She said she was doing research on a paper about vanity for one of your classes. She was rather outlandishly dressed in all white. Said her name was Maggie Hamilton."

I laughed. "I know who you mean," I said, "but her name isn't Margaret Hamilton."

"Well, she had me pull some microfilm for her from the local newspaper. She took it over to the machine, cued up the reel, and started reading through it. When I walked back over there a little later to see if she needed help, she was gone. I left the reel on the machine for a while in case she came back but she didn't. Before I took the reel off, out of curiosity, I glanced at the page she was on and the name Avramody jumped out at me."

"More about the honeyed knot?" I asked.

"Not exactly," she said. "Do you remember about six years ago a student who went to the college here who raped and murdered a little girl?"

I said nothing.

"Hello?" said Jean.

"I'm here," I finally said.

"The little girl's name was Melissa Avramody. I don't know what you can do with that," she said.

"Thanks," I said. "I remember now."

After I hung up, I got out of my chair and paced back and forth in the confines of the office. This pointless journey finally ended at the window that overlooked the empty parking lot. I leaned my forehead against the glass and looked out. The sun had nearly set and twilight was creeping out from the trees of the nature preserve that bounded the asphalt expanse. I saw my car sitting there like a lonely student who has stayed in class long after dismissal. A few seconds later my attention was drawn to something moving in the shadows by the edge of the woods. It stamped its hooves and, startled by the approach of night, turned to show me its rack of bone, one branch growing down into its jaw. At the sight of it, a feeling welled up from deep within me, and my own jaw opened to release a word made only of consonants.

When you are a teacher, you are ever vigilant to instruct, to correct, to lecture, to advise, to care. The residue of this responsibility accumulates around you through time and can serve to make you a poor student. That night in my office, in the last hours of the semester, I passed them all, Kevin Wheast, Melissa Avramody, Mrs. Apes, by setting myself an assignment to stand for those I never received. I did not ask how long it had to be or if I could have an extension but turned on my computer and began typing. Somewhere in all those words, I found the rhymes. Then the final loop of the honeyed knot tightened and drew me back into its jumbled heart.

*I've been a professor of writing and literature for the past twenty-five years, fifteen of that at Brookdale Community College in Lincroft, New Jersey. I know a lot of writers say that they would never want to teach writing for a living because it would deaden them to their own work. That hasn't been my experience. My students' writing has really helped me with my own. The idea for "The Honeyed Knot" was sparked by the fact that I actually did have a student in my class one semester who raped and murdered a little girl in his neighborhood. There was nothing I could have done to prevent it from happening, but for some reason I still felt a measure of responsibility for the tragedy. It haunted me for quite a while and left me cold to teaching for a time—something I had always loved. The story is not a confession, nor an expiation, nor an explanation, but merely an attempt to express what I was feeling about the situation. The strangest thing about it is that, I swear, it's 99.9 percent true.*

*Gordon Van Gelder accepted this story for* The Magazine of Fantasy & Science Fiction *and suggested some changes to certain parts, especially the ending. The story benefited from these changes, but still I was very wary of the piece because of the great emotional connection it had for me. I think Gordon had far more faith in the story than I did. Only when the piece was published and I reread it again in the magazine did I fully allow myself to like it. The process of writing it, editing it, and seeing it published helped me to exorcise some ghosts and reminded me about the importance of my work as a teacher.*

# MICHAEL LIBLING

# Timmy Gobel's Bug Jar

*Michael Libling lives in Montreal with his wife, Pat, a writer of children's books. He has three bright and beautiful daughters and a neurotic mutt named Woody. When he's not writing fiction, he makes his living writing other things. He's been a newspaper columnist, radio talk-show host, speechwriter, and creative director of an ad agency. Most recently, he's put the finishing touches on a new novel.*

*The author says: "The inspiration for 'Timmy Gobel's Bug Jar,' including Timmy and his buddies, can be traced back to the small, rural Ontario town I grew up in. Come summer, bug jars were as common as balls and bats. And more often than not, you never quite knew what you'd find inside once you unscrewed the lid. . . ."*

*The story was first published in* The Magazine of Fantasy & Science Fiction.

—E. D.

Nobody remembers Addison anymore. And not just because so much like misery has passed our way since. No, I blame the Russians. I mean, it was the same day they sent Yuri Gagarin into space, so Addison was pretty much pushed to the back pages. The whole world fell for the diversion. Who wouldn't? It's not like Addison was something anybody wanted to talk about, after all. I can vouch for that firsthand; I've told the whole story only once. But that doesn't mean I don't remember. Every time I turn on Brokaw or pick up a *Sun-Times* or think of my sister, Meggie, I remember. I sure as hell remember.

April 12, 1961. The three of us huddled about that bug jar as if it were a crystal ball, revealing the shape of our respective things to come. And though it was, in fact, neither made of crystal nor imbued with any mystic foresight, it did in its own way portend our futures. At the bottom of the jar, among the carcasses of crickets, grasshoppers and anonymous creepy-crawlies, lay the tiniest of skeletons—a human skeleton, too, so it appeared, though none of us had much of a handle on anatomy.

"Where's the head?" Werner wanted to know. "It doesn't have a friggin' head." Howie Werner. Three seconds on the scene and a total pain-in-the-ass as usual.

"By the moss," Timmy pointed. "It must've rolled away when I took it down." The jar had been sitting on a shelf in Timmy Gobel's shed since the previous summer. "See it? See it?"

"Wow, friggin' tiny, eh?"

"Yeah," said Timmy, "friggin' is right."

I nodded in agreement. I was tall even then, though a lot thinner, and splattered with more freckles than any single kid deserved. But being big didn't make any difference. The skeleton so creeped me out, I could not speak. Nor could I let on. Not with Werner around. If he sensed the slightest weakness, I would never hear the end of it. Still, I could not turn away from the jar.

"Wait a sec!" Werner snorted, eyes bulging like he'd just found the secret to life. "Wait just one friggin' second!" And there it was, that dreaded hee-haw, his lips and gums and teeth screwed up tight like some donkey snout in an overcinched bridle, that grating laugh that just begged to be silenced with a fist to the face. "You got us, Gobe. You got us good, man. So where'd you get it, anyhow? Cracker Jacks? Neat. Real neat."

"No, I swear. I thought that too—that somebody was pulling a fast one on me. Like it broke off a key chain or something. But it's real, I'm sure." Timmy raised his magnifying glass to the jar. It had come with the stamp collecting kit his grandmother had sent for his eleventh birthday, but this was the first time he had used it for anything other than barbecuing ants or branding hockey pads. "Look, around its middle, see. . . ."

I put my eye right up to it and pulled back just as fast; a tad slower and I might well have puked.

"And at the back of the head . . . see . . . see . . . ," Timmy directed.

"Jesus!" Werner didn't look too well himself. "Looks like . . . uh . . ." he gulped, "rotting guts . . . and . . . uh . . . Jesus . . . hair and stuff. . . . What the hell is it, Gobe? You bump off a friggin' leprechaun?"

Timmy shook his head, shrugged.

"Well, I'll tell you one thing, if it's an elf you got lyin' in there, you could be up for murder one, Gobe!" That was the good part about having Werner around—putting up with his crap was inevitably rewarded with his cockeyed take on things. If he wasn't getting on your nerves, Werner made you laugh. And even the slightest sign of approval would cause him to follow through with a litany of adlibbed hits and misses. One could almost hear his brain working, if not his sense of logic. "Or what if some headshrinker from the jungle or somewhere shrunk some guy's body? And then tossed it out of a plane flying over?"

"Huh?"

"Or maybe it's one of those African pygmies. Like in that dumb Tarzan movie."

"Anybody ever tell you you're nuts, Werner?" It was not the first time Timmy had posed the question. "Pygmies are small, but not that small. And headshrinkers? Jesus!"

"Besides," I said, voice barely above a whisper, "wouldn't there be a spear or something in there with him?"

"What if there is? Let's take a closer look. . . ." Werner reached for the jar, but Timmy fended him off.

"Back off, asshole! You'll wreck him up. Look what happened to his head."

"Maybe it didn't roll away," I suggested, every word a chore. "Maybe the grasshopper bit it off."

"Yeah!" Werner cut in. "Maybe you didn't see him, Gobe, 'cause he was *inside* the grasshopper. Maybe the grasshopper had swallowed him whole, just before you caught it."

"Except I don't think grasshoppers eat meat," I corrected, careful not to over-state the point.

"Then maybe it was a costume. Maybe he was dressed up like a grasshopper, you know, for Halloween or whatever?"

"You're saying he was going trick-or-treating, dressed like a grasshopper? Jesus, Werner, even if he could reach the doorbell, he'd no sooner ring it than some jerk would step on him." A moment of silence followed before we realized what Timmy had said. We collapsed onto the grass, aching with laughter.

"Or what . . . what . . . ," Werner howled, ". . . what if they're Martians . . . dressed up like . . . like . . . like friggin' grasshoppers to fool us?"

"It's a friggin' Martian grasshopper invasion!" cried Timmy. "Run! Run for your lives!" He flipped to his feet. "The Martians are coming! The Martians are coming!"

"Yeah," I grinned, "Martians."

It took a long while before we got back on track. Oddly, it was I who broke the silence, an occurrence only slightly less rare than finding a tiny skeleton at the bottom of a bug jar. Eyes riveted to my PF Flyers, heels perpendicular, I spoke softly, tentatively. "What if it's your conscience, Gobe?" I thought for sure we'd all crack up again—me included. I thought for sure I'd come up with one as good as any Werner could muster. But Timmy looked like he'd just been handed a fistful of liver.

"My what?"

"You know, your conscience," I repeated, hoping they'd pick up on my grin. Hell, it was a big grin too. "The little guy inside your head who tells you right from wrong." I swallowed, sighed. It wasn't the first time this had happened; people never seemed to catch on when I was pulling their leg.

"Huh? You mean like in cartoons? Like the little devil who sits on your shoulder?"

"Yeah, sort of, I guess. I was thinking that maybe he fell out of your ear when you were bug hunting or whatever." I was about to tell them I was only kidding, but then Werner jammed his thumbs up into his armpits and began flapping his elbows, squawking saliva into my face.

"Cuckoo! Cuckoo! Cuckoo!" I swatted him away. "Cuckoo! Cuckoo! Cuckoo!"

Timmy scratched his head, weighing the latest theory. "But if I don't have a conscience—I mean, if I've lost mine—and if I've been without one since that guy got stuck in the jar, wouldn't I have been doing a whole bunch of bad things since then? I don't think I have, have I?"

It had come this far, now I felt obliged to take it all the way. "That's just it, Gobe. If this little guy is your conscience, you wouldn't have any way of knowing if you've been doing bad things, because you wouldn't have any conscience to tell you."

"But you guys would know if I was doing bad stuff, 'cause I probably would've done some of it to you—and definitely to Werner. And have I? Have I been doing bad stuff?"

"Oh, yeah," Werner declared, slapping his sides, "tons of it. Robbed a bank. Spray-painted 'fuck you' all over the school. Swiped some cars. Jerked off on Meggie Patterson's boobs—"

"Shut up," I stammered, face red, fingers pressed into fists. I hated when they talked about my sister like that. Heck, I hated when they talked about her at all.

"Jesus, Gobe, you're not really listening to this nut case, are you? This conscience bullshit makes about as much sense as my pygmy."

"Shut up, will ya, Werner? For one friggin' second, just shut the hell up and let me think." Timmy might as well have been talking to the damn wall for all Werner seemed to care. The more you wanted him to clam up, the more he prattled on.

"Well, I can tell you one thing, Gobe, if there's some little guy running around inside my head, telling me what to do, I'm going to get me the biggest damn Q-tip I can find. . . ."

Perhaps it was in the delivery, maybe that's why the three of us were on the grass again, done in by Werner's latest quip. There was just something funny about *the way* Werner said things, not *what* he said.

After that, the theorizing and speculation pretty much withered away. We hit the wall, so to speak. Just plain stumped. Clearly, a higher authority was called for.

"Mr. Schwartz? Or how about Miss Corcoran?" Werner suggested.

Timmy shook his head. "Uh-uh. No teachers." School never did sit too well with Timmy. This was in the days before terms like "learning disability" and "attention deficit disorder" were bandied about—before Ritalin made the menu alongside milk and cookies. So it came down to your basic standoff on pretty much a daily basis; he didn't take to teachers and they didn't take to him. Hell, he didn't take to anyone over the age of twenty. Later, when hippies were warning us to never trust anyone over thirty, I'd often think of Timmy Gobel and how he was so far ahead of his time. "Uh-uh. No friggin' teachers."

That's when I offered up Meggie. Just like that. I hadn't meant to, swear to God. But the words were on my tongue and out of my mouth before I knew what I was saying. "She's really good at science and stuff. Got that scholarship and. . . ."

"Yeah, Meggie," Werner seconded, dancing around like he'd just scored a touchdown. Any excuse to be near Meggie was good enough for him. But to me, his enthusiasm was downright stomach-wrenching.

I was pretty sure that Timmy was excited about the prospect of Meggie too, but he had the good sense to keep his feelings in check. He also saw a downside. "I don't know if Meggie is such a good idea. Then your Mom will find out, and once parents get involved. . . ."

"Yeah," Werner groaned. "They'll mess everything up. That jar is ours."

"Mine," Timmy corrected. "It's my jar."

"Yeah, yeah. Whatever."

"My folks are away until Sunday," I said. "And I don't think Meggie will say a word. My Mom's always complaining how Meggie doesn't tell her anything."

"Yeah, okay then. Meggie it is." That was another thing I picked up about Timmy. He always seemed to worry about coming off looking like a kid in front of Meggie, even if that's what he was compared to her; we were barely into high school, whereas she was almost done. "What if it's just some bug skeleton that looks like a human? What if she thinks we're just being stupid?"

"Bugs don't have skeletons," I assured. "Besides, Gobe, Meggie already thinks we're stupid."

Meggie studied the jar, while Timmy and Werner studied Meggie, her yellow short-shorts, her polka-dot halter, her bare belly, her. . . . *If it came down to Connie Stevens or Meggie Patterson, who'd you choose? What about Debbie Reynolds—her or Meggie Patterson? Between Sandra Dee and Meggie Patterson? Hayley Mills or Meggie Patterson?* The way Timmy Gobel and Howie Werner saw it, it was no contest; Meggie came out on top, fantasy after fantasy. Heck, more than once, I had guys suck up to me just to get close to her. Sometimes I wondered if I would've had any friends at all if my sister weren't so damn pretty.

"So what is it, Meg?" I prodded. I wanted to get them the hell away from her fast.

"Or, more importantly, *who* is it?" Werner anted, working hard to impress.

But Meggie seemed not to hear a word; she brushed past us and set the jar upon the kitchen table. Her magnifying glass was a lot bigger than Timmy's. "Could be any number of things," she speculated quietly. "Extraterrestrial life form. A new species. A genetic mutation. The missing link. . . ."

"Shit. You saying it fell off some guy's friggin' shirtsleeve? Is that what you're saying?"

"Jeez, Werner!" Timmy moaned, hoping to distance himself, in Meggie's eyes, at least. "Not that kind of missing link, you idiot!"

Meggie remained oblivious, the contents of the jar continuing to mesmerize.

Werner blushed. "I knew that. I was just kidding. Cripes! Can't a guy joke around here? Everybody's so friggin' serious all of a sudden. . . ." That was the odd thing about Werner, with girls around, he was never particularly funny.

"It demands closer scrutiny," Meggie announced, primarily to herself. With the jar snugly against her, she marched with great care up the stairs to her bedroom, the three of us at her sandaled heels, me doing my best to obscure my friends' view of my sister's backside.

With Timmy's permission, Meggie tweezered the skull out of the jar and set it under her microscope. She was going to cure cancer some day; that's what she always said, anyhow.

I suggested we go play ball in the park until Meggie was done, but no one took me up on it. The closest Timmy and Werner had ever come to Meggie's bedroom was in their fantasies; they were not about to trade the moment for a game of pitch and catch.

Meggie went to work. First, she put her eye to the lens, then she'd jot down a note, then she'd go back to the lens, make an adjustment or two, and then jot down another note. She spoke only once, to scold Werner for sitting on her bed. "What'd I do?" he whined. "What'd I do?"

We were beginning to worry she might never be done, when she pushed back from the desk and swiveled her chair to face us. Eyebrows raised, blue eyes wide, ponytail bobbing, she shifted her gaze from me to Werner to the owner of the jar. "Tommy, isn't it? Tommy Gobel?"

Timmy nodded eagerly. *Meggie knew his name! Meggie knew his name!* Well, almost, anyhow.

"Now you said you found this where, Tommy?"

"I don't know. I was just going through some junk in our shed, when I came across the old bug jar. Heck, I don't even remember the last time I used it. Ages ago, maybe, I think. I mean, I'm way too old to collect bugs and—" I'd never thought of last summer as *ages ago*, but if that was the way Timmy saw it, I wasn't going to question him. Not in front of Meggie, anyhow.

"And the skeleton was in there, just like that?"

"Yeah. Weird, eh?"

" 'Weird' is a good word, all right. It's the strangest thing," she said, "but I've been observing your find for the last twenty minutes and—well . . . I . . . uh—I think you should see what I see."

Timmy peered into the microscope. "Has it changed or is it just me?"

"Oh, yes," Meggie said, "it has definitely changed."

"Lemme look." Werner pushed through to the microscope. "Holy friggin' cow! Holy friggin' cow!"

"What is it?" I said. "What's going on?"

"See for yourself," my sister urged.

"No. You tell me, Meg. What is it? What's changing?"

"The little man," she said. "I'm not sure how to say it, but it appears he's not decomposing, after all."

"What?" I had no idea what she was talking about.

Timmy swallowed. "We thought he was rotting, right? But that's not it at all, guys. He . . . he's. . . ."

"What the fuh—?"

"Huh?"

Meggie returned to the microscope. "His hair . . . his flesh . . . he's not losing it," she whispered, as if recording notes for future reference. "If anything, he appears to be regenerating."

"You mean like he's growing stuff back?"

"Exactly," Meggie nodded, the weight of the mystery squarely upon her shoulders. "Look, I don't know what we have here, but we'd better tell someone about it."

"Who? Who we gonna tell?" Timmy's defenses shot up around him like a bamboo stockade. "I just knew bringing it here was gonna be a mistake. . . ."

"Relax," Meggie chided. "I was just going to say we bring it to Miss Corcoran, her being a biology teacher and all."

Timmy folded his arms across his chest. "No way. No teachers. And especially not her."

Meggie looked to me for support. "What's his problem?"

Timmy answered for me. "I don't want any grown-ups in on this, okay? They'll just mess everything up."

"But this is serious," Meggie stressed. "I certainly don't know what to make of it. I don't think anybody's ever seen anything like this."

"How do you know?" Timmy fired back. "Maybe they see things like this all the time, and keep it from us. Maybe it's our turn to keep something from them."

"Well, I'm not about to merely sit here with it," Meggie stated firmly. "We are going to have to do something."

"Yeah," Werner cut in. "Let's eat. I'm starved."

I was reaching for my second slice of pizza when I caught the twitch out the corner of my eye. But I couldn't get the words out to tell the others. All I could do was point at the jar, saliva bubbles popping across my lips. Meggie frowned, certain I was just horsing around, but then she saw the twitch too. The skeleton's legs were moving, in slow wavy ripples, like tiny strips of bacon on a frying pan.

"Jesus!"

"Jesus!"

"Holy friggin' shit."

Meggie held her magnifying glass against the jar.

"Is it hatching or something?" Werner asked.

"It's already hatched, idiot," Timmy snapped. "Now we're waiting to see what it turns into."

"Maybe some friggin' butterfly."

"Maybe some loud-mouthed idiot."

"Up yours, Gobel."

"Up yours, Werner."

"My goodness," Meggie gasped. "It's not—not a—not a he."

"Huh?"

"It's a woman," Meggie announced.

"What? A girl?"

"A woman," Meggie repeated. "Your little man appears to be a woman."

"How can you tell?" asked Werner, but we all ignored him.

Meggie scurried back to the microscope. "Let me see if. . . . My God! The head! The head is gone! Where's the head? Where's the head?"

We must have looked quite the sight, leaping about in all directions, but Meggie stopped us cold. "Don't move, you idiots. You'll step on it. Just stay where you are and tell me if you see it."

Heads panned the room. The carpet. The bed. The desk. Dead silence. Except for Timmy, who had suddenly begun to wheeze. If the Heimlich maneuver had been around, surely one of us would have offered to perform it. But in those days, the choking either took care of itself or I guess you simply died.

"You okay?" I called to him. We were all concerned. Well, maybe not Meggie—not entirely; she probably figured he was just horsing around too.

Timmy rapped his chest a few times, coughed, and then shook his head, slapping his face as if there were water in his ear. "I'm okay," he said at last, voice ragged.

"That's what you get for bolting pizza," stated Meggie. "Now if it's all right with the rest of you clowns, I suggest we resume our search."

I spotted it almost immediately. I doubled over, cradling my gut. "Oh, Jesus! I'm going to be sick. It's there," I pointed. "There." The others followed my trembling finger to the jar and the tiny head sitting atop the lid. The now tiny and hairy head.

"Jesus!"

"How in the hell . . . ?"

Timmy grabbed Werner by the collar and parked his knuckles under his friend's chin. "Did you do this, asshole? Did you?"

"Nobody did this," said Meggie. "It did it on its own."

"Huh?"

"I think," she said, "it's trying to pull itself together. . . ."

"Be a good idea if you did the same," Werner cautioned Timmy, breaking free of his grip.

Meggie unscrewed the lid and carefully lowered the head into the jar, releasing it atop the now motionless torso. "I don't care what you say, I am taking this to Miss Corcoran now."

Timmy blocked the door.

"Out of my way, little boy," she ordered.

"Uh-uh."

"This is my house and my bedroom and you will get out of my way."

"Gimme my jar."

"You're not being reasonable, Tommy. You don't seem to understand what we have here. This could make us famous. Do you understand—famous? Maybe even rich."

"Gimme my jar."

Again, Meggie looked to me. "Would you please try to talk some sense into your friend?"

I shrugged. "Maybe you should just give him the jar," I said.

"Great." Meggie rolled her eyes. "Thank you for your help, brother dear. You are such a retard at times. . . ." Timmy saw his opening. He grabbed for the jar, but Meggie spun out of his way and deftly cached the trophy in no man's land—between her breasts. Timmy gawked before her, at a loss as to what to do next. But not Werner. He threw himself from the other side of the room, tackling Timmy waist high. The two of them smashed onto the floor and rolled through what was left of the pizza. They were still picking pepperoni off their shirts before they realized Meggie had made good her escape. By the time we got outside, her green Corvair was tearing round the corner.

"Where does she live?" Timmy demanded.

"My sister?" I thought he'd lost his marbles.

"Corcoran. Corcoran. Where does she live?"

"Oh . . . her. I don't know." I wish to hell I would've shut up then and there, instead of rattling on the way I did. It wasn't like me. Must've been nerves. I chalk it up to nerves. "She's probably still at school. Meggie says she stays real late most days, doing science things or whatever. Meggie's over there with her all the time. Drives my Mom nuts. That's how she got her scholarship. I. . . ." My tongue continued to flap in the breeze even after Timmy had pedaled off on his bike, his legs pumping furiously. I might yet be talking if Werner hadn't interrupted.

"Where the hell is he going?" Werner wondered. "School's the other way."

"Beats me," I said. "Maybe he's going to tell his Dad or something."

"His Dad?" Werner laughed. "Gobe tell his Dad? Yeah, right. Don't hold your breath on that one, pal. Looks to me like he's chickening out."

"Maybe," I said, not buying it for a second.

Werner and I continued on in Meggie's wake to Addison High. We were both curious as to what Miss Corcoran would have to say about the creepy little thing, and that led to fresh speculation. Werner asked if I'd ever seen the movie, *The Incredible Shrinking Man*, where this guy keeps getting smaller and smaller and smaller until he can slip through the holes in a window screen, and we wondered if that same fate hadn't befallen one of Timmy's neighbors, before Timmy scooped him or her into his bug jar. Finally, we decided that it was either a visitor from outer space or a time traveler from the future. How we arrived at these conclusions, I cannot say, but at the time they seemed to be the most logical. The school parking lot and Meggie's Corvair were in view when Werner took our conversation on a whole other tack: "Think your sister might go out with me now—on a date or something?"

"What?"

"You know, seeing how I got Gobe off her back and stuff . . . ?"

"There's a piece of pepperoni on your shoulder," I said.

Schools weren't the armed fortresses they are today. As I recall, Addison High didn't even have locks on the doors. But, I can tell you, the whole scene unfolded as mighty spooky, and not solely because a resurrection in miniature might be waiting for Werner and me up ahead. There's just something sacrilegious about a school after hours. Hollow corridors bled silent. Doomsday lighting, dying fluorescents stuttering overhead. Misshapen shadows on tired linoleum. And every tap, crack, and whisper booming back tenfold from battered lockers.

If Meggie's magnifying glass was big compared to Timmy's, you should have seen Miss Corcoran's. It was like something Jack might have swiped from the giant during one of his forays up the beanstalk. And there she was, looking up from her desk, peering at us through the glass as we shuffled into the classroom, her magnified right eye nailing us to the door. *Jesus! Werner and I must've jumped a mile.* "Yes?" she said, "is there something I can do for you?" Her voice was an ongoing experiment in elocution.

"It's my brother and his friend," Meggie explained.

"Oh, yes. Of course." The biology teacher pretended to recognize us, but her act wasn't overly convincing. "Well, you boys take a seat and be quiet about it. It seems we have quite the mystery on our hands."

Force of habit sent the two of us toward the rear of the room, but Corcoran swiftly added, "Where I can see you, if you don't mind, gentlemen?" We took our places in the first row.

Timmy's bug jar sat on the desk in the middle of Miss Corcoran's ink blotter. The two examined the jar together, Miss Corcoran in her oak swivel, Meggie standing behind and leaning over the teacher's shoulder. "And I'm telling you,"

Meggie noted, "not thirty minutes ago her head was completely detached. Completely."

"Her? It's not exactly a female, dear."

"But she was, Miss. I'm telling you she was. Honest."

"Odd. How very, very odd. And you say it was moving?"

"Just the legs. But only for a moment or two. The head too, I guess. But nobody saw how. One moment it was under my microscope, the next it was sitting on top of the jar."

"Well, the former simply may have been a trompe-l'oeil, dear, while the latter may indeed have a very sound explanation—grounded in mischief, perhaps?" This time, Miss Corcoran lowered her magnifying glass as she looked our way. Werner and I shrugged, our sense of guilt rising under the teacher's glare, despite our absolute innocence. I could hardly believe what she was doing. And I don't think Meggie could believe it either. Here, the teacher had something no one had ever seen before, sitting right on top of her desk, and she was taking time out to accuse Werner and me of mischief! The tension that followed was immediate. Miss Corcoran manipulated silence the way a conductor wields a baton. But the silence didn't last.

"Gimme my jar." How Timmy made his entrance without any of us seeing or hearing I do not know. But from my perspective, he had arrived in the nick of time. "Gimme my jar."

"Well, look what the dog dragged in," declared Miss Corcoran, folding her hands atop the desk, the tips of her pinkies grazing the jar. She glanced at the clock on the wall. "I don't believe I've seen you in school this late since your last detention, Mr. Gobel. Have you come for another?"

"Gimme my jar."

"I suggest you change your tone of voice, young man."

"Gimme my jar."

"In my thirty years of teaching, I have never once tolerated rudeness and you are making a very big mistake, young man, if you suspect that I am about to begin now."

"It's my jar," Timmy said, and from behind his back he pulled a gun. The German Luger his father had brought back from the War. The souvenir.

Meggie gasped, her hand at her mouth, looking to Miss Corcoran for guidance. But the teacher was unswayed—and perhaps severely near-sighted as well. "Now I'm going to say it once and only once, Mr. Gobel. You will turn around, you will quietly go out the door, and you will make yourself very scarce indeed, before you do something the two of us will surely regret."

Timmy pulled the trigger. Behind Miss Corcoran and Meggie, the blackboard exploded, shards of slate crashing to the floor.

"Jesus, Gobe!" Werner cried, as he ducked under the desk. "Are you out of your friggin' mind?"

Was I the only one who noticed? Was the creepy little thing in the jar not standing? Were its arms not above its head at full extension? *Look! Look!* I wanted to shout. *Look! Look! It's watching us.* But I could barely breathe, let alone speak. Timmy pulled the trigger again. Nothing happened. Once more. Again, nothing. He examined the gun and offhandedly placed it on a desk. The worst appeared over, *thank God.*

Miss Corcoran surveyed the damage, her finger wagging eternal damnation. "This is an outrage. Addison High School is no place for miscreants and vandals, Mr. Gobel, and this is indeed vandalism at its most extreme mindlessness. Do you know what it comes down to, Miss Patterson?" Meggie shook her head; she hadn't moved an inch, not even when the blackboard had shattered. "It's breeding. I've said it time and again, it all comes down to breeding."

Timmy turned his back. I relaxed, relieved at the retreat. There was still a chance for him, I thought. At best, I figured, he'd be suspended. At worst, a couple of months up at the boy's farm in Pepperell. But what none of us had noticed was the other item Timmy had brought with him, and left propped in the corner beside the door. He swung the shotgun up and around, leveled the barrels at Miss Corcoran and fired. *Boom! Boom!* Just like that, *Boom! Boom!* The biology teacher and my sister, Meggie, crumpled to the floor behind the desk. The wall where the blackboard had been was covered in blood and God-knows-what-else.

Seeing Meggie fall must have been more than Werner could stomach. He threw off the desk that was his shelter and stumbled to his feet, arms flailing, furniture toppling. "Are you out of your friggin' mind, Gobe? Are you, Gobe? Are you?" And using a chair as a shield, he flung himself at Timmy for the second time that day. Timmy side-stepped the chair, raised the shotgun and caught Werner mid-flight with the butt—the crack of impact at least as loud as the bullet that had struck the blackboard. *Massive head trauma is what they called it. Massive.*

The rest unreels for me as a film strip, one grisly frame of my long safeguarded insanity at a time. Forever distinct and isolated from every other frame.

I stand. I do not know what to do. But I know I cannot continue to do nothing.

Timmy removes the spent shells.

I drag myself to Miss Corcoran's desk. Meggie lies still. Most of Miss Corcoran's upper half is missing. But the jar remains in the middle of the desk, miraculously untouched, save for a smattering of blood about the lid. I remind myself to breathe.

Timmy reloads.

I gather up the jar in both hands and extend this offering to Timmy. His shotgun is pointed at my chest. I should expect to die, but I do not.

"It's mine, Patterson."

"I know, Gobe. Please. Take it." Tears stain my cheeks. I lick my lips, savor the salt.

As Timmy lets the shotgun fall to his side, the lid of the jar in my hand suddenly pops off. On edge, it rolls to Timmy's feet, rattling to a stop against the heel of Werner's sneaker. Our focus shifts to the inside of the jar.

It pulls itself up onto the rim, its face indistinct, its hair—if that's what you can call it—white, almost crystalline, like the frost on last week's ice cream. The skeleton may have once appeared human, but the skin that now contains it seems anything but. It is male. Then female. Then male, again. It is like a rainbow in an oil slick. A silverfish with two arms, two legs and a head. A toy soldier in a tinfoil jumpsuit. I hold it in my hands. I stare directly at it. But I cannot for the life of me establish what it looks like. It's here. And then it's not. It's there. And then it's not.

It turns its head right, then left, raises its tiny arms, bends it knees, then vanishes. I feel it on my fingers. I see it for an instant as it slithers across my palm. I lose it on my wrist. I spot it at my elbow. It is mercury run wild. *Jesus! Fishbait on the lam.* It is on my sleeve. My shoulder. My chin. I try to swat it away. The bug jar smashes to the floor. "Get off! Get off!" It's on my lips, for God's sake. And then it is in my nose. "Help me," I'm crying. "Help me."

And then I don't know where it is. But I do know that I want to hold Timmy's shotgun. I want to hold it very much. I want it like I have never wanted anything before.

Timmy levels the barrels at my head. "No, Patterson," he says. "Uh-uh. I told you, it's mine." He swings for the fences, my head his home run ball.

I go down, but I do not go out. I am whisked to the safety of our kitchen, a plate of fried chicken and mashed potatoes and creamed corn before me, and Meggie complaining to Mommy and Daddy that I am the hardest-headed little brat in all of Addison, if not the country. And an instant later I am returned to Miss Corcoran's biology class. My hands are bleeding, fragments of the bug jar imbedded in my palms.

Timmy is on his knees. The barrels of the shotgun are in his mouth.

I know even then that I will never forget the expression on his face. The fear. The loneliness. The hate—for himself and God-knows-who-or-what-else. *I'm sorry but I just couldn't help myself.* It is the same expression I will see again and again for the rest of my life. Watching Brokaw. Reading the *Sun-Times.* Whenever someone will ask about the scars on my palms. Whenever I will think of Meggie.

I see a flicker at the trigger—*a firefly on dayshift.* And then I don't.

I told them everything I knew. Everything that happened. Well, to be honest, I told them *everything* only once. After the first go-round and their reactions, I had the good sense not to mention that among the carcasses of crickets, grasshoppers and anonymous creepy-crawlies in Timmy Gobel's bug jar lay the tiniest of skeletons, a human skeleton too, so it appeared, though none of us—not Howie Werner, me, or Timmy—had much of a handle on anatomy. Odds are, if I'd stuck to the real version, I would have ended up in a padded cell somewhere upstate. Frankly, for as long as it lasted, I enjoyed playing the hero, being catered to and such, even though I knew damn well I didn't measure up. But I realized early on that most folks tend to be more comfortable with heroes than mere survivors, as long as they're not messed up too badly or shamelessly loony.

The only headline I ever saw was on the front page of the *Addison Weekly Register.*

## STUDENT GUNMAN KILLS THREE, THEN SELF
### Lone survivor describes massacre

But the nurse grabbed the paper away before I got a chance to read the story. Not that I needed to.

Like I said, I blame the Russians for the way it turned out. I mean, if they hadn't sent Yuri Gagarin into space that day, I'll bet you anything the investigation would have taken an entirely different route—and maybe we could have nipped this thing in the bud. This epidemic or whatever. *What did Timmy call it—the Martian grasshopper invasion?* Hell, wouldn't surprise me one damn bit if the Russians were in on it from the start. I mean, if not for their diversion, surely someone would have picked up on the fact that when the shotgun fired, when the back of Timmy Gobel's head blew off, his hands were in his pockets.

Even now, not a day goes by that I'm not certain I have glimpsed it. Not a day goes by that I don't wish it back inside my head.

# MICHAEL CHABON

# The God of Dark Laughter

*Michael Chabon was born in Washington, D.C. in 1963 and grew up in Columbia, Maryland. He is the author of* Werewolves in their Youth, Wonder Boys, A Model World and Other Stories, The Mysteries of Pittsburgh, *and the Pulitzer Prize–winning novel* The Amazing Adventures of Kavalier & Clay. *His short stories have appeared in* The New Yorker, Harper's, GQ, Playboy, *and* Esquire.

*Although Chabon is not generally considered a horror writer or fantasist he has occasionally made forays into Lovecraft country. His story "In the Black Mill" appeared in* The Year's Best Fantasy & Horror: Eleventh Annual Collection.

*"The God of Dark Laughter," another oddly powerful, dark piece, was first published in* The New Yorker.

—E. D., T. W.

Thirteen days after the Entwhistle-Ealing Bros. circus left Ashtown, beating a long retreat toward its winter headquarters in Peru, Indiana, two boys out hunting squirrels in the woods along Portwine Road stumbled on a body that was dressed in a mad suit of purple and orange velour. They found it at the end of a muddy strip of gravel that began, five miles to the west, as Yuggogheny County Road 22A. Another half mile farther to the east and it would have been left to my colleagues over in Fayette County to puzzle out the question of who had shot the man and skinned his head from chin to crown and clavicle to clavicle, taking ears, eyelids, lips, and scalp in a single grisly flap, like the cupped husk of a peeled orange. My name is Edward D. Satterlee, and for the last twelve years I have faithfully served Yuggogheny County as its district attorney, in cases that have all too often run to the outrageous and bizarre. I make the following report in no confidence that it, or I, will be believed, and beg the reader to consider this, at least in part, my letter of resignation.

The boys who found the body were themselves fresh from several hours' worth of bloody amusement with long knives and dead squirrels, and at first the investigating officers took them for the perpetrators of the crime. There was blood on the boys' cuffs, their shirttails, and the bills of their gray twill caps.

But the county detectives and I quickly moved beyond Joey Matuszak and Frankie Corro. For all their familiarity with gristle and sinew and the bright-purple discovered interior of a body, the boys had come into the station looking pale and bewildered, and we found ample evidence at the crime scene of their having lost the contents of their stomachs when confronted with the corpse.

Now, I have every intention of setting down the facts of this case as I understand and experienced them, without fear of the reader's doubting them (or my own sanity), but I see no point in mentioning any further *anatomical* details of the crime, except to say that our coroner, Dr. Sauer, though he labored at the problem with a sad fervor, was hard put to establish conclusively that the victim had been dead before his killer went to work on him with a very long, very sharp knife.

The dead man, as I have already mentioned, was attired in a curious suit—the trousers and jacket of threadbare purple velour, the waistcoat bright orange, the whole thing patched with outsized squares of fabric cut from a variety of loudly clashing plaids. It was on account of the patches, along with the victim's cracked and split-soled shoes and a certain undeniable shabbiness in the stuff of the suit, that the primary detective—a man not apt to see deeper than the outermost wrapper of the world (we do not attract, I must confess, the finest police talent in this doleful little corner of western Pennsylvania)—had already figured the victim for a vagrant, albeit one with extraordinarily big feet.

"Those cannot possibly be his real shoes, Ganz, you idiot," I gently suggested. The call, patched through to my boarding house from that gruesome clearing in the woods, had interrupted my supper, which by a grim coincidence had been a Brunswick stew (the specialty of my Virginia-born landlady) of pork and *squirrel*. "They're supposed to make you laugh."

"They *are* pretty funny," said Ganz. "Come to think of it." Detective John Ganz was a large-boned fellow, upholstered in a layer of ruddy flesh. He breathed through his mouth, and walked with a tall man's defeated stoop, and five times a day he took out his comb and ritually plastered his thinning blond hair to the top of his head with a dime-size dab of Tres Flores.

When I arrived at the clearing, having abandoned my solitary dinner, I found the corpse lying just as the young hunters had come upon it, supine, arms thrown up and to either side of the flayed face in a startled attitude that fuelled the hopes of poor Dr. Sauer that the victim's death by gunshot had preceded his mutilation. Ganz or one of the other investigators had kindly thrown a chamois cloth over the vandalized head. I took enough of a peek beneath it to provide me with everything that I or the reader could possibly need to know about the condition of the head—I will never forget the sight of that monstrous, fleshless grin—and to remark the dead man's unusual choice of cravat. It was a giant, floppy bow tie, white with orange and purple polka dots.

"Damn you, Ganz," I said, though I was not in truth addressing the poor fellow, who, I knew, would not be able to answer my question anytime soon. "What's a dead clown doing in my woods?"

We found no wallet on the corpse, nor any kind of identifying objects. My men, along with the better part of the Ashtown Police Department, went over and over the woods east of town, hourly widening the radius of their search. That day, when not attending to my other duties (I was then in the process of breaking up the Dushnyk cigarette-smuggling ring), I managed to work my way back along a chain of inferences to the Entwhistle-Ealing Bros. Circus, which, as I eventually recalled, had recently stayed on the eastern outskirts of Ashtown, at the fringe of the woods where the body was found.

The following day, I succeeded in reaching the circus's general manager, a man named Onheuser, at their winter headquarters in Peru. He informed me over the phone that the company had left Pennsylvania and was now en route to Peru, and I asked him if he had received any reports from the road manager of a clown's having suddenly gone missing.

"Missing?" he said. I wished that I could see his face, for I thought I heard the flatted note of something false in his tone. Perhaps he was merely nervous about talking to a county district attorney. The Entwhistle-Ealing Bros. Circus was a mangy affair, by all accounts, and probably no stranger to pursuit by officers of the court. "Why, I don't believe so, no."

I explained to him that a man who gave every indication of having once been a circus clown had turned up dead in a pinewood outside Ashtown, Pennsylvania.

"Oh, no," Onheuser said. "I truly hope he wasn't one of mine, Mr. Satterlee."

"Is it possible you might have left one of your clowns behind, Mr. Onheuser?"

"Clowns are special people," Onheuser replied, sounding a touch on the defensive. "They love their work, but sometimes it can get to be a little, well, too much for them." It developed that Mr. Onheuser had, in his younger days, performed as a clown, under the name of Mr. Wingo, in the circus of which he was now the general manager. "It's not unusual for a clown to drop out for a little while, cool his heels, you know, in some town where he can get a few months of well-earned rest. It isn't *common*, I wouldn't say, but it's not unusual. I will wire my road manager—they're in Canton, Ohio—and see what I can find out."

I gathered, reading between the lines, that clowns were high-strung types, and not above going off on the occasional bender. This poor fellow had probably jumped ship here two weeks ago, holing up somewhere with a case of rye, only to run afoul of a very nasty person, possibly one who harbored no great love of clowns. In fact, I had an odd feeling, nothing more than a hunch, really, that the ordinary citizens of Ashtown and its environs were safe, even though the killer was still at large. Once more, I picked up a slip of paper that I had tucked into my desk blotter that morning. It was something that Dr. Sauer had clipped from his files and passed along to me. *Coulrophobia: morbid, irrational fear of or aversion to clowns.*

"Er, listen, Mr. Satterlee," Onheuser went on. "I hope you won't mind my asking. That is, I hope it's not a, well, a confidential police matter, or something of the sort. But I know that when I do get through to them, out in Canton, they're going to want to know."

I guessed, somehow, what he was about to ask me. I could hear the prickling fear behind his curiosity, the note of dread in his voice. I waited him out.

"Did they—was there any—how did he die?"

"He was shot," I said, for the moment supplying only the least interesting part of the answer, tugging on that loose thread of fear. "In the head."

"And there was . . . forgive me. No . . . no harm done? To the body? Other than the gunshot wound, I mean to say."

"Well, yes, his head *was* rather savagely mutilated," I said brightly. "Is that what you mean to say?"

"Ah! No, no, I don't—"

"The killer or killers removed all the skin from the cranium. It was very skillfully done. Now, suppose you tell me what you know about it."

There was another pause, and a stream of agitated electrons burbled along between us.

"I don't know anything, Mr. District Attorney. I'm sorry. I really must go now. I'll wire you when I have some—"

The line went dead. He was so keen to hang up on me that he could not even wait to finish his sentence. I got up and went to the shelf where, in recent months, I had taken to keeping a bottle of whiskey tucked behind my bust of Daniel Webster. Carrying the bottle and a dusty glass back to my desk, I sat down and tried to reconcile myself to the thought that I was confronted—not, alas, for the first time in my tenure as chief law-enforcement officer of Yuggogheny County—with a crime whose explanation was going to involve not the usual amalgam of stupidity, meanness, and singularly poor judgment but the incalculable intentions of a being who was genuinely evil. What disheartened me was not that I viewed a crime committed out of the promptings of an evil nature as inherently less liable to solution than the misdeeds of the foolish, the unlucky, or the habitually cruel. On the contrary, evil often expresses itself through refreshingly discernible patterns, through schedules and syllogisms. But the presence of evil, once scented, tends to bring out all that is most irrational and uncontrollable in the public imagination. It is a catalyst for pea-brained theories, gimcrack scholarship, and the credulous cosmologies of hysteria.

At that moment, there was a knock on the door to my office, and Detective Ganz came in. At one time I would have tried to hide the glass of whiskey, behind the typewriter or the photo of my wife and son, but now it did not seem to be worth the effort. I was not fooling anyone. Ganz took note of the glass in my hand with a raised eyebrow and a school-marmish pursing of his lips.

"Well?" I said. There had been a brief period, following my son's death and the subsequent suicide of my dear wife, Mary, when I had indulged the pitying regard of my staff. I now found that I regretted having shown such weakness. "What is it, then? Has something turned up?"

"A cave," Ganz said. "The poor bastard was living in a cave."

The range of low hills and hollows separating lower Yuggogheny from Fayette County is rotten with caves. For many years, when I was a boy, a man named Colonel Earnshawe operated penny tours of the iridescent organ pipes and jagged stone teeth of Neighborsburg Caverns, before they collapsed in the mysterious earthquake of 1919, killing the Colonel and his sister Irene, and putting to rest many strange rumors about that eccentric old pair. My childhood friends and I, ranging in the woods, would from time to time come upon the root-choked mouth of a cave exhaling its cool plutonic breath, and dare one another to leave the sunshine and enter that world of shadow—that entrance, as it always seemed to me, to the legendary past itself, where the bones of Indians and Frenchmen might lie moldering. It was in one of these anterooms of buried history that the beam of a flashlight, wielded by a deputy sheriff from Plunkettsburg, had struck the silvery lip of a can of pork and beans. Calling to his companions, the deputy plunged through a curtain of spiderweb and found himself in the parlor, bedroom, and kitchen of the dead man. There were some cans of chili and hash, a Primus stove, a lantern, a bedroll, a mess kit, and an old Colt revolver, Army issue, loaded and apparently not fired for some time. And there were also books—a Scout guide to roughing it, a collected Blake, and a couple of odd texts, elderly and tattered: one in German called "Über das Finstere Lachen," by a man named Friedrich von Junzt, which appeared to be religious or philosophical in nature, and one a small volume bound in black leather and printed in no alphabet known to me, the letters sinuous and furred with wild diacritical marks.

"Pretty heavy reading for a clown," Ganz said.

"It's not all rubber chickens and hosing each other down with seltzer bottles, Jack."

"Oh, no?"

"No, sir. Clowns have unsuspected depths."

"I'm starting to get that impression, sir."

Propped against the straightest wall of the cave, just beside the lantern, there was a large mirror, still bearing the bent clasps and sheared bolts that had once, I inferred, held it to the wall of a filling-station men's room. At its foot was the item that had earlier confirmed to Detective Ganz—and now confirmed to me as I went to inspect it—the recent habitation of the cave by a painted circus clown: a large, padlocked wooden makeup kit, of heavy and rather elaborate construction. I directed Ganz to send for a Pittsburgh criminalist who had served us with discretion in the horrific Primm case, reminding him that nothing must be touched until this Mr. Espy and his black bag of dusts and luminous powders arrived.

The air in the cave had a sharp, briny tinge; beneath it there was a stale animal musk that reminded me, absurdly, of the smell inside a circus tent.

"Why was he living in a cave?" I said to Ganz. "We have a perfectly nice hotel in town."

"Maybe he was broke."

"Or maybe he thought that a hotel was the first place they would look for him."

Ganz looked confused, and a little annoyed, as if he thought I were being deliberately mysterious.

"*Who* was looking for him?"

"I don't know, Detective. Maybe no one. I'm just thinking out loud."

Impatience marred Ganz's fair, bland features. He could tell that I was in the grip of a hunch, and hunches were always among the first considerations ruled out by the procedural practices of Detective John Ganz. My hunches had, admittedly, an uneven record. In the Primm business, one had very nearly got both Ganz and me killed. As for the wayward hunch about my mother's old crony Thaddeus Craven and the strength of his will to quit drinking—I suppose I shall regret indulging that one for the rest of my life.

"If you'll excuse me, Jack . . ." I said. "I'm having a bit of a hard time with the stench in here."

"I was thinking he might have been keeping a pig." Ganz inclined his head to one side and gave an empirical sniff. "It smells like pig to me."

I covered my mouth and hurried outside into the cool, dank pinewood. I gathered in great lungfuls of air. The nausea passed, and I filled my pipe, walking up and down outside the mouth of the cave and trying to connect this new discovery to my talk with the circus man, Onheuser. Clearly, he had suspected that this clown might have met with a grisly end. Not only that, he had known that his fellow circus people would fear the very same thing—as if there were some coulrophobic madman with a knife who was as much a part of circus lore as the prohibition on whistling in the dressing room or on looking over your shoulder when you marched in the circus parade.

I got my pipe lit, and wandered down into the woods, toward the clearing where the boys had stumbled over the dead man, following a rough trail that the police had found. Really, it was not a trail so much as an impromptu alley of broken saplings and trampled ground that wound a convoluted course down the hill from the cave to the clearing. It appeared to have been blazed a few days before by the victim and his pursuer; near the bottom, where the trees gave way to open sky, there were grooves of plowed earth that corresponded neatly with encrustations on the heels of the clown's giant brogues. The killer must have caught the clown at the edge of the clearing, and then dragged him along by the hair, or by the collar of his shirt, for the last twenty-five yards, leaving this furrowed record of the panicked, slipping flight of the clown. The presumed killer's footprints were everywhere in evidence, and appeared to have been made by a pair of long and pointed boots. But the really puzzling thing was a third set of prints, which Ganz had noticed and mentioned to me, scattered here and there along the cold black mud of the path. They seemed to have been made by a barefoot child of eight or nine years. And damned, as Ganz had concluded his report to me, if that barefoot child did not appear to have been dancing!

I came into the clearing, a little short of breath, and stood listening to the wind in the pines and the distant rumble of the state highway, until my pipe went out. It was a cool afternoon, but the sky had been blue all day and the woods were peaceful and fragrant. Nevertheless, I was conscious of a mounting sense of disquiet as I stood over the bed of sodden leaves where the body had been found. I did not then, nor do I now, believe in ghosts, but as the sun dipped down behind the tops of the trees, lengthening the long shadows encompassing me, I became aware of an irresistible feeling that somebody was watching me. After a moment, the feeling intensified, and localized, as it were, so I was certain that to see who it was I need only turn around. Bravely—meaning not that I am a brave man but that I behaved as if I were—I took my matches from my jacket pocket and relit my pipe. Then I turned. I knew that when I glanced behind me I would not see Jack Ganz or one of the other policemen standing there; any of them would have said something to me by now. No, it was either going to be nothing at all or something that I could not even allow myself to imagine.

It was, in fact, a baboon, crouching on its hind legs in the middle of the trail, regarding me with close-set orange eyes, one hand cupped at its side. It had great puffed whiskers and a long canine snout. There was something in the barrel chest and the muttonchop sideburns that led me to conclude, correctly, as it turned out, that the specimen was male. For all his majestic bulk, the old fellow presented a rather sad spectacle. His fur was matted and caked with mud, and a sticky coating of pine needles clung to his feet. The expression in his eyes was unsettlingly forlorn, almost pleading, I would have said, and in his mute gaze I imagined I detected a hint of outraged dignity. This might, of course, have been due to the hat he was wearing. It was conical, particolored with orange and purple lozenges, and ornamented at the tip with a bright-orange pompom. Tied under his chin with a length of black ribbon, it hung from the side of his head at a humorous angle. I myself might have been tempted to kill the man who had tied it to my head.

"Was it you?" I said, thinking of Poe's story of the rampaging orang swinging a razor in a Parisian apartment. Had that story had any basis in fact? Could the dead clown have been killed by the pet or sidekick with whom, as the mystery of the animal smell in the cave now resolved itself, he had shared his fugitive existence?

The baboon declined to answer my question. After a moment, though, he raised his long crooked left arm and gestured vaguely toward his belly. The import of this message was unmistakable, and thus I had the answer to my question—if he could not open a can of franks and beans, he would not have been able to perform that awful surgery on his owner or partner.

"All right, old boy," I said. "Let's get you something to eat." I took a step toward him, watching for signs that he might bolt or, worse, throw himself at me. But he sat, looking miserable, clenching something in his right paw. I crossed the distance between us. His rancid-hair smell was unbearable. "You need a bath, don't you?" I spoke, by reflex, as if I were talking to somebody's tired old dog. "Were you and your friend in the habit of bathing together? Were you there when it happened, old boy? Any idea who did it?"

The animal gazed up at me, its eyes kindled with that luminous and sagacious sorrow that lends to the faces of apes and mandrills an air of cousinly reproach, as if we humans have betrayed the principles of our kind. Tentatively, I reached out to him with one hand. He grasped my fingers in his dry leather paw, and then the next instant he had leapt bodily into my arms, like a child seeking solace. The garbage-and-skunk stench of him burned my nose. I gagged and stumbled backward as the baboon scrambled to wrap his arms and legs around me. I must have cried out; a moment later a pair of iron lids seemed to slam against my skull, and the animal went slack, sliding, with a horrible, human sigh of disappointment, to the ground at my feet.

Ganz and two Ashtown policemen came running over and dragged the dead baboon away from me.

"He wasn't—he was just—" I was too outraged to form a coherent expression of my anger. "You could have hit *me!*"

Ganz closed the animal's eyes, and laid its arms out at its sides. The right paw was still clenched in a shaggy fist. Ganz, not without some difficulty, managed to pry it open. He uttered an unprintable oath.

In the baboon's palm lay a human finger. Ganz and I looked at each other, wordlessly confirming that the dead clown had been in possession of a full complement of digits.

"See that Espy gets that finger," I said. "Maybe we can find out whose it was."

"It's a woman's," Ganz said. "Look at that nail."

I took it from him, holding it by the chewed and bloody end so as not to dislodge any evidence that might be trapped under the long nail. Though rigid, it was strangely warm, perhaps from having spent a few days in the vengeful grip of the animal who had claimed it from his master's murderer. It appeared to be an index finger, with a manicured, pointed nail nearly three-quarters of an inch long. I shook my head.

"It isn't painted," I said. "Not even varnished. How many women wear their nails like that?"

"Maybe the paint rubbed off," one of the policemen suggested.

"Maybe," I said. I knelt on the ground beside the body of the baboon. There was, I noted, a wound on the back of his neck, long and deep and crusted over with dirt and dried blood. I now saw him in my mind's eye, dancing like a barefoot child around the murderer and the victim as they struggled down the path to the clearing. It would take a powerful man to fight such an animal off. "I can't believe you killed our only witness, Detective Ganz. The poor bastard was just giving me a hug."

This information seemed to amuse Ganz nearly as much as it puzzled him.

"He was a monkey, sir," Ganz said. "I doubt he—"

"He could make signs, you fool! He told me he was *hungry*."

Ganz blinked, trying, I supposed, to append to his personal operations manual this evidence of the potential usefulness of circus apes to police inquiries.

"If I had a dozen baboons like that one on my staff," I said, "I would never have to leave the office."

That evening, before going home, I stopped by the evidence room in the High Street annex and signed out the two books that had been found in the cave that morning. As I walked back into the corridor, I thought I detected an odd odor— odd, at any rate, for that dull expanse of linoleum and buzzing fluorescent tubes—of the sea: a sharp, salty, briny smell. I decided that it must be some new disinfectant being used by the custodian, but it reminded me of the smell of blood from the specimen bags and sealed containers in the evidence room. I turned the lock on the room's door and slipped the books, in their waxy protective envelopes, into my briefcase, and walked down High Street to Dennistoun Road, where the public library was. It stayed open late on Wednesday nights, and I would need a German-English dictionary if my college German and I were going to get anywhere with Herr von Junzt.

The librarian, Lucy Brand, returned my greeting with the circumspect air of one who hopes to be rewarded for her forbearance with a wealth of juicy tidbits. Word of the murder, denuded of most of the relevant details, had made the Ashtown *Ambler* yesterday morning, and though I had cautioned the unlucky young squirrel hunters against talking about the case, already conjectures, misprisions, and outright lies had begun wildly to coalesce; I knew the temper of my home town well enough to realize that if I did not close this case soon things might get out of hand. Ashtown, as the events surrounding the appearance of the so-called Green Man, in 1932, amply demonstrated, has a lamentable tendency toward municipal panic.

Having secured a copy of Köhler's Dictionary of the English and German Languages, I went, on an impulse, to the card catalogue and looked up von Junzt, Friedrich. There was no card for any work by this author—hardly surprising, perhaps, in a small-town library like ours. I returned to the reference shelf, and consulted an encyclopedia of philosophical biography and comparable volumes of philologic reference, but found no entry for any von Junzt—a diplomate, by the testimony of his title page, of the University of Tübingen and of the Sorbonne. It seemed that von Junzt had been dismissed, or expunged, from the dusty memory of his discipline.

It was as I was closing the Encyclopedia of Archaeo-Anthropological Research that a name suddenly leapt out at me, catching my eye just before the pages slammed together. It was a word that I had noticed in von Junzt's book: "Urartu." I barely managed to slip the edge of my thumb into the encyclopedia to mark the place; half a second later and the reference might have been lost to me. As it turned out, the name of von Junzt itself was also contained—sealed up—in the sarcophagus of this entry, a long and tedious one devoted to the work of an Oxford man by the name of St. Dennis T. R. Gladfellow, "a noted scholar," as the entry had it, "in the field of inquiry into the beliefs of the ancient, largely unknown peoples referred to conjecturally today as proto-Urartians." The reference lay buried in a column dense with comparisons among various bits of obsidian and broken bronze:

> G.'s analysis of the meaning of such ceremonial blades admittedly was aided by the earlier discoveries of Friedrich von Junzt, at the site of the former Temple of Yrrh, in north central Armenia, among them certain sacrificial artifacts pertaining to the worship of the proto-Urartian deity Yê-Heh, rather grandly (though regrettably without credible evidence) styled "the god of dark or mocking laughter" by the German, a notorious adventurer and fake whose work, nevertheless, in this instance, has managed to prove useful to science.

The prospect of spending the evening in the company of Herr von Junzt began to seem even less appealing. One of the most tedious human beings I have ever known was my own mother, who, early in my childhood, fell under the spell of Madame Blavatsky and her followers and proceeded to weary my youth and deplete my patrimony with her devotion to that indigestible caseation of balderdash and lies. Mother drew a number of local simpletons into her orbit, among them poor old drunken Thaddeus Craven, and burnt them up as thoroughly as the earth's atmosphere consumes asteroids. The most satisfying episodes of my career have been those which afforded me the opportunity to prosecute charlatans and frauds and those who preyed on the credulous; I did not now relish the thought of sitting at home with such a man all evening, in particular one who spoke only German.

Nevertheless, I could not ignore the undeniable novelty of a murdered circus clown who was familiar with scholarship—however spurious or misguided—concerning the religious beliefs of proto-Urartians. I carried the Köhler's over to the counter, where Lucy Brand waited eagerly for me to spill some small ration of beans. When I offered nothing for her delectation, she finally spoke.

"Was he a German?" she said, showing unaccustomed boldness, it seemed to me.

"Was *who* a German, my dear Miss Brand?"

"The victim." She lowered her voice to a textbook librarian's whisper, though there was no one in the building but old Bob Spherakis, asleep and snoring in the periodicals room over a copy of *Grit*.

"I—I don't know," I said, taken aback by the simplicity of her inference, or rather by its having escaped me. "I suppose he may have been, yes."

She slid the book across the counter toward me.

"There was another one of them in here this afternoon," she said. "At least, I think he was a German. A Jew, come to think of it. Somehow he managed to find the only book in Hebrew we have in our collection. It's one of the books old Mr. Vorzeichen donated when he died. A prayer book, I think it is. Tiny little thing. Black leather."

This information ought to have struck a chord in my memory, of course, but it did not. I settled my hat on my head, bid Miss Brand good night, and walked slowly home, with the dictionary under my arm, and, in my briefcase, von Junzt's stout tome and the little black-leather volume filled with sinuous mysterious script.

I will not tax the reader with an account of my struggles with Köhler's dictionary and the thorny bramble of von Junzt's overheated German prose. Suffice to say that it took me the better part of the evening to make my way through the introduction. It was well past midnight by the time I arrived at the first chapter, and nearing two o'clock before I had amassed the information that I will now pass along to the reader, with no endorsement beyond the testimony of these pages, nor any hope of its being believed.

It was a blustery night; I sat in the study on the top floor of my old house's round tower, listening to the windows rattle in their casements, as if a gang of intruders were seeking a way in. In this high room, in 1885, it was said, Howard Ash, the last living descendant of our town's founder, General Hannaniah Ash, had sealed the blank note of his life and dispatched himself, with postage due, to his Creator. A fugitive draft blew from time to time across my desk and stirred the pages of the dictionary by my left hand. I felt, as I read, as if the whole world were asleep—benighted, ignorant, and dreaming—while I had been left to man the crow's nest, standing lonely vigil in the teeth of a storm that was blowing in from a tropic of dread.

According to the scholar or charlatan Friedrich von Junzt, the regions around what is now northern Armenia had spawned, along with an entire cosmology, two competing cults of incalculable antiquity, which survived to the present day: that of Yê-Heh, the God of Dark Laughter, and that of Ai, the God of Unbearable and Ubiquitous Sorrow. The Yê-Hehists viewed the universe as a cosmic hoax, perpetrated by the father-god Yrrh for unknowable purposes: a place of calamity and cruel irony so overwhelming that the only possible response was a malevolent laughter like that, presumably, of Yrrh himself. The laughing followers of baboon-headed Yê-Heh created a sacred burlesque, mentioned by

Pausanias and by one of the travellers in Plutarch's dialogue "On the Passing of the Oracles," to express their mockery of life, death, and all human aspirations. The rite involved the flaying of a human head, severed from the shoulders of one who had died in battle or in the course of some other supposedly exalted endeavor. The clown-priest would don the bloodless mask and then dance, making a public travesty of the noble dead. Through generations of inbreeding, the worshippers of Yê-Heh had evolved into a virtual subspecies of humanity, characterized by distended grins and skin as white as chalk. Von Junzt even claimed that the tradition of painted circus clowns derived from the clumsy imitation, by noninitiates, of these ancient kooks.

The "immemorial foes" of the baboon boys, as the reader may have surmised, were the followers of Ai, the God Who Mourns. These gloomy fanatics saw the world as no less horrifying and cruel than did their archenemies, but their response to the whole mess was a more or less permanent wailing. Over the long millennia since the heyday of ancient Urartu, the Aiites had developed a complicated physical discipline, a sort of jujitsu or calisthenics of murder, which they chiefly employed in a ruthless hunt of followers of Yê-Heh. For they believed that Yrrh, the Absent One, the Silent Devisor who, an eternity ago, tossed the cosmos over his shoulder like a sheet of fish wrap and wandered away leaving not a clue as to his intentions, would not return to explain the meaning of his inexplicable and tragic creation until the progeny of Yê-Heh, along with all copies of the Yê-Hehist sacred book, "Khndzut Dzul," or "The Unfathomable Ruse," had been expunged from the face of the earth. Only then would Yrrh return from his primeval hiatus—"bringing what new horror or redemption," as the German intoned, "none can say."

All this struck me as a gamier variety of the same loony, Zoroastrian plonk that my mother had spent her life decanting, and I might have been inclined to set the whole business aside and leave the case to be swept under the administrative rug by Jack Ganz had it not been for the words with which Herr von Junzt concluded the second chapter of his tedious work:

> While the Yê-Hehist gospel of cynicism and ridicule has, quite obviously, spread around the world, the cult itself has largely died out, in part through the predations of foes and in part through chronic health problems brought about by inbreeding. Today [von Junzt's book carried a date of 1849] it is reported that there may be fewer than 150 of the Yê-Hehists left in the world. They have survived, for the most part, by taking on work in travelling circuses. While their existence is known to ordinary members of the circus world, their secret has, by and large, been kept. And in the sideshows they have gone to ground, awaiting the tread outside the wagon, the shadow on the tent-flap, the cruel knife that will, in a mockery of their own long-abandoned ritual of mockery, deprive them of the lily-white flesh of their skulls.

Here I put down the book, my hands trembling from fatigue, and took up the other one, printed in an unknown tongue. "The Unfathomable Ruse"? I hardly thought so; I was inclined to give as little credit as I reasonably could to Herr von Junzt's account. More than likely the small black volume was some inspirational text in the mother tongue of the dead man, a translation of the

Gospels, perhaps. And yet I must confess that there were a few tangential points in von Junzt's account that caused me some misgiving.

There was a scrape then just outside my window, as if a finger with a very long nail were being drawn almost lovingly along the glass. But the finger turned out to be one of the branches of a fine old horse-chestnut tree that stood outside the tower, scratching at the window in the wind. I was relieved and humiliated. Time to go to bed, I said to myself. Before I turned in, I went to the shelf and moved to one side the bust of Galen that I had inherited from my father, a country doctor. I took a quick snort of good Tennessee whiskey, a taste for which I had also inherited from the old man. Thus emboldened, I went over to the desk and picked up the books. To be frank, I would have preferred to leave them there—I would have preferred to burn them, to be really frank—but I felt that it was my duty to keep them about me while they were under my watch. So I slept with the books beneath my pillow, in their wax envelopes, and I had the worst dream of my life.

It was one of those dreams where you are a fly on the wall, a phantom bystander, disembodied, unable to speak or intervene. In it, I was treated to the spectacle of a man whose young son was going to die. The man lived in a corner of the world where, from time to time, evil seemed to bubble up from the rusty red earth like a black combustible compound of ancient things long dead. And yet, year after year, this man met each new outburst of horror, true to his code, with nothing but law books, statutes, and county ordinances, as if sheltering with only a sheet of newspaper those he had sworn to protect, insisting that the steaming black geyser pouring down on them was nothing but a light spring rain. That vision started me laughing, but the cream of the jest came when, seized by a spasm of forgiveness toward his late, mad mother, the man decided not to prosecute one of her old paramours, a rummy by the name of Craven, for driving under the influence. Shortly thereafter, Craven steered his old Hudson Terraplane the wrong way down a one-way street, where it encountered, with appropriate cartoon sound effects, an oncoming bicycle ridden by the man's heedless, darling, wildly pedalling son. That was the funniest thing of all, funnier than the amusing ironies of the man's profession, than his furtive drinking and his wordless, solitary suppers, funnier even than his having been widowed by suicide: the joke of a father's outliving his boy. It was so funny that, watching this ridiculous man in my dream, I could not catch my breath for laughing. I laughed so hard that my eyes popped from their sockets, and my smile stretched until it broke my aching jaw. I laughed until the husk of my head burst like a pod and fell away, and my skull and brains went floating off into the sky, white dandelion fluff, a cloud of fairy parasols.

Around four o'clock in the morning, I woke and was conscious of someone in the room with me. There was an unmistakable tang of the sea in the air. My eyesight is poor and it took me a while to make him out in the darkness, though he was standing just beside my bed, with his long thin arm snaked under my pillow, creeping around. I lay perfectly still, aware of the tips of this slender shadow's fingernails and the scrape of his scaly knuckles, as he rifled the contents of my head and absconded with them through the bedroom window, which was somehow also the mouth of the Neighborsburg Caverns, with tiny old Colonel Earnshaw taking tickets in the booth.

I awakened now in truth, and reached immediately under the pillow. The books were still there. I returned them to the evidence room at eight o'clock this morning. At nine, there was a call from Dolores and Victor Abbott, at their motor lodge out on the Plunkettsburg Pike. A guest had made an abrupt departure, leaving a mess. I got into a car with Ganz and we drove out to get a look. The Ashtown police were already there, going over the buildings and grounds of the Vista Dolores Lodge. The bathroom wastebasket of Room 201 was overflowing with blood-soaked bandages. There was evidence that the guest had been keeping some kind of live bird in the room; one of the neighboring guests reported that it had sounded like a crow. And over the whole room there hung a salt smell that I recognized immediately, a smell that some compared to the smell of the ocean, and others to that of blood. When the pillow, wringing wet, was sent up to Pittsburgh for analysis by Mr. Espy, it was found to have been saturated with human tears.

When I returned from court, late this afternoon, there was a message from Dr. Sauer. He had completed his postmortem and wondered if I would drop by. I took the bottle from behind Daniel Webster and headed on down to the county morgue.

"He was already dead, the poor son of a biscuit eater," Dr. Sauer said, looking less morose than he had the last time we spoke. Sauer was a gaunt old Methodist who avoided strong language but never, so long as I had known him, strong drink. I poured us each a tumbler, and then a second. "It took me a while to establish it because there was something about the fellow that I was missing."

"What was that?"

"Well, I'm reasonably sure that he was a hemophiliac. So my reckoning time of death by coagulation of the blood was all thrown off."

"Hemophilia," I said.

"Yes," Dr. Sauer said. "It is associated sometimes with inbreeding, as in the case of royal families of Europe."

*Inbreeding.* We stood there for a while, looking at the sad bulk of the dead man under the sheet.

"I also found a tattoo," Dr. Sauer added. "The head of a grinning baboon. On his left forearm. Oh, and one other thing. He suffered from some kind of vitiligo. There are white patches on his nape and throat."

Let the record show that the contents of the victim's makeup kit, when it was inventoried, included cold cream, rouge, red greasepaint, a powder puff, some brushes, cotton swabs, and five cans of foundation in a tint the label described as "Olive Male." There was no trace, however, of the white greasepaint with which clowns daub their grinning faces.

Here I conclude my report, and with it my tenure as district attorney for this blighted and unfortunate county. I have staked my career—my life itself—on the things I could see, on the stories I could credit, and on the eventual vindication, when the book was closed, of the reasonable and skeptical approach. In the face of twenty-five years of bloodshed, mayhem, criminality, and the universal human pastime of ruination, I have clung fiercely to Occam's razor, seeking always to keep my solutions unadorned and free of conjecture, and never to resort to conspiracy or any kind of prosecutorial woolgathering. My mother, whenever she was confronted by calamity or personal sorrow, invoked cosmic emanations, invisible empires, ancient prophecies, and intrigues; it has been the business of my life to reject such folderol and seek the simpler explanation. But we were fools, she and I, arrant blockheads, each of us blind to or heedless of the readiest explanation: that the world is an ungettable joke, and our human need to explain its wonders and horrors, our appalling genius for devising such explanations, is nothing more than the rim shot that accompanies the punch line.

I do not know if that nameless clown was the last, but in any case, with such pursuers, there can be few of his kind left. And if there is any truth in the grim doctrine of those hunters, then the return of our father Yrrh, with his inscrutable intentions, cannot be far off. But I fear that, in spite of their efforts over the last ten thousand years, the followers of Ai are going to be gravely disappointed when, at the end of all we know and everything we have ever lost or imagined, the rafters of the world are shaken by a single, a terrible guffaw.

# KURT LELAND

# The Adolescence of Orpheus

*"The Adolescence of Orpheus"* concerns the great musician of classical myth, best known for his journey to the underworld to rescue his wife, Eurydice, from death. This tour-de-force of contemporary mythic poetry comes from the Spring 2001 issue of The Beloit Poetry Journal.

Kurt Leland has published poetry in many venues, including Cottonwood, Stand, and The Christian Science Monitor. His work was honored with the 1993 Chad Walsh Award from The Beloit Poetry Journal. His long poem "Enemies" (about healing the rift between Germany and the United States caused by the Second World War) was published as a chapbook in Heidelberg, Germany; he is also the author of two books of speculative metaphysics.

About the following poem, the author writes: "In addition to being a poet I've trained for years as a classical musician—so I was speaking from experience when I wrote about how much practicing Orpheus has to do. Ancient Greek sources say that there really was a Musaios, although they disagree about whether he was a disciple of Orpheus or the latter's son. In 'The Adolescence of Orpheus' I've tried to clarify the point for scholars."

—T. W.

Fatherless, surrounded by women, with
the blood of his gift building the body
to house it, his mother, the Poem, said:
*Boy, even if everyone knows your myth,*
*it hasn't begun yet. That means you're free*
*awhile, before that trip down to the dead.*

*Your aunts and I think this home-schooling thing*
*goes only so far. We want to send you*
*down-mountain to socialize. I know what*
*you'll say—humans just aren't as amusing*
*as we are, and their horses can't fly. But who*
*better to teach you pain—not the mere cut.*

*or bruise: the kind that catches a god's ears*
*and might even bend them. You'll need that pain*
*or no one will listen—and the story*
*will be told of someone else, all those years*
*of practice wasted. Remember, the main*
*thing is not to disappoint History—*

*or I'll never hear the end of her*
*at-table I-told-you-sos.* So off he went
with no argument (hadn't she taught him
poetry *was* argument?—in other
words, he knew better that to argue meant
he'd have to know better words. He was slim,

handsome, a boy of fifteen with a tip-
to-toe tan. At first he slept on the loam
by the river, improvising each day.
A young man named Musaios heard him rip
through his riffs, asked: Would he mind coming home
to supper, his folks—would he sing, would he stay?

Well, he had to live somewhere, why not with
an angry old man who could vote, his wife,
the picture of badly aged vanity
and sudden miraculous kindness. The myth
would certainly forgive him if his life
stagnated awhile in the backcountry

as orphan, ephebe, and erstwhile elder
brother to a gangly, giggling tomboy
and budding herpetologist by the name
of Eurydice. It was no small matter
to keep his divinity secret. Ploy
after ploy was required so that his fame

rested merely on tireless practice. How,
after all, could he criticize the men
in masks trying to impersonate gods
in voices whose volume was meant to cow
the crowd and maintain concentration,
but couldn't prevent occasional nods?

Only he knew that the simplest word breathed
by his peers would thrill human nerves beyond
willfulness, fill them with service, command.
And the plays ridiculous dancing, wreathed
in smokes—Aunt Terpsichore was hardly fond
of their *To the right, stand to the left, stand . . .*

and all that murmuring that made it so hard
to keep count of anything complicated.
He liked small off-stage parts, though. One time—
*brek-kek-kek, koax, koax*—the poor bard
wanted frogs. Orpheus simply waited
till everyone else was on stage, said a rhyme

Pan had taught him for summoning what beast
he wished, and filled the outdoor theatre
with loud leaping green lumps of slime. Comic
beyond words, the piece was a hit—not least
for frog-happy Eurydice. Whether
anyone suspected the mantic

origins of this so-called coincidence,
its romantic impact had a certain
result—though not yet for Eurydice.
The only member of the audience
who saw him do it was her brother. Smitten
by the same charm that had drawn the frogs, he

obsessively followed the boy, listened
endless hours to his playing. Meanwhile,
Orpheus, in the cot beside him, would wake
from nightmares in which a half moon glistened
on a river, a rapt singer, the smile
on each face of several loves who would take

some part of him away, until only
the head remained, still singing, the passion
and sweetness of its song slowly dying
into discourse and dry philosophy.
When he screamed the whole household would run
to his aid—"Mom," Eurydice, stroking

his hands, the old man's *When I was his age. . . .*
He'd calm down, they'd leave, and then came the cure.
Musaios would discuss with him music
and painting, the "magic" arts of the stage,
would hold him and teach him a pleasure
no muse had yet hinted at. Athletic

training had accustomed him to naked
bodies in the gymnasium's plain air.
What they felt like in darkness made that world
a child's. But the best was lying in bed
afterwards, nose on his friend's neck, hair
in his hand, and the deep breathing that swirled

them both into sleep. He couldn't stay long
after that. He knew he'd forget where he

came from, not want to return. When he strode
back up to the Pierian Spring, the song
sung for his mother was surprisingly
sad. That was it: parting. His new abode

had worked its way through him like an illness.
Home—*either* place now—was where he was not.
Everything seen seemed like tarnishing brass.
His aunts cringed at the dissonance distress
pulled from the lyre. Even Apollo thought
his risks were ungodly extreme, the crass

noise of mortality the best human
singers tried to eliminate, and the worst
divinities would never fall prey to.
Orpheus left them, angry, confused. When
he got back to his step-family's in a burst
of speed and emotion, five years had passed. Mu-

saios was crazed from his absence. What he
tearfully told chilled Orpheus to the core—
how their home had been hit by disaster:
parents dead in a fire, Eurydice
safe with an uncle, the men called to war.
They embraced, found a place on the road where

they'd stay for the night. By dawn Musaios
had risen and drowned himself in the same
river they'd met by. The outcry of the ox-
drivers who found him was loud—and so close
that Orpheus reached them in minutes, a name
on his lips, and clasped his lover's wet locks

to his breast: *Why did he do it? Would no*
*kiss ever satisfy after a god's?*
*Or did fate or my myth make Musaios*
*irrelevant, our love a teenage show*
*of defiance? No, we weren't such clods,*
thought Orpheus. *We did just what Eros*

*demanded.* The corpse was placed on the bed
where they'd slept. All that day and the next he played,
the lyre in his bloodless white hands. He tore
at the strings, eyes closed so the tears he'd shed
would be pure pitches, unstrangled—afraid
at first of his dead love and loved ones. The more

grief entered his song, the closer they came:
He could feel their reach through the sinewed strings
each time the flesh of his fingertips struck.
They were there behind his eyelids—so tame

and obedient, with the large clipped wings
of their well-rehearsed pasts, or with luck

new flights imagination might lend them.
That was the meaning of music: late loves,
to bring them so close, bound in chords like sheaves
with an undertone to tie them and stem
the flow of tears—see, they scatter like doves
when the eyes come open or the chest heaves.

The myth began. He wed Eurydice,
had a son—Musaios—played endlessly,
was at home jamming just when his wife's field
studies turned deadly. Out hunting snakes, she
was grabbed from behind, fought free, turned to flee—
and dropped what she'd caught. It bit her. She reeled,

was dead when Orpheus found her. *No more
loss*, he thought. Was he god enough to raise
the dead? Poem, argument—he'd wield his
pain like both weapon and prayer. If the door
to Hell could be found and passed through, he'd praise
all of its powers and craze them—he'd quiz

even its king till his fingers bled. Art
made all of creation storm up in his strums.
Mad with grief, lost in his own music's long
maze, he failed: There's no Hades but the heart.
Nothing that has ever gone in there comes
out as itself—if at all, as a song.

# CHARLES DE LINT

# Trading Hearts at the Half Kaffe Café

Canadian author Charles de Lint has received the World Fantasy Award for his distinctive brand of mythic fiction, exploring mythological themes in a contemporary urban context. De Lint is best known for his interconnected stories set in the imaginary city of Newford, a place where indigenous North American myths collide with the tales and spirits brought here by various immigrant groups.

His Newford series includes the novels Memory and Dream, Forests of the Heart, *and* The Onion Girl, *and the story collections* Dreams Underfoot, The Ivory and the Horn, Moonlight and Vines, *and* Tapping the Dream Tree *(forthcoming). De Lint lives in Ottawa, Ontario, with his wife, artist MaryAnn Harris.*

*"Trading Hearts at the Half Kaffe Café" is an entertaining tale with darkness at its heart, rooted in traditional folklore. The story is reprinted from* Single White Vampire Seeks Same, *an anthology edited by Martin H. Greenberg and Brittiany A. Koren (DAW Books).*

— T. W.

**CHERISH EACH DAY**
Single male, professional, 30ish,
wants more out of life. Likes the
outdoors, animals. Seeking single
female with similar attributes and
aspirations. Ad# 6592

The problem is expectations.

We all buy so heavily into how we hope things will turn out, how society and our friends say it should be, that by the time we actually have a date, we're locked into those particular hopes and expectations and miss everything that could be. We end up stumbling our way through the forest, never seeing all the unexpected and wonderful possibilities and potentials because we're looking for the idea of a tree, instead of appreciating the actual trees in front of us.

At least that's the way it seems to me.

## Mona

"You already tried that dress on," Sue told me.

"With these shoes?"

Sue nodded. "As well as the red boots."

"And?"

"It's not a first-date dress," Sue said. "Unless you wear it with the green boots and that black jacket with the braided cuffs. And you don't take the jacket off."

"Too much cleavage?"

"It's not a matter of cleavage, so much as the cleavage combined with those little spaghetti straps. You're just so *there*. And it's pretty short."

I checked my reflection. She was right, of course. I looked a bit like a tart, and not in a good way. At least Sue had managed to tame my usually unruly hair so that it looked as though it had an actual style instead of the head topped with blonde spikes I normally saw looking back at me from the mirror.

"But the boots would definitely punk it up a little," Sue said. "You know, so it's not quite so 'come hither.' "

"This is hopeless," I said. "How late is it?"

Sue smiled. "Twenty minutes to showtime."

"Oh god. And I haven't even started on my make-up."

"With that dress and those heels, he won't be looking at your make-up."

"Wonderful."

I don't know how I'd gotten talked into this in the first place. Two years without a steady boyfriend, I guess, though by that criteria it should *still* have been Sue agonizing over what to wear and me lending the moral support. She's been much longer without a steady. Mind you, after Pete moved out, the longest relationship I'd been in was with this grotty little troll of a dwarf, and you had to lose points for that. Not that Nacky Wilde had been boyfriend material, but he *had* moved in on me for a few weeks.

"I think you should wear your lucky dress," Sue said.

"I met Pete in that dress."

"True. But only the ending was bad. You had a lot of good times together, too."

"I suppose . . ."

Sue grinned at me. "Eighteen minutes and counting."

"Will you stop with the Cape Canaveral bit already?"

## Lyle

"Just don't do the teeth thing and you'll be all right," Tyrone said.

"Teeth thing? What teeth thing?"

"You know, how when you get nervous, your teeth start to protrude like your muzzle's pushing out and you're about to shift your skin. It's not so pretty."

"Thanks for adding to the tension," I told him. "Now I've got that to worry about as well."

I stepped closer to the mirror and ran a finger across my teeth. Were they already pushing out?

"I don't even know why you're going through all of this," Tyrone said.

"I want to meet someone normal."

"You mean not like us."

"I mean someone who isn't as jaded as we are. Someone with a conventional lifespan for whom each day is important. And I know I'm not going to meet her when the clans gather, or in some bar."

Tyrone shook his head. "I still think it's like dating barnyard animals. Or getting a pet."

"Whatever made you so bitter?"

But Tyrone only grinned. "Just remember what mama said. Don't eat a girl on the first date."

## Mona

"Now don't forget," Sue said. "Build yourself up a little."

"You mean lie."

"Of course not. Well, not a lot. And it might help if you don't seem quite so bohemian right off the bat."

"Pete liked it."

Sue nodded. "And see where that got you. The bohemian artist type has this mysterious allure, especially to straight guys, but it wears off. So you have to show you have the corporate chops as well."

I had to laugh.

"I'm being serious here," Sue said.

"So who am I supposed to be?" I asked.

Sue started to tick the items off on her fingers. "Okay. To start with, you can't go wrong just getting him to talk about himself. You know, act sort of shy and listen a lot."

"I *am* shy."

"When it does come to what you do, don't bring up the fact that you write and draw a comic book for a living. Make it more like art's a hobby. Focus on the fact that you're involved in the publishing field—editing, proofing, book design. Everybody says they like bold and mysterious women, but the truth is, most of them like them from a distance. They like to dream about them. Actually having them sitting at a table with them is way too scary."

Sue had been reading a book on dating called *The Rules* recently, and she was full of all sorts of advice on how to make a relationship work. Maybe that was how they did it in the fifties, but it all seemed so demeaning to me entering the twenty-first century. I thought we'd come farther than that.

"In other words, lie," I repeated and turned back to the mirror to finish applying my mascara.

I couldn't remember the last time I'd worn any. On some other date gone awry, I supposed, then I mentally corrected myself. I should be more positive.

"Think of it as bending the truth," Sue said. "It's not like you're going to be pretending forever. It's just a little bit of manipulation for that all-important first impression. Once he realizes he likes you, he won't mind when it turns out you're this little boho comic book gal."

"Your uptown roots are showing," I told her.

"You know what I mean."

Unfortunately, I did. Everybody wanted to seem normal and to meet somebody normal, so first dates became these rather strained, staged affairs with both of you hoping that none of your little hang-ups and oddities were hanging out like an errant shirt-tail or a drooping slip.

"Ready?" Sue asked.

"No."

"Well, it's time to go anyway."

## Lyle

"So what are you going to tell her you do for a living?" Tyrone asked as we walked to the café. "The old hunter/gatherer line?"

"Which worked real well in Cro-Magnon times."

"Hey, some things never change."

"Like you."

Tyrone shrugged. "What can I say? If it works, don't fix it."

We stopped in front of The Half Kaffe. It was five minutes to.

"I'm of half a mind to sit in a corner," Tyrone said. "Just to see how things work out."

"You got the half a mind part right."

Tyrone shook his head with mock sadness. "Sometimes I find it hard to believe we came from the same litter," he said, then grinned.

When he reached over to straighten my tie, I gave him a little push to move him on his way.

"Give 'em hell," he told me. "Girl doesn't like you, she's not worth knowing."

"So now you've got a high opinion of me."

"Hey, you may be feeble-minded, but you're still my brother. That makes you prime."

I had to return that smile of his. Tyrone was just so . . . Tyrone. Always the wolf.

He headed off down the block before I could give him another shove. I checked my teeth in the reflection of the window—still normal—then opened the door and went inside.

## Mona

We were ten minutes late pulling up in front of The Half Kaffe.

"This is good," Sue said as I opened my door. "It doesn't make you look too eager."

"Another one of the 'Rules'?"

"Probably."

"Only probably?"

"Well, it's not like I've memorized them or done that well with them myself. You're the one with the date tonight."

I cut her some slack. If push came to shove, I knew she wouldn't take any grief from anyone, no matter what the rule book said.

I got out of the car. "Thanks for the ride, Sue."

"Remember," she said, holding up her phone. Folded up, it wasn't much bigger than a compact. "If things get uncomfortable or just plain weird, I'm only a cellphone call away."

"I'll remember."

I closed the door before she could give me more advice. I'd already decided I was just going to be myself—a dolled-up version of myself, mind you, but it actually felt kind of fun being all dressed up. I just wasn't going to pretend to be someone I wasn't.

Easy to promise to myself on the ride over, listening to Sue, but then my date had to be gorgeous, didn't he? I spotted him as soon as I opened the door, pausing in the threshold.

("I'll be holding a single rose," he'd told me.

("That is so romantic," Sue had said.)

Even with him sitting down, I knew he was tall. He had this shock of blue-black hair, brushed back from his forehead and skin the colour of espresso. He was wearing a suit that reminded me of the sky just as the dusk is fading and the single red rose lay on the table in front of him. He looked up when I came in—if it had been me, I'd have looked up every time the door opened, too—and I could have gone swimming in those dark, dark eyes of his.

I took a steadying breath. Walking over to his table, I held out my hand.

"You must be Lyle," I said. "I'm Mona."

## Lyle

She was cute as a button.

("Here's my prediction," Tyrone had said. "She'll be three-hundred pounds on a five-foot frame. Or ugly as sin. Hell, maybe both."

("I don't care how much she weighs or what she looks like," I told him. "Just so long as she's got a good heart."

(Tyrone smiled. "You're so pathetic," he said.)

And naturally I made a mess of trying to stand up, shake her hand and give her the rose, all at the same time. My chair fell down behind me. The sound of it startled me and I almost pulled her off her feet, but we managed to get it all straightened without anybody getting hurt.

I wanted to check my teeth, and forced myself not to run my tongue over them.

We were here for the obligatory before-dinner drink, having mutually decided earlier on a café rather than a bar, with the unspoken assumption that if things didn't go well here, we could call the dinner off, no hard feelings. After asking what she wanted, I went and got us each a latte.

"Look," she said when I got back. "I know this isn't the way it's supposed to go, first date and everything, but I decided that I'm not going to pretend to be more or different than I am. So here goes.

"I write and draw a comic book for living. I usually have ink stains on my fingers and you're more likely to see me in overalls, or jeans and a T-shirt. I know I told you I like the outdoors like you said you did in your ad, but I've never spent a night outside of a city. I've never had a regular job either, I don't like being anybody's pet boho girlfriend, and I'm way more shy than this is making me sound."

She was blushing as she spoke and looked a little breathless.

"Oh boy," she said. "That was really endearing, wasn't it?"

It actually was, but I didn't think she wanted to hear that. Searching for something to match her candor, I surprised myself as much as her.

"I'm sort of a werewolf myself," I told her.

"A werewolf," she repeated.

I nodded. "But only sort of. Not like in the movies with the full moon and hair sprouting all over my body. I'm just . . . they used to call us skinwalkers."

"Who did?"

I shrugged. "The first people to live here. Like the Kickaha, up on the rez. We're descended from what they call the animal people—the ones that were here when the world was made."

"Immortal wolves," she said.

I was surprised that she was taking this all so calmly. Surprised to be even talking about it in the first place, because it's never a good idea. Maybe Tyrone was right. We weren't supposed to mingle. But it was too late now and I felt I at least owed her a little more explanation.

"Not just wolves, but all kinds of animals," I said. "And we're not immortal. Only the first ones were and there aren't so many of them left anymore."

"And you can all take the shapes of animals."

I shook my head. "Usually it's only the ones who were born in their animal shape. The human genes are so strong that the change is easier. Those born human have some animal tributes, but most of them aren't skinwalkers."

"So if you bite me, I won't become a wolf."

"I don't know where those stories come from," I started, then sighed. "No, that's not true. I do know. These days most of us just like to fit in, live a bit in your world, a bit in the animal world. But it wasn't always like that. There have always been those among us who considered everyone else in the world their private prey. Humans and animals."

"Most of you?"

I sighed again. "There are still some that like to hunt."

## Mona

You're probably wondering why I was listening to all of this without much surprise. But you see, that grotty little dwarf I told you about earlier—the one that moved in on me—did I mention he also had the habit of just disappearing, poof, like magic? One moment you're talking to him, the next you're standing in a seemingly empty room. The disembodied voice was the hardest to get used to. He'd sit around and tell me all kinds of stories like this. You experience something like that on a regular basis and you end up with more tolerance for weirdness.

Not that I actually believed Lyle here was a werewolf. But the fact that he was talking about it actually made him kind of interesting, though I could see it getting old after awhile.

"So," I said. "What do you do when you're not dating human girls and running around as a wolf?"

"Do?"

"You know, to make a living. Or were you born wealthy as well as immortal."

"I'm not immortal."

"So what do you do?"

"I'm . . . an investment counselor."

"Hence the nice suit."

He started to nod, then sighed. When he looked down at his latte, I studied his jaw. It seemed to protrude a little more than I remembered, though I knew that was just my own imagination feeding on all his talk about clans of animals that walk around looking like people.

He lifted his head. "How come you're so calm about all of this?"

I shrugged. "I don't know. I like the way it all fits together, I suppose. You've obviously really thought it all through."

"Or I'm good at remembering the history of the clans."

"That, too. But the question that comes to my mind is, why tell me all of this?"

"I'm still asking myself that," he said. "I guess it came from your saying we should be honest with each other. It feels good to be able to talk about it to someone outside the clans."

He paused, those dark eyes studying me more closely. Oh why couldn't he have just been a normal guy? Why did he have to be either a loony, or some weird faerie creature?

"You don't believe me," he said.

"Well . . ."

"I didn't ask for proof when you were telling me about your comic books."

I couldn't believe this.

"It's hardly the same thing. Besides—"

I got up and fetched one of the freebie copies of *In the City* from their display bin by the door. Flipping almost to the back of the tabloid-sized newspaper, I laid open the page with my weekly strip "Spunky Grrl" on the table in front of him. This was the one where my heroine, the great and brave Spunky Grrl, was answering a personal ad. Write from your life, they always say. I guess that meant that next week's strip would have Spunky sitting in a café with a wolf dressed up as a man.

"It's not so hard to prove," I said, pointing at the by-line.

"Just because you have the same name—"

"Oh, please." I called over to the bar where the owner was reading one of those glossy British music magazines he likes so much. "Who am I, Jonathan?"

He looked up and gave the pair of us a once-over with that perpetually cool and slightly amused look he'd perfected once the café had become a success and he was no longer run ragged trying to keep up with everything.

"Mona Morgan," he said. "Who still owes me that page of original art from 'My Life As A Bird' that featured The Half Kaffe."

"It's coming," I said and turned back to my date. "There. You see? Now it's your turn. Make your hand change into a paw or something."

## Lyle

She was irrepressible and refreshing, but she was also driving me a little crazy and I could feel my teeth pressing up against my lips.

"Maybe some other time," I said.

She smiled. "Right. Never turn into a wolf on the first date."

"Something like that," I replied, remembering Tyrone's advice earlier in the evening. I wondered what she'd make of that, but decided not to find out. Instead I looked down at her comic strip.

It was one of those underground ones, not clean like a regular newspaper strip but with lots of scratchy lines and odd perspectives. There wasn't a joke either, just this wild-looking girl answering a personal ad. I looked up at my date.

"So I'm research?" I asked.

She shrugged. "Everything that happens to me ends up in one strip or another."

I pointed at the character in the strip. "And is this you?"

"Kind of an alter ego."

I could see myself appearing in an upcoming installment, turning into a wolf in the middle of the date. The idea bothered me. I mean, think about it. If you were a skinwalker, would you want the whole world to know it?

I lifted my gaze from the strip. This smart-looking woman bore no resemblance to her scruffy pen and ink alter ego.

"So who cleaned you up?" I asked.

I know the idea of showing up in her strip was troubling me, but that was still no excuse for what I'd just said. I regretted the words as soon as they spilled out of my mouth.

The hurt in her eyes was quickly replaced with anger. "A *human* being," she said and stood up.

I started to stand as well. "Look, I'm sorry—" I began but I was already talking to her back.

"You owe me for the lattes!" the barman called as I went to follow her.

I paid him and hurried outside, but she was already gone. Slowly I went back inside and stood at our table. I looked at the rose and the open paper. After a moment, I folded up the paper and went back outside. I left the rose there on the table.

I could've tracked her—the scent was still strong—but I went home instead to the apartment Tyrone and I were sharing. He wasn't back yet from wherever he'd gone tonight, which was just as well. I wasn't looking forward to telling him about how the evening had gone. Changing from my suit to jeans and a jersey, I sat down on the sofa and opened my copy of *In the City* to Mona's strip. I was still staring at the scruffy little blonde cartoon girl when the phone rang.

## Mona

As soon as I got outside, I made a quick bee-line down the alley that runs alongside the café, my boots clomping on the pavement. I didn't slow down until I got to the next street and had turned onto it. I didn't bother looking for a phonebooth. I knew Sue would pick me up, but I needed some down time first and it wasn't that long a walk back home. Misery's supposed to love company, but the way I was feeling it was still too immediate to share. For now, I needed to be alone.

I suppose I kind of deserved what he'd said—I had been acting all punky and pushing at him. But after awhile the animal people business had started to wear thin, feeling more like an excuse not to have a real conversation with me rather than fun. And then he'd been just plain mean.

Sue was going to love my report on tonight's fiasco. Not.

I'm normally pretty good about walking about on my own at night—not fearless like my friend Jilly, but I'm usually only going from my local subway stop or walking down well-frequented streets. Tonight, though . . .

The streets in this neighbourhood were quiet, and it was still relatively early, barely nine, but I couldn't shake the uneasy feeling that someone was following me. You know that prickle you can get at the nape of your neck—some leftover survival instinct from when we'd just climbed down the from the trees, I guess. A monkey buzz.

I kept looking back the way I'd come—expecting to see Mr. Wolf Man skulking about a block or so behind me—but there was never anybody there. It wasn't until I was on my own block and almost home that I saw the dog. Some kind of big husky, it seemed, from the glance I got before it slipped behind a parked car. Except its tail didn't go up in that trademark curl.

I kept walking towards my door, backwards, so that I could look down the street. The dog stuck its head out twice, ducking back when it saw me watching. The second time I bolted for my apartment, charged up the steps and onto the porch. I had my keys out, but I was so rattled, it took me a few moments to get the proper one in the lock. It didn't help that I spent more time staring down the street than at what I was doing. But I finally got the key in, unlocked the door, and was inside, closing and locking the door quickly behind me.

I leaned against the wall to catch my breath, positioned so that my gaze could go down the street. I didn't see the dog. But I did see a man, standing there in the general area of where the dog had been. He was looking down the street in my direction and I ducked back from the window. It was too far away to make out his features, but I could guess who he was.

This was what I'd been afraid of when I'd first seen the dog: That it wasn't a dog. That it was a wolf. That Mr. Wolf Man really *could* become a wolf and now he'd turned into Stalker Freak Man.

I was thinking in capitals like my superhero character Rocket Grrl always did when she was confronting evil doers like Can't Commit Man. Except I wasn't likely to go out and fight the good fight like she always was. I was more the hide-under-the-bed kind of person.

But I was kind of mad now.

I watched until the man turned away, then hurried up the stairs to my apartment. Once I was inside, I made sure the deadbolt was engaged. Ditto the lock on the window that led out onto the fire escape. I peered down at the street from behind the safety of the curtains in my living room, but saw no one out there.

I changed and paced around the apartment for awhile before I finally went into the kitchen and punched in Mr. Wolf Man's phone number. I lit into him the minute he answered.

"Maybe you think it's a big joke, following me home like that, but I didn't appreciate it."

"But I—" he started.

"And maybe you can turn into a wolf or a dog or whatever, or maybe you just have one trained to follow people, but I think it's horrible either way, and I just want you to know that we have an anti-stalking law in this city, and if I ever see you hanging around again, I'm going to phone the police."

Then I hung up.

I was hoping I'd feel better, but I just felt horrible instead. The thing is, I'd found myself sort of liking him before he got all rude and then did the stalking bit.

I guess I should have called Sue at this point, but it was still too freshly depressing to talk about. Instead I made myself some toast and tea, then went and sat in the living room, peeking through the curtains every couple of minutes to make sure there was no one out there. It was a miserable way to spend an evening that had held the potential of being so much more.

## Lyle

I hung up the phone feeling totally confused. What had she been talking about? But by the time Tyrone got home, I thought I had a clue.

"Did you follow her home?" I asked.

He just looked confused. "Follow who home?"

"My date."

"Why would I do that?"

"Because we got into a fight, and you're always stepping in to protect me or set people straight when you think they've treated me badly."

I could see that look come into his eyes—confirming my feelings, I thought, until he spoke.

"Your date went bad?" he asked.

"It went horribly—but you already know that."

Tyrone sighed. "I was nowhere near the café, or wherever you guys went after."

"We didn't have time to go anywhere after," I said, and then I told him about how the evening had gone.

"Let's see if I've got this straight," Tyrone said. "She tells you she likes to dress casually and draws comics for a living, so you tell her you're a skinwalker."

"We were sharing intimacies."

"Sounds more like lunacies on your part. What were you thinking?"

I sighed. "I don't know. I liked her. I liked the fact that she didn't want to start off with any B.S."

Tyrone shook his head. "Well, it's done now, I guess. With any luck she'll just think you're a little weird and leave it at that." He paused and fixed me with a considering look. "Tell me you didn't shift in front of her."

"No. But from this phone call . . ."

"Right. The phone call. I forgot. You don't think you put that idea into her head?"

"She sounded a little scared as well as pissed off. But if it wasn't you and it wasn't me, I guess her imagination must have been working overtime."

Tyrone shrugged. "Maybe. Except . . . did you touch her at all?"

"Not really. We just shook hands and I grabbed her shoulders when I stumbled and lost my balance."

"So your scent was on her."

I nodded. "I suppose."

I saw where he was going. We don't actually go out marking territory anymore—at least most of us don't. But if another wolf had caught my scent on her it might intrigue him enough to follow her. And if he was one of the old school, he might think it fun to do a little more than that.

"I've got to go to her place and check it out," I said.

"And you'll find it how?" Tyrone asked.

He was right. I didn't even know her phone number.

"That we can deal with," Tyrone said.

I'd forgotten what we can do with phones these days. Tyrone had gotten all the bells and whistles for ours and in moments he'd called up the digits of the last incoming call on the liquid display.

"It still doesn't tell us where she lives," I said. "And I doubt she'd appreciate a call from me right now. If ever."

"I can handle that as well," Tyrone told me and he went over to the computer.

I hadn't lied to Mona. I did deal with investments—online. I was on the computer for a few hours every day, but I wasn't the hacker Tyrone was. I watched as he hacked into the telephone company's billing database. Within minutes, he had an address match for the phone number. He wrote it down on a scrap of paper and stood up.

"This is my mess," I told him. "So I'll clean it up."

"You're sure?"

When I nodded, he handed me the address.

"Don't kill anybody unless you have to," he said. "But if you do, do it clean."

I wasn't sure if he meant Mona or her stalker, and I didn't want to ask.

## Mona

After I finished my toast and tea, I decided to go to bed. I wasn't really tired, but maybe I'd get lucky and fall asleep and when I woke up, it would be a whole new day. And it would sure beat sitting around feeling miserable tonight.

I washed up my dishes, then took one last look out the window. And froze. There wasn't one dog out there, but a half dozen, lounging on the sidewalk across the street like they hadn't a care in the world. And they weren't dogs. I've seen enough nature specials on PBS to know a wolf when I see one.

As I started to let the curtain drop, all their heads lifted and turned in my direction. One got to its feet and began to trot across the street, pausing halfway to look down the block. Its companions turned their gazes in that direction as well and I followed suit.

He was dressed more casually now—jeans and a windbreaker—but I had no trouble recognizing him. My date. Mr. Stalker Man. Oh, where was Rocket Grrl when you needed her?

I knew what I should be doing. Finding something to use as a weapon in case they got in. Dialing 9-1-1 for sure. Instead, all I could do was slide down to my knees by the window and stare down at the street.

## Lyle

It was worse than I'd thought. A pack of cousins had gathered outside the address I had for Mona. From the smell in the air, I knew they were out for fun. The trouble is, skinwalker fun invariably results in somebody getting hurt. We're the reason true wolves get such a bad rap. Whenever we're around, trouble follows.

The alpha-male rose up into a man shape at my approach. His pack formed a half-circle at his back, a couple more of them taking human shape. I could tell from the dark humour in their eyes that I'd just raised the ante on their night of fun. I realized I shouldn't have turned down Tyrone's offer to help, but it was too late now. I had to brave it out on my own.

"Thanks for the show of force," I said with way more confidence than I was feeling, "but I don't really need any help to see my girlfriend."

"She's not your girlfriend," the alpha-male said.

"Sure, she is."

"Bullshit. That little chickadee's so scared you can smell her fear a block away."

"Well, you're not exactly helping matters," I told him.

He gave me a toothy grin, dark humour flicking in his eyes.

"I was walking by the café when she dumped you," he said.

I shrugged. "We had a little tiff, no big deal. That's why I'm here now—to make up with her."

He shook his head. "She's as scared of you as she is of us. But tell you what, back off and you can have whatever's left over."

Some of us fit in as we can, some of us live a footloose life. Then there are the ones like these that went feral in the long ago and just stayed that way. Some are lone wolves, the others run in packs. Mostly they haunt the big cities now because in places this large, who's going to notice the odd missing person? People disappear every day.

"Time was," I said, "when we respected each other's territories. When we put someone under our protection, they stayed that way."

It was a long shot, but I had this going for me: we're a prideful people. And honour's a big thing between us. It has to be, or we'd have wiped each other out a long time ago.

He didn't like it. I don't know if I spoke to his honour, or whether it was because he couldn't place my clan affiliation and didn't know how big a pack he'd be calling down upon himself if he cut me down and went ahead and had his fun.

"You're saying she's your girlfriend?" he asked.

I nodded.

"Okay. Let's go up and ask her. If she lets you in, we'll back off. But if she doesn't . . ."

He let me fill in the blank for myself.

"No problem," I said.

Not like I had a choice in the matter. This was a win-win situation for him. If she let me in, he could back off without losing face. And if she didn't, no one in the clans would take my side because it would just look like I was honing in on their claim.

He stepped back, and I walked towards Mona's building. The pack fell in behind me, all of them in human shape now. I glanced up and caught a glimpse of Mona's terrified face in the window. I tried to look as harmless as possible.

Trust me, I told her, willing the thought up to her. It's your life that's hanging in the balance here.

But she only looked more scared.

Then we were on the stairs, and I couldn't see her anymore.

"Don't even think about trying to warn her," the alpha-male said from behind me. "She's got to accept you without a word from you or all bets are off."

The door to the front hall was locked when I tried it. The alpha-male reached past me and grabbed the knob, giving it a sharp twist. I heard the lock break, then the door swung open and we were moving inside.

Did I mention that we're stronger than we look?

## Mona

I was still trying to adjust to the fact that the wolves really had turned into people, when my stalker led them into the apartment building. He looked up at me just before they reached the stairs, his face all pretend sweetness and light, but it didn't fool me. I knew they were going to tear me to pieces.

Get up, get up, I told myself. Call the police. Sneak out onto the fire escape and run for it.

But all I could do was sit on the floor with my back to the window and stare at my front door, listening to their footsteps as they came up the stairs. When they stopped outside my door, I held my breath. Somebody knocked, and I just about jumped out of my skin. This uncontrollable urge to laugh rose up in me. Here they were, planning to kill me, yet they were just knocking politely on the door. I was hysterical.

"We can smell you in there."

That wasn't Lyle, but one of his friends.

I shivered and pressed up against the wall behind me.

"Come see us through the peephole," the voice went on. "Your boyfriend wants to know if you'll let him in. Or are you still too mad at him?"

I didn't want to move, but I slowly got to my feet.

"If you don't come soon, we'll huff and we'll puff, just see if we won't."

I stood swaying the middle of my living room, hugging myself. Wishing so desperately that I'd never left the apartment this evening.

"Or maybe," the mocking voice went on, "we'll go chew off the faces of the nice couple living below you. They do smell good."

I was moving again, shuffling forward, away from the phone, towards the door.

It was too late to call for help anyway. Nobody was going to get here in time. If they didn't just smash through my door, maybe they really would go kill the Andersons who had the downstairs apartment. And this wasn't their fault. I was the one stupid enough to go out on a blind date with a werewolf.

"That's it," the voice told me. "I can hear you coming. Show us what a good hostess you are. What a forgiving girlfriend."

I was close enough now to hear the chorus of sniggers and giggles that echoed on after the voice had finished. When I reached the door, I rose slowly up on my tiptoes and looked through the peephole.

They were all out there in the hall, my stalker and his pack of werewolf friends.

God, I thought, looking at Lyle, trying to read his face, to understand why he was doing this. How could I ever have thought that I liked him?

## Lyle

I knew it was over now. There was no way Mona was going to open the door—not if she had an ounce of sense in her—but at least I'd gotten the pack into a confined space. I couldn't take them all down, but maybe I could manage a few.

I could smell Mona the same as the pack did—smell her fear. She was numbed by it. But maybe once I set on the pack, it'd snap her out of her paralysis long enough to flee out onto the fire escape I'd noticed running up the side of the building. Or perhaps the noise would be enough for the neighbours to call the police. If they could get here before the pack battered down the door, there was still a chance she could survive.

She was on the other side of the door now. Looking out of the peephole. I tried to compose myself, to give her a look that she might read as hope. To convey that I meant her no harm.

But then the alpha-male gave me a shove. Without thinking, I snarled at him, face partially shifting, jaws snapping. He darted back, laughter triumphant in his eyes, and I knew what he'd done. He'd shown Mona that I was no different from them. Just another skinwalker. Another inhuman creature, hungry for her blood.

"All you have to do is answer a couple of questions," the alpha-male said, facing the door. "Do you forgive your boyfriend? Will you invite him in?"

There was a long silence.

"Why . . . why are you doing this?" Mona finally said, her voice muffled by the door. But we all had a wolf's hearing.

"Tut, tut," the alpha-male said. "You're not playing by the rules. You're not supposed to ask a question, only answer ours."

I knew she was still looking from the peephole.

"I'm sorry, Mona," I said. "For everything."

The alpha-male turned on me with a snarl. I drew him aside before he could speak, my back to the door.

"Come on," I told him, my voice pitched low. "You know we had a quarrel. How's this supposed to be fair with you scaring the crap out of her and here I haven't even apologized to her? I mean, take a vote on it or something."

He turned to his companions. I could see they didn't like it, but my argument made sense.

"Fine," he said. "You've made your apology."

He turned to the door and let his face go animal.

"Well?" he snarled. "What's your answer, little chickadee? Your boyfriend says he's sorry so can he come in and play now?"

## Mona

I almost died when Lyle's face did it's half-transformation. The wolfish features disappeared as fast as they had appeared. He turned to me with those beautiful dark eyes of his, and I couldn't see the same meanness and hunger in them that were in the eyes of the others. And I was looking for it, believe me. Then, while I was still caught in his gaze, he went and apologized to me, like none of this was his doing. Like he was sorry for everything, the same as I was. Not just for what he'd said to me in the café, but because we'd liked each other and then we'd let it all fell apart before we ever gave it a chance to be more.

Call me naïve, or maybe even stupider still, but I believed that apology of his was genuine. It was something he needed to say, or that I needed to hear. Maybe both.

I was so caught up in the thought of that, that I didn't even start when the other guy did his half-wolf face thing and began snarling at me. Instead, I flashed on something Lyle had said to me earlier in the evening, back at the café.

These days most of us just like to fit in, he'd told me. Live a bit in your world, a bit in the animal world. But it wasn't always like that. There have always been those among us who considered everyone else in the world their private prey.

Most of you? I'd asked.

I remember him sighing, almost like he was ashamed, when he'd shaken his head and added, But there are still some that like to hunt.

Like this guy with his animal face and snarl, with his pack of wolfish friends.

But I was done being afraid. I was Rocket Grrl, or at least I was trying to be. I concentrated on this question the wolf-faced leader of the pack kept asking, focusing exactly on what it was he was asking, and why. It felt like a fairy tale moment and I flashed on Beauty and the Beast, the prince turned into a frog, the nasty little dwarf who'd moved in on me until an act of kindness set him free. All those stories pivoted around the right thing being said.

That doesn't happen in real life, the rational part of my mind told me.

I knew that. Not usually. But sometimes it did, didn't it?

## Lyle

"Time's up, chickadee," the alpha-male said.

I got myself ready. First I'd try to knock as many of them down the stairs as I could, then I'd shift to wolf shape and give them a taste of what it felt like being hurt. I knew I didn't have a chance against all of them, but I'd still be able to kill a few before they took me down. I'd start with the alpha-male.

Except before I could leap, I heard the deadbolt disengage. The door swung open, and then she was standing there, small and blonde and human-frail, but with more backbone than all of this sorry pack of skinwalkers put together, me included. We all took a step back. Mona cleared her throat.

"So . . . so what you're asking," she said, "is do I forgive Lyle?"

The alpha-male straightened his shoulders. "That's it," he said. "Part one of a two-parter."

She didn't even look at him, her gaze going over his shoulder to me.

"I think we were both to blame," she said. "So of course I do. Do you forgive me?"

I couldn't believe what I was hearing. I wasn't even worrying about the pack at that moment. I was just so mesmerized with how brave she was. I think the pack was, too.

"Well?" she asked.

All I could do was nod my head.

"Then you can come in," she said. "But not your friends."

"They're not my friends," I told her.

The alpha-male growled with frustration until one of the pack touched his arm.

"That's it," the pack member said. "It's over."

The alpha-male shook off the hand, but he turned away and the pack trooped down the stairs. When I heard the front door close, I let out a breath I hadn't been aware I was holding.

"You were amazing," I told Mona.

She gave me a small smile. "I guess I have my moments."

"I'll say. I don't know how you knew to do it, but you gave them exactly the right answer."

"I wasn't doing it for them," she told me. "I was doing it for us."

I shook my head again. "It's been a weird night, but I'm glad I got to meet you all the same."

I started for the stairs.

"Where are you going?" she asked. "They could be waiting out there for you."

I turned back to look at her. "They won't. It's an honour thing. Maybe if I run into them some other time there'll be trouble, but there won't be any more tonight."

"We never finished our date," she said.

"You still want to go out somewhere with me?"

She shook her head. "But we could have a drink in here and talk awhile."

I waited a heartbeat, but when she stepped aside and ushered me inside, I didn't hesitate any longer.

"I was so scared," she said as she closed the door behind us.

"Me, too."

"Really?"

"There were six of them," I said. "They could have torn me apart at any time."

"Why didn't they?"

"I told them you were my girlfriend—that we'd just had a fight in the café. That way, in their eyes, I had a claim on you. The honour thing again. If you were under my protection, they couldn't hurt you."

"So that's what you meant about my giving them the exact right answer."

I nodded.

"And if I hadn't?" she asked.

"Let's not go there," I said. But I knew she could see the answer in my eyes.

"You'd do that even after what I said to you on the phone?"

"You had every right to feel the way you did."

"Are you for real?"

"I hope so." I thought about all she'd experienced tonight. "So are you going to put this in one of your strips?"

She laughed. "Maybe. But who'd believe it?"

## Mona

It's funny how things work. When I was leaving the café earlier, I could have happily given him a good bang on the ear. Later, when I thought he was stalking me, I was ready to have him put in jail. When the pack was outside my window and he joined them, I was so terrified I couldn't move or think straight.

And now I'm thinking of asking him to stay the night.

# KELLY LINK

## Louise's Ghost

*Kelly Link is one of the best new writers to emerge in the fantasy field in the last decade. Her stories are smart, sly, beautifully crafted, and thoroughly unique. Her fiction has appeared in* Century, Realms of Fantasy, Asimov's Science Fiction Magazine, Lady Churchill's Rosebud Wristlet, Event Horizon, *and previous volumes of* The Year's Best Fantasy & Horror—*as well as in the children's anthology* A Wolf at the Door.

*"Louise's Ghost" is reprinted from her excellent first collection,* Stranger Things Happen *(Small Beer Press). It's a delicious tale of ghosts and music— sad, funny, and surreal.*

*Link has won the World Fantasy Award and the James Tiptree, Jr. Award. She lives in Brooklyn, New York.*

—*T. W.*

Two women and a small child meet in a restaurant. The restaurant is nice— there are windows everywhere. The women have been here before. It's all that light that makes the food taste so good. The small child—a girl dressed all in green, hairy green sweater, green T-shirt, green corduroys and dirty sneakers with green-black laces—sniffs. She's a small child but she has a big nose. She might be smelling the food that people are eating. She might be smelling the warm light that lies on top of everything. None of her greens match except of course they are all green.

"Louise," one woman says to the other.

"Louise," the other woman says.

They kiss.

The maitre d' comes up to them. He says to the first woman, "Louise, how nice to see you. And look at Anna! You're so big. Last time I saw you, you were so small. This small." He holds his index finger and his thumb together as if pinching salt. He looks at the other woman.

Louise says, "This is my friend, Louise. My best friend. Since Girl Scout camp. Louise."

The maitre d' smiles. "Yes, Louise. Of course. How could I forget?"

Louise sits across from Louise. Anna sits between them. She has a notebook full of green paper, and a green crayon. She's drawing something, only it's difficult to see what, exactly. Maybe it's a house.

Louise says, "Sorry about you know who. Teacher's day. The sitter canceled at the last minute. And I had such a lot to tell you, too! About you know, number eight. Oh boy, I think I'm in love. Well, not in love."

She is sitting opposite a window, and all that rich soft light falls on her. She looks creamy with happiness, as if she's carved out of butter. The light loves Louise, the other Louise thinks. Of course it loves Louise. Who doesn't?

This is one thing about Louise. She doesn't like to sleep alone. She says that her bed is too big. There's too much space. She needs someone to roll up against, or she just rolls around all night. Some mornings she wakes up on the floor. Mostly she wakes up with other people.

When Anna was younger, she slept in the same bed as Louise. But now she has her own room, her own bed. Her walls are painted green. Her sheets are green. Green sheets of paper with green drawings are hung up on the wall. There's a green teddy bear on the green bed and a green duck. She has a green light in a green shade. Louise has been in that room. She helped Louise paint it. She wore sunglasses while she painted. This passion for greenness, Louise thinks, this longing for everything to be a variation on a theme, it might be hereditary.

This is the second thing about Louise. Louise likes cellists. For about four years, she has been sleeping with a cellist. Not the same cellist. Different cellists. Not all at once, of course. Consecutive cellists. Number eight is Louise's newest cellist. Numbers one through seven were cellists as well, although Anna's father was not. That was before the cellists. BC. In any case, according to Louise, cellists generally have low sperm counts.

Louise meets Louise for lunch every week. They go to nice restaurants. Louise knows all the maitre d's. Louise tells Louise about the cellists. Cellists are mysterious. Louise hasn't figured them out yet. It's something about the way they sit, with their legs open and their arms curled around, all hunched over their cellos. She says they look solid but inviting. Like a door. It opens and you walk in.

Doors are sexy. Wood is sexy, and bows strung with real hair. Also cellos don't have spit valves. Louise says that spit valves aren't sexy.

Louise is in public relations. She's a fundraiser for the symphony—she's good at what she does. It's hard to say no to Louise. She takes rich people out to dinner. She knows what kinds of wine they like to drink. She plans charity auctions and masquerades. She brings sponsors to the symphony to sit on stage and watch rehearsals. She takes the cellists home afterwards.

Louise looks a little bit like a cello herself. She's brown and curvy and tall. She has a long neck and her shiny hair stays pinned up during the day. Louise thinks that the cellists must take it down at night—Louise's hair—slowly, happily, gently.

At camp Louise used to brush Louise's hair.

Louise isn't perfect. Louise would never claim that her friend was perfect. Louise is a bit bow-legged and she has tiny little feet. She wears long, tight silky skirts. Never pants, never anything floral. She has a way of turning her head to look at you, very slowly. It doesn't matter that she's bowlegged.

The cellists want to sleep with Louise because she wants them to. The cellists don't fall in love with her, because Louise doesn't want them to fall in love with her. Louise always gets what she wants.

Louise doesn't know what she wants. Louise doesn't want to want things.

Louise and Louise have been friends since Girl Scout camp. How old were they? Too young to be away from home for so long. They were so small that some of their teeth weren't there yet. They were so young they wet the bed out of homesickness. Loneliness. Louise slept in the bunk bed above Louise. Girl Scout camp smelled like pee. Summer camp is how Louise knows Louise is bowlegged. At summer camp they wore each other's clothes.

Here is something else about Louise, a secret. Louise is the only one who knows. Not even the cellists know. Not even Anna.

Louise is tone deaf. Louise likes to watch Louise at concerts. She has this way of looking at the musicians. Her eyes get wide and she doesn't blink. There's this smile on her face as if she's being introduced to someone whose name she didn't quite catch. Louise thinks that's really why Louise ends up sleeping with them, with the cellists. It's because she doesn't know what else they're good for. Louise hates for things to go to waste.

A woman comes to their table to take their order. Louise orders the grilled chicken and a house salad and Louise orders salmon with lemon butter. The woman asks Anna what she would like. Anna looks at her mother.

Louise says, "She'll eat anything as long as it's green. Broccoli is good. Peas, lima beans, iceberg lettuce. Lime sherbet. Bread rolls. Mashed potatoes."

The woman looks down at Anna. "I'll see what we can do," she says.

Anna says, "Potatoes aren't green."

Louise says, "Wait and see."

Louise says, "If I had a kid—"

Louise says, "But you don't have a kid." She doesn't say this meanly. Louise is never mean, although sometimes she is not kind.

Louise and Anna glare at each other. They've never liked each other. They are polite in front of Louise. It is humiliating, Louise thinks, to hate someone so much younger. The child of a friend. I should feel sorry for her instead. She doesn't have a father. And soon enough, she'll grow up. Breasts. Zits. Boys. She'll see old pictures of herself and be embarrassed. She's short and she dresses like a Keebler Elf. She can't even read yet!

Louise says, "In any case, it's easier than the last thing. When she only ate dog food."

Anna says, "When I was a dog—"

Louise says, hating herself. "You were never a dog."

Anna says, "How do you know?"

Louise says, "I was there when you were born. When your mother was pregnant. I've known you since you were this big." She pinches her fingers together, the way the maitre d' pinched his, only harder.

Anna says, "It was before that. When I was a dog."

Louise says, "Stop fighting, you two. Louise, when Anna was a dog, that was when you were away. In Paris. Remember?"

"Right," Louise says. "When Anna was a dog, I was in Paris." Louise is a travel agent. She organizes package tours for senior citizens. Trips for old women. To Las Vegas, Rome, Belize, cruises to the Caribbean. She travels frequently herself and stays in three-star hotels. She tries to imagine herself as an old woman. What she would want.

Most of these women's husbands are in care or dead or living with younger women. The old women sleep two to a room. They like hotels with buffet lunches and saunas, clean pillows that smell good, chocolates on the pillows, firm mattresses. Louise can see herself wanting these things. Sometimes Louise imagines being old, waking up in the mornings, in unfamiliar countries, strange weather, foreign beds. Louise asleep in the bed beside her.

Last night Louise woke up. It was three in the morning. There was a man lying on the floor beside the bed. He was naked. He lay on his back, staring up at the ceiling, his eyes open, his mouth open, nothing coming out. He was bald. He had no eyelashes, no hair on his arms or legs. He was large, not fat but solid. Yes, he was solid. It was hard to tell how old he was. It was dark, but Louise doesn't think he was circumcised. "What are you doing here?" she said loudly.

The man wasn't there anymore. She turned on the lights. She looked under the bed. She found him in her bathroom, above the bathtub, flattened up against the ceiling, staring down, his hands and feet pressed along the ceiling, his penis drooping down, apparently the only part of him that obeyed the laws of gravity. He seemed smaller now. Deflated. She wasn't frightened. She was angry.

"What are you doing?" she said. He didn't answer. Fine, she thought. She went to the kitchen to get a broom. When she came back, he was gone. She looked under the bed again, but he was really gone this time. She looked in every room, checked to make sure that the front door was locked. It was.

Her arms creeped. She was freezing. She filled up her hot water bottle and got in bed. She left the light on and fell asleep sitting up. When she woke up in the morning, it might have been a dream, except she was holding the broom.

The woman brings their food. Anna gets a little dish of peas, brussel sprouts, and collard greens. Mashed potatoes and bread. The plate is green. Louise takes a vial of green food coloring out of her purse. She adds three drops to the mashed potatoes. "Stir it," she tells Anna.

Anna stirs the mashed potatoes until they are a waxy green. Louise mixes more green food coloring into a pat of butter and spreads it on the dinner roll.

"When I was a dog," Anna says, "I lived in a house with a swimming pool. And there was a tree in the living room. It grew right through the ceiling. I slept in the tree. But I wasn't allowed to swim in the pool. I was too hairy."

"I have a ghost," Louise says. She wasn't sure that she was going to say this. But if Anna can reminisce about her former life as a dog, then surely she, Louise, is allowed to mention her ghost. "I think it's a ghost. It was in my bedroom."

Anna says, "When I was a dog I bit ghosts."

Louise says, "Anna, be quiet for a minute. Eat your green food before it gets cold. Louise, what do you mean? I thought you had ladybugs."

"That was a while ago," Louise says. Last month she woke up because people were whispering in the corners of her room. Dead leaves were crawling on her face. The walls of her bedroom were alive. They heaved and dripped red. "What?" she said, and a ladybug walked into her mouth, bitter like soap. The floor crackled when she walked on it, like red cellophane. She opened up her windows. She swept ladybugs out with her broom. She vacuumed them up. More flew in the windows, down the chimney. She moved out for three days. When she came back, the ladybugs were gone—mostly gone—she still finds them tucked into her shoes, in the folds of her underwear, in her cereal bowls and her wine glasses and between the pages of her books.

Before that it was moths. Before the moths, an opossum. It shat on her bed and hissed at her when she cornered it in the pantry. She called an animal shelter and a man wearing a denim jacket and heavy gloves came and shot it with a tranquilizer dart. The opossum sneezed and shut its eyes. The man picked it up by the tail. He posed like that for a moment. Maybe she was supposed to take a picture. Man with opossum. She sniffed. He wasn't married. All she smelled was opossum.

"How did it get in here?" Louise said.

"How long have you been living here?" the man asked. Boxes of Louise's dishes and books were still stacked up against the walls of the rooms downstairs. She still hadn't put the legs on her mother's dining room table. It lay flat on its back on the floor, amputated.

"Two months," Louise said.

"Well, he's probably been living here longer than that," the man from the shelter said. He cradled the possum like a baby. "In the walls or the attic. Maybe in the chimney. Santa claws. Huh." He laughed at his own joke. "Get it?"

"Get that thing out of my house," Louise said.

"Your house!" the man said. He held out the opossum to her, as if she might want to reconsider. "You know what he thought? He thought this was his house."

"It's my house now," Louise said.

Louise says, "A ghost? Louise, it is someone you know? Is your mother okay?"

"My mother?" Louise says. "It wasn't my mother. It was a naked man. I'd never seen him before in my life."

"How naked?" Anna says. "A little naked or a lot?"

"None of your beeswax," Louise says.

"Was it green?" Anna says.

"Maybe it was someone that you went out with in high school," Louise says. "An old lover. Maybe they just killed themselves, or were in a horrible car accident. Was he covered in blood? Did he say anything? Maybe he wants to warn you about something."

"He didn't say anything," Louise says, "And then he vanished. First he got smaller and then he vanished."

Louise shivers and then so does Louise. For the first time she feels frightened. The ghost of a naked man was levitating in her bathtub. He could be anywhere. Maybe while she was sleeping, he was floating above her bed. Right above her nose, watching her sleep. She'll have to sleep with the broom from now on.

"Maybe he won't come back," Louise says, and Louise nods. What if he does? Who can she call? The rude man with the heavy gloves?

The woman comes to their table again. "Any dessert?" she wants to know. "Coffee?"

"If you had a ghost," Louise says, "How would you get rid of it?"

Louise kicks Louise under the table.

The woman thinks for a minute. "I'd go see a psychiatrist," she says. "Get some kind of prescription. Coffee?"

But Anna has to go to her tumble class. She's learning how to stand on her head. How to fall down and not be hurt. Louise gets the woman to put the leftover mashed green potatoes in a container, and she wraps up the dinner rolls in a napkin and bundles them into her purse along with a few packets of sugar.

They walk out of the restaurant together, Louise first. Behind her, Anna whispers something to Louise. "Louise?" Louise says.

"What?" Louise says, turning back.

"You need to walk behind me," Anna says. "You can't be first."

"Come back and talk to me," Louise says, patting the air. "Say thank you, Anna."

Anna doesn't say anything. She walks before them, slowly so that they have to walk slowly as well.

"So what should I do?" Louise says.

"About the ghost? I don't know. Is he cute? Maybe he'll creep in bed with you. Maybe he's your demon lover."

"Oh please," Louise says. "Yuck."

Louise says, "Sorry. You should call your mother."

"When I had the problem with the ladybugs," Louise says, "she said they would go away if I sang them that nursery rhyme. Ladybug, ladybug, fly away home."

"Well," Louise says, "they did go away, didn't they?"

"Not until I went away first," Louise says.

"Maybe it's someone who used to live in the house before you moved in. Maybe he's buried under the floor of your bedroom or in the wall or something."

"Just like the possum," Louise says. "Maybe it's Santa Claus."

Louise's mother lives in a retirement community two states away. Louise cleaned out her mother's basement and garage, put her mother's furniture in storage, sold her mother's house. Her mother wanted this. She gave Louise the money from the sale of the house so that Louise could buy her own house. But she won't come visit Louise in her new house. She won't let Louise send her on a package vacation. Sometimes she pretends not to recognize Louise when Louise calls. Or maybe she really doesn't recognize her. Maybe this is why Louise's clients travel. Settle down in one place and you get lazy. You don't bother to remember things like taking baths, or your daughter's name.

When you travel, everything's always new. If you don't speak the language, it isn't a big deal. Nobody expects you to understand everything they say. You can wear the same clothes every day and the other travelers will be impressed with your careful packing. When you wake up and you're not sure where you are. There's a perfectly good reason for that.

"Hello, Mom," Louise says when her mother picks up the phone.

"Who is this?" her mother says.

"Louise," Louise says.

"Oh yes," her mother says. "Louise, how nice to speak to you." There is an awkward pause and then her mother says, "If you're calling because it's your birthday, I'm sorry. I forgot."

"It isn't my birthday," Louise says. "Mom, remember the ladybugs?"

"Oh yes," her mother says. "You sent pictures. They were lovely."

"I have a ghost," Louise says, "and I was hoping that you would know how to get rid of it."

"A ghost!" her mother says. "It isn't your father, is it?"

"No!" Louise says. "This ghost doesn't have any clothes on, Mom. It's naked and I saw it for a minute and then it disappeared and then I saw it again in my bathtub. Well, sort of."

"Are you sure it's a ghost?" her mother says.

"Yes, positive." Louise says.

"And it isn't your father?"

"No, it's not Dad. It doesn't look like anyone I've ever seen before."

Her mother says, "Lucy—you don't know her—Mrs. Peterson's husband died two nights ago. Is it a short fat man with an ugly moustache? Dark-complected?"

"It isn't Mr. Peterson," Louise says.

"Have you asked what it wants?"

"Mom, I don't care what it wants," Louise says. "I just want it to go away."

"Well," her mother says. "Try hot water and salt. Scrub all the floors. You should polish them with lemon oil afterwards so they don't get streaky. Wash the windows too. Wash all the bed linens and beat all the rugs. And put the sheets back on the bed inside out. And turn all your clothes on the hangers inside out. Clean the bathroom."

"Inside out," Louise says.

"Inside out," her mother says. "Confuses them."

"I think it's pretty confused already. About clothes, anyway. Are you sure this works?"

"Positive," her mother says. "We're always having supernatural infestations around here. Sometimes it gets hard to tell who's alive and who's dead. If cleaning the house doesn't work, try hanging garlic up on strings. Ghosts hate garlic. Or they like it. It's either one or the other, love it, hate it. So what else is happening? When are you coming to visit?"

"I had lunch today with Louise," Louise says.

"Aren't you too old to have an imaginary friend?" her mother says.

"Mom, you know Louise. Remember? Girl Scouts? College? She has the little girl, Anna? Louise?"

"Of course I remember Louise," her mother says. "My own daughter. You're a very rude person." She hangs up.

Salt, Louise thinks. Salt and hot water. She should write these things down. Maybe she could send her mother a tape recorder. She sits down on the kitchen floor and cries. That's one kind of salt water. Then she scrubs floors, beats rugs, washes her sheets and her blankets. She washes her clothes and hangs them back up, inside out. While she works, the ghost lies half under the bed, feet and genitalia pointed at her accusingly. She scrubs around it. Him. It.

She is being squeamish, Louise thinks. Afraid to touch it. And that makes her angry, so she picks up her broom. Pokes at the fleshy thighs, and the ghost hisses under the bed like an angry cat. She jumps back and then it isn't there anymore. But she sleeps on the living room sofa. She keeps all the lights on in all the rooms of the house.

"Well?" Louise says.

"It isn't gone," Louise says. She's just come home from work. "I just don't know *where* it is. Maybe it's up in the attic. It might be standing behind me, for all I know, while I'm talking to you on the phone and every time I turn around, it vanishes. Jumps back in the mirror or wherever it is that it goes. You may hear me scream. By the time you get here, it will be too late."

"Sweetie," Louise says. "I'm sure it can't hurt you."

"It hissed at me," Louise says.

"Did it just hiss, or did you do something first?" Louise says.

"Kettles hiss. It just means the water's boiling."

"What about snakes?" Louise says. "I'm thinking it's more like a snake than a pot of tea."

"You could ask a priest to exorcise it. If you were Catholic. Or you could go to the library. They might have a book. Exorcism for dummies. Can you come to the symphony tonight? I have extra tickets."

"You've always got extra tickets," Louise says.

"Yes, but it will be good for you," Louise says. "Besides I haven't seen you for two days."

"Can't do it tonight," Louise says. "What about tomorrow night?"

"Well, okay," Louise says. "Have you tried reading the Bible to it?"

"What part of the Bible would I read?"

"How about the begetting part? That's official sounding," Louise says.

"What if it thinks I'm flirting? The guy at the gas station today said I should spit on the floor when I see it and say, 'In the name of God, what do you want?'"

"Have you tried that?"

"I don't know about spitting on the floor," Louise says. "I just cleaned it. What if it wants something gross, like my eyes? What if it wants me to kill someone?"

"Well," Louise says, "that would depend on who it wanted you to kill."

Louise goes to dinner with her married lover. After dinner, they will go to a motel and fuck. Then he'll take a shower and go home, and she'll spend the night at the motel. This is a *Louise*-style economy. It makes Louise feel slightly more virtuous. The ghost will have the house to himself.

Louise doesn't talk to Louise about her lover. He belongs to her, and to his wife, of course. There isn't enough left over to share. She met him at work. Before him she had another lover, another married man. She would like to believe that this is a charming quirk, like being bowlegged or sleeping with cellists.

But perhaps it's a character defect instead, like being tone deaf or refusing to eat food that isn't green.

Here is what Louise would tell Louise, if she told her. I'm just borrowing him—I don't want him to leave his wife. I'm glad he's married. Let someone else take care of him. It's the way he smells—the way married men smell. I can smell when a happily married man comes into a room, and they can smell me too, I think. So can the wives—that's why he has to take a shower when he leaves me.

But Louise doesn't tell Louise about her lovers. She doesn't want to sound as if she's competing with the cellists.

"What are you thinking about?" her lover says. The wine has made his teeth red.

It's the guiltiness that cracks them wide open. The guilt makes them taste so sweet, Louise thinks. "Do you believe in ghosts?" she says.

Her lover laughs. "Of course not."

If he were her husband, they would sleep in the same bed every night. And if she woke up and saw the ghost, she would wake up her husband. They would both see the ghost. They would share responsibility. It would be a piece of their marriage, part of the things they don't have (can't have) now, like breakfast or ski vacations or fights about toothpaste. Or maybe he would blame her. If she tells him now that she saw a naked man in her bedroom, he might say that it's her fault.

"Neither do I," Louise says. "But if you did believe in ghosts. Because you saw one. What would you do? How would you get rid of it?"

Her lover thinks for a minute. "I wouldn't get rid of it," he says. "I'd charge admission. I'd become famous. I'd be on *Oprah*. They would make a movie. Everyone wants to see a ghost."

"But what if there's a problem," Louise says. "Such as. What if the ghost is naked?"

Her lover says, "Well, that would be a problem. Unless you were the ghost. Then I would want you to be naked all the time."

But Louise can't fall asleep in the motel room. Her lover has gone home to his home which isn't haunted, to his wife who doesn't know about Louise. Louise is as unreal to her as a ghost. Louise lies awake and thinks about her ghost. The dark is not dark, she thinks, and there is something in the motel room with her. Something her lover has left behind. Something touches her face. There's something bitter in her mouth. In the room next door someone is walking up and down. A baby is crying somewhere, or a cat.

She gets dressed and drives home. She needs to know if the ghost is still there or if her mother's recipe worked. She wishes she'd tried to take a picture.

She looks all over the house. She takes her clothes off the hangers in the closet and hangs them back right-side out. The ghost isn't anywhere. She can't find him. She even sticks her face up the chimney.

She finds the ghost curled up in her underwear drawer. He lies face down, hands open and loose. He's naked and downy all over like a baby monkey.

Louise spits on the floor, feeling relieved. "In God's name," she says, "What do you want?"

The ghost doesn't say anything. He lies there, small and hairy and forlorn, face down in her underwear. Maybe he doesn't know what he wants any more than she does. "Clothes?" Louise says. "Do you want me to get you some clothes? It would be easier if you stayed the same size."

The ghost doesn't say anything. "Well," Louise says. "You think about it. Let me know." She closes the drawer.

Anna is in her green bed. The green light is on. Louise and the babysitter sit in the living room while Louise and Anna talk. "When I was a dog," Anna says, "I ate roses and raw meat and borscht. I wore silk dresses."

"When you were a dog," Louise hears Louise say, "you had big silky ears and four big feet and a long silky tail and you wore a collar made out of silk and a silk dress with a hole cut in it for your tail."

"A green dress," Anna says. "I could see in the dark."

"Good night, my green girl," Louise says, "good night, good night."

Louise comes into the living room. "Doesn't Louise look beautiful," she says, leaning against Louise's chair and looking in the mirror. "The two of us. Louise and Louise and Louise and Louise. All four of us."

"Mirror, mirror on the wall," the babysitter says, "who is the fairest Louise of all?" Patrick the babysitter doesn't let Louise pay him. He takes symphony tickets instead. He plays classical guitar and composes music himself. Louise and Louise would like to hear his compositions, but he's too shy to play for them. He brings his guitar sometimes, to play for Anna. He's teaching her the simple chords.

"How is your ghost?" Louise says. "Louise has a ghost," she tells Patrick.

"Smaller," Louise says. "Hairier." Louise doesn't really like Patrick. He's in love with Louise for one thing. It embarrasses Louise, the hopeless way he looks at Louise. He probably writes love songs for her. He's friendly with Anna. As if that will get him anywhere.

"You tried garlic?" Louise says. "Spitting? Holy water? The library?"

"Yes," Louise says, lying.

"How about country music?" Patrick says. "Johnny Cash, Patsy Cline, Hank Williams?"

"Country music?" Louise says. "Is that like holy water?"

"I read something about it," Patrick says. "In *New Scientist*, or *Guitar* magazine, or maybe it was *Martha Stewart Living*. It was something about the pitch, the frequencies. Yodeling is supposed to be effective. Makes sense when you think about it."

"I was thinking about summer camp," Louise says to Louise.

"Remember how the counselors used to tell us ghost stories?"

"Yeah," Louise says. "They did that thing with the flashlight. You made me go to the bathroom with you in the middle of the night. You were afraid to go by yourself."

"I wasn't afraid," Louise says. "You were afraid."

At the symphony, Louise watches the cellists and Louise watches Louise. The cellists watch the conductor and every now and then they look past him, over at Louise. Louise can feel them staring at Louise. Music goes everywhere, like light and, like light, music loves Louise. Louise doesn't know how she knows this—she can just feel the music, wrapping itself around Louise, insinuating itself into her beautiful ears, between her lips, collecting in her hair and in the little scoop between her legs. And what good does it do Louise, Louise thinks? The cellists might as well be playing jackhammers and spoons.

Well, maybe that isn't entirely true. Louise may be tone deaf, but she's explained to Louise that it doesn't mean she doesn't like music. She feels it in her bones and back behind her jaw. It scratches itches. It's like a crossword puzzle. Louise is trying to figure it out, and right next to her, Louise is trying to figure out Louise.

The music stops and starts and stops again. Louise and Louise clap at the intermission and then the lights come up and Louise says, "I've been thinking a lot. About something. I want another baby."

"What do you mean?" Louise says, stunned. "You mean like Anna?"

"I don't know," Louise says. "Just another one. You should have a baby too. We could go to Lamaze classes together. You could name yours Louise after me and I could name mine Louise after you. Wouldn't that be funny?"

"Anna would be jealous," Louise says.

"I think it would make me happy," Louise says. "I was so happy when Anna was a baby. Everything just tasted good, even the air. I even liked being pregnant."

Louise says, "Aren't you happy now?"

Louise says, "Of course I'm happy. But don't you know what I mean? Being happy like that?"

"Kind of," Louise says. "Like when we were kids. You mean like Girl Scout camp."

"Yeah," Louise says. "Like that. You would have to get rid of your ghost first. I don't think ghosts are very hygienic. I could introduce you to a very nice man. A cellist. Maybe not the highest sperm count, but very nice."

"Which number is he?" Louise says.

"I don't want to prejudice you," Louise says. "You haven't met him. I'm not sure you should think of him as a number. I'll point him out. Oh, and number eight, too. You have to meet my beautiful boy, number eight. We have to go out to lunch so I can tell you about him. He's smitten. I've smited him."

Louise goes to the bathroom and Louise stays in her seat. She thinks of her ghost. Why can't she have a ghost and a baby? Why is she always supposed to give up something? Why can't other people share?

Why does Louise want to have another baby anyway? What if this new baby hates Louise as much as Anna does? What if it used to be a dog? What if her own baby hates Louise?

When the musicians are back on stage, Louise leans over and whispers to Louise, "There he is. The one with big hands, over on the right."

It isn't clear to Louise which cellist Louise means. They all have big hands. And which cellist is she supposed to be looking for? The nice cellist she shouldn't be thinking of as a number? Number eight? She takes a closer look. All of the cellists are handsome from where Louise is sitting. How fragile they look, she thinks, in their serious black clothes, letting the music run down their strings like that and pour through their open fingers. It's careless of them. You have to hold onto things.

There are six cellists on stage. Perhaps Louise has slept with all of them.

Louise thinks, if I went to bed with them, with any of them, I would recognize the way they tasted, the things they liked and the ways they liked them. I would know which number they were. But they wouldn't know me.

The ghost is bigger again. He's prickly all over. He bristles with hair. The hair is reddish brown and sharp looking. Louise doesn't think it would be a good idea to touch the ghost now. All night he moves back and forth in front of her bed, sliding on his belly like a snake. His fingers dig into the floorboards and he pushes himself forward with his toes. His mouth stays open as if he's eating air.

Louise goes to the kitchen. She opens a can of beans, a can of pears, hearts of palm. She puts the different things on a plate and places the plate in front of the ghost. He moves around it. Maybe he's like Anna—picky. Louise doesn't know what he wants. Louise refuses to sleep in the living room again. It's her bedroom after all. She lies awake and listens to the ghost press himself against her clean floor, moving backwards and forwards before the foot of the bed all night long.

In the morning the ghost is in the closet, upside down against the wall. Enough, she thinks, and she goes to the mall and buys a stack of CDs. Patsy Cline, Emmylou Harris, Hank Williams, Johnny Cash, Lyle Lovett. She asks the clerk if he can recommend anything with yodeling on it, but he's young and not very helpful.

"Never mind," she says. "I'll just take these."

While he's running her credit card, she says, "Wait. Have you ever seen a ghost?"

"None of your business, lady," he says. "But if I had, I'd make it show me where it buried its treasure. And then I'd dig up the treasure and I'd be rich and then I wouldn't be selling you this stupid country shit. Unless the treasure had a curse on it."

"What if there wasn't any treasure?" Louise says.

"Then I'd stick the ghost in a bottle and sell it to a museum," the kid says. "A real live ghost. That's got to be worth something. I'd buy a hog and ride it to California. I'd go make my own music, and there wouldn't be any fucking yodeling."

The ghost seems to like Patsy Cline. It isn't that he says anything. But he doesn't disappear. He comes out of the closet. He lies on the floor so that Louise has to walk around him. He's thicker now, more solid. Maybe he was a Patsy Cline fan when he was alive. The hair stands up all over his body, and it moves gently, as if a breeze is blowing through it.

They both like Johnny Cash. Louise is pleased—they have something in common now.

"I'm onto Jackson," Louise sings. "You big talken man."

The phone rings in the middle of the night. Louise sits straight up in bed. "What?" she says. "Did you say something?" Is she in a hotel room? She orients herself quickly. The ghost is under the bed again, one hand sticking out as if flagging down a bedroom taxi. Louise picks up the phone.

"Number eight just told me the strangest thing," Louise says.

"Did you try the country music?"

"Yes," Louise says. "But it didn't work. I think he liked it."

"That's a relief," Louise says. "What are you doing on Friday?"

"Working," Louise says. "And then I don't know. I was going to rent a video or something. Want to come over and see the ghost?"

"I'd like to bring over a few people," Louise says. "After rehearsal. The cellists want to see the ghost, too. They want to play for it, actually. It's kind of complicated. Maybe you could fix dinner. Spaghetti's fine. Maybe some salad, some garlic bread. I'll bring wine."

"How many cellists?" Louise says.

"Eight," Louise says. "And Patrick's busy. I might have to bring Anna. It could be educational. Is the ghost still naked?"

"Yes," Louise says. "But it's okay. He got furry. You can tell her he's a dog. So what's going to happen?"

"That depends on the ghost," Louise says. "If he likes the cellists, he might leave with one of them. You know, go into one of the cellos. Apparently it's very good for the music. And it's good for the ghost too. Sort of like those little fish that live on the big fishes. Remoras. Number eight is explaining it to me. He said that haunted instruments aren't just instruments. It's like they have a soul. The musician doesn't play the instrument any more. He or she plays the ghost."

"I don't know if he'd fit," Louise says. "He's largish. At least part of the time."

Louise says, "Apparently cellos are a lot bigger on the inside than they look on the outside. Besides, it's not like you're using him for anything."

"I guess not," Louise says.

"If word gets out, you'll have musicians knocking on your door day and night, night and day," Louise says. "Trying to steal him. Don't tell anyone."

Gloria and Mary come to see Louise at work. They leave with a group in a week for Greece. They're going to all the islands. They've been working with Louise to organize the hotels, the tours, the passports, and the buses. They're fond of Louise. They tell her about their sons, show her pictures. They think she should get married and have a baby.

Louise says, "Have either of you ever seen a ghost?"

Gloria shakes her head. Mary says, "Oh honey, all the time when I was growing up. It runs in families sometimes, ghosts and stuff like that. Not as much now, of course. My eyesight isn't so good now."

"What do you do with them?" Louise says.

"Not much," Mary says. "You can't eat them and you can't talk to most of them and they aren't worth much."

"I played with a Ouija board once," Gloria says. "With some other girls. We asked it who we would marry, and it told us some names. I forget. I don't recall that it was accurate. Then we got scared. We asked it who we were talking to, and it spelled out Z-E-U-S. Then it was just a bunch of letters. Gibberish."

"What about music?" Louise says.

"I like music," Gloria says. "It makes me cry sometimes when I hear a pretty song. I saw Frank Sinatra sing once. He wasn't so special."

"It will bother a ghost," Mary says. "Some kinds of music will stir it up. Some kinds of music will lay a ghost. We used to catch ghosts in my brother's fiddle.

Like fishing, or catching fireflies in a jar. But my mother always said to leave them be."

"I have a ghost," Louise confesses.

"Would you ask it something?" Gloria says. "Ask it what it's like being dead. I like to know about a place before I get there. I don't mind going someplace new, but I like to know what it's going to be like. I like to have some idea."

Louise asks the ghost but he doesn't say anything. Maybe he can't remember what it was like to be alive. Maybe he's forgotten the language. He just lies on the bedroom floor, flat on his back, legs open, looking up at her like she's something special. Or maybe he's thinking of England.

Louise makes spaghetti. Louise is on the phone talking to caterers. "So you don't think we have enough champagne," she says.

"I know it's a gala, but I don't want them falling over. Just happy. Happy signs checks. Falling over doesn't do me any good. How much more do you think we need?"

Anna sits on the kitchen floor and watches Louise cutting up tomatoes. "You'll have to make me something green," she says. "Why don't you just eat your crayon," Louise says. "Your mother isn't going to have time to make you green food when she has another baby. You'll have to eat plain food like everybody else, or else eat grass like cows do."

"I'll make my own green food," Anna says.

"You're going to have a little brother or a little sister," Louise says. "You'll have to behave. You'll have to be responsible. You'll have to share your room and your toys—not just the regular ones, the green ones, too."

"I'm not going to have a sister," Anna says. "I'm going to have a dog."

"You know how it works, right?" Louise says, pushing the drippy tomatoes into the saucepan. "A man and a woman fall in love and they kiss and then the woman has a baby. First she gets fat and then she goes to the hospital. She comes home with a baby."

"You're lying," Anna says. "The man and the woman go to the pound. They pick out a dog. They bring the dog home and they feed it baby food. And then one day all the dog's hair falls out and it's pink. And it learns how to talk, and it has to wear clothes. And they give it a new name, not a dog name. They give it a baby name and it has to give the dog name back."

"Whatever," Louise says. "I'm going to have a baby, too. And it will have the same name as your mother and the same name as me. Louise. Louise will be the name of your mother's baby, too. The only person named Anna will be you."

"My dog name was Louise," Anna says. "But you're not allowed to call me that."

Louise comes in the kitchen. "So much for the caterers," she says. "So where is it?"

"Where's what?" Louise says.

"The you know what," Louise says, "you know."

"I haven't seen it today," Louise says. "Maybe this won't work. Maybe it would rather live here." All day long she's had the radio turned on, tuned to the country station. Maybe the ghost will take the hint and hide out somewhere until everyone leaves.

The cellists arrive. Seven men and a woman. Louise doesn't bother to remember their names. The woman is tall and thin. She has long arms and a long nose. She eats three plates of spaghetti. The cellists talk to each other. They don't talk about the ghost. They talk about music. They complain about acoustics. They tell Louise that her spaghetti is delicious. Louise just smiles. She stares at the woman cellist, sees Louise watching her. Louise shrugs, nods. She holds up five fingers.

Louise and the cellists seem comfortable. They tease each other. They tell stories. Do they know? Do they talk about Louise? Do they brag? Compare notes? How could they know Louise better than Louise knows her? Suddenly Louise feels as if this isn't her house after all. It belongs to Louise and the cellists. It's their ghost, not hers. They live here. After dinner they'll stay and she'll leave. Number five is the one who likes foreign films, Louise remembers. The one with the goldfish. Louise said number five had a great sense of humor.

Louise gets up and goes to the kitchen to get more wine, leaving Louise alone with the cellists. The one sitting next to Louise says, "You have the prettiest eyes. Have I seen you in the audience sometimes?"

"It's possible," Louise says.

"Louise talks about you all the time," the cellist says. He's young, maybe twenty-four or twenty-five. Louise wonders if he's the one with the big hands. He has pretty eyes, too. She tells him that.

"Louise doesn't know everything about me," she says, flirting.

Anna is hiding under the table. She growls and pretends to bite the cellists. The cellists know Anna. They're used to her. They probably think she's cute. They pass her bits of broccoli, lettuce.

The living room is full of cellos in black cases the cellists brought in, like sarcophaguses on little wheels. Sarcophabuses. Dead baby carriages. After dinner the cellists take their chairs into the living room. They take out their cellos and tune them. Anna insinuates herself between cellos, hanging on the backs of chairs. The house is full of sound.

Louise and Louise sit on chairs in the hall and look in. They can't talk. It's too loud. Louise reaches into her purse, pulls out a packet of earplugs. She gives two to Anna, two to Louise, keeps two for herself. Louise puts her earplugs in. Now the cellists sound as if they are underground, down in some underground lake, or in a cave. Louise fidgets.

The cellists play for almost an hour. When they take a break Louise feels tender, as if the cellists have been throwing things at her. Tiny lumps of sound. She almost expects to see bruises on her arms.

The cellists go outside to smoke cigarettes. Louise takes Louise aside. "You should tell me now if there isn't a ghost," she says. "I'll tell them to go home. I promise I won't be angry."

"There is a ghost," Louise says. "Really." But she doesn't try to sound too convincing. What she doesn't tell Louise is that she's stuck a Walkman in her closet. She's got the Patsy Cline CD on repeat with the volume turned way down.

Louise says, "So he was talking to you during dinner. What do you think?"

"Who?" Louise says. "Him? He was pretty nice."

Louise sighs. "Yeah. I think he's pretty nice, too."

The cellists come back inside. The young cellist with the glasses and the big hands looks over at both of them and smiles a big blissed smile. Maybe it wasn't cigarettes that they were smoking.

Anna has fallen asleep inside a cello case, like a fat green pea in a coffin.

Louise tries to imagine the cellists without their clothes. She tries to picture them naked and fucking Louise. No, *fucking* Louise, fucking her instead. Which one is number four? The one with the beard? Number four, she remembers, likes Louise to sit on top and bounce up and down. She does all the work while he waves his hand. He conducts her. Louise thinks it's funny.

Louise pictures all of the cellists, naked and in the same bed. She's in the bed. The one with the beard first. Lie on your back, she tells him. Close your eyes. Don't move. I'm in charge. I'm conducting this affair. The one with the skinny legs and the poochy stomach. The young one with curly black hair, bent over his cello as if he might fall in. Who was flirting with her. Do this, she tells a cellist. Do this, she tells another one. She can't figure out what to do with the woman. Number five. She can't even figure out how to take off number five's clothes. Number five sits on the edge of the bed, hands tucked under her buttocks. She's still in her bra and underwear.

Louise thinks about the underwear for a minute. It has little flowers on it. Periwinkles. Number five waits for Louise to tell her what to do. But Louise is having a hard enough time figuring out where everyone else goes. A mouth has fastened itself on her breast. Someone is tugging at her hair. She is holding onto someone's penis with both hands, someone else's penis is rubbing against her cunt. There are penises everywhere. Wait your turn, Louise thinks. Be patient.

Number five has pulled a cello out of her underwear. She's playing a sad little tune on it. It's distracting. It's not sexy at all. Another cellist stands up on the bed, jumps up and down. Soon they're all doing it. The bed creaks and groans, and the woman plays faster and faster on her fiddle. Stop it, Louise thinks, you'll wake the ghost.

"Shit!" Louise says—she's yanked Louise's earplug out, drops it in Louise's lap. "There he is under your chair. Look. Louise, you really do have a ghost."

The cellists don't look. Butter wouldn't melt in their mouths. They are fucking their cellos with their fingers, stroking music out, promising the ghost yodels and Patsy Cline and funeral marches and whole cities of music and music to eat and music to drink and music to put on and wear like clothes. It isn't music Louise has ever heard before. It sounds like a lullaby, and then it sounds like a pack of wolves, and then it sounds like a slaughterhouse, and then it sounds like a motel room and a married man saying I love you and the shower is running at the same time. It makes her teeth ache and her heart rattle.

It sounds like the color green. Anna wakes up. She's sitting in the cello case, hands over her ears.

This is too loud, Louise thinks. The neighbors will complain. She bends over and sees the ghost, small and unobjectionable as a lapdog, lying under her chair. Oh, my poor baby, she thinks. Don't be fooled. Don't fall for the song. They don't mean it.

But something is happening to the ghost. He shivers and twists and gapes.

He comes out from under the chair. He leaves all his fur behind, under the chair in a neat little pile. He drags himself along the floor with his strong beautiful hands, scissoring with his legs along the floor like a swimmer. He's planning to change, to leave her and go away. Louise pulls out her other earplug. She's going to give them to the ghost. "Stay here," she says out loud, "stay here with me and the real Patsy Cline. Don't go." She can't hear herself speak. The cellos roar like lions in cages and licks of fire. Louise opens her mouth to say it louder, but the ghost is going. Fine, okay, go comb your hair. See if I care.

Louise and Louise and Anna watch as the ghost climbs into a cello. He pulls himself up, shakes the air off like drops of water. He gets smaller. He gets fainter. He melts into the cello like spilled milk. All the other cellists pause. The cellist who has caught Louise's ghost plays a scale. "Well," he says. It doesn't sound any different to Louise but all the other cellists sigh.

It's the bearded cellist who's caught the ghost. He holds onto his cello as if it might grow legs and run away if he let go. He looks like he's discovered America. He plays something else. Something old-fashioned, Louise thinks, a pretty old-fashioned tune, and she wants to cry. She puts her ear plugs back in again. The cellist looks up at Louise as he plays and he smiles. You owe me, she thinks.

But it's the youngest cellist, the one who thinks Louise has pretty eyes, who stays. Louise isn't sure how this happens. She isn't sure that she has the right cellist. She isn't sure that the ghost went into the right cello. But the cellists pack up their cellos and they thank her and they drive away, leaving the dishes piled in the sink for Louise to wash.

The youngest cellist is still sitting in her living room. "I thought I had it," he says. "I thought for sure I could play that ghost."

"I'm leaving," Louise says. But she doesn't leave.

"Good night," Louise says.

"Do you want a ride?" Louise says to the cellist.

He says, "I thought I might hang around. See if there's another ghost in here. If that's okay with Louise."

Louise shrugs. "Good night," she says to Louise.

"Well," Louise says, "good night." She picks up Anna, who has fallen asleep on the couch. Anna was not impressed with the ghost. He wasn't a dog and he wasn't green.

"Good night," the cellist says, and the door slams shut behind Louise and Anna.

Louise inhales. He's not married, it isn't that smell. But it reminds her of something.

"What's your name?" she says, but before he can answer her, she puts her ear plugs back in again. They fuck in the closet and then in the bathtub and then he lies down on the bedroom floor and Louise sits on top of him. To exorcise the ghost, she thinks. Hotter in a chilly sprout.

The cellist's mouth moves when he comes. It looks like he's saying, "Louise, Louise," but she gives him the benefit of the doubt. He might be saying her name.

She nods encouragingly. "That's right," she says. "Louise."

The cellist falls asleep on the floor. Louise throws a blanket over him. She watches him breathe. It's been a while since she's watched a man sleep. She takes a shower and she does the dishes. She puts the chairs in the living room away. She gets an envelope and she picks up a handful of the ghost's hair. She puts it in the envelope and she sweeps the rest away. She takes her earplugs out but she doesn't throw them away.

In the morning, the cellist makes her pancakes. He sits down at the table and she stands up. She walks over and sniffs his neck. She recognizes that smell now. He smells like Louise. Burnt sugar and orange juice and talcum powder. She realizes that she's made a horrible mistake.

Louise is furious. Louise didn't know Louise knew how to be angry. Louise hangs up when Louise calls. Louise drives over to Louise's house and no one comes to the door. But Louise can see Anna looking out the window.

Louise writes a letter to Louise. "I'm so sorry," she writes. "I should have known. Why didn't you tell me? He doesn't love me. He was just drunk. Maybe he got confused. Please, please forgive me. You don't have to forgive me immediately. Tell me what I should do."

At the bottom she writes, "P.S. I'm not pregnant."

Three weeks later, Louise is walking a group of symphony patrons across the stage. They've all just eaten lunch. They drank wine. She is pointing out architectural details, rows of expensive spotlights. She is standing with her back to the theater. She is talking, she points up, she takes a step back into air. She falls off the stage.

A man—a lawyer—calls Louise at work. At first she thinks it must be her mother who has fallen. The lawyer explains. Louise is the one who is dead. She broke her neck.

While Louise is busy understanding this, the lawyer, Mr. Bostick, says something else. Louise is Anna's guardian now.

"Wait, wait," Louise says. "What do you mean? Louise is in the hospital? I have to take care of Anna for a while?"

No, Mr. Bostick says. Louise is dead.

"In the event of her death, Louise wanted you to adopt her daughter Anna Geary. I had assumed that my client Louise Geary had discussed this with you. She has no living family. Louise told me that you were her family."

"But I slept with her cellist," Louise said. "I didn't mean to. I didn't realize which number he was. I didn't know his name. I still don't. Louise is so angry with me."

But Louise isn't angry with Louise anymore. Or maybe now she will always be angry with Louise.

Louise picks Anna up at school. Anna is sitting on a chair in the school office. She doesn't look up when Louise opens the door. Louise goes and stands in front of her. She looks down at Anna and thinks, this is all that's left of Louise. This is all I've got now. A little girl who only likes things that are green, who used to be a dog. "Come on, Anna," Louise says. "You're going to come live with me."

Louise and Anna live together for a week. Louise avoids her married lover at work. She doesn't know how to explain things. First a ghost and now a little girl. That's the end of the motel rooms.

Louise and Anna go to Louise's funeral and throw dirt at Louise's coffin. Anna throws her dirt hard, like she's aiming for something. Louise holds on to her handful too tightly. When she lets go, there's dirt under her fingernails. She sticks a finger in her mouth.

All the cellists are there. They look amputated without their cellos, smaller, childlike. Anna, in her funereal green, looks older than they do. She holds Louise's hand grudgingly. Louise has promised that Anna can have a dog. No more motels for sure. She'll have to buy a bigger house, Louise thinks, with a yard. She'll sell her house and Louise's house and put the money in trust for Anna. She did this for her mother—this is what you have to do for family.

While the minister is still speaking, number eight lies down on the ground beside the grave. The cellists on either side each take an arm and pull him back up again. Louise sees that his nose is running. He doesn't look at her, and he doesn't wipe his nose, either. When the two cellists walk him away, there's grave dirt on the seat of his pants.

Patrick is there. His eyes are red. He waves his fingers at Anna, but he stays where he is. Loss is contagious—he's keeping a safe distance.

The woman cellist, number five, comes up to Louise after the funeral. She embraces Louise, Anna. She tells them that a special memorial concert has been arranged. Funds will be raised. One of the smaller concert halls will be named the Louise Geary Memorial Hall. Louise agrees that Louise would have been pleased. She and Anna leave before the other cellists can tell them how sorry they are, how much they will miss Louise.

In the evening Louise calls her mother and tells her that Louise is dead.

"Oh sweetie," her mother says. "I'm so sorry. She was such a pretty girl. I always liked to hear her laugh."

"She was angry with me," Louise says. "Her daughter Anna is staying with me now."

"What about Anna's father?" her mother says. "Did you get rid of that ghost? I'm not sure it's a good idea having a ghost in the same house as a small girl."

"The ghost is gone," Louise says.

There is a click on the line. "Someone's listening in," her mother says. "Don't say anything—they might be recording us. Call me back from a different phone."

Anna has come into the room. She stands behind Louise. She says, "I want to go live with my father."

"It's time to go to sleep," Louise says. She wants to take off her funeral clothes and go to bed. "We can talk about this in the morning."

Anna brushes her teeth and puts on her green pajamas. She does not want Louise to read to her. She does not want a glass of water. Louise says, "When I was a dog . . ."

Anna says, "You were never a dog—" and pulls the blanket, which is not green, up over her head and will not say anything else.

Mr. Bostick knows who Anna's father is. "He doesn't know about Anna," he tells Louise. "His name is George Candle and he lives in Oregon. He's married and has two kids. He has his own company—something to do with organic produce, I think, or maybe it was construction."

"I think it would be better for Anna if she were to live with a real parent,"

Louise says. "Easier. Someone who knows something about kids. I'm not cut out for this."

Mr. Bostick agrees to contact Anna's father. "He may not even admit he knew Louise," he says. "He may not be okay about this."

"Tell him she's a fantastic kid," Louise says. "Tell him she looks just like Louise."

In the end George Candle comes and collects Anna. Louise arranges his airline tickets and his hotel room. She books two return tickets out to Portland for Anna and her father and makes sure Anna has a window seat. "You'll like Oregon," she tells Anna. "It's green."

"You think you're smarter than me," Anna says. "You think you know all about me. When I was a dog, I was ten times smarter than you. I knew who my friends were because of how they smelled. I know things you don't."

But she doesn't say what they are. Louise doesn't ask.

George Candle cries when he meets his daughter. He's almost as hairy as the ghost. Louise can smell his marriage. She wonders what Anna smells.

"I loved your mother very much," George Candle says to Anna. "She was a very special person. She had a beautiful soul."

They go to see Louise's gravestone. The grass on her grave is greener than the other grass. You can see where it's been tipped in, like a bookplate. Louise briefly fantasizes her own funeral, her own gravestone, her own married lover standing beside her gravestone. She knows he would go straight home after the funeral to take a shower. If he went to the funeral.

The house without Anna is emptier than Louise is used to. Louise didn't expect to miss Anna. Now she has no best friend, no ghost, no adopted former dog. Her lover is home with his wife, sulking, and now George Candle is flying home to his wife. What will she think of Anna? Maybe Anna will miss Louise just a little.

That night Louise dreams of Louise endlessly falling off the stage. She falls and falls and falls. As Louise falls she slowly comes apart. Little bits of her fly away. She is made up of ladybugs.

Anna comes and sits on Louise's bed. She is a lot furrier than she was when she lived with Louise. "You're not a dog," Louise says.

Anna grins her possum teeth at Louise. She's holding a piece of okra. "The supernatural world has certain characteristics," Anna says. "You can recognize it by its color, which is green, and by its texture, which is hirsute. Those are its outside qualities. Inside the supernatural world things get sticky but you never get inside things, Louise. Did you know that George Candle is a werewolf? Look out for hairy men, Louise. Or do I mean married men? The other aspects of the green world include music and smell."

Anna pulls her pants down and squats. She pees on the bed, a long acrid stream that makes Louise's eyes water.

Louise wakes up sobbing. "Louise," Louise whispers. "Please come and lie on my floor. Please come haunt me. I'll play Patsy Cline for you and comb your hair. Please don't go away."

She keeps a vigil for three nights. She plays Patsy Cline. She sits by the phone because maybe Louise could call. Louise has never not called, not for so long.

If Louise doesn't forgive her, then she can come and be an angry ghost. She can make dishes break or make blood come out of the faucets. She can give Louise bad dreams. Louise will be grateful for broken things and blood and bad dreams. All of Louise's clothes are up on their hangers, hung right-side out. Louise puts little dishes of flowers out, plates with candles and candy. She calls her mother to ask how to make a ghost appear but her mother refuses to tell her. The line may be tapped. Louise will have to come down, she says, and she'll explain in person.

Louise wears the same dress she wore to the funeral. She sits up in the balcony. There are enormous pictures of Louise up on the stage. Influential people go up on the stage and tell funny stories about Louise. Members of the orchestra speak about Louise. Her charm, her beauty, her love of music. Louise looks through her opera glasses at the cellists. There is the young one, number eight, who caused all the trouble. There is the bearded cellist who caught the ghost. She stares through her glasses at his cello. Her ghost runs up and down the neck of his cello, frisky. It coils around the strings, hangs upside-down from a peg.

She examines number five's face for a long time. Why you, Louise thinks. If she wanted to sleep with a woman, why did she sleep with you? Did you tell her funny jokes? Did you go shopping together for clothes? When you saw her naked, did you see that she was bowlegged? Did you think that she was beautiful?

The cellist next to number five is holding his cello very carefully. He runs his fingers down the strings as if they were tangled and he were combing them. Louise stares through her opera glasses. There is something in his cello. Something small and bleached is looking back at her through the strings. Louise looks at Louise and then she slips back through the f hole, like a fish.

They are in the woods. The fire is low. It's night. All the little girls are in their sleeping bags. They've brushed their teeth and spit, they've washed their faces with water from the kettle, they've zipped up the zippers of their sleeping bags.

A counselor named Charlie is saying, "I am the ghost with the one black eye, I am the ghost with the one black eye."

Charlie holds her flashlight under her chin. Her eyes are two black holes in her face. Her mouth yawns open, the light shining through her teeth. Her shadow eats up the trunk of the tree she sits under.

During the daytime Charlie teaches horseback riding. She isn't much older than Louise or Louise. She's pretty and she lets them ride the horses bareback sometimes. But that's daytime Charlie. Nighttime Charlie is the one sitting next to the fire. Nighttime Charlie is the one who tells stories.

"Are you afraid?" Louise says.

"No," Louise says.

They hold hands. They don't look at each other. They keep their eyes on Charlie.

Louise says, "Are *you* afraid?"

"No," Louise says. "Not as long as you're here."

# ELLEN WERNECKE

# Fairy Tale Pantoum

*Ellen Wernecke is a young poet from Wisconsin. Her work has appeared in magazines including* Merlyn's Pen *and* Porcupine. *The following poem, rich in fairy tale symbolism, was first published in* The Louisville Review *(Vol. 49/50), a biannual journal from Spalding University in Kentucky.*

—T. W.

The queen died and then the king died
Of grief—isn't that how the story goes?
The sorcerer taps his silver stick
And out fly the bewildered doves

Of grief—isn't that how the story goes?
There weren't seven brides for seven brothers
And out fly the bewildered doves
To bring the foolish maidens home.

There weren't seven brides for seven brothers
But one scepter gold had blessed them all
To bring the foolish maidens home.
(Can we begrudge their pinwheel minds?)

The frosty sheep in mudrent fields
Shedding careful pricks of brackish blood
And the hero is endlessly questing—
He seeks approval, but finds only dark.

Shedding careful pricks of brackish blood
The sorcerer taps his silver stick
He seeks approval but finds only dark—
The queen died and then the king died.

# SCOTT THOMAS

## The Puppet and the Train

*Scott Thomas is a poet and an artist, as well as a writer of both fiction and nonfiction. He has written articles on topics ranging from prehistoric grave art and British megaliths to wassail and Sheela-na-Gigs.*

*His short stories have been published in numerous magazines, including* Leviathan #3, Redsine, Deathrealm, Lore, Haunts, The Urbanite, Flesh and Blood, *and* Penny Dreadful, *and in the anthologies* The Dead Inn, Strangewood Tales, Starry Nights, *and the late Karl Edward Wagner's* The Year's Best Horror #22. *His first collection,* The Shadow of Flesh *was published in 1997.*

*A lifelong New Englander, Thomas has long been fascinated by the cycle of the seasons. He lives with his wife, Nancy, and cat, Hamish. Their antique farmhouse in Massachusetts was the inspiration for the home of the protagonist in "The Puppet and the Train," a story that first appeared in the author's second collection,* Cobwebs and Whispers.

—E. D.

*Massachusetts, 1909*

Although there had been several known cases of human infestation, actinomycosis, more commonly known as lumpy jaw, preferred cattle by a notable margin. The insidious little fungus would steal into the body of an animal, more often than not the head, where it would inspire swelling and create an abscess within the inflamed area. Gabriel Burkett had seen untreated animals afflicted with tumors the size of coconuts.

Even when kneeling, Gabe seemed tall. He was down in the shadow of a barn, long gentle fingers moving over the jaw of a hulking milk cow. The animal shifted nervously, moved its large eye and snorted. The veterinarian leaned his face close to its head and whispered soothingly.

Joseph McDonald, the owner of the cow, stood by with his hands in his pockets, watching. He had seen Gabe at work before, observed his solemn precision. He trusted Gabriel Burkett implicitly.

Still kneeling, Gabe nodded to himself, thought a moment more and looked up. "It's lumpy jaw, all right," he said. "If we had caught it sooner, I'd have cut it out, but it might be into bone at this point and there are some good-sized blood vessels to consider . . ."

Gabe felt around some more, then stood. He patted the beast's great neck.

"Simple enough," Gabe concluded, "we'll give her iodide of potash in her drinking water for a week or so. That should do nicely."

McDonald grinned. He was expecting something more invasive, something more complicated. Gabe looked him in the eye, like a preacher would, and while a younger man at forty-six, he spoke in a fatherly fashion, "Now Joseph, if you should happen to notice this sort of thing again, don't wait so long to fetch me, all right?"

McDonald nodded. "I will, Gabe, I will."

The men stepped away from the barn into the warm June sun. They turned to the road, alerted by the sound of a mortorcar's horn. A Model T raced around the bend and came to a dusty stop. Gabe frowned. He hated "Tin Lizzies" and relied on a beloved horse for his personal transportation. Mankind, he felt, was not wise enough to responsibly wield the power of its technology. Bombs, guns and soaring, horseless vehicles demonstrated his point menacingly, succinctly.

Young Dan Muir, son of a lawyer and a neighbor of these men, sprang from the automobile, goggled and wind-haired. He seemed breathless, as if he had run the length of dirt road to the McDonald farm, rather than driven it in his expensive contraption of metal.

"Doctor Burkett," the man called, "you must come—there's been a terrible accident down where they're setting up the circus in Gaughan's field."

Gabe threw McDonald a woeful look before climbing reluctantly into the sputtering horseless machine.

They raced over the top of a hill and drove down to where a stretch of railroad tracks gleamed out from behind a dense wall of small trees and tall bushes. Gabe cursed quietly to himself. He thought the accident scene looked like a cross between a children's book illustration and a nightmare. A train had plowed into the side of an elephant.

Poor jousting partners, a locomotive and an elephant. The giant grey mammal, like some misplaced corporeal relic of prehistory, was on its side; the steaming black metal monster had simply tilted off its rails. There was a great dark wound on the left where the tusked beast had taken the blow. The man who had been leading the elephant across the tracks when the train came roaring out of the bushes had fared the worst. No need to check for a pulse there. Strangely, there was more blood from him than from the larger animal.

A small crowd had gathered; the motorcar stopped. Burkett could only stare until Dan Muir turned to him and said, "Can you help it? See there, the front legs are kicking; it's still alive!"

"I've never treated an elephant," Gabe muttered.

"But you're a veterinarian; you can help it, can't you?"

Gabe did not reply. He took up his bag, climbed out of the car and pushed his way through the crowd.

It was an Indian elephant, that much he knew. He could tell from the tusks, smaller and straighter than those of the larger African breed. There was an unpleasant burnt smell close to the creature. He leaned over the massive wrinkled head and gazed into the black eye, big as a fist. The eye did not seem to contain anything like a spark of life, yet a thick dry trunk coiled around Gabe's leg and quivered. Startled, Gabe took a step back, nearly tripping over the appendage, which, following its tremor, went limp. Perhaps it was an involuntary nervous reaction; he had seen animals move in curious ways at the point of death and shortly thereafter.

The elephant was cold to the touch, cooler than the air, as if it had been dead for some time, though the accident had happened just a quarter of an hour previous. Gabe put a hand in front of the mouth and felt no breath. He worked his way back. Its side was not moving; there was no evidence of breathing whatsoever. The front limbs had stopped the spastic motion he had observed from the car, looking down as they came over the top of the hill, looking out over the colorful spired circus tents with their stripes and flags and the clutter of wagons like an encampment of gypsies.

"Look there!" someone in the crowd called out suddenly, and Gabe turned, looking up as a thin, naked man with brownish skin pulled himself up out of the enormous, surprisingly bloodless wound in the elephant's side. The man had wild black hair and wild black eyes and threw the crowd a glance both feral and contemptuous before springing from the dead elephant and racing off into the thick greenery nearby.

"Dear God," Gabe hissed.

"Catch him," the shout went up, and after a baffled pause, some young men did charge off in pursuit.

Gabe climbed up the body and peered into the wound, through the pale bars of the elephant's ribs into a hollow space where one would have expected to find an assortment of organs. It was like a room, the roof darkened as if a fire had been lit inside, and there was a dry tree bark-colored floor. Gabe reached a trembling hand down into the thing and scooped up two pale objects, which appeared to be candles, slipping them into his pocket.

Below, a man with a pointed beard of silver, sporting the long coat and the tall hat of a circus master, was bemoaning the loss of Trevor the Talking Elephant. He seemed less concerned with the trainer, whose segments now lay beneath a pair of damp blankets.

Dizzy, Gabe sat on one of the mighty grey legs, as if on a bench, and stared at the earth. He heard the rushing hiss of steam from the big black engine and watched as an ant dragged off a small piece of the elephant trainer.

We find Gabriel Burkett at his humble home which overlooks an orchard in the southern hills of a small central Massachusetts town. Tired from interviewing members of the circus, the driver of the train, and having discussed the bizarre situation with the local police, he only let his wife Audrey hear the more mundane aspects of the case. He did not wish to disturb her with the whole story for even he, a man accustomed to seeing sad and distressing sights, was himself unnerved by that afternoon's events.

The days in June were long and they sat outside after eating and watched the sky over the town as it went to orange and pink and deep blue. Roofs and steeples poked up through the distant billowing green of trees. Gabe thought about the thin brown figure that had dashed into the brush. The men who had gone looking for him had not been successful.

Gabe, while a serious-looking man, did not appear stern. He had dark, somewhat wavy hair and dark, deep-set eyes. There was something melancholic about his face, the features both intense and gentle. A child had once told him that he looked more like an undertaker than a veterinarian. He gazed over at his wife who sat on the farmer's porch with him, her lap a tangle of knitting, and he made a mental note to himself that he should (uncharacteristically) lock the door that night.

Lying in bed, he thought about the train, like a great metal puppet caterpillar, racing along with men inside, and wondered if—though it seemed impossible— the elephant had served a similar purpose, transporting its lone passenger, or, more accurately, its pilot. It had to have been dead before the train hit it; no animal can live with the majority of its vital organs missing. And where had those gone? The train had ripped the wound in the thing's side and, having inspected the carcass, Gabe had not found any scars that would have indicated an earlier extraction of the poor behemoth's innards.

Unable to sleep, he quietly rose and bent over the bed to touch Audrey's cheek. Sometimes she spoke out in the darkness, especially when their large amber and white cat moved restlessly, repositioning himself to find the most comfortable spot, thus disturbing her. She would mutter from a place between sleep and the world. She did this now. "Crouching on a roof . . . black mist from the lips," she said, then settled back into soft, rhythmic breathing. Her husband brushed a strand of cidery hair from her face.

Gabe walked downstairs and found the two candles in the pocket where he had left them. He had not told anyone else about them, none of the other stupefied townsfolk, not even the police. In a way he was afraid to have others see them, for it would make it harder to deny that such a mystery could exist in the world if there were more than one witness.

One of the resident circus freaks, a woman from Mexico who was covered in long dark hair, had told Gabe that she had heard strange noises one night and had wandered out of her tent to see a strange brown woman inserting a small cloth doll, like a witch's poppet, into the birthing place of Trevor the Talking elephant. The elephant was known as Bessie then and performed in a ring and was also made to move heavy objects. That was before they discovered that the elephant could "talk," and it was only later that the name was changed to Trevor. Somehow the circus proprietor seemed taken with that bit of alliteration and felt that the public would respond better to a male elephant talking more so than they would a female. Besides, the creature spoke in a masculine voice.

Gabe sat for a time just holding the candles. They had a strange feel, as if they were made from pale flesh, and they smelled of rare and secretive herbs, from far-off lands where a New Englander ought not venture. When at last he lit one, and saw the images in the light around the flame, he blew it out and hid both candles away in his desk.

One might think that an enigmatically hollowed-out elephant would make for a fine sideshow attraction in a circus. It was not to be. For while the curious flocked, the owner of the traveling entertainment had ordered the burning of the body mere hours after its demise. Gabriel Burkett learned this the next day, when he returned in hopes of better examining the creature. What veterinarian or man of science could blame him for wanting to? He was sorely disappointed to find that the remains had been destroyed. As for the circus, it packed up and left in the middle of the night, days earlier than scheduled. Those seeking thrills and diversion found only a trampled field.

Windy pines framed the pasture where Gabe knelt by a sheep in sunny grass. A farmer and his sons hovered nearby and Gabe's horse was grazing. Idyllic as the sprawling farmland appeared, it was haunted by tiny monsters, such as that which had caused the blindness in the patient that the man was examining.

Felix Griffin had summoned Gabe because the sheep had taken to walking in circles and seemed incapable of straight, forward motion. Then its vision went.

Gabe stood above the others when he rose, wiping his hands on his trousers. His face was grim and his voice low, "It's not good, Felix. I believe it's a case of gid in sheep. Are you familiar with it?"

"No," the farmer said.

"Occasionally a sheep will ingest the eggs of a bladder worm—a tape-worm in an early stage, actually. Well, the eggs hatch in the stomach and the worm gets into the blood and lands up somewhere else in the body, maybe the lungs or the heart, or in this case, the brain." Gabe pointed to his own skull.

Absently stroking the back of the sheep, the doctor continued. "This walking in circles indicates that only one side is infected. The blindness is another indication of bladder worm. The condition is advanced enough for me to feel some softening of the skull . . ."

The farmer was staring at the animal, nodding as he listened.

One of Griffin's freckled boys looked up at Gabe and said, "Are you going to kill her?"

Gabe crouched down to face the boy. "This poor beast is very ill, son. Sometimes we have to put an animal down as an act of mercy, or to prevent it from spreading a condition to other animals."

"But this one is my favorite . . ."

"Your favorite, you say? Well then, maybe I'll try something. There's nothing to lose, really. But will you promise you won't hate me if I can't save her?"

"I promise," the boy said.

The sheep was moved back to the barn and prepared. Gabe located the soft spot on its skull and went to work with a trocar and a cannula. He used a syringe to draw the contents out of the cyst.

Following the procedure, Gabe and the farmer stood outside in the tilted afternoon light.

"What do you think, Doc?"

Gabe sighed. "Well, there is a risk of brain inflammation, and that could be fatal, as one might expect. There could even be another worm in there that I didn't get. I can't be certain. We'll hope for the best."

The young freckled boy came up to Gabe and shook his hand. "She's going to be fine, now, I know she is. Thank you, mister."

Gabe always looked both sad and hopeful when he smiled.

The tempo of Aileen McCutcheon's humming was usually dictated by the particular task she was involved with at any given time. There were slow wistful airs when she knelt weeding in a warm garden of summer herbs. Jaunty reels accompanied the husking of corn, a ritual performed in a creaking rocking chair beneath her favorite maple. Patching her husband's wounded farm clothes called for slow quiet tones and now, in the kitchen, hustling to get a meal on the table, a swiftly melodic country dance tune swirled with the smells and steam of cooking.

The chickens sounded outside. There was always the risk of foxes and occasionally a neighbor's dog, or even a group of dogs, would steal into the yard and wreak havoc. Aileen glanced out the window into the yard and gasped.

A naked man with brownish skin and tousled black hair was crouched over a dead rooster. The other chickens lay convulsing on the ground around him. Aileen screamed and the stranger lifted his head to look at the window. He smiled menacingly, his wild eyes agleam and wispy black mist hissed out between his teeth.

Aileen released a series of piercing shrieks which sent the man running and brought her husband and his brother from a close field. They found her standing in the yard with the dead birds.

Gabriel Burkett stood holding the rooster, absently stroking its dead feathers. He studied Aileen intensely, nodding along with her words as she pointed to the grassy hill behind the farmhouse, describing how the lithe brown man had sprung away like a startled deer.

Ronald McCutcheon had taken a rifle and gone over the hill behind the house, searching the edge of the woods that blurred to green and black shadows, while Ronald's brother had gone to fetch the veterinarian and Edgar Gould, the chief of police.

"Sounds like that fellow from the circus," the Chief said.

Gabe nodded; the thought had occurred to him, too. He set the rooster down and bent to examine a hen.

The Chief was tall, with silvery hair and spectacles. He turned a slow circle, squinting. A search of the farm buildings had been fruitless. He watched Gabe for a moment. It was unusual for him to see the animal doctor in a state of puzzlement.

"Did he break their necks?" The Chief asked.

"No. No signs of violence whatsoever," Gabe reported.

"What do you make of that black on the beaks? Looks like carbon from a fire . . ."

There was a strange burnt smell in the air.

"So it does," Gabe agreed.

Ronald McCutcheon poked at one of the birds with his boot. "So, you don't know how he killed them?"

Gabe shook his head. "I suggest you don't eat any of them, Ronald . . . he may have used some kind of poison. I'd like to take one with me to do a postmortem."

"A what?"

"An examination."

"Oh. Of course," Ronald said.

"Well," the Chief said, "let me know if you find anything, Gabe. I'm goin' home—all these dead birds are makin' me hungry."

"Don't stay up too late," Audrey said. She kissed Gabe's forehead and went upstairs to bed.

When he finished with the chicken, the man moved from his examination room with its silvery tools and tables, its jars and bottles and sharp chemical smells. He settled in the modest library that looked out on moon-haunted pines. The two candles he had taken from inside the elephant were still hidden in the desk. He wondered if they would tell him more than the body of the bird had.

The examination had mystified Gabe. The hen appeared normal but for two things: the dark scorch-like black on the beak, and the heart, which was brittle and shriveled, like a prune.

Following a moment of hesitation, Gabe lit one of the stout fleshy candles. He folded his arms tight against his chest, but a chill found him through his clothes. Soft images blurred out of the hazy nimbus around the flame. It was as if he were in a moving vehicle, watching through a watery window.

There were familiar fields and houses. Familiar roads. At one point he seemed to be witnessing a view from a neighbor's roof, then he was crossing the dark, slow waters of the Assabet River, where he had played as a boy. It was night and the visions came like living paintings, traveling north. Through Northborough, the western corner of Marlborough, into Berlin. A house loomed, a dark window close, then inside, up some stairs. A door opened. It was a closet. Clothing hung in darkness. Then the first candle burnt out and the air smelled scorched.

Trembling, Gabe lit the second candle, and its ghastly glow was full of ghostly motion. Outside that house in Berlin . . . a sweet-faced old dog looked up, then sagged to the ground. Moon-suggested roads passed. A raccoon; it fell over on the earth, kicked, lay still.

The candle was shrinking. There were only fields and woods now.

"Landmarks," Gabe whispered urgently, "show some landmarks!"

The candle was sputtering. The pictures in the air above his desk grew dim and faded.

"Damn!" Gabe pounded the desk. The images had only shown him the direction, not the destination.

There was a trail of dead animals, like bread crumbs, scattered from Eastborough to Berlin. Dead cows, dead wildlife, dead pets. Gabe's heart ached. He saw the faces of farmers, their eyes dark with woe as they observed fallen flocks, the wet eyes of children cradling limp kittens and loyal sightlessly staring hounds. Brooding with a thin old man in a pasture where sheep lay crumpled like shrapnel from an exploded cloud, Gabe turned to the fellow and asked, "Is there a gunsmith in this town?"

The Browning 1903 was a small, simple automatic. It was comfortable in the hand and flat for easy concealment in a pocket or a waistband. Gabe hated guns. Gabe handed the gunsmith some bills and turned to leave. A box of bullets and the weapon added alien weight to his coat. He pushed the door open and a bell on it jingled.

It was bright outside and he moved to his horse, Sarah, who was tied outside. He stepped around to her left and came face to face with the thin brownish man whom he had seen climb out of the dead elephant.

The man smiled. He was dressed in fine clothes and his hair was combed back, tame. He was handsome, charming in the way he carried himself, some might think.

"Hunting does not suit you, Doctor," the man said, his face too close. His breath had a burnt smell. "Shouldn't you be off helping some crippled duck or something?"

Gabe could not locate his voice at first.

The man reached up and stroked Sarah's warm brown neck.

"What are you?" Gabe's voice quavered.

"A puppet," the man said cheerily, "just like you. We're all puppets to our natures. Unfortunately our natures seem to be at odds. You're good at helping creatures, and I . . ."

The man turned so that his mouth was several inches from the horse's snout and he exhaled a burst of black mist.

Sarah gasped and collapsed sideways, her great weight thumping dead on the dusty street.

"No!" Gabe cried.

The brown man grinned, turned and darted away. Gabe fumbled his weapon out, tried to remember how to remove the clip from the bottom of the handle, finally managed that and, with quaking hands, attempted to slip bullets into the magazine, the way the gunsmith had shown him.

It was too late. The man had pranced like an antelope down Berlin's main street, past the big brick bank, the pale stone library and the shops with great gleaming windows, and was gone. Gabe dropped the gun and knelt by his horse in the road, running his hand over her face as tears ran down his own.

Summer passed and September came. The days growing cooler as the frost moved downward from Canada—slow and steady steps of ice. The days ever shorter, afternoon balanced on a quiet sense of expectation, and a growing sense of resignation.

Gabe had returned to a world of normalcy. For weeks he had gone into the woods to practice shooting with the small pistol, telling Audrey he was going for walks. He had gotten quite accurate, but now the gun sat in a drawer in his desk, in the library.

He no longer brooded over maps, speculating on where his enemy might have gone, or might be headed. The trail had ended in Concord. Some dairy cows had died mysteriously, he had heard, and their faces had borne the telltale scorching. But that was the last incident; there were no more reports of strange animal deaths. Perhaps it was for the best, he thought. That monster probably could have dropped him just as easily as it had dropped Sarah. It was a powerful opponent, and likely imbued with uncanny sensitivities, for it had recognized Gabe and even appeared to know his intentions.

Life seemed right, sitting there on the porch with his Audrey, watching the sky go from orange to pink, to cool September blue. She with her knitting and soft greying hair, the loose strands from her bun giving her a girlish look. Gabe looked out over the trees and knew there was a vast world out there, with great bustling cities, and exotic countries, each with their own marvels and charms, but he loved the simple things and the familiar. He did not hunger to roam and explore. The hills and fields, the old homes and stone walls, the orchards and woods of the town he loved were enough for him.

Gabe gazed over at Audrey as she rocked, humming. He smiled, and his smile was both hopeful and sad.

"Motorcars," Gabe muttered disdainfully, hunched over the injured pig.

Sam Maynard, the farmer, paced in the dirt, cursing beneath his breath. His twelve-year-old son, who had been learning to drive their year-old Indiana-made Black Crow, stood guiltily near, pouting.

The animal was well-behaved, under the circumstances. It lay on its side breathing nervously, kicked a bit at first, but did not struggle or try to escape. Gabe spoke to it in a comforting whisper as he worked, checking the injured leg for broken bones, of which fortunately, there were none.

At last the veterinarian looked up. "It might have been much worse, I should say. No breaks. The wound is not so bad; no need for stitches."

Maynard was relieved and smiled. "She made such a sound when he hit her . . . scared the Devil out of me!"

"That's because she was scared, more than hurt, I'd be willing to say," Gabe ventured.

Treatment was simple enough. He cleaned the wound and dusted it with powdered iodoform before bandaging.

Gabe rose, tall and straight, and clapped his hands together. He checked his pocket watch, slipped it back into his vest. "She'll be fine, Sam, just keep her out of the mud until that heals over."

The farmer barked at his son, "Get her into the hog house and clean yourself up for supper."

Turning to the doctor, the man spoke more softly, "You're welcome to stay and have a bite, Gabe. The missus is roasting a chicken . . ."

"You're kind to offer, Sam, but my missus is, too, and she's queen of the world when it comes to roast chicken." Gabe chuckled. "I best be off."

Sam walked Gabe to his new horse, Nipmuck. The tall man mounted and before heading off, asked, "Say, Sam, how's that prized hog of yours doing? Did that ginger clear up the indigestion?"

"It sure did, just like you said. In fact, we're taking her up to Derry, New Hampshire, come Saturday—there's a big fair up there, you know. You might want to take your Audrey up for the day; have yourself a good time. I hear there's to be an apple pie contest and an ox pull and even a talking cow, if you can believe a thing like that."

"A talking cow?"

"That's what they say." Sam chortled.

Gabe shivered. "Well, Sam, feels like it's going to be a cold night. I better be on my way . . ."

"A hundred dollars?" Dan Muir exclaimed. "Well sure, Doc, I'll drive you. Hell, I'll drive you to Timbuktu for a hundred dollars."

"Excellent," Gabe said stiffly. He left McTaggart's Pub, where he had known he'd find young Muir, and rode swiftly to his cozy home, which somehow felt warmer, filled with the smell of baked chicken. But Gabe's appetite had been compromised, and he could do little more than dream into the steam wisping up from his plate.

In the morning, after slipping into his library and fumbling in the desk, he told Audrey that he was going for a walk, to take in the changing foliage in the woods.

Muir came by the house shortly after nine o'clock and tooted his horn. Gabe thought the Model T looked like a cross between a coffin and an insect, black and gleaming in the September sunlight.

"Ready, Doc?" Dan Muir called.

Halfway between his porch and the idling metal monstrosity, Gabe turned and gazed back at Audrey, who stood smiling unsuspectingly. He wanted to have a good long look at her, in case it was his last.

Over roads of gravel and dirt, roads soft with mud and crisp with leaves, they traveled north. On through Middlesex County, through the city of Lowell with its great brick mills churning, up into Collinsville with green pastures, golden haystacks and rustling acres of corn. They crossed into New Hampshire, and the road was a lonely ribbon of brown through dark pine forest. Hawks hung like kites in the clear sky and hills of blue haze rose up.

Small villages passed, white churches brightly spired against changing maples and ragged spires of fir. Gabe, quiet and too distracted to focus on his own fear of traveling in the Ford, grinned when they came upon one of those motorized buggies, commonly called high-wheelers, stuck in the muddy road. Popular with farmers and built to negotiate such rural routes, this one's thin wheels were no match for the deep dark puddle that dominated a low point in the path. The farmer had hitched a massive quarter horse to his technological wonder. Gabe chuckled bitterly when the horse pulled the buggy free.

"All of these contraptions would be better off with horses pulling them," Gabe declared.

"Don't blame the machine," Muir said, "It's the driver's shortcomings that got him stuck." He maneuvered the Model T onto the grassy bank of the road, around the puddle and the embarrassed farmer, and sped onward.

Dan Muir gave Gabe a funny look when the veterinarian handed him the hundred dollars upon arriving at the county fair in Derry.

"You needn't pay me now, Doc. I figured you'd wait 'til we got home."

Gabe shrugged ambiguously and set off through the crowds.

There were tents and the smell of cooking, close laughter and great-eyed children. Gabe craned his neck, searching. His pulse was fast and dizziness came into his head, rose swiftly along the road from his heart. He reached into the pocket of his grey coat and clung to the cold metal there.

There was a large wooden structure erected for the occasion; a long steep roof supported only by beams. Much of the activity was centered there. Gabe worked his way over, excusing himself politely, numbly, as he stepped closer, moving through the throngs. It was shaded and cool beneath the roof and there were tables and more milling bodies. Prize-winning pumpkins, prize-winning apples, prize-winning grain on display. He could smell the corn, gold, pale and sweet.

There were household goods made by women and a section where men, with thumbs crooked in their suspenders, gazed eagerly upon newfangled labor-saving farm devices. Gabe moved along, floated tall in the crowd, the hum of his blood moving faster.

Exiting one of the mall's far ends, Gabe studied the field where the fair had been set up. He could see the rail pens with their show-beasts enclosed. Closer still and he could smell the warm, earthy animal smells. Bored and nervous creatures paced, chewed, or impossibly tried to become invisible, tucking themselves into hay or corners in their tight pens. There were ribbons tacked to the enclosures—best ewe, best heifer, best bull. Cows lowed. Where was the talking cow?

More tents stood ahead, beyond the livestock area. Here there was a touch of carnival atmosphere. A garish painting of a two-headed lamb loomed up. People had gathered around for a contest to award the woman with the smallest feet $2.00. A larger group stood outside a pale rippling tent from which came the scent of fresh hay and manure. Gabe saw the sign with big red letters, heard a boy out front, like a barker, calling, "Come see the magnificent talking cow! Come one and all and view this miraculous wonder. Hear it speak and answer your questions!"

Gabe stared at the crude painting of a black and white cow as people bumped against him, pushing past to join the human herd. He found himself in line, moving slowly toward the freckled boy, felt the offered money leave his hand.

It was dark inside and a man with a bushy white beard was addressing the group which faced the dully staring cow. The animal stood in a tiny pen up on a pedestal at the center of the enclosure. The beast looked innocuous enough.

The farmer, dressed handsomely in an expensive suit, thanks to his freak cow, chose from a small sea of raised hands; everyone wanted to ask the talking cow a question. "You there," the man said, pointing to a pretty young woman.

"What's your name?" the girl giggled, feeling rather foolish.

"Betsy," the cow replied in a voice that sounded rather masculine for a Betsy. A low murmur went through the crowd.

The farmer gave a big toothless smile. "Someone else?"

Again the hands went up and the farmer, gloating like a ringmaster, pointed to a tall solemn-looking man with dark, deep-set eyes. The man edged closer. He strained to see the side of the cow, which was marked strangely, as if the hide had been opened and melted shut.

Gabe was about to speak when a familiar voice assaulted him. "Hey, Gabe!"

It was Sam Maynard. He and his son stood nearby, and the farmer thrust out a blue ribbon which his pig had won.

"Look, Gabe, we got first prize!"

The sideshow's host sounded impatient now. "You had a question, mister?"

Gabe's concentration had been broken by the appearance of his neighbor. He turned back to the cow's head, large and close through the bars of its pen, and his hand slid back into the gun pocket. He felt the weight, the trigger, the sweat and heat in his palm.

"Yes, I have a question . . . Tell me, Betsy, how is it you can talk?"

The cow raised its skull to the man and the mouth moved and, looking into its eyes, Gabe could tell that the animal was not truly alive—not in the conventional sense.

The beast answered evenly, "My speech is a gift from God," it said.

Gabe edged closer still, in the cramped choking shadows of the tent. "What god might that be?"

"The very same god that gave you speech," the cow said.

The hand came up, the gun came up and it banged and flashed. Smoke and noise. Again and again. People screamed and stampeded to get out as Gabe fired into the head and body until the gun was empty and clicking. The cow shrieked as a man would shriek and toppled heavily onto its side.

"Son of a bitch!" the beast's owner cursed, rushing at Gabe.

Gabe spun to face the man, said, "It's a monster! A monster!"

The farmer struck Gabe in the face and he went down, dropping a crescent-bladed pruning knife he had pulled from his coat. Others, seeing that he was out of bullets, converged, kicking him. He looked up, saw Sam Maynard staring in horror and confusion.

Gabe called to him, "Sam, cut it open! The right side—cut it!"

Gabe curled on the ground as a flurry of feet thudded against him. He gasped and coughed. Sam hesitated for a moment, then grabbed the pruning knife with its cruel curved blade and pulled himself up into the cow's pen. He knelt beside it. Trembling, he sliced into the side of the animal, along the oddly mottled length of hide. It gave easily, opened wide and a burnt smell filled the tent. The men who had been beating Gabe stopped and watched as Sam pulled open the sides of the bloodless maw. There were no ribs on that side, and curled inside, like an unborn thing, was a naked brownish man with wild black hair and wild dying eyes. The bullets that had punched through the cow had found him, and now blood came snaking from a hole in his throat. Unable to speak, he let out a final breath, a hiss of black mist that went up into Sam's face. Sam gasped, shuddered and toppled from the platform. He lay beside Gabe on the hard dirt floor, dead.

Having been arrested for murder, Gabe sat in a cell for two days, bruised and cold, hugging his cracked ribs. He heard a pair of footsteps approach and looked up to see the chief of police and young Dan Muir. Muir's father had been hired to defend the veterinarian.

"You're all done, here," the officer said, unlocking the cell.

Gabe stared quizzically. "I don't understand . . ."

"The charges against you have been dropped, Doctor Burkett. Go home and try to forget this whole thing. That's what folks around here want to do, forget the whole ungodly mess."

Muir helped Gabe from his bunk, then out to the Model T which, under the circumstances, was a welcome sight.

———————

They drove down the quiet lanes of an autumn afternoon. The air was pleasantly cool and the sun shone bright. Hawks hung free and smaller birds pecked in the harvest fields, unaccosted for the time being.

It did not take Gabriel long to ask the question. "Why did they let me go?"

Dan Muir gave him a strange look. "They said I'm not supposed to say a word to anyone."

Gabe studied him. "But . . ."

"But I think you ought to know. They performed an autopsy on that man that was in the cow. He wasn't like a man in ways, from what I heard."

"What do you mean?" Gabe asked.

"Well, when they opened his head and looked in his skull, there was this thing in there where his brain should have been. Some kind of an animal, I guess, sort of like a cross between a human fetus and an insect in a larval stage. Its body was all shiny black and segmented, and it had these skinny tendrils running down into his spinal column, and into his major blood vessels."

Gabe stared at the road. "Dear God," he whispered.

"The fellow that did the autopsy wanted to take it to show a professor friend over at Harvard, but the police chief had it burned."

"Good man," Gabe said softly. "Good man."

The smell of roasting chicken was emanating from the house. Gabe sat on the porch watching as the sun mocked the colors of the ridge of trees it was setting behind. His chair creaked as he rocked and he could hear Audrey humming from inside.

The days were short now, and October was only hours away. Dreaming off into the deepening heavens, he caught movement from the corner of his eye. A moth had become entangled in a spider web up where one of the support beams of the farmer's porch met the overhanging roof. The moth struggled futilely and the spider poked out from a dark split in the wood and edged out.

Gabe stood, tall man that he was, and reached up. With gentle fingers, he worked delicately to pry the moth from the thin and sticky bands. The brown moth fluttered and went spinning free into the cool air. Gabe stood on the porch and watched as it made its way into the uncertain dusk. He smiled and his smile, as always, was hopeful and sad.

# CHRISTOPHER FOWLER

# Crocodile Lady

*Christopher Fowler lives and works in central London, where he runs the Soho film and design company, Creative Partnership, creating film campaigns. In his spare time he write novels and short stories.*

*Although he began his career writing humor books, he shifted into what he calls "dark urban." His first short story collection,* City Jitters, *featured interlinked tales of urban malevolence. Since then he's had seven further volumes of short stories published:* City Jitters Two, The Bureau of Lost Souls, Sharper Knives, Flesh Wounds, Personal Demons, *and* Uncut. *His most recent collection,* The Devil in Me, *was published in early 2002. He won the British Fantasy Society Award in 1998 for his story "Wageslaves."*

*His first novel,* Roofworld, *is being developed as a film. Other novels by Fowler are* Rune, Red Bride, Darkest Day, Spanky *(being scripted as a feature by director Guillermo Del Toro),* Psychoville, *(just cast as a film with Jude Law and Sadie Frost in the lead roles),* Disturbia, Soho Black, *and* Calabash. *His most recent novel,* Get Out of the House, *was published in the spring of 2002, and his next is called* Nothing Is Too Much Trouble. *"Crocodile Lady" originally appeared in* Crimewave: Dark Before Dawn.

—E. D.

## 1. Finchley Road to Swiss Cottage

*London has the oldest underground railway system in the world. Construction began in 1863 and was completed in 1884. Much later it was electrified, and since then has been periodically modified. A great many of the original stations have been abandoned, renamed or resited. A partial list of these would include Aldwych, British Museum, Brompton Road, York Road, St Mary's, Down Street, Marlborough Road, South Kentish Town, King William Street, North End and City Road. In many cases the maroon-tiled ticket halls remain, and so do the railway platforms. Even now, some of these tunnels are adorned with faded wartime signs and posters. Crusted with dry melanic silt produced by decades of still air, the walls boom softly as trains pass in nearby tunnels, but the stations themselves no longer have access from the streets above, and are only visited by scuttling brown mice. If you look hard, though, you can glimpse the past. For example, the eerie green and cream platform of the old Mark Lane station can be spotted from passing trains to the immediate west of the present Tower Hill Station.*

"You know what gets me through the day? Hatred. I hate the little bastards. Each and every one of them. Most of the time I wish they would all just disappear." Deborah fixed me with a cool eye. "Yeah, I know it's not the best attitude for a teacher to have, but when you know them as well as I do . . ."

"I think I do," I replied.

"Oh? I thought this work was new to you. Being your first day and all."

"Not new, no."

"My boyfriend just decided he wants us to have kids. He never liked them before. When he was made redundant he started picking me up from school in the afternoons, and saw them running around my legs in their boots and rain-macs asking endless questions, and suddenly he thought they were cute and wanted to have a baby, just when I was thinking of having my tubes tied. I don't want to bring my work home with me. We still haven't sorted it out. It's going to ruin our relationship. Hey, hey." Deborah broke off to shout at a boy who was trying to climb over the barrier. "Get back down there and wait for the man to open the gate." She turned back to me. "Christ, I could use a cigarette. Cover for me when we get there. I'll sneak a couple in while they're baiting the monkeys, that's what all the other teachers do."

Good teachers are like good nurses. They notice things ordinary people miss. Ask a nurse how much wine she has left in her glass and she'll be able to tell you the exact amount, because for her the measurement of liquids is a matter of occupational observation. The same with teachers. I can tell the age of any child to within six months because I've been around them so much. Then I got married, and I wasn't around them anymore.

But old habits die hard. You watch children constantly, even when you think you're not, and the reflex continues to operate even in civilian life. You bump into pupils in the supermarket. "Hello, Miss, we didn't know you ate food." They don't quite say that, but you know it's what they're thinking.

If there's one thing I know it's how children think. That was why I noticed there was something wrong at Baker Street. My senses had been caught off guard because of the tunnels. Actually, I sensed something even before then, as early as our arrival at Finchley Road tube station. I should have acted on my instincts then.

God knows, I was nervous enough to begin with. It was the first day of my first week back at work after twelve long years, and I hadn't expected to be have responsibility thrust at me like this, but the school was understaffed, teachers were off sick and the headmaster needed all the help he could get. The last time I had worked in the education system, the other teachers around me were of roughly the same age. Now I was old enough to be a mother to most of them, and a grandmother to their charges. I wouldn't have returned to Invicta Primary at all if my husband hadn't died. I wasn't surprised when the bank warned me that there would be no money. Peter wasn't exactly a rainy-day hoarder. I needed to earn, and have something to keep my mind occupied. Teaching was the only skill I was sure I still possessed.

Which was how I ended up shepherding twenty seven-to-eight-year-old boys and girls on a trip to the London Zoological Gardens, together with another teacher, Deborah, a girl with a tired young face and a hacking smoker's cough.

I hadn't been happy about handling the excursion on my first day back, especially when I heard that it involved going on the tube. I forced myself not to think about it. There were supposed to be three of us but the other teacher was off with flu, and delaying the trip meant dropping it from the term schedule altogether, so the headmaster had decreed that we should go ahead with the original plan. There was nothing unusual in this; the teaching shortage had reached its zenith and I'd been eagerly accepted back into the school where I'd worked before I was married. They put me on a refresher course, mostly to do with computer literacy, but the basic curriculum hadn't changed much. But things were very different from when I was a pupil myself. For a start, nobody walked to the school any more. Parents didn't think it was safe. I find parents exasperating—all teachers do. They're very protective about some things, and yet utterly blind to other, far more obvious problems. If they found out about the short-staffed outings, everybody would get it in the neck. The parents had been encouraged to vote against having their children driven around in a coach; it wasn't environmentally friendly. It didn't stop them from turning up at the school gates in people-carriers, though.

Outside the station the sky had lowered into muddy swirls of cloud, and it was starting to rain. Pupils are affected by the weather. They're always disruptive and excitable when it's windy. Rain makes them sluggish and inattentive. (In snow they go mad and you might as well close the school down.) You get an eye for the disruptives and outsiders, and I quickly spotted the ones in this group, straggling along at the rear of the tube station hall. In classrooms they sit at the back in the corners, especially on the left-hand side, the sneaky, quiet trouble-makers. They feel safe because you tend to look to the center of the class, so they think they're less visible. Kids who sit in the front row are either going to work very hard or fall in love with you. But the ones at the rear are the ones to watch, especially when you're turning back towards the blackboard.

There were four of them, a pair of hunched, whispering girls as close as Siamese twins, a cheeky ginger-haired noisebox with his hands in everything, and a skinny, melancholy little boy wearing his older brother's jacket. This last one had a shaved head, and the painful-looking nicks in it told me that his hair was cut at home to save money. He kept his shoulders hunched and his eyes on the ground at his feet, braced as though he was half-expecting something to fall on him. A pupil who hasn't done his homework will automatically look down at the desk when you ask the class a question about it, so that only the top of his head is visible (this being based on the 'if I can't see her, she can't see me' theory). If he is sitting in the back row, however, he will stare into your eyes with an earnest expression. This boy never looked up. Downcast eyes can hide a more personal guilt. Some children are born to be bullied. They seem marked for bad luck. Usually they have good reason to adopt such defensive body language. Contrary to what parents think, there's not a whole lot you can do about it.

"What's his name?" I asked.

"Oh that's Connor, he'll give you no trouble. Never says a word. I forget he's here sometimes." *I bet you do*, I thought. *You never notice him because he doesn't want you to.*

"Everybody hold up their right hand," I called. It's easier to count hands than heads when they're standing up, but still they'll try to trick you. Some kids will hold up both hands, others won't raise any. I had lowered my voice to speak to them; you have to speak an octave lower than your normal register if you want to impose discipline. Squeaky high voices, however loud, don't get results. They're a sign of weakness, indicating potential teacher hysteria. Children can scent deficiencies in teachers like sharks smell blood.

"Miss, I'm left handed." The ginger boy mimed limb-failure; I mentally transferred him from 'disruptive' to 'class clown.' They're exuberant but harmless, and usually sit in the middle of the back row.

"I want to see everybody's hand, now." *Sixteen*, and the four at the rear of the ticket hall. "Keep right under cover, out of the rain. You at the back, tuck in, let those people get past." *Seventeen*, the clown, *eighteen*, *nineteen*, the Siamese twins, *twenty*, the sad boy. "We're going to go through the barrier together in a group, so everybody stay very, very close." I noticed Deborah studying me as I marshalled the children. There was disapproval in her look. She appeared about to speak, then held herself in check. *I'm doing something wrong*, I thought, alarmed. But the entry gate was being opened by the station guard, and I had to push the sensation aside.

Getting our charges onto the escalator and making them stand on the right was an art in itself. Timson, the class clown, was determined to prove he could remount the stairs and keep pace with passengers travelling in the opposite direction. An astonishingly pretty black girl had decided to slide down on the rubber hand-rail.

"We step off at the end," I warned, "don't jump, that's how accidents happen." My voice had rediscovered its sharp old timber, but now there was less confidence behind it. London had changed while I had been away, and was barely recognizable to me now. There were so many tourists. Even at half past ten on a wintry Monday morning, Finchley Road tube station was crowded with teenagers in wet nylon coats, hoods and backpacks, some old ladies on a shopping trip, some puzzled Japanese businessmen, a lost-looking man in an old-fashioned navy blue raincoat. Deborah exuded an air of weary lassitude that suggested she wouldn't be too bothered if the kids got carried down to the platform and were swept onto the rails like lemmings going over a cliff.

"Stay away from the edge," I called, stirring my arms at them. "Move back against the wall to let people past." I saw the irritation in commuters' faces as they eyed the bubbling, chattering queue. Londoners don't like children. "We're going to be getting on the next train, but we must wait until it has stopped and its doors are open before we move forward. I want you to form a crocodile."

The children looked up at me blankly. "A crocodile shape, two, two, two, two, all the way along," I explained, chopping in their direction with the edges of my palms.

Deborah gave me a wry smile. "I don't think anyone's ever told them to do that before," she explained.

"Then how do you get them to stay in lines?" I asked.

"Oh, we don't, they just surge around. They never do what they're told. You can't do anything with them. The trouble with children is they're not, are they? Not children. Just grabby little adults."

No, I thought, *you're so wrong.* But I elected not to speak. I looked back at the children gamely organizing themselves into two wobbly columns. "They're not doing so badly."

Deborah wasn't interested. She turned away to watch the train arriving. "Crocodile, crocodile," the kids were chanting, making snappy-jawed movements to each other. The carriages of the train appeared to be already half-full. I had expected them to be almost empty. As the doors opened, we herded the children forward. I kept my eyes on the pairs at the back, feeding them in between my outstretched arms as though I was guiding unruly sheep into a pen. I tried not to think about the entrance to the tunnel, and the stifling, crushing darkness beyond it.

"Miss, Raj has fallen over." I looked down to find a minuscule Indian child bouncing up from his knees with a grin on his face. I noted that no damage had been done, then lifted his hands, scuffed them clean and wrapped them around the nearest carriage pole. "Hang on," I instructed as the doors closed.

"Miss, how many stops is it?" asked a little girl at my side.

"We go to Swiss Cottage, then St. John's Wood, then Baker Street, then we change from the Jubilee line to the Bakerloo line and go one stop to Regent's Park."

"Miss, is there a real cottage in Swiss Cottage?"

"Miss, are we going to Switzerland?"

"Miss, can you ski in Swiss Cottage?"

"Miss, are we going skiing?"

"We're going skiing! We're going skiing!"

The train pulled away and everyone screamed. For a moment I sympathized with Deborah. I looked out of the window as the platform vanished. When I married Peter we moved out to Amersham, at the end of the Metropolitan line, and stopped coming into central London. Peter was a lecturer. I was due for promotion at the school. In time I could have become the headmistress, but Peter didn't want me to work and that was that, so I had to give up my job and keep house for him. A year later, I discovered that I couldn't have children. Suddenly I began to miss my classroom very badly.

"Miss, make him get off me." Timson was sitting on top of a girl who had grabbed a seat. Without thinking, I lifted him off by his jacket collar.

"I wouldn't do that if I were you," said Deborah. "They'll have you up before the Court of Human Rights for maltreatment. Best not to touch them at all." She swung to the other side of the central pole and leaned closer. "How long has it been since you last taught?"

"Twelve years."

"You've been away a long time." It sounded suspiciously like a criticism. "Well, we don't manhandle them anymore. EEC ruling." Deborah peered out of the window. "Swiss Cottage coming up, watch out."

## 2. Swiss Cottage to St. John's Wood

*Many projects to build new tube lines were abandoned due to spiralling costs and sheer impracticability. An unfinished station tunnel at South Kensington served as a signalling school in the nineteen thirties, and was later equipped to record delayed-action bombs falling into the Thames which might damage the underwater tube tunnels. The Northern Heights project to extend the Northern Line to Alexandra Palace was halted by the Blitz. After this, the government built a number of deep-level air-raid shelters connected to existing tube stations, several of which were so far underground that they were leased after the war as secure archives. As late as the 1970s, many pedestrian tube subways still looked like passageways between bank vaults. Vast riveted doors could be used to seal off tunnels in the event of fire or flood. There was a subterranean acridity in the air. You saw the light rounding the dark bend ahead, heard the pinging of the albescent lines, perhaps glimpsed something long sealed away. Not all of the system has changed. Even now there are tunnels that lead nowhere, and platforms where only ghosts of the past wait for trains placed permanently out of service.*

Trying to make sure that nobody got off when the doors opened would have been easier if the children had been wearing school uniforms, but their casual clothes blended into a morass of bright colors, and I had to rely on Deborah keeping the head-count from her side of the carriage. In my earlier days at Invicta the pupils wore regulation navy blue with a single yellow stripe, and the only symbol of non-conformity you saw—apart from the standard array of faddish haircuts—was the arrangement of their socks, pulled down or the wrong color, small victories for little rebels.

I avoided thinking about the brick and soil pressing down on us, but was perspiring freely by now. I concentrated on the children, and had counted to fifteen when half a dozen jolly American matrons piled into the car, making it hard to finish the tally. I moved as many of the children as I could to one side, indicating that they should stay in crocodile formation. I instinctively knew that most of them were present, but I couldn't see the sad little boy. "Connor," I called, "Make yourself known please." An elliptical head popped out between two huge tourists. So unsmiling. I wondered if he had a nemesis, someone in the class who was making his life hell. Bullies are often small and aggressive because of their height. They go for the bigger, softer boys to enhance their reputation, and they're often popular with games teachers because of their bravado. There's not much I don't know about bullies. I was married to one for twelve years.

"I've got these new assignment books in my bag," said Deborah, relooping her hair through her scrunchie and checking her reflection in the glass. "Some government psychology group wants to test out a theory about how kids look at animals. More bloody paperwork. It's not rocket science, is it, the little sods just see it as a day off and a chance to piss about."

"You may be right," I admitted. "But children are shaped far more by their external environment than anyone cares to admit."

"How's that, then?"

"They recently carried out an experiment in a New York public school," I explained, "placing well-behaved kids and those with a history of disruption in two different teaching areas, one clean and bright, the other poorly lit and untidy. They found that children automatically misbehaved in surroundings of chaos—not just the troubled children but all of them, equally."

Deborah looked at me oddly, swaying with the movement of the train. Grey cables looped past the windows like stone garlands, or immense spiderwebs. "You don't miss much, don't you? Is that how you knew Connor was hiding behind those women?"

"No, that's just instinct. But I've been reading a bit about behavioral science. It's very interesting." I didn't tell her that before I was married I had been a teacher for nearly fourteen years. The only thing I didn't know about children was what it was like to have one.

"Well, I'm sorry, I know it's a vocation with some people, but not me. It's just a job. God, I'm dying for a fag." She hiked her bag further up her shoulder. "Didn't your old man want you to work, then?"

"Not really. But I would have come back earlier. Only . . ." I felt uncomfortable talking to this young woman in such a crowded place, knowing that I could be overheard.

"Only what?"

"After I'd been at home for a while, I found I had trouble going out."

"Agorophobia?"

"Not really. More like a loss of balance. A density of people. Disorienting architecture, shopping malls, exhibition halls, things like that."

"I thought you didn't look very comfortable back there on the platform. The tubes get so crowded now."

"With the tube it's different. It's not the crowds, it's the tunnels. The shapes they make. Circles. Spirals. The converging lines. Perhaps I've become allergic to buildings." Deborah wasn't listening, she was looking out of the window and unwrapping a piece of gum. Just as well, I thought. I didn't want her to get the impression that I wasn't up to the job. But I could feel the pressure in the air, the scented heat of the passengers, the proximity of the curving walls. An oversensitivity to public surroundings, that was what the doctor called it. I could tell what he was thinking, *oh god, another stir-crazy housewife.* He had started writing out a prescription while I was still telling him how I felt.

"We're coming into Baker Street. Christ, not again. There must have been delays earlier."

Through the windows I could see a solid wall of tourists waiting to board. We slowed to a halt and the doors opened.

## 3. Baker Street to Regent's Park

*The world's first tube railway, the Tower Subway, was opened in 1870, and ran between the banks of the Thames. The car was only ten feet long and five feet wide, and had no windows. This claustrophobic steel cylinder was an early materialization of a peculiar modern phenomenon; the idea that great discomfort could be endured for the purpose of efficiency, the desire to reach another place with greater speed. An appropriately satanic contraption for a nation of iron, steam and smoke.*

———————

"This is where we change," called Deborah. "Right, off, the lot of you."

"Can you see them all?" I asked.

"Are you kidding? I bet you there's something going on somewhere as well, all these people, some kind of festival." The adults on the platform were pushing their way into the carriage before we could alight. Suddenly we were being surrounded by red, white and green striped nylon backpacks. Everyone was speaking Italian. Some girls began shrieking with laughter and shoving against each other. Ignoring the building dizziness behind my eyes, I pushed back against the door, ushering children out, checking the interior of the carriage, trying to count heads.

"Deborah, keep them together on the platform, I'll see if there are any more." I could see she resented being told what to do, but she sullenly herded the class together. The guard looked out and closed the train doors, but I held mine back.

"How many?" I called.

"It's fine, they're all here. Come on, you'll get left behind."

I pushed my way through the children as Deborah started off toward the Bakerloo line. "You worry too much," she called over her shoulder. "I've done this trip loads of times, it's easy once you're used to it."

"Wait, I think we should do another head check—" But she had forged ahead with the children scudding around her, chattering, shouting, alert and alive to everything. I glanced back anxiously, trying to recall all of their faces.

I saw him then, but of course I didn't realize.

Four minutes before the next train calling at Regent's Park. I moved swiftly around them, corralling and counting. Deborah was bent over, listening to one of the girls. The twins were against the wall, searching for something in their bags. Timson, the class clown, was noisily jumping back and forth, violently swinging his arms. I couldn't find him. Couldn't find Connor. Perhaps he didn't want me to, like he didn't want Deborah to notice.

"Let's see you form a crocodile again," I said, keeping my voice low and calm.

"Miss, will we see crocodiles at the zoo?"

"Miss, are you the crocodile lady?"

Some of the children at the back moved forward, so I had to start the count over. I knew right then. *Nineteen.* One short. No Connor. "He's gone," I said. "He's gone."

"He can't have gone," said Deborah, shoving her hair out of her eyes. She was clearly exasperated with me now. "He tends to lag behind."

"I saw him on the train."

"You mean he didn't get off? You saw everyone off."

"I thought I did." It was getting difficult to keep the panic out of my voice. "There was—something odd."

"What are you talking about?" She turned around sharply. "Who is pulling my bag?" I saw that the children were listening to us. They miss very little, it's just that they often decide not to act on what they see or hear. I thought back, and recalled the old-fashioned navy blue raincoat. *An oversensitivity to everyday surroundings.* He had been following the children since Finchley Road. I had seen him in the crowd, standing slightly too close to them, listening to their laughter, watching out for the lonely ones, the quiet ones. Something had registered in me even then, but I had not acted upon my instincts. I tried to recall the interior of the carriage. Had he been on the train? I couldn't—

"He's probably not lost, just lagging behind."

"Then where is he?"

"We'll get him back, they don't go missing for long. I promise you, he'll turn up any second. It's quite impossible to lose a small child down here, unfortunately. Imagine if we did. We'd have a bugger of a job covering it up." Her throaty laugh turned into a cough. "Have to get all the kids to lie themselves blue in the face, pretend that none of us saw him come to school today."

"I'm going to look."

"Oh, for Christ's sake."

"Suppose something really has happened?"

"Well, what am I supposed to do?"

"Get the children onto the next train. I'll find Connor and bring him back. I'll meet you at the zoo. By the statue of Guy the gorilla."

"You can't just go off! You said yourself—"

"I have to, I know what to look for."

"We should go and tell the station guards, get someone in authority."

"There isn't time."

"This isn't your decision to make, you know."

"It's my responsibility."

"Why did you come back?"

Her question threw me for a second. "The children."

"This isn't your world now," she said furiously. "You had your turn. Couldn't you let someone else have theirs?"

"I was a damned good teacher." I studied her eyes, trying to see if she understood. "I didn't have my turn."

There was no more time to argue with her. I turned and pushed back through the passengers surging up from the platform. I caught the look of angry confusion on Deborah's face, as though this was something I had concocted deliberately to wreck her schedule. Then I made my way back to the platform.

I was carrying a mobile phone, but down here, of course, it was useless. Connor was bright and suspicious; he wouldn't go quietly without a reason. I tried to imagine what I would do if I wanted to get a child that wasn't mine out of the station with the minimum of fuss. I'd keep him occupied, find a way to stop him from asking questions. Heavier crowds meant more policing, more station staff, but it would be safer to stay lost among so many warm bodies. He'd either try to leave the station at once, and run the risk of me persuading the guards to keep watch at the escalator exits, or he'd travel to another line and leave by a different station. Suddenly I knew what he intended to do—but not where he intended to do it.

## 4. King's Cross to Euston

*There exists a strange photograph of Hammersmith Grove Road station taken four years after the service there ceased operation. It shows a curving platform of transverse wooden boards, and, facing each other, a pair of ornate deserted waiting rooms. The platform beyond this point fades away into the mist of a winter dusk. There is nothing human in the picture, no sign of life at all. It is as though the station existed at the edge of the world, or at the end of time.*

I tried to remember what I had noticed about Connor. There are things you automatically know just by looking at your pupils. You can tell a lot from the bags they carry. Big sports holdalls mean messy work and disorganization; the kid is probably carrying his books around all the time instead of keeping them in his locker, either because he doesn't remember his timetable or because he is using the locker to store cigarettes and contraband. A smart briefcase usually indicates an anal pupil with fussy parents. Graffitti and stickers on a knapsack means that someone is trying to be a rebel. Connor had a cheap plastic bag, the kind they sell at high street stores running sales all year round.

I pushed on through the platforms, checking arrival times on the indicator boards, searching the blank faces of passengers, trying not to think about the penumbral tunnels beyond. For a moment I caught sight of the silver rails curving away to the platform's tiled maw, and a fresh wave of nausea overcame me. I forced myself to think about the children.

You can usually trace the person who has graffittied their desk because you have a ready-made sample of their handwriting, and most kids are lousy at disguising their identities. Wooden pencil-boxes get used by quiet creative types. Metal tins with cartoon characters are for extroverts. Children who use psychedelic holders covered in graffitti usually think they're streetwise, but they're not.

You always used to be able to tell the ones who smoked because blazers were made of a peculiar wool-blend that trapped the smell of cigarettes. Now everyone's different. Spots around a child's nose and mouth often indicate a glue-sniffer, but now so many have spots from bad diets, from stress, from neglect. Some children never—

He was standing just a few yards away.

The navy blue raincoat was gabardine, like a fifties schoolchild's regulation school coat, but in an adult size. Below this were black trousers with creases and turn-ups, freshly polished Oxford toecap shoes. His hair was slicked smartly back, trimmed in classic short-back-and-sides fashion by a traditional barber who had tapered the hair at the nape and used an open razor on the neck. You always notice the haircuts.

He was holding the boy's hand. He turned his head and looked through me, scanning the platform. The air caught in my lungs as he brought his focus back to me, and matched my features in his memory. His deep-set eyes were framed by rimless spectacles that removed any readable emotion from his face. He defiantly held my gaze. We stood frozen on the concourse staring at each other as the other passengers surged around us, and as Connor's head slowly turned to follow his new friend's sightline, I saw that this man was exhilarated by the capture of his quarry, just as I knew that his initial elation would turn by degrees to sadness and then to anger, as deep and dark as the tunnels themselves.

The tension between their hands grew tighter. He began to move away, pulling the boy. I looked for someone to call to, searching faces to find anyone who might help, but found indifference as powerful as any enemy. Dull eyes reflected the platform lights, slack flesh settled on heavy bodies, exuding sour breath, and suddenly man and boy were moving fast, and I was pushing my way through an army of statues as I tried to keep the pair of them in my sight.

I heard the train before I saw it arriving at the end of the pedestrian causeway between us, the billow of heavy air resonating in the tunnel like a depth charge. I felt the pressure change in my ears and saw them move more quickly now. For a moment I thought he was going to push the boy beneath the wheels, but I knew he had barely begun with Connor yet.

I caught the doors just as they closed. Connor and the man had made it to the next carriage, and were standing between teenaged tourists, only becoming visible as the tunnel curved and the carriage swung into view, briefly aligning the windows. We remained in stasis, quarry, hunter and pursuer, as the train thundered on. My heart tightened as the driver applied the brakes and we began to slow down. Ahead, the silver lines twisted sinuously toward King's Cross, and another wall of bodies flashed into view.

As the doors opened, fresh swells of passengers surged from carriage to platform and platform to carriage, shifting and churning so much that I was almost lifted from my feet. I kept my eyes focussed on the man and the boy even though it meant stumbling against the human tide. Still he did not run, but moved firmly forward in a brisk walk, never slowing or stopping to look back. The carriage speakers were still barking inanely about delays and escalators. I could find no voice of my own that would rise above them, no power that would impede their escape. Wherever they went, I could only follow.

## 5. Euston to Camden Town

*Once, on the other side of that century of devastating change, Oscar Wilde could have taken the tube to West End. The underground was built before the invention of the telephone, before the invention of the fountain pen. Once, the platform walls were lined with advertisements for Bovril, Emu, Wrights Coal Tar Soap, for the Quantock Sanitary Laundry, Peckham, and the Blue Hall Cinema, Edgeware Road, for Virol, Camp Coffee and Lifebuoy, for Foster Clark's Soups and Cream Custards, and Eastman's Dyeing & Cleaning. These were replaced by pleas to Make Do And Mend, to remember that Loose Lips Sink Ships, that Walls Have Ears, that Coughs And Sneezes Spread Diseases. Urgent directional markers guided the way to bomb shelters, where huddled families and terrified eyes watched and flinched with each thunderous impact that shook and split the tiles above their heads.*

On through the tunnels and passages, miles of stained cream tiles, over the bridges that linked the lines. I watched the navy blue raincoat shifting from side to side until I could see nothing else, my own fears forgotten, my fury less latent than his, building with the passing crush of lives. Onto another section of the Northern Line, the so-called Misery Line, but now the battered decadence of its maroon rolling stock had been replaced with livery of dull grafitti-scrubbed silver, falsely modern, just ordinary. The maroon trains had matched the outside tiles of the stations, just as the traffic signs of London were once striped black and white. No such style left now, of course, just ugly-ordinary and invisible-ordinary. But he was not ordinary, he wanted something he could not have, something nobody was allowed to take. On through the gradually thinning populace to another standing train, this one waiting with its doors open. But they began to close as we reached them, and we barely made the jump, the three of us, before we were sealed inside.

What had he told the boy to make him believe? It did not matter what had been said, only that he had seen the child's weakness and known which role he had to play; anxious relative, urgent family friend, trusted guide, helpful teacher. To a child like Connor he could be anything as long as he reassured. Boys like Connor longed to reach up toward a strong clasping hand. They needed to believe.

Out onto the platform, weaving through the climbing passengers, across the concourse at Euston and back down where we had come from, toward another northbound train. We had been travelling on the Edgeware branch, but it wasn't where he wanted to go. Could he be anxious to catch a High Barnet train for some reason? By now I had deliberately passed several guards without calling out for help, because I felt sure they would only argue and question and hinder, and in the confusion to explain I would lose the boy forever. My decision was vindicated, because the seconds closed up on us as the High Barnet train slid into the station. By now I had gained pace enough to reach the same carriage, and I stood facing his back, no more than a dozen passengers away. And this time I was foolish enough to call out.

My breathless voice did not carry far. A few people turned to look at me with anxious curiosity. One girl appeared to be on the edge of offering her help, but the man I was pointing to had suddenly vanished from sight, and so had the boy, and suddenly I was just another crazy woman on the tube, screaming paranoia, accusing innocents.

At Camden Town the doors mercifully opened, releasing the nauseous crush that was closing in on me. I stuck out my head and checked along the platform, but they did not alight. I could not see them. What had happened? Could they have pushed through the connecting door and—God help the child—dropped down onto the track below? They had to be on board, and so I had to stay on. The doors closed once more and we pulled away again into the suffocating darkness.

## 6. Kentish Town to South Kentish Town

*The tunnels withstood the firestorms above. The tunnels protected. At the heart of the system was the Inner Circle, far from a circle in the Euclidian sense, instead an engineering marvel that navigated the damp earth and ferried its people through the sulphurous tunnels between iron cages, impervious to the world above, immune to harm. Appropriately, the great metal circles that protected workers as they hacked at the clay walls were known as shields. They protected then, and the strength of the system still protects. The tunnels still endure.*

He had dropped down to his knees beside the boy, whispering his poisons. I had missed him between the bodies of standing, rocking travellers, but I was ready as the train slowed to a halt at Kentish Town. I was surprised to see that the platform there was completely deserted. Suddenly the landscape had cleared. As he led the boy out I could tell that Connor was now in distress, pulling against the hand that held him, but it was no good; his captor had strength and leverage. No more than five or six other passengers alighted. I called out, but my voice was lost beneath the rumble and squeal of rolling steel. There were no guards. Someone must see us on the closed circuit cameras, I thought, but how would eyes trained for rowdy teenaged gangs see danger here? There was just a child, a man, and a frightened middle-aged woman.

I glanced back at the platform exit as the train pulled out, wondering how I could stop him if he tried to push past. When I looked back, he and Connor had vanished. He was below on the line, helping the child down, and then they were running, stumbling into the entrance of the tunnel.

We were about to move beyond the boundaries of the city, into a territory of shadows and dreams. As I approached the entrance I saw the silver lines slithering away into amber gloom, then darkness, and a wave of apprehension flushed through me. By dangling my legs over the platform and carefully lowering myself, I managed to slide down into the dust-caked gully. I knew that the tall rail with the ceramic studs was live, and that I would have to stay at the outer edge. I was also sure that the tunnel would reveal alcoves for workers to stand in when trains passed by. In the depth of my fear I was colder and more logical than I had been for years. Perhaps by not calling to the guards, by revealing myself in pursuit, I had in some way brought us here, so that now I was the child's only hope.

The boy was pulling hard against his stiff-legged warden, shouting something upwards, but his voice was distorted by the curving tunnel walls. They slowed to a walk, and I followed. The man was carrying some kind of torch; he had been to this place before, and had prepared himself accordingly. My eyes followed the dipping beam until we reached a division in the tunnel wall. He veered off sharply and began to pick a path through what appeared to be a disused section of the line. Somewhere in the distance a train rattled and reverberated in its concrete causeway. My feet were hurting, and I had scraped the back of my leg on the edge of the platform. I could feel a thin hot trickle of blood behind my knee. The thick brown air smelled of dust and desiccation, like the old newspapers you find under floorboards. It pressed against my lungs, so that my breath could only be reached in shallow catches. Ahead, the torchbeam shifted and hopped. He had climbed a platform and pulled the boy up after him.

As I came closer, his beam illuminated a damaged soot-grey-sign: SOUTH KENTISH TOWN. The station had been closed for almost eighty years. What remained had been preserved by the dry warm air. The platform walls were still lined to height of four feet with dark green tiles arranged in column patterns. Every movement Connor made could be heard clearly here. His shoes scuffed on the litter-strewn stone as he tried to yank his hand free. He made small mewling noises, like a hungry cat.

Suddenly the torch-beam illuminated a section of stairway tiled in cream and dark red. They turned into it. I stopped sharply and listened. He had stopped, too. I moved as quickly and and quietly as I could to the stairway entrance.

He was waiting for me at the foot of the stairs, his fingers glowing pink over the lens of the upright torch. Connor was by his side, pressed against the wall.

It was then I realized that Connor usually wore glasses—you can usually tell the children who do. I imagined they would be like the ones worn by his captor. Because I was suddenly struck by how very alike they looked, as though the man was the boy seen some years later. I knew then that something terrible had happened here before and could so easily happen again, that this damaged creature meant harm because he had been harmed himself, because he was fighting to recapture something pure, and that he knew it could never again be. He wanted his schooldays back but the past was denied to him, and he thought he could recapture the sensations of childhood by taking someone else's.

I would not let the boy have it stolen from him. Innocence is not lost; it is taken.

"You can't have him," I said, keeping my voice as clear and rational as I could. I had always known how to keep my fear from showing. It is one of the first things you learn as a teacher. He did not move. One hand remained over the torch, the other over the boy's right hand.

"I know you were happy then. But you're not in class anymore." I raised my tone to a punitive level. "He's not in your year. You belong somewhere different."

"Whose teacher are you?" He cocked his head on one side to study me, uncurling his fingers from the torch. Light flooded the stairway.

"I might have been yours," I admitted.

He dropped the boy's hand, and Connor fell to the floor in surprise.

"The past is gone," I said quietly, "Lessons are over. I really think you should go now." For a moment the air was only disturbed by my uneven breath and the sound of water dripping somewhere far above.

He made a small sound, like the one Connor had made earlier, but deeper, more painful. As he approached me I forced myself to stand my ground. It was essential to maintain a sense of authority. I felt sure he was going to hit me, but instead he stopped and studied my face in the beam of the torch, trying to place my features. I have one of those faces; I could be anyone's teacher. Then he lurched out of the stairwell and stumbled away along the platform. With my heart hammering, I held Connor to me until the sound of the man was lost in the labyrinth behind us.

"You're the Crocodile Lady," said Connor, looking up at me.

"I think I am," I agreed, wiping a smudge from his forehead.

Unable to face the tunnels again, I climbed the stairs with Connor until we reached a door, and I hammered on it until someone unlocked the damned thing. It was opened by a surprised Asian girl in a towel. We left the building via the basement of the Omega Sauna, Kentish Town Road, which still uses the station's old spiral staircase as part of its design. London has so many secrets.

The police think they know who he is now, but I'm not sure that they'll ever catch him. He's as lost to them as he is to everyone else. Despite his crimes— and they have uncovered quite a few—something inside me felt sorry for him, and sorry for the part he'd lost so violently that it had driven him to take the same from others. The hardest thing to learn is how to be strong.

Everyone calls me the Crocodile Lady.

# JANE YOLEN

# The Barbarian and the Queen: Thirteen Views

*Jane Yolen is a folklorist, teacher, editor, storyteller, and the author of more than two hundred books, primarily for young readers. She has been called "the Hans Christian Andersen of America" by* Newsweek *and "the Aesop of the twentieth century" by* The New York Times.

*In addition to her multi-award–winning children's books, she has written masterful works of adult fantasy including* Sister Light, Sister Dark; White Jenna; The One-Armed Queen; *and* Briar Rose. *Her adult short fiction has recently been collected in* Sister Emily's Lightship, *and she is the editor of the three-volume anthology series* Xanadu.

*Yolen has won the World Fantasy Award, two Nebula Awards, and three Mythopoeic Awards. She divides her time between homes in western Massachusetts and St. Andrews, Scotland. "The Barbarian and the Queen: Thirteen Views" is a stylish tale that first appeared in* Starlight 3, *edited by Patrick Nielsen Hayden (Tor Books).*

*—T. W.*

## 1.

Dax sat on the edge of his chair, uneasy with the cushion at the back. His people always said that "Comfort is the enemy of the warrior." He was always most careful when he felt most at ease.

He clutched the porcelain cup with one of his death grips. It was only by chance that he did not break the cup and spill the contents—a special blend of Angoran and Basilien tea flavored with tasmairn seeds—down his leather pants. They were his best leather, sewn by his favorite wife. He did not want to stain them.

This queen of the New People who invited him to drink, this old woman with the face of a frog. Did she mean him to come and discuss peace? Or did she mean to threaten more war?

He looked into the cup and saw the black leaves thick as bog at the bottom. She meant him to die, then.

*I will not*, he thought—slowly drawing out his long blade—*go to the dark lands alone.*

## 2.

Prince Henry sat next to his mother and stared at the barbarian who perched on the edge of his seat, one enormous hairy hand wrapped around a teacup.

*Rather like a vulture on a cliff's edge*, Prince Henry thought. *Except, of course, for the teacup.*

"Excuse me, sir," Prince Henry said, "but why don't you lean back in the chair. You look terribly uncomfortable."

The barbarian grunted, a sound quite like the sound Prince Henry's prize pig made in labor.

"Comfortable warrior," the barbarian said in his grunt voice, "dead warrior."

"Yes, of course. But no one here is actually trying to kill you," Prince Henry said sensibly.

The barbarian stood up suddenly and looked about with hooded eyes. His muscles bunched alarmingly.

"He means," Prince Henry's mother put in tactfully, "that he must at all times be on his guard so as not to get into bad habits. And Henry—you do know about bad habits, don't you?"

Satisfied that no enemies were coming up from behind, the barbarian sat again. On the edge of the chair.

The queen smiled and poured some of the tasmairn-laced tea into the cup. She never showed—even for a moment—that she feared the barbarian might crush the cup, and it one of an important set sent to her by her godmother, the Sultana.

"Sugar?"

Prince Henry was too young to be impressed with his mother's calm demeanor. But he knew better than to say anything more. Bad habits was a subject best left unexplored.

## 3.

She crossed and uncrossed her legs three times just to hear the stockings squeak. She'd never actually owned a pair before, having to make do with drawing lines down the back of her legs. But then all the girls did that. At least they'd done it through the war. No one had ever known the difference. And since she had the best-looking legs in her little town, she'd never actually felt the need for the real thing.

Before now, that is.

She made the squeak again.

Catching a glimpse of herself in the full-length mirror, she checked her shoulder-length blonde hair.

"Looking good, Babs," she said, and winked at the reflection and took a sip of tea from the little pink flower cup. God, how she could have used a slug of something stronger.

Just then the queen came into the room and Babs stood at once. They had taught her well, all those nameless servants. And she was a fast learner, as long as it wasn't school stuff.

She wobbled ever so slightly on the high heels. Those were new for her, too, the height of them. But with the money the servants had doled out, she knew she had to have them. It made her taller than the prince, but then he didn't seem to mind.

The queen stood at the door waiting for something. A bow maybe. But Babs knew her rights. She was an American and they didn't need to bow to any old queen. Still she gave a quick little bob just in case.

"So you are this Barbie character," the queen said, looking down her long nose. "The girl my son has been seeing. The girl everyone is talking about." She said the word *everyone* as if it were dirty somehow. But necessary.

"I'm called Babs, your majesty."

"Babs? Don't be ridiculous. Babs is a cow's name." The queen signaled for her tea to be served. "I shall call you Barbie." She sat down on a chair that was covered with a fine raw silk the color of old milk.

Babs caught another glimpse of herself in the mirror before sitting. Every golden hair was in place and her mouth was drawn on perfectly. On the other hand, the queen—with her long nose and bulging eyes, her dowdy dress and her blue hair—the queen was a mess.

*And who's the cow here?* Babs thought, crossing her legs slowly so that the queen could hear every little squeak.

## 4.

Queen Victoria stared over the flowered teacup at her new Prime Minister. Her nose twitched but she did not sniff at him. It would not do. *He* was the barbarian, not she. All Jews were barbarians. Eastern, oily, brilliant, full of dark unpronounceable magic. However long they lived in England, they remained different, apart, unknowable. She did not trust him. She *could* not trust him. But she would never say so.

"More tea, Mr. Disraeli?"

Disraeli smiled an alarmingly brilliant smile, and nodded. His lips moved but no words—no English words—could be heard. Across the rosewood table the queen slowly melted like butter on a hot skillet. A few more cabalistic phrases and she reformed into a toad.

"Yes, please, ma'am," Disraeli answered.

The toad, wearing a single crown jewel in her head, poured the tea.

"Ribbet," she said clearly.

"I agree, ma'am," said Disraeli. "I entirely agree." With a single word he turned her back. It was not an improvement. Such small distractions amused him on these state visits. He could not say as much for the queen.

## 5.

The queen had turned three that morning and had not gotten what she wanted for her birthday. At the moment she was lying on the floor and holding her royal breath and turning quite blue.

In any other household, Nanny Brown would have paddled her charge swiftly on her lovely pink bottom. Such a tempting target right now, on the Caucasian Dragon carpet. But one does not paddle a royal bottom whatever the cause.

Nanny Brown sighed and, holding the dimity cup filled with tasmairn tea—the best thing for her headaches—leaned back against the rocker waiting for the tantrum to wear itself out.

"I . . . want . . . a . . . barbarian," the little queen had screamed before flinging herself down.

Nanny Brown knew that tame barbarians from the Eastern Steppes were all the rage these days. Most castles had one or two. But the regent had said no.

And when that piece of "ordure" ("Best say shite where one means shite," Mr. Livermore, the butler, had told her, but she could never let such a word pass her lips) said no to something that the little queen wanted . . .

"Well, he does not have to deal with her tantrums," Nanny Brown said under her breath.

The tantrum finally passed, of course. They always did. The queen sat up, her face the color of one of her dear dead mother's prize roses. Her golden ringlets, so lovingly twirled around Nanny Brown's finger not an hour since, were now wet little yellow tangles. The lower lip stuck out more than was strictly necessary.

"Oh, Nanny," she cried. "My tummy hurts. I think I am going to swallow up again."

"Come to Nanny," Nanny Brown said. She put down the cup, the tasmairn having once again worked wonders, and held her arms out wide. "And I shall tell you a story about a big bad wolf. So much better than any old smelly barbarian, don't you think?" That was safe. They had a wolf down in the private zoo and she could spin out the tale till the little queen fell asleep and they could visit it after her nap. Wolves always went down well with this one.

The little queen stood up and wriggled into Nanny Brown's ample lap, her big, blue eyes still pooling.

"A story, Nanny," she said, "I want my story."

"And so you shall have it, my dove," said Nanny Brown, setting the rocker into motion.

The queen put her thumb in her mouth, like a stopper in a perfume bottle.

The barbarian was forgotten.

## 6.

The Barbarian, waist a solid 44, pecs nicely sculpted by recent days at the Uptown Gym, this week's special at $25 if you sign up the full year and use the coupons from Safeway, wrapped his hamfist around the dimity cup of tea carefully because the cup was frigging hot. He could smell the mint leaves and something else as well, maybe a touch of tasmairn? Good for what ails you and then some, as his old aunt used to say, his mother's sister still in the old country or cuntry as Cappy put it. He'd always drink tasmairn tea. As long as there was nothing else added. Nothing—you know—illegal. Like some guys always wanted you to try. They tested you these days after every match. He couldn't afford to be ruled off. Not with the house payment coming due. And wanting to buy Jolie a real ring for putting up with him without complaints or at least not a lot for so many years.

But this Queen dame who was fronting money for his training was—Cappy said—an angel come from somewhere real far away, Connecticut maybe, or Maine. Wanting to be part of the action. And he had to see her for tea. She said a drink but Cappy said not during training though he longed for a single malt something from Scotland where his mother—God rest her—had come from and even eighty years later had a brogue could flay the skin off your cheeks. The ones both sides of your nose and the other ones as well.

This Queen character wanted to know what she was buying for her cash, touch the bod a bit, he guessed, the dames who came to watch him always wanted that. Jolie didn't mind; she was used to it as long as it wasn't anywhere serious. An arm, a calf, maybe even a thigh, though not higher or Jolie really would kill him and if she left what would become of him he didn't know but probably like some old cauliflower fighter just hang around the gym not knowing his ass from . . . from a teacup.

He smiled, glad he'd put in the new bridge so the spaces between his teeth didn't show. And the colored lenses which he wore out of the ring but not in since a good blow to the head could lose them and them worth a small fortune being colored and all not like glasses which were twelve bucks at Safeway if you could find one to fit. Turned his head slightly to look at her, the Queen character, out of the corner of his eye. Jolie liked that, said it was cute which given he weighed in at 388 was something he supposed.

And the Queen smiled back, only her teeth were odd—even pointed like, even filed if he didn't know better. Not Connecticut then, or Maine. Somewhere across the pond maybe. Her accent was strange. Maybe Brooklyn, maybe further away. And he didn't or wouldn't ever know better because she leaned into him, over him, those teeth in his throat and razoring down to his belly, slitting him open, the hot intestines falling out like so many sausages, her eyes glittering, and he never laid a hand, Jolie, he swore. Or a hold. Nothing serious at all, so who was the barbarian now?

## 7.

Since coming from East Jersey, the barbarian had been forced to be tea-total, and never more so than when he had drinks with the Queen. She, poor mad thing, was once again AA-ed and—he knew—that meant T. Really, things were better before alphabet soup had been invented. He remembered fondly his illiterate days on the steppes and the fermented yak dung. It was why he liked Lapsang Souchong, it had the same slightly smoky, yakky taste. Not this tasmairn stuff. Crap with a capital K.

"Drink up, Queenie," he said to her, lifting the cup, the one with all the letters on it.

She raised her flower-sprigged cup back at him. It did—he thought—suit her to a T.

## 8.

Boobs the Barbarian sat and spread her thighs to let in a little breeze. Leather was hot this time of year, but the customers demanded it.

She'd been weeks without a paying gig, and this one—dancing for Randy Queen's birthday party—was easily a C-note, not counting tips, and could pay off her week's rent and with some over. Maybe get some new hardware. Her sword was looking a bit thin. The costumer who'd made it for her three years ago was out of business now. But a new place had opened up just down the street, promising fine edges and light-weights. She could do with a lighter blade.

The tea in her floral cup had gone cold, but she drank it anyway. Then she swirled her finger in the sugar at the bottom and sucked on the finger. A good sugar high right now was what she needed to get through the next couple of hours.

Behind the door the music started.

Usually she liked to dance to *Carmina Burana*, but this was a strictly bump-and-grind crowd, the men already well oiled and eager for some hot stuff. Which she could do, of course.

Hot.

The leather.

The tea.

*And me*, she thought.

Flinging the cup over her shoulder for luck—she hated those little sprigged flowers anyway—she stood and started for the kitchen door. As she walked, already swaying to the music, she began to loosen the strings on her jerkin.

When she strode into the room, the roar of the men was nearly overpowering. But with a smile, she drew her sword and quieted them all.

## 9.

The sky over Venice was the deep blue of a glass bead. No stars. No moon.

Ned Robertson shrugged his shoulders, and the costume he was wearing felt heavy and ill-fitting. *Like an old boot*, he thought.

When he had complained, the costumer had smiled a gap-tooth smile and said, "All barbarian costumes fit like dis, signor. Otherwise they would not be barbary. You capice?" Though of course his English was atrocious and Ned had had to talk rather more loudly to make him understand.

*I should have worn a Pierrot*, he thought. *Chalk to cheese*. Instead he had let Sofia talk him into the leather. She'd run her hand over his shoulder, down his back, and whispered in his ear, "I love the feel of this stuff."

He should have let *her* wear the leather.

Venice was too hot for such a costume on a man.

Sofia, of course, was dressed like Marie Antoinette, in a wig that made her almost as tall as he was. She was such a pretty little thing, a pocket Venus as his mother used to say.

He cursed the leather costume, the heat of Venice, his new wife's towering wig.

*But what's a man to do?*

He put on the mask with its permanent smile and went downstairs.

There were at least ten Marie Antoinettes in the milling tour group, and a dozen Pierrots. He could not see Sofia in the crowd.

But evidently all the Marie Antoinettes could see him. Or some part of him, anyway. For suddenly they were all laughing behind their fans and pointing and the Pierrots made a series of awful jokes at his expense.

*Bugger this*, he thought, and ran back upstairs where he shed the leather skins and swore he would not go back down there again.

*Not for all the tasmairn tea in China.*

## 10.

Dar sat uneasily by the northern queen and stared at the black spot high up on her cheekbone. It was not a god-spot, which all his wives had. It looked like a bit of a petal stuck there. He wondered if he should point it out to her. He wondered if such things mattered to these brittle creatures from the north.

She lowered one eyelid at him.

Among his people, such a thing meant she wanted to fuck. But did it mean the same here? He did not want to offend. Not now. Not when his people and hers were deep in negotiations for the passage across the Great River. The cattle were unsettled and lowing their misery. As were his wives. He had to be certain.

There. She did it again.

Dar hesitated.

But then her unshod foot touched his under the table, the toes slowly rubbing up his leg, past the calf, along the inside of the thigh.

There was no mistaking her desire.

Dar stood up quickly, upended the table, teapot, flowered cups, and sachets of tea. Reaching the queen in a single step, he grabbed her up, flipped her over, slammed her onto the ground, and raised the massive skirts over her head. Momentarily flummoxed by the thing that hid her bum, he solved that problem by ripping the soft material apart.

Then he entered her.

She was harder than his wives, harder than any of his sheep. But she opened to him at last and let out only one stifled cry.

Dar was sure it was a cry of pleasure.

## 11.

EXT: HAMPTON COURT, day, 17th century

A COACH comes up the drive, driven by two HORSES. FOOTMEN run out and open the door. TWO COURTIERS in capes descend. They help out a YOUNG WOMAN dressed in the latest Elizabethan fashion. She is dark skinned. Her black hair is in braids. The COURTIERS, of

course, are powdered whiter than white and wear wigs. The COURTI-
ERS and YOUNG WOMAN all enter the building.

INT: PRESENCE ROOM. Even though it is day, there are torches and
candles everywhere. QUEEN ELIZABETH I, well past middle age, her
face whitened with powder, sits on a high carved chair on a dais, a large
goblet decorated with flowers in her hand. She is speaking to SIR ROB-
ERT CECIL, a middle-aged scribe/politician.

ELIZABETH

Is she a barbarian?

CECIL<br>(Cautiously)

How does one measure barbarity, Majesty?

ELIZABETH<br>(Testily)

Do not play words with me, Cecil. You will not win the game. Does she wear
skins? Does she have a bone through her nose? Does she eat her enemies?

CECIL<br>(Bowing slowly, languidly)

She wears skins in her own home, Majesty. Here she is dressed in the latest
fashion. There is no bone through her nose. And as far as I know, she does not
cannibalize her neighbors.

ELIZABETH<br>(She sighs, looks bored, takes a sip from the cup)

CECIL

She does, however, use bear grease in her hair.

ELIZABETH<br>(Looking up eagerly)

Does she smell?

DOOR bursts open and TWO COURTIERS from the carriage march
in, stop, bow. FIRST COURTIER waves in the dark-skinned YOUNG
WOMAN to stand by him. He takes her by the hand and forces her to
bow.

ELIZABETH<br>(Looking interested, leans forward)

Come here. Come here, child.

FIRST COURTIER pushes the young woman forward. The SECOND
COURTIER with a flourish and bow, speaks.

SECOND COURTIER

She is a princess in her own country, Majesty.

ELIZABETH
(Aside to Cecil)

Better and better, Cecil. You did not tell me she was a barbarian princess.

CECIL
(Recovering quickly; clearly this is news to him)

It was meant to be a surprise, Majesty. I see we have been successful.

ELIZABETH
(Putting the goblet down on a side table)

What is your name, my lady?

YOUNG WOMAN
(Turns and looks at the two men for translation)

FIRST COURTIER
(He speaks in her own language a quick sentence)

YOUNG WOMAN
(Speaking directly to Elizabeth)

Pocahontas.

ELIZABETH
(Bringing a pomander ball to her nose)

Have her come closer. I would smell her.

FIRST COURTIER
(Speaking to Young Woman)

Go. Forward. Now.

YOUNG WOMAN goes reluctantly up to the steps of the dais and when
signaled by ELIZABETH, goes up the three steps to stand by the queen.
ELIZABETH takes the pomander from her nose for a moment, then
sniffs YOUNG WOMAN, who, in turn, sniffs her.

YOUNG WOMAN
(Turns and speaks to the First Courtier)

Feh! Feh! Feh!

ELIZABETH

What did she say? What did she say?

CECIL
(Trying hard not to laugh)

Oh, I think she was perfectly clear, Majesty. She says you smell!

<Note to Producer—Pocahontas was actually brought to England during the reign of King James I, several years after Elizabeth died. But I doubt the public will know this. Or care.>

## 12.

Do not, I beg thee, make me wait too long.
True love should yield the ground with little fight.
We stand here taking count of what is wrong,
When all but sense and reason have ta'em flight.
Then send them off, thy soldiers standing guard,
That all unrobed, thy beauty might be seen,
Till crying pax I come across your sward,
Barbarian to his unresisting queen.
Fling now the castle gates full open wide,
And with your fingers, offer up the store
That others have all cautioned you to hide;
Your royal jewels I richly will adore.
Pray let me roam your countryside full free
So that by love alone I ravage thee.

## 13.

Grax sat uneasily on the synth-hide stool waiting for the queen. He drank tea because, after a night of bar-hopping, from the Wet End to the White Horse, his stomach was tied up, knotted as neatly as a sailor's rope.

Running his fingers over the tensed muscles, he groaned. He could hear the tea gurgling inside, complaining like the river Dee in full flood. In the diner's mirror, his face was reflected back with a green tinge.

The queen would notice such things. *Mean and green*, she'd probably say. If he was lucky she wouldn't sing.

He took another sip out of the chipped white cup with the flower decals all along the rim. By-the-Powers-Tetley, he could have used something stronger. Blackberry maybe. He whispered to himself:

"Blackberry,
Bayberry,
Thistle and thorn.
You'll rue the day
That you were born."

But she'd smell it on him and say something. Her word alone could make his stomachache last a full month.

When he took his third sip, she was there, sitting on a stool next to him as if it were a throne. Her hair was gold today and piled in a high crown, her lips rowanberry red.

"New in town, sailor?" she asked lightly. "What's a nice barbarian like you doing in a place like this?"

He knew she didn't expect an answer. Not from a barbarian.

"Give us a kiss."

He did what was expected, on the cheek. But her cheek was rough, the beard already beginning to show through the rouge. It surprised him. She never used to be so careless.

"By the Green, Mab!" he said, incautiously. "I thought you could do a better job than that."

She smiled sadly at him. "The grid is going, Grax. The Magic is failing. An old queen just doesn't have the power to fool anymore."

He put down his cup and held her hands. "It doesn't matter," he said, and meant it. "It doesn't matter to me."

But of course it did matter, which is why Mab had come to him.

"You shall put the grid aright," she said. "A day's work."

A *week at least*, he knew. *And an eternity if I get it wrong*. But he didn't say it aloud. Some things were best left unsaid, lest the wrong ears hear them. He said only what was expected. "I will go, my queen."

She smiled at him. There was a gap between her top front teeth that hadn't been there before. And a pimple on the side of her nose.

*Oh-oh*, mused Grax, *the grid is in worse shape than I thought*. He stood, bowed quickly, and was gone.

Mab watched him till he was no more than a point on the horizon, then sighed.

The counterman leaned over and said, "Mab, he's not the best any more."

She turned and raised an eyebrow. "He's all there is, Sil."

The counterman ran a nervous hand through his shaggy locks and rubbed one of his button horns. "What about Dar? What about Babs? What about . . ."

"Gone," she said with an awful sigh that fluttered the wings of three pigeons in a nearby park. "All gone." Then she put her head on the counter and cried, her tears making deep runnels in her makeup, for once something was gone from her, it was gone from all the world.

# BOB HICOK

# Becoming Bird

*Bob Hicok's poetry has appeared in* The Iowa Review, The Kenyon Review, The Southern Review, Ploughshares, Poetry, Prairie Schooner, *and other journals. He has won a Felix Pollak Poetry Prize Citation, and his work has been included in* Best American Poetry 1997 *and two Pushcart Prize anthologies. His books are* Plus Shipping, The Legend of Light, *and, most recently,* Animal Soul *(Invisible Cities Press, 2001), which was a finalist for the National Book Critics Circle Award. His fourth book,* Insomnia Diary, *will be published by Pitt in 2004.*

*"Becoming Bird" is reprinted from the Winter 2001 issue of* Quarterly West.

—*T. W.*

It began with a tattoo gun to his back.
Face down, he sniffed the skin of dead men
on an execution table the artist bought
from a guard who pinched it from the trash

at Jackson Prison. It was to be one feather
outside each scapula, an idea
that arrived while he flipped *Art
Through the Ages* past the side view

of *Kristos Boy*, who, without arms and confined
to the appetite of marble, still seemed
poised for air, to lift through the roof
of the Acropolis Museum into the polluted sky

of Athens, bound for translucence. But healed,
turning left, right in a sandwich of mirrors,
the lonely feathers asked to be plucked,
the black ink grew from a root of dusk

to charcoal tip, they'd have fluttered
if wind arrived, reflex to join the rush,
but alone seemed less symbolic than forgotten.
So he returned to the *Cunning Needle*,

to Martha of pierced tongue and navel, said
wings and she slapped the table, added
coverts and scapulars, secondaries
and tertials, for a year needles chewed

his skin closer to hawk, to dove, injected
acrylic through tiny pearls of blood.
Then with a back that belonged to the sky
he couldn't stop, sprouted feathers

to collarline, down thighs, past knees
and his feet became scaled, claws gripped
the tops of his toes, she turned him over
for the fine work of down, he laid arms

on the syringe-wings of the table,
a model of crucifixion dreaming flight
through the pricks. So now, by day's end
he can barely hold back the confidence

of his wings. At home, naked with eyes
closed, he feels wind as music
and dreams his body toward a mouse
skimming the woven grass, not considering

but inhabiting the attack, falling hard
as hunger teasing the reach of land,
while from the ink of the first tattoo
a real feather grows, useless but patient.

# MILBRE BURCH

# Sop Doll

*Milbre Burch is an award-winning oral storyteller and recording artist. Specializing in traditional folktales, she has performed at "spoken word" festivals in twenty-two states, as well as in twelve European cities. She has recorded Jane Yolen's stories on the popular audio cassette* Touch Magic, Pass it On *and has published her own stories and poems in* Ready-to-Tell Tales, More Ready-to-Tell Tales, Xanadu II, *and* Ruby Slippers, Golden Tears. *She lives in Chapel Hill, North Carolina, with her husband and two daughters.*

*"Sop Doll" is an original story that reads like an old traditional tale, rooted in "Jack" stories and other lore of the American south. This charmingly spooky story is reprinted from the April issue of* Realms of Fantasy *magazine.*

—*T. W.*

Jack left his Mama's house and set out to seek his fortune. Lookin' for a job of work took him to a small village where the men looked right mean and the women looked right hungry. He stopped at a house standin' near a mill at the edge of a pond. At the door he met a dark-eyed miller and his young wife. The woman was unnatural thin, hardly enough meat on her hand to keep her weddin' ring on. Still, her copper-colored hair and pretty green eyes bewitched Jack.

"So you're Jack, are ye?" asked the miller. "I heard tell of you before. Could use me a man like you to rid me of a problem." And he offered for Jack to be his hired man, runnin' the mill and caretakin' it at night.

Drawin' in a breath, the miller's wife said, "You're sendin' the boy to his death and him not long gone from his mammy. That's a pity already but seein' as how he's so handsome and hardy, it's a shame as well." Then she blushed to the very roots of her red hair, and Jack blushed, too.

The miller smiled strangely, seemed to take pleasure in his wife's fears. He told Jack that the last two hired men had ended up dead the first night lyin' by the mill wheel, with their throats tore out. When he said this, smilin' and fiddlin' with his heavy gold weddin' band, his wife paled and turned away. Pale as she was, though, Jack liked her look, wouldn't mind a chance to bring back a little color to her cheeks his own self.

The miller said, "Them other boys couldn't keep they minds on they business or they hands to theyselves once they saw Sary here. She's one of 12, all dark but her, and every one of um's a looker. I took her off her daddy's hands, last of the litter, and the runt. When you got a pretty wife, who's simple, the way Sary is, the night can be long and botherin', wonderin' each time you stir whether she's abed or out on the road meetin' some boy a'travelin' through. On top of that, they say my mill is haunted by witches, gonna suck out your breath, tear out your throat, make you twitch like you got salt under your skin."

He turned his eyes to his wife and his look was mean. Then he spoke again sayin', "I got a suspicion them witches are just a batch of women, what don't know how to please they husbands, rather please theyselves, and I aim to be done with them, either way. Go work my mill and guard it too, Jack, and I'll pay you in copper. They's a cot and a lantern and a fry pan for ye there. You grind the grain the townfolk bring you, so I kin stay here to make sure what belongs to me stays mine." The miller's wife shivered when he said that, and it made Jack wonder.

Well, the short of it was that Jack agreed to take the job, and some salt pork and cider and some kindlin' and went by his self to the mill down the way. As he was leavin' the miller's house, Sary asked him, "My man here says you're a giant killer. But don't you need no weapon to protect you, Jack?"

"No, Ma'am," he said. "Long as I've got my wits."

The day was long with grindin', grindin' whatever grain the townsfolk brought, till the dusk set in, and Jack thought he'd close up the mill. But down the road, a strange woman came, walkin' slowly. And when she came into the yard, Jack was surprised to see she weren't no hag, but a woman in her prime. She had clearly seen some hard times, for one side of a once-purty face bore a long scar and the eye on that side was covered with a patch. Her hair was black and her good eye was a golden one, and she had a grain bag full of seed heads waitin' to be ground. Another man might have turned her away without a thought as she was comin' so late. T'other might have been frightened by her, feral-lookin' as a panther and maybe tetched in the head. Still another might have tried to get her alone in the mill; even a homely woman's got her uses.

But Jack was real polite and respectful. "Evenin', Ma'am," he said. "You come just in time; there's still water comin' in the sluice." She did not speak, stopped short of the door, and gave over the sack of seed kernels. Jack took and ground the grain, then filled her sack with the meal and carried it back to her waitin' in the dooryard.

Her voice reminded him of Sary's when she finally spoke, sayin', "You been good to me, Jack, where others have done me harm." Her hand reached to touch the side of her face where the eye was covered. "Sary said you was a good'un, so I grant you this boon," and she clapped her hand on his, and he felt somethin' in his palm, cold and steely. It was a fine silver knife.

When he looked up again, slow movin' as she'd seemed, the woman was gone. The bag of cornmeal lay at his feet, and there was nothin' on the road but a one-eyed cat sauntering into the brush. He shrugged, picked up the meal bag, and went on back inside.

The sunset painted the mill in twilight colors through 12 small windows, up under the roof line, three to each wall. There, in the gatherin' shadows with no more grain to grind till mornin', Jack began to slice the salt pork into the fry pan usin' the little silver knife. Workin' all day had piqued his thirst so he set down that pretty silver knife and reached for the cider jug, took several long swigs. The boy wasn't used to hard cider and it knocked ol' Jack clean out and sprawled him on the floor. He woke up, still hungry, with his head a'poundin' and a'spinnin'. He thought for a moment that the room was full of cats but once it came to rest again, he found he was alone. Jack looked up at the windows above him and saw a full Moon sittin' in the star-studded quilt of the sky.

Now Jack was not much one to ponder about all that had happened that day, so he just lit the lantern and a small fire, and commenced to cook him his dinner. As the salt pork was sizzlin', givin' off grease, Jack made corn fritters the way his Mama taught him. Suddenly, he heard the thump of cat's paws landin' on a sill. Lookin' up, he saw a cat in the window frame above him and her fur gleamed like burnished copper. She jumped down from the window and padded across the floor toward Jack and the sizzlin' pan of meat and fritters. As she came close, he saw how she was rail thin, with her ribs showin' through. She stopped and sat right up next to him as he tended his dinner. Jack was turnin' the meat, usin' the silver knife. Three times she reached a paw out toward the pan, mewlin' in a strange voice, "Sop doll," and each time he warned her away by brandishin' the knife.

Till at last Jack said: "Don't you go soppin' in the pan. Keep your ol' sop doll out of the supper. It's bad enough to be hungry without bein' burned to boot. I'll give ye some, just let me cook it through." When the meat was done on both sides, and the fritters was golden brown, Jack, he kept his word and served half to the cat. "Can't offer ye nothin' to drink," he said, "the cider's got a wallop." The cat rubbed her chin over the back of his hand and they ate together in silence. When she was done, she licked her paws and washed her whiskers. Last of all, she brushed her sleek body past him and flicked his cheek with the tip of her tail before skitterin' off into the shadows.

Jack yawned and stretched lithe as a tom cat, pulled the cot over by the dyin' fire, turned down the lantern, wrapped up in his raggedy coat, and lay down to wait for day. He had hardly closed his eyes when he sensed someone close by, heard the soft mewlin' of a cat, and opened his eyes to see Sary there with roses in her cheeks, tuckin' a quilt around him. "I thank you for your kindness, Jack, to me and to my black-haired sister. Say nothin' of what you might see tonight, keep your wits and your silver knife sharp till you need 'em, and you may live." She pulled back away from him, her green eyes movin' to the windows up under the roof line.

Jack looked up to see what Sary saw: 11 dark shapes congregatin' in those small windows high above. The 12th window was empty, but a low shape came again out of the shadows and into the center of the room. As the moonlight fell on her, a copper cat moved on all fours. She greeted her sisters with a great "merow" and they answered her with a chorus of cat calls. Then the largest one, black as midnight with one golden eye, spoke aloud in a familiar voice, sayin' "Little sister, your husband is determined to plague us, maybe even kill us for this little time we spend together. And now he's done sent another boy to shoo us away and get his self killed for his trouble."

The copper cat answered in Sary's voice, "No, this one's different. This here's Jack, the giant-killer. He knows how to hold his temper and his tongue. And he won't let his self be hounded, won't have no hissy fit over a host of house pets. You'll see."

"Well, he's got the knife, so we've done what we can, I reckon," said the one with the night sky fur. "Your man'll come directly with his hound dogs to worry us. He feeds 'em better'n he feeds you, but they got a taste for blood. By now he's missed you at home and will come and loose them dogs on Jack like he always done before. Once they've killed the boy, he'll search Jack's pockets for gold. It's the miller his self who haunts this mill."

"Help me then, sisters," said Sary, her fur shiny like a penny givin' back the Moon's light. "Let's see if we can't change the way this story's told." The cats looked one to the other and then jumped down from their window perches, and moved toward Jack like heavy fog comin' in across the highlands. They circled round and round the cot, purrin' a prayer-spell for his protection.

He lay still, wide-eyed, and when the copper one jumped upon the foot of his cot, Jack asked her, "So do you be witches, Sary?"

"Shape-shifters mostly, it runs in our family," she said. "But Jack, ye should know that my sister's right. My man is probably headed here now, and you might do well to run while you can, you see, he's. . . ."

The night was split with the noisy howlin' of a pack of dogs, and 11 cats scattered and scrambled back up the walls to the windowsills above. Only the copper one stayed by Jack's side. She looked up to him and said, "I'm simple, Jack, not like you. But even if I had my wits for a weapon, tonight I'd use the knife. Cut him, Jack. Cut him with the silver knife. It's the only way to stop him for good." Jack reached down and scooped the knife up out of the fry pan, slid it clean against his trouser leg, and slipped it into his pocket, as the cat jumped up to her perch. Last thing he did was to gather the bag full of cornmeal up next to him on the bed.

The door opened with a long, slow creak and the miller with near a dozen dogs padded into the room and stood at bay. The dark-eyed man seemed to sniff the air, his dogs ranged round him in a pack, their teeth bared, their noses high. "Where is she, Jack?" he asked. "I can smell she's been here. Her and her sisters."

"Don't know what you mean," says Jack, yawnin' and stretchin', but otherwise lyin' still. He saw no need to move too quick and startle them dogs. "I been asleep since supper."

The miller advanced on Jack and his hounds circled round the narrow bed. "Don't lie to me, boy. I see she brought our weddin' quilt to warm you, and I smell your fear. Yessir, it smells real sweet to me and my dogs." Jack heard a rumble in the throats of the hounds. "Didn't my Sary come to you, tell you she was hungry 'cause I like to keep her weak? What she really wanted was to get you in the dark, kiss your mouth, suck your breath, tear out your throat like she did them other boys."

His tone made Jack shiver and sit up slowly, one hand movin' into his pocket to close around the knife, t'other tightenin' on the collar of the meal bag. The copper cat was just above him in the window. Now just 'cause you've killed a giant doesn't mean you never get afraid, and Jack knew to pay attention to his own gooseflesh. With the miller comin' toward him and the witch-cat at his back, he wasn't sure where to turn. Then he remembered that prayer ring them cats had made for him. "I reckon you got Sary wrong," Jack said softly. "Why don't you try to gentle up on her 'stead of bein' so mean and suspicious? She'd be a right good wife to a good husband."

As Jack spoke he heard the man make a low sound deep in his throat and saw him bend his body and start to crouch as he moved the last few feet to the bed. By the time the miller reached Jack's side, he was movin' on all fours, a great, slaverin' hound o' hell with sharp teeth and powerful jaws. The creature sniffed the pan left by the bed. "Sop doll," he said in a voice like thunder gatherin' at the edge of the night. "Is that what she said to you? Well, I'm gonna sop your blood tonight, Jack. Come on now, I'm hungry for you. I'll tear your throat and sop your blood and the dogs'll get the rest."

The moment the miller sprang at Jack with his fangs bared, Jack slit the meal bag wide open and hefted that cornmeal into the air between them. The miller got a face full, and a gritty cloud of meal descended on the rest of the dogs. The strangled sounds of coughin' and chokin' filled the room.

That's when Sary and her sisters sprang as well. Pourin' out of the windows like a cascade of water made somehow sharp, each one landed astride a dog to scratch out his eyes or bite off an ear or rake his snout to ribbons while she rode him round the room and out the door. The night outside was full of yaps and yelps as the cats herded them dogs home.

Sary leapt down upon the miller's shoulders even as he managed to pin Jack to the bed with his great front paws. Jack's forearm was deep in his jaws, and the hand holdin' the knife was trapped against the straw mattress. So Sary scrabbled backways down the miller's spine, and reachin' round his tail, she scratched at him hard beneath it. The hound's throaty growlin' changed to a cry of pain and surprise and grief, as Jack got aloose from him and slashin' against him with the silver knife, lopped off one of his big front paws.

The hound stumbled backward off the cot. Jack heard Sary's "merow" as she skidded off the miller's back and across the floor. The wounded dog staggered and rolled on his back in a hot spreadin' pool of his own blood, before crawlin' on three legs to the door and out into the night. "Sary?" Jack called softly, "Are ye all right?"

"Better'n that, Jack, thanks to you," said Sary walkin' toward him on two feet. She bent and lit the lantern. Jack stood up quick when he saw what lay at his feet: a man's hand, dusted in cornmeal, with the miller's weddin' band glintin' on one finger. "I scratched him up good, but you cut him with the silver knife, Jack. Now he can't come back to bein' a man. Won't make much of a huntin' dog neither I reckon. You keep the knife, Jack," she said, "in case you need to use it again."

Then she sopped the miller's blood in the quilt's scalloped hem. When she was done, she slipped her own weddin' band off and dropped it into her husband's open palm. She wrapped the bloody thing in the slit meal sack and laid it deep in the bedclothes, banked the fire, and burned the bundle clear to ash.

Jack stayed on some time at that house, till Sary's sisters had learned the mill trade real good. Some of the men in town, stayed away from that place, but most folks used the mill right often. At night, Jack sometimes heard a howlin'—mournful, though, not threatenin' atall. The three-legged hound dog was scarcely ever seen, and ever time he was, he had his tail between his legs.

Once Sary's sisters was set, Jack hit the road again to seek more adventures. Some even say one time, he married a king's daughter. But since she don't show up in any of the other tales, I don't put no stock in that. Still, I did hear tell, that wherever he went and whatever he did, Jack always kep' a copper-colored cat close by his side.

# CHRISTOPHER BARZAK

# Plenty

*Christopher Barzak is a member of a talented group of young midwestern writers whose works have been recently collected in* Rabid Transit: New Fiction by the Ratbastards. *His stories have appeared in science fiction, fantasy, and literary magazines including* Nerve, Strange Horizons, Lady Churchill's Rosebud Wristlet, Icon, *and* The Penguin Review. *He lives in Youngstown, Ohio, where he is pursuing a Master's degree in English at Youngstown State University.*

*At the Wiscon SF/Fantasy convention last year there was a lively, heated debate about the nature of "working class" genre fiction. "Plenty" is a fine, deceptively quiet story that falls in that realm. Barzak explores what it takes, and what it costs, to cross over boundaries: between mundane life and magic, and between one social class and another. It first appeared in* Strange Horizons, *an online journal, in the May 28th edition.*

—*T. W.*

Although I hadn't seen my friend Gerith in years, I wasn't surprised to receive a letter from him, asking me to come home. Gerith had been sending me these requests every year or so after I left Youngstown, most of them chronicling the misfortunes of the old neighborhood where we grew up. From Gerith's descriptions, not much had changed for the better. Each day the city disintegrated a little further. People who had once been important to us disappeared without warning. Often he would ask about my life now that I no longer lived there. *Are you okay?* he wondered. *Are you happy?* And each time I would answer: *I have a secure job, I live in a great city, I have a girlfriend who loves me more than I love myself. I have plenty.*

No matter how I answered them, though, Gerith's letters filled me with a sense of guilt. Whenever one of his letters arrived in the mail, I'd put it in the pocket of my jacket for a while and forget about it. Then, after I got up the nerve to read it, I'd sit down and laugh or cry with nostalgia for the old neighborhood. Even though I'd spent most of my life trying to escape Youngstown, the place was still my home. Gerith's letters reminded me of that.

This time, as always, I hoped Gerith would allow me to finally make a clean escape. I wanted him to tell me that the South Side had received funding for rebeautification, that the shelter where he worked had enough food and beds, and that life in general was an eternal flame of mercy and generosity.

Instead, his news left me reeling: "Mrs. Burroway has died, David. The funeral is Saturday. I hope you'll come home for it."

Immediately I had a vision of houses, stripped and gutted, left behind by the dead.

I'd already made plans for the weekend, so I spent a few minutes unmaking them. There was the financiers' dinner on Friday, and on Saturday I'd promised to meet Karen for lunch. She'd been wanting to speak to me about our relationship. I called her answering machine and canceled our date. Then I phoned the office and explained that an old friend had died. The boss was generous, asked no questions, and told me to be careful if I planned to drive all that way. I packed an overnight bag and left Chicago for Youngstown.

There was another reason for going home as well. I'd been keeping a secret for far too long, and now I needed to tell someone about it. The secret involved a small amount of magic, although these days magic is not something in which everyone can afford to believe. There is a suspicious absence of miracles. But sometimes impossible things happen when no one is looking.

It happened in Youngstown, during my last year of college. Fall arrived early that year and spattered the few trees on our street rust red and wax yellow, cinnamon brown, and orange. The leaves were a welcome relief from the sight of our crumbling surroundings: boarded-up warehouses, empty storefronts with cardboard covering the windows, and walls tattooed with strange but banal graffiti. I remember the Market Street bridge in particular, and the words YOU HAVE CROSSED THE LINE scrawled on both sides of it in black spray paint. I passed under that banner each day, as I walked to and from school. It bothered me no end. I wanted to know what line. And who, exactly, had power over the geography of my life?

Gerith and I bought a house together that year. We'd finally decided to cut the umbilical cords that tied us to our parents. Both of us had grown up in that post-industrial shell of a former steel town, a place steeped in a depression that no one knew how to relieve. In the end, most people affected indifference to the situation. No one in our town wanted to be re-educated for alternative careers. Instead, they'd spend their unemployment checks on the lottery and whiskey. We felt the world owed us some obscure inheritance. This strange psychology had been passed down by our parents and grandparents, who actually did lose their jobs during the seventies. We were children of the dispossessed who wanted to be the dispossessed.

The house we bought was an old Victorian on Chalmers Street, and it cost us only six thousand dollars. Houses were cheap in Youngstown because most of the city was a ghetto. The only profitable business nearby was the university. Our house had two floors, a basement, an attic, and a front porch spread wide and deep as a cave. There was a turret that rose out of one corner of the roof—we thought we had our very own castle.

After using what money we'd saved to buy the place, Gerith and I were broke. We'd both won grants and taken out loans to pay for college, so that left us with a little extra cash each quarter, but that money never seemed to arrive at the right times. For the first few months we had electricity and water but no telephone or heat. When the autumn chill grew strong and the wind rattled our windows, we wrapped ourselves in the afghans our mothers had crocheted for us.

Whatever other luxuries we did without, the one that hurt most was food. We ate peanut butter sandwiches and ramen, drank tap water that tasted of chlorine, and sometimes splurged on a packet of Kool-Aid. On our kitchen table we kept a wooden fruit bowl that was always empty. After a few months, my taste buds began to deteriorate.

We didn't know much about our neighbors. We knew that a black family lived on one side of us: a mother with two teenage girls, one of whom had a son of her own. On the other side was a Puerto Rican couple, Rosa and Manuel, who screamed at each other in Spanish until four in the morning sometimes. And across the street, in a Victorian like ours, lived Mrs. Burroway, a white-haired old lady who walked hunched over and carried a black cane with a silver horse head for a handle.

She seemed ancient to me even then, bone-thin, her skin hanging loose on her frame. She wore a pair of thick black-rimmed glasses that exaggerated her cloudy cataracts and the blue of her eyes. Almost every day she sat on her porch, alone, her cane laid across her lap. Sometimes I'd see her carrying a brown bag, overfull with groceries, to a neighbor's house. And this was how we finally met.

One morning, as I gathered my schoolbooks, I heard a thump outside the front door. Then the doorbell rang repeatedly, loud and annoying. I pulled my backpack over my shoulder and opened the door.

Outside, at my feet, was a bag of groceries. A stalk of celery jutted out of the top, and tin cans and a bunch of bananas were visible beneath it. I looked up and saw Mrs. Burroway crossing the street, hunched over as though several sacks of grain were piled on her back. I picked up the bag and ran off the porch to stop her.

I caught her on the other side of the street and said, "I'm sorry, but why did you leave these groceries on my porch?"

She turned those blue, cloud-ridden eyes on me as I spoke, looking a little startled, and licked her lips before she replied. "You boys are looking a bit slight," she said, uncovering her teeth to smile.

"But surely you can't afford to buy groceries for us," I said. I smiled and held the bag out for her to take.

"No, no." She waved her hands at the bag as if it were cursed. "Those are yours. Besides, I have plenty."

"Well," I said, and stood mute for a moment. "Well, thank you."

"My pleasure," she said. Then she turned around and continued on to her house.

Gerith and I spent that day at home instead of school. We opened cans of soup, stripped bananas out of their skins, ate stalks of celery with cream cheese spread in the grooves. We drank a six-pack of grape soda we found at the bottom of the bag. We smoked marijuana, which Gerith supplied, and wondered aloud at what I had missed in my computer literacy class, what Gerith had missed in his philosophy of eco-feminism lecture. By evening, most of the food was gone. One banana lay curled on its side in the fruit bowl and two cans of clam chowder stocked our pantry shelves.

"So," said Gerith. We sat cross-legged on the braided rug in the living room. "Do you think Mrs. Burroway is crazy, or just very generous?"

I took a hit off the pipe and passed it to him, holding the smoke inside my lungs until it began to hurt. I took another gulp of air before exhaling. "Very generous," I answered. "Though that doesn't exclude the possibility of a mental disorder."

"Wow," Gerith shook his head. "That's pretty amazing."

I nodded, and chuckled a little at Gerith's astonishment.

"What?" he said, but I told him it was nothing, just the pot. I waved away his question with an expansive gesture and then we both laughed for several minutes.

Winter in Ohio that year filled the streets with snow and ice. The city became an audience for weather reports—streets were slick, drifts grew large enough for children to play on, and temperatures dropped below zero. Winter that year, I had an International Finance class, Human Impacts on the Environment, and Ballroom Dancing. I couldn't write an essay on acid rain that made any sense, but I learned how to waltz. It didn't matter anyway; the finance course was where I directed all of my energy. It drained me, doing the work for that class, but I kept reminding myself that it would be worth it one day.

Gerith, on the other hand, dropped his courses that quarter. He said he'd finish them in the summer instead. He started volunteering at the shelter, and soon everything he did revolved around that.

One night in December, while I sat at my desk and studied the effects of chemical treatments on city water, Gerith appeared in my doorway, ringing a bell. He clanged it back and forth lazily several times, then smiled in a way that I knew meant he wanted something.

"I'm going to the grocery story to collect money for the Salvation Army," he said. "You should come."

"I have a final in two days," I said, tapping the book spread out in front of me.

"Come on," he said. "What are you going to learn tonight that you can't cram in tomorrow?" He moved into my room and put his hand on my desk, tapping his fingers near the edge of my book.

"I can't cram," I said. "You know that."

"Do something worthwhile for once," he said.

"I think I am. I'm trying to graduate."

He flipped my book closed and grabbed my leather jacket off the doorknob. "No arguing," he said. "You're coming. This will be food for your soul."

We stood outside the grocery store fifteen minutes later, in a swirl of snow. Christmas lights lined the awning and filled the store's front window, blinking on and off in time to Christmas music—"Jingle Bells," I think. The Salvation Army bucket stood propped between us, and Gerith rang his bell continuously. He clanged it louder whenever anyone approached from the parking lot, or whenever the electric doors behind us slid open. I had a bell, too, but I rang it reluctantly, until Gerith shot me a stern look.

"I should be studying," I said.

"You're going to do fine," Gerith assured me. "You can take that test without opening a book."

"Easy for you to say. You've already had this class, and I have a C going into the final."

The doors slid open behind us. A woman wearing a black wool coat and carrying two plastic bags of groceries exited the store. Gerith rang his bell in the air and looked intently at her. "Merry Christmas!" he said.

The woman nodded and returned the greeting. She moved one of her bags into her other hand and dug into her purse for money. She threw a handful of copper and silver into the bucket and walked away.

"Thank you," Gerith called after her. "See," he said. "You just have to call attention to the cause."

"Yeah," I said. I looked at my watch. "How long do I have to do this?"

"Three more hours," Gerith said. He raised his bell and rang it a few times to accent his answer.

"I'm going now," I said. I set my bell down on the bucket, heard the tongue choke inside it, and started to leave.

"You can't go now," Gerith yelled after me. "David, I mean—"

I turned back around, hands stuffed deep in my pockets, and yelled, "What? Just what do you mean?"

He rolled his eyes and stamped his feet on the snow-packed ground, pulled his hair away from his face.

"I mean, God, why don't you just care about something for once in your life? Something outside of yourself."

"You've got a lot of nerve," I told him. "You're just as selfish as I am. Don't think I buy into your Gerith-the-all-giving act. You do that for yourself as much as I study my ass off to graduate." I kicked at a drift of snow and a chunk broke off and burst into powder.

The doors behind Gerith slid open. Mrs. Burroway came toddling out, holding a bag of groceries in her arms. She looked at me and smiled, then looked at Gerith and asked, "When did you boys start ringing the bell? It was a nice old man when I went in."

"We just started half an hour ago," Gerith told her.

"Just missed you, then," said Mrs. Burroway. "Here, hold this for me." She handed Gerith her bag, opened her purse and took out a few bills. She stuffed them into the bucket, hand shaking as she pushed them in. "Were you leaving just now?" she asked me.

"Yes," I said. "I'm leaving."

"Good. I have some food at home to send home with you. Can you carry my bag for me?"

I nodded. By now, Gerith and I were accustomed to accepting food from Mrs. Burroway. She brought us a sack every week. Sometimes two sacks. We never knew how she afforded it. She did the same for all of our neighbors, and Gerith mentioned that she brought food to the shelter several times a week as well. I had always assumed she was a well-off widow who lived modestly, but Rosa, the

Puerto Rican woman next door, said Mrs. Burroway was as poor as anyone else on the street. "Mrs. Burroway," Rosa said, "she's a good woman, a saint. But you wouldn't catch me spending too much time on her porch." I'd asked Rosa to elaborate, but she'd only said, "No white woman can cook like that."

It was a strange and vague answer that puzzled me as much as some of the graffiti on the streets.

When I took hold of Mrs. Burroway's bag that night in December, I didn't notice any food in it. Mostly furniture polish and toiletries, soap and hair spray.

"Thank you, David," she told me. She swung a scarf around her neck with a little flourish, then put her horse-head cane out in front of her feet and propelled herself forward.

I didn't look back at Gerith as we left. I couldn't. If I did, I might succumb to guilt, and I had too much pride for that. I couldn't let him beat me down for wanting something for myself.

Mrs. Burroway chattered beside me about the winter cold she'd just gotten over, about how terrible the weather was this year. We walked the few blocks to our street, and as we walked and spoke in that lunar landscape, I thought I could hear Gerith, ringing his bell behind us.

Gerith and I didn't speak much after that. We moved around our home like ghosts or shadows, slipping out of the peripheries of each other's vision. I kept to my room, planted at my desk, and Gerith continued to work at the shelter. He started classes again, so he could finish his degree in social work. During the late hours of the night, I'd hear him come home from the shelter and try to ease the front door closed as soundlessly as possible. That never worked, though, because the front door always creaked no matter how much you oiled it. I'd hear him pace the hardwood floor outside my room. I made myself believe he was getting on fine without me.

In early April, I was notified about a job in Chicago. I could start after graduation if I liked. I was ecstatic. A real job, real money for once in my life. With the salary I'd be earning, I could pay back my school loans in two years. I called my parents to tell them the news, to show them that my schooling had paid off.

I had two months to tie up loose strings and to graduate. There were few problems, really. In fact, the only person in my life who could cause me grief at that point was Gerith.

I couldn't tell him. All through April and halfway through May, I tried to gather the obstinacy I thought I'd need to counter his own. I knew he'd be angry with me for leaving, especially since half the house was mine.

The day I confronted him arrived in the last week of May, when I had only three weeks left before leaving. I waited for Gerith on our front porch, on an old rotten sofa we'd propped out there the summer before. A clay pot filled with dirt but no plant sat beside me, and I wondered if we had ever tried growing anything in it. It was Sunday, and Gerith had pulled an all-nighter at the shelter the night before. When I finally saw him turn onto our street, carrying his overnight bag, walking sluggishly, I entertained the idea of not telling him at all. Just leave and forget about him, I told myself. Forget about Youngstown. The future was my destination.

He greeted me as he approached the porch, a half salute that trailed off into a wave. His hair was bound behind his neck in a ponytail, and the skin beneath his eyes looked puffy and gray.

"Hey there," he said, climbing the porch steps. "How are things going?"

I shrugged.

"Something wrong?"

"I'm leaving," I said. There, it was out.

"Leaving?" Gerith arched his eyebrows and held one of his hands out, palm up. "What do you mean?"

"I have a job," I said. I looked over at the dirt-filled pot beside me, stuffed my fingers in it and played with the dirt. "It's in Chicago."

Gerith didn't say anything right off. I kept playing with the dirt so I wouldn't have to look at him. Finally, though, I looked up.

His head was lowered, his eyes fixed on the peeling floorboards of the porch. He'd let his carryall slip out from under his arm, and he clung to it by its strap. He looked a little bewildered.

"Well," he said. He looked up as he spoke. "Guess you'll want me to buy your half of the house."

"No," I told him. "It's yours."

He nodded and stared at me and finally said, "I hope you don't like it. The job, I mean. You belong here, David. You'll always have a room here."

"Thanks," I said, "but I don't think I'll be coming back."

"It'll be here," he repeated. Then he went into the house.

I sat outside and wondered why he'd let me off so easy. It wasn't like Gerith to not put up a fight. Maybe I'd caught him when he was too tired. Maybe he'd realized that arguing about this would have been futile.

I didn't move from the sofa for hours. The sun moved across the sky like a hand on a watch, and a pale crescent moon rose up to replace it. I noticed that the Puerto Rican couple's house next door was for sale, although the prospect of it selling was low. Rosa and Manuel had moved out two weeks before, and within a week of their leaving, the neighborhood had picked their house clean. During the night, people had come—neighbors and people from nearby streets— and removed the aluminum siding, the copper pipes, brass doorknobs, leftover furniture, and anything else that could be turned over for money. The house sparkled in the twilight now, a house with silver insulation wrap exposed on all sides. It looked as though it had been covered in chewing gum wrappers. I'd seen this several times before, over the year on Chalmers Street. Houses people left behind, house of the recently dead, were veins to be mined.

Two days before I left, an ice storm hit Youngstown. It started as rain, but then the temperature dropped, and soon the city was encased in ice. I watched the whole affair from my bedroom window, until the storm glazed it over with a sheet of corrugated ice. My bags were packed; my room was empty. Anyone could have lived there, or no one.

The electricity shut off sometime during the evening, and I wandered through the house with a flashlight, sweeping through the dark with its swathe of light. The house creaked under the weight of the ice, and I wanted to be in Chicago already, as if in Chicago there would never be any ice. Gerith was at the shelter— he'd called earlier to say he'd be spending the night there.

It wasn't until later that evening, after night gathered and the storm receded, that I thought to check on Mrs. Burroway. All alone in her ramshackle house, she could have fallen in the dark of the blackout. I put on my jacket and broke a seal of ice off the front door as I pushed out.

Immediately I slipped and fell. The porch was glazed with ice. So were the front lawn, the sidewalks, the streetlights. Tree limbs sagged under the extra weight, grazing the ground. The whole world sparkled under the white light of the moon and stars. A world made of blown glass.

I picked myself up and moved cautiously across the yard, across the street, onto Mrs. Burroway's porch. I couldn't see any light through the windowpane on her front door. No candles or lamps or flashlights. I knocked and ice slid away from where my knuckles hit. After a few moments, when no answer came, I knocked again. Still no answer.

I stepped back down to the lawn. The grass crunched beneath my shoes. I circled around to the side of the house and wiped some ice away from one of the windows, so I could peer in between cupped hands. With my face pressed against the chill of Mrs. Burroway's kitchen window, all I could see was darkness at first. Then, suddenly, light entered the room, a small candle flame that shuddered and winked in the dark, throwing shards of light around the room, breaking the shadows. Behind it was Mrs. Burroway. The flame spun and guttered because the hand she held it in shook. She set it down on her kitchen table, and I saw a feast there, spread across the surface.

The table was made of dark wood, mahogany maybe, and it shone in the candlelight. The food on the table seemed to radiate warmth. There were oranges that shone like globes of gold, a turkey that steamed and sweated glistening juice, pies with cherry gel and peach slices bursting out of their crusts, round chocolate cakes, cans of soup, jugs of milk, boxes of cereal.

Mrs. Burroway moved away from the table and disappeared into the shadows. A moment later she crept back into the light with a stack of brown paper bags in her hands. She set the bags down on a chair, unfolded one, and began to pack fruit, cans of soup, jars of peanut butter, and cartons of eggs into it. She sliced the turkey and slid generous cuts into baggies and included those in the grocery bags as well. My mouth watered at the sight of it all.

She continued to pack bag after bag full of food. When the table was clear, she set the bags on the floor around it. Then she wiped it down with a towel.

I realized I'd become enchanted by this almost religious ritual of hers. I was about to knock on the window when I saw something I have never told anyone about.

After Mrs. Burroway wiped down her table, the air shimmered faintly above the table's surface, and more food, other kinds of food, materialized on it.

Soon an abundance of grapes, Cornish hens, bags of rice, and jars of golden-brown honey filled the space.

I fogged the window with my breath and wiped it away. But as I wiped at the window my hand squeaked against the glass and Mrs. Burroway turned her head and saw me. At first she looked frightened, her eyes wide and her jaw slack. Then she recognized me and, very slowly, lifted one gnarled finger to her pursed lips.

I nodded dumbly and her mouth bloomed into a smile. She waved at me, and then I turned and left, and went back to my house.

---

I left Youngstown still in possession of that secret image, of the table and the feast spread over it. Now the thought of Mrs. Burroway's house stripped to gleaming insulation wrap reminded me of what I needed to do. The neighborhood would take from her house what they could, but I had to make sure the table would survive.

I spent the night before the funeral with my parents, rather than go to the old house on Chalmers Street. I needed a night to myself before I could face Gerith. I called my answering machine back in Chicago; I had only one message, from Karen. She told me she was sorry to hear about my friend and to call as soon as I could.

In the morning I woke and dressed for the funeral. I drove to the cemetery in a downpour. Soon the caravan of mourners arrived. I waited in my car until everyone else got out of theirs and hurried under purses and umbrellas to the chapel. I saw Gerith, in the line of pallbearers, grab one handle of Mrs. Burroway's casket and lift it out of the hearse. His hair was combed back into a neat ponytail, and he wore a black suit. It was the first time I'd ever seen him wear one.

After the priest blessed Mrs. Burroway and delivered his sermon, we all left the chapel. Gerith stopped me at the door and put an arm around me. "It's good to see you," he said. I patted him on the back and nodded.

"I'm sorry," I said. I'm sure he thought I was talking about Mrs. Burroway's death. I wasn't, though, not really. It was an apology for not visiting earlier, and for leaving and not keeping in touch. For not telling him about the table. For that night in front of the grocery store.

"I found her," Gerith told me. "No one had seen her for a couple of days, so I went over. I'd been going over to talk to her every so often for the past few years. She was on her kitchen floor—a stroke, the doctor says. There was all this food on her table. She'd been cooking enough for an army again."

"I have to show you something," I said. I led Gerith to my car and told him to get in. "Trust me," I said. "It's important."

We drove back to Chalmers Street. The old neighborhood had changed some, of course, but most things remained the same. The Puerto Rican couple's house had been torn down and now it was an empty lot. Our house, though, Gerith's and my house, looked the same.

"It's in Mrs. Burroway's house," I told Gerith. He looked at me and furrowed his brow.

"What are you talking about, David?" he said.

I opened the car door and ran through the sheets of rain to Mrs. Burroway's front porch. Luckily it seemed no one had touched it yet. I imagined this might be out of some obscure loyalty to Mrs. Burroway, although how long that loyalty would last was uncertain.

Gerith followed behind me, jingling keys in his hands. "What is it?" he asked again, as he opened her door. I brought him through the front rooms of her house, which smelled of medicine and dust, and into her kitchen. It was still there—the table, filled with a preserved feast. "This is it," I said. And I finally told Gerith what I'd witnessed.

After we cleared the table of food, Gerith and I lifted it at both ends and moved it awkwardly through her house, bumping into walls and lamps. Then we carried it across the street in the rain, to our house.

We moved Gerith's wobbly-legged table into a side room, and then I said, "Let's see what's what." We stood one on either side of Mrs. Burroway's table, which I now saw had been inlaid with a lighter stained wood as a border. Tiny runes of some sort were scrawled along the border, burned into the wood. I took a damp dish towel and said, "Here we go."

But as I wiped and wiped her shining table, nothing happened. There was no shimmering in the air just over the surface, no ghostly smells preceding the transported food. Gerith looked up at me skeptically. "It's okay, David," he said. "It's still a nice table."

"But—" I said. "But I know what I saw." Then I had an idea. I handed the damp towel over the table to Gerith. "You try," I said.

He must have been pitying me, because he began to wipe the table down with a sigh. "We can't do this forever," he said. "People are coming here for the memorial."

But even as he spoke, it was working. "Look, Gerith," I said, and he moved his hand from the table. Already the air danced with tiny blue sparks. Then the food began to take shape, first transparent as a film projection, then suddenly solid. The roasts, the fruit, the boxes of cereal and cans of soup. Gerith laughed, a little surprised sound, and looked at me with unbelieving eyes.

"It's how she did it," I said. "All those years."

We talked for the rest of the day, about old times, about Chalmers Street and the shelter. Neighbors came and we all shared stories about Mrs. Burroway, although I kept my story about her to myself. I decided to stay for a few more days so Gerith and I could catch up properly. I told Gerith about Karen, and called her to let her know everything was all right. And all of this time—while the neighbors visited, while Gerith and I reacquainted ourselves—we sat around the table and its feast. We sent bags of food home with everyone.

It was enough, I told myself. I knew the table would be in the best of hands with Gerith, the kind of hands that were like Mrs. Burroway's. Open from the start.

I left for Chicago a few days later. On the way out of the city, I passed under the Market Street bridge again. It still said, YOU HAVE CROSSED THE LINE.

# URSULA K. LE GUIN

# The Bones of the Earth

*Ursula K. Le Guin is, quite simply, one of the greatest fantasists of our age, as well as a distinguished writer of science fiction, realist fiction, nonfiction, and poetry. Among her many honors are a National Book Award, the World Fantasy Award, five Hugo Awards, five Nebula Awards, the Kafka Award, a Pushcart Prize, and the Harold D. Vursell Memorial Award from the American Academy of Arts and Letters. She lives in Portland, Oregon, and describes herself as "a feminist, a conservationist, and a western American, passionately involved with West Coast literature, landscape, and life."*

*2001 was a good year for fans of Le Guin's great fantasy masterwork: the novels and stories set in the magical archipelego of Earthsea. She not only published a fine new Earthsea novel,* The Other Wind, *but also a new collection,* Tales of Earthsea. *It was a difficult task indeed to choose just one story to reprint here, for they all can be counted among the year's best. "The Bones of the Earth" is a quiet tale, and all the more powerful for it.*

—T. W.

It was raining again, and the wizard of Re Albi was sorely tempted to make a weather spell, just a little, small spell, to send the rain on round the mountain. His bones ached. They ached for the sun to come out and shine through his flesh and dry them out. Of course he could say a pain spell, but all that would do was hide the ache for a while. There was no cure for what ailed him. Old bones need the sun. The wizard stood still in the doorway of his house, between the dark room and the rain-streaked open air, preventing himself from making a spell, and angry at himself for preventing himself and for having to be prevented.

He never swore—men of power do not swear, it is not safe—but he cleared his throat with a coughing growl, like a bear. A moment later a thunderclap rolled off the hidden upper slopes of Gont Mountain, echoing round from north to south, dying away in the cloud-filled forests.

A good sign, thunder, Dulse thought. It would stop raining soon. He pulled up his hood and went out into the rain to feed the chickens.

He checked the henhouse, finding three eggs. Red Bucca was setting. Her eggs were about due to hatch. The mites were bothering her, and she looked scruffy and jaded. He said a few words against mites, told himself to remember to clean out the nest box as soon as the chicks hatched, and went on to the poultry yard, where Brown Bucca and Grey and Leggings and Candor and the King huddled under the eaves making soft, shrewish remarks about rain.

"It'll stop by midday," the wizard told the chickens. He fed them and squelched back to the house with three warm eggs. When he was a child he had liked to walk in mud. He remembered enjoying the cool of it rising between his toes. He still liked to go barefoot, but no longer enjoyed mud; it was sticky stuff, and he disliked stooping to clean his feet before going into the house. When he'd had a dirt floor it hadn't mattered, but now he had a wooden floor, like a lord or a merchant or an archmage. To keep the cold and damp out of his bones. Not his own notion. Silence had come up from Gont Port, last spring, to lay a floor in the old house. They had had one of their arguments about it. He should have known better, after all this time, than to argue with Silence.

"I've walked on dirt for seventy-five years," Dulse had said. "A few more won't kill me!"

To which Silence of course made no reply, letting him hear what he had said and feel its foolishness thoroughly.

"Dirt's easier to keep clean," he said, knowing the struggle already lost. It was true that all you had to do with a good hard-packed clay floor was sweep it and now and then sprinkle it to keep the dust down. But it sounded silly all the same.

"Who's to lay this floor?" he said, now merely querulous.

Silence nodded, meaning himself.

The boy was in fact a workman of the first order, carpenter, cabinetmaker, stonelayer, roofer; he had proved that when he lived up here as Dulse's student, and his life with the rich folk of Gont Port had not softened his hands. He brought the boards from Sixth's mill in Re Albi, driving Gammer's ox team; he laid the floor and polished it the next day, while the old wizard was up at Bog Lake gathering simples. When Dulse came home there it was, shining like a dark lake itself. "Have to wash my feet every time I come in," he grumbled. He walked in gingerly. The wood was so smooth it seemed soft to the bare sole. "Satin," he said. "You didn't do all that in one day without a spell or two. A village hut with a palace floor. Well, it'll be a sight, come winter, to see the fire shine in that! Or do I have to get me a carpet now? A fleecefell, on a golden warp?"

Silence smiled. He was pleased with himself.

He had turned up on Dulse's doorstep a few years ago. Well, no, twenty years ago it must be, or twenty-five. A while ago now. He had been truly a boy then, long-legged, rough-haired, soft-faced. A set mouth, clear eyes. "What do you want?" the wizard had asked, knowing what he wanted, what they all wanted, and keeping his eyes from those clear eyes. He was a good teacher, the best on Gont, he knew that. But he was tired of teaching, didn't want another prentice underfoot. And he sensed danger.

"To learn," the boy whispered.

"Go to Roke," the wizard said. The boy wore shoes and a good leather vest. He could afford or earn ship's passage to the school.

"I've been there."

At that Dulse looked him over again. No cloak, no staff.

"Failed? Sent away? Ran away?"

The boy shook his head at each question. He shut his eyes; his mouth was already shut. He stood there, intensely gathered, suffering: drew breath: looked straight into the wizard's eyes.

"My mastery is here, on Gont," he said, still speaking hardly above a whisper. "My master is Heleth."

At that the wizard whose true name was Heleth stood as still as he did, looking back at him, till the boy's gaze dropped.

In silence Dulse sought the boy's name, and saw two things: a fir cone, and the rune of the Closed Mouth. Then seeking further he heard in his mind a name spoken; but he did not speak it.

"I'm tired of teaching and talking," he said. "I need silence. Is that enough for you?"

The boy nodded once.

"Then to me you are Silence," the wizard said. "You can sleep in the nook under the west window. There's an old pallet in the woodhouse. Air it. Don't bring mice in with it." And he stalked off towards the Overfell, angry with the boy for coming and with himself for giving in; but it was not anger that made his heart pound. Striding along—he could stride, then—with the sea wind pushing at him always from the left and the early sunlight on the sea out past the vast shadow of the mountain, he thought of the Mages of Roke, the masters of the art magic, the professors of mystery and power. "He was too much for 'em, was he? And he'll be too much for me," he thought, and smiled. He was a peaceful man, but he did not mind a bit of danger.

He stopped then and felt the dirt under his feet. He was barefoot, as usual. When he was a student on Roke, he had worn shoes. But he had come back home to Gont, to Re Albi, with his wizard's staff, and kicked his shoes off. He stood still and felt the dust and rock of the cliff-top path under his feet, and the cliffs under that, and the roots of the island in the dark under that. In the dark under the waters all islands touched and were one. So his teacher Ard had said, and so his teachers on Roke had said. But this was his island, his rock, his dirt. His wizardly grew out of it. "My mastery is here," the boy had said, but it went deeper than mastery. That, perhaps, was something Dulse could teach him: what went deeper than mastery. What he had learned here, on Gont, before he ever went to Roke.

And the boy must have a staff. Why had Nemmerle let him leave Roke without one, empty-handed as a prentice or a witch? Power like that shouldn't go wandering about unchanneled and unsignaled.

My teacher had no staff, Dulse thought, and at the same moment thought, The boy wants his staff from me. Gontish oak, from the hands of a Gontish wizard. Well, if he earns it I'll make him one. If he can keep his mouth closed. And I'll leave him my lore-books. If he can clean out a henhouse, and understand the Glosses of Danemer, and keep his mouth closed.

The new student cleaned out the henhouse and hoed the bean patch, learned the meaning of the Glosses of Danemer and the Arcana of the Enlades, and kept his mouth closed. He listened. He heard what Dulse said; sometimes he heard what Dulse thought. He did what Dulse wanted and what Dulse did not know he wanted. His gift was far beyond Dulse's guidance, yet he had been right to come to Re Albi, and they both knew it.

Dulse thought sometimes in those years about sons and fathers. He had quarreled with his own father, a sorcerer-prospector, over his choice of Ard as his teacher. His father had shouted that a student of Ard's was no son of his, had nursed his rage, died unforgiving.

Dulse had seen young men weep for joy at the birth of a first son. He had seen poor men pay witches a year's earnings for the promise of a healthy boy, and a rich man touch his gold-bedizened baby's face and whisper, adoring, "My immortality!" He had seen men beat their sons, bully and humiliate them, spite and thwart them, hating the death they saw in them. He had seen the answering hatred in the sons' eyes, the threat, the pitiless contempt. And seeing it, Dulse knew why he had never sought reconciliation with his father.

He had seen a father and son work together from daybreak to sundown, the old man guiding a blind ox, the middle-aged man driving the iron-bladed plough, never a word spoken. As they started home the old man laid his hand a moment on the son's shoulder.

He had always remembered that. He remembered it now, when he looked across the hearth, winter evenings, at the dark face bent above a lore-book or a shirt that needed mending. The eyes cast down, the mouth closed, the spirit listening.

"Once in his lifetime, if he's lucky, a wizard finds somebody he can talk to." Nemmerle had said that to Dulse a night or two before Dulse left Roke, a year or two before Nemmerle was chosen Archmage. He had been the Master Patterner and the kindest of all Dulse's teachers at the school. "I think, if you stayed, Heleth, we could talk."

Dulse had been unable to answer at all for a while. Then, stammering, guilty at his ingratitude and incredulous at his obstinacy—"Master, I would stay, but my work is on Gont. I wish it was here, with you—"

"It's a rare gift, to know where you need to be, before you've been to all the places you don't need to be. Well, send me a student now and then. Roke needs Gontish wizardry. I think we're leaving things out, here, things worth knowing . . ."

Dulse had sent students on to the school, three or four of them, nice lads with a gift for this or that; but the one Nemmerle waited for had come and gone of his own will, and what they had thought of him on Roke Dulse did not know. And Silence, of course, did not say. It was evident that he had learned there in two or three years what some boys learned in six or seven and many never learned at all. To him it had been mere groundwork.

"Why didn't you come to me first?" Dulse had demanded. "And then go to Roke, to put a polish on it?"

"I didn't want to waste your time."

"Did Nemmerle know you were coming to work with me?"

Silence shook his head.

"If you'd deigned to tell him your intentions, he might have sent a message to me."

Silence looked stricken. "Was he your friend?"

Dulse paused. "He was my master. Would have been my friend, perhaps, if I'd stayed on Roke. Have wizards friends? No more than they have wives, or sons, I suppose . . . Once he said to me that in our trade it's a lucky man who finds someone to talk to . . . Keep that in mind. If you're lucky, one day you'll have to open your mouth."

Silence bowed his rough, thoughtful head.

"If it hasn't rusted shut," Dulse added.

"If you ask me to, I'll talk," the young man said, so earnest, so willing to deny his whole nature at Dulse's request that the wizard had to laugh.

"I asked you not to," he said. "And it's not my need I spoke of. I talk enough for two. Never mind. You'll know what to say when the time comes. That's the art, eh? What to say, and when to say it. And the rest is silence."

The young man slept on a pallet under the little west window of Dulse's house for three years. He learned wizardry, fed the chickens, milked the cow. He suggested, once, that Dulse keep goats. He had not said anything for a week or so, a cold, wet week of autumn. He said, "You might keep some goats."

Dulse had the big lore-book open on the table. He had been trying to reweave one of the Acastan Spells, much broken and made powerless by the Emanations of Fundaur centuries ago. He had just begun to get a sense of the missing word that might fill one of the gaps, he almost had it, and—"You might keep some goats," Silence said.

Dulse considered himself a wordy, impatient man with a short temper. The necessity of not swearing had been a burden to him in his youth, and for thirty years the imbecility of prentices, clients, cows, and chickens had tried him sorely. Prentices and clients were afraid of his tongue, though cows and chickens paid no attention to his outbursts. He had never been angry at Silence before. There was a very long pause.

"What for?"

Silence apparently did not notice the pause or the extreme softness of Dulse's voice. "Milk, cheese, roast kid, company," he said.

"Have you ever kept goats?" Dulse asked, in the same soft, polite voice.

Silence shook his head.

He was in fact a town boy, born in Gont Port. He had said nothing about himself, but Dulse had asked around a bit. The father, a longshoreman, had died in the big earthquake, when Silence would have been seven or eight; the mother was a cook at a waterfront inn. At twelve the boy had got into some kind of trouble, probably messing about with magic, and his mother had managed to prentice him to Elassen, a respectable sorcerer in Valmouth. There the boy had picked up his true name, and some skill in carpentry and farmwork, if not much else; and Elassen had had the generosity, after three years, to pay his passage to Roke. That was all Dulse knew about him.

"I dislike goat cheese," Dulse said.

Silence nodded, acceptant as always.

From time to time in the years since then, Dulse remembered how he hadn't lost his temper when Silence asked about keeping goats; and each time the memory gave him a quiet satisfaction, like that of finishing the last bite of a perfectly ripe pear.

After spending the next several days trying to recapture the missing word, he had set Silence to studying the Acastan Spells. Together they finally worked it out, a long toil. "Like ploughing with a blind ox," Dulse said.

Not long after that he gave Silence the staff he had made for him of Gontish oak.

And the Lord of Gont Port had tried once again to get Dulse to come down to do what needed doing in Gont Port, and Dulse had sent Silence down instead, and there he had stayed.

And Dulse was standing on his own doorstep, three eggs in his hand and the rain running cold down his back.

How long had he been standing here? Why was he standing here? He had been thinking about mud, about the floor, about Silence. Had he been out walking on the path above the Overfell? No, that was years ago, years ago, in the sunlight. It was raining. He had fed the chickens, and come back to the house with three eggs, they were still warm in his hand, silky brown lukewarm eggs, and the sound of thunder was still in his mind, the vibration of thunder was in his bones, in his feet. Thunder?

No. There had been a thunderclap, a while ago. This was not thunder. He had had this queer feeling and had not recognised it, back—when? long ago, back before all the days and years he had been thinking of. When, when had it been?—before the earthquake. Just before the earthquake. Just before a half mile of the coast at Essary slumped into the sea, and the people died crushed in the ruins of their villages, and a great wave swamped the wharfs at Gont Port.

He stepped down from the doorstep onto the dirt so that he could feel the ground with the nerves of his soles, but the mud slimed and fouled any messages the dirt had for him. He set the eggs down on the doorstep, sat down beside them, cleaned his feet with rainwater from the pot by the step, wiped them dry with the rag that hung on the handle of the pot, rinsed and wrung out the rag and hung it on the handle of the pot, picked up the eggs, stood up slowly, and went into his house.

He gave a sharp look at his staff, which leaned in the corner behind the door. He put the eggs in the larder, ate an apple quickly because he was hungry, and took up his staff. It was yew, bound at the foot with copper, worn to satin at the grip. Nemmerle had given it to him.

"Stand!" he said to it in its language, and let go of it. It stood as if he had driven it into a socket.

"To the root," he said impatiently, in the Language of the Making. "To the root!"

He watched the staff that stood on the shining floor. In a little while he saw it quiver very slightly, a shiver, a tremble.

"Ah, ah, ah," said the old wizard.

"What should I do?" he said aloud after a while.

The staff swayed, was still, shivered again.

"Enough of that, my dear," Dulse said, laying his hand on it. "Come now. No wonder I kept thinking about Silence. I should send for him . . . send to him . . . No. What did Ard say? Find the center, find the center. That's the question to ask. That's what to do . . ." As he muttered on to himself, routing out his heavy cloak, setting water to boil on the small fire he had lighted earlier, he wondered if he had always talked to himself, if he had talked all the time when Silence lived with him. No. It had become a habit after Silence left, he thought, with the bit of his mind that went on thinking the ordinary thoughts of life, while the rest of it made preparations for terror and destruction.

He hard-boiled the three new eggs and one already in the larder and put them into a pouch along with four apples and a bladder of resinated wine, in case he had to stay out all night. He shrugged arthritically into his heavy cloak, took up his staff, told the fire to go out, and left.

He no longer kept a cow. He stood looking into the poultry yard, considering. The fox had been visiting the orchard lately. But the chickens would have to forage if he stayed away. They must take their chances, like everyone else. He opened their gate a little. Though the rain was no more than a misty drizzle now, they stayed hunched up under the henhouse eaves, disconsolate. The King had not crowed once this morning.

"Have you anything to tell me?" Dulse asked them.

Brown Bucca, his favorite, shook herself and said her name a few times. The others said nothing.

"Well, take care. I saw the fox on the full-moon night," Dulse said, and went on his way.

As he walked he thought; he thought hard; he recalled. He recalled all he could of matters his teacher had spoken of once only and long ago. Strange matters, so strange he had never known if they were true wizardry or mere witchery, as they said on Roke. Matters he certainly had never heard about on Roke, nor had he ever spoken about them there, maybe fearing the Masters would despise him for taking such things seriously, maybe knowing they would not understand them, because they were Gontish matters, truths of Gont. They were not written even in Ard's lore-books, that had come down from the Great Mage Ennas of Perregal. They were all word of mouth. They were home truths.

"If you need to read the Mountain," his teacher had told him, "go to the Dark Pond at the top of Semere's cow pasture. You can see the ways from there. You need to find the center. See where to go in."

"Go in?" the boy Dulse had whispered.

"What could you do from outside?"

Dulse was silent for a long time, and then said, "How?"

"Thus." And Ard's long arms stretched out and upward in the invocation of what Dulse would know later was a great spell of Transforming. Ard spoke the words of the spell awry, as teachers of wizardry must do lest the spell operate. Dulse knew the trick of hearing them aright and remembering them. When Ard was done, Dulse had repeated the words in his mind in silence, half-sketching the strange, awkward gestures that were part of them. All at once his hand stopped.

"But you can't undo this!" he said aloud.

Ard nodded. "It is irrevocable."

Dulse knew no transformation that was irrevocable, no spell that could not be unsaid, except the Word of Unbinding, which is spoken only once.

"But why—?"

"At need," Ard said.

Dulse knew better than to ask for explanation. The need to speak such a spell could not come often; the chance of his ever having to use it was very slight.

He let the terrible spell sink down in his mind and be hidden and layered over with a thousand useful or beautiful or enlightening mageries and charms, all the lore and rules of Roke, all the wisdom of the books Ard had bequeathed him. Crude, monstrous, useless, it lay in the dark of his mind for sixty years, like the cornerstone of an earlier, forgotten house down in the cellar of a mansion full of lights and treasures and children.

The rain had ceased, though mist still hid the peak and shreds of cloud drifted through the high forests. Though not a tireless walker like Silence, who would have spent his life wandering in the forests of Gont Mountain if he could, Dulse had been born in Re Albi and knew the roads and ways around it as part of himself. He took the shortcut at Rissi's well and came out before midday on Semere's high pasture, a level step on the mountainside. A mile below it, all in sunlight now, the farm buildings stood in the lee of a hill across which a flock of sheep moved like a cloud-shadow. Gont Port and its bay were hidden under the steep, knotted hills that stood inland above the city.

Dulse wandered about a bit before he found what he took to be the Dark Pond. It was small, half mud and reeds, with one vague, boggy path to the water, and no tracks on that but goat hoofs. The water was dark, though it lay out under the bright sky and far above the peat soils. Dulse followed the goat tracks, growling when his foot slipped in the mud and he wrenched his ankle to keep from falling. At the brink of the water he stood still. He stooped to rub his ankle. He listened.

It was absolutely silent.

No wind. No birdcall. No distant lowing or bleating or call of voice. As if all the island had gone still. Not a fly buzzed.

He looked at the dark water. It reflected nothing.

Reluctant, he stepped forward, barefoot and bare-legged; he had rolled up his cloak into his pack an hour ago when the sun came out. Reeds brushed his legs. The mud was soft and sucking under his feet, full of tangling reed-roots. He made no noise as he moved slowly out into the pool, and the circles of ripples from his movement were slight and small. It was shallow for a long way. Then his cautious foot felt no bottom, and he paused.

The water shivered. He felt it first on his thighs, a lapping like the tickling touch of fur; then he saw it, the trembling of the surface all over the pond. Not the round ripples he made, which had already died away, but a ruffling, a roughening, a shudder, again, and again.

"Where?" he whispered, and then said the word aloud in the language all things understand that have no other language.

There was the silence. Then a fish leapt from the black, shaking water, a white-grey fish the length of his hand, and as it leapt it cried out in a small, clear voice, in that same language, "Yaved!"

The old wizard stood there. He recollected all he knew of the names of Gont, brought all its slopes and cliffs and ravines into his mind, and in a minute he saw where Yaved was. It was the place where the ridges parted, just inland from Gont Port, deep in the knot of hills above the city. It was the place of the fault. An earthquake centered there could shake the city down, bring avalanche and tidal wave, close the cliffs of the bay together like hands clapping. Dulse shivered, shuddered all over like the water of the pool.

He turned and made for the shore, hasty, careless where he set his feet and not caring if he broke the silence by splashing and breathing hard. He slogged back up the path through the reeds till he reached dry ground and coarse grass, and heard the buzz of midges and crickets. He sat down then on the ground, hard, for his legs were shaking.

"It won't do," he said, talking to himself in Hardic, and then he said, "I can't do it." Then he said, "I can't do it by myself."

He was so distraught that when he made up his mind to call Silence he could not think of the opening of the spell, which he had known for sixty years; then when he thought he had it, he began to speak a Summoning instead, and the spell had begun to work before he realised what he was doing and stopped and undid it word by word.

He pulled up some grass and rubbed at the slimy mud on his feet and legs. It was not dry yet, and only smeared about on his skin. "I hate mud," he whispered. Then he snapped his jaws and stopped trying to clean his legs. "Dirt, dirt," he said, gently patting the ground he sat on. Then, very slow, very careful, he began to speak the spell of calling.

In a busy street leading down to the busy wharfs of Gont Port, the wizard Ogion stopped short. The ships' captain beside him walked on several steps and turned to see Ogion talking to the air.

"But I will come, master!" he said. And then after a pause, "How soon?" And after a longer pause, he told the air something in a language the ship's captain did not understand, and made a gesture that darkened the air about him for an instant.

"Captain," he said, "I'm sorry, I must wait to spell your sails. An earthquake is near. I must warn the city. Do you tell them down there, every ship that can sail make for the open sea. Clear out past the Armed Cliffs! Good luck to you." And he turned and ran back up the street, a tall, strong man with rough greying hair, running now like a stag.

Gont Port lies at the inner end of a long narrow bay between steep shores. Its entrance from the sea is between two great headlands, the Gates of the Port, the Armed Cliffs, not a hundred feet apart. The people of Gont Port are safe from sea-pirates. But their safety is their danger: the long bay follows a fault in the earth, and jaws that have opened may shut.

When he had done what he could to warn the city, and seen all the gate guards and port guards doing what they could to keep the few roads out from becoming choked and murderous with panicky people, Ogion shut himself into a room in the signal tower of the Port, locked the door, for everybody wanted him at once, and sent a sending to the Dark Pond in Semere's cow pasture up on the Mountain.

His old master was sitting in the grass near the pond, eating an apple. Bits of eggshell flecked the ground near his legs, which were caked with drying mud. When he looked up and saw Ogion's sending he smiled a wide, sweet smile. But he looked old. He had never looked so old. Ogion had not seen him for over a year, having been busy; he was always busy in Gont Port, doing the business of the lords and people, never a chance to walk in the forests on the mountainside or to come sit with Heleth in the little house at Re Albi and listen and be still. Heleth was an old man, near eighty now; and he was frightened. He smiled with joy to see Ogion, but he was frightened.

"I think what we have to do," he said without preamble, "is try to hold the fault from slipping much. You at the Gates and me at the inner end, in the Mountain. Working together, you know. We might be able to. I can feel it building up, can you?"

Ogion shook his head. He let his sending sit down in the grass near Heleth, though it did not bend the stems of the grass where it stepped or sat. "I've done nothing but set the city in a panic and send the ships out of the bay," he said. "What is it you feel? How do you feel it?"

They were technical questions, mage to mage. Heleth hesitated before answering.

"I learned about this from Ard," he said, and paused again.

He had never told Ogion anything about his first teacher, a sorcerer of no fame even in Gont, and perhaps of ill fame. Ogion knew only that Ard had never gone to Roke, had been trained on Perregal, and that some mystery or shame darkened the name. Though he was talkative, for a wizard, Heleth was silent as a stone about some things. And so Ogion, who respected silence, had never asked him about his teacher.

"It's not Roke magic," the old man said. His voice was dry, a little forced. "Nothing against the balance, though. Nothing sticky."

That had always been his word for evil doings, spells for gain, curses, black magic: "sticky stuff."

After a while, searching for words, he went on: "Dirt. Rocks. It's a dirty magic. Old. Very old. As old as Gont Island."

"The Old Powers?" Ogion murmured.

Heleth said, "I'm not sure."

"Will it control the earth itself?"

"More a matter of getting in with it, I think. Inside." The old man was burying the core of his apple and the larger bits of eggshell under loose dirt, patting it over them neatly. "Of course I know the words, but I'll have to learn what to do as I go. That's the trouble with the big spells, isn't it? You learn what you're doing while you do it. No chance to practice." He looked up. "Ah—there! You feel that?"

Ogion shook his head.

"Straining," Heleth said, his hand still absently, gently patting the dirt as one might pat a scared cow. "Quite soon now, I think. Can you hold the Gates open, my dear?"

"Tell me what you'll be doing—"

But Heleth was shaking his head: "No," he said. "No time. Not your kind of thing." He was more and more distracted by whatever it was he sensed in the earth or air, and through him Ogion too felt that gathering, intolerable tension.

They sat unspeaking. The crisis passed. Heleth relaxed a little and even smiled. "Very old stuff," he said, "what I'll be doing. I wish now I'd thought about it more. Passed it on to you. But it seemed a bit crude. Heavy-handed . . . She didn't say where she'd learned it. Here, of course . . . There are different kinds of knowledge, after all."

"She?"

"Ard. My teacher." Heleth looked up, his face unreadable, its expression possibly sly. "You didn't know that? No, I suppose I never mentioned it. I wonder what difference it made to her wizardry, her being a woman. Or to mine, my being a man . . . What matters, it seems to me, is whose house we live in. And who we let enter the house. This kind of thing—There! There again—"

His sudden tension and immobility, the strained face and inward look, were like those of a woman in labor when her womb contracts. That was Ogion's thought, even as he asked, "What did you mean, 'in the Mountain'?"

The spasm passed; Heleth answered, "Inside it. There at Yaved." He pointed to the knotted hills below them. "I'll go in, try to keep things from sliding around, eh? I'll find out how when I'm doing it, no doubt. I think you should be getting back to yourself. Things are tightening up." He stopped again, looking as if he were in intense pain, hunched and clenched. He struggled to stand up. Unthinking, Ogion held out his hand to help him.

"No use," said the old wizard, grinning, "you're only wind and sunlight. Now I'm going to be dirt and stone. You'd best go on. Farewell, Aihal. Keep the— keep the mouth open, for once, eh?"

Ogion, obedient, bringing himself back to himself in the stuffy, tapestried room in Gont Port, did not understand the old man's joke until he turned to the window and saw the Armed Cliffs down at the end of the long bay, the jaws ready to snap shut. "I will," he said, and set to it.

"What I have to do, you see," the old wizard said, still talking to Silence because it was a comfort to talk to him even if he was no longer there, "is get into the mountain, right inside. But not the way a sorcerer-prospector does, not just slipping about between things and looking and tasting. Deeper. All the way in. Not the veins, but the bones. So," and standing there alone in the high pasture, in the noon light, Heleth opened his arms wide in the gesture of invocation that opens all the greater spells; and he spoke.

Nothing happened as he said the words Ard had taught him, his old witch-teacher with her bitter mouth and her long, lean arms, the words spoken awry then, spoken truly now.

Nothing happened, and he had time to regret the sunlight and the sea wind, and to doubt the spell, and to doubt himself, before the earth rose up around him, dry, warm, and dark.

In there he knew he should hurry, that the bones of the earth ached to move, and that he must become them to guide them, but he could not hurry. There was on him the bewilderment of any transformation. He had in his day been fox, and bull, and dragonfly, and knew what it was to change being. But this was different, this slow enlargement. I am vastening, he thought.

He reached out towards Yaved, towards the ache, the suffering. As he came closer to it he felt a great strength flow into him from the west, as if Silence had taken him by the hand after all. Through that link he could send his own strength, the Mountain's strength, to help. I didn't tell him I wasn't coming back, he thought, his last words in Hardic, his last grief, for he was in the bones of the mountain now. He knew the arteries of fire, and the beat of the great heart. He knew what to do. It was in no tongue of man that he said, "Be quiet, be easy. There now, there. Hold fast. So, there. We can be easy."

And he was easy, he was still, he held fast, rock in rock and earth in earth in the fiery dark of the mountain.

It was their mage Ogion whom the people saw stand alone on the roof of the signal tower on the wharf, when the streets ran up and down in waves, the cobbles bursting out of them, and walls of clay brick puffed into dust, and the Armed Cliffs leaned together, groaning. It was Ogion they saw, his hands held out before him, straining, parting: and the cliffs parted with them, and stood straight, unmoved. The city shuddered and stood still. It was Ogion who stopped the earthquake. They saw it, they said it.

"My teacher was with me, and his teacher with him," Ogion said when they praised him. "I could hold the Gate open because he held the Mountain still." They praised his modesty and did not listen to him. Listening is a rare gift, and men will have their heroes.

When the city was in order again, and the ships had all come back, and the walls were being rebuilt, Ogion escaped from praise and went up into the hills above Gont Port. He found the queer little valley called Trimmer's Dell, the true name of which in the Language of the Making was Yaved, as Ogion's true name was Aihal. He walked about there all one day, as if seeking something. In the evening he lay down on the ground and talked to it. "You should have told me. I could have said goodbye," he said. He wept then, and his tears fell on the dry dirt among the grass stems and made little spots of mud, little sticky spots.

He slept there on the ground, with no pallet or blanket between him and the dirt. At sunrise he got up and walked by the high road over to Re Albi. He did not go into the village, but past it to the house that stood alone north of the other houses at the beginning of the Overfell. The door stood open.

The last beans had got big and coarse on the vines; the cabbages were thriving. Three hens came clucking and pecking around the dusty dooryard, a red, a brown, a white; a grey hen was setting her clutch in the henhouse. There were no chicks, and no sign of the cock, the King, Heleth had called him. The king is dead, Ogion thought. Maybe a chick is hatching even now to take his place. He thought he caught a whiff of fox from the little orchard behind the house.

He swept out the dust and leaves that had blown in the open doorway across the floor of polished wood. He set Heleth's mattress and blanket in the sun to air. "I'll stay here a while," he thought. "It's a good house." After a while he thought, "I might keep some goats."

# TERRY BLACKHAWK

# What the Story Weaves, the Spinner Tells

*Terry Blackhawk received her B.A. from Antioch College and taught English and Creative Writing in the Detroit public schools for twenty-eight years—where she founded InsideOut, a literary arts project for Detroit students. Her poetry has appeared in journals including* The Michigan Quarterly Review, Nimrod, Passages North, Poet Lore, Spoon River, Yankee, *and* Artful Dodge, *and has been collected in* Body & Field *(Michigan State University, 1999).*

*She has received the Foley Poetry Award, a Distinguished Merit Award from Poetry Atlanta, and two Pushcart Prizes, among other honors. She lives in Detroit, where she is poet-in-residence and director of InsideOut.*

*Blackhawk's poem "What the Story Weaves, the Spinner Tells" comes from* Calyx, Vol. 20, #2.

—T. W.

When I look out from inside
the dream and the space of the dream
shines between us, I see you there, shining

on the other side. The dream is a tale,
a story I tell, drawing us in to a new space,
encircling us in common light.

When everything vanishes but the light
of memory, what will protect us inside
our lines, this darkly echoing space?

Will it be the red handprint of our dreams
hovering over our heads, this thread of a tale
raveling, or the way I see your eyes shining?

Fisherman, you haul your nets in the shining
evening, your straining limbs pollinated by light.
Princess, you descend from the tower into the tale,

crumple, rise, redressed, victorious. Inside
our story, we do not live in grace but dream
of transformation, a new path to that open space

in the grasses where we reassemble our bones, pace
backward, then reclaim the panther whose shining
teeth dismembered the dimensions of our dream.

Third child, Grimm's little girl had it right: light
is the only way to fill us from the inside
out, the match in her apron pocket, the tale

a bright window against the dark forest. We tell
and grow new with every telling, amazed by the space
we shape, the way we regard one another inside it.

You, listener, are the story I see which I step, shining,
into, where I become this hologram of myself, a sleight
of mind and words I speak but do not own.

# CAITLÍN R. KIERNAN

# Onion

*Caitlín R. Kiernan's short fiction has been collected in* Candles for Elizabeth, Tales of Pain and Wonder, Wrong Things *(with Poppy Z. Brite), and most recently in* From Weird and Distant Shores. *She has also published two novels,* Silk *and* Threshold, *and scripted graphic novels for DC/Vertigo (*The Dreaming, The Girl Who Would Be Death, *and the forthcoming* Bast: Eternity Game*).*

*About "Onion" she says:*

*"The possibility of invisible worlds existing parallel to our own, or worlds that are almost invisible, has been on my mind a great deal the last couple of years. "Onion" occurred to me while reading Christiaan Huygens'* The Celestial Worlds Discovered, *from which I took the closing epigraph."*

*"Onion" was first published in the collection* Wrong Things, *Subterranean Press.*

—E. D.

Frank was seven years old when he found the fields of red grass growing behind the basement wall. The building on St. Mark's where his parents lived after his father took a job in Manhattan and moved them from the New Jersey suburbs across the wide, gray Hudson. And of course he'd been told to stay out of the basement, no place for a child to play because there were rats down there, his mother said, and rats could give you tetanus and rabies. Rats might even be carrying plague, she said, but the sooty blackness at the foot of the stairs was too much temptation for any seven-year-old, the long, long hallway past the door to the super's apartment and sometimes a single naked bulb burned way down at the end of that hall. Dirty, whiteyellow stain that only seemed to emphasize the gloom, drawing attention to just how very dark dark could be, and after school Frank would stand at the bottom of the stairs for an hour at a time, peering into the hall that led down to the basement.

"Does your mama know you're always hanging around down here?" Mr. Sweeney would ask whenever he came out and found Frank lurking in the shadows. Frank would squint at the flood of light from Mr. Sweeney's open door, would shrug or mumble the most noncommittal response he could come up with.

"I bet you she don't," Mr. Sweeney would say. "I bet you she *don't* know."

"Are there really rats down there?" Frank might ask and Mr. Sweeney would nod his head, point towards the long hall and say "You better *believe* there's rats. Boy, there's rats under this dump big as German shepherd puppies. They got eyes like acetylene blow torches and teeth like carving knives. Can chew straight through concrete, these rats we got."

"Then why don't you get a cat?" Frank asked once and Mr. Sweeney laughed, phlegmy old man laugh, and "Oh, we had some cats, boy," he said. "We had whole goddamn cat *armies*, but when these rats get done, ain't never anything left but some gnawed-up bones and whiskers."

"I don't believe that," Frank said. "Rats don't get that big. Rats don't eat cats."

"You better get your skinny rump back upstairs, or they're gonna eat you too," and then Mr. Sweeney laughed again and slammed his door, left Frank alone in the dark, his heart thumping loud and his head filled with visions of the voracious, giant rats that tunneled through masonry and dined on any cat unlucky enough to get in their way.

And that's the way it went, week after week, month after month, until one snowblind February afternoon, too cold and wet to go outside and his mother didn't notice when he slipped quietly downstairs with the flashlight she kept in a kitchen drawer. Mr. Sweeney was busy with a busted radiator on the third floor, so nobody around this time to tell him scary stories and chase him home again, and Frank walked right on past the super's door, stood shivering in the chilly, mildewstinking air of the hallway. The unsteady beam of his flashlight to show narrow walls that might have been blue or green a long time ago, little black-and-white, six-sided ceramic tiles on the floor, but half of them missing and he could see the rotting boards underneath. There were doors along the length of the hall, some of them boarded up, nailed shut, one door frame without any door at all and he stepped very fast past that one.

*Indiana Jones wouldn't be afraid*, he thought, counting his footsteps in case that might be important later on, listening to the winter wind yowling raw along the street as it swept past the building on its way to Tompkins Square Park and the East River. Twenty steps, twenty-five, thirty-three and then he was standing below the dangling bulb and for the first time Frank stopped and looked back the way he'd come. And maybe he'd counted wrong, because it seemed a lot farther than only thirty-three steps back to the dim and postage-stamp-sized splotch of day at the other end of the hall.

Only ten steps more down to the basement door, heavy, gray steel door with a rusted hasp and a Yale padlock, but standing wide open like it was waiting for him and maybe Mr. Sweeney only forgot to lock it the last time he came down to check the furnace or wrap the pipes. And later, Frank wouldn't remember much about crossing the threshold into the deeper night of the basement, the soupthick stench and taste of dust and rot and mushrooms, picking his way through the maze of sagging shelves and wooden crates, decaying heaps of rags and newspapers, past the ancient furnace crouched in one corner like a cast-iron octopus. Angry, orangered glow from the furnace grate like the eyes of the super's cat-eating rats—he *would* remember that—and then Frank heard the dry, rustling sound coming from one corner of the basement.

Years later, through high school and college and the slow purgatory of his twenties, *this* is where the bad dreams would always begin, the moment that he lifted the flashlight and saw the wide and jagged crack in the concrete wall. A faint draft from that corner that smelled of cinnamon and ammonia, and he *knew* better than to look, knew he should turn and run all the way back because it wasn't ever really rats that he was supposed to be afraid of. The rats just a silly, grown-up lie to keep him safe, smaller, kinder nightmare for his own good, and *Run, boy*, Mr Sweeney whispered inside his head. *Run fast while you still can, while you still don't know.*

But Frank didn't run away, and when he pressed his face to the crack in the wall, he could see that the fields stretched away for miles and miles, crimson meadows beneath a sky the yellowgreen of an old bruise. The white trees that writhed and rustled in the choking, spicy breeze, and far, far away, the black thing striding slowly through the grass on bandy, stiltlong legs.

Frank and Willa share the tiny apartment on Mott Street, roachy Chinatown hovel one floor above an apothecary so the place always stinks of ginseng and jasmine and the powdered husks of dried sea creatures. Four walls, a gas range, an ancient Frigidaire that only works when it feels like it, but together they can afford the rent, most of the time, and the month or two they've come up short Mrs. Wu has let them slide. His job at a copy shop and hers waiting tables and sometimes they talk about moving out of the city, packing up their raggedy-ass belongings and riding a Greyhound all the way to Florida, all the way to the Keys, and then it'll be summer all year long. But not this sticky, sweltering New York summer, no, it would be clean ocean air and rum drinks, sunwarm sand and the lullaby roll and crash of waves at night.

Frank is still in bed when Willa comes out of the closet that passes as their bathroom, naked and dripping from the shower, her hair wrapped up in a towel that used to be white and he stops staring at the tattered Cézanne print thumb-tacked over the television and stares at her instead. Willa is tall and her skin so pale he thought she might be sick the first time they met, so skinny that he can see intimations of her skeleton beneath that skin like milk and pearls. Can trace the bluegreen network of veins and capillaries in her throat, between her small breasts, winding like hesitant, watercolor brush strokes down her arms. He's pretty sure that one day Willa will finally figure out she can do a hell of lot better than him and move on, but he tries not to let that ruin whatever it is they have now.

"It's all yours," she says, his turn even though the water won't be hot again for at least half an hour, and Willa sits down in a chair near the foot of the bed. She leans forward and rubs vigorously at her hair trapped inside the dingy towel.

"We could both play hooky," Frank says hopefully, watching her, imagining how much better sex would be than the chugging, headache drone of Xerox machines, the endless dissatisfaction of clients. "You could come back to bed and we could lie here all day. We could just lie here and sweat and watch television."

"Jesus, Frank, how am I supposed to resist an offer like *that?*"

"Okay, so we could screw and sweat and watch television."

She stops drying her hair and glares at him, shakes her head and frowns, but the sort of frown that says *I wish I could* more than it says anything else.

"That new girl isn't working out," she says.

"The fat chick from Kazakhstan?" Frank asks and he rolls over onto his back, easier to forget the fantasies of a lazy day alone with Willa if he isn't looking at her sitting there naked.

"Fucking *Kazakhstan*. I mean, what the hell were Ted and Daniel thinking? She can't even speak enough English to tell someone where the toilet is, much less take an order."

"Maybe they felt sorry for her," Frank says unhelpfully and now he's staring up at his favorite crack on the waterstained ceiling, the one that always makes him think of a Viking orbiter photo of the Valles Marineris from one of his old astronomy books. "I've heard that people do that sometimes, feel sorry for people."

"Well, they'd probably lose less money if they just sent the bitch to college, the way she's been pissing off customers."

"Maybe you should suggest that today," and a moment later Willa's wet towel smacks him in the face, steamydamp terry cloth that smells like her black hair dye and the cheap baby shampoo she uses. It covers his eyes, obscuring his view of the Martian rift valley overhead, but Frank doesn't move the towel immediately, better to lie there a moment longer, breathing her in.

"Is it still supposed to rain today?" Willa asks and he mumbles through the wet towel that he doesn't know.

"They keep promising it's going to rain and it keeps not raining."

Frank sits up and the towel slides off his face and into his lap, lies there as the dampness begins to soak through his boxers.

"I don't know," he says again; Willa has her back turned to him and she doesn't reply or make any sign to show that she's heard. She's pulling a bright yellow T-shirt on over her head, the Curious George shirt he gave her for Christmas, has put on a pair of yellow panties, too.

"I'm sorry," she says. "It's the heat. The heat's driving me crazy."

Frank glances towards the window, the sash up but the chintzy curtains hanging limp and lifeless in the stagnant July air; he'd have to get out of bed, walk all the way across the room, lean over the sill and peer up past the walls and rooftops to see if there are any clouds. "It might rain today," he says, instead.

"I don't think it's ever going to rain again as long as I live," Willa says and steps into her jeans. "I think we've broken this goddamn planet and it's never going to rain anywhere ever again."

Frank rubs his fingers through his stiff, dirty hair and looks back at the Cézanne still life above the television—a tabletop, the absinthe bottle and a carafe of water, an empty glass, the fruit that might be peaches.

"You'll be at the meeting tonight?" he asks and Frank keeps his eyes on the print because he doesn't like the sullen, secretive expression Willa gets whenever they have to talk about the meetings.

"Yeah," she says, sighs, and then there's the clothmetal sound of her zipper. "Of course I'll be at the meeting. Where the hell else would I be?"

And then she goes back into the bathroom and shuts the door behind her, leaves Frank alone with Cézanne and the exotic reek of the apothecary downstairs, Valles Marineris and the bright day spilling uninvited through the window above Mott Street.

———

Half past two and Frank sits on a plastic milk crate in the stockroom of Gotham Kwick Kopy, trying to decide whether or not to eat the peanut butter and honey sandwich he brought for lunch. The air conditioning's on the blink again and he thinks it might actually be hotter inside the shop than out on the street; a few merciful degrees cooler in the stockroom, though, shadowy refuge stacked high with cardboard boxes of copy paper in a dozen shades of white and all the colors of the rainbow. He peels back the top of his sandwich, the doughy Mill-brook bread that Willa likes, and frowns at the mess underneath. So hot out front that the peanut butter has melted, oily mess to leak straight through wax paper and the brown bag and he's trying to remember if peanut butter and honey can spoil.

Both the stockroom doors swing open and Frank looks up, blinks and squints at the sunframed silhouette, Joe Manske letting in the heat and "Hey, don't do that," Frank says as Joe switches on the lights. The fluorescents buzz and flicker uncertainly, chasing away the shadows, drenching the stockroom in their bland, indifferent glare.

"Dude, why are you sitting back here in the dark?" Joe asks and for a moment Frank considers throwing the sandwich at him.

"Why aren't you working on that Mac?" Frank asks right back and "It's fixed, good as new," Joe says, grins his big, stupid grin, and sits down on a box of laser print paper near the door.

"That fucker won't *ever* be good as new again."

"Well, at least it's stopped making that sound. That's good enough for me," and Joe takes out a pack of Camels, offers one to Frank and Frank shakes his head no. A month now since his last cigarette, quitting because Willa's step-mother is dying of lung cancer, quitting because cigarettes cost too goddamn much, anyhow, and "Thanks, though," he says.

"Whatever," Joe Manske mumbles around the filter of his Camel, thumb on the strike wheel of his silver lighter and in a moment the air is filled with the pungent aroma of burning tobacco. Frank gives up on the dubious sandwich, drops it back into the brown bag and crumples the bag into a greasy ball.

"I fuckin' hate this fuckin' job," Joe says, disgusted, smoky cloud of words about his head, and he points at the stockroom doors with his cigarette. "You just missed a real piece of work, man."

"Yeah?" and Frank tosses the sandwich ball towards the big plastic garbage can sitting a few feet away, misses and it rolls behind the busted Canon 2400 color copier that's been sitting in the same spot since he started this job a year ago.

"Yeah," Joe says. "I was trying to finish that pet store job and this dude comes in, little bitty old man looks like he just got off the boat from Poland or Armenia or some shit—"

"My grandfather was Polish," Frank says and Joe sighs loudly, long impatient sigh and he flicks ash onto the cement floor. "You *know* what I mean."

"So what'd he want, anyway?" Frank asks, not because he cares but the short-est way through any conversation with Joe Manske is usually right down the middle, just be quiet and listen and sooner or later he'll probably come to the end and shut up.

"He had this *old* book with him. The damned thing must have been even older than him and it was falling apart. I don't think you could so much as look at it without the pages crumbling. Had it tied together with some string and he kept askin' me all these questions, real technical shit about the machines, you know."

"Yeah? Like what?"

"Dude, I don't know. I can't remember half of it, techie shit, like I was friggin' Mr. Wizard or somethin'. I finally just told him we couldn't be responsible if the copiers messed up his old book, but he still kept on askin' these questions. Lucky for me, one of the self-service machines jammed and I told him I had to go fix it. By the time I was finished, he was gone."

"You live to serve," Frank says, wondering if Willa would be able to tell if he had just one cigarette. "The customer is always right."

"Fuck that shit," Joe Manske says. "I don't get paid enough to have to listen to some senile old fart jabberin' at me all day."

"Yes sir, helpful is your middle name."

"Fuck you."

Frank laughs and gets up, pushes the milk crate towards the wall with the toe of one shoe so no one's going to come along later and trip over it, break their neck and have him to blame. "I better get back to work," he says and "You do that," Joe grumbles and puffs his Camel.

Through the stockroom doors and back out into the stifling, noisy clutter of the shop, and it must be at least ten degrees warmer out here, he thinks. There's a line at the register and the phone's ringing, no one out front but Maggie and she glowers at him across the chaos. "I'm on it," Frank says; she shakes her head doubtfully and turns to help a woman wearing a dark purple dress and matching beret. Frank's reaching across the counter for the telephone receiver when he notices the business card lying near a display of Liquid Paper. Black sans serif print on an expensive, white cotton card stock and what appears to be an infinity symbol in the lower left-hand corner. FOUND: LOST WORLDS centered at the top, TERRAE NOVUM ET TERRA INDETERMINATA on the next line down in smaller letters. Then a name and an address—Dr. Solomon Monalisa, Ph.D., 43 W. 61st St., Manhattan—but no number or e-mail, and Frank picks up the card, holds it so Maggie can see.

"Where'd this come from?" he asks but she only shrugs, annoyed but still smiling her strained and weary smile for the woman in the purple beret. "Beats me. Ask Joe, if he ever comes back. Now, will you *please* answer the phone?"

He apologizes, lifts the receiver, "Gotham Kwick Kopy, Frank speaking. How may I help you?" and slips the white card into his back pocket.

The group meets in the basement of a synagogue on Eldridge Street. Once a month, eight o'clock until everyone who wants to talk has taken his or her turn, coffee and stale doughnuts before and afterwards. Metal folding chairs and a lectern down front, a microphone and crackly PA system even though the room isn't really large enough to need one. Never more than fourteen or fifteen people, occasionally as few as six or seven, and Frank and Willa always sit at the very back, near the door. Sometimes Willa doesn't make it all the way through a meeting and she says she hates the way they all watch her if she gets up to leave early, like she's done something wrong, she says, like this is all her fault, some-how. So they sit by the door, which is fine with Frank; he'd rather not have everyone staring at the back of his head, anyway.

He's sipping at a styrofoam cup of the bitter, black coffee, three sugars and it's still bitter, watching the others, all their familiar, telltale quirks and peculi-arities, their equivocal glances, when Willa comes in. First the sound of her clunky motorcycle boots on the concrete steps and then she stands in the door-way a moment, that expression like it's always the first time for her and it can never be any other way.

"Hey," Frank says quietly. "I made it," she replies and sits down beside him. There's a stain on the front of her Curious George T-shirt that looks like choc-olate sauce.

"How was your day?" he asks her, talking so she doesn't lock up before things even get started.

"Same as ever. It sucked. They didn't fire Miss Kazakhstan."

"That's good, dear. Would you like a martini?" and he jabs a thumb towards the free-coffee-and-stale-doughnut table. "I think I'll pass," Willa says humor-lessly, rubs her hands together and stares at the floor between her feet. "I think my stomach hurts enough already."

"Would you rather just go home? We can miss one night. I sure as hell don't care—"

"No," she says, answering too fast, too emphatic, so he knows she means yes. "That would be silly. I'll be fine when things get started."

And then Mr. Zaroba stands, stocky man with skin like tea-stained muslin, salt-and-pepper hair and beard and his bushy, gray eyebrows. Kindly blue grand-father eyes and he raises one hand to get everyone's attention, as if they aren't all looking at him already, as if they haven't all been waiting for him to open his mouth and break the tense, uncertain silence.

"Good evening, everyone," he says, and Willa sits up a little straighter in her chair, expectant arch of her back as though she's getting ready to run.

"Before we begin," Mr. Zaroba continues, "there's something I wanted to share. I came across this last week," and he takes a piece of paper from his shirt pocket, unfolds it, and begins to read. An item from the New York Tribune, February 17th, 1901; reports by an Indian tribe in Alaska of a city in the sky that was seen sometimes, and a prospector named Willoughby who claimed to have witnessed the thing himself in 1897, claimed to have tried to photograph it on several occasions and succeeded, finally.

"And now this," Zaroba says and he pulls a second folded sheet of paper from his shirt pocket, presto, bottomless bag of tricks, that pocket, and this time he reads from a book, Alaska by Miner Bruce, page 107, he says. Someone else who saw the city suspended in the arctic sky, a Mr. C. W. Thornton of Seattle, and " 'It required no effort of the imagination to liken it to a city,' " Mr. Zaroba reads, " 'but was so distinct that it required, instead, faith to believe that it was not in reality a city.' "

People shift nervously in their seats, scuff their feet, and someone whispers too loudly.

"I have the prospector's photograph," Zaroba says. "It's only a xerox from the book, of course. It isn't very clear, but I thought some of you might like to see it," and he hands one of the sheets of paper to the person sitting nearest him.

"Damn, I need a cigarette," Willa whispers and "You and me both," Frank whispers back. It takes almost five minutes for the sheet of paper to make its way to the rear of the room, passed along from hand to hand to hand while Zaroba stands patiently at the front, his head bowed solemn as if leading a prayer. Some hold onto it as long as they dare and others hardly seem to want to touch it. A man three rows in front of them gets up and brings it back to Willa.

"I don't see nothing but clouds," he says, sounding disappointed.

And neither does Frank, fuzzy photograph of a mirage, deceit of sunlight in the collision of warm and freezing air high above a glacier, but Willa must see more. She holds the paper tight and chews at her lower lip, traces the distorted peaks and cumulonimbus towers with the tip of an index finger.

"My god," she whispers.

In a moment Zaroba comes up the aisle and takes the picture away, leaves Willa staring at her empty hands, her eyes wet like she might start crying. Frank puts an arm around her bony shoulders, but she immediately wiggles free and scoots her chair a few inches farther away.

"So, who wants to get us started tonight?" Mr. Zaroba asks when he gets back to the lectern. At first no one moves or speaks or raises a hand, each looking at the others or trying hard to look nowhere at all. And then a young woman stands up, younger than Willa, filthy clothes and bruisedark circles under her eyes, hair that hasn't been combed or washed in ages. Her name is Janice and Frank thinks that she's a junky, probably a heroin addict because she always wears long sleeves.

"Janice? Very good, then," and Mr. Zaroba returns to his seat in the first row. Everyone watches Janice as she walks slowly to the front of the room, or they pretend not to watch her. There's a small hole in the seat of her dirty, threadbare jeans and Frank can see that she isn't wearing underwear. She stands behind the lectern, coughs once, twice, and brushes her shaggy bangs out of her face. She looks anxiously at Mr. Zaroba and "It's all right, Janice," he says. "Take all the time you need. No one's going to rush you."

"Bullshit," Willa mutters, loud enough that the man sitting three rows in front of them turns and scowls. "What the hell are you staring at," she growls and he turns back towards the lectern.

"It's okay, baby," Frank says and takes her hand, squeezes hard enough that she can't shake him loose this time. "We can leave anytime you want."

Janice coughs again and there's a faint feedback whine from the mike. She wipes her nose with the back of her hand and "I was only fourteen years old," she begins. "I still lived with my foster parents in Trenton and there was this old cemetery near our house, Riverview Cemetery. Me and my sister, my foster sister, we used to go there to smoke and talk, you know, just to get away from the house."

Janice looks at the basement ceiling while she speaks, or down at the lectern, but never at the others. She pauses and wipes her nose again.

"We went there all the time. Wasn't anything out there to be afraid of, not like at home. Just dead people, and me and Nadine weren't afraid of dead people.

Dead people don't hurt anyone, right? We could sit there under the trees in the summer and it was almost like things weren't so bad. Nadine was a year older than me."

Willa tries to pull her hand free, digs her nails into Frank's palm but he doesn't let go. They both know where this is going, have both heard Janice's story so many times they could recite it backwards, same tired old horror story, and "It's okay," he says out loud, to Willa or to himself.

"Mostly it was just regular headstones, but there were a few big crypts set way back near the water. I didn't like being around them. I told her that, over and over, but Nadine said they were like little castles, like something out of fairy tales.

"One day one of them was open, like maybe someone had busted into it, and Nadine had to see if there were still bones inside. I begged her not to, said whoever broke it open might still be hanging around somewhere and we ought to go home and come back later. But she wouldn't listen to me.

"I didn't want to look inside. I swear to God, I didn't."

"*Liar,*" Willa whispers, so low now that the man three rows in front of them doesn't hear, but Frank does. Her nails are digging deeper into his palm, and his eyes are beginning to water from the pain. "*You* wanted to see," she says. "Just like the rest of us, you wanted to see."

"I said, 'What if someone's still in there?' but she wouldn't listen. She wasn't ever afraid of anything. She used to lay down on train tracks just to piss me off."

"What did you see in the crypt, Janice, when you and Nadine looked inside?" Mr. Zaroba asks, but no hint of impatience in his voice, not hurrying her or prompting, only helping her find a path across the words as though they were slippery rocks in a cold stream. "Can you tell us?"

Janice takes a very deep breath, swallows, and "Stairs," she says. "Stairs going down into the ground. There was a light way down at the bottom, a blue light, like a cop car light. Only it wasn't flashing. And we could hear something moving around down there, and something else that sounded like a dog panting. I tried to get Nadine to come back to the house with me then, but she wouldn't. She said 'Those stairs might go *anywhere*, Jan. Don't you want to *see*? Don't you want to *know*?' "

Another pause and "I couldn't stop her," Janice says.

Willa mutters something Frank doesn't understand, then, something vicious, and he lets go of her hand, rubs at the four crescent-shaped wounds her nails leave behind. Blood drawn, crimson tattoos to mark the wild and irreparable tear in her soul by marking him, and he presses his palm to his black work pants, no matter if it stains, no one will ever notice.

"I waited at the top of the stairs until dark," Janice says. "I kept on calling her. I called her until my throat hurt. When the sun started going down, the blue light at the bottom got brighter and once or twice I thought I could see someone moving around down there, someone standing between me and the light. Finally, I yelled I was going to get the goddamn cops if she didn't come back . . ." and Janice trails off, hugs herself like she's cold and gazes straight ahead, but Frank knows she doesn't see any of them sitting there, watching her, waiting for the next word, waiting for *their* turns at the lectern.

"You don't have to say any more tonight," Zaroba says. "You know we'll all understand if you can't."

"No," Janice says. "I *can* . . . I really *need* to," and she squeezes her eyes shut tight. Mr. Zaroba stands, takes one reassuring step towards the lectern.

"We're all right here," he says, and "We're *listening*," Willa mumbles mockingly. "We're listening," Zaroba says a second later.

"I didn't go get the police. I didn't tell anyone anything until the next day. My foster parents, they just thought she'd run away again. No one would believe me when I told them about the crypt, when I told them where Nadine had really gone. Finally, they made me show them, though, the cops did, so I took them out to Riverview."

"Why do we always have to fucking start with her?" Willa whispers. "I can't remember a single time she didn't go first."

Someone sneezes and "It was sealed up again," Janice says, her small and brittle voice made big and brittle by the PA speakers. "But they opened it. The cemetery people didn't want them to, but they did anyway. I swore I'd kill myself if they didn't open it and get Nadine out of there."

"Can *you* remember a time she didn't go first?" Willa asks and Frank looks at her, but he doesn't answer.

"All they found inside was a coffin. The cops even pulled up part of the marble floor, but there wasn't anything under it, just dirt."

A few more minutes, a few more details, and Janice is done. Mr. Zaroba hugs her and she goes back to her seat. "Who wants to be next?" he asks them and it's the man who calls himself Charlie Jones, though they all know that's not his real name. Every month he apologizes because he can't use his real name at the meetings, too afraid someone at work might find out, and then he tells them about the time he opened a bedroom door in his house in Hartford and there was nothing on the other side but stars. When he's done, Zaroba shakes his hand, pats him on the back, and now it's time for the woman who got lost once on the subway, two hours just to get from South Ferry to the Houston Street Station, alone in an empty train that rushed along through a darkness filled with the sound of children crying. Then a timid Colombian woman named Juanita Lazarte, the night she watched two moons cross the sky above Peekskill, the morning the sun rose in the south.

And all the others, each in his or her turn, as the big wall clock behind the lectern ticks and the night fills up with the weight and absurdity of their stories, glimpses of impossible geographies, entire worlds hidden in plain view if you're unlucky enough to see them. "If you're damned," Juanita Lazarte once said and quickly crossed herself. Mr. Zaroba there whenever anyone locks up, his blue eyes and gentle ministrations, Zaroba who was once an atmospheric scientist and pilot for the Navy. He's seen something too, of course, the summer of 1969, flying supplies in a Hercules C-130 from Christchurch, New Zealand to Mc-Murdo Station. A freak storm, whiteout conditions and instrument malfunction, and when they finally found a break in the clouds somewhere over the Transantarctic Mountains the entire crew saw the ruins of a vast city, glittering obsidian towers and shattered, crystal spires, crumbling walls carved from the mountains themselves. At least that's what Zaroba says. He also says the Navy pressured the other men into signing papers agreeing never to talk about the flight and when he refused, he was pronounced mentally unsound by a military psychiatrist and discharged.

When Willa's turn comes, she glances at Frank, not a word but all the terrible things right there in her eyes for him to see, unspoken resignation, surrender, and then she goes down the aisle and stands behind the lectern.

Frank wakes up from a dream of rain and thunder and Willa's sitting crosslegged at the foot of their bed, nothing on but her pajama bottoms, watching television with the sound off and smoking a cigarette. "Where the hell'd you get that?" he asks, blinks sleepily and points at the cigarette.

"I bought a pack on my break today," she replies, not taking her eyes off the screen. She takes a long drag and the smoke leaks slowly from her nostrils.

"I thought we had an agreement."

"I'm sorry," but she doesn't sound sorry at all, and Frank sits up and blinks at the TV screen, rubs his eyes, and now he can see it's Jimmy Stewart and Katharine Hepburn, *The Philadelphia Story*.

"You can turn the sound up, if you want to," he says. "It won't bother me."

"No, that's okay. I know it by heart, anyway."

And then neither of them says anything else for a few minutes, sit watching the television, and when Willa has smoked the cigarette down to the filter she stubs it out in a saucer.

"I don't think I want to go to the meetings anymore," she says. "I think they're only making it worse for me."

Frank waits a moment before he replies, waiting to be sure that she's finished, and then, "That's your decision, Willa. If that's what you want."

"Of course it's my decision."

"You know what I meant."

"I can't keep reciting it over and over like the rest of you. There's no fucking point. I could talk about it from now till doomsday and it still wouldn't make sense and I'd still be afraid. Nothing Zaroba and that bunch of freaks has to say is going to change that, Frank."

Willa picks up the pack of Camels off the bed, lights another cigarette with a disposable lighter that looks pink by the flickering, grainy light from the TV screen.

"I'm sorry," Frank says.

"Does it help you?" she asks and now there's an angrysharp edge in her voice, Willa's switchblade mood swings, sullen to pissed in the space between heartbeats. "Has it *ever* helped you at all?"

Frank doesn't want to fight with her tonight, wants to close his eyes and slip back down to sleep, back to his raincool dreams. Too hot for an argument, and "I don't know," he says, and that's almost not a lie.

"Yeah, well, whatever," Willa mumbles and takes another drag off her cigarette.

"We'll talk about it in the morning if you want," Frank says and he lies back down, turns to face the open window and the noise of Mott Street at two A.M., the blinking orange neon from a noodle shop across the street.

"I'm not going to change my mind, if that's what you mean," Willa says.

"You can turn the sound up," Frank tells her again and concentrates on the soothing rhythm of the noodle shop sign, orange pulse like campfire light, much, much better than counting imaginary sheep. In a moment he's almost asleep again, scant inches from sleep, and "Did you ever see *Return to Oz?*" Willa asks him.

"What?"

"*Return to Oz*, the one where Fairuza Balk plays Dorothy and Laurie Piper plays Auntie Em."

"No," Frank replies. "I never did," and he rolls over onto his back and stares at the ceiling instead of the neon sign. In the dark and the gray light from the television, his favorite crack looks even more like the Valles Marineris.

"It wasn't anything like *The Wizard of Oz*. I was just a little kid, but I re-member it. It scared the hell out of me."

"Your mother let you see scary movies when you were a little kid?"

Willa ignores the question, her eyes still fixed on *The Philadelphia Story* if they're fixed anywhere, and she exhales a cloud of smoke that swirls and drifts about above the bed.

"When the film begins, Auntie Em and Uncle Henry think Dorothy's sick," she says. "They think she's crazy, because she talks about Oz all the time, be-cause she won't believe it was only a nightmare. They finally send her off to a sanitarium for electric shock treatment—"

"Jesus," Frank says, not entirely sure that Willa isn't making all this up. "That's horrible."

"Yeah, but it's true, isn't it? It's what really happens to little girls who see places that aren't supposed to be there. People aren't ever so glad you didn't die in a twister that they want to listen to crazy shit about talking scarecrows and emerald cities."

And Frank doesn't answer because he knows he isn't supposed to, knows that she would rather he didn't even try, so he sweats and stares at his surrogate, plaster Mars instead, at the shadow play from the television screen; she doesn't say anything else, and in a little while more, he's asleep.

In this dream there is still thunder, no rain from the ocher sky but the crack and rumble of thunder so loud that the air shimmers and could splinter like ice. The tall red grass almost as high as his waist, rippling gently in the wind, and Frank wishes that Willa wouldn't get so close to the fleshy, white trees. She thinks they might have fruit, peaches and she's never eaten a white peach before, she said. Giants fighting in the sky and Willa picking up windfall fruit from the rocky ground beneath the trees; Frank looks over his shoulder, back towards the fissure in the basement wall, back the way they came, but it's vanished.

*I should be sacred*, he thinks. *No, I should be* scared.

And now Willa is coming back towards him through the crimson waves of grass, her skirt for a linen basket to hold all the pale fruit she's gathered. She's smiling and he tries to remember the last time he saw her smile, *really* smile, not just a smirk or a sneer. She smiles and steps through the murmuring grass that seems to part to let her pass, her bare arms and legs safe from the blades grown sharp as straight razors.

"They *are* peaches," she beams.

But the fruit is the color of school-room chalk, its skin smooth and slick and glistening with tiny, pinhead beads of nectar seeping out through minute pores. "Take one," she says, but his stomach lurches and rolls at the thought, loath to even touch one of the things and then she sighs and dumps them all into the grass at his feet.

"I used to know a story about peaches," Willa says. "It was a Japanese story, I think. Or maybe it was Chinese."

"I'm pretty sure those *aren't* peaches," Frank says, and he takes a step backwards, away from the pile of sweating, albino fruit.

"I heard the pits are poisonous," she says. "Arsenic, or maybe it's cyanide."

A brilliant flash of chartreuse lightning then and the sky sizzles and smells like charred meat. Willa bends and retrieves a piece of the fruit, takes a bite before he can stop her; the sound of her teeth sinking through its skin, tearing through the colorless pulp inside, is louder than the thunder, and milky juice rolls down her chin and stains her Curious George T-shirt. Something wriggles from between her lips, falls to the grass, and when Willa opens her jaws wide to take another bite Frank can see that her mouth is filled with wriggling things.

"They have to be careful you don't swallow your tongue," she says, mumbling around the white peach. "If you swallow your tongue you'll choke to death."

Frank snatches the fruit away from her, grabs it quick before she puts any more of it in her belly, and she frowns and wipes the juice staining her hands off onto her skirt. The half-eaten thing feels warm and he tosses it away.

"Jesus, that was fucking silly, Frank. The harm's already done, *you* know that. The harm was done the day you looked through that hole in the wall."

And then the sky booms its symphony of gangrene and sepsis and lightning stabs down at the world with electric claws, thunder then lightning but that's only the wrong way round if he pretends Willa isn't right, if he pretends that he's seven again and this time he doesn't take the flashlight from the kitchen drawer. This time he does what his mother says and doesn't go sneaking off the minute she turns her back.

Frank stands alone beneath the restless trees, his aching, dizzy head too full of all the time that can't be redeemed, now or then or ever, and he watches as Willa walks alone across the red fields towards the endless deserts of scrap iron and bone, towards the bloated, scarletpurple sun. The black things have noticed her and creep along close behind, stalking silent on ebony, mantis legs.

This time, he wakes up before they catch her.

The long weekend, then, hotter and drier, the sky more white than blue and the air on Mott Street and everywhere else that Frank has any reason to go has grown so ripe, so redolent, that sometimes he pulls the collars of his T-shirts up over his mouth and nose, breathes through the cotton like a surgeon or a wild west bandit, but the smell always gets through anyway. On the news there are people dying of heat stroke and dehydration, people dying in the streets and ERs, but fresh-faced weathermen still promise that it will rain very soon. He's stopped believing them and maybe that means that Willa's right and it never will rain again.

Frank hasn't shown the white card—FOUND: LOST WORLDS—to Willa, keeps it hidden in his wallet, only taking it out when he's alone and no one will see, no one to ask where or what or who. He's read it over and over again, has each line committed to memory, and Monday morning he almost calls Mr. Zaroba about it. The half hour between Willa leaving for the cafe and the time that he has to leave for the copy shop if he isn't going to be late, and he holds the telephone receiver and stares at Dr. Solomon Monalisa's card lying there on the table in front of him. The sound of his heart, the dial-tone drone, and the traffic down on Mott Street, the spice-and-dried-fish odor of the apothecary leaking up through the floorboards, and a fat drop of sweat slides down his forehead and spreads itself painfully across his left eyeball. By the time he's finished rubbing at his eye, calling Zaroba no longer seems like such a good idea after all, and Frank puts the white card back into his wallet, slips it in safe between his driver's license and a dog-eared, expired MetroCard.

Instead he calls in sick, gets Maggie and she doesn't believe for one moment that there's anything at all wrong with him.

"I fucking swear, I can't even get up off the toilet long enough to make a phone call. I'm calling *you* from the head," only half an effort at sounding sincere because they both know this is only going through the motions.

"As we speak—" he starts, but Maggie cuts him off.

"That's enough, Frank. But I'm telling you, man, if you wanna keep this job, you better get your slacker ass down here tomorrow morning."

"Right," Frank says. "I hear you," and she hangs up first.

And then Frank stares at the open window, the sun beating down like the Voice of God out there, and it takes him almost five minutes to remember where to find the next number he has to call.

Sidney McAvoy stopped coming to the meetings at the synagogue on Eldridge Street almost a year ago, not long after Frank's first time. Small, hawk-nosed man with nervous, ferrety eyes, and he's always reminded Frank a little of Dustin Hoffman in *Papillon*. Some sort of tension or wound between Sidney and Mr. Zaroba that Frank never fully understood, but he saw it from the start, the way their eyes never met and Sidney never took his turn at the lectern, sat silent, brooding, chewing the stem of a cheap, unlit pipe. And then an argument after one of the meetings, the same night that Zaroba told Janice that she shouldn't ever go back to the cemetery in Trenton, that she should never try to find the staircase and the blue light again. Both men speaking in urgent, angry whispers, Zaroba looking up occasionally to smile a sheepish, embarrassed, apologetic smile. Everyone pretending not to see or hear, talking among themselves, occupied with their stale doughnuts and tiny packets of non-dairy creamer, and then Sidney McAvoy left and never came back.

Frank would've forgotten all about him, almost had forgotten, and then one night he and Willa were coming home late from a bar where they drink sometimes, whenever they're feeling irresponsible enough to spend money on booze. Cheap vodka or cheaper beer, a few hours wasted just trying to feel like everyone else, the way they imagined other, normal people might feel, and they ran into Sidney McAvoy a few blocks from their apartment. He was wearing a ratty green raincoat, even though it wasn't raining, and chewing on one of his pipes, carrying a large box wrapped in white butcher's paper, tied up tight and neat with twine.

"Shit," Willa whispered. "Make like you don't see him," but Sidney had already noticed them and he was busy clumsily trying to hide the big package behind his back.

"I *know* you two," he declared, talking loudly, a suspicious, accusatory glint to his quavering voice. "You're both with Zaroba, aren't you? You still go to his *meetings*." That last word a sneer and he pointed a short, grubby finger at the center of Frank's chest.

"That's really none of your goddamn business, is it?" Willa growled and Frank stepped quickly between them; she mumbled and spit curses behind his back and Sidney McAvoy glared up at Frank with his beadydark eyes. A whole lifetime's worth of bitterness and distrust trapped inside those eyes, eyes that have seen far too much or far too little, and "How have you been, Mr. McAvoy," Frank said, straining to sound friendly, and he managed the sickly ghost of a smile.

Sidney grunted and almost dropped his carefully-wrapped package.

"If you *care* about that girl there," he said, speaking around the stem of the pipe clenched between his yellowed teeth, "you'll keep her away from Zaroba. And you'll both stop *telling* him things, if you know what's good for you. There are more useful answers in a road atlas than you're ever going to get out of that old phony."

"What makes you say that?" Frank asked. "What were you guys fighting about?" but Sidney was already scuttling away down Canal Street, his white package hugged close to his chest. He turned a corner without looking back and was gone.

"Fucking nut job," Willa mumbled. "What the hell's his problem, anyway?"

"Maybe the less we know about him the better," Frank said and he put an arm around Willa's small waist, holding her close to him, trying hard not to think about what could have been in the box but unable to think of anything else.

And two weeks later, dim and snowy last day before Thanksgiving, Frank found Sidney McAvoy's number in the phone book and called him.

A wet comb through his hair, cleaner shirt and socks, and Frank goes out into the sizzling day; across Columbus Park to the Canal Street Station and he takes the M to Grand Street, rides the B line all the way to the subway stop beneath the Museum of Natural History. Rumbling along through the honeycombed earth, the diesel and dust and garbage scented darkness and him swaddled inside steel and unsteady fluorescent light. Time to think that he'd rather not have, unwelcome luxury of second thoughts, and when the train finally reaches the museum he's almost ready to turn right around and head back downtown. Almost, but Dr. Solomon Monalisa's card is in his wallet to keep him moving, get him off the train and up the concrete steps to the museum entrance. Ten dollars he can't spare to get inside, but Sidney McAvoy will never agree to meet him anywhere outside, too paranoid for a walk in Central Park or a quiet booth in a deli or a coffee shop somewhere.

"People are always listening," he says, whenever Frank has suggested or asked that they meet somewhere without an entrance fee. "You never know what they might overhear."

So sometimes it's the long marble bench in front of the *Apatosaurus*, or the abyssal, blueblack gloom of the Hall of Fishes, seats beneath a planetarium constellation sky, whichever spot happens to strike Sidney's fancy that particular day. His fancy or his cabalistic fantasies, if there's any difference, and today Frank finds him in the Hall of Asiatic Mammals, short and rumpled man in a threadbare tweed jacket and red tennis shoes standing alone before the Indian leopard diorama, gazing intently in at the pocket of counterfeit jungle and the taxidermied cats. Frank waits behind him for a minute or two, waiting to be noticed, and when Sidney looks up and speaks, he speaks to Frank's reflection.

"I'm very busy today," he says, brusque, impatient. "I hope this isn't going to take long."

And no, Frank says, it won't take long at all, I promise, but Sidney's doubtful expression to show just how much he believes that. He sighs and looks back to the stuffed leopards, papier-mâché trees and wax leaves, a painted flock of peafowl rising to hang forever beneath a painted forest canopy. Snapshot moment of another world and the walls of the dimly-lit hall lined with a dozen or more such scenes.

"You want to know about Monalisa," Sidney says. "That's why you came here, because you think I can tell you who he is."

"Yeah," and Frank reaches into his pocket for his wallet. "He came into the place where I work last week and left this." He takes out the card and Sidney turns around only long enough to get it from him.

"So, you talked to him?"

"No, I didn't. I was eating my lunch in the stockroom. I didn't actually see him for myself."

Sidney stares at the card, seems to read it carefully three or four times and then he hands it back to Frank, goes back to staring at the leopards.

"Why didn't you show this to Zaroba?" he asks sarcastically, taunting, but Frank answers him anyway, not in the mood today for Sidney's grudges and intrigues.

"Because I didn't think he'd tell me anything. You know he's more interested in the mysteries than ever finding answers." And Frank pauses, silent for a moment and Sidney's silent, too, both men watching the big cats now—glass eyes, freeze-frame talons, and taut, spectacled haunches—as though the leopards might suddenly spring towards them, all this stillness just a clever ruse for the tourists and the kiddies; maybe dead leopards know the nervous, wary faces of men who have seen things that they never should have seen.

"He knows the truth would swallow him whole," Sidney says. The leopards don't pounce and he adds, "He knows he's a coward."

"So who is Dr. Monalisa?"

"A bit of something the truth already swallowed and spat back up," and Sidney chuckles sourly to himself and produces one of his pipes from a jacket pocket. "He's a navigator, a pilot, a cartographer . . ."

Frank notices that one of the two leopards has captured a stuffed peacock, holds it fast between velvet, razored paws, and he can't remember if it was that way only a moment before.

"He draws maps," Sidney says. "He catalogs doors and windows and culverts."

"That's bullshit," Frank whispers, his voice low now so the old woman staring in at the giant panda exhibit won't hear him. "You're trying to tell me he can *find* places?"

"He isn't a sane man, Frank," Sidney says and now he holds up his left hand and presses his palm firmly against the glass, as if he's testing the invisible barrier, gauging its integrity. "He has answers, but he has prices, too. You think *this* is Hell, you see how it feels to be in debt to Dr. Solomon Monalisa."

"It isn't me. It's Willa. I think she's starting to lose it."

"We all lost 'it' a long time ago, Frank."

"I'm afraid she's going to do something. I'm afraid she'll hurt herself."

And Sidney turns his back on the leopards then, takes the pipe from his mouth, and glares up at Frank.

But some of the anger, some of the bitterness has gone from his eyes, and "He *might* keep her alive," he says, "but you wouldn't want her back when he was done. If she'd even *come* back. No, Frank. You two stay away from Monalisa. Look for your own answers. You don't think you found that card by accident, do you? You don't really think there are such things as coincidences? That's not even his real address—"

"She can't sleep anymore," Frank says, but now Sidney McAvoy isn't listening, glances back over his shoulder at the Indian rain forest, incandescent daylight, illusory distances, and "I have to go now," he says. "I'm very busy today."

"I think she's fucking *dying*, man," Franks says as Sidney straightens his tie and puts the pipe back into his pocket; the old woman looks up from the panda in its unreal bamboo thicket and frowns at them both.

"I'm very busy today, Frank. Call me next week. I think I can meet you at the Guggenheim next week."

And he walks quickly away towards the Roosevelt Rotunda, past the Siberian tiger and the Sumatran rhinoceros, leaving Frank alone with the frowning woman. When Sidney has vanished into the shadows behind a small herd of Indian elephants, Frank turns back to the leopards and the smudgy hand print Sidney McAvoy has left on their glass.

Hours and hours later, past sunset to the other side of the wasted day, the night that seems even hotter than the scorching afternoon, and Frank is dreaming that the crack in the basement wall on St. Mark's Place is much too narrow for him to squeeze through. Maybe the way it really happened after all, and then he hears a small, anguished sound from somewhere close behind him, something hurting or lost, and when he turns to see, Frank opens his eyes and there's only the tangerine glow of the noodle shop sign outside the apartment window. He blinks once, twice, but this stubborn world doesn't go away, doesn't break apart into random, kaleidoscopic shards to become some other place entirely. So he sits up, head full of the familiar disappointment, this incontestable solidity, and it takes him a moment to realize that Willa isn't in bed. Faint outline of her body left in the wrinkled sheets and the bathroom light is burning, the door open, so she's probably just taking a piss.

"You okay in there?" he asks, but no reply. The soft drip, drip, drip of the kitchenette faucet, tick of the wind-up alarm clock on the table next to Willa's side of the bed, street noise, but no answer. "Did you fall in or something?" he shouts. "Did you drown?"

And still no response, but his senses waking up, picking out more than the ordinary, everynight sounds, a trilling whine pitched so high he feels it more than hears it, and now he notices the way that the air in the apartment smells.

*Go back to sleep*, he thinks, but both legs already over the edge of the bed, both feet already on the dusty floor. *When you wake up again it'll be over.*

The trill worming its way beneath his skin, soaking in, pricking gently at the hairs on his arms and the back of his neck, and all the silver fillings in his teeth have begun to hum along sympathetically. Where he's standing, Frank can see into the bathroom, just barely, a narrow slice of linoleum, slice of porcelain toilet tank, a mildew and polyurethane fold of shower curtain. And he thinks that the air has started to shimmer, an almost imperceptible warping of the light escaping from the open door, but that might only be his imagination. He takes one small step towards the foot of the bed and there's Willa, standing naked before the tiny mirror above the bathroom sink. The jut of her shoulder blades and hip bones, the anorexic swell of her rib cage, all the minute details of her painful thinness seem even more pronounced in the harsh and curving light.

"Hey. Is something wrong? Are you sick?" and she turns her head slowly to look at him, or maybe only looking towards him because there's nothing much like recognition on her face. Her wide, unblinking eyes, blind woman's stare, and "Can't you hear me, Willa?" he asks as she turns slowly back to the mirror. Her lips move, shaping rough, inaudible words.

The trilling grows infinitesimally louder, climbs another half-octave, and there's a warm, wet trickle across Frank's lips and he realizes that his nose is bleeding.

Behind Willa the bathroom wall, the shower, the low ceiling—everything— ripples and dissolves and there's a sudden, staccato *pop* as the bulb above the sink blows. And after an instant of perfect darkness, perfect nothing, dull and yellowgreen shafts of light from somewhere far, far above, flickering light from an alien sun shining down through the waters of an alien sea; dim, translucent shapes dart and flash through those depths, bodies more insubstantial than jel- lyfish, more sinuous than eels, and Willa rises to meet them, arms outstretched, her hair drifting about her face like a halo of seaweed and algae. In the ocean- filtered light, Willa's pale skin seems sleek and smooth as dolphinflesh. Air rushes from her lips, her nostrils, and flows eagerly away in a glassy swirl of bubbles.

The trilling has filled Frank's head so full, and his aching skull, his brain, seem only an instant from merciful implosion, fragile, eggshell bone collapsed by the terrible, lonely sound and the weight of all that water stacked above him. He staggers, takes a step backwards, and now Willa's face is turned up to meet the sunlight streaming down, and she's more beautiful than anyone or anything he's ever seen or dreamt.

Down on Mott Street, the screech of tires, the angry blat of a car horn and someone begins shouting very loudly in Chinese.

And now the bathroom is only a bathroom again, and Willa lies in a limp, strangling heap on the floor, her wet hair and skin glistening in the light from the bulb above the sink. The water rolls off her back, her thighs, spreads across the floor in a widening puddle, and Frank realizes that the trilling has finally stopped, only the memory of it left in his ringing ears and bleeding nose. When the dizziness has passed, he goes to her, sits down on the wet floor and holds her while she coughs and pukes up gouts of salt water and snotty strands of something the color of verdigris. Her skin so cold it hurts to touch, cold coming off her like a fever, and something small and chitinous slips from her hair and scuttles away behind the toilet on long, jointed legs.

"Did you *see*?" she asks him, desperate, rheumy words gurgling out with all the water that she's swallowed. "Did you, Frank? Did you *see* it?"

"Yes," he tells her, just like every time before. "Yes, baby. I did. I saw it all," and Willa smiles, closes her eyes, and in a little while she's asleep. He carries her, dripping, back to their bed and holds her until the sun rises and she's warm again.

The next day neither of them goes to work, and some small, niggling part of Frank manages to worry about what will happen to them if he loses the shit job at Gotham Kwick Kopy, if Willa gets fired from the cafe, obstinate shred of himself still capable of caring about such things. How the rent will be paid, how they'll eat, everything that hasn't really seemed to matter in more years than he wants to count. Half the morning in bed and his nosebleed keeps coming back, a roll of toilet paper and then one of their towels stained all the shades of dried and drying blood; Willa wearing her winter coat despite the heat, and she keeps trying to get him to go to a doctor, but no, he says. That might lead to questions, and besides, it'll stop sooner or later. It's always stopped before.

By twelve o'clock, Willa's traded the coat for her pink cardigan, feels good enough that she makes them peanut butter and grape jelly sandwiches, black coffee and stale potato chips, and after he eats Frank begins to feel better, too. But going to the park is Willa's idea, because the apartment still smells faintly of silt and dead fish, muddy, low-tide stink that'll take hours more to disappear completely. He knows the odor makes her nervous, so he agrees, even though he'd rather spend the afternoon sleeping off his headache. Maybe a cold shower, another cup of Willa's bitterstrong coffee, and if he's lucky he could doze for hours without dreaming.

They take the subway up to Fifth, follow the eastern edge of the park north, past the zoo and East Green all the way to Pilgrim Hill and the Conservatory Pond. It's not so very hot that there aren't a few model sailing ships on the pond, just enough breeze to keep their miniature Bermuda sails standing tall and taut as shark fins. Frank and Willa sit in the shade near the Alice in Wonderland statue, her favorite spot in all of Central Park, rocky place near the tea party, granite and rustling leaves, the clean laughter of children climbing about on the huge, bronze mushrooms. A little girl with frizzy black hair and red and white peppermint-striped tights is petting the kitten in Alice's lap, stroking its metal fur and meowling loudly, and "I can't ever remember her name," Willa says.

"What?" Frank asks. "Whose name?" not sure if she means the little girl or the kitten or something else entirely.

"Alice's kitten. I know it had a name, but I never can remember it."

Frank watches the little girl for a moment, and "Dinah," he says. "I think the kitten's name was Dinah."

"Oh, yeah, Dinah. That's it," and he knows that she's just thinking out loud, whatever comes to mind so that she won't have to talk about last night, so the conversation won't accidentally find its own way back to those few drowning moments of chartreuse light and eel shadows. Trying so hard to pretend and he almost decides they're both better off if he plays along and doesn't show her Dr. Solomon Monalisa's white calling card.

"That's a good name for a cat," she says. "If we ever get a kitten, I think I'll name it Dinah."

"Mrs. Wu doesn't like cats."

"Well, we're not going to spend the rest of our lives in that dump. Next time, we'll get an apartment that allows cats."

Frank takes the card out and lays his wallet on the grass, but Willa hasn't even noticed, too busy watching the children clambering about on Alice, too busy dreaming about kittens. The card is creased and smudged from a week riding around in his back pocket and all the handling it's suffered, the edges beginning to fray, and he gives it to her without any explanation.

"What's this?" she asks and he tells her to read it first, just read it, so she does. Reads it two or three times and then Willa returns the card, goes back to watching the children. But her expression has changed, the labored, make-believe smile gone and now she just looks like herself again, plain old Willa, the distance in her eyes, the hard angles at the corners of her mouth that aren't quite a frown.

"Sidney says he's for real," half the truth, at best, and Frank glances down at the card, reading it again for the hundredth or two-hundredth time.

"Sidney McAvoy's a fucking lunatic."

"He says this guy has maps—"

"Christ, Frank. What do you want me to say? You want me to give you *permission* to go talk to some crackpot? You don't need my permission."

"I was hoping you'd come with me," he says so softly that he's almost whispering, and he puts the card back into his wallet where neither of them will have to look at it, stuffs the wallet back into his jeans pocket.

"Well, I won't. I go to your goddamn meetings. I already have to listen to that asshole Zaroba. That's enough for me, thank you very much. That's more than enough."

The little girl petting Dinah slips, loses her footing and almost slides backwards off the edge of the sculpture, but her mother catches her and sets her safely on the ground.

"I see what it's doing to you," Frank says. "I have to watch. How much longer do you think you can go on like this?"

She doesn't answer him, opens her purse and takes out a pack of cigarettes, only one left and she crumbles the empty package and tosses it over her shoulder into the bushes.

"What if this guy really can help you? What if he can make it *stop*?"

Willa is digging noisily around in her purse, trying to find her lighter or a book of matches, and she turns and stares at Frank, the cigarette hanging unlit from her lips. Her eyes shining bright as broken gemstones, shattered crystal eyes, furious, resentful, and he knows then that she could hate him, that she could leave him here and never look back. She takes the cigarette from her mouth, licks her upper lip, and for a long moment Willa holds the tip of her tongue trapped tight between her teeth.

"What the hell makes you think I want it to stop?"

And silence as what she's said sinks in and he begins to understand that he's never understood her at all. "It's killing you," he says, finally, the only thing he can think to say, and Willa's eyes seem to flash and grow brighter, more broken, more eager to slice.

"No, Frank, it's the only thing keeping me *alive*. Knowing that it's out there, that I'll see it again, and someday maybe it won't make me come back *here*."

And then she gets up and walks quickly away towards the pond, brisk, determined steps to put more distance between them. She stops long enough to bum a light from an old black man with a dachshund, then ducks around one corner of the boathouse and he can't see her anymore. Frank doesn't follow, sits watching the tiny sailboats and yachts gliding gracefully across the mossdark surface of the water, their silent choreography of wakes and ripples. He decides maybe it's better not to worry about Willa for now, plenty enough time for that later, and he wonders what he'll say to Monalisa when he finds him.

We shall be less apt to admire what this World calls great, shall nobly despise those Trifles the generality of Men set their Affections on, when we know that there are a multitude of such Earths inhabited and adorn'd as well as our own.

CHRISTIAAN HUYGENS (c. 1690)

# NORMAN PARTRIDGE

# Where the Woodbine Twineth

*Norman Partridge has worked in many genres—"sometimes all in one story,"
says his friend Joe R. Lansdale. Partridge's novels include mysteries (Saguaro
Riptide and The Ten-Ounce Siesta), psychological horror (Slippin' into
Darkness), and supernatural noir (Wildest Dreams). In addition to his longer
works, Partridge has produced three volumes of short fiction, including the
Stoker Award–winning Mr. Fox and Other Feral Tales. "Where the Woodbine
Twineth" first appeared in the author's most recent collection, The Man with
the Barbed-Wire Fists, published by Night Shade Books.*

*"One night I got to thinking about all the horror stories that are rooted in
the Civil War," Partridge says. "There are actually quite a few of them.
Ambrose Bierce started the ball rolling, and you can follow it through Rod
Serling's Twilight Zone right up to the present day. For my story I wanted a
strong psychological component, but I also was after the resonance of folklore.
The latter is one reason the story is dedicated to Manly Wade Wellman
(another being that I cribbed the title from one of his stories)."*

*—E. D.*

When the war was over the living came home. Not a rifle among them
but those that had been transformed into crutches or canes, but rifles
would not have mattered to men who were tired of war and wounds
and death. Their bellies were empty and they broke their swords into
plowshares, and they embraced a land they remembered and people they could
not forget and wished the simple wish that they had never gone to war.

Of course, the dead came home, too. They came at night, and warily . . . their
bellies bloated with grave worms, their hearts as heavy as fallen fruit. They
marched in tattered battalions beneath willows that whispered in the sultry summer wind, and they paused at forgotten crossroads bordered by thorny brush
and bayonet bramble, and they marched on and made their camps in cemeteries
where mortal footfalls were seldom heard, far past the place where the woodbine
twineth.

That was how it was with the living and the dead. But others came home,
too. Men like John Barter. Barter had seen many places since leaving the South.

Places to the north, places with names that he could never forget. Gettysburg . . . Cemetery Ridge . . . Devil's Den. . . .

But John Barter did not speak of those places. He spoke hardly at all. He came home with a mouthful of bone buttons that he had sliced off a Union sergeant's uniform. He chewed and sucked those buttons all the way from Virginia, tramping the lonely miles in sunshine and in shadow, and he came home with rags on his feet and seven toes, and he came home with a sword that was as sharp as an officer's tongue.

He came home with a fiddle, too, an instrument given him by his wife on the day of his enlistment. A single nail pierced the fiddle's neck, the wood scissored around it like the slivered hand of Jesus on a crucifix. Still, the fiddle made sweet music. All Barter's comrades said so . . . both the living and the dead. Even a Yankee at a distant outpost could be moved to tears by the sound of Barter playing "Aura Lee" on the eve of battle.

So Barter brought the fiddle home, just as his wife knew he would. He carried it all the way from Virginia wrapped in a mildewed regimental flag, and her heart beat a little faster at the sight of the instrument in her husband's hands. Of course, the nail that pierced the fiddle's neck had rusted since she had driven it home on that far-off day, but she had expected that. Time rusted all things.

Her name was Loreena, and she was a woman only seven years gone from a country very different than this one. That was the reason she knew the things she did. In Loreena's country, the land was so very green and the shadows so very long that in the end everything was nearly black. Heavy clouds held the people to the land and did not let them stray, but the clouds could have been as heavy as iron and still they would have been unable to hold Loreena. She was a woman made for other places, and she did not fear the heavens and she did not fear the earth.

Loreena did not fear much of anything. Not the living. Not the dead. As a girl she had learned many secrets from her grandmother, a woman who spoke only in whispers. Loreena kept those whispered words in her head and in her heart. She listened to them still, as she practiced the craft her grandmother had taught her. The old woman's whispers told her that the world held a place for all things, and Loreena wanted nothing more than to stake one small corner of it for her husband and herself, for she loved John Barter as she could love no other.

When Barter's ragged feet crossed the threshold of their cabin, Loreena took the fiddle from his hands. Even before they embraced, she took it. Barter's picture hung on the wall, secured by a nail grown nearly as rusty as the one that pierced the fiddle. Barter hardly recognized himself, for the picture had been made before the war.

Loreena took that picture off the wall as if it were something dead and threw it into the fireplace. Then she grabbed Barter's fiddle by the neck—as if it were something alive—and she nailed it to the wall in the picture's place. Finally she parted her husband's lips with gentle fingers and, one by one, took the bone buttons from his mouth and placed them on the mantelpiece.

Still, John Barter did not say a word, so Loreena kissed him deeply, and she kissed him long. And when their lips parted she stripped the ragged uniform off her husband's back and tossed it into the blazing fireplace, and then she took off her clothes and guided her husband's fingers over her naked flesh until they found the tight circle of silk around her neck.

Barter's hands circled that ribbon and his fingers disappeared in Loreena's long black hair, and beneath that hair at the back of her neck his fingers found a black velvet bag knotted to that silk ribbon, and in that bag were eleven nails— just a little rusty—that pricked Loreena's neck on moonless nights and brought bad dreams.

But now those bad dreams were banished . . . or so Loreena thought. For she believed in magic. And she believed in a twelfth nail that had bound a portrait to a wall of the home she shared with John Barter, just as she believed in the power of a thirteenth nail that was driven through a fiddle's neck.

A thirteenth nail now driven into that very same wall.

A nail that bound a fiddle to that wall.

Yes. Loreena believed in magic.

Just as she believed in a man's soul.

One that had never been allowed to wander.

But Barter was a different man now. He didn't want to be different at all, but he was. He wanted to sleep with the dark wings of Loreena's hair brushing his face and the wild scent of her on his lips . . . and yet he did not want to sleep at all, wanted instead to steal his fiddle from the wall and serenade his fallen comrades by a blazing campfire, slicing the bow back and forth while Yankee blood gleamed on his fingernails in the firelight.

Barter wanted to share these strange thoughts with his wife, but he could not do that. When he tried he found that his words had gone, and yet sometimes he was afraid that they would spill from his lips before he could stop them. So he took a few bone buttons from the mantelpiece and put them in his mouth, and then he could not speak a word.

But he could listen well enough, and he found that there were many things to hear. The voices of the living, telling him that he needed to forget. The voices of the dead, telling him that he had forgotten too much already. He heard these things clearly, the same way his wife heard the whispers of her dead grand- mother.

And in this way one year passed, and then another, and then a third. And in that time Barter discovered that there were many things he could not do. He could not beat his sword into a plowshare. He could not drive its sharp blade into the earth. And he could not keep his eyes from the fiddle nailed to the wall, just as he could not keep his fingers from the nail that held it there, a nail with a flat head that flaked rust like dead skin.

Though he touched it—gently, the way one would touch the stem of a flower—Barter never tested the strength of that nail. He knew what it meant to his wife.

One day Barter carried his sword to the livestock pen. He was surprised to find that the pen was full of Yankees, smart and tall in the crisp blue uniform of the victor.

The Yankees taunted him, making sport of his tattered clothes and his tattered ways. Barter wanted to ignore them, but that was impossible. Their blue suits shone like the night, and their brass buttons gleamed like the sun. Their pink faces were rosy with laughter, but their words lashed Barter like his own memories.

Barter sucked bone buttons and tried not to listen, but he could no more do that than escape his own thoughts. Finally he could stand no more. He charged the Yankees with a rebel yell, and he struck them down with a terrible swift sword no Northerner's hand would ever hold, and when he had finished with them he sliced the gleaming buttons off their blue uniforms and stuffed those buttons into his mouth along with the buttons of bone.

The taste of brass was very much like the taste of blood. Something sharp, a slap to the face, a trumpet call to a sleeping man. The taste set Barter's senses on edge. Soon he noticed that many of the fallen Yankees had faces like pigs. Their officer, a captain, was as big as a bull. Most of the Yankees were dead, but some of them still breathed. Barter spit buttons of brass and bone from his mouth and asked the Yankees if they were men or animals, but they only screamed and screamed and screamed.

Loreena ran to her husband's side, the silk ribbon tight around her neck, the nails in the velvet bag pricking her spine. She screamed, too, but Barter did not hear her. He only heard the music of eleven nails dancing, a sound like rainfall going to rust.

Loreena grasped his bloodstained hand, but Barter could not feel her fingers. Her fingers fell away like rust, like rainfall.

Twilight had come and gone, but Barter felt that he was knee-deep in it. That was all he felt. But it was not all he saw, or heard. Dead soldiers marched through scarlet shadows. He heard their every step. They came—their bellies bloated with grave worms, their hearts as heavy as fallen fruit—and they ringed the livestock pen, and they stared at Barter and they stared at his sword, and they saw that both were stained with the blood of pigs and cattle.

"That is a poor use of good steel," said one of the soldiers, and Barter nodded in agreement.

He knew the soldier was right. Everyone knew. The truth of the soldier's words was reflected in the faces of his fallen comrades. Pity shone in their dead eyes. Barter tried to look away, but found he could not. He stood there with the sword in his hand, with slain beasts at his feet, and he knew that his comrades saw him for what he had become.

There were no buttons in Barter's mouth. He looked for words there, but found none.

But his comrades had words. One of them stepped into the livestock pen and took Barter's hand.

"Come with us," the soldier said.

Barter nodded, but he could not move. He wanted to go with the men, even though he knew he did not belong with them any more than he belonged with Loreena. His portrait had tasted flame a long time ago, and his fiddle had been nailed to the wall for three long years. Barter could barely remember "Aura Lee." Sometimes he tried to hum it around the buttons in his mouth, but it never sounded the same, and Barter knew that it never would—

The dead men turned away.

The moment had passed, and they could wait no longer.

"Goodbye," was all they said.

In the livestock pen, dying Yankees screamed their last. In the woods, just past a forgotten crossroads bordered by thorny brush and bayonet bramble, dead men sang "Aura Lee" as they marched to a cemetery camp where mortal footfalls were seldom heard.

In John Barter's cabin, Loreena placed her husband's hands flat on the table that stood beneath the fiddle. A hammer lay above Barter's bloodstained finger-tips. Loreena took the silk ribbon from around her neck. She opened the velvet bag that was attached to it, spilling eleven nails into her open palm. But all that remained of the nails were brittle shards and rusted flakes, and they sifted through Loreena's fingers like sand.

Loreena started to cry, because time rusted all things.

Even magic. Even men.

But Barter smiled at his wife. He took the fiddle from the wall. That was not hard to do, for the nail that held it in place was very weak.

Barter tossed the fiddle into the fireplace. He watched it burn the way he had watched his unfamiliar portrait burn, and he took the last of the bone buttons from the mantelpiece and placed them in his mouth and sucked on them with Loreena standing close by his side but so far away, and he didn't say a word as the fiddle popped and sizzled in the flames.

He listened, instead, to the sound of a flickering campfire . . . far, far away.

Far past the place where the woodbine twineth.

(For Manly Wade Wellman)

# GLEN HIRSHBERG

# Struwwelpeter

Glen Hirshberg lives in Los Angeles with his wife and son. His novella, "Mr. Dark's Carnival," which appeared in The Year's Best Fantasy & Horror: Fourteenth Annual Collection was nominated for both the International Horror Guild Award and the World Fantasy Award. His first novel, The Snowman's Children, will be published by Carroll and Graf this fall. Currently, he is putting the final touches on a collection of ghost stories and working on a new novel.

"Struwwelpeter" made its debut on SCIFI.COM and marks the author's second consecutive publication in The Year's Best Fantasy and Horror series.

About this story, Hirshberg notes: "Ballard is an actual section of Seattle, but the neighborhood portrayed here bears little resemblance to it, except for the rain and the duplexes and the lutefisk smell. This story is dedicated to Phil Bednarz, wherever he is, for taking me bell-ringing."

—E. D.

"The dead are not altogether powerless."
—CHIEF SEATTLE

This was before we knew about Peter, or at least before we understood what we knew, and my mother says it's impossible to know a thing like that anyway. She's wrong, though, and she doesn't need me to tell her she is, either.

Back then, we still gathered, afterschool afternoons, at the Andersz's house, because it was close to the Locks. If it wasn't raining, we'd drop our books and grab Ho Hos out of the tin Mr. Andersz always left on the table for us and head immediately toward the water. Gulls spun in the sunlight overhead, their cries urgent, taunting, telling us, you're missing it, you're missing it. We'd sprint between the rows of low stone duplexes, the sad little gardens with their flowers battered by the rain until the petals looked bent and forgotten like discarded training wheels, the splintery, sagging blue walls of the Black Anchor restaurant where Mr. Paars used to hunker alone and murmuring over his plates of reeking lutefisk when he wasn't stalking 15th Street, knocking pigeons and homeless people out of the way with his dog-head cane. Finally, we'd burst into the park, pour down the avenue of fir trees like a mudslide, scattering people, bugs, and birds before us until we hit the water.

For hours we'd prowl the green hillsides, watching the sailors yell at the invading seals from the top of the Locks while the seals ignored them, skimming for fish and sometimes rolling on their backs and flipping their fins. We watched the rich-people sailboats with their masts rusting, the big grey fishing boats from Alaska and Japan and Russia with the fishermen bored on deck, smoking, throwing butts at the seals and leaning on the rails while the gulls shrieked overhead. As long as the rain held off, we stayed and threw stones to see how high up the opposing bank we could get them, and Peter would wait for ships to drift in front of us and then throw low over their bows. The sailors would scream curses in other languages or sometimes ours, and Peter would throw bigger stones at the boathulls. When they hit with a thunk, we'd flop on our backs on the wet grass and flip our feet in the air like the seals. It was the rudest gesture we knew.

Of course, most days it was raining, and we stayed in the Andersz's basement until Mr. Andersz and the Serbians came home. Down there, in the damp—Mr. Andersz claimed his was one of three basements in all of Ballard—you could hear the wetness rising in the grass outside like lock-water. The first thing Peter did when we got downstairs was flick on the gas fireplace (not for heat, it didn't throw any), and we'd toss in stuff: pencils, a tinfoil ball, a plastic cup, and once a broken old 45 which formed blisters on its surface and then spit black goo into the air like a fleeing octopus dumping ink before it slid into a notch in the logs to melt. Once, Peter went upstairs and came back with one of Mr. Andersz's red spiral photo albums and tossed it into the flames, and when one of the Mack sisters asked him what was in it, he told her, "No idea. Didn't look."

The burning never lasted long, five minutes, maybe. Then we'd eat Ho Hos and play the Atari Mr. Andersz had bought Peter years before at a yardsale, and it wasn't like you think, not always. Mostly, Peter flopped in his orange beanbag chair with his long legs stretched in front of him and his too-long black bangs splayed across his forehead like the talons of some horrible, giant bird gripping him to lift him away. He let me and the Mack sisters take turns on the machine, and Kenny London and Steve Rourke, too, back in the days when they would come. I was the best at the basic games, *Asteroids* and *Pong*, but Jenny Mack could stay on *Dig Dug* forever and not get grabbed by the floating grabby-things in the ground. Even when we asked Peter to take his turn, he wouldn't. He'd say, "Go ahead," or, "Too tired," or, "Fuck off," and once I even turned around in the middle of losing to Jenny and found him watching us, sort of, the rainy window and us, not the TV screen at all. He reminded me a little of my grandfather before he died, all folded up in his chair and not wanting to go anywhere and kind of happy to have us there. Always, Peter seemed happy to have us there.

When Mr. Andersz got home, he'd fish a Ho Ho out of the tin for himself if we'd left him one—we tried to, most days—and then come downstairs, and when he peered out of the stairwell, his black wool hat still stuck to his head like melted wax, he already looked different than when we saw him at school. At school, even with his hands covered in yellow chalk and his transparencies full of fractions and decimals scattered all over his desk and the pears he carried with him and never seemed to eat, he was just Mr. Andersz, fifth-grade math teacher, funny accent, funny to get angry. At school, it never occurred to any of us to feel sorry for him.

"Well, hello, all of you," he'd say, as if talking to a litter of puppies he'd found, and we'd pause our game and hold our breaths and wait for Peter. Sometimes—most times—Peter said, "Hey" back, or even, "Hey Dad." Then we'd all chime in like a clock tolling the hour, "Hey Mr. Andersz," "Thanks for the Ho Hos," "You're hat's all wet again," and he'd smile and nod and go upstairs.

There were the other days, too. A few, that's all. On most of those, Peter just didn't answer, wouldn't look at his father. It was only the one time that he said, "Hello, Dipshit-Dad," and Jenny froze at the Atari and one of the floating grabby things swallowed her digger, and the rest of us stared, but not at Peter, and not at Mr. Andersz, either. Anywhere but there.

For a few seconds, Mr. Andersz seemed to be deciding, and rain-rivers wriggled down the walls and windows like transparent snakes, and we held our breath. But all he said, in the end, was, "We'll talk later, Struwwelpeter," which was only a little different from what he usually said when Peter got this way. Usually, he said, "Oh. It's you, then. Hello, Struwwelpeter." I never liked the way he said that, as though he was greeting someone else entirely, not his son. Eventually, Jenny or her sister Kelly would say, "Hi, Mr. Andersz," and he'd glance around at us as though he'd forgotten we were there, and then he'd go upstairs and invite the Serbians in, and we wouldn't see him again until we left.

The Serbians made Steve Rourke nervous, which is almost funny, in retrospect. They were big and dark, both of them, two brothers who looked at their hands whenever they saw children. One was a car mechanic, the other worked at the Locks, and they sat all afternoon, most afternoons, in Mr. Andersz's study, sipping tea and speaking Serbian in low whispers. The words made their whispers harsh, full of Zs and ground-up Ss, as though they'd swallowed glass. "They could be planning things in there," Steve used to say. "My dad says both those guys were badass soldiers." Mostly, as far as I could tell, they looked at Mr. Andersz's giant library of photo albums and listened to records. Judy Collins, Joan Baez. Almost funny, like I said.

Of course, by this last Halloween—my last night at the Andersz house—both Serbians were dead, run down by a drunken driver while walking across Fremont Bridge, and Kenny London had moved away, and Steve Rourke didn't come anymore. He said his parents wouldn't let him, and I bet they wouldn't, but that isn't why he stopped coming. I knew it, and I think Peter knew it, too, and that worried me, a little, in ways I couldn't explain.

I almost didn't get to go, either. I was out the door, blinking in the surprising sunlight and the wind rolling off the Sound through the streets, when my mother yelled, "ANDREW!" and stopped me. I turned to find her in the open screen door of our duplex, arms folded over the long, grey coat she wore inside and out from October to May, sunlight or no, brown-grey curls bunched on top of her scalp as though trying to crawl over her head out of the wind. She seemed to be wiggling in mid-air, like a salmon trying to hold itself still against a current. Rarely did she take what she called her "frustrations" out on me, but she'd been crabby all day, and now she looked furious, despite the fact that I'd stayed in my room, out of her way, from the second I got home from school, because I knew she didn't really want me out tonight. Not with Peter. Not after last year.

"That's a costume?" She gestured with her chin at my jeans, my everyday black sweater, too-small brown mac she'd promised to replace this year.

I shrugged.

"You're not going trick-or-treating?"

The truth was, no one went trick-or-treating much in our section of Ballard, not like in Bellingham where we'd lived when we lived with my dad. Too wet and dismal, most days, and there were too many drunks lurking around places like the Black Anchor and sometimes stumbling down the duplexes, shouting curses at the dripping trees.

"Trick-or-treating's for babies," I said.

"Hmm, I wonder which of your friends taught you that," my mother said, and then a look flashed across her face, different than the one she usually got at times like this. She still looked sad, but not about me. She looked sad for me.

I took a step toward her, and her image wavered in my glasses. "I won't sleep there. I'll be home by eleven," I said.

"You'll be home by ten, or you won't be going anywhere again anytime soon. Got it? How old do you think you are, anyway?"

"Twelve," I said, with as much conviction as I could muster, and my mother flashed the sad look again.

"If Peter tells you to jump off a bridge . . ."

"Push him off."

My mother nodded. "If I didn't feel so bad for him . . ." she said, and I thought she meant Peter, and then I wasn't sure. But she didn't say anything else, and after a few seconds, I couldn't stand there anymore, not with the wind crawling down the neck of my jacket and my mother still looking like that. I left her in the doorway.

Even in bright sunlight, mine was a dreary neighborhood. The gusts of wind herded paper scraps and street-grit down the overflowing gutters and yanked the last leaves off the trees like a gleeful gang on a vandalism rampage. I saw a few parents—new to the area, obviously—hunched into rain-slickers, leading little kids from house to house. The kids wore drug-store clown costumes, Darth Vader masks, sailor caps. They all looked edgy, miserable. At most of the houses, no one answered the doorbell.

Outside the Andersz's place, I stopped for just a minute, watching the leaves leaping from their branches like lemmings and tumbling down the wind, trying to figure out what was different, what felt wrong. Then I had it: the Mountain was out. The endless Fall rain had rolled in early that year, and it had been weeks, maybe months, since I'd last seen Mount Rainier. Seeing it now gave me the same unsettled sensation as always. "It's because you're looking south, not west," people always say, as if that explains how the mountain gets to that spot on the horizon, on the wrong side of the city, not where it actually is but out to sea, seemingly bobbing on the waves, not the land.

How many times, I wondered abruptly, had some adult in my life asked why I liked Peter? I wasn't cruel, and despite my size, I wasn't easily cowed, and I did okay in school—not as well as Peter, but okay—and I had "a gentleness, most days," as Mrs. Corbett (Whore Butt, to Peter) had written on my report card last year. "If he learns to exercise judgment—and perhaps gives some thought to his choice of companions—he could go far."

I wanted to go far from Ballard, anyway, and the Locks, and the smell of lutefisk, and the rain. I liked doorbell ditching, but I didn't get much charge out of throwing stones through windows. And if people were home when we did it, came out and shook their fists or worse, just stood there, looking at us the way you would a wind or an earthquake, nothing you could slow or stop, I'd freeze, feeling bad, until Peter screamed at me or yanked me so hard that I had no choice but to follow.

I could say I liked how smart Peter was, and I did. He could sit dead still for twenty-seven minutes of a thirty-minute comprehension test, then scan the reading and answer every question right before the teacher, furious, hovering over him and watching the clock, could snatch the paper away without the rest of us screaming foul. He could recite the periodic table of elements backwards, complete with atomic weights. He could build skyscrapers five feet high out of chalk and rubber cement jars and toothpicks and crayons that always stayed standing until anyone who wasn't him tried to touch them.

I could say I liked the way he treated everyone the same, which he did, in a way. He'd been the first in my grade—the only one, for a year or so—to hang out with the Mack sisters, who were still, at that point, the only African Americans in our school. But he wasn't all that nice to the Macks, really. Just no nastier than he was to the rest of us.

No. I liked Peter for exactly the reason my mother and my teachers feared I did: because he was fearless, because he was cruel—although mostly to people who deserved it when it wasn't Halloween—and most of all, because he really did seem capable of anything. So many of the people I knew seemed capable of nothing, for whatever reason. Capable of nothing.

Out on the whitecap-riddled sound, the sun sank, and the Mountain turned red. It was like looking inside it, seeing it living. Shivering slightly in the wind, I hopped the Andersz's three stone steps and rang the bell.

"Just come in, fuck!" I heard Peter yell from the basement, and I started to open the door, and Mr. Andersz opened it for me. He had his grey cardigan straight on his waist for once and his black hat was gone and his black-grey hair was wet and combed on his forehead, and I had the horrible, hilarious idea that he was going on a date.

"Andrew, come in," he said, sounding funny, too formal, the way he did at school. He didn't step back right away, either, and when he did, he put his hand against the mirror on the hallway wall, as though the house was rocking underneath him.

"Hey, Mr. Andersz," I said, wiping my feet on the shredded green mat that said something in Serbian. Downstairs, I could hear the burbling of the *Dig Dug* game, and I knew the Mack sisters had arrived. I flung my coat over Peter's green slicker on the coatrack, took a couple steps toward the basement door, turned around, stopped.

Mr. Andersz had not moved, hadn't even taken his hand off the mirror, and now he was staring at it as though it was a spider frozen there.

"Are you all right, Mr. Andersz?" I asked, and he didn't respond. Then he made a sound, a sort of hiss, like a radiator when you switch it off.

"How many?" he muttered. I could barely hear him. "How many chances? As a teacher, you know there won't be many. You get two, maybe three moments in an entire year . . . Something's happened, there's been a fight or someone's sick or the soccer team won or something, and you're looking at a student . . ." His voice trailed off, leaving me with the way he said 'student.' He pronounced it 'stuDENT.' It was one of the things we all made fun of, not mean fun, just fun. "You're looking at them," he said, "and suddenly, there they are. And it's them, and it's thrilling, terrifying, because you know you might have a chance . . . an opportunity. You can say something."

On the mirror, Mr. Andersz's hand twitched, and I noticed the sweat beading under the hair on his forehead. It reminded me of my dad, and I wondered if Mr. Andersz was drunk. Then I wondered if my dad was drunk, wherever he was. Downstairs, Jenny Mack yelled, "Get off," in her fighting voice, happy-loud, and Kelly Mack said, "Good, come on, this is boring."

"And as parent . . ." Mr. Andersz muttered. "How many? And what happens . . . the moment comes . . . but you're missing your wife. Just right then, just for a while. Or your friends. Maybe you're tired. It's just that day. It's rainy, you have meals to make, you're tired . . . There'll be another moment. Surely. You have years. Right? You have years . . ."

So fast and so silent was Peter's arrival in the basement doorway that I mistook him for a shadow from outside, didn't even realize he was there until he pushed me in the chest. "What's your deal?" he said.

I started to gesture at Mr. Andersz, thought better of it, shrugged. Footsteps clattered on the basement stairs, and then the Macks were in the room. Kelly had her tightly braided hair stuffed under a black, backward baseball cap. Her bare arms were covered in paste-on snake tattoos, and her face was dusted in white powder. Jenny wore a red sweater, black jeans. Her hair hung straight and shiny and dark, hovering just off her head and neck like a bird's crest, and I understood, for the first time, that she was pretty. Her eyes were bright green, wet and watchful.

"What are you supposed to be?" I said to Kelly, because suddenly I was uncomfortable looking at Jenny.

Kelly flung her arm out to point and did a quick, ridiculous shoulder-wriggle. It was nothing like her typical movements; I'd seen her dance. "Vanilla Ice," she said, and spun around.

"Let's go," Peter said, stepping past me and his father and tossing my mac on the floor so he could get to his slicker.

"You want candy, Andy?" Jenny teased, her voice sing-songy.

"Ho Ho?" I asked. I was talking, I suppose, to Mr. Andersz, who was still staring at his hand on the mirror. I didn't want him to be in the way. It made me nervous for him.

The word 'Ho Ho' seemed to rouse him, though. He shoved himself free of the wall, shook his head as if awakening, and said, "Just a minute," very quietly.

Peter opened the front door, letting in the wind, and Mr. Andersz pushed it closed, not hard. But he leaned against it, and the Mack sisters stopped with their coats half on. Peter just stood beside him, his black hair sharp and pointy on his forehead like the tips of a spiked fence. But he looked more curious than angry.

Mr. Andersz lifted a hand to his eyes, squeezed them shut, opened them. Then he said, "Turn out your pockets."

Still, Peter's face registered nothing. He didn't respond to his father or glance at us. Neither Kelly nor I moved, either. Beside me, Jenny took a long, slow breath, as though she was clipping a wire on a bomb, and then she said, "Here, Mr. A," and she pulled the pockets of her grey coat inside out, revealing two sticks of Dentyne, two cigarettes, a ring of keys with a Seahawks whistle dangling amongst them, and a ticket-stub. I couldn't see what from.

"Thank you, Jenny," Mr. Andersz said, but he didn't take the cigarettes, hardly even looked at her. He watched his son.

Very slowly, after a long time, Peter smiled. "Look at you," he said. "Being daddy." He pulled out the liner of his coat-pockets. There was nothing in them at all.

"Pants," said Mr. Andersz.

"What do you think you're looking for, Big Bad Daddy?" Peter asked. "What do you think you're going to find?"

"Pants," Mr. Andersz said.

"And what will you do, do you think, if you find it?" But he turned out his pants pockets. There was nothing in those, either, not even keys or money.

For the first time since Peter had come upstairs, Mr. Andersz looked at the rest of us, and I shuddered. His face looked the same way my mother's had when I left the house: a little scared, but mostly sad. Permanently, stupidly sad.

"I want to tell you something," he said. If he spoke like this in the classroom, I thought, no one would wedge unbent paperclips in his chalkboard erasers anymore. "I won't have it. There will be no windows broken. There will be no little children terrorized—"

"That wasn't our fault," said Jenny, and she was right, in a way. We hadn't known anyone was hiding in those bushes when we toilet-papered them, and Peter had meant to light his cigarette, not the roll of toilet paper.

"Nothing lit on fire. No one bullied or hurt. I won't have it, because it's beneath you, do you understand? You're the smartest children I know." Abruptly, Mr. Andersz's hands flashed out and grabbed his son's shoulders. "Do you hear me? You're the smartest child I've ever seen."

For a second, they just stood there, Mr. Andersz clutching Peter's shoulders as though trying to steer a runaway truck, Peter completely blank.

Then, very slowly, Peter smiled. "Thanks, Dad," he said.

"Please," Mr. Andersz said, and Peter opened his mouth, and we all cringed.

But what he said was, "Okay," and he slipped past his father and out the door. I looked at the Mack sisters. Together, we watched Mr. Andersz in the doorway with his head tilted forward on his neck and his hands tight at his sides, like a diver at the Olympics getting ready for a backflip. He never moved, though, and eventually, we followed Peter out. I was last, and I thought I felt Mr. Andersz's hand on my back as I went by, but I wasn't sure, and when I glanced around, he was still just standing there, and the door swung shut.

I'd been inside the Andersz's house fifteen minutes, maybe less, but the wind had whipped the late afternoon light over the horizon, and the Mountain had faded from red to grey-black, motionless now on the surface of the water like an oil tanker, one of those massive, passing ships on which no people were visible, ever. I never liked my neighborhood, but I hated it after sundown, the city gone, the Sound indistinguishable from the black, starless sky, no one walking. It was like we were someone's toy set that had been closed up in its box and snapped shut for the night.

"Where are we going?" Kelly Mack said, her voice sharp, fed up. She'd been sick of us, lately. Sick of Peter.

"Yeah," I said, rousing myself. I didn't want to soap car windows or throw rocks at streetsigns or put on rubber masks and scare trick-or-treaters, exactly, but those were the things we did. And we had no supplies.

Peter closed his eyes, leaned his head back, took a deep breath of the rushing air and held it. He looked almost peaceful. I couldn't remember seeing him that way. It was startling. Then he stuck one trembling arm out in front of him, pointed at me, and his eyes sprung open.

"Do you know . . ." he said, his voice deep, accented, a perfect imitation, "what that bell does?"

I clapped my hands. "That bell . . ." I said, in the closest I could get to the same voice, and the Mack sisters stared at us, baffled, which made me grin even harder, "raises the dead."

"What are you babbling about?" said Kelly to Peter, but Jenny was looking at me, seawater-eyes curious and strange.

"You know Mr. Paars?" I asked her.

But of course she didn't. The Macks had moved here less than a year and a half ago, and I hadn't seen Mr. Paars, I realized, in considerably longer. Not since the night of the bell, in fact. I looked at Peter. His grin was as wide as mine felt. He nodded at me. We'd been friends a long time, I realized. Almost half my life.

Of course, I didn't say that. "A long time ago," I told the Macks, feeling like a longshoreman, a lighthouse keeper, someone with stories who lived by the sea, "there was this man. An old, white haired-man. He ate lutefisk—it's fish, it smells awful, I don't really know what it is—and stalked around the neighborhood, scaring everybody."

"He had this cane," Peter said, and I waited for him to go on, join me in the telling, but he didn't.

"All black," I said. "Kind of scaly. Ribbed, or something. It didn't look like a cane. And it had this silver dog's head on it, with fangs. A doberman—"

"Anyway . . ." said Kelly Mack, though Jenny seemed to be enjoying listening.

"He used to bop people with it. Kids. Homeless people. Whoever got in his way. He stomped around 15th Street terrorizing everyone. Two years ago, on the first Halloween we were allowed out alone, right about this time of night, Peter and I spotted him coming out of the hardware store. It's not there anymore, it's that empty space next to the place where the movie theatre used to be. Anyway, we saw him there, and we followed him home."

Peter waved us out of his yard, toward the Locks. Again, I waited, but when he glanced at me, the grin was gone. His face was normal, neutral, maybe, and he didn't say anything.

"He lives down there," I said, gesturing to the south toward the Sound. "Way past all the other houses. Past the end of the street. Practically in the water."

Despite what Peter had said, we didn't head that way. Not then. We wandered toward the Locks, into the park. The avenue between the pine trees was empty except for a scatter of solitary bums on benches, wrapping themselves in shredded jackets and newspapers as the night nailed itself down and the dark billowed around us in the wind gusts like the sides of a tent. In the roiling trees, black birds perched on the branches, silent as gargoyles.

"There aren't any other houses that close to Mr. Paars's," I said. "The street turns to dirt, and it's always wet because it's down by the water. There are these long, empty lots full of weeds, and a couple sheds, I don't know what's in them or who would own them. Anyway, right where the pavement ends, Peter and I dropped back and just kind of hung out near the last house until Mr. Paars made it to his yard. God, Peter, you remember his yard?"

Instead of answering, Peter led us between the low stone buildings to the canal, where we watched the water swallow the last streaks of daylight like some monstrous whale gulping plankton. The only boats in the slips were two sailboats, sails furled, rocking as the waves slapped against them. The only person I saw on either stood at the stern of the boat closest to us, head hooded in a green oil-slicker, face aimed out to sea.

"Think I could hit him from here?" said Peter, and I flinched, looked at his fists expecting to see stones, but he was just asking. "Tell them the rest," he said.

I glanced at the Macks, was startled to see them holding hands, leaning against the rail over the canal, though they were watching us, not the water. "Come on, already," Kelly said, but Jenny just raised her eyebrows at me. Behind her, seagulls dipped and tumbled on the wind like shreds of cloud that had been ripped loose.

"We waited, I don't know, a while. It was cold. Remember how cold it was? We were wearing winter coats and mittens. It wasn't windy like this, but it was freezing. At least that made the dirt less muddy when we finally went down there. We passed the sheds and the trees, and there was no one, I mean no one, around. Too cold for any trick-or-treating anywhere around here, even if anyone was going to. And there wasn't anywhere to go on that street, regardless.

"Anyway. It's weird. Everything's all flat down there, and then right as you get near the Paars place, this little forest springs up, all these thick firs. We couldn't really see anything."

"Except that it was light," Peter murmured.

"Yeah. Bright light. Mr. Paars had his yard floodlit, for intruders, we figured. We thought he was probably paranoid. So we snuck off the road when we got close and went into the trees. In there, it was wet. Muddy, too. My mom was so mad when I got home. Pine needles sticking to me everywhere. She said I looked like I'd been tarred and feathered. We hid in this little grove, looked into the lawn, and we saw the bell."

Now Peter turned around, his hands flung wide to either side. "Biggest fucking bell you've ever seen in your life," he said.

"What are you talking about?" said Kelly.

"It was in this . . . pavilion," I started, not sure how to describe it. "Gazebo, I guess. All white and round, like a carousel, except the only thing inside was this giant white bell, like a church bell, hanging from the ceiling on a chain. And all the lights in the yard were aimed at it."

"Weird," said Jenny, leaning against her sister.

"Yeah. And that house. It's real dark, and real old. Black wood or something, all sort of falling apart. Two stories, kind of big. It looked like four or five of the sheds we passed sort of stacked on top of each other and squashed together. But the lawn was beautiful. Green, mowed perfectly, like a baseball stadium."

"Kind of," Peter whispered. He turned from the canal and wandered away again, back between buildings down the tree-lined lane.

A shiver swept up the skin on my back as I realized, finally, why we were going back to the Paars's house. I'd forgotten, until that moment, how scared we'd been. How scared Peter had been. Probably, Peter had been thinking about this for two years.

"It was all so strange," I said to the Macks, all of us watching the bums in their rattling paper blankets and the birds clinging by their talons to the branches and eyeing us as we passed. "All that outside light, the house falling apart and no lights on in there, no car in the driveway, that huge bell. So we just looked for a long time. Then Peter said—I remember this, exactly—'He just leaves something shaped like that hanging there. And he expects us not to ring it.'

"Then, finally, we realized what was in the grass."

By now, we were out of the park, back among the duplexes, and the wind had turned colder, though it wasn't freezing, exactly. In a way, it felt good, fresh, like a hard slap in the face.

"I want a shrimp-and-chips," Kelly said, gesturing over her shoulder toward 15th Street, where the little fry-stand still stayed open next to the Dairy Queen, although the Dairy Queen had been abandoned.

"I want to go see this Paars house," said Jenny. "Stop your whining." She sounded cheerful, fierce, the way she did when she played *Dig Dug* or threw her hand in the air at school. She was smart, too, not Peter-smart, but as smart as me, at least. And I think she'd seen the trace of fear in Peter, barely there but visible in his skin like a fossil, something long dead and never before seen, and it fascinated her. That's what I was thinking when she reached out casually and grabbed my hand. Then I stopped thinking at all. "Tell me about the grass," she said.

"It was like a circle," I said, my fingers still, my palm flat against hers. Even when she squeezed, I held still. I didn't know what to do, and I didn't want Peter to turn around. If Kelly had noticed, she didn't say anything. "Cut right in the grass. A pattern. A circle, with this upside down triangle inside it, and—"

"How do you know it was upside down?" Jenny asked.

"What?"

"How do you know you were even looking at it the right way?"

"Shut up," said Peter, quick and hard, not turning around, leading us onto the street that dropped down to the Sound, to the Paars house. Then he did turn around, and he saw our hands. But he didn't say anything. When he was facing forward again, Jenny squeezed once more, and I gave a feeble squeeze back.

We walked half a block in silence, but that just made me more nervous. I could feel Jenny's thumb sliding along the outside of mine, and it made me tingly, terrified. I said, "Upside down. Right-side up. Whatever. It was a symbol, a weird one. It looked like an eye."

"Old dude must have had a hell of a lawn-mower," Kelly muttered, glanced at Peter's back, and stopped talking, just in time, I thought. Mr. Andersz was right. She was smart, too.

"It kind of made you not want to put your foot in the grass," I continued. "I don't know why. It just looked wrong. Like it really could see you. I can't explain."

"Didn't make me want not to put my foot in the grass," Peter said.

I felt Jenny look at me. Her mouth was six inches or so from my hair, my ear. It was too much. My hand twitched and I let go.

Blushing, I glanced at her. She looked surprised, and she drifted away toward her sister.

"That's true," I said, wishing I could call Jenny back. "Peter stepped right out."

On our left, the last of the duplexes slid away, and we came to the end of the pavement. In front of us, the dirt road rolled down the hill, red-brown and wet and bumpy, like some stretched, cut-out tongue on the ground. I remembered the way Peter's duck-boots had seemed to float on the surface of Mr. Paars's floodlit green lawn, as though he was walking on water.

"Hey," I said, though Peter had already stepped onto the dirt and was strolling, fast and purposeful, down the hill. "Peter," I called after him, though I followed, of course. The Macks were beside but no longer near me. "When's the last time you saw him? Mr. Paars?"

He turned around, and he was smiling, now, the smile that scared me. "Same time you did, Bubba," he said. "Two years ago tonight."

I blinked, stood still, and the wind lashed me like the end of a twisted-up towel. "How do you know when I last saw him?" I said.

Peter shrugged. "Am I wrong?"

I didn't answer. I watched Peter's face, the dark swirling around and over it, shaping it, like rushing water over stone.

"He hasn't been anywhere. Not on 15th Street. Not at the Black Anchor. Nowhere. I've been watching."

"Maybe he doesn't live there anymore," Jenny said carefully. She was watching Peter, too.

"There's a car," Peter said. "A Lincoln. Long and black. Practically a limo."

"I've seen that car," I said. "I've seen it drive by my house, right at dinner time."

"It goes down there," said Peter, gesturing toward the trees, the water, the Paars house. "Like I said, I've been watching."

And of course, he had been, I thought. If his father had let him, he'd probably have camped right here, or in the gazebo under the bell. In fact, it seemed impossible to me, given everything I knew about Peter, that he'd let two years go by.

"Exactly what happened to you two down there?" Kelly asked.

"Tell them now," said Peter. "There isn't going to be any talking once we get down there. Not until we're all finished." Dropping into a crouch, he picked at the cold, wet dirt with his fingers, watched the ferries drifting out of downtown toward Bainbridge Island, Vashon. You couldn't really make out the boats from there, just the clusters of lights on the water like clouds of lost, doomed fireflies.

"Even the grass was weird," I said, remembering the weight of my sopping pants against my legs. "It was so wet. I mean, everywhere was wet, as usual, but this was like wading in a pond. You put your foot down and the whole lawn rippled. It made the eye look like it was winking. At first we were kind of hunched over, sort of hiding, which was ridiculous in all that light. I didn't want to walk in the circle, but Peter just strolled right through it. He called me a baby because I went the long way around."

"I called you a baby because you were being one," Peter said, but not meanly, really.

"We kept expecting lights to fly on in the house. Or dogs to come out. It just seemed like there would be dogs. But there weren't. We got up to the gazebo, which was the only place in the whole yard with shadows, because it was surrounded by all these trees. Weird trees. They were kind of stunted. Not pines, either, they're like birch trees, I guess. But short. And their bark is black."

"Felt weird, too," Peter muttered, straightening up, wiping his hands down his coat. "It just crumbled when you rubbed it in your hands, like one of those soft block-erasers, you know what I mean?"

"We must have stood there ten minutes. More. It was so quiet. You could hear the Sound, a little, although there aren't any waves there or anything. You could hear the pine trees dripping, or maybe it was the lawn. But there weren't any birds. And there wasn't anything moving in that house. Finally, Peter started toward the bell. He took exactly one step into the gazebo, and one of those dwarf-trees walked right off its roots into his path, and both of us started screaming."

"What?" said Jenny.

"I didn't scream," said Peter. "And he hit me."

"He didn't hit you," I said.

"Yes he did."

"Could you shut up and let Andrew finish?" said Kelly, and Peter lunged, grabbing her slicker in his fists and shoving her hard and then yanking her forward so that her head snapped back on its stalk like a decapitated flower and then snapped into place again.

It had happened so fast that neither Jenny or I had moved, but Jenny hurtled forward now, raking her nails down Peter's face, and he said, "OW!" and fell back, and she threw her arms around Kelly's shoulders. For a few seconds, they stood like that, and then Kelly put her own arms up and eased Jenny away. To my astonishment, I saw that she was laughing.

"I don't think I'd do that again, if I were you," she said to Peter, her laughter quick and hard, as though she was spitting teeth.

Peter put a hand to his cheek, gazing at the blood that came away on his fingers. "Ow," he said again.

"Let's go home," Jenny said to her sister.

No one answered right away. Then Peter said, "Don't." After a few seconds, when no one reacted, he said, "You've got to see the house." He was going to say more, I think, but what else was there to say? I felt bad, without knowing why. He was like a planet we visited, cold and rocky and probably lifeless, and we kept coming because it was all so strange, so different than what we knew. He looked at me, and what I was thinking must have flashed in my face, because he blinked in surprise, turned away, and started down the road without looking back. We all followed. Planet, dark star, whatever he was, he created orbits.

"So the tree hit Peter," Jenny Mack said quietly when we were halfway down the hill, almost to the sheds.

"It wasn't a tree. It just seemed like a tree. I don't know how we didn't see him there. He had to have been watching us the whole time. Maybe he knew we'd followed him. He just stepped out of the shadows and kind of whacked Peter across the chest with his cane. That black dog-head cane. He did kind of look like a tree. His skin was all gnarly, kind of dark. If you rubbed him between your fingers, he'd probably have crumbled, too. And his hair was so white. A tree that was way too old.

"And his voice. It was like a bullfrog, even deeper. He spoke real slow. He said, 'Boy. Do you know what that bell does?' And then he did the most amazing thing of all. The scariest thing. He looked at both of us, real slow. Then he dropped his cane. Just dropped it to his side. And he smiled, like he was daring us to go ahead. 'That bell raises the dead. Right up out of the ground.' "

"Look at these," Kelly Mack murmured as we walked between the sheds.

"Raises the dead," I said.

"Yeah, I heard you. These are amazing."

And they were. I'd forgotten. The most startling thing, really, was that they were still standing. They'd all sunk into the swampy grass on at least one side, and none of them had roofs, not whole roofs, anyway, and the window-slots gaped, and the wind made a rattle as it rolled through them, like waves over seashells, empty things that hadn't been empty always. They were too small to have been boat sheds, I thought, had to have been for tools and things. But tools to do what?

In a matter of steps, they were behind us, between us and the homes we knew, the streets we walked. We reached the ring of pines around the Paars house, and it was different, worse. I didn't realize how, but Peter did.

"No lights," he said.

For a while, we just stood in the blackness while saltwater and pine-resin smells glided over us like a mist. There wasn't any moon, but the water beyond the house reflected what light there was, so we could see the long, black Lincoln in the dirt driveway, the house and the gazebo beyond it. After a minute or so, we could make out the bell, too, hanging like some bloated, white bat from the gazebo ceiling.

"It *is* creepy," Jenny said.

"Ya think?" I said, but I didn't mean to, it was just what I imagined Peter would have said if he were saying anything. "Peter, I think Mr. Paars is gone. Moved, or something."

"Good," he said. "Then he won't mind." He stepped out onto the lawn and said, "Fuck."

"What?" I asked, shoulders hunching, but Peter just shook his head.

"Grass. It's a lot longer. And it's wet as hell."

"What happened after 'That bell raises the dead?' " Jenny asked.

I didn't answer right away. I wasn't sure what Peter wanted me to say. But he just squinted at the house, didn't even seem to be listening. I almost took Jenny's hand. I wanted to. "We ran."

"Both of you? Hey, Kell . . ."

But Kelly was already out on the grass next to Peter, smirking as her feet sank. Peter glanced at her, cautiously, I thought. Uncertain. "You would have, too," he said.

"I might have," said Kelly.

Then we were all on the grass, holding still, listening. The wind rushed through the trees as though filling a vacuum. I thought I could hear the Sound, not waves, just the dead, heavy wet. But there were no gulls, no bugs.

Once more, Peter strolled straight for that embedded circle in the grass, still visible despite the depth of the lawn, like a manta-ray half-buried in seaweed. When Peter's feet crossed the corners of the upside-down triangle—the tear-ducts of the eye—I winced, then felt silly. For all I knew, it was a corporate logo; it looked about that menacing. I started forward, too. The Macks came with me. I walked in the circle, though I skirted the edge of the triangle. Step on a crack and all. I didn't look behind to see what the Macks did, I was too busy watching Peter as his pace picked up. He was practically running, straight for the gazebo, and then he stopped.

"Hey," he said.

I'd seen it, too, I thought, feeling my knees lock as my nervousness intensified. In the lone upstairs window, there'd been a flicker. Maybe. Just one, for a single second, and then it was gone again. "I saw it," I called, but Peter wasn't listening to me. He was moving straight toward the front door. And anyway, I realized, he hadn't been looking upstairs.

What the hell's he doing?" Kelly said as she strolled past me, but she didn't stop for an answer. Jenny did, though.

"Andrew, what's going on?" she said, and I looked at her eyes, green and shadowy as the grass, but that just made me edgier, still.

I shook my head. For a moment, Jenny stood beside me. Finally, she shrugged and followed her sister. None of them looked back, which meant, I thought, that there really hadn't been rustling behind us just now, back in the pines. When I whipped my head around, I saw nothing but trees and twitching shadows.

"Here, puss-puss-puss," Peter called softly. If the grass had been less wet and I'd been less unsettled, I'd have flopped on my back and flipped my feet in the air at him, the seal's send-off. Instead, I came forward.

The house, like the sheds, seemed to have sunk sideways into the ground. With its filthy windows and rotting planks, it looked like the abandoned hull of a beached ship. Around it, the leafless branches of the dwarf-trees danced like the limbs of paper skeletons.

"Now, class," said Peter, still very quietly. "What's wrong with this picture?"

I assume you mean other than giant bells, weird eyeballs in the grass, empty sheds, and these whammy-ass trees," Kelly said, but Peter ignored her.

"He means the front door," said Jenny, and of course she was right.

I don't even know how Peter noticed. It was under an overhang, so that the only light that reached it reflected off the ground. But there was no doubt. The door was open. Six inches, tops. The scratched brass of the knob glinted dully, like an eye.

"Okay," I said. "So the door didn't catch when he went in, and he didn't notice."

"When who went in?" said Peter, mocking. "Thought you said he moved."

The wind kicked up, and the door glided back another few inches, then sucked itself shut with a click.

"Guess that settles that," I said, knowing it didn't even before the curtains came streaming out the single front window, grey and gauzy as cigarette smoke as they floated on the breeze. They hung there a few seconds, then glided to rest against the side of the house when the wind expired.

"Guess it does," said Peter softly, and he marched straight up the steps, pushed open the door, and disappeared into the Paars house.

None of the rest of us moved or spoke. Around us, tree-branches tapped against each other, the side of the house. For the second time I sensed someone behind me and spun around. Night-dew sparkled in the lawn like broken glass, and one of the shadows of the towering pines seemed to shiver back, as though the trees had inhaled it. Otherwise, there was nothing. I thought about Mr. Paars, that dog-head cane with its silver fangs.

What's he trying to prove?" Kelly asked, a silly question where Peter was concerned, really. It wasn't about proving. We all knew that.

Jenny said, "He's been in there a long time," and Peter stuck his head out the window, the curtain floating away from him.

"Come see this," he said, and ducked back inside.

Hesitating, I knew, was pointless. We all knew it. We went up the stairs together, and the door drifted open before we even touched it. "Wow," said Kelly staring straight ahead, and Jenny took my hand again, and then we were all inside. "Wow," Kelly said again.

Except for a long, wooden table folded and propped against the staircase like a lifeboat, all the furniture we could see had been draped in white sheets. The sheets rose and rearranged themselves in the breeze, which was constant and everywhere, because all the windows had been flung wide open. Leaves chased each other across the dirt-crusted hardwood floor, and scraps of paper flapped in mid-air like giant moths before settling on the staircase or the backs of chairs or blowing out the windows.

Peter appeared in a doorway across the foyer from us, his black hair bright against the deeper blackness of the rooms behind him. "Don't miss the den," he said. "I'm going to go look at the kitchen." Then he was gone again.

Kelly had started away, now, too, wandering into the living room to our right, running her fingers over the tops of a covered couch as she passed it. One of the paintings on the wall, I noticed, had been covered rather than removed, and I wondered what it was. Kelly drew up the cover, peered beneath it, then dropped it and stepped deeper into the house. I started to follow, but Jenny pulled me the other way, and we went left into what must have been Mr. Paars's den.

"Whoa," Jenny said, and her fingers slid between mine and tightened.

In the dead center of the room, amidst discarded file folders that lay where they'd been tossed and empty envelopes with plastic address-windows that flapped and chattered when the wind filled them, sat an enormous, oak, rolltop desk. The top was gone, broken away, and it lay against the room's lone window like the cracked shell of a dinosaur egg. On the surface of the desk, in black, felt frames, a set of six photographs had been arranged in a semicircle.

"It's like the top of a tombstone," Jenny murmured. "You know what I mean? Like a . . . what do you call it?"

"Family vault," I said. "Mausoleum."

"One of those."

Somehow, the fact that two of the frames turned out to be empty made the array even more unsettling. The other four held individual pictures of what had to be brothers and one sister—they all had flying white hair, razor-blue eyes— standing, each in turn, on the top step of the gazebo outside, with the great bell looming behind them, bright white and all out of proportion, like the Mountain on a too-clear day.

"Andrew," Jenny said, her voice nearly a whisper, and in spite of the faces in the photographs and the room we were in, I felt it all over me. "Why Struwwelpeter?"

"What?" I said, mostly just to make her speak again.

"Struwwelpeter. Why does Mr. Andersz call him that?"

"Oh. It's from some kids' book. My mom actually had it when she was little. She said it was about some boy who got in trouble because he wouldn't cut his hair or cut his nails."

Jenny narrowed her eyes. "What does that have to do with anything?"

"I don't know. Except my mom said the pictures in the book were really scary. She said Struwwelpeter looked like Freddy Krueger with a 'fro."

Jenny burst out laughing, but she stopped fast. Neither of us, I think, liked the way laughter sounded in that room, in that house, with those black-bordered faces staring at us. "Struwwelpeter," she said, rolling the name carefully on her tongue, like a little kid daring to lick a frozen flagpole.

"It's what my mom called me when I was little," said Peter from the doorway, and Jenny's fingers clenched hard and then fell free of mine. Peter didn't move toward us. He just stood there while we watched, paralyzed. After a few, long seconds, he added, "When I kicked the shit out of barbers, because I hated having my haircut. Then when I was just being bad. She'd say that instead of screaming at me. It made me cry." From across the foyer, in the living room, maybe, we heard a single, soft bump, as though something had fallen over.

With a shrug, Peter released us and stepped past us back into the foyer. We followed, not touching, now, not even looking at each other. I felt guilty, amazed, strange. When we passed the windows the curtains billowed up and brushed across us.

"Hey, Kelly," Peter whispered loudly into the living room. He whispered it again, then abruptly turned our way and said, "You think he's dead?"

"Looks like it," I answered, glancing down the hallway toward the kitchen, into the shadows in the living room, which seemed to have shifted, somehow, the sheet some way different as it lay across the couch. I couldn't place the feeling, it was like watching an actor playing a corpse, knowing he was alive, trying to catch him breathing.

"But the car's here," Peter said. "The Lincoln. Hey, KELLY!" His shout made me wince, and Jenny cringed back toward the front door, but she shouted, too.

"Kell? KELL?"

"Oh, what is *that*?" I murmured, my whole spine twitching like a severed electrical wire, and when Jenny and Peter looked at me, I pointed upstairs.

"Wh—" Jenny started, and then it happened again, and both of them saw it. From under the half-closed door at the top of the staircase—the only door we could see from where we were—came a sudden slash of light which disappeared instantly, like a snake's tongue flashing in and out.

We stood there at least a minute, maybe more. Even Peter looked uncertain, not scared, quite, but something had happened to his face. I couldn't place it right then. It made me nervous, though. And it made me like him more than I had in a long, long time.

Then, without warning, Peter was halfway up the stairs, his feet stomping dust out of each step as he slammed them down, saying, "Fucking hilarious, Kelly. Here I come. Ready or not." He stopped halfway up and turned to glare at us. Mostly at me. "Come on."

"Let's go," I said to Jenny, reached out on my own for the first time and touched her elbow, but to my surprise she jerked it away from me. "Jenny, she's up there."

"I don't think so," she whispered.

"Come *on*," Peter hissed.

"Andrew, something's wrong. Stay here."

I looked into her face, smart, steely Jenny Mack, first girl ever to look at me like that, first girl I'd ever wanted to, and right then, for the only time in my life, I felt—within me—the horrible thrill of Peter's power, knew the secret of it. It wasn't bravery and it wasn't smarts, although he had both those things in spades. It was simply the willingness to trade. At any given moment, Peter Andersz would trade anyone for anything, or at least could convince people that he would. Knowing you could do that, I thought, would be like holding a grenade, tossing it back and forth in the terrified face of the world.

I looked at Jenny's eyes, filling with tears, and I wanted to kiss her, though I couldn't even imagine how to initiate something like that. What I said, in my best Peter voice, was, "I'm going upstairs. Coming or staying?"

I can't explain. I didn't mean anything. It felt like playacting, no more real than holding her hand had been. We were just throwing on costumes, dancing around each other, scaring each other. Trick or treat.

"KELLY?" Jenny called past me, blinking, crying openly, now, and I started to reach for her again, and she shoved me, hard, toward the stairs.

"Hurry up," said Peter, with none of the triumph I might have expected in his voice.

I went up, and we clumped, side by side, to the top of the stairs. When we reached the landing, I looked back at Jenny. She was propped in the front door, one hand on the doorknob and the other wiping at her eyes as she jerked her head from side to side, looking for her sister.

At our feet, light licked under the door again. Peter held up a hand, and we stood together and listened. We heard wind, low and hungry, and now I was sure I could hear the Sound lapping against the edge of the continent, crawling over the lip of it.

"OnetwothreeBOO!" Peter screamed and flung open the door, which banged against a wall inside and bounced back. Peter kicked it open again, and we lunged through into what must have been a bedroom, once, and was now just a room, a blank space, with nothing in it at all.

Even before the light swept over us again, from outside, from the window, I realized what it was. "Lighthouse," I said, breathless. "Greenpoint Light."

Peter grinned. "Oh, yeah. Halloween."

Every year, the suburbs north of us set Greenpoint Light running again on Halloween, just for fun. One year, they'd even rented ferries and decked them out with seaweed and parents in pirate costumes and floated them just offshore, ghost-ships for the kiddies. We'd seen them skirting our suburb on their way up the coast.

"Do you think—" I started, and Peter grabbed me hard by the elbow. "Ow," I said.

"*Listen*," snapped Peter.

I heard the house groan as it shifted. I heard paper flapping somewhere downstairs, the front door tapping against its frame or the inside wall as it swung on the wind.

"*Listen*," Peter whispered, and this time I heard it. Very low. Very faint, like a finger rubbed along the lip of a glass, but unmistakable once you realized what it was. Outside, in the yard, someone had just lifted the tongue of the bell and tapped it, oh so gently, against the side.

I stared at Peter, and he stared back. Then he leapt to the window, peering down. I thought he was going to punch the glass loose from the way his shoulders jerked.

"Well?" I said.

"All I can see is the roof." He shoved the window even further open than it already was. "CLEVER GIRLS!" he screamed, and waited, for laughter, maybe, a full-on bong of the bell, something. Abruptly, he turned to me, and the light rolled across him, waist-high, and when it receded, he looked different, damp with it. "Clever girls," he said.

I whirled, stepped into the hall, looked down. The front door was open, and Jenny was gone. "Peter?" I whispered, and I heard him swear as he emerged onto the landing beside me. "You think they're outside?"

Peter didn't answer right away. He had his hands jammed in his pockets, his eyes cast down at the floor. He shuffled in place. "The thing is, Andrew," he said, "there's nothing to do."

"What are you talking about?"

"There's nothing to do."

"Find the girls?"

He shrugged.

"Ring the bell?"

"They rang it."

"You're the one who brought us out here. What were you expecting?"

He glanced back at the bedroom's bare walls, the rectangular, dustless space in the floor where, until very recently, a bed or rug must have been, the empty light fixture overhead. Struwwelpeter. My friend. "Opposition," he said, and shuffled off down the hall.

"Where are you going?" I called after him.

He turned, and the look on his face stunned me, it had been years since I'd seen it. The last time was in second grade, right after he punched Robert Case, who was twice his size, in the face and ground one of Robert's eyeglass lenses into his eye. The last time anyone who knew him had dared to fight him. He looked . . . sorry.

"Coming?" he said.

I almost followed him. But I felt bad about leaving Jenny. And I wanted to see her and Kelly out on the lawn, pointing through the window at us and laughing. And I didn't want to be in that house anymore. And it was exhausting being with Peter, trying to read him, dancing clear of him.

"I'll be outside," I said.

He shrugged and disappeared through the last unopened door at the end of the hall. I listened for a few seconds, heard nothing, turned, and started downstairs. "Hey, Jenny?" I called, got no answer. I was three steps from the bottom before I realized what was wrong.

In the middle of the foyer floor, amidst a swirl of leaves and paper, Kelly Mack's black baseball cap lay upside down like an empty tortoise shell. "Um," I said to no one, to myself, took one more uncertain step down, and the front door swung back on its hinges.

I just stared, at first. I couldn't even breathe, let alone scream, it was like I had an apple-core lodged in my throat. I just stared into the white spray-paint on the front door, the triangle-within-a-circle. A wet, wide-open eye. My legs wobbled, and I grabbed for the banister, slipped down to the bottom step, held myself still. I should scream, I thought. I should get Peter down here, and both of us should run. I didn't even see the hand until it clamped hard around my mouth.

For a second, I couldn't do anything at all, and that was way too long, because before I could lunge away or bite down, a second hand snaked around my waist, and I was yanked off my feet into the blackness to my left and slammed against the living room wall.

I wasn't sure when I'd closed my eyes, but now I couldn't make them open. My head rang, and my skin felt tingly, tickly, as though it was dissolving into the atoms that made it up, all of them racing in a billion different directions, and soon there'd be nothing left of me, just a scatter of energy and a spot on Mr. Paars's dusty, decaying floor.

"Did I hurt you?" whispered a voice I knew, close to my ears. It still took me a long time to open my eyes. "Just nod or shake your head."

Slowly, forcing my eyes open, I nodded.

"Good. Now sssh," said Mr. Andersz, and released me.

Behind him, both Mack sisters stood grinning.

"You like the cap?" Kelly said. "The cap's a good touch, no?"

"Sssh," Mr. Andersz said. "Please. I beg you."

"You should see you," Jenny whispered, sliding up close. "You look so damn scared."

"What's—"

"He followed us to see if we were doing anything horrible. He saw us come in here, and he had this idea to get back at Peter."

I gaped at Jenny, then Mr. Andersz, who was peering, very carefully, around the corner, up the stairs.

"Not to get back," he said, so serious. It was the same voice he'd used in his own front hallway earlier that evening. He'd never looked more like his son than he did right then. "To reach out. Reach him. Someone's got to do something. He's a good boy. He could be. Now, please. Don't spoil this."

Everything about Mr. Andersz at that moment astounded me. But watching him revealed nothing further. He stood at the edge of the living room, shoulders hunched, hair tucked tight under his dock-worker's cap, waiting. Slowly, my gaze swung back to Jenny, who continued to grin in my direction, but not at me, certainly not with me. And I knew I'd lost her.

"This was about Peter," I said. "You could have just stuck your head out and waved me down."

"Yep," said Jenny, and watched Mr. Andersz, not me. Upstairs, a door creaked, and Peter's voice rang out. "Hey, Andrew."

To Jenny's surprise and Mr. Andersz's horror, I almost answered. I stepped forward, opened my mouth. I'm sure Jenny thought I was getting back at her, turning the tables again, but mostly, I didn't like what Mr. Andersz was doing. I think I sensed the danger in it. I might have been the only one.

But I was twelve. And Peter certainly deserved it. And Mr. Andersz was my teacher, and my friend's father. I closed my mouth, sank back into the shadows, and did not move again until it was over.

"ANDREW, I KNOW YOU CAN HEAR ME!" Peter shouted, stepping onto the landing. He came, clomp clomp clomp, toward the stairs. "ANNN-DREW!" Then, abruptly, we heard him laugh. Down he came, his shoes clattering over the steps. I thought he might charge past us, but he stopped, right where I did.

Beside the couch, under the draped painting, Kelly Mack pointed at her own hatless head and mouthed, "Oh, yeah."

But it was the eye on the door, I thought, not the cap. Only the eye would have stopped him, because like me—and faster than me—Peter would have realized that neither Mack sister, smart as they were, would have thought of it. Even if they'd had spray paint. Mr. Andersz had brought spray paint? Clearly, he'd been planning this—or something like this—for quite some time. If he was the one who'd done it, that is.

"What the fuck," Peter muttered. He came down a step. Another. His feet touched flat floor, and still Mr. Andersz held his post.

Then, very quietly, he said, "Boo."

It was as if he'd punched an ejector-seat button. Peter flew through the front door, hands flung up to ward off the eye as he sailed past it. He was fifteen feet from the house, still flying, when he realized what he'd heard. We all saw it hit him. He jerked in midair like a hooked marlin reaching the end of a harpoon rope.

For a few seconds, he just stood in the wet grass with his back to us, quivering. Kelly had sauntered past Mr. Andersz onto the front porch, laughing. Mr. Andersz, I noticed, was smiling, too, weakly. Even Jenny was laughing quietly beside me.

But I was watching Peter's back, his whole body vibrating like an imploded building after the charge has gone off, right at the moment of collapse. "No," I said.

When Peter finally turned around, though, his face was his regular face, inscrutable, a little pale. The spikes in his hair looked almost silly in the shadows, and made him look younger. A naughty little boy. Calvin with no Hobbes.

"So he *is* dead," Peter said.

Mr. Andersz stepped outside. Kelly was slapping her leg, but no one paid her any attention.

"Son," said Mr. Andersz, and he stretched one hand out, as though to call Peter to him. "I'm sorry. It was . . . I thought you might laugh."

"He's dead, right?"

The smile was gone from Mr. Andersz's face now, and from Jenny's, I noted when I glanced her way. "Kelly, shut up," I heard her say to her sister, and Kelly stopped giggling.

"Did you know he used to teach at the school?" Mr. Andersz asked, startling me.

"Mr. Paars?"

"Sixth grade science. Biology, especially. Years ago. Kids didn't like him. Yes, Peter, he died a week or so ago. He'd been very sick. We got a notice about it at school."

"Then he won't mind," said Peter, too quietly, "if I go ahead and ring that bell. Right?"

Mr. Andersz didn't know about the bell, I realized. He didn't understand. I watched him look at his son, watched the weight he always seemed to be carrying settle back around his shoulders, lock into place like a yoke. He bent forward, a little.

"My son," he said. Uselessly.

So I shoved past him. I didn't mean to push him, I just needed him out of the way, and anyway, he gave no resistance, bent back like a plant.

"Peter, don't do it," I said.

The eyes, black and mesmerizing, swung down on me. "Oh. Andrew. Forgot you were here."

It was, of course, the cruelest thing he could have said, the source of his power over me and the reason I was with him—other than the fact that I liked him, I mean. It was the thing I feared most, in general, no matter where I was.

"That bell . . ." I said, thinking of the dog's head-cane, that deep and frozen voice, but thinking more, somehow, about my friend, rocketing away from us now at incomprehensible speed. Because that's what he seemed to be doing, to me.

"Wouldn't it be great?" said Peter. And then, unexpectedly, he grinned at me. He would never forget I was there, I realized. Couldn't. I was all he had.

He turned and walked straight across the grass. The Mack sisters and Mr. Andersz followed, all of them seeming to float in the long, wet green like seabirds skimming the surface of the ocean. I did not go with them. I had the feel of Jenny's fingers in mine, and the sounds of flapping paper and whirling leaves in my ears, and Peter's last, surprising smile floating in front of my eyes, and it was enough, too much, an astonishing Halloween.

"This thing's freezing," I heard Peter say, while his father and the Macks fanned out around him, facing the house and me. He was facing away, toward the trees. "Feel this." He held the tongue of the bell toward Kelly Mack, but she'd gone silent, now, watching him, and she shook her head.

"Ready or not," he said. Then he reared back and rammed the bell-tongue home.

Instinctively, I flung my hands up to my ears, but the effect was disappointing, particularly to Peter. It sounded like a dinner bell, high, a little tinny, something that might call kids or a dog out of the water or the woods at bedtime. Peter slammed the tongue against the side of the bell one more time, dropped it, and the peal floated away over the Sound, dissipating into the salt air like seagull-cry.

For a few breaths, barely any time at all, we all stood where we were. Then Jenny Mack said, "Oh." I saw her hand snake out, grab her sister's, and her sister looked up, right at me, I thought. The two Macks stared at each other. Then they were gone, hurtling across the yard, straight across that wide-open white eye, flying toward the forest.

Peter whirled, looked at me, and his mouth opened, a little. I couldn't hear him, but I saw him murmur, "Wow," and a new smile exploded, one I couldn't even fathom, and he was gone, too, sprinting for the trees, passing the Macks as they all vanished into the shadows.

"Uh," said Mr. Andersz, backing, backing, and his expression confused me most of all. He was almost laughing. "I'm so sorry," he said. "We didn't realize . . ." He turned and chased after his son. And still, somehow, I thought they'd all been looking at me, until I heard the single, sharp thud from the porch behind me. Wood hitting wood. Cane-into-wood.

I didn't turn around. Not then. What for? I knew what was behind me. Even so, I couldn't get my legs to move, quite, not until I heard a second thud, closer, this time, as though the thing on the porch had stepped fully out of the house, making its slow, steady way toward me. Stumbling, I kicked myself forward, put a hand down in the wet grass and the mud closed over it like a mouth. When I jerked it free, it made a disappointed, sucking sort of sound, and I heard a sort of sigh behind me, another thud, and I ran, all the way to the woods.

Hours later, we were still huddled together in the Andersz's kitchen, wolfing down Ho Hos and hot chocolate. Jenny and Kelly and Peter kept laughing, erupting into cloudbursts of excited conversation, laughing some more. Mr. Andersz laughed, too, as he boiled more water and spooned marshmallows into our mugs and told us.

The man the bell had called forth, he said, was Mr. Paars's brother. He'd been coming for years, taking care of Mr. Paars after he got too sick to look after himself, because he refused to move into a resthome or even his brother's home.

"The Lincoln," Peter said, and Mr. Andersz nodded.

"God, poor man. He must have been inside when you all got there. He must have thought you were coming to rob the place, or vandalize it, and he went out back."

"We must have scared the living shit out of him," Peter said happily.

"Almost as much as we did you," said Kelly, and everyone was shouting, pointing, laughing again.

"Mr. Paars had been dead for days when they found him," Mr. Andersz told us. "The brother had to go away, and he left a nurse in charge, but the nurse got sick, I guess, or Mr. Paars wouldn't let her in, or something. Anyway, it was pretty awful when the brother came back. That's why the windows were all open. It'll take weeks, I bet, to air that place out."

I sat, and I sipped my cocoa, and I watched my friends chatter and eat and laugh and wave their arms around, and it dawned on me, slowly, that none of them had seen. None of them had heard. Not really. I almost said something five different times, but I never quite did, I think because of the way we all were, just for that hour, that last, magic night: triumphant, and windswept, and defiant, and together. Like real friends. Almost.

That was the last time, of course. The next summer, the Macks moved to Vancouver, although they'd slowly slipped away from Peter and me anyway by then. Mr. Andersz lost his job—there was an incident, apparently, he just stopped teaching and sat down on the floor in the front of his classroom and swallowed an entire box of chalk, stick by stick—and wound up working in the little caged-in accounting office at the used car lot in the wasteland down by the Ballard Bridge. And slowly, over a long period of time, it became more exciting, even for me, to talk about Peter than it was to be with him.

Soon, I think, my mother is going to get sick of staring at the images repeating over and over on our TV screen, the live reports from the rubble of my school and the yearbook photo of Peter and the video of him being stuffed into a police car and the names streaming across the bottom of the screen like a tornado warning, except too late. For the fifteenth time, at least, I see Steve Rourke's name go by. I should have told him, I thought, should have warned him. But he should have known. I wonder why my name isn't up there, why Peter didn't come after me. The answer, though, is obvious. He forgot I was there. Or he wants me to think he did.

It doesn't matter. Any minute, my mother's going to get up and go to bed, and she's going to tell me I should, too, and that we'll leave here, we'll get away and never come back.

"Yes," I'll say. "Soon."

"All those children," she'll say. Again. "Sweet Jesus, I can't believe it. Andrew." She'll drop her head on my shoulder and throw her arms around me and cry.

But by then, I won't be thinking about the streaming names, the people I knew who are people no longer, or what Peter might have been thinking tonight. I'll be thinking, just as I am now, about Peter in the grass outside the Paars house, at the moment he realized what we'd done to him. The way he stood there, vibrating. We didn't make him what he was. Not the Macks, not his dad, not me—none of us. But it's like he said: God puts something shaped like that in the world, and then He expects us not to ring it.

And now there's only one thing left to do. As soon as my mom finally lets go, stops sobbing, and stumbles off to sleep, I'm going to sneak outside, and I'm going to go straight down the hill to the Paars house. I haven't been there since that night. I have no idea if the sheds or the house or the bell even exists, anymore.

But if they do, and if that eye in the grass, or any of its power, is still there . . . well, then. I'll give a little ring. And then we'll know, once and for all, whether I really did see two old men, with matching canes, on the porch of the

Paars house when I glanced back right as I fled into the woods. Whether I really did hear rustling from all those sideways sheds as I flew past, as though, in each, something was sliding out of the ground. I wonder if the bell works only on the Paars family, or if it affects any recently deceased in the vicinity. Maybe the dead really can be called back, for a while, like kids from recess. And if they do come back—and if they're angry, and they go looking for Peter, and they find him—well. Let the poor, brilliant, fucked-up bastard get what he deserves.

# GALA BLAU

# Outfangthief

*Gala Blau was born in Berlin in August 1975. She divides her time between Germany and England and designs jewelry when she is not writing. "Outfangthief" is her first published short story. She is now at work on a novel.*

*"Outfangthief" was originally published in* The Mammoth Book of Vampire Stories by Women, *edited by Stephen Jones for Constable and Robinson Ltd. in the U.K. and Carroll & Graf in the U.S.*

—E. D.

At the moment the car slid out of control, Sarah Running had been trying to find a radio station that might carry some news of her crime. She had been driving for hours, risking the M6 all the way from Preston. Though she had seen a number of police vehicles, the traffic had been sufficiently busy to allow her to blend in, and anyway, Manser would hardly have guessed she would take her ex-husband's car. Michael was away on business in Stockholm and would not know of the theft for at least another week.

But Manser was not stupid. It would not be long before he latched on to her deceit.

As the traffic thinned, and night closed in on the motorway, Sarah's panic grew. She was convinced that her disappearance had been reported and she would be brought to book. When a police Range Rover tailed her from Walsall to the M42 turn-off, she almost sent her own car into the crash barriers at the centre of the road.

Desperate for cover, she followed the signs for the A14. Perhaps she could make the 130 miles to Felixstowe tonight and sell the car, try to find passage on a boat, lose herself and her daughter on the Continent. In a day they could be in Dresden, where her grandmother had lived; a battered city that would recognize some of its own and allow them some anonymity.

"Are you all right back there, Laura?"

In the rear-view mirror, her daughter might well have been a mannequin. Her features were glacial; her sunglasses formed tiny screens of animation as the sodium lights fizzed off them. A slight flattening of the lips was the only indication that all was well. Sarah bore down on her frustration. Did she understand what she had been rescued from? Sarah tried to remember what things had been like for herself as a child, but reasoned that her own relationship with her mother had not been fraught with the same problems.

"It's all okay, Laura. We'll not have any more worries in this family. I promise you."

All that before she spotted the flashing blue and red lights of three police vehicles blocking her progress east. She turned left on to another A road bound for Leicester. There must have been an accident; they wouldn't go to the lengths of forming a roadblock for her, would they? The road sucked her deep into darkness; on either side wild hedgerows and vast oily swells of countryside muscled into them. Headlamps on full beam, she could pick nothing out beyond the winding road apart from the ghostly dusting of insects attracted by the light. Sarah, though, felt anything but alone. She could see, in the corner of her eye, something blurred by speed, keeping pace with the car as it fled the police cordon. She took occasional glances to her right, but could not define their fellow traveller for the dense tangle of vegetation that bordered the road.

"Can you see that, Laura?" she asked. "What is it?"

It could have been a trick of the light, or something silver reflecting the shape of their car. Maybe it was the police. The needle on the speedometer edged up to eighty. They would have to dump the car somewhere soon, if the police were closing in on them.

"Keep a lookout for a B&B, okay?" She checked in the mirror; Laura's hand was splayed against the window, spreading mist from the star her fingers made. She was watching the obliteration of her view intently.

Sarah fumbled with the radio button. Static filled the car at an excruciating volume. Peering into the dashboard of the unfamiliar car, trying to locate the volume control, she perceived a darkening in the cone of light ahead. When she looked up, the car was drifting off the road, aiming for a tree. Righting the swerve only took the car more violently in the other direction. They were still on the road, but only just, as the wheels began to rise on the passenger side.

*but i wasn't drifting off the road, was i?*

Sarah caught sight of Laura, expressionless, as she was jerked from one side of the car to the other and hoped the crack she heard was not caused by her head slamming against the window.

*i thought it was a tree big and black it looked just like a tree but but but*

And then she couldn't see much because the car went into a roll and everything became part of a violent, circular blur and at the centre of it were the misted, friendly eyes of a woman dipping into her field of view.

*But but but how can a tree have a face?*

She was conscious of the cold and the darkness. There was the hiss of traffic from the motorway, soughing over the fields. Her face was sticky and at first she thought it was blood, but now she smelled a lime tree and knew it was its sap being sweated on to her. Forty metres away, the road she had just left glistened with dew. She tried to move and blacked out.

Fingers sought her face. She tried to bat them away but there were many fingers, many hands. She feared they might try to pluck her eyes out and opened her mouth to scream and that was when a rat was pushed deep into her throat.

Sarah came out of the dream, smothering on the sodden jumper of her daughter, who had tipped over the driver's seat and was pressed against her mother. The flavor of blood filled her mouth. The dead weight of the child carried an inflexibility about it that shocked her. She tried to move away from the crushing bulk and the pain drew grey veils across her eyes. She gritted her teeth, knowing that to succumb now was to die, and worked at unbuckling the seat-belt that had saved her life. Once free, she slumped to her left and her daughter filled the space she had occupied. Able to breath again, she was pondering the position in which the car had come to rest, and trying to reach Laura's hand, when she heard footsteps.

When she saw Manser lean over, his big, toothy grin seeming to fill the shattered window frame, she wished she had not dodged the police; they were preferable to this monster. But then she saw how this wasn't Manser after all. She couldn't understand how she had made the mistake. Manser was a stunted, dark man with a face like chewed tobacco. This face was smooth as soapstone and framed by thick, red tresses: a woman's face.

Other faces, less defined, swept across her vision. Everyone seemed to be moving very fast.

She said, falteringly, "Ambulance?" But they ignored her.

They lifted Laura out of the window to a cacophony of whistles and cheers. There must have been a hundred people. At least they had been rescued. Sarah would take her chances with the police. Anything was better than going home.

The faces retreated. Only the night stared in on her now, through the various rents in the car. It was cold, lonely and painful. Her face in the rear-view mirror: all smiles.

He closed the door and locked it. Cocked his head against the jamb, listened for a few seconds. Still breathing.

Downstairs, he read the newspaper, ringing a few horses for the afternoon races. He placed thousand pound bets with his bookies. In the ground-floor washroom, he took a scalding shower followed by an ice-cold one, just like James Bond. Rolex Oyster, Turnbull & Asser shirt, Armani. He made four more phone calls: Jez Knowlden, his driver, to drop by in the Jag in twenty minutes; Pamela, his wife, to say that he would be away for the weekend; Jade, his mistress, to ask her if she'd meet him in London. And then Chandos, his police mole, to see if that bitch Sarah Running had been found yet.

Sarah dragged herself out of the car just as dawn was turning the skyline milky. She had drifted in and out of consciousness all night, but the sleet that had arrived within the last half-hour was the spur she needed to try to escape. She sat a few feet away from the car, taking care not to make any extreme movements, and began to assess the damage to herself. A deep wound in her shoulder had caused most of the bleeding. Other than that, which would need stitches, she had got away with pretty superficial injuries. Her head was pounding, and dried blood formed a crust above her left eyebrow, but nothing seemed to be broken.

After quelling a moment of nausea when she tried to stand, Sarah breathed deeply of the chill morning air and looked around her. A farmhouse nestled within a crowd of trees seemed the best bet; it was too early for road users. Cautiously at first, but with gathering confidence, she trudged across the muddy, furrowed field towards the house, staring all the while at its black, arched windows, for all the world like a series of open mouths, shocked by the coming of the sun.

She had met Andrew in 1985, in the Preston library they both shared. A relationship had started, more or less, on their hands bumping each other while reaching for the same book. They had married a year later and Sarah gave birth to Laura then, too. Both of them had steady, if unspectacular work. Andrew was a security guard and she cleaned at the local school and for a few favored neighbors. They eventually took out a mortgage on their council house on the right-to-buy scheme and bought a car, a washing machine and a television on the never-never. Then they both lost their jobs within weeks of each other. They owed seventeen thousand pounds. When the law center they depended on heavily for advice lost its funding and closed down, Sarah had to go to hospital when she began laughing so hysterically she could not catch her breath. It was as Andrew drove her back from the hospital that they met Malcolm Manser for the first time.

His back to them, he stepped out in front of their car at a set of traffic lights and did not move when they changed in Andrew's favor. When Andrew sounded the horn, Manser turned around. He was wearing a long, nubuck trenchcoat, black Levi's, black boots and a black T-shirt without an inch of give in it. His hair was black save for wild slashes of grey above his temples. His sunglasses appeared to be sculpted from his face, so seamlessly did they sit on his nose. From the trenchcoat he pulled a car jack and proceeded to smash every piece of glass and dent every panel on the car. It took about twenty seconds.

"Mind if I talk to you for a sec?" he asked, genially, leaning against the crumbled remains of the driver's side window. Andrew was too shocked to say anything. His mouth was very wet. Tiny cubes of glass glittered in his hair. Sarah was whimpering, trying to open her door, which was sealed shut by the warp of metal.

Manser went on: "You have 206 pieces of bone in your body, fine sir. If my client, Mr Anders, does not receive seventeen grand, plus interest at ten per cent a day—which is pretty bloody generous if you ask me—by the end of the week, I will guarantee that after half an hour with me, your bone tally will be double that. And that yummy piece of bitch you've got ripening back home. Laura? I'll have her. You test me. I dare you."

He walked away, magicking the car jack into the jacket and giving them an insouciant wave.

A week later, Andrew set himself on fire in the car which he had locked inside the garage. By the time the fire services got to him he was a black shape, thrashing in the back seat. *Set himself on fire.* Sarah refused to believe that. She was sure that Manser had murdered him. Despite their onerous circumstances, Andrew was not the suicidal type. Laura was everything to him; he'd not leave this world without securing a little piece of it for her.

What then? A nightmare time. A series of safe houses that were anything but. Early morning flits from dingy addresses in Bradford, Cardiff, Bristol and Walsall. He was stickier than anything Bostik might produce. "Bug out," they'd tell her, these kind old men and women, having settled on a code once used by soldiers in some war or another. "Bug out." Manser had contacts everywhere. Arriving in a town that seemed too sleepy even to acknowledge her presence, she'd notice someone out of whack with the place, someone who patently did not fit in but had been planted to watch out for her. Was she so transparent? Her migrations had been random; there was no pattern to unpick. And yet she had stayed no longer than two days in any of these towns. Sarah had hoped that returning to Preston might work for her in a number of ways. Manser wouldn't be expecting it for one thing; for another, Michael, her ex-husband, might be of some help. When she went to visit him though, he paid her short shrift.

"You still owe me fifteen hundred quid," he barked at her. "Pay that off before you come grovelling at my door." She asked if she could use his toilet and passed any number of photographs of Gabrielle, his new squeeze. On the way, she stole from a hook on the wall the spare set of keys to his Alfa Romeo.

It took twenty minutes to negotiate the treacherous field. A light frost had hardened some of the furrows while other grooves were boggy. Sarah scuffed and skidded as best she could, clambering over the token fence that bordered an overgrown garden someone had used as an unauthorized tipping area. She picked her way through sofa skeletons, shattered TV sets, collapsed flat-pack wardrobes and decaying, pungent black bin-bags.

It was obvious that nobody was living here.

Nevertheless, she stabbed the doorbell with a bloody finger. Nothing appeared to ring from within the building. She rapped on the door with her knuckles, but half-heartedly. Already she was scrutinizing the windows, looking for another way in. A narrow path strangled by brambles led around the edge of the house to a woefully neglected rear garden. Scorched colors bled into each other, thorns and convulvulus savaged her ankles as she pushed her way through the tangle. All the windows at the back of the house had been broken, probably by thrown stones. A yellow spray of paint on a set of storm doors that presumably led directly into the cellar picked out a word she didn't understand: *scheintod*. What was that? German? She cursed herself for not knowing the language of her elders, not that it mattered. Someone had tried to obscure the word, scratching it out of the wood with a knife, but the paint was reluctant. She tried the door but it was locked.

Sarah finally gained access via a tiny window that she had to squeeze through. The bruises and gashes on her body cried out as she toppled into a gloomy larder. Mingled into the dust was an acrid, spicy smell; racks of ancient jars and pots were labelled in an extravagant hand: *cumin, coriander, harissa, chili powder*. There were packs of flour and malt that had been ravaged by vermin. Dried herbs dusted her with a strange, slow rain as she brushed past them. Pickling jars held back their pale secrets within dull, lusterless glass.

She moved through the larder, arms outstretched, her eyes becoming accustomed to the gloom. Something arrested the door as she swung it outwards. A dead dog, its fur shaved from its body, lay stiffly in the hallway. At first she thought it was covered in insects, but the black beads were unmoving. They were nicks and slashes in the flesh. The poor thing had been drained. Sarah recoiled from the corpse and staggered further along the corridor. Evidence of squatters lay around her in the shape of fast-food packets, cigarette ends, beer cans and names signed in the ceiling by the sooty flames of candles. A rising stairwell vanished into darkness. Her shoes crunched and squealed on plaster fallen from the bare walls.

"Hello?" she said, querulously. Her voice made as much impact on the house as a candyfloss mallet. It died on the walls, absorbed so swiftly it was as if the house was sucking her in, having been starved of human company for so long. She ascended to the first floor. The carpet that hugged the risers near the bottom gave way to bare wood. Her heels sent dull echoes ringing through the house. If anyone lived here, they would know they were not alone now. The doors opened on to still bedrooms shrouded by dust. There was nothing up here.

"Laura?" And then more stridently, as if volume alone could lend her more spine: "*Laura!*"

Downstairs she found a cozy living room with a hearth filled with ashes. She peeled back a dust cover from one of the sofas and lay down. Her head pounded with delayed shock from the crash and the mustiness of her surroundings. She thought of her baby.

It didn't help that Laura seemed to be going off the rails at the time of their crisis. Also her inability, or reluctance, to talk of her father's death worried Sarah almost as much as the evidence of booze and drug use. At each of the safe houses, it seemed there was a Laura trap in the shape of a young misfit, eager to drag someone down with him or her. Laura gave herself to them all, as if glad of a mate to hasten her downward spiral. There had been one boy in particular, Edgar—a difficult name to forget—whose influence had been particularly invidious. They had been holed up in a Toxteth bedsit. Sarah had been listening to City FM. A talk-show full of languid, catarrhal Liverpool accents that was making her drowsy. The sound of a window smashing had dragged her from slumber. She caught the boy trying to drag her daughter through the glass. She had shrieked at him and hauled him into the room. He could have been no older than ten or eleven. His eyes were rifle green and would not stay still. They darted around like steel bearings in a bagatelle game. Sarah had drilled him, asking him if he had been sent from Manser. Panicked, she had also been firing off instructions to Laura, that they must pack immediately and be ready to go within the hour. It was no longer safe.

And then: Laura, crawling across the floor, holding on to Edgar's leg, pulling herself up, her eyes fogged with what could only be ecstasy. Burying her face in Edgar's crotch. Sarah had shrank from her daughter, horrified. She watched as Laura's free hand travelled beneath her skirt and began to massage at the gusset of her knickers while animal sounds came from her throat. Edgar had grinned at her, showing off a range of tiny, brilliant white teeth. Then he had bent low, whispering something in Laura's ear before charging out of the window with a speed that Sarah thought could only end in tragedy. But when she rushed to the opening, she couldn't see him anywhere.

It had been the devil's own job trying to get her ready to flee Liverpool. She had grown wan and weak and couldn't keep her eyes off the window. Dragging her on to a dawn coach from Mount Pleasant, Laura had been unable to stop crying and as the day wore on, complained of terrible thirst and unbearable pain behind her eyes. She vomited twice and the driver threatened to throw them off the coach unless Laura calmed down. Somehow, Sarah was able to pacify her. She found that shading her from the sunlight helped. A little later, slumped under the seat, Laura fell asleep.

Sarah had begun to question ever leaving Preston in the first place. At least there she had the strength that comes with knowing your environment. Manser had been a problem in Preston but the trouble was that he remained a problem. At least back there, it was just him that she needed to be wary of. Now it seemed Laura's adolescence was going to cause her more of a problem than she believed could be possible. But at the back of her mind, Sarah knew she could never have stayed in her home town. What Manser had proposed, sidling up to her at Andrew's funeral, was that she allow Laura to work for him, whoring. He guaranteed an excellent price for such a perfectly toned, *tight* bit of girl.

"Men go for that," he'd whispered, as she tossed a fistful of soil on to her husband's coffin. "She's got cracking tits for a thirteen-year-old. High. Firm. Nipples up top. Quids in, I promise you. You could have your debt sorted out in a couple of years. And I'll break her in for you. Just so's you know it won't be some stranger nicking her cherry."

That night, they were out of their house, a suitcase full of clothes between them.

"You fucking *beauty*."

Manser depressed the call-end button on his Motorola and slipped the phone into his jacket. Leaning forward, he tapped his driver on the shoulder. "Jez. Get this. Cops found the bitch's car in a fucking field outside Leicester. She'd totalled it."

He slumped back in his seat. The radio masts at Rugby swung by on his left, lights glinting through a thin fog. "Fuck London. You want the A5199. Warp Factor two. And when we catch the minging little tart, we'll show her how to have a road accident. Do the job properly for her. Laura though, Laura comes with us. Nothing happens to Laura. Got it?"

At Knowlden's assent, Manser closed his eyes. This year's number three had died just before he left home. It had been a pity. He liked that one. The sutures on her legs had healed in such a way as to chafe his thigh as he thrust into her. But there had been an infection that he couldn't treat. Pouring antibiotics down her hadn't done an awful lot of good. Gangrene set in. Maybe Laura could be his number four. Once Doctor Losh had done his bit, he would ask him the best way to prevent infection. He knew what Losh's response would be: *let it heal*. But he liked his meat so very rare when he was fucking it. He liked to see a little blood.

---

Sarah woke up to find that her right eye had puffed closed. She caught sight of herself in a shard of broken mirror on the wall. Blood caked half her face and the other half was black with bruises. Her hair was matted. Not for the first time, she wondered if her conviction that Laura had died was misplaced. Yet in the same breath, she couldn't bear to think that she might now be suffering with similar, or worse, injuries. Her thoughts turned to her saviors—if that was what they were. And if so, then why hadn't she been rescued?

She relived the warmth and protection that had enveloped her when those willowy figures had reached inside the car and plucked out her child. Her panic at the thought of Laura either dead or as good as had been ironed flat. She felt safe and, inexplicably, had not raged at this outrageous kidnap; indeed, she had virtually sanctioned it. Perhaps it had been the craziness inspired by the accident, or endorphins stifling her pain that had brought about her indifference. Still, what should have been anger and guilt was neutralized by the compulsion that Laura was in safe hands. What she didn't want to examine too minutely was the feeling that she missed the rescue party more than she did her own daughter.

Refreshed a little by her sleep, but appalled at the catalogue of new aches and pains that jarred each movement, Sarah made her way back to the larder where she found some crackers in an airtight tin. Chewing on these, she revisited the hallway and dragged open the heavy curtains, allowing some of the late afternoon light to invade. Almost immediately she saw the door under the stairs. She saw how she had missed it earlier; it was hewn from the same dark wood and there was no door handle as such, just a little recess to hook your fingers into. She tried it but it wouldn't budge. Which meant it was locked from the inside. Which meant that somebody must be down there.

"Laura?" she called, tapping on the wood with her fingernails. "Laura, it's Mum. Are you in there?"

She listened hard, her ear flush against the crack of the jamb. All she could hear was the gust of subterranean breezes moving through what ought to be the cellar. She must check it out; Laura could be down there, bleeding her last.

Sarah hunted down the kitchen. A large pine table sat at one end of the room, a dried orange with a heart of mold at its center. She found a stack of old newspapers bound up with twine from the early 1970s by a back door that was forbiddingly black and excessively padlocked. Ransacking the drawers and cupboards brought scant reward. She was about to give in when the suck of air from the last yanked cupboard door brought a small screwdriver rolling into view. She grabbed the tool and scurried back to the cellar door.

Manser stayed Knowlden with a finger curled around his lapel. "Are you carrying?"

Knowlden had parked the car off the road on the opposite side to the crash site. Now the two men were standing by the wreck of the Alfa. Knowlden had spotted the house and suggested they check it out. If Sarah and her daughter had survived the crash—and the empty car suggested that they had—then they might have found some neighborly help.

"I hope you fucking are," Manser warned.

"I'm carrying okay. Don't sweat it."

Manser's eyebrows went north. "Don't tell me to not sweat it, pup. Or you'll find yourself doing seventy back up the motorway without a fucking car underneath you."

The sun sinking fast, they hurried across the field, constantly checking the road behind them as they did so. Happy that nobody had seen them, Manser nodded his head in the direction of the front door. "Kick the mud off your boots on that bastard," he said.

It was 5:14 p.m.

Sarah was halfway down the cellar stairs and wishing she had a flashlight with her when she heard the first blows raining down on the door. She was about to return to the hallway when she heard movement from below. A *lot* of movement. Creaks and whispers and hisses. There was a sound as of soot trickling down a flue. A chatter: teeth in the cold? A sigh.

"Laura?"

A chuckle.

The door gave in just before Knowlden was about to. His face was greasy with sweat and hoops of dampness spoiled his otherwise pristine shirt.

"Gun," Manser said, holding his hand out. Knowlden passed him the weapon, barely disguising his disdain for his boss. "You want to get some muesli down you, mate," Manser said. "Get yourself fit." He checked the piece was loaded and entered the house, muzzle pointing ahead of him, cocked horizontally. Something he'd done since seeing Brad Pitt do the same thing in *Seven*.

"Knock, knock," he called out. "Daddy's home."

Sarah heard, just before all hell broke loose, Laura's voice, firm and even, say: "Do not touch her." Then she was knocked back on the stairs by a flurry of black leather and she was aware only of bloody-eyed, pale-skinned figures flocking past her. And teeth. She saw each leering mouth as if in slow motion, dark lips peeled back to reveal teeth so white they might have been sculpted from ice.

She thought she saw Laura among them and tried to grab hold of her jumper but she was left clutching air as the scrum piled into the hallway, whooping and screaming like a gang of kids let out early from school. When the shooting started she couldn't tell if the screaming had changed in pitch at all, whether it had become more panicked. But at the top of the stairs she realized she was responsible for most of it. There appeared to be some kind of stand-off. Manser, the fetid little sniffer dog of a man, was waving a gun around while his henchman clenched and unclenched his hands, eyeing up the opposition, which was substantial. Sarah studied them properly for the first time, these women who had rescued her baby and left her to die in the car. And yet proper examination was beyond her. There were four of them, she thought. Maybe five. They moved around and against each other so swiftly, so lissomely that she couldn't be sure. They were like a flesh knot. Eyes fast on their enemy, they guarded each other with this mesmerizing display. It was so seamless it could have been choreographed.

But now she saw that they were not just protecting each other. There was someone at the heart of the knot, appearing and disappearing in little ribbons and teasers of colour. Sarah need see only a portion of face to know they were wrapped around her daughter.

"Laura," she said again.

Manser said, "Who the fuck are these clowns? Have we just walked into Goth night down the local student bar, or what?"

"Laura," Sarah said again, ignoring her pursuer. "Come here."

"Everyone just stand back. I'm having the girl. And to show you I'm not just pissing in my paddling pool . . ." Manser took aim and shot one of the women through the forehead.

Sarah covered her mouth as the woman dropped. The three others seemed to fade somewhat, as if their strength had been affected.

"Jez," said Manser. "Get the girl."

Sarah leaped at Knowlden as he strode into the pack but a stiff arm across her chest knocked her back against the wall, winding her. He extricated Laura from her guardians and dragged her kicking back to his boss.

Manser was nodding his head. "Nice work, Jez. You can have jelly for afters tonight. Get her outside."

To Sarah he said, "Give her up." And then he was gone.

Slumped on the floor, Sarah tried to blink a fresh trickle of blood from her eyes. Through the fluid, she thought she could see the women crowding around their companion. She thought she could see them lifting her head as they positioned themselves around her. But no. No. She couldn't accept that she was seeing what they began to do to her then.

Knowlden fell off the pace as they ran towards the car. Manser was half dragging, half carrying Laura who was thrashing around in his arms.

"I'm nearly ready," she said. "I'll bite you! I'll bite you, I swear to God."

"And I'll scratch your eyes out," Manser retorted. "Now shut the fuck up. Jesus, can't you do what girls your age do in the movies? Faint, or something?"

At the car, he bundled her into the trunk and locked it shut. Then he fell against the side of the car and tried to control his breathing. He could just see Knowlden plodding towards him in the dark. Manser could hear his squealing lungs even though he had another forty meters or so to cover.

"Come on Jez, for fuck's sake! I've seen mascara run faster than that."

At thirty meters, Manser had a clearer view of his driver as he died.

One of the women they had left behind in the house was moving across the field at a speed that defied logic. Her hands were outstretched and her nails glinted like polished arrowheads. Manser moved quickly himself when he saw how she slammed into his chauffeur. He was in third gear before he realized he hadn't taken the handbrake off and he was laughing harder than he had ever laughed in his life. Knowlden's heart had been skewered on the end of her claws like a piece of meat on a kebab. He didn't stop laughing until he hit the M1, southbound.

Knowlden was forgotten. All he had on his mind now was Laura, naked on the slab, her body marked out like the charts on a butcher's wall.

Dazed, Sarah was helped to her feet. Their hands held her everywhere and nowhere, moving along her body as soft as silk. She tried to talk but whenever she opened her mouth, someone's hand, cold and rank, slipped over it. She saw the pattern in the curtains travel by in a blur though she could not feel her feet on the floor. Then the night was upon them, and the frost in the air sang around her ears as she was swept into the sky, embedded at the center of their slippery mesh of bodies, smelling their clothes and the scent of something ageless and black, lifting off the skin like forbidden perfume. *Is she all right now?* she wanted to ask, but her words wouldn't form in the ceaseless blast of cold air. Sarah couldn't count the women that cavorted around her. She drifted into unconsciousness thinking of how they had opened the veins in their chests for her, how the charge of fluid had engulfed her face, bubbling on her tongue and nostrils like dark wine. How her eyes had flicked open and rolled back into their sockets with the unspeakable rapture of it all.

Having phoned ahead, Manser parked the car at midnight on South Wharf Road, just by the junction with Praed Street. He was early, so instead of going directly to the dilapidated pub on the corner he sauntered to the bridge over Paddington Basin and stared up at the Westway, hoping for calm. The sounds emanating from that elevated sweep were anything but soothing. The mechanical sigh of speeding vehicles reminded him only of the way those witches' mouths had breathed, snake-like jaws unhinged as though in readiness to swallow him whole. The hiss of tires on rain-soaked tarmac put him in mind of nothing but the wet air that had sped from Knowlden's chest when he was torn open.

By the time he returned, he saw in the pub a low-wattage bulb turning the glass of an upstairs window milky. He went to the door and tapped on it with a coin in a prearranged code. Then he went back to the car and opened the boot. He wrestled with Laura and managed to clamp a hand over her mouth, which she bit, hard. Swearing, he dragged a handkerchief from his pocket and stuffed it in her mouth, punching her twice to get her still. The pain in his hand was mammoth. She had teeth like razors. Flaps of skin hung off his palm; he was bleeding badly. Woozy at the sight of the wound, he staggered with Laura to the door, which was now open. He went through it and kicked it shut, checking the street to make sure he hadn't been seen. Upstairs, Losh was sitting in a chair containing more holes than stuffing.

"This was a good boozer before it was closed down," Manser said, his excitement unfolding deep within him.

"Was," Losh said, keeping his eyes on him. He wore a butcher's apron that was slathered with blood. He smoked a cigarette, the end of which was patterned with bloody prints from his fingers. A comma of blood could be mistaken for a kiss-curl on his forehead. "Everything changes."

"You don't," Manser said. "Christ. Don't you ever wash?"

"What's the point? I'm a busy man."

"How many years you been struck off?"

Losh smiled. "Didn't anybody ever warn you not to piss off the people you need help from?"

Manser swallowed his distaste of the smaller man. "Nobody warns me nothing," he spat. "Can't we get on?"

Losh stood up and stretched. "Cash," he said, luxuriously.

Manser pulled a wad from his jacket. "There's six grand there. As always."

"I believe you. I'd count it but the bank get a bit miffed if they get blood on their bills."

"Why don't you wear gloves?"

"The magic. It's all in the fingers." Losh gestured towards Laura. "This the one?"

"Of course."

"Pretty thing. Nice legs." Losh laughed. Manser closed his eyes. Losh said, "What you after?"

Manser said, "The works."

Wide eyes from Losh. "Then let's call it eight thou."

A pause. Manser said, "I don't have it with me. I can get it tomorrow. Keep the car tonight. As collateral."

Losh said, "Done."

The first incision. Blood squirted up the apron, much brighter than the stains already painted upon it. A coppery smell filled the room. The pockets of the pool table upon which Laura was spread were filled with beer towels.

"Soft tissue?"

Manser's voice was dry. He needed a drink. His cock was as hard as a house brick. "As much off as possible."

"She won't last long," Losh said.

Manser stared at him. "She'll last long enough."

Losh said, "Got a number five in mind already?"

Manser didn't say a word. Losh reached behind him and picked up a Samsonite suitcase. He opened it and pulled out a hacksaw. Its teeth entertained the light and flung it in every direction. At least Losh kept his tools clean.

The operation took four hours. Manser fell asleep at one point and dreamed of his hand overpowering the rest of his body, dragging him around the city while the mouth that slavered and snarled at the center of his palm cupped itself around the stomachs of passers-by and devoured them.

He wakened, rimed with perspiration, to see Losh chewing an errant hangnail and tossing his instruments back into the suitcase. Laura was wrapped in white bath towels. They were crimson now.

"Is she okay?" Manser asked. Losh's laughter in reply was infectious and soon he was at it too.

"Do you want the offcuts?" Losh asked, wiping his eyes and jerking a thumb at a bucket tastefully covered with a dishcloth.

"You keep them," Manser said. "I've got to be off."

Losh said, "Who opened the window?"

Nobody had opened the window; the lace curtains fluttering inward were being pushed by the bulge of glass. Losh tore them back just as the glass shattered in his face. He screamed and fell backwards, tripping on the bucket and sprawling on to the floor.

To Manser it seemed that strips of the night were pouring in through the broken window. They fastened themselves to Losh's face and neck and munched through the flesh like a caterpillar at a leaf. His screams were low and already being disguised by blood as his throat filled. He began to choke but managed one last, hearty shriek as a major blood vessel parted, spraying color all around the room with the abandon of an unmanned hosepipe.

*How can they breathe with their heads so deep inside him?* Manser thought, hypnotized by the violence. He felt something dripping on his brow. Touching his face with his fingers, he brought them away to find them awash with blood. He had time to register, as he looked up at the ceiling, the mouth as it yawned, dribbling with lymph, the head as it vibrated with unfettered anticipation. And then the woman dropped on him, ploughing her jaws through the meat of his throat and ripping clear. He saw his flesh disappear down her gullet with a spasm that was almost beautiful. But then his sight filled with red and he could understand no more.

She had been back home for a day. She couldn't understand how she had got here. She remembered being born from the warmth of her companions and standing up to find both men little more than pink froth filling their suits. One of the men had blood on his hands and a cigarette smouldered between his fingers. The hand was on the other side of the room, though.

She saw the bloody, tiny mound of towels on the pool table. She saw the bucket; the dishcloth had shifted, revealing enough to tell her the game. Two toes was enough. She didn't need to be drawn a picture.

And then somehow she found herself outside. And then on Edgware Road where a pretty young woman with dark hair and a woven shoulder bag gave her a couple of pounds so that she could get the tube to Euston. And then a man smelling of milk and boot polish she fucked in a shop doorway for her fare north. And then Preston, freezing around her in the early morning as if it were formed from winter itself. She had half expected Andrew to poke his head around the corner of their living-room to say hello, the tea's on, go and sit by the fire and I'll bring some to you.

But the living room was cold and bare. She found sleep at the time she needed it most, just as her thoughts were about to coalesce around the broken image of her baby. She was crying because she couldn't remember what her face looked like.

When she revived, it was dark again. It was as if daylight had forsaken her. She heard movement towards the back of the house. Outside, in the tiny, scruffy garden, a cardboard box, no bigger than the type used to store shoes, made a stark shape amid the surrounding frost. The women were hunched on the back fence, regarding her with owlish eyes. They didn't speak. Maybe they couldn't.

One of them swooped down and landed by the box. She nudged it forward with her hand, as a deer might coax a newborn to its feet. Sarah felt another burst of unconditional love and security fill the gap between them all. Then they were gone, whipping and twisting far into the sky, the consistency, the trickiness of smoke.

Sarah took the box into the living room with her and waited. Hours passed; she felt herself become more and more peaceful. She loved her daughter and she hoped Laura knew that. As dawn began to brush away the soot from the sky, Sarah leaned over and touched the lid. She wanted so much to open it and say a few words, but she couldn't bring herself to do it.

In the end, she didn't need to. Whatever remained inside the box managed to do it for her.

# Rites: Cleaning the Last Bones

Gavin J. Grant was born and raised in Scotland, and now lives in Brooklyn, New York. He is publisher of Small Beer Press, editor of the literary fantasy/ sf/surrealism journal Lady Churchill's Rosebud Wristlet, and works for booksense.com, the independent bookstore online portal. He is also a fiction writer and poet whose work has appeared in Altair, Aberrations, The Urban Pantheist, and online at SCIFI.COM.

His story "Ship, Sea, Mountain, Sky," cowritten with Kelly Link, appeared in last year's volume of The Year's Best Fantasy & Horror. The following poem is a dark fantasia reprinted from the Dark Planet online journal—www.sfsite.com/darkplanet/poetry/.

—T. W.

Crow hopped forward and plucked the eye,
Held it high for all to see.
With a jerk, swallowed it whole.

Lion padded quietly up through accustomed space,
Left the ribs neatly to the side.
Choked the tough heart down.

Softer parts vanished in a sharp-toothed liquid rush of fur,
Insects rose and fell, fell and rose.
—Waves on a disappearing beach.

Monkey took a rock
And soon was feeding alone
On delicate gray matter.

Cat watched, licking one paw, then the other.
Dog watched, a deeper silence.

Something worried at tendons, ligaments,
Something sucked at the long cracked bones,
Interwoven, footprints mapped the human form.

A gentle breeze blew a dry
brown sycamore leaf over the skeleton.
Night came.

# JEAN-CLAUDE DUNYACH

# Watch Me When I Sleep

*Jean-Claude Dunyach, born in 1957, has a Ph.D. in applied mathematics and supercomputing. He works for Airbus in Toulouse. He has been writing science fiction since the beginning of the 1980s, and has published seven novels and five collections of short stories.*

*His latest novel, Etoiles Mourantes (Dying Stars), written in collaboration with the French writer Ayerdhal, won the Grand Prix de la Tour Eiffel in 1999 as well as the Prix Ozone. He also writes lyrics for several French singers—this experience served as an inspiration for one of his novels about a rock and roll singer touring in Antarctica with a zombie philharmonic orchestra.*

*The author would like to thank Sheryl Curtis, his translator, for making his story read better in English than he feels it does in French.*

*"Watch Me When I Sleep" was first published in* Interzone.

—E. D.

I swallowed my fairy when I was twelve years old. It was an accident. It was too hot to watch the goats and I fell asleep at the edge of the rushing stream, my head on a piece of sun-warmed shale. I guess my mouth was open—I do snore sometimes. And I was dreaming. Fairies can hear unspoken wishes, desires and curses, but dreams attract them more than anything else.

I felt her slip between my lips, the cutting edge of her wings slicing my tongue. I bit down, by reflex, but it was too late. My cry frightened the herd. My mouth sticky with blood, I called my dog to help me bring back the goats. I drank the icy water that raced down from the mountains until my teeth ached.

As I walked back along the rushing stream to the farm, I felt the fairy gently tickle my innards. She was preparing her nest in the acid cavity of my stomach. Somehow, none of this frightened me.

My father's anger did, though.

I prepared the meal—my mother died giving birth to me and my aunt has difficulty walking when it's hot out. So she settles for giving orders and waving her cane about. Since she was never able to have children to pass the farm on to, she's not terribly fond of me. She bombarded me with questions when I came back earlier than expected with the goats still hungry. She shook her head as she examined the cuts on my lips before sending me off to the kitchen.

I heard my father and my uncle come in from the fields, then my aunt's voice even sharper than usual, "Your idiot son was sleeping instead of watching the flock. He caught a fairy!"

The kitchen door opened. My uncle held back, supporting his wife against him. My father walked toward me, a leather belt in his hand.

"You'll leave for town this evening," he murmured, looking me straight in the eye. "But before you go, I'll teach you to daydream when there's work to be done!"

He wasn't a bad man. And if it had been just the two of us, his punishment would have been just. I made no effort to get away, even when my aunt started to egg him on in her strident voice. The fairy was starting to secrete her poison in my innards and I didn't really feel his blows. I should have pretended to suffer, I guess, faking pain as in the old stories. But I was too young to know any better.

Since I didn't cry, my uncle joined in as well, picking up the broom. The handle broke against my leg and I heard the bone splinter. Then the pain hit me, so strong that I cried out before fainting away in front of the fireplace.

When I awoke, I was lying on the kitchen table, my fractured leg held straight by a makeshift splint. The two pieces of the broom handle were secured to my leg, stretching along either side of my knee, tufts of heather still tied to the end. Nothing is allowed to go to waste in my uncle's house. The pain that radiated from my fracture mingled with the burning caused by the lacerations on my back and in my mouth.

"I'm sorry, son," said a voice above me.

My father bent over my leg, without touching it. The house was silent.

"Your uncle has gone to fetch the blacksmith. I set the bone myself. It was a clean break—you'll walk again."

I blinked, exhausted by the pain. Bundles of herbs hung from the ceiling, their odour long gone. Shadows formed bruises along the smoke-blackened beams.

"You can't leave here," my father added in a weary voice. "It will be a month before your leg heals and you can bear the trip. That's too long. You have to be brave."

"What about the fairy?" I asked, overwhelmed as my memories returned.

"Don't say that word! She'll hear you."

He placed a large hand, smelling of dirt and the stable, over my mouth.

"That filth could hatch any time and get away from you. Do you know what will happen next?" His eyes bored into mine. "Do you?"

I nodded and groaned despite the gag. The pain gradually ebbed, proof that the fairy was there, in my stomach, weaving her cocoon. My stomach acids were working on her, transforming her. When she was ready, she would fly out of me, if I allowed her to, and the link woven between us would never be broken after that. She would respond to my call and dance before me, invisible to anyone else. Fairies change those who host them. Every child knows that.

During my sole visit to town, for the Fall fair the year I turned ten, my uncle had taken me to see a boy with unkempt hair, who was almost twice my age. Imprisoned in a cage, locked with a simple latch, he spoke to his fingers as he wriggled them in the light, like a puppet play filled with princes and birds. The stories he stammered were too fleeting to be understood. His eyes had been burned from staring at the sun without blinking.

My uncle gave the boy's mother two piece of copper so I could get a close look at him. This unexpected generosity struck me as much as the spectacle of the cage and its occupant.

"You'll be brave when the blacksmith arrives," my father pressed me. It was both an order and a plea. I groaned under his hand, not understanding. He bent down close to me and with the few words he had he explained what they were going to do to me. What they were forced to do to me. For my own good.

I believe I screamed. I passed out again when the blacksmith used his tongs. My father wouldn't let anyone hold me while they pulled out several of my teeth.

When I awoke again, lying in the bed that had belonged to my mother, two closed rings had been inserted at the corners of my mouth preventing me from opening it. A muzzle, forged in haste, forced its way through my teeth in holes drilled with a red-hot nail. Iron fangs held my jaws closed, while I groaned constantly with the suffering. My entire body hurt. Waves, first hot then icy, rolled up my leg, coiling in my belly and exploding through my lips like an aborted cry. With each breath, a thick, ashy-tasting foam filled my mouth with bitterness.

At the beginning, they tied my hands to the bedposts, so I couldn't hurt myself trying to tear the rings out. But after a week I was so weak I could barely move. Eventually, they untied me. To prevent me from starving to death, the blacksmith had pulled two of my top teeth. The hole was just large enough to allow a little goat's milk, broth and all the wine my father could get his hands on through. Before setting off for the fields each morning, he patiently fed me, deaf to my aunt's complaints that he would be late. Then I lay there alone until nightfall when he would come and talk to me about the herd and the scent of hay, as he washed me with a ball of straw dipped in water.

They left me something to chew on but I could no longer bite down. During the early hours of the day, when the pain left me alone, I imagined all kinds of curses, without being able to utter them. The rest of the time, I listened to the blood pound in the cavern of my mouth and waited for my bones to knit.

I was twelve years old and knew nothing of silence. I lost weight. I was in pain. Time passed. In my mind's eye, I drew on the whitewashed walls, rubbing the rings that muzzled me with my fingertips. My fracture was slow to heal and my father spent every evening at my bedside. There was less wine and more milk in the drink he spooned through the hole in my teeth, sometimes even a meat broth or a beaten egg. Towards the end, I could feed myself—my hands had almost stopped shaking—but I couldn't make him understand that.

"Save your breath," he murmured, wiping the dirt off my chin.

The fairy was transforming in my belly and my dreams were tinted with bright colours. But I always woke up alone, without the slightest memory, and the muzzle prevented me from crying out in my sleep.

I started by posing my foot gently on the floor, in a careful effort to walk over to the chamber pot that my aunt always left at the other end of the room. Then, one day, I managed to walk with the crutch my father had made for me out of pieces of ash. The wood, carved green, creaked with every step. Traces of sap stuck to my skin, like some poorly healed wound oozing under my fingers. In the basin of water that sat on the windowsill, my reflection stared back at me like a rebellious horse. The laugh that this vision brought to my lips filled my eyes with tears.

The evening I was able to go down the stairs on my own to sit at the dinner table, my uncle set down the grey loaf of bread he was cutting and glanced heavily towards his wife.

"We'll leave tomorrow."

Nodding, I took the bowl of goat's milk my father held out to me. I poured the liquid carefully between my teeth. A rivulet dribbled down my chin and into a puddle on the table. The metal muzzle clicked against the bowl, like a clock. No one else was eating. I turned towards my aunt and she backed away, eyes wide with fear.

"It's already too late," she murmured, crossing her fingers in front of her. "There's evil in that child!"

My father railed against her and my uncle cursed me. As for me, I no longer listened to them. Inside my head, the fairy had started to talk.

"I'll teach you stories," the voice said.

I lay stretched out on sacks of potatoes, at the back of the cart. It was drizzling and my lips were wet. I could neither answer the fairy nor complain. My uncle was afraid of the storm. "Your muzzle will attract lightning," he grumbled, cracking the whip.

So I kept watch as the dark clouds approached. The town was a day's travel away. Since we wouldn't arrive until sunset, we'd either have to pay for a night at the inn or sleep in the mud, under the cart. Stories don't keep the rain off.

"I'll tell you secrets," the voice started in again.

I thought about the goats I'd left alone, about my dog who had run off because no one had bothered to feed him while I was healing. There are no secrets, only things no one has time to take care of.

"You'll do better than you'd think by looking at you," insisted the fairy.

I could see my face reflected in my uncle's eyes. I know how he saw me. When he'd harnessed the horse, he had looked at the leather straps and the rings in my mouth, shaking his head. Appearances may be deceiving, but the truth is often worse.

The fairy fidgeted in my stomach. During the night, she had threaded her way up to the impassable barrier of my teeth and I had heard her weep. Her sobs sounded like a waterfall in winter, when the last threads of water crack the ice. I would have liked to tell her that none of this was my choosing, but my words came up short against the muzzle. Finally, I groaned out the only song I knew, as best I could, until she stopped.

"I don't want you to be different from us," my father had told me before locking my jaw. I only wish I had never wanted that either.

I finally managed to sleep, despite the voice and the rain, waking with the clop clop clop of horseshoes on pavement. The lightning had spared me and the muddy trail had changed into a decent road. We were approaching the wooden ramparts. The odour of smoke and rot hung in the air, with traces of other scents I couldn't identify—some sweet, others painfully spicy. Guards stopped us, then rummaged through the hay with their pitchforks. My uncle paid them, grumbling the whole time, and they let us through the gates. Above us, ferns burned in stone troughs along the rampart walk. The first stars were just coming out and the shopkeepers had already closed the shutters that protected their stands. Yet, people were still out in the streets. The town was a closed world, a world with different rules that my uncle barely understood and never discussed. Yet, when I saw how the townspeople looked me up and down, I knew that the differences did not run deep.

"I'll give you whatever you want," begged the fairy.

I sat down, my back against the hay, and stared back at the passers-by. My uncle could have had them pay to stare at my strangeness, but I quickly realized that he was too ashamed to even think of it. I didn't dare ask for anything either. My dreams were too simple and I wasn't sure that what I wanted really existed.

"You'll guard the cart," my uncle said as he unhooked the horses. "I'll be back tomorrow at dawn. If someone comes up to the cart, show yourself. Your mug would scare any thief away!"

He took care of the horse, placing the blanket I had brought over its back. Then he walked off, leading the horse by its bridle into the shadows at the end of street. I couldn't make out where he was headed.

We had stopped in a small square surrounded by houses with closed shutters through which the scent of hot soup and cabbage escaped into the night. I burrowed into the hay, not daring to wander off from the cart. The night was damp and cool. The fairy was silent. I watched the moon hiding behind the clouds for a long time. Her pockmarked face was even uglier than mine, but she smiled, safe from the grasp of the world.

I wasn't really sleepy. The town sung with a thousand new sounds that prevented me from finding any peace. I rubbed my swollen gums gently, listening to the clink of the rings on my muzzle. The cluster of buildings crowded in around me, more houses, streets and walls than I had ever seen in my life. The line of the rooftops formed an alphabet against the sky punctuated by the moving lights of the guards who protected us from the outside. The outside world was vast beyond all reason. Enclosed in my cage of iron and hay, I thought about my uncle's farm and the pasture trails I knew by heart. The pain in my teeth would soon be gone. Even my leg was healing.

In the pit of my stomach, I suddenly felt the fairy stir and I understood just how alone I felt. I would have liked my father to come with us to town, but my uncle would never have allowed it. I listened, in case the voice in my head started to speak again. She was a prisoner too and we each had cause to hate the other.

I groaned and stretched, not rousing the fairy. In my stomach, the cocoon had opened and the fairy had taken refuge in it. I imagined her draped with the strips of her former refuge, in the depths of a dark cavern that must appear as incomprehensible to her as the world. My uncle had told me that she would tempt me in every way possible. I hadn't realized there would be so few.

"Are you sleeping?"

I had to spit out every syllable, stretching my jaws as far as I could. Hands on my stomach, I waited for an answer that took a long time coming.

"You don't want me," the voice said.

I shook my head, metal clanking. The night amplified the sounds, making them even sharper. I couldn't tell her just how much I understood her, or why both her destiny and mine were sealed in the same manner. All that came out of my mouth was a terrible gurgling.

Three times, I scraped my lips and tongue against the rings, trying to shape the words that haunted me. What I wanted was too simple for her. No kingdoms, no treasures, no extraordinary powers for me. Just something I wasn't even sure I could enjoy.

"Watch me when I sleep," I begged, unable to make myself understood.

Then I wiped the bloody slobber from my chin and waited.

"I had so much to give," said the fairy, "And I had to happen on you."

I thought she was going to start crying again, but her store of tears had been exhausted. She said good night to me in a weary voice and I counted stars until everything blurred before my eyes.

The roosters woke me at dawn. My uncle arrived shortly after that, leading the horse behind him. The sound of shutters being opened mingled with the shouts of the first merchants and the chirping of the birds. The air smelled of smoke. I was hungry.

"I lost two handfuls of coins to the guards," my uncle said, without looking at me. "Their dice are so loaded they can't even roll them. This whole situation has cost me a fortune. I hope you remember that!"

He harnessed the horse and gave him a sharp crack on the rump. The cart started forward with a grinding of axles. A window opened above us and I just barely escaped the contents of a chamber pot.

"Old Grimlich is waiting for us. You'll do exactly what he tells you to. He's seen more fairies blown that he has hairs on his head."

My uncle snorted briefly and drew a heel of bread from under his tunic. I was so hungry I couldn't keep my mouth from watering. The rings were rusting against my tongue and I licked them to ease the pain. The clack of hooves on cobblestone rattled my teeth.

I smelled the glassblower's shop before I saw it. The odour of molten glass and burning seaweed filled the street. The house was long and narrow, with a workshop at the back and a flat for apprentices in the loft. There was even a ring for tying up a horse, as in the rich houses my father had told me about to help me sleep.

My uncle took up the tongs and helped me out of the cart, roughly brushing the hay off my breeches. I leaned on my crutch and followed him inside. A young servant who was coming out of the shop turned away, appeared to change her mind, and gave me an encouraging smile. I smiled back as well as I could, scraping my lips on the rings. She remained on the doorstep, watching me, until I went behind the counter. In the very back, a door led to the glass shop.

The heat struck me like a club. In the middle of the room, stood a crucible filled with a molten paste, suspended over a furnace. A stunted old man, wearing a leather apron, was busy with the flames. Behind him, hooks and blades of all kinds lay on a workbench, along with flattened flasks that reflected the flames. A metal rod with a flared end stood in a bucket of ashy water. It was taller than I was and as thick as a snake. I had never seen anything like it.

In the pit of my stomach the fairy started to wriggle about.

Pushed by my uncle, I walked towards the fire. The ground crackled under my clogs and burning grit flared out from under the crucible. I had left the crutch against the door so it wouldn't catch fire.

"Your son?" the old man asked, without looking up. "He knows what to do?"

"My brother's son. Yes, he knows. He'll obey." Looking at me sideways, he added, "All in all, he's not a bad boy."

"The money?"

My uncle dug through his purse. Old Grimlich bit each coin before placing it in the pocket of his apron. Then he spat on his fingers and picked up the rod.

"If you want help selling it, I'll take a third of what you get," he said as he plunged the end of the tube into the crucible of molten glass. "That's a lot, but my clients are rich enough to satisfy both of us. Prepare the boy!"

Suddenly nauseous, I bent over. My uncle pressed his large hand against the nape of my neck, forcing me to straighten up.

"You'll be free soon enough," he said as he brought the tongs up towards my face. "I'm going to break the rings so you can open your jaw. But don't open your mouth until I tell you to. Then and only then you have to blow with all your might into the tube . . ."

"You must blow from deep, deep inside," said Grimlich. "Like when you shout."

"Are you ready?"

An ocean of acid filled me. The fairy was quiet, but I could feel her blindly hitting against the walls of my stomach. I couldn't stop myself from sobbing as I thought of the suffering I would be inflicting on her. My uncle sniffed in fury and caught my head under his arm. The tongs bit into the metal. With a crack, the first ring broke. Then the second. The fangs of the muzzle gave way next and my gums started to bleed.

"Keep your mouth closed, boy!" ordered the old man. "And look at me!"

The metal rod came up out of the crucible, a globe of molten glass wobbling at the end. The old man puffed up his cheeks and raised the end of the tube to his lips. By the light of the flames, I could see the veins in his forehead swell as he blew with everything he had.

Once the glass ball had swollen to the size of my two clenched fists, he turned it above the flames. My uncle released me, still waving the tongs about in front of my eyes. The pain in my mouth had never been so intense.

"Now!" shouted Grimlich.

He placed the end of the tube against my swollen lips.

My stomach churned as I tasted his saliva. Like an echo, a cry rose up from deep within me. There were no words. Nothing but pure terror resonating within my bones. My uncle held me by the shoulders and the old man held the cane over the crucible. Just as I was about to start screaming myself, he struck me forcefully in the stomach. A flood of bile filled my mouth and I blew with all my might to keep from choking.

The fairy blew out of me.

In the shop with its reddish shadows, she shone like the sun. Crumpled by my breath, she flew out curled up in a ball, into the molten glass. She tried to spread her wings despite the horrible heat, despite the pain. Iridescent reflections spun in a whirlpool in the heart of the glass. Her cry was drowned in the molten mass. Finally, I no longer heard her.

"Easy, there," said Grimlich, as he took the rod from my hands. "I'll do the rest." My uncle released me. I fell to my knees and vomited again. Heaving, I expelled the cocoon like the placenta of a stillborn baby. I didn't dare raise my eyes to look at what was left of the fairy.

"I'll get a good price for this," my uncle exulted. "All those colours!" "She'll be cool enough to touch soon," said the glassblower. "It's curious, but it's almost as if these filthy things absorb all the heat from within. Look at her, it's as if she's still moving."

I felt my temples pound. Groaning, I stood up, grabbed the tongs from my uncle's hand and struck the glass ball hanging from the end of the tube. It cracked with a dry tinkling, then burst open and shattered. My uncle roared, but I waved the tongs at him and he backed away, protecting his face.

The fairy spun like a leaf towards the ground. Fine needles of crystal pierced through her torso and her transparent wings crumbled to dust between my fingers as I tried to hold on to her. Sparks rained down from the fire, igniting her hair.

She burned like a rainbow.

Since that time, the wind whistles through the holes in my teeth and I smile less frequently. I never left the farm again. When I stretch out along the river, the sky is immense and empty above me. The clouds no longer write their white poems and I no longer know how to read the symbols in the water. I either digested my dreams from that time, or vomited them out.

My uncle died first. Then my father. My aunt had an attack that left her unable to speak. Sometimes I sit in front of her, beyond the reach of her cane, so that she can watch my face and try to respond with her eyes. She's the only family I have, after all.

I still snore with my mouth open. But now I sleep inside, safe behind locked windows. No fairy has ever come to watch me when I sleep.

# PATRICK ROSCOE

## The Tattoo Artist

*Patrick Roscoe was born in Spain and now divides his time between Spain and Vancouver. He is the author of numerous books, including* God's Peculiar Care, The Lost Oasis, *and* Love is Starving Itself.

*"The Tattoo Artist" is a mysterious, evocative tale first published in the Canadian literary journal* Descant *(Fall 2001 edition). It also appears in Roscoe's splendid new collection* The Truth About Love.

—T. W.

It was not easy to find the tattoo artist, though his skill was renowned throughout the town and far beyond. Away from boulevards and cafes, away from lights and crowds, he lived among the narrow, twisting alleys behind the *quartier portugais*. These were lit only by weak lamps attached infrequently to cold stone walls, and often dark rats roamed freely within the gutters and the waste. Few people passed over the rough cobblestones then; occupants were silent, if not sleeping, behind closed doors to either side; the doors were unnumbered as the alleys were not named. Except for a cat's sudden scream, or the squeak of a bat, there were no sounds except my footstep and heartbeat echoing against stone. I knew it was possible to find the tattoo artist only on a night without stars, when he did not prick coloured constellations upon the black skin of the sky.

Yet a sign did not hang helpfully upon the artist's door; nor did the door stand open in invitation. Within the labyrinth the tattoo artist's location itself remained as elusively unfixed as a fugitive's, though it was purported that his room was always the same bare, cement space illuminated by a candle, half-burned, whose light transformed the ancient dyes and needles into substances sheened with gold. If you could discover the secret way to the tattoo artist, the path of your life would be forever changed, it was averred in the tone of absolute certainty only ignorance can evoke: nothing and everything was known about this man whom the mute would describe in clear, precise detail if only they could speak. Perhaps he strolled through the *souk*, unrecognized but not disguised, to hear the stories told about him—all contradictory, all unproven—when we wearied of discussing the sixty lessons of the Koran or the reason for changing tides.

In the town we all grew up with mother's dire warnings that if we were not careful the tattoo artist would etch hideous, permanent pictures upon our sleeping skin. Later we learned that possibly his designs could attract the ideal lover who would not waver, who would not stray. Some said he substituted poison for ink when sought out by an evil man and some suggested that in certain worthy cases his handiwork could cure sickness and even extend life. There were those too who claimed that his instruments were the tools of Allah, and his images the Prophet's revelation. It was agreed that one needed to seek the tattoo artist at the correct time of life: overly tender skin would fester, blister and scar beneath his needles, while tough and weathered flesh would break them. The tattoo artist was a Jew from Essaouira, a *marabout* from Tarfaya, a Berber murderer or thief. Perhaps he was a distant cousin on your mother's side, the beggar disintegrating with leprosy before the Cinema Le Paris, that pilgrim glimpsed yesterday on the road to Azammour. Stories shifted like Sahara sand blowing through the *derbs*, and changed shape and form from one day to the next, according to the wind. I did not puzzle at never seeing an example of the tattoo artist's work during my yearning youth: by the time I grew into a man and felt compelled one starless night to seek him for myself, I had come to believe his design remained invisible upon a subject until that being stretched his soul into a canvas tight and strong and broad enough to display the beauty that it held.

I had to ask infrequent strangers hurrying through the alleys for directions. Often they would not pause to answer, or only muttered brusquely that they didn't know; many spoke a dialect I hadn't heard before and couldn't understand, as if they came from the other side of the Atlas Mountains, or far beyond the Rif. If I knocked on a door to ask my way, those inside remained silent, or with a shout warned me away. Increasingly, I remembered how it was said that numerous people had vanished in search of the tattoo artist; whenever some restless, dissatisfied soul disappeared from our town the presumption was that he had passed through the gates of the *quartier portugais* and had not emerged again. Some said these narrow alleys, dark even during day, teemed with lost spirits who on starless nights reached out with hungry bones of fingers for anyone foolish enough to seek the tattoo artist they had failed to find. This was home, it was rumoured, to countless beings fallen into disappointment and despair, and that they sought consolation in narcotic and carnal pleasures was evidenced in sweet smoke and moans rising into the blue sky above our sensible town. "See what happens," mothers warned their discontented children, hoping one day these offspring would grow to feel happy with the prospect of a perfectly satisfactory, harmless tattoo of the kind offered every day and at reasonable price in the market; for example, a green cross of Islam, or a yellow star of hope.

I wandered until north and south became indistinct, and time and distance without proportion, before I found someone who would help. She looked at me with cold, suspicious eyes under the lamp where we met, and appeared undecided whether to speak or not. Slowly a knowing smile twisted her face, which was scarred and disfigured beneath heavy powder. "The next crossing," she finally said, placing ironic emphasis upon each word. "The third door to the left." Then she turned and walked swiftly away, drawing a scarf more closely around her head, leaving light, mocking laughter behind.

The tattoo artist did not answer my knock, but when I pushed the door it opened. In a room off the entrance he sat on a wooden bench between the small table which held his instruments and colours and the chair in which his clients sat when not required to lie upon the floor or to stand erect to receive his mark. He was looking in my direction as I entered but did not rise to greet me. The old man wore a dark robe, with a hood concealing whether his hair was black or white or disappeared, and partly obscuring his eyes. The garment made it difficult to know his size or shape; his fingers, unadorned with rings, were long and thin. No tattoos were visible upon the skin left uncovered by the hooded robe. Appearing absorbed in thought, and scarcely conscious of my presence, the tattoo artist did not speak.

I sat in the chair and explained that I wanted a tattoo unlike any other in the world. Commonplace tattoos—a lover's name or initials; an eagle, snake or lion—did not interest me, less the heart, the arrow; the bolt of lightning; nor did I desire even a rare symbol of obscure significance. I wanted a unique tattoo, a singular tattoo: a shape that would clearly reveal to the world exactly who I was, and how the design of my being was in many minute ways, indicted in his etching, different from all others. If I did not know how it looked or what it was named, this was because the mark I wished for did not yet exist except within the tattoo artist's imagination. There was only one thing I knew for certain: it should be imprinted upon my heart.

The tattoo artist listened, then left the room by a door at its rear. He returned to set a tray holding a small silver teapot and three glasses on the floor. After a moment he poured pale tea into two of the glasses. Steam began to rise. Suddenly I wanted to tell the tattoo artist many things about myself: where I had come from, what I had seen and done, whom I had loved. I needed him to know how long I had been anticipating this moment, and how difficult it had been to find him, and how the doubts I had once felt about receiving his mark were vanished. He should hear me and see me, I believed, in order to know exactly what tattoo to place upon my skin; but the artist only watched the rising steam, seemingly uninterested in the material he had to work with, and I could not interrupt his silence. He turned to shift the candle slightly, then studied the shadow it cast upon the wall. He signed once. Removing a small square of paper from the folds of his robe, he untwisted it above one glass, spilling white powder. He handed me the glass. I drank its hot contents quickly, then loosened my shirt and lay on my back. The cement below me warmed as I fell asleep.

It was cold when I awoke. The candle still burned halfway down. The tray that held the teapot still lay on the floor. One glass was empty, one glass was full, the third was gone. There was a burning sensation at my heart. I bent my neck and saw my tattoo. At once I knew I had never seen this shape before. It was unique. I did not know what the small shape symbolized; it called nothing definite to my mind, yet seemed at once to suit me and to describe me. Was there a suggestion of a wave, a hint of an eye, an allusion to an outstretched wing? Fastening the buttons of my shirt, I watched the tattoo artist use a wet cloth to wipe his needles of dye. When they were clean, he replaced them exactly in their former position on the table. He stared at his instruments with an expression that contained amazement or horror or pleasure, or a combination of these three emotions. He was unable to hear my thanks or to receive my offered payment, and I left his room.

For several years I was pleased with my unique tattoo, though long after the pricked skin healed it continued to burn in such a way that I could never forget its presence. When exposed it caused astonishment and envy, and those with apparently ordinary tattoos sought my companionship and approval. My mark became famous in the town and occupied a central place in conversation. On the corners old men argued endlessly over its meaning and at the shore small children tried to trace its outline with sticks upon the sand. Seers used the shape to predict the future. Holy men proclaimed it visible evidence of Allah's touch. In the dark, lovers pressed lips against those brilliant colours; tongues travelled its contours, and tried to lick it off my skin. There was a season too when many youths attempted to have my tattoo copied onto themselves by the everyday tattoo artists in the market; these imitations, however skilled, were always inexact, and appeared somehow grotesque. During this time I felt that even with my shirt buttoned to my neck it was possible for passers to see through cloth to the colours stained upon my heart.

Later, though unchanged itself, my tattoo seemed to evoke a different response, such as distrust or pity or fear. My fellow townspeople fell silent when I approached down the street, and mothers placed hands over children's eyes to shield them from the sight. No longer did lovers line up to lie with me upon the sand; perhaps they realized their kisses would not erase my mark, less swallow it inside themselves. Now I was lonely, and separated from those around me by what I had once hoped would permit them to see me clearly and know me intimately. I tried to keep my tattoo hidden, as if it were ugly or obscene, wearing a heavy burnoose as armour even during the hottest season. "I hope you got what you wanted," my mother said, as another wedding procession wound past our door with its bright song of union. Ashamed of my mark, I wished it to fade or wash away, or to alter into an unremarkable design. At night, dreams concerning an undistinguished existence, with an unbranded aspect, afforded me brief release; awakening at morning brought more bitter disappointment. When I offered tattoo artists in the market large sums to remove my mark, their refusals were nervously adamant, and I was driven to prowl the dark alleys behind the quartier portugais once more. Hoping its creator could alter or eliminate the unwanted design, I searched for him on many starless nights, yet in those narrow passages encountered only yearning youths with blank, unmarked skin. "Go home," I told them.

One day my tattoo suddenly began to burn more searingly, as if freshly pricked upon my skin. Now the pain was so sharp that it would not permit me to sleep or dream or pray. At this time I gradually began to wonder about the tattoo artist himself, seeking to recall every detail of my experience with him, and to find in that memory some clue to the meaning of my mark or a way of living with it. I mused upon the possible landscape of his past and the likely contours of his present. What were his intentions when faced with the canvas of my skin? What desires urged him to use dyes and needles upon me in one way and not another? This was the period when I hoped to understand the implications of my mark by knowing the being who had placed it there, as we turn our eyes above the clouds to contemplate the force that works upon us here below.

In this way my long journey began. First I roamed the town itself and then the towns nearby in search of someone with the same tattoo as mine. I had faith that at least one other being in the world wore that brilliant shape that hovered over my heart; even accidentally, even a single time, it must have been created before. It had to have a twin. As years went by and my search did not end, I journeyed farther from the town, crossing mountains and valleys, deserts and plains, rivers and oceans and streams. In distant lands, I saw many things and met many people, but the single shape I hunted for did not appear before my eyes. I believed, still, that when it finally occurred our meeting would possess the symmetry and grace of a balanced equation: my mark would vanish beneath his gaze as his would dissolve under mine, and we would no longer each feel the same constant pain. "One glass was empty, one glass was full, the third was gone," I repeated as the road stretched far before me.

Though my end is growing near. I continue to roam from place to place in hope of discovering someone marked like me. The tattoo still burns above my heart; I have not grown used to its ache. While the colours of the world have faded, and stars dimmed with my faith, the tattoo still flames as brightly as in the beginning. Now it is many years since I have been to my town, and I do not know if my family and friends still live. I do not know if the tattoo artist still hides within the dark alleys behind the *quartier portugais*. I do not know if he still pricks his stained needle into flesh, scarring it differently each time, leaving upon our hearts the unique designs from which we seek release.

# ELIZABETH HAND

# Cleopatra Brimstone

*Elizabeth Hand is the author of six novels, including* Waking the Moon, Winterlong, *and* Glimmering, *and a short story collection,* Last Summer at Mars Hill. *Her work has received numerous honors, including the Nebula, World Fantasy, and Tiptree Awards, and in 2001 she was the recipient of an Individual Artist's Fellowship in Literature from the Maine Arts Commission and the National Endowment for the Arts. Her critical essays and reviews appear regularly in the* Washington Post Book World, Village Voice, *and* Fantasy & Science Fiction.

*Hand's fiction roams the genres with grace and ease—my only complaint is that she doesn't write enough short fiction.*

*"Cleopatra Brimstone," a darkly brilliant tale, was originally published in* Redshift.

—E. D.

Her earliest memory was of wings. Luminous red and blue, yellow and green and orange; a black so rich it appeared liquid, edible. They moved above her, and the sunlight made them glow as though they were themselves made of light, fragments of another, brighter world falling to earth about her crib. Her tiny hands stretched upward to grasp them but could not: they were too elusive, too radiant, too much of the air.

Could they ever have been real?

For years she thought she must have dreamed them. But one afternoon when she was ten she went into the attic, searching for old clothes to wear to a Halloween party. In a corner beneath a cobwebbed window she found a box of her baby things. Yellow-stained bibs and tiny fuzzy jumpers blued from bleaching, a much-nibbled stuffed dog that she had no memory of whatsoever.

And at the very bottom of the carton, something else. Wings flattened and twisted out of shape, wires bent and strings frayed: a mobile. Six plastic butterflies, colors faded and their wings giving off a musty smell, no longer eidolons of Eden but crude representations of monarch, zebra swallowtail, red admiral, sulphur, an unnaturally elongated skipper and *Agrias narcissus*. Except for the *narcissus*, all were common New World species that any child might see in a suburban garden. They hung limply from their wires, antennae long since broken off; when she touched one wing it felt cold and stiff as metal.

The afternoon had been overcast, tending to rain. But as she held the mobile to the window, a shaft of sun broke through the darkness to ignite the plastic wings, bloodred, ivy green, the pure burning yellow of an August field. In that instant it was as though her entire being were burned away, skin hair lips fingers all ash; and nothing remained but the butterflies and her awareness of them, orange and black fluid filling her mouth, the edges of her eyes scored by wings.

As a girl she had always worn glasses. A mild childhood astigmatism worsened when she was thirteen: she started bumping into things and found it increasingly difficult to concentrate on the entomological textbooks and journals that she read voraciously. Growing pains, her mother thought; but after two months, Janie's clumsiness and concomitant headaches became so severe that her mother admitted that this was perhaps something more serious, and took her to the family physician.

"Janie's fine," Dr. Gordon announced after peering into her ears and eyes. "She needs to see the optometrist, that's all. Sometimes our eyes change when we hit puberty." He gave her mother the name of an eye doctor nearby.

Her mother was relieved, and so was Jane—she had overheard her parents talking the night before her appointment, and the words CAT *scan* and *brain tumor* figured in their hushed conversation. Actually, Jane had been more concerned about another odd physical manifestation, one that no one but herself seemed to have noticed. She had started menstruating several months earlier: nothing unusual in that. Everything she had read about it mentioned the usual things—mood swings, growth spurts, acne, pubic hair.

But nothing was said about eyebrows. Janie first noticed something strange about hers when she got her period for the second time. She had retreated to the bathtub, where she spent a good half hour reading an article in *Nature* about oriental ladybug swarms. When she finished the article, she got out of the tub, dressed, and brushed her teeth, and then spent a minute frowning at the mirror.

Something was different about her face. She turned sideways, squinting. Had her chin broken out? No; but something had changed. Her hair color? Her teeth? She leaned over the sink until she was almost nose-to-nose with her reflection.

That was when she saw that her eyebrows had undergone a growth spurt of their own. At the inner edge of each eyebrow, above the bridge of her nose, three hairs had grown remarkably long. They furled back toward her temple, entwined in a sort of loose braid. She had not noticed them sooner because she seldom looked in a mirror, and also because the hairs did not arch above the eyebrows, but instead blended in with them, the way a bittersweet vine twines around a branch.

Still, they seemed bizarre enough that she wanted no one, not even her parents, to notice. She found her mother's tweezers, neatly plucked the six hairs, and flushed them down the toilet. They did not grow back.

At the optometrist's, Jane opted for heavy tortoiseshell frames rather than contacts. The optometrist, and her mother, thought she was crazy, but it was a very deliberate choice. Janie was not one of those homely B-movie adolescent girls, driven to science as a last resort. She had always been a tomboy, skinny as a rail, with long slanted violet-blue eyes; a small rosy mouth; long, straight black hair that ran like oil between her fingers; skin so pale it had the periwinkle shimmer of skim milk.

When she hit puberty, all of these conspired to beauty. And Jane hated it. Hated the attention, hated being looked at, hated that the other girls hated her. She was quiet, not shy but impatient to focus on her schoolwork, and this was mistaken for arrogance by her peers. All through high school she had few friends. She learned early the perils of befriending boys, even earnest boys who professed an interest in genetic mutations and intricate computer simulations of hive activity. Janie could trust them not to touch her, but she couldn't trust them not to fall in love. As a result of having none of the usual distractions of high school—sex, social life, mindless employment—she received an Intel-Westinghouse Science Scholarship for a computer-generated schematic of possible mutations in a small population of viceroy butterflies exposed to genetically engineered crops. She graduated in her junior year, took her scholarship money, and ran.

She had been accepted at Stanford and MIT, but chose to attend a small, highly prestigious women's college in a big city several hundred miles away. Her parents were apprehensive about her being on her own at the tender age of seventeen, but the college, with its elegant, cloister-like buildings and lushly wooded grounds, put them at ease. That and the dean's assurances that the neighborhood was completely safe, as long as students were sensible about not walking alone at night. Thus mollified, and at Janie's urging—she was desperate to move away from home—her father signed a very large check for the first semester's tuition. That September she started school.

She studied entomology, spending her first year examining the genitalia of male and female scarce wormwood shark moths, a species found on the Siberian steppes. Her hours in the zoology lab were rapturous, hunched over a microscope with a pair of tweezers so minute they were themselves like some delicate portion of her specimen's physiognomy. She would remove the butterflies' genitalia, tiny and geometrically precise as diatoms, and dip them first into glycerine, which acted as a preservative, and next into a mixture of water and alcohol. Then she observed them under the microscope. Her glasses interfered with this work— they bumped into the microscope's viewing lens—and so she switched to wearing contact lenses. In retrospect, she thought that this was probably a mistake.

At Argus College she still had no close friends, but neither was she the solitary creature she had been at home. She respected her fellow students and grew to appreciate the company of women. She could go for days at a time seeing no men besides her professors or the commuters driving past the school's wrought-iron gates.

And she was not the school's only beauty. Argus College specialized in young women like Jane: elegant, diffident girls who studied the burial customs of Mongol women or the mating habits of rare antipodean birds; girls who composed concertos for violin and gamelan orchestra, or wrote computer programs that charted the progress of potentially dangerous celestial objects through the Oort cloud. Within this educational greenhouse, Janie was not so much orchid as sturdy milkweed blossom. She thrived.

Her first three years at Argus passed in a bright-winged blur with her butterflies. Summers were given to museum internships, where she spent months cleaning and mounting specimens in solitary delight. In her senior year Janie received permission to design her own thesis project, involving her beloved shark moths. She was given a corner in a dusty anteroom off the zoology lab, and there she set up her microscope and laptop. There was no window in her corner, indeed there was no window in the anteroom at all, though the adjoining lab was pleasantly old-fashioned, with high-arched windows set between Victorian cabinetry displaying Lepidoptera, neon-carapaced beetles, unusual tree fungi, and (she found these slightly tragic) numerous exotic finches, their brilliant plumage dimmed to dusty hues. Since she often worked late into the night, she requested and received her own set of keys. Most evenings she could be found beneath the glare of the small halogen lamp, entering data into her computer, scanning images of genetic mutations involving female shark moths exposed to dioxane, corresponding with other researchers in Melbourne and Kyoto, Siberia and London.

The rape occurred around ten o'clock one Friday night in early March. She had locked the door to her office, leaving her laptop behind, and started to walk to the subway station a few blocks away. It was a cold, clear night, the yellow glow of the crime lights giving dead grass and leafless trees an eerie autumn glow. She hurried across the campus, seeing no one, and then hesitated at Seventh Street. It was a longer walk, but safer, if she went down Seventh Street and then over to Michigan Avenue. The shortcut was much quicker, but Argus authorities and the local police discouraged students from taking it after dark. Jane stood for a moment, staring across the road to where the desolate park lay; then, staring resolutely straight ahead and walking briskly, she crossed Seventh and took the shortcut.

A crumbling sidewalk passed through a weedy expanse of vacant lot, strewn with broken bottles and the spindly forms of half a dozen dusty-limbed oak trees. Where the grass ended, a narrow road skirted a block of abandoned row houses, intermittently lit by crime lights. Most of the lights had been vandalized, and one had been knocked down in a car accident—the car's fender was still there, twisted around the lamppost. Jane picked her way carefully among shards of shattered glass, reached the sidewalk in front of the boarded-up houses, and began to walk more quickly, toward the brightly lit Michigan Avenue intersection where the subway waited.

She never saw him. He was *there*, she knew that; knew he had a face, and clothing; but afterwards she could recall none of it. Not the feel of him, not his smell; only the knife he held—awkwardly, she realized later, she probably could have wrested it from him—and the few words he spoke to her. He said nothing at first, just grabbed her and pulled her into an alley between the row houses, his fingers covering her mouth, the heel of his hand pressing against her windpipe so that she gagged. He pushed her onto the dead leaves and wads of matted windblown newspaper, yanked her pants down, ripped open her jacket, and then tore her shirt open. She heard one of the buttons strike back and roll away. She thought desperately of what she had read once, in a Rape Awareness brochure: not to struggle, not to fight, not to do anything that might cause her attacker to kill her.

Janie did not fight. Instead, she divided into three parts. One part knelt nearby and prayed the way she had done as a child, not intently but automatically, trying to get through the strings of words as quickly as possible. The second part submitted blindly and silently to the man in the alley. And the third hovered above the other two, her hands wafting slowly up and down to keep her aloft as she watched.

"Try to get away," the man whispered. She could not see him or feel him though his hands were there. "Try to get away."

She remembered that she ought not to struggle, but from the noises he made and the way he tugged at her realized that was what aroused him. She did not want to anger him; she made a small sound deep in her throat and tried to push him from her chest. Almost immediately he groaned, and seconds later rolled off her. Only his hand lingered for a moment upon her cheek. Then he stumbled to his feet—she could hear him fumbling with his zipper—and fled.

The praying girl and the girl in the air also disappeared then. Only Janie was left, yanking her ruined clothes around her as she lurched from the alley and began to run, screaming and staggering back and forth across the road, toward the subway.

The police came, an ambulance. She was taken first to the police station and then to the City General Hospital, a hellish place, starkly lit, with endless underground corridors that led into darkened rooms where solitary figures lay on narrow beds like gurneys. Her pubic hair was combed and stray hairs placed into sterile envelopes; semen samples were taken, and she was advised to be tested for HIV and other diseases. She spent the entire night in the hospital, waiting and undergoing various examinations. She refused to give the police or hospital staff her parents' phone number or anyone else's. Just before dawn they finally released her, with an envelope full of brochures from the local Rape Crisis Center, New Hope for Women, Planned Parenthood, and a business card from the police detective who was overseeing her case. The detective drove her to her apartment in his squad car; when he stopped in front of her building, she was suddenly terrified that he would know where she lived, that he would come back, that he had been her assailant.

But, of course, he had not been. He walked her to the door and waited for her to go inside. "Call your parents," he said right before he left.

"I will."

She pulled aside the bamboo window shade, watching until the squad car pulled away. Then she threw out the brochures she'd received, flung off her clothes and stuffed them into the trash. She showered and changed, packed a bag full of clothes and another of books. Then she called a cab. When it arrived, she directed it to the Argus campus, where she retrieved her laptop and her research on tiger moths, and then had the cab bring her to Union Station.

She bought a train ticket home. Only after she arrived and told her parents what had happened did she finally start to cry. Even then, she could not remember what the man had looked like.

She lived at home for three months. Her parents insisted that she get psychiatric counseling and join a therapy group for rape survivors. She did so, reluctantly, but stopped attending after three weeks. The rape was something that had happened to her, but it was over.

"It was fifteen minutes out of my life," she said once at group. "That's all. It's not the rest of my life."

This didn't go over very well. Other women thought she was in denial; the therapist thought Jane would suffer later if she did not confront her fears now.

"But I'm not afraid," said Jane.

"Why not?" demanded a woman whose eyebrows had fallen out.

*Because lightning doesn't strike twice*, Jane thought grimly, but she said nothing. That was the last time she attended group.

That night her father had a phone call. He took the phone and sat at the dining table, listening; after a moment stood and walked into his study, giving a quick backward glance at his daughter before closing the door behind him. Jane felt as though her chest had suddenly frozen, but after some minutes she heard her father's laugh; he was not, after all, talking to the police detective. When after half an hour he returned, he gave Janie another quick look, more thoughtful this time.

"That was Andrew." Andrew was a doctor friend of his, an Englishman. "He and Fred are going to Provence for three months. They were wondering if you might want to house-sit for them."

"In *London*?" Jane's mother shook her head. "I don't think—"

"I said we'd think about it."

"*I'll* think about it," Janie corrected him. She stared at both her parents, absently ran a finger along one eyebrow. "Just let me think about it."

And she went to bed.

She went to London. She already had a passport, from visiting Andrew with her parents when she was in high school. Before she left there were countless arguments with her mother and father, and phone calls back and forth to Andrew. He assured them that the flat was secure, there was a very nice reliable older woman who lived upstairs, that it would be a good idea for Janie to get out on her own again.

"So you don't get gun-shy," he said to her one night on the phone. He was a doctor, after all: a homeopath not an allopath, which Janie found reassuring. "It's important for you to get on with our life. You won't be able to get a real job here as a visitor, but I'll see what I can do."

It was on the plane to Heathrow that she made a discovery. She had splashed water onto her face, and was beginning to comb her hair when she blinked and stared into the mirror.

Above her eyebrows, the long hairs had grown back. They followed the contours of her brow, sweeping back toward her temples; still entwined, still difficult to make out unless she drew her face close to her reflection and tilted her head just so. Tentatively she touched one braided strand. It was stiff yet oddly pliant; but as she ran her finger along its length a sudden *surge* flowed through her. Not an electrical shock: more like the thrill of pain when a dentist's drill touches a nerve, or an elbow rams against a stone. She gasped; but immediately the pain was gone. Instead there was a thrumming behind her forehead, a spreading warmth that trickled into her throat like sweet syrup. She opened her mouth, her gasp turning into an uncontrollable yawn, the yawn into a spike of such profound physical ecstasy that she grabbed the edge of the sink and thrust forward, striking her head against the mirror. She was dimly aware of someone knocking at the lavatory door as she clutched the sink and, shuddering, climaxed.

"Hello?" someone called softly. "Hello, is this occupied?"

"Right out," Janie gasped. She caught her breath, still trembling; ran a hand across her face, her finger halting before they could touch the hairs above her eyebrows. There was the faintest tingling, a temblor of sensation that faded as she grabbed her cosmetic bag, pulled the door open, and stumbled back into the cabin.

Andrew and Fred lived in an old Georgian row house just west of Camden Town, overlooking the Regent's Canal. Their flat occupied the first floor and basement; there was a hexagonal solarium out back, with glass walls and heated stone floor, and beyond that a stepped terrace leading down to the canal. The bedroom had an old wooden four-poster piled high with duvets and down pillows, and French doors that also opened onto the terrace. Andrew showed her how to operate the elaborate sliding security doors that unfolded from the walls, and gave her the keys to the barred window guards.

"You're completely safe here," he said, smiling. "Tomorrow we'll introduce you to Kendra upstairs and show you how to get around. Camden Market's just down that way, and *that* way—"

He stepped out onto the terrace, pointing to where the canal coiled and disappeared beneath an arched stone bridge. "—that way's the Regent's Park Zoo. I've given you a membership—"

"Oh! Thank you!" Janie looked around delighted. "This is *wonderful.*"

"It is." Andrew put an arm around her and drew her close. "You're going to have a wonderful time, Janie. I thought you'd like the zoo—there's a new exhibit there, 'The World Within' or words to that effect—it's about insects. I thought perhaps you might want to volunteer there—they have an active docent program, and you're so knowledgeable about that sort of thing."

"Sure. It sounds great—really great." She grinned and smoothed her hair back from her face, the wind sending up the rank scent of stagnant water from the canal, the sweetly poisonous smell of hawthorn blossom. As she stood gazing down past the potted geraniums and Fred's rosemary trees, the hairs upon her brow trembled, and she laughed out loud, giddily, with anticipation.

Fred and Andrew left two days later. It was enough time for Janie to get over her jet lag and begin to get barely acclimated to the city, and to its smell. London had an acrid scent: damp ashes, the softer underlying fetor of rot that oozed from ancient bricks and stone buildings, the thick vegetative smell of the canal, sharpened with urine and spilled beer. So many thousands of people descended on Camden Town on the weekend that the tube station was restricted to incoming passengers, and the canal path became almost impassable. Even late on a weeknight she could hear voices from the other side of the canal, harsh London voices echoing beneath the bridges or shouting to be heard above the din of the Northern Line trains passing overhead.

Those first days Janie did not venture far from the flat. She unpacked her clothes, which did not take much time, and then unpacked her collecting box, which did. The sturdy wooden case had come through the overseas flight and customs seemingly unscathed, but Janie found herself holding her breath as she undid the metal hinges, afraid of what she'd find inside.

"*Oh!*" she exclaimed. Relief, not chagrin: nothing had been damaged. The small glass vials of ethyl alcohol and gel shellac were intact, and the pillboxes where she kept the tiny #2 pins she used for mounting. Fighting her own eagerness, she carefully removed packets of stiff archival paper; a block of Styrofoam covered with pinholes; two bottles of clear Maybelline nail polish and a small container of Elmer's Glue-All; more pillboxes, empty, and empty gelatine capsules for very small specimens; and last of all a small glass-fronted display box, framed in mahogany and holding her most precious specimen: a hybrid *Celerio harmuthi kordesch*, the male crossbreed of the spurge and elephant hawkmoths. As long as the first joint of her thumb, it had the hawkmoth's typically streamlined wings but exquisitely delicate coloring, fuchsia bands shading to a soft rich brown, its thorax thick and seemingly feathered. Only a handful of these hybrid moths had ever existed, bred by the Prague entomologist Jan Pokorny in 1961; a few years afterward, both the spurge hawkmoth and the elephant hawkmoth had become extinct.

Janie had found this one for sale on the Internet three months ago. It was a former museum specimen and cost a fortune; she had a few bad nights, worrying whether it had actually been a legal purchase. Now she held the display box in her cupped palms and gazed at it raptly. Behind her eyes she felt a prickle, like sleep or unshed tears; then a slow thrumming warmth crept from her brows, spreading to her temples, down her neck and through her breasts, spreading like a stain. She swallowed, leaned back against the sofa, and let the display box rest back within the larger case; slid first one hand and then the other beneath her sweater and began to stroke her nipples. When some time later she came it was with stabbing force and a thunderous sensation above her eyes, as though she had struck her forehead against the floor.

She had not; gasping, she pushed the hair from her face, zipped her jeans, and reflexively leaned forward, to make certain the hawkmoth in its glass box was safe.

Over the following days she made a few brief forays to the news-agent and greengrocer, trying to eke out the supplies Fred and Andrew had left in the kitchen. She sat in the solarium, her bare feet warm against the heated stone floor, and drank chamomile tea or claret, staring down to where the ceaseless stream of people passed along the canal path, and watching the narrow boats as they piled their way slowly between Camden Lock and Little Venice, two miles to the west in Paddington. By the following Wednesday she felt brave enough, and bored enough, to leave her refuge and visit the zoo.

It was a short walk along the canal, dodging bicyclists who jingled their bells impatiently when she forgot to stay on the proper side of the path. She passed beneath several arching bridges, their undersides pleated with slime and moss. Drunks sprawled against the stones and stared at her blearily or challengingly by turns; well-dressed couples walked dogs, and there were excited knots of children, tugging their parents on to the zoo.

Fred had walked here with Janie, to show her the way. But it all looked unfamiliar now. She kept a few strides behind a family, her head down, trying not to look as though she was following them; and felt a pulse of relief when they reached a twisting stair with an arrowed sign at its top.

Regent's Park Zoo

There was an old old church across the street, its yellow stone walls overgrown with ivy, and down and around the corner a long stretch of hedges with high iron walls fronting them, and at last a huge set of gates, crammed with children and vendors selling balloons and banners and London guidebooks. Janie lifted her head and walked quickly past the family that had led her here, showed her membership card at the entrance, and went inside.

She wasted no time on the seals or tigers or monkeys, but went straight to the newly renovated structure where a multicolored banner flapped in the late-morning breeze.

An Alternate Universe: Secrets of the Insect World

Inside, crowds of schoolchildren and harassed-looking adults formed a ragged queue that trailed through a brightly lit corridor, its walls covered with huge glossy color photos and computer-enhanced images of hissing cockroaches, hellgrammites, morpho butterflies, deathwatch beetles, polyphemous moths. Janie dutifully joined the queue, but when the corridor opened into a vast sunlit atrium she strode off on her own, leaving the children and teachers to gape at monarchs in butterfly cages and an interactive display of honeybees dancing. Instead she found a relatively quiet display at the far end of the exhibition space, a floor-to-ceiling cylinder of transparent net, perhaps six feet in diameter. Inside, buckthorn bushes and blooming hawthorn vied for sunlight with a slender beech sapling, and dozens of butterflies flitted upward through the new yellow leaves, or sat with wings outstretched upon the beech tree. They were a type of Pieridae, the butterflies known as whites; though these were not white at all. The females had creamy yellow-green wings, very pale, their wingspans perhaps an inch and a half. The males were the same size; when they were at rest their flattened wings were a dull, rather sulphurous color. But when the males lit into the air, their wings revealed vivid, spectral yellow undersides. Janie caught her breath in delight, her neck prickling with that same atavistic joy she'd felt as a child in the attic.

"Wow," she breathed, and pressed up against the netting. It felt like wings against her face, soft, webbed; but as she stared at the insects inside, her brow began to ache as with migraine. She shoved her glasses onto her nose, closed her eyes, and drew a long breath; then she took a step away from the cage. After a minute she opened her eyes. The headache had diminished to a dull throb; when she hesitantly touched one eyebrow, she could feel the entwined hairs there, stiff as wire. They were vibrating, but at her touch the vibrations, like the headache, dulled. She stared at the floor, the tiles sticky with contraband juice and gum; then she looked up once again at the cage. There was a display sign off to one side; she walked over to it, slowly, and read.

*Cleopatra Brimstone*
## Gonepteryx Rhamni Cleopatra

This popular and subtly colored species has a range that extends throughout the northern hemisphere, with the exception of arctic regions and several remote islands. In Europe, the brimstone is a harbinger of spring, often emerging from its winter hibernation under dead leaves to revel in the countryside while there is still snow upon the ground.

"I must ask you please not to touch the cages."

Janie turned to see a man, perhaps fifty, standing a few feet away. A net was jammed under his arm; in his hand he held a clear plastic jar with several butterflies at the bottom, apparently dead.

"Oh. Sorry," said Jane. The man edged past her. He set his jar on the floor, opened a small door at the base of the cylindrical cage, and deftly angled the net inside. Butterflies lifted in a yellow-green blur from leaves and branches; the man swept the net carefully across the bottom of the cage and then withdrew it. Three dead butterflies, like scraps of colored paper, drifted from the net into the open jar.

"Housecleaning," he said, and once more thrust his arm into the cage. He was slender and wiry, not much taller than she was, his face hawkish and burnt brown from the sun, his thick straight hair iron-streaked and pulled back into a long braid. He wore black jeans and a dark-blue hooded jersey, with an ID badge clipped to the collar.

"You work here," said Janie. The man glanced at her, his arm still in the cage; she could see him sizing her up. After a moment he glanced away again. A few minutes later he emptied the net for the last time, closed the cage and the jar, and stepped over to a waste bin, pulling bits of dead leaves from the net and dropping them into the container.

"I'm one of the curatorial staff. You American?"

Janie nodded. "Yeah. Actually, I—I wanted to see about volunteering here."

"Lifewatch desk at the main entrance." The man cocked his head toward the door. "They can get you signed up and registered, see what's available."

"No—I mean, I want to volunteer here. With the insects—"

"Butterfly collector, are you?" The man smiled, his tone mocking. He had hazel eyes, deep-set; his thin mouth made the smile seem perhaps more cruel than intended. "We get a lot of those."

Janie flushed. "No. I am not a *collector*," she said coldly, adjusting her glasses. "I'm doing a thesis on dioxane genital mutation in *Cucullia artemisia*." She didn't add that it was an undergraduate thesis. "I've been doing independent research for seven years now." She hesitated, thinking of her Intel scholarship, and added, "I've received several grants for my work."

The man regarded her appraisingly. "Are you studying here, then?"

"Yes," she lied again. "At Oxford. I'm on sabbatical right now. But I live near here, and so I thought I might—"

She shrugged, opening her hands, looked over at him, and smiled tentatively. "Make myself useful?"

The man waited a moment, nodded. "Well. Do you have a few minutes now? I've got to do something with these, but if you want you can come with me and wait, and then we can see what we can do. Maybe circumvent some paperwork."

He turned and started across the room. He had a graceful, bouncing gait, like a gymnast or circus acrobat: impatient with the ground beneath him. "Shouldn't take long," he called over his shoulder as Janie hurried to catch up.

She followed him through a door marked AUTHORISED PERSONS ONLY, into the exhibit laboratory, a reassuringly familiar place with its display cases and smells of shellac and camphor, acetone and ethyl alcohol. There were more cages here, but smaller ones, sheltering live specimens—pupating butterflies and moths, stick insects, leaf insects, dung beetles. The man dropped his net onto a desk, took the jar to a long table against one wall, blindingly lit by long fluorescent tubes. There were scores of bottles here, some empty, others filled with paper and tiny inert figures.

"Have a seat," said the man, gesturing at two folding chairs. He settled into one, grabbed an empty jar and a roll of absorbent paper. "I'm David Bierce. So where're you staying? Camden Town?"

"Janie Kendall. Yes—"

"The High Street?"

Janie sat in the other chair, pulling it a few inches away from him. The questions made her uneasy, but she only nodded, lying again, and said, "Closer, actually. Off Gloucester Road. With friends."

"Mm." Bierce tore off a piece of absorbent paper, leaned across to a stainless-steel sink and dampened the paper. Then he dropped it into the empty jar. He paused, turned to her and gestured at the table, smiling. "Care to join in?"

Janie shrugged. "Sure—"

She pulled her chair closer, found another empty jar and did as Bierce had, dampening a piece of paper towel and dropping it inside. Then she took the jar containing the dead brimstones and carefully shook one onto the counter. It was a female, its coloring more muted than the males'; she scooped it up very gently, careful not to disturb the scales like dull green glitter upon its wings, dropped it into the jar and replaced the top.

"Very nice." Bierce nodded, raising his eyebrows. "You seem to know what you're doing. Work with other insects? Soft-bodied ones?"

"Sometimes. Mostly moths, though. And butterflies."

"Right." He inclined his head to a recessed shelf. "How would you label that, then? Go ahead."

On the shelf she found a notepad and a case of Rapidograph pens. She began to write, conscious of Bierce staring at her. "We usually just put all this into the computer, of course, and print it out," he said. "I just want to see the benefits of an American education in the sciences."

Janie fought the urge to look at him. Instead she wrote out the information, making her printing as tiny as possible.

*Gonepteryx rhamni cleopatra*
UNITED KINGDOM: LONDON
*Regent's Park Zoo*
*Lat/Long unknown*
*21.IV.2001*
*D. Bierce*
*Net/caged specimen*

She handed it to Bierce. "I don't know the proper coordinates for London."

Bierce scrutinized the paper. "It's actually the Royal Zoological Society," he said. He looked at her, and then smiled. "But you'll do."

"Great!" She grinned, the first time she'd really felt happy since arriving here. "When do you want me to start?"

"How about Monday?"

Janie hesitated: this was only Friday. "I could come in tomorrow—"

"I don't work on the weekend, and you'll need to be trained. Also they have to process the paperwork. Right—"

He stood and went to a desk, pulling open drawers until he found a clipboard holding sheafs of triplicate forms. "Here. Fill all this out, leave it with me, and I'll pass it on to Carolyn—she's the head volunteer coordinator. They usually want to interview you, but I'll tell them we've done all that already."

"What time should I come in Monday?"

"Come at nine. Everything opens at ten; that way you'll avoid the crowds. Use the staff entrance, someone there will have an ID waiting for you to pick up when you sign in—"

She nodded and began filling out the forms.

"All right then." David Bierce leaned against the desk and again fixed her with that sly, almost taunting gaze. "Know how to find your way home?"

Janie lifted her chin defiantly. "Yes."

"Enjoying London? Going to go out tonight and do Camden Town with all the yobs?"

"Maybe. I haven't been out much yet."

"Mm. Beautiful American girl—they'll eat you alive. Just kidding." He straightened, started across the room toward the door. "I'll you see Monday then."

He held the door for her. "You really should check out the clubs. You're too young not to see the city by night." He smiled, the fluorescent light slanting sideways into his hazel eyes and making them suddenly glow icy blue. "Bye then."

"Bye," said Janie, and hurried quickly from the lab toward home.

That night, for the first time, she went out. She told herself she would have gone anyway, no matter what Bierce had said. She had no idea where the clubs were; Andrew had pointed out the Electric Ballroom to her, right up from the tube station, but he'd also warned her that was where the tourists flocked on weekends.

"They do a disco thing on Saturday nights—Saturday Night Fever, everyone gets all done up in vintage clothes. Quite a fashion show," he'd said, smiling and shaking his head.

Janie had no interest in that. She ate a quick supper, vindaloo from the take-away down the street from the flat; then she dressed. She hadn't brought a huge amount of clothes—at home she'd never bothered much with clothes at all, making do with thrift-shop finds and whatever her mother gave her for Christmas. But now she found herself sitting on the edge of the four-poster, staring with pursed lips at the sparse contents of two bureau drawers. Finally she pulled out a pair of black corduroy jeans and a black turtleneck and pulled on her sneakers. She removed her glasses and for the first time in weeks inserted her contact lenses. Then she shrugged into her old navy peacoat and left.

It was after ten o'clock. On the canal path, throngs of people stood, drinking from pints of canned lager. She made her way through them, ignoring catcalls and whispered invitations, stepping to avoid where kids lay making out against the brick wall that ran alongside the path or pissing in the bushes. The bridge over the canal at Camden Lock was clogged with several dozen kids in mohawks or varicolored hair, shouting at each other above the din of a boom box and swigging from bottles of Spanish champagne.

A boy with a champagne bottle leered, lunging at her.

" 'Ere, sweetheart, 'ep youseff—"

Janie ducked, and he careered against the ledge, his arm striking brick and the bottle shattering in a starburst of black and gold.

"Fucking cunt!" he shrieked after her. "Fucking bloody *cunt!*"

People glanced at her, but Janie kept her head down, making a quick turn into the vast cobbled courtyard of Camden Market. The place had a desolate air: the vendors would not arrive until early next morning, and now only stray cats and bits of windblown trash moved in the shadows. In the surrounding buildings people spilled out onto balconies, drinking and calling back and forth, their voices hollow and their long shadows twisting across the ill-lit central courtyard. Janie hurried to the far end, but there found only brick walls, closed-up shop doors, and a young woman huddled within the folds of a filthy sleeping bag.

"*Couldya—couldya—*" the woman murmured.

Janie turned and followed the wall until she found a door leading into a short passage. She entered it, hoping she was going in the direction of Camden High Street. She felt like Alice trying to find her way through the garden in Wonderland: arched doorways led not into the street but headshops and brightly lit piercing parlors, open for business; other doors opened onto enclosed courtyards, dark and smelling of piss and marijuana. Finally from the corner of her eye she glimpsed what looked like the end of the passage, headlights piercing through the gloom like landing lights. Doggedly she made her way toward them.

"Ay watchowt watchowt," someone yelled as she emerged from the passage onto the sidewalk and ran the last few steps to the curb.

She was on the High Street—rather, in that block or two of curving no-man's-land where it turned into Chalk Farm Road. The sidewalks were still crowded, but everyone was heading toward Camden Lock and not away from it. Janie waited for the light to change and raced across the street, to where a cobble-stoned alley snaked off between a shop selling leather underwear and another advertising "Fine French Country Furniture."

For several minutes she stood there. She watched the crowds heading toward

Camden Town, the steady stream of minicabs and taxis and buses heading up Chalk Farm Road toward Hampstead. Overhead, dull orange clouds moved across a night sky the color of charred wood; there was the steady low thunder of jets circling after takeoff at Heathrow. At last she tugged her collar up around her neck, letting her hair fall in loose waves down her back, shoved her hands into her coat pockets, and turned to walk purposefully down the alley.

Before her the cobblestone path turned sharply to the right. She couldn't see what was beyond, but she could hear voices: a girl laughing, a man's sibilant retort. A moment later the alley spilled out onto a cul-de-sac. A couple stood a few yards away, before a doorway with a small copper awning above it. The young woman glanced sideways at Janie, quickly looked away again. A silhouette filled the doorway; the young man pulled out a wallet. His hand disappeared within the silhouette, reemerged, and the couple walked inside. Janie waited until the shadowy figure withdrew. She looked over her shoulder and then approached the building.

There was a heavy metal door, black, with graffiti scratched into it and pale blurred spots where painted graffiti had been effaced. The door was set back several feet into a brick recess; there was a grilled metal slot at the top that could be slid back, so that one could peer out into the courtyard. To the right of the door, on the brick wall within the recess, was a small brass plaque with a single word on it.

Hive

There was no doorbell or any other way to signal that you wanted to enter. Janie stood, wondering what was inside; feeling a small tingling unease that was less fear than the knowledge that even if she were to confront the figure who'd let that other couple inside, she herself would certainly be turned away.

With a *skreek* of metal on stone the door suddenly shot open. Janie looked up, into the sharp, raggedly handsome face of a tall, still youngish man with very short blond hair, a line of gleaming gold beads like drops of sweat piercing the edge of his left jaw.

"Good evening," he said, glancing past her to the alley. He wore a black sleeveless T-shirt with a small golden bee embroidered upon the breast. His bare arms were muscular, striated with long sweeping scars: black, red, white. "Are you waiting for Hannah?"

"No." Quickly Janie pulled out a handful of five-pound notes. "Just me tonight."

"That'll be twenty then." The man held his hand out, still gazing at the alley; when Janie slipped the notes to him he looked down and flashed her a vulpine smile. "Enjoy yourself." She darted past him into the building.

Abruptly it was as though some darker night had fallen. Thunderously so, since the enfolding blackness was slashed with music so loud it was itself like light: Janie hesitated, closing her eyes, and white flashes streaked across her eyelids like sleet, pulsing in time to the music. She opened her eyes, giving them a chance to adjust to the darkness, and tried to get a sense of where she was. A few feet away a blurry grayish lozenge sharpened into the window of a coat-check room. Janie walked past it, toward the source of the music. Immediately the floor slanted steeply beneath her feet. She steadied herself with one hand against the wall, following the incline until it opened onto a cavernous dance floor.

She gazed inside, disappointed. It looked like any other club, crowded, strobe-lit, turquoise smoke and silver glitter coiling between hundreds of whirling bodies clad in candy pink, sky blue, neon red, rainslicker yellow. Baby colors, Janie thought. There was a boy who was almost naked, except for shorts, a transparent water bottle strapped to his chest and long tubes snaking into his mouth. Another boy had hair the color of lime Jell-O, his face corrugated with glitter and sweat; he swayed near the edge of the dance floor, turned to stare at Janie, and then beamed, beckoning her to join him.

Janie gave him a quick smile, shaking her head; when the boy opened his arms to her in mock pleading she shouted "No!"

But she continued to smile, though she felt as though her head would crack like an egg from the throbbing music. Shoving her hands into her pockets she skirted the dance floor, pushed her way to the bar and bought a drink, something pink with no ice in a plastic cup. It smelled like Gatorade and lighter fluid. She gulped it down and then carried the cup held before her like a torch as she continued on her circuit of the room. There was nothing else of interest, just long queues for the lavatories and another bar, numerous doors and stairwells where kids clustered, drinking and smoking. Now and then beeps and whistles like birdsong or insect cries came through the stuttering electronic din, whoops and trilling laughter from the dancers. But mostly they moved in near silence, eyes rolled ceiling-ward, bodies exploding into Catherine wheels of flesh and plastic and nylon, but all without a word.

It gave Janie a headache—a *real* headache, the back of her skull bruised, tender to the touch. She dropped her plastic cup and started looking for a way out. She could see past the dance floor to where she had entered, but it seemed as though another hundred people had arrived in the few minutes since then: kids were standing six deep at both bars, and the action on the floor had spread, amoebalike, toward the corridors angling back up toward the street.

"Sorry—"

A fat woman in an Arsenal jersey jostled her as she hurried by, leaving a smear of oily sweat on Janie's wrist. Janie grimaced and wiped her hand on the bottom of her coat. She gave one last look at the dance floor, but nothing had changed within the intricate lattice of dancers and smoke, braids of glow-lights and spotlit faces surging up and down, up and down, while more dancers fought their way to the center.

"Shit." She turned and strode off, heading to where the huge room curved off into relative emptiness. Here, scores of tables were scattered, some over-turned, others stacked against the wall. A few people sat, talking; a girl lay curled on the floor, her head pillowed on a Barbie knapsack. Janie crossed to the wall and found first a door that led to a bare brick wall, then a second door that held a broom closet. The next was dark-red, metal, official-looking: the kind of door that Janie associated with school fire drills.

A fire door. It would lead outside, or into a hall that would lead there. Without hesitating she pushed it open and entered. A short corridor lit by EXIT signs stretched ahead of her, with another door at the end. She hurried toward it, already reaching reflexively for the keys to the flat, pushed the door-bar, and stepped inside.

For an instant she thought she had somehow stumbled into a hospital emergency room. There was the glitter of halogen light on steel, distorted reflections thrown back at her from curved glass surfaces; the abrasive odor of isopropyl alcohol and the fainter tinny scent of blood, like metal in the mouth.

And bodies: everywhere, bodies, splayed on gurneys or suspended from gleaming metal hooks, laced with black electrical cord and pinned upright onto smooth rubber mats. She stared openmouthed, neither appalled nor frightened but fascinated by the conundrum before her: how did *that* hand fit *there*, and whose leg was *that*? She inched backwards, pressing herself against the door and trying to stay in the shadows—just inches ahead of her ribbons of luminous bluish light streamed from lamps hung high overhead. The chiaroscuro of pallid bodies and black furniture, shiny with sweat and here and there red-streaked, or brown; the mere sight of so many bodies, real bodies—flesh spilling over the edge of tabletops, too much hair or none at all, eyes squeezed shut in ecstasy or terror and mouths open to reveal stained teeth, pale gums—the sheer *fluidity* of it all enthralled her. She felt as she had, once, pulling aside a rotted log to disclose the ant's nest beneath, masses of minute fleeing bodies, soldiers carrying eggs and larvae in their jaws, tunnels spiraling into the center of another world. Her brow tingled, warmth flushed her from brow to breast . . .

Another world, that's what she had found then, and discovered again now.

"*Out.*"

Janie sucked her breath in sharply. Fingers dug into her shoulder, yanked her back through the metal door so roughly that she cut her wrist against it.

"No lurkers, what the fuck—"

A man flung her against the wall. She gasped, turned to run, but he grabbed her shoulder again. "Christ, a fucking girl."

He sounded angry but relieved. She looked up: a huge man, more fat than muscle. He wore very tight leather briefs and the same black sleeveless shirt with a golden bee embroidered upon it. "How the hell'd you get in like *that*?" he demanded, cocking a thumb at her.

She shook her head, then realized he meant her clothes. "I was just trying to find my way out."

"Well you found your way in. In like fucking Flynn." He laughed: he had goldcapped teeth, and gold wires threading the tip of his tongue. "You want to join the party, you know the rules. No exceptions."

Before she could reply he turned and was gone, the door thudding softly behind him. She waited, heart pounding, then reached and pushed the bar on the door.

Locked. She was out, not in; she was nowhere at all. For a long time she stood there, trying to hear anything from the other side of the door, waiting to see if anyone would come back looking for her. At last she turned, and began to find her way home.

Next morning she woke early, to the sound of delivery trucks in the street and children on the canal path, laughing and squabbling on their way to the zoo.

She sat up with a pang, remembering David Bierce and her volunteer job; then she recalled this was Saturday, not Monday.

"Wow," she said aloud. The extra days seemed like a gift.

For a few minutes she lay in Fred and Andrew's great four-poster, staring abstractedly at where she had rested her mounted specimens atop the wainscoting—the hybrid hawkmoth; a beautiful Honduran owl butterfly, *Caligo atreus*; a mourning cloak she had caught and mounted herself years ago. She thought of the club last night, mentally retracing her steps to the hidden back room, thought of the man who had thrown her out, the interplay of light and shadow upon the bodies pinned to mats and tables. She had slept in her clothes; now she rolled out of bed and pulled her sneakers on, forgoing breakfast but stuffing her pocket with ten- and twenty-pound notes before she left.

It was a clear, cool morning, with a high pale-blue sky and the young leaves of nettles and hawthorn still glistening with dew. Someone had thrown a shopping cart from the nearby Sainsbury's into the canal; it edged sideways up out of the shallow water, like a frozen shipwreck. A boy stood a few yards down from it, fishing, an absent, placid expression on his face.

She crossed over the bridge to the canal path and headed for the High Street. With every step she took the day grew older, noisier, trains rattling on the bridge behind her and voices harsh as gulls rising from the other side of the brick wall that separated the canal path from the street.

At Camden Lock she had to fight her way through the market. There were tens of thousands of tourists, swarming from the maze of shops to pick their way between scores of vendors selling old and new clothes, bootleg CDs, cheap silver jewelry, kilims, feather boas, handcuffs, cell phones, mass-produced furniture and puppets from Indonesia, Morocco, Guyana, Wales. The fug of burning incense and cheap candles choked her; she hurried to where a young woman was turning samosas in a vat of sputtering oil and dug into her pocket for a handful of change, standing so that the smells of hot grease and scorched chickpea batter canceled out patchouli and Caribbean Nights.

"Two, please," Janie shouted.

She ate and almost immediately felt better; then she walked a few steps to where a spike-haired girl sat behind a table covered with cheap clothes made of ripstop fabric in Jell-O shades.

"Everything five pounds," the girl announced. She stood, smiling helpfully as Janie began to sort through pairs of hugely baggy pants. They were cross-seamed with Velcro and deep zippered pockets. Janie held up a pair, frowning as the legs billowed, lavender and green, in the wind.

"It's so you can make them into shorts," the girl explained. She stepped around the table and took the pants from Janie, deftly tugging at the legs so that they detached. "See? Or a skirt." The girl replaced the pants, picked up another pair, screaming orange with black trim, and a matching windbreaker. "This color would look nice on you."

"Okay." Janie paid for them, waited for the girl to put the clothes in a plastic bag. "Thanks."

"Bye now."

She went out into Camden High Street. Shopkeepers stood guard over the tables spilling out from their storefronts, heaped with leather clothes and souvenir T-shirts: MIND THE GAP, LONDON UNDERGROUND, shirts emblazoned with the Cat in the Hat toking on a cheroot. THE CAT IN THE HAT SMOKES BLACK. Every three or four feet someone had set up a boom box, deafening sound bites of salsa, techno, "The Hustle," Bob Marley, "Anarchy in the UK," Radiohead. On the corner of Inverness and the High Street a few punks squatted in a doorway, looking over the postcards they'd bought. A sign in a smoked-glass window said ALL HAIRCUTS 10£, MEN WOMEN CHILDREN.

"Sorry," one of the punks said as Janie stepped over them and into the shop.

The barber was sitting in an old-fashioned chair, his back to her, reading the *Sun*. At the sound of her footsteps he turned, smiling automatically. "Can I help you?"

"Yes please. I'd like my hair cut. All of it."

He nodded, gesturing to the chair. "Please."

Janie had thought she might have to convince him that she was serious. She had beautiful hair, well below her shoulders—the kind of hair people would kill for, she'd been hearing that her whole life. But the barber just hummed and chopped it off, the *snick snick* of his shears interspersed with kindly questions about whether she was enjoying her visit and his account of a vacation to Disney World ten years earlier.

"Dear, do we want it shaved or buzz-cut?"

In the mirror a huge-eyed creature gazed at Janie, like a tarsier or one of the owlish caligo moths. She stared at it, entranced, and then nodded. "Shaved. Please."

When he was finished she got out of the chair, dazed, and ran her hand across her scalp. It was smooth and cool as an apple. There were a few tiny nicks that stung beneath her fingers. She paid the barber, tipping him two pounds. He smiled and held the door open for her.

"Now when you want a touch-up, you come see us, dear. Only five pounds for a touch-up."

She went next to find new shoes. There were more shoe shops in Camden Town than she had ever seen anywhere in her life; she checked out four of them on one block before deciding on a discounted pair of twenty-hole black Doc Martens. They were no longer fashionable, but they had blunted steel caps on the toes. She bought them, giving the salesgirl her old sneakers to toss into the waste bin. When she went back onto the street it was like walking in wet cement—the shoes were so heavy, the leather so stiff that she ducked back into the shoe shop and bought a pair of heavy wool socks and put them on. She returned outside, hesitating on the front step before crossing the street and heading back in the direction of Chalk Farm Road. There was a shop here that Fred had shown her before he left.

"Now, that's where you get your fetish gear, Janie," he said, pointing to a shop window painted matte black. THE PLACE, it said in red letters, with two linked circles beneath. Fred had grinned and rapped his knuckles against the glass as they walked by. "I've never been in; you'll have to tell me what it's like." They'd both laughed at the thought.

Now Janie walked slowly, the wind chill against her bare skull. When she could make out the shop, sun glinting off the crimson letters and a sad-eyed dog tied to a post out front, she began to hurry, her new boots making a hollow thump as she pushed through the door.

There was a security gate inside, a thin, sallow young man with dreadlocks nodding at her silently as she approached.

"You'll have to check that." He pointed at the bag with her new clothes in it. She handed it to him, reading the warning posted behind the counter.

> Shoplifters will be Beaten,
> Flayed, Spanked, Birched, Bled,
> and then Prosecuted
> to the Full Extent of the Law

The shop was well lit. It smelled strongly of new leather and coconut oil and pine-scented disinfectant. She seemed to be the only customer this early in the day, although she counted seven employees manning cash registers, unpacking cartons, watching to make sure she didn't try to nick anything. A CD of dance music played, and the phone rang constantly.

She spent a good half hour just walking through the place, impressed by the range of merchandise. Electrified wands to deliver shocks, things like meat cleavers made of stainless steel with rubber tips. Velcro dog collars, Velcro hoods, black rubber balls and balls in neon shades; a mat embedded with three-inch spikes that could be conveniently rolled up and came with its own lightweight carrying case. As she wandered about more customers arrived, some of them greeting the clerks by name, others furtive, making a quick circuit of the shelves before darting outside again. At last Janie knew what she wanted. A set of wristcuffs and one of anklecuffs, both of very heavy black leather with stainless steel hardware; four adjustable nylon leashes, also black, with clips on either end that could be fastened to cuffs or looped around a post; a few spare S-clips.

"That it?"

Janie nodded, and the register clerk began scanning her purchases. She felt almost guilty, buying so few things, not taking advantage of the vast Meccano glory of all those shelves full of gleaming, somber contrivances.

"There you go." He handed her the receipt, then inclined his head at her. "Nice touch, that—"

He pointed at her eyebrows. Janie drew her hand up, felt the long pliant hairs uncoiling like baby ferns. "Thanks," she murmured. She retrieved her bag and went home to wait for evening.

It was nearly midnight when she left the flat. She had slept for most of the afternoon, a deep but restless sleep, with anxious dreams of flight, falling, her hands encased in metal gloves, a shadowy figure crouching above her. She woke in the dark, heart pounding, terrified for a moment that she had slept all the way through till Sunday night.

But, of course, she had not. She showered, then dressed in a tight, low-cut black shirt and pulled on her new nylon pants and heavy boots. She seldom wore makeup, but tonight after putting in her contacts she carefully outlined her eyes with black and then chose a very pale lavender lipstick. She surveyed herself in the mirror critically. With her white skin, huge violet eyes, and hairless skull, she resembled one of the Balinese puppets for sale in the market—beautiful but vacant, faintly ominous. She grabbed her keys and money, pulled on her wind-breaker, and headed out.

When she reached the alley that led to the club, she entered it, walked about halfway, and stopped. After glancing back and forth to make sure no one was coming, she detached the legs from her nylon pants, stuffing them into a pocket, and then adjusted the Velcro tabs so that the pants became a very short orange-and-black skirt. Her long legs were sheathed in black tights. She bent to tighten the laces on her metal-toed boots and hurried to the club entrance.

Tonight there was a line of people waiting to get in. Janie took her place, fastidiously avoiding looking at any of the others. They waited for thirty minutes, Janie shivering in her thin nylon windbreaker, before the door opened and the same gaunt blond man appeared to take their money. Janie felt her heart beat faster when it was her turn, wondering if he would recognize her. But he only scanned the courtyard, and, when the last of them darted inside, closed the door with a booming *clang*.

Inside, all was as it had been, only far more crowded. Janie bought a drink, orange squash, no alcohol. It was horribly sweet, with a bitter, curdled aftertaste. Still, it had cost two pounds: she drank it all. She had just started on her way down to the dance floor when someone came up from behind to tap her shoulder, shouting into her ear.

"Wanna?"

It was a tall, broad-shouldered boy a few years older than she was, perhaps twenty-four, with a lean ruddy face, loose shoulder-length blond hair streaked green, and deep-set, very dark blue eyes. He swayed dreamily, gazing at the dance floor and hardly looking at her at all.

"Sure," Janie shouted back. He looped an arm around her shoulder, pulling her with him; his striped V-neck shirt smelled of talc and sweat. They danced for a long time, Janie moving with calculated abandon, the boy heaving and leaping as though a dog were biting at his shins.

"You're beautiful," he shouted. There was an almost imperceptible instant of silence as the DJ changed tracks. "What's your name?"

"Cleopatra Brimstone."

The shattering music grew deafening once more. The boy grinned. "Well, Cleopatra. Want something to drink?"

Janie nodded in time with the beat, so fast her head spun. He took her hand and she raced to keep up with him, threading their way toward the bar.

"Actually," she yelled, pausing so that he stopped short and bumped up against her. "I think I'd rather go outside. Want to come?"

He stared at her, half-smiling, and shrugged. "Aw right. Let me get a drink first—"

They went outside. In the alley the wind sent eddies of dead leaves and news-paper flying up into their faces. Janie laughed and pressed herself against the boy's side. He grinned down at her, finished his drink, and tossed the can aside; then he put his arm around her. "Do you want to go get a drink, then?" he asked.

They stumbled out onto the sidewalk, turned and began walking. People filled the High Street, lines snaking out from the entrances of pubs and restaurants. A blue glow surrounded the streetlights, and clouds of small white moths beat themselves against the globes; vapor and banners of gray smoke hung above the punks blocking the sidewalk by Camden Lock. Janie and the boy dipped down into the street. He pointed to a pub occupying the corner a few blocks down, a large old green-painted building with baskets of flowers hanging beneath its windows and a large sign swinging back and forth in the wind: THE END OF THE WORLD. "In there, then?"

Janie shook her head. "I live right here, by the canal. We could go to my place if you want. We could have a few drinks there."

The boy glanced down at her. "Aw right," he said—very quickly, so she wouldn't change her mind. "That'd be awright."

It was quieter on the back street leading to the flat. An old drunk huddled in a doorway, cadging change; Janie looked away from him and got out her keys, while the boy stood restlessly, giving the drunk a belligerent look.

"Here we are," she announced, pushing the door open. "Home again, home again."

"Nice place." The boy followed her, gazing around admiringly. "You live here alone?"

"Yup." After she spoke Janie had a flash of unease, admitting that. But the boy only ambled into the kitchen, running a hand along the antique French farmhouse cupboard and nodding.

"You're American, right? Studying here?"

"Uh-huh. What would you like to drink? Brandy?"

He made a face, then laughed. "Aw right! You got expensive taste. Goes with the name, I'd guess." Janie looked puzzled, and he went on, "Cleopatra—fancy name for a girl."

"Fancier for a boy," Janie retorted, and he laughed again.

She got the brandy, stood in the living room unlacing her boots. "Why don't we go in there?" she said, gesturing toward the bedroom. "It's kind of cold out here."

The boy ran a hand across his head, his blond hair streaming through his fingers. "Yeah, aw right." He looked around. "Um, that the toilet there?" Janie nodded. "Right back, then . . ."

She went into the bedroom, set the brandy and two glasses on a night table, and took off her windbreaker. On another table, several tall candles, creamy white and thick as her wrist, were set into ornate brass holders. She lit these— the room filled with the sweet scent of beeswax—and sat on the floor, leaning against the bed. A few minutes later the toilet flushed and the boy reappeared. His hands and face were damp, redder than they had been. He smiled and sank onto the floor beside her. Janie handed him a glass of brandy.

"Cheers," he said, and drank it all in one gulp.

"Cheers," said Janie. She took a sip from hers, then refilled his glass. He drank again, more slowly this time. The candles threw a soft yellow haze over the four-poster bed with its green velvet duvet, the mounds of pillows, forest-green, crimson, saffron yellow. They sat without speaking for several minutes. Then the boy set his glass on the floor. He turned to face Janie, extending one arm around her shoulder and drawing his face near hers.

"Well, then," he said.

His mouth tasted acrid, nicotine and cheap gin beneath the blunter taste of brandy. His hand sliding under her shirt was cold; Janie felt goose pimples rising across her breast, her nipple shrinking beneath his touch. He pressed against her, his cock already hard, and reached down to unzip his jeans.

"Wait," Janie murmured. "Let's get on the bed. . . ."

She slid from his grasp and onto the bed, crawling to the heaps of pillow and feeling beneath one until she found what she had placed there earlier. "Let's have a little fun first."

"*This* is fun," the boy said, a bit plaintively. But he slung himself onto the bed beside her, pulling off his shoes and letting them fall to the floor with a thud. "What you got there?"

Smiling, Janie turned and held up the wristcuffs. The boy looked at them, then at her, grinning. "Oh, ho. Been in the back room, then—"

Janie arched her shoulders and unbuttoned her shirt. He reached for one of the cuffs, but she shook her head. "No. Not me, yet."

"Ladies first."

"Gentleman's pleasure."

The boy's grin widened. "Won't argue with that."

She took his hand and pulled him, gently, to the middle of the bed. "Lie on your back," she whispered.

He did, watching as she removed first his shirt and then his jeans and underwear. His cock lay nudged against his thigh, not quite hard; when she brushed her fingers against it he moaned softly, took her hand and tried to press it against him.

"No," she whispered. "Not yet. Give me your hand."

She placed the cuffs around each wrist, and his ankles; fastened the nylon leash to each one and then began tying the bonds around each bedpost. It took longer than she had expected; it was difficult to get the bonds taut enough that the boy could not move. He lay there watchfully, his eyes glimmering in the candlelight as he craned his head to stare at her, his breath shallow, quickening.

"There." She sat back upon her haunches, staring at him. His cock was hard now, the hair on his chest and groin tawny in the half-light. He gazed back at her, his tongue pale as he licked his lips. "Try to get away," she whispered.

He moved slightly, his arms and legs a white X against a deep green field. "Can't," he said hoarsely.

She pulled her shirt off, then her nylon skirt. She had nothing on beneath. She leaned forward, letting her fingers trail from the cleft in his throat to his chest, cupping her palm atop his nipple and then sliding her hand down to his thigh. The flesh was warm, the little hairs soft and moist. Her own breath quickened; sudden heat flooded her, a honeyed liquid in her mouth. Above her brow the long hairs stiffened and furled straight out to either side: when she lifted her head to the candlelight she could see them from the corner of her eyes, twin barbs black and glistening like wire.

"You're so sexy." The boy's voice was hoarse. "God, you're—"

She placed her hand over his mouth. "Try to get away," she said, commandingly this time. "*Try to get away.*"

His torso writhed, the duvet bunching up around him in dark folds. She raked her fingernails down his chest, and he cried out, moaning "Fuck me, god, fuck me . . ."

"Try to get away."

She stroked his cock, her fingers barely grazing its swollen head. With a moan he came, struggling helplessly to thrust his groin toward her. At the same moment Janie gasped, a fiery rush arrowing down from her brow to her breasts, her cunt. She rocked forward, crying out, her head brushing against the boy's side as she sprawled back across the bed. For a minute she lay there, the room around her seeming to pulse and swirl into myriad crystalline shapes, each bearing within it the same line of candles, the long curve of the boy's thigh swelling up into the hollow of his hip. She drew breath shakily, the flush of heat fading from her brow; then pushed herself up until she was sitting beside him. His eyes were shut. A thread of saliva traced the furrow between mouth and chin. Without thinking she drew her face down to his, and kissed his cheek.

Immediately he began to grow smaller. Janie reared back, smacking into one of the bedposts, and stared at the figure in front of her, shaking her head.

"No," she whispered. "No, no."

He was shrinking: so fast it was like watching water dissolve into dry sand. Man-size, child-size, large dog, small. His eyes flew open and for a fraction of a second stared horrified into her own. His hands and feet slipped like mercury from his bonds, wriggling until they met his torso and were absorbed into it. Janie's fingers kneaded the duvet; six inches away the boy was no larger than her hand, then smaller, smaller still. She blinked, for a heart-shredding instant thought he had disappeared completely.

Then she saw something crawling between folds of velvet. The length of her middle finger, its thorax black, yellow-striped, its lower wings elongated into frilled arabesques like those of a festoon, deep yellow, charcoal black, with indigo eyespots, its upper wings a chiaroscuro of black and white stripes.

*Bhutanitis lidderdalii.* A native of the eastern Himalayas, rarely glimpsed: it lived among the crowns of trees in mountain valleys, its caterpillars feeding on lianas. Janie held her breath, watching as its wings beat feebly. Without warning it lifted into the air. Janie cried out, falling onto her knees as she sprawled across the bed, cupping it quickly but carefully between her hands.

"Beautiful, beautiful," she crooned. She stepped from the bed, not daring to pause and examine it, and hurried into the kitchen. In the cupboard she found an empty jar, set it down, and gingerly angled the lid from it, holding one hand with the butterfly against her breast. She swore, feeling its wings fluttering against her fingers, then quickly brought her hand to the jar's mouth, dropped the butterfly inside, and screwed the lid back in place. It fluttered helplessly inside; she could see where the scales had already been scraped from its wing. Still swearing she ran back into the bedroom, putting the lights on and dragging her collection box from under the bed. She grabbed a vial of ethyl alcohol, went back into the kitchen and tore a bit of paper towel from the rack. She opened the vial, poured a few drops of ethyl alcohol onto the paper, opened the jar and gently tilted it onto its side. She slipped the paper inside, very slowly tipping the jar upright once more, until the paper had settled on the bottom, the butterfly on top of it. Its wings beat frantically for a few moments, then stopped. Its proboscis uncoiled, finer than a hair. Slowly Janie drew her own hand to her brow and ran it along the length of the antennae there. She sat there staring at it until the sun leaked through the wooden shutters in the kitchen window. The butterfly did not move again.

The next day passed in a metallic gray haze, the only color the saturated blues and yellows of the *lidderdalii's* wings, burned upon Janie's eyes as though she had looked into the sun. When she finally roused herself, she felt a spasm of panic at the sight of the boy's clothes on the bedroom floor.

"Shit." She ran her hand across her head, was momentarily startled to recall she had no hair. "Now what?"

She stood there for a few minutes, thinking; then she gathered the clothes—striped V-neck sweater, jeans, socks, Jockey shorts, Timberland knockoff shoes—and dumped them into a plastic Sainsbury's bag. There was a wallet in the jeans pocket. She opened it, gazed impassively at a driver's license—KENNETH REED, WOLVERHAMPTON—and a few five-pound notes. She pocketed the money, took the license into the bathroom, and burned it, letting the ashes drop into the toilet. Then she went outside.

It was early Sunday morning, no one about except for a young mother pushing a baby in a stroller. In the neighboring doorway the same drunk old man sprawled surrounded by empty bottles and rubbish. He stared blearily up at Janie as she approached.

"Here," she said. She bent and dropped the five-pound notes into his scabby hand.

"God bless you, darlin'." He coughed, his eyes focusing on neither Janie nor the notes. "God bless you."

She turned and walked briskly back toward the canal path. There were few waste bins in Camden Town, and so each day trash accumulated in rank heaps along the path, beneath streetlights, in vacant alleys. Street cleaners and sweeping machines then daily cleared it all away again. Like elves, Janie thought. As she walked along the canal path she dropped the shoes in one pile of rubbish, tossed the sweater alongside a single high-heeled shoe in the market, stuffed the underwear and socks into a collapsing cardboard box filled with rotting lettuce, and left the jeans beside a stack of papers outside an unopened newsagent's shop. The wallet she tied into the Sainsbury's bag and dropped into an overflowing trash bag outside of Boots. Then she retraced her steps, stopping in front of a shop window filled with tatty polyester lingerie in large sizes and boldly artificial-looking wigs: pink Afros, platinum blond falls, black-and-white Cruella De Vil tresses.

The door was propped open; Schubert lieder played softly on 3 2. Janie stuck her head in and looked around, saw a beefy man behind the register, cashing out. He had orange lipstick smeared around his mouth and delicate silver fish hanging from his ears.

"We're not open yet. Eleven on Sunday," he said without looking up.

"I'm just looking." Janie sidled over to a glass shelf where four wigs sat on Styrofoam heads. One had very glossy black hair in a chin-length flapper bob. Janie tried it on, eyeing herself in a grimy mirror. "How much is this one?"

"Fifteen. But we're not—"

"Here. Thanks!" Janie stuck a twenty-pound note on the counter and ran from the shop. When she reached the corner she slowed, pirouetted to catch her reflection in a shop window. She stared at herself, grinning, then walked the rest of the way home, exhilarated and faintly dizzy.

Monday morning she went to the zoo to begin her volunteer work. She had mounted the *Bhutanitis lidderdalii*, on a piece of Styrofoam with a piece of paper on it, to keep the butterfly's legs from becoming embedded in the Styrofoam. She'd softened it first, putting it into a jar with damp paper, removed it and placed it on the mounting platform, neatly spearing its thorax—a little to the right—with a #2 pin. She propped it carefully on the wainscoting beside the hawkmoth, and left.

She arrived and found her ID badge waiting for her at the staff entrance. It was a clear morning, warmer than it had been for a week; the long hairs on her brow vibrated as though they were wires that had been plucked. Beneath the wig her shaved head felt hot and moist, the first new hairs starting to prickle across her scalp. Her nose itched where her glasses pressed against it. Janie walked, smiling, past the gibbons howling in their habitat and the pygmy hippos floating calmly in their pool, their eyes shut, green bubbles breaking around them like little fish. In front of the insect zoo a uniformed woman was unloading sacks of meal from a golf cart.

"Morning," Janie called cheerfully, and went inside.

She found David Bierce standing in front of a temperature gauge beside a glass cage holding the hissing cockroaches.

"Something happened last night, the damn things got too cold." He glanced over, handed her a clipboard, and began to remove the top of the gauge. "I called Operations but they're at their fucking morning meeting. Fucking computers—"

He stuck his hand inside the control box and flicked angrily at the gauge. "You know anything about computers?"

"Not this kind." Janie brought her face up to the cage's glass front. Inside were half a dozen glossy roaches, five inches long and the color of pale maple syrup. They lay, unmoving, near a glass petri dish filled with what looked like damp brown sugar. "Are they dead?"

"Those things? They're fucking immortal. You could stamp on one, and it wouldn't die. Believe me, I've done it." He continued to fiddle with the gauge, finally sighed, and replaced the lid. "Well, let's let the boys over in Ops handle it. Come on, I'll get you started."

He gave her a brief tour of the lab, opening drawers full of dissecting instruments, mounting platforms, pins; showing her where the food for the various insects was kept in a series of small refrigerators. Sugar syrup, cornstarch, plastic containers full of smaller insects, grubs and mealworms, tiny gray beetles. "Mostly we just keep on top of replacing the ones that die," David explained, "that and making sure the plants don't develop the wrong kind of fungus. Nature takes her course, and we just goose her along when she needs it. School groups are here constantly, but the docents handle that. You're more than welcome to talk to them, if that's the sort of thing you want to do."

He turned from where he'd been washing empty jars at a small sink, dried his hands, and walked over to sit on top of a desk. "It's not terribly glamorous work here." He reached down for a Styrofoam cup of coffee and sipped from it, gazing at her coolly. "We're none of us working on our Ph.D.'s anymore."

Janie shrugged. "That's all right."

"It's not even all that interesting. I mean, it can be very repetitive. Tedious."

"I don't mind." A sudden pang of anxiety made Janie's voice break. She could feel her face growing hot, and quickly looked away. "Really," she said sullenly.

"Suit yourself. Coffee's over there; you'll probably have to clean yourself a cup, though." He cocked his head, staring at her curiously, and then said, "Did you do something different with your hair?"

She nodded once, brushing the edge of her bangs with a finger. "Yeah."

"Nice. Very Louise Brooks." He hopped from the desk and crossed to a computer set up in the corner. "You can use my computer if you need to, I'll give you the password later."

Janie nodded, her flush fading into relief. "How many people work here?"

"Actually, we're short-staffed here right now—no money for hiring and our grant's run out. It's pretty much just me and whoever Carolyn sends over from the docents. Sweet little bluehairs mostly; they don't much like bugs. So it's providential you turned up, *Jane*."

He said her name mockingly, gave her a crooked grin. "You said you have experience mounting? Well, I try to save as many of the dead specimens as I can, and when there's any slow days, which there never are, I mount them and use them for the workshops I do with the schools that come in. What would be nice would be if we had enough specimens that I could give some to the teachers, to take back to their classrooms. We have a nice Web site and we might be able to work up some interactive programs. No schools are scheduled today, Monday's usually slow here. So if you could work on some of *those*—" He gestured to where several dozen cardboard boxes and glass jars were strewn across a countertop. "—that would be really brilliant," he ended, and turned to his computer screen.

She spent the morning mounting insects. Few were interesting or unusual: a number of brown hairstreaks, some Camberwell beauties, three hissing cockroaches, several brimstones. But there was a single *Acherontia atropos*, the death's-head hawkmoth, the pattern of gray and brown and pale yellow scales on the back of its thorax forming the image of a human skull. Its proboscis was unfurled, the twin points sharp enough to pierce a finger: Janie touched it gingerly, wincing delightedly as a pinprick of blood appeared on her fingertip.

"You bring lunch?"

She looked away from the bright magnifying light she'd been using and blinked in surprise. "Lunch?"

David Bierce laughed. "Enjoying yourself? Well, that's good, makes the day go faster. Yes, lunch!" He rubbed his hands together, the harsh light making him look gnomelike, his sharp features malevolent and leering. "They have some decent fish and chips at the stall over by the cats. Come on, I'll treat you. Your first day."

They sat at a picnic table beside the food booth and ate. David pulled a bottle of ale from his knapsack and shared it with Janie. Overhead scattered clouds like smoke moved swiftly southward. An Indian woman with three small boys sat at another table, the boys tossing fries at seagulls that swept down, shrieking, and made the smallest boy wail.

"Rain later," David said, staring at the sky. "Too bad." He sprinkled vinegar on his fried haddock and looked at Janie. "So did you go out over the weekend?"

She stared at the table and smiled. "Yeah, I did. It was fun."

"Where'd you go? The Electric Ballroom?"

"God, no. This other place." She glanced at his hand resting on the table beside her. He had long fingers, the knuckles slightly enlarged; but the back of his hand was smooth, the same soft brown as the *Acherontia's* wingtips. Her brows prickled, warmth trickling from them like water. When she lifted her head she could smell him, some kind of musky soap, salt; the bittersweet ale on his breath.

"Yeah? Where? I haven't been out in months, I'd be lost in Camden Town these days."

"I dunno. The Hive?"

She couldn't imagine he would have heard of it—far too old. But he swiveled on the bench, his eyebrows arching with feigned shock. "You went to *Hive?* And they let you in?"

"Yes," Janie stammered. "I mean, I didn't know—it was just a dance club. I just—danced."

"Did you." David Bierce's gaze sharpened, his hazel eyes catching the sun and sending back an icy emerald glitter. "Did you."

She picked up the bottle of ale and began to peel the label from it. "Yes."

"Have a boyfriend, then?"

She shook her head, rolled a fragment of label into a tiny pill. "No."

"Stop that." His hand closed over hers. He drew it away from the bottle, letting it rest against the table edge. She swallowed: he kept his hand on top of hers, pressing it against the metal edge until she felt her scored palm began to ache. Her eyes closed: she could feel herself floating, and see a dozen feet below her own form, slender, the wig beetle-black upon her skull, her wrist like a bent stalk. Abruptly his hand slid away and beneath the table, brushing her leg as he stooped to retrieve his knapsack.

"Time to get back to work," he said lightly, sliding from the bench and slinging his bag over his shoulder. The breeze lifted his long graying hair as he turned away. "I'll see you back there."

Overhead the gulls screamed and flapped, dropping bits of fried fish on the sidewalk. She stared at the table in front of her, the cardboard trays that held the remnants of lunch, and watched as a yellow jacket landed on a fleck of grease, its golden thorax swollen with moisture as it began to feed.

She did not return to Hive that night. Instead she wore a patchwork dress over her jeans and Doc Martens, stuffed the wig inside a drawer, and headed to a small bar on Inverness Street. The fair day had turned to rain, black puddles like molten metal capturing the amber glow of traffic signals and streetlights.

There were only a handful of tables at Bar Ganza. Most of the customers stood on the sidewalk outside, drinking and shouting to be heard above the sound of wailing Spanish love songs. Janie fought her way inside, got a glass of red wine, and miraculously found an empty stool alongside the wall. She climbed onto it, wrapped her long legs around the pedestal, and sipped her wine.

"Hey. Nice hair." A man in his early thirties, his own head shaved, sidled up to Janie's stool. He held a cigarette, smoking it with quick, nervous gestures as he stared at her. He thrust his cigarette toward the ceiling, indicating a booming speaker. "You like the music?"

"Not particularly."

"Hey, you're American? Me, too. Chicago. Good bud of mine, works for Citibank, he told me about this place. Food's not bad. Tapas. Baby octopus. You like octopus?"

Janie's eyes narrowed. The man wore expensive-looking corduroy trousers, a rumpled jacket of nubby charcoal-colored linen. "No," she said, but didn't turn away.

"Me neither. Like eating great big slimy bugs. Geoff Lanning—"

He stuck his hand out. She touched it, lightly, and smiled. "Nice to meet you, Geoff."

For the next half hour or so she pretended to listen to him, nodding and smiling brilliantly whenever he looked up at her. The bar grew louder and more crowded, and people began eyeing Janie's stool covetously.

"I think I'd better hand over this seat," she announced, hopping down and elbowing her way to the door. "Before they eat me."

Geoff Lanning hurried after her. "Hey, you want to get dinner? The Camden Brasserie's just up here—"

"No thanks." She hesitated on the curb, gazing demurely at her Doc Martens. "But would you like to come in for a drink?"

He was very impressed by her apartment. "Man, this place'd probably go for a half mil, easy! That's three quarters of a million American." He opened and closed cupboards, ran a hand lovingly across the slate sink. "Nice hardwood floors, high-speed access—you never told me what you do."

Janie laughed. "As little as possible. Here—"

She handed him a brandy snifter, let her finger trace the back of his wrist. "You look like kind of an adventurous sort of guy."

"Hey, big adventure, that's me." He lifted his glass to her. "What exactly did you have in mind? Big-game hunting?"

"Mmm. Maybe."

It was more of a struggle this time, not for Geoff Lanning but for Janie. He lay complacently in his bonds, his stocky torso wriggling obediently when Janie commanded. Her head ached from the cheap wine at Bar Ganza; the long hairs above her eyes lay sleek against her skull, and did not move at all until she closed her eyes and, unbidden, the image of David Bierce's hand covering hers appeared.

"Try to get away," she whispered.

"Whoa, Nellie," Geoff Lanning gasped.

"Try to get away," she repeated, her voice hoarser.

"Oh." The man whimpered softly. "Jesus Christ, what—oh, my God, *what*—"

Quickly she bent and kissed his fingertips, saw where the leather cuff had bitten into his pudgy wrist. This time she was prepared when with a keening sound he began to twist upon the bed, his arms and legs shriveling and then coiling in upon themselves, his shaven head withdrawing into his tiny torso like a snail within its shell.

But she was not prepared for the creature that remained, its feathery antennae a trembling echo of her own, its extraordinarily elongated hind spurs nearly four inches long.

"*Oh,*" she gasped.

She didn't dare touch it until it took to the air: the slender spurs fragile as icicles, scarlet, their saffron tips curling like Christmas ribbon, its large delicate wings saffron with slate-blue and scarlet eyespots, and spanning nearly six inches. A Madagascan moon moth, one of the loveliest and rarest silk moths, and almost impossible to find as an intact specimen.

"What do I do with you, what do I do?" she crooned as it spread its wings and lifted from the bed. It flew in short sweeping arcs; she scrambled to blow out the candles before it could get near them. She pulled on a bathrobe and left the lights off, closed the bedroom door and hurried into the kitchen, looking for a flashlight. She found nothing, but recalled Andrew telling her there was a large torch in the basement.

She hadn't been down there since her initial tour of the flat. It was brightly lit, with long neat cabinets against both walls, a floor-to-ceiling wine rack filled with bottles of claret and vintage burgundy, compact washer and dryer, small refrigerator, buckets and brooms waiting for the cleaning lady's weekly visit. She found the flashlight sitting on top of the refrigerator, a container of extra batteries beside it. She switched it on and off a few times, then glanced down at the refrigerator and absently opened it.

Seeing all that wine had made her think the little refrigerator might be filled with beer. Instead it held only a long plastic box, with a red lid and a red biohazard sticker on the side. Janie put the flashlight down and stooped, carefully removing the box and setting it on the floor. A label with Andrew's neat architectural handwriting was on the top.

> Dr. Andrew Filderman
> St. Martin's Hospice

"Huh," she said, and opened it.

Inside there was a small red biohazard waste container and scores of plastic bags filled with disposable hypodermics, ampules, and suppositories. All contained morphine at varying dosages. Janie stared, marveling, then opened one of the bags. She shook half a dozen morphine ampules into her palm, carefully reclosed the bag, put it back into the box, and returned the box to the refrigerator. Then she grabbed the flashlight and ran upstairs.

It took her a while to capture the moon moth. First she had to find a killing jar large enough, and then she had to very carefully lure it inside, so that its frail wing spurs wouldn't be damaged. She did this by positioning the jar on its side and placing a gooseneck lamp directly behind it, so that the bare bulb shone through the glass. After about fifteen minutes, the moth landed on top of the jar, its tiny legs slipping as it struggled on the smooth curved surface. Another few minutes and it had crawled inside, nestled on the wad of tissues Janie had set there, moist with ethyl alcohol. She screwed the lid on tightly, left the jar on its side, and waited for it to die.

Over the next week she acquired three more specimens. *Papilio demetrius*, a Japanese swallowtail with elegant orange eyespots on a velvety black ground; a scarce copper, not scarce at all, really, but with lovely pumpkin-colored wings; and *Graphium agamemnon*, a Malaysian species with vivid green spots and chrome-yellow strips on its somber brown wings. She'd ventured away from Camden Town, capturing the swallowtail in a private room in an SM club in Islington and the *Graphium agamemnon* in a parked car behind a noisy pub in Crouch End. The scarce copper came from a vacant lot near the Tottenham Court Road tube station very late one night, where the wreckage of a chain-link fence stood in for her bedposts. She found the morphine to be useful, although she had to wait until immediately after the man ejaculated before pressing the ampule against his throat, aiming for the carotid artery. This way the butterflies emerged already sedated, and in minutes died with no damage to their wings. Leftover clothing was easily disposed of, but she had to be more careful with wallets, stuffing them deep within rubbish bins, when she could, or burying them in her own trash bags and then watching as the waste trucks came by on their rounds.

In South Kensington she discovered an entomological supply store. There she bought more mounting supplies and inquired casually as to whether the owner might be interested in purchasing some specimens.

He shrugged. "Depends. What you got?"

"Well, right now I have only one *Argema mittrei*." Janie adjusted her glasses and glanced around the shop. A lot of morphos, an Atlas moth: nothing too unusual. "But I might be getting another, in which case . . ."

"Moon moth, eh? How'd you come by that, I wonder?" The man raised his eyebrows, and Janie flushed. "Don't worry, I'm not going to turn you in. Christ, I'd go out of business. Well, obviously I can't display those in the shop, but if you want to part with one, let me know. I'm always scouting for my customers."

She began volunteering three days a week at the insect zoo. One Wednesday, the night after she'd gotten a gorgeous *Urania leilus*, its wings sadly damaged by rain, she arrived to see David Bierce reading that morning's *Camden New Journal*. He peered above the newspaper and frowned.

"You still going out alone at night?"

She froze, her mouth dry, turned, and hurried over to the coffee-maker. "Why?" she said, fighting to keep her tone even.

"Because there's an article about some of the clubs around here. Apparently a few people have gone missing."

"Really?" Janie got her coffee, wiping up a spill with the side of her hand. "What happened?"

"Nobody knows. Two blokes reported gone, family frantic, that sort of thing. Probably just runaways. Camden Town eats them alive, kids." He handed the paper to Janie. "Although one of them was last seen near Highbury Fields, some sex club there."

She scanned the article. There was no mention of any suspects. And no bodies had been found, although foul play was suspected. (*"Ken would never have gone away without notifying us or his employer. . . ."*)

Anyone with any information was urged to contact the police.

"I don't go to sex clubs," Janie said flatly. "Plus those are both guys."

"Mmm." David leaned back in his chair, regarding her coolly. "You're the one hitting Hive your first weekend in London."

"It's a *dance* club!" Janie retorted. She laughed, rolled the newspaper into a tube, and batted him gently on the shoulder. "Don't worry. I'll be careful."

David continued to stare at her, hazel eyes glittering. "Who says it's you I'm worried about?"

She smiled, her mouth tight as she turned and began cleaning bottles in the sink.

It was a raw day, more late November than mid-May. Only two school groups were scheduled; otherwise the usual stream of visitors was reduced to a handful of elderly women who shook their heads over the cockroaches and gave barely a glance to the butterflies before shuffling on to another building. David Bierce paced restlessly through the lab on his way to clean the cages and make more complaints to the Operations Division. Janie cleaned and mounted two stag beetles, their spiny legs pricking her fingertips as she tried to force the pins through their glossy chestnut-colored shells. Afterwards she busied herself with straightening the clutter of cabinets and drawers stuffed with requisition forms and microscopes, computer parts and dissection kits.

It was well past two when David reappeared, his anorak slick with rain, his hair tucked beneath the hood. "Come on," he announced, standing impatiently by the open door. "Let's go to lunch."

Janie looked up from the computer where she'd been updating a specimen list. "I'm really not very hungry," she said, giving him an apologetic smile. "You go ahead."

"Oh, for Christ's sake." David let the door slam shut as he crossed to her, his sneakers leaving wet smears on the tiled floor. "That can wait till tomorrow. Come on, there's not a fucking thing here that needs doing."

"But—" She gazed up at him. The hood slid from his head; his gray-streaked hair hung loose to his shoulders, and the sheen of rain on his sharp cheekbones made him look carved from oiled wood. "What if somebody comes?"

"A very nice docent named Mrs. Eleanor Feltwell is out there, *even as we speak*, in the unlikely event that we have a single visitor."

He stooped so that his head was beside hers, scowling as he stared at the computer screen. A lock of his hair fell to brush against her neck. Beneath the wig her scalp burned, as though stung by tiny ants; she breathed in the warm acrid smell of his sweat and something else, a sharper scent, like crushed oak-mast or fresh-sawn wood. Above her brows the antennae suddenly quivered. Sweetness coated her tongue like burnt syrup. With a rush of panic she turned her head so he wouldn't see her face.

"I—I should finish this—"

"Oh, just *fuck* it, Jane! It's not like we're *paying* you. Come on, now, there's a good girl—"

He took her hand and pulled her to her feet, Janie still looking away. The bangs of her cheap wig scraped her forehead, and she batted at them feebly. "Get your things. What, don't you ever take days off in the States?"

"All right, all right." She turned and gathered her black vinyl raincoat and knapsack, pulled on the coat, and waited for him by the door. "Jeez, you must be hungry," she said crossly.

"No. Just fucking bored out of my skull. Have you been to Ruby in the Dust? No? I'll take you then, let's go—"

The restaurant was down the High Street, a small, cheerfully claptrap place, dim in the gray afternoon, its small wooden tables scattered with abandoned newspapers and overflowing ashtrays. David Bierce ordered a steak and a pint. Janie had a small salad, nasturtium blossoms strewn across pale green lettuce, and a glass of red wine. She lacked an appetite lately, living on vitamin-enhanced, fruity bottled drinks from the health food store and baklava from a Greek bakery near the tube station.

"So." David Bierce stabbed a piece of steak, peering at her sideways. "Don't tell me you really haven't been here before."

"I haven't!" Despite her unease at being with him, she laughed, and caught her reflection in the wall-length mirror. A thin plain young woman in shapeless Peruvian sweater and jeans, bad haircut, and ugly glasses. Gazing at herself she felt suddenly stronger, invisible. She tilted her head and smiled at Bierce. "The food's good."

"So you don't have someone taking you out to dinner every night? Cooking for you? I thought you American girls all had adoring men at your feet. Adoring slaves," he added dryly. "Or slave girls, I suppose. If that's your thing."

"No." She stared at her salad, shook her head demurely, and took a sip of wine. It made her feel even more invulnerable. "No, I—"

"Boyfriend back home, right?" He finished his pint, flagged the waiter to order another, and turned back to Janie. "Well, that's nice. That's very nice—for him," he added, and gave a short harsh laugh.

The waiter brought another pint, and more wine for Janie. "Oh really, I better—"

"Just drink it, Jane." Under the table, she felt a sharp pressure on her foot. She wasn't wearing her Doc Martens today but a pair of red plastic jellies. David Bierce had planted his heel firmly atop her toes; she sucked in her breath in shock and pain, the bones of her foot crackling as she tried to pull it from beneath him. Her antennae rippled, then stiffened, and heat burst like a seed inside her.

"Go ahead," he said softly, pushing the wineglass toward her. "Just a sip, that's right—"

She grabbed the glass, spilling wine on her sweater as she gulped at it. The vicious pressure on her foot subsided, but as the wine ran down her throat she could feel the heat thrusting her into the air, currents rushing beneath her as the girl at the table below set down her wineglass with trembling fingers.

"There." David Bierce smiled, leaning forward to gently cup her hand between his. "Now this is better than working. Right, Jane?"

He walked her home along the canal path. Janie tried to dissuade him, but he'd had a third pint by then; it didn't seem to make him drunk but coldly obdurate, and she finally gave in. The rain had turned to a fine drizzle, the canal's usually murky water silvered and softly gleaming in the twilight. They passed few other people, and Janie found herself wishing someone else would appear, so that she'd have an excuse to move closer to David Bierce. He kept close to the canal itself, several feet from Janie; when the breeze lifted she could catch his oaky scent again, rising above the dank reek of stagnant water and decaying hawthorn blossom.

They crossed over the bridge to approach her flat by the street. At the front sidewalk Janie stopped, smiled shyly, and said, "Thanks. That was nice."

David nodded. "Glad I finally got you out of your cage." He lifted his head to gaze appraisingly at the row house. "Christ, this where you're staying? You split the rent with someone?"

"No." She hesitated: she couldn't remember what she had told him about her living arrangements. But before she could blurt something out he stepped past her to the front door, peeking into the window and bobbing impatiently up and down.

"Mind if I have a look? Professional entomologists don't often get the chance to see how the quality live."

Janie hesitated, her stomach clenching; decided it would be safer to have him in rather than continue to put him off.

"All right," she said reluctantly, and opened the door.

"Mmmm. Nice, nice, very nice." He swept around the living room, spinning on his heel and making a show of admiring the elaborate molding, the tribal rugs, the fireplace mantel with its thick ecclesiastical candles and ormolu mirror. "Goodness, all this for a wee thing like you? You're a clever cat, landing on your feet here, Lady Jane."

She blushed. He bounded past her on his way into the bedroom, touching her shoulder; she had to close her eyes as a fiery wave surged through her and her antennae trembled.

"Wow," he exclaimed.

Slowly she followed him into the bedroom. He stood in front of the wall where her specimens were balanced in a neat line across the wainscoting. His eyes were wide, his mouth open in genuine astonishment.

"Are these *yours*?" he marveled, his gaze fixed on the butterflies. "You didn't actually catch them—?"

She shrugged.

"These are incredible!" He picked up the *Graphium agamemnon* and tilted it to the pewter-colored light falling through the French doors. "Did you mount them, too?"

She nodded, crossing to stand beside him. "Yeah. You can tell, with that one—" She pointed at the *Urania leilus* in its oak-framed box. "It got rained on."

David Bierce replaced the *Graphium agamemnon* and began to read the labels on the others.

*Papilio demetrius*
UNITED KINGDOM: LONDON
*Highbury Fields, Islington*

7.V.2001
J. Kendall

*Isopa katinka*
UNITED KINGDOM: LONDON
Finsbury Park
09.V.2001
J. Kendall

*Argema mittrei*
UNITED KINGDOM: LONDON
Camden Town
13.IV.2001
J. Kendall

He shook his head. "You screwed up, though—you wrote *London* for all of them." He turned to her, grinning wryly. "Can't think of the last time I saw a moon moth in Camden Town."

She forced a laugh. "Oh—right."

"And, I mean, you can't have actually *caught* them—"

He held up the *Isopa katinka*, a butter-yellow Emperor moth, its peacock's-eyes russet and jet-black. "I haven't seen any of these around lately. Not even in Finsbury."

Janie made a little grimace of apology. "Yeah. I meant, that's where I found them—where I bought them."

"Mmmm." He set the moth back on its ledge. "You'll have to share your sources with me. I can never find things like these in North London."

He turned and headed out of the bedroom. Janie hurriedly straightened the specimens, her hands shaking now as well, and followed him.

"Well, Lady Jane." For the first time he looked at her without his usual mocking arrogance, his green-flecked eyes bemused, almost regretful. "I think we managed to salvage something from the day."

He turned, gazing one last time at the flat's glazed walls and highly waxed floors, the imported cabinetry and jewel-toned carpets. "I was going to say, when I walked you home, that you needed someone to take care of you. But it looks like you've managed that on your own."

Janie stared at her feet. He took a step toward her, the fragrance of oak-mast and honey filling her nostrils, crushed acorns, new fern. She grew dizzy, her hand lifting to find him; but he only reached to graze her cheek with his finger.

"Night then, Janie," he said softly, and walked back out into the misty evening.

When he was gone she raced to the windows and pulled all the velvet curtains, then tore the wig from her head and threw it onto the couch along with her glasses. Her heart was pounding, her face slick with sweat—from fear or rage or disappointment, she didn't know. She yanked off her sweater and jeans, left them on the living room floor and stomped into the bathroom. She stood in the shower for twenty minutes, head upturned as the water sluiced the smells of bracken and leafmold from her skin.

Finally she got out. She dried herself, let the towel drop, and went into the kitchen. Abruptly she was famished. She tore open cupboards and drawers until she found a half-full jar of lavender honey from Provence. She opened it, the top spinning off into the sink, and frantically spooned honey into her mouth with her fingers. When she was finished she grabbed a jar of lemon curd and ate most of that, until she felt as though she might be sick. She stuck her head into the sink, letting water run from the faucet into her mouth, and at last walked, surfeited, into the bedroom.

She dressed, feeling warm and drowsy, almost dreamlike; pulling on red-and-yellow-striped stockings, her nylon skirt, a tight red T-shirt. No bra, no panties. She put in her contacts, then examined herself in the mirror. Her hair had begun to grow back, a scant velvety stubble, bluish in the dim light. She drew a sweeping black line across each eyelid, on a whim took the liner and extended the curve of each antenna until they touched her temples. She painted her lips black as well and went to find her black vinyl raincoat.

It was early when she went out, far too early for any of the clubs to be open. The rain had stopped, but a thick greasy fog hung over everything, coating windshields and shop windows, making Janie's face feel as though it were encased in a clammy shell. For hours she wandered Camden Town, huge violet eyes turning to stare back at the men who watched her, dismissing each of them. Once she thought she saw David Bierce, coming out of Ruby in the Dust; but when she stopped to watch him cross the street saw it was not David at all but someone else. Much younger, his long dark hair in a thick braid, his feet clad in knee-high boots. He crossed. High Street, heading toward the tube station. Janie hesitated, then darted after him.

He went to the Electric Ballroom. Fifteen or so people stood out front, talking quietly. The man she'd followed joined the line, standing by himself. Janie waited across the street, until the door opened and the little crowd began to shuffle inside. After the long-haired young man had entered she counted to one hundred, crossed the street, paid her cover, and went inside.

The club had three levels; she finally tracked him down on the uppermost one. Even on a rainy Wednesday night it was crowded, the sound system blaring Idris Mohammed and Jimmy Cliff. He was standing alone near the bar, drinking bottled water.

"Hi!" she shouted, swaying up to him with her best First Day of School Smile. "Want to dance?"

He was older than she'd thought—thirtyish, still not as old as Bierce. He stared at her, puzzled, and then shrugged. "Sure."

They danced, passing the water bottle between them. "What's your name?" he shouted.

"Cleopatra Brimstone."

"You're kidding!" he yelled back. The song ended in a bleat of feedback, and they walked, panting, back to the bar.

"What, you know another Cleopatra?" Janie asked teasingly.

"No. It's just a crazy name, that's all." He smiled. He was handsomer than David Bierce, his features softer, more rounded, his eyes dark brown, his manner a bit reticent. "I'm Thomas Raybourne. Tom."

He bought another bottle of Pellegrino and one for Janie. She drank it quickly, trying to get his measure. When she finished she set the empty bottle on the floor and fanned herself with her hand.

"It's hot in here." Her throat hurt from shouting over the music. "I think I'm going to take a walk. Feel like coming?"

He hesitated, glancing around the club. "I was supposed to meet a friend here. . . ." he began, frowning. "But—"

"Oh." Disappointment filled her, spiking into desperation. "Well, that's okay. I guess."

"Oh, what the hell." He smiled: he had nice eyes, a more stolid, reassuring gaze than Bierce. "I can always come back."

Outside she turned right, in the direction of the canal. "I live pretty close by. Feel like coming in for a drink?"

He shrugged again. "I don't drink, actually."

"Something to eat then? It's not far—just along the canal path a few blocks past Camden Lock—"

"Yeah, sure."

They made desultory conversation. "You should be careful," he said as they crossed the bridge. "Did you read about those people who've gone missing in Camden Town?"

Janie nodded but said nothing. She felt anxious and clumsy—as though she'd drunk too much, although she'd had nothing alcoholic since the two glasses of wine with David Bierce. Her companion also seemed ill at ease; he kept glancing back, as though looking for someone on the canal path behind them.

"I should have tried to call," he explained ruefully. "But I forgot to recharge my mobile."

"You could call from my place."

"No, that's all right."

She could tell from his tone that he was figuring how he could leave, gracefully, as soon as possible.

Inside the flat he settled on the couch, picked up a copy of *Time Out* and flipped through it, pretending to read. Janie went immediately into the kitchen and poured herself a glass of brandy. She downed it, poured a second one, and joined him on the couch.

"So." She kicked off her Doc Martens, drew her stockinged foot slowly up his leg, from calf to thigh. "Where you from?"

He was passive, so passive she wondered if he would get aroused at all. But after a while they were lying on the couch, both their shirts on the floor, his pants unzipped and his cock stiff, pressing against her bare belly.

"Let's go in there," Janie whispered hoarsely. She took his hand and led him into the bedroom.

She only bothered lighting a single candle before lying beside him on the bed. His eyes were half-closed, his breathing shallow. When she ran a fingernail around one nipple he made a small surprised sound, then quickly turned and pinned her to the bed.

"Wait! Slow down," Janie said, and wriggled from beneath him. For the last week she'd left the bonds attached to the bedposts, hiding them beneath the covers when not in use. Now she grabbed one of the wrist-cuffs and pulled it free. Before he could see what she was doing it was around his wrist.

"Hey!"

She dived for the foot of the bed, his leg narrowly missing her as it thrashed against the covers. It was more difficult to get this in place, but she made a great show of giggling and stroking his thigh, which seemed to calm him. The other leg was next, and finally she leapt from the bed and darted to the headboard, slipping from his grasp when he tried to grab her shoulder.

"This is not consensual," he said. She couldn't tell if he was serious or not.

"What about this, then?" she murmured, sliding down between his legs and cupping his erect penis between her hands. "This seems to be enjoying itself."

He groaned softly, shutting his eyes. "Try to get away," she said. "Try to get away."

He tried to lunge upward, his body arcing so violently that she drew back in alarm. The bonds held; he arched again, and again, but now she remained beside him, her hands on his cock, his breath coming faster and faster and her own breath keeping pace with it, her heart pounding and the tingling above her eyes almost unbearable.

"Try to get away," she gasped. "Try to get away—"

When he came he cried out, his voice harsh, as though in pain, and Janie cried out as well, squeezing her eyes shut as spasms shook her from head to groin. Quickly her head dipped to kiss his chest; then she shuddered and drew back, watching.

His voice rose again, ended suddenly in a shrill wail, as his limbs knotted and shriveled like burning rope. She had a final glimpse of him, a homunculus sprouting too many legs. Then on the bed before her a perfectly formed *Papilio krishna* swallowtail crawled across the rumpled duvet, its wings twitching to display glittering green scales amidst spectral washes of violet and crimson and gold.

"Oh, you're beautiful, beautiful," she whispered.

From across the room echoed a sound: soft, the rustle of her kimono falling from its hook as the door swung open. She snatched her hand from the butterfly and stared, through the door to the living room.

In her haste to get Thomas Raybourne inside she had forgotten to latch the front door. She scrambled to her feet, naked, staring wildly at the shadow looming in front of her, its features taking shape as it approached the candle, brown and black, light glinting across his face.

It was David Bierce. The scent of oak and bracken swelled, suffocating, fragrant, cut by the bitter odor of ethyl alcohol. He forced her gently onto the bed, heat piercing her breast and thighs, her antennae bursting out like quills from her brow and wings exploding everywhere around her as she struggled fruitlessly.

"Now. Try to get away," he said.

*For Mike Harrison*

# LAWRENCE MILES

# Grass

*Lawrence Miles is a writer and artist who lives in a suburb of London. He is the author of several popular TV tie-in novels, and the creator, editor, and cowriter of* The Book of War. *As an artist, he has exhibited in the Barbican in London and other venues.*

*The following story is Miles's first publication in* The Magazine of Fantasy & Science Fiction: *a sparkling "alternate history" tale concerning Thomas Jefferson, mammoths, and the exploration of the American frontier. "Grass" is reprinted from the September issue of the magazine.*

—*T. W.*

"Only in the context of a *totality* of the sciences do Jefferson's achievements make sense. This would for instance explain the apparent contradiction of how a man now famed for his contribution to the political sciences . . . [was also] purportedly the first westerner to fully reconstruct the remains of a prehistoric mammoth. It's more the failing of an over-enthusiastic age than of the man himself that Jefferson seriously believed such antediluvian beasts could have survived until the 1800s in the wilds of the unexplored midwest. . . ."

—D. P. MANN, *THE WORLDS OF THOMAS JEFFERSON* (1958).

It starts with the President of the United States of America, although we should be clear on exactly what kind of *gentleman* we're discussing here. Sitting behind the Presidential desk (rosewood, as it happens, and very nice too) is a man whom later generations will call a polymath, a statesman-philosopher, a true product of the enlightenment. Oh yes, this particular President is a *creator*, with a portfolio that begins "We, the people" and works its way up to a big climax from there. He's also a man who distrusts priests of just about every denomination, which explains much of what's about to happen here: he's got a lot of time for the divine, this one, but mere mortal authority figures get his back up like nothing else on God's Earth. Now, we can't be sure that what we're about to see in this room is *bona fide* true, because the affairs of the President are traditionally left behind closed doors, and there are some rules even we're expected to follow. But we can put the scene together out of the pieces we know. Call it listening at keyholes. Call it history by degrees.

Mr. Jefferson—Mr. President—sits behind the aforementioned desk, in front of a vast window that looks out onto a garden of grass and cat's-ears, a garden quite specifically designed so as to in no way resemble the three million square miles of hostile territory beyond it. The light's flooding through the window onto the parquet-and-polish floor, while the President himself is leaning over the books with which he surrounds himself (this being a less literate time, how-ever, "surrounds" makes the number of books involved sound greater than it really is), reaching for his little box of joy. The box is small and off-white, a gift from a visitor whose exact name and purpose Mr. Jefferson can't quite recall: he seems to recollect that it was a woman, probably French (he has no difficulty remembering this, as he's had a head for Frenchwomen ever since a certain remarkable incident in a brothel in Paris . . . this is another story, and not the only "another story" which will be intercepting us today). History doesn't record what he keeps *inside* the box, though as we've imagined Mr. Jefferson as a free-thinking nineteenth century gentleman it could be anything from snuff to hash-ish. Let's give him the benefit of the doubt, and assume it's chewing tobacco. Undignified as it may seem.

"It has to be done—it *must* be done—it is our duty," he says, as he starts picking at the box's contents. He talks the way he writes, with far too many hyphens and pauses, and he's addressing the two men standing on the other side of his desk. "If we're to claim these lands for the good of our nation—if we're to prevent them being overrun by jackals and opportunists—if we're to have room in which to breathe, and not fall upon each other as they do in Europe. . . ."

Now, it so happens that Mr. Jefferson's domain has recently grown, thanks to a certain land deal which is not only due to increase his running total of United States, but which will also give him vast tracts of what he believes to be lush and verdant farmland, possibly including that mythical easy route to the Pacific. And the two men who now stand in Mr. Jefferson's office, nodding in solemn agreement, will go down in history as the first men to travel into the heart of this new terrain: or the first to take notes anyway, which is the way history works. Their names are, from left to right, Meriwether Lewis and William Clark. As expected.

(This is all quite ridiculous, of course. At least one of these men already belongs to the President's inner circle. If Jefferson wants to brief them on their mission, then he's more likely to do it in a cozy drawing room with a bottle of Cognac, swapping stories as Lewis lounges on a chaise lounge and Clark leans nonchalantly against the fireplace. But how can we resist imagining it this way? The two of them standing to attention before the Presidential desk, being in-structed to journey into the dark heart of the Northwest and bring the land under control. No doubt you're already imagining these two great explorers, these two grizzled veterans of the wilderness, walking into the President's office dressed in furs and racoon-skin hats. We need to believe they're going to step out of the briefing and, without even pausing for breath, stride off into the jungles of uncharted America. Such is history.)

Mr. Jefferson is telling the explorers that nobody can say for sure what they'll find in the Northwestern territories. The French who sold him the land have hardly been forthcoming, and the Indians aren't likely to be much help either.

The President expects every form of terrain imaginable, from the tropical to the simply peculiar. He's read the greatest naturalists of the age. He has plans to meet with Alexander von Humboldt himself. He's even heard the theories of the Englishman Frere, who claims to have found human remains which blatantly defy the book of Genesis, something Mr. Jefferson greatly appreciates. Oh, yes indeed. As an enlightened gentleman, the President knows the *terra incognita* Lewis and Clark will find is no Biblical wasteland. It's to be an altogether more rational landscape, filled with all the wonders that biology and geology can produce. A new world, untouched by Church dogma, governed only by the laws of Nature and Nature's God.

This is the point when Mr. Jefferson tells Lewis and Clark about the mammoths. Oddly—seeing as most of this patchwork conversation will be lost to posterity—the part about the mammoths is the one thing the history books *do* record.

It starts with the President, but in purely chronological terms the briefing in the office isn't the first thing to actually *happen*. Just look at this landscape, for example. Nothing behind-closed-doors here. The sky's a color which later generations will be unable to imagine as anything other than a kind of paint, a deep blue, a *dark* blue, that makes the green, green grass look as though it's glaring in the sunlight. The air's fresh, pre-industrial fresh, the kind of fresh you only get once it's been filtered through the lungs of several million herd animals and a couple of dozen Indian tribes (this is as fresh as nature gets, no doubt about it). The grass clings to the slopes, sticks close to the curves of the land, so the green's only broken up by the dirt-paths where animals have left their scents behind them like breadcrumb-trails. And mountains? Oh, there are mountains. Just waiting on the horizon, looking as if they'll *always* be just waiting on the horizon, wherever you stand on the surface of the Earth. Perfect idyll. Perfect Montana.

Timeless, we'd say. But from the President's point of view, we'd have to call it the past. Months before the briefing of Mr. Lewis and Mr. Clark, the white race has already set foot in the Land of the Shining Mountains.

Here she comes now.

Her name's Lucia Cailloux, and at this moment she's running barefoot through the grass, up the side of a slope which seems to have been put there just to warn travelers that the Rockies will be starting soon, and that they'd better get used to moving uphill. An observer would point out that Lucia— whose manner of dress is unusually masculine, but then, that's probably what you'd expect from someone who's spent so much time talking to damned heathen Indians—is technically wearing *boots*. But that's not how it feels to Lucia. No, she can feel the warm, warm earth between her naked toes, because in her head she's suddenly become an eight-year-old. As a twenty-year-old woman in the service of her government, this is hardly what she's being paid for, but right now her superiors are more than eight thousand miles away and Lucia can't help but feel she's going to get away with it.

You see, right now she believes she's *going* somewhere. When she was young, she once ran all the way up the Rue Viande, something of an achievement when you've got child-sized legs and no shoes, because the Rue Viande is a perfect slope and the sheer amount of dirt on it (in those days, anyway, before Napoleon started cleaning it all up) made the road feel like mud in the summer. On that day—running all the way to the tannery, right at the highest point of the street, where the skins were strung up like flags at the top of the world—the junior Lucia could feel the whole world cracking like glass behind her, with the wind ripping through her dirt-blonde hair and the sheer speed (all of, oh, two miles an hour) tearing at her little dress. And as she headed for the tip of that slope, she knew—*she knew*—she'd look down and see something big and wonderful on the other side, as her reward for running all the way. She knew she'd see the whole world, in all its truth and majesty. The face, if you will, of Nature's God.

She was right, as well. Young Lucia always *was* a perceptive little witch.

Now the older Lucia, barefoot and booted, knows the same thing. She can quite literally smell it on the wind. At the top of the slope, she stops, so this is the point when we finally see her face in closeup. Dirt-blonde hair ragged around her shoulders, pasty little freckles blistering in the sunlight, the pupils in her big, big eyes getting smaller as she brushes the last few drops of sweat and sunshine away from her forehead. It doesn't really matter whether we're looking at Lucia *now* or watching the eight-year-old flashback version, because as it turns out her hair's naturally dirt-blonde in color. Twelve years after the Rue Viande, even a clean Lucia looks that way.

Lucia can hear her co-traveler, the Indian, thumping his way up the slope behind her. He calls out to her: "*Quelque chose?*"

And Lucia calls back: "*Tout.*" (But that's pretty much the last time we'll be hearing her words in their natural spoken tongue.)

So the world spins around us, vertigo-wise, until we can look down on the great grass-covered crater beyond the slope. The dimple in the world, where Nature's God herself has reached down and left a whacking great fingerprint on the landscape. A gentle pit, with slopes of green sunning themselves in the midday heat, letting troughs of rainwater simmer and merge on their skin.

And there at the bottom of it all, the mammoths.

Now Lucia finds herself running again, and for a moment she isn't sure whether it's *now* her running or *then* her, until she remembers that on the Rue Viande she never went down the other side of the slope. At the bottom of the basin, the mammoths are grazing. It'd be almost abstract, like seeing drawings of fluffy brown clouds on a painted backdrop, if it weren't for the smell.

(Of course, when the eight-year-old Lucia stood on the *other* slope, the view was quite different. What she saw was a cartload of corpses, blocking the street while the horseman stopped to flirt with one of the local girls, as if having a cartload of corpses was some kind of aphrodisiac. But then, that was the Revolution for you. *C'est la vie*, as they say everywhere except Paris.)

That smell's starting to bother Lucia now, because she's remembering the smell of dung on the Rue Viande. She's so busy separating the horse-smell from the mammoth-smell that she doesn't even realize how far inertia's taking her. Gravity drags her to the bottom of the crater, then keeps her going, so before she can think about it she's stumbling over the ridges where the beasts have chewed and trampled away the grass. Pity the poor woman. The second most momentous moment of her life so far, and all she perceives is a series of confusing, ragged-edged images. The red-brown blurs that she knows are impossible animals. The smears of green that mark the walls of the crater, plastered with spoor and crushed plants: and is that a baby there, a baby mammoth, a little smudge of hair trying to stick close to its bigger smudge of a mother . . . ?

This is when things get slightly out of hand. It's when Lucia turns, nearly falling arse over tit in the process, and finds herself staring at the absurdly huge shape which is even now bearing down on her. The bull-mammoth weighs just over seven tons, not that Lucia will ever know it, and when rising up on its hind legs (as it is now) it must be all of fifteen feet high. When it raises its trunk, and opens its mouth, and flexes its massive lungs, you know it's quite capable of destroying anything that threatens its own stomping ground.

Nonetheless, the first thing Lucia does when faced with this monstrosity is "protect" herself by putting her arms up in front of her face. And they call this the Age of Reason.

There was an Indian. You might have forgotten about him.

He's now standing on the crest of the slope, watching the great beast rear up over the woman who's nominally his employer, though as a product of a non-market culture the Indian considers this "employer" business to be a pile of deershit. The Indian's name (for our purposes, anyway) is Broken Nose, which is not, of course, a "real" Indian name. It was given to him by a group of Frenchmen with especially fat faces, and it was earned after a confrontation at a French trading post, during which—predictably—the Indian broke a French official's nose. The friends of the unfortunate fat-faced man, being typically European, found this amusing. Being *very* typically European, "Broken Nose" was their idea of irony. It's apparently supposed to sound like an authentic Indian title, although Broken Nose himself considers it just a good excuse to punch future fat-faced men without them being surprised. Besides, his original Shoshoni name was even more embarrassing.

It has to be said, Broken Nose doesn't have a great interest in the aesthetic. Below him are creatures the American settlers would find unbelievable, which would probably trigger a religious spasm in the Catholics or the Jesuits whom Mr. Jefferson distrusts so much. However, Broken Nose simply finds the beasts stupid-looking, wearing thick wool all over their bodies despite the sunshine. Broken Nose is *slightly* concerned for his "employer," but he's well aware that she can look after herself.

On the first night of the expedition, when Broken Nose and Mademoiselle Cailloux made camp on the trail from Louisiana—where the Frenchwoman had arrived under the name of "Lucy Pebbles," and bartered for supplies in what sounded to the Indian like a perfect local accent—the two of them talked at length. Or as much as was possible, anyway, given that Broken Nose had been taught French by men who only needed to prime him for certain tasks. Without any due modesty, Broken Nose showed Mme. Cailloux the scar which had been ritually inflicted across his inner thigh (*not* by his own tribe, but that's another "another story"). And with less regard for her integrity than Broken Nose would have expected from a European woman, Mme. Cailloux bared her torso from her neck to her waist, revealing a scab left by a bullet which she claimed *should* have killed her, by all the known laws of Nature and science. This began a discussion about the great wars in Europe, about the little tribal elder called

Napoleon and the weapons he could muster: guns like those Mme. Cailloux herself carried, but grown so large that they needed huge boats of their own. Broken Nose asked why the Europeans always insisted on fighting with each other, and that gave the Mademoiselle pause for thought.

"*Your* people fight, don't they?" she said.

Broken Nose told her that this was indeed the case.

"Then why do *you* do it?" the woman asked.

The obvious answer was "because you tell us to," naturally, but Broken Nose suspected this was missing the point. The reasons seemed to him to be to do with territory, with possessions, with differences in gods. . . .

"No," said Mme. Cailloux. "We fight to stop the other tribes becoming *whole*."

Broken Nose didn't understand that. He still doesn't, although Mme. Cailloux has assured him that he will, before their mission here is complete. That is, if she doesn't get herself killed by the bull-mammoth.

In all probability, it's impossible to describe how it feels to have a mammoth rearing up over you. Maybe it's like the feeling you get when you lie on your back and watch the stars, and for a moment—*just for a moment*—you suddenly realize the true size of what you're staring at, as your brain suddenly forgets to force your usual scale of perception onto things. Maybe. It might be interesting to ask Lucia, even though she has even less conception of the distances of stars than the rest of us (but she's probably wise enough to know that Uranus, the furthest-flung of the seven planets, is seventeen hundred million miles farther away than she'll ever travel).

For the record, the mammoth *isn't* going to trample her to death. But looking up at the beast now, seeing its great brown-black outline framed against the perfect blue, Lucia feels she's watching the very countenance of Nature's God. As with the cart of corpses on the Rue Viande, it's the little details that really bother her. The strands of crushed grass on the bottom of its big round feet. The curve of its maw, the upturned V-shape that she knows could swallow a man, if not whole, then certainly in no more than *two* mouthfuls. The chips in its tusks, tiny imperfections in arcs of ivory so long that no matter which way she turns her head, she knows she won't be able to see both tips at once. And then there's its breath. Its terrible and ancient mammoth-breath, washing over her as the animal bellows into her face (one of those things Lucia's never considered until now, and which she's sure the academics who study the bones of these beasts have never considered either).

Yes, these are the things Lucia has trouble coping with. So many little creases and flaws, more than she could catalogue in half a lifetime, let alone in the raw seconds she believes she has left. The beast's stubby-but-oh-so-big front legs pedal the air in front of its body, and then it suddenly finds itself falling.

It doesn't push itself forward as it falls. It doesn't, as it were, *attack*. It drops to the ground in front of Lucia, not on top of her, and the impact would surely crack the Earth open if the ground here weren't so used to the abuse. This is the way a bull-mammoth warns off the opposition. Lucia's realizing that even as she peels her heart from the roof of her mouth and tries to stop herself falling over (noticing, as an incidental detail, that the smell of sweat which is starting to blot out the dung-scent is *hers* and not the fault of the herd).

The bull-mammoth is exhausted. It's not a creature built for rearing up on its hind legs, and the only conclusion we—like Lucia—can reach is that it expects strangers to be so intimidated by its mass that it doesn't actually need to follow up the threat. Having made its point, having bellowed its great beef-heart out, it can't do anything more than stand still and get its breath back. Lungs the size of fat children inflate and deflate, inflate and deflate, under a heavy pelt that must be home to entire empires of insects. From four feet above her head, those huge black eyes are staring down at Lucia, as if the thing's daring her to try anything else.

Easy to call it the face of Nature's God. So big, so blatant, that we can only assume it's been put there for a purpose. Which it has, as Lucia well knows. *All* animals are there for a purpose. Horses are for riding, pigs are for eating. As far as she's concerned, the mammoths are here as a kind of metaphor. These are *political* animals, hence Mr. Jefferson's interest.

(You must have been wondering, for example, where this herd originates: woolly skins and elephant-blubber hardly seem to fit in around here. The best explanation we can hope for is that a number of mammoths were once the property of Catherine of Russia, she who was known as "The Great" before some idiot in her court started spreading that God-awful story about the horse. Horse or no horse, Catherine had something of a reputation as a witch . . . a label applied to most efficient female rulers, it's true, but even before her death there were fabulous and revolting stories about the company she liked to keep, and the animal rites they used to perform. Horses for riding, pigs for eating, trained monkeys for ritual. It's not entirely clear what the link is between the Empress of Russia being a witch and the existence of live mammoths here in what will one day be the State of Montana, although Lucia has heard it said, with maddening vagueness, that one can easily lead to the other. History is full of these logical gaps. Certainly, it's rumored that one such hairy beast was given by Catherine as a gift to George III of England, but that George—half-crazed brute that he was—destroyed the thing in a fight with pit dogs without even realizing its value. Lucia is secretly of the opinion that if Russia had given such a gift to the French, they probably would have eaten it.)

But Lucia's mammoth just keeps gasping. It's vulnerable now. With its show of strength over, it's got nothing to protect it but its dignity. Gravity has not been kind to these creatures, which probably explains why they're ripping up the grass on the crater floor when there are so many nice fresh trees just a couple of hundred yards over the rim. So when Lucia takes a step forward, the mammoth doesn't even blink: it's impossible to imagine such a blink being anything but a major task, and taking anything less than an afternoon to complete. From the look on its face, we could almost believe it's *indignant*.

How can we help but try to read its expression? If the mammoths were put here as metaphors, then we can read them any way we like. It's hard not to find meaning in something that big.

There's a stillness now, Lucia regarding the mammoth, the mammoth regarding Lucia. It's only once Lucia has paid her respects to the silence that she raises her hand. The trunk is close enough to touch, and touch it she does. Her fingers run through the tiny brown hairs, across the leathery old skin, over the wrinkles and the patches of dirt. She almost expects the beast to flinch, or to purr like a cat.

It's vulnerable, anybody can see that. Now, and only now, Lucia gets her one big chance to touch the impossible.

This is what passed between Mme. Cailloux and Broken Nose that morning, after they pulled themselves to their feet at dawn and began the final trek to the place of the mammoths:

Mme. Cailloux spoke of a man called Jefferson, the leader of the colonists who lived off in the eastern lands. Mme. Cailloux explained to Broken Nose that her own tribal leader, Napoleon Short-Arse, had agreed to *sell* a portion of the land to the aforementioned Jefferson (a notion which, like the "employer" idea, Broken Nose finds profoundly stupid).

"We're afraid," said the Mademoiselle. "All of us. Your people. My people."

Broken Nose told her that his people weren't afraid of anything, which was, in his experience, what the French expected to hear from a stupid Indian.

"There's a saying in Europe," Mme. Cailloux went on. " 'The other man's grass is always greener.' We fight for territory. We start wars to acquire the other man's land. Why?"

Broken Nose shrugged. "More room. For cattle."

"No," the Frenchwoman told him. "It's because we think . . . we secretly believe . . . that the other man's land is a paradise. We start to believe there are great secrets there. Secrets we have to know for ourselves. And when we take the land away from him, and we find there's no paradise there . . . then we tell ourselves it was the *other* man's kind of paradise. Not ours. You understand?"

"Your people are stupid," said Broken Nose. (Not entirely true: this is what he believes he said, *after the fact*, although his training in the French tongue doesn't cover the possibility of him insulting his "employers." In his head, *after the fact*, he hears the words in his own language.)

"Perhaps," he imagines that Mme. Cailloux said. "But it's a matter of warfare. In war, we attack the enemy's resources. If an enemy has supply lines, we cut them. If an enemy has a better kind of weapon, we rid him of it."

This sounded to Broken Nose like the first sensible thing she'd said.

She went on to explain many things which Broken Nose had either no understanding of or no interest in. She told him, for example, that in the possession of Napoleon Short-Arse there was a length of metal, which purportedly came from a weapon that had been used to cut the flesh of one of the white man's gods "while he hung on the cross," this metal having the power to induce divine visions (of the spirit-world, Broken Nose guessed) in anyone who was scratched by it.

"Imagine such a thing in the power of the Vatican," the Mademoiselle said, although Broken Nose had no idea what marked these Vatican out from any of the other European tribes. "The relic would prove them correct. It would show them to be justified in all their beliefs. Thus would their grass become greener, and their state grow stronger. They might even become *whole*."

"Whole?" queried Broken Nose.

"I saw the Revolution," replied Mme. Cailloux. "I know what happens when people get what they want. Or when they *believe* they do."

None of which told Broken Nose anything remotely useful, or even explained the woman's mission to find the mammoths before the land gets passed on to Mr. Jefferson. But now, in what we have to call the *present*, Broken Nose is trying not to trip over his skin-shod heels as he tumbles down the slope of the crater. Up ahead, he can see Mme. Cailloux, facing the largest of all the mammoths (or is it just the closest?). He can see the woman resting her hand on the monster's trunk, and he can see the beast keeping quite still, something which his fellow Shoshoni would probably take as proof of the foreign witch's powers over the animal kingdom. But Broken Nose has little time for the wonders of nature, and sees her only as being lucky.

He pulls himself to a halt as the ground levels out under his feet, stopping just a few yards from the bulk of the bull-mammoth. Its eyes are fixed on the woman, and it makes pained groaning noises when it breathes. Slowly, and with some reluctance, Mme. Cailloux lowers her hand.

"*Tout*," she says. (This is the original French, of course, but somehow it makes more sense that way.)

Broken Nose isn't really sure where he should look. It seems disrespectful, somehow, to disturb this union. There they stand, woman and monster, in a communion that would seem almost obscene if it weren't so unlikely. For some reason, Broken Nose remembers a folk tale from his childhood about a father who had an improper relationship with his daughter, and who was swallowed up by the Earth as a punishment. After a few moments more, he speaks.

"The cargo," he says, using a word he's more than familiar with even though it's not entirely the right one. "Our *tools.* . . ."

It's then that Mme. Cailloux regains her senses, preternatural or otherwise, and turns away from the beast. The mammoth never blinks, though, and never moves its head. The Mademoiselle looks up toward the top of the slope, presumably remembering the packs which she and Broken Nose have left over the rise, the equipment her own "employers" issued her before transporting her here to the Land of the Shining Mountains. (And just as we imagined Lewis and Clark standing to attention before Jefferson, so Broken Nose imagines Mme. Cailloux standing before Napoleon Short-Arse himself, although he's imagining Napoleon sitting in a position of honor around a roaring fire rather than sitting behind a desk: there is, of course, no Shoshoni word for "furniture.")

So it is that Mme. Cailloux draws away from the mammoth, to begin her slow climb back up the slope, with Broken Nose at her heels. Mme. Cailloux doesn't look back at the mammoth as she walks, something Broken Nose interprets as an almost incestuous shame. And the mammoth doesn't watch her go, simply continuing to stare at the spot where she once stood. So it's left to Broken Nose to glance over his shoulder on the way up the slope, to watch the woolly monster recover its strength after its four seconds' worth of rabid activity, while the rest of the herd-animals go on bellowing and sniffing at each other. He wonders if the bull-mammoth even understands the difference between its human visitors and the other beasts of the wilderness.

"These are Mr. Jefferson's animals," he hears Mme. Cailloux say, halfway up the rise. "They feed on Mr. Jefferson's grass."

He *still* doesn't know what she's talking about. Broken Nose is starting to feel that even the mammoths understand this mission better than he does, but then again, wouldn't you expect him to think that way? Being Shoshoni, when *he* uses the mammoths as a metaphor the results aren't particularly literary.

Which leads us back to the President of the United States of America himself, as he sits behind his rosewood desk in his rose-tinted office, picking snuff or hashish or chewing tobacco out of his little carved box. This is some months in what might be called Lucia's future, so Lewis and Clark have in the last few minutes dutifully marched out of the office in their unlikely racoonskin hats. No doubt a kayak is waiting for them outside.

But now Mr. Jefferson's alone with his thoughts, and we can make the usual array of guesses as to what those thoughts might be. The President is hoping that his explorers will bring him back news of a Northwest Passage, a trade route that could turn his republic into an empire almost overnight (not that he *wants* an empire, as such, but . . . well, you know how it is). And then, of course, there's the prospect of mammoths. If such things are found, they're sure to be given a place of honor in the new American mythology. He briefly wonders if there's room for a mammoth on the national crest: possibly he can put one in place of the eagle. A beast which proves, by its very nature, that the Church is full of asses and the world runs to the will of the new sciences. Just for a second, for a stupid childish second, he imagines riding the back of such an animal in a parade along Pennsylvania Avenue, celebrating his second—oh, to hell with precedent, make it his third—term in office. Jefferson's monsters, that's what the Church would say. He imagines the mammoths' backs being draped in flags, decked out in the red-and-white stripes and the seventeen stars (although the flag which hangs above the window in this particular office only has sixteen, those artisans who handle such things being a little slower than the expansion of the new republic).

All this makes Mr. Jefferson consider the box again. He tries to remember the name of the woman who presented it to him, the well-spoken Mademoiselle who appeared in this very office just a few short months ago, her skins and furs making her look like an Indian coming home from a trek in the great forests. Naturally, it's ludicrous to think that a complete stranger, and such an ill-dressed one, should be allowed to stroll into the Presidential office without even officially presenting herself . . . but the notion's as hard to resist as all the other things we've seen inside this virtual room. Whether or not the woman *did* introduce herself, the one thing Mr. Jefferson can remember is what she told him when she placed the little off-white box on his desk.

"Your new world, *Monsieur* President," she said. Well, maybe she didn't say "mister" in the French style, maybe Jefferson's just remembering it that way because he likes the accent, but the point remains that when he slid the box open he found inside it just a few blades of green, green grass. Mr. Jefferson fails to remember how he responded to this, or even whether he asked his visitor to explain herself: she may well have vanished from his office before he could so much as speak (after all, a mysterious entrance should always be complemented by a mysterious exit.).

Here and now, the President believes the contents of the box to have been a kind of message, sent by some agency he has yet to identify. In fact, he's only half-right.

And this is Jefferson's future. More precisely, this is 1805, halfway through Lewis and Clark's two-year excursion into the wildlands, the point at which the two men (and all their followers, though right now they're gloriously irrelevant) finally stumble across a certain indentation in a certain grassland. A crater, if you will. It's here that the two explorers, being consummate outdoorsmen, find trampled ground and traces of spoor which suggest the trail of some grand animal herd. At first they conclude that the Indians have driven their cattle through the area, though this theory falters when they arrive at the bottom of the basin, where the graves have been dug. They *assume* there are graves here, anyway, given that the ground's been broken from one side of the crater to the other. Now, as not even the Shoshoni would do something as bizarre as grazing their animals on top of their dead—and as a quick search of the area uncovers European shell-casings in the grass—there's obviously some kind of mystery here.

Sadly, it's not one the explorers feel they have time to solve. Besides, even by this stage they're starting to learn that digging up native graves is a bad move, tactically speaking. There's some discussion about what might be called the "central" grave, the fifteen-foot-long tract of broken earth which, from its size, must surely indicate the last resting place of a great leader (proving to the leader-obsessed white men that the people who performed these burials must have been *partly* civilized, even though the Shoshoni contingent in the expedition claims not to recognize the style). Lewis and Clark steer well clear, deciding to give the mysterious fallen chief the respect he must surely deserve.

Later, in the oh-so-short years between the end of the expedition and Lewis's highly dubious suicide, the duo will theorize that the site was deliberately desecrated by rogue Frenchmen as some kind of political maneuver. A stampede must have taken place at some point, so the large animals, whatever they may have been, were probably used by the French as weapons of destruction.

Like Jefferson, these people excel at being only partly correct.

And however far into the future we go, Mr. Jefferson, President of the United States of America, fails to understand the significance of any of this. Well, what can we expect? Polymath and philosopher he may be, but he doesn't even understand the significance of the box. The little off-white box which remains in his possession for the rest of his term in office, a gift from one of the very few people who understood exactly what he wanted from his glorious new territory, and knew precisely why he couldn't be allowed to get it. A box Mr. Jefferson might have used for snuff, or hashish, or tobacco, which a French woman once claimed was all that remained of his virtual paradise, and which just happened to be made out of ivory.

# SANDRA J. LINDOW

# If Death, A Preprimer

*Sandra Lindow, fifty-something, takes her role of apprentice crone seriously. She works in a residential treatment center teaching reading and writing to emotionally disturbed adolescents from which she has learned patience and gained considerable inspiration.*

*She hopes that her poetry will disturb the comfortable and comfort the disturbed. She lives in Eau Claire, Wisconsin, with her husband and daughter.*

*Her most recent book is* A Celebration of Bones *(Jazz Police). "If Death, A Preprimer" was first published in* The Magazine of Speculative Poetry.

—E. D., T. W.

If death were a book,
I would shelve it
high and to the back
where I wouldn't see it often,
having read the cover blurbs
and decided that infinite chapters
of ultimate silence disenchant
when there are so many other books
to be read and written.

If death were a lamp,
I would soften its glare
with a white Victorian satin shade
braided and tasseled and bent
to illuminate the words of poets,
who die young at every age.
Then I'd set it behind the couch
of my heart's desiring
where it wouldn't intrude
on livelier exertions.

If death were a language,
I would wait to learn it

until I saw it writ indelibly
behind my eyes, a novel
right brain experience, reading
the unfamiliar vowels and consonants
on pages of failing flesh,
making sense of it finally
and just in time.

If death were a door,
I would enter by necessity,
pressing the key of my failed flesh
into its forgiving lock, opening,
then closing firmly on the pain
and indignity of dying. Vaulting
the sanctuary of the penultimate
church, I would rise beyond
the small imprisonment of the flesh,
returning to the center.

# S. P. SOMTOW

# The Bird Catcher

*The* International Herald Tribune *recently referred to S. P. Somtow as "the most well-known expatriate Thai in the world." He has published forty-five books, including the groundbreaking horror novel* Vampire Junction *and the semi-autobiographical work* Jasmine Nights, *and has won numerous awards for his writing. He is also a composer of note, whose most recent large-scale work was a requiem commissioned by the government of Thailand to express Thailand's sympathy for the victims of the 9/11 tragedy and its aftermath.*

*"The Bird Catcher" was originally published in* The Museum of Horrors.

—E. D.

There was this other boy in the internment camp. His name was Jim. After the war, he made something of a name for himself. He wrote books, even a memoir of the camp that got turned into a Spielberg movie. It didn't turn out that gloriously for me.

My grandson will never know what it's like to be consumed with hunger, hunger that is heartache, hunger that can propel you past insanity. But I know. I've been there. So has that boy Jim; that's why I really don't envy him his Spielberg movie.

After the war, my mother and I were stranded in China for a few more years. She was penniless, a lady journalist in a time when lady journalists only covered church bazaars, a single mother at a time when "bastard" was more than a bad word.

You might think that at least we had each other, but my mother and I never intersected. Not as mother and son, not even as Americans awash in great events and oceans of Asian faces. We were both loners. We were both vulnerable.

That's how I became the bogeyman's friend.

He's long dead now, but they keep him, you know, in the Museum of Horrors. Once in a generation, I visit him. Yesterday, I took my grandson Corey. Just as I took his father before him.

The destination stays the same, but the road changes every generation. The first time I had gone by boat, along the quiet back canals of the old city. Now there was an expressway. The toll was forty baht—a dollar—a month's salary that would have been, back in the '50s, in old Siam.

My son's in love with Bangkok, the insane skyline, the high tech blending with the low tech, the skyscraper shaped like a giant robot, the palatial shopping malls, the kinky sex bars, the bootleg software arcades, the whole tossed salad. And he doesn't mind the heat. He's a big-time entrepreneur here, owns a taco chain.

I live in Manhattan. It's quieter.

I can be anonymous. I can be alone. I can nurse my hunger in secret.

Christmases, though, I go to Bangkok; this Christmas, my grandson's eleventh birthday, I told my son it was time. He nodded and told me to take the chauffeur for the day.

So, to get to the place, you zigzag through the world's raunchiest traffic, then you fly along this madcap figure-eight expressway, cross the river where stone demons stand guard on the parapets of the Temple of Dawn, and then you're suddenly in this sleazy alley. Vendors hawk bowls of soup and pickled guavas. The directions are on a handwritten placard attached to a street sign with duct tape.

It's the Police Museum, upstairs from the local morgue. One wall is covered with photographs of corpses. That's not part of the museum; it's a public service display for people with missing family members to check if any of them have turned up dead. Corey didn't pay attention to the photographs; he was busy with Pokémon.

Upstairs, the feeling changed. The stairs creaked. The upstairs room was garishly lit. Glass cases along the walls were filled with medical oddities, two-headed babies and the like, each one in a jar of formaldehyde, each one meticulously labeled in Thai and English. The labels weren't printed, mind you. Handwritten. There was definitely a middle school show-and-tell feel about the exhibits. No air-conditioning. And no more breeze from the river like in the old days; skyscrapers had stifled the city's breath.

There was a uniform, sick-yellow tinge to all the displays . . . the neutral cream paint was edged with yellow . . . the deformed livers, misshappen brains, tumorous embryos all floating in a dull yellow fluid . . . the heaps of dry bones an orange-yellow, the rows of skulls yellowing in the cracks . . . and then there were the young novices, shaven-headed little boys in yellow robes, staring in a heat-induced stupor as their mentor droned on about the transience of all existence, the quintessence of Buddhist philosophy.

And then there was Si Ui.

He had his own glass cabinet, like a phone booth, in the middle of the room. Naked. Desiccated. A mummy. Skinny. Mud-colored, from the embalming process, I think. A sign (handwritten, of course) explained who he was. See Ui. Devourer of children's livers in the 1950s. My grandson reads Thai more fluently than I do. He sounded out the name right away.

*Si Sui Sae Ung.*

"It's the bogeyman, isn't it?" Corey said. But he showed little more than a passing interest. It was the year Pokémon Gold and Silver came out. So many new monsters to catch, so many names to learn.

"He hated cages," I said.

"Got him!" Corey squealed. Then, not looking up at the dead man, "I know who he was. They did a documentary on him. Can we go now?"

"Didn't your maid tell you stories at night? To frighten you? 'Be a good boy, or Si Ui will eat your liver?' "

"Gimme a break, Grandpa. I'm too old for that shit." He paused. Still wouldn't look up at him. There were other glass booths in the room, other mummified criminals: a serial rapist down the way. But Si Ui was the star of the show. "Okay," Corey said, "she did try to scare me once. Well, I was like five, okay? Si Ui. You watch out, he'll eat your liver, be a good boy now. Sure, I heard that before. Well, he's not gonna eat my liver now, is he? I mean, that's probably not even him; it's probably like wax or something."

He smiled at me. The dead man did not.

"I knew him," I said. "He was my friend."

"I get it!" Corey said, back to his Gameboy. "You're like me in this Pokémon game. You caught a monster once. And tamed him. You caught the most famous monster in Thailand."

"And tamed him?" I shook my head. "No, not tamed."

"Can we go to McDonald's now?"

"You're hungry."

"I could eat the world!"

"After I tell you the whole story."

"You're gonna talk about the Chinese camp again, Grandpa? And that kid Jim, and the Spielberg movie?"

"No, Corey, this is something I've never told you about before. But I'm telling you so when I'm gone, you'll know to tell your son. And your grandson."

"Okay, Grandpa."

And finally, tearing himself away from the video game, he willed himself to look.

The dead man had no eyes; he could not stare back.

*He hated cages. But his whole life was a long imprisonment . . . without a cage, he did not even exist.*

Listen, Corey. I'll tell you how I met the bogeyman.

Imagine I'm eleven years old, same as you are now, running wild on a leaky ship crammed with coolies. They're packed into the lower deck. We can't afford the upper deck, but when they saw we were white, they waved us on up without checking our tickets. It looks more interesting down there. And the food's got to be better. I can smell a Chinese breakfast. That oily fried bread, so crunchy on the outside, dripping with pig fat . . . yeah.

It's hot. It's boring. Mom's on the prowl. A job or a husband, whichever comes first. Everyone's fleeing the communists. We're some of the last white people to get out of China.

Someone's got a portable charcoal stove on the lower deck, and there's a toothless old woman cooking congee, fanning the stove. A whiff of opium in the air blends with the rich gingerly broth. Everyone down there's clustered around the food. Except this one man. Harmless-looking. Before the Japs came, we had a gardener who looked like that. Shirtless, thin, by the railing. Stiller than a statue. And a bird on the railing. Also unmoving. The other coolies are ridiculing him, making fun of his Hakka accent, calling him simpleton.

I watch him.

"Look at the idiot," the toothless woman says. "Hasn't said a word since we left Swatow."

The man has his arms stretched out, his hands cupped. Frozen. Concentrated. I suddenly realize I've snuck down the steps myself, pushed my way through all the Chinese around the cooking pot, and I'm halfway there. Mesmerized. The man is stalking the bird, the boy stalking the man. I try not to breathe as I creep up.

He pounces. Wrings the bird's neck . . . in one swift liquid movement, a twist of the wrist, and he's already plucking the feathers with the other hand, ignoring the death-spasms. And I'm real close now. I can smell him. Mud and sweat. Behind him, the open sea. On the deck, the feathers, a bloody snowfall.

He bites off the head and I hear the skull crunch.

I scream. He whirls. I try to cover it up with a childish giggle.

He speaks in a monotone. Slowly. Sounding out each syllable, but he seems to have picked up a little pidgin. "Little white boy. You go upstairs. No belong here."

"I go where I want. They don't care."

He offers me a raw wing.

"Boy hungry?"

"Man hungry?"

I fish in my pocket, find half a liverwurst sandwich. I hold it out to him. He shakes his head. We both laugh a little. We've both known this hunger that consumes you; the agony of China is in our bones.

I say, "Me and Mom are going to Siam. On account of my dad getting killed by the Japs and we can't live in Shanghai anymore. We were in a camp and everything." He stares blankly and so I bark in Japanese, like the guards used to. And he goes crazy.

He mutters to himself in Hakka which I don't understand that well, but it's something like, "Don't look 'em in the eye. They chop off your head. You stare at the ground, they leave you alone." He is chewing away at raw bird flesh the whole time. He adds in English, "Si Ui no like Japan man."

"Makes two of us," I say.

I've seen too much. Before the internment camp, there was Nanking. Mom was gonna do an article about the atrocities. I saw them. You think a two-year-old doesn't see anything? She carried me on her back the whole time, papoose-style.

When you've seen a river clogged with corpses, when you've looked at piles of human heads, and human livers roasting on spits, and women raped and set on fire, well, Santa and the Tooth Fairy just don't cut it. I pretended about the Tooth Fairy, though, for a long time. Because, in the camp, the ladies would pool their resources to bribe Mr. Tooth Fairy Sakamoto for a little piece of fish.

"I'm Nicholas," I say.

"Si Ui." I don't know if it's his name or something in Hakka.

I hear my mother calling from the upper deck. I turn from the strange man, the raw bird's blood trailing from his lips. "Gotta go." I turn to him, pointing at my chest, and I say, "Nicholas."

Even the upper deck is cramped. It's hotter than Shanghai, hotter even than the internment camp. We share a cabin with two Catholic priests who let us hide out there after suspecting we didn't have tickets.

Night doesn't get any cooler, and the priests snore. I'm down to a pair of shorts and I still can't sleep. So I slip away. It's easy. Nobody cares. Millions of people have been dying and I'm just some skinny kid on the wrong side of the ocean. Me and my mom have been adrift for as long as I can remember.

The ship groans and clanks. I take the steep metal stairwell down to the coolies' level. I'm wondering about the birdcatcher. Down below, the smells are a lot more comforting. The smell of sweat and soy-stained clothing masks the odor of the sea. The charcoal stove is still burning. The old woman is simmering some stew. Maybe something magical . . . a bit of snake's blood to revive some-one's limp dick . . . crushed tiger bones, powdered rhinoceros horn, to heal pretty much anything. People are starving, but you can still get those kind of ingredi-ents. I'm eleven, and I already know too much.

They are sleeping every which way, but it's easy for me to step over them even in the dark. The camp was even more crowded than this, and a misstep could get you hurt. There's a little bit of light from the little clay stove.

I don't know what I'm looking for. Just to be alone, I guess. I can be more alone in a crowd of Chinese than up there. Mom says things will be better in Siam. I don't know.

I've threaded my way past all of them. And I'm leaning against the railing. There isn't much moonlight. It's probably past midnight but the metal is still hot. There's a warm wind, though, and it dries away my sweat. China's too far away to see, and I can't even imagine Boston anymore.

He pounces.

Leather hands rasp my shoulders. Strong hands. Not big, but I can't squirm out of their grip. The hands twirl me around and I'm looking into Si Ui's eyes. The moonlight is in them. I'm scared. I don't know why, really, all I'd have to do is scream and they'll pull him off me. But I can't get the scream out.

I look into his eyes and I see fire. A burning village. Maybe it's just the opium haze that clings to this deck, making me feel all weird inside, seeing things. And the sounds. I think it must be the whispering of the sea, but it's not, it's voices. *Hungry, you little chink?* And those leering, buck-toothed faces. Like comic book Japs. Barking. The fire blazes. And then, abruptly, it dissolves. And there's a kid standing in the smoky ruins. Me. And I'm holding out a liverwurst sandwich. Am I really that skinny, that pathetic? But the vision fades. And Si Ui's eyes become empty. Soulless.

"Si Ui catch anything," he says. "See, catch bird, catch boy. All same." And smiles, a curiously captivating smile.

"As long as you don't eat me," I say.

"Si Ui never eat Nicholas," he says. "Nicholas friend."

Friend? In the burning wasteland of China, an angel holding out a liverwurst sandwich? It makes me smile. And suddenly angry. The anger hits me so sud-denly I don't even have time to figure out what it is. It's the war, the maggots in the millet, the commandant kicking me across the yard, but more than that it's my mom, clinging to her journalist fantasies while I dug for earthworms, letting my dad walk out to his death. I'm crying and the bird catcher is stroking my cheek, saying, "You no cry now. Soon go back America. No one cry there." And it's the first time someone has touched me with some kind of tenderness in, in, in, I dunno, since before the invasion. Because Mom doesn't hug, she kind of encircles, and her arms are like the bars of a cage.

So, I'm thinking this will be my last glimpse of Si Ui. It's in the harbor at Klong Toei. You know, where Anna landed in *The King and I*. And where Joseph Conrad landed in *Youth*.

So all these coolies, and all these trapped Americans and Europeans, they're all stampeding down the gangplank, with cargo being hoisted, workmen trundling, fleets of those bicycle pedicabs called *samlors*, itinerant merchants with bales of silk and fruits that seem to have hair or claws, and then there's the smell that socks you in the face, gasoline and jasmine and decay and incense. Pungent salt squid drying on racks. The ever-present fish sauce, blending with the odor of fresh papaya and pineapple and coconut and human sweat.

And my mother's off and running, with me barely keeping up, chasing after some waxed-mustache British doctor guy with one of those accents you think's a joke until you realize that's really how they talk.

So I'm just carried along by the mob.

"You buy bird, little boy?" I look up. It's a wall of sparrows, each one in a cramped wooden cage. Rows and rows of cages, stacked up from the concrete high as a man, more cages hanging from wires, stuffed into the branch-crooks of a mango tree. I see others buying the birds for a few coins, releasing them into the air.

"Why are they doing that?"

"Good for your karma. Buy bird, set bird free, shorten your suffering in your next life."

"Swell," I say.

Farther off, the vendor's boy is catching them, coaxing them back into cages. That's got to be wrong, I'm thinking as the boy comes back with ten little cages hanging on each arm. The birds haven't gotten far. They can barely fly. Answering my unspoken thought, the bird seller says, "Oh, we clip wings. Must make living too, you know."

That's when I hear a sound like the thunder of a thousand wings. I think I must be dreaming. I look up. The crowd has parted. And there's a skinny little shirtless man standing in the clearing, his arms spread wide like a Jesus statue, only you can barely see a square inch of him because he's all covered in sparrows. Perched all over his arms like they're telegraph wires or something, and squatting on his head, and clinging to his baggy homespun shorts with their claws. And the birds are all chattering at once, drowning out the cacophony of the mob.

Si Ui looks at me. And in his eyes I see . . . bars. Bars of light, maybe. Prison bars. The man's trying to tell me something. *I'm trapped.*

The crowd that parted all of sudden comes together and he's gone. I wonder if I'm the only one who saw. I wonder if it's just another aftereffect of the opium that clogged the walkways on the ship.

But it's too late to wonder; my mom has found me, she's got me by the arm and she's yanking me back into the stream of people. And in the next few weeks I don't think about Si Ui at all. Until he shows up, just like that, in a village called Thapsakae.

After the museum, I took Corey to Baskin-Robbins and popped into Starbucks next door for a frappuccino. Visiting the bogeyman is a draining thing. I wanted to let him down easy. But Corey didn't want to let go right away.

"Can we take a boat ride or something?" he said. "You know I never get to come to this part of town." It's true. The traffic in Bangkok is so bad that they sell little car toilets so you can go while you're stuck at a red light for an hour. This side of town, Thonburi, the old capital, is a lot more like the past. But no one bothers to come. The traffic, they say, always the traffic.

We left the car by a local pier, hailed a river taxi, just told him to go, anywhere, told him we wanted to ride around. Overpaid him. It served me right for being me, an old white guy in baggy slacks, with a backwards-facing-Yankees-hatted blond kid in tow.

When you leave the river behind, there's a network of canals, called *klongs*, that used to be the arteries and capillaries of the old city. In Bangkok proper, they've all been filled in. But not here. The farther from the main waterway we floated, the further back in time. Now the *klongs* were fragrant with jasmine, with stilted houses rearing up behind thickets of banana and bamboo. And I was remembering more.

Rain jars by the landing docks . . . lizards basking in the sun . . . young boys leaping into the water.

"The water was a lot clearer," I told my grandson. "And the swimmers weren't wearing those little trunks . . . they were naked." Recently, fearing to offend the sensibilities of tourists, the Thai government made a fuss about little boys skinny-dipping along the tourist riverboat routes. But the river is so polluted now, one wonders what difference it makes.

They were bobbing up and down around the boat. Shouting in fractured English. Wanting a lick of Corey's Baskin-Robbins. When Corey spoke to them in Thai, they swam away. Tourists who speak the language aren't tourists anymore.

"You used to do that, huh, Grandpa."

"Yes," I said.

"I like the Sports Club better. The water's clean. And they make a mean chicken sandwich at the poolside bar."

I only went to the Sports Club once in my life. A week after we landed in Bangkok, a week of sleeping in a pew at a missionary church, a week of wringing out the same clothes and ironing them over and over.

"I never thought much of the Sports Club," I said.

"Oh, Grandpa, you're such a prole." One of his father's words, I thought, smiling.

"Well, I did grow up in *Red* China," I said.

"Yeah," he said. "So what was it like, the Sports Club?"

. . . a little piece of England in the midst of all this tropical stuff. The horse races. Cricket. My mother has a rendezvous with the doctor, the one she's been flirting with on the ship. They have tea and crumpets. They talk about the

Bangkok Chinatown riots, and about money. I am reading a battered EC comic that I found in the reading room.

"Well, if you don't mind going native," the doctor says, "there's a clinic, down south a bit; pay wouldn't be much, and you'll have to live with the benighted buggers, but I daresay you'll cope."

"Oh, I'll go native," Mom says, "as long as I can keep writing. I'll do anything for that. I'd give you a blowjob if that's what it takes."

"Heavens," says the doctor. "More tea?"

And so, a month later, we come to a fishing village nestled in the western crook of the Gulf of Siam, and I swear it's paradise. There's a village school taught by monks, and a little clinic where Mom works, dressing wounds, jabbing penicillin into people's buttocks; I think she's working on a novel. That doctor she was flirting with got her this job because she speaks Chinese, and the village is full of Chinese immigrants, smuggled across the sea, looking for some measure of freedom.

Thapsakae . . . it rhymes with Tupperware . . . it's always warm, but never stifling like in Bangkok . . . always a breeze from the unseen sea, shaking the ripe coconuts from the trees . . . a town of stilted dwellings, a tiny main street with storefront rowhouses, fields of neon green rice as far as the eye can see, lazy waterbuffalo wallowing, and always the canals running alongside the half-paved road, women beating their wet laundry with rocks in the dawn, boys diving in the noonday heat . . . the second day I'm there, I meet these kids, Lek and Sombun. They're my age. I can't understand a word they're saying at first. I'm watching them, leaning against a dragon-glazed rain jar, as they shuck their school uniforms and leap in. They're laughing a lot, splashing, one time they're throwing a catfish back and forth like it's some kind of volleyball, but they're like fishes themselves, silvery-brown sleek things chattering in a singsong language. And I'm alone, like I was at the camp, flinging stones into the water. Except I'm not scared like I was there. There's no time I have to be home. I can reach into just about any thicket and pluck out something good to eat: bananas, mangoes, little pink sour-apples. My shorts are all torn (I still only have one pair) and my shirt is stained with the juices of exotic fruits, and I let my hair grow as long as I want.

Today I'm thinking of the birds.

You buy a bird to free yourself from the cage of karma. You free the bird, but its wings are clipped and it's inside another cage, a cage circumscribed by the fact that it can't fly far. And the boy that catches it is in another cage, apprenticed to that vendor, unable to fly free. Cages within cages within cages. I've been in a cage before; one time in the camp they hung me up in one in the commandant's office and told me to sing.

Here, I don't feel caged at all.

The Thai kids have noticed me and they pop up from the depths right next to me, staring curiously. They're not hostile. I don't know what they're saying, but I know I'm soon going to absorb this musical language. Meanwhile, they're splashing me, daring me to dive in, and in the end I throw off these filthy clothes and I'm in the water and it's clear and warm and full of fish. And we're laughing and chasing each other. And they do know a few words of English; they've picked it up in that village school, where the monks have been ramming a weird anti-quated English phrase-book down their throats.

But later, after we dry off in the sun and they try to show me how to ride a waterbuffalo, later we sneak across the *gailan* field and I see him again. The bird catcher, I mean. *Gailan* is a Chinese vegetable like broccoli only without the bushy part. The Chinese immigrants grow it here. They all work for this rich Chinese man named Tae Pak, the one who had the refugees shipped to this town as cheap labor.

"You want to watch TV?" Sombun asks me.

I haven't had much of a chance to see TV. He takes me by the hand and pulls me along, with Lek behind him, giggling. Night has fallen. It happens really suddenly in the tropics, boom and it's dark. In the distance, past a wall of bamboo trees, we see glimmering lights. Tae Pak has electricity. Not that many private homes do. Mom and I use kerosene lamps at night. I've never been to his house, but I know we're going there. Villagers are zeroing in on the house now, walking surefootedly in the moonlight. The stench of night-blooming jas-mine is almost choking in the compound. A little shrine to the Mother of Mercy stands by the entrance, and ahead we see what passes for a mansion here; the wooden stilts and the thatched roof with the pointed eaves, like everyone else's house, but spread out over three sides of a quadrangle, and in the center a ruined pagoda whose origin no one remembers.

The usual pigs and chickens are running around in the space under the house, but the stairway up to the veranda is packed with people, kids mostly, and they're all gazing upward. The object of their devotion is a television set, the images on it ghostly, the sound staticky and in Thai in any case . . . but I recognize the show . . . it's *I Love Lucy*. And I'm just staring and staring. Sombun pushes me up the steps. I barely remember to remove my sandals and step in the trough at the bottom of the steps to wash the river mud off my feet. It's really true. I can't understand a word of it but it's still funny. The kids are laughing along with the laugh track.

Well . . . that's when I see Si Ui. I point at him. I try to attract his attention, but he too, sitting cross-legged on the veranda, is riveted to the screen. And when I try to whisper to Sombun that hey, I know this guy, what a weird co-incidence, Sombun just whispers back, "*Jek, jek,*" which I know is a putdown word for a Chinaman.

"I know him," I whisper. "He catches birds. And eats them. Alive." I try to attract Si Ui's attention. But he won't look at me. He's too busy staring at Lucille Ball. I'm a little bit afraid to look at him directly, scared of what his eyes might disclose, our shared and brutal past.

Lek, whose nickname just means "tiny," shudders.

"*Jek, jek,*" Sombun says. The laugh track kicks in.

Everything has changed now that I know he's here. On my reed mat, under the mosquito nets every night, I toss and turn, and I see things. I don't think they're dreams. I think it's like the time I looked into Si Ui's eyes and saw the fire. I see a Chinese boy running through a field of dead people. It's sort of all in black and white and he's screaming and behind him a village is burning.

At first it's the Chinese boy but somehow it's me too, and I'm running, with my bare feet squishing into dead men's bowels, running over a sea of blood and shit. And I run right into someone's arms. Hard. The comic-book Japanese villain face. A human heart, still beating, in his hand.

"Hungry, you little chink?" he says.

Little chink. Little *jek*.

Intestines are writhing up out of disemboweled bodies like snakes. I saw a lot of disemboweled Japs. Their officers did it in groups, quietly, stony-faced. The honorable thing to do.

I'm screaming myself awake. And then, from the veranda, maybe, I hear the tap of my mom's battered typewriter, an old Hermes she bought in the Sunday market in Bangkok for a hundred baht.

I crawl out of bed. It's already dawn.

"Hi, Mom," I say, as I breeze past her, an old *phakhomah* wrapped around my loins.

"Wow. It talks."

"Mom, I'm going over to Sombun's house to play."

"You're getting the hang of the place, I take it."

"Yeah."

"Pick up some food, Nicholas."

"Okay." Around here, a dollar will feed me and her three square meals. But it won't take away the other hunger.

Another lazy day of running myself ragged, gorging on papaya and coconut milk, another day in paradise.

It's time to meet the serpent, I decide.

Sombun tells me someone's been killed, and we sneak over to the police station. Si Ui is there, sitting at a desk, staring at a wall. I think he's just doing some kind of alien registration thing. He has a Thai interpreter, the same toothless woman I saw on the boat. And a policeman is writing stuff down in a ledger.

There's a woman sitting on a bench, rocking back and forth. She's talking to everyone in sight. Even me and Sombun.

Sombun whispers, "That woman Daeng. Daughter die."

Daeng mumbles, "My daughter. By the railway tracks. All she was doing was running down the street for an ice coffee. Oh, my terrible karma." She collars a passing inspector. "Help me. My daughter. Strangled, raped."

"That Inspector Jed," Sombun whispers to me. "Head of the whole place."

Inspector Jed is being polite, compassionate and efficient at the same time. I like him. My mom should hang out with people like that instead of the losers who are just looking for a quick lay.

The woman continues muttering to herself. "*Nit, nit, nit, nit, nit,*" she says. That must be the girl's name. They all have nicknames like that. Nit means "tiny," too, like Lek. "Dead, strangled," she says. "And this town is supposed to be heaven on earth. The sea, the palm trees, the sun always bright. This town has a dark heart."

Suddenly, Si Ui looks up. Stares at her. As though remembering something. Daeng is sobbing. And the policeman who's been interviewing him says, "Watch yourself, chink. Everyone smiles here. Food falls from the trees. If a little girl's murdered, they'll file it away; they won't try to find out who did it. Because this is a perfect place, and no one gets murdered. We all love each other here . . . you little *jek*."

Si Ui has this weird look in his eye. Mesmerized. My mother looks that way sometimes . . . when a man catches her eye and she's zeroing in for the kill. The woman's mumbling that she's going to go be a nun now, she has nothing left to live for.

"Watch your back, *jek*," says the policeman. He's trying, I realize, to help this man, who he probably thinks is some kind of village idiot type. "Someone'll murder you just for being a stupid little chink. And no one will bother to find out who did it."

"Si Ui hungry," says Si Ui.

I realize that I speak his language, and my friends do not.

"Si Ui!" I call out to him.

He freezes in his tracks and slowly turns, and I look into his eyes for the second time, and I know that it was no illusion before.

Somehow we've seen through each other's eyes.

I am a misfit kid in a picture-perfect town with a dark heart, but I understand what he's saying, because though I look all different I come from where he comes from. I've experienced what it's like to be Chinese. You can torture them and kill them by the millions, like the Japs did, and still they endure. They just shake it off. They've outlasted everyone so far. And will till the end of time. Right now in Siam they're the coolies and the laborers, and soon they're going to end up owning the whole country. They endure. I saw their severed heads piled up like battlements, and the river choked with their corpses, and they outlasted it all.

These Thai kids will never understand.

"Si Ui hungry!" the man cries.

That afternoon, I slip away from my friends at the river, and I go to the *gailan* field where I know he works. He never acknowledges my presence, but later, he strides farther and farther from the house of his rich patron, toward a more densely wooded area past the fields. It's all banana trees, the little bananas that have seeds in them, you chew the whole banana and spit out the seeds, rat-tat-tat, like a machine gun. There's bamboo, too, and the jasmine bushes that grow wild, and mango trees. Si Ui doesn't talk to me, doesn't look back, but somehow I know I'm supposed to follow him.

And I do.

Through the thicket, into a private clearing, the ground overgrown with weeds, the whole thing surrounded by vegetation, and in the middle of it a tumbledown house, the thatch unpatched in places, the stilts decaying and carved with old graffiti. The steps are lined with wooden cages. There's birdshit all over the decking, over the wooden railings, even around the foot trough. Birds are chattering from the cages, from the air around us. The sun has been searing and sweat is running down my face, my chest, soaking my *phakhomah*.

We don't go up into the house. Instead, Si Ui leads me past it, toward a clump of rubber trees. He doesn't talk, just keeps beckoning me, the curious way they have of beckoning, palm pointing toward the ground.

I feel dizzy. He's standing there. Swaying a little. Then he makes a little clucking, chattering sound, barely opening his lips. The birds are gathering. He seems to know their language. They're answering him. The chirping around us grows to a screeching cacophony. Above, they're circling. They're blocking out the sun and it's suddenly chilly. I'm scared now. But I don't dare say anything. In the camp, if you said anything, they always hurt you. Si Ui keeps beckoning me: nearer, come nearer. And I creep up. The birds are shrieking. And now they're swooping down, landing, gathering at Si Ui's feet, their heads moving to and fro in a regular rhythm, like they're listening to . . . a heartbeat. Si Ui's heartbeat. My own.

An image flashes into my head. A little Chinese boy hiding in a closet . . . listening to footsteps . . . breathing nervously.

He's poised. Like a snake, coiled up, ready to pounce. And then, without warning, he drops to a crouch, pulls a bird out of the sea of birds, puts it to his lips, snaps its neck with his teeth, and the blood just spurts, all over his bare skin, over the homespun wrapped around his loins, an impossible crimson. And he smiles. And throws me the bird.

I recoil. He laughs again when I let the dead bird slip through my fingers. Pounces again and gets me another.

"Birds are easy to trap," he says to me in Chinese, "easy as children, sometimes; you just have to know their language." He rips one open, pulls out a slippery liver. "You don't like them raw, I know," he says, "but come, little brother, we'll make a fire."

He waves his hand, dismisses the birds; all at once they're gone and the air is steaming again, In the heat, we make a bonfire and grill the birds' livers over it. He has become, I guess, my friend. Because he's become all talkative. "I didn't rape her," he says.

Then he talks about fleeing through the rice fields. There's a war going on around him. I guess he's my age in his story, but in Chinese they don't use past or future, everything happens in a kind of abstract now-time. I don't understand his dialect that well, but what he says matches the waking dreams I've had tossing and turning under that mosquito net. There was a Japanese soldier. He seemed kinder than the others. They were roasting something over a fire. He was handing Si Ui a morsel. A piece of liver.

*Hungry, little chink?*

Hungry. I understand hungry.

*Human liver.*

In Asia they believe that everything that will ever happen has already happened. Is that what Si Ui is doing with me, forging a karmic chain with his own childhood, the Japanese soldier?

There's so much I want to ask him, but I can't form the thoughts, especially not in Chinese. I'm young, Corey. I'm not thinking karmic cycles. What are you trying to ask me?

"I thought Si Ui ate children's livers," said Corey. "Not some dumb old birds'."

We were still on the *klong*, turning back now toward civilization; on either side of us were crumbling temples, old houses with pointed eaves, each one with its little totemic spirit house by the front gate, pouring sweet incense into the air, the air itself dripping with humidity. But ahead, just beyond a turn in the *klong*, a series of eighty-story condos reared up over the banana trees.

"Yes, he did," I said, "and we'll get to that part, in time. Don't be impatient."

"Grandpa, Si Ui ate children's livers. Just like Dracula bit women in the neck. Well, like, it's the main part of the story. How long are you gonna make me wait?"

"So you know more than you told me before. About the maid trying to scare you one time, when you were five."

"Well, yeah, Grandpa, I saw the miniseries. It never mentioned you."

"I'm part of the secret history, Corey."

"Cool." He contemplated his Pokémon, but decided not to go back to monster trapping. "When we get back to the Bangkok side, can I get caramel frappuccino at Starbucks?"

"Decaf," I said.

That evening I go back to the house and find Mom in bed with Jed, the police inspector. Suddenly, I don't like Jed anymore.

She barely looks up at me; Jed is pounding away and oblivious to it all; I don't know if Mom really knows I'm there, or just a shadow flitting beyond the mosquito netting. I know why she's doing it; she'll say that it's all about getting information for this great novel she's planning to write, or research for a major magazine article, but the truth is that it's about survival; it's no different from that concentration camp.

I think she finally does realize I'm there; she mouths the words "I'm sorry" and then turns back to her work. At that moment, I hear someone tapping at the entrance, and I crawl over the squeaky floorplanks, Siamese-style (children learn to move around on their knees so that their head isn't accidentally higher than someone of higher rank) to see Sombun on the step.

"Can you come out?" he says. "There's a *ngaan wat*."

I don't know what that is, but I don't want to stay in the house. So I throw on a shirt and go with him. I soon find out that a *ngaan wat* is a temple fair, sort of a cross between a carnival and a church bazaar and a theatrical night out.

Even from a mile or two away we hear the music, the tinkling of marimbas and the thud of drums, the wail of the Javanese oboe. By the time we get there, the air is drenched with the fragrance of pickled guava, peanut pork skewers, and green papaya tossed in fish sauce. A makeshift dance floor has been spread over the muddy ground and there are dancers with rhinestone court costumes and pagoda hats, their hands bent back at an impossible angle. There's a Chinese opera troupe like I've seen in Shanghai, glittering costumes, masks painted on the faces in garish colors, boys dressed as monkeys leaping to and fro; the Thai and the Chinese striving to outdo each other in noise and brilliance. And on a grill, being tended by a fat woman, pigeons are barbecuing, each one on a mini-spear of steel. And I'm reminded of the open fire and the sizzling of half-plucked feathers.

"You got money?" Sombun says. He thinks that all *farangs* are rich. I fish in my pocket and pull out a few *saleungs*, and we stuff ourselves with pan-fried *roti* swimming in sweet condensed milk.

The thick juice is dripping from our lips. This really is paradise. The music, the mingled scents, the warm wind. Then I see Si Ui. There aren't any birds nearby, not unless you count the pigeons charring on the grill. Si Ui is muttering to himself, but I understand Chinese, and he's saying, over and over again, "Si Ui hungry, Si Ui hungry." He says it in a little voice and it's almost like baby talk.

We wander over to the Chinese opera troupe. They're doing something about monkeys invading heaven and stealing the apples of the gods. All these kids are somersaulting, tumbling, cartwheeling, and climbing up onto each other's shoulders. There's a little girl, nine or ten maybe, and she's watching the show. And Si Ui is watching her. And I'm watching him.

I've seen her before, know her from that night we squatted on the veranda staring at American TV shows. Was Si Ui watching her even then? I tried to remember. Couldn't be sure. Her name's Juk.

Those Chinese cymbals, with their annoying "boing-boing-boing" sound, are clashing. A man is intoning in a weird singsong. The monkeys are leaping. Suddenly I see, in Si Ui's face, the same expression I saw on the ship. He's utterly still inside, utterly quiet, beyond feeling. The war did that to him. I know. Just like it made my mom into a whore, and me into . . . I don't know . . . a bird without a nesting place . . . a lost boy.

And then I get this . . . *irrational* feeling. That the little girl is a bird, chirping to herself, hopping along the ground, not noticing the stalker.

So many people here. So much jangling, so much laughter. The town's dilapidated pagodas sparkle with reflected colors, like stone Christmas trees. Chinese opera rings in my ears. I look away, when I look back they are gone . . . Sombun is preoccupied now, playing with a two-*saleung* top that he just bought. Somehow I feel impelled to follow. To stalk the stalker.

I duck behind a fruit stand and then I see a golden deer. It's a toy, on four wheels, pulled along a string. I can't help following it with my eyes as it darts between hampers full of rambutans and pomelos.

The deer darts toward the cupped hands of the little girl. I see her disappear into the crowd, but then I see Si Ui's face, too; you can't mistake the cold fire in his eyes.

She follows the toy. Si Ui pulls. I follow, too, not really knowing why it's so fascinating. The toy deer weaves through the ocean of feet. Bare feet of monks and novices, their saffron robes skimming the mud. Feet in rubber flipflops, in the wooden sandals the *Jek* call *kiah*. I hear a voice: *Juk, Juk!* And I know there's someone else looking for the girl, too. It's a weird quartet, each one in the sequence known only to the next one. I can see Si Ui now, his head bobbing up and down in the throng because he's a little taller than the average Thai even though he's so skinny. He's intent. Concentrated. He seems to be on wheels himself, he glides through the crowd like the toy deer. The woman's voice, calling for Juk, is faint and distant; she hears it, I'm sure, but she's ignoring her mother or her big sister. I only hear it because my senses are sharp now, it's like the rest of the temple fair's all out of focus now, all blurry, and there's just the four of us. I see the woman now, it must be a mother or aunt, too old for a sister, collaring a *roti* vendor and asking if he's seen the child. The vendor shakes his head, laughs. And suddenly we're all next to the pigeon barbecue, and if the woman was only looking in the right place she'd see the little girl, giggling as she clambers through the forest of legs, as the toy zigzags over the dirt aisles. And now the deer has been yanked right up to Si Ui's feet. And the girl crawls all the way after it, seizes it, laughs, looks solemnly up at the face of the Chinaman—

"It's him! It's the chink!" Sombun is pointing, laughing. I'd forgotten he was even with me.

Si Ui is startled. His concentration snaps. He lashes out. There's a blind rage in his eyes. Dead pigeons are flying everywhere.

"Hungry!" he screams in Chinese. "Si Ui hungry!"

He turns. There is a cloth stall nearby. Suddenly he and the girl are gone amid a flurry of billowing sarongs. And I follow.

Incense in the air, stinging my eyes. A shaman gets possessed in a side aisle, his followers hushed. A flash of red. A red sarong, embroidered with gold, a year's wages, twisting through the crowd. I follow. I see the girl's terrified eyes. I see Si Ui with the red cloth wrapped around his arms, around the girl. I see something glistening, a knife maybe. And no one sees. No one but me.

*Juk! Juk!*

I've lost Sombun somewhere. I don't care. I thread my way through a bevy of *ramwong* dancers, through men dressed as women and women dressed as men. Fireworks are going off. There's an ancient wall, the temple boundary, crumbling . . . and the trail of red funnels into black night . . . and I'm standing on the other side of the wall now, watching Si Ui ride away in a pedicab, into the night. There's moonlight on him. He's saying something; even from far off I can read his lips; he's saying it over and over: *Si Ui hungry, Si Ui hungry.*

So they find her by the side of the road with her internal organs missing. And I'm there, too, all the boys are at dawn, peering down, daring each other to touch. It's not a rape or anything, they tell us. Nothing like the other girl. Someone has seen a cowherd near the site, and he's the one they arrest. He's an Indian, you see. If there's anyone the locals despise more than the Chinese, it's the Indians. They have a saying: If you see a snake and an Indian, kill the *baby.*

Later, in the market, Inspector Jed is escorting the Indian to the police station, and they start pelting him with stones, and they call him a dirty Indian and a cowshit eater. They beat him up pretty badly in the jail. The country's under martial law in these days, you know. They can beat up anyone they want. Or shoot them.

But most people don't really notice, or care. After all, it is paradise. To say that it is not, aloud, risks making it true. That's why my mom will never belong to Thailand; she doesn't understand that everything there resides in what is left unsaid.

That afternoon I go back to the rubber orchard. He is standing patiently. There's a bird on a branch. Si Ui is poised. Waiting. I think he is about to pounce. But I'm too excited to wait. "The girl," I say. "The girl, she's dead, did you know?"

Si Ui whirls around in a murderous fury, and then, just as suddenly, he's smiling.

"I didn't mean to break your concentration," I say.

"Girl soft," Si Ui says. "Tender." He laughs a little. I don't see a vicious killer. All I see is loneliness and hunger.

"Did you kill her?" I say.

"Kill?" he says. "I don't know. Si Ui hungry." He beckons me closer. I'm not afraid of him. "Do like me," he says. He crouches. I crouch, too. He stares at the bird. And so do I. "Make like a tree now," he says, and I say, "Yes. I'm a tree." He's behind me. He's breathing down my neck. Am I the next bird? But somehow I know he won't hurt me.

"Now!" he shrieks. Blindly, instinctively, I grab the sparrow in both hands. I can feel the quick heart grow cold as the bones crunch. Blood and birdshit squirt into my fists. It feels exciting, you know, down there, inside me. I killed it. The shock of death is amazing, joyous. I wonder if this is what grown-ups feel when they do things to each other in the night.

He laughs. "You and me," he says, "now we same-same."

He shows me how to lick the warm blood as it spurts. It's hotter than you think. It pulses, it quivers, the whole bird trembles as it yields up its spirit to me.

And then there's the weirdest thing. You know that hunger, the one that's gnawed at me, like a wound that won't close up, since we were dragged to that camp . . . it's suddenly gone. In its place there's a kind of nothing.

The Buddhists here say that heaven itself is a kind of nothing. That the goal of all existence is to become as nothing.

And I feel it. For all of a second or two, I feel it. "I know why you do it," I say. "I won't tell anyone, I swear."

"Si Ui knows that already."

Yes, he does. We have stood on common ground. We have shared communion flesh. Once a month, a Chinese priest used to come to the camp and celebrate mass with a hunk of maggoty *man to*, but he never made me feel one with anyone, let alone God.

The blood bathes my lips. The liver is succulent and bursting with juices.

Perhaps this is the first person I've ever loved.

The feeling lasts a few minutes. But then comes the hunger, swooping down on me, hunger clawed and ravenous. It will never go away, not completely.

They have called in an exorcist to pray over the railway tracks. The mother of the girl they found there has become a nun, and she stands on the gravel pathway lamenting her karma. The most recent victim has few to grieve for her. I overhear Inspector Jed talking to my mother. He tells her there are two killers. The second one had her throat cut and her internal organs removed . . . the first one, strangulation, all different . . . he's been studying these cases, these ritual killers, in American psychiatry books. And the cowherd has an alibi for the first victim.

I'm only half-listening to Jed, who drones on and on about famous mad killers in Europe. Like the butcher of Hanover, Jack the Ripper. How their victims were always chosen in a special way. How they killed over and over, always a certain way, a ritual. How they always got careless after a while, because part of what they were doing came from a hunger, a desperate need to be found out. How after a while they might leave clues . . . confide in someone . . . how he thought he had one of these cases on his hands, but the authorities in Bangkok weren't buying the idea. The village of Thapsakae just wasn't grand enough to play host to a reincarnation of Jack the Ripper.

I listen to him, but I've never been to Europe, and it's all just talk to me. I'm much more interested in the exorcist, who's a Brahmin, in white robes, hair down to his feet, all nappy and filthy, a dozen flower garlands around his neck, and amulets tinkling all over him.

"The killer might confide in someone," says Jed, "someone he thinks is in no position to betray him, someone perhaps too simpleminded to understand. Remember, the killer doesn't know he's evil. In a sense, he really can't help himself. He doesn't think the way we think. To himself, he's an innocent."

The exorcist enters his trance and sways and mumbles in unknown tongues. The villagers don't believe the killer's an innocent. They want to lynch him.

Women washing clothes find a young girl's hand bobbing up and down, and her head a few yards downstream. Women are panicking in the marketplace. They're lynching Indians, Chinese, anyone alien. But not Si Ui, he's a simpleton, after all. The village idiot is immune from persecution because every village needs an idiot.

The exorcist gets quite a workout, capturing spirits into baskets and jars.

Meanwhile, Si Ui has become the trusted *Jek*, the one who cuts the *gailan* in the fields and never cheats anyone of their two-*saleung* bundle of Chinese broccoli.

I keep his secret. Evenings, after I'm exhausted from swimming all day with Sombun and Lek, or lazing on the back of a waterbuffalo, I go to the rubber orchard and catch birds as the sun sets. I'm almost as good as him now. Sometimes he says nothing, though he'll share with me a piece of meat, cooked or uncooked; sometimes he talks up a storm. When he talks pidgin, he sounds like he's a half-wit. When he talks Thai, it's the same way, I think. But when he goes on and on in his Hakka dialect, he's as lucid as they come. I think. Because I'm only getting it in patches.

One day he says to me, "The young ones taste the best because it's the taste of childhood. You and I, we have no childhood. Only the taste."

A bird flies onto his shoulder, head tilted, chirps a friendly song. Perhaps he will soon be dinner.

Another day, Si Ui says, "Children's livers are the sweetest, they're bursting with young life. I weep for them. They're with me always. They're my friends. Like you."

Around us, paradise is crumbling. Everyone suspects someone else. Fights are breaking out in the marketplace. One day it's the Indians, another day the chinks, the Burmese. Hatred hangs in the air like the smell of rotten mangoes.

And Si Ui is getting hungrier.

My mother is working on her book now, thinking it'll make her fortune; she waits for the mail, which gets here sometimes by train, sometimes by oxcart. She's waiting for some letter from Simon & Schuster. It never comes, but she's having a ball, in her own way. She stumbles her way through the language, commits appalling solecisms, points her feet, even touches a monk one time, a total sacrilege ... but they let her get away with everything. *Farangs*, after all, are touched by a divine madness. You can expect nothing normal from them.

She questions every villager, pores over every clue. It never occurs to her to ask me what I know.

We glut ourselves on papaya and curried catfish.

"Nicholas," my mother tells me one evening, after she's offered me a hit of opium, her latest affection, "this really is the Garden of Eden."

I don't tell her that I've already met the serpent.

Here's how the day of reckoning happened, Corey:

It's midmorning and I'm wandering aimlessly. My mother has taken the train to Bangkok with Inspector Jed. He's decided that her untouchable *farang*-ness might get him an audience with some major official in the police department. I don't see my friends at the river or in the marketplace. But it's not planting season, and there's no school. So I'm playing by myself, but you can only flip so many pebbles into the river and tease so many waterbuffaloes.

After a while I decide to go and look for Sombun. We're not close, he and I, but we're thrown together a lot; things don't seem right without him.

I go to Sombun's house; it's a shabby place, but immaculate, a row house in the more "citified" part of the village, if you can call it that. Sombun's mother is making chili paste, pounding the spices in a stone mortar. You can smell the sweet basil and the lemongrass in the air. And the betelnut, too; she's chewing on the intoxicant; her teeth are stained red-black from long use.

"Oh," she says, "the *farang* boy."

"Where's Sombun?"

She doesn't know quite what to make of my Thai, which has been getting better for months. "He's not home, Little Mouse," she says. "He went to the *Jek*'s house to buy broccoli. Do you want to eat?"

"I've eaten, thanks, auntie," I say, but for politeness' sake I'm forced to nibble on bright green *sali* pastry.

"He's been gone a long time," she said, as she pounded. "I wonder if the chink's going to teach him to catch birds."

"Birds?"

And I start to get this weird feeling. Because *I'm* the one who catches birds with the Chinaman, I'm the one who's shared his past, who understands his hunger. Not just any kid.

"Sombun told me the chink was going to show him a special trick for catching them. Something about putting yourself into a deep state of *samadhi*, reaching out with your mind, plucking the life-force with your mind. It sounds very spiritual, doesn't it? I always took the chink for a moron, but maybe I'm misjudging him; Sombun seems to do a much better job," she said. "I never liked it when they came to our village, but they do work hard."

Well, when I leave Sombun's house, I'm starting to get a little mad. It's jealousy, of course, childish jealousy; I see that now. But I don't want to go there and disrupt their little bird-catching session. I'm not a spoilsport. I'm just going to pace up and down by the side of the *klong*, doing a slow burn.

The serpent came to *me!* I was the only one who could see through his madness and his pain, the only one who truly knew the hunger that drove him! That's what I'm thinking. And I go back to tossing pebbles, and I tease the gibbon chained by the temple's gate, and I kick a waterbuffalo around. And, before I knew it, this twinge of jealousy has grown into a kind of rage. It's like I was one of those birds, only in a really big cage, and I'd been flying and flying and thinking I was free, and now I've banged into the prison bars for the first time. I'm so mad I could burst.

I'm playing by myself by the railway tracks when I see my mom and the inspector walking out of the station. And that's the last straw. I want to hurt someone. I want to hurt my mom for shutting me out and letting strangers into her mosquito net at night. I want to punish Jed for thinking he knows everything. I want someone to notice me.

So that's when I run up to them and I say, "I'm the one! He confided in *me!* You said he was going to give himself away to someone and it was *me*, it was *me!*"

My mom just stares at me, but Jed becomes very quiet. "The Chinaman?" he asks me.

I say, "He told me children's livers are the sweetest. I think he's after Sombun." I don't tell him that he's only going to teach Sombun to catch birds, that he taught me, too, that boys are safe from him because like the inspector told us, we're not the special kind of victim he seeks out. "In his house, in the rubber orchard, you'll find everything," I say. "Bones. He makes the feet into a stew," I add, improvising now, because I've never been inside that house. "He cuts off their faces and dries them on a jerky rack. And Sombun's with him."

The truth is, I'm just making trouble. I don't believe there's dried faces in the house or human bones. I know Sombun's going to be safe, that Si Ui's only teaching him how to squeeze the life force from the birds, how to blunt the ancient hunger. Him instead of me. They're not going to find anything but dead birds.

There's a scream. I turn. I see Sombun's mother with a basket of fish, coming from the market. She's overheard me, and she cries, "The chink is killing my son!" Faster than thought, the street is full of people, screaming their anti-chink epithets and pulling out butcher knives. Jed's calling for reinforcements. Street vendors are tightening their *phakhomas* around their waists.

"Which way?" Jed asks, and suddenly I'm at the head of an army, racing full tilt toward the rubber orchard, along the neon green of the young rice paddies, beside the canals teeming with catfish, through thickets of banana trees, around the walls of the old temple, through the fields of *gailan* . . . and this too feeds my hunger. It's ugly. He's a Chinaman. He's the village idiot. He's different. He's an alien. Anything is possible.

We're converging on the *gailan* field now. They're waving sticks. Harvesting sickles. Fish knives. They're shouting, "Kill the chink, kill the chink." Sombun's mother is shrieking and wailing, and Inspector Jed has his gun out. Tae Pak, the village rich man, is vainly trying to stop the mob from trampling his broccoli. The army is unstoppable. And I'm their leader, I brought them here with my little lie. Even my mother is finally in awe.

I push through the bamboo thicket and we're standing in the clearing in the rubber orchard now. They're screaming for the *Jek's* blood. And I'm screaming with them.

Si Ui is nowhere to be found. They're beating on the ground now, slicing it with their scythes, smashing their clubs against the trees. Sombun's mother is hysterical. The other women have caught her mood, and they're all screaming now, because someone is holding up a sandal . . . Sombun's.

*...a little Chinese boy hiding in a closet...*

The images flashes again. I must go up into the house. I steal away, sneak up the steps, respectfully removing my sandals at the veranda, and I slip into the house.

A kerosene lamp burns. Light and shadows dance. There is a low wooden platform for a bed, a mosquito net, a woven rush mat for sleeping; off in a corner, there is a closet.

Birds everywhere. Dead birds pinned to the walls. Birds' heads piled up on plates. Blood spatters on the floor planks. Feathers wafting. On a charcoal stove in one corner, there's a wok with some hot oil and garlic, and sizzling in that oil is a heart, too big to be the heart of a bird. . . .

My eyes get used to the darkness. I see human bones in a pail. I see a young girl's head in a jar, the skull sawn open, half the brain gone. I see a bowl of pickled eyes.

I'm not afraid. These are familiar sights. This horror is a spectral echo of Nanking, nothing more.

"Si Ui," I whisper. "I lied to them. I know you didn't do anything to Sombun. You're one of the killers who does the same thing over and over. You don't eat boys. I know I've always been safe with you. I've always trusted you."

I hear someone crying. The whimper of a child.

"Hungry," says the voice. "Hungry."

A voice from behind the closet door . . .

The door opens. Si Ui is there, huddled, bone-thin, his *phakhomah*, about his loins, weeping, rocking.

Noises now. Angry voices. They're clambering up the steps. They're breaking down the wall planks. Light streams in.

"I'm sorry," I whisper. I see fire flicker in his eyes, then drain away as the mob sweeps into the room.

My grandson was hungry, too. When he said he could eat the world, he wasn't kidding. After the second decaf frappuccino, there was Italian ice in the Oriental's coffee shop, and then, riding back on the Skytrain to join the chauffeur who had conveniently parked at the Sogo mall, there was a box of Smarties. Corey's mother always told me to watch the sugar, and she had plenty of Ritalin in stock—no prescription needed here—but it was always my pleasure to defy my daughter-in-law and leave her to deal with the consequences.

Corey ran wild in the Skytrain station, whooping up the staircases, yelling at old ladies. No one minded. Kids are indulged in Babylon East; little blond boys are too cute to do wrong. For some, this noisy, polluted, chaotic city is still a kind of paradise.

My day of revelations ended at my son's townhouse in Sukhumvit, where maids and nannies fussed over little Corey and undressed him and got him in his Pokémon pajamas as I drained a glass of Beaujolais. My son was rarely home; the taco chain consumed all his time. My daughter-in-law was a social butterfly; she had already gone out for the evening, all pearls and Thai silk. So it fell to me to go into my grandson's room and to kiss him goodnight and good-bye.

Corey's bedroom was little piece of America, with its *Phantom Menace* drapes and its Playstation. But on a high niche, an image of the Buddha looked down;

a decaying garland still perfumed the air with a whiff of jasmine. The air-conditioning was chilly; the Bangkok of the rich is a cold city; the more conspicuous the consumption, the lower the thermostat setting. I shivered, even as I missed Manhattan in January.

"Tell me a story, Grandpa?" Corey said.

"I told you one already," I said.

"Yeah, you did," he said wistfully. "About you in the Garden of Eden, and the serpent who was really a kid-eating monster."

All true. But as the years passed I had come to see that perhaps I was the serpent. I was the one who mixed lies with the truth, and took away his innocence. He was a child, really, a hungry child. And so was I.

"Tell me what happened to him," Corey said. "Did the people lynch him?"

"No. The court ruled that he was a madman, and sentenced him to a mental home. But the military government of Field Marshall Sarit reversed the decision, and they took him away and shot him. And he didn't even kill half the kids they said he killed."

"Like the first girl, the one who was raped and strangled," Corey said. "but she didn't get eaten. Maybe that other killer's still around." So he had been paying attention after all. I know he loves me, though he rarely says so; he had suffered an old man's ramblings for one long air-conditioning-free day, without complaint. I'm proud of him, can barely believe I've held on to life long enough to get to know him.

I leaned down to kiss him. He clung to me; and, as he let go, he asked me sleepily, "Do you ever feel that hungry, Grandpa?"

I didn't want to answer him; so, without another word, I slipped quietly away.

That night, I wandered in my dreams through fields of the dead; the hunger raged; I killed, I swallowed children whole and spat them out; I burned down cities; I stood aflame in my self-made inferno, howling with elemental grief; and in the morning, without leaving a note, I took a taxi to the airport and flew back to New York.

To face the hunger.

# GRAHAM JOYCE

# Black Dust

Graham Joyce is a British writer whose work falls into the interesting interstitial realm at the intersection of horror, contemporary fantasy, and mainstream fiction. His novels include Requiem, Dark Sister, Indigo, The Tooth Fairy, and, most recently, Smoking Poppy, all of which are highly recommended. His short fiction has been collected in Partial Eclipse and Other Stories (Subterranean Press). Joyce lives in Leicester, England, and has won two British Fantasy Awards.

The ghost story that follows is an affecting tale without sentimentality, both brutal and compassionate, and beautifully written. "Black Dust" first appeared in 2001 as a chapbook from Subterranean Press, then in the February 2002 issue of The Magazine of Fantasy & Science Fiction.

—T. W.

Half hidden behind a thicket of hawthorn and holly bushes was a second cave. It astonished him to see it there. As a kid Andy had scrambled over every boulder, probed every fissure and crevice, and swung from the exposed roots of every tree clinging to the face of Corley Rocks. Yet here was a new cave, quite unlike the one in which he'd been holed up for the afternoon. After feeling the mild tremor, Andy needed to get home. But something in this new cave called to him.

Unlike the first cave, a mere split in the rock face that had always been there, this one was dome-shaped, with an arched chamber as an entrance. He drew closer. As he squeezed between the hawthorn and prickly holly to get into the cave, it became obvious to him that this second cave went back much deeper. He could see well enough for the first few yards, but after that the cave shadows set hard in a resinous black diamond.

Still it called.

He wanted to move deeper in, but his throat dried and his breathing came short. He rolled his foot in the blackness. A pebble crunched under his shoe.

There was a tiny light, no bigger than a glow-worm, swinging at the rear of the cave. It flickered and went out. Then it appeared again. The light shimmered, still swinging slightly from left to right. He heard footsteps shuffling toward him, and then there appeared in the gloom a second light, smaller than the first, and nearer the cave floor. The lights were approaching. Then there was a sound like the low growl of an animal, and it made him think of that dog.

That dog, slavering and throwing itself at the fence, chewing the thick wire mesh. A brute of an Alsatian, but the drooling jaws and yellow teeth had Andy convinced it was part wolf. Andy always kept one eye peeled for the dog while the other, of course, was alert for Bryn's father.

Bryn appeared in his socks. "It's all right," he said. "He's not here."

Andy crossed the swarthy yard and removed his shoes at the threshold of the kitchen. Shoes off at the door because of the coal dust. Everyone. The house and yard once belonged to a coal merchant who'd gone bust, and the cinder path leading to Bryn's house was black. The yard was black. The gate was black. The coal dust had even pointed up the cement between the black-red bricks. They had to take off their shoes so as not to trail black dust into the house. Bryn had developed a lazy habit of not bothering to put on his shoes merely to cross the yard, even though his father, with a bunched fist, had once made his ear bleed for this offense.

"Twenty minutes before he gets back."

The boys went through the kitchen. Bryn's mother Jean looked up from her ironing. "Still down there then, your dad."

"Yes," said Andy.

"Twenty-four hours now."

"Yes."

"They got oxygen. They got food to them. They'll get him out." She pressed her iron into a collar and a jet of steam wheezed into the air.

The two boys went upstairs to Bryn's room, where they got the rope, the water bottle, and the tiny brass compass. They didn't want to hang around. Important not to be there when Ike got back off shift. Sometimes when they played table football or lounged in Bryn's bedroom, the door would open quietly and Bryn's mother would whisper, "He's back. Make yourself scarce." And with that they always would.

Once when Andy awaited Bryn in the kitchen, Ike had come in from work and imposed himself in the doorway, glowering. Andy had felt compelled to look away. Without saying a word to Bryn's mum, the big man slumped in an armchair before the fire, and how the chair-springs had groaned. Ike's skin glowed pink with the scrubbing from a recent shower at the pit, but his body still leaked the odor of coal. A smell like a sulfurous gas, streaming off the man as he stared moodily into the fire. He snorted at the coal-dust irritating his sinuses, hawked and spat into the fire, and this movement released a fresh wave of hostile gas.

Andy had on that occasion feared that even breathing might cause offense. Finally Bryn appeared, beckoning him away. Outside the door they had both vented huge sighs.

Of course they didn't need the compass to find their way to Corley Rocks. A matter of a mile and half from the mining estate, Corley Rocks was the highest natural point in the old county of Warwickshire. The ploughed earthworks of an Iron Age encampment moldered on the flat field above an outcrop of red sandstone rock, and from there you could take in the green belt of land all around. To the south stood the two giant wheels of the pit-head winding gear, and beyond that the spires and smoking chimneys of Coventry.

The dog started up again.

"Shut it," Bryn growled as they left the house. "Shut it." It was exactly the way Andy had heard Bryn's old man speak to the dog, half song, half warning, and it was always effective in subduing the animal. Except when Andy or anyone else tried, in which case the dog simply became more inflamed, hurling itself with stupid energy against the mesh fence.

"Do you think that dog is a killer?" Andy said as they walked up the black cinder path away from the house.

"Probably." Bryn hooped the rope across one shoulder. "You carry the water bottle."

The rope was usually for display only. They'd never done any real climbing at Corley Rocks. Everywhere was accessible by scrambling over the smooth, rounded edges of the sandstone. There was only one place where a rope might be helpful, at the sheer face of the rock above the cave, and Bryn was keen to try it. And it had to be admitted: looped across the torso from left collarbone to right hip, the rope looked a treat.

Andy was envious, because carrying the water bottle was shit. But the rope was Bryn's after all.

They had to pass the entrance to the mine, with its weighbridges and security gates. "Don't think about it," Bryn said. "They've got air. And food. They'll get him out."

It was a hot afternoon in August, and by the time they reached the rocks they were sweating and had drunk all of the water. The cave was merely a fissure, a crack opened in the rock face, but it could be reached by the means of small cavities scooped out of the soft stone, ancient handholds and toegrips. They climbed up and retreated to the back of the cave, welcoming the shade.

Their schoolteacher had said that traces of prehistoric habitation had been found at the cave: flints, stone tools, bones. Someone had even unearthed a huge sabre-tooth, currently being examined by experts at Coventry museum. People had always lived there, it was said, and before that the rocks themselves had been pushed up by fault lines in the vast coal reservoirs under the ground: the very coal that Andy and Bryn's fathers now mined on a daily basis.

Bryn lifted the rope from his shoulders, causing his T-shirt to ride up. Andy saw below Bryn's ribcage the flowering of a huge blue and yellow bruise. It looked like one of the purple-leaf cabbages his own dad grew in the garden. He said nothing. He knew. Bryn knew he knew. And it was none of his business, that's what Andy's mother had said to his father.

"Not your business, Stan, to go getting tangled up in," Nina warned her husband. "Not your business at all."

Andy's father had wanted to go down to Bryn's house to have words. Bryn had turned up one afternoon while Andy's dad dribbled water from the garden hose on his prize-winning leeks. For the old giggle Andy's dad put his finger over the hose and jet-sprayed the two boys. The giggling stopped when the lads stripped off their wet T-shirts.

"Hell, you've been in the wars, haven't you?" Stan said, turning back to his leeks. Then he did a double-take, looked harder, and laid down the hose. Taking in the multiple bruises on the lad's body, he stepped closer. "Let's have a look at you, son."

Bryn danced away. "Nothing. Fell off a ladder."

"Come here, I said. Stand still. Christ, son! Hell's bells!" He brushed the wounds gently with his callused fingertips. Then he said, very quietly, "Must have been a good few times you fell off that ladder."

"Yeah," Bryn sniffed.

Andy's mother, who'd seen all of this, came out with a clean T-shirt apiece for the lads. Stan was already halfway down the path. She chased after him. "You're not going down there. Not your business!"

Stan had himself once clouted Andy with a closed fist, but only once, and some years ago. Not a single day had passed when he hadn't regretted it. "I'll be back sharpish."

"You're not going down there!"

Stan pulled up short. "I said I'll be back sharp," he whispered in a way that settled the argument. Andy's mum returned to the back garden, where the boys had their heads down and hose was still dribbling water onto the leek-bed.

With the dog going berserk behind the mesh fence Stan had knocked on the door and had taken a step back. It was some moments before Ike Thompson appeared blinking in the doorway, puff-eyed, looking like he'd just been disturbed from a nap. His eyes were lined with coal-dust like a woman's mascara. He sniffed. "Stan," he said.

"A word in the yard, Ike?" Stan turned his back and walked into the open expanse of the disused coal merchant's yard.

Ike shuffled in the doorway, slipped on his boots without lacing them, and followed Stan across the yard.

The men knew each other well enough. They'd mined the same districts, notably the 42s and the 56s; they nodded to each other whenever their paths crossed, they'd even once been part of the same Mine Rescue Team, and they knew that their boys were good pals. They just didn't like each other.

The two miners stood in the cinder-black yard at a distance of about five paces. The dog was barking mad, flinging itself at the fence. "Your Bryn's up at our house just now."

Ike was a big man. His grizzled face bore the blue signature scars of coal mining, like someone had scribbled on his face with a ballpoint pen. He stood a head taller than Stan. But Stan was trunk-necked with a barrel of a chest and muscle packed like coiled wire. He had his own mining scar, a blue and white star right in the middle of his forehead, like a bullet wound.

Ike lifted a hand to his mouth, squeezing his bottom lip between a coal-ingrained thumb and a coal-ingrained forefinger. "Yup."

"Says he fell off of a ladder."

Ike let his hand drop now he knew what this was about. He glanced to the side, and then back at Stan. "Yup."

The Alsatian barked, and slavered, and seemed to try to chew its way through the mesh fence. "He won't be falling off that ladder again, now will he, Ike?"

Ike turned to the dog, and in a low, throaty voice, almost a hiss, said, "Shut iiiiiiiiiiitttttttttt." The dog lowered its head and crept back into its kennel. "That it?" said Ike.

"That's about it."

"Right. You can go now."

"Happen I will go. But if that lad should fall off another ladder, then I'll come down here again. And we'll have another talk. More serious."

"Oh aye?"

"Too right, we will. Too right."

The two men stood off each other for another minute. Then Stan said, "I'll be seeing you, Ike."

Stan retraced his steps along the cinder path. He felt Ike's gaze drilling into him at every step.

"Stop thinking about it," Bryn said. "They'll get him out. My old man will get him out."

Andy knew they would get his dad out all right. He just wished everyone would stop telling him. He hadn't been allowed to go up to the pit-head, where the wives and grown-up sons and daughters and the rescue teams and the camera crews all congregated, waiting. It had been twenty-fours hours since a roof had collapsed half a mile underground, trapping seven miners, one of whom was Stan. The rescue teams had made an early breakthrough, piping air and passing food through to the trapped men, but the rescue efforts had hit a snag when a second roof-fall had threatened. Ike was on one of the rescue teams.

"They're right under here," Bryn said. "Right under this spot."

"How do you know that?"

"My old man told me. He said the seam runs north and under these rocks."

Andy thought about his own dad half a mile directly below him, waiting.

"You're not *crying* are you?" Bryn said. "Not *crying*."

"Dust in my eye. Dust." Andy's fingers found a flake of red stone. He flung it from the back of the cave into the crack of light, and it dropped, skittering down the slope. "Anyway you wouldn't care if anything happened to your old man."

Andy wished he hadn't said that. Bryn started whipping the end of his rope. "He might be a shit but at least he. . . ."

"At least he what?"

"Nah. Come on. Let's climb the Edge."

The boys scrambled out of the cave and walked up to an outcrop of red stone known as the Witch's Face. Bryn hoisted himself over the chin and nose of the Face and wanted to use the rope to get Andy up. Andy objected on grounds of pointlessness. From there they proceeded to the Edge, a cliff overhang directly above the cave.

*At least he what?* Andy thought as they clambered up the steep sandstone slopes, between ragged clumps of hawthorn and holly. One day Stan had brought home a second-hand guitar. Andy had pestered Stan for this guitar, but when it arrived he soon found out that the strings cut his fingers to shreds. He'd taken the guitar down to Bryn's house, and he was exhibiting it to Bryn when Ike appeared unexpectedly, standing in the kitchen doorway, sniffing back coal-dust. His eyes fell on the guitar.

Ike walked across the kitchen without removing his boots, gently lifting the guitar from the lad. "What you got here then, lovely boy? Let's have a look, then."

Ike sat, effeminately crossed his legs, positioned the guitar across his thigh, and gently thumbed the strings. He played a chord or two and the dog in the yard howled. Ike laughed. "Hear that?" He strummed a few more chords and then picked out a tune. "Christ, these strings stand too high off the frets. You'll never play this, lovely boy. Nice tone, but it's a piece of rubbish."·

"My dad got it for me," Andy said, meaning to sound defensive.

Ike laid the guitar down. "Come on lads, get in the car."

"Where you going?" Jean had protested.

"Get in the car, boys!"

Where they went, in Ike's beat-up old Ford Zephyr, was Chaplin's music store. Ike spent most of the journey explaining to Andy how he used to have a guitar—two guitars, even—but when Bryn and his sister had come along, why, there was no time, no bloody time to play them, and he'd always regretted selling the instruments, and now he was going to put that right. He talked like that all the way round the music shop, non-stop; he insulted the shop manager; tried out every second-hand guitar in the store, crooned passionately to other customers; purchased right off two decent instruments for the boys; and had a twenty-minute bash on a Premiere Drum Kit before leaving.

"Where's the swining money coming for those, then?" Jean shouted when they got back.

Ike was all sweetness. He squeezed his wife and kissed her angry mouth. "Music before butter," he said. "Remember that, lovely boys. Music before butter."

Stan and Nina had something to say about it, too. They made Andy take his guitar back. Stan went with him. Stan and Andy stood in the kitchen, with their shoes on this time.

"Why can't I buy the lads an instrument apiece?" Ike said. "Why can't I?"

"It's too generous," Stan said.

"Rubbish. How's that anybody's concern but mine?"

"It's my swining-well concern, too," said Jean. "Where's the money coming from?"

The lads watched all this intently. "Boys, sod off into the other room, will you?" Stan said. Bryn and Andy filed out, both still clutching the new guitars by the necks, and closed the door behind them. "Look, Ike, you can't make up for things by throwing money at them."

"What's that? You've lost me."

"The guitars. You can't make other things right."

Ike suddenly understood Stan's point. His face clouded. "I see. I see what this is about, and I don't like it. Tell me, how does one thing touch the other?"

"I'm just saying."

"How the bloody hell does one thing touch the other? If I want to buy the boys instruments apiece, I buy the bloody instruments apiece! Christ, man!"

Stan was man enough to sense he might have made a mistake. "I don't know, Ike, it's too much."

But Ike had soured now. He called the boys back, and while he waited for them, he said, "Your lad can carry his guitar home with him or I'll take it in the yard and split it into matchwood, now!"

"He will, as well," Jean put in.

Stan sighed. "Come on," he said to the bewildered Andy. "Bring your guitar."

Ike followed them out. The dog growled from its kennel but Ike silenced it with a thunderous look. "One thing does not touch another," he said, almost in a whisper. "You should know that, Stan. One thing does not touch another."

"Happen."

They'd not gone twelve yards before Ike softly called to Andy. "Practice every day, mind," he said softly, and with a terrifying squint to his eye. "Practice every day."

"I will," said Andy.

On the top of the Edge Bryn fumbled with the rope, securing a Pig's Ear knot as he looped it round a spindly clump of rooted hawthorn. Andy was supposed then to loop the rope around his own waist while Bryn lowered himself over the Edge, preparing to descend to the cave that way—a mere matter of nine or ten feet below the lip of the Edge.

Bryn duly disappeared over the lip, negotiating toeholds and fingergrips, grunting occasionally and chattering happily. Andy meanwhile stood with his hands in his pockets, anxiously gazing across at the twin wheels of the pit-head winding gear, wondering how the rescue was proceeding. It was possible to superimpose on the landscape the giant ghost of an old lady crouched at those black wheels, spinning away with some dark and concealed purpose. And it was while Andy gazed across the fields to the distant mineworks that he heard a yelp and felt the rope tighten round his waist.

Andy grabbed the branch of a nearby tree. The rope jagged against the feeble hawthorn, lifting it out by its roots. Bryn yelped again as the rope dropped him another six feet. Then the hawthorn root popped out of the sandy soil, like a pulled tooth. The rope whiplashed at Andy, turning him in a complete circle, losing its purchase on his body. The bush lashed at Andy's face as it went past him. It snagged on two fingers of exposed tree-root, and Bryn was dumped another six feet. Then the bush tore free and whistled as it went over the Edge.

Andy didn't stop to look over. Instead he hurried down past the Witch's Face and round to the slope in front of the cave, where Bryn lay in a crumpled heap. Blood bubbled at the corner of his mouth.

"Yawlright?" Andy said.

"Of course I'm not all right."

"You're all right."

Bryn groaned. He'd been badly winded by the fall, and he'd scraped his hands and his knees. He'd also bitten his tongue, which accounted for the blood. In the end he'd fallen no more than about twelve feet, and had bounced down the sandstone slope beneath the cave mouth. He sat up, holding his head.

"Hey," said Andy. "Not *crying*, are you."

"You shit. Why didn't you hold on to me?"

"You must be joking. You were gone before I knew it."

"Useless. You're useless." Bryn was on his feet.

"It was your stupid idea. Tying the rope to that bush. Stupid. Where are you going?"

"I'm going home."

"Wait. I'll come with you."

"Sod off."

Bryn shrugged off his friend's advances and limped away. Within a minute he was out of sight. "Wasn't my fault," Andy shouted. He slumped onto the slope beneath the cave, knowing he should have gone home with Bryn. While Andy's mother was spending every anxious moment waiting at the pit-head for news of the rescue, Bryn's mother had told him to come for tea. Just as he'd done the previous night, munching on sardine sandwiches when Ike had turned up.

Ike had broken shifts to be part of the rescue team. He'd stood in the doorway, kicking his boots off, all-in. He drew a chair to the table where the boys sat, and without a word to anyone laid his head down by the plates and the butter, leaking the odor of coal and exhaustion. The boys munched on their sandwiches, looking at him. After a while Jean placed a steaming mug of tea on the table and Ike lifted his head. He blinked sleepily at the boys.

"Well," Jean had said.

"Not much," Ike said. He slurped his tea noisily. Then he turned to Andy. "Thing is, lovely boy, he's a in a corner with the other blokes and the ceiling is pressed down on 'em, see. And we can't get."

A flat, opened sardine can lay on the table, next to the butter. He picked up the can. "See how you get this bit of fish stuck in the corner and you can't get your knife into it? Well, that bit of sardine's your dad. In there, look? And the top of this tin is the roof come down on him. Now if we pull out what's holding up the roof, see?" He pressed down a huge, coal-ingrained thumb, crumpling the flimsy metal sheet of the sardine can. Tomato sauce and fish oil bubbled around the scythed edges of the can. "Well. There you are."

Ike carefully replaced the sardine can next to the butter. "Don't you worry, lovely boy. Ike will get him out." Then he put his head back on the table and closed his eyes.

Jean had made a silent gesture that they should leave the table.

Recalling all of this, Andy felt a sob break free deep in his chest and force its way into his throat. He wiped his eyes and tossed another pebble down the sandstone slope. There was nothing he could do. They wouldn't let him wait up at the pit-head and there was no one at home.

Then the ground shook. Very slightly. The mild tremor made him grab at the earth, and he thought he heard a muffled thump. Just for a second he'd felt the shock of earth dislodging, and he knew he hadn't imagined it because a couple of tiny pebbles broke loose from the cave and went bouncing down the slope. He wondered if it had anything to do with the pit rescue.

He decided to hurry home. He got up and picked his way down the slope, barely keeping his footing. He knew that if he went back up to the Edge he could cut across fields and get home faster. His hands trembled. He was clambering between boulders, over the exposed roots of trees, when he stumbled. That's when he saw the second cave.

———

Inside the cave, the dog-like growl subsided. Then it came again, only this time it sounded like a man trying to clear his throat of coal-dust. The two tiny lights continued to swing from side to side. Another distressed throaty growl made Andy want to get out.

But as the lights floated toward him out of the gloom he recognized the bowl of a miner's helmet. The upper light was a helmet lamp. A miner, face blackened with coal-dust, approached him from the dark end of the cave. Hanging from the miner's belt was a Davey lamp, with its tiny flame alive.

The miner stopped, and leaned against the wall. Breathing heavily, he tried to clear his throat again. He was struggling. "Hello Andy. Where's my lovely boy, then?"

Ike blinked at him in the darkness, his face caked with sweat and black dust. All Andy could see of his features were his teeth and the whites of his eyes. Ike had a rope looped over his shoulder; identical to the one he and Bryn had played with earlier. "Bryn went home."

Ike seemed confused. He closed his eyes and leaned his head against the cave wall. Ike was breathing asthmatically. He seemed to have trouble getting his words out. "Oh. Came to have a word with him, I did. See."

Now Andy could see and hear industrious activity taking place deeper in the cave behind Ike. He tried to look beyond the miner. "Where's my Dad?"

"Your old man's all right. I got him out." Ike unhooked the rope from his shoulder and flung it to the cave entrance. "Told you I would."

Andy tried to push past Ike, to get to his Dad. "Let me through."

Ike stopped him. Struggling to draw himself up to his full height, he placed a big blackened paw on Andy's shoulder. "No, no, no. That's not for you back there. Nothing to concern you back there. I just came to see my lovely boy. But you say he's not here, then?"

"No. He went home."

Ike slowly lifted a sooty hand to wipe back the sweat from his brow. Even in the darkness Andy could see it bubbling black and coursing dust into Ike's eyes. He was out of breath. "Tell him I came. Now you run along home, son. Go and see your old man." Andy nodded as the miner turned and retreated, with slow heavy steps, the lamp swinging at his side, deeper into the blackness of the cave. "And tell your old man," Ike called softly.

"Tell him what?"

"Just tell him."

Andy escaped from the cave into the bright summer light. There, lying on the floor was the rope Ike had flung at the cave entrance. Andy picked it up. It was black from the coal, and the gritty dust immediately transferred itself to the boy's hands. He was already blackened from the paw print Ike had left on his shirt, so he hooked the rope over his shoulder and hastened home.

When Andy persuaded the gatekeeper to let him through to the pithead, he found his mother there, and his father. Stan had already been brought up with the other rescued men. They were all in good shape, but there was no celebration and no rejoicing because one of the rescue team had been killed in the effort of getting the men out.

Andy didn't see Bryn for some weeks afterward. His mother had taken him, along with his sister, to stay with her family in Wales. When Bryn did return Andy tried to pass on the message Ike had given him.

"What?"

"He came looking for you. Up at the rocks. Your old man."

"What?"

"He left the rope. Do you want it? The rope?"

Bryn wrinkled his nose in contempt. "No."

"But you must."

"Shut it, will you? Shut it."

Eventually, Bryn and his mother and sister moved permanently to Wales.

Andy never said anything about it to his own father. One afternoon he said to Stan, "So Bryn's dad saved your life then, didn't he?"

"That's what they say, son. That's what they say."

That was the closest they ever got to discussing the matter.

More than once Andy went back up to Corley Rocks to try to find the second cave. He looked hard for it. He never did find it. Though he did have the rope. He hung it on a nail in the garden shed, where it remained untouched for many years, black with coal-dust.

# TIM PRATT

# Annabelle's Alphabet

*Tim Pratt is a recent graduate of the Clarion Writers Workshop, and an emerging writer in the fantasy field, with short fiction scheduled to appear in upcoming issues of* Realms of Fantasy *and other magazines. He lives in Oakland, California, where he is an editorial assistant and book reviewer for* Locus, *as well as the editor of the small press poetry journal* Star\*Line.

*"Annabelle's Alphabet" is a brief, bright, and chilling piece that falls into the interstitial realm between story and prose poem, between fantasy and horror. It is reprinted from* Lady Churchill's Rosebud Wristlet 9, *an edgy little magazine edited by Gavin J. Grant and Kelly Link in Brooklyn, New York.*

—T. W.

*A is for Annabelle*, who turned ten today. She is on a birthday picnic with her parents, wearing what her mother calls her Alice-in-Wonderland dress, and the warm air smells of summer. Annabelle hears chimes in the wind, but her parents, arguing on a blanket, don't seem to notice. Annabelle might follow the music, later, through the yellow and blue field of wildflowers, into the woods. The chimes seem to call her name, three syllables: "Ann-a-belle." She laughs and claps her hands. Her parents murmur.

*B is for Butterflies*. Annabelle sees one now, yellow wings fluttering through the long grass over the hills. She chases it until it lands, then leans over to watch it resting on a blossom. Annabelle thinks it might be looking at her, but she isn't sure if butterflies have eyes.

Her father collects butterflies, pins them down and seals them under glass. She's seen him in the garage, where he keeps his collection, looking at them. Sometimes, when he doesn't know she's there, he rips off their wings, and that frightens her.

Annabelle shivers and waves her hand at the butterfly. "Go on," she whispers. "Fly away." It does.

*C is for Cages*. Once at another girl's birthday party Annabelle saw parakeets, yellow and blue, singing in a cage. She looked at them for a minute and decided to set them free. She tugged at the cage door, but a broad soft woman in a flowered dress stopped her. "No, dear," she said. "Don't let them out."

"I want them to fly," Annabelle said, her eyes suddenly hot and full of tears.

"No," the woman repeated, leading Annabelle back to cake and ice cream. "Their wings are clipped. They couldn't fly anyway."

"Do their wings ever grow back?" Annabelle asked, but the woman didn't answer.

*D is for Dreams*, of course. Annabelle dreams of green places, and she often dreams of flying, soaring over woods and water, singing as she goes. One morning, when she was five years old, she said "I flied, Mommy, last night I flied!" Her mother's eyes went wide and she made a squeaking noise, as if choking on her eggs.

"In her dreams," her father said sharply, looking up from his paper. "She means in her dreams. Everyone has that dream."

Annabelle's mother nodded and looked down at her plate.

Annabelle remembers that, even five years later. She has a very good memory, but far enough back it turns to mist and shadows and pine trees.

*E is for Earthworms*. Annabelle's father is a weekend fisherman, and there's a patch of black dirt behind the house where he digs for worms. Once, young and dirty-kneed, Annabelle watched him dig.

"Catypillars," she said when he pulled up a long worm, wiggling, and dropped it in the bucket.

"Not caterpillars," her father said. "Worms."

"Worms?" Annabelle said, scrunching up her face.

"Yes. Caterpillars are fuzzy, and they turn into butterflies. Worms are slimy, and they don't turn into anything. But." He raised his finger in front of Annabelle's wide gold-flecked eyes. "If you cut a worm in half, both halves go on living." He took out his pocketknife, laid a worm on a shattered piece of cinderblock, and sliced it neatly in half. There was no blood, and both halves wriggled wildly. "See?"

Annabelle looked for a moment, solemn, and then said "Put it back together, Daddy."

He frowned, picking up the two wiggling half-worms and dropping them in his bucket. "I can't, Annabelle. There's no way to put them together again."

"Oh," she said in a quiet voice. But she wondered.

*F is for Fairies*. Annabelle's mother is religious, and there are pictures and statues of angels all over the house, with their white wings and pale, pretty faces. When Annabelle was younger, she called them fairies. "No," her mother said sternly. "They're angels."

"But they got wings," Annabelle said.

Her mother embraced her in freckled arms. "I know, darling, but they're angels. I promise. And you're my little angel."

"I don't got wings," Annabelle said scornfully.

*G is for Garden*. Annabelle's mother has one, with roses and posies and tulips and other blossoms, and in the summer they buzz with bees. Once Annabelle was sent to pull weeds, but instead she took up flowers and wove them into her red hair, and made chains for her wrists. Her mother squawked and shouted when she saw, but Annabelle was serene, sitting on the lawn with her skirts spread around her. She was a flower.

*H is for Hair*, sunset-red on Annabelle's head. Her father's hair is sandy blonde and short, her mother's is flat brown and cut in a bob. Annabelle's hair falls in curly waves, nearly to her knees. It has never been cut.

When Annabelle's mother brushes her daughter's hair, as she does every morning, it never snags or tangles. Her mother tells herself it must be the shampoo she uses, but it certainly doesn't do that for her own hair. She chooses not to think about it. Annabelle's mother chooses not to think about a great many things.

*I is for Innocence*, and today as every day Annabelle is drifting farther from that state. Her father watches her sometimes as she plays, frowning, and sometimes he grins like a jack o' lantern, but he's never laid a hand on her, even to punish. Sometimes he seems nervous when he hugs her, and he never touches her back for long. Annabelle's innocence is still complete, but today she turned ten and as she grows through double digits that innocence will disappear. For some things, some reconnections, time is growing short.

*J is for Joy*, and that's what Annabelle was for her parents, or was meant to be, or could have been. "She's a gift from God," Annabelle's mother said when they got their newfound daughter home, but she was hesitant, trembling. She put her hands across her belly. "We—I wanted a baby so much."

From the kitchen she heard a rasp and her young husband said "She is. You did. There's just something to take care of first." Another rasp, metal on stone, and Annabelle's mother closed her eyes. "Get it sharp," she said. "Very sharp, so it doesn't hurt much. I'll boil some water."

Somewhere in the house, far from the green places she'd known, baby Annabelle lay on her stomach and cried.

*K is for Knives*. Annabelle has dim memories, masquerading as nightmares. Even at ten years old, her father has to cut her food; she can't stand to touch a knife. She doesn't like meat anyway, because it reminds her too much of her own muscles, moving under the skin. She has muscles in her back that she can flex, but they don't move anything at all.

She stares at the wall as her father saws away at the food on her plate. She can't stand to look at the knife. Or at him, wielding it.

*L is for Lost things*. Annabelle loses things a lot, but her father almost never does; he's only once lost anything, that she can remember. Listening from the top of the stairs, Annabelle heard him shout at her mother. "They're gone! They were wrapped in cloth and locked in the chest and now they're gone! What did you do with them?"

*M is for Music and for Mystery*, and this is both. Those chimes: "Ann—a—belle," ringing over the hills from the trees. They aren't birdsong, and they aren't bells, and Annabelle's parents, just a few feet away on the blanket, don't hear a thing. It is Annabelle's birthday, and she got a pink bike with a basket and a new kite to fly. The kite is in the grass, forgotten, and her bike is back at home.

Annabelle wonders if she'll be getting another gift.

*N is for Normal,* and some things aren't, and those things need to be cut right out. Annabelle's father knows that, and so does her mother, though it hurts her more.

Annabelle doesn't think about it. Normal is what things are, and only things that aren't what they are can be wrong.

*O is for Outside,* and that's Annabelle's earliest memory, of being outside, tiny in the forest, looking up at stars and pine trees. Lost. Like the baby in the rhyme, that came tumbling down when the bough broke and the cradle fell. Then came voices, and two tall people, scooping her from the forest floor, exclaiming, turning her over. Annabelle doesn't know what the memory means, but her mother sings lullabies and that's one of the voices, and her father tells stories in measured tones, and that's the other.

Sometimes Annabelle sneaks out of the house and lies down in her back yard and looks up at the sky, through the pines.

*P is for Picnic,* and what a wonderful idea that was. "Annabelle would love a birthday picnic," her mother said, "and it's such a pretty day. But where should we go?"

"There's a field I know, by a nice stretch of woods," her father said thoughtfully.

They packed the car and took Annabelle, and her new kite, to the field. Neither of her parents seemed to remember this place, though they'd often taken walks in the woods here, when they were younger. A strange cloud covers their memories, filling their heads. They'd last seen this field on a summer night like this one, exactly ten years before. They'd come to watch the butterflies.

This was before he started dipping the butterflies, wings and all, in chloroform. Before he locked them under glass.

Before (but only just before, a matter of minutes, perhaps) they found Annabelle.

*Q is for Quiet,* and Annabelle is that. Even the soughing of the wind has stopped, and her parents are murmuring, sipping lemonade. She can still hear the chimes if she holds her breath, but they're fading. Even the beating of her heart is enough to make her miss notes: "Ann—belle—a—belle." Yes, the chimes are fading, and if she intends to follow them, she must do so soon.

*R is for Ripping,* when the knife went dull, when things weren't quite severed and man hands pulled and blood welled up, R is for the Rasp of the knife on the whetstone, but some things are too attached to be cut neatly, no matter how sharp the blade, and they tear.

*S is for Scars.* Annabelle has two on her back, shiny and wide, running vertically down her shoulder blades. Her mother told her that she stumbled and fell on a board with nails in it, and that's where the scars come from. Her father told her she was scratched by a dog when she was a baby, and that's where she got them. Sometimes her muscles spasm beneath the scars. And often in the morning, after a dream of flying, her shoulders ache.

*T is for Time*, and Annabelle feels it shortening and shortening as the shadows lengthen and the sun slides west.

*U is for Umbilicus*, the first connection between mother and daughter, which leaves its mark on the child's belly forever. But Annabelle has no navel, her stomach is as smooth as the skin of a peach, unmarked and untouched. Annabelle's mother thinks sometimes of umbilical cords being cut with scissors, of that fundamental severance, which she and Annabelle never had. Instead of scissors, there was a knife, and it wasn't a cord that was cut, not the connection between mother and daughter that was severed, but a different connection altogether.

And now Annabelle is in the field on her birthday, and it seems that while some connections must remain sundered forever, others can be rejoined.

*V is for Vigilant*, and Annabelle's mother is that, she always keeps an eye out for her daughter. She can't have more children, that thought is always on top of her mind, and she rarely lets Annabelle out of her sight. But now her attention wanders, she even forgets Annabelle for a moment, the thoughts fly out of her head and she's back in her girlhood, laughing with her new husband. Laughing, before Annabelle, and knives, and grisly silky mementos that mysteriously disappear, just as Annabelle is now disappearing over the hills toward the forest.

*W is for Worried*, and Annabelle knows her parents will be, but the chiming is louder now, a part of her is calling her and that's more important than anything, and she runs across the fields into the trees, the song in her head like her own voice, her own song, calling her home, and as she runs she can almost feel herself flying.

*X is for Xenophobia*, the hate of the stranger, and Annabelle doesn't know that word, and neither does her mother, and while her father does know it, he would never ascribe it to himself.

Yet his daughter is a stranger, and his wife also in many ways, and himself most of all, and he hates them all, really. When he sits in the basement tearing the wings from butterflies and remembering the night they found Annabelle, hate fills him. You can't turn something into something it's not, he thinks at the picnic, looking at the fat clouds float effortlessly by. Flying.

And then his wife says "Where's Annabelle?" and things happen very fast.

*Y is for Yell*, which Annabelle's mother does, she stands on the blanket and shouts her daughter's name. Her husband stands, frowning, hands clenched on a napkin that he rips in half, and they both shout for their daughter, who is gone, gone, and they look for the flutter of a blue dress, for curly red hair, but there's nothing, not even in the trees, there's only

*Z is for Zephyr*, the gentle west wind, coming up suddenly strong over the field from the trees, blowing into the shouting faces of Annabelle's mother and father, but only the wind answers them, blowing as though buffeted by a million wings and then, like apple blossoms blowing free, like silk streamers in the air, a hundred thousand sunset red and golden butterflies burst from the trees in the forest, flying.

And after it all Annabelle knows she is not a worm, or an angel, or a flower. She is something else, something of the green, something like a butterfly that lost its wings but, after a time, regained them.

# SUSANNA CLARKE

# Tom Brightwind, or, How the Fairy Bridge Was Built at Thoresby

*Susanna Clarke is a British writer published in America, where she has developed something of a cult following for her arch, delightful tales set in an England that never was. She draws inspiration from Jane Austen, Charles Dickens, Neil Gaiman, and G. K. Chesterton ("pretty much in that order," she says)—and fans of Sylvia Townsend Warner's elegant fantasies (Kingdoms of Elfin, etc.) will also find much to savor in the wry fairy story that follows.*

*Since Clarke began publishing fiction in 1996, her stories have appeared in the* Starlight *anthologies, various Datlow-Windling fairy-tale anthologies, and in four previous volumes of* The Year's Best Fantasy & Horror. *She lives in the medieval city of Cambridge, England, where she is at work on her first novel,* Jonathan Strange and Mr. Norrell. *"Tom Brightwind, or, How the Fairy Bridge Was Built at Thoresby" is reprinted from* Starlight 3, *edited by Patrick Nielsen Hayden (Tor Books).*

—T. W.

*The friendship between the eighteenth-century Jewish physician David Montefiore and the fairy Tom Brightwind is remarkably well documented. In addition to Montefiore's own journals and family papers, we have numerous descriptions of encounters with Montefiore and Brightwind by eighteenth- and early nineteenth-century letter writers, diarists and essayists. Montefiore and Brightwind seem, at one time or another, to have met most of the great men of the period. They discussed slavery with Boswell and Johnson, played dominoes with Diderot, got drunk with Richard Brinsley Sheridan and, upon one famous occasion, surprised Thomas Jefferson in his garden at Monticello.[1]*

---

[1] Poor David Montefiore was entirely mortified to be discovered trespassing upon another gentleman's property and could scarcely apologise enough. He told Thomas Jefferson that they had heard so much of the beauty of Monticello

*Yet, fascinating as these contemporary accounts are, our most vivid portrait of this unusual friendship comes from the plays, stories and songs which it inspired. In the early nineteenth-century "Tom and David" stories were immensely popular both here and in Faerie Minor, but in the latter half of the century they fell out of favour in Europe and the United States. It became fashionable among Europeans and Americans to picture fairies as small, defenceless creatures. Tom Brightwind— loud, egotistical, and six feet tall—was most emphatically not the sort of fairy that Arthur Conan Doyle and Charles Dodgson hoped to find at the bottom of their gardens.*

*The following story first appeared in* Blackwood's Magazine *(Edinburgh: September 1820) and was reprinted in* Silenus's Review *(Faerie Minor: April 1821). Considered as literature it is deeply unremarkable. It suffers from all the usual defects of second-rate early nineteenth-century writing. Nevertheless, if read with proper attention, it uncovers a great many facts about this enigmatic race and is particularly enlightening on the troublesome relationship between fairies and their children.*

*Professor James Sutherland*
*Research Institute of Sidhe Studies*
*University of Aberdeen*
*October 1999*

## How the Fairy Bridge was Built at Thoresby

For most of its length Shoe-lane in the City of London follows a gentle curve and it never occurs to most people to wonder why. Yet if they were only to look up (and they never do) they would see the ancient wall of an immense round tower and it would immediately become apparent how the lane curves to accommodate the tower.

This is only one of the towers that guard Tom Brightwind's house. From his earliest youth Tom was fond of traveling about and seeing everything and, in order that he might do this more conveniently, he had placed each tower in a different part of the world. From one tower you step out into Shoe-lane; another occupies the greater part of a small island in the middle of a Scottish loch; a third looks out upon the dismal beauty of an Algerian desert; a fourth stands upon DryingGreen-street in a city in *Faerie Minor*; and so on. With characteristic exuberance Tom named this curiously constructed house *Castel des Tours saunz Nowmbre*, which means the Castle of Innumerable Towers. David Montefiore had counted the innumerable towers in 1764. There were fourteen of them.

On a morning in June in 1780 David Montefiore knocked upon the door of the Shoe-lane tower. He inquired of the porter where Tom might be found and was told that the master was in his library.

As David walked along dim, echoing corridors and trotted up immense stone staircases, he bade a cheerful "Good Morning! Good Morning!" to everyone he passed. But the only answers that he got were doubtful nods and curious stares,

---

that they had been entirely unable to resist coming to see it for themselves. This polite explanation went a good way towards pacifying the President (who was inclined to be angry). Unfortunately Tom Brightwind immediately began to describe the many ways in which his own gardens were superior to Thomas Jefferson's. Thomas Jefferson promptly had them both turned off his property.

for no matter how often he visited the house, the inhabitants could never get used to him. His face was neither dazzlingly handsome nor twisted and repulsive. His figure was similarly undistinguished. His countenance expressed neither withering scorn, nor irresistible fascination, but only good humour and a disposition to think well of everyone. It was a mystery to the fairy inhabitants of *Castel des Tours saunz Nowmbre* why anyone should wish to wear such an expression upon his face.

Tom was not in the library. The room was occupied by nine fairy princesses. Nine exquisite heads turned in perfect unison to stare at David. Nine silk gowns bewildered the eye with their different colors. Nine different perfumes mingled in the air and made thinking difficult.

They were a few of Tom Brightwind's grand-daughters. Princess Caritas, Princess Bellona, Princess Alba Perfecta, Princess Lachrima and Princess Flammifera were one set of sisters; Princess Honey-of-the-Wild-Bees, Princess Lament-from-across-the-Water, Princess Kiss-upon-a-True-Love's-Grave and Princess Bird-in-the-Hand were another.

"O David ben Israel!" said Princess Caritas, "How completely charming!" and offered him her hand.

"You are busy, Highnesses," he said, "I fear I disturb you."

"Not really," said Princess Caritas, "We are writing letters to our cousins. Duty letters, that is all. Be seated, O David ben Israel."

"You did not say that they are our female cousins," said Princess Honey-of-the-Wild-Bees. "You did not make that plain. I should not like the Jewish doctor to run away with the idea that we write to any other sort of cousin."

"To our female cousins *naturally*," said Princess Caritas.

"We do not know our male cousins," Princess Flammifera informed David.

"We do not even know their names," added Princess Lament-from-across-the-Water.

"And even if we did, we would not *dream* of writing to them," remarked Princess Alba Perfecta.

"Though we are told they are very handsome," said Princess Lachrima.

"Handsome?" said Princess Caritas. "Whatever gave you that idea? I am sure I do not know whether they are handsome or not. I do not care to know. I never think of such things."

"Oh now, *really* my sweet!" replied Princess Lachrima with a brittle laugh. "Tell the truth, do! You scarcely ever think of anything else."

Princess Caritas gave her sister a vicious look.

"And to which of your cousins are you writing?" asked David quickly.

"To Igraine . . ."

"Nimue . . ."

"Elaine . . ."

"And Morgana."

"Ugly girls," remarked Princess Caritas.

"Not their fault," said Princess Honey-of-the-Wild-Bees generously.

"And will they be away long?" asked David.

"Oh!" said Princess Flammifera.

"Oh!" said Princess Caritas.

"Oh!" said Princess Honey-of-the-Wild-Bees.

"They have been sent away," said Princess Bellona.

"Forever . . ." said Princess Lament-from-across-the-Water.

". . . and a day," added Princess Flammifera.

"We thought everybody knew that," said Princess Alba Perfecta.

"Grandfather sent them away," said Princess Kiss-upon-a-True-Love's-Grave.

"They offended Grandfather," said Princess Bird-in-the-Hand.

"Grandfather is most displeased with them," said Princess Lament-from-across-the-Water.

"They have been sent to live in a house," said Princess Caritas.

"Not a nice house," warned Princess Alba Perfecta.

"A nasty house!" warned Princess Lachrima, with sparkling eyes. "With nothing but male servants! Nasty, dirty male servants with thick ugly fingers and hair on the knuckles! Male servants who will doubtless show them no respect!" Lachrima put on a knowing, amused look. "Though perhaps they may show them something else!" she said.

Caritas laughed. David blushed.

"The house is in a wood," continued Princess Bird-in-the-Hand.

"Not a nice wood," added Princess Bellona.

"A nasty wood!" said Princess Lachrima excitedly. "A thoroughly damp and dark wood, full of spiders and creepy, slimy, foul-smelling . . ."

"And why did your grandfather send them to this wood?" asked David quickly.

"Oh! Igraine got married," said Princess Caritas.

"Secretly," said Princess Lament-from-across-the-Water.

"We thought everyone knew that," said Princess Kiss-upon-a-True-Love's-Grave.

"She married a Christian man," explained Princess Caritas.

"Her harpsichord master!" said Princess Bellona, beginning to giggle.

"He played such beautiful concertos," said Princess Alba Perfecta.

"He had such beautiful . . ." began Princess Lachrima.

"Rima! Will you desist?" said Princess Caritas.

"Cousins," said Princess Honey-of-the-Wild-Bees sweetly, "when you are banished to a dark, damp wood, we will write to *you*."

"I did wonder, you know," said Princess Kiss-upon-a-True-Love's-Grave, "when she began to take harpsichord lessons every day. For she was never so fond of music till Mr. Cartwright came. Then they took to shutting the door—which, I may say, I was very sorry for, the harpsichord being a particular favorite of mine. And so, you know, I used to creep to the door to listen, but a quarter of an hour might go by and I would not hear a single note—except perhaps the odd discordant plink as if one of them had accidentally leaned upon the instrument. Once I thought I would go in to see what they were doing, but when I tried the handle of the door I discovered that they had turned the key in the lock . . ."

"Be quiet, Kiss!" said Princess Lament-from-across-the-Water.

"She's only called Kiss," explained Princess Lachrima to David helpfully, "she's never *actually* kissed anyone."

"But I do not quite understand," said David. "If Princess Igraine married without her grandfather's permission, then that of course is very bad. Upon important matters children ought always to consult their parents, or those who stand in the place of parents. Likewise parents—or as we have in this case, grandparents—ought to consider not only the financial aspects of a marriage and the rank of the prospective bride of bridegroom but also the child's character and likely chances of happiness with that person. The inclinations of the child's heart ought to be of paramount importance. . . ."

As David continued meditating out loud upon the various reciprocal duties and responsibilities of parents and children, Princess Honey-of-the-Wild-Bees stared at him with an expression of mingled disbelief and distaste, Princess Caritas yawned loudly, and Princess Lachrima mimed someone fainting with boredom.

". . . But even if Princess Igraine offended her grandfather in this way," said David, "Why were her sisters punished with her?"

"Because they did not stop her, of course," said Princess Alba Perfecta.

"Because they did not tell Grandfather what she was about," said Princess Lament-from-across-the-Water.

"We thought everybody knew that," said Princess Bird-in-the-Hand.

"What happened to the harpsichord master?" asked David.

Princess Lachrima opened her large violet blue eyes and leaned forward with great eagerness, but at that moment a voice was heard in the corridor.

". . . but when I had shot the third crow and plucked and skinned it, I discovered that it had a heart of solid diamond—just as the old woman had said— so, as you see, the afternoon was not entirely wasted."

Tom Brightwind had a bad habit of beginning to talk long before he entered a room, so that the people whom he addressed only ever heard the end of what he wished to say to them.

"What?" said David.

"Not entirely wasted," repeated Tom.

Tom was about six feet tall and unusually handsome even for a fairy prince (for it must be said that in fairy society the upper ranks generally make it their business to be better-looking than the commoners). His complexion gleamed with such extraordinary good health that it seemed to possess a faint opalescence, slightly unnerving to behold. He had recently put off his wig and taken to wearing his natural hair, which was long and straight and a vivid chestnut-brown color. His eyes were blue, and he looked (as he had looked for the last three or four thousand years) about thirty years of age. He glanced about him, raised one perfect fairy eyebrow, and muttered sourly, "Oak and Ash, but there are a lot of women in this room!"

There was a rustle of nine silk gowns, the slight click of door, a final exhalation of perfume, and suddenly there were no princesses at all.

"So where have you been?" said Tom, throwing himself into a chair and taking up a newspaper. "I expected you yesterday. Did you not get my message?"

"I could not come. I had to attend to my patients. Indeed I cannot stay long this morning. I am on my way to see Mr. Monkton."

Mr. Monkton was a rich old gentleman who lived in Lincoln. He wrote David letters describing a curious pain in his left side and David wrote back with advice upon medicines and treatments.

"Not that he places any faith in what I tell him," said David cheerfully. "He also corresponds with a physician in Edinburgh and a sort of sorcerer in Dublin. Then there is the apothecary in Lincoln who visits him. We all contradict one another but it does not matter because he trusts none of us. Now he has written to say he is dying and at this crisis we are summoned to attend him in person. The Scottish physician, the Irish wizard, the English apothecary and me! I am quite looking forward to it! Nothing is so pleasant or instructive as the society and conversation of one's peers. Do not you agree?"

Tom shrugged.[2] "Is the old man really ill?" he asked.

"I do not know. I never saw him."

Tom glanced at his newspaper again, put it down again in irritation, yawned and said, "I believe I shall come with you." He waited for David to express his rapture at this news.

What in the world, wondered David, did Tom think there would be at Lincoln to amuse him? Long medical conversations in which he could take no part, a querulous sick old gentleman, and the putrid airs and hush of a sickroom! David was on the point of saying something to this effect when it occurred to him that, actually, it would be no bad thing for Tom to come to Lincoln. David was the son of a famous Venetian rabbi. From his youth he had been accustomed to debate good principles and right conduct with all sorts of grave Jewish persons. These conversations had formed his own character and he naturally supposed that a small measure of the same could not help but improve other people's. In short he had come to believe that if only one talks long enough and expresses oneself properly, it is perfectly possible to argue people into being good and happy. With this aim he generally took it upon himself to quarrel with Tom Brightwind several times a week—all without noticeable effect. But just now he had a great deal to say about the unhappy fate of the harpsichord master's bride and her sisters, and a long ride north was the perfect opportunity to say it.

So the horses were fetched from the stables, and David and Tom got on them. They had not gone far before David began.

"Who?" asked Tom, not much interested.

"The Princesses Igraine, Nimue, Elaine and Morgana."

"Oh! Yes, I sent them to live in . . . What do you call that wood on the far side of Pity-Me? What is the name that you put upon it? No, it escapes me. Anyway, there."

"But eternal banishment!" cried David in horror. "Those poor girls! How can you bear the thought of them in such torment?"

"I bear it very well, as you see," said Tom. "But thank you for your concern. To own the truth, I am thankful for any measure that reduces the number of women in my house. David, I tell you, those girls talk *constantly*. Obviously I talk a great deal too. But then I am always doing things. I have my library. I am the patron of three theaters, two orchestras and a university. I have numerous interests in *Faerie Major*. I have seneschals, magistrates, and proctors in all the various lands of which I am sovereign, who are obliged to consult my pleasure constantly. I am involved in . . ." Tom counted quickly on his long, white fingers. ". . . thirteen wars which are being prosecuted in *Faerie Major*. In one particularly

---

[2]Fairy princes do not often trouble to seek out other fairy princes, and on the rare occasions that they do meet, it is surprising with what regularity one of them will die—suddenly, mysteriously, and in great pain.

complicated case I have allied myself with the Millstone Beast and with his enemy, La Dame d'Aprigny, and sent armies to both of them. . . ." Tom paused here and frowned at his horse's ears. "Which means, I suppose, that I am at war with myself. Now why did I do that?" He seemed to consider a moment or two, but making no progress he shook his head and continued. "What was I saying? Oh, yes! So *naturally* I have a great deal to say. But those girls do nothing. Absolutely nothing! A little embroidery, a few music lessons. Oh! and they read English novels! David! Did you ever look into an English novel? Well, do not trouble yourself. It is nothing but a lot of nonsense about girls with fanciful names getting married."

"But this is precisely the point I wish to make," said David. "Your children lack proper occupation. Of course they will find some mischief to get up to. What do you expect?"

David often lectured Tom upon the responsibilities of parenthood, which annoyed Tom, who considered himself to be a quite exemplary fairy parent. He provided generously for his children and grandchildren and only in exceptional circumstances had any of them put to death.[3] "Young women must stay at home quietly until they marry," said Tom. "What else would you have?"

"I admit that I cannot imagine any other system for regulating the behavior of young Christian and Jewish women. But in their case the interval between the schoolroom and marriage is only a few years. For fairy women it may stretch into centuries. Have you no other way of managing your female relations? Must you imitate Christians in everything you do? Why! You even dress as if you were a Christian!"

"As do you," countered Tom.

"And you have trimmed your long fairy eyebrows."

"At least I still have eyebrows," retorted Tom, "Where is your beard, Jew? Did Moses wear a little grey wig?" He gave David's wig of neat curls a contemptuous flip. "I do not think so."

"You do not even speak your own language!" said David, straightening his wig.

"Neither do you," said Tom.

David immediately replied that Jews, unlike fairies, honored their past, spoke Hebrew in their prayers and upon all sorts of ritual occasions. "But to return to the problem of your daughters and grand-daughters, what did you do when you were in the *brugh*?"

This was tactless. The word "*brugh*" was deeply offensive to Tom. No one who customarily dresses in spotless white linen and a midnight-blue coat, whose nails are exquisitely manicured, whose hair gleams like polished mahogany—in

---

[3]Fairies exceed even Christians and Jews in their enthusiasm for babies and young children, and think nothing of adding to their brood by stealing a pretty Christian child or two.

Yet in this, as in so many things, fairies rarely give much thought to the consequences of their actions. They procreate or steal other people's children, and twenty years later they are amazed to discover that they have a house full of grown men and women. The problem is how to provide for them all. Unlike the sons and daughters of Christians and Jews, fairy children do not live in confident expectation of one day inheriting all their parents' wealth, lands and power, since their parents are very unlikely ever to die.

It is a puzzle that few fairies manage to solve satisfactorily and it is unsurprising that many of their children eventually rebel. For over seven centuries Tom Brightwind had been involved in a vicious and bloody war against his own firstborn son, a person called Prince Rialobran.

short, no one of such refined tastes and delicate habits—likes to be reminded that he spent the first two or three thousand years of his existence in a damp dark hole, wearing (when he took the trouble to wear anything at all) a kilt of coarse, undyed wool and a moldering rabbitskin cloak.[4]

"In the *brugh*," said Tom, lingering on the word with ironic emphasis to shew that it was a subject polite people did not mention, "the problem did not arise. Children were born and grew up in complete ignorance of their paternity. I have not the least idea who my father was. I never felt any curiosity on the matter."

By two o'clock Tom and David had reached Nottinghamshire,[5] a county which is famous for the greenwood which once spread over it. Of course at this late date the forest was no longer a hundredth part of what it once had been, but there were still a number of very ancient trees and Tom was determined to pay his respects to those he considered his particular friends and to shew his disdain of those who had not behaved well towards him.[6] So long was Tom in greeting his friends, that David began to be concerned about Mr. Monkton.

"But you said he was not really ill," said Tom.

---

[4]The *brugh* was for countless centuries the common habitation of the fairy race. It is the original of all the fairy palaces one reads of in folktales. Indeed the tendency of Christian writers to glamorize the *brugh* seems to have increased with the centuries. It has been described as a "fairy palace of gold and crystal, in the heart of the hill" (Lady Wilde, *Ancient Legends, Mystic Charms and Superstitions of Ireland*, Ward & Downey, London, 1887). Another chronicler of fairy history wrote of "a steep-sided grassy hill, round as a pudding-basin . . . A small lake on its summit had a crystal floor, which served as a skylight." (Sylvia Townsend Warner, *The Kingdoms of Elfin*, Chatto & Windus, London, 1977).

The truth is that the *brugh* was a hole or series of interconnecting holes that was dug into a barrow, very like a rabbit's warren or badger's set. To paraphrase a writer of fanciful stories for children, this was not a comfortable hole, it was not even a dry, bare sandy hole; it was a nasty, dirty, wet hole.

Fairies, who are nothing if not resilient, were able to bear with equanimity the damp, the dark and the airlessness, but stolen Christian children brought to the *brugh* died, as often as not, of suffocation.

[5]In the late eighteenth century a journey from London to Nottinghamshire might be expected to take two or three days. Tom and David seem to have arrived after a couple of hours: this presumably is one of the advantages of choosing as your traveling companion a powerful fairy prince.

[6]Fairies born in the last eight centuries or so—sophisticated, literate, and consorting all their lives with Christians— have no more difficulty than Christians themselves in distinguishing between the animate and the inanimate. But to members of older generations (such as Tom) the distinction is quite unintelligible.

Several magical theorists and commentators have noted that fairies who retain this old belief in the souls of stones, doors, trees, fire, clouds, etc., are more adept at magic than the younger generation and their magic is generally much stronger.

The following incident clearly shows how, given the right circumstances, fairies come to regard perfectly ordinary objects with a strange awe. In 1697 an attempt was made to kill the Old Man of the White Tower, one of the lesser princes of Faerie. The would-be assassin was a fairy called Broc (he had stripes of black and white fur upon his face). Broc had been greatly impressed by what he had heard of a wonderful new weapon which Christians had invented to kill each other. Consequently he forsook all magical means of killing the Old Man of the White Tower (which had some chance of success) and purchased instead a pistol and some shot (which had none). Poor Broc made his attempt, was captured, and the Old Man of the White Tower locked him up in a windowless stone room deep in the earth. In the next room the Old Man imprisoned the pistol, and in a third room the shot. Broc died sometime around the beginning of the twentieth century (after three centuries without a bite to eat, a drop to drink, or a sight of the sun, even fairies grow weaker). The pistol and the shot, on the other hand, are still there, still considered by the Old Man as equally culpable, still deserving punishment for their wickedness. Several other fairies who wished to kill the Old Man of the White Tower have begun by devising elaborate plans to steal the pistol and the shot, which have attained a strange significance in the minds of the Old Man's enemies. It is well known to fairies that metal, stone and wood have stubborn natures; the gun and shot were set upon killing the Old Man in 1697 and it is quite inconceivable to the fairy mind that they could have wavered in the intervening centuries. To the Old Man's enemies it is quite clear that one day the gun and the shot will achieve their purpose.

"That was not what I said at all! But whether he is or not, I have a duty to reach him as soon as I can."

"Very well! Very well! How cross you are!" said Tom. "Where are you going? The road is just over there."

"But we came from the other direction."

"No, we did not. Well, perhaps. I do not know. But both roads join up later on so it cannot matter in the least which we chuse."

Tom's road soon dwindled into a narrow and poorly marked track which led to the banks of a broad river. A small, desolate-looking town stood upon the opposite bank. The road reappeared on the other side of the town and it was odd to see how it grew broader and more confident as it left the town and traveled on to happier places.

"How peculiar!" said Tom, "Where is the bridge?"

"There does not seem to be one."

"Then how are we to get across?"

"There is a ferry," said David.

A long iron chain stretched between a stone pillar on this side of the river and another pillar on the opposite bank. Also on the other side of the river was an ancient flat-bottomed boat attached to the chain by two iron brackets. An ancient ferryman appeared and hauled the boat across the river by means of the chain. Then Tom and David led the horses onto the boat and the ancient ferryman hauled them back over.

David asked the ferryman what the town was called.

"Thoresby, sir," said the man.

Thoresby proved to be nothing more than a few streets of shabby houses with soiled, dusty windows and broken roofs. An ancient cart was abandoned in the middle of what appeared to be the principal street. There was a market cross and a marketplace of sorts—but weeds and thorns grew there in abundance, suggesting there had been no actual market for several years. There was only one gentleman's residence to be seen: a tall old-fashioned house built of grey limestone, with a great many tall gables and chimneys. This at least was a respectable-looking place though in a decidedly provincial style.

Thoresby's only inn was called the Wheel of Fortune. The sign showed a number of people bound to a great wheel which was being turned by Fortune, represented here by a bright pink lady wearing nothing but a blindfold. In keeping with the town's dejected air the artist had chosen to omit the customary figures representing good fortune and had instead shown all the people bound to Fortune's wheel in the process of being crushed to pieces or being hurled into the air to their deaths.

With such sights as these to encourage them, the Jew and the fairy rode through Thoresby at a smart trot. The open road was just in sight when David heard a cry of "Gentlemen! Gentlemen!" and the sound of rapid footsteps. So he halted his horse and turned to see what was the matter.

A man came running up.

He was a most odd-looking creature. His eyes were small and practically colorless. His nose was the shape of a small bread roll, and his ears—which were round and pink—might have been attractive on a baby, but in no way suited him. But what was most peculiar was the way in which eyes and nose huddled together at the top of his face, having presumably quarreled with his mouth, which had set up a separate establishment for itself halfway down his chin. He was very shabbily dressed and his bare head had a thin covering of pale stubble upon it.

"You have not paid the toll, sirs!" he cried.

"What toll?" asked David.

"Why! The ferry toll! The toll for crossing the river."

"Yes. Yes, we have," said David. "We paid the man who carried us across the river."

The odd-looking man smiled. "No, sir!" he said. "You paid the fee, the ferryman's penny! But the toll is quite another thing. The toll is levied upon everyone who crosses the river. It is owed to Mr. Winstanley and I collect it. A man and a horse is sixpence. Two men and two horses is twelvepence."

"Do you mean to say," said David in astonishment, "that a person must pay *twice* to come to this miserable place?"

"There is no toll, David," said Tom airily. "This scoundrel merely wishes us to give him twelvepence."

The odd-looking man continued to smile, although the expression of his eyes had rather a malicious sparkle to it. "The gentleman may insult me if he wishes," he said, "Insults are free. But I beg leave to inform the gentleman that I am very far from being a scoundrel. I am a lawyer. Oh, yes! An attorney consulted by people as far afield as Southwell. But my chief occupation is as Mr. Winstanley's land agent and man of business. My name, sir, is Pewley Witts!"

"A lawyer?" said David. "Oh, I do beg your pardon!"

"David!" cried Tom. "When did you ever see a lawyer that looked like that? Look at him! His rascally shoes are broken all to bits. There are great holes in his vagabond's coat and he has no wig! Of *course* he is a scoundrel!" He leaned down from his tall horse. "We are leaving now, scoundrel. Good-bye!"

"These are my sloppy clothes," said Pewley Witts sullenly. "My wig and good coat are at home. I had no time to put them on when Peter Dawkins came and told me that two gentlemen had crossed by the ferry and were leaving Thoresby without paying the toll—which, by the bye, is still twelvepence, gentlemen, and I would be much obliged if you would pay it."

A devout Jew must discharge his debts promptly—however inadvertently those debts might have been incurred; a gentleman ought never to procrastinate in such matters; and, as David considered himself to be both those things, he was most anxious to pay Pewley Witts twelvepence. A fairy, on the other hand, sees things differently. Tom was determined not to pay. Tom would have endured years of torment rather than pay.

Pewley Witts watched them argue the point back and forth. Finally he shrugged. "Under the circumstances, gentlemen," he said, "I think you had better talk to Mr. Winstanley."

He led them to the tall stone house they had noticed before. A high stone wall surrounded the house and there was a little stone yard which was quite bare except for two small stone lions. They were crudely made things, with round, surprised eyes, snarls full of triangular teeth, and fanciful manes that more resembled foliage than fur.

A pretty maidservant answered the door. She glanced briefly at Pewley Witts and David Montefiore, but finding nothing to interest her there, her gaze traveled on to Tom Brightwind, who was staring down at the lions.

"Good morning, Lucy!" said Pewley Witts. "Is your master within?"

"Where else would he be?" said Lucy, still gazing at Tom.

"These two gentlemen object to paying the toll, and so I have brought them here to argue it out with Mr. Winstanley. Go and tell him that we are here. And be quick about it, Lucy. I am wanted at home. We are killing the spotted pig today."

Despite Pewley Witt's urging, it seemed that Lucy did not immediately deliver the message to her master. A few moments later from an open window above his head, David heard a sort of interrogatory murmur followed by Lucy's voice exclaiming, "A beautiful gentleman! Oh, madam! The most beautiful gentleman you ever saw in your life!"

"What is happening?" asked Tom, drifting back from his examination of the lions.

"The maid is describing me to her mistress," said David.

"Oh," said Tom, and drifted away again.

A face appeared briefly at the window.

"Oh, yes," came Lucy's voice again, "and Mr. Witts and another person are with him."

Lucy reappeared and conducted Tom, David and Pewley Witts through a succession of remarkably empty chambers and passageways to an apartment at the back of the house. It was odd to see how, in contrast to the other rooms, this was comfortably furnished with red carpets, gilded mirrors and blue-and-white china. Yet it was still a little somber. The walls were paneled in dark wood and the curtains were half drawn across two tall windows to create a sort of twilight. The walls were hung with engravings but, far from enlivening the gloom, they only added to it. They were portraits of worthy and historical personages, all of whom appeared to have been in an extremely bad temper when they sat for their likenesses. Here were more scowls, frowns and stares than David had seen in a long time.

At the far end of the room a gentleman lay upon a sofa piled with cushions. He wore an elegant green-and-white chintz morning gown and loose Turkish slippers upon his feet. A lady, presumably Mrs. Winstanley, sat in a chair at his side.

As there was no one else to do it for them, Tom and David were obliged to introduce themselves (an awkward ceremony at the best of times). David told Mr. and Mrs. Winstanley his profession, and Tom was able to convey merely by his way of saying his name that he was someone of quite unimaginable importance.

Mr. Winstanley received them with great politeness, welcoming them to his house (which he called Mickelgrave House). They found it a little odd, however, that he did not trouble to rise from the sofa—or indeed move any of his limbs in the slightest degree. His voice was soft and his smile was gentle. He had pleasant, regular features and an unusually white complexion—the complexion of someone who hardly ever ventured out of doors.

Mrs. Winstanley (who rose and curtsied) wore a plain gown of blackberry-colored silk with the merest edging of white lace. She had dark hair and dark eyes. Had she only smiled a little, she would have been extremely lovely.

Pewley Witts explained that Mr. Brightwind refused to pay the toll.

"Oh no, Witts! No!" cried Mr. Winstanley upon the instant, "These gentlemen need pay no toll. The sublimity of their conversation will be payment enough, I am certain." He turned to Tom and David. "Gentlemen! For reasons which I will explain to you in a moment, I rarely go abroad. Truth to own I do not often leave this room and consequently my daily society is confined to men of inferior rank and education, such as Witts. I can scarcely express my pleasure at seeing you here!" He regarded David's dark, un-English face with mild interest. "Montefiore is an Italian name, I think. You are Italian, sir?"

"My father was born in Venice," said David, "but that city, sadly, has hardened its heart towards the Jews. My family is now settled in London. We hope in time to be English."

Mr. Winstanley nodded gently. There was, after all, nothing in the world so natural as people wishing to be English. "You are welcome too, sir. I am glad to say that I am completely indifferent to a man's having a different religion from mine."

Mrs. Winstanley leaned over and murmured something in her husband's ear.

"No," answered Mr. Winstanley softly, "I will not get dressed today."

"You are ill, sir?" asked David. "If there is anything I can—"

Mr. Winstanley laughed as if this were highly amusing. "No, no, physician! You cannot earn your fee quite as easily as that. You cannot persuade me that I feel unwell when I do not." He turned to Tom Brightwind with a smile. "The foreigner can never quite comprehend that there are more important considerations than money. He can never quite understand that there is a time to leave off doing business."

"I did not mean . . ." began David, coloring.

Mr. Winstanley smiled and waved his hand to indicate that whatever David might have meant was of very little significance. "I am not offended in the least. I make allowances for you. Dottore." He leant back delicately against the cushions. "Gentlemen, I am a man who might achieve remarkable things. I have within me a capacity for greatness. But I am prevented from accomplishing even the least of my ambitions by the peculiar circumstances of this town. You have seen Thoresby. I daresay you are shocked at its wretched appearance and the astonishing idleness of the townspeople. Why, look at Witts! In other towns lawyers are respectable people. A lawyer in another town would not slaughter his own pig. A lawyer in another town would wear a velvet coat. His shirt would not be stained with gray."

"Precisely," said Tom, looking with great disdain at the lawyer.

David was quite disgusted that anyone should speak to his inferiors in so rude a manner and he looked at Witts to see how he bore with this treatment. But Witts only smiled and David could almost have fancied he was simple, had it not been for the malice in his eyes.

"And yet," continued Mr. Winstanley, "I would not have you think that Witts is solely to blame for his slovenly appearance and lack of industry. Witts's life is blighted by Thoresby's difficulties, which are caused by what? Why, the lack of a bridge!"

Pewley Witts nudged Mr. Winstanley with his elbow. "Tell them about Julius Caesar."

"Oh!" said Mrs. Winstanley, looking up in alarm. "I do not think these gentlemen wish to be troubled with Julius Caesar. I dare say they heard enough of him in their schoolrooms."

"On the contrary, madam!" said Tom, in accents of mild reproach. "I for one can never grow tired of hearing of that illustrious and courageous gentleman. Pray go on, sir."[7] Tom sat back, his head supported on his hand and his eyes fixed upon Mrs. Winstanley's elegant form and sweet face.

"You should know, gentlemen," began Mr. Winstanley, "that I have looked into the history of this town and it seems our difficulties began with the Romans—whom you may see represented in this room by Julius Caesar. His portrait hangs between the door and that pot of hyacinths. The Romans, as I daresay you know, built roads in England that were remarkable for both their excellence and their straightness. A Roman road passes very close to Thoresby. Indeed, had the Romans followed their own self-imposed principle of straightness, they ought by rights to have crossed the river here, at Thoresby. But they allowed themselves to be deterred. There was some problem—a certain marshiness of the land, I believe—and so they deviated from their course and crossed the river at Newark. At Newark they built a town with temples and markets and I do not know what else, while Thoresby remained a desolate marsh. This was the first of many occasions upon which Thoresby suffered for other people's moral failings."

"Lady Anne Lutterell," prompted Pewley Witts.

"Oh, Mr. Winstanley!" said his wife, with a little forced laugh, "I must protest. Indeed I must. Mr. Brightwind and Mr. Montefiore do not wish to concern themselves with Lady Anne. I feel certain that they do not care for history at all."

"Oh! quite, madam!" said Tom. "What passes for history these days is extraordinary. Kings who are remembered more for their long dull speeches than for anything they did upon the battlefield, governments full of fat old men with grey hair, all looking the same—who cares about such stuff? But if you are speaking of real history, true history—by which of course I mean the spirited description of heroic personages of ancient times—Why, there is nothing which delights me more!"

"Lady Anne Lutterell," said Mr. Winstanley, taking no notice of either of them, "was a rich widow who lived at Ossington." (Mrs. Winstanley looked down at her folded hands in her lap.) "There is a picture of her ladyship between that little writing table and the longcase clock. It was widely known that she intended to leave a large sum of money as an act of piety to build a bridge in this exact spot. The bridge was promised and in anticipation of this promised the town of Thoresby was built. But at the last moment she changed her mind and built a

---

[7]Tom Brightwind was not the only member of his race who was passionately devoted to the memory of Julius Caesar. Many fairies claim descent from him and there was a medieval Christian legend that Oberon (the wholly fictitious king of the fairies) was Julius Caesar's son.

chantry instead. I dare say, Mr. Montefiore, you will not know what that is. A chantry is a sort of chapel where priests say mass for the dead. Such—though I am ashamed to admit it—were the superstitious practices of our ancestors."

"Queen Elizabeth," said Pewley Witts, winking at David and Tom. It was becoming clear how he revenged himself for all the slights and insults which he received from Mr. Winstanley. It seemed unlikely that Mr. Winstanley would have made quite so many foolish speeches without Witts to encourage him.

"Queen Elizabeth indeed, Witts," said Mr. Winstanley pleasantly.

"Queen Elizabeth!" cried Mrs. Winstanley in alarm. "Oh! But she was a most disagreeable person! If we must talk of queens, there are several more respectable examples. What do you say to Matilda? Or Anne?"

Tom leaned as closely as he conveniently could to Mrs. Winstanley. His face shewed that he had a great many opinions upon Queen Matilda and Queen Anne which he wished to communicate to her immediately, but before he could begin, Mr. Winstanley said, "You will find Elizabeth, Mr. Brightwind, between the window and the looking-glass. In Elizabeth's time the people of Thoresby earned their living by making playing cards. But the Queen granted a Royal Patent for a monopoly for the manufacture of playing-cards to a young man. He had written a poem praising her beauty. She was, I believe, about sixty-five years old at the time. As a consequence no one in England was allowed to make playing-cards except for this young man. He became rich and the people of Thoresby became destitute."

Mr. Winstanley continued his little history of people who might have built a bridge at Thoresby and had not done so, or who had injured the town in some other way. His wife tried to hide his foolishness as much as was in her power by protesting vigorously at the introduction of each fresh character, but he paid her not the slightest attention.

His special contempt was reserved for Oliver Cromwell, whose picture hung in pride of place over the mantelpiece. Oliver Cromwell had contemplated fighting an important battle at Thoresby but had eventually decided against it, thereby denying Thoresby the distinction of being blown up and laid to waste by two opposing armies.

"But surely," said David at last, "your best course is to build the bridge yourself."

"Ah!" Mr. Winstanley smiled. "You would think so, wouldn't you? And I have spoken to two gentlemen who are in the habit of lending money to other gentlemen for their enterprises. A Mr. Blackwell of London and a Mr. Crumfield of Bath. Mr. Witts and I described to both men the benefits that would accrue to them were they to build my bridge, the quite extraordinary amounts of money they would make. But both ended by declining to lend me the money." Mr. Winstanley glanced up at an empty space on the wall as if he would have liked to see it graced by portraits of Mr. Blackwell and Mr. Crumfield and so complete his museum of failure.

"But it was a very great sum," said Mrs. Winstanley. "You do not tell Mr. Brightwind and Mr. Montefiore what a very great sum it was. I do not believe I ever heard such a large figure named in my life before."

"Bridges are expensive," agreed David.

Then Mrs. Winstanley, who seemed to think that the subject of bridges had been exhausted among them, asked David several questions about himself. Where had he studied medicine? How many patients had he? Did he attend ladies as well as gentlemen? From speaking of professional matters David was soon led to talk of his domestic happiness—of his wife and four little children.

"And are you married, sir?" Mrs. Winstanley asked Tom.

"Oh, no, madam!" said Tom.

"Yes," David reminded him. "You are, you know."

Tom made a motion with his hand to suggest that it was a situation susceptible to different interpretations.

The truth was that he had a Christian wife. At fifteen she had a wicked little face, almond-shaped eyes and a most capricious nature. Tom had constantly compared her to a kitten. In her twenties she had been a swan; in her thirties a vixen; and then in rapid succession a bitch, a viper, a cockatrice and, finally, a pig. What animals he might have compared her to now no one knew. She was well past ninety and for forty years or more she had been confined to a set of apartments in a distant part of the *Castel des Tours saunz Nowmbre* under strict instructions not to show herself, while her husband waited impatiently for someone to come and tell him she was dead.

By now Tom and David had given the half hour to the Winstanleys which politeness demanded and David began to think of Mr. Monkton in Lincoln and of his anxiousness to reach him. But Mr. Winstanley could not quite bring himself to accept that his two new friends were about to leave him and he made several speeches urging them to stay for a week or two. It was left to Mrs. Winstanley to bid them farewell in a more rational manner.

They were not, however, able to leave immediately. There was some delay about fetching the horses and while they were waiting in the yard Lucy came out and looked nervously from one to the other. "If you please, sir, Mrs. Winstanley wishes to speak to you privately!"

"Ah ha!" said Tom, as if he half-expected such a summons.

"No, sir! Not you, sir!" Lucy curtsied her apologies. "It is the Jewish doctor that is wanted."

Mrs. Winstanley was waiting in her bedchamber. The room was large, but somewhat sparsely furnished. It contained nothing but a chair, a chest and a large four-poster bed with green brocade hangings. Mrs. Winstanley stood by the bed. Everything about her—rigid bearing, strained look, the way in which she continually twisted her hands together—betrayed the greatest uneasiness.

She apologized for troubling him.

"It is no trouble," said David, "Not the least in the world. There is something you wish to ask me?"

She looked down. "Mr. Winstanley and I have been married for four years, but as yet we have no children."

"Oh!" He thought for a moment. "And there is no dislike upon either side to the conjugal act?"

"No." Mrs. Winstanley sighed. "No. That is one duty at least that my husband does not shirk."

So David asked all the usual questions that a physician generally asks in such a situation and she answered without any false shame.

"There is nothing wrong as far as I can see," David told her. "There is no reason why you should not bear a child. Be in good health, Mrs. Winstanley. That is my advice to you. Be cheerful and then—"

"Oh! But I had hoped that . . ." She hesitated. "I had hoped that, as a foreign gentleman, you might know something our English doctors do not. I am not the least afraid of anything you might suggest. I can bear any pain for the sake of a child. It is all I ever think of. Lucy thinks that I ought to eat carrots and parsnips that have odd shapes, and that I ought to persuade Mr. Winstanley to eat them too."

"Why?"

"Because they look like little people."

"Oh! Yes, of course. I see. Well, I suppose it can do no harm."

David took as affectionate a leave of Mrs. Winstanley as was consistent with so brief an acquaintance. He pressed her hand warmly and told her how sincerely he hoped she might soon have everything she wished for. He was sure that no one could deserve it more.

Tom was seated upon his horse. David's horse stood at his side. "Well?" said Tom, "What did she want?"

"It is a lack of children," said David.

"What is?"

"That afflicts the lady. The reason she never smiles."

"Children are a great nuisance," said Tom, reverting immediately to his own concerns.

"To you, perhaps. But a human woman feels differently. Children are our posterity. Besides, all women, fairy, Christian, or Jew, crave a proper object to love. And I do not think she can love her husband."

David was in the act of mounting his horse as he said this, an operation which invariably cost him a little trouble. He was somewhat surprised, on arriving upon the horse's back, to discover that Tom was nowhere to be seen.

*Now wherever has he gone?* he wondered. *Well, if he expects me to wait for him, he will be disappointed! I have told him half a dozen times today that I must go to Lincoln!*

David set off in the direction of Lincoln, but just as he reached the end of the town he heard a sound behind him and he looked round, expecting to see Tom.

It was Pewley Witts mounted on a horse which seemed to have been chosen for its great resemblance to himself in point of gauntness, paleness, and ugliness. "Mr. Montefiore!" he said. "Mr. Winstanley is most anxious that you and Mr. Brightwind should see his property and he has appointed me your guide. I have just spoken to Mr. Brightwind, but he has something important to do in Thoresby and cannot spare the time. He says that you will go for both!"

"Oh, does he indeed?" said David.

Pewley Witts smiled confidentially. "Mr. Winstanley thinks that you will build his bridge for him!"

"Why in the world should he think that?"

"Come, come! What sort of fools do you take us for in Thoresby? An English lord and a Jew traveling about the country together! Two of the richest devils in all creation! What can you be doing, but seeking opportunities to lengthen your long purses?"

"Well, I fear you will be disappointed. He is not an English lord and I am the wrong sort of Jew. And I am not traveling about the country, as you put it. I am going to Lincoln."

"As you wish. But it so happens that Mr. Winstanley's property lies on either side of the Lincoln road. You cannot help but see it, if you go that way." He grinned, and said helpfully, "I will come with you and point out the places of interest."

In Mr. Winstanley's fields the weeds stood as thick as the corn. A number of thin, sad-looking men, women, and children were scaring the birds away.

*Poor wretches!* thought David. *They do indeed suffer for other people's moral failings. How I wish that I could persuade Tom to build the bridge for their sakes! But what hope is there of that? I cannot even persuade him into loving his own children.*

While David indulged these gloomy reflections, Pewley Witts named the yields of Mr. Winstanley's lands (so many bushels per acre) and described how those yields would be doubled and tripled should Mr. Winstanley ever trouble to drain his waterlogged fields or enrich his soil with manure.

A little farther on Pewley Witts pointed out some grassy hillocks beneath which, he said, was a thick layer of clay. He described how Mr. Winstanley could, if he wished, establish a manufactory to make pots and vases out of the clay.

"I believe," said Pewley Witts, "that earthenware pots and vases are quite the thing nowadays and that some gentlemen make a great deal of money from their manufacture."

"Yes," said David with a sigh, "I have heard that."

In another place they looked at a thin wood of birch trees on a windblown, sunny hillside. Pewley Witts said that there was a rich seam of coal beneath the wood, and Mr. Winstanley could, if he felt at all inclined to it, mine the coal and sell it in Nottingham or London.

"Answer me this, then!" cried David in exasperation. "Why does he not do these things? Sell the coal! Make the pots! Grow more corn! Why does he do nothing?"

"Oh!" said Pewley Witts with his malicious smile. "I have advised him against it. I have advised him that until the bridge is built he ought not to attempt anything. For how would he carry the corn or pots or coal to the people who wanted them? He would lose half his profit to carriers and barge-owners."

The more David saw of Mr. Winstanley's neglected lands, the more he began to doubt the propriety of going to Lincoln.

*After all,* he thought, *Mr. Monkton already has two doctors to attend him, not counting the Irish wizard. Whereas the poor souls of Thoresby have no one at all to be their friend. Do I not perhaps have a superior duty to stay and help them if I can by convincing Tom to build the bridge? But what in the world could I say to make him do it?*

To this last question he had no answer just at present, but in the meantime: "Mr. Witts!" he cried. "We must go back. I too have something important to do in Thoresby!"

As soon as they arrived at Mickelgrave House David jumped off his horse and set about looking for Tom. He was walking down one of the empty stone passageways when he happened to notice, through an open door, Mrs. Winstanley and Lucy in the garden. They appeared to be in a state of some excitement and were exclaiming to each other in tones of amazement. David, wondering what in the world the matter could be, went out into the garden, and arrived there just as Lucy was climbing up upon a stone bench in order to look over the wall.

"It has reached Mr. Witts's house!" she said.

"What is it? What is wrong?" cried David.

"We have just had a visit from three little boys!" said Mrs. Winstanley in a wondering tone.

"They were singing," said Lucy.

"Oh! Boys like to sing," said David. "My own two little sons—Ishmael and Jonah—know a comic song about a milkmaid and a cow which—"

"Yes, I daresay," interrupted Mrs. Winstanley. "But this was quite different! These boys had wings growing out of their backs. They were sailing through the air in a tiny gilded ship rigged with silken ribbons and they were casting out rose petals on either hand."

David climbed up beside Lucy and looked over the wall. Far off in a bright blue sky, a small golden ship was just sailing out of sight behind the church tower. David made out three little figures with lutes in their hands; their heads were thrown back in song.

"What were they singing?" he asked.

"I do not know," said Mrs. Winstanley, in perplexity. "It was in a language I did not know. Italian, I think."

In the drawing room the curtains had been pulled across the windows to shut out the golden light of early evening. Mr. Winstanley was lying upon the sofa with his hand thrown across his eyes.

"Mr. Winstanley!" cried his wife. "The most extraordinary thing . . ."

Mr. Winstanley opened his eyes and smiled to see David before him. "Ah! Mr. Montefiore!" he said.

"Lucy and I were in the garden when—"

"My love," said Mr. Winstanley in tones of mild reproach, "I am trying to speak to Mr. Montefiore." He smiled at David. "And how did you enjoy your ride? I confess that I think our surroundings not unattractive. Witts said he believed you were mightily entertained."

"It was most . . . enlightening. Where is Mr. Brightwind?"

The door was suddenly flung open and Tom walked in.

"Mr. Winstanley," he said, "I have decided to build your bridge!"

Tom was always fond of amazing a roomful of people and of having everyone stare at him in speechless wonder, and upon this particular occasion he must have been peculiarly gratified.

Then Mr. Winstanley began to speak his joy and his gratitude. "I have looked into the matter," he said, "or rather Mr. Witts has done it on my account—and I believe that you can expect a return on your investment of so many percent— that is to say, Mr. Witts can tell you all about it . . ." He began to leaf rapidly through some papers which David was quite certain he had never looked at before.

"You may spare yourself the trouble," said Tom, "I have no thought of any reward. Mr. Montefiore has been lecturing me today upon the necessity of providing useful employment for one's children and it occurs to me, Mr. Winstanley, that unless this bridge is built your descendants will have nothing to do. They will be idle. They will never achieve that greatness of spirit, that decisiveness of action which ought to be theirs."

"Oh, Indeed! Quite so!" said Mr. Winstanley. "Then all that remains is to draw up plans for the bridge. I have made sketches of my ideas. I have them somewhere in this room. Witts estimates that two years should be enough to complete the work—perhaps less!"

"Oh!" said Tom. "I have no patience for a long undertaking. I shall build the bridge tonight between midnight and sunrise. I have just one condition." He held up a long finger. "One. Mr. Winstanley, you and all your servants, and Mr. Montefiore too, must go and stand upon the riverbank tonight and witness the building of my bridge."

Mr. Winstanley eagerly assured him that not only he and Mrs. Winstanley and all their servants would be there, but the entire population of the town.

As soon as Mr. Winstanley had stopped talking, David took the opportunity to tell Tom how glad he was that Tom was going to build the bridge, but Tom (who was generally very fond of being thanked for things) did not seem greatly interested. He left the room almost immediately, pausing only to speak to Mrs. Winstanley. David heard him say in a low voice, "I hope, madam, that you liked the Italian music!"

As David was now obliged to stay in Thoresby until the following morning, Mr. Winstanley sent one of his servants to Lincoln to tell Mr. Monkton that Mr. Montefiore was on his way and would be at his house the next day.

Just before midnight the people of Thoresby gathered at the Wheel of Fortune. In honor of the occasion Mr. Winstanley had got dressed. Oddly enough he was somehow less impressive in his clothes. The air of tragedy and romance which he commonly possessed seemed to have disappeared entirely when he put his coat and breeches on. He stood upon a three-legged stool and told the wretched, ragged crowd how grateful they should be to the great, good, and generous gentleman who was going to build them a bridge. This gentleman, said Mr. Winstanley, would soon appear among them to receive their thanks.

But Tom did not appear. Nor was Mrs. Winstanley present, which made her husband very angry, and so he sent Lucy back to Mickelgrave House to fetch her.

Mr. Winstanley said to David, "I am greatly intrigued by Mr. Brightwind's proposal of building the bridge in one night. Is it to be an *iron* bridge, I wonder? I believe that someone has recently built an iron bridge in Shropshire. Quite astonishing. Perhaps an iron bridge can be erected very quickly. Or a wooden bridge? There is a wooden bridge at Cambridge. . . ."

Just then Lucy appeared, white-faced and frightened.

"Oh, there you are!" said Mr. Winstanley. "Where is your mistress?"

"What is the matter, Lucy?" asked David. "What in the world has happened to you?"

"Oh, sir!" cried Lucy. "I ran up the high street to find my mistress, but when I reached the gate of the house two lions came out and roared at me!"

"Lions?" said David.

"Yes, sir! They were running about beneath my feet and snapping at me with their sharp teeth. I thought that if they did not bite me to death they were sure to trip me up!"

"What nonsense this is!" cried Mr. Winstanley. "There are no lions in Thoresby. If your mistress chooses to absent herself from tonight's proceedings then that is her concern. Though frankly I am not at all pleased at her behavior. This is, after all, probably the most important event in Thoresby's history." He walked off.

"Lucy, how big were these lions?" asked David.

"A little larger than a spaniel, I suppose."

"Well, that is most odd. Lions are generally larger than that. Are you quite sure—"

"Oh! What does it matter what size the horrible creatures had grown to?" cried Lucy impatiently. "They had teeth enough and snarls enough for animals thrice the size! And so, Lord forgive me, I was frightened and I ran away! And supposing my poor mistress should come out of the house and the lions jump up at her! Supposing she does not see them in the dark until it is too late!" She began to cry.

"Hush, child," said David. "Do not fret. I will go and find your mistress."

"But it was not just the lions," said Lucy. "The whole town is peculiar. There are flowers everywhere and all the birds are singing."

David went out of the inn by the front door and immediately struck his head against something. It was a branch. There was a tree which stood next to the Wheel of Fortune. In the morning it had been of a reasonable size, but it had suddenly grown so large that most of the inn was hidden from sight.

"That's odd!" thought David.

The tree was heavy with apples.

"Apples in June," thought David, "That's odder still!"

He looked again.

"Apples on a horse-chestnut tree! That's oddest of all!"

In the moonlight David saw that Thoresby had become very peculiar indeed. Figs nestled among the leaves of beech-trees. Elder-trees were bowed down with pomegranates. Ivy was almost torn from walls by the weight of ripe blackberries growing upon it. Anything which had ever possessed any sort of life had sprung into fruitfulness. Ancient, dried-up window frames had become swollen with sap and were putting out twigs, leaves, blossoms and fruit.

Door-frames and doors were so distorted that bricks had been pushed out of place and some houses were in danger of collapsing altogether. The cart in the middle of the high street was a grove of silver birches. Its broken wheels put forth briar roses and nightingales sang in it.

"What in the world is Tom doing?" wondered David.

He reached Mickelgrave House and two very small lions trotted out of the gate. In the moonlight they looked more stony than ever.

"I assume," thought David, "that, as these lions are of Tom's creating, they will not harm me."

The lions opened their mouths and a rather horrible sound issued forth—not unlike blocks of marble being rent in pieces. David took a step or two towards the house. Both lions leaped at him, snarling and snapping and snatching at the air with their stone claws.

David turned and ran. As he reached the Wheel of Fortune he heard the clock strike midnight.

Eighty miles away in Cambridge an undergraduate awoke from a dream. The undergraduate (whose name was Henry Cornelius) tried to go back to sleep again, but discovered that the dream (which was of a bridge) had somehow got lodged in his head. He got out of bed, lit his candle, and sat down at a table. He tried to draw the bridge, but he could not get it exactly (though he knew he had seen it somewhere quite recently).

So he put on his breeches, boots and coat and went out into the night to think. He had not gone far when he saw a very odd sight. Edward Jackson, the bookseller, was standing in the doorway of his shop in his nightgown. There was no respectable grey wig on his head, but only a greasy old nightcap. He held a quarto volume in one hand and a brass candlestick in the other.

"Here!" he said the moment he clapped eyes upon Henry Cornelius. "This is what you are looking for!" And he pushed the book into Cornelius's hands. Cornelius was surprised because he owed Jackson money and Jackson had sworn never to let him have another book.

The moon was so bright that Cornelius was able very easily to begin examining his book. After a while he glanced up and found he was looking into the stable-yard of an inn. There, in a shaft of moonlight, was Jupiter, the handsomest and fastest horse in Cambridge. Jupiter was saddled and ready, and seemed to wait patiently for someone. So, without giving any further consideration to the matter, Cornelius got upon his back. Jupiter galloped away.

Cornelius sat calmly turning the pages of his book. Indeed, so absorbed was he in what he found there, that he did not pay a great deal of attention to the journey. Once he looked down and saw complicated patterns of silver and blue etched on the dark ground. At first he supposed them to be made by the frost, but then it occurred to him that the month was June and the air was warm. Besides, the patterns more resembled moonlit fields and farms and woods and lanes seen from very high up and very far away. But, whatever the truth of it, it did not seem to be of any great importance and so he continued to examine his book. Jupiter sped on beneath the moon and the stars and his hooves made no sound whatsoever.

"Oh! Here it is," said Cornelius once.

And then, "I see."

And a little later, "But it will take a great deal of stone!"

A few minutes later Cornelius and Jupiter stood upon the riverbank opposite Thoresby.

"So!" said Cornelius softly. "Just as I supposed! It is not built yet."

The scene before Cornelius was one of the most frantic industry imaginable. Massive timbers and blocks of stones lay strewn about on the bank and teams of horses were bringing more every minute. There were workmen everywhere one looked. Some drove or pulled the horses. Others shouted orders. Yet more brought lights and stuck them in the trees. What was very extraordinary about these men was that they were dressed in the oddest assortment of nightgowns, coats, breeches, nightcaps and hats. One fellow had been in such a hurry to get to Thoresby that he had put his wife's gown and bonnet on, but he hitched up his skirts and carried on regardless.

Amidst all this activity two men were standing still, deep in conversation. "Are you the architect?" cried one of them, striding up to Cornelius. "My name is John Alfreton, master mason of Nottingham. This is Mr. Wakeley, a very famous engineer. We have been waiting for you to come and tell us what we are to build."

"I have it here," said Cornelius, showing them the book (which was Giambattista Piranesi's *Carceri d'Invenzione*).

"Oh! It's a prison, is it?"

"No, it is only the bridge that is needed," said Cornelius, pointing to a massive bridge lodged within a dreary prison. He looked up and suddenly caught sight of an eerie, silent crowd on the opposite bank. "Who are all those people?" he asked.

Mr. Alfreton shrugged. "Whenever industrious folk have work to do, idle folk are sure to gather round to watch them. You will find it best, sir, to pay them no attention."

By one o'clock a huge mass of wooden scaffolding filled the river. The scaffolding was stuffed full of torches, lanterns and candles and cast a strange, flickering light over the houses of Thoresby and the watching crowd. It was as if a firefly the size of St. Paul's Cathedral had sat down next to the town.

By two o'clock Henry Cornelius was in despair. The river was not deep enough to accommodate Piranesi's bridge. He could not build as high as he wished. But Mr. Alfreton, the master mason, was unconcerned. "Do not vex yourself, sir," he said. "Mr. Wakeley is going to make some adjustments."

Mr. Wakeley stood a few paces off. His wig was pushed over to one side so that he might more conveniently scratch his head and he scribbled frantically in a little pocket book.

"Mr. Wakeley has a great many ideas as to how we shall accomplish it," continued Alfreton. "Mr. Wakeley has built famous navigations and viaducts in the north. He has a most extraordinary talent. He is not a very talkative gentleman but he admits that he is pleased with our progress. Oh! It shall soon be done!"

By four o'clock the bridge was built. Two massive semicircular arches spanned the river. Each arch was edged with great rough-hewn blocks of stone. The effect was classical, Italianate, monumental. It would have been striking in London; in Thoresby it dominated everything. It seemed unlikely that any one would ever look at the town again; henceforth all that people would see was the bridge. Between the arches was a stone tablet with the following inscription in very large letters:

## Thomas Brightwind Me Fecit
## Anno Domini MDCCLXXX[8]

David had spent the night inquiring of the townspeople if any of them knew where Tom had got to. As soon as the bridge was built he crossed over and put the same question to the workmen. But an odd change had come over them. They were more than half-asleep and David could get no sense out of any of them. One man sighed and murmured sleepily, "Mary, the baby is crying." Another, a fashionably dressed young man, lifted his drooping head, and said, "Pass the port, Davenfield. There's a good fellow." And a third in a battered grey wig would only mutter mathematical equations and recite the lengths and heights of various bridges and viaducts in the neighborhood of Manchester.

As the first strong golden rays of the new day struck the river and turned the water all to silver, David looked up and saw Tom striding across the bridge. His hands were stuffed into his breeches pockets and he was looking about him with a self-satisfied air. "She is very fine, my bridge, is she not?" he said. "Though I was thinking that perhaps I ought to add a sort of sculpture in *alto rilievo* showing God sending zephyrs and cherubim and manticores and unicorns and lions and hypogriffs to destroy my enemies. What is your opinion?"

"No," said David, "the bridge is perfect. It wants no further embellishment. You have done a good thing for these people."

"Have I?" asked Tom, not much interested. "To own the truth, I have been thinking about what you said yesterday. My children are certainly all very foolish and most of them are good-for-nothing, but perhaps in future it would be gracious of me to provide them with responsibilities, useful occupation, etc., etc. Who knows? Perhaps they will derive some advantage from it."[9]

"It would be very gracious," said David, taking Tom's hand and kissing it. "And entirely like you. When you are ready to begin educating your sons and daughters upon this new model, let you and me sit down together and discuss what might be done."

"Oh," said Tom, "but I have begun already!"

On returning to Thoresby to fetch their horses, they learned that Mr. Winstanley's servant had returned from Lincoln with the news that Mr. Monkton had died in the night. ("There, you see," said Tom airily, "I told you he was ill.") The servant also reported that the English apothecary, the Scottish physician and the Irish wizard had not permitted Mr. Monkton's dying to interfere with a very pleasant day spent chatting, playing cards, and drinking sherry-wine together in a corner of the parlor.

---

[8]Thomas Brightwind made me, the year of our Lord 1780.

[9]Despite Tom's low opinion of his offspring, some of his sons and daughters contrived to have quite successful careers without any help from him. A few years after the period of this tale, at more or less the same time, several scholarly gentlemen made a number of important discoveries about electricity. Among them was a shy, retiring sort of person who lived in the town of Dresden in Saxony. The name of this person was Prince Valentine Brightwind. Tom was most interested to learn that this person was his own son, born in 1511. Tom told Miriam Montefiore (David's wife), "This is the first instance that I recall of any of my children doing anything in the least remarkable. Several of them have spent remarkably large amounts of money and some of them have waged wars against me for remarkably long periods of time, but that is all. I could not be more delighted or surprised. Several people have tried to persuade me that I remember him—but I do not."

"Anyway," said Tom, regarding David's disappointed countenance, "what do you say to some breakfast?"

The fairy and the Jew got on their horses and rode across the bridge. Rather to David's surprise they immediately found themselves in a long, sunlit *piazza* full of fashionably-dressed people taking the morning air and greeting each other in Italian. Houses and churches with elegant façades surrounded them. Fountains with statues representing Neptune and other allegorical persons cast bright plumes of water into marble basins. Roses tumbled delightfully out of stone urns and there was a delicious smell of coffee and freshly baked bread. But what was truly remarkable was the light, as bright as crystal and as warm as honey.

"Rome! The Piazza Navona!" cried David, delighted to find himself in his native Italy. He looked back across the bridge to Thoresby and England. It was as if a very dirty piece of glass had been interposed between one place and the other. "But will that happen to everyone who crosses the bridge?" he asked.

Tom said something in Sidhe[10], a language David did not know. However the extravagant shrug which accompanied the remark suggested that it might be roughly translated as "Who cares?"

After several years of pleading and arguing on David's part Tom agreed to forgive Igraine for getting married and her three sisters for concealing the fact. Igraine and Mr. Cartwright were given a house in Camden Place in Bath and a pension to live on. Two of Igraine's sisters, the Princesses Nimue and Elaine, returned to the *Castel des Tours saunz Nowmbre*. Unfortunately something had happened to Princess Morgana in the nasty house in the dark, damp wood and she was never seen again. Try as he might David was entirely unable to interest anyone in her fate. Tom could not have been more bored by the subject, and Nimue and Elaine, who were anxious not to offend their grandfather again, thought it wisest to forget that they had ever had a sister of that name.

The fairy bridge at Thoresby did not, in and of itself, bring prosperity to the town, for Mr. Winstanley still neglected to do anything that might have made money for himself or the townspeople. However two years after Tom and David's visit, Mr. Winstanley was shewing the bridge to some visitors when, very mysteriously, part of the parapet was seen to move and Mr. Winstanley fell into the river and drowned. His lands, clay and coal all became the possessions of his baby son, Lucius. Under the energetic direction first of Mrs. Winstanley and later of Lucius himself the lands were improved, the clay was dug up, and the coal was mined. Pewley Witts had the handling of a great deal of the business which went forward, and grew very rich. Unfortunately this did not suit him. The dull satisfaction of being rich himself was nothing to the vivid pleasure he had drawn from contemplating the misery and degradation of his friends and neighbors.

And so nothing remains but to make a few observations upon the character of Lucius Winstanley. I daresay the reader will not be particularly surprised to learn that he was a most unusual person, quite extraordinarily handsome and possessed of a highly peculiar temper. He behaved more like Thoresby's king than its chief landowner and ruled over the townspeople with a mixture of un-

---

[10]The language of the fairies of the *brugh*.

reliable charm, exhausting capriciousness, and absolute tyranny which would have been entirely familiar to anyone at all acquainted with Tom Brightwind.

He had besides some quite remarkable talents. In the journal of a clergyman we find an entry for the summer of 1806. It describes how he and his companion arrived at Thoresby Bridge (as the town was now called) on horseback and found the town so still, so eerily silent that they could only suppose that every creature in the place must be either dead or gone away. In the yard of the New Bridge Inn the clergyman found an ostler and asked him why the town was as quiet as any tomb.

"Oh!" said the ostler. "Speak more softly, if you please, sir. Lucius Winstanley, a very noble and learned gentleman—you may see his house just yonder—was drunk last night and has a headache. On mornings after he has been drinking he forbids the birds to sing, the horses to bray and the dogs to bark. The pigs must eat quietly. The wind must take care not to rustle the leaves and the river must flow smoothly in its bed and not make a sound."

The clergyman noted in his journal, ". . . the entire town seems possessed of the same strange mania. All the inhabitants go in awe of Mr. Lucius Winstanley. They believe he can work wonders and does so almost every hour."[11]

But though the people of Thoresby Bridge were proud of Lucius, he made them uncomfortable. Around the middle of the nineteenth century they were forced to admit to themselves that there was something a little odd about him; although forty or so years had passed since his thirtieth birthday he did not appear to have aged a single day. As for Lucius himself, it was inevitable that he should eventually get bored of Thoresby even if he did enliven it for himself by having great ladies fall in love with him, changing the weather to suit his moods and—as once he did—making all the cats and dogs talk perfect English while the townspeople could only mew and bark at each other.

On a spring morning in 1852 Lucius got on his horse, rode on to his father's bridge and was never seen again.

---

[11]Journals of the Reverend James Havers-Galsworthy, 1804–1823.

# SUSAN PALWICK

# Gestella

*Susan Palwick is an assistant professor of English at the University of Nevada,
Reno, where she teaches writing and literature. Her first novel,* Flying in Place
*won the International Association of the Fantastic in the Arts William
Crawford Award; her second novel,* Shelter, *is forthcoming from Tor. In 1997,
her* Starlight 1 *story "GI Jesus" was a finalist for the World Fantasy Award;
her story "Going After Bobo," which originally appeared in* Asimov's Science
Fiction Magazine, *was reprinted in Gardner Dozois'* The Year's Best Science
Fiction: Eighteenth Annual Collection. *Other recent short fiction has been
published in* Not of Woman Born, The Horns of Elfland, The Magazine of
Fantasy & Science Fiction, *and on the* SCIFICTION *Web site.*

*She describes "Gestella," originally published in* Starlight 3, *as
"undoubtedly the darkest thing I've ever written." Readers familiar with her
other work will know that this is no mean feat.*

—E. D.

Time's the problem. Time and arithmetic. You've known from the beginning that the numbers would cause trouble, but you were much younger
then—much, much younger—and far less wise. And there's culture shock,
too. Where you come from, it's okay for women to have wrinkles. Where
you come from, youth's not the only commodity.

You met Jonathan back home. Call it a forest somewhere, near an Alp. Call
it a village on the edge of the woods. Call it old. You weren't old, then: you
were fourteen on two feet and a mere two years old on four, although already
fully grown. Your kind are fully grown at two years, on four feet. And experienced: oh, yes. You knew how to howl at the moon. You knew what to do when
somebody howled back. If your four-footed form hadn't been sterile, you'd have
had litters by then—but it was, and on two feet, you'd been just smart enough,
or lucky enough, to avoid continuing your line.

But it wasn't as if you hadn't had plenty of opportunities, enthusiastically
taken. Jonathan liked that. A lot. Jonathan was older than you were: thirty-five,
then. Jonathan loved fucking a girl who looked fourteen and acted older, who
acted feral, who *was* feral for three to five days a month, centered on the full

moon. Jonathan didn't mind the mess that went with it, either: all that fur, say, sprouting at one end of the process and shedding on the other, or the aches and pains from various joints pivoting, changing shape, redistributing weight, or your poor gums bleeding all the time from the monthly growth and recession of your fangs. "At least that's the only blood," he told you, sometime during that first year.

You remember this very clearly: you were roughly halfway through the four-to-two transition, and Jonathan was sitting next to you in bed, massaging your sore shoulder blades as you sipped mint tea with hands still nearly as clumsy as paws, hands like mittens. Jonathan had just filled two hot water bottles, one for your aching tailbone and one for your aching knees. Now you know he wanted to get you in shape for a major sportfuck—he loved sex even more than usual, after you'd just changed back—but at the time, you thought he was a real prince, the kind of prince girls like you weren't supposed to be allowed to get, and a stab of pain shot through you at his words. "I didn't kill anything," you told him, your lower lip trembling. "I didn't even hunt."

"Gestella, darling, I know. That wasn't what I meant." He stroked your hair. He'd been feeding you raw meat during the four-foot phase, but not anything you'd killed yourself. He'd taught you to eat little pieces out of his hand, gently, without biting him. He'd taught you to wag your tail, and he was teaching you to chase a ball, because that's what good four-foots did where he came from. "I was talking about—"

"Normal women," you told him. "The ones who bleed so they can have babies. You shouldn't make fun of them. They're lucky." You like children and puppies; you're good with them, gentle. You know it's unwise for you to have any of your own, but you can't help but watch them, wistfully.

"*I* don't want kids," he says. "I had that operation. I told you."

"Are you sure it took?" you ask. You're still very young. You've never known anyone who's had an operation like that, and you're worried about whether Jonathan really understands your condition. Most people don't. Most people think all kinds of crazy things. Your condition isn't communicable, for instance, by biting or any other way, but it is hereditary, which is why it's good that you've been so smart and lucky, even if you're just fourteen.

Well, no, not fourteen anymore. It's about halfway through Jonathan's year of folklore research—he's already promised not to write you up for any of the journals, and keeps assuring you he won't tell anybody, although later you'll realize that's for his protection, not yours—so that would make you, oh, seventeen or eighteen. Jonathan's still thirty-five. At the end of the year, when he flies you back to the United States with him so the two of you can get married, he'll be thirty-six. You'll be twenty-one on two feet, three years old on four.

Seven to one. That's the ratio. You've made sure Jonathan understands this. "Oh, sure," he says. "Just like for dogs. One year is seven human years. Everybody knows that. But how can it be a problem, darling, when we love each other so much?" And even though you aren't fourteen anymore, you're still young enough to believe him.

At first it's fun. The secret's a bond between you, a game. You speak in code. Jonathan splits your name in half, calling you Jessie on four feet and Stella on two. You're Stella to all his friends, and most of them don't even know that he has a dog one week a month. The two of you scrupulously avoid scheduling social commitments for the week of the full moon, but no one seems to notice the pattern, and if anyone does notice, no one cares. Occasionally someone you know sees Jessie, when you and Jonathan are out in the park playing with balls, and Jonathan always says that he's taking care of his sister's dog while she's away on business. His sister travels a lot, he explains. Oh, no, Stella doesn't *mind*, but she's always been a bit nervous around dogs—even though Jessie's such a *good* dog—so she stays home during the walks.

Sometimes strangers come up, shyly. "What a beautiful dog!" they say. "What a *big* dog! What kind of dog is that?"

"Husky-Wolfhound cross," Jonathan says airily. Most people accept this. Most people know as much about dogs as dogs know about the space shuttle. Some people know better, though. Some people look at you, and frown a little, and say, "Looks like a wolf to me. Is she part wolf?"

"Could be," Jonathan always says with a shrug, his tone as breezy as ever. And he spins a little story about how his sister adopted you from the pound because you were the runt of the litter and no one else wanted you, and now look at you! No one would ever take you for a runt now! And the strangers smile and look encouraged and pat you on the head, because they like stories about dogs being rescued from the pound.

You sit and down and stay during these conversations; you do whatever Jonathan says. You wag your tail and cock your head and act charming. You let people scratch you behind the ears. You're a *good* dog. The other dogs in the park, who know more about their own species than most people do, aren't fooled by any of this; you make them nervous, and they tend to avoid you, or to act supremely submissive if avoidance isn't possible. They grovel on their bellies, on their backs; they crawl away backwards, whining.

Jonathan loves this. Jonathan loves it that you're the alpha with the other dogs—and, of course, he loves it that he's your alpha. Because that's another thing people don't understand about your condition: they think you're vicious, a ravening beast, a fanged monster from hell. In fact, you're no more bloodthirsty than any dog not trained to mayhem. You haven't been trained to mayhem: you've been trained to chase balls. You're a pack animal, an animal who craves hierarchy, and you, Jessie, are a one-man dog. Your man's Jonathan. You adore him. You'd do anything for him, even let strangers who wouldn't know a wolf from a wolfhound scratch you behind the ears.

The only fight you and Jonathan have, that first year in the States, is about the collar. Jonathan insists that Jessie wear a collar. Otherwise, he says, he could be fined. There are policemen in the park. Jessie needs a collar and an ID tag and rabies shots.

Jessie, you say on two feet, needs so such thing. You, Stella, are bristling as you say this, even though you don't have fur at the moment. "Jonathan," you tell him, "ID tags are for dogs who wander. Jessie will never leave your side, unless you throw a ball for her. And I'm not going to get rabies. All I eat is Alpo, not dead raccoons: how am I going to get rabies?"

"It's the law," he says gently. "It's not worth the risk, Stella."

And then he comes and rubs your head and shoulders *that* way, the way you've never been able to resist, and soon the two of you are in bed having a lovely sportfuck, and somehow by the end of the evening, Jonathan's won. Well, of course he has: he's the alpha.

So the next time you're on four feet, Jonathan puts a strong chain choke collar and an ID tag around your neck, and then you go to the vet and get your shots. You don't like the vet's office much, because it smells of too much fear and pain, but the people there pat you and give you milk bones and tell you how beautiful you are, and the vet's hands are gentle and kind.

The vet likes dogs. She also knows wolves from wolf-hounds. She looks at you, hard, and then looks at Jonathan. "Gray wolf?" she asks.

"I don't know," says Jonathan. "She could be a hybrid."

"She doesn't look like a hybrid to me." So Jonathan launches into his breezy story about how you were the runt of the litter at the pound: you wag your tail and lick the vet's hand and act utterly adoring.

The vet's not having any of it. She strokes your head; her hands are kind, but she smells disgusted. "Mr. Argent, gray wolves are endangered."

"At least one of her parents was a dog," Jonathan says. He's starting to sweat. "Now, *she* doesn't look endangered, does she?"

"There are laws about keeping exotics as pets," the vet says. She's still stroking your head; you're still wagging your tail, but now you start to whine, because the vet smells angry and Jonathan smells afraid. "Especially endangered exotics."

"She's a dog," Jonathan says.

"If she's a dog," the vet says, "may I ask why you haven't had her spayed?" Jonathan splutters. "Ex*cuse* me?"

"You got her from the pound. Do you know how animals wind up at the pound, Mr. Argent? They land there because people breed them and then don't want to take care of all those puppies or kittens. They land there—"

"We're here for a rabies shot," Jonathan says. "Can we get our rabies shot, please?"

"Mr. Argent, there are regulations about breeding endangered species—"

"I understand that," Jonathan says. "There are also regulations about rabies shots. If you don't give my *dog* her rabies shot—"

The vet shakes her head, but she gives you the rabies shot, and then Jonathan gets you out of there, fast. "Bitch," he says on the way home. He's shaking. "Animal-rights fascist bitch! Who the hell does she think she is?"

She thinks she's a vet. She thinks she's somebody who's supposed to take care of animals. You can't say any of this, because you're on four legs. You lie in the back seat of the car, on the special sheepskin cover Jonathan bought to protect the upholstery from your fur, and whine. You're scared. You liked the vet, but you're afraid of what she might do. She doesn't understand your condition; how could she?

The following week, after you're fully changed back, there's a knock at the door while Jonathan's at work. You put down your copy of *Elle* and pad, bare-footed, over to the door. You open it to find a woman in uniform; a white truck with "Animal Control" written on it is parked in the driveway.

"Good morning," the officer says. "We've received a report that there may be an exotic animal on this property. May I come in, please?"

"Of course," you tell her. You let her in. You offer her coffee, which she doesn't want, and you tell her that there aren't any exotic animals here. You invite her to look around and see for herself.

Of course there's no sign of a dog, but she's not satisfied. "According to our records, Jonathan Argent of this address had a dog vaccinated last Saturday. We've been told that the dog looked very much like a wolf. Can you tell me where that dog is now?"

"We don't have her anymore," you say. "She got loose and jumped the fence on Monday. It's a shame; she was a lovely animal."

The animal-control lady scowls. "Did she have ID?"

"Of course," you say. "A collar with tags. If you find her, you'll call us, won't you?"

She's looking at you, hard, as hard as the vet did. "Of course. We recommend that you check the pound at least every few days, too. And you might want to put up flyers, put an ad in the paper."

"Thank you," you tell her. "We'll do that." She leaves; you go back to reading *Elle*, secure in the knowledge that your collar's tucked into your underwear drawer upstairs and that Jessie will never show up at the pound.

Jonathan's incensed when he hears about this. He reels off a string of curses about the vet. "Do you think you could rip her throat out?" he asks.

"No," you say, annoyed. "I don't want to, Jonathan. I liked her. She's doing her job. Wolves don't just attack people: you know better than that. And it wouldn't be smart even if I wanted to: it would just mean people would have to track me down and kill me. Now, look, relax. We'll go to a different vet next time, that's all."

"We'll do better than that," Jonathan says. "We'll move."

So you move to the next county over, to a larger house with a larger yard. There's even some wild land nearby, forest and meadows, and that's where you and Jonathan go for walks now. When it's time for your rabies shot the following year, you go to a male vet, an older man who's been recommended by some friends of friends of Jonathan's, people who do a lot of hunting. This vet raises his eyebrows when he sees you. "She's quite large," he says pleasantly. "Fish and Wildlife might be interested in such a large dog. Her size will add another, oh, hundred dollars to the bill, Johnny."

"I see." Jonathan's voice is icy. You growl, and the vet laughs.

"Loyal, isn't she? You're planning to breed her, of course."

"Of course," Jonathan snaps.

"Lucrative business, that. Her pups will pay for her rabies shot, believe me. Do you have a sire lined up?"

"Not yet." Jonathan sounds like he's strangling.

The vet strokes your shoulders. You don't like his hands. You don't like the way he touches you. You growl again, and again the vet laughs. "Well, give me a call when she goes into heat. I know some people who might be interested."

"Slimy bastard," Jonathan says when you're back home again. "You didn't like him, Jessie, did you? I'm sorry."

You lick his hand. The important thing is that you have your rabies shot, that your license is up to date, that this vet won't be reporting you to Animal Control. You're legal. You're a *good* dog.

You're a good wife, too. As Stella, you cook for Jonathan, clean for him, shop.

You practice your English while devouring *Cosmopolitan* and *Martha Stewart Living*, in addition to *Elle*. You can't work or go to school, because the week of the full moon would keep getting in the way, but you keep yourself busy. You learn to drive and you learn to entertain; you learn to shave your legs and pluck your eyebrows, to mask your natural odor with harsh chemicals, to walk in high heels. You learn the artful uses of cosmetics and clothing, so that you'll be even more beautiful than you are *au naturel*. You're stunning, everyone says so: tall and slim with long silver hair and pale, piercing blue eyes. Your skin's smooth, your complexion flawless, your muscles lean and taut: you're a good cook, a great fuck, the perfect trophy wife. But of course, during that first year, while Jonathan's thirty-six going on thirty-seven, you're only twenty-one going on twenty-eight. You can keep the accelerated aging from showing: you eat right, get plenty of exercise, become even more skillful with the cosmetics. You and Jonathan are blissfully happy, and his colleagues, the old fogies in the Anthropology Department, are jealous. They stare at you when they think no one's looking. "They'd all love to fuck you," Jonathan gloats after every party, and after every party, he does just that.

Most of Jonathan's colleagues are men. Most of their wives don't like you, although a few make resolute efforts to be friendly, to ask you to lunch. Twenty-one going on twenty-eight, you wonder if they somehow sense that you aren't one of them, that there's another side to you, one with four feet. Later you'll realize that even if they knew about Jessie, they couldn't hate and fear you any more than they already do. They fear you because you're young, because you're beautiful and speak English with an exotic accent, because their husbands can't stop staring at you. They know their husbands want to fuck you. The wives may not be young and beautiful any more, but they're no fools. They lost the luxury of innocence when they lost their smooth skin and flawless complexions.

The only person who asks you to lunch and seems to mean it is Diane Harvey. She's forty-five, with thin grey hair and a wide face that's always smiling. She runs her own computer repair business, and she doesn't hate you. This may be related to the fact that her husband Glen never stares at you, never gets too close to you during conversation; he seems to have no desire to fuck you at all. He looks at Diane the way all the other men look at you: as if she's the most desirable creature on earth, as if just being in the same room with her renders him scarcely able to breathe. He adores his wife, even though they've been married for fifteen years, even though he's five years younger than she is and handsome enough to seduce a younger, more beautiful woman. Jonathan says that Glen must stay with Diane for her salary, which is considerably more than his. You think Jonathan's wrong; you think Glen stays with Diane for herself.

Over lunch, as you gnaw an overcooked steak in a bland fern bar, all glass and wood, Diane asks you kindly when you last saw your family, if you're homesick, whether you and Jonathan have any plans to visit Europe again soon. These questions bring a lump to your throat, because Diane's the only one who's ever asked them. You don't, in fact, miss your family—the parents who taught you to hunt, who taught you the dangers of continuing the line, or the siblings with whom you tussled and fought over scraps of meat—because you've transferred all your loyalty to Jonathan. But two is an awfully small pack, and you're starting to wish Jonathan hadn't had that operation. You're starting to wish you could continue the line, even though you know it would be a foolish thing to do. You wonder if that's why your parents mated, even though they knew the dangers.

"I miss the smells back home," you tell Diane, and immediately you blush, because it seems like such a strange thing to say, and you desperately want this kind woman to like you. As much as you love Jonathan, you yearn for someone else to talk to.

But Diane doesn't think it's strange. "Yes," she says, nodding, and tells you about how homesick she still gets for her grandmother's kitchen, which had a signature smell for each season: basil and tomatoes in the summer, apples in the fall, nutmeg and cinnamon in winter, thyme and lavender in the spring. She tells you that she's growing thyme and lavender in her own garden; she tells you about her tomatoes.

She asks you if you garden. You say no. In truth, you're not a big fan of vegetables, although you enjoy the smell of flowers, because you enjoy the smell of almost anything. Even on two legs, you have a far better sense of smell than most people do; you live in a world rich with aroma, and even the scents most people consider noxious are interesting to you. As you sit in the sterile fern bar, which smells only of burned meat and rancid grease and the harsh chemicals the people around you have put on their skin and hair, you realize that you really do miss the smells of home, where even the gardens smell older and wilder than the woods and meadows here.

You tell Diane, shyly, that you'd like to learn to garden. Could she teach you?

So she does. One Saturday afternoon, much to Jonathan's bemusement, Diane comes over with topsoil and trowels and flower seeds, and the two of you measure out a plot in the backyard, and plant and water and get dirt under your nails, and it's quite wonderful, really, about the best fun you've had on two legs, aside from sportfucks with Jonathan. Over dinner, after Diane's left, you try to tell Jonathan how much fun it was, but he doesn't seem particularly interested. He's glad you had a good time, but really, he doesn't want to hear about seeds. He wants to go upstairs and have sex.

So you do.

Afterwards, you go through all of your old issues of *Martha Stewart Living*, looking for gardening tips.

You're ecstatic. You have a hobby now, something you can talk to the other wives about. Surely some of them garden. Maybe, now, they won't hate you. So at the next party, you chatter brightly about gardening, but somehow all the wives are still across the room, huddled around a table, occasionally glaring in your direction, while the men cluster around you, their eyes bright, nodding eagerly at your descriptions of weeds and aphids.

You know something's wrong here. Men don't like gardening, do they? Jonathan certainly doesn't. Finally one of the wives, a tall blonde with a tennis tan and good bones, stalks over and pulls her husband away by the sleeve. "Time to go home now," she tells him, and curls her lip at you.

You know that look. You know a snarl when you see it, even if the wife's too civilized to produce an actual growl.

You ask Diane about this the following week, while you're in her garden, admiring her tomato plants. "Why do they hate me?" you ask Diane.

"Oh, Stella," she says, and sighs. "You really don't know, do you?" You shake your head, and she goes on. "They hate you because you're young and beautiful, even though that's not your fault. The ones who have to work hate you because you don't, and the ones who don't have to work, whose husbands support them, hate you because they're afraid their husbands will leave them for younger, more beautiful women. Do you understand?"

You don't, not really, even though you're now twenty-eight going on thirty-five. "Their husbands can't leave them for me," you tell Diane. "I'm married to Jonathan. I don't *want* any of their husbands." But even as you say it, you know that's not the point.

A few weeks later, you learn that the tall blonde's husband has indeed left her, for an aerobics instructor twenty years his junior. "He showed me a picture," Jonathan says, laughing. "She's a big-hair bimbo. She's not *half* as beautiful as you are."

"What does that have to do with it?" you ask him. You're angry, and you aren't sure why. You barely know the blonde, and it's not as if she's been nice to you. "His poor wife! That was a terrible thing for him to do!"

"Of course it was," Jonathan says soothingly.

"Would you leave me if I wasn't beautiful anymore?" you ask him.

"Nonsense, Stella. You'll always be beautiful."

But that's when Jonathan's going on thirty-eight and you're going on thirty-five. The following year, the balance begins to shift. He's going on thirty-nine; you're going on forty-two. You take exquisite care of yourself, and really, you're as beautiful as ever, but there are a few wrinkles now, and it takes hours of crunches to keep your stomach as flat as it used to be.

Doing crunches, weeding in the garden, you have plenty of time to think. In a year, two at the most, you'll be old enough to be Jonathan's mother, and you're starting to think he might not like that. And you've already gotten wind of catty faculty-wife gossip about how quickly you're showing your age. The faculty wives see every wrinkle, even through artfully applied cosmetics.

During that thirty-five to forty-two year, Diane and her husband move away, so now you have no one with whom to discuss your wrinkles or the catty faculty wives. You don't want to talk to Jonathan about any of it. He still tells you how beautiful you are, and you still have satisfying sportfucks. You don't want to give him any ideas about declining desirability.

You do a lot of gardening that year: flowers—especially roses—and herbs, and some tomatoes in honor of Diane, and because Jonathan likes them. Your best times are the two-foot times in the garden and the four-foot times in the forest, and you think it's no coincidence that both of these involve digging around in the dirt. You write long letters to Diane, on e-mail or, sometimes, when you're saying something you don't want Jonathan to find on the computer, on old-fashioned paper. Diane doesn't have much time to write back, but does send the occasional e-mail note, the even rarer postcard. You read a lot, too, everything you can find: newspapers and novels and political analysis, literary criticism, true crime, ethnographic studies. You startle some of Jonathan's colleagues by casually dropping odd bits of information about their field, about other fields, about fields they've never heard of: forensic geography, agricultural ethics, post-structuralist mining. You think it's no coincidence that the obscure disciplines you're most interested in involve digging around in the dirt.

Some of Jonathan's colleagues begin to comment not only on your beauty but on your intelligence. Some of them back away a little bit. Some of the wives, although not many, become a little friendlier, and you start going out to lunch again, although not with anyone you like as much as Diane.

The following year, the trouble starts. Jonathan's going on forty; you're going on forty-nine. You both work out a lot; you both eat right. But Jonathan's hardly wrinkled at all yet, and your wrinkles are getting harder to hide. Your stomach refuses to stay completely flat no matter how many crunches you do; you've developed the merest hint of cottage-cheese thighs. You forgo your old look, the slinky, skintight look, for long flowing skirts and dresses, accented with plenty of silver. You're going for exotic, elegant, and you're getting there just fine; heads still turn to follow you in the supermarket. But the sportfucks are less frequent, and you don't know how much of this is normal aging and how much is lack of interest on Jonathan's part. He doesn't seem quite as enthusiastic as he once did. He no longer brings you herbal tea and hot water bottles during your transitions; the walks in the woods are a little shorter than they used to be, the ball-throwing sessions in the meadows more perfunctory.

And then one of your new friends, over lunch, asks you tactfully if anything's wrong, if you're ill, because, well, you don't look quite yourself. Even as you assure her that you're fine, you know she means that you look a lot older than you did last year.

At home, you try to discuss this with Jonathan. "We knew it would be a problem eventually," you yell him. "I'm afraid that other people are going to notice, that someone's going to figure it out—"

"Stella, sweetheart, no one's going to figure it out." He's annoyed, impatient. "Even if they think you're aging unusually quickly, they won't make the leap to Jessie. It's not in their worldview. It wouldn't occur to them even if you were aging a hundred years for every one of theirs. They'd just think you had some unfortunate metabolic condition, that's all."

Which, in a manner of speaking, you do. You wince. It's been five weeks since the last sportfuck. "Does it bother you that I look older?" you ask Jonathan.

"Of *course* not, Stella!" But since he rolls his eyes when he says this, you're not reassured. You can tell from his voice that he doesn't want to be having this conversation, that he wants to be somewhere else, maybe watching TV. You recognize that tone. You've heard Jonathan's colleagues use it on their wives, usually while staring at you.

You get through the year. You increase your workout schedule, mine *Cosmo*, for bedroom tricks to pique Jonathan's flagging interest, consider and reject liposuction for your thighs. You wish you could have a facelift, but the recovery period's a bit too long, and you're not sure how it would work with your transitions. You read and read and read, and command an increasingly subtle grasp of the implications of, the interconnections between, different areas of knowledge: ecotourism, Third World famine relief, art history, automobile design. Your lunchtime conversations become richer, your friendships with the faculty wives more genuine.

You know that your growing wisdom is the benefit of aging, the compensation for your wrinkles and for your fading—although fading slowly, as yet—beauty.

You also know that Jonathan didn't marry you for wisdom.

And now it's the following year, the year you're old enough to be Jonathan's mother, although an unwed teenage one: you're going on fifty-six while he's going on forty-one. Your silver hair's losing its luster, becoming merely gray. Sportfucks coincide, more or less, with major national holidays. Your thighs begin to jiggle when you walk, so you go ahead and have the liposuction, but Jonathan doesn't seem to notice anything but the outrageous cost of the procedure.

You redecorate the house. You take up painting, with enough success to sell some pieces in a local gallery. You start writing a book about gardening as a cure for ecotourism and agricultural abuses, and you negotiate a contract with a prestigious university press. Jonathan doesn't pay much attention to any of this. You're starting to think that Jonathan would only pay attention to a full-fledged Lon Chaney imitation, complete with bloody fangs, but if that was ever in your nature, it certainly isn't now. Jonathan and Martha Stewart have civilized you.

On four legs, you're still magnificent, eliciting exclamations of wonder from other pet owners when you meet them in the woods. But Jonathan hardly ever plays ball in the meadow with you anymore; sometimes he doesn't even take you to the forest. Your walks, once measured in hours and miles, now clock in at minutes and suburban blocks. Sometimes Jonathan doesn't even walk you. Sometimes he just shoos you out into the backyard to do your business. He never cleans up after you, either. You have to do that yourself, scooping old poop after you've returned to two legs.

A few times you yell at Jonathan about this, but he just walks away, even more annoyed than usual. You know you have to do something to remind him that he loves you, or loved you once; you know you have to do something to reinsert yourself into his field of vision. But you can't imagine what. You've already tried everything you can think of.

There are nights when you cry yourself to sleep. Once, Jonathan would have held you; now he rolls over, turning his back to you, and scoots to the farthest edge of the mattress.

During that terrible time, the two of you go to a faculty party. There's a new professor there, a female professor, the first one the Anthropology Department has hired in ten years. She's in her twenties, with long black hair and perfect skin, and the men cluster around her the way they used to cluster around you.

Jonathan's one of them.

Standing with the other wives, pretending to talk about new films, you watch Jonathan's face. He's rapt, attentive, totally focused on the lovely young woman, who's talking about her research into ritual scarification in New Guinea. You see Jonathan's eyes stray surreptitiously, when he thinks no one will notice, to her breasts, her thighs, her ass.

You know Jonathan wants to fuck her. And you know it's not her fault, any more than it was ever yours. She can't help being young and pretty. But you hate her anyway. Over the next few days, you discover that what you hate most, hate even more than Jonathan wanting to fuck this young woman, is what your hate is doing to you: to your dreams, to your insides. The hate's your problem, you know; it's not Jonathan's fault, any more than his lust for the young professor is hers. But you can't seem to get rid of it, and you can sense it making your wrinkles deeper, shriveling you as if you're a piece of newspaper thrown into a fire.

You write Diane a long, anguished letter about as much of this as you can safely tell her. Of course, since she hasn't been around for a few years, she doesn't know how much older you look, so you simply say that you think Jonathan's fallen out of love with you since you're over forty now. You write the letter on paper, and send it through the mail.

Diane writes back, and not a postcard this time: she sends five single-spaced pages. She says that Jonathan's probably going through a midlife crisis. She agrees that his treatment of you is, in her words, "barbaric." "Stella, you're a beautiful, brilliant, accomplished woman. I've never known anyone who's grown so much, or in such interesting ways, in such a short time. If Jonathan doesn't appreciate that, then he's an ass, and maybe it's time to ask yourself if you'd be happier elsewhere. I hate to recommend divorce, but I also hate to see you suffering so much. The problem, of course, is economic: can you support yourself if you leave? Is Jonathan likely to be reliable with alimony? At least—small comfort, I know—there are no children who need to be considered in all this. I'm assuming that you've already tried couples therapy. If you haven't, you should."

This letter plunges you into despair. No, Jonathan isn't likely to be reliable with alimony. Jonathan isn't likely to agree to couples therapy, either. Some of your lunchtime friends have gone that route, and the only way they ever got their husbands into the therapist's office was by threatening divorce on the spot. If you tried this, it would be a hollow threat. Your unfortunate metabolic condition won't allow you to hold any kind of normal job, and your writing and painting income won't support you, and Jonathan knows all that as well as you do. And your continued safety's in his hands. If he exposed you—

You shudder. In the old country, the stories ran to peasants with torches. Here, you know, laboratories and scalpels would be more likely. Neither option's attractive.

You go to the art museum, because the bright, high, echoing rooms have always made it easier for you to think. You wander among abstract sculpture and Impressionist paintings, among still lifes and landscapes, among portraits. One of the portraits is of an old woman. She has white hair and many wrinkles; her shoulders stoop as she pours a cup of tea. The flowers on the china are the same pale, luminous blue as her eyes, which are, you realize, the same blue as your own.

The painting takes your breath away. This old woman is beautiful. You know the painter, a nineteenth-century English duke, thought so too.

You know Jonathan wouldn't.

You decide, once again, to try to talk to Jonathan. You make him his favorite meal, serve him his favorite wine, wear your most becoming outfit, gray silk with heavy silver jewelry. Your silver hair and blue eyes gleam in the candlelight, and the candlelight, you know, hides your wrinkles.

This kind of production, at least, Jonathan still notices. When he comes into the dining room for dinner, he looks at you and raises his eyebrows. "What's the occasion?"

"The occasion's that I'm worried," you tell him. You tell him how much it hurts you when he turns away from your tears. You tell him how much you miss the sportfucks. You tell him that since you clean up his messes more than three weeks out of every month, he can damn well clean up yours when you're on four legs. And you tell him that if he doesn't love you any more, doesn't want you any more, you'll leave. You'll go back home, to the village on the edge of the forest near an Alp, and try to make a life for yourself.

"Oh, Stella," he says. "Of course I still love you!" You can't tell if he sounds impatient or contrite, and it terrifies you that you might not know the difference. "How could you even *think* of leaving me? After everything I've given you, everything I've done for you—"

"That's been changing," you tell him, your throat raw. "The changes are the *problem*. Jonathan—"

"I can't believe you'd try to hurt me like this! I can't believe—"

"Jonathan, I'm *not* trying to hurt you! I'm reacting to the fact that you're hurting me! Are you going to stop hurting me, or not?"

He glares at you, pouting, and it strikes you that after all, he's very young, much younger than you are. "Do you have any idea how ungrateful you're being? Not many men would put up with a woman like you!"

"*Jonathan!*"

"I mean, do you have any idea how hard it's been for *me*? All the secrecy, all the lying, having to walk the damn dog—"

"You used to enjoy walking the damn dog." You struggle to control your breathing, struggle not to cry. "All right, look you've made yourself clear. I'll leave. I'll go home."

"You'll do no such thing!"

You close your eyes. "Then what do you want me to do? Stay here, knowing you hate me?"

"I don't hate you! You hate me! If you didn't hate me, you wouldn't be threatening to leave!" He gets up and throws his napkin down on the table; it lands in the gravy boat. Before leaving the room, he turns and says, "I'm sleeping in the guestroom tonight."

"Fine," you tell him dully. He leaves, and you discover that you're trembling, shaking the way a terrier would, or a poodle. Not a wolf.

Well. He's made himself very plain. You get up, clear away the uneaten dinner you spent all afternoon cooking, and go upstairs to your bedroom. Yours, now: not Jonathan's anymore. You change into jeans and a sweatshirt. You think about taking a hot bath, because all your bones ache, but if you allow yourself to relax into warm water, you'll fall apart; you'll dissolve into tears, and there are things you have to do. Your bones aren't aching just because your marriage has ended; they're aching because the transition is coming up, and you need to make plans before it starts.

So you go into your study, turn on the computer, call up an Internet travel agency. You book a flight back home for ten days from today, when you'll definitely be back on two feet again. You charge the ticket to your credit card. The bill will arrive here in another month, but by then you'll be long gone. Let Jonathan pay it.

Money. You have to think about how you'll make money, how much money you'll take with you—but you can't think about it now. Booking the flight has hit you like a blow. Tomorrow, when Jonathan's at work, you'll call Diane and ask her advice on all of this. You'll tell her you're going home. She'll probably ask you to come stay with her, but you can't, because of the transitions. Diane, of all the people you know, might understand, but you can't imagine summoning the energy to explain.

It takes all the energy you have to get yourself out of the study, back into your bedroom. You cry yourself to sleep, and this time Jonathan's not even across the mattress from you. You find yourself wondering if you should have handled the dinner conversation differently, if you should have kept yourself from yelling at him about the turds in the yard, if you should have tried to seduce him first, if—

The ifs could go on forever. You know that. You think about going home. You wonder if you'll still know anyone there. You realize how much you'll miss your garden, and you start crying again.

Tomorrow, first thing, you'll call Diane.

But when tomorrow comes, you can barely get out of bed. The transition has arrived early, and it's a horrible one, the worst ever. You're in so much pain you can hardly move. You're in so much pain that you moan aloud, but if Jonathan hears, he doesn't come in. During the brief pain-free intervals when you can think lucidly, you're grateful that you booked your flight as soon as you did. And then you realize that the bedroom door is closed, and that Jessie won't be able to open it herself. You need to get out of bed. You need to open the door.

You can't. The transition's too far advanced. It's never been this fast; that must be why it hurts so much. But the pain, paradoxically, makes the transition seem longer than a normal one, rather than shorter. You moan, and whimper, and lose all track of time, and finally howl, and then, blessedly, the transition's over. You're on four feet.

You can get out of bed now, and you do, but you can't leave the room. You howl, but if Jonathan's here, if he hears you, he doesn't come.

There's no food in the room. You left the master bathroom toilet seat up, by chance, so there's water, full of interesting smells. That's good. And there are shoes to chew on, but they offer neither nourishment nor any real comfort. You're hungry. You're lonely. You're afraid. You can smell Jonathan in the room—in the shoes, in the sheets, in the clothing in the closet—but Jonathan himself won't come, no matter how much you howl.

And then, finally, the door opens. It's Jonathan. "Jessie," he says. "Poor Jessie. You must be so hungry; I'm sorry." He's carrying your leash; he takes your collar out of your underwear drawer and puts it on you and attaches the leash, and you think you're going for a walk now. You're ecstatic. Jonathan's going to walk you again. Jonathan still loves you.

"Let's go outside, Jess," he says, and you dutifully trot down the stairs to the front door. But instead he says, "Jessie, this way. Come on, girl," and leads you on your leash to the family room at the back of the house, to the sliding glass doors that open onto the back yard. You're confused, but you do what Jonathan says. You're desperate to please him. Even if he's no longer quite Stella's husband, he's still Jessie's alpha.

He leads you into the backyard. There's a metal pole in the middle of the backyard. That didn't used to be there. Your canine mind wonders if it's a new toy. You trot up and sniff it, cautiously, and as you do, Jonathan clips one end of your leash onto a ring in the top of the pole.

You yip in alarm. You can't move far; it's not that long a leash. You strain against the pole, the leash, the collar, but none of them give; the harder you pull, the harder the choke collar makes it for you to breathe. Jonathan's still next to you, stroking you, calm, reassuring. "It's okay, Jess. I'll bring you food and water, all right? You'll be fine out here. It's just for tonight. Tomorrow we'll go for a nice long walk, I promise."

Your ears perk up at "walk," but you still whimper. Jonathan brings your food and water bowls outside and puts them within reach.

You're so glad to have the food that you can't think about being lonely or afraid. You gobble your Alpo, and Jonathan strokes your fur and tells you what a good dog you are, what a beautiful dog, and you think maybe everything's going to be all right, because he hasn't stroked you this much in months, hasn't spent so much time talking to you, admiring you.

Then he goes inside again. You strain towards the house, as much as the choke collar will let you. You catch occasional glimpses of Jonathan, who seems to be cleaning. Here he is dusting the picture frames: here he is running the vacuum cleaner. Now he's cooking—beef stroganoff, you can smell it—and now he's lighting candles in the dining room.

You start to whimper. You whimper even more loudly when a car pulls into the driveway on the other side of the house, but you stop when you hear a female voice, because you want to hear what it says.

"So terrible that your wife left you. You must be devastated."

"Yes, I am. But I'm sure she's back in Europe now, with her family. Here, let me show you the house." And when he shows her the family room, you see her: in her twenties, with long black hair and perfect skin. And you see how Jonathan looks at her, and you start to howl in earnest.

"Jesus," Jonathan's guest says, peering out at you through the dusk. "What the hell *is* that? A wolf?"

"My sister's dog," Jonathan says. "Husky-Wolfhound mix. I'm taking care of her while my sister's away on business. She can't hurt you: don't be afraid." And he touches the woman's shoulder to silence her fear, and she turns towards him, and they walk into the dining room. And then, after a while, the bedroom light flicks on, and you hear laughter and other noises, and you start to howl again.

You howl all night, but Jonathan doesn't come outside. The neighbors yell at Jonathan a few times—*Shut that dog up, goddammit!*—but Jonathan will never come outside again. You're going to die here, tethered to this stake.

But you don't. Towards dawn you finally stop howling; you curl up and sleep, exhausted, and when you wake up the sun's higher and Jonathan's coming through the open glass doors. He's carrying another dish of Alpo, and he smells of soap and shampoo. You can't smell the woman on him.

You growl anyway, because you're hurt and confused. "Jessie," he says. "Jessie, it's all right. Poor beautiful Jessie. I've been mean to you, haven't I? I'm so sorry."

He does sound sorry, truly sorry. You eat the Alpo, and he strokes you, the same way he did last night, and then he unsnaps your leash from the pole and says, "Okay, Jess, through the gate into the driveway, okay? We're going for a ride."

You don't want to go for a ride. You want to go for a walk. Jonathan promised you a walk. You growl.

"Jessie! Into the car, *now*! We're going to another meadow, Jess. It's farther away than our old one, but someone told me he saw rabbits there, and he said it's really big. You'd like to explore a new place, wouldn't you?"

You don't want to go to a new meadow. You want to go to the old meadow, the one where you know the smell of every tree and rock. You growl again.

"Jessie, you're being a *very bad dog*! Now get in the car. Don't make me call Animal Control."

You whine. You're scared of Animal Control, the people who wanted to take you away so long ago, when you lived in that other county. You know that Animal Control kills a lot of animals, in that county and in this one, and if you die as a wolf, you'll stay a wolf. They'd never know about Stella. As Jessie, you'd have no way to protect yourself except your teeth, and that would only get you killed faster.

So you get into the car, although you're trembling.

In the car, Jonathan seems more cheerful. "Good Jessie. Good girl. We'll go to the new meadow and chase balls now, eh? It's a big meadow. You'll be able to run a long way." And he tosses a new tennis ball into the backseat, and you chew on it, happily, and the car drives along, traffic whizzing past it. When you lift your head from chewing on the ball, you can see trees, so you put your head back down, satisfied, and resume chewing. And then the car stops, and Jonathan opens the door for you, and you hop out, holding your ball in your mouth.

This isn't a meadow. You're in the parking lot of a low concrete building that reeks of excrement and disinfectant and fear, fear, and from the building you hear barking and howling, screams of misery, and in the parking lot are parked two white Animal Control trucks.

You panic. You drop your tennis ball and try to run, but Jonathan has the leash, and he starts dragging you inside the building, and you can't breathe because of the choke collar. You cough, gasping, trying to howl. "Don't fight, Jessie. Don't fight me. Everything's all right."

Everything's not all right. You can smell Jonathan's desperation, can taste your own, and you should be stronger than he is but you can't breathe, and he's saying "Jessie, don't bite me, it will be worse if you bite me, Jessie," and the screams of horror still swirl from the building and you're at the door now, someone's opened the door for Jonathan, someone says, "Let me help you with that dog," and you're scrabbling on the concrete, trying to dig your claws into the sidewalk just outside the door, but there's no purchase, and they've dragged you inside, onto the linoleum, and everywhere are the smells and sounds of terror. Above your own whimpering you hear Jonathan saying, "She jumped the fence and threatened my girlfriend, and then she tried to bite me, so I have no choice, it's such a shame, she's always been such a good dog, but in good conscience I can't—"

You start to howl, because he's lying, *lying*, you never did any of that!

Now you're surrounded by people, a man and two women, all wearing colorful cotton smocks that smell, although faintly, of dog shit and cat pee. They're putting a muzzle on you, and even though you can hardly think through your fear—and your pain, because Jonathan's walked back out the door, gotten into the car and driven away, Jonathan's *left* you here—even with all of that, you know you don't dare bite or snap. You know your only hope is in being a good dog, in acting as submissive as possible. So you whimper, crawl along on your stomach, try to roll over on your back to show your belly, but you can't, because of the leash.

"Hey," one of the women says. The man's left. She bends down to stroke you. "Oh, God, she's so scared. Look at her."

"Poor thing," the other woman says. "She's *beautiful*."

"I know."

"Looks like a wolf mix."

"I know." The first woman sighs and scratches your ears, and you whimper and wag your tail and try to lick her hand through the muzzle. Take me home, you'd tell her if you could talk. Take me home with you. You'll be my alpha, and I'll love you forever. I'm a *good* dog.

The woman who's scratching you says wistfully, "We could adopt her out in a minute, I bet."

"Not with that history. Not if she's a biter. Not even if we had room. You know that."

"I know." The voice is very quiet. "Wish I could take her myself, though."

"Take home a biter? Lily, you have kids!"

Lily sighs. "Yeah, I know. Makes me sick, that's all."

"You don't need to tell me that. Come on, let's get this over with. Did Mark go to get the room ready?"

"Yeah."

"Okay. What'd the owner say her name was?"

"Stella."

"Okay. Here, give me the leash. Stella, come. Come on, Stella."

The voice is sad, gentle, loving, and you want to follow it, but you fight every step, anyway, until Lily and her friend have to drag you past the cages of other dogs, who start barking and howling again, whose cries are pure terror, pure loss. You can hear cats grieving, somewhere else in the building, and you can smell the room at the end of the hall, the room to which you're getting inexorably closer. You smell the man named Mark behind the door, and you smell medicine, and you smell the fear of the animals who've been taken to that room before you. But overpowering everything else is the worst smell, the smell that makes you bare your teeth in the muzzle and pull against the choke collar and scrabble again, helplessly, for a purchase you can't get on the concrete floor: the pervasive, metallic stench of death.

# RAY GONZALEZ

## The Legend

*Ray Gonzalez was born in El Paso, Texas, and is now an associate professor in the MFA Creative Writing Program at The University of Minnesota. He has published many volumes of short fiction, essays, and poetry, including* Memory Fever, Turtle Pictures *(winner of the 2001 Minnesota Book Award for Poetry),* The Underground Heart: Essays From Hidden Landscapes, The Heat of Arrivals *(winner of the 1997 PEN/Oakland Josephine Miles Book Award),* Cabato Sentora, *and* Circling the Tortilla Dragon. *His poetry has appeared in two volumes of* The Best American Poetry *and one* Pushcart Prize *volume; his nonfiction was included in the second edition of* The Norton Anthology of Nature Writing. *In addition, he is the editor of twelve anthologies, most recently* Touching the Fire: Fifteen Poets of the Latino Renaissance. *He has served as Poetry Editor of* The Bloomsbury Review *for twenty-two years, and founded LUNA, a poetry journal, in 1998. Among his awards are a 2000 Loft Literary Center Career Initiative Fellowship, a 1998 Illinois Arts Council Fellowship in Poetry, a 1993 Before Columbus Foundation American Book Award for Excellence in Editing, and a 1988 Colorado Governor's Award for Excellence in the Arts.*

*The following story comes from Gonzalez's excellent new story collection* The Ghost of John Wayne *(University of Arizona Press), winner of the 2002 Western Heritage Award. "The Legend" is an eerily magical tale, vivid and haunting despite its brevity.*

—T. W.

The legend says Martita rose from the dead and gave Pentito his shadow. She came into his room one night with a fistful of flowers from her grave. She blessed his sleeping head and made sure his shadow was secure in mind and spirit. She waved the yellow petals over his closed eyes and prayed to Cristo to take care of his family. Pentito's brother was missing in Vietnam, and she had to bless Pentito's shadow so that his brother would return to his family without harm. Three months before this night, Martita was shot and killed in a drive-by shooting in the neighborhood. Pentito was the gunman, aiming at Cinto, Martita's boy. Martita knows this as she stands over the sleeping young man. She waves the driest flower over his mouth, holds it two inches from his chubby face, the tattoos on his arms glowing in the dark. The legend has it that Martita had come to Pentito's bedside every night since her murder. It says Pentito awoke one time to the blackest night he had ever seen. He stumbled for the lamp. When he turned it on, furniture in his room had been moved. He reached for his gun, went to the window, and looked out at the blackest trees and a street with no lights. Even his car in his father's driveway was painted black. Pentito rubbed his eyes and saw his shadow get in and out of the car. Out of impulse, he raised the gun but knew he was watching himself. He blinked and there was nothing there. The tale says Pentito participated in four other drive-bys, wounding six people and killing two before being caught and sent to prison. His shadow escaped from prison after three years. It made its way back to the neighborhood but hesitated to enter any houses on Pentito's block because the shadow could sense Martita's presence. It wandered the streets at night, but no one saw it or noticed how the street lamps kept burning out that year. Martita's flowers floated across the cool summer night and landed in the cactus gardens of several neighbors, that season of the shadow's escape. By the time the neighbors watered their plants that rarely needed watering, Martita's petals were dust, her fingertips tracing rows of dirt in the clay pots. The myth is built around Martita haunting the neighborhood boys without giving them their shadows, except for Pentito, the chosen one. Some of them stayed in the gang, others got shot, a couple survived high school to get drafted and sent to Vietnam. One of them was killed only four days into his tour. The other made it for seven months and one week before stepping on a booby trap and returning home with one leg and the inability to speak. The legend points out how Pentito's brother was never found and is officially listed as an MIA. It insists Martita eventually gave her silence to the wind and let Pentito stay incarcerated, surviving prison until the age of thirty-four. After seventeen years in a cell, he was stabbed in the showers. By then, the guards and other inmates were used to the strange drawings Pentito had created on his cell walls over the years—the image of a thin, worried-looking woman's face. The day before he was killed, Pentito drew the largest figure of all, the woman holding a bouquet of flowers in one of her bony hands. This entire legend is carved in microscopic print on Martita's headstone. You can read the whole story if you rub the dirt off her name and birth and death dates, then get down on all fours and look closely where the worn stone meets the grass on either side of the crypt. There are shadows in the dark grass, several feet of green and continuously damp grass growing in an odd island of prosperity that stands out from the rest of the dry, disintegrating rows of tombstones in the cemetery.

# TANYA HUFF

# Oh, Glorious Sight

*Tanya Huff is the author of over fifteen popular fantasy and science fiction novels, including the "Keepers of the Chronicles" series, and the Victoria Nelson "vampire detective" books. Her most recent books are* The Better Part of Valor *and* Long Hot Summoning. *She lives in rural Canada.*

*"Oh, Glorious Sight" marks Huff's debut appearance in* The Year's Best Fantasy & Horror *series. The story is an imagistic and rather poignant work of historical fantasy. It comes from* Oceans of Magic, *an anthology of adventure tales set on the high seas, edited by Brian M. Thomsen and Martin H. Greenberg (DAW Books).*

—*T. W.*

Will Hennet, first mate on *The Matthew*, stood at the rail and watched her master cross the dock, talking with great animation to the man by his side.

"So the Frenchman goes with you?"

"Aye."

"He a sailor, then?"

"He tells me he's sailed."

"And that man, the Italian?"

"Master Cabot's barber."

The river pilot spat into the harbor, scoring a direct hit on the floating corpse of a rat, his opinion of traveling with barbers clear. "Good to have clean cheeks when the sirens call you over the edge of the world."

"So they say." Only a sailor who'd never left the confines of the Bristol Channel could still believe the world was flat, but Hennet had no intention of arguing with a man whose expert guidance they needed if they were to reach the anchorage at King's Road on this tide.

"Seems like Master Cabot's taking his time to board."

That, Hennet could agree with wholeheartedly.

"By God's grace, this time tomorrow we'll be on the open sea."

Gaylor Roubaix laughed at the excitement in his friend's voice. "And this time a month hence, we'll be in Cathay sleeping in the arms of sloe-eyed maidens."

"*What* kind of maidens?"

"You aren't the only one to have read the stories of Marco Polo; it isn't my fault if you only remember silk and spice. Slow down," he added with a laugh. "It's unseemly for the master of the ship to run across the docks."

"Slow down?" Zoane Cabatto—now John Cabot by grace of the letters patent granted by the English king—threw open his arms. "How? When the wind brings me the scent of far off lands and I hear . . ." His voice trailed off, and he stopped so suddenly Roubaix had gone another six steps before he realized he was alone.

"Zoane!"

"*Ascoltare*. Listen." Head down, he charged around a stack of baled wool.

Before Roubaix—who'd heard nothing at all—could follow, angry shouting in both Italian and English rose over the ambient noise of the docks. The shouting stopped, suddenly punctuated by a splash, and the mariner reappeared.

"A dockside tough was beating a child," he said by way of explanation. "I put a stop to it."

Roubaix sighed and closed the distance between them. "Why? It was none of your concern."

"Perhaps, but I leave three sons in God's grace until we return, and it seemed a bad omen to let it continue." He stepped forward and paused again at Roubaix's expression. "What is it?"

In answer, the other man pointed.

Cabot turned.

The boy was small, a little older than a child but undernourished by poverty. Dark hair, matted into filthy clumps, had recently been dusted with ash, purple-and-green bruises gave the grime on the thin arms some color, and the recent winter, colder than any in living memory, had frozen a toe off one bare foot. An old cut, reopened on his cheek, bled sluggishly.

His eyes were a brilliant blue, a startling color in the thin face, quickly shuttered as he dropped his gaze to the toes of Cabot's boots.

"Go on, boy, you're safe now!"

Roubaix snorted. "Safe until the man who was beating him is out of the water, then he'll take his anger at you out on the boy."

Beginning to regret his impulsive action, Cabot spread his hands. "What can I do?"

"Take him with us."

"Are you mad?"

"There is a saying, the farther from shore, the farther from God. We go a long way from shore. A little charity might convince God to stay longer." Roubaix's shrug held layers of meaning. "Or you can leave him to die. Your choice."

Cabot looked across the docks to the alleys and tenements of dockside, dark in spite of early morning sunlight that danced across the harbor swells and murmured, "Your father was right, Gaylor, you should have been a priest." After a long moment, he turned his attention back to the boy. "What is your name?" he asked, switching to accented English.

"Tam." His voice sounded rusty, unused.

"I am John Cabot, Master of *The Matthew*."

The brilliant blue gaze flicked to the harbor and back with a question.

"Sí. That ship. We sail today for the new world. If you wish, you sail with us."

He hadn't expected to be noticed. He'd followed only because the man had been kind to him, he'd wanted to hold the feeling a little longer. When the man turned, he nearly bolted. When he was actually spoken to, his heart began beating so hard he could hardly hear his own answer.

And now this.

He knew, for he'd been told it time and time again, that ships were not crewed by such as he, that sailors had legitimate sons to find a place for, that there'd never be a place for some sailor's get off a tuppenny whore.

"Well, boy? Do you come?"

He swallowed hard, and nodded.

"Is Master Cabot actually bringing that boy on board?"

"Seems to be," Hennet answered grimly.

"A Frenchman, a barber, and a piece of dockside trash." The river pilot spat again. "He'll sail you off the edge of the world, you mark my words."

"Mister Hennet, are we ready to sail?"

"Aye, sir." Hennet stepped forward to meet Cabot at the top of the gangplank, the river pilot by his side. "This is Jack Pyatt. He'll be seeing us safe to King's Road."

"Mister Pyatt." Cabot clapped the man's outstretched hand in both of his in the English style. "I thank you for lending us your skill this day."

"Lending?" The pilot's prominent brows went up. "I'm paid well for this, Master Cabot."

"Yes, of course." Dropping the man's hand, Cabot started toward the fo'c'sle. "If you are ready, the tide does not wait. Mister Hennet, cast off."

"Zoane . . ."

Brows up, Cabot turned. "Oh, yes, the boy. Mister Hennet, this is Tam. Make him a sailor. Happy now?" he asked Roubaix pointedly in French.

"Totally," Roubaix replied. "And when you have done making him a sailor," he murmured in English to Hennet as he passed, "you may make a silk purse from a sow's ear."

"Aye, sir."

He wanted to follow Master Cabot, but the sudden realization that a dozen pairs of eyes had him locked in their sight froze him in place. It wasn't good, it wasn't safe to be the center of attention.

Hennet watched the worship in the strange blue eyes replaced by fear, saw the bony shoulders hunch in on themselves to make a smaller target and looked around to find the source. It took him a moment to realize that nothing more than the curiosity of the crew was evoking such terror.

"Right, then!" Fists on his hips, he turned in place. "You heard the master!"

"We're to make him a sailor, then?" Rennie McAlonie called out before any-one could move.

"You're to cast off the lines, you poxy Scots bastard."

"Aye, that's what I thought."

"And you . . ." The boy cringed and Hennet softened his voice to a growl. "For now, stay out of the way."

He didn't know where out of the way was. After he'd been cursed at twice and cuffed once, the big man the master called Hennet shoved him down beside the chicken coop and told him to stay put. He could see a bit of Master Cabot's leg, so he hugged his knees to his chest and chewed on a stalk of wilted greens he'd taken from an indignant hen.

The tenders rowed *The Matthew* down the channel and left her at King's Road, riding at anchor with half a dozen other ships waiting for an east wind to fill the sail.

"Where's the boy?"

"Now that's a right good question, Mister Hennet." Rennie pulled the ratline tight and tested his knot. "Off somewhere dark and safe's my guess."

The mate snorted. "We've ballast enough. Master Cabot wants him taught."

"It'd be like teachin' one of the wee folk. He's here, but he's not a part of us. It's like the only other livin' thing he sees is Master Cabot."

"It's right like havin' a stray dog around," offered another of the crew, "the kind what runs off with his tail 'tween his legs when ya tries to make friends."

Hennet glanced toward the shore. "If he's to be put off, it has to be soon, before the wind changes. I'll speak with Master Cabot."

"Come now, it's only been three days." Rope wrapped around his fist, Rennie turned to face the mate. "This is right strange to him. Give the poor scrawny thing a chance."

"You think you can win him?"

"Aye, I do."

The boy's eyes were the same color as the piece of Venetian glass he'd brought back for his mother from his first voyage. Wondering why he remembered that now, Hennet nodded. "All right. You've got one more day."

Master Cabot wanted him to be a sailor, and he tried, he truly did. But he couldn't be a sailor hiding in dark corners and he couldn't tell when it was safe to come out and he didn't know any other way to live.

He felt safest after sunset when no one moved around much and it was easier to disappear. Back pressed up against the aftcastle wall, as close to Master Cabot as possible, he settled into a triangle of deep shadow and cupped his hand protectively over the biscuits he'd tied into the tattered edge of his shirt. So far, there'd been food twice a day but who knew how long it would keep coming.

Shivering a little, for the nights were still cold, he closed his eyes.

And opened them again.

What was that sound?

"Ren, look there."

Rennie, who'd replaced the shepherd's pipe with a leather mug of beer, peered over the edge of the mug. Eyes that gleamed as brilliant a blue by moon as by sun, stared back at him.

"He crept up while you was playin'," John Jack murmured, leaning in to his ear. "Play sumptin' else."

Without looking aside, Rennie set down the last of his beer, put the pipe between his lips and blew a bit of a jig. Every note drew the boy closer. When he blew the last swirl of notes, the boy was an arm's reach away. He could feel the others holding their breath, could feel the weight of the boy's strange eyes. It was like something out of story had crept out of the shadows. Moving slowly, he held out the pipe.

"Rennie . . . !"

"Shut up. Go on, boy."

Thin fingers closed around the offered end and tentatively pulled it from his grasp.

He stroked the wood, amazed such sounds could come out of something so plain, then he put it in his mouth the way he'd seen the red-haired man do.

The first noise was breathy, unsure. The second had an unexpected purity of tone.

"Cover and uncover the holes: it makes the tune." Rennie wiggled his fingers, grinned as the boy wiggled his in imitation, and smacked John Jack as he did the same.

He covered each hole in turn, listening. Brows drawn in, he began to put the sounds together.

Toes that hadn't tapped to Rennie's jig moved of their own accord.

When he ran out of sounds and stopped playing, he nearly bolted at the roar of approval that rose up from the men, but he couldn't take the pipe away and he wouldn't leave it behind.

Rennie tapped his front teeth with a fingernail. "You've played before?" he asked at last.

Tam shook his head.

"You played what I played, just from hearing?"

He nodded.

"Do you want to keep the pipe?"

He nodded again, fingers white around the wooden shaft, afraid to breathe in case he shattered.

"If you stay out where you can seen, be a part of the crew, you can keep it."

"Rennie!"

"Shut up, John Jack, I've another. And," he jabbed a finger at the boy, "you let us teach you to be a sailor."

Recoiling from the finger, Tam froze. He looked around at the semicircle of men then down at the pipe. The music made it safe to come out, so as long as he had the pipe he was safe. Master Cabot wanted him to be a sailor. When he lifted his head, he saw that the red-haired man still watched him. He nodded a third time.

———

By the fifth day of waiting, the shrouds and ratlines were done and the crew had been reduced to bitching about the delay, every one of them aware it could last for weeks.

"Hey, you!"

Tam jerked around and nearly fell over as he leaped back from John Jack looming over him.

"You bin up ta crow's nest yet?"

He shook his head.

"Well, get yer arse up there, then."

It was higher than it looked and he'd have quit halfway, but Master Cabot was standing in his usual place on the fo'c'sle not watching but there, so he ignored the trembling in his arms and legs and kept going, finally falling over the rail and collapsing on the small round of planking.

After he got his breath back, he sat up and peered through the slats.

He could see to the ends of the earth, but no one could see him. He didn't have words to describe how it made him feel.

Breezes danced around the nest that couldn't be felt down on the deck. They chased each other through the rigging, playing a tune against the ropes.

Tam pulled out his pipe and played the tune back at them.

The breezes blew harder.

"Did you send him up there, McAlonie?"

"No, Mister Hennet, I did not." Head craned back, Rennie grinned. "But still, it's best he does the climb first when we're ridin' steady."

"True." Denying the temptation to stare aloft at nothing, the mate frowned. "That doesn't make the nest his own private minstrel's gallery, though. Get him down."

"He's not hurtin' aught and it's right nice to be serenaded like."

"MISTER HENNET!" The master's bellow turned all heads.

"I don't think Master Cabot agrees," Hennet pointed out dryly.

The breezes tried to trip him up by changing direction. Fingers flying, Tam followed.

Although the Frenchman seemed to be enjoying the music, Master Cabot did not. Lips pressed into a thin line, Hennet climbed onto the fo'c'sle.

He barely had his feet under him when Master Cabot pointed toward the nest and opened his mouth.

Another voice filled the space.

"East wind rising, sir!"

Tam's song rose triumphantly from the top of the ship.

"Get him down now, McAlonie!" Hennet bellowed as he raced aft.

"Aye, sir!" But Rennie spent another moment listening to the song, and a moment more watching the way the rigging moved in the wind.

———

Once out of the channel and sailing hard toward the Irish coast, the crew waited expectantly for Tam to show the first signs of seasickness, but, with the pipe tied tight in his shirt, the dockside brat clambered up and down the pitching decks like he'd never left land.

Fortunately, Master Cabot's Genoese barber provided amusement enough.

*"Merciful Father, why must I wait so for the touch of your Grace on this, your most wretched of children?"*

Tam didn't understand the words, but he understood the emotion—the man had thrown his guts into the sea both before and after the declaration. Legs crossed, back against the aftcastle wall, he frowned thoughtfully. The shivering little man looked miserable.

"Seasickness won't kill ya," yelled down one of the mast hands, "but you'll be wishing it did."

Tam understood that, too. There'd been many times in his life when he'd wished he was dead.

He played to make the barber feel better. He never intended to make him cry.

"What do you mean, you could see Genoa as the boy played?"

The barber feathered the razor along Cabot's jaw. "What I said, patron. The boy played, I saw Genoa. I was sick no more."

"From his twiddling?"

"Yes."

"That is ridiculous. You got your sea legs, nothing more."

"As you say, patron."

"What happened to your head, boy?"

Braced against the rolling of the ship, Tam touched his bare scalp and risked a shrug. "Shaved."

Hennet turned to a snickering John Jack for further explanation.

"Barber did it ta thank him, I reckon. Can't understand his jabbering."

"It's an improvement," the mate allowed. "Or will be when those sores heal."

"That the new world?"

"Don't be daft, boy, 'tis Ireland. We'll be puttin' in to top the water casks."

"We can sail no closer to the wind than we are," Cabot glared up at an overcast sky and then into the shallow bell of the lanteen sail. "It has been blowing from the west since we left Ireland! Columbus had an east wind, but me, I am mocked by God."

Roubaix spread his hands, then grabbed for a rope as the bow dipped unexpectedly deep into a trough. "Columbus sailed in the south."

*"Stupido!* Tell me something I don't know!" Spinning on one heel, balance perfected by years at sea, Cabot stomped across to the ladder and slid down into the waist.

Exchanging a glance with the bow watch that needed no common language, Roubaix followed. At the bottom of the ladder, he nearly tripped over a bare leg. The direction of the sprawl and the heartbroken look still directed at Cabot's back told as much of the story as necessary.

"He is not angry at you, Tam." The intensity of joy that replaced the hurt in the boy's stare gave him pause. He doubted Zoane had any idea how much his dockside brat adored him. "He only pushes you because he cannot push the winds around to where he needs them. Do you understand?"

Tam nodded. It was enough to understand that he'd done nothing wrong in the master's sight.

"What's he playing?" Hennet muttered, joining Rennie and John Jack at the bow. "There's no tune to it."

"I figure that depends on who's listenin'," Rennie answered with a grin. He jerked his head toward where Tam was leaning over the rail. "Have a look, Mister Hennet."

Brows drawn in, Hennet leaned over by the boy and looked down at the sea. Seven sleek gray bodies rode the bow wave.

"He's playing for the dolphins," he said, straightening and turning back toward the two men.

"Aye. And you can't ask for better luck."

The mate sighed. Arms folded, he squinted into the wind. "We could use a bit of luck."

"Master Cabot still in a foul mood, is he?"

"Better than he be in a mood for fowl," John Jack cackled. Two days before, a line squall had snapped the mainstay sail halberd belaying pin and dropped the full weight of the sail right on the chicken coop. The surviving hens had been so hysterical, they'd all been killed, cooked, and eaten.

A little surprised John Jack had brains enough for such a play on words, Hennet granted him a snort before answering Rennie. "If the winds don't change . . ."

There was no need to finish.

Tam had stopped playing at the sound of the master's name and now, pipe tightly clutched, he crossed to Hennet's side. "We needs . . ." he began, then froze when the mate turned toward him.

"We need what?"

He shot a panicked glance at Rennie who nodded encouragingly. He licked salt off his lips and tried again. "We needs ta go north."

"We need to go west, boy."

His heart beat so violently he could feel his ribs shake. Pushing the pipe against his belly to keep from throwing up his guts, Tam shook his head. "No. North."

Impressed—in spite of the contradiction—by obvious fear overcome, Hennet snorted again. "And who tells you that, boy?"

Tam pointed over the side.

"The dolphins?" When Tam nodded, Hennet turned on the two crewman, about to demand which of them had been filling the boy's head with nonsense. The look on Rennie's face stopped him. "What?"

"I fished the Iceland banks, Mister Hennet, outa the islands with me da when I were a boy. Current runs west from there and far enough north, the blow's east, northeast."

"You told the boy?"

"Swear to you, not a word."

The three men stared at Tam and then, at a sound from the sea, at each other. The dolphins were laughing.

"North." Cabot glanced down at his charts, shook his head, and was smiling when he looked up again at the mate. "Good work."

Hennet drew in a long breath and let it out slowly. He didn't like taking credit for another's idea but he liked even less the thought of telling the ship's master they were changing course because Tam had played pipes for a pod of dolphins. "Thank you, sir."

"Make the course change."

"Aye, sir." As he turned on his heel to leave the room, he didn't like the way the Frenchman was looking at him.

"He was hiding something, Zoane."

"What?"

"I don't know." Smiling at little at his own suspicion, Roubaix shook his head. "But I'll wager it has to do with the boy. There's something about those eyes."

Cabot paused at the cabin door, astrolabe in hand. "Whose eyes?"

"The boy's."

"What boy?"

"Tam." When no comprehension dawned, he sighed. "The dockside boy you saved from a beating and brought with us . . . What latitude are we at, Zoane?"

Face brightening, Cabot pointed to the map. "Roughly forty-eight degrees. Give me a moment to take a reading and I can be more exact. Why?"

"Not important. You'd better go before you lose the sun." Alone in the room, he rubbed his chin and stared down at the charts. "If he was drawn here, you'd remember him, wouldn't you?"

" 'S cold."

"We're still north, ain't we; though the current's run us more south than we was." John Jack handed the boy a second mug of beer. "Careful, yer hands'll be sticky."

He'd spent the afternoon tarring the mast to keep the wood from rotting where the yard had rubbed and had almost enjoyed the messy job. Holding both mugs carefully as warned, he joined Rennie at the south rail.

"Ta. lad."

They leaned quietly beside each other for a moment, staring out at a sea so flat and black the stars looked like they continued above and below without a break.

"You done good work today," Rennie said at last, wiping his beard with his free hand. He could feel Tam's pleasure, and he smiled. "I'll make you a sailor yet." When he saw the boy turn from the corner of one eye, he turned as well, following his line of sight, squinting up onto the darkness on the fo'c'sle. There could be no mistaking the silhouette of the master. "Give it up, boy," he sighed. "The likes of him don't see the likes of us unless we gets in their way."

Shoulders slumped, Tam turned all the way around, and froze. A moment later, he was racing across the waist and throwing himself against the north rail.

Curious, Rennie followed. "I don't know what he's seen, do I?" he snarled at a question. "I've not asked him yet." He didn't have to ask—the boy's entire body pointed up at the flash of green light in the sky. " 'Tis the *Fir Chlis*, the souls of fallen angles God caught before they reached earthly realms. Call 'em also the Merry Dancers—though they ain't dancing much this time of year."

When Tam scrambled up a ratline without either speaking or taking his eyes from the sky, Rennie snorted and returned to the beer barrel. John Jack had just lifted the jug when the first note sounded.

The pipe had been his before it was Tam's, but he'd never heard it make that sound. Beer poured unheeded over his wrist as he turned to the north.

The light in the sky was joined by another.

For every note, another light.

When a vast sweep of sky had been lit, the notes began to join each other in a tune.

"I'll be buggered," John Jack breathed. "He's playin' fer the Dancers."

Rennie nodded. "Fast dance brings bad weather, boy!" he called. "Slow dance for fair!"

The tune slowed, the dance with it.

The lights dipped down, touched their reflections in the water, and whirled away.

"I ain't never seen them so close."

"I ain't never seen them so . . ." Although he couldn't think of the right word, Rennie saw it reflected in the awe on every uplifted face. It was like, like watching angels dance.

The sails gleamed green and blue and orange and red.

All at once, the music stopped, cut off in mid note. The dancers lingered for a heartbeat and then the sky was dark again, the stars dimmer than they'd been before.

Blinking away the afterimages, Rennie ran to the north rail only to find another man there before him. As there had been no mistaking the master's silhouette, so there was no mistaking the master.

Tam lay stunned on the deck, yanked down from the ratlines.

Cabot bent and picked up the pipe. Chest heaving, he lifted his fist, the pipe clenched within it, into the air. "I will not have this witchcraft on my ship!"

"Master Cabot . . ."

He whirled around and jabbed a finger of his freehand toward the mate. "*Tacere!* Did you know of this?"

Hennet raised both hands but did not back away. "He's just a boy."

"And damned!" Drawing back his upraised arm, he flung the pipe as hard as he could into the night, turned to glare down at Tam . . . "Play one more note and you will follow it!" . . . in the same motion strode off and into his cabin.

Hennet barely managed to stop John Jack's charge.

In the silence that followed, Roubaix stepped forward, looked down at Tam cradled in Rennie's arms, then went after Cabot.

"Let me go," John Jack growled.

Hennet started, as though he hadn't even realized he still held the man's shoulders. He opened his hands and knelt by Rennie's side. "How's the boy?"

"Did you ever hear the sound of a heart breaking, Mister Hennet?" The Scot's eyes were wet as he shifted the limp weight in his arms. "I heard it tonight, and I pray to God I never hear such a sound again."

Cabot was bent over the charts when Roubaix came into the cabin. The slam of the door jerked him upright and around.

"You are a fool, Zoane!"

"Watch your tongue," Cabot growled. "I am still master here."

Roubaix shook his head, too angry to be cautious. "Master of what?" he demanded. "Timber and canvas and hemp! You ignore the hearts of your men!"

"I save them from damnation. Such witchery will condemn their souls . . ."

"It was not witchcraft!"

"Then what?" Cabot demanded, eyes narrowed, his fingers clenched into fists by his sides.

"I don't know." Roubaix drew in a deep breath and released it slowly. "I do know this," he said quietly, "there is no evil in that boy in spite of a life that should have destroyed him. And, although the loss of his pipe dealt him a blow, that it was by your hand, the hand of the man who took him from darkness, the man he adored and only ever wanted to please, that was the greater blow."

"I cannot believe that."

Roubaix stared across the cabin for a long moment, watched the lamp swing once, twice, a third time painting shadows across the other man's face. "Then I am sorry for you," he said at last.

He would have retreated again to dark corners, but he couldn't find them anymore, he'd been too long away. Instead, he wrapped shadows tightly around him, thick enough to hide the memory of the master's face.

"He spoke yet?"

"No." Arms folded, Rennie stared across at the slight figure who sat slumped at the base of the aftcastle wall.

"Ain't like he ever said much," John Jack sighed. "You give 'em yer other pipe?"

"I tried yesterday. He won't take it."

They watched Cabot's barber emerge from below and wrap a blanket around the boy murmuring softly in Italian the whole while.

John Jack snorted. "I'd not be sittin' in Master Cabot's chair when that one has a razor in his hand, thought I reckon he hasn't brains to know his danger."

"I don't want to hear any more of that talk."

Both men whirled around to see Hennet standing an arm's length away.

"And if ya stopped sneakin' up on folk, ya wouldn't," John Jack sputtered around a coughing fit.

Hennet ignored him. "There's fog coming in and bow watch saw icebergs in the distance. I want you two up the lines, port and starboard."

"Ain't never been near bergs when we couldn't drop anchor and wait till we could see."

"Nothing to drop anchor on," the mate reminded them. "Not out here. Now go, before it gets any worse."

It got much worse.

Hennet dropped all the canvas he could and still keep *The Matthew* turned into the swell, but they were doing better than two knots when the fog closed in. It crawled over the deck, soaking everything in its path, dripping from the lashes of silent men peering desperately into the night. They couldn't see, but over the groans of rope and canvas and timber, they could hear waves breaking against the ice.

No one saw the berg that lightly kissed the port side.

The ship shuddered, rolled starboard, and they were by.

"That were too buggerin' close."

Terror wrapped them closer than the fog.

"I hear another! To port!"

"Are you daft? Listen! Ice dead ahead!"

"Be silent! All of you." Cabot's command sank into the fog. "How long to dawn, Mister Hennet?"

Hennet turned to follow the chill and unseen passage of a mountain of ice. "Too long, sir."

"We must have light!"

The first note from the crow's nest backlit the fog with brilliant blue.

Cabot moved to the edge of the fo'c'sle and glared down into the waist. "Get him down from there, Mister Hennet."

Hennet folded his arms. "No, sir. I won't."

The second note streaked the fog with green.

"I gave you an order!"

"Aye, sir."

"Follow it!"

"No, sir."

"You!" Cabot pointed up at a crewman straddling the yard. "Get him down."

John Jack snorted. "Won't."

The third note was golden and at its edge, a sliver of night sky.

"Then I'll do it myself!" But when he reached for a line, Roubaix was there before him.

"Leave him alone, Zoane."

"It is witchcraft!"

"No." He switched to English so everyone would understand. "You asked for light, he does this for you."

The dance moved slow and stately across the sky.

Cabot looked around, saw nothing but closed and angry faces. "He sends you to hell!"

"Better than sending us to the bottom," Rennie told him. "Slow dance brings fair weather. He's piping away the fog."

Tam stopped when he could see the path through glittering green/white palaces of ice. He leaned over, tossed the pipe gently, and watched it drop into Rennie's outstretched hands. Then he stepped up onto the rail, and scanned the upturned faces for the master's. When he found it, he took a deep breath, and jumped out as hard as he was able.

No one spoke. No one so much as shouted a protest or moaned a denial.

The small body arced out, farther than should have been possible, then disappeared in the darkness. . . .

The silence lingered.

"You killed him." Hennet stepped toward Cabot, hands forming fists at his side. "You said if he played another note, he'd follow his pipe. And he did. And you killed him."

Still blinded by the brilliant blue of the boy's eyes, Cabot stepped back. "No . . ."

John Jack dropped down out of the lines. "Yes."

"No." As all heads turned toward him, Rennie palmed salt off his cheeks. "He didn't hit the water."

"Impossible."

"Did you hear a splash? Anything?" He swept a burning gaze over the rest of the crew. "Did any of you? No one called man overboard, no one even ran to the rails to look for a body. There is no body. He didn't hit the water. Look."

Slowly, as though on one line, all eyes turned to the north where a brilliant blue wisp of light danced between heaven and Earth.

"Fallen angels. He fell a little farther than the rest, is all; now he's back with his own."

Then the light went out, and all the sounds of a ship at sea rushed in to fill the silence.

"Mister Hennet, iceberg off the port bow!"

Hennet leaped to the port rail and leaned out. "Helmsman, two degrees starboard! All hands to the mainsail!"

As *The Matthew* began to turn to safety, Roubaix took Cabot's arm and moved him unprotesting out of the way of the crew.

"Gaylor," he whispered. "Do you believe?"

Roubaix looked up at the sky and then down at his friend. "You are a skilled and well-traveled mariner, Zoane Cabatto, and an unparalleled cartographer, but sometimes you forget that there are things in life you cannot map and wonders you will not find on any chart."

*The Matthew* took thirty-five days to travel from Bristol to the new land John Cabot named Bona Vista. It took only fifteen days for her to travel back home again and for every one of those days the sky was a more brilliant blue than any man on board had ever seen and the wind played almost familiar tunes in the rigging.

# DANIEL ULANOVSKY SACK

## Home Cooking

*Daniel Ulanovsky Sack was born, raised, and educated in Argentina, then went on to continue his studies in Paris, and at Harvard University. Currently he is a journalist with* Clarín, *a newspaper in Buenos Aires, and the editor of* Latido, *a journal of cultural exploration. He is the author of one book,* Los Desafíos del Nuevo Milenio, *published in Buenos Aires. "Home Cooking" appeared in* With Signs and Wonders, *an anthology of Jewish fabulist fiction from around the world, edited by Daniel M. Jaffe (Invisible Cities Press).*

*"Home Cooking" was translated from the Spanish by Louise Popkin, a lecturer at the Harvard University Division of Continuing Education. Popkin's translations of prose, poetry, and drama have appeared in numerous anthologies and journals. She divides her time between Massachusetts and Montevideo, Uruguay.*

—T. W.

Eustaquia was the first to sense something odd. Just the day before, as she dusted the mirror in the dining room, she had thought her Indian complexion looked lighter and that her wrinkles were almost gone. Her hair no longer hung straight down to her waist: it was fluffy and held its shape, as if she had been to the beauty shop downtown. What a peculiar feeling: nobody was around, yet somebody was. Good Lord, she had better cross herself. And the scent of magnolias . . . but wait a minute, it's too early . . . Why, yes, they had been in bloom the day that everyone sat there looking at the poor *señora*, the women drinking tea, and the men coffee.

And then that very evening little Miss Fanny, still in black, mentioned the kidneys in wine sauce Mama used to make. The best part was that sweetish taste from the onions. Not onions, green garlic, Raquel insisted. And Don David said I'd do anything to make them happy, and he promised to ask Aunt Sarita for the recipe or, if she doesn't have it, Simona Finkel, that lady who takes orders for knishes.

After dinner it was time for their nightly ritual. They listened to their favorite soap opera on a local radio station, read a few pages in their books, then okay, how about a kiss now, and you're off to bed. At eleven all the lights went out in the big old house and in the faint glow of the crescent moon, you could barely see the linen still hanging on the clothesline in the rear courtyard, the one the maid's rooms opened onto. Eustaquia really disliked the idea of leaving the sheets out there all night, but they were still damp and she wasn't about to bring them in so they could get all musty. Not that I'm superstitious, but everything gets so clean in the sun and Lord only knows what might be out there at night.

Once David saw that the girls were asleep, he could let down his guard. Better they should go out, he told himself, that way they can't see me cry. But why am I crying, when it feels like she's still around? And Eustaquia tossed and turned in her bed. With a little garlic and a bit of onion, too—all finely chopped—a dash of red wine, some lemon juice and two teaspoons of sugar. You dice up the kidneys real small . . . Oh, and use the clay pot, Eustaquia, and keep the cover on, so they'll soak up the sauce. And don't overcook them; more than half an hour and they're as tough as shoe leather. No, ma'am, no more than half an hour. And I won't forget the salt. Salty like my sweat, water . . . there now, let me get up . . . Yes, of course I'll fix them.

As soon as the sun was up she rinsed out the sheets again without explaining why. It's a gorgeous, sunny day, my dears, and I've got a surprise for you. Go get your papa, he'll be taking you to the park for a walk. And I'm off to the butcher shop: Don Andrés, you make sure those kidneys aren't too big, now; and I don't want them swimming in blood, either.

Fanny and Raquel had a fabulous time. Their walk began at the flower bed with the calendar, the one where they write each day's date with tiny plants that jump around like magic. There's a man who comes at night, Papa said. I don't believe you; how can they keep moving them, when they take so long to grow? With their father's permission, the two girls were all dolled up: Instead of their usual black, they had on pale pink chiffon dresses and little tan straw hats. Their shoes weren't ideal for the park, but they just loved the sheen of the patent leather. And how can I say no to them, isn't it bad enough they have no mother? To the pond? Okay, but keep your hands out of that filthy water; three tickets for the boat ride, please. Oooh, look at that little monkey; wow, there are two of them. Watch out, they might have rabies, and what if they bite? Oh, come on, Papa, just one little bag. I told you, it's almost time for lunch. Well, okay, but don't overdo it; that candied popcorn is no good for you; it'll just give you a tummyache.

When they got back to the house, Don David tried his best to be mistaken: that smell couldn't possibly be what knew it was. Darling, don't do this to me, why won't you understand? But the girls were ecstatic: "It's Mama's dish, those kidneys with all that yummy gravy to soak up." But Eustaquia, you said you didn't know how to make them, that the *señora* never taught you. And may I die and go to hell if I lied, sir. I got up today and bought the kidneys, and this is how they turned out . . . And that's the honest truth—I swear by the Father, the Son, and the Holy Ghost—so please, Don David, don't scold me. No, I didn't read it anywhere; I don't even know how to read.

They ate the kidneys in silence. The grown-ups, that is. The girls, on the other hand, were in high spirits and gulped down two whole servings apiece, 'cause Mama told me when we were all grown up she'd teach us how, only we were still too little. For now, she'd say, just the caramel candies.

After a few weeks that kidney dish was back on their weekly menu. Every Tuesday and Saturday Eustaquia would fix it, and when they smelled the sweetish aroma of the onion and green garlic, no one remembered that the recipe had simply reappeared out of the blue. And little by little life in the Berstein household seemed to return to normal. Although David held on to his dark ties and handkerchiefs, Fanny and Raquel stopped wearing black for good. School took up a major part of the girls' time, each first in her class, just as Mama would have liked. And every Saturday, there were movies and every Sunday, tea over at Aunt Sarita's, since she was all alone in life.

I hadn't given it any thought until now, but it isn't good for the girls to grow up without a mother; and you really loved your sister, so why not? Besides, embarrassing as it is to say this, I'm attracted to you; you're so much like her. As for Sarita, well, she wasn't saying yes or no, and that was driving David mad. Please God, I can't deal with bringing the girls up on my own. And I'd sooner die than admit it to anyone, but, well . . . a man has his needs, and at this stage in life I'm not about to go running around.

Sarita was terrified but she knew that in due time, she'd say yes. Even the rabbi from the Paraguay Street synagogue approved of the match; he didn't see anything wrong with her having her first man at age forty-something. Dear God, why were pleasure and fear always so inseparable?

That afternoon she had promised to help Raquel and Fanny with their homework. The three of them were in the dining room learning that Argentina extended from Jujuy all the way down to the Southern Territories. And thanks for the hot chocolate, Eustaquia, and those warm teacakes with the poppy seeds. But for heaven's sake put down that tray, your hand is shaking.

"Do you feel sick? You're looking a little peaked."

"It's just that while I was dusting, I was sure I saw something. It reminded me of when . . . No, don't mind me, Miss Sarita. I must be tired, there's been too much to do. That's all it is."

Why, Eustaquia, whatever is the matter with you? Why are you getting so worked up talking about this? Look, my dear, go have a cup of tea and lie down for a while. I'm sure your blood pressure is down. And don't worry about dinner, I'll see to it. No, ma'am, please don't send me to my room, there's something I have to tell you. Let me explain. Whenever I look in the big mirror, I feel like I'm out of my mind. And maybe I really am. Because my head shakes on its own, as if I were saying no. Is that me shaking it? I say no, but my reflection in the mirror says yes. But it's saying no, Miss Sarita.

"You're talking nonsense, my dear. And, look, you're burning up with fever. Now, you go straight to bed; by tomorrow you'll calm down, and you'll feel much better. I've told David that this house is too big for you to take care of by yourself. Nobody can stretch themselves that thin."

Raquel and Fanny went on with their homework. And Sarita started dreaming up dinner. Why not make a real feast and prove that she, too, could be a housewife? Down with the idea that single women are okay at baking teacakes but next to useless when it comes to real cooking, because after all, if it's only me, I may as well keep it nice and simple.

By now the aroma of chopped basil was wafting into the dining room, where the girls sat gabbing away. So was the sound of the chicken frying with the onions and a red pepper. Something felt familiar, though they weren't sure just what. For all that was left of Mama was their fondness for those kidneys, thanks to Eustaquia, who had learned to cook them. Hunger, that hunger mingled with their homework, and the enigmatic flavors.

"Papa, Eustaquia's sick and she's got a fever. She's burning up. Aunt Sarita's sent her to bed and started dinner."

David didn't notice what was happening. In his eagerness, his mind failed to recognize those familiar smells; he figured she was cooking up some new dish. Of course, he was happy. Why, he was even glad when Eustaquia got sick: he assumed she had done it on purpose, to give Sarita a chance and let them be a family of four again. And so he dressed for the occasion, going up to his room to put on a colorful tie.

In the kitchen the banging of the pots and pans resounded to the rhythm of obsession. She had to prove she could do it, that everything would work out for the best. The chicken was crisp; the carrots and sweet potatoes were browning in a cast-iron skillet in the oven; and the cream, mixed with the basil, was all ready to be poured over the platter, right before it was served.

David came into the kitchen with a mischievous look about him. For the first time he dared to touch her the way a man touches a woman. Just on the arm, to be sure, but how good it felt. Shhh, just for a little while, let me get the feel of your skin. And she said okay, but I'm scared. Don't look at me: the rush of adrenaline, all those hangups. And right then and there, that first kiss. Stolen, yes, but the real thing.

All at once David came back to his senses. Why, it's that chicken in basil cream sauce she used to make for our birthdays. Now I recognize it, Sarita, it smells exactly the same. Thank you. And then it was come on, everyone, let's eat. How odd: The girls were hungry one minute, and full the next. David, torn between his compassion and his queasiness. Sarita, still in a festive mood, and still oblivious. Then Fanny took the plunge: Aunt Sarita, this tastes really bitter. My tummy hurts.

"I wonder if the cream spoiled. Or maybe the chicken they sold us was bad."

The breasts and drumsticks started turning black. Only David tried to eat another mouthful, and he couldn't swallow it. He hid it under the tablecloth so he wouldn't hurt her feelings. But Sarita was already in tears, a mixture of stifled sobs and retching; she had to spit out what didn't belong to her.

Meanwhile, in her room facing the rear courtyard, Eustaquia babbled on in her sleep. And be sure not to pour the cream over it until after you've added the basil; otherwise, it'll all turn bitter. Don't worry, ma'am, I understand perfectly; they mustn't be mixed. Why, yes, of course, I'll make it, *señora*.

# GENE WOLFE

# Queen

*Gene Wolfe is deservedly one of the most acclaimed writers in the fantasy field and the winner of three* World Fantasy Awards, *the British Fantasy Award, and two Nebula Awards. He is best known for his extraordinary fantasy masterwork* The Shadow of the Torturer, *which has been published in twelve languages. Other excellent novels include* The Fifth Head of Cerberus, The Urth of the New Sun, On Blue's Waters, In Green's Jungles, *and* Return to the Whorl. *His short fiction has been collected in* Strange Travelers, Endangered Species, *and* The Island of Doctor Death and Other Stories and Other Stories. *Born in Brooklyn, New York, Wolfe and his wife now live outside Chicago.*

*In his short fiction, Wolfe has explored a wide variety of themes and styles, ranging from flowery "Arabian Nights" stories to sharp works of contemporary horror. The following piece is a skillful little fable that draws its symbolism from one of the best-known stories in the world. It comes from the December issue of* Realms of Fantasy *magazine.*

—T. W.

It was late afternoon when the travelers reached the village. The taller of the two led the way to the well, and they sat there to wait as travelers do who hope that someone will offer them a roof for the night. As it chanced the richest man in the village hurried by, then stopped compelled by something he glimpsed in their faces. Something he could not have explained.

"I'll be back this way quite soon," he told them. "We have a room for guests, and can offer you a good supper."

The taller thanked him. "We were only hoping for directions. What is the name of your village?"

The richest man told him.

"We have come to the right place then." He named the old woman.

"She's poor," the richest man said.

They said nothing it was as though they had not heard.

"She hasn't a lot. Are you relatives? Maybe you could buy something and take it to her, then she could cook it for you. A lamb."

"Where does she live?" the taller asked.

"Over there." The richest man pointed. "At the edge of the village." He hesitated. "Come with me. I'll show you."

They followed him, walking side by side so silently that he looked behind him thinking they might have gone. Neither had a staff. That seemed strange; he tried to recall when he had last seen a traveler who had no staff to help him walk, no staff to defend his life, if defense of life were needed.

The old woman was still at her spinning, which surprised him. She let them in and invited them to sit. The travelers did, but he did not, saying, "There are things I have to do. I only brought them here because they didn't know how to find your house. Are they relations of yours?"

She shook her head.

"Do you know them? It might not be safe."

She considered, her head to one side, remembering. "I think I know that one. Or perhaps not. It's been so long."

"You're not going to hurt her, I hope?" the richest man asked. "She has nothing."

Speaking for the first time, the smaller of the two said, "We have come to take her to the coronation."

"Well." The richest man cleared his throat. "She is a, er, um, descendant of the royal line. I had forgotten. However . . ."

"However?"

He coughed. "However, a great many people are, and she has little with which to make you welcome."

"A little oil," the old woman said. "Some flour."

"So why don't I, ah, provide a bit of food? I could have my servants bring something, and dine with you myself." Suddenly unsure, he looked at the old woman. "Would that be all right?"

"I would like it," the old woman assured him.

When his servants had spread a cloth for them and loaded her small table with dishes, he dismissed them and sat down.

"I don't know that all this is good," he said. "Likely some of it won't be. But some of it's bound to be good."

"Do you want to go now?" the smaller traveler asked the old woman. "Or would you rather eat first? It's up to you." She smiled. "Is it a long way?"

The taller said, "Very long indeed. The place is very far from here."

"Then I would like to eat first." She prayed over the food the richest man had provided, and as he listened to her it came to him that he had never heard such prayers before, and then that he had never heard prayer at all. He was like a man who had seen only bad coin all his life, he thought, and after a great many years receives a purse of real silver, fresh from the mint.

"That is true," the taller said when the old woman had finished her prayer, "but food is good, too." It seemed to the richest man that this had been said in an answer to his thought, though he could not be sure.

"I was about to say that I never expected to go to a coronation," the old woman told the smaller, smiling, "but now that I think about it, I realize it isn't really true. I used to dream that I'd see my son's coronation—that my son would be a king, and someday I would see him crowned. It was silly of me."

"Her son was a teacher," the richest man explained.

They ate olives, bread, and mutton and drank wine.

"You won't be leaving in the morning, I hope?" The richest man had discovered that he did not want them to go; he would suggest they sleep in his house, as he had first proposed. They could rejoin the old woman in the morning.

"No," the taller said.

"That's good. You must be tired, since you've come a long way. You really ought to stay here for a fortnight or more recruiting your strength. This is an interesting part of the country, agriculturally and historically. I can show you around and introduce you to all the people you ought to meet. Believe me, it never hurts to be introduced, to have connections in various parts of the country. Too many people think that they can do everything through relatives, their families, and their wives' relations. It never works out."

No one spoke.

"I'll see to it that you're welcomed everywhere."

The old woman said, "If we're really going to go to a coronation . . ."

"I can find a donkey for you," the richest man told her, "and I will. You couldn't keep up with these two fellows for an hour. I'm sure you realize it, and they're going to have to realize it, too."

She was looking at the taller. "Weren't you the one who came to tell me about my son?"

He nodded.

"I knew I'd seen you somewhere. Yes, that was it. You don't look a day older."

The richest man coughed apologetically. "You're not relatives of hers, I take it."

"No," the taller said. "We're messengers."

"Well, you're welcome just the same. I hope you'll stay until the new moon, at least."

"We will leave when she has eaten as much as she wants," the smaller told him.

"Tonight?" It was insane. He thought the smaller might be joking.

"Oh, I've had all I want," the old woman said. "It doesn't take much to fill me up these days."

The taller said, "Then we should go."

"I want to thank you," the old woman told the richest man. "What you've done for me tonight was very kind. I'll always remember it."

He wished that it had been a great deal more, and tried to say he was sorry that he had never befriended her during all the years she had lived in the village, and that it would be otherwise in the future.

She looked at the taller when he said these things, and the taller nodded assent.

"You're a messenger," she said. "You said so. Just a messenger."

The taller nodded again. "A servant."

"Sent to get me." A shadow, as of fear, crossed her face. "You're not the messenger of death?"

"No," the taller told her. "I'm not."

"What about him?" She indicated the smaller.

"We should go now." The taller stood as he spoke.

The richest man felt that all three had forgotten him. More diffidently than he had intended, he asked whether he might go with them.

"To the coronation?" The taller shook his head. "You may not. It's by invitation only."

"Just to the edge of the village."

The taller smiled and nodded. "Since we are there now, yes, you may."

"You'll tell others," the smaller said when they were outside. "That's good. Because you're rich, they'll have to listen to you. But some won't believe you, because you're dishonest. That should be perfect."

"I am not dishonest," the richest man said.

They walked on.

"I've done some dishonest things, perhaps. Those things were dishonest, but not I."

The sun had set behind the hills, but its light still filled the sky. A breeze sprang up, swaying the lofty palm at the edge of his new pasture. The taller had been walking on the old woman's right; now the smaller took her left arm as if to assist her.

"Right here, I think," the smaller said. "There's a bit of a climb, but you won't find it tiring."

The taller spoke to the richest man. "This is where we part company. We wish you well."

The old woman stopped when he said that, and when she turned back to face the richest man, he saw that she was standing upon nothing, that she and they had climbed, as it appeared, a hummock of air. "Good-bye," she said. "Thank you again. Please tell everyone I'll miss them terribly, and that I'll come back just as soon as I can."

The richest man managed to nod, became aware that he was gaping, and closed his mouth.

"I suppose we ought to go on now," she said to the taller, and he nodded.

The richest man stood watching them follow a path he could not see up a hill he could not see—a hill that he could not see, he thought, because it had no summit. Only hills with summits were visible to his eyes. He had not known that before! When they had gone so high that the sun's light found them again, they halted; and he heard the taller say, "Do you want to take a last look? This would be a good place to do it."

"It's really quite little, isn't it?" The old woman's voice carried strangely. "It's precious, and yet it's not important."

"It used to be important," the smaller said; and it seemed to the richest man that it was the breeze that spoke.

The old woman laughed a girl's laugh. "Perhaps we'd better hurry. Do you know, I feel like running."

"We'll run if you like," the taller told her, "but we can't promise to run as fast as you can."

"We'll just walk briskly," the richest man heard the old woman say, "but it had better be very briskly. We wouldn't want to be late for the coronation."

"Oh, we won't be." (The richest man could not be sure which of her companions had replied.) "I can guarantee that. The coronation won't begin until you get there."

Night came as the richest man watched them climb higher, and at last one of his servants came too, and asked what he was looking at.

"Right there." The richest man pointed. "Look there, and look carefully. What do you see?"

The servant looked, rubbed his eyes, and looked again; and at last he said, "Three stars, master."

"Exactly," the richest man said. "Exactly."

Together they returned to the old woman's house. There was a great deal of food still on the table, and the richest man told his servant to fetch the cook and the scullion, to gather everything up, and to return it to his kitchen.

"Is this your house now, master?" his servant asked.

"Certainly not." The richest man paused, thinking. "But I'm going to take care of it for her while she's away."

The servant left, and the richest man found the figs, selected a fig, and ate it. Some people would want to tear this house down, and time and weather would do it for them, if they were allowed to. He would see that they did not: that nothing was stolen or destroyed. That necessary repairs were made. He would keep it for her. It would be his trust, and suddenly he was filled with a satisfaction near to love at being thus trusted.

# CAROL EMSHWILLER

# The Project

*Carol Emshwiller is the author of* Verging on the Pertinent, The Start of the End of It All, *and other books. Her unusual, thought-provoking stories have appeared in a wide variety of both genre and literary magazines. She has won the World Fantasy Award, and received a National Endowment for the Arts grant, two New York State grants, and a Pushcart Prize. She grew up in Michigan and France, and now teaches fiction writing at New York University School of Continuing Education.*

*"The Project" is classic Emshwiller: smart, stylish, and mysterious. It comes from the August issue of* The Magazine of Fantasy & Science Fiction.

*—T. W.*

For Generations our wives have said, "What? What! Why are you men always adoing and adoing, such that you are hither and thither all the time while we harvest and chop, set the traps, make the ropes for the bridges and the ropes for the slings and nets—we even make the ropes for the Project?"

I always answer, "Men are adoing."

This is the second project. The first failed. The remnants of it lie in the canyons. Only our grandfathers remember. Our boys think the grandfathers failed because they didn't know as much as we know now, but I think they had tricks and theories. Easy to see they were as smart as we are. I've seen their shattered boulders. Some are even larger than our largest, or were before they fell. We no longer attempt to raise boulders of that size.

This has been a part of our lives for as long as even our oldest can remember. We can't think back to when the Project was not our main concern. Nor conceive of such a time. And why would we want to? Those days must have been useless days.

We are a strong people. You can see it in our noses. None but the strong could have stayed and lived here. Our hair is bleached by altitude. Our legs are stringy.

Even our old ladies still jump from stone to stone. Our songs, unlike those of any other peoples, are full of hohs. Some say we don't sing at all, but only shout and growl.

First we built a fortress. This was so long ago we no longer understand its purpose. (We live within its crumbling walls.) Except for the mountain lion we have no enemies. And who but us would want land such as this with hardly a single flat spot larger than a split boulder?

That lion took our baby daughter. That's why my wife keeps saying, "What? *What!*" She blames me. "Had you been . . . ! Had you but been . . . ! Had you!"

I say, and I say it slowly, "*As. It. Is.* We've hardly enough men for the Project." There are but eighty. We need every single one on the ropes. The stone we raise now is the largest so far. Couldn't be done, they said and said, but we are doing it.

The evening our baby was taken, the owl flew low, looking huge in the moonlight. I thought I could reach up and touch its white underbelly. First I heard the flap of wings. First I thought it was a ghost. Then I thought, It's just an owl, not knowing that it really was a ghost, or soon would be.

As to the lion, my baby daughter must have made but a single mouthful.

I'm not the only one who has lost a child. This happens when game is scarce. It had been a dry winter. The pine nuts were few, so rodents are few. Grouse, hares, the sweet, gray foxes, few. Our wild mountain sheep, eaten to the last of them. We have to depend on our goats for everything now. (Would that my daughter had been penned up with the kids.)

(The blanket my wife was knitting is now for someone else's child.)

Since we lost our little girl my wife has been blaming me even for the lack of radishes.

"Not even trim the wicks," she says. "It's little enough," she says. "Do I shout?" she says. "Do I sit? Tired as I am, do I sit?"

I say, "Tired as *I* am. Look how my eyes are shutting." I say, "Until you work at raising boulders, you will never understand such a tiredness as this."

Radishes! Wicks! Who would care but somebody's wife?

They said the stones are too big, the mountain top too high, lightning will strike, boulders will turn red, glow, and then crack as if to deafen. I say, "Yes, yes! *Of course!*"

Say what they wish, but it's easy to see all paths lead to our village. One has only to climb to our highest places and look down to see how true that is. We're not a way station alongside some path that goes someplace else. Therefore it's clear there is no need to go to some lower place and look for other happenings, so we have never gone.

Our catamount prowls wherever she wishes. Sometimes at night, I see her eyes shine. Disembodied. Steady on. Then a sudden freezing along the backbone, as if I saw a child on the brink of the brink.

The lion is young. We think she's only recently left the den of her birth. She's thin. It's the young ones, don't yet know what they're about, so all the more dangerous. She's the color of our boulders. She belongs—as much as we do. In fact more.

I'm a strong man. A big man. The biggest. Except for me we don't look like the people of the valley. We're smaller and wirier. I have never been down there, but now and then one of them climbs up here. We recognize them right away and not just because we know everybody who lives up here, but by their cheek-bones and their wide open eyes. We know they're used to shadows because when we look down there, into their valley, we see how, every afternoon, our mountains shade them. We wonder what they're up to here in the up instead of down in their the down.

Down there they call us, "The people of the goats, or of the mountain sheep." They even call us, "The people of the catamount." We are more likely the people of the dinner of the catamount.

My wife says, "Shouldn't the Project be the lion? Shouldn't the lion be first so our little ones can sleep in peace or play capture the peak? If you'll not make the lion your project, then I'll make it mine."

How can she? She can't even draw the bow. And as to the spear . . . Women use spears as canes to steady themselves as they climb over rocks.

(One evening I saw our house cat leap up and pull a bat out of the air. I know what my wife will have to deal with.)

"If you don't go, I go. What do I have to wait for here waiting and waiting? For the cabbages to grow?"

Is she really going out to hunt lion, small as she is and always cold without me to warm her?

"Go," I say, "I'm busy with the Project. There will always be a beast, if not this one then another."

Yet I will follow. Even though I'm not only the foreman, but the most important puller and checker and the finest fitter of all, and my voice echoes out over the canyons louder than any, I will follow. My pockmarked face has made her my one and only. Even my size was against me with the women.

We men of the mountains are not like me. I'm teased that my father was not my father but that my mother was raped by some valley man and never confessed it. "Out picking berries, one can not only come across a bear." Though they also say my father was a bear—a bald-headed bear. I'd rather that than some valley man.

My wife . . . even she would hardly be a mouthful for the lion. She's as small as I am large. Her name is Wren and she's like a wren.

Our women are named Lark, Titmouse, Towhee, Quail, Redstart, Killdeer. . . . (Killdeer because we so admire the broken wing trick and hope to see the same in the mothers of our children.) Our men are named for raptors: Vulture, Eagle, Hawk, Goshawk, Kestrel, Falcon, and such.

(Not Owl. We would never name anyone Owl.)

My name is Harrier. We named our baby Sparrow. Now I can hardly think that word.

I say, "It's the lion that will be stalking you."

"I will be adoing."

Always. . . . *Always* the women take our time from what's important. The Project will last for generations. Centuries. Perhaps forever. Even as long as our mountain remains a mountain. Women's thoughts are on the everyday. I want to say, "What about the monumental? Have you ever thought of that?" And I would say it except I already have and more times than I can count.

What I think as I follow my woman down and then up, and then up and down and down and up again, is: How fortunate to be alive so far! The turkey vulture soars. One tiny cloud. For a while a raven family keeps one step ahead. I'm thinking how the Milky Way is still up there shining all across the sky, there, even though you can't see it in the daytime. I'm needed elsewhere, but I will enjoy the day as it is right now, though my wife, my wren, hurries away from me with all my weapons.

Whenever I top a rise and look back I see them struggling. My group at the top—all the strongest pullers. I see skids and ramps and wedges, pulleys. . . . They won't make much headway without me. (I didn't ask leave to come, I just came. Who would want a wife out here in The Nowhere, much less in The Down?)

Did Wren look back and see I wasn't there? I would have been easy to spot because of my bulk. Now, as I look I can see that all are, just as they are, mountain men and small. No wonder they joke that I'm the bastard of a bald-headed bear.

She's easy to follow. We wear red, the mountain color. The better to be seen. She wears a red bonnet and her fuzzy red sweater. She has her boots and her mittens tied on the back of her pack. She wears moccasins, but crosses the streams barefoot and wipes her feet with a red towel. But I wear the color of the lion and stay well behind. The black straps of my pack across my chest, my wide black hat, imitate the cracks of the mountains and make me even more like a piece of half-split rock.

She goes lower, then climbs up again into a cozy pass, cozy black basalt cliffs on one side and tawny, more rounded granite on the other. Behind the black side, an iron oxide peak looms orange. There's several patches of frazzle ice to chew on. There are overhanging rocks. I'm thinking this is a good place for a lioness. Then I know this *is* the place. I don't know how I know but I can almost smell her.

Here is where my wife, my lion's mouthful, decides to spend the night. I guess if the lion finds it inviting, everyone would.

She doesn't look frightened as she settles in. I suppose one who has just lost a baby doesn't feel any fear for a long time afterward. Perhaps never.

I stay close. Then I come closer. I watch my wife sleep in the moonlight. All the nights since the baby died she hasn't slept much but now she does. As if the very danger is comforting. As if what has eaten our baby might eat her so the owl would fly again.

I take back my weapons, dress myself in a leather apron. Surely the lion will come. Surely the lion is here already.

———

I see her—first just eyes reflecting moonlight, then a shadow. She comes out from a low overhang, exactly where I thought she'd come from. I'd never have seen her if I hadn't suspected she'd come from there. She stands still and looks at me. Even though I knew . . . even though I hoped she'd be there, I feel that edge-of-a-cliff feeling, myself, about to fall. Or the Project about to come loose and crash down on us.

I want to lure her away from my wife, so, like the killdeer, I limp. Down from the cozy pass, down into the switchbacks below, behind boulders, away and lower. I don't want even the sounds . . . neither my sounds nor cat sounds . . . But if we're this far down, why would my wife think they had anything to do with me? Many's the times we've awakened to the lion's midnight yowls, howls, screeches, caterwauling, up there near our village, and turned to each other, and said, "It's only the young lion, fresh out of her mother's den."

Why would my wife think anything of it except to reach for me and find me not there?

When we're far down, lioness and I, and in a flat clear place where trees are few and the moon shines through and I can see clearly, I turn.

It's this leather apron between me and claws that saves me. And, of course, the inexperience of the lioness.

She had a look in her eyes of wondering about the world. My daughter had the same. And when I killed her she had a look as if to say: I can't be, and already, dead. No doubt my daughter had the same when that moment came to her. When I saw that, I hesitated, but it was too late.

I carry her carcass to the side of the clearing. No doubt about it, she was starving. No doubt about it, she'd have come after my wife. Perhaps my wife wanted her to. Warmth to warmth, fur to skin, as lovers. Or herself as gift. Or simply to close a circle.

I limp back—this time the limping is real. I expected worse. I brought herbs and bandages in case. Back under the lioness's overhang, I bandage myself. I stow my weapons and the leather apron in a corner.

Then I go lie down, again not far from my wife to guard her. As I had told her, there will always be a beast somewhere out there at the edges of our lives.

Pain keeps me from sleeping. One can't get close to any sort of cat without having wounds.

I had thought my wife would turn around and go back, but she goes on. She doesn't know the lion is dead. Should I stop her? Try to? Tell her the lion will be gone to the buzzards before midday? Show myself? But one look at me and she'd know all there is to know. I'll not yet show myself.

I chafe with all this hithering and thithering. I regret every minute I spend away from the Project. We say, "What's worth the doing is worth dying for or why be adoing." I might well have died here in the middle of nowhere. I had always thought to die for the Project, not from cat scratchings.

My wife goes on down, not knowing she's stalking nothing. Might as well be following her own stepped-on mosses. Might as well look up and back and over her left shoulder for the special place where dead babies congregate for each other's company—all the dead babies who have just smiled their first smiles.

None of us know anything about The Down, and proud of it. There'll be bear. There'll be snakes and bugs and goodness knows what. Things we never heard of. Trees and bushes are already changing. And they grow closer together.

From here I get a good view of this flat land. Flat as far as you can see. We know nothing about it nor care to. We don't ponder fields, or horses or cows or plows. We say, "That which is highest is its own reward."

Those big ugly men, hunking around down there. Altitude makes them puff. Their lips turn blue. We offer them our best food knowing they'll refuse. Always halfway along that last and steepest climb to our fortress, they throw up.

If they can't see the importance of the Project then there's no explaining it, neither to them nor to our women who keep saying, "What in the world!" and, "Why! Why ever!"

I told her and I told her, you can't stalk a cat. Where does she think she's on the way to? Does she want to see for herself all that we are proud not knowing? Or is it that (curious as a wife) she simply wants to find something different?

And she already has. I never saw flowers as large as these. I see her peer and sniff. I see her stroke the velvet of the petals. She leans as she leaned over our baby.

I do. I do love her.

I climb a mound and look back (mound is all one can call these lumps of The Down. These silly hills make me even more proud to be a mountain man.) I can't see my men anymore, nor pulleys nor ropes, but the Project is clear, bright white against the sky. Exactly as we planned it. When we cap it with the last and largest boulder, we'll have done the impossible.

My wife stands and looks and listens. She imitates the call of a bird I never heard before. (She can imitate all the bird calls in the mountains, but this is a new sound to us.) I see she's here for whatever she can find that's different. There'll be no stopping her. She studies the ground and then steps carefully so as not to crush anything, even something small.

I'm beginning to feel as she must be feeling, that this is to be seen and known about. I look around as she looks around. The sky is flatter than I thought. Distances are different. I'll have to walk it to understand it.

And there the horned cows. Without them I'd not have had a leather apron tough enough to save me.

But this is our water. It all comes from us. As we climbed down, always we heard rushing water sounds and thought nothing of it because, up in our village, it is the sound of our daily life. Here they've forced it into straight lines all across their land. Until now, I had wondered what those straight lines were. Nothing is as straight up there except split rocks. When the sun shined all the way down here, I had thought the waterways were of silver and that that is where our bracelets came from.

My wife has hurried on as though to reach some new thing before some other new thing, but it'll be dark soon. She will have to find a bedding down place even here in this pasture land. Once away from the mounds, there's not a single boulder. None have rolled this far. But now and then there are trees and sometimes bushes, especially along the ditches that tame our water. My wife finds a place to hide. She has already taken off all her red, back in the lower hills.

What will they be thinking of her here, where everything is large? And what will they think of her trousers and her fine bleached hair? I, being the size I am, could hide as one of them, whereas she could never. Except I wouldn't know how to live here. What do you say to a horse? What do you whistle to send a dog off and around? And what of bulls? I've heard things of bulls.

They say time is different down here. It goes at a faster walk. In The Up our steps are slower because the ground is rough. But even these people of The Down can't walk away from time.

Before she goes to hide in her bushes she studies the moon. I see that she sees as I do—how life depends on water and on sky. She gestures, one palm up. She seems to make a wish. We say to children, catch a moon beam, make a wish, but you need a pinch of mountain aster for it to come true.

I lie down, next bush to her. This time I do sleep. Though I wonder, what of bulls? And what of dogs and how large do they grow down here?

This time, when I finally wake, she's stepping away from the shelter of the trees. She's in red again, showing herself on purpose. Nearby, at the edge of the field, there's what I know is a plow. We have none such. She stands beside it. I'm so stiff and sore I can hardly get up but I do.

Here, already, there's a flatland man coming straight toward her. The man is riding sideways on one of those horse things. I had not known there'd be so much hair at the ankles. All kinds of straps hang down. So many one wonders how he knows to hook them up. He jumps off and leads the horse to the plow and to my wife.

They stand one to one. They speak. He, with the swallowed Rs of the Down and no clicks on the Ks. He calls her, Little Lady. "Little Lady of the mountains." He reaches out his fingers. Is it as if to be smelled? Does he think she's an animal?

I can see he looks like me. Except no pock marks. (I could never grow a decent beard because of that. His is decent.) For a moment I see myself as if a long time ago when I hated my size as everyone else did, and said so to my face. There came a time, though, when I won every fistfight. Then they hated me even more, but that all changed when I was old enough to work on the Project. I was foreman at seventeen. This man would scare every mountain man but me. He's even larger than I am, but my muscles are the muscles of those who lift boulders.

He and my wife reach out slowly. Touch hands as if the other is a miracle of strangeness. Then he reaches as if to touch her bleached hair. Reaches but doesn't touch, though almost. Her hair has hardly any color, not enough to call it yellow.

Something is happening between them. Something instant of the instant.

"I want to see," my wife says, "all the things of here."

I will show myself. I will risk as Wren does, whatever it is they do to people from Up, but mostly risk so my wife will see my miserable condition and know that I've saved her. I look at myself . . . my bandages leaking, my shredded sleeves and trousers, shredded everywhere where the apron didn't cover. My limp is not a pretense. My legs wobble. If I fall it won't be on purpose. Will either of them notice?

Does she understand what we add up to, I and my sweet Wren? That I've saved her and all the village and the children can play capture the peak? For now until some other beast comes around.

I will speak. I will say, As to the two of us. As to us . . .

And I do speak, but what I say is, "As to myself and the Project and the meaning of it . . ." For a moment it's as if the Project is before me, just as it has been every day and all the days of my life until now, shining, polished white against our sky, which is of a darker blue than this pale blue of the Down. The Project as hub of all paths. I think to say more of the things that are important, but I start to shake. I go down on my knees.

They turn to me. I see my wife seeing what I wanted her to see. She says, "Oh!"

But he says, "*You!*" and again, "*You!*"

It's he who comes to me, lifts me and hugs me as if a brother found at last, kisses each cheek before I have time to think to pull away. I haven't the strength to anyway. This is not the mountain people's way. The horse leans and noses me. I don't know if he'll bite or not. His head is much bigger than I thought a horse's head would be and bonier.

Though I'm almost as big as this man, he lifts me over his shoulder and then pushes me up upon the creature. Sits me sideways. (The creature is warm as a wife. Warm as the lion was when I carried her away from the trail.) The man walks us toward the village. The movement of the horse is painful to my scratches. I gasp, but my wife is looking up at this man, not at me. She walks beside him as though it was the most natural thing in the world to be crossing this flat land with grass all over it, with a stranger, and with me on a horse.

Other men, sideways on their horses are coming out, one by one and two by two, to their fields. As we meet the first, the man says, "Here's our long lost bastard half brother. We've waited all this time for him to come back to us. And doesn't he look just like his father?"

I want to say, A bear! A bear was my father, but I'm too tired and sick to protest. I think my wife should do it for me considering the state I'm in. I want her to say how I'm a mountain man; how, if could I walk, you would see it in my walk; and if I spoke, you would hear it in my words, but I fear she may no longer be proud of our mountains, though she knows full well the mountains are where everything begins, where even this very water, here in this very roadside ditch, rolls down from, even where the weather is engendered, else why would clouds hang at their tops? How can it be that one look in one single moment to one man almost as ugly as I am, is enough to change her mind?

I must protest. I don't know how much these people know of important things. Perhaps there's no such thing as marriage as we know it up there. We always say they're in need of speeches down here, so I begin, even just to these two men and these two horses who swivel their ears toward me, listening. I had not thought to mention the Project, but I do. I say, "How would we know anything without the Project be the reasons for it? How figure elevations so as to know the highest and therefore most important of all the mountains?"

But my wife interrupts me right in the middle of it, "What are you saying! Even here among the strangers of the Down, you speak of such things! Here, sick and bloodied, and having done it for my sake, even as you faint, you speak of unimportant things!"

I say, "You speak as if of turnips."

"Make a speech if you must, but you would miss my turnips if I never grew them."

If she loves me still, or ever has, it's for everyday things that amount to very little. I lose hope. I, the foreman of the Project, the killer of the lion, having made everybody safer, fall.

I must have fainted at that very moment of losing heart, because of it in fact. Next thing I know I'm in a bed and a large dog is licking my face.

I've been washed and rebandaged. My scratches no longer hurt. I'm covered with a quilt the likes of which I've never seen. It's as light as if a froth. There's a smell of stew. I had not thought the Down would be as comfortable as this.

A woman sits near me. She's dressed in long skirts and no red at all unless you count her rough red hands. They're as large as mine, and are in her lap with her darning. Her face is wide and flat as the wide flat land that must have made it so.

And here's my wife, also wearing the skirts of the Down and no red. (Those skirts must snag and tangle in their legs. They will have to be holding them out of the way.) She looks so odd I have the thought that she'll even talk as they do. I wonder what she's been doing as I've been lying here unconscious.

She comes to me from stirring pots, still holding a wooden spoon. She pushes the dog aside so that he licks my hand instead, and tries to get under the bandages. "So," she says, "and after all this time."

I don't know if she means that I've finally awakened or that I've finally killed the lion.

"The catamount! The catamount!"

The way she looks at me. . . . Her eyes must seem strange to the people down here, they are the bleached blue of us mountain people (except for mine), but she looks at me as though *I* am the stranger. She says, "So you finally."

I think to tell her something of my love so I say, "I have feelings for more than just the Project."

She shakes her head, disgusted. She's still . . . even *still*, put out with me. Is there no gratefulness? From anyone? Lions can roam great distances, even in a single night, and they're not easy to kill. It not only takes skill, but also a willingness to end up with scratches and gashes, top to bottom. Our lioness may well have taken children from here also. All peoples will have profited from my daring.

"I have risked the killing of it."

"Did you know, all this time, your name isn't Harrier? Has never been? They've kept track of you down here. You're easily seen from halfway up. The large in you belongs to them. Look how this chair is large. Look at the bed. Look how even their pots and pans are large." She waves the spoon at me. "Here, look, a spoon as if for a giant."

"I have risked," I say and then I turn away. She turns away, too, and lets the dog lick my face again. At least the dog. At least him.

Time goes along here as there and I recover some. First I can do little more than sit outside, I and the dog, his big wide flatland head on my lap. It's just as I used to sit of an evening up home with a dog all the way on my lap. I sit and learn things of the Down. I hadn't thought there'd be so much noise down here. Even all night long, cows and horses, dogs running off barking at things yipping with high voices. We don't have coyotes up there.

Later I walk around and see things. There's both more and less mystery to it. I see how a plow works, how to yell out to cattle and yet keep them calm. "Curious as a cow," they say down here, and it's true, every time I hobble down their road, cows come to see what I'm about and then follow me.

The people call me Hosh. It has no relationship to any bird that I know of.

It seems Wren has become a sort of personage down here. I think because of her eyes and her size and that she's bleached all over and that her fingers are long and graceful. Since she has few skills besides knitting and cooking and looking out for goats, what other reason can there be? Her grace should be for my eyes and none other. Her hair also, for me only. Her cheeks. . . . (I saw that first man we met, he's called Boffin . . . I saw him touch her cheeks, one forefinger on each side of her face, as if he thought to measure her.)

(Why have they named me something without one of their endings on it, as Boffin, Duggan, Mawlin, and Algun? Is it to insult me? Do they laugh behind their hands at the shortness of my name every time they say it?) I'll not be brother to the likes of them who look at Wren the way they do.

So then I look at these women swishing around in their skirts (as Wren is swishing now also). They've fed me, spoonful by spoonful, washed me. . . . They have salves for my lacerations. They've been doing all the things, that Wren should have been doing. They even look at me as Wren looks at Boffin, but everything about them only reminds me of myself. Even their necks are as wide as my own. I could borrow their shoes.

Every day I wonder, where is Wren? When I see her in the distance, I always take her for one of their children at first, before I see it's her. There's always several men around her. I've killed the lion only for her.

There comes a day of bad weather. Thunder and lightning, off and on hail even, right here in the Down as if on the mountains. *Our* weather—they say so themselves—come all the way down here, just as our water does.

Rain is so rare everybody is out to see it and feel it protected only by their sun hats. Even I, though I've already seen more of it than I need to. Clouds roil. The light is as if twilight. We all stand outside looking toward the mountains.

And then, out from under thunderheads, *exactly* over the Project, only there, the weather suddenly clears. It's as if the Project had done it. There's only that one place with blue sky, and I see. . . . Yes, it is! The capstone *is* raised. *Perpen-*

*dicular!* Atop the eight holding stones. Around it, a circle of clear weather, as though caused by it. And why not? With that last boulder the Project is the highest of all the peaks surrounding it.

In my wildest speculations I hadn't thought such beauty. I'd thought: monumental, majestic, exalted even, but not this loveliness. And from down here, such delicacy. And with the sun on it, such sparkle. This will show my wife the importance of important things, and the need. What would the sky be without it? Just look at the faces of the people. And my wife, as wide-eyed as any of them.

"There!" I say, "That's what we mean. Look! That's what I've always meant. Can you say it wasn't worth it?"

Even so, wide-eyed as she is, and all glittery with the look of *our Project*. . . . Even so, she leans toward me and whispers, "But Sparrow."

"And I'm not there," I say. I know I sound as though I don't care about Sparrow. It's that I don't know what to say. What can I say? What should I answer? I say, "But I'm not even there."

She says, shouting, "Don't shout!"

Everybody looking up. Every single one of them—stunned at first, rain and tears flowing down their faces. Then the lightning lights their grins. They're saying, "Well, well, *well!*" and, "The little brothers of the Up have done it," and other things of that nature. They pat me on the back. Little pat, pat, pats. *Pats!* As if it hadn't taken years. Generations. As if it wasn't a grand and noble, even an impossible thing. Do they realize the Project will be there longer than their little lives? Do they know I was the foreman?

I limp away, I and the dog. I've done with them.

They have their arms around each other's shoulders. They're in a circle doing a skipping sort of dance, which, seeing how big they are, makes them look more ridiculous than ever.

(They'll be dancing up there, too, stamping, jumping, also in a circle, though not touching. There was a special beer saved for just this day.)

"Hosh," they say, and they open a space for me in their dance. "Little brother. Come."

To have more pats?

They say I'm not well enough to return, but I'm done with their over-watered fields (wasting *our* water), their slippery grass where even the horse skid and go down, let alone the people. On the mountain we have more dangerous dangers, but they're dangers more to my taste.

If, for instance, some night we should steal a horse and ride out, fast, through the long straight flat places. . . . (I have said to myself and long before, that I wouldn't return without Wren.)

I'll tell her I've loved her just as if she was the Project and for as long. Since she's finally seen it as it should be seen, she'll understand the importance of my love. How it sparkles. How it will last beyond either of us.

But she won't come. I know it ahead of time. Yet again she'll say, "What, *what!*"

I'll say, "I killed the lioness only for you."

She'll humpf.

(It's the dog will follow me as a wife should. Try to. He's old and arthritic. He likes somebody who limps. We'll be two of a kind.)

I'll say, you stay for the love of radishes the size of turnips, for chairs too big to sit on, for spoons that don't fit your mouth. I risked my life, I'll say. I say it, "I risked myself."

This is the beginning of everything that happens afterward. This and lightning, and hail, as it's falling now, big as walnuts. I look up straight into it. They've all run inside, even Wren, but I'm used to worse. I suppose they're afraid of ruining their hats. *Hats!* The meaning of the meaning of life, nor beauty either, has nothing to do with hats.

# LIZ LOCHHEAD

## The Man in the Comic Strip

*Scottish poet Liz Lochhead makes deft use of fantasy, horror, and fairy tale imagery in quite a number of her poems. Her collection* Dreaming Frankenstein *is particularly recommended to fantasy readers in this regard (particularly for the arch poem inspired by the magical ballad "Tam Lin").*

*A longtime resident of Glasgow, Lochhead is also acclaimed as a playwright, performer, and broadcaster. Her plays include* Mary Queen of Scots Got Her Head Chopped Off, Shanghaied, The Big Picture, *and* Perfect Days.

*Her poetry has been published in* Blood and Ice, Three Scottish Poets, *and other volumes. "The Man in the Comic Strip" first appeared in the Winter 2001 edition of* Poetry Review. *It is a pleasure to reprint Lochhead's wistful fantasia here.*

—T. W.

For the man in the comic strip
Things are not funny.
In the land of the unreadable signs
And ambiguous symbols
He exists between the hache and the ampersand
Between the ankh and the ziggurar
Between the fylfot and the fleur de lys
Between the cross and the crescent
Between the twinned sigrunes and the swastika and the *sauvastika*
Its mirror-image, its opposite (meaning darkness/light, whichever)
Under the flag with the crucially five
(Or six or seven) pointed star
Running whichever direction his pisspoor
Piston legs are facing
Getting nowhere fast.

If only he had the sense he was born with
He'd know there is a world of difference
Between the thinks bubble and the speech balloon
And when to keep it zipped, so, with a visible fastener—

But his mouth is always getting him into trouble.
Fistfights blossom round him.
There are flowers explode when the punches connect.
A good idea is a lightbulb, but too seldom.
When he curses, spirals
And asterisks and exclamation marks
Whizz around his head like his always palpable distress.
Fear comes off him like petals from a daisy.
Anger brings lightning down on his head and
Has him hopping.

Hunger fills the space around him
With floating ideograms of roasted chickens
And iced buns like maidens' breasts the way
The scent of money fills his eyes with dollar signs.

For him the heart is always a beating heart,
True love—
Always comically unrequired.
The unmistakable silhouette of his one-and-only
Will always be kissing another
Behind the shades at her window
And, down-at-the-mouth, he'll
Always have to watch it from the graphic
Lamplit street.

He never knows what is around the corner
Although we can see it coming.
When he is shocked his hair stands perfectly on end

But his scream is a total zero and he knows it.
Knows to beware of the zigzags of danger.
Knows how very different from
The beeline of zees that is a hostile horizontal buzzing
Of single-minded insects swarming after him
Are the gorgeous big haphazard zeds of sleep.

# SCOTT THOMAS

# Strange Things About Birds

*In "Strange Things about Birds," despite its brevity, the author paints a vivid, powerfully strange tale, proving that sometimes what's left unsaid can be as important as the rest of a conversation.*

*—E. D.*

### England, 1911

A little wine is good this time of night," the old woman said. "It quiets my nerves."

Wilkens looked up from his book and smiled politely. "Yes, I should think it would," the man said gently, turning his eyes back down.

The spinster Thacker held a glass of dark liquid up to her face and peered into it; the fireplace seeded it with beads of light, and reflected a false blush on her pallor.

"Did I tell you of my experiences with birds, Mr. Wilkens?" the woman asked.

Wilkens lowered his book. "No, I don't believe so . . ."

The old woman chuckled, squirming deeper into her wing chair. "Oh, it's late and I'm a bore; perhaps some other time . . ."

"No, please," Wilkens, a dignified looking gentleman of middle age, a new arrival at the bed and breakfast, leaned closer, "a story before bed is just the thing—this book is a bore, Miss Thacker."

The woman straightened, pleased, and set her wine glass down on a table.

"Well, birds are strange things, Mr. Wilkens, least in my experience; they've always come at odd times and done odd things. I recall as a babe hearing their morning chatter, outside my window. I don't have any recollection of human voices, mind you, but those piercing cacophonous bird noises have nested in my brain these many years. My cousin Edith once told me I was spouting bird-sounds long before uttering 'mummy' and 'daddy'."

The woman laughed, a trace of bitterness rasping in her throat. Mr. Wilkens smiled quizzically. "You don't say?"

"I learned to speak eventually, unfortunately. I tend to talk a bit much at times. It's the wine, I think."

"I don't mind, Miss Thacker."

"You're kind to say, dear. Once in Spring, I think, I was visiting my mother in hospital—poor thing was always in and out of the hospital in those days—and she took me up against her, intending to breast feed me. She was ever so warm and she opened her robe and this little beaked head poked out where there ought to have been a breast. A grackle, I think it was, and it snapped at my lower lip and took it off like that!"

The woman clicked the fingers of a gnarled hand.

"Then this head, with my lip hanging from its beak like a worm, retreated back into Mum's robe. I was bleeding something terrible and made a mess of the bedding, and Mum scolded me and claimed I'd bit her and the nurse came. But, as you can see, my mouth healed nicely."

The woman reached up to her lips, bruised with wine.

"Yes, I see." Wilkens muttered, eyeing her.

"Ahhh, I'm boring you. I should be off to bed. I'm a chatty old girl, Mr. Wilkens . . ."

"No, no. Please continue, good woman."

The storyteller sipped from her drink, closing her faded eyes, sitting back in her chair. Strands of white hair had fallen from her bun, like webs on her forehead.

"I hated birds entirely as a girl. They taunted me in the orchard down the road from our house and laughed at me in the school yard, and one night one flew into my bedroom window and I cried terribly until Daddy came and caught it. I told him to kill it, but he wouldn't. It was a queer sort of bird, greenish-grey and the room smelled like sage when it fluttered about, thumping into walls and rapping against the window glass before Daddy took it in his hands.

"My parents kept it in a box in the pantry. It had leaves for feathers, you see, and Mummy would pluck them to use in stews and stuffing when she cooked poultry. We were always eating birds then.

"My brother Kenneth, rest his soul, had a rather peculiar interest in birds. He used to draw them, but they were always featherless beasts, the way he depicted them, much like dinosaurs, I should think. He drew birds with breasts. Big breasts, pointy breasts, breasts like eggs and some with beaks rather than nipples. Every so often I'd spy him up in his room standing naked by his desk with a plucked goose atop, like it was an altar, and he'd be moving in and out of the carcass and caressing its clammy flesh. He did it to a turkey, too, slapping it like Daddy slapped me when I was naughty.

"Once I asked him what he was doing and he said he was helping Mum make the stuffing."

Wilkens quickly reversed his frown when the woman opened her eyes and gazed at him. He chuckled nervously. "The stuffing, you say?"

"Yes. I never eat stuffing any more, though—I rather lost my taste for it after that.

"There were even birds in church when I was growing up. Crows, and a raven with terrible black eyes, and a great beak, and claws. They tried to hide, of course, but I saw them in the shadows and I heard them whisper about me, and I feared them so.

"When I began to mature, I noticed a soft dark growth down about my privates, and ohhh, such horror gripped me. No one had ever told me that people grow hair down there, you understand, so I mistook it for feathers. Well, straightaway I cut it off and when it grew back I cut it again. Naturally my parents neglected to inform me that young women have their, you know, cycles and all. So when I began to bleed I was quite beside myself. Heavens, I thought, a bird must have stolen inside me! So I went to the priest and he said he would look to see if a bird had indeed made a nest of me. He lifted up my skirt and then his black robe and a raven was there and it pecked and pecked and I screamed until he held his hand over my mouth."

Several moments passed before Wilkens found his voice. "How horrible for you."

The woman nodded, clutching her glass of wine in her lap, staring into its purple depths.

"Birds are strange creatures, Mr. Wilkens. Very intelligent, too. One Summer after Mummy died, we went on holiday and stayed at a cottage not far from the sea, and I was afraid to go out, because I had grown breasts, you see, and the gulls would stare at them when I was on the beach. So I stayed inside as much as possible, and I made certain that the windows in my room were closed and locked and the door too and only Daddy had a key, besides the one underneath my pillow.

"Wouldn't you know, those gulls got in my room somehow, a flock of them fluttering about my bed, and they took away my covers and ripped my sleeping gown to pieces and put their white wings all over me, like great hands, and I grabbed a candleholder from the bed stand and went to beat them off, and there was blood splashing about and the gulls were screaming . . ."

Wilkens flinched when the wine glass struck the floor, spilling. He leapt up from his seat and went to fetch a damp towel. He knelt by the old woman's chair, dabbing at the stain.

"When the screaming stopped," spinster Thacker said, "I saw Daddy across the bottom of my bed, and he was a mess with blood. He had chased the gulls away, but they had killed him."

Wilkens looked up and his face was sad. "Poor thing," he muttered.

"Daddy had chased them off, those nasty gulls, but he was dead. So they took me to a special place where I was safe. Ahh, but it's late and here I am going on and on about silly birds, my poor Mr. Wilkens, and you must be ever so tired."

"Tired in good company, dear woman," Wilkens said, and he saw her to her room.

"How was your stay?" Judith asked as they motored south from the rail station.

Wilkens smiled gently at his wife and put a hand on hers.

"It was quite nice," he said, but he seemed distant, she thought.

Wilkens gazed about as they drove through the village, taking in the school with birds pecking about the yard, and the church where birds perched amidst shadowy outcrops of brick and he looked at birds dotting along the telegraph wires. He felt something sad move through him, observing the buildings and the scurrying vehicles and the people of the Earth, and he felt a tenderness for the wild things, winged and otherwise.

"Innocent creatures," he mumbled to himself.

"What's that?" Judith asked.

"Nothing," Wilkens said.

# KATHE KOJA AND BARRY N. MALZBERG

# What We Did That Summer

Barry N. Malzberg is the author of about thirty science fiction novels, a dozen collections of science fiction short stories, and one book of essays (Engines of the Night).

His most recent novel, The Remaking of Sigmund Freud, was published in 1985, although there were about 100 short stories in the period between 1988 and 1993—only a few short stories in the years since then, but he hopes to be a little more productive in the years ahead. He has done about twenty-five stories in collaboration with Kathe Koja, five to ten of which he feels to be the best work with which he has ever been involved.

To which, Kathe Koja adds "Amen." Solo, Kathe Koja is the author of Extremities, a short fiction collection, and various novels. Her latest novel is Straydog.

"What We Did That Summer" straddles the genres of science fiction and horror. It was originally published in the anthology Redshift.

—E. D.

Boy, I sure miss those aliens, he said.

What? She had to put down her beer for that one but there was nothing stronger than amusement now; she was not surprised; it was not possible any longer to surprise her. Say that again, she said, leaning into the metal ladderback of the kitchen chair, the one with the crooked leg that when it moved scraped that red linoleum with the textbook sound of discontent. Say it again and then explain it.

Nothing to explain, he said, I just miss them. We called them aliens, those girls, it was our word for them, they would have done anything. Anything, you wouldn't believe, he said, nodding and nodding in that way he had. Not for money, you know, they didn't want money or presents, whatever. It was like a contest they were having between themselves. Almost like we weren't there at all, he said, and sighed, scratched himself in memory as she watched without contempt, watched all this from some secret part of herself that was not a failed madam, not a woman whom he had once paid, regularly though never well, to fuck; not a woman whose home now permitted no yielding surface whatsoever, nothing soft or warm or pleasant to the touch, no plush sofas and certainly no beds; she herself slept on a cot like a board and ate macaroni and cheese and potpies that she bought at the supermarket when they were on sale. Tell me, she said. Tell me about those aliens, why not. Let me get another beer first, though.

Get one for me, too, he said, and scratched again; there was an annoying dry patch between his legs, just behind the dangle of his scrotum, not an easy place to scratch in public but at her place, well. Well well well. It had never mattered what he did here, not in the old days, the brisk wild days in which she had absorbed without delight the greater part of his pay, or that strange hallucinatory period in which he had decided he was into S&M and she had proved so thoroughly and with such élan that he was not; not during his divorce from Deborah and the unraveling that followed, and the rewinding of the skein which followed *that*; she was in some ways the best friend he had ever had, and it was for that reason he suspected without knowing or caring to admit that he had begun to tell her this story, this night, in this comfortless kitchen with its piles of old yellow pages and its warped unclosable window presenting its endless, disheartening view of the faraway river and all points east.

All right, she said, setting down both cans of beer; they did not use glasses; glasses were both effete and a bother with beer like this. Go on, tell me. So they fucked your heads off, you and your gang, those dumb boys you ran with, and they never took your dollar bills or the flowers you picked yourselves. Queen Anne's lace, am I right, from the side of the road? past the beer cans in the ditches? Or the candy you bought from the drugstore, three Hershey bars for them to split? What charity, she said, laughing although not directly at him or even the boy he had been. What princes, she said, what royalty you must have been.

If you're going to make fun, he said, subtly ashamed at the sound of his own petulance but unwilling to correct it, I won't tell the story.

Oh yes you will, she said, not laughing now but smiling. Of course you will. Go on ahead and tell it, I won't laugh. Much.

All right then, he said, and scratched again, but thus invited was somehow at a loss for a true beginning: he drank some of the beer, set down the can. Well, he said. You remember John Regard?

John Regard, she said. I remember he was an asshole, yes.

Well, think what you want, but he was a good friend to me, he used to let me borrow his car, that black-and-yellow Barracuda. Remember that?

No, she said; they both knew she was lying. If there's going to be a lot about John Regard in this story, I don't think I want to hear it after all.

Oh, just shut up, he said, and listen. Anyway, it was John who found them, out in the field that night; it was behind where the factories used to be, all those tool-and-die places. We were drinking beer, but we weren't drunk, stopping the narrative there, pointing with the hand holding the can; neither of them if they noticed remarked on this irony. We were not drunk and I want you to remember that.

I will, she said.

Anyway, John said he heard voices or saw a flashlight or something, and we headed over there, and we found these girls and they were naked. Three of them, bare-ass naked.

She scraped the chair leg a little, leaning with all her weight. What were they doing? she said.

Nothing, I don't know. Even from this distance, time and age, and geography she saw his wistfulness, the depth and slow passion of his wonder. They were just sitting there, he said, talking. And John said—

I know what John said. Meat on the hoof, that's what John—

Will you quit? he said, with a sudden sad ferocity that silenced them both; they sat in the silence as in the middle of a large and formal room and finally he said, Just let me tell it, all right? Just let me tell the fucking thing and get it over with, and then you can say whatever the hell you want. All right? Is that all right with you, milady?

Yes, she said. Yes, it's fine. Go on.

Well. Not sullen but disturbed, as if he had lost his place in chronology itself and would take his own time finding it. Well, anyway, he said. They were sitting there naked and John said (daring her with a look to mock) Do you ladies need some help? And they didn't say anything at first but finally they did, one of them, she seemed like the oldest or the smartest or something, and she said, in this way that was like an accent but not really an accent, you know what I mean? Like the person is from somewhere but you can't place where. And she said We're having a bet. That's what she said. We're having a bet and we can't decide who's right.

And John said (leaning back a little as if back in the field, taking his time, measuring his place) Well what's the bet? Now you have to remember we were both kids, then, you know, we were sixteen or so, and we both had pretty good rods on, looking at these naked girls there in the dirt and the weeds and so on. They weren't really beautiful girls, they were kind of a little fat or out of shape— what's the word? misshapen? Is that a word?—but they were definitely girls and they were naked girls and that was good enough for us. So John said What's your bet, and they said We are trying to bet which one of us can have the most boys.

It was very still in the kitchen; she did not say anything though he thought she would, until the silence told him that she was not going to comment on this and so Well, he said. That was all we needed to hear and, well, John said you can start with me, ladies, and so there we were. Us and those three girls.

She still did not say anything until she saw that he would not continue without some kind of comment or response from her, something to keep the story moving like rollers under a ponderous piano, or someone's obese and terrible aunt. Well, she said. There you were, like you say. I can guess what happened next. Then what?

Well that was the thing, he said. After we were done and getting dressed I asked them their names, you know, and they wouldn't tell us, not like they were shy or something but as if they weren't sure what we wanted. And so they wouldn't say anything and finally I left.

You? she said. What happened to John?

He was, he had to go piss or something. I don't remember, crossly. Anyway that was it for that night but the next night we went out there, you know, again (in that field with its weeds and chunked metal, scrap and dirt and the oily smell of the tool-and-die shops, its moonlessness and its absence of mystery) and there they were. Only this time only one of them was naked and the other two were wearing these dresses, weird dresses, you know, like old ladies or something would wear. And the smart one said She doesn't want to make a baby, about the naked one, you know? She doesn't want to make a baby so do something different this time.

Well, she said, and could not help smiling; and he smiled, too, and they both laughed a little, a laugh not wholly comfortable but without true embarrassment, and she said Get me another beer, will you? and he did. So anyway, he said. We did it all different ways with that girl, and the other two sat in their old-lady dresses and watched us like they were kids in school and never said a word or made any sound at all. Just sat there in the dirt and watched us do their sister, you know, until we were tired.

How long did that take? she said.

A lot longer than it does now, he said, and she smiled, and he did, too. So they talked to each other in little voices and John said How about tomorrow? and they said no, not tomorrow but that they would see us soon. And then we left.

So what happened then? she said. Incidentally, you're going to knock that beer over if you keep—

I see it, it's okay. So we went back anyway (and from his face she could see he was less present in the kitchen than in that midnight field, picking his way with lust and hope through the clutter and debris, searching for three misshapen naked girls who would perform with him acts he had never dreamed of suggesting, who would do whatever he asked for as long as he could without demanding recompense or return; it was some men's idea of heaven, she knew) but they weren't there. We waited around and waited around and they didn't show and so finally we left. And John went back the next night and—

John did? What about you?

I didn't have a car, he said shortly; they both knew what that meant and neither remarked on it, John's well-known selfishness and duplicity, John sneaking back alone in the yellow-and-black Barracuda to have them all for himself. Anyway, he said, John went back but he didn't find them, and so we figured maybe they were gone for good. But then one night about two weeks later they came back. It was raining, we had to do it in the car. John was in back—

With two of them, she said.

Yes. With two of them. You want to tell my story or should I? (But it was mere rote irritation, only physical pain could have stopped this story now; it was like the last drive to orgasm, you needed a baseball bat and room to swing it if you wanted to make it stop.) So I was up front with the other one, and it rained and rained, water like crazy down the windshield and the windows. And every once in a while I would try to get her to drink some beer, you know, but she never would, she said she didn't want any. And we kept at it all night, it was about four o'clock when finally they said they would see us later and they got out of the car and walked away in the rain, the three of them side by side like they were in a marching band or something, they kept walking until I couldn't see them anymore.

And then what? she said, imagining him sore and drunk and triumphant, prince in a circus of carnality and stretched imagination, after fucking and sucking and dog-style and what have you, what else is there, what else is left for a sixteen-year-old boy who has not yet perfected the angles and declensions of true desire? Even with her, as a man both matured and stunted by the pressure of his needs, there had come a limiting and it had come from him. Then what happened? she said again, but gently, to lead and not to prod.

He did not answer at first; he seemed not to have heard her. Then he sighed and drank the rest of the beer in the can, one melancholy swallow. Well, he said. I was all for finding out their names and where they lived and so on and so on, but John said they were probably foreigners and their fathers would shoot our heads off or cut off our balls or something if we tried. So all we did was go back to the field, and sit there, and wait.

And did they come back? she said.

Well, he said, that's the interesting part. One of the interesting parts, I guess. They did and they didn't. What I mean is that the next night out in the field we waited and waited until we had got past the point where the beer meant anything, you know that kind of drunk where every new one just seems to bring you down, make you less drunk and sadder? We sat there in the field drinking and talking about pussy and what the aliens had been like and all the time the sky seemed to be lightening up like dawn except that it wasn't near morning and we weren't getting anywhere at all. The fucking had seemed good at first but the longer we talked and waited the sadder it got until I had a whole new look on the situation: we were a couple of sixteen-year-old kids humping these naked girls who didn't know any better and in a way, when you looked at it, it could have been maybe even rape. Like they were feeble-minded or something or just out from an institution, they sure didn't act normal. How the hell did we know? How did we know? he said with a shudder, looking now as if the field in memory had become a bleak and dangerous place, a place of pain and not of happiness; and she looked at him not for the first time in a way that went past his old face, his sunken shoulders, his dumb, dragging features, and she thought You took his money and let him climb on top of you, and then you didn't want to feel like a whore anymore, so you stopped taking his money and then sooner or later you stopped taking him and what the hell was that, now? What did that come to? Are you happy now? Never mind him: what about you?

Well, he said, the sluice of beer problematic down his throat, he swallowed as if it were his own trapped saliva, as if it was something he needed but did not want. Well just about four in the morning or something like that, John and I were so drunk and so sick we were ready to give up and go home and then all of a sudden this guy comes out of the bushes, a tall thin guy as naked as the girls had been except for this big hat he was wearing and something around his neck like a medal or a badge, it was hard to tell in the light. But he was naked as hell and I just want to tell you this part, you can believe it or not, but he didn't have any cock or balls. He had nothing in that place, just smoothness, and he was about the scariest fellow we had ever seen, drunk or sober, because of that empty place there and a look in his eyes which even then we could tell. You're the ones, aren't you? he said to John and me, the same way the girls talked, that foreigner-talk, only from him it was mean. You're the ones they've been doing it with.

We looked at him, and there was nothing to say. I mean, what could we say? Yes, we were doing it? Doing what? While we were trying to figure that one out he made a motion and the girls were there, except this time they weren't naked. They must have come from the bushes, too, but it was hard to tell. Maybe they dropped from the sky. You got to understand, we were so drunk by now and the whole situation was so peculiar that we couldn't get a handle on it. You follow me? But those girls were chittering away and poking each other like animals and then they pointed at me and John, raised their fingers and just pointed them down. We felt pretty damned foolish, I want you to know, and scared, too; here's some guy without a cock and balls and three girls pointing at you, it would scare anybody. Even you, he said.

She said nothing. The beer in the can had gone flat, but she did not move, to drink it, to replace it. The refrigerator buzzed and buzzed like a large and sorry insect trapped in a greasy jar.

Maybe it wouldn't scare you, he said. Who knows what scares you, anyway, but it sure scared us. No one said anything for a minute, and then I said, All right. All right, I said, we did it. They wanted us to, John said, and you can say what you want about John, but that was a brave thing to say, in that field at that moment, to that guy. They wanted us to, he said, and they asked for everything and if they tell you different, it's a lie. We gave them whatever they wanted, and if you got any quarrel, take it up with them.

I don't have a quarrel, the guy said, I only want facts. The girls were still chittering, and I could see that John was starting to shake, but I have to tell you that for me it was different. I might've been more scared than any of them, but whether it was the beer or not, I just didn't give a damn. I mean, it looked like some kind of farmer's daughter scam, you know what I mean? Like he was going to charge us for having devirginated his precious daughters and who the hell was he, anyway, and where was he when they were being fucked? All right, I said, John's right. We did it because they begged for it and wanted it worse than us and that's all there is to it. You got any problems you take it up with them.

I already have, the guy said, and made a motion, and the three girls turned around and moved away from there. That's already been achieved, the guy said. Now it comes to you. You've done this and you're going to have to pay. That's all. This is what they call the iron law of the universe, and you are caught up in it.

A pause less silence than memory's clench, he was so far back in that night it was as if she spoke to two people, man and boy and neither truly listening. Why are you telling me this now? she said. You never told me any of this all these years. I lay under you for ten years and you treated me like shit and then you left and now you tell me this story? I don't understand you, she said. I never understood you, realizing as she said this that it was only part of the truth: the real thing was that she had never understood anything. So why do you come back to tell me this now? she said. You were sixteen, you and John, that was, what, twenty-five, thirty years ago? What does this have to do with anything?

Maybe you should just get out of here, take your ass down the hollow and split. I never liked it, she said, leaning slightly toward him, her elbows on the table as if she sighted him down the barrel of some strange and heinous gun. I have to tell you that now. You tell me about aliens? You're an alien. You never made me feel like a woman, you never made me feel anything at all except bad. I felt like a cornhole, is that what you call it? A gloryhole? A place to stick it into until it made come and you yelped, that was a hell of a thing. I don't like you much for that.

Well, he said, wincing, staring at her, dragged at least halfway back from the field. Well, now, I don't like that either. I'm almost finished now, why don't you let me finish? I got started so let me finish and shut your mouth. All right? She said nothing. Well, he said, in such a way that made her wonder if he had heard more than every third word she had said, well this guy says again You have to pay. That is the first and only law of the universe, of time and density. If you do something you pay for it but you pay double and if you don't understand what you were doing, well then it is triple. Here you are now, the guy said, you pay triple. Three times. Then he made some kind of motion like he was shooing us off, and the next thing I knew the field was on fire. It was fire outside like the fucking had been fire inside and everything was scorched black and then he was gone. That was the end of it—girls, guy without a cock, the whole thing. They never came back again. John was standing in the same place when the fire went out and looked about the same, but who knows, inside and outside, who can tell? He had nothing to say and I had nothing to say either. You have to pay, the guy said, that was the deal. So we had to pay, that was all.

So then what? she said.

So nothing, he said. We left the field and that was the end of it for thirty years. It's thirty years tonight, you want to know, he said. So it's an anniversary. I'm telling you on the anniversary. That was a decision John and I made, that with what we knew and what had happened we'd wait twenty-five years and then tell. Maybe that sounds dumb, but there's a lot of dumb stuff around. The whole thing, I figure, was pretty much dumb from the start; that's another iron law of the universe.

Twenty-five years, she said, or thirty? Make up your mind.

It's thirty tonight, he said.

So what's the point? she said. Are you going to tell me that John died and now you're going to? Is that the payoff, that on the thirtieth anniversary of the guy without a cock telling you you had to pay, you cash in? That's a bunch of crap, she said. You were always full of crap. In bed, out of bed, you told more lies than any man I ever knew. Enough, she said, and stood, picked up the beer cans. I've heard enough for now. You're not getting any ever again, anniversary or no anniversary, cock or no cock. Just go home.

John didn't die just now, he said. He was staring up at her without any true expression, as if his features could not form the picture his mind wanted to show. John died a long time ago, six, seven years, he got hit by a bus. In Fayetteville. I thought you knew that, didn't you know that?

No, she said, I didn't know. I don't keep up with things so good anymore, I live in a shack and try to stay away from all of that stuff. I was never much for news. So John is dead, all right. And where does that leave you?

The iron law, he said, I had to tell you about that because of the anniversary. I would have told John, we would have told each other but he was dead, he got the bus up his behind first and there was nobody to tell. Maybe he took the bus up his behind, who knows? Look at me, he said. He reached for her, touched her face, dragged her face to attention. Do you see me? he said. Do you know what I got? Do you know what really went on there in that field, what it came to?

Crazy, she thought, he was crazy like the rest of them, they'd tell you one thing, anything to get inside you and then they'd yank that one gob of come out, barking and moaning and then go back to being cute until the next time. Except that this one had always been crazy, with his cowboy boots and his bondage stories and his divorce from Deborah, always mooning around, it was different for him, she knew, an entirely different thing.

They let us do everything, he said. Everything we wanted. But everything means everything, it means all of it, do you understand? He seemed very sad, as if he might begin to curse or cry. Like you used to be, he said. Just like you.

I never was, she said, simply, without heat or cruelty. I never was anything you wanted, don't you know that? Don't you know that by now?

You take, he said, you take and take and take and then it's all inside you and you have to give it back. I'm not talking about one squirt, he said, not jism. This is something else.

Take and take, so what else is new? she said. Just don't give it to me. The beer cans were still in her hands; her hands were sweating. I don't want it. Don't you give it to me. She felt if she looked too closely at him she would see inside his skull, see his brain, the soft and desperate jelly within the cage: see the memories and thoughts, foaming, dead foam like scum on the water, polluted scum at the beach that burns your ankles when you walk too close, burns your skin like the field, burning, burning.

So now we have to give it back, he said. John's dead. If you take, you give, if you give you take. His breathing was ragged, uneven; I want to show you, he said through that breathing like a gag against his mouth, like gauze. I want you to see what I mean. What I got.

I don't want to see anything, she said, get out of here now, but it was too late, he was pulling at his pants, pulling at himself and for one moment she thought in simple terror: *They took it*, it's all gone, it's all going to be smooth there like the guy in the story but it was not smooth, it was a general circulation cock and balls just like she remembered except somewhat looser and wrinkled, half-erect there in his hand, his hand was shaking as if in some vast vibration. As if his body existed in some other room than this.

What comes out, he said, breathing, shaking. You have to see. I want you to see this thing. It was not spunk of which he was speaking, he had warned her of that, and she knew it was true. Take and take, he said, give and give. Give and take. He was getting it harder, the cock springing straight; in the empty place where the aliens had marked him the iron law was working, clamping, squeezing as his hand squeezed, as he wheezed and breathed, as he lazed and hazed, as he shook and took. She backed against the sink, turned her face away. His breath in crescendo, the refrigerator buzz, her own heart; oh, boy, you have to see this, he said. Turn around and look at this.

She said nothing.

Turn around and look, he said. Look at me.

The cracked edge of the counter pressed her belly, her hip. Around her the field was burning; the air was filled with the smell of scorching grass. Awaiting landfall, awaiting the impact of metal on earth she put up one alien hand to shield her face from the sight of him, from the worst of what was to come: the mounting boys, their simple, screaming, wondering faces, the stink of grass, the fiery closure of her thighs: all their detritus poured into her cup of reparation. Alien she fell, alien she waited: alien the great locks of the ship slammed open. In that riveting metal clutch: nothing. The clinging contact, the groans of the boys. The heart in his hand: but nothing.

# RYAN G. VAN CLEAVE

## Aesculapius in the Underworld

*Ryan G. Van Cleave is a poet and freelance photojournalist originally from Chicago. He has published eleven books, including* Like Thunder: Poets Respond to Violence in America, American Diaspora: Poetry of Displacement, *and* Say Hello. *His work has appeared in a number of venues including* Arts & Letters, Ploughshares, TriQuarterly, The Antioch Review, Wicked Mystic, Fantasy Magazine, Little Green Men, *and* Cabal Asylum. *The poem that follows is reprinted from the May 2001 edition of* Poem, *a biannual journal published in Huntsville, Alabama.*

*In classical myth, Aesculapius was the son of Apollo and the god of medicine. He became such a gifted healer that he was able to restore the dead to life. This angered Pluto, lord of the Realm of the Dead, who urged Zeus to destroy him. After his death, Aesculapius was placed among the stars.*

—T. W.

Tonight, on the deck of Charon's death-barge,
Aesculapius sees a woman he once danced
with under the moonlight in bluish sea-surge
of the Mediterranean—this is a story the
loremasters swear is true—he puts his hands
to hers, cold as a long-buried fossil, and the
whorls of their fingerprints merge as her body
tells him, in Braille, via osmosis, how to unknit
the hurts that took her breath, her sense of touch.
The sinew of flesh, the dark resonance of bone
sings to him, a wind of answers sluicing through
ruined apple trees, jack pines, every secret to
the mending of mortality and beyond; death isn't
a barrier, the stop-and-shift-into-reverse cry that
it is for others. Her wrist will burn for a month,

but she shudders then awakens, her golden eyelids
moving fast as the bark of Cerberus at the bone-and-mortar
gate jar her truly awake, aware of one more chance,
the opportunity to throw the past like a half-empty sack
into the back of a wagon going the opposite direction;
smaller and moving out of sight, her old life, her old ways.
She plants a kiss soft on Aesculapius' parchment-thin cheek,
then swims for the far shore, where the long reeds
wave darkly in the breeze, goodbye, goodbye.

# GREGORY MAGUIRE

# Scarecrow

*Gregory Maguire is the author of the bestselling novels* Wicked: The Life and Times of the Wicked Witch of the West *(inspired by L. Frank Baum's "Oz" books) and* Confessions of an Ugly Stepsister *(a literary reworking of Cinderella). His most recent novel,* Lost, *is a terrific ghost tale involving Charles Dickens and Jack the Ripper. In addition to these books for adults, he has also published many books for children (such as the popular "Hamlet Chronicles" series), as well as short stories and poetry. Maguire teaches creative writing, lectures as a critic of children's literature across America, and has served as artist-in-residence at the Blue Mountain Center, the Isabella Stewart Gardner Museum, and the Hambidge Center. He lives in Concord, Massachusetts.*

*"Scarecrow" is a wickedly clever tale rooted in classic American fantasy. It comes from* Half-Human, *a young-adult anthology edited by Bruce Coville (Scholastic).*

—T. W.

What's the first thing you know in life? Even before you know words? Sun in the sky. Heart of gold in a field of blue, and the world cracks open. You are knowing something. There you are.

As with all of us, the Scarecrow awoke knowing he had *been* for some time already, though unwoken. There was a sense of vanishing splendor in the world about him, an echo of a lost sound even before he knew what *sound* or *echo* meant. The backward crush of time and, also, time's forward rush. The knife of light between his eyes. The wound of hollowness behind his forehead. There was motion, sound, color; there was scent, depth, hope. There was already, in the first fifteen seconds, *then* and *now*.

Before him were two fields. One was filled with ripening corn. The other was shorn clean, and grew only a gallows tree in the dead center.

Beyond the fields huddled a low farmhouse, painted blue. And beyond the farmhouse rose a hill, also painted blue, or was that just the color of shadow when the cloud passed over?

A tribe of Crows sank from a point too high above for the Scarecrow to see or imagine. Their voices brayed insult at him as they fell to the field, ears of green-husked sweetcorn breaking beneath their attack. "Hey, there," cried the Scarecrow, "well then!" More instinct than anything else, and not to frighten them away, necessarily. More to announce his notice of them. But they were startled, and wheeled around, and disappeared.

Who am I? he said to himself, and then he said it aloud. The sky refused to answer, as did the corn, the wind, the light—or if they were answering, he couldn't understand the language.

The Crows returned to blot the field before him. With weapons of beak and claw and mighty wing, they beat at the corn, feasting.

"Welcome!" called the Scarecrow.

They laughed at him.

One Crow flew nearer. She seemed less interested in the corn than the others. She wore a rhinestone necklace. Her wings were infested with fleas and her eyes, he noticed, rheumy. She was an old Crow and not in the best of health.

"What's wrong with you? You're supposed to scare us," she said.

"Oh, I didn't realize."

She waggled her head. "Brainless fool."

"Brainless? What do you mean?" he said.

"Think about it. Brainless. No brain."

"How can I think about it if I haven't got a brain?" he murmured.

"You haven't got a brain, haven't got a clue, so you haven't got a chance to keep us from the corn. You're supposed to be *protecting the corn*."

Was she being kind, in telling him his life's work, or was she taunting him for being so stupid? She flew nearer, though her cousins were ambushing the ranks of corn with fiercer strength than ever. The Scarecrow wondered if she was too old to attack the corn as fiercely as her kin. Or was she too old to be that hungry? Maybe she just preferred gossip to gluttony.

"Most creatures who can talk can figure out a little," she said. "What's your problem, brother, that you're so dim-witted?"

"My arms hurt. Maybe if they didn't hurt I would be able to think. I need to be able to think. How did I get here?" he said. "At least tell me that."

The Crow hopped onto a fence rail nearby and settled her head at an angle. She looked at him with one black eye, bright as the back of a beetle. "This is my field, I live here," she said, "I notice what goes on. But where to start?"

"The beginning," begged the Scarecrow.

"A farmer sowed a field not far away, some time ago, and from the seeds he scattered there grew a great lot of hay. Every day he watched the rain water it, and the sun nourish it, and he kept the Cows from tramping it down. It grew up bright as a field of bronzy-green swords. He was proud of that field of hay! And just before the rains at the end of summer, his heart bursting with pride, the farmer swept along the field with a huge scythe, and cut the hay to the ground."

The Scarecrow gasped. "He killed it!"

"We call it harvest," said the Crow, "but it looks mighty like killing, I agree. Anyway, the hay lay in fine thick patterns across the field. The farmer picked it up with a fork and loaded it onto a wagon. Later he bound it with twine, and stored the bales in a barn. Most of it he fed to his Cows."

"Cannibals!" snorted the Scarecrow. "He sacrificed his field for the Cows!"

"We call it farming," said the Crow. "And hay cannot talk or think like you and me. But will you pay attention? Sometimes farmers stuff some of their hay into a pair of trousers and a bright red shirt. Then a farmer might put some more into an old farm sack, and paint a face upon it. A farmer could set the sack upon the neck of the shirt, and tie it together with a moldy bit of rope good for little else."

"And then what?" said the Scarecrow.

"Well, that's you," said the Crow.

"Hay and straw and some moldy rope and some secondhand clothes? That's all I am?" said the Scarecrow. "The farmer made me? Did he teach me to talk, did he sing me to sleep, did he bless my forehead? But where did the clothes come from?"

"I don't know if the farmer made you," said the Crow, cagily, hiding something. "But he intended to, as he had set aside enough hay for your limbs, and he had chosen the sack and painted your face upon it. And those are his clothes, anyway, so in a sense he is your father."

"Didn't he need them?" asked the Scarecrow.

"No," said the Crow. "Not after a while. Before he could finish you, he fell sick. I suppose he must have died. No man needs his clothes after he's died."

"What does *after* mean?" said the Scarecrow, who was too new to understand befores and afters.

"It means the *next* that follows the *now*, or the *now* that follows the *once*."

"I wish I had a brain," said the Scarecrow. "I understand a man falling sick and dying, but I do not understand befores and afters."

"The last time I laid eyes on him, I was perched on his windowsill, being nosy. I saw him tossing and turning with a fever. It seemed bad. I know he must have died, for if he had not, he would be running to berate you for letting us Crows eat all the corn. But he is dead, and you are all alone. That's too bad, but it can't be helped. I suppose his farmer neighbors took the clothes off his dead body and finished dressing you, and set you on your stake to do the job you were made to do. Too bad you can't do it very well. And now I will stop chatting and go eat some corn myself." Off she flew, in a fluttery, palsied manner, her jewelry flashing in the sun like splashes of fountain. The Scarecrow could see that she had been waiting to peck at ears of corn already cut open by the stronger crows.

"Stop," called the Scarecrow, "stop!" He did not mean for her to stop eating the corn, for he did not care. He meant to stop her from leaving. But she didn't listen.

The Crows made a mess of the cornfield. The Scarecrow knew that the old Crow must have been telling the truth, for no farmer came running from the nearby house to scold him for the damage. But even more damage lay in store. The next day the sky turned hugely purple. Mountainous clouds swept over, dragging along the ground a smoky funnel of wind. The remaining stalks were flattened. When the Crows returned, they had to settle their spiky pronged feet in the complicated floor of leaves and stalks, and hunt with lowered heads for what corn could still be found.

"Stop," cried the Scarecrow, "look out! Beware!" But he was not trying to protect the corn. He had seen a different danger approaching his friend the Crow. Her hearing was not what it once must have been so she wasn't aware. Her head was down, hunched in her collar of fine glints, digging for an especially rich ear of corn. From a hump of green rubble launched a missile of red fur and black leather boots, and teeth as sharp as the points of rhinestones. Sharper even. The other Crows escaped in an explosion of noisy wings and terrified cries, but the old Crow was too slow. She fell beneath clever paws and hungry jaws, and the jewelry made a bright exclamation mark in the air before it dropped to the ground.

"Yum," said the Fox, after he had finished his meal. "Yes, she was good. But I feel like a little something more." He tried his teeth on the necklace, but it did not appeal to his taste. So the Fox stood up in his black leather boots, and though he could see farther than he would have had the corn not fallen in the wind, he still could not find a suitable sweet morsel to finish his meal. "Straw-head," said the Fox, "you are higher than I. Can you see anything sweet for me to go after?" He licked his chops.

"What do you mean, *after*?" said the Scarecrow, a bit wary, but still curious.

"After?" said the Fox. "*After*? After means *toward*. I go after the Crow, and I get her. I go after my Vixen, and I get her. I go after what I want. What do you want?"

"To understand," said the Scarecrow, sighing.

"Ah, knowledge is sweet, too," said the Fox. He resigned himself to conversation rather than dessert, and he circled himself into a coil of Fox, where he could see how his hind legs ended so magnificently in black leather boots. He settled his bush over himself like a blanket. Then he put his chin upon his front paws and looked up at the Scarecrow. His eyes began to close.

"It seems a brutal world," said the Scarecrow.

"Doesn't it though," said the Fox appreciatively.

"You speak as if you know me," said the Scarecrow.

"I believe I know your clothes," said the Fox. "I recognize them. Your clothes make you seem quite familiar. I am happy not to be running from the farmer who used to wear them. When he would see me in his henhouse he would run for a weapon. But now the clothes have survived the man, for he must be dead. Otherwise he would be out here harvesting what is left of his flattened crop of corn. I notice that his clothes are capable of nothing more than housing straw— rather chatty straw, to my surprise, but straw nonetheless."

"He died of a terrible illness, I hear," said the Scarecrow.

"Is that so? Not what I heard." The Fox purred softly at the thought of treachery. "In all likelihood he died over there on the gallows tree. He was to be hung by the neck until he was dead," said the Fox. "The farmer's friendly neighbors intended to break his neck just as I broke the neck of Madame Crow a few minutes ago."

"But why?" said the Scarecrow, alarmed.

"Before you were born, the farmer had gone off to another village to buy some seedcorn," said the Fox. "When he came back he fell deeply ill. Folks round here are afraid of the plague, and none of them would tend him. He tossed and turned in a raging fever. But somehow he survived, and believed himself to be recovered. He went to the well in the center of the village and greeted all his neighbors—thought somewhat coldly. I'll wager, since they had not come to his help. Then a terrible misfortune occurred. Within days the villagers he met succumbed to fevers and fits, and some of them died. The ones who survived blamed him for the outbreak of sickness. They went after him."

"After him," said the Scarecrow, trying hard to understand.

"They said he had caused the death of their loved ones," said the Fox. "They said he had infected them on purpose, so that other families would not have the help to bring in their corn, and he alone would prosper with a good crop. They came after him with pitchforks and accusations. The farmer was not yet well enough to run away with any speed. They caught him in the middle of the corn. I saw them trap him; I was hiding in the weevily shadows, watching. They went to hang him, much as you are hung there on your stake. I would have stayed to watch the execution, but a sudden summer storm came up, and I fled to my hole. But I suppose they did their job and gave him his death."

"Did he not ask for their charity?" said the Scarecrow.

"Oh, anyone can ask," said the Fox. "No doubt the Crow would have asked for my charity if she'd been able to squeeze breath through her gullet. But charity doesn't satisfy the stomach, does it?"

The Scarecrow didn't know. He tried to close his eyes to squeeze out the sight of the gallows tree in the next field over, but his eyes were painted open. He tried not to listen to the Fox, but his ears were painted open. He tried to still the beating in his chest, but he couldn't; this was because a family of Mice had discovered the Scarecrow and were exploring him as a possible home. It was both uncomfortable and slightly embarrassing to have Mice capering about inside his clothes.

"I suggest you should look for lodging elsewhere," said the Scarecrow in as low a voice as he could manage, "for there is a Fox nearby who likes to go after small creatures."

The Mice took heed and removed themselves to a safer neighborhood. The Fox, nearly asleep, began to laugh softly. "Charity is so appealing in the young," he said. Soon thereafter he began to snore.

The Scarecrow had no choice but to look at the farmhouse, the fields, the gallows tree, the hill beyond them all. The world seemed a bitter place, arranged just so: fields, gallows, house, and hill.

Then around the edge of the hill came a girl and a dog. They were both walking briskly, with a little skip in their step, and from time to time the dog would run ahead and sniff at the seams of the world here and there. The Fox was deep in his dream and the dog would soon be upon him. "Stop!" cried the Scarecrow.

The Fox bolted upright from his sleep and his neck twisted around so his ruff stood out like a brush. He saw the child and the dog. Instinctively ready to flee, the Fox took just enough time to glance up at the Scarecrow as if to say: *Why? Why do you save me, when you disapprove of how I am, when you disapprove of how the world is? Why do you bother?*

But he could not take the time to voice the questions, for the dog was almost upon him, and the Fox disappeared in a streak of smoke-red against the green-

and-gold wreckage of the cornfield. He vanished so quickly that he left behind his pair of handsome black leather boots.

The dog barked. It seemed unable to make a sensible remark, and the Scarecrow by now was not inclined to question it anyway. The Scarecrow did not know why he had alerted the Fox to danger. Were the clothes that the Scarecrow was born into the clothes of a kindly man or a terrible one? Did it matter who the farmer had been, did that shape who the Scarecrow might be? What manner of creature, what quality of spirit, what variety of soul?

It was very troubling. The Scarecrow merely watched as the girl approached. By now he was not sure that he cared to know any more about the world.

The girl wore her hair in pigtails. She was clothed in a sensible dress with an apron tied neatly behind in a bow. She wore neither rhinestone necklace nor black leather boots, but her shoes were glittering in the afternoon sun. "What's that, then?" she said to the dog in a fond voice. "Did you smell something of interest?"

The dog circled about beneath the Scarecrow's pillar, and looked up and barked.

"Why, a Scarecrow," said the girl. "What do you know?"

Since the Scarecrow knew very little indeed, he did not answer.

"I should like to know which is the best way to proceed," said the girl, almost to herself. "The road divides here, and we could go this way, or that way."

The Scarecrow knew only the house, the fields, the gallows tree, the hill.

"Perhaps it doesn't matter, though," continued the girl, musing. "We didn't choose to come here, after all, so perhaps any choice we make from here has the chance of being the right one."

"What does that mean?" said the Scarecrow.

The girl gave a little start and the dog went and cowered behind the basket she had set down. "I'm a foreigner," she said, "an accidental visitor, and I do not know my way."

"I mean, *after all*," said the Scarecrow. "I do not understand befores and afters. What does *after all* mean? It sounds important."

"After all?" said the girl. She put her head to one side. "It means, when everything is thought about, what you can then conclude."

"If you can't think," said the Scarecrow, "can you have an after all?"

"Of course," said the girl, "but thinking helps."

"I should like to learn to think," said the Scarecrow. "I should like to know about this more, before the world seems too dark to bear."

"Would you like to get down?" said the girl.

This had never occurred to the Scarecrow yet. "May I?" he said.

"I will loosen you off your hook if I can reach," said the girl, but she couldn't. Still, she didn't give up. She wandered across the field to the farmhouse. The Scarecrow watched her knock on the door, and when there was no answer, he saw her enter. Before long she returned with a little chair. She stood on it and worked at the nail on which the Scarecrow hung. She managed to bend it down, and off he slid, into a heap on the ground.

It felt good to move!

"Whyever did you help me?" he asked.

"Whyever not?" she said, and he didn't know the answer since he didn't know much. But he grinned, for it was fun to be asked, and maybe if she asked him again someday, he would have an answer ready.

"How do you come to be a talking Scarecrow?" she said.

"I don't know," he said. "How do you come to be a talking girl?"

"I'm sure I have no idea," said the girl. "I was born this way."

"So was I," said the Scarecrow. "But my clothes were given me by a dead man, I hear."

He told the girl the story of the farmer who had been treacherously ill, and then had shared his disease with his neighbors, though by chance or intention it could not be said for sure. The Scarecrow told how the neighbors had fallen upon the farmer and killed him for the crime.

The girl looked doubtful. "Who tells you such a grim tale?" she said.

"A Crow, rest her soul, and a Fox, luck preserve him," said the Scarecrow.

The girl looked sadly at the Scarecrow. "You believe everything you're told?" she said.

"I haven't been told a whole lot yet," the Scarecrow admitted. "I'm only two days old, I think."

The girl said, "Wait here while I return the chair to where I found it." And off she went with a thoughtful expression on her face. Her dog followed her with a cheery wag of his tail.

The Scarecrow trusted that she would return. And return she did. She had a calmer look on her face. "The Crow did not know and the Fox did not know," she said warmly. "But I can read, and I do know. I saw a letter on the table in the farmhouse. It was a letter written by the farmer."

"Yes?" said the Scarecrow.

"The letter said, 'To my neighbors: You will think that I have died. But I have not. This spring when I went over the hill to buy my seedcorn, I fell in love with a woman there. On my return, I had hoped to sow my fields quickly and then go back to marry her, and bring her here to live, but my sickness prevented my traveling. When you caught me and brought me so close to death on the gallows tree, I thought that was the end. But fate would have it otherwise. The storm came up and you all ran for safety. Then appeared my beloved, who had worried because I hadn't returned to her. She had come to find out why, and she had seen you gather, and hid herself in the corn. Seizing her chance, she leapt up and cut me down. So today I am going to marry her. I will not come back to this farm, for I need to make myself a happily ever after somewhere far from here. I have dressed myself in brand-new clothes to make her pleased with her choice. Here are my old clothes. Please use them for the public good and make a Scarecrow to protect the corn from the Crows. It is your corn now, as it always would have been whenever you needed it. Good-bye.' "

The Scarecrow felt his spirits lift up. "So the owner of these clothes was a man who cared for the well-being of his neighbors, even those who had tried to kill him?"

"I do believe," said the girl, "an unusual man with a good heart."

"We should go tear down the gallows tree in the middle of the next field," said the Scarecrow, "so the neighbors may not try such a scheme again."

The girl peered at it with her hand over her eye. "That is not usually a gallows tree," she decided. "It is really just a pole for you to rest upon when that field is ready to be planted with another crop of corn."

The Scarecrow said, "So the stories of the Crow and the Fox were wrong."

"The Crow and Fox were not wrong," said the girl, "they just did not know what came after." She smiled at the Scarecrow and began to play with bits of corn husk. She made a dolly from an ear of corn, and twisted the leaves of cornstalks to make arms and legs. She dressed it in a rhinestone necklace and a pair of black leather boots.

The Scarecrow waited for the dolly to speak. It was no less than he was, some dead agricultural matter dressed up in human clothes. But it did not speak or move as he did.

"Why does it not tell us something?" he asked the girl. "Why am I alive and it is not?"

"I do not know," said the girl. "I am young too. I do not know why I have arrived here in this strange land, where Scarecrows can talk. There is a lot I don't know. It was all winds and noises when I came—"

This reminded the Scarecrow of the day of his awakening—the day before yesterday. He nodded, for the first time knowing something to be true because of his own experience of it. "And lights," he said.

"Yes, and lights," said the girl. "Lights and darks. And suddenly I was here, where everything seems strange. And I don't know why. Like the Fox and the Crow, I don't know the whole story yet. But that's a good reason to go on, don't you think?"

"Go where?" said the Scarecrow.

"Go forward," said the girl. "See something. Learn something. Figure it out. We won't ever get the whole thing, I bet, but we'll get something. And then we'll have something to tell when we're old about what happened to us when we were young."

"Now?" said the Scarecrow. "Can you tell it now?"

"After," said the girl. "We have to have the *before* first, and that's life."

"And what's life?" said the Scarecrow.

"Moving," said the girl. "Moving on. Shall we move on? Will you come with me?"

"Yes," said the Scarecrow. "For the sake of knowing some more about this, of developing my brains so I can bear this mystery better." Straw limbs and human clothes, perhaps, but still hungry for a life to live before so that there could be a story to tell after.

"Which way shall we go?" said the girl.

"Not toward the fields, the house, the hill, the gallows tree," said the Scarecrow. "Let's go in the direction we have not yet gone."

"Good enough for me," said the girl. She left the corn dolly for some other child to find. Then she picked up her basket and the dog came running to her heels. Now that the Scarecrow was down on the ground, he could see that the two fields that made up his world so far were divided by a road paved with yellow brick.

"This way," said the girl. And she and the Scarecrow turned their heads toward the west.

# MELISSA HARDY

# The Bockles

*Melissa Hardy is a Canadian writer whose stories have gained a following both in the fantasy genre and in the literary mainstream. Winner of the 1994 Journey Prize, she is the author of* A Cry of Bees, Constant Fire, *and, most recently,* The Uncharted Heart. *Her short fiction has appeared in a wide variety of magazines, small press magazines, and literary journals.*

*This story marks Hardy's first appearance in the* The Year's Best Fantasy & Horror, *although her work has previously been listed in the Honorable Mentions section. "The Bockles" is a richly atmospheric tale about a miner's fateful bargain with the faeries. It was inspired by the author's grandfather, a Cornishman recruited by the agent of a Canadian gold-mining company. "The Bockles" is reprinted from Hardy's new collection,* The Uncharted Heart *(Alfred A. Knopf, Canada). The entire collection is wonderful and well worth seeking out.*

*—T. W.*

For three hundred years, Pulglases had worked the South Crofty mine, which lies between Camborne and Redruth on the Connor, or the Red River, so called because of the residue of tin that washes down from the mine and turns the water a rusty color before it dumps it into St. Ives Bay. And before the tinners went underground, Pulglases streamed for ore in that same region, down there towards the south of the County of Cornwall and inland, on the road between Truro and Penzance. South Crofty was a deep mine: four hundred fathoms blasted through hard granite. Not that this was unusual. All the mines in Cornwall were deep, for the ore is borne in fissures running vertically through the rock, and each of these fissures must be shafted separately if it is to be worked. The tin they mined in South Crofty was sweetness itself, like moon parings, but it didn't dig easy. The deeper they drilled, the more water seeped into the shaft, for saving that short piece of land north of the Tamar, Cornwall is an island, afloat in the Atlantic like a boat. So the South Crofty miners worked a donkey-powered rag and a chain operation to de-water the mine, and that was a job to which Pulglases took—driving the donkey and, later, working the pump in the engine house—with the result that, as long as anyone could remember, a Pulglases had been in charge of drying the shaft while other, lesser Pulglases had worked deep in the mine, drilling and mucking or working the 303 machine.

There was something that set the Pulglases apart from other folk. Way back, a Pulglase man had married a changeling (for piskies, like mockingbirds, are wont to creep into a mortal's house by night and abscond with whatever babies they can lay their hands on, leaving one of their own very peculiar offspring in their stead—and these changelings are not only odd-looking, but also difficult to keep clothed, as piskies prefer to rush around buck naked in all kinds of weather, with only their long hair for a covering). From that union on, not only were the Pulglases short-legged, but they also possessed the ability to converse with piskies. Moreover, though it made for a draft, they built their houses of granite or greenstone with holes strategically placed in the walls so that the piskies could enter and leave at will. "To bar them from the hearth would be to drive away good luck," they explained to dubious neighbours. Still, it had to be admitted that the Pulglases had no need to place those knobs of lead known as piskies' paws on the roofs of their houses to prevent the piskies from dancing on them and thereby souring the milk, and that as a family, they tended to thrive, living longer lives than most and their children scarcely ever dying, provided the child was not born at the interval between the old and new moons and its head was not washed before the requisite twelve months specified by those wise in these matters.

Now it happened that there were bockles in the South Crofty mine—bockles or knackers, it was unclear which. Knackers are the spirits of tinners who died unexpectedly in underground accidents. They are malevolent-looking—gnarled, with oversized heads, squinting eyes and mouths that stretch from ear to ear. They stand no taller than three feet and have long grey beards. Bockles, on the other hand, are that breed of pisky that lives underground. No matter what level of South Crofty a miner was working on, he could hear piskies knocking at the rock from some nearby point within the earth with little picks and axes and hammers—sometimes a tinner would even uncover some child-sized tool hidden away in a rock cranny—but just where they were digging was impossible to make out. Moreover, the sound was most clearly discerned at the very deepest part of the shaft. This led the miners to conclude that somewhere a way far down lay a rich lode, for it is a well, known fact that both knackers and bockles can actually smell copper, tin and silver the way a man can smell his dinner as he comes over the moor towards home. However, everyone was afraid to stray into such unfamiliar territory—there was no telling what reception they might get. Knackers are almost always cantankerous, and piskies are, at best, capricious, friendly one moment and devilish the next. Everyone, that is, except for Kevern Pulglase, who maintained the pumps at the engine house as his father had before him, and his son, Digory, just turned seventeen and in charge of clearing the gutters that ran along the train track inside the mine.

Now Kevern, in his time, had been an inquisitive boy and quick, or so his teachers had said before he quit school at the age of nine to work underground. He was always poking about by himself amid the scrub and gorse on the moor, trapping rabbits for his mother and shooting plover and woodcock to take home, and so he had come to have some direct experience of piskies, having encountered them a number of times and observed their dances. That, plus, of course, his pisky blood. His son, Digory, on the other hand, was a thick sort of boy, loutish and slow. Like all the Pulglases, he had short, bowed legs, big ears and a long, pulled face. Like those in his mother's family, he was rheumy, weak-eyed and tended to leak at the nose. The most interesting thing Digory had done to date was to overturn his friend Jacca's backhouse when Jacca's uncle Ythel was in it. As for piskies, Digory had never knowingly encountered one, though his nan had often told him that she had seen them dance around his head as an infant. "That could be a good thing . . . or a bad one," she advised him. (Digory's nan could cure warts, pox, whooping cough and hernias and so was widely sought after as a charmer.)

"We'll fetch us out tonight," his father told him one fair midsummer's Saturday, "and see what we can see. It's a full moon, and that's favored time for pisky-spotting. If they be bockles and not knackers, they'll be out tonight. But listen to me, son—you cannot breathe a word of this to anyone. Not to your nan or your ma or that Jacca fellow or that Loveday lass you've been courting, with the mouth on her like an open trap. And especially not to the boys on your shift or any miner at South Crofty. For if my plan succeeds, we'll make of ourselves rich men, but t'will be at the expense of the others, and they won't like us too well if they know what we're up to. So can you keep a tight lid on it, lad?"

"Why, yes, Da," Digory replied, uncomprehending.

Accordingly, father and son left their house, which was on the main road leading out of Redruth, just as the moon was rising over the hill. In Kevern's packsack were a couple of pasties, sticks of yellow and black barley and two Mason jars of that Cornish mead made from clear honey and seasoned with root ginger and rosemary (this was on account of it being the full Mead Moon). They sat down under a yew tree outside the entrance of the South Crofty and waited. Sure enough, just after midnight, a whole pack of bockles came swarming out of the mine's entrance, dragging bags twice their size behind them—Kevern saw at once that they were bockles and not knackers because of the likeness they bore to moor piskies. These bags the bockles carried off to a place about a mile north of town on the moor's edge, with Digory and Kevern scrambling through the bracken and bramble behind them. There, beside a quaking pool edged with lady's smock and ragged robin, they spilled the big sacks onto the dewy sedge to make a pile of shining ore, which they proceeded (being piskies) to dance merrily about. Kevern and Digory, somewhat fuddled by drink by this time, secreted themselves behind an outcrop of weathered, lichenous granite to watch. "Would you look at that!" Digory exclaimed to his father under his breath. "They're as small as my . . ." He paused in consternation, for when it came down to it, he couldn't say how small the bockles actually were. And this was quite to be expected, for although piskies give the impression of being very small folk, it is impossible to say whether they are this big or that big because 1) they tend to fluctuate in size; 2) they gutter and flicker like candles in a wind; and 3) most people who see them are at least a little drunk.

In the case of bockles, they are earthen in hue, stained brown with mossy undertones. They are slight of build, boneless in appearance and go about entirely naked except that their long, tangled hair reaches frequently to their knees, concealing such private parts as they posses. They emit the slightest phosphorescent glow, smell of honeysuckle after a rain, and when they speak or sing, there is a peculiar resonance to the sound, as if the listener's ears were ringing. Those who encounter them frequently experience vertigo.

"Whoa!" muttered Digory, clinging to the rock for support, for he suddenly felt dizzy and not a little nauseous.

"Stay here and keep quiet," his father advised him. Then, to Digory's amazement and somewhat to his alarm, Kevern squared his shoulders, took a deep breath and stepped out from behind the rock into the spill of moonlight and the very midst of the frolicking bockles. The piskies froze. Then one of them, a little taller than the others and having about him a somewhat regal air, said something to the rest in a slippery-eel voice the meaning of which Digory could almost but not quite grasp. All the bockles laughed and clapped their little hands—their laughter sounded like silver bells, their clapping like dry seed pods crushed by little feet.

"We meet again, cousin," the head of the bockles continued, turning back to Digory's father. "Only you are somewhat more gigantic than before. What is it you want from the bockles?"

"That's a lot of ore you have there, cousin!" observed Kevern. "You must have worked hard to break up so much with your little hammers."

"You know how we bockles like pretty things," replied the pisky. "Things that glitter and shine."

"I remember," Kevern assured him. "So I was thinking that we might make a deal."

The bockles murmured. A twittering sound like birds make in the rain.

"What kind of deal?" inquired the head bockle shrewdly.

"You tell me where to dig for the ore, and I and my son will bring you a tenth of the richest ore we find, properly dressed, so that you won't even have the trouble of breaking it up," offered Kevern.

"Is that your son standing over there behind that rock?"

"Yes," Kevern admitted.

"Let him stand up so the bockles may see his face."

"Digory, stand up!"

Digory shuffled to his feet, cap in hand, gulping.

The head bockle gazed at him intently and stroked his little chin. "Hmmmm . . ." he murmured.

"We can bring it here, to this very place, if you like." Kevern sweetened the deal.

"Aha!" The bockle considered the offer.

"It will give you more time to dance," Digory blurted out.

"Digory!" his father warned him.

"The boy makes a good point." The bockle interceded on Digory's behalf. "Very well, then. You will bring us the ore on the night of the full moon. A new load every full moon. Those are our terms."

"You have my word on it," Kevern swore.

"We'll have more than that if you are forsworn," the bockle reminded him, glancing at Digory.

Kevern nodded. "I know," he said. "I do not make this promise lightly. I know the consequences of failing to comply with the terms of a deal struck with piskies."

"I know you do," acknowledged the bockle. "My auntie, your nan, taught you well. We shall accept your offer. Go down into the mine tomorrow, when everyone else is at church. Go down to the very deepest level, where there is standing water. Listen carefully. I, on my side, shall strike my hammer against the rock three times. Dig in that spot and you will not be disappointed."

"I will do as you say," replied Kevern. "We shall both benefit from this arrangement. You will see."

"That we shall," concluded the bockle, turning back to the dance.

"We shall be rich men!" Kevern told his son excitedly as they stumbled back to their village. But Digory was so confounded by drink and the actual physical effect that the bockles have upon mortals (not only did he have less pisky blood than his father, but his body weight was also less) that he remembered the encounter as one would a peculiarly compelling dream—vividly, but in snatches and blurts.

From that day on, for the next seven years, the Pulglases, father and son, crept down to the mine of a Sunday morning, just as the bells of the little Wesleyan chapel were beginning to call folks into church and dug wherever the bockles' hammers directed them. One tenth of the broken-up and dressed ore Kevern set out for the bockles on the night of the full moon; the other nine-tenths he sold to a man who traded in black-market ore. As Kevern had predicted, the Pulglases became wealthy men in this way, able to buy a farm in the country and pigs and sheep and to build a fine stone house on their land, with holes worked right into the walls for the piskies to come and go at will and full of all sorts of exotic treasures—a Royal Doulton figurine of a French lady on the mantelpiece, a tea caddy that came straight from India and an engraving of Dick Turpin on horseback that had once belonged to the local gentry. Kevern's mother and wife had not only a vegetable garden for growing parsnips, carrots and turnips, but also a cutting garden that Digory's mother planted with wallflowers and Canterbury bells. A hired boy cut pukes of turf and faggots of furze and kept their turbary filled to the top, and a girl from the neighbouring farm helped out with the cooking. As for food, the Pulglases wanted for nothing. There was always a ham hock in the boil, or a fat roast of beef dripping with suet, or a big fish brought up from Gwithian wrapped in newspaper and lambasted with butter and then dredged in vinegar to be eaten with mustard.

Indeed, the Pulglases became so prosperous that no one could figure out why they continued to work in the mine. "It's in our blood," Kevern explained. "The Pulglases have always been tinners." The truth was that they had not yet grown quite rich enough to quit and so kept on postponing their retirement, for at that time, they would loose access to their underground treasure.

One day, when Kevern was riding the hoist down to the bottom of the mine to check the water level (for they had recently drilled down an additional twenty-six feet and experienced a bad run of flooding as a result), the rod snapped. Kevern and thirty other men hurtled to their deaths 2,400 feet below. Digory had just ridden the hoist up a few moments before and was in the punch room clocking out from his shift. The sound of the men screaming as they fell was muted by the roar of the drills from below and the noisy suck of the big pump.

It sounded distant, wadded up like a piece of paper, unconnected to his life and experience. The mine was closed for three days while they removed the bodies, which were little more than pulp and were unrecognizable. "Like straining a stew," as one miner on the burial detail commented.

Digory was on his own.

Now, there were never two more different men than Digory Pulglase and his father. Kevern Pulglase was smart; Digory was stupid. Kevern was prudently cautious; Digory, careless and feckless. The first full moon after his father died, Digory delivered a tenth of his spoils to the bockles as usual, but the next full moon after that, he skimmed a little off the top of the tenth, figuring that the bockles would not notice the slight discrepancy. Every full moon for a year thereafter, he skimmed a little bit more and a little bit more off the piskies' portion until finally, at the rising of the Blood Moon in October (so called for pig-sticking), he got so drunk down at Davy Jones's Locker that he forgot to leave the bockles their tithe at all. When the milk did not sour in the days that followed and the baby's first tooth did not come in snaggled—by this time, Digory had married his lumpish sweetheart, Loveday Carvyth, and had two great walloping sons on her—he figured that either the bockles didn't care about the bargain he had failed to keep or, very possibly, their power was less than his father had imagined. He even began to wonder if the bockles existed at all. Perhaps the mead had caused him to see things that weren't there—mead could do that if left too long in the fermenting.

The Snow Moon came and went, then the Oak Moon. Again Digory got drunk at the pub and did not leave the bockles their tithe. No harm befell him or his family. That Sunday, however, when he had descended deep into the mine, as was his wont, there was no bockle hammer to tell him where to dig. He sat there in the cold, quaky dark on an empty carbide tin for two hours, but the bockles did not signal him. "Well, that's that," he said to himself and the next day retired from the mine and went up village to live on his farm.

A whole half-year came and went. Then, in July, on the Mead Moon, the same moon that had shone when Kevern and Digory had made their original pact with the bockles, Digory celebrated by riding his bicycle into Redruth and closing the pub there some seven hours later. With no thought of piskies, he made his weaving way home—five miles up and down narrow roads through the moon-bathed countryside—to discover that his fine stone house had fallen into a hole twice its size and one and a half storeys deep.

Apparently, his father had built it over some mine workings abandoned so long before that no one had remembered exactly where they were located, and the ground had finally given way under the immense weight. Everyone who had been inside the house when the cave-in occurred died, of course, buried in a heap of square granite blocks and heavy oaken beams—this included Digory's wife, his two babies, his mother and an as-yet-unmarried sister. The only survivors were his dog, Alfie, who had been asleep in the barn at the time, and his old nan, his father's mother, who had been availing herself of the backhouse when the ground stove in. "A terrible rumbling, like the earth was opening up to let the dead rise up," was how she described it. "Then the most fearful silence. Oh, I should have known it was coming when I heard the owl hoot and then that hen of your ma's actually crowing." Later she tried to comfort her distraught grandson. "It was not your fault, boy," she told him. "Nor your father's neither. Who was to know there was a great bloody hole under the house?" But Digory knew full well that it was his fault, that the bockles were punishing him for not keeping his part of the bargain struck on that long-ago night. He had been a fool to think that they had not noticed or did not care. He had been a fool to think them powerless or—more foolish still—non-existent. Digory was convinced that the bockles had either dug the hole under the house or, more likely, used their pisky powers to induce Kevern to build on that very spot, in case they should at some point require easy access to retribution.

Digory took to drink—that is, he took to drink more than he had previously taken to drink. Over the space of a year, he lost everything his father and he had acquired as a result of their deal with the bockles. The sheep died of giddie, the hogs of mumps and the horse of staggers. The corn took a mold on it and withered in the fields. Once again he was compelled to take up lodgings in Redruth and seek employment at the South Crofty mine. However, it was not the same as it had once been down in the shaft. The other men kept their distance, even his old friend Jacca, for if good luck had a tendency to rub off, bad luck was downright contagious. No man in his right mind wanted Digory on his shift or in the hoist bucket with him, for fear of cave-ins or missed holes or snapped cables. So Digory moved his nan into her sister's cottage and went west to Penwith, near Cape Cornwall, where he signed on to work at the Botallack mine. The Botallack's engine house was set high on a peak of granite overlooking the Atlantic, the ocean foaming at its base. The mine's underground workings extended out under the seabed, several fathoms deep. Digory was not used to working with the weight of the sea squeezing the rock over his head, making it creak and buckle. It was hot down the shaft and the air was leaden with heavy moisture—a man had to gulp for air and then strain his lungs just to breathe it. The roar of the waves breaking against the cliffs above him rang in his ears, making him dizzy, and salt water seeped into the rock crannies where he worked and clung to him like spray.

About this time, an agent in the employ of the Hollinger mine arrived at the Pomery Hotel in nearby St. Just—Colonel Putherbough, formerly of His Majesty's Army in India. Colonel Putherbough was an avuncular sort of man, lionine in aspect, with a big, well-made head and a mane of bright white hair; his manner was simultaneously hearty and smooth. He had been charged with recruiting as many Cornish tin and copper miners as he could muster, for skilled miners were at a premium in the Porcupine region of Northern Ontario, where the Hollinger was located, the frontier region being populated, in so far as it was populated, by feral French trappers, red Indians and what Cornishmen call woosers, wild men of the wood. Colonel Putherbough rented a hall and posted a notice, inviting the miners to attend a lecture on a Thursday evening. Seventy miners attended—already there had been talk of the Botallack being mined out, of the need to move on.

"The Hollinger is the largest gold mine in the British Empire. Why, did you know that it has more than one hundred miles of underground tunnels?" Colonel Putherbough astounded his audience. "Last year alone, the Hollinger produced $68,000 of gold ore each and every month of the year! And easy to drill and blast. No fear of the ocean coming down on top of you if you hit a missed hole.

No, sir. As for Canada . . . well, let me tell you, my friends, it's the most beautiful country in the world. Rugged. No doubt about that. And cold, I'll grant you, but bracing." He thumped his barrel chest, then coughed. "Not damp and drizzly as it is here." Taking a snowy white hanky from his pocket, he blew his nose loudly. "As for the wages! Eighty-five Canadian dollars a month . . . and that's before your bonus, gentlemen. Plus, if you have a wife or get yourself one, the company will give you a house of your very own."

Later, Digory travelled to Redruth to see his nan. "Would there be piskies in Canada?" he asked her.

She just shook her woolly grey head. "Not Cornish piskies, I shouldn't think," she averred. "Why do you ask?"

"Oh, naught," Digory reassured her hastily. Although in most matters, a loose-lipped man Digory had kept his word to his father in one respect—he had not breathed a word of their compact with the bockles to anyone. Nor was he about to break his promise now that he had gone and lost everything through his sloth and his greed; he could not bear for his nan, the only person left in the world who had any regard for him, to know that he was responsible for all their misfortune. "Would you come with me to Canada, then, Nan . . . if I decide to go?"

"Oh, no," Nan said, pouring her grandson a cup of tea and dribbling condensed milk from the can into it. "Too old. I'm happy enough here with Great-Auntie Lowena."

So three months later, Digory Pulglase went to Padstow, where the air smelled of tar, rope, rusted chain and tidal water, and set sail for Canada on a ship called the *Restless*, with a letter of employment signed by Colonel Putherbough in his jacket pocket. He made landfall at the Port of Quebec, along with ninety-nine other Cornishmen sponsored by the Hollinger, and from there he travelled by rail to Toronto and from Toronto to Northern Ontario, arriving in Timmins at the peak of the blackfly season in 1922. The township was not ten years old and still resembled the rough camp that it had so recently been, despite the fact that it boasted all the amenities of a typical Ontario town its size—a piggery, a bakery, a dairy, a dry-goods store and a shoemaker's, an ice-cream parlor, two hotels, two theatres, a barber shop, a pool room, a feed store, a livery, a lockup, a newspaper of record (the *Porcupine Advance*) and a firehall. The streets ran with mud; there was no grass to be found anywhere, but only raw, upturned earth and patches of sedge, and where there wasn't new construction, there were stumps and stacks of wood haphazardly piled and heaps of refuse.

Digory put up at the Old Boston Hotel, a two-storey clapboard, ramshackle affair of a building piled up on the corner of Pine and Second. Despite its designation, it was really a sort of rooming house catering to bachelor miners. For sixty cents a day, he shared a bed with a mucker called Romanian John who stood six foot five, weighed in at well over 250 pounds, spoke little English and had fleas. Digory did not like sleeping with Romanian John. The only way around it was to find himself a wife, thereby qualifying for a Hollinger house. This was easier said than done. As it turned out, there were not many women unspoken for in Northern Ontario. Not only could a man not afford to be choosy, he also could not afford to wait if and when an opportunity to snag a wife presented itself. That was how the Cornishman found himself proposing to Moira Flannery a mere half an hour after meeting her at the Moneta (the local blind pig) and moments before impregnating her in the heap of rubble out back of it (if, indeed, he was the father of her baby, which was a matter of some speculation). Moira was eighteen, just off the boat herself from Cork, a big, blowsy girl, all pink and white, with reddish hair that did not so much grow from her head as sizzle from it and snapping blue eyes. She was in the employ of a prominent local physician at the time, Dr. Kirby. A strict man, he let the housemaid go when she confessed to being pregnant, but he gave her a decent sum of money by way of severance, realizing that she would have need of it in her straitened circumstances. Later he discovered that the housemaid had pawned numerous pieces of family silver over the short term of her employment, as well as some expensive jewellery belonging to his wife, and pocketed the money. When the physician threatened to call the constable, Moira countered with threats of an intimate nature. Upon reflection, Dr. Kirby contented himself with redeeming the pawned goods and hiring a Chinese houseboy to replace the Irish girl.

No doubt about it: Moira Flannery was a cunning opportunist, as mendacious as she was spirited and as insolent as she was indolent. But all Digory saw was a plump young bride . . . and a Hollinger house. The Hollinger houses were narrow, two-storey structures consisting, for the most part, of tarpaper tacked onto a wooden frame. They were a dark green in color, trimmed with white, and all of them were exactly alike. If there was a thing that could be counted upon, it was that no man would get a finer house than his fellow miner or a bigger one or even one that differed so much as one iota in its layout. On the first floor of a Hollinger house was a tiny parlor dominated by a tin stove—this parlor was so small that many a pregnant woman coming onto her time became stuck in it trying to turn around. There was also a kitchen that opened onto a lean-to. The second storey, where two small bedrooms crowded in under the eaves, was obtained by means of a precipitous flight of stairs. There were no halls or vestibules or mud rooms or even closets in a Hollinger house. There were considered superfluous luxuries. There was a sort of rough cellar that could serve a family as a cold room in which to store barrels of apples; sacks of potatoes, onions and turnips; old traps, fishlines and the like. They were cold, frail husks of houses compared with the fine, sturdy domicile his father had built back in Cornwall, but they were four walls a man could call his own, at least for the duration of his employment, and they were free. Moreover, Digory was lucky in that he put his name in at a time when the foundations of an entire block's worth of Hollinger houses had already been laid down on Borden Street. As soon as the ground thawed, miners working for extra dollars after their shifts underground would frame the houses and tack up the tarpaper and slap a roof on them in three weeks, and Digory and Moira would have their spanking new Hollinger house.

In the meantime, Digory rented a basement apartment that Moira had found for them down in the Young Street and Wilson Avenue area, not far from the Mattagami River. This was where their twin sons, Kevern and Elwyn, were born on a stormy February morning of that same year. These names, which Digory had picked out, were the very same as those borne by his and Loveday's sons. Needless to say, he did not tell Moira this . . . no, nor anything else about his first family and the terrible fate that had befallen them. He did not want her to think that he was unlucky or, worse (if she were to discover the real truth), stupidly venal. But who was there in this remote place to tell her? No one. Surely his secret was safe. He had been right to come so far away, to leave his guilty secret buried in a hold in Cornwall, mixed together with the blood and bones of his unfortunate family, dead through his fault, and therefore almost as if by his hand. For no matter how much Digory drank to forget, he had never forgotten this: that he had killed his mother and his sister, his wife and his sons as surely as if he had taken that old muzzle-loader down from over the mantlepiece and shot them, or lit a faggot of furze and hurled it through an open window into the sleeping house, or beaten their heads in with the backside of a shovel. Now he began not so much to forget that he had killed them as to forget that they were dead in the first place. He did this consciously in the beginning, telling himself that the first Kevern and Elwyn had been reborn (in some ineffable way that he was hard put to understand but nevertheless felt certain was the case) in the identical bodies of their half-brothers. In addition, he took to calling Moira by his first wife's name: Loveday. "T'is a term of endearment," he reassured his new bride. "Like calling you darling or pet. For I love you all the day long." Not knowing that Loveday was, in fact, an old Cornish name, Moira took his pretty explanation at face value. As time wore on, the break between his old life and his new one knit up like a badly set bone, crooked and lumpy, but in its way intact. Cornwall and all that had passed there settled deeper into the mists that rolled across his mind, and there were times when he wondered if he and his father had ever made a compact with the bockles in the first place, and if what had befallen his family had taken place in reality or in a dream.

Moira did not share her husband's burgeoning sense of well-being. Being holed up in a dark and icy basement flat all day with two squalling babies and no money but what her poor dullard of a husband reluctantly doled out was not what she had in mind when she travelled all the way across the Atlantic to Canada, then signed on to go to this remote frontier town. It was true that she had hoped to marry, but marry well. A rich man, an important man. Perhaps a prospector just off selling a rich claim. That was what she had wanted. That was what she had intended. And not only was Digory poor, with no prospects of being anything but poor, he was no prize either, with his big ears and his homely face and the start of a gut on him too, not to mention what he had for brains which was what you did in the backhouse provided you could dig your way back there through all the snow. Moira had married Digory only because he had asked her, and because of course, she was pregnant, though counting back, she was pretty sure that the twins weren't Digory's but belonged to that fellow who worked for the livery up on Third Street for a couple of months before heading west to Manitoba. Frenchy had been his name, or at least that was what he had told her. And that was another thing: it was not as if she had wanted children. She had been the oldest of twelve; sure but she had had her fill of mewling babies and snot-nosed toddlers back in County Cork. "If I never have to wipe another nose or bottom, I will be a happy woman," she had declared before bursting into tears. "How could I have let this happen to me? How? How?" But this story is not about Moira.

There's no gold camp in the world—nor any other camp where precious minerals are mined—without its high-graders. High-graders in Timmins were those who pocketed a few nuggets on a shift and then stole, shaking in their boots, down to the Moneta to sell them to the man known far and wide as Père Henri. Père Henri was so short in stature that, had he been any shorter, he might have been considered a dwarf. He had a big, craggy head upon which was perched a black beret; small, squinty eyes that always appeared red and sore; a wide, mobile mouth; and a wispy grey goatee. Rumor had it that Père Henri had been a Catholic priest before he was defrocked, that he had come to this part of the North from Quebec to be a missionary to the Ojibwa but had somehow strayed. Certainly he affected a priest's collar, together with a priest's rusty black suit, and his manner was both solemn and sanctimonious. Père Henri always sat at a table in the back of the Moneta, right next to the rear door, to facilitate escape, should that prove necessary. It was his table. He sat in a special chair with an elevated seat that the blind pig's owner, Arthur McNab, had had made for him. McNab did not allow anyone else to sit there (Père Henri was good for business), and anyone who had been in Timmins for more than a fortnight knew better than to try, for if a miner was to earn that little bit extra, if he was to buy that new dress for his wife or those skates for his kids or a bicycle or a fiddle or a dogsled, his best recourse was Père Henri. Sinner though he undoubtedly was, the ex-clergyman always paid a fair price for gold.

At the time, Digory was on the night shift. One of the good things about being on the night shift was that a man could take more liberties during the hours of darkness than in the daylight, when there were not only more eyes to see what a body was up to, but also better visibility. Digory found that it was an easy thing to stroll up through one of the raises that opened out onto the golf course that Hollinger had built for its employees and toss a chunk of ore over the barbed-wire fence surrounding the compound. Later, after he had got off his shift, he would stroll over to that same fence, pocket the nugget and head home. The next evening, just before punching in, he would stop by the blind pig for a pint and conduct his business with Père Henri.

"You have a good eye for free gold, my friend," Père Henri complimented Digory. His smile was broad, his teeth green.

Digory shrugged but could not resist informing the high-grader, "I come by it naturally. My whole family . . . miners for generations."

"Mine too," Père Henri assured him smoothly. "For centuries."

It struck Digory then that Père Henri had a kind of mossy look to him that he found deeply suspicious. Perhaps it was because the room was smoky, or perhaps because he had begun to drink rather earlier than usual that day. That might account for the fact that the ex-priest seemed now to loom, now to shrink in his vision. He reminded Digory of someone. Just whom he could not quite remember, but the notion disturbed him at some fundamental level. He could not shake it, and from that time on, the Cornishman took his business elsewhere, selling his purloined nuggets to another entrepreneur, freshly arrived from the silver fields in Cobalt, despite the fact that this new high-grader consistently cheated him.

That year the thaw came much too quickly. In a matter of only ten short days, all the snow that had been shovelled up against the houses in the course of along, hard winter and piled into banks as high as one-storey buildings and packed down on top of all the thoroughfares in town until street level stood three feet higher than it did in summer—all of this snow melted. The earth underneath people's feet turned sodden and spongy, and water levels soared in all the rivers and creeks and lakes of the district. The lower-lying areas along the river flooded to a depth of eighteen inches. Some houses in these areas listed tipsily. A barn collapsed into a heap of weathered lumber, then broke apart like a raft, boards spinning in the current, and an outhouse overturned and floated half way downstream before getting wedged in a culvert. Town Creek, which begins in northeast Timmins and meanders through large culverts to its outlet on the Mattagami River, not far from where the Mountjoy River joins the larger waterway, oozed and slopped over its banks. Things better left frozen un-thawed—a winter's worth of odure, animal carcasses and viscera tossed out back of the butcher's shop or piggery to freeze in a heap, not to mention corpses kept in the undertaker's cold room until the earth could be worked with a shovel. Earthworms erupted from the soil in purplish pink handfuls, wild with joy, and the streets ran with thick, rank ooze. *The Porcupine Advance* had predicted rain that May 3, but no one was prepared for how much it would rain on that glowering, tempestuous day. During Digory's eight-hour shift alone, 6.7 inches fell. The sudden increase in water levels, coupled with the blockage of Town Creek at several points owing to debris from previous flooding, caused a flash flood that overflowed the Mattagami's banks, ripping the wooden bridge from its moorings, collapsing corduroy roads and inundating the area of Wilson and Young with churning, muddy water. Digory stopped off at the Moneta for a pint before heading home, only to find McNab closing up early. The Scot was a bearishly big man with a curly russet beard streaked with white. He wore round wire spectacles and every second tooth in his head flashed gold. "Haven't you heard?" he asked Digory. "That whole area down by the river is flooded. Every-body's gone down to help. That's where I'm heading now. Say, don't you live down there yourself?"

"Wilson and Young," Digory confirmed.

"Well, I'd get home if I were you," McNab advised him, pulling on his mack-intosh. "Père Henri was in here not a half-hour ago. Said Wilson was under tow feet of water."

Suddenly, Digory felt dizzy. His stomach flipped over, blackness swam before his eyes and his knees buckled beneath him; he had to grab hold of McNab's arm to keep on his feet.

"Are you all right, Pulglase?" McNab snapped irritably. He was anxious to go.

"My wife and boys . . ." Digory gasped. The ringing in his ears and the rush of blood to his head was so loud that he could barely hear himself speak. "We're in a basement apartment. Just till they build our new Hollinger house. Jesus Christ! The basement! They'll drown like puppies in a barrel!"

"Like I said, man. You'd better get down there," said McNab, impatient to be gone himself. Then, when Digory continued to cling to his arm, sagging against him, he sighed with exasperation and offered, "Come on, then. We'll go together."

Taking Digory by the arm, the Scotsman hauled him outside and half dragged, half pushed him down the hill towards the river. It was hard going. The rain was steady in their faces, cold and hard, and the streets ran thick with slippery mud. Twice, Digory, who had yet to regain his equilibrium, pitched forward onto his hands and knees, only to have McNab haul him, streaming ooze and whimpering, roughly to his feet again and drive him forward like a farmer would a recalcitrant, disoriented beast. When they finally made it to the corner of Wilson and Young, it was just as Père Henri had said: the entire area was submerged under an expanse of brown, churning water that lapped up to the windowsills of the houses' first storeys. Together the two men waded through chest-high water out to a low barge onto which volunteer firemen were loading bodies.

"How many have you got?" McNab called out to one of the firemen. "Seven so far," the fireman responded.

"Any women and children?"

"Babies, all right. Over here." The fireman pointed.

There, piled into a corner, lay Moira and the two infants. They looked like broken dolls, with their limbs akimbo, their skin rubbery and too white. "They yours?" the fireman inquired of McNab. He shook his head and pointed to Digory. "Are they yours, then?" the fireman repeated, this time to Digory, who nodded, unable to speak for choking back a sob. "Didn't know what hit them, fellow," the fireman explained softly. Then he shook his head and spat off to one side, into the churning water. "Woman who owns the house remembered they were down there only when it was too late. Too busy worrying about getting her furniture to higher ground." He reached out from the barge and patted Digory awkwardly on the back—by now, Digory was blubbering. "Anyway, buddy, we got to get them up to Buckovetsky's stockroom. Temporary morgue. They're not the only ones. There'll be more before we're through."

"Come on," McNab urged him. "No point standing here in all this water. Not doing anybody any good. Let these men do their job." He led Digory back up onto dry land, where the Cornishman collapsed in a heap on the ground. "Get up now, man. Get up," the Scot chided. "No point in carrying on this way. God's will, you know."

"No! No! You don't understand," Digory sobbed. "God had nothing to do with it. I killed them. They died because of me."

"They drowned in the flood, man. You had nothing to do with it!" McNab attempted to reason with him.

"No! No!" Digory insisted. "It's all my fault. I thought an ocean was far enough, but I was wrong—*wrong!*—and now they're dead, just like the others!" Glancing up, he spotted Père Henri standing at the top of the street, a small, dark figure clothed in swirling rain. He was overcome with another attack of vertigo. His stomach heaved and his head spun. "Oooh!" he moaned and ducked his head between his knees.

"Enough of that. Come on. On your feet," McNab said. "I tell you what. We'll got to the Moneta. Get you a nice whisky. On the house." He dragged Digory to his feet. "There we go. Come along, now. Why it's Père Henri! Hello, Henri. We were just going back to the Moneta. Our friend here . . ." McNab lowered his voice. "Well, he's had some very bad news."

"Very!" Digory corroborated thickly. He tried to look at the ex-priest, but it was impossible. First he loomed in his vision, then he shrunk, then he guttered like a candle.

"I'm sorry to hear that," the high-grader said.

"You are?" Digory whispered, clinging to McNab.

"Of course," replied the ex-priest.

"My whole family," Digory choked out the words. "Dead! Wiped out!"

"A tragedy," Père Henri agreed. "Well"—and he patted Digory on the shoulder—"perhaps there's a lesson in all this."

"Coming, Henri?" McNab asked.

"Thank you, no. Not tonight. I've done enough work for one day," Père Henri demurred, and turning on his heel, the diminutive Frenchman headed off down the street towards the east. That was the last anyone ever saw of Père Henri. He told no one where he was going; he simply disappeared. When anyone spoke of it, McNab, who, with his slight acquaintance, had known the high-grader better than anyone else, would shrug and say, "Probably went back to where he came from. Wherever that was." As for Digory Pulglase, he never remarried. He lived in the Old Boston Hotel, sharing a sagging bed with a succession of verminous miners, until one May afternoon, nearly sixteen years to the day when he and his father had struck their fateful deal with the bockles, he bit his drill into the side of a drift, hit a bootleg hole and the rock exploded, killing him instantly, as well as the four men working alongside him.

# JAMES P. BLAYLOCK

# His Own Back Yard

*James P. Blaylock is one of the finest writers of what* Library Journal *calls "American magical realism," and it's a privilege to welcome him to the pages of* The Year's Best Fantasy & Horror. *Blaylock lives in California, which provides the setting for much of his work—such as the fine novels* Land of Dreams, The Last Coin, The Paper Grail, Night Relics, All the Bells on Earth, The Rainy Season, *and* Winter Tides, *all highly recommended. He is also the author of "imaginary world" fantasy novels, children's fiction, and short stories published in a variety of magazines and small press editions.*

*"His Own Back Yard" is a classic Blaylock tale: thoughtful, moving, and unsettling. It comes from the Scifiction section of the SCIFI.COM Web site, edited by Ellen Datlow.*

—T. W.

The abandoned house was boarded up, its chimney fallen, the white paint on the clapboards weathered to the color of an old ghost. It was hidden from the street by two low-limbed sycamores in the front yard and by an overgrown oleander hedge covered in pink and white flowers. Alan stood by his car in the driveway, sheltered from the street in the empty and melancholy afternoon, half listening to the drone of an unseen airplane and to the staccato clamor of a jack hammer, that stopped and started in a muted racket somewhere blocks away in the nearby neighborhood.

More than twenty years had passed since Alan had last driven out to his childhood home. A year or so after he had married Susan the two of them had stopped on the road, and he had climbed out of the car with no real idea what he hoped to find. A new family had moved in by then—his own parents having sold the house and moved north a year before—and the unrecognizable children's toys on the lawn were disconcerting to him, and so he had climbed back into the car and driven away.

His marriage to Susan was one of the few things in his life that he had done without hesitation, and that had turned out absolutely right. A few days ago she had gone back east for two weeks to visit her aunts in Michigan, taking along their son Tyler, who was starting college in two months in Ann Arbor. Alan had stayed home looking forward to the peace and quiet, a commodity that had grown scarce over the years. But somewhere along the line he had lost his talent for solitude, and the days of empty stillness had filled him with a sense of loss that was almost irrational, as if Susan and Tyler been gone months instead of days, or as if, like the old house in front of him now, he was coming to the end of something.

He walked into the back yard and tried the rear door, which of course was locked, and then tried without success to peer through a boarded-up kitchen window. He looked back up the driveway to make sure he was unseen, but just then a man came into view, walking along the shoulder of the road, heading uphill past the house. Alan moved back out of sight, waiting for an interminable couple of minutes before looking out once more. Hurrying now, he pried two of the boards off with his hands, wiggling the nails loose and setting the boards aside on the ground. He put his face to the dusty glass and peered through, letting his eyes adjust to the darkness within. There was a skylight overhead, which, like the oleander hedge out front, hadn't been part of the house twenty years ago. Filtered sunlight shone through its litter of leaves and dirt so that the interior of the kitchen slowly appeared out of the darkness like a photograph soaking in developer. He had been afraid that he would find the house depressingly vandalized, but it wasn't; and he stared nostalgically at the familiar chrome cabinet pulls and the white-painted woodwork and the scalloped moldings, remembering the breakfast nook and curio shelves, the dining room beyond, the knotty pine bookshelves topped with turned posts that screened the hallway leading to his bedroom.

He stepped away from the window and walked along the side of the property, between the house and the fence, toward where his bedroom stood—or what had been his bedroom all those years ago. There were no boards on the window, but the view was hidden by curtains. He rejected the idea of breaking the window, and instead retraced his steps, his hands in his pockets, careful not to look over the fence, beyond which lay the back yards of houses built a decade ago. In his day there had been a farm house on several acres, belonging to an old childless couple named Prentice who had the remnants of a grove of walnuts and a chicken coop and goats. There had been fruit trees on their property, peaches and Santa Rosa plums that he had eaten his share of.

He paused in the shade of a big silk oak tree near the garden shed in the back yard and stood listening to the breeze rustle the leaves, hearing again the distant clattering echo of the jack hammer. The heavy grapevines along the fence hadn't been pruned back in years, and the air was weighted with the smell of concord grapes, overripe and falling in among the vines to dry in the summer heat. The August afternoon was lonesome and empty, and the rich smell of the grapes filled him with the recollection of a time when he'd had no real knowledge that the hours and days were quietly slipping away, bartered for memories.

The shed at the back of the garage was ramshackle and empty except for scattered junk, its door long ago fallen off and only a single rusted hinge left as a reminder that it had once had a door at all. He remembered that there had been a brick pad in front of the door, but the bricks were gone, and there was nothing but compressed dirt. Inside, a short wooden shelf held a couple of broken clay pots, and on the wall below the shelf hung a single ancient aluminum lawn chair with a woven nylon seat. Alan was certain he remembered that very chair, in considerably better shape, hanging in this same place thirty years ago. On impulse he stepped into the shed, took the chair down, and unfolded it, wiping off dust and cobwebs before walking out under the tree, where he put the chair down in the shade and sat in it, letting his weight down carefully. The nylon webbing was frayed with age, and the aluminum was bent and weakened at the joints, but the seat held, and he relaxed and surveyed the back yard, feeling a sense of invitation, of growing familiarity. Now that the house was sold and abandoned, soon to be torn down, it was his as much as it was anyone's, and it seemed to him as if the years had passed in the blink of an eye, the house having waited patiently for his return.

The quarter acre yard was smaller than he remembered, although it was immense by southern California standards, and the untended Bermuda grass lawn, flanked by now-weedy flowerbeds, stretched away toward the back fence and garden as ever, with the same orange trees and the big avocado tree that had shaded it since as early as he could remember. On impulse he stood up and walked to the edge of the lawn, where he pushed aside the high brown grass with the toe of his shoe until he found the first of the brick stepping stones that led out to the back garden. He recalled the countless times he had clipped away the grass that had overgrown the bricks, like a gardener edging headstones in a cemetery—an idea that was almost funny, since he had in fact buried something beneath this very stepping stone, which had seemed to him as a child to be permanently set in the lawn, like a benchmark.

When he was a kid he had put together little treasures, collections of marbles and pieces of quartz crystal and small toys that he buried inside foil-wrapped coffee cans around the back yard. The first of his treasures he had buried right here. And now, within a matter of weeks, bulldozers would level the house and grade the yard, and that would be the end of any buried treasures.

He bent over and yanked at the Bermuda grass, pulling out tufts of it in order to expose the edges of the brick. The roots were heavy, a tangled mass that had grown between and around the bricks, packing them together so tightly that they might have been set in concrete. He walked back to the garden shed and looked at the remains of old tools that lay scattered inside: a broken spade, the blade of a hoe, a bamboo rake with most of the tines snapped off.

He picked up the spade, which had about a foot of splintered handles, and went back out to the stepping stone where he slipped the blade in along the edge of the brick, leaning into it, pushing with his foot until he levered the brick out of its hole. The other bricks followed easily now, leaving a three inch deep square, walled and floored and criss-crossed with tangled white roots. Grasping the broken shovel handle he hacked through them, tearing clumps of roots and grass away with his hands, exposing the packed dirt underneath.

After scraping and hacking away an inch or so of soil he unearthed a rusty ring of metal—the top of a coffee can. A big shred of foil, stained gold, lay three-quarters buried in the orange-brown dirt, and he pulled it loose, the dirt collapsing into what must have been the vacancy left when the can had rusted away. Almost immediately he found a tiny porcelain dog—a basset hound that his mother had bought for him as a remembrance of their own basset, which had died when Alan was four or five years old. He tried to recall the dog's name, but it wouldn't come to him, and his losing the name filled him with sadness. It occurred to him that he couldn't actually recall the living dog at all, but had only a memory built up out of a few of his parents' stories, which had themselves been only memories.

He polished the dirt from the porcelain and set the figurine aside on the lawn. The wind rose just then, and the leaves overhead stirred with a sibilant whispering, and for a time the afternoon was utterly silent aside from the wind-animated noises. Fallen leaves rose from the lawn and tumbled toward the fence, and he heard a distant creaking noise, like a door opening, and the low muttering sound of animals from somewhere off to the east.

When he peered into the hole again he saw a tarnished silver coin smashed flat, and instantly he recalled the morning that he and his parents had laid pennies and nickels and dimes on the train tracks near the beach in Santa Barbara, and how this dime had been flattened into a perfect oval, with the image still clear and clean, and had become his good luck coin. It reminded him now of the buffalo nickel that he carried for luck, one of his old childhood habits that he hadn't given up. He found three more objects: the lens from a magnifying glass, a carved wooden tiki with tiny ball bearings for eyes, brown with their own rust, and a pint-sized glass marble, a light, opaque blue with pink swirls.

He scraped the hole out a little deeper, getting well down beneath the rusty soil, but if there were other pieces of buried treasure lying around he couldn't find them. He pushed the soil and dug-up roots back in, rubbing the grass to disperse the leftover dirt, and then refit the bricks into their original positions as best he could, patting the edges back down before blowing the bricks clean. He sat down and polished the objects with the tail of his shirt, arranging them finally on the arms of the chair, remembering the day his father had come up with the idea of burying treasures and had helped him pick out these several trinkets from the scattered junk on the shelves of his bedroom. The two of them had made an elaborate map and burned the edges with a candle flame, but over the years he had lost track of the map, just as he had forgotten about the treasure itself.

He was vaguely aware again of the barnyard muttering from beyond the fence to the east. He closed his eyes, listening carefully, trying to puzzle out the eerily familiar noise, which faded now, seemingly as soon as he paid attention to it. He opened his eyes, looking toward the fence. A heat haze rippled across the old redwood boards and for one disconcerting moment it seemed to him that he saw right through the shingled rooftops of the tract homes beyond the fence. He blinked the illusion away and looked around uneasily, listening now to the ghostly whispering of the wind in the leaves. It seemed to him that something was pending, like the smell of ozone rising from concrete just before a summer rainfall.

He moved the treasure pieces around idly, letting each of them call up memories of his childhood. He recalled quite clearly his father's telling him that a buried treasure was better than a treasure that you held in your hand, that sometimes it was better that your birds stayed in the bushes, a constant and prevailing mystery.

In his reverie he heard a hissing noise, interrupted by a ratcheting clack, and in the very instant that he identified it as the sound of a Rainbird sprinkler, he felt a spray of drops on his arm. He looked up in surprise, at the empty dead lawn and the deserted house, but the sound had already faded, and his arm was dry. He turned his attention back to the objects, suddenly recalling the name of their basset hound, Hasbro; but no sooner had he formed the name in his mind, and recalled with it a memory of the dog itself, than a blast of wind shook the garden shed behind him, and the limbs of the silk oak flailed overhead so that a storm of leaves blew down. He half stood up in surprise, leaning heavily against the chair arm to steady himself, and the flimsy aluminum frame collapsed beneath him. He fell sideways, dumping the dug-up trinkets onto the lawn, and lay there for a moment, too dizzy to stand, listening to the wind, the tree and clouds spinning around him. There was a glittering before his eyes, like a swarm of fireflies rising from the lawn straight up into the sky, and his face and arms were stung by blowing dust as the wind gusted, its noise a deep basso profundo that seemed to shake his bones. He covered his face with his forearm and struggled to his knees, turning his back to the wind, which died now as suddenly as it had arisen. When he opened his eyes he saw that the aluminum chair had been lifted by the wind and tossed into the grapevines.

He stood staring at the chair and the vines, uncomprehending: the vines were carefully pruned now, stretched out along tight wires affixed to the fence. And he realized that the silk oak beside him was a sapling, maybe twelve feet high, its little bit of foliage sufficient to shade a cat. A car throttled past on the street, and he looked in that direction, feeling exposed, standing in plain sight, a trespasser. The oleander hedge was gone. The sycamores stood as ever, but where the hedge had been was the dirt shoulder of an irrigation ditch. Another car passed on the road, an old Ford truck.

He stepped back out of sight, hidden from the street by the garage and shed, dizzy and faint and hearing from beyond the fence the muttering sounds again: goats, the muttering of goats and chickens from the old Prentice farm. The smell of the sun-hot grapes was cloying, and he had the displaced confusion of waking up from a vivid dream. He heard the ratcheting noise and once more was swept with water droplets that felt as warm as blood against his skin. The lawn was green, and cut short. A hose stretched across from a spigot in the garden to where the Rainbird played water over the grass, the spray advancing toward him.

He saw then that the gate they shared with the Prentices—had shared with the Prentices—stood halfway open. The rooftops of the tract houses that had occupied the old Prentice property were gone, replaced by the dark canopy of a grove of walnut trees that stretched away east like billowing green clouds. The limbs of a plum tree, heavy with fruit, hung over the fence. The windows of his own house were no longer boarded up, the chimney no longer fallen. He remembered the treasure now, lying out on the lawn, and he looked around in a new panic, gripped by the idea that he would want those five objects, that unearthing the treasure was somehow connected to his being here. Getting down onto his hands and knees, he ran his fingers through the grass, but there was no sign of them, the trinkets had simply vanished.

He recalled the little firefly swarm that had lifted from the lawn and blown away in the wind, and he was filled with the certainty that his treasure had decomposed, metamorphosed into some sort of glittering dust. And blown away with it was his return ticket home.

He stepped between the vines and the rear wall of the shed and sat down in the dirt, his mind roaring with the dark suspicion that he was alone in the world, that there was no place in it where he wasn't a stranger. With a surging hope he recalled the faces of old childhood friends; surely he could find his way to their houses. But what sort of greeting would he get, looming up out of the hazy afternoon, a forty-year-old man babbling about being displaced in time? He thought about Susan and Tyler, and his throat constricted. He swallowed hard, forcing himself to think, to concentrate.

An idea came to him with the force of an epiphany: the five objects, his small treasure, might still be buried in the ground. After all, he had dug them up twenty-odd years from now. He walked to the stepping stones, the grass around them now neatly clipped away, and without too much effort lifted one of the bricks out of its depression. He went back to the shed, opening the door and finding a trowel, returning to the hole and hacking into the soil underneath. The trowel sank nearly to its handle. There were fewer entangled roots, and the ground was wet from the recent watering. He wiggled out another brick and jammed the trowel into the dirt in a different place, but again the blade sank without contacting any resistance. He tried a third time, and a fourth and then simply hacked away at the soil until he forced himself to give up the futile search. There was no can, no treasure. Clearly it hadn't been buried yet. When would it be buried? A week from now? A year?

Methodically now, he tamped the soil flat and re-fitted the bricks, tossing the trowel onto the lawn near the base of the tree and stepping across to where the lawn was wet in order to wipe the mud off his hands. He heard a screen door slam, and, turning, he saw movement next door through the narrow gaps between the fence boards: someone—Mrs. Prentice?—walking toward the gate. He ran back toward the shed, and slipped inside, pulling the door shut after him, tripping over the junk on the shed floor and groping in the darkness for something to hold onto.

The objects roundabout him appeared out of the darkness as his eyes adjusted. He recognized them from when he was a kid, doing chores: the rakes and shovels and pruning saws, the old lawn mower, the edger that he used to push around the edges of the stepping stones. Hanging on a peg was the aluminum lawn chair.

He peered out through an open knothole in one of the redwood boards, seeing that old Mrs. Prentice had just come in through the gate. She crossed toward the back of the yard and turned off the sprinkler, then came straight down the stepping stones and passed out of sight. He heard her footsteps on the concrete walk adjacent to the shed, receding down past the garage toward the front of the house, and he pushed the shed door open far enough to step out. Wafering himself against the wall, he edged toward the corner until he could look carefully past it.

She was out on the driveway now, stooping over to pick up a newspaper. She straightened up, looked at the front of the house, and started up the walk in his direction, reading the newspaper headline. He ducked back, hurriedly re-entering the shed and pulling the door silently shut. Her footsteps drew near, then were silent as if she were standing there thinking.

The trowel! Of course she saw it tossed onto the lawn. He caught his breath. *Don't open the door!* he thought, and he grabbed a coat hook screwed into the top of the shed door and held onto it, bracing his other hand against the door jamb in order to stop her from looking in. A couple of seconds passed, and then she tugged on the door handle, managing to open the door a quarter of an inch before he reacted and jerked it back. Again she pulled on it, but he held it tight this time. His heart slammed in his chest, and the wild idea came into his head to throw the door open himself, and simply tell her who he was, that he was Alan, believe it or not. But he didn't let go of the hook. Finally, he heard her walk away. He peered out through the knothole, watching her retrace her steps across the lawn and through the gate, swinging it shut after her. When her screen door slammed, he stepped out into the sunlight. The trowel lay near the tree again, where she had returned it.

He hurried toward the house, keeping low. No one but a lunatic would assume that the shed door was *latched* from the inside. Along with the tossed-aside trowel it would add up to evidence. Would she call the police? Surely not now—not in the innocent middle of the century. He couldn't remember if Mr. Prentice had a day job: perhaps he was home, and she had gone to fetch him. He glanced at the driveway and the street and was struck with the latent realization that his car was gone. *Of course* it was gone, left behind, sitting in that other driveway thirty years in the future. There was no car at all in this driveway, his or the family's car. He looked around more attentively, forcing himself to slow down, to work things out. He saw that there were still puddles of water in the flowerbeds along the driveway, eighty feet from where the Rainbird had been chattering away before Mrs. Prentice had turned it off. The garden was wet, too. She had apparently watered the entire yard over the course of the day, which argued that maybe she wouldn't be back, that she was finished with her work.

And she had picked up the newspaper, too, which made it likely that the family—his family—was away, and must have been away for a while, long enough for it to have fallen to the Prentices to watch over the house and yard. Which meant what?—probably one of their two-week summer trips to Colorado or Iowa or Wisconsin.

Listening hard for the sound of the screen door slamming, he stepped to the back stoop, climbed the three stairs in a crouch in order to remain unseen, and tried the door knob. Again it was locked. *Again?*—the idea of it baffled him, and he was once more swept with a dizzying confusion. This wasn't the second time today he had tried the knob; it was the first time. Although his own fingerprints might already be on it, they would be prints from a smaller hand. . . .

It dawned on him that the objects might be in the house right now, not yet buried. He had no real idea at what age he had buried them—ten, twelve? He heard the Prentice's screen door slam, and almost before he knew he had thought of it, he was heading up along the side of the house toward the front. There, right at the corner of the house, just where he remembered it, stood a big juniper, growing nearly up into the eaves. He felt around on its trunk, waist high, his hand closing on the hidden house key hanging on a nail. The cold metal sent a thrill of relief through him, and a few seconds later he was on the front porch, glancing back at the empty street and sliding the key into the lock. He opened the door and stepped into the dim interior of the living room, recalling the smell of the place, the furniture, the books in the bookcase.

He locked the door carefully behind him and pocketed the key, then moved through the house, into the kitchen, keeping low. Through the window in the door he saw that old Mr. Prentice was in the back yard now. Mrs. Prentice stood at the open gate, watching her husband. He walked to the shed, looking around him. Cautiously he tried the door, which swung open. He looked in, then picked up the trowel from the lawn and put it away. He closed the shed door, and then walked back toward the grapevines. There was nowhere in the yard for a person to hide, except perhaps out in the back corner, where the limbs of the avocado tree hung almost to the ground, creating an enclosed bower. He walked in that direction now, cocking his head, peering into the shadows. But apparently there was enough sunlight through the leaves for him to see that no one at all was hiding there, because he turned and walked back toward the open gate, saying something to his wife.

Then he stopped and looked straight at the house. Alan ducked out of sight, scuttling back across the kitchen floor and into the dining room, wondering wildly where he would hide if the man came in. He heard a step on the back stoop, and the back door rattled as Mr. Prentice tried the bolt. Alan glanced toward the dark hallway. Could he even *fit* under his bed now? But Mr. Prentice descended the wooden steps again, and by the time Alan crept back into the kitchen and looked out the window, the gate was already swinging shut. For another five minutes he stood there watching, relaxing a little more as time passed. Probably old man Prentice would simply think his wife was nuts, that it was just like a woman not to be able to open a shed door.

The several hours before night fell passed slowly. The newspaper beside the living-room couch revealed that it was July of 1968. He was, in this other life, ten years old. Hesitantly he made his way up the hall and looked into his old bedroom. Although it seemed to him impossible, it was utterly familiar. He knew every single thing—the toys, the tossed pieces of clothing, the window curtains, the bedspread, the bubbling aquarium on the dresser—as if he had carried with him a thousand scattered and individualized memories all these years, like the trinkets in the coffee can. He picked up a small net and scooped a dead angel fish out of the aquarium, taking it into the bathroom where he flushed it down the toilet. Then he returned to the room, possessed by the urge to lie down on the bed, draw the curtains across the windows, and stare at the lighted aquarium as he had done so many times so long ago. But he caught himself, feeling oddly like a trespasser despite his memories.

Still, he could be forgiven for borrowing a few things. He looked around, spotting the porcelain basset hound immediately, and then recalling in a rush of memory that the lens of the magnifying glass lay in the top drawer of his old oak desk. He opened the drawer and spotted it, right there in plain sight. The blue marble lay in the drawer too, rolled into the corner. It took him a little longer to find the tiki, which had fallen to the floor beside the dresser. He picked it up and cleaned the dust off it, noting that the ball bearing eyes were train-flattened dime eluded him, though, until he spotted a small metal tray with a flamingo painted on it lying on the night stand, where, before bed, he used to put the odds and ends from his pockets. Seeing the tray reminded him that Alan would be carrying the dime in his pocket back in these days, just as he was carrying the buffalo nickel in his own pocket. So where would the dime be? Wisconsin? Colorado? Or homeward bound in the old Plymouth Fury, driving through the southwest desert? Maybe closer yet, coming down over the Cajon Pass, forty-five minutes away. . . .

He moved the four objects around on the desktop, arranging and rearranging them, waiting for the telltale rising of the wind, the sound of a door creaking open, signifying sounds. But nothing happened.

He thought about keeping the items with him, in his pocket, but in the end he set the tiki on the desktop, put the porcelain dog back on the shelf, and returned the lens and the marble to the drawer, where he could retrieve them all in an instant. He stepped to the window and unlatched it, pushing it open easily. There was no screen, so he could be out the window quickly. Their family had never traveled at night; they were motel travelers—five hundred miles a day and then a Travel Lodge with a pool and Coke machine and, later in the evening, gin rummy around the motel room table. By nine or ten o'clock tonight he could safely fall asleep and then take up his worries tomorrow.

He spent the rest of the afternoon and evening reading his mother's copy of Steinbeck's *The Long Valley*. The book was in his own library at home now—whatever now constituted. The heavy paper pages and brown cloth binding had the same dusty, reassuring smell that he remembered, both as a boy and later as a man, and the stories in the book, existing as they did outside of time, felt like a safe and stable haven to him, a good place to wait things out.

He became aware that it was quickly growing too dark to read, and at the same time he realized that he was ravenously hungry. He walked into the dim kitchen and opened the refrigerator. In the freezer he found a stack of Van de Camp TV dinners, and picked out the Mexican dinner—enchiladas, beans, and rice—and in a moment of stupidity looked around for a microwave oven. Smiling at his own foolishness, he turned on the oven in the O'Keefe and Merritt range, slid the foil-wrapped dinner onto the top rack, and then went back to the refrigerator where he found a hunk of cheddar cheese to snack on. He opened a bottle of Coke to wash it down with and stood at the kitchen sink, watching the glow of sunset fade over the rooftops to the east.

The house was dark when he took his dinner out of the oven, removed the foil, and ate it at the kitchen table, thinking that the enchilada tasted better in his memory than it did now. Although this was something he had already come to expect over the years, it was still a disappointment. It occurred to him that he should look around for a flashlight: he couldn't turn on a brighter light to read by, not with the Prentices next door, probably still spooked over the garden shed mystery. And he wondered idly about the trash: the Coke bottle and the foil tray and wrapper. Who knew what-all he would accumulate if he had to wait out a week here? And what would his mother say when she discovered that the TV dinners in the freezer had vanished? If he was here for the long haul, he would work his way through the refrigerator and freezer and half the cupboard, too.

Thinking about it made him feel more desperately alone, and his shoulders sagged as the enormity of his problem dropped on him like a weight. The empty house around him was true to his memory, and yet it wasn't his anymore. He was reminded of the decades that had passed away, of the first happy years of his marriage when he and Susan had spent their money traveling, of Tyler's childhood, of his mother's death a few short years after she and his father had moved out of the house and retired up the coast in Cambria.

He breathed deeply and looked out the window, trying to focus on the night landscape. The lantern in the driveway illuminated part of the wall of the garage before it faded into darkness. A pair of headlights appeared out on the street, the car swinging around the uphill curve in the road, the noise of its engine dwindling with distance. At least, he thought, there was the happy coincidence of Susan and Tyler being away in Michigan. They might wonder why he wasn't answering the phone at home, but it would likely be days before they began to worry about his absence. Then his mind revolved treacherously back around to his dilemma, and he recalled that Susan and Tyler weren't away in the east at all, not now, not in this century. Tyler was a decade away from being born. Susan was a twelve-year-old girl, living in Anaheim, oblivious to his existence.

What if he couldn't get back? Simply never returned? He saw himself living as a transient, as a ghost, waiting for the years to drag by until he could catch up with them again, drifting on the edges of Susan's life and then of Susan and Tyler's life—of his own life—haunting the same restaurants, hanging around the Little League field, watching the three of them from a distance. But he could never insinuate himself into their lives. A strange interloper—particularly a copy of himself—would never be welcome, not by Susan and not by Tyler and most of all not by him, by Alan, who wasn't really the same *him* at all now that the years had passed, despite the blood that ran in his veins.

Of course on that far-off day when Susan and Tyler would travel back to Michigan, and Alan, feeling lonely and maudlin, would once again dig up the treasure, then a door would open and he could step in and fill his own shoes, literally, if he chose to. He could simply walk back into his old life, answer the long distance calls when they came, prepare himself to tell his phenomenal story to Tyler, whose father had now disappeared, and to Susan, whose husband had aged thirty years overnight, and might as well be her own grandfather.

This time he didn't hear the sound of the car engine or see the headlights, but he heard the car door slam, heard a boy's voice—his own voice!—shout something, his own father shouting back, telling him to carry his own suitcase. Without a second thought, Alan was on his feet, starting toward his bedroom. He stopped himself and turned back toward the kitchen table, picking up the TV tray and shoving it into the trash under the sink, cramming the empty Coke bottle in after it and wiping his hand across the table to clean up a smear of enchilada sauce. The *back* door, he thought, but even as he turned toward the service porch he heard his father coming up along the side of the house, headed for the back yard, and through the kitchen window he saw the shadowy figure carrying an ice chest. He ducked out of sight, hearing the clatter of a key in the front door lock, and slipped into the hallway, heading straight into his bedroom, sliding up the window. He stopped, hearing his mother's voice in the livingroom now, followed by his own voice complaining about something. But there was no time to listen. He grabbed the porcelain dog and the tiki and slipped them into his pocket, then opened the drawer and snatched up the lens and the marble, shoving the drawer shut even as he was pulling the window curtains aside. He swung his foot over the sill and simply rolled out sideways into the flowerbed, scrambled to his feet, and quietly shut the window. He crouched there catching his breath, and watched as the bedroom light blinked on and he heard the suitcase drop to the floor.

As silently as possible he walked up the side of the house, trying to stop himself from trembling. He was relatively safe right where he was as long as he made no noise: there was no reason on earth for his father to come out here to the side of the house. He heard a sound now—the shed door closing, the ice chest no doubt returned to its place on the shelf—and he peered out past the corner of the service porch to see his father head back down the driveway toward the car. He looked at his watch. It was just eight o'clock, early yet, and he recalled the familiar nightly routine, the Sunday evening television, probably ice cream and cookies. But first Alan would have put on his pajamas so that he was ready for bed, which would mean either emptying his pockets into the tray if he was feeling organized, or, equally likely, simply throwing his pants onto the bedroom floor.

Impatient, he walked silently back down toward the bedroom, where the light still shone through the curtains. Whatever he was going to do, he had to do it tonight. It wouldn't get any easier. And what was the alternative? Spend his days and nights hiding in the garden shed, drinking water out of the hose, waiting for another chance? As soon as it was safe he would reenter the room, find the dime, and go back out the window. In the back yard he could take his time arranging the five items; he could take the rest of his life arranging and rearranging them until whatever had happened to him happened once more.

The moon had risen over the mountains to the east, and shone now on the wall of the house. He stood listening at the closed window, standing aside so that his moon shadow was cast on the wall and not on the curtains. The seconds passed in silence. It was impossible to tell whether Alan was still in the room or had gone out, leaving the light on. But then he heard the sound of the television in the livingroom, the channels changing. Had it been Alan who had turned it on? He held his breath, focusing on the silence, listening for movement.

Making up his mind, he put his hand softly against the top of the window sash and pushed on it gently and evenly. Just then the bedroom light blinked out, plunging the room into darkness. He ducked away from the window, his heart racing. Minutes passed and nothing happened, the night silent but for the sound of crickets and the muted chatter on the television. He stood up again, took a deep breath, and pushed the window open as far as it would go. After listening to the silence, he boosted himself up onto the sill, overbalancing and sliding into the room. He stood up, hearing voices—his mother and father, talking quietly but urgently.

He saw the smashed dime in the tray along with some other coins, and in an instant it was in his hand and he turned back toward the window, crawling through, his shoes bumping against the sill as he tumbled onto the ground. He clambered to his feet, grabbing the window to shut it. The bedroom light came on, and he froze in a crouch, the window not quite shut, the curtain hitched open an inch where it had caught on the latch. He hesitated, drawing his hand slowly away from the window frame, certain they knew someone had been in the house. And yet he couldn't bring himself to move: getting away—getting back—meant nothing to him.

"Don't say anything to him," his father said, close by now. "There's no use making him worry." Alan saw him briefly as he crossed the bedroom, disappearing beyond the edge of the curtain.

"But the oven is still *warm*," his mother said, following him in. "And sauce on the tray in the trash isn't even dried out. I think he was here when we came home. What if he's still in the house?"

Alan bent toward the window until he could see her face. Somehow it hadn't occurred to him how young she would be, probably thirty-five or six. He had known that she was pretty, but over the years he had lost track of how absolutely lovely she had been, and he found that his memory of her was shaped by her last years, when she was older and fighting with the cancer.

"He's not in the house," his father said. "I've been all through it, putting things away. If he's not in *here*, which he's obviously not, then he's gone. I'll check the garage and the shed just to make sure. For now, though, let's just keep this to ourselves."

"But what did he want? This is too weird. He was reading one of my *books*. Who would break into a house to read the books?"

"I don't know. I don't think anything's missing. There was money on the dresser in the bedroom, and it's still there. Your jewelry box hasn't been touched. . . ."

There was a sudden silence now, and Alan realized that the curtains were moving gently in the breeze through the open window. He ducked away down the side of the house as quickly and silently as he could, half expecting to hear the window slide open behind him or the sound of hurrying footsteps in the house. Without hesitating he set straight out across the back lawn toward the garden shed, looking back at the kitchen window and back door. The light was on in the kitchen, but there was still no one visible.

Should he get the chair out of the shed? Be sitting down for this? Reenact the whole thing exactly? He dug the five objects out of his pocket and held them in one hand, hopefully anticipating the disorienting shift, the rising of the wind, the rippling air. But nothing happened. He was simply alone in the moonlit night, the crickets chirping around him. His father appeared in the kitchen now, clearly heading toward the back door, and Alan moved back toward the grapevines, out of sight. He heard the door open as he sat down on the lawn, laying the objects on his knees, compelling himself to concentrate on them and not on the approaching footsteps, which stopped close by. He opened his eyes and looked up, feeling like an idiot. His father stood a few feet away, a golf club in his hands, staring down at him. Alan stared back in momentary confusion. He might have been looking at his own brother.

"Why don't you just stay there," his father said, "so I don't have to bean you with this driver."

"Sure."

"What were you doing in the house?"

For a time Alan couldn't answer. When he found his voice he said simply, "I'm Alan."

"Okay. I'm Phil. Pardon me if I don't shake your hand. What the hell were you doing in my house? What were you looking for?"

Alan smiled at the question, which was no easier to answer than the last one. "My past," he said. "I was looking for my past. You don't recognize me, do you? You can't."

"What do you mean, your past? Did you used to live here or something? This is some kind of nostalgia thing?"

"Yeah. I used to live here."

"So what are you doing with my son's stuff? That's from his room, isn't it? That dog and the tiki?"

"It's from his room. But I didn't steal it."

"You're just borrowing it?"

"Yes," Alan said softly. Then, "No, it's mine, too. I *am* Alan . . . Dad." He had to force himself to say it out loud, and he found that there were tears welling in his eyes. His father still stood staring at him, his own face like a mask.

Alan went on, pulling random bits from his memory: "You bought me the aquarium at that place in Garden Grove, off Magnolia Street. We got a bunch of fish, and they all ate each other, and we had to go back down there and buy more. And you know the cracked shade on the lamp in the livingroom? Me and Eddie Landers did that by accident after school on Halloween day when we were waiting for Mom to come home. That was probably last Halloween, or maybe two years ago at the most. I was the mummy, remember? Eddie was Count Dracula. He was staying here because his parents were out of town. Let me show you something," he said, carefully laying the five trinkets on the brick pad in front of the shed door and then shifting forward to get to his feet. His father took a step back, and the head of the golf club rose where it had been resting on the lawn. Alan stopped moving. "Can I get up?"

"Okay. Slowly, eh?"

"Sure. Just getting my wallet." Alan stood, reaching into his back pocket. He took his drivers license out of his wallet and held it out. "Look at the date." He pocketed the wallet, and his father took the card, turning it so that it was illuminated by moonlight. "Above the picture," Alan told him. He heard laughter from inside the house now, and realized that it was himself, probably watching television, still oblivious to everything going on outside here.

After glancing at it his father handed the license back. "I guess I don't get it," he said. But clearly he did get it; he simply couldn't believe it.

Alan put the license into his shirt pocket. "I came back from—from thirty years from now. In the future." He pointed at the objects lying on the bricks. "You and I buried this stuff in a coffee can, like a treasure, under the first stepping stone, right there."

"We did, eh? We buried them? When was that?"

Alan shrugged. "Any day now, I guess. Next month? I don't know, but we buried them. We will, anyway. I came back and dug them up."

There was the sound of the back door opening, and his mother came out onto the back stoop, looking in their direction. "What are you doing, dear?" she asked with feigned cheerfulness. "Is everything all right?" Probably she was ready to call the police.

"Yeah, it's fine," Alan's father said back to her. "Just . . . putting some stuff away." She stepped back into the house and shut the door, but then reappeared in the kitchen, where she stood at the window, watching. His father was still staring at him, but puzzled, less suspicious now.

"You remember the time we were up at Irvine Park," Alan asked, "and we found those old bottle caps with the cork on the back, and you got the corks out and put the bottle caps on my shirt, with the cork holding them on from the other side? And I picked up that cactus apple and got all the needles in my hand? And it started to rain, and we got under the tree, and you said that the pitcher of lemonade would get wet, and Mom ran back to the table to cover it?"

His father dropped the golf club to the lawn, letting it lie there. "That was thirty years ago," Alan said. "Can you imagine? It's still funny, though. And there was that time when Mom lost her purse, remember, and she looked all over for it, and you came home from work and found it in the refrigerator?"

"She put it away with the groceries," his father said. "That was last month."

Alan nodded. "I guess it could have been." He realized now that his father's silence was no longer disbelief, and he stepped forward, opening his arms. His father hugged him, and for a time they stood there, listening to the night, saying nothing. Alan stepped away finally, and his father squeezed him on the shoulder, smiling crookedly, looking hard at his face.

Alan reached into his pocket and took out the odds and ends that he carried, the buffalo nickel, his pocket knife. He showed his father the little antler-handled knife. "Recognize this? It's just like the one you gave me, except I lost that one. I found this one just like it at the hardware store and bought it about a year ago."

"I didn't give you a pocket knife like that."

"You know what? I guess maybe you haven't given it to me yet."

"Then I guess I don't need to bother, if you're just going to lose the damned thing."

Alan smiled at him. "But if you don't, then how am I going to know to buy this one at the hardware store?"

They listened in silence to the crickets for a moment. "How old would you be now?" his father asked him.

"Forty-two," Alan said. "How about you?"

"Forty. That's pretty funny. Married?"

"Yeah. Take a look at this." He dug in his wallet again, removing a picture of Tyler, his high school graduation picture. He looked at it fondly, but abruptly felt dizzy, disoriented. He nearly sat down to keep himself from falling. His father took the picture, and the dizziness passed. "That's Tyler," Alan said, taking a deep breath and focusing his thoughts. But he heard his own voice as an echo, as if through a tube. "Your grandson. Susan and I gave him Mom's maiden name."

Alan's father studied the picture. "He looks like your mother, doesn't he?"

"A lot. I didn't realize it until tonight, when she was standing in my bedroom. You must have seen that the window was open . . . ?"

"*Your* bedroom," his father said, as if wondering at the notion. "Here." Alan took his keys out of his other pocket. Among them was the loose house key that he had removed from the nail in the juniper. "That's how I got into the house."

Still holding Tyler's picture, his father took the key. He nodded at the other keys on Alan's key ring. "What's that one?"

Alan held out his car key. "Car key. One of the buttons is for the door locks and the other pops the trunk open from a distance. There's a little battery in it. It puts out an FM radio wave. Push the door button a couple of times, and an alarm goes off." Alan pushed it twice, recalling that his own car, in some distant space and time, was sitting just thirty feet away, and he found himself listening to hear a ghostly car alarm. But what he heard, aside from the crickets and the muted sound of the television, was a far-off clanking noise, like rocks cascading onto a steel plate. The night wind ruffled his hair. And from beyond the fence, just for a split second, the dark canopy of walnut leaves looked hard-edged and rectilinear to him, like rooftops. Then it was a dark, slowly moving mass again, and he heard laughter and the sound of the television.

"Thirty years?"

"It seems like a long time, but I swear it's not."

"No, I don't guess it is. What's the date back where you come from? Just out of curiosity."

Alan thought about it. "Eighth of July, 2001." He found himself thinking about his mother, doing the math in his head. What did she have? Twenty years or so? His father hadn't ever remarried. Alan glanced toward the house where his mother still stood at the window, looking out at the night.

His father followed his gaze. "Tell me something," he said after a moment. "Were you happy? You know, growing up?"

"I was happy," Alan said truthfully. "It was a good time."

"You found your heart's desire?"

"Yeah, I married her."

"And how about your boy Tyler? You think he's happy?" He held the picture up.

"I think so. Sure. I know it."

"Uh huh. Look, I think maybe it's better if you go back now, before your Mom flips. Can you? It's getting late."

"Yeah," Alan said, realizing absolutely that the clanking noise he had heard was the sound of a jackhammer. He took the pocket knife and nickel out of his pocket again, and held them in his hand with his keys, then reached into his shirt pocket to retrieve his drivers license.

"I'd invite you in, you know, for ice cream and cookies, but your mother—I don't know what she'd do. I don't think it would . . ."

"I know. Alan, too. . . ." He nodded at the house. "We might as well let him watch TV."

"Right. It would be like . . . a disturbance, or something. I guess we don't need that. We're doing pretty good on our own."

"And it's going to stay good," Alan said. "Is there anything? . . ."

"That I want to know?" His father shook his head. "No. I'm happy with things like they are. I'm looking forward to meeting Tyler, though." He handed the picture back.

"If you can ever find some way to do it," Alan said, taking the picture, "let Mom know that. . . ."

But he felt himself falling backward. And although it came to him later as only a dim memory, he recalled putting out his hand to stop his fall, dropping the stuff that he held. He found himself now in bright sunlight, lying on the dead Bermuda grass, the words of his half-finished sentence lost to him, the onrushing wind already dying away and the smell of grapes heavy on the sun-warmed air. The telltale glitter shimmered before his eyes, and he sat up dizzily, looking around, squinting in the brightness, hearing the clanging of the jack-hammer, which cut off sharply, casting the afternoon into silence. He saw that the shed was dilapidated and doorless now, the house once again boarded up. His car, thank God, sat as ever in the driveway.

His keys! He stood up dizzily, looking down at his feet. With his keys gone he had no way of . . .

"Hey."

At the sound of the voice, Alan shouted in surprise and reeled away into the wall of the shed, turning around and putting out his hands. He saw that a man sat in the dilapidated aluminum lawn chair beneath the silk oak—his father, smiling at him. With the sun shining on his face, he might have been a young man. Alan lowered his hands and smiled back.

"Welcome home," his father said to him.

# Honorable Mentions: 2001

Abraham, Daniel, "As Sweet," *Realms of Fantasy*, December.

———, "The Lesson Half-Learned," *Asimov's Science Fiction Magazine*, May.

Addison, Linda D., "Fiery Oracle" (poem), *Consumed, Reduced to Beautiful Grey Ashes*.

———, "The Hunt" (poem), Ibid.

———, "The Next Time" (poem), Ibid.

Aguirre, Forrest, "The Universal Language of Silence," *Twilight Showcase*, January.

Alexander, Maria, "The King of Shadows," gothic.net, December.

Allen, Brady, "Six Miles From Earth," *Crimewave 5: Dark Before Dawn*.

Anderson, Kevin J., "Redmond's Private Screening," *Realms of Fantasy*, April.

Anderson, Poul, "The Lady of the Winds," *Fantasy & Science Fiction*, October/November.

Aprile, Emma, "Fairy Story" (poem), *Poem*, November.

Aridjis, Homero, translated by George McWhirter, "Six Senses of Death" (poem), *Conjunctions* 36.

Baker, Kage, "The Applesauce Monster," *Asimov's SF*, December.

———, "What the Tyger Told Her," *Realms of Fantasy*, June.

Banker, Ashok, "Devi Ations," gothic.net, December.

———, "Devi Darshan," *Weird Tales* 326.

———, "In the Shadow of Her Wings," *Interzone*, April.

Barker, Lawrence, "Gurian," *Not One of Us* 26.

Barker, Trey R., "Cage," *Talebones* 21.

———, "How Still Her Eyes," *Crime Spree*.

———, "Needle and Blood," *The Dead Inn*.

Barron, Laird, "Shiva, Open Your Eye," *Fantasy & Science Fiction*, September.

Bauer, Chris, "Downsizing," *Kimota* 14.

Beal, Steve, "Following Fitzgerald," *Extremes 3: Terror on the High Seas*.

Bennett, Nancy, "Jane, the Giant's Wife" (poem), Dark Planet CD-Rom.

———, "Meeting Death" (poem), *Frisson*, Spring.

———, "Widow's Walk" (poem), *Penny Dreadful* 14.

Berman, Ruth, "Renting the Overgrown Grounds" (poem), *Asimov's SF*, January.

Berne, Henry, "Oedipus Again" (poem), *Frisson*, Summer.

Bewick, Simon, "Somewhere Down the River," *Strange Horizons*, September.

Blaylock, James P., "Small Houses," scifi.com, October 10.

Bloom, Reginald, "Your Infection," *Chiaroscuro* 10.

Bloomingdale, Judith, "The Woman in the Moon" (poem), *The Texas Review*, Vol. XXII, #3/4.

Boston, Bruce, "Arbitrary Night in the University Lab" (poem), *White Space*.

———, "Curse of the Succubus' Husband" (poem), Ibid.

———, "Embracing the Singularity," *Masque of Dreams*.

———, "Raucous World" (poem), *White Space*.

Bowes, Richard, "For Innocent Children," *My Life in Speculative Fiction*.

———, "The Quicksilver Kid," scifi.com, January 17.

Bradburn-Ruster, Michael, "Language of the Crow" (poem), *The Antigonish Review* 125.

Bradbury, Ray, "Fore!" *Fantasy & Science Fiction*, October/November.

Branseum, John, "The Boys Under the Bridge" (poem), *Flesh & Blood* 7.

Braunbeck, Gary A., "Curtain Call," *Dracula in London*.

———, "The Fields, the Sky," *Creature Fantastic*.

———, "In the Direction of Summers Coming," *Escaping Purgatory: Fables in Words and Pictures*.

Braunbeck, Gary A., & Snyder, Lucy A., "Souls to Take," *Villains Victorious*.

Brite, Poppy Z., "The Crystal Empire," *Wrong Things*.

———, "O Death, Where Is Thy Spatula," thespook.com, July.

Brooke, Keith, "Memesis," *Strange Pleasures*.

Broster, D. K., "The Taste of Pomegranates," *Couching at the Door*.

Brown, Eric, "A Writer's Life" (novella), PS Publishing.

Brown, Warren & Brown, Lana, "Sifting Out the Hearts of Men," *The Book of All Flesh*.

Bucknell, Tobias S., "Trinkets," Ibid.

Burns, Cliff, "Windigo," *Roadworks* 12.

Cacek, P. D., "The Christmas Ghost," Christmas Card from Wormhole Books.

———, "Go Get the Doctor and the Doctor Said," *Bloodtype*.

Cadnum, Michael, "Elf Trap," *Fantasy & Science Fiction*, April.

Calder, Richard, "Espiritu Santo," *Interzone*, August.

———, "The Nephilim," *Interzone*, February.

Campbell, Ramsey, "All for Sale," *gothic.net*, December.

———, "Raised by the Moon," thespook.com, July.

———, "Tatters," thespook.com, October.

———, "Worse Than Bones," *The Museum of Horrors*.

Cancilla, Dominick, "The Execution Trick," thespook.com, July.

Carter, Stuart, "Spectacle of Nothing," *Kimota* 14.

Castle, Mort, "I Am Your Need," *Brain Box: Son of Brainbox*.

Castro, Adam-Troy, "The Juggler," *A Desperate, Decaying Darkness*.

———, "Toy," Ibid.

Charles, Renée M., "Opening the Veins of Jade," *Wicked Words* 5.

Chiang, Ted, "Hell is the Absence of God," *Starlight* 3.

Chislett, Michael, "The Waif," *Supernatural Tales* 1.

———, "You'll Never Walk Alone," *Ghosts & Scholars* 33.

Choo, Mary E., "The Language of Crows," World Fantasy Convention CD-Rom.

Christie, Antony, "Caliban's Island" (poem), *The Antigonish Review* 126.

Clark, Simon, "Goblin City Lights," *Urban Gothic*.

Claverie, Ezra, "Burcham Is Unrelenting," *Crimson Online Magazine* 14.

Cole, Henri, "Myself With Cats" (poem), *The New Yorker*, October 10.

Collins, Paul, "Whispers," *Stalking Midnight*.

Conrad, C. A., "The Franks" (poem), *Strange Horizons*, November 19.

Conrad, Roxanne Longstreet, "The Dark Downstairs," *Dracula in London*.

Conway, Jason, "Broken," *Darkness Rising: Hideous Dreams*.

Cooper, Geoff, "Badgetree: A Brackard's Point Story," *A Darker Dawning*.

Coover, Robert, "Punch," *Conjunctions* 36.

Coville, Bruce, "The Hardest, Kindest Gift," *Half-human*.

Coward, Mat, "One Box of Books," "Broadcast From Bath" series, BBC Radio.

Cowdall, David, "Caressed," *Peep Show* 2.

Cowdrey, Albert E., "The King of New Orleans," *Fantasy & Science Fiction*, February.

———, "Nature 2000," *Fantasy & Science Fiction*, April.

———, "Queen for a Day," *Fantasy & Science Fiction*, October/November.

Cox, F. Brett, "What They Did to My Father," *Black Gate*, Summer.

Crowther, Peter, "Barnard Boyce Bennington and the American Dream," *SWV*. . . .

Curnow, Fiona, "The Protection," deathlings.com.

D'Ammassa, Don, "Delayed Departure," *Extremes* 2.

Dann, Jack, "The Diamond Pit" (novella), *Fantasy & Science Fiction*, June.

De Lint, Charles, "Refinerytown," Triskell Press (chapbook).

Deja, Thomas, "The Judgment of the Unicorn," *Bare Bones* 1.

Del Vento, A., "Released," *Indigenous Fiction*, February.

DeNiro, Alan, "Cuttlefish," *Lady Churchill's Rosebud Wristlet* 8.

———, "The Excavation," *Minnesota Monthly*, June.

———, "The Friendly Giants," *3rd Bed* 4.

Disch, Thomas M., "Jour de Fête," *Fantasy & Science Fiction*, May.

———, "The Shadow," *Fantasy & Science Fiction*, December.

Dixit, Shikhar, "Spontaneous Generation," *Strange Horizons*, March 3.

Dodds, John, "Dr. North's Wound," *Fantastic Metropolis* (webzine), December.

Doig, James, "Friends of the Dead," *Ghosts & Scholars* 33.

———, "The Visit," *All Hallows* 26.

Donati, Stefano, "Johnny Click Latelies," *Poddities*.

Doolittle, Sean, "A Kick in the Lunchbucket," *Crimewave 5: Dark Before Dawn*.

Dorr, James S., "Dust," *Strange Mistresses*.

———, "The Madwoman of Pontneuf" (poem), *Chiaroscuro* 8.

———, "Rat Girl," *Dark Regions* 16.

———, "The Riverman's Daughter," *Strange Mistresses*.

———, "Swarms," *Bloodtype*.

Douglas, Kay, "Lock 27," *All Hallows* 26.

Duffy, Steve, "Better Than One," *The Five Quarters*.

———, "Forever and a Day," Ibid.

———, "Old as the Hills," *Ghosts & Scholars* 33.

Duncan, Andy, "Premature Burials," *Realms of Fantasy*, April.

———, "Senator Bilbo," *Starlight* 3.

Dungate, Pauline E., "Nina," *Villains Victorious*.

Dunn, Dawn, "Never Say Die," *Pink Marble and Never Say Die* (chapbook).

———, "Pink Marble," Ibid.

Durbin, Frederic S., "The Place of Roots," *Fantasy & Science Fiction*, February.

Dyer, Lawrence, "The Gravedigger," *Nemonymous*, November.

Earle, Steve, "Jaguar Dance," *Doghouse Roses*.

Edelman, Scott, "Do the Dead Care?" *These Words are Haunted*.

——, "Live People Don't Understand," *The Book of All Flesh*.

Edghill, Rosemary, "Child of Ocean," *Oceans of Magic*.

Eekhout, Greg van, "Runaway with No Tags," *Maelstrom*, October.

Eller, Steve, "Consumption," Ibid.

——, "Facets," *Extremes* 2.

Ellison, Harlan, "From A to Z, in the Sarsaparilla Alphabet," *Fantasy & Science Fiction*, February.

Emory, Jon-Michel, "The Restoration Man," *New Genre* 2.

Emshwiller, Carol, "As If," *Lady Churchill's Rosebud Wristlet* 8.

Eschbach, Andreas, trans. by Doryl Jensen, "The Carpetmaker's Son," *Fantasy & Science Fiction*, January.

Etchemendy, Nancy, "Demolition," *Fantasy & Science Fiction*, April.

Etchison, Dennis, "Kill Them All," *Cemetery Dance* 34.

——, "One of Us," thespook.com, September.

——, "Red Dog Down," *Talking in the Dark*.

Faulkner, Ian M., "Emmy," *All Hallows* 28.

Feeley, Gregory, "Spirit of Place" (novella), ipublish.com.

Files, Gemma, "Folly," World Fantasy Convention CD-Rom.

——, "No Darkness But Ours," *Twilight Showcase*, Nov.–Jan. 2002.

——, "Year Zero," *The Mammoth Book of Vampire Stories by Women*.

Finch, Paul, "The Extremist," horrorfind.com. June.

——, "Flibbertigibbet" (novella), *Mammoth Book of Historical Whodunnits*.

——, "The Knock at the Cellar Door," *After Shocks*.

——, "September," Ibid.

Fintushel, Eliot, "Drought," *Lady Churchill's Rosebud Wristlet* 9.

Fishler, Barry, "Song for Edna," *The Third Alternative* 29.

Forbes, Amy Beth, "A is for Apple," *Lady Churchill's Rosebud Wristlet* 9.

Ford, Jeffrey, "Out of the Canyon," *Fantastic Metropolis* (webzine), October 15.

Fox, Derek M., "Downfall," *Through Dark Eyes*.

——, "Family Ties," Ibid.

——, "Salt Wind," Ibid.

——, "Shapes," Ibid.

——, "Walking on Shadows," *Bare Bones* 1.

Franklin, Aaron, "All Burnt to Ashes," *All Hallows* 26.

Franks, Jason, "The Third Sigil," deathlings.com.

Frazer, Shamus, "Khorassim," *Where Human Pathways End*.

——, "Mr. Nicholas Loses His Grip," Ibid.

——, "Walking on Air," Ibid.

Friesner, Esther M., "Warts and All," *Fantasy and Science Fiction*, March.

Fry, Susan, "The Impressionists in Winter," *The Museum of Horrors*.

Fu, Shelley, "The Heavenly River," *Ho Yi the Archer*.

G. Jon, "Straw-Clutching," *Roadworks* 12.

Gagliani, William D., "Port of Call," *Extremes 3: Terror on the High Seas*.

——, "Starbird," *The Midnighters Club*.

Gaiman, Neil, "Other People," *Fantasy & Science Fiction*, October/November.

Gallagher, Stephen, "Feeding Frenzy," *Walking in Eternity*.

———, "My Repeater," *Fantasy and Science Fiction*, January.

Gardner, C.A., "Triptych," *Horror Garage* 4.

Gates-Grimwood, Terry, "The Friends of Mike Santini," *Nemonymous*, November.

Gifune, Greg F., "Malevolent Night," *Bloodtype*.

———, "Past Tense," *Heretics*.

Glass, Alexander, "The Necropolis Line," *The Third Alternative* 26.

———, "Violin Road," *The Third Alternative* 28.

Glassco, Bruce, "If I Never Get Back," *Realms of Fantasy*, June.

Godfrey, Darren O., "Inland, Shoreline," *The Museum of Horrors*.

Gonzalez, Ray, "The Garden of Padre Anselmo," *The Ghost of John Wayne and Other Stories*.

Gorman, Ed, "I Know What the Night Knows," *Cemetery Dance* 34.

Goss, Theodora, "Chrysanthemums" (poem), *Lady Churchill's Rosebud Wristlet* 8.

———, "Helen in Sparta" (poem), Ibid.

———, "The Ophelia Cantos" (poem), *Lady Churchill's Rosebud Wristlet* 9.

Gould, Jason, "Human Nature," *Masters of Terror 2001 Anthology* (Web site).

Grant, Charles L., "Whose Ghosts These Are," *The Museum of Horrors*.

Grant, John, "Snare," *Strange Pleasures*.

Grave, P. K., "Winter Feed," *Dark Horizons* 39 (Spring).

Gray, Muriel, "Shite Hawks," *The Third Alternative* 27.

Gray, T. M., "Beyond the Mist," *Extremes 3: Terror on the High Seas*.

Greenberg, David, "Minotaur" (poem), *Colorado Review*, Fall/Winter.

Greenland, Colin, "Wings," *Starlight* 3.

Greenwood, Ed, "One Last, Little Revenge," *The Book of All Flesh*.

Gross, Daniel, "Other Moments," *Strange Horizons*, December 10.

Grow, M. E., "The Donner Party—Christmas Eve" (poem), *The New York Quarterly* 57.

Gullen, David, "the red painted metal felt cool and smooth in his grip . . ." *Roadworks* 12.

Haldeman, Joe, "January Fires" (poem), *Asimov's SF*, January.

Hall, Hazel, "Maker of Songs" (poem), *Calyx*, Summer.

Hambly, Barbara, "Til Death," *Bending the Landscape: Horror*.

Hardy, K. S., "The Conjurer of Storms" (poem), *Penny Dreadful* 14.

———, "Hell Gate" (poem), *The Bible of Hell*.

Hardy, Melissa, "The Unchartered Heart," *The Unchartered Heart*.

Harman, Christopher, "Laughing Matter," *Dark Horizons* 40.

Harness, Charles L., "The Dome," *Weird Tales* 326.

Harrington, Janice N., "Superstitions that the Mulatto Passed on to Her Daughter" (poem), *Beloit Poetry Journal*, Winter.

Hartley, James L., "The Children of Temujin," *The Rare Anthology*.

Hartman, Keith, "Waltz of the Epileptic Penguins," *Bending the Landscape: Horror*.

Hautala, Rick, "Miss Henry's Bottles" (novella), *Trick or Treat*.

Hemmingson, Michael, "American Scenes of Affection," *Delirium* (webzine) 5.

———, "Pup," *Bare Bones* 1.

Henderson, Eoin, "Hound Dog Blues," *Roadworks* 12.

Hernández, Gary G., "Lilith's Dance," *Fantasmas*.

Higgins, John, "Present Tense," *Aurealis* 27/28.

Hines, Jim C., "Inspecting the Workers," *The Book of All Flesh*.

Hoffman, Nina Kiriki, "Star Song," *A Constellation of Cats*.

———, "The Mouse's Song" (poem), *Out of Avalon*.

Holder, Nancy, "Dead Devil in the Freezer," *Cemetery Dance* 36.

Holland, Jane, "Love Song for a Gargoyle" (poem), *Poetry Review*, Summer.

Hood, Robert, "Rotten Times," *Aurealis* 27/28.

Hook, Andrew, "April Syrup," *Roadworks* 12.

Hopkins, Brian A., "Diving the Coolidge," *Historical Hauntings*.

———, "These Are The Moments I Live For," *These I Know By Heart*.

Hopkins, Brian A., & Van Pelt, James, "In the Days Still Left," *Bending the Landscape: Horror*.

Hopkinson, Nalo, "And The Lilies—Them A-Blow," *Skin Folk*.

———, "Snake," Ibid.

———, "Something to Hitch Meat To," Ibid.

———, "Under Glass," Ibid.

Houarner, Gerard, "Here Come the Whistle Men," *Horror Garage* 4.

———, "A Kiss to Build a Dream," *Bloodtype*.

———, "When Mom Changed," *Scars*.

Houarner, Gerard Daniel, "Smoking Mirror Reflection," *Rogue Worlds*, October 1.

Howard, Jonathan L., "Between the River and the Road," *Realms of Fantasy*, June.

Howe, Harrison, "On Borrowed Time," *Poddities*.

Howkins, Elizabeth, "The Lacemaker" (poem), *Penny Dreadful* 14.

———, "The Scavengers" (poem), Ibid.

Hoyt, Sarah A., "Another George," *Dark Regions* 15 Winter/Spring.

Humphrey, Andrew, "Family Game," *Crimewave 5: Dark Before Dawn*.

———, "Open the Box," *The Third Alternative* 29.

Hunt, Deborah, "The Kiss," *Bare Bones* 1.

Hunter, Ian, "The Sand is Always Waiting," horrorfind.com.

———, "The Woman with the Hair," *Human*.

Hyck, Michael T., Jr., "Harvesting Sorrow," 4×4.

Hyde, Gregory R., "Flesh Wound," *A Pound of Ezra*.

———, "Just Another Blue," Ibid.

———, "Old in Asia," Ibid.

———, "A Pound of Ezra," Ibid.

Ings, Simon, "Ménage," *Asimov's SF*, October/November.

Jacob, Charlee, "Baby," *The Dead Inn*.

———, "Child of Ocean," *Extremes 3: Terror on the High Seas*.

———, "Dreamspike," *Brain Box: Son of Brainbox*.

———, "Hanoi Halloween" (poem), *Bare Bones* 1.

———, "A Soothing, Yet Penetrating Poetry," *Extremes 2*

———, "Taunting the Minotaur" (poem), *Taunting the Minotaur*.

———, "Upon the Genesis Board" (poem), *The Bible of Hell*.

Jacobs, Harvey, "Fish Story," *Fantasy and Science Fiction*, February.

Jones, Gwyneth, "A North Light," *The Mammoth Book of Vampire. Stories by Women*.

Jones, Mark Howard, "Wishful Thinking," *Roadworks* 12.

Joyce, Paul, "Burning Angels Down," *Kimota* 15.

Kandel, Michael, "Mayhem Tours," *Fantasy and Science Fiction*, September.

Kane, Mary, "Yellow Chair," *Beloit Poetry Journal*, Winter.

Katz, Joy, "From the Tree, You Must Not Eat" (poem), *South West Review*, Vol. 86, #2/3.

Kay, Guy Gavriel, "At the Root of Her Tree" (poem), World Fantasy Convention CD-Rom.

Keene, Brian, "Earthworm Gods" (novella), *No Rest for the Wicked*.

———, "Lest Ye Become," *Poddities*.

Keene, Brian & Olivieri, Michael, "Crazy for You," *Crime Spree*.

———, "To Fight with Monsters," *4×4*.

Keene, Jarret, "Conjure Me," *Louisiana Literature*, Spring.

Kelly, Michael, "The Melancholy Taste of Metal," *Twilight Showcase*, November.

Keohane, Dan, "The Doll Wagon," *Poddities*.

Kennedy, Jake, "Motif," *Descant* 112.

Ketchum, Jack, "The Haunt," *Cemetery Dance* 34.

———, "Mother + Daughter," thespook.com, August.

———, "The Passenger" (novella), *Night Visions* 10.

———, "Sheep Meadow Story" (novella), *Triage*.

Kidd, Chico, "Mark of the Beast," *Second Sight and Other Stories*.

———, "Pandora's Box," Ibid.

———, "Past Acquaintances," Ibid.

———, "Second Sight," Ibid.

Kiernan, Caitlín R., "So Runs the World Away," *The M. B. of Vampire Stories by Women*.

Kiernan, Caitlín R. & Brite, Poppy Z., "The Rest of the Wrong Thing," *Wrong Things*.

Kilpatrick, Nancy, "Cold Comfort," *Cold Comfort*.

———, "The Middle of Nowhere," Ibid.

Klages, Ellen, "Triangle," *Bending the Landscape: Horror*.

Klaus, Annette Curtis, "Summer of Love," *The Color of Absence*.

Knight, Damon, "The Fourth Wish," thespook.com, October.

Kopel, Stephen, "bly-blessed" (poem), *The Antigonish Review* 126.

Koskinen, Marjatta, (tran. from Finnish by Jill Timbers) "Dies Irae," *With Signs & Wonders*.

Laimo, Michael, "Last Resort," *The Book of All Flesh*.

Lake, Paul, "Saint Nick" (poem), *Cumberland Poetry Review*, Spring.

Landis, Geoffrey, "Gulliver's Boots" (poem), *Asimov's SF*, March.

Lane, Joel, "A Hairline Crack," *Roadworks* 11.

———, "The Last Cry," *Roadworks* 12.

Langan, John, "On Skua Island," *Fantasy and Science Fiction*, August.

Lannes, Roberta, "Turkish Delight," *The M. B. of Vampire Stories by Women*.

Larbalestier, Justine, "Cruel Brother," www.strangehorizons.com, October 10.

Larkin, Tanya, "Penelope" (poem), *Quarterly West*, Autumn/Winter.

Laws, Robin D., "Susan," *The Book of All Flesh*.

Laymon, Richard, "The Keeper," Chapbook *Gauntlet* premium.

———, "Pick-up on Highway One," *Cemetery Dance* 34.

———, "Triage" (novella), *Triage*.

Le Guin, Ursula K., "The Finder," *Tales from Earthsea*.

———, "On the High Marsh," Ibid.

Lebbon, Tim, "Kissing at Shadows," *Cemetery Dance* 36.

———, "Last Exit for the Lost," *Phantoms of Venice*.

———, "Loving Memory," *Poddities*.

Lee, Mary Soon, "City of Mercy," *Winter Shadows and Other Tales*.

———, "The Fall of the Kingdom," Ibid.

———, "The Winter of the Rats," Ibid.

Lee, Tanith, "La Vampiresse," *Weird Tales* 324.

———, "Where all Things Perish" (novella), *Weird Tales* 325.

Lestewka, Pat, "El Burro Loco," *Bloodtype*.

Lethem, Jonathan, "This Shape We're In" (novella), *This Shape We're In*.
Lewis, Paul, "In Her Eyes," *Dark Horizons* 40.
———, "One Last Wish," *Dark Horizons* 39.
Ligotti, Thomas, "My Case for Retributive Action," *Weird Tales* 324.
———, "Our Temporary Supervisor," *Weird Tales* 325.
Lindberg, Seth, "23 Snapshots of San Francisco," *Twilight Showcase*, August.
Link, Kelly, "Most of my Friends Are Two-Thirds Water," *Stranger Things Happen*.
Linville, Susan Urbanek, "Light," *Sword and Sorceress XVIII*.
Little, Bentley, "The Move," *Cemetery Dance* 34.
———, "The Riders," *Cemetery Dance* 36.
Locascio, Phil, "Quietus," *Kinships*, September.
———, "The Letter of Timothy Devingham," *Extremes 3: Terror on the High Seas*.
Longhorn, David, "The Glyphs," *Ghosts & Scholars* 32.
Longmuir, Chris, "The Ghost Train," *Dark Horizons* 39.
Lord, Nancy, "The Man Who Swam with Beavers," *The Man Who Swam with Beavers*.
Lovegrove, James, "Running," *The Third Alternative* 26.
MacAllister, Carol, "Jump Rope" (poem), *Flesh & Blood* 7.
MacLeod, Loren, "Children of Fortune," *Dark Horizons* 39.
Maistros, Louis, "The Print Man," *The Midnighters Club*.
Malenky, Barbara, "Gold Nuggets," *Darkness Rising: Night's Soft Pains*.
Malniczek, Paul, "Devil Man of the Hollow," *Darkness Rising: Hideous Dreams*.
Marano, Michael, "Little Round Head," *gothic.net*, July.
Marillier, Juliet, "Otherling," *Realms of Fantasy*, April.
Massie, Elizabeth, "Day is Done, Gone the Sun," *Chiaroscuro* 9.
Masterton, Graham, "The Scrawler," *Gauntlet Chapbook / Urban Gothic*.
Matter, Holly Wade, "Memorabilia," *Bending the Landscape: Horror*.
Matthews, Patricia, "The Ghost of Twombley Hall," *Extremes 2*.
McConnon, James, "Innocence Gained," *Roadworks* 12.
McDermott, Kirstyn, "Smile for Me," *Redsine* 6.
McFarland, Michael James, "The Hypnotist," *Twilight Showcase*, November–January 2002.
McGarry, Terry, "Limnery in Cursive," *Realms of Fantasy*, October.
McGrath, Campbell, "Archimedes," *Colorado Review*, Summer.
———, "Xena, Warrior Princess" (poem), *Pleiades*, Vol. 21, #1.
McLaughlin, Mark, "A Beauty Treatment for Mrs. Hamogeorgakis," *Terror Tales*, Spring.
———, "The Groveler in the Grotto," *The Night the Lights Went Out in Arkham*.
———, "When We Was Flab," horrorfind.com. July.
McNaughton, Brian, "Congratulations," *Nasty Stories*.
———, "The Hole," Ibid.
Melniczek, Paul, "Companion," *Frightful Fiction*, November 30.
Meloy, Paul, "Raiders," *The Third Alternative* 27.
Mileman, Tony, "Across the Hills," *Nemonymous*, November.
Minier, Samuel, "Figments and Other Bedtime Friends" (poem), *Flesh & Blood* 7.
Minnion, Keith, "It's for You," *Cemetery Dance* 34.
Monk, Devon, "Last Tour of Duty," *Realms of Fantasy*, December.
Moore, Ralph Robert, "Visibility," *Roadworks* 11.
Moore, Nancy Jane, "Three O'Clock In The Morning," *Lady Churchill's Rosebud Wristlet* 8.
Morden, Simon, "Hollow," *Extremes 3: Terror on the High Seas*.
———, "Whitebone Street," *Masters of Terror 2001 Anthology* (Web site).

Morgan, Christine, "Dawn of the Living-Impaired," *The Book of All Flesh*.

Morlan, A. R., "Dark Ladonna," *Crimson Online Magazine* 14.

————, "Dora's Trunk," *Challenging Destiny*, April.

————, "Opening the Veins of Jade," *Wicked Words* 5.

Morressy, John, "About Face," *Fantasy & Science Fiction*, October/November.

Morris, Roger, "The Devil's Drum," *Darkness Rising: Night's Soft Pains*.

Moss, Barbara Klein, "Interpreters," *The Missouri Review*, Vol. XXIV, #2.

Murakami, Haruki, "A Poor-Aunt Story," translated from the Japanese by Jay Rubin, *The New Yorker*, 12/3.

Murphy, Joe, "La Carrera de la Muerte," *The Book of All Flesh*.

Murphy, M. J., "The Line I Walk," *New Genre* 2.

Newton, Kurt, "Butter Red and Diamond Eyes," *Delirium*.

————, "The Mole Trap," *Crime Spree*.

————, "The Pit," *Poddities*.

Nicholson, Scott, "Murdermouth," *The Book of All Flesh*.

Nickle, David, "The Lodge," World Fantasy Convention CD-Rom.

Nix, Garth, "Under the Lake," *Fantasy & Science Fiction*, February.

Noecker, Shane, "Between the Lines," *All Hallows* 27.

Nolan, William F., "In Real Life," *The Museum of Horrors*.

O'Connell, Jack, "Legerdemain," *Fantasy & Science Fiction*, October/November.

O'Rourke, Monica J., "Loathsome in New York," *Scars*.

Oates, Joyce Carol, "Angel of Mercy," thespook.com, October.

————, "Commencement," *Redshift*.

————, "The Museum of Dr. Moses," *The Museum of Horrors*.

Ochse, Weston, "Into the Darkness, Gently," *The Dead Inn*.

————, "Natural Selection" (chapbook), Dark Tales Publications.

Oldknow, Antony, "The Damusters' March," *All Hallows* 27.

Olivas, Daniel A., "Devil's Talk," *Facets*, April.

Oliveri, Michael, "Hell Hath no Fury," *4X4*.

————, "Shades of Red," *Dark Fluidity*.

Oliveri, Michael and Hyck, Michael T., Jr., "Engaging Entropy," *4×4*.

Otis, Martha, "Mole," *Indiana Review*, Fall.

Otto, Lon, "The Old Truth in Costa Rica," *Colorado Review*, Summer.

Outram, Richard, "Grief Tree" (poem), *The Antigonish Review* 125.

Park, Carma, "Poppies" (poem), *Dark Regions* 16.

Partridge, Norman, "Blood Money," *The Man with the Barbed Wire Fists*.

————, "Red Rover, Red Rover," thespook.com, August.

Pas, Lia, "Crow" (poem), World Fantasy Convention CD-Rom.

Patterson, Meredith L., "Pale Foxes," strangehorizons.com, March 3.

Pearlman, Daniel, "The Colonel's Jeep," *Extremes* 2.

Pence, Amy, "The Nettle House" (poem), *Poem*, May.

Phillips, Holly, "Last One," *On Spec*, Fall.

Piccirilli, Tom, "A Square Wedge of Vanilla," *Dark Fluidity*.

Pierce, Tamora, "Elder Brother," *Half-human*.

Platt, John R., "Waiting," strangehorizons.com, May 21.

Popkes, Steven, "Tom Kelley's Ghost," *Fantasy & Science Fiction*, July.

Porte, Barbara Ann, "Beauty and the Serpent," *Beauty and the Serpent: Thirteen Tales of Unnatural Animals*.

Porter, Karen R., "Behind the Sky" (poem), *The Bible of Hell*.

Pratt, Tim, "Behemoth," *Brain Box: Son of Brainbox*.

————, "Mask" (poem), strangehorizons.com, June 18.

Pugmire, W. H., "Ides of March" (poem), *Songs of Sesqua Valley*.

————, "Mother" (poem), Ibid.

————, "The Phantom of Beguilement," *Tales of Love and Death*.

————, "The Zanies of Sorrow," *Tales of Love and Death*.

Pulver, Joe, "I, Like the Coyote" (poem), *Dreams & Nightmares* 58.

Rae, Mary, "In the Night" (poem), *Penny Dreadful* 14.

Ratner, Austin, "Nine Worthy and the Best that Ever Were," *Missouri Review*, Vol. XXVI, #1.

Rath, Tina, "The Co-Walker," *Darkness Rising: Hideous Dreams*.

Reed, Kit, "Playmate," *Fantasy & Science Fiction*, May.

Reed, Robert, "Crooked Creek," *Fantasy & Science Fiction*, January.

————, "The Last Game," *Fantasy & Science Fiction*, August.

————, "Market Day," *Fantasy & Science Fiction*, March.

————, "Past Imperfect," *Asimov's SF*, March.

————, "Season to Taste," *Fantasy & Science Fiction*, April.

Rendell, Ruth "Piranha to Scurfy" (novella), *Ellery Queen's Mystery Magazine*, September/
   October.

Rice, Ben, "The Specks in the Sky," *The New Yorker*, December 24 and 31.

Richards, Tony, "Going Back," *The Third Alternative* 29.

Richerson, Carrie, "Love on a Stick," *Bending the Landscape: Horror*.

————, "The Golden Chain," *Fantasy & Science Fiction*, April.

Rickert, M., "Moorina," *Fantasy & Science Fiction*, February.

Riedel, Kate, "Neighbors," *On Spec*, Spring.

————, "To Others we Know Not of," *Weird Tales* 323.

Robertson, R. Garcia y, "Firebird," *Fantasy & Science Fiction*, May.

Robson, Nicky, "Airtight," *Blood & Donuts*.

Roderick, David, "Owl Night," *Quarterly West*.

Rogers, Bruce Holland, "The Spires," *Flaming Arrows*.

Rohrig, Judi, "Blind Mouths," *Cemetery Dance* 35.

Rose, Rhea, "The Lemonade Stand," *Talebones* 22.

Rosen, Barbara, "The Muttering," *Mooreeffoc*, Summer.

Rosenman, John, "Steam Heat," *The Dead Inn*.

Rowlands, David G., "Lord of the Flies," *Supernatural Tales* 1.

————, "Pua Mana (Sea Breeze)," *Ghosts & Scholars* 33.

Rozic, Edward R., "Dear Air," *Bloodtype*.

Rusch, Kristine Kathryn, "Star," *A Constellation of Cats*.

Rutale, Patricia, "Creatures," *Tales of the Unanticipated*, April.

Ryan, Paul, "Claw," *Nor of Human*.

Saavedra, Pedro J., "Mordred on the Couch" (poem), *The N.Y. Quarterly* 57.

Sallee, Wayne Allen, "This Old Man Came Rolling Home," *Blood & Donuts*.

Sallis, James, "Day's Heat," *Asimov's SF*, February.

Salmonson, Jessica Amanda, "The Apartment," *World Horror Convention Program Book*.

San Giovanni, Mary, "Skincatchers," horrorfind.com. May.

Saplak, Charles M., "Meatloaf is Monday," *AHMM*, December.

Sarrantonio, Al, "Hornets," *Trick or Treat*.

Savile, Steve, "Angels in the Snow," *Similar Monsters*.

———, "The Fragrance of You," Ibid.

Savory, Brett A., "The Distance Travelled" (chapbook), *Prime*.

Schofield, Neil A., "Fat Chance," *AHMM*, April.

Schow, David J., "Entr'acte," *Eye*.

———, "Quebradora," Ibid.

———, "Scoop Goes Rectosonic," Ibid.

Schwader, Ann K., "Confessions of the White Acolyte" (poem), Ibid.

———, "Charles Dexter Unwarded" (five sonnets) *The Worms Remember*.

———, "False Hope" (poem), *Penny Dreadful* 14.

———, "Ophelia's Moon" (poem), Ibid.

———, "Pompelo's Doom (A Dream of Chaugnar Faugn)" (poem), Ibid.

———, "Survivals" (poem), Ibid.

Schweitzer, Darrell, "I Dreamed that I Sailed in a Ship of Heroes" (poem), *Mooreeffoc*, Summer.

———, "Song of a Forgotten God" (poem), *Talebones* 21.

Searle, Antony, "Flap," *Nor of Human*.

Searles, Vera, "The Lanterns," *Crimson Online Magazine* 14.

Setton, Ruth Knafo, "The Cat Garden," *With Signs and Wonders*.

Shannon, Lorelei, "Brownies with Nuts," *Vermifuge, and other Toxic Cocktails*.

———, "The Little Spark," *Horror Garage* 4.

———, "The Menfolks Come for Dinner," *Vermifuge, and Other Toxic Cocktails*.

Sharma, Akhil, "Surrounded by Sleep," *The New Yorker*, December 10.

Sheckley, Robert, "A Trick Worth Two of That," *Fantasy & Science Fiction*, May.

Shepard, Lucius, "Eternity and Afterward" (novella), *Fantasy & Science Fiction*, March.

Shepard, Reginald, "Apollo Steps in Daphne's Footprints" (poem), *TriQuarterly*, Fall.

Shipp, Jeremy C. "Just Another Vampire Story," *Darkness Rising: Hideous Dreams*.

Shirley, John "The Claw Spur," *Horror Garage* 3.

———, "In the Road," *Darkness Divided*.

———, "My Victim," *Cemetery Dance* 34.

———, "One Stick, Both Ends Sharpened," *Horror Garage* 4.

———, "Talisman," thespook.com, September.

———, "Tighter," *Darkness Divided*.

———, "Whisperers," Ibid.

———, "Your Servants in Hell," Ibid.

Shouse, Deborah, "A Portrait of Angels," *With Signs and Wonders*.

Sidor, Steven, "Mopping Up," horrorfind.com. June.

Silva, David B., "Memory's Weave," *Night Visions* 10.

———, "Small Talk Dies in Agonies," Ibid.

———, "The Sum of a Man," Ibid.

———, "Whose Puppets Best and Worst Are We?" *Cemetery Dance* 35.

Simmons, William P., "The Wind, When it Comes," *Darkness Rising: Hideous Dreams*.

Simner, Janni Lee, "Water's Edge," *Half-human*.

Simpson, Martin, "Laying on Hands," *The Third Alternative* 28.

Singleton, Sarah, "The Magpie," *Strange Pleasures*.

Slay, Jack, Jr., "Once," *Realms of Fantasy*, October.

Smale, Alan, "Bridges," *Dark Regions* 16.

Smart, Alexi, "Broken Canes," *Bending the Landscape: Horror*.

Smith, Douglas, "By Her Hand, She Draws You Down," *The Third Alternative* 28.

Snyder, Lucy A., "Through Thy Bounty," *The Midnighter's Club*.

Soles, Caro, "Reunion," World Fantasy Convention CD-Rom.

Sorescu, Marin, "The Dragon" (poem), translated from the Romanian by Adam J. Sorkin and Lidia Vianu, *The American Poetry Review*, September/October.

Spriggs, Robin, "Cinema Surrendari," *Wondrous Strange*.

Springer, Nancy, "Becoming," *Half-human*.

Stevens, Bryce, "Forever by his Side," *Stalking the Demon*.

———, "The Wise Woman and the Snow Leopard," Ibid.

Stover, Matthew, Woodring, "Br'er Robert," *Fantastic Metropolis*, October 28.

Stuart, Kiel, "Are You Now or Have You Ever Been?" *Mooreeffoc*, Fall.

Sturges, Matthew, "The Horizon's Far Margin," *Beneath the Skin and other Stories*.

———, "The Odd Within," Ibid.

Tarr, Judith, "Finding the Grail," *Out of Avalon*.

Taylor, John Alfred, "The Game of Nine," *Asimv's SF*, September.

Taylor, Larry, "Annie," Writers of Earth Story Competition 2001 (Web site).

Teare, Brian, "Sleeping Beauty and the Prince: Self-Portrait as Victim and Perpetrator" (poem), *Pleiades*, Vol. 21, #1.

Tem, Melanie, "Lunch at Charon's," *The M. B. of Vampire Stories by Women*.

Tem, Steve Rasnic, "The Far Side of the Lake," *The Far Side of the Lake*.

Tem, Steve and Melanie, "North," *Extremes 2*.

Thomas, Jeffrey, "Working Stiffs," *The Dead Inn*.

Thomas, Lee, "The Estranged," *neverworlds.com*, December.

Thomas, Scott, "Cobwebs," *Cobwebs and Whispers*.

———, "The Harvest of War," Ibid.

———, "Her Fine Mouth," *Penny Dreadful* 14.

———, "Hunter of Gulls," *Cobwebs and Whispers*.

———, "Joseph Warren's Invention," Ibid.

———, "Marcy Waters," Ibid.

———, "Sharp Medicine," Ibid.

———, "The Thorn Dance," Ibid.

———, "Vale of the White Horse," Ibid.

———, "Whispers," Ibid.

Thompson, Philip, "Father to Son," *All Hallows* 27.

Thon, Melanie Rae, "Instructions for Extinction," *Colorado Review*, Summer.

Tiedemann, Mark W., "Passing," *Bending the Landscape: Horror*.

Tilton, Lois, "Prisoner Exchange," *Asimv's SF*, September.

Tourney, Anne, "Body Care," *Dark Regions* 16.

Travis, John, "Cuticles," *Dark Horizons* 40.

Travis, Tia V., "A Gift with Hollow Spaces," thespook.com. December.

Tremblay, Paul G., "King Bee," *The Dead Inn*.

Triton, Jennifer, "In Fear of Angels" (poem), *The Bible of Hell*.

Trojan, Kurt von, "The House," *Aurealis* 27/28.

Tullis, S. D., "The Weird Ways," *The Third Alternative* 29.

Tumosonis, Don, "What Goes Down," *Ghosts & Scholars* 32.

Turzillo, Mary A., "The Need of Her Flesh" (poem), *Asimov's SF*, August.

———, "When Gretchen was Human," *The M. B. of Vampire Stories by Women*.

Urbancik, John, "Lapse of Vengeance," *Indigenous Fiction*, June.

———, "Snow Sparrow," *Dark Fluidity*.

Vagle, Rob, "Messages," *Realms of Fantasy*, April.

Valentine, Jean, "Eleventh Brother" (poem), *Colorado Review*, Spring.

Van Belkom, Edo, "Gummy Worms," *Six Inch Spikes*.

——, "Organ Music," *Blood & Donuts*.

——, "The Starlet," Ibid.

Van Cleave, Ryan G., "The Danaides" (poem), *TriQuarterly*, Fall.

Van Leff, Valerie, "The Flying Camel Spin," *The Antioch Review*, Winter.

Van Pelt, James, "The Stars Underfoot," *Realms of Fantasy*, August.

——, "The Yard God," *Talebones* 22.

Vande Velde, Vivian, "Being Dead," *Being Dead*.

VanderMeer, Jeff, "The Exchange by Nicholas Sporlender" (chapbook), *Hogbotton and Sons*.

——, "The Florida Freshwater Squid," *Fantastic Metropolis* (Web site).

Volk, Stephen, "The Fall Children," *All Hallows* 26.

Volpe, Steve, "Night Game," *Night Terrors* 9.

Vukcevich, Ray, "Beatnicks with Banjos," *Meet Me in the Moon Room*.

——, "In the Refrigerator," Ibid.

——, "Pretending," *Lady Churchill's Rosebud Wristlet* 8.

——, "Whisper," *Fantasy & Science Fiction*, January.

Wadholm, Richard, "From Here you can See the Sunquists," *Asimov's SF*, January.

Waggoner, Tim, "Fixer-Upper," *Single White Vampire Seeks Same*.

Wallace, David Foster, "Another Pioneer," *Colorado Review*, Summer.

Walsh, Jane, "State of the Art," *All Hallows* 28.

Walsh, Pat, "The Pumpkin Field," Ibid.

Walter, Victor, "Flight of Time," *New England Review*, Spring.

Warburton, Geoffrey, "Dunn's Pictures," *Dark Horizons* 39, Spring.

——, "The Maze," *All Hallows* 27.

Ward, C. E., "The Particular," *Ghosts & Scholars* 32.

Warrington, Freda, "Little Goose," *F20* 2.

Wasserman, Jamie, "Why I Believe in Ghosts" (poem), *Flesh & Blood* 7.

Watkins, William Jon, "Under the Sand," *Extremes 3: Terror on the High Seas*.

Weaver, Delice D., "Less than Objective," Ibid.

Webb, Don, "The Jest of Yig," *Weird Tales* 322.

Weinberg, Robert, "Three Steps Back," *Dial Your Dreams*.

What, Leslie, "Goyles in the Hood," *Black Gate* 2.

——, "That Jellyfish Man Keeps A-Rollin," *The Third Alternative* 29.

——, "Those Taunted Lips," *Historical Hauntings*.

White, Edward Lucas, "Canea," *Sesta and other Strange Stories*.

——, "Gertrude," Ibid.

——, "The Tooth," Ibid.

——, "The Voices," Ibid.

Whitman, David, "Deadfellas" (novella), *Dark Tales* (chapbook).

——, "Dust in the Wind," *Frightful Fiction/Fangoria online*, September.

William, Conrad, "Imbroglio," *The Museum of Horrors*.

——, "Nearly People" (novella), PS Publishing.

Williams, Liz, "The Sea of Time and Space," *Realms of Fantasy*, October.

Wilson, Mehitobel, "Blind in the House of the Headman," *Brain Box: Son of Brainbox*.

——, "Jacks," *Peep Show* 2.

Winfield, Mason C., "The Hunters," *feoamante.com*.

Wood, Simon, "The Hoarder," *Not One of Us* 26.

Wright, Richard, "Bulemia Daemonica," *Brain Box: Son of Brainbox*.

Yolen, Jane, "Centaur Field," *Half-human*.

———, "Impedimenta" (poem), *Peregrine*.

Zipper, Gerald, "Blind Doors" (poem), *Frisson*, Winter 2000.

Zucker, Rachel, "Letter (Demeter to Persephone)" (poem), *Colorado Review*, Spring.

# The People Behind the Book

Horror editor ELLEN DATLOW is the fiction editor of SCIFI.COM. She was the fiction editor for *Omni* magazine for over a decade, and has edited numerous anthologies, including *Vanishing Acts*. She has also collaborated with Terri Windling on a number of anthologies besides *The Year's Best Fantasy and Horror* series, including *A Wolf at the Door*. She has won six World Fantasy Awards for her editing. She lives in New York City.

Fantasy editor TERRI WINDLING has been a passionate advocate of Fantasy Literature for more than two decades, winning six World Fantasy Awards for her work. She is a consulting fantasy editor for Tor Books, and she has published numerous anthologies including *The Armless Maiden*, the *Borderland* series for teenagers, and the *Snow White, Blood Red* adult fairy-tale series (the latter co-edited with Ellen Datlow). Her own fiction includes *The Wood Wife* (winner of the Mythopoeic Award), *A Midsummer Night's Faery Tale* and *The Winter Child*; she has also written extensively about mythology and folklore. As a painter, she has exhibited her art in the U.S. and U.K. She divides her time between homes in Devon, England, and Tucson, Arizona.

Media Critic ED BRYANT is an award-winning author of science fiction, fantasy, and horror, having published short fiction in countless anthologies and magazines. He's won the Nebula Award for his science fiction, and other works of his short fiction have been nominated for many other awards. He's also written for television. He lives in Denver, Colorado.

Comics critic CHARLES VESS's award-winning art has graced the pages of numerous comic books for over twenty years. In 1991, Charles shared the World Fantasy Award for Best Short Story with Neil Gaiman for their collaboration on *Sandman #19*, the first and only time a comic book has won this honor. In 1997, Charles won the Will Eisner Comic Industry Award for best penciler/inker for his work on *The Book of Ballads and Sagas* (which he self-publishes through his own Green Man Press) as well as *Sandman #75*. In 1999, he received the World Fantasy Award for Best Artist. For current information, visit his Web site: www.greenmanpress.com. He lives amid the Appalachian mountains in southwest Virginia.

Anime and manga critic JOAN D. VINGE is the two-time Hugo Award-winning author of the *Snow Queen* cycle and the Cat books. She has had stories published in all the major SF magazines, and has written adaptations of more than a dozen films. Her most recent book is *Tangled Up in Blue*, a novel in the Snow Queen universe. She's working on *LadySmith*, a novel set in bronze-age Western Europe. She lives in Madison, Wisconsin.

Jacket artist THOMAS CANTY has won the World Fantasy Award for Best Artist. He has painted and/or designed jackets and covers for many books, and has art-directed many other books covers, over an art and design career that spans more than twenty years. He's produced the art for *The Year's Best Fantasy and Horror* series since its inception. He lives outside Boston, Massachusetts.

Packager JAMES FRENKEL has worked as an editor for over thirty years, at a number of publishing houses. He was the publisher of Bluejay Books. He has edited anthologies, including *True Names and the Opening of the Cyberspace Frontier*. Presently he is Senior Editor at Tor Books, where he's worked since 1987. Aided by JESSE VOGEL, STEPHEN SMITH, and a legion of interns from the University of Wisconsin, he edits and packages books in Madison, Wisconsin.